Wh-a-at wantest thou with me at this hour of the night?" stammer'd the Jew.

THE HEBREW MAIDEN;

OR,

THE LOST DIAMOND.

A TALE OF CHIVALRY.

BY THE AUTHOR OF "FATHERLESS FANNY;" "TALES
OF THE DRAMA;" &c. &c.

Success, the mark no mortal wit,
Of surest hand can always hit:
For whatsoe'er we perpetrate,
We do but row, we're steered by Fate,
Which in success oft disinherits,
For spurious causes, noblest merits.
BUTLER.

LONDON:

PUBLISHED BY E. LLOYD, 231, SHOREDITCH.

MDCCCXLI.

THE
HEBREW MAIDEN;
OR,
THE LOST DIAMOND.

CHAPTER I.

> " Girl, thine evil star is in th' ascendant,
>   And the dark cloud of dire adversity
>   Frowns loweringly upon thee."
>
> THE VESPER BELL.

MAY the God of Israel shield and protect thee, my child; may He watch over thee as one of his chosen people, and may'st thou, through His divine assistance, escape those snares that are daily spread for the destruction of youthful innocence."

These words were addressed by Isaac, the Jew of Tadcaster, to his only and beloved daughter, the gentle and dark-eyed Rebecca, who had thrown herself upon her knees at his feet, to receive his blessing, ere she retired to her chamber for the night. A smile of pride and exultation spread over the countenance of the old man as he gazed on the beauteous being before him, and, imprinting a kiss upon her forehead, he raised her

No. 1

from the lowly posture she had assumed. Somewhat surprised at the melancholy of her father, the maiden turned her love-inspired gaze towards him, and throwing one arm fondly round his neck, she enquired anxiously the cause of his present lowliness of spirits.

"Alas, my child," he replied, "thou little knowest the miseries to which the children of our tribe are subjected. Hitherto thou hast passed thy life in comparative quiet, but a change has taken place in the destinies of our people, and I fear, ere many days have glided over us, the persecutions of those who hate our creed will burst forth with redoubled violence."

"And wherefore thinkest thou so, my father?" asked Rebecca in a cheerful tone, that was intended to raise the heart of him to whom she had addressed herself.

"Thou knowest," replied the old man, "that our good king, Henry the Second, is departed from the glory which was his inheritance upon earth. He was friendly to,—or at least not an oppressor of the Hebrew nation, and I fear there is but too much reason to expect that his successor to the throne will prove a heavy task-master to those who all sects conspire to trample upon. This they call christian charity, forgetting that their own religion commands them to love all men as their brothers."

"Nay, dearest father, you are unjust towards the young king;" cried Rebecca, ardently :—"Report speaks of Richard Cour de Lion as the very soul of chivalry and honour ; he hath ever been magnanimous, even to his enemies, and surely he will not stain his fair name by any act that might bring upon him a charge of cruelty or injustice."

"That, my child, will depend on circumstances," answered Isaac ;—"if we bribe him with rich presents, we shall have protection, but should we fail in that our lot will be most grievous."

"Then, knowing that, should we not purchase security upon those terms?" demanded the maiden,—"you are rich—"

"Hush !" exclaimed the Jew, glancing eagerly around him to see that there were no listeners :—"speak not of riches, girl,—speak not of them, I say, for we live in troublesome times, and were any of our people known to possess the world's idol—gold, it would bring upon them the fierce persecution of those who loathe and execrate them for their religion sake !—No, no, child—I am not rich—I am poor,—very, very poor, and yet thou would call down upon me the fierce vengeance of those who would torture those aged limbs, did they but think, that by doing so, they could extract from me the smallest particle of that dross which the world regards as of so much value. But I have no gold, child, none—none, and they who filled thy mind with such folly have foully misled thee."

"Nay, thou hast thyself misled me then," cried Rebecca.

"I, girl !"

"Yes, even yourself, dearest father; have you not promised my affianced husband, Reuben Grenard, a marriage portion, that few, even among the nobles of this land could give."

"True,—true,—but I was a vain boaster, child,—a braggart, without the means of performing even a twentieth part of my promise."

"You have deceived Reuben, then ?"

"Yes, yes,—that is, I—I—"

"Enough, enough, my father," interrupted Rebecca,—"I was wrong to press this foolish matter so far—very wrong—but forgive me, and I will away to my bed."

Again the old man pressed his lips to the blooming cheek of his beloved daughter, and, happy in the consciousness of virtue, she was about to pass through the door which led to her chamber when a loud knocking was heard without, and ere she could effect her retreat, a stranger, muffled up in a capacious riding cloak, strode into the apartment.

"Wh—a—t wantest thou with me at this late hour of the night?" stammered the Jew, trembling with anxiety, and thinking only of his money bag, and the treacherous designs that might be entertained against them by the intruder;—"speak—what would'st thou with thy poor servant?"

"Thou art Isaac of Tadcaster, if I mistake not?"

"The same, at your honour's service."

"And," resumed the intruder, "one of the richest rogues in all Christendom, unless rumour proves to be a liar."

"Of a verity, rumour lies most foully," answered the Jew, with a faltering tongue :—"I am not rich, though the world gives me credit for possessing that which all men so eagerly covet."

"Psha! quibble not to me, old man," exclaimed the stranger, impatiently. "I know thy craft and am prepared to cope with it, so now, tell me plainly and honestly, wilt thou advance me a sum of money, supposing I place in thy hands that which is worth double the price I ask for it."

"That will depend upon circumstances," answered Isaac, whose curiosity was now somewhat excited;—"in all honour and firmness I will purchase what thou speakest of—I will give thee a fair price for it—that is,—supposing it to be honestly thine own."

"Why, whose else should it be?" demanded the stranger, in no very good humour at the doubt which had been thus raised; "the article is a diamond ring, worth two hundred pieces of gold at the very least, and yet I offer it thee for one hundred."

"Indeed!" exclaimed Isaac, examining the jewel minutely;—"it may be, as you say, worth two hundred pieces of gold, but I am no judge of such things, and might be grievously imposed upon were I to purchase it."

"You refuse to have it then?"

"No—no," eagerly exclaimed the Hebrew—"I don't exactly refuse to have it,—but I know not its real value,—and money is so scarce, and——"

"Ugh!" cried the stranger, snatching the glittering jewel from the old man, and handing it to Rebecca; "if you are no judge of it yourself, here's one who knows whether the price I ask for it is too much or not. By St. Nicholas, old man, this is a fair wench of yours, and I know not which shine brightest—her eyes, or the diamonds that sparkle in the bauble."

"Rebecca, leave the room, girl—leave us, I charge thee," cried her father, in accents of alarm,—"this is no place for thee, my child, and as thou lovest me begone!"

"By thy leave no," exclaimed the stranger, advancing, and seizing the hand of the retreating maiden;—"it is not my fortune every day to fall into such fair company, and thy beauteous daughter shall stay to be a witness of this business between us."

"How!" ejaculated Isaac angrily;" dost thou come to insult us?"

"I come to deal with thee as one man should deal with another," answered the stranger; "I am here to exchange this bauble for the gold which I need, and surely it is not too much to ask that this maiden should honour me with her presence."

"Wilt thou release her," cried the old man, clutching the handle of the dagger he wore beneath his vest,—"wilt thou suffer her to depart, or must I spill thy Christian blood even upon my own hearth?"

"Mercy, mercy, dear father!" screamed Rebecca, suddenly releasing herself from the stranger's grasp, and throwing herself at the feet of the old man:—"do not shed the blood of one who hath entered your house in all confidence, spare him, and I will be content to obey your behest."

Isaac gazed upon her, and his heart relented; with a trembling hand he returned the poniard to its sheathe, and then fixing his eyes sternly upon the countenance of the intruder, he bade him instantly quit the place.

"Not till we have concluded the business that brought me hither," answered the other, with the easy confidence of one who knew his own superior strength. "I came hither to obtain gold for this diamond, and I shall not leave your presence till some sort of bargain has been concluded between us."

"I tell thee I want it not," answered Isaac;—"in truth I have not the sum by me you have asked for it."

"Tush, man! that is but a trick of thy craft," returned the other doggedly. "The gem is well worth thy having; the price I have set upon it is far under its real value, and as to thy saying thou hast not wherewithal to purchase it, why, between thee and me old man, I have heard it whispered, that thou coulds't, if thou likest, buy half the estates of the needy nobles, who hover like gaudy butterflies about the court."

"They speak falsely of me," cried the Jew, with a feeling of alarm that he could not conceal;—"I am a penniless beggar, and they only scoff at me who say I am rich."

"Then thou cans't not purchase this trifle of me?"

"Stay, I will recollect myself;—I have a small sum of gold belonging to a friend who has gone abroad; if I might use that for a few days, till I could sell the jewel at a trifling profit, your wishes might be complied with."

"That will do," exclaimed the stranger, "provided the sum is any where near what I ask for it."

"Then I fear we must part even as we met," returned Isaac;—"I have but eighty pieces of gold in the house, and you have but just now demanded an hundred."

"Give me the eighty, and the ring is yours," cried the other. "I am not over nice to a few pieces of gold, and if ever we happen to bargain again, you must remember to throw the advantage a little more in my favour. And now maiden," he continued, addressing himself to Rebecca, "the affair between your father and myself is settled, and therefore will I leave the jewel upon your finger, to be worn by one of the higher price than all the diamonds that were ever dug from the bowels of the Golconda."

During this, Isaac had been engaged in counting out the required sum from a small box which he had fetched from a closet, and having told it over and over again to be sure that he had not given a gold piece more than he agreed for, he advanced towards the stranger, who he regarded with a scrutinizing look. as he said:—

"You appear anxious to dispose of this for a sum that I will now tell you is far below its real value. This ring could only have belonged to some great noble, and therefore do I require to be informed how you became possessed of it, and what your motive is for parting with it."

"Dost thou know that I am not a noble?" demanded the stranger.

"On the contrary, I should believe that thou art," answered Isaac; "for the rudeness of thy manner, and the freedom of speech assures me that thou art one of the privileged class."

"Thou hast guessed marvellously near the mark then," returned the other with easy composure;—" But I have not yet answered thine other questions :—Thou would'st know how I became possessed of the bauble—know then that it was left me by my maternal grandmother, and as for the reason of my parting with it, why faith, I believe my reason for getting rid of the jewel, is the same that drives many an honest man to act against his conscience,—In fact, friend Jew, I want money."

"And to raise that trifling sum you would part with that which you say was a family relic ?"

"Psha! family relics, as you call them, will not satisfy the vile harpies of the law, when they are cadging close at your heels," answered the other.

"Thou art in debt then ?"

"Over head and ears. Nay, I have with difficulty escaped the hounds that are in search of me, and ——"

Here a tremendous hammering was heard at the outer door, and loud shouts were heard demanding instant admittance. At this the stranger became violently agitated, and grasping the Jew's hand convulsively, he implored to be concealed in some place of safety, till his pursuers should have completed the search they were making for him.

"And why should thou hide thyself, now that thou hast the money in thy possession to satisfy their demands?" asked the Hebrew. "Pay them out of the eighty pieces of gold I have just given thee, and they will depart satisfied."

"It is not half enough for the purpose," answered the stranger, "and they would not only rob me of all I have, but the greedy knaves would threw me into a prison till the rest of the debt is satisfied. Hark! they are battering in the door, and in a few moments I shall be in their hands, unless you aid me in escaping from their vengeance."

"And if it should be known I haddone so, their rage would fall upon me as well as thyself."

"Thou wilt not avoid their fury if they find me here," answered the stranger. "Nay, thou wilt suffer even more severely if they have reason to expect that thou hast harboured me in thy house. Thy daughter, too, whom thou lovest, will share the perils of the father, and thou pretty well knowest the sort of mercy thou hast to expect if once their suspicions are fixed upon thee. Hark! the door yields to their repeated blows;—now tell me, old man, whether I shall have protection, or thyself and yonder maiden a dungeon."

"Thou hast prevailed over me, and I will shield thee even at the hazard of my life," exclaimed Isaac, and then raising a trap door in the middle of the chamber, he revealed a dark vault, down which a flight of stone steps led to a subterranean apartment beneath.

"Descend quickly," cried the old man in a tone of alarm: "thou will find a spacious chamber beneath, from which a passage will lead thee to another flight of stone steps. I will send my servant to open the door, and thou cans't then escape the perils that now environ thee. Away—give me no thanks, thy foes are already in the house, and there is barely time to effect thy retreat undiscovered."

Thus adjured, the stranger hastily vanished through the trap door, which being immediately closed, and the place covered over with a rug, it seemed that the safety of the stranger had been completely effected. Scarcely, however, had this been done, when Jonah, the Hebrew's serving man rushed into the room, announcing that the officers of justice had effected a forcible entry into the house, and that they were at present occupied in searching the adjoining apartment.

"So! not an instant is to be lost then," exclaimed the Jew,—"take this key, Jonah, and open the door which leads from the court yard behind our house; a stranger will issue from it, whom thou must assist to escape. When that is done, lock the door, and put the key in some secure hiding place where these men will hardly chance to find it."

In obedience to this injunction, the man hastened from his master's presence, and scarcely had he disappeared on his errand when a couple of constables, followed by a rabble of men rushed unceremoniously into the room. Rebecca sank terrified upon a seat, but her father, indignant at the outrage that had been committed against him, stood up with a bold front before the intruders, and demanded the cause of ther tumultuous proceedings against an old and harmless man.

"Hear me, exclaimed Master Simon Snout, one of the constables, "we are here in the name of his most excellent majesty, Richard the First, King of England, to comprehend and make prisoner a certain fellow who, to our certain knowledge, is revealed somewhere in your house."

"If you mean that any body is concealed in my house you are greatly mistaken friend," answered the Jew, firmly.

"You hear the old dog of a Hebrew!" cried Snout, looking round upon his companions. "He resumes to correct my language, as if a constable was obliged to speak after the fashion of common individuals! But his tricks are discovered;—we know what we're about, and if he don't give up the prisoner we'll pull his house down about his ears for him."

"Oh, in mercy spare my father!" cried Rebecca, aroused by this threat, and throwing herself on her knees before the self-important constable. "He is innocent of any crime, and surely you would not heap injuries upon the head of one, whom age has rendered helpless."

"Don't talk to me, woman," exclaimed Simon Snout, with an air of supreme contempt;—"ain't I the king's self in my own person, and shall I be spoken to by one that's no better than a Turk or infidel? Go to, silly wench, and leave me to perform the duty according to my office."

"To the point then," interposed Isaac, impatiently; "if you have business here, despatch it quickly, for the hour grows late, and I would retire to my couch."

"Hurry no man's cattle," cried the constable haughtily;—"I am a man in office;—I serve the king—and if you consult me, you consult the king's most gracious majesty, which is an offence to be punished with death, and the loss of all your property."

"I neither wish to insult you nor yet to be undutiful to my king;" answered Isaac, meekly; "yet would I know the reason why my house has been entered at this hour of the night, as if I had been guilty of some great offence."

"Well then, to come to the point," said Snout; "the most illustrious knight Templar, Sir Gaston de Neville, hath this day been attacked, near Enfield Chase, by that renowned robber, Black Ivan, and his followers; who stripped him of all the valuables he had about him, and then bound their victim to a tree, while they made clear off with their booty."

"And what have I to do with that?" demanded the Jew. "Is my house to be thus broken open by a rabble because a great man happens to have been robbed on the highway?"

"Do you dare to dispute the law?" cried the man of authority, striking his long staff of office violently on the ground. " Hath not the robber been traced to this house, and shall we depart from it till we have brought the defender to justice ?"

" The offender is not here I again tell you," cried the Jew with trepidation.

" Then he hath been here, and you have suffered him to escape—and that's treason by the law of the land."

" Go thy ways," exclaimed Isaac, " I know nothing of the robber of whom you are in search."

" No, no, indeed, indeed, we know nothing of him !" cried Rebecca, clasping her hands in despair.

" Hah ! now I have predicted thee of falsehood, maiden !" exclaimed the constable, darting forward and snatching from her finger the ring which had been placed there by the stranger. " Thou say'st thou knowest nothing of the robber, and yet here is the lost diamond for which we were told to make a particular search."

" Lost diamond ! what mean you ?" demanded Isaac.

" That your daughter has on her finger, the very diamond ring that was stolen from Sir Gaston de Neville a few hours since," answered Simon Snout. " Oh! you may well look comflusticated, for it's a fact that I've been telling you, and what's more, this pretty maiden must away with us to the castle of Sir Gaston, in Moorfields."

" Oh, in mercy spare me !" cried Rebecca, as the officer seized her arm and dragged her violently towards the door.

" Don't ask me to spare you," replied the constable ; " for, though I have the honour to represent his gracious majesty, I have no power to let you off till you have been carried before Sir Gaston de Neville, who will himself decide whether you shall be set at liberty or committed to a dungeon."

" Hear me !" exclaimed Isaac, in accents of despair ;—" Sir Gaston de Neville—whom men have surnamed the " Terrible," for his many cruelties, is a bitter enemy of ours. He has long sought to obtain favour with my daughter, but when she spurned his unholy addresses, he vowed to be deeply revenged, unless she would purchase his forbearance by becoming the minion to his base passions. He will exult in thus getting us into his power, and my poor child will sink in that infamy which her soul abhors !"

" Can't help it," returned the constable, with cold indifference ;— " justice is blind, you know, and if people will harbour rogues and vagabonds, they may suffer for it according to law."

" I will confess all, on condition that you let my daughter go free," cried the almost frenzied Israelite.

" You can profess whatever you please," replied Simon Snout ;—" but it will depend upon my excretion afterwards, whether I think her a proper object for the royal mercy. Go on, friend Isaac, and make a clear conscience, by delivering up this robber into the hands of justice— that's myself."

" The truth is then," replied the Hebrew, " about half an hour since, a stranger, closely muffled up in his cloak, presented himself before us. In answer to my questions, he said that he was closely pursued by his creditors, and as the only alternative that remained, offered that diamond ring for sale, stating that the proceeds would be the means of saving him from the horrors of a gaol."

" A very likely story, indeed ;—but go on, and let me hear what became of the vagrum."

" With my assistance he escaped; while you were battering down my door," answered Isaac. "He told me that my own life, and that of my daughter, would be endangered if he should be found in the house; and, instigated by terror on her account, I suffered him to pass through a subterranean way, that leads from this room."

"Good!" ejaculated the constable; "then, now, Master Isaac, with your assistance, we'll proceed to unearth the fox; show us the place where he is concealed, and perhaps you and this trembling maiden may gain your own pardon."

"Here is the vault," cried the Hebrew, raising the trap-door and showing the grim abyss beneath. "He passed down these steps, and doubtless you will find him, if you take the trouble to search the place."

"Oh, that shall be done in no time," answered Snout, seizing hold of a torch from the hands of one of his followers, and preparing to descend. But suddenly recollecting himself, he ordered half-a dozen of the men to accompany him, while the rest remained in the room to guard the Jew and his daughter, and at the same time to prevent any act of treachery that might be meditated against him. This done, he disappeared with his men down the steps, leaving Isaac to appease the terrors of his child, who had thrown herself upon a seat, where she gave way to those tears of anguish, which this unforeseen event had given rise to.

But it was in vain that he strove to assure her that all would turn out well;—Rebecca knew the eager perseverance with which their enemies ever delighted to oppress the sons and daughters of Israel and rejecting the consolations of her venerable parent she continued to bewail the heavy calamity which had thus unexpectedly threatened to annihilate the happiness they had hitherto enjoyed. In the midst of these lamentations, the footsteps of Simon Snout and his companions were heard returning, and in a few seconds afterwards the ignorant functionary of the law once more presented himself before them.

'So!" he exclaimed angrily, "a very pretty trick you have played me truly! I, the representative of majesty, have been fooled into searching through a filthy dark vault, for a robber that is not there, while you, no doubt,—if it had not been for my wonderful sagacity,—thought to escape from my clutches."

"By the heaven above us, I swear the stranger went to conceal himself in the vault you have just left, scarcely a minute before you burst so unceremoniously upon us."

"Aye, aye, thou'lt stick to thy story, no doubt," cried the incensed officer of justice. "Thou wilt not confess the truth, I dare say; yet, nevertheless, we must find a way to force a confession, and there is no place that I can think of, will be better for the purpose, than to carry thy daughter with us to the castle of Sir Gaston de Neville."

"Oh, no—no,—spare her—spare her, I implore thee," cried Isaac, in an agony of terror. "If thou needest a victim, take me;—rack my old limbs,—torture me as thou wilt, and I will bless thee, so long as I know that my beloved daughter is safe from injury."

"Oh, as for that, you know," answered Snout, "we men in office can do as we like, so long as the king's interest is properly looked after."

"Then you will release her?"

"No,—she must go with us to Sir Gaston; he is the best judge of what ought to be done to her, and if his right honourable favour should be bestowed upon the maiden, why then I shall have done my duty, and then, old Isaac, of Tadcaster, wilt have nothing to grumble about."

"Villain! release your hold," exclaimed the aged Israelite, rushing forward to his daughter's rescue.

But his effort was unavailing, for he was violently thrust back by me of the rabble who had followed the constables, and ere the almost frenzied father could again throw himself into the midst of the crowd, the terror-stricken Rebecca was carried shrieking from the house. At this moment a dizziness seized upon the brain of Isaac, his senses left him, and reeling heavily to the floor, he lay for some time unconscious of the miseries that had thus befallen him.

CHAPTER II.

" I, under fair pretence of friendly ends,
  And well-placed words of glazing courtesy,
  Baited with reasons not unplausible,
  Wind me into easy-hearted man,
  And hug him into snares."   MILTON.

ON leaving the house of her father, the unconscious Rebecca was hurried along by the constable until they reached a place where a horse-litter was in waiting for her reception. As they approached, a young man, attired in the splendid garb of a page, stepped towards them, and tapping Simon Snout upon the shoulder, inquired whether all was right,

" Right, quotha !" exclaimed the constable; " aye, marry is it, fair Master Adrian, and thy master,—the most mighty Sir Gaston de Neville,—will this night possess the prize he hath so long sighed for."

No. 2.

"Thou hast performed thine errand marvellously well," rejoined the page, "and great will be thy reward."

"If it be not, he may do his own dirty work the next time himself," answered the officer of the law, as he placed the still insensible Rebecca in the litter. "I have brought away the maiden on a charge of felony, and unless he keep her safely in his own stronghold, the fault will be his own—not mine."

"By Our Lady, but thou hast done well in securing her," cried Adrian;—"my master hardly expected so much of thee, and when he finds thou hast thus agreeably disappointed him, thou wilt be in favour enough to help thy friends. But is she so very handsome, Master Snout, as the world reports her to be?"

"Humph! I should say she is very beautiful," replied the constable; "but perhaps I am no judge, and these are matters that I always leave to the opinion of my superiors."

"Can you not let me have a glimpse at her face?" cried Adrian, standing on tip-toe, and trying to look over the shoulder of Master Snout. "I am allowed to be a judge of female beauty, and perhaps my opinion may be of service to a man of thine obtuse intellect."

"Marry I know not what thou meanest by abstruse intellect," exclaimed Snout, "but if it be meant in the way of compliment, I can tell thee it will not obtain for thee a sight of the maiden. She is a feast for thy master's eyes, sirrah, and none beneath the rank of a knight at least, shall look upon her till I have delivered her safe into the hands of Sir Gaston de Neville."

And with these words Master Simon Snout ordered the litter to be put in motion, and then taking his place on one side of it, to prevent any attempt at escape, he directed the bearers to move on with what speed they could. By this time they had left what was then the outskirts of London, and having reached a lonely, desolate-looking place, the whole cavalcade hurried onwards across that wild portion of the city suburbs known as Moorfields. On reaching this spot, they proceeded more slowly, when Adrian, stepping up to the constable, who still kept his place by the side of the litter, whispered another inquiry, relative to the fair burden they were thus carrying to the abode of his master. By this time Simon Snout had grown a little more communicative, for he was in expectation of being in high favour with Sir Gaston de Neville, and consequently his heart was more open towards those who had the honour of serving the knight templar. Drawing himself therefore up to the highest standard he could assume, the officer of the law condescended to cast a gracious look upon the page, and placing his mouth close to the ear of his companion, he asked whether he could keep a secret.

"If it is of consequence, I can," answered Adrian, "and especially so when my master's gallantry with the fair sex is concerned."

"Humph!—you suspect then that the Jewess is brought hither for other purposes than that of charging her with having in her possession the lost diamond of your master?"

"I know the knight loves her," returned Adrian; "and moreover do I know that when once his heart is set upon an object, he is not very nice as to the means he employs to gain his ends. But, touching this lost diamond,—it seems Sir Gaston was robbed of it on Enfield Chase, and the next thing we hear is, that the jewel is found in the possession of this girl."

"And a lucky chance too," observed the constable;—"Sir Gaston will be well pleased at the opportunity it gives him, and this Jewess— between ourselves,—will not find it a very easy task to release herself from the hands of a man who has long been scheming to get her into his power."

"And how happened it," asked Adrian, "that your sagacity led to the discovery of this property?"

"Oh, leave me alone for nosing out a piece of mischief," replied Master Simon Snout. "Immediately after the robbery, Sir Gaston galloped up to London, and sought me out as a man that could be depended on when matters of importance are to be performed. From his *prescription*, I at once knew who the robber was—"

"His description, you mean, master constable."

"Well, description, if you like it better," cried the other testily, "though, for the life of me I can see no difference between the two words. But to *presume* my story—I knew in a moment that the robbery had been committed by no one else than Black Ivan, the Bandit, and as he always comes up to London to sell whatever he has taken from the traveller he meets with, I laid in wait for him, and sure enough, the rogue passed by me disguised in a large cloak, that he thought would be sufficient to conceal him from his enemies. But I was not to be put off the scent in that way, and following him through the streets of London, I traced him to the house of Isaac of Tadcaster."

"Hah!" exclaimed Adrian; "then doubtless there is some connection between the robber and the Jew!"

"That's what I should like to prove," answered Simon Snout.—"However, I got all the assistance I could, and with a dozen or so of stout fellows, I forced my way into the house, in hopes of securing the robber. But the bird had flown, Master Adrian, and for once, Simon Snout was cheated out of the best chance I ever had of gaining a rich reward."

"And so," observed the page. "being foiled in your design of capturing the robber, you, in your mighty wisdom, made a prisoner of the Jew's beauteous daughter?"

"Aye, and not without good reason, too," answered Master Snout, with a chuckle of self-approbation;—"the girl had got Sir Gaston's diamond ring on her finger, and knowing that the knight had long sought an opportunity to obtain possession of the maiden, I took her in custody on a charge of being a party in the robbery; and now, as you perceive, she is on her way to the stronghold of your noble master."

"And, doubtless, you expect a fair reward for your foul practices against the poor girl?" exclaimed Adrian in a tone of disgust at the heartlessness of his companion.

"Thou hast guessed rightly for once, friend Adrian," answered the constable exultingly. "The noble knight, thy master, is no niggard when his humour has been gratified, and seeing the trouble he has already had to obtain possession of the girl, I do certainly expect something very liberal from his hands in the way of reward."

"If I had my will, thy reward should be the bastinadō," exclaimed Adrian, in disgust.

"And wherefore, most valorous page?" cried the other with surprise.

"Because of thine officiousness," answered Adrian;—"hast thou not done thine utmost to bring wretchedness and endless sorrow upon one who never harmed thee? Of a verity, thou art a knave of the first water, and if I had my way, thou shouldst taste the scourge for thy pains, ere thou wert half an hour older."

The constable listened to this harangue of the page's with a mixture of astonishment and rage which he could not conceal. He eyed his youthful monitor with supreme contempt, and there is no knowing whether Master Simon Snout might not have been guilty of a breach of the king's peace, had they not at that moment found themselves at the gate of Sir Gaston de Neville's castellated mansion, near Moorfields. Seeing this, the constable suppressed his rising indignation as well as he could, and having summoned the porter to the gate, he demanded instant admittance to the presence of his knightly master.

"Nay, that were impossible," answered Janus Bolter, the keeper of the gate. "I have strict orders to be upon the watch to night, and it would be worth more than my poor life, were I to quit my post to go on thy fool's errands. Besides, Sir Gaston has gone to rest, and ere he went he left strict orders that no one should disturb him to-night on any pretence."

"Then thou wilt not go, Master Janus Bolter?"

"Haven't I already told you I would not?"

"True, but I knew not that thou wert such an errant fool till now," answered Simon Snout. "I tell thee, man, thou mayst make money by this job. Thy lord will easily pardon thee for disobeying his commands on this occasion, and what is more, I can promise thee a reward for thy pains, if thou wilt but choose to risk of waking him for this once."

"And have I no man's word for this but thine?" asked the warder with an ill-suppressed sneer.

"Marry, what better man's woulds't thou have?" demanded the other, in no very good humour at Bolter's perversity;—"have I ever deceived thee in my life, unbelieving dog?"

"Never," answered the other; "and for a most especial good reason; which is, that I would never trust thee."

"Nay, Master James, thou art rather too hard upon the constable," interposed Adrian, who had been enjoying this brief parley between the janitor and the man of law;—"it seems that Simon Snout hath arrived here on special business, which concerns our master, and therefore it may gravely offend Sir Gaston if this knave should be sent away without informing him of the success that has attended his errand. Besides, this litter contains a female prisoner, who stands charged with a heavy offence against the knight, our master, who will be sorely displeased should he not be informed of her being brought hither."

"Then be it thy task to announce it to him," exclaimed the warder; "thou knowest his chamber, and, being a favourite, may chance to escape the anger that would be aroused against any other man. So hie thee away, good Adrian, and the prisoner, attended by the constable, shall wait thy return in my lodge."

Upon this, Adrian left the place, and took his way towards that part of the edifice which was appropriated to the use of his master. The building was an extremely large and strongly built one, having been erected by a former owner as much for a place of security against his more powerful enemies, as for a residence during the few days he was suffered to live in peace. In the centre were the principal chambers allotted for the especial use of the noble owner, while at each corner rose a frowning tower, far above the ordinary height of the remainder of the building, in which were numerous apartments, and beneath whose tower chambers it was said were horrible subterraneous dungeons, where many an unhappy prisoner had been suffered to languish and perish, under the cruel mandates of the haughty possessor.

It was towards the centre compartment of this baronial residence, that Adrian took his way, and having passed through the principal entrance, and ascended a flight of stone stairs, he wound his way through three or four narrow and circuitous passages, which finally brought him to the sleeping chamber of his imperious master. Sir Gaston was asleep, but even the light foot-fall of his trusty page roused him from his slumbers, and starting from the couch on which he had thrown himself, he eagerly demanded the occasion of this unusual visit.

"How now, Adrian?" he exclaimed; "what means this intrusion? Speak, sirrah, and if thy news be bad, let the recital of it be brief that I may the sooner know the worst that I have to expect."

"Pardon me, most noble knight," answered the page, "but the tidings I bear thee, though urgent, are of evil omen. The Hebrew Maiden, Rebecca, has been arrested by one of the officers of justice, and is now waiting thy further commands."

"Hah!" exclaimed the Knight Templar, starting from his couch; "by all my hopes, but this is beyond my fondest expectations! Yet say, Adrian, how is it thou hast contrived to do me this great, this unparalled service?"

"This service, Sir Knight, was none of my performing," answered Adrian modestly. "By chance, Master Simon Snout, the constable, contrived to trace the brigand who robbed you, to the house of the maiden's father, and your diamond ring being found upon her finger, gave him a plausible pretext for arresting, and bringing her before you."

"The man shall be rewarded for his pains," exclaimed the knight; "he hath admirably performed my office, and shall henceforth revel in my favour. But, prithee tell me, Adrian, what says the pretty maiden to the dilemma into which she has fallen?—does she not weep, that after all, she has thus fallen into the snares of the very man she hath so long and proudly shunned?"

"So far, I believe," replied Adrian, "the poor wench knows not the misfortune that hath overtaken her. On being accused of having some share in the robbery, she fell into a state of insensibility, and up to the moment of my leaving her to inform your favour of her arrival, she had not recovered from her state of death like stupor."

"Well, well," muttered Sir Gaston, as he strode thoughtfully through his chamber; "it is perhaps better that it should be so, for otherwise she might have excited by her cries the pity of some passing fool who would have ventured life and limb to rescue her from our clutches. Now, however, she is mine, and no power of earth, heaven, or hell, shall ever wrest her from my grasp!"

"Shall I order her to be brought into your presence?" asked Adrian, "or will you defer the interview till the morning, when probably she will have recovered from her fit?"

"I will restrain my impatience for a few hours," answered the knight, "and in the morning, when her spirits are somewhat revived, I will present myself before the maiden, and by the ardour of my language obtain her pardon for the violence with which she has been torn from home."

"Methinks that will prove a harder task than you imagine," muttered Adrian, half aside;—but the words were overheard by Sir Gaston de Neville, who, far from being offended with their boldness, replied with earnestness:—

"To a youth like yourself, Adrian, whose knowledge of the world at present scarce exceeds that of a child, the task may, as you say, prove no easy one. But remember, I possess over her power that she cannot resist. As a Jewess, she will find little favour in the eyes of those who execrate and utterly contemn her creed;—the world will not pity her, and in spite of any appeals she may make to those who profess to love virtue, she must yield herself to the arms of one who has sworn to make her his prize."

"But should the king hear of it may not the affair take an awkward turn against yourself?" asked Adrian. "Nay, Sir Knight, you frown and think me over bold,—yet what I say is intended in all honesty, and your poor dependant only seeks to warn you against perils that might afterwards burst with terrific fury on your head."

"By St. Paul, but thou art a forward boy!" exclaimed the knight, "and had any other, save thyself, uttered those words, he might have felt that Gaston De Neville is not slower in his wrath, than he is impetuous in his love. Thou speakest of the king, boy, but Richard is no friend of the Jew's, and even if he were, have I not proof of my ring being found in Rebecca's possession, and would not that of itself be sufficient to hurry her to an ignominious fate in the event of her refusing to become my light o' love?"

"And must one so fair and beautiful become the victim of a cruel persecution?" cried Adrian despondingly.

"Thou art bold, sirrah page!" exclaimed Sir Gaston, angrily. "By St. George, thou presumest on my love for thee, but now I warn thee, thou art treading on dangerous ground, and another word such has thou hast just uttered, might lose for thee for ever the favour that may one one day serve to raise thee to eminence and honour."

"Pardon me, Sir Knight, but ——"

"Be silent, and urge me no further with thy foolish speech," interrupted the haughty baron;—"leave me, Adrian, and say to my attendants that it is my will that the Hebrew Maiden be conveyed to those apartments which adjoin the eastern tower. There let her remain till the morning, and bid her prepare to receive me with that courtesy which can alone rescue her from the shame and disgrace of public trial, the issue of which may effect her life. Nay, answer me not, Adrian, away and do my bidding faithfully, or thou losest that portion of my esteem with which I was wont to regard thee."

Bowing submissively to the austere knight, the youth slowly and reluctantly quitted the apartment of his lord, and then hastening his steps, he proceeded to the lodge where Rebecca had been sheltered until his return from Sir Gaston. By this time the maiden had recovered from the stupor which had for so long a period bound her senses, and having fully ascertained the situation in which she was placed, she gave way to the bitter anguish which filled her heart almost to bursting. In the midst of this, Adrian returned with the orders that had just been given by the Knight Templar, and so terrified was she at the dangers which were thus thickly pressing around her, that throwing herself upon her knees before the page, she earnestly implored him to aid an oppressed maiden in escaping from the snares in which she had thus unfortunately fallen. This, however, was more than Adrian could undertake to do, but assuring her that he would seek by every means in his power to render her situation less irksome, he led her towards those apartments which had been expressly set apart for her use by his imperious master.

Left to herself, Rebecca gave free vent to the torrent of her griefs, and weeping at the miseries she would yet have to undergo she threw herself upon her knees, and uttered fervent players to the Maker of the universe for protection for herself and father. Somewhat restored to firmness by these holy aspirations, she next began to think whether there was no way of escaping from her prison, ere the morning's dawn should render such an attempt abortive. With the eagerness of newly awakened hope, she snatched the lamp from the table, and searched round the gloomy chamber, but here all appeared to defy any attempt that might be made, and with a sigh, she was again yielding herself to despair, when the torn and delapidated condition of the tapestry in one part of the room, convinced her that a door somewhere thereabout would in all probability conduct her to some other part of the edifice, which had now become her prison. Full of this idea, she hastily threw aside the hangings which concealed the wall, and on passing the light of her lamp over the place, she at length to her inexpressible joy, beheld the object she had so anxiously sought for. Unfortunately, however, the door was locked in the inside, and she was about once more to give way to despair, when a sudden gust of wind forced it so violently against the lock as almost to burst it off its rusty hinges. This again revived her drooping spirits, and with an effort of desperation, she exerted all her strength against the frail work, and presently afterwards, to her extreme joy, the door gradually gave way, and she beheld before her another chamber, whose darkness forbade her ascertaining correctly either its peculiar use or to what other part of the place it might lead.

But situated as she was, Rebecca summoned up all her resolution, and resolving to effect her escape or perish in the attempt, she once more grasped the lamp, and stepping boldly forward, she examined as accurately as the light would permit her the dark and dreary apartment in which she thus found herself. By its octangular shape she could plainly enough perceive that it belonged to one of the turrets which she had observed when conducted by the page across the court-yard, and taking courage from the success that had so far favoured her, she next began to look around; the walls to discover whether there was no place of egress by which she might continue her flight. In this, however, she was doomed to be disappointed—nothing but solid masonry met her eyes in whatever direction they were turned, and she was about to yield once more to all the horrors of black despair, when she observed something shining upon the floor at no great distance from where she stood. Stooping to ascertain what this was, she perceived an iron ring, evidently placed there for the purpose of raising a trap door, and seizing hold of this, she found, no less to her pleasure than surprise, that it was to be moved with more ease than she had at first anticipated. Inspired, therefore, with fresh courage, she applied both hands to the task of raising what she fondly believed to be the only barrier to her escape. In a few moments the trap yielded to her efforts, but the gust of confined air that now rushed through the aperture had nearly extinguished her lamp, and thus rendered futile all the labour she had been at.

Somewhat warned by this circumstance, Rebecca advanced cautiously towards the opening in the floor, and, with the aid of her lamp, discovered a flight of broken steps that led into a dark and chilly vault beneath. Undismayed, however, by the frightful scene before her, she commenced her descent slowly and cautiously, and on reaching the bottom of the steps, she found herself in a rude chamber, which, from certain appearances, was, no doubt, a subterranean dungeon intended for the place of imprisonment for those who chanced to fall under the displeasure of the haughty lord of the mansion.

The walls were rugged, as if hewn out of the rock, and the flooring so uneven that it was with difficulty our heroine could make her way from one part of the place to another without being precipitated over the numerous obstacles that met her footsteps at every turn. Again she had to search about narrowly for some place of exit from this wretched place, and it was not until she had searched long and labouriously that her light at length fell upon a small aperture in the wall near the ground, but so low was this rough place of communication, that it was impossible to pass into the next chamber without crawling on the hands and knees. Resolved not to be thwarted by any obstacles, Rebecca stooped to pass onwards, but as she did so, she beheld in the small passage, through which she had to make her way, numerous toads, lizards, and other crawling reptiles, which seemed to have assembled themselves together as if for the purpose of opposing her further progress towards escape. Shuddering at the sight of these filthy vermin, she started back for a moment unable to conquer her repugnance; but again she remembered how much depended upon her resolution, she hurriedly made her way through this loathsome barrier.

Rebecca now found herself in a larger and more lofty chamber than any she had yet passed through. Indeed the feeble light of her lamp was insufficient to penetrate the deep shades of darkness with which she was on every side surrounded, and for a few moments she paused, uncertain which way to direct her steps. But when she remembered the dangers that threatened her unless a desperate effort was made to escape from the stronghold of her foe, she once more continued her way, and paused not until the rugged wall of the dungeon effectually resisted her further progress. By this time her lamp, the oil of which was nearly consumed, gave but too evident tokens of speedily expiring, and thus depriving her of the trifling assistance its feeble flame had thus far afforded. Hurrying round the dungeon, therefore, she eagerly looked for some place of egress, but though she had performed more than half the circuit of the chamber, she had hitherto discovered no sign of any communication with any other cell. At length, however, she perceived a door thickly studded with large nails, whose massive iron heads seemed to defy any attempts that might be made to force a passage whilst the portal itself remained fastened on the inside. Upon more closely examining the heavy portal she found that it was secured by a spring-lock which, after some time had been spent in endeavouring to discover the secret by which the door might be opened, she had the mortification to find still defeated all her efforts to secure her retreat from this place. In her despair, however, Rebecca still continued to pass her hand over th rough surface of the portal, and in the end she was rewarded by finding that what appeared to be one of the iron-headed nails, yielded to the touch. Delighted at this discovery, she pressed her finger more vigorously to the part, and to her extreme gratification, the door flew open with a sudden bound, leaving her at liberty to proceed onwards on her way to liberty.

By the faint light with which she was supplied, our heroine could perceive that this dungeon possessed more architectural pretentions than any of the others through which she had passed. The massive pillars and the low semi-circular arches proclaimed the era to which this part of the edifice owed its origin, and from a quantity of straw with which the place was littered, it was pretty evident that the chamber had been used at some period or other, as a prison to one of those unfortunate beings who had fallen under the displeasure of the lord of the castle. Rebecca shuddered as she reflected upon the miseries that had been endured in this lone spot, and she would have passed hurriedly forward, but by this time her lamp was nearly extinguished, and it was only with extreme caution, that she was able to move about from one part of the place to another. All within was as silent as the grave, but on the outside of this cheerless dungeon she could hear the ceaseless roar of a terrific tempest, whose violence shook even the strong masonry of which the castle was constructed. Each moment, too, the feeble light of her lamp

threw a fainter beam around, and in spite of all her efforts to resuscitate the expiring flame, it become but too evident that ere long she would be left to perish in a place from whence she saw but little probability of escaping.

Rendered desperate by the hopelessness of her situation Rebecca now strode fearfully round the dungeon, and perceiving what appeared to be a narrow passage leading to an inner cell, she was hurrying towards it, when her foot struck against something, and lowering her lamp to discover what it was that impeded her progress, she beheld, to her horror, a skeleton seated upon the ground, and chained to one of the pillars to which, as a prisoner, he had been secured during the unhappy moments of his captivity. At the same moment too, the door behind was closed with a heavy sound, and thus was all retreat cut off, and the hapless maiden found herself shut up in a living tomb, with the hideous object that had before met her view. Terror-striken, Rebecca sank fainting on the floor,—her lamp was extinguished, and thus was she left to perish in the darksome dungeon, which had already became the grave of the miserable captive, whose bones lay scattered and bleaching on the ground.

CHAPTER III.

" Oh, my lord, in pity hear me ;
Restore my child to her fond old father's arms,
And I will bless thee." THE SANCTUARY.

WITH the earliest dawn of the morning, Reuben Grenard hastened to the house of the Jew in the joyful anticipation of once more meeting
No. 3.

his belóved Rebecca, who, in a few days henee, was, with her father's approbation, to become his bride. With heart elate he knocked at the door, expecting to be instantly admitted, but to his surprise his well-known signal was repeated several times, and yet not a sound was heard in the house, to assure him that Isaac was preparing to give him admittance. At length, becoming alarmed, he knocked yet louder and more frequently, till becoming more convinced that something must have happened amiss, he hastened round to the back part of the premises, where, without any great effort, he forced his way into the place and rushed up stairs to see what had occurred to render his kind old friend so deaf to his repeated summonses for admittance. To his surprise, however, Isaac was not there, and it was also painfully evident that he had not that night sought his couch, as every thing remained in the same state as on the preceding evening.

Alarmed at this circumstance, he hastened once more to the lower part of the house, and no sooner had he entered the room, than the still insensible form of Isaac, lying upon the floor, met his view. Blood was flowing from a wound in his temple, and in the first moment of his terror, Reuben imagined that his venerable friend had been assassinated by some villain for the sake of plunder.

In an agony of alarm he threw himself upon his knees, by the side of the still insensible Isaac, and gently raising his head, gazed earnestly in his countenance to see whether any signs of life yet remained. At this moment a low, suppressed groan escaped the lips of the old man, and presently afterwards, opening his eyes, he gazed wildly round the room, as if in search of some object which he almost despaired of seeing.

" Where,—where is she ?" he exclaimed faintly ;—" tell me of my child—my Rebecca ;—alas ? have they torn her from me—never—never more to meet."

" Father of mercies ! what mean you ?" cried Reuben, in a paroxysm of alarm, produced by these words of the old man. " You speak of Rebecca ;—she is in danger, and perhaps her life depends upon my flying instantly to her rescue. Say, old man—who has torn her from thee, and were it my own brother that has committed this cowardly act, his blood should answer it."

Thus adjured, Isaac, as soon as he was sufficiently recovered, related all that had taken place on the preceding night. He minutely described the visit of Black Ivan, the robber, and the object that had brought him there; the subsequent arrival of the constable and his force was next alluded to, as well as the suspicion that had fallen on Rebecca, in consequence of the diamond ring being found upon her finger. He then described the terrible scene that took place when she was torn from him, and in reply to Reuben's inquiry, he explained the reasons he had for supposing she had been carried off to the fortified mansion of Sir Gaston de Neville.

The young man listened to the narrative with impatience, frequently breaking in upon the recital, and as often vowing to release her from the hands of the Knight Templar, or perish in the attempt. Reuben's soul was on fire as he heard the old man's tale of the preceding night's adventure, and as Isaac brought his story to a conclusion, he eagerly asked him if he was willing to accompany him to the house of Sir Gaston de Neville. At this suggestion the old man's eyes grew bright with hope, for he knew that Reuben had resolution enough to accomplish any design he might set his mind upon, and he felt confident that if once he commenced the task of rescuing Rebecca from the hands of the villain, his object would be accomplished, or he himself would perish in the attempt at preserving her from the criminal intentions of those who had torn her from her father's roof.

"My son," cried the old man, firmly grasping the hand of Reuben Grenard, "thou hast asked me if I will join with thee in hunting villany to its lair. I am old, but my heart will not quail at danger, and thou shalt yet see what a father dares do in behalf of his beloved daughter. I will accompany thee, and may the God of our fathers aid us in our just cause."

"He will," exclaimed Reuben, ardently, "the innocent will not be suffered to fall through the vile artifices of the wicked, and the right hand of heaven will be stretched forth to assist those who go forth to fight in a righteous cause."

"But, Sir Gaston is a foe whom there is but too much reason to dread," answered Isaac, doubtingly. "Cruel towards all whom he calls his foes, he hath raised for himself a name that is regarded with dread and apprehension. His enemies he never spares, and each one that offends him is in turn hurled down at his feet to be trampled upon and scorned."

"Yet his star will not always rise triumphant," cried Reuben; "the time will come when clouds will gather round the planet, and whenever that period arrives, then must the haughty Sir Gaston look in vain for the compassion of those who will exult in his downfall."

"We must be wary, my son," answered Isaac, "or we may bring down ruin on our own heads before we have accomplished the task we have set ourselves. Sir Gaston de Neville was in high favour with the late king, and if the one who has just ascended the throne esteems him in the same degree, it would bring ruin upon us were our schemes to be too early detected."

"King Richard esteems few of those who were his father's friends," exclaimed the young man, "and noble as he is reported to be by nature, there is little fear of his ever encouraging this recreant Knight Templar in his shameless acts. No, in Richard Cœur de Lion the oppressed will ever find a sure friend, and should all other schemes fail, I will throw myself at the foot of the throne and demand justice from the sovereign under whom I live."

"And dost thou believe that as a Jew —as one of that despised race, whom all Christians shun as they would contamination—thou would'st obtain the justice thou mightest seek?"

"I hope that justice will be done to one class of his subjects as well as to another," answered Reuben. "That our people have long and most unjustly suffered through the cruel injustice of their fellow-men is indeed true, but a better feeling will one day or other display itself, and then shall the Hebrew be allowed to claim citizenship with those who have so long considered the children of Israel as hardly better than the beasts of the fields. Yes, my father, the king who now rules the nation is a lover of justice, and if need be, we will appeal to him for the preservation of Rebecca from the hands of her heartless oppressor."

"Then let us now seek her in the strong fortress of Sir Gaston de Neville," exclaimed Isaac, impatiently; "let us follow her thither, and demand an audience with the haughty knight, who, if he denies her being under his roof, will no longer be worthy of honourable treatment, and therefore must he fall into the snare that will be laid for his destruction."

"Come, Reuben," cried the old man with anxious earnestness; "let us hasten our departure ere they remove my beloved child to some on or other of the numerous other castles possessed by this recreant knight.

Let us away, and woe unto those who may dare refuse to restore a virtuous daughter to the arms of her fond and doating father."

Reuben was too anxious to put their scheme in execution to offer any opposition to this design, and following the aged Israelite from the house, they first secured the doors and then took their way towards the fortress of Sir Gaston de Neville. It was in somewhat less than an hour that they stood before the principal portal of the huge stone mansion, and having summoned the warder, they demanded instant admittance to his master on an affair of pressing emergency.

"Begone about thy business, old man," exclaimed the surly janitor, growling at having been disturbed by those whom he conceived could have no business with a person of the knight's consequence; "leave the place, will you, or I may chance to let loose a brace of blood-hounds who will send thee scampering across the country at the peril of thy worthless life."

"Let me see thy master, and I shall be the sooner gone," answered Isaac. "I have business of deep and serious import to confer with him about, and never will I quit these gates until I have been satisfied for the wrongs he has done me."

"Dost thou dare to bandy words with me?" demanded the warder, in a tone of fierceness.

"I dare speak my mind to all men, whether they be richer or poorer, equal or superior to myself," answered the old man firmly. "Nay, more, I come hither to see the knight, Sir Gaston de Neville, and I have already told you that I will remain at his gates till he hath given orders for my admittance to his presence."

"Then art thou an insolent knave for thy pains," cried the incensed warder, and unsheathing the long and ponderous sword from his side, he made a rush towards the old man with the intention of punishing his temerity upon the spot. Luckily, however, Reuben perceived the design of the ruffian, and throwing himself between the warder and his intended victim, he arrested the fatal blow just as the weapon was descending with terrific force on the Hebrew's head. Enraged at this unexpected interference, the ruffian now turned his weapon against the younger man, and there is a little doubt but that his superior strength and dexterity would have proved more than a match for Reuben had not succour arrived at the moment in a manner the most unexpected. In fact, drawn to the spot by the uproar, Adrian, the page of Sir Gaston de Neville, quickly saw the disadvantage under which one of the combatants was struggling, and placing himself on his side, he charged the warder with such resolution and vigour, that the latter was fain to beat a hasty retreat after having called out lustily for quarter.

"Oh, as for thy worthless carcase, it shall be safe for this once," exclaimed Adrian, smiling at the terrors of the man he had thus overcome. "I want not to injure thee, Master Janus, but by the virgin thou shall not assault these strangers, who thou seest are not armed sufficiently to guard themselves against thy villanous attacks."

He now inquired of Isaac the business that had brought him to Sir Gaston's castle, and having discovered that he was the father of the maiden who had been brought in as a captive on the night before, he resolved to obtain for the two strangers an interview with the knight who had so cruelly wronged them.

"It seems," he said, "that you have pressing business with my noble master, Sir Gaston de Neville, and if I have your word for it, that you will depart as soon as your message is delivered, I will undertake to obtain for you the required interview."

" I will but demand my daughter," replied Isaac, " and if your knight chooses to deliver her unharmed into my hands, I will depart in all peace."

" Then follow me," exclaimed Adrian, and then directing his footsteps across the court-yard, accompanied by the two strangers, he led them through the principal entrance of the building, and from thence to the room where they found Sir Gaston de Neville, pacing up and down with all the frantic gestures of a madman.

" Hah! who art thou?" he exclaimed, as Isaac of Tadcaster and his young friend made their appearance;—" speak, sirrahs,—what wouldst thou with me, and why come thus unbidden into my presence?"

" We are here to demand justice," answered the elder Hebrew, undismayed by the haughty salutation of the knight;—" thou hast wronged me grievously, Sir Gaston, and a wretched father comes to solicit back from thee the virtuous child thou hast torn shrieking from his arms."

" Humph!" muttered the Templar, " you are here about the wench who was brought hither last night?"

" Aye, who was brought hither by force and fraud," answered the old man, unabashed by the presence of his haughty superior. " The maiden came to this, thy strong-hold, a shrieking victim, and I—her father,—old, and standing upon the verge of the grave, come to rescue her from destruction."

" Then thine errand is a fruitless one," replied Sir Gaston, " for she whom thou seekest is no longer an inmate within these walls."

" 'Tis false!" exclaimed Isaac, trembling with passion.

" 'Tis well these words were uttered by an old man, and one too, who belongs to a class that I regard as being so utterly beneath me," cried the knight fiercely. " Less words, old man, have produced bloodshed and death, and thou mightest perhaps have received thy just reward, had it not been that I can in some degree feel for the sorrow with which thou mournest the loss of thy beauteous daughter."

" If thou feelest as a man and father, restore her to me," cried Isaac, in a paroxysm of grief. " I love her beyond all other creatures on God's earth, and to lose her now under such circumstances would be the greatest affliction with which my spirit could be bowed down."

" Psha! wilt thou leave me Jew?" exclaimed the Templar furiously; —" wilt thou begone, I say, or must I order thee to be bastinaded in the presence of my retinue, as a warning to all others who may at any future time force their way into my presence."

" Restore my daughter, and I will depart blessing thee," cried the Hebrew, clasping his hands convulsively together.

" Have I not already told thee the maiden is not here?" replied the knight.

" And yet," groaned Isaac, " it is but a few hours since she was dragged from my arms by a heartless ruffian, who accused her of a heinous offence and declared his intention of bringing her to your strong-hold."

" All which I grant was done," answered Sir Gaston, " and yet, as I have told thee before, the maiden is no longer beneath my roof."

" Thou hast sent her then to another of thy castles."

" Nay," returned the Knight Templar. " I could fain wish it had been as thou sayst. But the truth is, the wench has contrived to give me the slip;—she has escaped from the quarters that were assigned to her, and, driven almost to madness at the defeat of my plans, I could find it in my heart to hang every rogue of them who has been in any way concerned in suffering her to leave the castle."

" Nay, this is some fiction invented to get rid of a father's importunities," exclaimed Isaac. "Thou still holdest my daughter as thy captive, and here I demand her at thy hands, pure and innocent as she first entered these accursed walls."

" Fool!" exclaimed Sir Gaston, " I again tell thee thy daughter is no longer here.   Hence!—or feel the vengeance your own wilful conduct hath provoked."

" I will not leave thee," answered Isaac, " unless it be to wait upon King Richard, and to pour into his ears the tale of thy falsehood and perjury. Ere now, a knights' spurs have been hacked from his heels by the kitchen scullion, for a less offence than thine, and it shall go hard if I disgrace thee not, unless thou restorest back to me my daughter."

" By heaven! this is no longer to be borne!" cried Sir Gaston, fiercely, and drawing a poniard from his vest, he would have plunged it into the bosom of the old man had not Reuben at that moment rushed forward and prevented the meditated blow. At this juncture, too, Adrian hastily approached, and at a signal from his imperious master led Isaac and his younger companion from the castle precincts. This done, he returned to the presence of Sir Gaston.

" And now that we are once more alone," cried the Templar, " we will go in search of this girl, who you tell me, has quitted the chamber which was allotted to her use. I can pretty well guess that she has wandered through some of the subterranean dungeons, and should we not go in search of her, she will in all probability lose herself among the mazes of the place, and thus perish through the folly that has tempted her to attempt her escape from the castle.

So saying, the knight, followed by Adrian, took his way towards that part of the building which had been given for the use of Rebecca, and then directing his steps towards the chapel, a stone was raised, and the two descended into the vault beneath,

---

CHAPTER IV.

" Taking their way through low, dark, frowning vaults,
    Horrors assail them both at every turn,
    At which the blood turns cold."
                                        VICENZIO.

AIDED by the light of the torch which the page had brought with him, the knight groped his way along numerous subterranean chambers which were connected with each other through a long range, and of the doors of which he was provided with the keys through the foresight of Adrian who was previously aware of the place which it was the will of his imperious master to search through. As they proceeded along these narrow passages, hollow gusts of wind swept by them, like the moaning of disturbed spirits, threatening every instant to extinguish the only light with which they were furnished, and supplying the superstitious Adrian with ample food to fill his soul with dread, lest some of the apparitions, with which the castle was said to be haunted, should emerge from behind the antique pillars, in order to claim as their victims, those who had thus dared to encroach on their wild and gloomy domains. Agitated by a thousand fears, the page could scarcely venture to follow his master, without looking round him at every step, to see whether any unhallowed spirit was ready to pounce upon them, and it was not till his master had repeatedly upbraided him for his want of courage that he at last ventured to enter a dismal looking chamber, the door of which had given him a great deal of trouble to unlock. In fact, it was with extreme reluctance that he at last obeyed the mandates of his superior, and no sooner had he mustered up courage enough to advance a step into the much dreaded chamber, than starting back, he had nearly overthrown his master in his haste to retreat from some horrible object that his fears had conjured up. Enraged at this cowardice, Sir Gaston could no longer repress his fury, and seizing the trembling page in his iron grasp, he demanded in a voice of indignation, what had occasioned his precipitate retreat.

"Oh, good Sir Knight, don't ask me!" he cried in a voice that showed the extreme terror that had taken possession of him;—"don't ask me what I have seen, for it was too terrible for description, and—and——"

"Fool! what hast thou to fear?" demanded Sir Gaston de Neville, with increased passion. "What hast thou seen, I again ask, to cause all this trembling and alarm?"

"What have I seen?" retorted Adrian:—"oh, sir! enough to appal the stoutest heart. I have seen a gigantic apparition, and if your knightship will but take one peep into the vault, you will be convinced of the truth of what I have said!"

"Prating idiot!" cried the infuriated knight, "this is some trick of thine, to put me off this search upon which my soul is bent. But it shall not serve thee, slave;—I am resolved to discover this girl, and if thou dost not instantly precede me through these vaults, I will despatch thee with my dagger, and leave thy vile carcase to be companion to the toads and lizards that thou knowest are the only tenants of these dreary cells."

"Don't! oh, pray don't talk so," exclaimed Adrian, in a paroxysm of alarm. "The very thought of it is enough to kill me with downright fright:—to be perhaps only half slain, and thus to be left here as a companion to the horrible looking figure I just now saw."

"What figure dost thou speak of, boy?" demanded Sir Gaston.

"The tall dev—gentleman, I mean, whom I just now beheld," answered Adrian, checking himself, lest any disrespectful remarks of the person he alluded to, should bring down upon him the vengeance of some infuriated inhabitant of another world.

"Psha! thou art beside thyself, Adrian," exclaimed his master.

"There was one in that chamber just now, beside myself," answered the page, glancing uneasily towards the half-opened door. "I saw it as plainly as I now see your excellency, and a more ill-favoured hobgoblin I never had the misfortune to set eyes upon."

"Indeed!" exclaimed Sir Gaston, "then if thou saw so much of this apparition, perhaps thou canst describe it to me."

"Ah, sir!" groaned the page, "I caught but a momentary glance of it, but in that moment I was able to see that it was of such a gigantic height that its head reached to the very ceiling of the vaulted chamber."

"So much for the height," observed Sir Gaston," "and now tell me, boy whether thou didst observe aught beside?"

"I did sir," answered Adrian; "I particularly noticed that its colour was very black, and that it seemed to grow taller, the further I advanced into the chamber."

"Then," cried Sir Gaston, "I have discovered a key to all this mystery. Enter the room again, boy, and at my bidding, thou shalt again behold this apparition that has so much terrified you."

"I—I—I— would rather not run so great a risk," stammered Adrian,

retreating with tottering footsteps from the door. "It would be a wilful tempting of evil spirits to do me an injury, and I would rather perish
by your sword than again run the risk of beholding that fearful spirit."

"Coward !" muttered the knight, "dost thou dare refuse to do my
bidding ?"

"N—n—n—no," again stammered the alarmed page ;—" I—I—don't
exactly refuse, only I would much rather not rashly run myself into
danger."

"Thy danger will be greater if this delay lasts any longer," exclaimed
the knight, impatiently. "Too long already has this trifling lasted, and
now thou shalt either execute my commands, or this dagger shall enter
thy recreant heart !"

Adrian started as he saw saw the gleam of the poniard glancing in
the light of the torch, and knowing the fearful impetuosity of his master's temper, he at length staggered a few paces towards the door, and
then precipitately rushed back again, as the same fearful vision again
met his view.

"There !—there it is again !" he cried with excessive terror. "I
have seen it once more, and all the threats in the world shall not induce
me to face it a third time. It has grown to twice the size it was before,
and if I must perish, let it be by your hand, rather than be torn piecemeal by a monster so terrible as that !"

"Idiot !" roared Sir Gaston ; "I have now discovered the source of
all this groundless terror. The apparition, as I imagined, has turned
out to be perfectly harmless ;—in fact, slave, thou hast been frightened
with nothing more terrible than thine own shadow."

"My own shadow !—impossible !" cried the page ; "why the apparition I beheld, was at least three times my own height."

"That may be true," answered the knight, "and yet what I have
told thee is the truth. Behold, and convince thyself.—Now look again,
as I hold the torch behind thee, and thou wilt once more see the same
grim shadow against the wall, which has caused thee so much needless
terror."

Though unwilling to do so, Adrian was obliged to comply with his
master's injunctions, and after making many attempts, he at length
gained courage enough to do his master's bidding. This time, the thing
was palpable enough, and being convinced that all his terrors had been
utterly groundless, he began to stammer out the best excuse for the
cowardice he had exhibited. For a wonder, Sir Gaston was, or at least
appeared to be, satisfied with his explanation, and then once more placing the torch in the hands of the still trembling page, he bade him go
before and light him on his way through the remainder of the subterranean vaults. This command Adrian was obliged to comply with, but
all his terrors were not yet removed, and it was not without some terror
that he slowly proceeded on his way, looking timidly round him every
moment, as if again expecting to behold some horrible sight in the
gloomy vaults through which they were slowly wending their way. At
length he again again paused, and lowering his torch towards the ground,
and picking up a piece of armour, gazed upon it with a look that showed
the terror that had again taken possession of his soul. The steel breast-
plate was rusted in many parts; a hole, as if formed with a dagger, was
pierced through the middle, and to his horror, he discovered that the
inside of it was spotted and stained with blood !

Sir Gaston witnessed his perturbation, and darting angrily forward,
he snatched the iron corselet from his hand, and hurled it with terrific
force to the other end of the chamber.

"What hast thou found now to excite thy wonder?" he cried wrathfully. Canst thou not pass a piece of armour but thou must pause to gaze upon it as if there was any marvel in it?"

"Did'st thou not see where a dagger had pierced it?" cried Adrian, timidly.

"I did—and is there anything surprising in that?"

"None," answered Adrian, "but the inside of it was covered with blood, and that appears to me to be ——"

"Peace, babbler! and learn to speak only of matters that concern thee," cried the knight, interrupting him. "The blow that slew the wearer of that corslet was probably dealt in the midst of some battle's strife, and the owner honourably yielded up his life in defence of his country's liberty."

"True," replied Adrian, "I forgot that, and yet finding the bloodstained relic in this horrible place, would almost make one believe that some foul crime had been committed here."

"Dog! dost thou dare imagine ought so evil as that a murder has been committed beneath the roof that calls me master?" cried Sir Gaston, turning pale with rage. "Knowest thou not the deference due to thy lord but thou must prate of things that so closely touch his honour."

"Pardon me," exclaimed the page; "it was but a passing thought, and I am now convinced of my foolish error. And yet," he continued, "deeds of blood have been committed in such places as this ere now, and ——"

"Lead on, sirrah!" interrupted the knight, impatiently; "speech ill-becomes a menial to his master, and I would have thee know that dan-

No. 4

ger lurks around thee whilst thou dost speak of things that concern thee not. Lead on, I say, or we may be too late to find this wench who has so unaccountably disappeared from her chamber."

Adrian dreaded the gathering storm which he plainly saw was ready to burst forth with terrific fury, and trimming his torch so as to afford as much light as possible, he once more moved forward, opening a number of doors that communicated from one to another, each of which they carefully searched in the expectation that Rebecca might have strayed thus far in her efforts to escape. All their labour was, however, thus far, in vain, and they were about to return by the way they had come, when another door met their view, which had hitherto escaped their notice. At the command of Sir Gaston the page endeavoured to open it, but the massive iron-studded portal refused to move before the puny efforts of the stripling, and being unprovided with any key that would fit the lock, they were about to abandon the task as hopeless, when the knight bethought himself of a plan that would most likely accomplish the design he had in view.

Seizing, therefore, an immense fragment of stone that he saw lying at his feet, he hurled the ponderous missile with all his force again the door. The effect, though not immediately successful, was evident; the portal slightly yielded to the tremendous blow it had received, and encouraged by this circumstance, Sir Gaston repeated the experiment with such success, that ultimately the door flew open with a heavy crash, and the next moment the knight and his attendant found themselves in the dungeon it had been their object to reach. Upon this an immediate search was commenced round the vaulted dungeon, and at last, attracted by some white object upon the floor, they discovered Rebecca lying pale and insensible on the spot where she had fallen as described in a former chapter.

Having thus succeeded in effecting the design that had brought him thither, Sir Gaston bade the page precede him with the light, and then taking the insensate form of the lovely Hebrew Maiden in his arms, he returned by the way which had led her to the place, and this being a much nearer way, he shortly afterwards reached the armoury where his lovely burden was carefully placed upon a couch, and every means resorted to, that might once more restore her to life and consciousness.

CHAPTER V.

" Art thou of human kind,
Who thus can triumph o'er a woman's fears,
Mocking her grief with ribaldry and jeers ?"

MARIANNA.

IT was some time, however, before the hapless Rebecca could be revived from the dreadful lethargy into which she had fallen, and when at last she opened her languid eyes, and beheld the hated form of Sir Gaston de Neville bending over her, she started as if some horrible beast of prey was about to spring upon her, and, uttering a cry of terror, sank back trembling and aghast.

Sir Gaston saw the dread with which he was regarded, and calling hypocrisy to his aid, he endeavoured by every means in his power, to assure her that she had nothing to dread for her safety; that he loved her far better than any other mortal he had ever seen before, and that it now only remained with herself to choose whether her future life should be rendered supremely blessed, or, on the contrary, whether she would, by her obstinate rejection of his love, bring upon herself that misery which would never terminate but with her life.

Rebecca heard his words, and as he proceeded, her heart loathed him more and more for the villany with which he had sought to deprive her of a father's protection. Gazing upon him with a look of intense hatred, she, with her arm, motioned for him to leave her, but Sir Gaston took no heed of this, and grasping one of her hands within his own, he again earnestly implored her to listen with patience, ere she resolved upon a step that would irrevocably lead to her destruction. But the indignant maiden disregarded this threat, and assuming all the firmness she could call to her aid, she exclaimed with more than her wonted energy :—

"Avaunt, thou fiend of darkness and mischief—leave me, Sir Gaston, for here I swear before high heaven, never to pardon one who has thus sought to wreck the peace of her who never injured him. Leave me, I say, and thus afford the only reparation in your power to injured innocence."

"Sweet maid, thy words move me not," answered Sir Gaston, with seeming calmness. "That I love thee is no fault of my own ; thy beauteous face is alone to blame, and if I have sought forcible means to get thee into my power, let my ardent passion plead my excuse and melt thee into compassion."

"Monster!" cried the Jewess, "thy words do but add to the infamy of the course thou hast pursued towards a wretched girl, whom thou hast doomed to misery and despair. Quit my sight, and never again dare to present thyself before me, unless thou wouldst hear the curses and imprecations I will heap upon thy devoted head."

"Girl!—wouldst thou drive me to desperation?"

"Nay, I would rather seek to drive thee to repentance," answered Rebecca. "I would have thee remember that there is vengeance in heaven against the evil doer, and that thine own crimes must sooner or later bring thee to that dreadful punishment which is the portion of the wicked!"

"To what wouldst thou urge me, girl?"

"Askest thou to what I would urge thee?" cried Rebecca, with surprise. "Know then, thou man of crime, that I would urge thee to make the only reparation in thy power to injured innocence. I would have thee restore me to a fond father's arms. Do this;—suffer the remainder of my days to pass in peace, and I will freely forgive thee the artifice with which thou hast brought me to this accursed place!"

"Nay, thou dost ask me of that which it is impossible to grant," answered Sir Gaston. "Thy charms have captivated my soul,—nay more,—I love thee as man never before loved woman;—I would die for thee Rebecca, and yet thou canst coldly reject one who has already endured so much."

"Dost thou call this passion by the name of love?" asked Rebecca scornfully.

"I do, dear girl."

"Then dost thou most foully miscall it," she replied, "for love would rather have prompted thee to leave me in my former happiness, than thus to drive me to the very verge of madness and despair. Thou hast deeply injured me, Sir Gaston de Neville, but be assured I am not so friendless, but one, at least, will be found to hurl retribution upon thy guilty head."

"Thou alludest to thy Jewish lover, Reuben," answered the knight scornfully.

"I do," she replied with maidenly pride, "and one in whose bosom more honour abounds, is not to be found among those who call themselves Christians.—He is the lover chosen by a father for his daughter's future husband, and yet thou hast dared to separate us in furtherance of thine own most vile and wicked deeds."

"If I have done so, love must plead my excuse," answered the knight. Reuben has no wealth to bestow upon thee, whilst I can offer to thee countless sums of gold that will render thy station equal to that of an Eastern Princess."

"Thy gold, sir knight, will rot in its coffers, ere I accept of it," answered Rebecca firmly. "My heart is pledged to Reuben Grenard, and never will I break that sacred pledge whilst life shall be vouchsafed to me."

"Foolish girl!" exclaimed Sir Gaston, "knowest thou not that thou art now in my power, and that I can force thee to my will."

"Nay, thou dar'st not!"

"How, Rebecca,—dare not!"

"I repeat it," she replied,—"thou dar'st not; "for so surely as I am not restored to my father's arms by a certain time, he will proceeed to the court, and lay his complaints against thee at the foot of the good King Richard's throne."

"Richard of the Lion's Heart, would not listen to the complaints of a despised Jew," answered Sir Gaston. "Nay, even if he did so, I have interest enough with my sovereign to bring down upon your whole tribe such a burst of terrible wrath, as should be remembered to the very end of time. At my slightest word the sword of the avenger should be plucked forth, and few of thy Hebrew tribe would survive to hand down the terrible tale of retribution to their children!"

"It is enough," exclaimed Rebecca, "thy words have but confirmed my hate, and I now tell thee, for the last time, thy suit is utterly in vain."

"Then force shall compel thee to my arms!" cried Sir Gaston fiercely. "I have sought to make thee yield by pouring into thine ear the story of my strong, impetuous love; thou hast rejected me, and thus I seize upon and claim my promised victim!"

Uttering these words, the knight was about to drag her from the chamber, but at that moment Rebecca snatched a dagger from his girdle, and then retreating a pace or two, she raised the threatening weapon towards her own bosom, and thus addressed him:—

"Sir Gaston de Neville, behold how utterly I can despise thy efforts to destroy me. Thou would add violence to thine other injuries!—But I am now armed as thou seest—my hand grasps within it the fatal steel, and so surely as thou advancest but one single step towards me, I will bury this poniard in my bosom!"

"Nay, Rebecca, hear me!" cried the alarmed Templar.

"Avaunt! for I will not listen to thee!" cried the maiden resolutely. "Too well already do I know thy treacherous heart, and now thou beholdest the weapon ready to deprive thy victim of life. Leave me I say again, or in the madness of my despair thou wilt behold me fall a bleeding corse at thy feet!"

"Rebecca! for heaven's sake forbear!" exclaimed the knight with alarm. "I will leave thee for the present, girl; thou shall have thy way for once, mad wench, and perhaps, upon cooler reflection, thou wilt not reject with scorn him who would perish rather than lose so fair a prize. In the meantime I will send a female attendant to conduct thee to thine apartment, and perhaps when next we meet, thou wilt look more kindly upon him who would be thy friend—thy protector."

With these words, the knight strode from the room, leaving Rebecca a prey to the harrowing thoughts produced by the baseness of her cruel persecutor. She was not, however, suffered to remain long in solitude, for in a very few minutes afterwards she was startled at hearing the door open, and looking round, she discovered the promised female attendant, who stood for a second or two, uncertain whether to advance or not, until our heroine, pleased with the air of innocence exhibited by the girl, bade her reproach. This invitation the other readily accepted, and tripping lightly into the room she said :—

" Please, young lady, I have been sent by master to show you to the new chamber, instead of the one you managed so cleverly to escape from. To be sure, Sir Gaston seemed to be in a terrible passion, as if something had happened to ruffle him, and so I hurried off as soon as ever I could, to see whether you were in as great a rage as he was."

"Alas! girl, I have need of a companion in my misfortunes," cried Rebecca. " Doomed to be the prisoner of your tyrant master, my thoughts are full of sadness and despair, and I will gladly accept your offered services, as some solace in the midst of my afflictions."

"Ah!" exclaimed the girl, "that's just what I expected, from master's being in such a confounded passion. He's always making love to the girls, and somehow or other, I couldn't help fancying there was some mischief going on, when I first heard of your being brought to the castle in that mysterious fashion. Then, too, just now his conduct was so queer and outlandish, for striding up to me in the hall, and looking at me as fierce as a lion, ' Edith,' he said, ' go instantly to the armoury; you will find a female there, who you will henceforth regard as your mistress. Hasten to her, and take her to the apartment which has been prepared for her reception in the north turret.' With that, away I bustled with all my heart, and now, young lady, you have only to say when you will go to your new apartment, and I am ready to lead you there."

"Let us seek the chamber instantly," replied Rebecca. " There, perhaps, I may be suffered to remain, unmolested from the hated visits of. Sir Gaston de Neville."

"Why, I don't know how that may be," answered Edith, " for the truth is, our master has a terrible character among the girls. He's what they call a general lover, and I dare say you will not be more free from his visits in one part of the castle than another. However, we will go there without delay, and it shall be no fault of mine, I can assure you, if the place seems dull when once you begin to hear some of the many marvellous stories I can relate about this great wilderness of a place."

Without making any reply, Rebecca followed her attendant to the north turret, where she found an apartment had been fitted up for her, according to the fashion of that by-gone time. On arriving here, she dismissed Edith for the present, and then falling upon her knees, offered up a fervent prayer to heaven for aid and protection under the trying difficulties in which she was placed.

CHAPTER VI.

" Give but thy word to make the maiden mine ;
Promise but this, old man, and, as I live,
To-morrow's sun shall see her safe from harm."
                                    THE RIVAL CHIEFTAINS.

WITH a heavy heart, and foreboding the most fatal consequences to his own peace, Isaac and the faithful Reuben left the lordly halls of Sir Gaston de Neville, from whence they had been repulsed by the command of the haughty Knight Templar. That Rebecca was still in the power of her betrayer, the unhappy father was but too well assured, and knowing as he did, the influence possessed by Sir Gaston, there was too much reason to fear that she would fall a prey to the demoniacal arts which had thus far been successful in violently tearing her from the protection of a parent.

As Isaac once more entered that dwelling which had hitherto yielded him so large a share of happiness, he gazed round him as if seeking the beloved object who had hitherto welcomed his return with smiles of innocence and joy. But alas! how changed was the present occasion! No daughter was there to greet him with the kiss of peace,—the chair she usually occupied stood empty by the window, and all semed to wear an air of gloom, that struck like an ice-bolt to the heart of the bereft old man. His brain reeled as he beheld this desolation that had come upon him ;—reason for a brief period forsook her throne, and, uttering a groan of anguish and despair, he sank into a seat overcome by the intensity of his own mental sufferings.

Equally afflicted, but resolving to master his own feelings for the present, Reuben Grenard now devoted all his care towards aiding the recovery of his venerable friend and benefactor. With words of comfort he sought to assure Isaac that there was yet a probability of snatching her from the hands of her cruel persecutor; but the aged Hebrew was deaf to the consolation thus offered, and it was some time ere he replied to his faithful comrade in misfortune. At last, however, raising his eyes from the ground, and looking with a stedfast gaze into the countenance of his young companion, he said, in a tone choked with emotion :—

" For thy zeal, Reuben, in my behalf, I thank thee from my very soul. But thou art young in years, my friend, and little knowest thou the art with which evil men seek to conceal their guilt from the eyes of the world. Sir Gaston de Neville hath sought the ruin of our peace ;—he hath succeeded in robbing an old man of his beloved child, and who is there, thinkest thou, who will dare to rob him of a prize he has been at so much pains to obtain ?"

" Thou knowest slightly of my love, or that question had never been asked," exclaimed Reuben, with generous warmth.

" Nay, there thou wrongest me," answered Isaac, " for thy noble worth has not passed unheeded, nor have I failed to approve the union, which, ere long was to have taken place between thee and my beloved child. With a father's joy, I beheld the promised happiness of my Rebecca, and believing that peace and content would be her future destiny, I thought not that the ruin of all my hopes could be so near at hand. But thou seest the oppression cast upon us by these Christians ; we are regarded by them, not as brothers, but as objects upon whom to exercise their blind, infuriate hate."

"Then let us seek to cast off the odious yoke that binds us," cried Reuben, ardently. "We are not powerless in the land, and one vigorous effort might at least compel our enemies to treat us as brethren."

"Boy!" exclaimed Isaac, reprovingly, "thy words show how little experience thou hast yet gathered. I tell thee we must remain passive sufferers for a time; endurance of evil is the lot of our people till the God of our fathers shall see fit to bring us forth from darkness into light."

"Then thou counsellest quiet submission to tyranny?"

"I do."

Reuben heard these words with surprise, but, accustomed as he was to pay deference to the words of his venerable friend, he suffered this part of the subject to drop without further comment or remark. Still, however, he was resolved not to let Rebecca fall a prey to her foe without an effort being made to rescue the hapless maiden, and once more addressing the old man he said :—

"Thou hast seen the wolf fall upon thy fold, and seize upon the lamb thou dids't so much love. Thou hast felt the power of an oppressor, as I now ask of thee whether we shall endure this heavy wrong without making one effort to wrest the maiden from the hands of a villain?"

"No!" answered the aged Israelite, with sudden ardour;—the evil must be redressed,—the wrong-doer must be punished!"

"Then let mine be the hand to avenge the deed!"

"Thine, Reuben!—knowest thou the difficulties that must stand in the way of such an enterprize?"

"I have weighed them all, and my mind is made up to overcome all obstacles," answered the youth, ardently. "Remember, father, in whose cause I am thus called upon to exert myself, and then doubt not the zeal which will direct my efforts."

"I doubt not thine ardour, boy," answered Isaac;—"but knowing whom thou hast to contend against, I fear thy rash attempt to rescue Rebecca would be met with ruin and despair."

"Who then cans't thou look to for succour in this hour of peril?" demanded Reuben Grenard.

"Upon me let your hopes rest!" exclaimed a voice behind them, and on turning round they beheld the gigantic form of Black Ivan, who had that moment entered the apartment. His person was completely concealed in the ample folds of a large riding cloak that he wore, but as he advanced he threw aside the covering, and laying his hand upon the palsied arm of the venerable Jew, he said carelessly :—

"Thou art doubtless surprised at seeing one whom thou regardest with fear and dread. Perhaps thou thinkest me an enemy, old man, and yet, ere we part, I will prove how deep an interest I have taken in thy welfare."

"What meanest thou?", demanded Isaac, with fear and trembling;—"thy presence was most unexpected, and I fear the business that brings thee hither betokeneth no good either to me or mine!"

"Now thou art looking to bags of gold old man!" exclaimed the robber, with a smile of contempt;—"thou knowest me to be a robber by profession, and thy suspicions prompt thee to regard my presence with dread."

"For what art thou here, if money be not thy object?" demanded Reuben.

"To serve this old man, and rescue his lovely daughter from the hands of a villain," answered Black Ivan haughtily.

"Hah!" cried the Jew with surprise," woulds't thou indeed restore a hapless daughter to her father's arms?"

"Aye, on certain conditions the girl shall be snatched from the fate that threatens her."

"And those conditions ——"

"Are that she shall be my reward," interrupted the robber.

"Aye, thou startest with amazement, old man, and perhaps thou will reject my terms, but I ask thee which thou woulds't rather see,—her,—the mistress of yon pampered knight, or the wife of one whose crimes are not so great as they have been represented by his enemies?"

"Wretch!" exclaimed Reuben, wildly, "knowest thou not that her father will never consent to one of Israel's daughter's becoming the bride of a Christian?"

"Psha! I know nothing of the old man's prejudices, neither do I care for them," answered Ivan. "I am here to make the only proposition by which Rebecca can be saved, and it now remains for her father to say whether or not she shall become an object for the world's scorn and contempt."

"Then hear me," cried Isaac, resolutely,—"that I love my child,—far, very far, beyond my own existence is known to all whose good opinion is worth preserving;—I would sacrifice my own useless life in her defence,—would throw away the last coin I possess in the world, but never will I consent to yield one so pure—so excellent, to become the bride of a man whose crimes have rendered him an outcast from his fellow creatures. This is my resolve, Ivan, and whether it be for good or harm, I will remain steadfast in it till the last hour of my existence!"

"And this," exclaimed the robber, "is done that you may afterwards bestow her upon the puny rival who now stands before me!"

"He hath at least the virtue of honesty to recommed him to my favour," answered the Jew, with scorn, "and that is more than you can advance in your behalf."

"And what is it that has driven me to become what I am?" demanded Black Ivan. "Oppressed by my fellow creatures I long ago learnt to hate and loathe those whom at one time in my life I could have loved. For a slight fault I was punished by what your tyrants are pleased to call the law. Imprisonment I bore,—aye, and bore it patiently till the period to which I was doomed had expired; but when I again came forth from my dungeon, it was with a soul burning for vengeance, and panting to hurl revenge upon those who had made me a mark for the world's scorn. I had vowed in the dreary hours of my captivity to make my oppressor's smart for the wrongs I had endured, and, in some degree I have not been unmindful of my oath. Some have met death from my hands, and it shall not be long ere others fall beneath the poiniard of the man they ruined and trampled upon."

"Nay, repent, I conjure thee," cried Isaac, horror-struck at the fearful violence with which these words were uttered; "be satisfied with the vengeance thou has already taken, and return once again to society from which thou hast banished thyself."

"Ha! ha! ha!" shouted the robber wildly, "and who, thinkest thou would henceforth become the associate of a man branded and driven forth by the malice of his foes?—Who, I ask thee, would hold out the right hand of fellowship to be grasped by one whose soul is said to be stained with every crime at which human nature shudders. No—no—they have made me what I am:—as a robber I am not without friends and associates; among them I have thrown myself, nay, am now their leader, and never will I quit their society to mix again with men who flatter only to deceive."

"Thou hast said enough," answered Isaac;—"thou art resolved to persist in a career of crime and bloodshed, and yet thou wouldst fain persuade me to yield up a beloved daughter as thy bride."

"Remember, old man!—it is thy only way to save her from the villain who has torn her from thine arms."

"Thou hast judged me wrong," cried Reuben, "if thou believest that Rebecca will fall a prey to the knight whilst I have power to raise a sword in her defence. I am her betrothed husband, and Sir Gaston de Neville will yet find that the despised Jew is not to be trampled upon with impunity."

"Then my interference in this maiden's behalf is rejected?"

"It is."

"Even as you please," answered the robber fiercely; "thou hast seen thy promised bride torn from her father's arms, without an effort made to rescue her, and yet, with all thy boasted love, thou wouldst suffer her to remain a captive to him who has dared to commit the outrage. However, thou hast yet to learn that Black Ivan is a rival not to be scorned, and perhaps, ere many days have passed away he may exult in having cheated thee of thy beauteous girl, for whose sake thou professest so much."

Again the robber threw around him his huge cloak, and ere Reuben had time to seize upon the intruder, he had disappeared from the room. Enraged at the contempt manifested for him by the robber, he would have followed him from the house, but Isaac foresaw the consequences of such an attempt and taking the hand of his youthful friend he implored him to desist from a project that must only bring upon them consequences

No. 5

more disastrous than those they were already suffering from.   Thus adjured, Reuben became more calm, and as news had reached them that King Richard was to arrive in London early on the following morning from the north of England, it was arranged between them that they should meet the procession at the village of Charing, where they would throw themselves at the feet of the monarch, and implore his assistance in rescuing Rebecca from the hands of Sir Gaston de Neville.   Some-what re-assured by the hope thus held out, they retired to their several sleeping apartments, resolving, in the event of being disappointed in this expectation, to seek other and more violent means to snatch the maiden from that destruction with which she was threatened.

CHAPTER VII.

" Gaily the glittering band pursues its route,
    But soon a host appears to stop their course,
    And war's wild uproar presently succeeds."

MIRANDA.

ACCORDING to the previous appointment, the gallant King Richard the First set our from the castle of the Lord Scroope,—where he and his retinue had slept on the previous night,—in order to reach London where busi-ness of pressing emergence required his immediate attendance.   It was a noble sight to the chivalrous monarch and his numerous train of Lords and Knights as they pursued their way, marching as they did in all the gorgeous panoply of state, and exhibiting a splendid array, such as in these days we may vainly look for.   Immediately in advance of the king marched a goodly array of stout English bowmen, celebrated for dex-terity in their craft, and exhibiting all that cool courage and determina-tion, for which they were so justly renowned wherever they had been called upon to exhibit their dexterity in behalf of their country.   Around the person of the sovereign were assembled many of the chief men of the nation, all of whom wore the splendid armour of the period, and were mounted upon magnificent war-steeds, whose rich caparisons added not a little to the extraordinary brilliancy of the cavalcade.   Then came the men-at-arms, veterans who had 'served under Richard in the hot plains of Palestine, and whose deeds of bravery had won for them the confidence and approbation of their sovereign.

The sun had scarcely risen when the king, thus attended, rode forth from the strongly fortified castle of Lord Scroope, and as it was the only resting place between that point and London, Richard was impatient to proceeded with what haste they could in order that he might reach his palace where a conference had been appointed to take place with the chief of his nobility on matters of pressing and immediate consequence. In fact so anxious was the king to reach the place of destination with as little delay as possible, that, whispering Lord Scroope to follow him, he put spurs to his horse and dashed onwards, soon leaving the remain-der of his retinue some distance behind him.   At length, however, the prudence and forethought of Lord Scroope came to his aid, and checking the speed of his impatient charger, he exclaimed :—

" Pardon me, your majesty, for thus venturing to thwart your pleasure, but much risk is incurred by thus riding without a sufficient guard ;— the robber whom they call Black Ivan, lurks in the neighbourhood, and he will hardly let so rich a prize escape him if the rumour should have reached his ears that King Richard passes thus near his haunts."

" The knave will hardly dare show himself if he learns at the same time the numerous band of friends by whom I am accompanied," answered the king smiling at the alarm of his companion.

" But your guards are now far behind us," replied Lord Scroope, " and should we chance to meet the robber we may fall an easy prey to him and his ruffians long ere assistance could reach us."

" Thou forgettest my trusty battle-axe, and the good service it hath often done me in worse straits than such a one as thou seemst to fear," answered the king, brandishing the weapon he spoke of, and at the same time urging his horse to greater speed.

Lord Scroope saw that it was in vain to throw out any further obstacles, and following the king closely they proceeded a short distance till reaching the summit of a hill, from whence they obtained a distant view of London, and the noble river on the banks of which it stands. Struck with the sight and wishing to relieve his horse for a moment or two, the king paused, and pointing towards the metropolis of his dominions, he exclaimed with exultation :—

" Behold, my lord, the proud city which even now is the centre of civilization and liberty. The sight of it always fills my soul with pride, and now that I am king, it shall teach me so to rule my people that they shall become greater and greater until the whole world shall admit the superiority of our little island."

" England," answered Scroope, " has already obtained the admiration even of her enemies."

" True," returned the king, " but I can venture to prophecy that the time will come, when our country shall far outstrip all other in the race for superiority. Its people are brave and energetic, and with good laws for their government the palm of eminence shall be decreed to England."

" With a king, brave and wise as your majesty, our country may indeed become the envy of the world," exclaimed Lord Scroope, approvingly.

" Nay, my lord," cried the king sharply, " thou knowest I despise flattery. Speak the honest truth, man, for, though a monarch, I hate the silvered words with which courtiers ever seek to render themselves acceptible. And now, my lord, forward, for I already hear the approach of our retinue, who, having missed us, are doubtless hurrying on with a lspeed."

" The sounds your majesty speaks of," replied the nobleman, " proceed not from the direction in which we should expect our friends. Horsemen are about to meet us, and should they belong to the band of Black Ivan, we may yet repent the rashness that impelled us to ride so much in advance of our friends."

" By heaven, you are right, Scroope," cried the king, " the riders, whoever they are, are coming through yonder valley ; and from the cloud of dust that rises just below us, I should imagine thy advance in no inconsiderable number."

" Had we not better stay till our own friends are in sight ?" suggested the nobleman.

" Rather would I perish by the ignoble hands of Black Ivan himself, than betray so much fear of one whom I despise !" answered Richard fearlessly. " No, my lord, we are both armed, and if the worst comes, we must teach these rascals that two men in an honourable cause are far more than a match for all the numbers they can bring against us.

"Your majesty," answered Scroope, "shall have no cause to accuse me of cowardice, in the event of our coming to blows. If I was for a moment apprehensive, it was only lest my king should be placed in danger, but, having so fair an example to follow, I promise to give these fellows a reception such as they perhaps little anticipate."

By this time the king and his companion had slowly ridden to the bottom of the hill, where they had hardly arrived, when a numerous body of horsemen appeared in sight, one of whom, advancing before the rest, approached the king, and seizing his bridle, commanded him in a peremptory tone to stop.

"At whose orders am I thus delayed in my journey?" demanded Richard, spurring his noble charger, and with the suddenness of the movement disengaging himself from the hold of his antagonist. "Now, sirrah, speak, and tell me who thou art that darest thus interrupt a passenger on the king's highway?"

"One who claims to be as great as the king himself," answered the other.

"Insolent ruffian!" exclaimed Scroope, drawing his sword, and riding forward to cut the man who had thus dared to interrupt them on their way. But the king motioned him back, and then addressing himself to the other, he said:—

"Thou claimest to be as great as Richard himself;—perhaps thy courtesy will not refuse to inform me who I have thus the honour of addressing?"

"Black Ivan, the robber!"

"I thought as much," answered the lion-hearted monarch, "and now in return, perhaps thou wouldst like to know who it is thou hast so incautiously delayed on his journey?"

"In that matter," returned the other, raising his cap respectfully, "I can save your majesty all further trouble. Ivan, the robber, has now the honour of being in the presence of Richard, King of England!"

"How," exclaimed the monarch, knowing my rank, "dost thou dare to hold me longer in parley?"

"Nay," replied the robber, "for once in our lives a king and a brigand are upon equal terms. Thou hast ventured hither without thy usual escort, and must be content to pay the penalty of thine imprudence."

"Villain!" cried Lord Scroope, "thy presumption shall cost thee thy life!"

"Forbear, Scroope, I command thee!" interposed the king. "This knave speaks truly; I have indeed acted unwisely, and would now learn from him what penalty it is his will to demand of me."

"In the first place I must have thy purse?"

"A most modest request truly!" answered Richard, "but Black Ivan has to earn it ere he obtains the reward he seeks. So much for thy first demand, now for thy second."

"My next," answered the robber, "is that thou wilt extend thy pardon towards me and all those under my command."

"By St. George! thou shalt have my life first!" exclaimed the king impatiently.

"Does your majesty see the force that surrounds me?"

"I do, and fear them not!"

"But at my bidding your life would be the sacrifice of such temerity."

"Am I threatened by a caitiff such as thou!" cried the king, wrathfully, and wielding his terrible battle axe, he aimed a blow at the robber, with such precision, that Black Ivan must have fallen a victim to his own rashness, had he not suddenly turned his horse's head, and thus escaped with a slighter wound, that brought him bleeding to the earth. Upon this the king leaped from his charger, and rushed forward to complete the work he had been thus foiled in, but ere he could reach the object of his vengeance, Black Ivan had risen from the ground, and stood ready to receive the attack with which he was threatened.

The conflict that now ensued was terrific; blow succeeded blow with the greatest rapidity, and from the resolution evinced by the robber, not to yield till the last moment, it became but too evident that Richard was placed in a situation of the most imminent peril. But Lord Scroope had seen the danger in which his sovereign was placed, and applying a bugle to his lips, he succeeded in sounding it with such good effect, that almost immediately afterwards, the retinue was seen galloping down the hill to the rescue of their royal master.

Taken thus by surprise, the robbers now commenced a hasty retreat, leaving their leader still engaged in deadly strife with his valorous opponent. Indeed they were still fighting foot to foot when the attendants of the king arrived; and several of them rushing forward, would have sacrificed the brigand on the spot, had not Richard commanded them to spare his life, and to take him with them to London, where he might afterwards meet the punishment his crimes seemed to merit. As for Lord Scroope, he was found to have been so severely wounded, that it was necessary to form a litter for him, and in that state he was conveyed to London. This being done, Black Ivan was placed on the horse of the wounded nobleman, and when a sufficient guard was raised around him, the whole cavalcade set forth once more towards their place of destination.

CHAPTER VIII.

" Hither the heroes and the nymphs resort,
To taste awhile the pleasures of a court."—POPE.

LONG before the hour appointed for the arrival of King Richard and his train in London, Isaac of Tadcaster, attended by Reuben Grenard, had directed his footsteps towards the then small suburban village of Charing, through which it was expected the royal procession would pass. Here our two Hebrews found a great crowd of idlers already assembled in anticipation of witnessing the sight, and, desirous of avoiding mixing themselves with those who usually treated of their religion with contumely and insult, they stood a little apart, resolving to wait till a favourable moment should arrive to present themselves before the king.

But even this humility was insufficient to protect them from the laughter and jeers of those whose bigotry and intollerance induced them to regard a Jew as an object worthy only of their ill-usage. A cry of "Down with the unbelieving dogs!" was presently raised; stones and other missiles were hurled at the two unfortunate objects of their unjust rage, and from the loud cries of fierce anger that were raised, there is little doubt but that a still serious attack would have been made had not a report at the moment been raised that the royal procession was now just appearing in the distance. This instantly turned the tide of events; the two Jews were suffered to remain in peace for a short time, and the rabble began pressing forward, each man being anxious to displace his neighbour, in order that he might himself obtain a sight of all that was going forward.

Thus relieved from any immediate danger, Isaac and his companion ventured to advance a little nearer without being observed, and so anxious were they to reach a place from whence they might throw themselves at the feet of the king, that they had forced their way through a part of the crowd, before they were aware of the danger such an act was likely to bring them into. At last, however, a stout young city apprentice chanced to observe them, as they were anxiously urging their way through the thickest of the rabble, and, thinking it an excellent joke to ill-use a harmless inoffensive Jew, he seized Isaac by the beard, and pulling him with all his might, shouted out to his comrades to assist in maltreating the defenceless old man. But Reuben's ire was excited to the highest pitch, by the unprovoked insult which had thus been offered to his aged friend, and, reckless of the consequences to himself. he dealt the youngster a blow, which at once released Isaac from his grasp, and sent the cowardly assailant reeling backwards among his companions.

This served as the signal for an immediate onset. The wrath of all who had witnessed the transaction was, as a matter of course, excited against the two Hebrews, and no doubt they would have suffered for their temerity, had not the advanced guard of the king at that moment galloped up to the spot, and compelled the crowd to flee in all directions. By this movement Isaac and Reuben were separated from the parties who had just manifested such hostile intentions towards them, and at the same time they fortunately obtained a place in the front rank of the crowd, from whence they could easily throw themselves at the feet of the sovereign, and implore that justice they had come to seek.

In the meanwhile the procession passed on increasing in magnificence as it proceeded, until the majestic form of Richard himself appeared at no great distance off. The appearance of the king at once inspired the heart of Isaac with hope, for the countenance of the monarch bore the impress of virtue and true nobility, and the air of extreme affability with which he acknowledged the loyal shouts of his subjects, gave fair promise that his ear would not be deaf to those who ventured to pour forth their complaints. As he approached still nearer, his attention seemed to be rivetted upon the venerable countenance of the Hebrew, and seizing that favourable moment, Isaac threw himself upon his knees, and held up the petition with which he had come prepared.

But this daring act had nearly cost the Israelite his life, for no sooner had he, thus thrown himself forward, than one of the attendants sprang from his horse, and, uplifting his poignard, would have struck the point to his heart, had not the voice of King Richard been heard at the moment, commanding him to desist.

" Hold, knave !" he exclaimed, angrily, " wouldst thou convert the joy of this day into curses for thy blood fury ? He whom thou wouldst strike with death is old and ill able to contend against thy youth and strength."

" My liege," answered the attendant, " he is a Jew, and——"

" Therefore does he still more need our protection against the tyranny of his fellow creatures!" exclaimed the king, impatiently, interrupting the attendant. " He belongs, sirrah, to a persecuted race of men, and, though his creed may differ from our own, heaven preserve me from the crime of persecuting those, who have so much need of our consideration. Give me the scroll, Hugh Tiptoft, that he would present, and if his wrongs do indeed demand redress, Jew though he be, he shall have it, even if it were against my best loved friend."

With evident reluctance Hugh Tiptoft took the petition from the Hebrew's hand, and presented it to the king amidst the murmurs of the crowd, who stood wondering and dissatisfied that the monarch should thus condescend so much, as to give ear to the complaints of one belonging to a tribe so greatly abhorred and despised. The king, however, took no heed of this, but having carefully perused the petition he refolded and handed it to Ralph de Glanville, his Chief Justiciary who rode beside him.

"My lord," he said, " this paper contains a heavy grievance alleged to have been committed by Sir Gaston de Neville against this old man. A lovely and virtuous maiden hath been beguiled from her father's protecting care, and, by the bones of my ancestors! justice shall instantly be done, or Sir Gaston will lose that favour which can alone maintain him in his present envied state of exaltation."

"Your Grace has but to command, and your will shall be obeyed," answered the Chief Justiciary. "And yet, methinks," he continued, " it would be rash to condemn Sir Gaston de Neville upon the unsupported charge of this old man. Let proof be brought of the truth, and I pledge myself to aid your majesty as far as my power will permit."

"Alas! alas! all is true that I have there written down," said Isaac, in a voice almost choked with grief. " I have been foully wronged by this Knight Templar, and my only hope of justice, rests now upon his majesty."

"Thou shalt have the justice thou demandest," answered the king. " I will protect equally all my subjects, whether they be Jew or Gentile, and woe unto this knight if he proves guilty of the charge brought against him."

"Nay, sire," cried Isaac, " believe me, I seek not vengeance on my foe. All I ask for is the restoration of my daughter, pure and innocent as when she was stolen from my care ;—let her be given to me as I have said, and the evil-doer shall obtain the prayers and forgiveness of her father."

"At present," interposed the Chief Justiciary, " the charge is altogether unsupported. Sir Gaston de Neville may be wholly innocent of the crime alleged against him, and till it is proved that he took away this old man's daughter, we must continue to give him the benefit of our most favourable constructions."

"His guilt or innocence, my lord, may be soon ascertained," answered the king; " for see where yonder Sir Gaston de Neville rides towards us, and surely he will not stain 'his knighthood with dishonour, as to so far cover the crime with falsehood if he be indeed guilty."

To this the Chief Justiciary assented, though he knew well enough in his own mind that the Knight Templar would deny any knowledge of the girl; and, reining his horse a little in the rear, he made way for Sir Gaston, who at that moment advanced to pay his respects to the king. Richard, however, received him with marked coolness, and when the knight had finished his expressions of loyalty and respect with which he greeted the sovereign, the latter, pointing to the venerable Hebrew, demanded whether he knew ought of the person to whom he directed his attention. For a moment or two Sir Gaston was confounded at the suddenness with which this question had been put, but at last recovering his usual self-command, he answered :—

"Were I to deny all knowledge of the person your majesty has alluded to, I should utter a falsehood unworthy the honour the late king, your illustrious predecessor, was pleased to bestow upon me. I do indeed know the man, sire, and that too, for one of the most unconscionable extortioners throughout your majesty's dominions."

"Do you know him then only as a money-lender?"

"That is the extent of my acquaintance with him;" answered Sir Gaston de Neville. "Having occasion for a sum of money not many weeks since, I applied to him, and, after a hard bargain, the advance was made."

"Jew!" exclaimed Richard, "thou hast heard what this knight hath said;—he disclaims all knowledge of thee, except that which took place in consequence of certain dealings which took place between ye."

"Sir Gaston de Neville hath good cause to be careful how he acknowledges too much," replied Isaac. "He fears lest the penalty of shame should fall upon him for the crime he hath committed against a weak, defenceless old man, and therefore will he deny any further acquaintance with the miserable victim that has fallen into his snare."

"Peace! thou old doting idiot,—peace, I say!" exclaimed Sir Gaston, furiously;—"thou wouldst fain ruin me in the estimation of my king, and, by the heaven above us! thou shalt bitterly rue this hour unless instantly thou deniest any charge thou mayst have brought against me."

"Nay, proud sir," replied the Jew, calmly, "I am not to be browbeaten by thee, in addition to the many other wrongs I have endured at thy hands. To thy teeth I tell thee thou hast robbed me of my child, and, villain, though thou art, thou dar'st not deny my charge!"

"Thou hearest what the old man says, Sir Gaston," cried the king!—"he charges thee with having stolen his child, and it is now for thee to show thine innocence."

"Pardon me, sire," answered Sir Gaston, "but it is rather for my accuser to prove his base assertion. Command him to make good his words, and then it will be for me to endure whatever punishment your majesty may think proper to inflict."

"The knight speaks fairly, Jew," exclaimed the king. "Convict him clearly of what thou hast urged against him, and I swear,—despite his lofty station,—to deal forth that justice which the urgency of the case demands."

"My charge rests chiefly upon presumptive evidence," replied Isaac, "because the knight hath taken care to play his part with care and dissimulation. A few weeks since he introduced himself to me as one whom extravagance had well-nigh ruined, and who required the loan of a sum of money to relieve him from pressing difficulties. I would have got rid of him with a churlish answer, but he persisted in urging me to pity his adverse fortune;—spoke of the ruin and disgrace that would follow an exposure of his affairs, and offered to make heavy sacrifices on condition that I would for once release him from his dilemma. But I soon found that his real object in visiting my house was to rob me of an only and beloved daughter, and then, breaking off all further negociations with him, I forbade him ever to enter my doors again."

"So far thou didst act wisely," observed the king. "Sir Gaston, of course, obeyed your injunctions, and any other charge must consequently be founded on suspicion."

"Not entirely," answered Isaac, "for from that time he hath been seen constantly watching about my house at those hours when I am usually absent from home. I was, however, aware of his designs, and fortunately frustrated them until two nights since, when he found an excuse to obtain forcible entrance to my house, from whence she was violently carried away on a charge of being in possession of a diamond ring beloguing to Sir Gaston de Neville."

"And that the charge was not a false one thou well knowest," replied the Knight Templar, insolently. "The truth is, your majesty," he continued, addressing himself to the king, "that two days ago I happened to be robbed in the neighbourhood of Enfield Chase by the notorious brigand Black Ivan and his band. Alarmed, however, at hearing the approach of the travellers they fled in dismay, upon which a faithful retainer of mine followed Black Ivan to London, and continued to keep a careful watch upon him, until he saw him enter the house of this Jew. Upon that the assistance of some constables was procured, and on reaching the place they found my diamond ring upon the finger of this man's daughter."

"Hah!" exclaimed the king, "if this be true the affair begins to wear another aspect. What say'st thou, old man, thou hast heard Sir Gaston, and can contradict him in ought that is false."

"Alas!" groaned Isaac, "the knight has spoken truly. "The ring. l admit, was found on her finger."

"You hear, sire," whispered the Chief Justiciary, "this old man confesses to have been a participator in the robbery."

"My Lord Justice," exclaimed Isaac, who had overheard these words, "thou dost wrong me most foully. I confess to no guilty knowledge concerning the jewel of which I became possessed. A stranger,—who I afterwards found was Black Ivan, presented himself before me, and offered me the ring for a sum of gold. I hesitated, and upon that he assured me that he was induced to part with it in consequence of being urgently pressed by his creditors for the payment of debts due to them. At length I yielded, and in a moment of thoughtlessness placed the ring on my daughter's finger, where it was found by the officers, and on

No. 6

which was founded the charge upon which she was dragged off to the castle of Sir Gaston de Neville."

"There is some mystery in this that must be cleared up," exclaimed the king, and then addressing himself to the Knight Templar he desired to be informed whether the Hebrew Maiden was still detained within his castle.

"She is not, sire," answered Sir Gaston;—"she escaped shortly after her arrival there, and all our efforts to find her again have been in vain."

The king looked incredulously at the knight as he made this bold assertion, but refraining from saying anything further on the subject, he whispered some directions to one of his attendants, and almost imme-diately afterwards the robber, Black Ivan, was brought from the rear and placed near the sovereign.

"You see, Sir Gaston," said the monarch, smiling, "that fortune has been pleased to throw black Ivan into my power. I have made him pri-soner, and it is now my pleasure that you hold him securely in your own custody until I demand him to be restored to me for the purpose of rendering him up to justice. Guard him carefully, Sir Knight, and see that he escapes not with the same ease with which you permitted your female captive to elude your clutches."

"Nay, sire ——"

"Tut, tut!—Sir Gaston, we need no apologies," interrupted the king. "You have had my charge to keep the prisoner safely, and remember I shall speedily demand him at your hands. As for you," he continued, addressing himself to Isaac,—"your case requires consideration. I will bethink me what is best to be done, and when arrangements have been made you shall hear further from me. And now, my good lords, let us once more set forward to our palace at Westminster!"

With these words the cavalcade moved on, and Isaac followed by Reuben, left the place to consult further how they might best seek for the immediate restoration of Rebecca. Sir Gaston, too, was not in the best humour at having been appointed gaoler over Black Ivan, but knowing there was no alternative, he commanded his attendants to look after the prisoner, and then set forward on his return to the castle.

CHAPTER IX.

"Howe'er 'tis well, that while mankind
Though fate's fantastic mazes errs,
They can imagined pleasures find,
To combat against real cares."—PRIOR.

IN the meantime Rebecca set griefworn and spiritless, for she had expected that ere now her father or Rebecca would have found some means to discover the place of her imprisonment, and rescue her from the terrible situation into which she had so unexpectedly fallen. It is true Edith the attendant who had been appointed to wait upon her, was un-ceasing in her endeavours to turn her thoughts from all painful subjects, but the girl was too talkative by half, and the more Edith chattered upon various uninteresting subjects, the more heartily tired did our heroine become of her society. At last, however, she resolved to assume a more cheerful air, in hopes that her attendant would think her society less needful; but, as it happened, this had just the contrary effect, for Edith no sooner saw that the young mistress was more cheerful than,—expecting, no doubt,—to have a willing auditor,—she poured forth the whole torrent of her volubility, entering not only into her own history, but into that of all the people with whose she happened to be acquainted. But her favourite topic was that of her master's failings in regard to his excessive fondness for the fair sex. This subject seemed to her inexhaustible; but, occasionally, when Rebecca expressed herself as being weary of listening to so much depravity, she would adroitly change the conversation, and by way of raising the spirits of our fair captive, she would relate all the ghost stories that were prevalent among the servants belonging to Sir Gaston's household. But this was quite as distasteful to Rebecca as the other subject, and, finding that there was no chance of getting rid of the girl, she asked whether there were no other matters upon which she could contrive to make herself entertaing without being at the same time either personal or a retailer of petty scandal.

"Lor' ma'am," said the loquacious girl, "I should have thought now, you would have liked to hear what a monster Sir Gaston is, because it might make you aware of his evil doings and prepare you to avoid his artifices."

"That," answered Rebecca, "I can do quite as well without listening to these idle tales."

"Well," cried Edith with surprise, "when I began to tell you about the sprites, and the apparitions, and the hobgoblins, and the ghostesses that haunt this crazy old castle, you seemed to be just in as great a fidget, and ask me if I cannot find something more entertaining to relate; —as if anything in the world could be more entertaining than a good ghost story."

"Perhaps so," replied Rebecca, "but I am dull enough already, and would feign avoid everything that tends to fill the mind with fear or trepidation."

"Well then," suppose I tell you what I heard from our young page Julian," observed Edith,—"you have never seen Julian, I believe?— Oh, he's a little duck of a fellow! and if you were once to hear him talk as I do, you would perhaps think with me,—that he beats all the rest of the male folks in the castle to nothing."

"Humph!" ejaculated Rebecca, who could scarcely forbear smiling in spite of her sorrows;—this Julian seems to be an especial favorite,— a lover perhaps?"

"There ma'am you must excuse me," answered Edith. "Dear little Julian tells me its wrong to kiss and tell, so I shall not say a word about how often he snatches nectar from my lips, as he calls it; nor how often he has promised to name a day for our marriage, nor how often he has broken his promise, nor how often——"

"Really if you go on thus I shall know all the secrets of your courtship before you are aware of it," cried Rebecca. Be prudent, girl, if you wish to keep your own counsel, and once more change the conversation to some topic that may be equally entertaining, and yet less dangerous to yourself."

"Well then, suppose I tell you the story that was related to me by Julian, who heard it from the groom, who was informed of it by the falconer, and who declared that he had been told the story by a person whose word was not to be doubted not on no account whatsomever."

"It must be highly interesting," observed Rebecca, "to be considered worthy of such a careful transmission among the domestics of Sir Gaston de Neville."

"Will you hear it and judge for yourself?"

"That," answered Rebecca, "must depend upon whether the narrative involves any of the family secrets connected with the owner of this castle. Unfavourable rumours are, I know, current against him, but I am unfortunately already aware of enough of his baseness, and to hear more of it would only serve to sicken me at the recital of his enormities."

"But there are neither secrets, nor enormities, nor anything else that you need be afraid of listening to," replied Edith. "The fact is that Sir Gaston de Neville may, or may not be rightful owner of this, and other castles held by him. Ah! you may well stare, but the time may yet come when somebody else will arrive to push him off the stool, and I, for one, should not be very sorry for it, seeing that we cannot well have a much worse master in his place."

"You speak in riddles, girl," cried the wondering Rebecca. " Sir Gaston de Neville, as the lawful heir, succeeded his father in these estates, and who, think you, is to dispossess him of them in the manner you seem to think so easy?"

"One that has more right to them than he has," answered the girl. Ah, you don't believe me I see, and yet more improbable things have come to pass before now."

"Silly girl!" cried our heroine, "this is some idle tale invented by the evil wishers of Sir Gaston de Neville. Men in power and affluence have ever such enemies, but rest assured you will never see the change you seem so much to wish."

"You have never heard then, I suppose, that our master has an elder brother, if folks only knew where to find him."

"Such a rumour I must confess has never reached me," answered Rebecca. "Nay, even if it had, I should have regarded it only as one of those idle reports that are generated, nobody knows by whom or for what reason."

"You are wrong, depend upon it," cried Edith, "because Julian told me all about it, and I know he would not tell me a falsehood for all the world. He says that Sir Gaston had an elder brother,—that that elder brother was somehow or another stolen away in his infancy;—that nobody knows who took him away, nor where he was taken to. Of course, a great fuss was made about the loss of the young heir to the house of Neville;—people were dispatched in every direction to find him;—large rewards were offered for his restoration, but when all was done, the child could never be heard of. It was a strange thing how the matter could have been managed so cleverly, but so it was, and Sir Gaston never knows what it is to have a happy moment, seeing that, when least expected, he may be called upon to give up all he possesses in the world, to a brother that he dont care a straw about.

"This is a wild story of yours, Edith," exclaimed our heroine; "and yet, even if there should be any truth in it, the elder brother you speak of may be dead, and then all cause for Sir Gaston's uneasiness be entirely removed."

"Why, that may be to be sure," replied Edith, "and yet it's pretty plain Sir Gaston don't think so, for they say that is the reason he never has married, seeing that he might bring beggary and ruin upon his wife and family."

"Of course," observed Rebecca, "he has ceased to make any farther enquiries after the lapse of so many years."

"He has," answered the girl, "and woe be unto any luckless wight that dares say a word to him upon the subject. Julian says he once heard a particular friend—*particular friend*, you know, Miss, are always *particularly* kind; he once heard, I say, this particular friend mention the subject very slightly, and then to see how Sir Gaston stormed and raved would have done your heart good."

"Were *you* present on the occasion?" asked our heroine.

"No, but Julian was, and that's just the same thing you know."

"Well," smiled Rebecca, "this Julian, whoever he is, may think himself very highly honoured to be so constantly favoured with a place in your memory. We have now been conversing together but a quarter of an hour, and I verily believe his name has been mentioned at least a dozen times."

"Ah!" sighed Edith, "if you did but know him you would not wonder at my partiality for him. He's the best looking young man in the household—comes of a good family—is liberal in his compliments to me —dances like an angel, and is never so happy as when he can steal half-an-hour to walk out with me, and talk all about love and all other such like interesting subjects."

"And among his other qualifications," observed Rebecca, "he seems to know a vast deal about his master's affairs."

"Aye, a great deal more than I have told you of," answered the girl. "He knows all Sir Gaston's love matters; can repeat by heart the whole list of girls that have been made the victims of his master's roving habits —giving their birth, parentage, age and education, together with all other particulars that are most interesting to your true lover of the marvellous."

"And do you think he never imposes upon your weakness in listening to all this nonsense?"

"Impose upon me!"

"Aye, do you not think it very possible?"

"If I only caught him doing such a thing, see how I would serve him out for it," answered Edith, indignantly. "Impose upon me, indeed! only let him attempt to do such a thing, and if I didn't scratch his face for him, say my name's not what it is, that's all!"

"Trust me, Edith, he is not to be depended upon," exclaimed Rebecca. "He makes himself too busy in his master's affairs, and a person of that description is never to be regarded with any other feelings than those of suspicion and distrust."

"Upon my word!" cried the girl, "you seem to stick up for Sir Gaston as if you didn't dislike him so much as you pretended to do at first."

"Edith, no more of this," exclaimed our heroine. I have but too much reason to dread even the bare mention of his name, and the misery occasioned by my present unfortunate situation might well have obtained for me some share of your pity and commisseration."

"Well, I declare now! if you ain't quite huffish with a poor lady!" cried Edith, instantly changing her tone. "Not but what I ought to be ashamed of myself for saying you could ever fancy a man that has been guilty of bringing misery on so many girls. Besides, they say he has a good many other wicked doings to answer for; things that would make your blood run cold to hear. Nay, I have heard for a fact that he has even been guilty of the crime of mur——"

At this instant the door of the chamber was violently thrown open, and Sir Gaston, pale and disordered, strode with rapid steps into the room. Towards Edith, in particular, he cast a look of fierce displeasure, and then motioning with his hand towards the door, he commanded her instantly to retire. This the girl did eagerly enough, and running with terror from the room she left Rebecca alone and unprotected with the fierce and vindictive Sir Gaston de Neville.

CHAPTER X.

" What may this mean,
That thou, dead corse, again, in complete steel,
Revisit'st thus the glimpse of the moon,
Making night hideous ? ——"   SHAKSPERE.

THE dark frown that had gathered on the countenance of the Knight Templar was sufficient to convince Rebecca of the danger that now threatened her through the violence of her cruel persecutor. That he had overheard the latter charges brought against him by the garrulous Edith, there was but too much reason to expect; whether the report was true or false, he, at any rate, had now learnt the opinion entertained against him by the world, and the probability was that he would seek to avenge himself by the perpetration of fresh acts of violence.

Full of dread, Rebecca had sunk upon a seat at his approach, but the knight was not to be moved by her terrors, and stepping fiercely towards her, he demanded in a voice agitated with passion, whether she had yet made up her mind to save herself and her father from destruction by yielding to him that love which hitherto he had solicited in vain. But the maiden turned from him with disgust, and it was not without a violent effort that she was at length able to implore time ere she gave an answer to his base proposition.

" Not an instant !" he replied, hoarsely; " I am here to demand a reply, and again I warn you, that your own life, and that of your father, depend upon the decision you may now choose to come to."

" Nay," she replied, firmly, " over my own destiny you can have no control. There is a power above to protect the innocent from the guilty, and upon that do I rely for aid, even against the machinations of Sir Gaston de Neville."

" Indeed !" exclaimed the knight, " and yet I have only to stretch forth my hand, and thy promised aid would avail thee little."

" This dagger, then, will at least rescue me from the power of a hated villain !" cried Rebecca, drawing the weapon she had named from beneath the folds of her mantle, and holding it in a threatening attitude towards her own bosom. " With this, I can release myself, even upon the instant, aye, proud knight, and will do so, if you advance but one step nearer to put your fiendish threat into execution !"

" Hold ! I implore you, hold !" exclaimed Sir Gaston, terrified by the vehemence with which these words were uttered. " Return that poniard to the place from whence thou didst take it, and I pledge myself to offer no further violence, until thou hast again refused to hear my earnest prayers for pity."

" Pity !" cried Rebecca, " dost thou ask for pity from one whom thou hast betrayed beneath thy hated roof ? Base as thou art, I scorn all thy prayers and supplications. I loathe thee as the serpent who would beguile the innocent, and rather than make terms with such as thee, will cheerfully lay down my life by those means which chance has thus thrown in my way."

" By heavens, this is frenzy !" exclaimed Sir Gaston ; " I would reason calmly with thee, and yet thou dost obstinately reject all my entreaties that peace may be between us."

" Remain at the distance at which thou now standest, and I will answer thee," replied the Hebrew Maiden, gathering renewed firmness.

"Say,—what wouldst thou with me? Dost thou repent; and may I now return to the broken-hearted old man whom thou wouldst render harmless?"

"There thou askest more than I can grant," replied the knight. "I have said how much I love thee;—have played a desperate game to get thee into my power, and it is scarcely now to be expected that I will yield thee up, when thus safe within my grasp!"

"Thou art deceived!" replied Rebecca; "thou knowest I am not in thy power, whilst this dagger remains in my possession. Nay, I see by thy threatening looks thou would advance to snatch from me this instrument of protection. But I am bold and resolute, Sir Gaston;—death has no terrors for me, and so surely as thou dost approach me, even though but a single step, so surely wilt thou see me lie a breathless, bleeding corse at thy feet."

"Rebecca!" for mercy's sake, throw aside that fatal weapon!"

"Never, while I have aught to dread from thee," she replied. It is the only friend thy vile practices have left me, and shall never quit my possession whilst life remains to me."

"Girl! this rashness will but serve to injure those whom thou dost most love," exclaimed the Templar. "Remember, it is in my power to deliver both thy father and Reuben Grenard into the hands of the executioner."

"Thou canst not," she replied; "they have neither of them broken the laws of the country, and, until they have committed some foul crime, it is beyond thy weak artifice to deliver them up to destruction."

"But charges are easily invented, and not quite so easily disproved.

"Villain! villain!" exclaimed Rebecca, trembling with emotion; "thou wouldst purchase blood with falsehood;—wouldst send an old man, who never injured thee, to perish beneath the hands of the executioner, in revenge for the daughter's virtue in casting thee from her feet with scorn."

"It is thine own obstinacy thou hast to blame for any evil that may befal," answered Sir Gaston. "By yielding to me thy love, Isaac of Tadcaster may spend the short remainder of thy days in peace, and even my rival, Reuben Grenard, may yet avoid the certain destruction that must otherwise overtake him.

"Thinkest thou either of them would purchase thy favour at the expense of my happiness?" demanded Rebecca. "No; like me, they would spurn all your promised good-will, and die exulting in the thought that their oppressor had failed in his demoniac schemes against the peace of a hapless girl,—the intended victim of his baseness."

"Dost thou brave my power, Rebecca?"

"I do."

"Dost thou know I can yet conquer thee?"

"Not whilst I am thus armed with this instrument of death!"

"Psha!" with one single bound I could rush upon and deprive thee of that poor defence."

"Put thy boast into execution, and witness its results. I am on my guard against any sudden surprise;—my eye watches thine, proud knight, and were I to suspect that such a thought lurked in thy brain, the weapon should do its work of death, and thus snatch me from the fate thou meditatest!"

As she spoke thus, the Jewess clutched the handle of the poniard more firmly, and by the look of resolution with which she regarded her persecutor, he saw plainly enough that she was fully prepared to carry her threat into effect.   He, therefore, once more assumed a milder bearing towards her, and affecting to treat the affair lightly, he said :—

"Come, come, girl, what I have said was only done to try thee;—I like the noble spirit that actuates thy soul, and, by heaven, from this moment, we must be better friends."

"Friends, Sir Gaston de Neville, we can never be," answered Rebecca ;—"thou hast laid bare thy soul, and, knowing the infamy of thy designs against a helpless girl, I can never regard thee with any other feeling save that of abhorrence."

"Thou art too severe, maiden," returned the knight. "I may have erred, but will no act of mine, serve to render us better friends."

"One act alone can wipe away thine offence.—Release me from this accursed place; — restore me to the arms of a fond, broken-hearted father, and I will endeavour to forget that thou hast ever sought to injure me."

"Thou art asking that which is utterly impossible," replied Sir Gaston. "To make thee mine has cost much time and patience; I have watched and waited for an opportunity to snatch thee from thy father's roof till hope had well nigh vanished, and in my despair I had given up all idea of gaining my wished-for prize as utterly vain. At last, however, the circumstance of finding that ring in thy possession, gave me the wished-for chance. Through that, thou art now in my strong hold, from whence all the fiends of hell shall not drag thee !"

"And yet thou mayst, ere long, be compelled to restore me to my much-loved home."

"Who shall compel me, maiden ?"

"The king."

"Hah ! dost thou threaten me with his interference ?"

"I do," answered Rebecca, "for people say he is good and will render justice to the humblest of his subjects. My father will throw himself at his feet, and demand justice against the cruel persecutor of his child."

"Thy father has already done so, and failed in the attempt," replied Sir Gaston.

"Merciful father !" cried the maiden, despairingly ;—"am I then forsaken in my utmost extremity ?"

"As surely as thou dost stand there."

"'Tis false !" exclaimed Rebecca ; "this is some invention of thine own, to fright me to thy purpose. —Avaunt fiend, for thy evil deeds are but too well known to me !"

"By my soul, I have spoken the truth," answered the knight, earnestly, "But a few hours since the king entered London for the purpose of making immediate preparations for his coronation. At the village of Charing,—which thou knowest is not far from the palace,—he was accosted by Isaac of Tadcaster, who, on his knees, presented a petition, praying for what he was pleased to term *justice* against me."

"And what said King Richard ?" demanded the maiden, with breathless anxiety ;—"did he not listen to an old man weeping at his feet for the loss of a beloved child ?"

"Why, at first," answered Sir Gaston, "the king certainly did seem inclined to think the Jew had some just cause of complaint against the person he had demanded an explanation of all that had taken place."

"And *you*," exclaimed Rebecca, with scorn ;—"*you* were base enough to give the lie to an old man's just complaints !"

"I certainly endeavoured to turn matters, as much as possible, in my own favour," answered the recreant knight. "I told his majesty the

story of my being robbed by Black Ivan;—of his being watched to the house of Isaac of Tadcaster;—and of officers being sent there to seize upon all who were in any way connected with the robbery."

"And thus implicated my father in a crime of which he had no knowledge !" cried Rebecca, trembling with emotion.

"Nay, I aimed at a higher game than that," replied Sir Gaston, unmoved by her fears. "Thy father was not required to become a victim to my projects, and therefore no charge was brought against him. I, however, related the circumstance of the diamond ring being found on your finger and pressed upon the king's notice the suspicion that such an incident must consequently bring upon yourself."

" Then King Richard believes me to be the guilty wretch thou hast described !" groaned the Hebrew Maiden.

" He does, girl."

" Villain !" she exclaimed, " thine infamy shall ere long recoil upon thine own head. But 'tis well, perhaps, that it should be so, for Richard will doubtless demand me at thy hands, and thus shall I, ere long, be released from the custody of my cruel oppressor."

"Such might have been the case had I not taken means to prevent it," answered the knight. " I told the king thou hadst secretly fled from my castle, and, as the assertion was not disbelieved, of course, the affair will cease to excite any attention. Thus you see, Rebecca, how superior cunning is to force since it has, by rendering you powerless, give me an advantage that it will be in vain for you to strive against."

" Still, monster, thou hast not deprived me of the power to seek my own destruction !" cried Rebecca, in despair, at the difficulties that presented themselves at every turn. As she spoke thus, she raised the glittering blade that was still grasped in her hand, and turning the point towards herself, she was about to plunge it in her heart, when the tapestry before her was seen to shake violently, and in an, instant afterwards, the spectral form of a warrior strode solemnly into the room.   As Rebecca saw the pale, cadaverous countenance of the helmetted apparition, she uttered a scream of terror—the poniard dropped from her grasp, and sinking to the ground, she became for a time insensible to the miseries of her present hapless situation.

Amazed at the suddenness with which all this had occurred, Sir Gaston turned round to discover the cause of all her terror, and as he did so, his eye fell upon the same figure, which was now gliding away towards the wall of the chamber, behind the tapestry of which it instantly disappeared.

It was in vain that Sir Gaston endeavoured to find out some secret door by which the fearful intruder had made its exit.   Every part appeared to be firm and unyielding, and after having fruitlessly sought to unravel the mystery, he hurried from the room,—despatched Edith to look after her young mistress, and then proceeded to the dungeon of Black Ivan.

CHAPTER XI.

" Here, stand behind this bulk. Straight will he come,
      Wear thy good rapier bare, and put it home ;
      Quick, quick, fear nothing ;—I'll be at thy elbow."—SHAKSPERE.

CONFINED in one of the deepest dungeons of the castle, without air or light, except the small portion admitted through a small hole in the roof ; — with the cold, damp floor only for a resting place, and deprived of every comfort, lay Black Ivan, brooding over his misfortunes, and devising a thousand wild schemes by which to effect his escape, and hurl his heaviest vengeance upon the author of all his present suffering.   Madly he shook his chains, when, after various efforts had been made to release himself from them, he found that he was still subject to their dominion, and that not a single chance remained to obtain that freedom for which his soul yearned.

Cursing the chance that had thus thrown him into the power of his enemies, Black Ivan at length started upon his feet, and jerking the massive iron chain that bound him to the wall with terrific violence, he endeavoured to rend the links, and thus release his limbs from the bondage that had already become so galling to him.   But as well might he have endeavoured to overturn the strong foundation of the castle itself, for the chain was of such strength as to defy all his efforts, and at last, overpowered with exertion, he again threw himself upon the ground, howling like a wild and infuriated animal at the utter frustration of all his hopes.

In the midst of all this, however, his attention was arrested by a sound just without his dungeon door ;—chains fell heavily as, one after the other, they were removed by the person seeking for admittance, and then came the noise of rusty bolts which were with difficulty forced from the staples by which they were secured.   Wondering who his visitor was, Black Ivan sprang once more upon his feet, and scarcely had he done so, than the door opened, and Sir Gaston de Neville, bearing a lighted lamp in his hand, entered the dreary dungeon of his captive.

" Hah! is it thou, base knight?" exclaimed the robber, as the light fell upon the pale and care-worn countenance of Sir Gaston. "But 'tis well," he continued, "thy foe is chained and manacled, and safely may'st thou now approach where, at any other time, it might cost thee thy miserable life."

" Hear me patiently, and then reproach me if thou wilt, Ivan," cried Sir Gaston, soothingly. " Thou takest me for an enemy, but perhaps, ere we part, thou wilt acknowledge me for thy friend."

" My friend!" exclaimed the brigand; "dost thou come then to give me liberty?"

" That," replied the knight, " will depend upon thyself.

" Hah!—thou comest to ask a favour?"

" I come, returned the other, " both to ask and to perform a favour. Thou hast it in thy power, Ivan, to do me a great service."

" Indeed!—and the reward?"

" Will be thine own liberty; dost thou agree to my terms?"

" Humph! that requires some little consideration."

" On the contrary," answered the knight, " I should have imagined it scarcely required any. This darksome dungeon is no place for a man to choose as his future residence, and trust me, thou hast not much chance of leaving it again, unless under the terms I have proposed."

" I see," exclaimed Black Ivan, after a brief pause; " the blood of some enemy is to be the price of my liberty?"

" True, thou hast guessed my thoughts. I would, indeed, have a rival removed, and who so fit to undertake the task as Black Ivan the Out-law?"

"And yet Black Ivan the Outlaw may be less sanguinary than thy-self. He is no shedder of blood, Sir Gaston de Neville, excepting in cases of sheer necessity, nor will he be so now, unless good cause is shown why he should seek the life of thine enemy."

" Thou shalt have sufficient reason shown thee," replied the Templar. "In fact, this man of whom I speak, stands between me and happiness; remove him, and I may chance to obtain the prize I seek."

" I must first know the name of the unfortunate wretch who has thus fallen under thy displeasure. Who is it that I am required to slay?"

" Reuben Grenard."

" Reuben Grenard!—what, he who is the chosen lover of the pretty Rebecca?"

" The same."

" Then here our treaty ends," exclaimed Ivan; "thou may'st believe me bloodthirsty, cruel, and vindictive, but I must have cause to strike ere my hand can inflict the blow that is to rob a fellow-creature of life. Reuben Grenard never injured me, and therefore mine shall not be the act that sends him unprepared into another world."

" Then hast thou sealed thine own doom to perpetual imprisonment in this miserable vault!" cried Sir Gaston. " A single blow made at the heart of my detested rival would have obtained deliverance for thee, and yet thou hast thrown away the only chance of liberty for a mere scruple of conscience."

" Thank heaven my conscience, bad as it is, has not quite so heavy a load upon it as your own," answered the robber. " That I have long followed a life of crime and violence is true, but I war only against the purses, not the lives of his majesty's subjects."

" Hast thou always avoided shedding blood?"

" Always," replied Ivan, " except in two or three extreme cases where I must either perish myself or deprive my enemy of the means of injuring me.   But even then my foe has been armed as well as myself, for would scorn to slay a man who had not an opportunity of defendin himself."

"Then thou refusest to earn liberty at the price I have named?" exclaimed Sir Gaston, enraged at the unexpected obstacle that had thus been thrown in his way.

"Thou hast my answer, Sir Knight," replied Black Ivan.   "Reuben Grenard, never injured me by thoughts or deed ; the world accounts him an honourable man, and I see no reason for stabbing him in the dark because he happens to have won more favour from the pretty Rebecca than thou hast been able to do."

"Fool !" exclaimed Sir Gaston, "thy hesitation might cost thee dear. Knowest thou not that thou art in my power, and that I have those about me who would not hesitate, at my bidding, to punish thy perverseness with death ?"

"Why, for that matter," answered Ivan, with cool indifference.   "I believe thou hast many about thee who would not stay for a second command to execute a deed of blood.   For instance, there is Bertrand le Noir, thy henchman—he is reckless of shedding human blood and therefore is a fit instrument for thy purpose."

"But if he should be discovered it would be known that I was the party who set him to do the deed ?"

"True, but that is no reason why I should rob a fellow creature of life.   In truth, I have made up my mind to remain a prisoner here rather than obey your commands."

"Have your wish then," exclaimed Sir Gaston, preparing to leave the dungeon ; "here thou must remain a captive, and be assured that no chance exists of thy ever regaining thy liberty."

"Stay," cried the robber, as he saw the knight was about to leave him ; "my wrists are galled with these manacles with which they are encircled—relieve me of them, Sir Knight, and I will learn to bear the rest of my punishment without repining."

"'Tis done," answered the Templar, "to add to thy security."

"But the chain round my body is sufficient to do that," replied Ivan; "release me of these, I again implore, and I will ask no other favour at thy hands."

Sir Gaston looked at the massive fetters that bound the prisoner to the wall of his dungeon, and fancying him sufficiently secured by them, he took a small key from his girdle, and at once removed the manacles from the wrists of his captive.   As he did this, however, Black Ivan, with a loud cry of triumph, rushed upon him, and ere the knight could avoid the danger, he was grasped firmly in the arms of his antagonist, and then, after a short but severe struggle, was dashed with terrific violence to the ground.   It was at this moment, and whilst the knight was still stunned with the force of the blow, that Ivan contrived to possess himself of the remaining keys, and then unfastening the iron girdle which encircled his 'waist, he snatched up the lamp and rushed out of the dungeon, leaving Sir Gaston still lying insensible on the ground.

CHAPTER XII.

"Speed, Malise, speed ! such cause of haste
  Thine active sinews never braced."— LADY OF THE LAKE.

REGARDLESS of all, save the liberty he was resolved upon attaining, Black Ivan proceeded rapidly through a long chain of low, winding passages that, from their extreme length, seemed interminable. Guided however, by the feeble rays of the light with which he had provided himself, he dashed recklessly forward, determined in his own mind to escape from the castle or perish in the attempt. But the further he penetrated the mazes with which he was surrounded, the more hopeless seemed the task he had undertaken, for each dungeon had been constructed with peculiar care to prevent the possibility of a prisoner's escape, for the single window with which each was provided, had been strongly secured with iron bars, placed both within and without the thickness of the walls, so that had he succeeded in removing one of these barriers, another still remained bidding defiance to his utmost strength. The doors, too, were of immense substance, and the fastenings with which they had been secured were of such an enormous size, as to render all chance of escape through any of them utterly hopeless. Thus situated, he was compelled to continue his way along the subterranean pasages which, as if to increase his difficulties, branched out in so many directions as completely to bewilder him.

Black Ivan had been placed in many a dangerous position before, but his soul had always scorned to yield even in the most pressing exigencies; now, however, he bitterly cursed the fate that kept him in the power of a hated enemy. He knew that a certain and ignominious doom awaited him unless he could find some mode of egress from the castle, and this thought urged him to renewed exertions even though the possibility of escape seemed to be growing less and less the farther he advanced in his way through the gloomy vaults amidst which he had lost his way.

At length, turning through a small low door he found himself in a dungeon larger and of much greater height than any which he had yet seen, and on the opposite side of which was another entrance which seemed to connect it with an extensive chain of dungeons that had apparently been used as prisons for the unfortunate at no very distant period. In one was a chair and table, both of which were lying overturned upon the ground, as if left there after some fearful struggle that had taken place between the wretched captive and the fierce ruffians who had been sent to take him to his doom.

As the fugitive held down the light to look upon this silent narrative of a crime that had been perpetrated upon the very spot where he stood, a sparkling object upon the ground caught his sight and, stretching forth his hand to ascertain what it was, he grasped a sword which had no doubt fallen from the hold of one of the ruffians who had been sent to execute the murderous design against a helpless captive. Be that as it might, the robber seized the weapon with a cry of satisfaction, and for the first time since his escape, he felt secure against the attacks of any who might be sent in pursuit of him.

At that moment his attention was arrested by hearing voices at no great distance, and looking back in the direction from whence he had come, he saw the glare of torches, and presently afterwards, three men were seen making their way along the passages as if in pursuit of him. In this dilemma he placed his own lamp in such a situation as to prevent its serving as a beacon to his enemies, and then grasping his sword yet more firmly, he stood prepared to defend himself to the very last, resolving to sell his life dearly, or overcome those who might attempt to frustrate his projected escape. But fortunately his pursuers took another turning that led them in a direction exactly opposite to the one that would have conducted them to the spot where stood the person of whom they were in search.

Breathing more freely, Ivan now continued his way, and having proceeded some distance further, he entered a dungeon, the roof of which was so low as to prevent his walking upright, though, with respect to extent, it appeared to be larger than any through which he had yet passed. Undaunted by difficulties, he proceeded onwards to the opposite side, where, contrary to his expectations, he found there was no doorway, by which to continue his search after liberty. This seemed a death blow to all his hopes of liberty; further progress seemed to be entirely cut off, and the only alternative that remained, was that of returning to the passage from whence he had branched off, and there seek some other track that might lead him from the gloomy dungeons in which he was imprisoned.

Yet in doing this, new dangers awaited him, that must be avoided if possible. There was every certainty of meeting the knights' retainers that had been sent in search of him, and wearied as he was with the exertion he had already undergone, he could hardly expect to cope against the superior strength of three against one. To remain where he was would be equally impracticable, for the close air of the low dungeon was already oppressive to him, and by remaining much longer in the place he must fall a victim to the poisonous atmosphere, thus pent up and confined within its narrow limits.

Thus reduced to the utmost extremity, Ivan hurried round the dungeon, carefully examining the walls to see whether there was no other place of exit than the one by which he had so lately come. Nor were his efforts long unavailing, for, to his great joy, he presently discovered a small door, so much decayed, that by the exertion of all his remaining strength he was enabled to force it open and thus gain access to another much more larger chamber than the one he was so anxious to escape from.

And now occurred fresh cause for trepidation, for at the moment when he forced open the door, he was startled by a loud and piercing shriek, as if proceeding from the chamber immediately above him. The voice was evidently that of a female, and so far he had nothing to apprehend, but he feared lest the outcry should have been overheard by those who had been sent in search of him and thus lead his enemies to the very spot where he was to be found.

In this extremity nothing remained for him to do but to make the best of his way from the place with all speed, and in furtherance of this design he hastened through the opening he had made, and immediately afterwards found himself in a subterranean apartment of vast extent, well lighted by numerous apertures, near the roof, all of which were carefully secured with iron stauncheons to prevent the possibility of escape by their means. Somewhat inspirited by this change, Black Ivan renewed his search and with little trouble, found, in one of the angles, a small portal which opened at the bottom of a flight of winding stone steps, up which he proceeded, and on gaining the summit he found, to his great joy, another door standing partly open, and which led into the court-yard near the outer gate of the castle.

Gratified at the prospect of escape that now opened to him, the fugitive now ventured to look round him, in order to ascertain the chances of getting clear off without fear of interruption. The entrance gate, he could see, was closed, but a small wicket remained open, and only a single sentinel was left to guard the place by which, with little difficulty, he might once more set himself at liberty.

This the robber determined to do at every hazard, but just as he was about to make a sudden spring upon the man who had charge of the entry, his thoughts recurred to the scream he had heard in the dungeon, and thinking it might perhaps be the Hebrew Maiden, whose voice had thus broken upon his ear, he determined to retrace his steps, and, if possible, make her the companion of his flight. No sooner, then, had this thought struck him, than hastening down the flight of steps, he once more returned to the dungeon he had just left, and from thence pursued his way to the vault which was beneath the apartment from whence the scream seemed to have proceeded. Upon his arrival there, he carefully examined the roof by means of the light he still carried, and having for some time diligently searched without any good effect, he at last perceived a trap door, which evidently communicated between the place where he was and the chamber immediately above. Inspired with hope by this sight he was about to force it open by main strength, but at that moment he heard the voice of Rebecca, and then pausing for a moment, he stood listening to a conversation that was then taking place between our heroine and her female attendant.

CHAPTER XIII.

" Away! away! the covey's fled the cover,
Put forth the dogs, and let the falcon fly—
I'll pend some leisure in the keen pursuit,
Nor longer waste my hours in sluggish quiet."

ANON.

WHEN Sir Gaston de Neville fled immediately after the mysterious disappearance of the armed apparition, he left, as we have previously observed, our heroine in a state of temporary insensibilty, from the terror she had experienced at the horrible sight that had met her view. Fortunately, however, Edith had been immediately sent to her assistance, and no sooner did the faithful attendant reach the apartment of her young mistress than she began to try every means in her power to restore her once more to life and consciousness. Nor were her efforts unavailing, for ere long Rebecca began to exhibit symptoms of returning consciousness, and once more opening her eyes, she gazed round her with a wild look of alarm, as if seeking some object that she dreaded tomeet. Edith observed her terror, and little guessing the real cause of her violent excitement, anxiously enquired what it was that had occasioned such painful trepidation.

" A sight, Edith, that, once seen, can never be erased from the memory," answered our heroine, sobbing convulsively, and burying her face in her hands.

" But what was it?" demanded the girl, whose curiosity was now highly excited. " It's all very well to talk in that dark, mysterious manner, but how am I ever to come at the facts, unless you condescend to be a little more explicit?"

" Let it suffice to tell thee, that I have seen that which filled my soul with agony and dread," replied Rebecca. " To tell thee more, would only serve to terrify thee, and I have myself experienced too much alarm to say aught that might fill thy soul with superstitious terrors."

" Lor', how you talk to be sure!" exclaimed Edith, half angry at the hesitation of her young mistress. " One would suppose that I was a perfect simpleton, and unfit to be trusted with a secret, that I dare say, after all, is no such great things to hear."

" Let it content thee to know," answered our heroine, " that I have within this hour, seen that which I hope never to meet with again."

" Ah !" cried the girl; " now I can guess what you mean ; you have just had an interview with Sir Gaston,—he is the terrible sight that has so much alarmed;—and to tell you the truth, I don't much wonder at it either, for he is sad fellow with the girls, as many have found to their cost."

" I have indeed seen Sir Gaston de Neville," cried Rebecca; " but even he,—bad as he is,—was not the worst sight that met my startled vision, a few minutes since. I have been visited by an unearthly guest,—aye, girl, by one whose presence was too terrible, even for the more iron nerves of your haughty lord."

" Gracious goodness !" cried Edith, " why you don't mean to say that you have seen a—a—a—what-d'ye-call-it ?"

" I see you guess my meaning, Edith, answered Rebecca. " Your faultering tongue tells me I need explain myself no further, and now all I ask of you is to keep the secret to yourself, and on no account, to whisper even the slightest hint of what I have somewhat foolishly betrayed."

" Oh, I'll be as mum as a mouse, depend on it," replied Edith. " I'm a famous one to keep a secret, only I wish you would just allow me to tell it to old deaf Mabel, because, poor soul! she tells me every thing she knows."

" As you would retain my favour," speak not a word of it to a single soul," exclaimed our heroine. " In truth I begin to think it must have been some strange delusion of my brain, since how else can I account for that which I have always laughed at as being the result of ignorance and superstition combined together."

" I don't know how you can account for it," answered Edith, " but whether it may be owing to ignorance and superstition or not, all I can say about it is, that a great many other people in the world believe in such things, and why should not I ? I'm sure I have heard my old grandmother tell such stories about ghosts and hobgoblins, that—Oh! mercy upon me ? — what was that ? — Something moved behind the tapestry, I am certain !"

" Nonsense, Edith !" exclaimed the Hebrew Maiden, half alarmed at the terrors of her companion. " I heard no other voice than that occasioned by the wind as it rustles through the arras."

" And was that all, do you think, ma'am ?" asked the girl, looking timidly around as dreading lest she might see some terrible object standing before her.

" Nay, I am sure it was all," answered Rebecca. " My folly in relating my own terrors has inspired you with dread, and now every trifling sound you hear is magnified into something very terrible. So come, Edith, let us change the conversation, and thus seek to turn our thoughts into a more cheerful channel."

" Oh, ma'am !" cried Edith, " it's all very fine to talk, but how do you suppose I can be cheerful when you have just now acknowledged seeing something that—that—"

" That was purely imaginary, perhaps," interrupted Rebecca. " At any rate I am willing to believe that the whole was a mere deception, and that I have been frightened without any real cause for it. Such, at least, is my present opinion, and I would fain persuade you to adopt a simular notion."

" But I tell you I can't do any such thing, ma'am," cried Edith, growing more and more alarmed. This horrible old castle is haunted by evil spirits, I know; there are all sorts of hobgoblins roaming and rambling

about it, just to frighten honest poor creatures like us out of our wits, and I know it will be the death of me if I stay here much longer."

"Peace, Edith, I entreat," exclaimed our heroine; "this folly is, I am aware, caused by my own want of discretion. I ought to have known your weakness, and avoided saying anything about my own groundless terrors."

"Ah!" cried the girl, "now you want to turn it off, and make me believe there was nothing in it; though, when I came into the room, you had fainted away as dead as a door nail, and the first thing you did on recovering, was to look round the place, as if expecting to see the same horrible sight that had before sent you into fits. Nay, you acknowledged as much at first, and yet now you want to persuade me that there is no such things as ghosts and hobgoblins."

"I merely wish to persuade you against giving way to a parcel of idle fears and fancies," answered Rebecca. "You are aware that Sir Gaston de Neville left me just before you came to my assistance, and his conduct it was that took the effect upon me which you just now witnessed."

"The wicked fellow!" exclaimed the girl. "He is enough to frighten any decent female out of her senses, and, for my own part, I only wonder he has not got his deserts from some of them before now. He ought to have his face well scratched;—aye, and he should have it too, if he only dared to speak improperly to me."

"And you would have me serve him so as well?"

"Most assuredly I would."

"Alas!" cried Rebecca, "you forget how helpless I am rendered. He has made me a prisoner in his castle, and both my father and my lover are in his power. With a word,—false though that word may be, —he could bring them under the displeasure of the king, and ruin,— nay, even death itself, might be the consequence."

" Well," exclaimed Edith, "Sir Gaston is a great villain I know, but if he would destroy a whole family merely out of revenge, I should say he is a greater monster than I thought him."

"He has taunted me that it is in his power to do so," answered Rebecca. "Like a fiend triumphing over a victim, he exults in the ruin he can bring upon an old and helpless man, and as if to add to my other pangs, he tells me that it is in my power to save a father from destruction! It was a sore trial, Edith, and yet I treated his base proposition in a manner it so justly merited."

"Is there no vengeance in heaven for so great a villain?" cried Edith, with indignation.

"There is, and it will yet light upon him," replied the Jewess. "Nay, more, the hour of retribution draws nigh, when he shall be made to feel the bitterness of adversity, even as he hath made others endure it before him. The king shall learn the baseness of his unworthy subject, and if the world speaks truly of Richard, he will not fail to punish this false knight even to the utmost of his deserts."

"And I shall be one to rejoice at it," cried Edith, "but for all that, I have not forgot all about the apparition you saw just now,—so tell me what it was like, and——"

At this moment a loud voice was heard, apparently underneath the apartment in which they were sitting, which so alarmed them both, that uttering a loud shriek of terror, they rose from their seats, and were making towards the door, when Bertrand le Noir suddenly entered the chamber.

"How now!" he exclaimed, sullenly, "what means that scream I heard just now?"

"It means nothing at all, good Bertrand," replied the terrified Edith, —"the—the—the fact is we just this minute heard a most unaccountable noise, and thinking that it must be a spirit, or something of that sort, we couldn't help making a noise—indeed we couldn't."

"Faugh! this is some more of your folly, girl," exclaimed the ruffian, angrily. "Your conscience is perhaps a little bit uneasy, and the least sound makes you imagine the devil is coming to carry you off in a flame of fire."

"I never had the pleasure of seeing the *gentleman* you have named till now," said Edith, glancing slyly at Bertrand.

"Humph!" growled the other, "and that I suppose you intend to pass as a bit of tolerable wit."

"I didn't intend anything of the sort," replied the girl, "for to tell you the truth, all the wits I happen to possess were frightened away as soon as ever you put your face inside that door."

"Come, come, this will not do, wench," exclaimed Bertrand. "I have been sent to see that you quit this chamber immediately. Black Ivan has somehow contrived to escape from his cell, and Sir Gaston is coming here in no very good humour I promise you."

"Has Black Ivan escaped?" cried Rebecca, with surprise.

"Why, he has not exactly escaped, young lady," answered the man, "because we feel pretty certain that he must be wandering somewhere among the vaults below, where he must soon again fall into our hands. He has made a desperate attempt though, which, instead of doing him any good, will teach us to look after him more carefully for the future."

"Are you sure he has not escaped from the castle?" asked Rebecca, eagerly.

"Quite certain," replied Bertrand le Noir; "he must now be wandering about the passages and dungeons beneath, and as two or three parties have been despatched, there's no doubt he will be safely lodged again before long."

"Well," cried Edith, "all I hope is that he may contrive to disappoint you all; for I am sure there is no place for any body to stay in by their own choice, and I dare say if Sir Gaston should happen to get hold of him again, the poor wretch will be put out of the way with as much dispatch as possible."

"Indeed!" muttered Bertrand, "and who, pray, do you suppose, would be guilty of so foul a crime as murder?"

"*Yourself*, as likely as any body," answered Edith, fearlessly.

"This insolence, girl, will not serve you," cried Bertrand. "So come, follow me from this room, or Sir Gaston will arrive before I have performed the duty I was sent to execute."

It would have been in vain for Edith to resist a command like this, and having entreated Rebecca to bear up with what fortitude she could against the oppression of a heartless tyrant, she followed Bertrand le Noir, leaving our heroine to reflect in solitude on the events which had thus placed her in the power of Sir Gaston de Neville.

Left to herself, Rebecca now became a prey to the terrors inspired by the expected visit of her cruel persecutor. She dreaded his coming as that of some fiend, that was about to claim his helpless victim; but again she remembered the poniard, with which she was still armed, and offering up a prayer to heaven for firmness, she resolved to sacrifice her own life, rather than fall beneath the insidious art of a villain.

As Rebecca rose from her knees, she was startled by hearing a slight noise close by, and the next instant a trap door, in the midst of her chamber, was violently thrown up, and the form of Black Ivan was seen slowly emerging from the vault beneath. Terrified at this unexpected meeting with the robber, she was about to retreat towards the door, but ere she could do so, Ivan had grasped her arm, and drawing her towards the place from whence he had effected his entrance, he whispered:—

"As thou wouldst save thyself, speak not a word above thy breath. I am here to rescue thee, Rebecca, and it will be thine own fault, if another half hour sees thee in the castle of thy vile betrayer."

"Alas!" cried Rebecca, "what confidence can I place in the word of a robber and an outlaw?"

"The robber and the outlaw, as thou callest him," answered Ivan, "can, at least, boast of more honour, than he who has made thee his prisoner. From beneath thy chamber I heard what passed between thee and Bertrand le Noir. It seems the knight will be here presently, and I ask to whom wilt thou rather trust thyself—to Black Ivan, or Sir Gaston de Neville?"

"In either case," answered Rebecca, "I am in fearful peril;—and yet if thou wilt give thy word to deliver me safely into the hands of my father, I will rely upon thy honour, rather than again meet that fearful man, whose perfidy I have seen so much reason to dread. Say then, have I thy promise that thou wilt immediately convey me from hence to the house from whence I have been so ruthlessly torn?"

"Wouldst thou make terms, with me when I offer thee liberty?" demanded Black Ivan, impatiently.

"I would, for therein is my only chance of safety."

"Nay, thou doest me an injustice, girl. I war against the purses of the rich, but a helpless woman shall ever find a protector in Black Ivan, the Outlaw."

" Be it as thou hast said," answered Rebecca. " Thus circumstanced I have no choice left, for either I must follow thee, or become the hopeless slave of the recreant knight, into whose hands I have fallen. Such is my fate, and therefore do I accept that which I believe to be the least evil of the two."

" Sir Gaston de Neville shall yet answer for his evil deeds towards both of us," whispered Black Ivan, fiercely. " Hitherto, the triumph hath been his, but perhaps the next time we chance to meet, fortune will not desert me as she did on the last occasion. I have been his captive, Rebecca ; the horrors of torture even were preparing, by which he might rack my limbs to agony, but ere long the foe he hath raised up against himself, may amply secure that revenge for which his soul eagerly thirsts. Yes, girl, I have sworn to vengeance, and seldom has Ivan failed in executing his projects, even though he may sometimes have waited for years, ere the moment of his triumph arrived."

" Nay, let me intreat you to begone," cried Rebecca. " Each moment that is lost may be invaluable to us. Sir Gaston has sent people out in quest of you, and there is but too much reason to dread they will be successful."

" I have made my escape sure, or I would not now be wasting moments that might be precious to us," answered the robber. " Already I have traversed the whole of the vaults beneath this castle, and with much labour and difficulty, have succeeded in discovering a free outlet from our prison."

" Still," cried our heroine, " we may be seen by some of the many retainers belonging to Sir Gaston de Neville. In that case our escape would be frustrated, and our fates rendered utterly hopeless."

" All that I have ascertained," answered Black Ivan ; " the principal gate is at present guarded by a single soldier,—I am armed as you see, and death to the fool if he dares interrupt our progress. So come, Rebecca, rely firmly upon me, and you will yet escape the base design of this most treacherous villain."

At this moment the footsteps of Sir Gaston were heard approaching, upon which Ivan sprang from the side of Rebecca, and ere the knight had gained admittance, the door of the apartment was securely fastened against him, and in defiance of the threats vociferated by Sir Gaston, they descended into the vault beneath, and having secured the trap-door, the brigand led his trembling charge to the flight of steps that were to lead them once more to liberty.

Agitated by a thousand fears, lest the project should fail, Rebecca paused at the entrance of the court-yard, unwilling to run the risk of being intercepted in the meditated escape, by which she would throw herself more than ever into the power of her ruthless enemy. But Ivan guessed the cause of her alarm, and whispering a few hurried words in her ear, he entreated her to summon all her fortitude for the few moments that were necessary to get them clear through the gate. Rebecca yielded to him as well as she could, and, scarcely had she acquiesced than, taking advantage of the sentinel's back being turned towards them, Ivan darted upon him with the speed of an arrow, and ere any resistance could be offered, the guard was completely mastered, and at the mercy of his antagonist. To gag and bind him was but the work of a minute, and no sooner was this done, than, returning to the place where he had left our heroine, he snatched her up in his arms, and rushed through the still open portal before any assistance could arrive to prevent the daring act that was to procure an escape for the two prisoners. This effected, Ivan flew, with Rebecca in his arms, towards a clump of trees that stood at no great distance off, and where he expected to find a small party of his men ready to protect him in case of an immediate pursuit. Nor were his hopes in this respect disappointed, for as they approached the spot, several of the robbers, with two spare horses, rode forth to meet them; when, Rebecca being mounted on one of the steeds, and Ivan on the other, they took their departure at a rapid rate, though not before they had been assured that their escape had been discovered and that a number of the knight's retainers we in full pursuit of them.

Thus threatened with danger by a party that would most likely prove too much for them in case of an engagement taking place between them, the robbers and their female companion dashed onwards with all possible speed, and leaving London behind them they had soon so far outstripped their pursuers, as no longer to feel any anxiety with regard to the superior numbers by which they had just been threatened.

It was in vain that Rebecca entreated to be informed whither they were conveyed; the robbers maintained a strict silence in spite of her earnest entreaties, and at length her worst fears were fearfully reallized by finding herself at the entrance of the robber's cave. With a feeling of intense horror, our unfortunate heroine now foresaw the doom for which she had been reserved; still, however, she tried the effect of tears and remonstrances at the cruel deception that had been practised upon her, but Ivan was immoveable, and on a signal being given by the chief, she was borne shrieking into the principal apartment of the brigand's cave.

CHAPTER XIV.

" 'Torn from the friends she loves,—lone, desolate,
    And lost to every hope, the maiden stands
    'Midst those whose crimes have rendered them the mark
    For good men's scorn and execration."

THE REPROBATE.

UPON being carried into the cave, Rebecca soon found herself in a spacious apartment, the walls of which appeared to have been hewed out of the solid rock, whilst the inequalities of the flooring was, in some degree, obviated by a vast quantity of rushes which had been strewed over it, answering the same purpose as a carpet in these more luxurious days. In the centre of the apartment stood a long oaken table, upon which remained cup and trenchers, whilst all around were strewed empty wine flaggons, denoting the wild scene of riot and debauchery of which this place had been the scene on the preceding night. From the roof hung three lamps, by means of which the otherwise darksome place was illuminated by day as well as night.

For some cause or other, Rebecca had been left entirely to herself, almost as soon as she had been conveyed to this dreary chamber. Even Black Ivan himself had disappeared after whispering his commands to the lieutenant, that a strict watch was to be kept in the entrance passage to the cave, in order to prevent the escape of our heroine.

Thus left to herself, the Hebrew Maiden gave way to those tears and heart-felt sufferings with which she was oppressed. She now saw the full extent of her sufferings, looking forward with dread to the life she was doomed to pass in this horrible abode, and devising a thousand wild and impracticable shemes to release herself from the captivity into which she had thus unhappily fallen. But even frantic as she was at the thought of her present afflictions, those schemes, one by one failed her, and when at length she felt convinced that all hope had failed her, she made up her mind to seek death by an act of violence rather than become the mistress of a man whose many crimes had brought upon him the sentence of outlawry. This thought—terrible as it would have been at any other time—afforded her some consolation amidst the mis. fortunes that so heavily pressed upon her, and having ascertained that she still bore about her the concealed poniard, she sank upon her knees and fervently entreated pardon of heaven in case she should be compelled to put this last fearful resolution into effect.

Wholly occupied in her own solemn reflections, Rebecca was not conscious of the approach of a visitor until a slight touch of the arm roused her from these meditations, and then starting from her knees she beheld an aged female whose countenance—wrinkled and careworn as it was—seemed not wholly destitute of kindness and humanity. Taken by surprise, Rebecca's first impulse was to fly, but as she was about to hurry from the chamber, the old woman gently seized her arm, saying in ac. cents of pity :—

"Stay, dear young lady—stay, I implore you. In me you behold no enemy, but rather one who would cheerfully lay down the brief remnant of a miserable existence to serve you."

"Canst thou release me from this dreadful place?" demanded Re. becca; "say but thou canst do that, and I will myself become a beggar to enrich thee."

"Patience, sweet maiden, and hear me," answered the old woman.— "That which thou hast asked passes my power to accomplish. Hither thou hast been brought by Black Ivan, and the vigilance of the guards he has set over thee, will defeat any attempt that may be made to escape from the cavern."

"Cruel doom!" sighed Rebecca; "thou wouldst have me understand then that there is no hope?"

"None whatever," replied Maud, for such was the old woman's name. "Fifty stout followers own the sway of Black Ivan, and well do they all know that the escape of a prisoner would be followed by the instant death of him who suffered it."

"Alas!" cried Rebecca; "is there not one among them who would aid my escape on the certainty of receiving a large reward from the hands of my father?"

"I fear there is not one who would risk the fierce wrath of his leader even for the riches of a monarch," answered Maud. "The vengeance of Black Ivan is like the sweeping of an impetuous hurricane—every thing falls beneath it, and no inducement would prevail upon any of the band to provoke a doom that would be certain to follow the discovery of their perfidy."

"Then," exclaimed the Jewess, "it must be attempted without the as. sistance I would have sought."

"To do so would be madness," answered Maud; "the entrance is strongly guarded by men upon whom the greatest reliance can be placed, and the attempt—ending as it must in defeat— would only subject you to the deadly rage of your persecutor."

"Am I then to understand," cried Rebecca, "that there is no hope for me; that I am doomed to pass the remainder of my days in wretched. ness and captivity?"

"Such, lady," replied the old woman, "is, I fear, the only prospect that is before you. Once within this place, and the world has closed upon you for ever!"

"But," exclaimed Rebecca, "it may remain with myself to say how long my enemy shall triumph in the captivity of his victim. He hath succeeded, it is true, in forcing me to this den of crime, but my own hands may yet save me from the foul dishonour he meditates."

"Girl! girl!" cried Maud, "thy speech grows wild and fearful; thou wouldst make me believe that with thine own hands thou wouldst rush unbidden into the presence of thy Maker."

"Fear may make even the most timid desperate," exclaimed our heroine, firmly. "In a moment of calmness I should shudder at such a thought, but the threats and exultations of that man would serve to banish all other considerations from my mind, save that of preserving myself from the dishonour he so basely meditates. Here I stand alone and unprotected, for even those who could serve me will shrink from the dreaded vengeance of their imperious master."

"I would that it were in my power to aid thee," answered Maud, compassionately. "My heart bleeds to behold thy sufferings, and yet one, aged and infirm as myself, cannot hope to rescue the victim from the snares of her betrayer."

"Is there no other entrance to the cavern, besides the one by which I was conducted hither?" asked Rebecca.

"None that I have ever seen or heard of."

"Does the whole of the band ever leave the place at once?"

"Never on any occasion since I have been here. Six, at least, are always left behind in case any surprise should be attempted by those who are always anxious to overthrow a horde of robbers whose deeds have brought upon themselves the enmity of all peaceful men."

"And yet," replied Rebecca, "six appears to be very few in the event of an attack being made by a strong body."

"It would be enough to repel any force that might be sent against them," answered Maud. "The entrance to the cave has been so constructed as to give every possible advantage to the besieged; and, desperate as the brigands are, they would never yield whilst life or strength remained to bid defiance to their enemies."

"Then I am indeed lost!" sighed Rebecca, in the agony of despair. "Removed from those who would gladly protect me with their lives, the only alternative that remains is to meet that death which can alone preserve me from the arts of this hated villain!"

"Be not rash, I beseech thee, young maiden," exclaimed Maud, earnestly. "The innocent will not be forsaken by heaven, and even in this moment of trial there may be some hope which at present thou dost not see."

"True," answered Rebecca, "thou hast counselled me well, old woman, and, bearing thy words in remembrance, I will not seek death until all chance of succour has completely failed me. Ivan's heart may yet be turned to pity towards the helpless girl he would have betrayed; he may not be deaf to the prayers and entreaties of one who never injured him."

"Be resolute, and he will respect thy firmness," exclaimed Maud. "At all events thou mayst reckon me as a friend, though much I fear the aid of one so aged as myself would avail thee little among the fierce and lawless men by whom we are surrounded."

"Heaven's blessings be upon thee for the pity thou hast shown for one who so much needs it!" cried the Jewess, fervently.

"Alas!" exclaimed Maud, "the scenes I have witnessed in this abode of infamy, have been enough to render my heart callous to all the better feelings of humanity. Thy beauty and innocence have, however, excited my pity and respect, and even though my own life should be the forfeit, I will yet throw myself between thee and danger."

"Thanks!—a thousand thanks for thy good offices," exclaimed Rebecca, overcome by the tender commisseration of the old woman; and then suddenly overcoming her agitation, she enquired of Maud how long she had been an inmate of the robbe 's cave.

"Eight-and-twenty years come next Hallowmass eve," answered the other. "It has been a weary time of captivity, but use hath now somewhat reconciled me to the life, so that all wish to leave it hath now fled for ever."

"Do I hear aright?" cried Rebecca, with surprise. "Has crime grown so familiar to thee, that thou carest not to quit this scene for the world from which thou hast been severed?"

"Alas! maiden, what have I to do with a world where all around would prove my loneliness and desolation?" asked the old woman, mournfully. "Those whom I loved are dead or far removed from the spot that was once dear to me. Strangers dwell beneath the roof where my happiest years were passed, and I should live neglected and despised by those who would know the lawless society in which so long a period of my existence has been passed."

"Thou judgest harshly of mankind," exclaimed Rebecca; "some, it is true, may prove harsh and unjust towards thee, but there are others who would pity the misfortunes in which thou hast been involved by a hapless fate."

"I would not try them, maiden," answered the old woman. "My days are drawing to a close, and here I am willing to remain until death closes my earthly pilgrimage for ever."

"Is it possible," exclaimed the Jewess, "that thou canst choose a destiny I so much shudder at?"

"Aye," answered Maud, "but thy situation and mine are widely different. Thou art young and full of hopes—hast friends too whom thou lovest, and a home for which thy heart yearneth. I have none of these, and therefore it matters little where the brief remainder of my days may be passed."

"Would that I were far from hence!" sighed Rebecca; "to quit this place I would cheerfully resign all that wealth which I have reason to believe will one day be mine—aye, even though it should compel me to become a wandering mendicant, begging from door to door a morsel of bread to sustain a lingering existence."

"Truly, my heart bleeds for thee," exclaimed Maud, in a tone of compassion. "I know the agony that must torture thy young soul, and yet cannot offer thee the consolation of hope. Once within this place, thou art here for ever—the doomed victim of a man ruthless by nature, and without compassion for the sufferings of others."

"Nay," cried Rebecca, with firmness, "obdurate as this Ivan is, he shall yet be baulked of the prey he has thus dared to seize upon. Here I will not remain a prisoner since it is in my own power to seek that haven of rest to which he cannot follow me."

"Oh! speak not thus, maiden, I implore thee," eagerly exclaimed the elder female. "It grieves me to hear thee speak thus, for the calm resolution with which thou utterest that threat assures me thou wilt not hesitate to strike the blow which will lay that fair form mangled and bleeding at the feet of thy persecutor."

"Thou hast judged me rightly, Maud; death, even by my own hand, before dishonour!"

"Oh, be not rash, dear girl, I implore you," cried Maud;—"Ivan loves, and therefore may not be so cruel as your fears anticipate. He will offer you honourable marriage, and it therefore remains with yourself to accept or reject the proposal he will make."

"Become the willing bride of a robber—outcast,—never!" exclaimed Rebecca, with sudden resolution. "Sooner would I perish by the most horrid tortures, than link my destinies with one whom I execrate and abhor!"

"And yet," cried Black Ivan, who at that moment abruptly entered the chamber, "the gentle Rebecca may find her advantage in coming to a different conclusion. Here she is not at present exactly her own mistress, though it will be her own fault if she is not, ere long, the happy wife of him who loves her to distraction."

Rebecca turned a look of withering scorn upon the robber as he uttered these words, but Ivan was unabashed by this manifestation of her hatred, and motioning for Maud to withdraw, he exclaimed :—

"It is in vain, Rebecca, that you thus scorn the addresses of one who knows his own power, and will, if need be, exert it."

"Why am I thus to be persecuted by the man who of all others I loathe and detest?" asked the maiden, unawed by the robber's presence. "You have taken a foul advantage to bring me hither, and I now appeal to you, by all your hopes of mercy from above, to restore me to that father whose life perhaps depends upon my speedy return."

"Psha!", cried the brigand, "what care I for the life of an old man, who would doubtless procure my immediate punishment, if he had it in his power to do so? I have ever hated him, girl, and he may thank the

No. 9

love I bore his daughter, that he has not ere now fallen into the hands of one from whom he would have experienced no mercy."

"Villain!" exclaimed Rebecca, "ruthless as thou art, thou durst not injure the grey hairs of one who never did thee harm."

"If I am the villain thou callest me, what is to hinder thy father becoming a sacrifice for his child's perverseness?" demanded Black Ivan. "Is it not through him that thou hatest me, and might I not well revenge myself upon him for the evil service he has done me?"

"Leave me!—leave me!" cried the Jewess, in a paroxysm of agony;—"begone monster, and do not tempt me to call down the vengeance of offended heaven upon thy recreant head!"

"Bah!" growled Black Ivan, "all these heroics will not serve either thee or thy father. Thou art in my power, girl, and the old man is not so far off, but that he is yet within reach of my poniard."

"Mercy!—mercy!" shrieked the horrified maiden.

"Mercy!" reiterated Ivan, with scorn;—"and what mercy I prithee dost thou ask of thy captor?"

"Death for myself;—life for my poor, old afflicted father!"

"Ha! ha! ha!" vociferated the robber, with exultation;—"dost thou condescend to ask thus much of me?"

"On my knees I implore it!" cried Rebecca, throwing herself at the feet of the outlaw. "Grant my earnest prayer, Ivan—say but you will spare my father's life, and I will become thy slave for ever!"

"Wilt thou become my wife, girl?"

"Never!—never!"

"Then force shall drag thee to the altar!" he replied. "Remember thou art here helpless and alone;—I give thee the choice of becoming my bride or my mistress, and now do I wait the decision upon which rests thy future destiny."

"Be not thus precipitate," cried Rebecca, "and I will endeavour to think over the proposals you have made."

"Hah!" returned Ivan, with a bitter sneer;—"you want to frame some device for your escape. But be assured that all hope of rescue is vain;—two offers have I made you, and one of them must be instantly accepted."

"I ask but time," cried our heroine, despairingly;—"grant me but a brief space, and I will reply to thee."

"Nay," roared Black Ivan, fiercely, "it is not thus thou wouldst have answered Reuben Grenard. Had he stood whining forth his love-sick nonsense in thine ear, thou woulds't have replied to him without delay."

"Reuben Grenard is the accepted lover of my heart's choice," answered our heroine, earnestly. "We have been playmates from our earliest infancy;—his religion is that of my father's, who have so long withstood the cruel persecutions of those who would trample our people into the very dirt. I acknowledge my love for Reuben Grenard, and sooner will I perish than give my hand to any other than him."

"Indeed!" muttered the robber;—"'tis well thou hast so much resolution Rebecca, for thine obstinacy promises to bring upon thee persecutions and trials that thou little dreamest of."

"All shall be borne with fortitude," answered the maiden, "for rather can I endure thy tyranny, than the reflection of having been false to those vows I have given to Reuben."

"Yet even he," returned Ivan, "is not safe whilst thou art obstinate. With ease I can make him captive as well as thyself, and thou wouldst perhaps in that case have the affliction of seeing him perish before thine eyes."

"Robber!—villain!" exclaimed Rebecca, retreating from him with horror; "dost thou not expect the avenging fires of heaven to lay thee low for crimes like thine? Can thy heart,—black as it is, prompt thee to the commission of deeds such as even fiends would shrink from?"

"Thou seest that I am unmoved," answered Ivan, with cool indifference;—"long have I been used to deeds that most men would shudder at, and it is hardly to be expected that my soul would quail at shedding the blood of one who I regard as a hated rival."

"Thine own heart might prompt thee to the evil deed," replied Rebecca, "yet is there one above all to shield the innocent from the foul deeds of the assassin."

"There thou speakest to me of matters that I rarely think of," exclaimed Ivan. "And yet, girl, I am not quite the hardened villain thou takest me for. I have been offered a bribe to slay thy lover, but rejected the terms, because I knew not then that thou wouldst refuse to become my bride."

"Alas!" cried the Jewess, "what other enemy have I who would thus seek the death of one I so dearly love?"

"Sir Gaston de Neville," answered the robber.

"Sir Gaston de Neville!—and yet I might have expected it," sighed Rebecca, "since he, like thyself, is reckless of blood whenever his own interest requires that it should be shed."

"He professes to love thee," answered the robber, "and wishing to get rid of his rival, he offered me both liberty and gold on condition that I would take the life of Reuben Grenard. I, however, rejected his terms, and the youth might yet have lived in safety, had not thine own obstinacy brought upon him the wrath of Black Ivan, the outlaw."

"If one spark of human feeling yet remains in thy bosom, I intreat thee to spare him!" cried Rebecca, driven almost to madness by the danger with which her lover was threatened. "Remember, Ivan, he hath never injured thee either in word or deed."

"I tell thee, girl, he hath," answered the robber, sternly; "has he not deprived me of thy love?—Thou knowest he hath, and for that he dies!"

"No,—no,—indeed,—indeed, he has not!" exclaimed the Hebrew Maiden, half frantic with her terrors. "Reuben is guiltless of having injured thee, for, had I never known him my heart would still have rejected thee. Spare him then, I entreat thee, and if thou wouldst have the prayers and blessings of those thou wouldst have injured, grant me that liberty of which thou wouldst unjustly deprive me."

"Rebecca!" exclaimed the brigand, "thou little knowest the fixed purpose of him to whom thou pleadest for mercy. I have been at some pains to bring thee hither, and be assured no power on earth shall ever release thee from the strong grasp of Black Ivan, the outlaw."

"Hear me, robber," cried the Jewess, with desperation;—"thou art a seeker after gold and treasures of other men. It is the only god of thine idolatry, and I now, in my father's name, promise thee whatever sum thou mayst demand as a ransom, on condition of receiving thy solemn pledge never again to seek the injury of those, who, on their part, will not do aught to place thee in peril."

"A fair offer, by Jove; but one that will not very readily be closed with!" returned Ivan. "Thy tribe, fair wench, I have often heard is famous for driving bargains, but thou hast met with one who is proof against any offer that may be made for thy liberty. Within this cave I hold thee securely, and never shalt thou depart from it with life."

"Then listen to me, Ivan," cried Rebecca, "whilst I tell thee thy plans will fail even at the moment when thou believest them to be most secure. For a time thou mayest perchance hold me in captivity, and I will even wear thy chains without complaint or reproach;—yet be assured I never will become thy bride even though thou boasteth of possessing fifty daring followers equal in villany to thyself."

" Dost thou defy my power, mad wench?"

" I do."

" 'Tis well," he replied; " for the present I will leave thee to thyself, but be assured that ere many hours have elapsed, thou wilt be dragged by main force to the altar, where I shall make thee mine for ever."

" Nay, thou shalt not!" returned Rebecca, firmly.

" Hah! am I defied?—and by a woman too!"

" Thou art, villain!" answered the Jewess. " Strong in the consciousness of right and virtue I can yet bid thee defiance!"

" Thou art a silly girl and art forgetful of my power."

" Nay, I know thy power, and scorn it!" she replied. " True, thou mayst drag me to the altar, before which I worship not, but life would no longer be of value to me, and in the desperation of despair, my own hand should rid me of a hated existence."

As Black Ivan was about to reply, one of the robbers hastily entered, and beckoning to his chieftain, withdrew him on one side and whispered in his ear a hurried message. With intense anxiety Rebecca watched them, and by the look of satisfaction that beamed in the countenance of her persecutor, she could perceive that the news he had received was highly gratifying. In an instant afterwards he dismissed the ruffian, and then approaching our heroine, he said :—

" Rebecca, thou hast defied my power, but even at this moment, when least expected, chance has given me an advantage that will serve my purpose admirably. Hear me, girl;—thy lover, Reuben Grenard, hath fallen into the hands of my men, and even now the stripling waits my further commands in another chamber ——"

Rebecca heard not the whole of this fatal intelligence ; a giddyness seized upon her brain, and with a faint cry of agony she sank senseless on the floor. At this moment Maud entered to the assistance of the captive, and having given a few directions to the old woman, Black Ivan hurried away to that part of the cavern to which he had been informed Reuben Grenard was conveyed.

CHAPTER XV.

" Where are thy countless hoards ?—
The heaps on heaps of gold of which report
Declares thou art the master ?"

ST. JOHN'S EVE.

NOTHING could exceed the rage of Sir Gaston de Neville, when he discovered the means by which he had been foiled. With violence he battered against the door, which had been fastened agianst him by Black Ivan in order to facilitate his escape, but it was not till the robber had completely succeeded in effecting his retreat, that, with the assistance of some of his retainers, he at last obtained an entrance to the chamber. Then commenced a hasty search in every place where the fugitives were likely to have found shelter, and when this proved unavailing, the knight ordered a few of his most trusty followers to accompany him, and issuing from the portal of his castle, he reached the exterior in time only to perceive that they were already mounted, and so far a-head as to bid defiance to any attempts that might be made to overtake them. Enraged at this, Sir Gaston followed them some distance, and then finding that further pursuit would be useless, he returned home, and selecting Bertrand le Noir, and three or four others to attend him, he set forth for the Jew's house, resolving to avenge himself on the old man for the escape of his daughter.

On reaching his place of destination, the door was opened by Isaac of Tadcaster, and ere the aged Israelite could well demand the cause of so unexpected a visit, he was roughly seized by Bertrand and carried to the apartment he had just left, whither he was quickly followed by Sir Gaston and those who had accompanied him. Sinking with fear, Isaac demanded the reason of his being thus surrounded and ill-used beneath the sacred roof of his own house:—

"Dog of a Jew!" exclaimed the knight, fiercely, "thou hast leagued thyself with those who have plotted their escape from my castle;— thou art in the secret, and I am resolved never to rest satisfied till thy life has been sacrificed to the rage thine own villany hath inspired."

"Sir Knight," answered Isaac, "if it is my life thou seekest, thou art welcome to it, on one condition;—spare my child, and, whenever it is thy will, rid me of an existence that is prized only whilst I can behold her in safety."

"Jew!—this hypocrisy will not save thee," cried Sir Gaston, fiercely. "Thou wouldst affect to know nothing of Rebecca's escape with the outlaw, Black Ivan."

"I would feign nothing to one I dread not," replied Isaac; "on the contrary, thou hast the name of being a recreant knight, and thou hast only to add to thy other crimes, by shortening the few remaining days of an aged man who never harmed thee. Strike, Sir Gaston, my bosom is bare before thee, and I will not shink from a blow that will rid me of thine accursed tyranny."

"Humph!" muttered the Templar, "this is the bravado of insolence, and will but serve to increase my fury against thee."

"Nay," answered Isaac, "that is impossible. Thine eye glances its deadly lightnings upon me, and yet thou seest I quail not at thy fearful presence."

"But thou mayst, old man, and that ere long," retorted the knight, stung by the cool indifference of the man he intended to intimidate. "Remember, the Christian has it in his power to crush the friendless Jew, whenever he may be inclined."

"Methinks, proud knight," exclaimed Isaac, bitterly, "inclination among thy people, is rarely wanting to hew down and crush a tribe whose only crime consists in differing with thee in religion. We have endured much from our lordly rulers, but perhaps a better period is already dawning upon us, for, if report speaks truly, Richard Cœur de Lion is above the unjust prejudices that impel his people to oppress those whom they should regard as brothers."

"Richard will be no friend to the Hebrews," cried Sir Gaston. "He knows that they have the wealth of the country in their hands, and depend on it, he will not spare those wherever their coffers are needed to be emptied for his necessities."

"Thou hast miscalculated the wealth of our people," answered Isaac. "For years they have been daily plundered by the Christian oppressors, and now there is not a Hebrew in the country, who can any longer produce that gold which your avarice would extort."

"That we will presently see," exclaimed Sir Gaston:—"report gives thee the credit of not being the poorest of thy tribe, and I therefore now demand of thee fifty purses of gold as the price of thy life, which will else become forfeited."

"Fifty purses of gold!" cried the alarmed Jew.

"Aye:—that is the sum I demand."

"Then thou hast demanded it in vain," replied Isaac, "for I am poor, and even to save my life, I could not raise a quarter of the sum thou hast named."

"Liar!" exclaimed the knight, fiercely;—"thou wouldst deceive me with false protestations of thy poverty."

"Nay, I deceive thee not," replied the Jew, earnestly. "Poverty is now become our only inheritance, for the nobles of England have basely wrung from us our gold, until we are reduced to absolute poverty and despair."

"Hah!" cried the Templar, wrathfully, "dost thou still persist in denying the possession of the sum I demand?"

"I do,—I do!—"

"Then torture shall wring from thee the confession of the hoards thou hast laid up," answered Sir Gaston. "I will try whether the dungeons beneath my castle will not change thy tone from defiance to submission!"

"Do with me as thou wilt," cried Isaac, in despair; "heap injury on injury upon thine aged victim, yet will he perish, and thou become ne'er the richer."

"But torture may effect what threats have failed in," replied Sir Gaston, doggedly. "I have, ere now, had to do with Jews, fully as perverse as thyself: men who vowed that they were as poor as Job, and yet, when the rack came to be applied, they were glad to purchase a miserable existence at whatever price I chose to put on it."

"And this thou callest Christianity!" retorted Isaac, with bitter emphasis.

"Dog!" exclaimed the knight, wrathfully, "dost thou dare cast thine irreverent sneers upon our holy faith? Hast thou forgotten the pains and penalties attached to such an offence as that thou hast just uttered?"

"I know thou canst put me to death for it," replied Isaac, unmoved at the violence of Sir Gaston; "I am moreover aware, Sir Knight, that we are expected to be dumb under all provocations, even though thou mayst be pleased to call me—'dog of a Jew!'"

"Shall I slay the prating idiot?" exclaimed Bertrand le Noir, half unsheathing his sword, and glancing inquiringly at his master, as if willing to obey his slightest command.

"Be not precipitate in thy wrath," cried Sir Gaston, with assumed calmness. "The old man has not yet, perhaps, made up his mind whether to grant or refuse the gift I have demanded at his hands; he may think better of this, and therefore, out of pure mercy, I grant him five minutes to determine whether I shall have his life, or the paltry sum of gold I have demanded."

"Dost thou call fifty purses of gold a small sum?" cried Isaac, in a tone of mingled reproach and alarm. "Such a sum would take the labour of years to amass together, and yet,—even granting I had it,—it is to be given up to the first person who thinks fit to demand it?"

"Turn Christian then," exclaimed Sir Gaston, "and thy hoards will be safe."

"Never!" cried the old man, resolutely; "seventy summers and winters have I lived in the faith of my fathers, and it is not at thy bidding, false knight, that I will turn apostate."

"Fool!—thou rejectest all terms, then?"

"I do."

"And dost thou recollect with what horrible tortures thy fellows have been destroyed; and that, too, upon the word of one, who, like me, thought fit to satiate his own revenge, and at the same time, rid the world of a man belonging to thy proscribed race?"

"I have both seen and heard much of the cruelties inflicted by one class of mankind upon another," replied Isaac. "Nay, my own father, —though standing on the very brink of the grave,—was thrown into a cauldron of boiling oil, as a punishment for the high crime of resisting the extortionate demands of a fiend, who,—like thyself,—called himself a Christian knight."

"And such a doom, Isaac, awaits thy father's son," exclaimed Sir Gaston, with a theatening scowl. "Nay, more, thy daughter shall be first re-captured, and the last moment of thy life shall be yet further tortured with the knowledge that she is once more in the power of the man ye both affect to despise."

"Thou wilt not," replied the Jew, endeavouring to assume an appearance of composure he was far from feeling, "demon as thou art, thou wilt not dare to offend high heaven with such a cruel, dastardly crime as that thou hast threatened me with!"

"And what, old man, is to hinder me?"

"Thine own terrors of future punishment," answered the Hebrew, "thou hast a soul to lose, and surely would not risk it by the commission of a crime like that."

"Psha!" cried the knight, contemptuously, "that would not be the greatest crime I have ever yet committed. Besides, I have long ceased to think of such idle terrors, which are suited only to excite alarm in the minds of the most weak and timid."

"Dost thou then dare to boast of thine infidelity?"

"At least," exclaimed the knight, endeavouring to turn the conversation into another channel, "I dare boast of having thee in my strong grasp. Thou art my prisoner, Isaac, and the slightest motion,—nay, the mere nodding of my head, is sufficient to cause a dozen daggers to be buried in thy heart."

"Give the word, Sir Gaston," whispered Bertrand le Noir, impatiently; "give but the word, I say, and the Jew shall not insult thee long with his bold speeches."

"Presently, good Bertrand, presently," answered the Templar: "I can well afford to hear his insults, since it is in my power to retaliate with tenfold vengeance."

"Of a verity, thy serving man is possessed of far more humanity than thyself," cried Isaac. "He would strike the deadly blow at once, whilst thou wouldst have me live on in torture and uncertainty."

"By the holy Virgin! thou hast afforded me a hint that is well worth the acting on," exclaimed Sir Gaston. "Death would indeed be a mercy to thee, and therefore thou shalt live on to wail and weep over the misfortunes it is my pleasure to crush thee with."

"Spare my daughter, and I will bear all without repining," cried Isaac, earnestly. "Say but that she shall be free from thy further persecutions, and I will endure any torments it may be thy pleasure to inflict without repining or reproach."

"Hah! dost thou still feel the wound there?" exclaimed the Templar, with exultation;—"by heaven it pleases me well to see that thou art not invulnerable, and rest assured I will not fail to make the most of my advantage."

"False knight! thou art deprived of thy vengeance," replied Isaac, with triumph;—"she whom thou wouldst rob me of is now far beyond thy reach."

"Aye, but for a brief time though, old man. She hath escaped me, it is true, but does it not mar thy triumph to know that she is now in the hands of Black Ivan, the brigand?"

"Ivan can scarcely be so great a villain as thyself," answered the Hebrew, fearlessly. "He may respect female virtue, and restore her once more to that society from which she hath been dragged."

"Or, which is still more probable, both she and her lover, Reuben Grenard, will perish together by the hands of the outlaw," observed Sir Gaston.

"Reuben Grenard is so far safe," replied the Hebrew:—"nay more, he hath heard of the maiden's peril, and is even now on his way to the robber's cave, in order to rescue her from their hands."

"Hah!" exclaimed Sir Gaston, "and how knew the youth of her being carried off by Black Ivan?"

"Ill news flies apace," answered the old man;—"in fact, scarcely half an hour since, a neighbour, who had seen the bandits and their terrified victim on their road from your castle, hastened hither to bring the intelligence of my daughter's peril. I would have fled to her rescue, but Reuben insisted upon my remaining here, promising either to bring her home in safety, or nobly fall in the defence of female helplessness."

"Truly," answered Sir Gaston, with a sneer, "his knight-errantry is deserving of a better fate than he is likely to meet with. Black Ivan, I dare say, will be well pleased to get his rival into his power, and if such an awkward affair should happen to occur, heaven only knows whether you will ever see this much favoured youth again."

"Thou, at least, for one, wouldst triumph in the fall of Reuben Grenard," exclaimed Isaac.

"Thou hast guessed marvellously near the truth," answered the Templar;—"the youth, as thou rightly thinkest, is no favourite of mine, and I should be glad to hear that he had fallen beneath Black Ivan's poniard, seeing that it will save me a task I have long meditated."

"Do I hear aright?" cried the Jew, with amazement; "hath the youth's life been in danger from thee?"

"Aye, marry hath it, old man."

"Villain!" exclaimed the Jew; "may the curses of heaven light upon thee for entertaining so base a thought!"

"Oh, spare thy rage, old man,,' returned Sir Gaston, with provoking coolness. "These storms of passion will serve thee but little, and as for thy daughter and her hated lover, I here swear that, if they should by any chance escape from Ivan and his band of desperadoes, I will myself hunt them through the world until I have slain one, and compelled the other to become my mistress."

"Then thus will a father seek to avenge himself on one who would destroy all that he holds most dear!" cried Isaac, and rushing with the madness of despair upon the Templar, he would have seized him by the

throat, had not Bertrand le Noir at the moment interposed himself, and caught the old man's arm as it was extended to carry his design into execution. In an instant the ruffian's hand plucked forth a dagger, which was raised with deadly aim towards the old man's heart, when the voice of Sir Gaston arrested the meditated blow.

"Hold! Bertrand," he exclaimed; "thy ready zeal pleases me well, and yet I would spare the old man's miserable life a little longer. He must be made to feel the heavy vengeance he hath excited in my breast, and when human torture can go no further, I will then call in thy aid to rid me of one who I regard only as I would a crawling reptile beneath my feet."

"Shall the Jew live then?" demanded Bertrand, in no very good humour at the interruption.

"For the present he may," replied the knight, "but it shall be under such circumstances as will render existence a torture hardly to be borne."

"I understand," answered Bertrand, "you will have him conveyed to one of your castle's dungeons, where he will have time to repent the insolence he hath this day manifested to a Knight of the Crusade."

"Such, good Bertrand, is indeed my intention," replied Sir Gaston; "the shades of evening have now closed in, and as by this time the streets are deserted, we can convey him to my mansion without interruption."

"But if he should cry aloud for assistance?" said the ruffian.

"Why, in that case, poniard him without remorse," exclaimed the other, hoarsely. "At the first cry that he raises let your dagger reach his heart; and then, having first assured yourself of his death, let every one retreat from the spot with what speed they can, and seek refuge by

No. 10

different routes, beneath my roof. Remember my injunctions, Bertrand, and see that they are strictly complied with.''

"All shall be as you have said," replied the other ; " but surely my noble master will not leave the Jew's house without helping himself to some of the gold the old man seems so unwilling to part with.''

"At present, let nothing be touched," exclaimed Sir Gaston. "Content yourself with carrying the old man off, and to-morrow I will give you further instructions.''

" Let your murderous weapons do their worst now,'' cried Isaac, fearlessly; '' slay me at once, and thus——''

Here his further speech was interrupted by Bertrand, who, throwing his own heavy riding cloak over the Hebrew's head, thus effectually prevented his raising any outcry for assistance. Having tied this securely round his victim, the ruffian next rushed to to the fire-place, and snatching from the hearth a burning brand, he applied it to the hangings with which the walls were surrounded, and in an instant the whole place was in a blaze. All this was effected before Sir Gaston had time to prevent the deed, and as the mischief was now past remedy, the party hastily retreated from the scene of conflagration, bearing with them the unfortunate Jew, who had thus drawn upon himself the vindictive rage of his powerful enemies.

CHAPTER XVI.

" Hark ! heard you not that cry ?—
The wail of feeble age, calling for help
Against some ruffian's arm ;—follow me, friends,
Or aid will come too late.'' THE SANCTUARY.

RENDERED desperate by the danger that threatened him, Isaac strove with all his little remaining strength to free himself from the grasp of Bertrand le Noir. It was in vain, however, that he made the attempt, for escape was utterly hopeless, and he was just abandoning himself to despair, when the cloak which covered his head became loosened in the struggle, and he was thus enabled to cry out lustily for assistance, ere Bertrand could prevent it. In an instant, however, he was again gagged as before, but the mischief had already been done, and scarcely had they began to move onwards once more, when footsteps were heard hastily approaching, and in an instant afterwards Sir Gaston and his party were attacked by six men, who, with drawn swords, commenced a furious attack upon them. Indeed, so unexpectedly had this attack been made, that the knight and his retainers were disarmed and struck to the earth almost as soon as the onset had been commenced. No attempt, however, was made to slay any of the vanquished party, for no sooner had they been rendered harmless, than the foremost of the rescuers stepped up to the Knight Templar, and assisted him to rise, whispering in his ear :—

"Sir Gaston de Neville will not find us vindictive enemies, but rather men who are resolved to aid the distressed, even though the oppressor may happen to rank himself amongst the king's friends.''

" Hah !'' exclaimed the knight, with surprise ; " thou knowest me, it seems ?''

" I do,'' replied the stranger, " and this, our last meeting, places thee in no very favourable light before mine eyes.''

The whole party hastily retreated from the scene of conflagration bearing
with them the unfortunate Jew.

ғ " Indeed !" muttered the Templar, "and perhaps it matters very little to me how I appear to thee, seeing that I was engaged in an affair that concerns no one but myself."

"Nay, there, Sir Gaston, thou art wrong," answered the stranger, "for when the great and powerful seek to oppress their humbler neighbours, it becomes everybody's concern, and he is no less than a villain himself who would stand by and see tyranny exercised against the helpless, without raising an arm in defence of the weaker party."

"Thou art insolent, sirrah !" exclaimed the knight, fiercely.

"And thou," returned the other, " art—a coward !"

"A coward !"

"Aye, that is the fitting term by which I call thee," answered the stranger. "Have I not found thee, with half-a-dozen willing slaves at thy heels, overwhelming this poor Jew with the most unjust oppression?—Hast thou not set fire to the roof that has sheltered him from the storms of many winters? Hast thou not done these things, and—having done them art thou not a coward?"

"Sirrah !" exclaimed Sir Gaston, fiercely, "had I arms in my hand thou wouldst not have dared to call me thus !"

"Oh ! if that is all, thou shalt not be long without thy weapon," replied the stranger, handing Sir Gaston de Neville the sword he had just taken from him. "I would not deprive thee of thine arms when thou wouldst use them in an honourable way, but, as an Englishman, I cannot stand by and see one poor old man set upon by thee and thy myrmidons."

"Draw and defend thyself," cried the enraged Templar, "for, as there is a heaven above us, I will neither give nor ask quarter in the coming combat between us."

"Hold !" exclaimed the other, "for in the first place I would know whether the Jew is in safety; and secondly, whether his house is saved of the flames, to which it was left by you and your base colleagues. That done, I shall be willing to give Sir Gaston de Neville the revenge for which he pants."

Then beckoning to one of the men who had accompanied him, he withdrew him a little aside, and having ascertained that the conflagration had been stopped, and the Jew once more restored to his home, he turned to Sir Gaston and again addressed him.

"Sir Knight," he said, "a few seconds since you offered me battle, which I deferred till some necessary inquiries had been made ; I have now learnt that the victim of your tyranny is safe, and having thus far done my duty to a fellow-creature, I am now equally ready to try my prowess against yours."

"But first," answered Sir Gaston, with scorn, "I must know who it is that I am about to measure swords with. Thou mayst be some adventurer without rank or title; nay, for aught I know, a follower of the renowned Black Ivan himself."

"Thou hast guessed wide of the mark this time, Sir Gaston," exclaimed the stranger, in a tone of easy confidence, that gave him the superiority over his antagonist. "I am no follower of Black Ivan,—neither am I without rank or title superior to thine own."

"Be who thou wilt," exclaimed Sir Gaston de Neville, goaded on to rage by the indifference with which the other treated him, "thou shalt not escape chastisement for the insult thou hast this night passed upon me. Declare thy name and style, if thou art not ashamed of them, and then prepare to leave the settlement of this quarrel to our good swords.

Again, I ask thee, who art thou, that hast thus dared to interfere be-twixt me and my own affairs ?"

"Will nothing less than my name satisfy thee?" demanded the stranger.

"Nothing less," answered the Templar, throwing himself into an atti-tude for defence or attack. according to circumstances. The stranger, however, with his own weapon struck down that of his antagonist, and then throwing aside his capacious cloak, and raising his slouched hat, which had been used for the purpose of disguise, he said :—

"Sir Gaston de Neville, thou hast thy will ;—look at me stedfastly, and see whether thou dost not recognize me."

"The king!" exclaimed Sir Gaston and his attendants, falling upon their knees in deep humility; this was an attitude, however, which the knight was not suffered to remain in for any long time by the good-na-tured monarch, who, having cast aside his sternness, said :—

"Thine eyes have not deceived thee, Sir Gaston; it is, indeed, Richard Cœur de Lion, who has thus been a witness of your harshness towards yonder poor unoffending Jew. Luckily I was at hand to rescue the unfortunate man, or thou mightest have had the crime of murder to answer for, instead of merely receiving a rebuke for the past offence, and a caution not to injure the unoffending Israelite again."

"Your Grace's goodness is accepted with thanks," cried Sir Gaston, with affected humility. " I am aware that I acted somewhat severely towards this Hebrew, but if you knew——"

"I seek to know nothing further," interrupted the king, "and if thou art wise, thou wilt suffer the affair to drop at this point. Depart home-wards, Sir Knight, and let not the present warning be thrown away."

"Will not your highness suffer me to escort you to the palace?" asked Sir Gaston; "it is reported that thieves and other disorderly rabble infest the streets and neighbourhood of London at this part of the evening, and I would therefore gladly accompany your majesty, lest some of the villains should meet, and perchance maltreat the king."

"Nay," answered Richard, carelessly, "I am aware of the rogues that are about, and have not only come out well armed myself, but have brought, as you see, a few friends upon whom I can depend, in case of an awkward rencontre. I have heard that the streets of our good City of London are not guarded quite so well as they might be, and, re-solving to convince myself of the fact, I disguised myself as you see, and, accompanied by these gentlemen, came forth in search of adven-tures. Nor have I beeen altogether disappointed, seeing that I have been the means of saving an old man from falling a victim to ——"

"Your majesty will pardon the interruption," cried Sir Gaston, "but I have retainers about, and——"

"Aye, aye," exclaimed the king; "thou wouldst not have them hear their master railed at even by a king. Be it so. Thou hast had thy reproof, and now, all I ask of thee, is that thou wilt suffer this old Israelite to pass the remainder of his days in peace and quietness."

"Your majesty then," observed the knight, with ill-concealed sar-casm, "is pleased to bestow your protection upon a tribe that has ever been the fair prey of the true believer."

"Hark'ye, Sir Gaston," exclaimed the king; "it is my will and pleasure to shield these people from the tyranny of those who have too long been their oppressors, and until you can give me a sufficient reason why they should not have a share of the law's protection, I will con-tinue to guard them and to punish those who see their injury."

"But your majesty has forgotten that I have good reason for the course I have adopted against this man," returned the knight. "I have been robbed of a diamond ring of great value; the jewel was found in the possession of Isaac's daughter, and with such evidence of their guilt, I am fully authorized in bringing them to punishment."

"Appeal to the law and thou shalt have justice," exclaimed Richard; "so far there is nothing but suspicion against the maiden, but if thou canst bring proof of her guilt, then will I fully warrant thee in bringing her to justice."

"Nay, sire, at present she is out of my reach," answered Sir Gaston de Neville. "The robber, Black Ivan, hath this day borne her off to some of his secret fortresses, and thus have the ends of justice been for a time defeated."

"And didst thou not pursue the outlaw?" demanded the monarch, with surprise.

"For a short distance," replied the Templar, "and then, finding that further efforts would be in vain, we hastened hither in order to prosecute our further enquiries of Isaac of Tadcaster concerning the robbery of which I complain."

"And so," exclaimed the king, "because you could not otherwise revenge yourself upon a helpless old man, you drag him away like a convicted felon, and then give his house to the flames by way of retaliation for a crime which is not yet proved against him. This, to say the least of it, is tyrannical, more especially since the object of your unjust persecution is one who has not the means to protect himself against a man of power and influence like yourself."

"But hear me, sire ——"

"I will hear nothing," interrupted Richard, "since nought that you can say will convince me of the act being one of justice. Enough, however, it is to be hoped, has been said to prevent a repetition of the outrage, and I now, therefore, command you to return home, where you may seek fairer means to bring the really guilty parties to justice."

The latter part of this conversation had been purposely carried on in so low a tone, as to be inaudible to those for whose ears it was not intended. It was, however, quite evident that the king was in earnest with respect to his intended protection of the hitherto persecuted Jews, and as Richard's temper was known to be warm and impetuous, the knight thought fit to promise implicit obedience to the royal commands. Upon this assurance being given, the sovereign departed, though not before he had left one of his attendants behind to watch the Jew's house until Sir Gaston had left the place, which he did in a few minutes afterwards, bitterly cursing the chance that had rescued Isaac at the very moment when he appeared to be so completely in his power.

CHAPTER XVII.

"What wond'rous sign is this?
What means this portent sent by heaven itself
To warn me 'gainst some ill?"

THE BLACK TOWER.

SULLENLY turning away from the place where he had been so unexpectedly defeated in the project he had formed against the Jew, Sir Gaston motioned for his retainers to follow, and then urging his way with what speed he could, he returned to his own stronghold; resolving, in his own mind, to execute some daring deed by which both the Israelite and his virtuous daughter should fall into a snare from which it would not be very easy to extricate themselves.

It is true there was danger of losing the king's favour if the plot should chance to be discovered, but then he hoped, with Bertrand's aid, to conduct his designs so secretly, that the mischief he was hatching should not only succeed to his utmost hopes, but that, at the same time, all should be managed with so much circumspection that, though people might suspect the share he had in the transaction, no one should be able to fix upon him a charge that would bring down the monarch's fiercest displeasure. Indeed, so determined was he not to be thwarted, that he resolved upon running the risks, and no sooner, therefore, had he re-turned home, than hastening to the armoury, he ordered Bertrand le Noir instantly to attend him to confer on an affair of much importance.

Bertrand knew well enough the nature of the business on which he was thus summoned, and instantly obeying the command, he at once presented himself before his master, who he found impatiently pacing up and down the apartments.

"Hah, Bertrand!" exclaimed the knight, pausing abruptly as the at-tendant made his appearance; "by Our Lady but thou art ever ready to obey the first summons of thy master, and greatly do I commend the zeal which prompts such faithful service. I greatly need thee now, man, and desire thy patient attention to what I am about to disclose."

"Sir Gaston," replied the other, "has ever found me anxious to obey even his slightest bidding."

"True," exclaimed the knight, "but now thou wilt be required to go further than on any former occasion. Thou knowest my heart is set upon possessing the Jewess, and being once resolved, no obstacle must be suffered to stand in my way."

"But the wench," observed Bertrand, "is at this moment in the hands of Black Ivan, the Outlaw."

"Well!" exclaimed the Templar, fiercely; "and shall Ivan thwart the will of Gaston de Neville, who hath ever made himself conspicuous by the certainty with which he overcomes all obstacles? Shall he suffer a rival like this Outlaw to possess himself of a treasure to purchase which he would sacrifice both body and soul?"

"Not if it was possible to prevent it," answered the retainer; "but Ivan is no common enemy to deal with—his haunt is not easily accessi-ble, and ere you can attack him with a sufficient force he would have borne this Rebecca to a place we may never find."

"Caitiff!" exclaimed Sir Gaston, with anger, "thou art growing cowardly in behalf. Once I could have relied upon thy zealous activity in the cause of thy master, and now, on a sudden, thou hast grown cold, leaving me to compass my own designs when thou shouldst be actively engaged in serving me."

"Hast thou ever found me shrink from my duty?" asked Bertrand, in a tone of sullen ill-humour.

"Nay," retorted the Templar, "thou has not dared openly to rebel against my commands because thou knowest my dagger was ever ready to punish thy slightest act of disobedience. As my slave thou hast done my bidding, or death had been thy certain portion!"

"Thy slave!" exclaimed Bertrand, wrathfully,

"Aye, as my slave," replied Sir Gaston. "Art thou not bound to me by ties thou canst not loosen; dost thou not owe thy very existence to me, since a word of mine could send thee to expiate thy crimes upon the gallows?"

"Sir Gaston de Neville forgets that the *slave* possesses some power over the destinies of his *master!*"

"Dost thou threaten me, Bertrand?"

"No," answered the other, "I use no threats; thine own rebukes have drawn forth whatever I have said; and now, having spoken thus boldly, I would suggest that we part ere any further anger arises out of this difference between us."

"Art thou mad to think of parting from me?" exclaimed the Knight Templar. "Are not our destinies in some degree mixed up together, and wouldst thou now think of leaving me when most thy services are required?"

"It is in thine own power to keep me ever about thee," replied Bertrand le Noir. "Call me not thy slave or threaten me with the consequences of thy displeasure, and I will remain with thee even until death."

"Well, well," exclaimed the knight, "thou must forget my warmth, or at least attribute it to the perplexity that at present surrounds me on every hand. The loss of this girl hath well nigh maddened me; her father, too, hath escaped the well-imagined plans I had laid for his destruction; and now, as if to drive me quite to despair, the king himself grows cold towards me, and I am threatened with his heavy displeasure."

"And yet," observed Bertrand, "all may be easily averted."

"How so?"

"By placing a curb upon your own impetuous passions," answered the retainer. "Give up all hopes of this girl, who seems to have crazed your brain; cease persecuting her father, and the king's friendship will remain yours as firmly as ever."

"Nay, you suggest to me an impossibility," replied the knight. "This Rebecca must be mine, however great the sacrifice—I have sworn it, Bertrand, and even though I had to pursue her to the lowest depths of hell, yet would I fearlessly dare all rather than relinquish a hope that nought but death itself shall ever frustrate."

"Then you are ready to risk even the anger of our good King Richard?"

Richard has no right to interfere between a subject and his will."

"And yet," replied Bertrand, "it has been already discovered that the king is most resolute in the strict exaction of obedience from all classes of his subjects. High rank gives no protection now, as it used to do formerly; all now are judged by their actions; and even the very Jews, —people who, till this time, have been the mark for general ill-usage,— are now shielded with the same care that is extended to all other classes of the people."

"That, perhaps," observed Sir Gaston, "is only done to excite temporary popularity among a people from whom he hopes to borrow a few thousand golden pieces. These Israelites will readily enough open the coffers for one they may believe to be a friend, but only let his own treasury be well replenished, and we shall then see how much longer he will prove friendly to the Jews of England."

"Yet such is not the general opinion entertained of our young king," replied Bertrand.

"Perhaps not, because it will better serve his own purpose, to maintain the favourable impression he has already made upon his subjects," answered the knight. "King Richard knows the value of a people's love, and will make good use of the opportunity he now has of furthering his ambitious projects. In a short time he will grow rich upon the offerings they will lay at his feet, and then we shall see how much longer he) will play the part self-interest now induces him to adopt. But I am speaking of matters that concern thee not; my present business is with this Isaac of Tadcaster and his fair daughter, both of whom must be enclosed within the meshes I have prepared for them, and thou, Bertrand, must be the instrument by which my designs are to to be executed."

"And in return," answered the retainer, sullenly, "I am still to be called thy *slave!*"

"Thou shall be my friend if this affair is managed skilfully," replied Sir Gaston. "I will raise thee from thy present low estate, and wealth to any amount shall be the reward of thy services."

"A tempting offer, truly!" exclaimed Bertrand le Noir, somewhat relaxing from his former sullenness, "and one that thou knowest I am hardly likely to resist."

"Thou will grant me all the assistance in thy power then?"

"Humph!" ejaculated the retainer;—"that would be promising more than I should afterwards like to fulfil. If I accept thy gold, I bind myself to do all that may be commanded, and already have I more blood to answer for than all the prayers and repentance of an after life may be able to propitiate. I am sick of crime, and would gladly obtain thy reward by any other means than my dagger."

"'Psha!" exclaimed Sir Gaston; "dost thou again whine as if this was the first step to crime?"

"Nay," answered Bertrand, after a momentary pause, "thou shalt find me all that thou desirest;—name the service I am expected to perform, and it shall be done, even though it may be to plunge my poniard into the hearts of this unfortunate Jew and his daughter."

"That, Bertrand," exclaimed the Templar, "is an act thou mayst be spared, for yet some time to come. At present my object is to get this Hebrew Maiden into my power, and then, by exciting her fears for the old man's safety, to compel her to accede to those terms which she has hitherto rejected with scorn. Aid me in this, and even thy most ambitious wishes shall be gratified."

"Tell me first how all this is to be accomplished?"

"Why," answered Sir Gaston de Neville, "that there is some difficulty in the affair is to be acknowledged, yet the reward shall be fully equal to it, and therefore thou will have nothing to complain of on that score."

"I understand you,"—cried Bertrand;—"it will be necessary for me to get Rebecca, in the first place, from the custody of this robber and his band."

"A task," returned his master, "which will be attended with some danger unless carefully executed. In order, however, to avoid peril, you must disguise yourself, and proceed to some place where you will be certain to meet with these brigands. They will probably carry you with them as their prisoner to the cavern; an opportunity will thus offer itself to carry our design into execution, and by cautiously watching till some chance arises in your favour, it may be possible to escape with Rebecca from the robbers den, and of course she will thus be once more thrown into my power."

"Of a verity," exclaimed Bertrand le Noir, "all this appears easy enough to talk about, and yet I suspect it will prove difficult to put into execution."

"Not if thou art cautious, good Bertrand."

"Cautious or not, the robbers will not be very likely to let two prisoners escape from their custody," answered the retainer. "Report

says, that beneath their caverns are dungeons from which it would be impossible to make your way, and that when once immured in them, a prisoner is entirely cut off from every hope of relief."

"But it will be thine own fault if they imprison thee," exclaimed the knight. "Thou canst pretend to like their wild course of life;—it would save thee from the terrors thou hast just spoken of, and at the same time give thee a fair opportunity to release Rebecca from the captivity she now endures."

"Nay, would she not guess my motive?"

"It is not necessary that she should know thee," answered Sir Gaston. "Thy disguise would effectually prevent her doing so, and thus I should make sure of your project being brought to a successful termination."

"Well," exclaimed Bertrand, "I am not over nice in these matters, it must be confessed, and yet, somehow or other I feel half ashamed of taking so much pains to injure a poor girl that never gave me cause to plunge her into so much misery. 'Tis a fiendish course, Sir Gaston, nor is it lessened by making the poor old man a victim to the same snares that are laid for the destruction of the daughter."

"Fool!—dost thou dare to preach to me?" muttered Sir Gaston de Neville through his closed teeth.

"I dare," answered the other, "because for once in my life time, I find myself on the right side of the question."

"Then thou art no longer to be depended on," exclaimed the knight, wrathfully. "From henceforth thou art no servant of mine. Leave me, Bertrand, that some one, upon whose fidelity I can rely, may fulfil the task I would have entrusted to thee."

No. 11

Bertrand le Noir turned away in obedience to the command of his master, but suddenly recollecting that the office he had refused might be given to some other of the knight's retainers, who would be less scrupulous than himself, he turned back, and with a softened expression of countenance, said :—

"Pardon me, Sir Gaston, if I have appeared unwilling to execute your behest, for, even though the command was one against human nature was likely to recoil, I would not willingly disobey the wishes of a master whom I have so long and zealously served."

"Hah!—this is as I expected," cried the knight, relaxing from his former sternness. "I knew thy fidelity, Bertrand, and relied on it, even when most thou didst seem to oppose my wishes. Thou wilt perform the business upon which I just now proposed to send thee?"

"I will."

"Good!" exclaimed Sir Gaston;—"now thou art thyself again, and I could almost venture to swear, that even were I to command thee to stab these two persons to the heart, thou wouldst not hesitate to execute my bidding?"

"In all things thou shalt find me faithful," replied Bertrand;—"aye, even though it should be to shed more of thy victim's blood!"

At this moment a vivid flash of lightning shot across the chamber, and scarcely had the vivid light passed away, when a peal of thunder followed, so loud, that Sir Gaston and Bertrand le Noir, hardened as their hearts were, felt horrified at the awful sound with which their ears were assailed. Then the wind rose with terrific violence; rushing through various chinks and crevices in the walls, and moving the heavy tapestry and the banners with which the walls were decorated, with a sound that served to increase the apprehension of the guilty knight and his attendant. Sir Gaston, however, was the first to recover his courage, and affecting to laugh at an occurrence which had, in fact, filled his soul with terror, he enquired of Bertrand, whether he was alarmed at a phenomenon, such as he had frequently heard before and disregarded.

"Never heard I such a one as this, Sir Gaston," returned the retainer, scarcely able to speak from terror. "The very castle seemed to rock to its foundation, and for a moment I believed it to have been set on fire by the lightning. And then the moaning of the wind as it swept through the chamber, seemed like the voices of a thousand demons, calling to, and warning us of the punishment that will follow the fulfilment of our present designs."

"Pooh!—what foolery is this?" demanded the knight, angrily. "It was not thus you were wont to regard what, after all, is nothing more than a mere summer's storm."

"That may be, Sir Gaston" answered the man, "but storms do not always happen to burst forth at just such a moment as this. If you remember, we were talking about a crime that was to be committed, and just at that very juncture it was, that the roaring thunder came like the voice of heaven, to warn us of our danger."

"How provoking is this stupidity," exclaimed the knight, with increasing anger. "I had believed, Bertrand, that you were above this superstitious folly, and yet I now find you yielding to it like some timid female."

"And not without sufficient cause," answered the other, glancing fearfully around him. As he did so, another flash, more violent even than the first, darted through the window of the armoury, and then came a clap of thunder, so loud, that the whole castle seemed to have been laid in ruins by the avenging stroke of heaven. Even the knight was awe-struck at the increasing fury of the tempest, and for a few seconds a death-like silence reigned between them. At that moment a deep groan seemed to issue from the suit of armour that stood close behind Sir Gaston de Neville, upon which the knight startled from his seat, and gazing with fixed eyes upon the figure before him, he remained for some few seconds utterly unable either to remove from the spot, or address himself to the supposed apparition before which he stood. At length, however, grasping the arm of Bertrand le Noir, to prevent his flight, he summoned all the resolution he could, and exclaimed:—

"If the spirit of an ancestor has taken refuge within this steel armour, I command it to speak the mission for which it hath visited me. Let me know thine errand, I charge thee, and by my soul I swear to obey whatever commands thou mayst give, even though it place my own life in instant jeopardy. Speak then, unhallowed spirit—speak, I adjure thee."

As Sir Gaston concluded speaking, a violent motion was perceptible in the figure, which seemed ready to step from the pediment upon which it stood, and ere the knight and his attendant could effect their retreat, the figure fell with a heavy crash to the ground at their feet, where it lay without further motion.

This was enough for Bertrand, whose terrors had been already excited to the utmost, and bursting from the firm grasp with which he had been held by Sir Gaston, he rushed with terror from the armoury, uttering cries of alarm. that quickly brought a number of the retainers to the assistance of their master. For some time, however, he was deaf to all their enquiries as to the cause of the uproar they had heard; but at length Sir Gaston recovered himself sufficiently to answer some of their questions, and then pointing to the suit of armour that lay at their feet, he bade them raise, and place it upon the pedestal from whence it had so mysteriously fallen. But this they found it impossible to do, as the armour, when they sought to move it, fell into a thousand pieces, as if it had been purposely destroyed by the hammer of a smith.

Sir Gaston de Neville pondered deeply and fearfully over the warning that this seemed to convey. It appeared, indeed, as if the spirit of his ancestors had appeared in his presence, to warn him of the danger he was about to incur;—this was the only construction he could put upon the mysterious affair, and turning from the spot, with a pale and care-worn countenance, he beckoned his attendants to follow him to another apartment. As one of the men, however, was passing the still scattered remains of the armour, his eye rested upon a dagger, which, on picking up from the ground, was discovered to be reeking with recent blood!

How to account for this little circumstance, Sir Gaston knew not, but snatching the murderous weapon from the man's hand, he rushed to his sleeping apartment, where in silence and privacy he might meditate over the events that had just occurred.

CHAPTER XVIII.

"Spare him—
But for a day—an hour—and I will bless thee
Even with my latest breath." THE CONFESSIONAL.

IT will be remembered that at the last interview that took place in the cavern between Black Ivan and Rebecca, news was brought that

84 THETHE HEBREW MAIDEN; OR,

Reuben Grenard had been captured, by a part of the band, and was then waiting in another part of the cave, until the pleasure of the brigand chief should be known as to his ultimate fate. Ivan, it may be recollected, exulted with fiendish triumph, at thus finding his rival in his power, and no sooner had our heroine fallen insensible, through the shock she had received at the danger in which her lover had been placed, than he hurried away to visit the prisoner.

As the robber chief entered the place where the young Jew was seated upon a stone bench, the quick glance of his eye showed the exultation with which he regarded this lucky chance by which a hated rival had been thrown into his power. But Reuben was undaunted, in spite of the alarming situation in which he was placed, and maintaining his composure, he awaited in silence the communication he was about to receive.

" By Saint Nicholas, the patron of thieves, but this meeting fills me with joy," cried Black Ivan, in a tone of exultatation. " To get thee in my power was the first wish of my soul, and lo, here thou art, a prisoner in my hands."

" I am," answered Reuben, calmly. " Fortune has thus far favoured thee, and if thou art not cruel as rumour has painted thee, thou wilt at once end my miseries with death."

" Oh, thou shalt have thy wish, believe me," exclaimed the robber, " Reuben Grenard is two much hated by his captor, to receive any other doom than that he has asked for."

" Then lead me forth at once," cried the young Jew. " I am ready, as thou seest, to meet my fate; and can endure any torture now that I have lost her, upon whom all my earthly affections were set."

" Indeed !"

" Why dost thou doubt me ?"

" Because it is easy to exhibit an air of bravery and defiance," answered Black Ivan. " Thou canst talk largely now, Reuben Grenard, but when thou standest on the threshold of death, thou wilt change thy tone."

" Never !"

" 'Psha ! thy youth must make life dear to thee," replied the other. " Few men are mad enough to wish for death, and I should imagine that thou, of all men, would be one of the last who wish for that change which will separate thee from the maiden of thy love."

" Hah !" exclaimed Reuben, " thou hast touched upon a subject that does indeed move me. For Rebecca's sake I would wish to live ;—but she, alas ! is in the power of a ruthless destroyer, and since all hope of rescuing her has vanished for ever, I would gladly perish rather than live to know of her dishonour."

" And prithee, where didst thou learn this romantic nonsense ?" asked the robber, with scorn ;—" who, in the name of all the saints, ever put such folly into thy crazy brain, as this thou hast been talking about ?"

" I had forgotten myself," answered Reuben, after a momentary pause ;—" thou, I ought to have known, art little likely to appreciate aught that agrees not with thine own fierce thoughts. To thee, life is everything, even though it might be burdened with the most harrowing reflections."

" Granted," returned the brigand; " I would indeed live as long as possible, and so methinks wouldst thou, if thy stubborn heart could be brought to supplicate me for mercy."

" Mercy from thee !" cried Reuben, scornfully ;—" from a black and hardened villain like thyself ?"

" Aye, aye," returned the other, " rail on, and call me by whatever name thou likest. Thine, young Jew, is a desperate situation, and thou mayst as well speak thy mind freely, seeing that nothing thou canst say or do will now injure thee. I have thee in my strong grasp, Reuben, and a single word will be sufficient to give thee the death thou desirest."

" Then pronounce the word, and keep me no longer in the suspense that is far worse than death itself."

" Hast thou no request to urge ?"

" None whatever ;—at least, none from thee."

" Hast thou considerd thine answer carefully ?"

" I have."

" Why, that is strange too, for I believed thou wouldst have asked for a parting interview with thy beloved."

" Would it have been granted ?"

" Aye,—that is to say, upon certain conditions," replied the robber.

" And what are those conditions ?"

" That you renounce the girl in my favour, and that you do all you can to prevail upon her to make no more fuss about becoming the mistress of Black Ivan. Tell her that she is only making matters worse by this obstinacy, and if you succeed in talking her into reason, I'll not only spare your life, but you shall be at liberty to join our band if you think fit to do so."

" Wretch !" exclaimed the indignant Reuben, " dost thou believe I am so destitute of honour as to accept life upon the base terms thou hast offered ? No !—the God of Israel hath thus far supported me, and I can still look unmoved upon death, rather than urge an innocent maiden to become the mistress of one so infamous."

" Well,—as you please," answered Ivan, in a tone of indifference,— " you can, of course, do as you think proper in the matter, though I believe there are few men that would be so mad, when a fair chance is offered them to escape."

" Of me, at least, it shall never be said that I preferred my own life to the honour of a maiden I love," answered the young Israelite. " My own existence is valueless, and freely shall it be given for the benefit of the helpless Rebecca."

" Why this is the veriest frenzy I ever heard of !" exclaimed the brigand. " Here have you fallen a captive to a rival ;—your life itself is in peril, and yet you obstinately refuse to purchase mercy on the easy terms I have offered."

" Aye," replied Reuben, " and am firm in that refusal. For my own part I fear not your threats, and can die cheerfully, rather than a single word of mine should be the means of destroying the poor maiden's peace for ever."

" Then you forget," cried Ivan, exultingly, " that the girl will still remain in my power ;—that she must be mine in spite of every thing, and that you are consequently throwing away your life without doing her any good ?"

" Monster !" exclaimed Reuben, with vehemence, " wouldst thou add torture by thus reminding me of the fate which thou hast doomed her ? Kill me with thy sword where I now stand, but do not stab me with words that must add tenfold bitterness to the last moments of existence."

" 'Psha !—live thy time patiently, man," retorted the robber, " and do not seek to shorten the period of thine existence until we have seen whether it will indeed be necessary to rid the band of a dangerous enemy. Think again of the offer I have made thee, and if, upon further reflection, thou art still obstinate, I'll warrant me thou shalt have little cause to complain of being kept in suspense."

"Nay, I have but one request to make," answered Reuben;—"release the maiden from this place, and I can die content, so that I know she is restored to the arms of a fond and doating father."

"Upon my word, young man," cried the robber, "you seem to have formed a very favourable opinion of my humanity, or such a favour as that you have asked had never been contemplated.—And so you can seriously ask me to give up possession of the girl when I have been at such pains to bring her here."

"You have," replied the young man, with a sigh, "yet I knew not till now, that your heart was utterly incapable of harbouring a generous feeling towards the helpless."

"Nonsense, man, I love the girl, and therefore cannot part with her so easily."

"Love!" cried Reuben, with scorn;—"call you that *love* which prompts you to an act of cruelty and oppression?"

"Why, the fact is," answered Black Ivan, "that I was never taught to distinguish between my own desires, and what others might call morality. I have passed the greater part of my time among the rough fellows that form this band, and having made laws for the government of ourselves, it is hardly likely that we should trouble our heads about those we break every day of our lives."

"Then you have resolved to sacrifice both of us on the altar of your own unhallowed inclinations?"

"Oh, you may call my determination by any name you please," retorted Black Ivan, with indifference. "In this place, I rule as supremely, as King Richard does upon the throne of England. My own wishes guide me in all things, and woe be unto him who dares to foil me!"

"It is useless then to argue any further," exclaimed Reuben, "my fate is already sealed, and all I now ask is that you will instantly, give me over to death."

"Well, captain, can't you accommodate the young man in the way he hints at?" asked a gruff voice close by. "We are not very nice about trifles here, and if he wishes to be dispatched quickly, I've eight or nine inches of cold steel at his service, that will soon will put an end to his grumbling."

"Peace, Hubert," vociferated the brigand leader. "I am master here, remember, and if a hand is raised against the prisoner till I have given the word, it will be met with the punishment of death without orm or trial."

"By all the saints in the calendar, he may go free for aught I care," returned Hubert, in a tone of pique. "I merely gave a little friendly hint, and since that has been thrown away, I shall remain silent from this time forward."

"Thou hast said wisely, Hubert," exclaimed the robber-chef, "my will is not to be frustrated, and it will be at his own risk if any one dares to interfere in a matter that concerns only myself."

"Am I threatened!" muttered Hubert, gloomily; "by'r Lady then, we have been too long together, and the sooner I take myself off from this place, the better."

"That you may give my enemies a clue to find me," cried Black Ivan, with a sneer.

"No," answered the other, boldly, "as one of your band, you have never yet had occasion to tax me with cowardice, nor shall you do so now. I may fall into the hands of those who have long sought to hunt us out, but neither torture, nor the threat of death itself, shall ever make me turn traitor against those that have been as friends and brothers to me."

"Give me your hand, Hubert," exclaimed the chieftain, somewhat softened by these words. "I may have judged you rather harshly, and from this moment we will learn to know each other better."

"Why, I thought you were a little hasty, captain," answered the other; "you spoke sharper than usual, but perhaps that is to be accounted for by something that has passed between you and the prisoner."

"He is obstinate," replied Ivan, "and refuses to aid me in prevailing upon our female captive to accept me as her lover in his room."

"Then why not punish him as you well know how?" asked Hubert. "You are master here, remember, and a word or a sign would be sufficient to rid you of him for ever."

"I have seen enough blood flow," answered the chief, "and would have spared his if he would have listened to my proposition."

"That I will never do," cried Reuben, who had hitherto remained a silent auditor of their conversation; "you have already heard me declare my readiness to die, and I therefore now beseech you to let your poniard do the work of death."

"He braves us rarely, at any rate," exclaimed Hubert, "and if I had my own way in this business, he should not have to ask a second time for that which would rid us of an enemy we have every reason to dread."

"What have we to dread from him?" demanded Black Ivan.

"Treachery!" answered the other. "Reuben Grenard will not fail to make a desperate effort to escape, and should he succeed in doing so, he now knows sufficiently of this place to guide a party of our foes hither."

"Hah!" cried the robber chief, "that is indeed possible, and our care must be exerted to prevent so dangerous an event taking place. Hubert, you have touched upon the right chord, and the Jew shall die, lest any mercy extended towards him should lead to our own speedy destruction."

"In the name of heaven spare him!" cried Rebecca, who at that moment rushed into the part of the cavern were they were assembled.

"Remove that maniac!" exclaimed the chieftain, fiercely, "remove her, I say, and let more care be taken that she again breaks not upon us thus abruptly."

"I will not go," replied Rebecca, struggling, and at length breaking from the ruffian who had seized hold of her. "I am now free, and the first that dares advance towards me will perish by a woman's hand!"

While speaking, Rebecca had snatched a dagger from the robber who had seized upon her, and then placing her back against the wall, she stood in an attitude that plainly showed it would be dangerous to approach her with any hostile intention. In fact, the robbers, all of them, stood aloof, and it was not until Hubert, laughing scornfully at the fears of his comrades, made a sudden rush towards her, that she was disarmed of the weapon with which she had so unexpectedly prepared herself.

"Fools!" he cried, "are ye afraid of a woman, that thus ye hang back like trembling cowards as ye are? Behold! she is now helpless, and it is your captain's command that she be immediately conveyed to her own chamber, there to await his further orders."

It was in vain that Rebecca prayed and entreated of them not to remove her until she had been allowed a brief intercourse with her lover. Those who heard the supplications of the maiden were deaf to her almost frantic cries for the permission she had solicited, and after a violent, but ineffectual struggle to break once more from them, she was dragged away by main force from the place, and conveyed to her own chamber, where she was left under the charge of old Maud.

"Fiends!" exclaimed Reuben, as soon as he could sufficiently recover himself from the horror into which he had been thrown;—"can ye thus act violently to a woman, whose sex and helplessness should at least afford some protection against your unmanly conduct?"

"Helplessness!" muttered one of the robbers;—"I can only say that I feel the effects of her nails, and if you call that being helpless, why it will be no use to say anything further upon the subject."

"Oh, she has got spirit enough to take care of herself, I warrant you," observed Hubert. "Leave the girl alone, and I dare venture to say she will do very well without the interference of you or any body else."

"Cowards as you are, you have prevented my doing anything in her behalf," exclaimed Reuben Grenard. "You have bound my limbs with fetters, but if you will give me the free use of my arms, and a sword to wield, I will yet show you that numbers should not deter me from making one desperate attempt to rescue her from the hands of villany."

"A tolerably modest proposal, truly," answered Herbert, with a sneer. "And so you would like us to give you a sword, in order that we might have the opportunity of witnessing with what prowess you can use it."

"The favour I ask is but a trifling one," replied Reuben;—"your numbers would be sure to overpower me, and the only consolation I should derive would be in the reflection that I had died in the defence of the maiden of my love."

"Then, by your leave, we would rather decline giving you an opportunity of so distinguishing yourself," cried Black Ivan, who had for some time had been turning over in his mind various plans for ridding himself of his rival, and thus securing the maiden who was thus thrown entirely upon his mercy. "Not," he continued, "but what I like to see a lad of mettle very well, but as I might chance to lose one of my men in the conflict, the most prudent course is to forbid them giving you any such advantage as you have requested."

"Besides" added Hubert, "it is not usual with us to permit a prisoner to pass a single night in our cavern. We have laws made to govern us, and, among other things, the captain is bound to give his captives over to death immediately after they have been brought to the cavern."

"You have reminded me of a duty that I had almost forgotten," exclaimed Black Ivan. "The prisoner must indeed die to-night, unless he chooses to take the required oath, and thus become one of our band."

"Never!" cried Reuben, firmly. "Chance has delivered me into your hands, but I will, at least, die without the taint of having connected myself with a society of desperate ruffians, whose crimes have long since rendered them the terror of nearly the whole kingdom. Death I can meet without fear, but dishonour never!"

"Well, as you please," replied Hubert. "Every man can, of course, follow the bent of his own inclination, and, since you prefer death, we, of course, will not attempt to disappoint your wishes;—so let your prayers be brief, for you have but a short time longer to remain in this world."

"I am ready now," cried Reuben;—"if your daggers are ready here

is my bared bosom to receive the blows that shall for ever release me from your tyranny."

"Not quite so fast, young sir, if you please," interrupted the robber chief. "It is for me to decide what death you shall die, and hitherto I have not given any commands to my men upon the subject."

"Let him swing on the nearest tree then," exclaimed Hubert; "the fellow is but a Jew, and that death will be quite good enough for one of his tribe."

"Nay, I am not to be moved from my purpose," returned Black Ivan. "Hanging is a punishment I never mean to inflict upon any one, seeing that it may chance to be my own fate some of these days. And, now I think of it, let our choicest bowmen be ordered out with as little delay as possible, for he shall be shot to death with arrows, and that, too, ere yonder sun sinks into his western home."

"Well said, captain," exclaimed Hubert; "this promptness is pleasing to us all, though, in my humble opinion, the death you have doomed him to, is far too honourable a one for an Israelite."

"Why, what matters it?" demanded the captain. "Death is the same thing, come in what shape it may, and therefore I have chosen this method rather than see the body hanging from its gibbet these many days to come, and thus being reminded what my own fate may be whenever Dame Fortune may think fit to desert us."

"S'death, captain, don't talk in that way!" cried Hubert, emphatically; "Fortune is a slippery jade I know, but let us hope she won't so far forsake us minions of the moon, as to leave us to such a fate as that. Between ourselves, hanging is fit only for dogs, and I always pray to the

No. 12

Holy Virgin that she will intercede to procure something better than such a doom for me."

At this moment another of the robbers entered, bringing in with him Bertrand le Noir, the favourite and confidant of Sir Gaston de Neville. Upon their making their appearance, the robber chief advanced a step or two to meet them, and having eyed the newly arrived visitor, he whispered to his fellow, enquiring where he had contrived to pick up this other prisoner.

"May it please you, noble captain," answered the man, "this is no prisoner unless you may think fit to make him so when you have heard the reason that has brought him to seek out our cavern."

"Hah! not a prisoner, say you?" exclaimed Black Ivan, "then what in the devil's name is the cause of his coming among us?"

"That," answered the man, "he will be best able to tell you himself."

"True," returned Ivan, and then addressing himself to the attendant of Sir Gaston de Neville, he enquired what business had brought him there to seek an interview with one whom almost all men conspired to shun.

"My noble master, Sir Gaston de Neville," answered the other, "has been pleased to entrust me with this message to Black Ivan, the Outlaw. It has been reported to him that Rebecca, the Hebrew Maiden, and daughter of old Isaac, Jew of Tadcaster, has been forcibly carried away, and as there appears to be good reason to suspect that she hath fallen into your hands, I am commissioned to seek you out and demand her instant liberation."

"Indeed!" exclaimed Black Ivan, "and perhaps you have also come to enforce your demand?"

"At present that is unnecessary," answered Bertrand le Noir. "My master believes you will not refuse his request, and therefore I am now only charged to make known his desire. and, in case you comply with it, to convey the fair Hebrew back to him in safety."

"Sir Gaston de Neville has been over gracious," returned the robber, "seeing that he could bring out so great a force to back his demands. However, it may be that he fears a defeat from my men, and to that circumstance it is probable I owe his present courtesy."

"My noble master entertains no evil designs against you," replied Bertrand, "and as a proof of it I have been despatched hither on my present errand of peace."

"Humph!" ejaculated the robber, "and yet, methinks his modesty is somewhat startling too.—Sir Gaston knows I love the wench, and——"

"Craving your pardon," interrupted Bertrand, "my master knows no such thing. He suspects the girl is not quite safe in your custody, and therefore——"

"Would rather have her in his own?"

"You have said truly."

"I thought so," exclaimed Black Ivan; "and now, since we understand one another so far, hear the message you are to carry back. Tell Sir Gaston I cannot treat with him through any second person, but that

he thinks fit to come here instead of sending a messenger, I dare say we shall very shortly understand one another. Say that to him, and doubtless he will not be long in accepting my invitation."

"If Sir Gaston listens to my advice he will think twice ere he ventures so near the lion's den."

"Ha! ha! ha!" laughed the brigand, "you begin to suspect, then, that his reception would not be quite so cordial as he would wish?"

"Why, for my own part," answered Bertrand, "I should consider, as a faithful retainer, that it was my duty to warn him against treachery. I have heard of Black Ivan before now, and common report gives him no great credit for hospitality towards those whom it may be convenient to keep safely under lock and key. There are ugly rumours, too, abroad that you have a knack of putting your captives out of the way in a quiet manner, and as I have no inclination to lose a good master, I shall certainly take the liberty to prevail upon him to remain as long as he can out of your reach."

"Well, I have heard you patiently," exclaimed Black Ivan, "and therefore I expect from you the same courtesy. You have spoken of rumours touching my conduct towards the prisoners whom chance throws in my way, nor do I think it worth my while to contradict them, since I dare say there may be a good deal of truth mixed up with a great many falsehoods. However, yonder sits one of my captives, who has already been doomed to die, and a very few minutes will serve to carry that sentence into execution. You will tell him that, and at the same time warn him that should he by any chance fall into my hands, he will meet a fate exactly similar to that of Reuben Grenard. And now, Bertrand, speed on thy way, for I swear that if thou remainest here but another five minutes, thou shalt be hung up to one of the trees, near our cavern, as a warning to all those who would endeavour to track Black Ivan to his retreat."

This was spoken with a tone and gesture that plainly showed there was no doubting the words that had been uttered, and Bertrand was but too happy to effect his escape to waste any time in useless parley. He therefore directed his footsteps in the direction pointed out, and in a few moments was once more on the outside of the cavern.

"A good riddance at any rate," exclaimed Hubert, "and now, having seen him fairly out, what, captain, is your pleasure with respect to our prisoner?"

"Let him have one hour," answered Black Ivan, "and at the end of that time, be it your task to see him led out to death!"

CHAPTER XIX.

"Lose not a moment in delay,
But let your troops march forth with utmost speed,
Or all your labour will be lost."

ISABELLA.

BERTRAND LE NOIR proceeded some distance from the cavern with the greatest caution, looking round to see whether his motions were being watched by any of the robbers, from whom he had so luckily escaped with his life. Finding, however, that his footsteps had not been dogged, he at once stuck into another path and directed his way towards a copse which stood a distance of about a mile-and-a-half from the robbers' cave. As he advanced nearer, he could see the forms of several persons who had evidently sought concealment there, and who were anxiously looking out to convey the first news of his approach to their superior. A few minutes more served to bring Bertrand to the boundary of the copse, and on arriving at that place he was accosted by a couple of men who greeted him with all the warmth of old friendship.

" By 'r Lady, but I am glad to see thee back with whole bones in thy skin, Bertrand," exclaimed one of the men, shaking him roughly by the hand.

" Didst thou expect me to have my bones broken, then ?" demanded Bertrand.

" Aye, marry did I," answered the other, " for rumour gives no great deal of credit to Black Ivan for humanity towards those that fall in his way, and as thy business with him was rather awkward, I would have wagered great odds that he paid thee in a coin far from acceptible."

" And doubtless he would have done so," replied Bertrand, " had he not known that my master is not one likely to put up with an injury, and that any wrong done to me would have been repaid with heavy interest before he was many hours older. In truth, Ivan knows his own security depends upon restraining the violence of his passions under certain circumstances, and to that, perhaps, more than to anything else do I owe ficed by my safety after entering the den of this raging lion."

" And did he use no threats ?"

" None that I valued," answered Bertrand le Noir,—" to be sure he talked rather largely, but as I knew that he would be no match for my master and his band of retainers whenever they came to close quarters, I laughed at his threats, and ventured to beard him still further though he was surrounded at the time by a number of as fierce looking fellows as ever you saw in your life."

" Then you may thank your lucky stars for getting off so well," observed his companion. " It is said that Black Ivan rarely submits to contradiction, and though Sir Gaston would most assuredly have avenged any violence that might have been committed against you, it would, in my opinion, have proved but sorry satisfaction for being sacrithe robber and his companions."

As the man concluded these words, the low note of a bugle was heard at no great distance off, and then suddenly recollecting himself, he continued :—

" That, friend Bertrand, is our master's signal, that he is impatient to see you, in order that he may learn what success has attended your late mission to the brigand. So come, let us away, or we may have as much to fear from his anger, as from the wrath of the much-dreaded Black Ivan himself."

Without making any reply to this, Bertrand followed the last speaker, and having made their way through the intricacies of the wood, they presently afterwards found themselves in a place that had been cleared away by the woodman's axe, and in the midst of which had been erected a pavilion, above which floated the banner of Sir Gaston de Neville. In the front, walked two sentinels; but as Bertrand was so well known and the object of his present visit perfectly understood, he was permitted to enter the tent without challenge from those who had been placed there to prevent the intrusion of any person whose business was not most urgent. As Bertrand entered, he perceived that the knight was seated in such profound meditation as not at first to be aware that any one had broken in upon his privacy. At length, however, he raised his eyes, and thus recognizing the well known form of his favourite attendant, his countenance become animated, and rising from his seat, he inquired, in an anxious voice, the success of his recent enterprise.

" We are but little indebted to fortune on the present occasion," answered Bertrand, " for though I was lucky enough to obtain an interview with Black Ivan, yet so bent is he upon keeping the Hebrew Maiden in his possession, that I have been unable to prevail upon him to yield her up at your demand."

"How!" exclaimed the knight, fiercely;—"dares the dog refuse the commands of one who has both the power and the inclination to crush him?"

"He received your message with scorn," answered Bertrand. "Nay, he even defies all that you may do to rescue the girl from his clutches, and I am sent back with a message in which insult and scorn are equally blended?"

"Hah! what says the robber to my demands?"

"That he regards them no more than the winds that blow," answered Bertrand le Noir.

"And did you threaten him that I would presently bring a sufficient force with me to humble him to the very dust?"

"I did."

"And was that also treated with scorn?"

"It was, Sir Knight. Nay, more, he pointed out to me a prisoner, who was bound as if for immediate execution, and after informing me that the man was to die immediately, he bade me say that, should chance ever throw you into his hands, he would have no more mercy than he felt for the poor wretch that was then waiting the word which was to deliver him over to death."

"Let him beware how he come in my way," exclaimed Sir Gaston de Neville, "for I swear that should he ever trust himself within my reach, to strike off his head with my hand, and place it above the highest tower of my castle, as a warning to all other evil-doers."

"Such an end to the villain is indeed to be desired," replied Bertrand, "and yet so wary has he grown, that I almost fear he will bid defiance to every attempt that may be made to finish his foul and excerable career."

"In me, at least," answered Sir Gaston, "he will find that he has provoked an enemy, not to be easily quieted, until he has paid the just forfeit of his life. Once already he has found means to effect his escape, when I thought him most safe, but if ever such an opportunity arrives again, he must invoke the assistance of the great fiend himself, ere he can hope to elude the doom his many heinous crimes have merited."

"But, in the meanwhile, Sir Knight," observed Bertrand, "he is going on with his crimes, and it is not impossible but he may seize upon your person, and fulfil the threat he has made, ere we have time to guard against the dark scheming of his subtle brain. Even now the maiden is in his power, and much I fear we shall not be able to rescue her, until she has fallen a victim to his unlawful passions."

"By heavens, then we must march against him without loss of time!" cried the knight, impatiently. "Our troops outnumber his, and it will be hard indeed, if we cannot rout this nest of miscreants, whose crimes have rendered them the terror and scourge of the whole country round."

"That your troops will cheerfully do their best to destroy the horde of robbers, I can readily believe," replied Bertrand. "They are faithful to their master, and will readily shed the last drop of their blood in his service, but the followers of Black Ivan are also brave, and their cause, being one of desperation and danger, will prompt them to fight to the very last, rather than yield with a certainty of meeting an ignominious death upon the gallows."

"You seem to fear them, Bertrand."

"No other man than my master would dare tell me so," replied the retainer, in a tone that plainly manifested his displeasure. "I care not for life, as many a well fought battle may convince you, nor should I now have spoken my mind so freely, had I not believed that you were about to risk the lives of yourself and faithful followers, merely to rescue a girl, who, after all, is not worth the trouble you have taken to get her in your power."

"Slave!" exclaimed the knight, fiercely, "do you dare to give an opinion in a matter that concerns only myself?"

"If I have done so," replied Bertrand, undaunted, "it has been to serve him who I call master."

"What!—by thwarting me in my will?"

"That," replied the retainer, "is only because I can foresee mischief should you fail in destroying this notorious brigand. In fact, if Black Ivan escapes, he will never rest until he has found means amply to re-venge himself for any wrongs he may conceive he has received at your hands."

"Tush, man! we will not give him a chance of escaping," answered Sir Gaston, impatiently striding up and down the pavillion. "We know well the consequences of a failure in this enterprise, and therefore it behoves every man to exert himself to the utmost, in order to secure an advantage over this most dangerous enemy."

"That all will do for their own sake," replied Bertrand. "We know the consequences of falling into the hands of Ivan, and sooner would we perish than meet an ignoble death from a villain who would glory in having the opportunity of having us mercilessly butchered before his eyes. I have now, however, said enough upon this subject, and it only remains for me to say that, as you have found me faithful on all former occasions, so shall you now find me willing to engage in any enterprise you may think proper to command."

"Well spoke, my gallant Bertrand!" exclaimed Sir Gaston de Neville. "Your words have served to remove whatever doubts I may have entertained, and as a proof of my confidence, it is my pleasure that you take the command immediately under myself."

"You have resolved then to attack these brigands?"

"Aye, and without the loss of any further time. The girl is unfortu-nately still in his power, and since you can guide us to his lurking place, we will march at once to her rescue."

"And the young Jew, her lover," observed Bertrand,—"he also I suppose is to be released from a doom that, in my opinion, he justly merits?"

"Why, that I have no particular liking for him, you may pretty well imagine," replied Sir Gaston. "He is, as you are aware, my rival in this maiden's love, and therefore would I gladly know that he had fal-len by the hands of these robbers. It is however necessary that we should march directly towards the cavern, and should the Israelite fall alive into my power, it will be a matter for after consideration, whether I shall hold him in captivity, or restore him to liberty under certain conditions."

"That is to say," observed Bertrand, "you will not wish to keep him as your prisoner, after he consents to give up all further pretensions to the hand of his betrothed."

"You have exactly guessed my meaning, good Bertrand. Reuben Grenard is too humble a foe to give me much uneasiness, and he may therefore be at large from the moment that he has pledged his word no longer to oppose me in this one point?"

"But what of the girl?" asked Bertrand;—"may it not happen that she will refuse to be a party to any such agreement."

"Oh;" answered the knight, "her scruples will have very little weight with me, I can assure you. Once secure in my castle, she will have no alternative, and must therefore consent to become the mistress of the man who holds her in his power."

"I see," replied the retainer; "the wench is likely to gain but little by her change from a robber's cavern to the castle of a wealthy and powerful knight."

"Leave me," exclaimed Sir Gaston, "for I begin to perceive that you are not the friend I have ever taken you for. I have permitted too much freedom to grow up in one whom I believed to be faithful, but it is now time you should learn that I am resolved to enforce obedience, even though it may not be in my power to command your reverence. Go, Bertrand, and show your diligence in assembling my troops for an immediate march towards the secret retreat of the robbers."

Bertrand sullenly took his departure, and, within half an hour returned to inform the knight that every thing was in readiness as he had commanded. Upon this, Sir Gaston hastily quitted the pavilion, and placing himself at the head of his retainers, took his way through the wood, guided by Bertrand le Noir, who had undertaken to conduct them to the bandit's cave.

CHAPTER XX.

"Mercy,—I crave your mercy!
Spare him, I do beseech you, or let me
Die with him." LOCHIEL'S DOOM.

AT the end of the hour, which had been granted by Black Ivan to his prisoner for preparation, Hubert once more presented himself before his chieftain, in order to inform him that every thing was now in readiness, and that he only awaited further commands, to march Reuben Grenard to the spot where the execution was appointed to take place. At this intimation the brigand smiled grimly, and hastily rising from the table where he had been indulging freely, he expressed his approbation at the punctuality with which every thing had been conducted. Then recollecting himself, he inquired whether Rebecca was guarded in her own apartment, so as to prevent her quitting it until after the fatal tragedy had been completed."

"She was safe there but a few minutes since," answered Hubert, "and judging what your wishes would be, I have desired old Maud not to leave her, nor on any account to suffer her to quit her sight until she had received permission from yourself to do so."

"'Tis well," cried Ivan; "but now tell me how the girl seems;—does she appear to be more reconciled to her fate, or shall I be compelled to use force in order to bend her stubborn spirit to my will?"

"Why, at present," answered Hubert, "she appears to be as obstinate as ever. But time, I dare say, will perform wonders: and when she learns that her lover has perished, I am inclined to think she will not make quite so many scruples as she has done."

"Nay, Hubert, thou knowest I am not one to be thwarted when once I have made up my mind. This girl I have resolved to have, and the more she opposes, the more determined am I to conquer, in spite of her aversion."

"For my own part," observed Herbert, "I could never see the use o humouring women to their vagaries. She has stuck out quite long enough, in my opinion, and I only wonder that you have been so patient with her."

"Well, well," cried Ivan, "if that has been a fault, it shall be so no longer. Reuben Grenard will soon be out of my way, and if she has any more scruples about uniting herself to a robber, why the only way will be to get rid of her, by the same means that have been used against her lover."

"True, captain," answered the other;—"a poniard is an excellent remedy for such as her, and, between ourselves, if there should be any occasion to put her out of the way, there is one, who I need not name, that will be happy to obey the commands of his captain, whenever he may think proper to test him."

"Thou art a faithful fellow, Hubert," exclaimed the chieftain, "and some day or other, shall meet the reward thou so well meritest. But a truce to compliments now, for we have business of importance to occupy our attention;—in a few minutes my rival will have ceased to live, and I will then hasten from the scene of execution, to urge my claims for the hand of my fairer captive, So come with me, Hubert, and share with me the pleasure I shall enjoy, in witnessing the death of him who has too long stood between me and my happiness."

With these words, he despatched Hubert to conduct his prisoner to the place appointed for the execution, and following himself shortly afterwards, he found Reuben securely bound to a tree, whilst a body of archers were drawn up in front of the unfortunate captive, ready to despatch him immediately, upon the word to do so being given. Ivan could not conceal the satisfaction he experienced, at thus beholding his rival on the point of receiving his doom, and striding hastily towards the victim of his hatred, he said in a low tone:—

"At last then, Reuben Grenard, I behold thee about to receive that fate which will for ever remove thee from my path. For a time, indeed, thou didst exult in the certainty that my suit was rejected, because thine own had been successful, and I therefore have thee to judge, how great must be my satisfaction, at seeing thee within a few moments of terminating a career that will leave Rebecca entirely at my disposal."

"That thou dost triumph, villain, is not to be denied," answered Reuben, firmly, "and yet, were it not for the bitter reflection that I leave the maiden unprotected, thou shouldst see how little terror I feel at the death to which thou hast sent me. But the period of thine exultation will not last long, for so sure as there is an avenging heaven above, so surely wilt thou, ere long, be made to repent the baseness that has hurried thee on to this act of cruelty. Tremble, therefore, Ivan, and repent if thou canst, the many iniquities of which thou hast been guilty."

"By my soul, Jew, thou wilt prove a false prophet in this matter, at least," answered the robber, in a careless tone;—"hitherto I have gone on without let or hindrance, and for my own part, I can see no reason for entertaining any alarm for the future."

"And yet," returned Reuben, "the avenging arm may be ready to strike even while thou speakest. The ways of heaven are dark and mysterious, and no man knoweth how soon he will be arrested in his wickedness."

"Be that as it may," returned Black Ivan, "thou hast thyself alone to thank for the death to which thou hast been adjudged;—I offered thee liberty, and thou hast been mad enough to reject the terms."

"Because thou woulds't have had me pollute my soul with guilt," answered Reuben. "That I might have lived is true, but it would have

leen to see Rebecca thy victim, together with the curse of knowing that she had delivered herself up to thee through my means."

"And now thou hast the comfortable reflection, that thy death is entirely owing to thine own obstinacy," returned the robber. "Besides, thou seest how I exult in thy fate, and surely that must add some bitterness to the last moments of thine existence."

"If thy bosom contains one single particle of feeilng, I pray thee end my miseries at once, by giving the word, that yonder archers are so impatiently looking for. It is my last and only request, and surely you cannot wish to prolong those miseries, of which I have already had more than my full share."

"Oh, fear not that I shall delay the signal much longer," answered Ivan. "I am impatient to carry the news of thy death to Rebecca, because when she hears of what has taken place, it is not unlikely that she will be ready enough to exchange a dead lover for a living one."

"Wretch!" exclaimed Reuben, "darest thou taunt me thus in this dread hour of trial!"

"Thou hast heard that I dare do so," answered the robber chief;— "thou hast found by this time that I have not much mercy for a hated rival, and yet thou canst affect surprise and indignation."

"Again I warn thee to be speedy with this execution," cried the prisoner;—"be speedy, I say, for a something assures me that if thou delayest much longer, thy victim will be snatched from the fate to which he has been doomed."

"Oh, if that is the case," replied Black Ivan, "thy wish shall at once be gratified. Archers—take your places—draw your arrows to their very points, and, as ye will answer it with your own lives, see that not one of you miss the heart of your victim. Stand firmly to your places, and when I raise my hand above my head, let your messengers of death speed forth on their fatal errand."

Ivan now paused for a moment, to mark whether any fear was visible in the countenance of his victim. To his disappointment, however, he saw that Reuben maintained his wonted firmness. and, enraged at this circumstance, he was in the act of raising his hand, to give the preconcerted signal, when a piercing shriek of anguish was heard, and the next moment Rebecca, pale, and with her hair hanging loosely about, rushed distractedly from the cavern, and threw herself between Reuben and the arrows, which at this instant were aimed towards his heart.

"Hold!" she exclaimed, in accents of despair;—"hold, I implore ye, or, if ye will slay him, let every weapon reach him through my heart."

"Remove her!" roared Black Ivan, furiously;—"drag her away, I say, and let the execution proceed without further interruption."

"I will not stir from this spot!" cried Rebecca, clasping her arms convulsively round Reuben, as she perceived some of the ruffians advancing to tear her away. "Ye seek the life of one who is most dear to me; and, since he must perish, I also will fall a victim to the heartless cruelty of yonder villain."

"Dost thou hear me, fellows?" again shouted the enraged captain; —"drag her from the place, I say, or the man who refuses to advance shall die by my hand."

"It is in vain that you set your blood hounds upon me," cried Rebecca, firmly, "for I can brave death and will meet it here rather than be torn from him ye are about to murder."

"Then thou shalt have thy wish," exclaimed Ivan, and once more addressing himself to the archers, he said:—"It is now my will that they both die;—remember men—let your aim be steady, and now, let your instruments of death do their bloody work!"

But ere this command could be carried into effect, a tremendous shower of arrows flew amongst the brigand archers, and the next moment saw more than half of them lying wounded upon the ground. Taken thus by surprise, those who were not wounded were unable to return the discharge, and before they could recover themselves, Sir Gaston de Neville, at the head of his numerous retainers, rushed forward, and, with their swords, commenced such a desperate attack, that the robbers were soon compelled to throw down their arms and sue for mercy. Black Ivan alone attempted to escape, but ere he could effect his object Bertand le Noir rushed forward, and after a brief struggle succeeded in making him his prisoner.

Reuben was then released from the tree to which he had been bound, a litter was formed to convey Rebecca from the place, and when the prisoners and wounded had been properly secured, Sir Gaston de Neville gave the word to march homewards, leaving a sufficient number of his own men behind to whom was committed the task of searching the cave, and seizing any stragglers who might still be lurking about.

CHAPTER XXI.

"Art thou the hag
Whose name makes peasants tremble, and whose arts
Are practised 'gainst mankind?"

THE BEGGAR'S LAMENT.

OPPRESSED in spirit and almost maddened by the loss of his beloved child, Isaac of Tadcaster returned home after having made an ineffectual search for the maiden whose loss he so bitterly deplored. In the agony of his soul he yielded himself to the despair that had gathered around his heart, and desiring his faithful attendant Jonah to go forth and make inquiry after his lost child, he threw himself upon his couch, where he lay for hours unconscious of all, save the deep affliction that had fallen like a withering blight upon those hopes which had once been so bright and fair. At last, however, he was aroused by a gentle footstep near him, and raising his head, he perceived Jonah, who having returned, was now standing and watching the prostrate form of his master with a countenance that showed the intense concern that the sorrows of the good old man occasioned him. The presence of his servant seemed to inspire Isaac with a momentary gleam of hope, and starting up from his recumbent position he inquired with breathless anxiety whether he was the bearer of any news more favourable to his expectations.

"Alas!" answered Jonah, "everything seems to confirm our fear that the maiden is for ever torn from the protection of her father."

"Hah!" cried the old man, "thou hast heard evil tidings of her, then?"

"I have;—in fact she is now again confined in the strong castle of Sir Gaston, the Terrible."

"Father of mercies!" cried the heart-broken Israelite, "then is she indeed in the power of the fiend of darkness!"

"Nay, good master, do not despair," exclaimed Jonah, in a soothing tone. "Great, indeed, is the cause of thy grief, and yet it is sinful to believe that the Father who watches over his meanest creatures, has deserted thy beloved child."

"Thou art right, Jonah," answered the old man. "It was wrong I admit, but the lacerated heart cannot restrain its moanings in moments such as this, nor can comfort ever reach my heart whilst the lamb, I have watched with a shepherd's care, is absent from her fold."

"Dost thou think then there is no chance of wresting her from the power of this base libertine?"

"Alas!" groaned the old man, "my heart tells me there is no hope."

"Not even from the king," asked Jonah, "whose love of justice and tenderness towards all his subjects is the theme of universal admiration?"

"Richard is a great and glorious monarch," answered the Israelite, "but we belong to a despised race, and our prayers will be unheeded."

"Not if you can gain access to the royal presence," exclaimed Jonah, in a tone of confidence. "All his subjects, whether they be Jews or Christians, equally claim his protection, and even the mighty Sir Gaston de Neville will be called to a severe account, were his conduct in this affair to be laid before him."

"It is in vain to expect it," exclaimed Isaac of Tadcaster;—"the villain has drawn his snares tightly around us, and my heart assures me that we are utterly at his mercy. Besides, how are we to obtain an audience of the king, when there are so many about him to use their influence against me?"

"Still, there is one chance left," returned the domestic, after a few moments' consideration; "Ralph de Glanville, the Chief Justiciary, possesses, it is said, the confidence of the king, and a bribe offered in that quarter is hardly likely to be rejected, even though it may come from the hands of one of our despised race."

"Will justice stoop so low," asked the old man, "as to yield for gold that which he would refuse to the poor and helpless supplicant?"

"Such, at least, is the character I have heard of him."

"We will try him then, at all events," returned the aged Israelite.— "I will offer him money and jewels, to obtain this interview with Richard, and should I succeed in releasing Rebecca, my whole fortune should be sacrificed even to the last coin I possess in the world."

"Nay, master," exclaimed Jonah, "thou needst not beggar thyself and the maiden; thou wilt hear what sum the Chief Justiciary will require for obtaining the interview with Richard, and I will dare be sworn his majesty will listen patiently to thy complaints without exacting from thee the hard earnings of a long and toilsome life."

"Thou forgettest," replied Isaac, "that the king is a Christian, and as such will not fail to extort, as his predecessors have done, all that he can from one who belongs to hated and persecuted tribe."

"Thou forgettest," returned the other, "that our present sovereign glories in his love of strict and impartial justice."

"Aye—when the parties believe in the same creed that he does," answered the old man, with bitter emphasis.

"Then would he cease to be a just monarch," returned Jonah, quickly. "By such a course Richard would forfeit the good name he has been at such pains to obtain, and from that time his honour would become tainted."

"Well, well, good Jonah," exclaimed the old man, "thou hast much confidence in our present ruler, and I will not reject the counsel thou hast given. As a last and desperate effort I will seek to obtain an audience, and, if that fails, I care not how soon death puts an end to my sufferings."

"Wilt thou see the Justiciary to-day?"

"Aye, this very hour," answered the afflicted father. "Moments are now too precious to be wasted in idleness, and I cannot rest until I have assured myself whether happiness or misery is to be my future doom."

"Thou wilt repair to the palace then?"

"I will."

"Alone?"

"No; thou shalt go with me, Jonah. I shall need a faithful friend, and in thee can I rely when all the world besides hath forsaken me."

"Nor shall thy confidence be abused, dear master," answered Jonah, earnestly. "From infancy I have lived with thee, and, if need be, thou shalt find that I can cheerfully die either with or for thee."

"Nay," returned the old man, "thy life, I hope, will at least be safe. Thou art poor, good Jonah, and therefore may escape persecution, since it is only for our gold that these Christians persecute us even to death. I, however, am suspected of having amassed a store of wealth, and I fear never will they restore my child to me until they have made the thing of scorn I dread to think of."

"Hast thou so soon forgotten thy promise to see the king?" asked the faithful domestic.

"I have not forgotten it," replied the Jew, "but my heart tells me the effort will be made in vain. I am old and feeble—the king powerful and young. I may plead to him upon my knees, but will he hearken to my prayers when they have for their object the punishment and disgrace of a great and favourite noble?"

"As a father," answered Jonah, "your heart will prompt you to make every effort."

"It does—it does," exclaimed the old man. "I feel that it must be done, and my resolution is formed accordingly. I will therefore depart instantly, earnestly imploring heaven to aid me in a cause so just."

"Whither goest thou, old man?" cried a female voice, as he was turning to leave the place, and at the same moment a tall gaunt figure presented herself, supported by a pair of crutches with which she had contrived to drag herself to the spot where she now stood. "Whither goest thou, I ask?" she repeated in a querulous voice; "speak—I charge thee, for cripple as I am, thou mayst yet find that I am not without power to serve thee."

"Tell me first," answered Isaac, gazing upon her with surprise, "who it is that has thus asked me the question?"

"Hah!—hast thou not heard of me, old man?"

"I may," he replied, "but know thee not."

"Indeed!—then I will enlighten thee; a cripple, as you see, yet one who may serve thee in thine utmost need. Say, wilt thou make a friend of her who all men shun for her dealings with beings of another world?"

"Avaunt, hag!" exclaimed the Jew, turning from her with disgust; "avaunt, I say, and leave me to fulfil, without interruption, the task I am engaged in."

"Dost thou despise my power?"

"I do."

"And dreadest not the heavy afflictions that I can bring upon thee and thine?"

"Thou canst not increase the grief that weighs down my oppressed soul," answered Isaac. "Already have the heaviest afflictions befallen me, and now can I defy thee to increase them."

"I know thy meaning well," returned the Pythoness, directing a scrutinizing glance towards the old man. "Thou hast lost a child, and, in her, all that thy heart holds dearest?"

"I have."

"And now thou relyest on the king's magnanimity for her restoration?"

"Thou hast spoken truly, woman," answered Isaac. "Report speaks favourably of his generosity, and I have made up my mind to pour forth a father's complaints at the feet of his majesty."

"And thou expectest that he will listen to thee with compassion?"

"It is at least worth the trial," replied the Jew. "A maiden's honour is threatened by a base knight, and I would demand the safety of one and the just punishment of the other."

"The knight," observed Meg, "is Sir Gaston de Neville?"

"It is."

"And dost thou believe Richard Cœur de Lion, will punish one of his bravest adherents at the bidding of one so humble as thyself?"

"I ask not for a severe punishment," replied the Jew, "but as a father I demand the restoration of my child."

"And dost thou not know," resumed the Weird woman, "that Sir Gaston de Neville will meet thy charge with another that may prove fatal to the daughter of thy love?"

"Hah!" exclaimed the startled old man, "thou speakest as if thou knewest of some impending evil. I implore thee, tell me, if thou knowest aught that threatens the safety of her who is far dearer to me than life itself."

"Nay, thou wilt laugh to scorn a warning that is produced by my power, and knowledge of necromancy?"

"Oh, if there is danger, speak, I conjure you!" cried Isaac, in an agony of terror.

"Wilt thou believe me when I speak?"

"I will,—I will!"

"Then, hear me," resumed Meg, limping nearer with the aid of her crutches; "thou knowest that Sir Gaston de Neville lost a valuable diamond, which was stolen from him by Black Ivan, the Outlaw, and afterwards found in the possession of thy daughter?"

"True;—but it was an accident," answered the startled Jew. "Black Ivan presented himself to me as a perfect stranger, and offered the diamond ring of which thou speakest, for a certain sum of gold. I advanced the money he required, and when the jewel had thus, by fair means, come into my possession, placed it upon the finger of my daughter for safety, intending it for a present to the king, on the occasion of his approaching coronation."

"A well told story, and probable enough," answered the old woman, "yet I doubt greatly whether Richard will be as inclined to believe it as I am."

"What!" exclaimed Isaac, "will he believe that I had any share in the robbery?"

"It will be Sir Gaston's care to make such a story plausible," answered the Weird Woman. "By so doing, he will deprive thee of any pity the king might otherwise feel for thee, and thy supposed participation in the robbery, will effectually bar thee from that justice thou thinkest to obtain."

"Alas! alas!" groaned the afflicted father, "then am I indeed encompassed by the snares of a wicked foe."

"To be sure thou art," she replied. "The power I possess enables me to warn thee of the evil thou hast to expect, and it was to serve thee, that I came unbidden into thy presence."

"For thy kindness, I repay thee with this sum of gold," exclaimed Isaac, offering her a purse which he had just unfastened from his girdle; "take it woman, and if thou wilt aid me in rescuing an innocent maiden from the evil designs of our enemies, I will beggar myself to enrich thee."

"I will accept thy present offer, old man," she replied, "because I am poor, and need a small portion of that wealth, which the world say thou possessest."

"But may I depend upon thy zeal?"

"At least thy daughter may."

"Ah!—thou speakest as if thou wouldst indeed befriend her," cried the old man.

"And so I would," answered Meg, earnestly. "I was perishing one bitter cold winter's night, when she came like an angel from heaven to my relief; I was starving, and she gave me food!"

"Then 'tis gratitude," observed Isaac, "that has prompted thee to step betwixt her and destruction?"

"It is," she replied: "I owe my life to her, and though I cannot now serve her to the extent of my wishes, I would so warn thee, as to give her some chance of escaping from the doom with which she is threatened."

"Speak, woman, I charge thee, speak !" cried Isaac, in an agony of terror. "What danger threatens her, and how may it be averted ?"

"The former question I may answer," she replied, "but the other will require time to reply to."

"Woman, you drive me mad with this fearful suspense ! What peril is it of which you speak?"

"The peril of death,—of shame—of ignominy !"

"Hah !—and may not all these be averted ?"

"Perhaps so, but all will depend on circumstances ;" replied the old woman, after a brief pause. "Sir Gaston, as I have already warned you, will not fail to insist upon it that she is guilty of having some share in the robbery of his diamond, and she will be condemned to death, unless you are present to demand trial by ordeal."

"Trial by ordeal !" groaned the hapless father, "then—then is she indeed lost !"

"It will, at least, afford her a chance of escape," replied Meg. "There is a power above to protect innocence, and it is not for man to doubt, even in those moments when danger seems to be nearest. Arouse thee, then,—take good heart, and perhaps, ere many hours have passed away, she will be once more restored to thine arms."

"Thy words afford me some consolation," answered Isaac, "and I will yield myself to thy bidding, even on the instant. My faithful domestic and I will instantly repair to the palace of king Richard, and demand the restoration of my child from the vile libertine who has snatched her from my arms."

"Let it be even as thou hast said," returned the Weird Woman; "hie thee forth, old man, and should my further counsel or aid be required, I will not fail to hasten to thee. Farewell, Jew, and may thy righteous errand meet the success I so much wish thee."

As she pronounced these words, she again dragged herself away with the assistance of her crutches, and having entirely disappeared, the woe-oppressed Israelite and his faithful attendant set forth, taking their way towards Westminster, where was situated the princely residence of the gallant monarch, Richard Cœur de Lion.

CHAPTER XXII.

"I would be just,
And therefore, in this case, inflexible ;—
Proceed, and let fair justice be dealt out
Between both parties."—THE ENVOY.

NEVER did Isaac of Tadcaster feel more oppressed in spirit than during his progress towards the palace; the words of the Weird Woman of the Heath, had fallen like daggers upon his heart, and the consolation offered by the faithful Jonah, had the effect only of convincing him more and more, that Rebecca was doomed to undergo sufferings, far more poignant than any she had yet endured. In imagination, he already beheld her under the dreadful torture to which she would be doomed, and as he thought of the excruciating agonies to which her tender frame would be subjected, his heart sickened ; and inwardly he prayed heaven to release both her and himself, rather than that they should live to become the sport of those who would glory in being spectators of their horrible agonies.

At length, finding that his good intentions were without effect, Jonah forbore to say anything further upon the subject, and for some time longer they walked on in silence, uninterrupted, except by the heavy groans and lamentations of the unfortunate parent, whose oppressive griefs were too heavy for endurance. Still, however, he uttered not a word of complaint; and, indeed, so absorbed did he seem to be in his own mental reflections, that they had reached the principal gateway leading to the palace, before he was aware that they had accomplished half the journey. On arriving there, he was aroused by a voice that fell gratingly upon his ear, and looking up, he beheld one of the king's body guard, who, having placed his javelin across the entrance, so as to impede their further progress, exclaimed tauntingly:—

"Hollo! thou villain Jew, whither goest thou in such speed, I should like to know?"

"To see him, who both thou and I are proud to call master," answered Isaac, undaunted by the martial appearance of the fellow.

"What!" exclaimed the man at arms, "art thou fool enough, then, to believe that admittance will be given to one of thy accursed tribe?"

"If my tribe is accursed, friend," answered the old man, mildly, "it is only by such as thyself;—by man whose blindness makes them believe that the Great Father of the Universe has created one class of men better than another."

"Hah!" cried the other, with fury, "hast thou the insolence to exalt thy people, and place them on a level with Christians?"

"He is unworthy to be called a Christian, who endeavours to create a difference betwixt any classes who worship the same Supreme Ruler," answered the Israelite. "All men belong to one family, and, though a difference may exist amongst them, it follows not that one portion of them shall take upon themselves to declare their own superiority."

"Why audacious slave," cried the soldier, "were it not for thine age, I would have struck thee down with the handle of my weapon long ere this. Knowest thou not that thou art within the precincts of the king's palace, where 'tis death for any one to be found lurking, unless introduced by one of his majestiy's chief favourites."

"I am here upon a holy errand," cried the Jew, in an imploring tone. "My daughter is in danger, and I would throw myself at the feet of my sovereign, to implore his intercession in her behalf?"

"Humph!—and dost thou believe King Richard has nothing else to do than to listen to the complaints of such as thee?" demanded the fellow, roughly.

"I believe," answered Isaac, with hesitation, "that his highness entertains equal compassion towards all his subjects, whether they be rich or poor. Oppression will find in time a ready corrector, and all I ask of thee, is that thou wilt obtain for me the audience I require."·

"And who would be the fool then, I should like to know?" growled the guard. "My place here would be forfeited, and perhaps my life too for the matter of that."

"Nay," replied the Israelite, "I will answer for it, thou shalt lose neither. The narrative of my wrongs will fully warrant thee for what thou doest, and instead of anger, thou wilt receive the commendation of thy royal master."

"Thou mayst tell me so, because it is to thine interest to do so," returned the man at arms. "I, however, happen to know that I should make a bad day's work of it, and therefore shall refuse to have any hand in it."

"What shall we do now, master?" whispered Jonah, who had been listening uneasily to this conversation.

"Why, get thee away with all the speed thou canst," replied the man "So turn your steps homewards again, for I can promise thee thou wilt get no admittance here whilst I am on duty."

"Alas! alas!" groaned the afflicted old man, "will nothing move thee to compassion?"

"Nothing," answered the guard,—"that is to say," he continued, "nothing short of a good round sum."

"Hah!" exclaimed Isaac!—"name thine own terms then;—say,— what amount of gold will prevail upon thee to obtain for me an audience of the king?"

"Humph!" answered the other,—"let me hear what thine own conscience will offer."

"Hah!" exclaimed a voice close by, that made them start at its proximity,. "who is it that dares to receive a bribe in this place besides myself?"

"Pardon me, my Lord Chief Justiciary," stammered the soldier, with terror;—"this man is to blame, and not me, since he it was who offered to purchase my services at a price that I could scarcely be expected to resist."

"Is this true, sirrah?" demanded Ralph de Glanville, sternly;— "hast thou indeed dared to trifle with one of the king's body guard?"

"I did but ask him to do me a favour, my Lord Judge," replied the Israelite, "and in doing so, had no intention to offend either his majesty or yourself."

"'Thou liest, base slave that thou art," vociferated the other, angrily. "This, for ought I know, is some scheme to assassinate the king, and

No. 14

thou must to the rack, that we may extort from thee a confession of thy guilt."

"I am innocent of such evil intention,—indeed, indeed I am!" cried the old man, in an agony of terror. "In me you behold a hapless father, anxious only for the preservation of his child, who, could he but be convinced of her safety, would cheerfully lay down his life, and breathe forth his last words in thankfulness and joy."

"This is some subterfuge to hide thy crime," answered the Chief Justiciary. "The tribe thou belongest to is enough to prove thy designs to be dangerous, and therefore it is my duty to commit thee to prison, until my gracious master's further pleasure is known as to the degree of punishment that shall be meted out to thee."

"Spare me but for a little time," exclaimed the old man, earnestly; "grant me but till I have succeeded in rescuing my daughter from danger, and I will bless thee."

"Fool!" exclaimed the other, "thinkest thee I require the blessings of a Jew? Knowest thou not the difference that is between us, and that I can deliver thee over to death without submitting thee to the form of a trial?"

"I know thy power, and mine own weakness," answered Isaac, meekly. "At present it is the will of heaven that our people shall bow to the yoke of the oppressor. Of this I am aware, but I warn you not to commit an act of injustice, even though it may be against one who has not the power to resist thee."

"Thou art insolent."

"I am firm, my lord, in the justice of my own cause," answered the afflicted Israelite. "That I am unfortunate is the fault of those who belong to thy creed."

"Hah! darest thou speak thus of Christians?"

"As men, my lord, I am fully justified in speaking of them as I have. Do they not glory in oppressing and injuring men whose only crime consists in following a creed that has been handed down to them from generation to generation, by their forefathers? Are we not made a mark for every indignity, and yet can it be proved that we were ever otherwise than loyal subjects,—cheerfully paying more than our share towards the maintenance of the sovereign who does not even afford us his protection in return?"

"This insolence is not to be borne!" cried Ralph de Glanville;— "not content with the liberty that is granted thee, thou must needs raise thy rebellious voice against the king, whose mercy thou hast so much reason to praise."

"Of Richard, I have not spoken one word in disparagement," replied the Jew, with humility. "He hath but lately come to the throne of this fair realm, and it yet remains to be proved whether he will follow in the blood-stained steps of those princes who have preceded him."

"Were he to take my advice," replied the Justiciary, "he would not much longer suffer one of your cursed tribe to taint the air of this Christian land."

"And wherefore," demanded Isaac, "dost thou speak thus of men whom God hath made your brethren?"

"Slave!" vociferated Ralph de Glanville, "dost thou dare to place thyself in the same rank with those who profess to be true believers?"

"I dare assert the dignity of men," answered the Israelite, "whose only crime consists in believing differently to yourself. If we are wrong, God alone should punish us, since none but He can weigh us in the impartial balance of justice."

"Shall the Jew speak thus, and live?" demanded the man-at-arms, plucking forth his dagger, and advancing to receive permission to lay the old man a bleeding corse at his feet. "Shall he dare utter his blasphemies, and not receive the punishment he deserves?"

"Hold!" interposed the Justiciary;—"shed not the blood of this man until thou hast received orders from the king himself. That he merits the fate thou wouldst bring upon him, is not to be denied, and yet our royal master might not be best pleased were we to take upon ourselves the task you have suggested."

"Then will England soon swarm with Jews if once they find our laws grow merciful towards them," answered the man-at-arms. "For my own part, I remember the time when a Jew's life was considered of no value; but I suppose they are to flourish in this reign, and fatten upon the gold they extort from us."

"Thou dost wrong us by such an insinuation," replied Isaac, firmly. "Where dost thou find more loyal subjects than amongst those who thou wouldst see ground into the very dust at thy feet? Do we not cheerfully pay our share towards the support of the state, and shall we not in return receive that protection which is afforded to others?"

"By heaven, thine insolence is not to be borne!" cried the Chief Justiciary, furiously. "Already hast thou received more protection than thou hast any right to expect, and yet now thou hast the effrontery to seek for more."

"I know not what you call protection," answered the old man, "but this I have learnt to my sorrow—a father may be robbed of his only—his darling child, and yet there is no help for him, because his creed happens to be different to thine own."

"'Tis false!" vociferated Ralph de Glanville.

"Nay," answered the Jew, "there is proof of what I have said in the unhappy person who now stands before you. I have been robbed of my daughter by a foul villain, and he refuses to restore her to my arms, even though I have implored him to do so on my knees."

"What," asked the Justiciary, "is the name of him against whom you make this complaint?"

"Sir Gaston de Neville."

"Hah!" exclaimed the other, "a brave man hast thou charged, and one, moreover, who happens to be high in favour with the king."

"And therefore," groaned the Israelite, "I am to have justice withheld from me!"

"Thou complainest without just cause," answered the other. "Richard will own no friendship with the man against whom a charge is preferred, nor is he ever deaf to the supplications of his subjects, even though they may chance to belong to thy people."

"May I then be permitted to see his grace?" demanded Isaac, eagerly.

"At present thou canst not," returned de Glanville; "but if thou wilt wait with patience, it is not unlikely that in a few days he may grant thee an interview."

"Alas!" groaned the old man, "a few days hence will be too late! My child is now in the power of a villain, and she will become the loathed wretch my poor old heart bleeds to think of!"

"Canst thou think of no way to save her you profess to love so much?" asked the Justiciary.

"I have," replied Isaac; "the king, they say, is no respecter of persons when they transgress. I am willing to believe what I have heard, and therefore did I come hither, in order to throw myself at his feet, and implore his interference in my behalf."

"An admirable method truly!" exclaimed the other, with a sneer. "Richard owes thee thanks for the good opinion thou hast formed of him, and yet, between ourselves, Jew, it is no easy matter to gain access to the royal presence, unless thou hast friends about the court."

"Then do thou be my friend," exclaimed the old man;—"take me before the king, our master, and my thanks—my eternal gratitude shall be thine."

"Nay, thanks and gratitude," returned the Justiciary, "are but poor coin to pass current about a court. Favours require more satisfactory payment, and thou wilt find thyself grievously mistaken, unless thou canst make up thy mind to part with some of the gold thou hast been at such pains to store up."

"Gold!" groaned the Israelite;—"alas! my lord,—I am poor,—very, ry poor, and the gold you speak of, it is not in my power to give."

"Then your daughter is lost to you for ever."

"Ah!" exclaimed the old man;—"now I think of it, I brought with me a purse of money;—it is all I have been able to scrape together after years of toil and hardship, yet it shall be yours, on condition that you obtain for me an audience with the king. There it is, my lord—take it —take it, and in return, perform the favour I have asked."

"Here is no great deal," observed De Glanville, weighing the purse in his hand. "'Tis light, old man, and scarcely worth the acceptance of one who is not in absolute need of thy money."

"Ah! you reject it then?"

"Why no, I said not that either," answered the other;—"I will take what thou hast offered, but it must be on condition that I receive a larger sum after the fulfilment of my promise. In fact, you shall see the king, and I will give you credit for a further sum, depending on your word to bring it, ere a week from this time shall have elapsed."

"Nay, ask me not for more, my lord," cried the Jew, imploringly. "I am a poor, a very poor old man, and all I possess in the world has been given to you already. Be content, therefore, with what you have, and in pity grant the request I have so earnestly made."

"Thou art sure thou hast no more?"

"Quite sure."

"Well, I do not believe thee," replied the Justiciary, "and yet I have scarcely the heart to refuse the pleadings of a broken-hearted father. Thou shalt see the king, old man, and let that suffice."

"When—when shall I see him, my lord?"

"Presently."

"For that word, I thank thee," cried Isaac, in a tumult of rapture;— "thou hast taken a load off my heart, and I now feel assured, that the task which has brought me hither will not prove in vain."

"Be not too sure of that," returned De Glanville. "The king may not give credit to thy story, and in that case, thou wilt be lucky to escape from his presence with thy life."

"He will—he will believe me," answered the old man. "A father's pleadings cannot be received with indifference, and when good King Richard hears my tale of sorrow, he will take speedy means to give me restitution."

"You forget," answered De Glanville, "that the person you come to complain against, is the friend and companion of the king. They fought together in the field, and rumour says, that on one occasion our monarch owed his life to the gallantry of Sir Gaston de Neville."

"Still he will not refuse to hear my complaint," returned Isaac. "I will not ask him to punish or degrade the man who has injured me.

All that I implore is, the restoration of my child, and if that is accomplished, my enmity towards Sir Gaston de Neville ceases for ever."

"Methinks Sir Gaston will be much beholden to thee for your forbearance," sneered the man-at-arms, who was yet standing hard by. "The knight must indeed, be badly off, if he requires the kindly consideration of a poor crawling worm like thyself."

"Peace, sirrah," exclaimed de Glanville, sharply, "and let us have no more of this unseemly interference. Hence, slave, to the king's chamber;—say that Ralph de Glanville wishes to introduce a poor supplicant to his presence, and bring me back word when his highness will be pleased to grant us an interview."

The man-at-arms departed, grumbling at the errand on which he was sent, and then, the Justiciary, turning once more to Isaac, continued in a tone of more kindness than he had at first used:—

"Thou wonderest, perhaps, at seeing the change in my deportment towards thee. The truth is, however, that I have a daughter, young, innocent, and beloved as thine own, and the remembrance of her, and the danger she may some day be subjected to, has served to soften my heart in thy favour. That reflection has determined the course I am about to adopt, and may heaven speed the errand upon which thou now goest!"

"Thanks!—a thousand thanks for thy kindness!" cried the old man, with fervour. "Thou hast already raised me from the lowest depths of despair, and never whilst I live, will I omit any act by which my gratitude may be made manifest."

"Has thy daughter no lover," asked the Chief Justiciary, "from whom she might have looked for aid, in this great hour of her peril?"

"She has," answered Isaac, "but Reuben Grenard belongs to the same persecuted race as herself."

"And, therefore," cried De Glanville, "he leaves her to her fate, rather than run any risk, by seeking to obtain her deliverance from the hands of a rival?"

"Alas!" exclaimed the old man, "Reuben set out in search of her, and has himself, I fear, fallen into the hands of the fierce and inexorable Sir Gaston de Neville. Be that as it may, however, I have never seen him since, and there is but too much reason to fear, that he will be either basely destroyed, or imprisoned during the remainder of his days, in a dreary dungeon."

"Nay, your prejudice runs too strong against the knight," answered De Glanville. "True, you have suffered much from his persecution, but depend on it, Sir Gaston would not foolishly risk the loss of the king's favour, by an act of tyranny such as you have mentioned."

"But Reuben Grenard is a Jew," replied the old man, "and, therefore, may be oppressed without fear of the consequences."

"There thou dost the king a great wrong," exclaimed De Glanville. "He is just towards all who demand his interference, and though thou belongest to a race abhorred by Christians, he will not fail to see thee righted."

At this moment, the man-at-arms returned, and, advancing towards de Glanville, whispered in his ear, that the king required his immediate presence in the audience chamber.

"And did he desire this Jew to accompany me thither?" demanded the Justiciary.

"After some hesitation, he did," replied the other.

"And is he alone?"

"He is; for Sir Gaston de Neville quitted his presence at the same moment that I presented myself."

"That affords but a bad omen for yourself," observed the Chief Justiciary, addressing himself to Isaac. "The knight has, doubtless, anticipated your present application for an audience, and has been beforehand with you, in order that he may be the first to give his own version of the story."

"Let him say or do what he will," answered the Jew, "he cannot deny the plain, unvarnished tale of a poor, broken-hearted father. He dares not deny that he has stolen my child, and surely, in that case, Richard cannot be so unjust as to refuse me his aid and support."

"He will deny it, though," exclaimed the other, "and that, too, in a manner that will go far towards satisfying the king of his innocence. You will, therefore, be prepared for the worst, and act accordingly."

"Let us begone, then," cried the old man, impatiently; "conduct me to the soveriegn's presence, and if I fail in the hopes I have formed, may heaven, in its mercy, release me from a life, which will then have become a heavy burden and an affliction."

Thus adjured, Ralph de Glanville was proceeding towards the door which led to the king's private apartment; but, perceiving that Jonah was also accompanying them, he paused, and commanded him to remain where he was, until his master returned. This order, the faithful domestic obeyed reluctantly enough, but a gesture from the Jew was sufficient to ensure his obedience, and as he slowly retired, the others left the place to execute the mission on which they were engaged.

At length, after passing through numerous rooms, they reached the one in which the king was seated, where, pausing for a few minutes, they waited until it should please their royal master to command their further advance. Presently, Richard seemed to start from the reverie into which he had fallen, and no sooner did he recognise the person of his Chief Justiciary, than, half rising from his seat, he bade him welcome, desiring him at the same time, to approach and relate the business which had brought him thither.

"Your highness," replied the other, "will, I am sure, pardon me, when you have learnt the nature of my errand. A father, most gracious sire, entreats your assistance, to restore to him a daughter, who, it appears, has been stolen from him, by one who relies for safety on the kindness you have ever been pleased to bestow upon him."

"Hah!" exclaimed the king. "Is there, then, one among my friends who has dared to commit an act of oppression, under the impression that I will shield him from the consequences?"

"There is," replied the Justiciary, "and the old man is here to lay before you the complaint he has to make."

"Stand forward, Jew," exclaimed Richard: "nay, tremble not in my presence, for as I live, I will see equal justice done between thee and the evil-doer."

"My liege," cried Isaac, "you see before you a broken-hearted father, whose misfortunes have well nigh brought his grey hairs with sorrow to the grave. My child,—my fair and innocent child, has been basely stolen from me, and the fiend who hath done this, derides my suffering, and refuses to restore her to my arms."

"Indeed!" exclaimed Cœur de Lion, with startling vehemence, "and who, pray, is it that has dared to do as thou sayest?"

"Sir Gaston de Neville."

"Hah! by Our Lady, the knight you mention has scarcely left our presence these five minutes. Nay, more, he himself was a supplicant in some such case as this, and has just now declared that he only detained the girl until he has had restored to him a valuable diamond, which he charges her with having some share in stealing."

"It is a false charge, my liege, indeed it is," cried the old man, in a paroxysm of grief. "Sir Gaston may have been robbed, but my child is innocent of the crime."

"Dost thou know her to be innocent?"

"I do,—nay, I myself purchased the diamond of a man, who afterwards proved to be Black Ivan, the Outlaw."

"I remember something of this case before," observed the king; "you pleaded for my intercession not long since, as I was passing through the village of Charing. I then promised you my protection, and believed that the affair had ended from that moment. It seems, however, I am deceived, and that Sir Gaston de Neville is determined to draw down upon himself the anger that will crush him!"

"I ask not for his punishment," replied Isaac. "The restitution of my child, is all I supplicate, and if that wish should be accomplished, I shall rest content."

"Robert," exclaimed the king, beckoning to a page, "follow Sir Gaston de Neville, and tell him I command his immediate presence. Answer no questions, however, that he may ask, but let him return in ignorance of the affair I wish to see him on."

Then as the page departed, Richard once more addressed himself to Isaac of Tadcaster.

"Thou shalt have justice done thee, old man, unless thy charge can be answered by him that it has been brought against. My court shall be no harbour for villany, nor should my own brother escape punishment, were he to commit a crime meriting my displeasure."

"Pardon me, sire," cried Isaac, "but I ask for nothing more than that my daughter may be instantly restored. Grant me but this favour, and 'tis all I seek."

At this juncture, Sir Gaston de Neville entered the audience chamber, and no sooner did he perceive that the Jew was there before him, than he would have effected his retreat. Richard, however, perceived his design, and rising hastily from his seat, exclaimed in a tone of authority :—

"Ho, Sir Knight, stay, I command you! Here is a charge brought against you, and we will not part until the matter has been thoroughly and rigidly investigated."

"I see my accuser," answered De Neville, "and can well understand the artful tale he has invented to deprive me of your royal favour. He accuses me of having taken away his daughter, but I answer it by charging her with the crime of robbery."

"And have you evidence to support such a charge?" asked the king.

"I have," replied Sir Gaston. "My followers, as well as myself, saw the diamond ring, which had been stolen from me, upon her finger, within a few hours after I had been robbed of it."

"You hear what the knight says," exclaimed Richard, addressing himself to the old man. "He has brought a heavy accusation against your daughter, and unless you can prove her innocence, I cannot so far stretch my power as to wrest the prisoner from his grasp."

"I deny the charge," cried Isaac; "the ring was purchased by me from a stranger, who told me that he was pursued by his creditors, and that he required the money to save himself from a prison. Thus the diamond came into my possession, and I placed it on the girl's finger, where it was afterwards found by Sir Gaston de Neville, when he traced the robber to my house."

"You hear him, my gracious liege!" exclaimed the knight, in a tone of exultation. "He denies not that his daughter had the ring in her possession, and this is but a lame story that he has invented to convince you of her innocence."

"As heaven shall be my judge, it is the truth," cried the old man, trembling with apprehension.

"Can you prove that the jewel was obtained in the way you have stated?" demanded the king.

"I have no evidence," answered the Jew, "unless Black Ivan was here, to add his testimony to my own."

"Black Ivan knows the value of his own neck too well for that," returned King Richard. "He is aware that I have little mercy on robbers like himself, and will, therefore, wisely keep himself beyond my reach."

"Nay," answered Sir Gaston, "the outlaw is already in safe custody within one of the strongest dungeons of my castle. I have succeeded in dispersing his band from their place of concealment, and it shall go hard indeed if ever he has it in his power to commit any further depredations on your majesty's subjects."

"Will you not bring him forward," asked the old man, "to give testimony to clear my child from the foul charge you have brought against her?"

"If I were to do so, it would be of no use," replied the knight. "Black Ivan is in no very good humour at the misfortunes that have befallen him, and he will not be prevailed upon to say one word to save your daughter from the consequences of her crime."

"She is innocent!—she is innocent!" cried the old Israelite, in despair.

"At present," observed Richard, "we want evidence to prove her innocence. Sir Gaston de Neville, an honourable knight, and a soldier of worthy fame, has directly charged her with being concerned in the robbery of this diamond. You can offer no proof to show that she is guiltless, and therefore, much as I may regret the necessity, her life becomes forfeited, unless within two days she can establish the falsehood of the accusation."

"Mercy! Mercy!" groaned the heart-stricken father, falling upon his knees, at the king's feet and clasping his hands in agony. "Spare her, my liege, I entreat you,—spare her, and do not send one so young and innocent to suffer for a crime she has not committed."

"It is in vain to plead, old man," exclaimed the king;—"I can pity her, but guilt cannot be suffered to go unpunished."

"Lost! lost!" cried Isaac, and sinking upon the floor he became unconscious of the terrible sufferings, which had thus fallen upon him with their overpowering weight. At last, however, he once more revived, and then, slowly rising from the place where he had sunk down, he again earnestly implored the king to command the release of his daughter from the power of her persecutor.

"It is impossible," answered Richard, who had been engaged in a conference with Sir Gaston de Neville;—"the knight insists upon her receiving the punishment due to her crimes, and the only mercy I can show, is to grant her the trial by ordeal. If she can pass through unscathed, her life shall not only by spared, but I give my kingly word that she shall be restored to her home."

"I accept your offer, my liege," exclaimed Isaac, remembering at that

moment the words of Meg of Finchley. " She shall submit to the ordeal, and, I doubt not, heaven will grant a miracle by which to save her from the doom her cruel persecutor so much desires to bring upon his innocent victim."

" Then on the second day from hence let her be brought hither," exclaimed the king. " She shall be tried by the ordeal of boiling water, and should she indeed escape that unharmed, I will grant her my free pardon. And now, old man, depart;—return home, and remember, on the appointed day, thou wilt be looked for here, as a witness to the proceedings that must either save thy child, or give her to an ignominious death."

With these words the king rose and took his departure, leaving Isaac a prey to the bitter thoughts that rushed through his tortured brain. Presently, however, the old man slowly left the room, and having once more met with Jonah, he accompanied him home, brooding over the afflictions that had thus befallen him in his declining days.

CHAPTER XXIII.

"Nay, not another instant shall he live,—
Drag him away, I say,—the gibbet is his doom,
And justly does he merit it."

HALIFAX GIBBET LAW.

SIR GASTON DE NEVILLE having thus, as he imagined, secured one of his victims, resolved to execute summary vengeance upon the other, and accordingly on arriving home he summoned Bertrand le Noir to his presence, and commanded him to see that a gallows was immediately erected on the outside of the castle walls, without, however, naming the culprit, on whom he was about to execute summary justice. This done, he retired to his chamber, not, perhaps, to sleep, but to meditate upon those future plans that were either to end in the death of Rebecca, or compel her to yield herself to his unlawful love.

The next morning he arose feverish and unrefreshed, and desiring one of his attendants to desire Bertrand le Noir to come to him im-mediately, he proceeded to the esplanade on the battlements, where he paced up and down with impatient steps until his retainer, Bertrand, at length made his appearance.

" And now," he exclaimed, after the salutations had passed between them, " tell me, good Bertrand, whether my commands have been obeyed, according to the instructions I gave you last night."

" You mean, Sir Gaston," answered the other, " whether the— the ——"

" Aye, aye," returned the other, impatiently, " your unwillingness to mention the word ' gallows,' convinces me that my meaning is perfectly understood."

" Why, to speak the truth," replied the other, " that word, some-how or other, sticks in my throat, and seems to give a sudden stiffness in the neck. However, sir, your orders have been obeyed, and the in-strument of death only waits its victim, whoever he may be."

" And canst thou not guess for whom it has been erected ?" asked the knight, hoarsely.

" I have scarcely given a thought on the subject," answered Ber-trand, " because it is the duty of a faithful servant, to perform his master's bidding, without pausing to inquire into his motives. I am sa-tisfied with the certainty that it is not for myself, and that being the case I care not who else may be the victim."

" Canst thou not give a guess at who it is that I intend to send to his long account ?"

" Aye, marry can I," answered the fellow, " and I would wager my best silver-hilted dagger, that the first name I mention, shall be that of him, whose hours are so nearly numbered."

" Let me hear, then, if thou art as shrewd as I have ever given thee the credit for :—who sayst thou is the man that I would next rid my-self of ?"

" Black Ivan, the bold Outlaw."

" Right ;—he it is who will suffer death, ere another hour shall have elapsed. He dies, Bertrand, and, since thou hast already guessed so well, perhaps you can next tell me why it is that I am anxious to rid myself of him without loss of time ?"

" I think I can," answered the ruffian. " He is in your way, and must be removed. In short, he has once enabled the girl, yonder, to effect her escape from your custody, and you have resolved to take cer-tain measures, in order to prevent a repetition of his offence."

" So far, thou art right again," replied Sir Gaston de Neville, chuck-ling with inward satisfaction. " I would, indeed, prevent his defeating my hopes a second time, but that is not the only object I now have in view ;—Black Ivan himself presumes to love this Hebrew Maiden, and I thus adopt a remedy that will effectually relieve me from all future fears of his rivalry."

" And a very admirable preventive, too, in my opinion," answered Bertrand, merrily, in spite of the serious subject they were engaged upon. "There is nothing like putting a man out of the way when we wish to avoid his doing us an injury, and perhaps the sooner this job is done the better it will be for yourself. Ivan is a slippery dog, as he has proved before now, and, since all is ready, why not despatch him with as little delay as possible?"

"In one hour he will cease to live," exclaimed Sir Gaston. "See, therefore, that my men are drawn up in front of the gallows, and when that is done, bring the prisoner before me that I may see him once more before he leaves this world for ever."

"And yet methinks that is running into unnecessary danger," exclaimed Bertrand. "This Outlaw is a dangerous fellow, and if he has made up his mind to have vengeance, it is not the cords that bind his limbs that will prevent his fulfilling his design."

"Do as I have commanded thee!" exclaimed Sir Gaston, angrily;—"bring him before me, I say, and I will put his boasted prowess to the proof."

Thus silenced, Bertrand le Noir departed without offering any further reply, and Sir Gaston being thus left to himself, continued to pace up and down, occasionally giving utterance to the dark thoughts that agitated and almost maddened his brain.

"I will now have vengeance for all I have endured," he muttered fiercely; "Ivan himself will ere long have parted with his worthless life, and she who hath hitherto scorned my earnest prayers, shall either perish or purchase her existence by becoming the mistress of the man she most loathes and despises. Aye, this is indeed revenge, and to obtain it I would bring upon myself an eternity of misery in the world to come."

Here he paused, and dark ruminations seemed to disturb him, but at length the sound of approaching footsteps fell upon his ears, and raising his eyes he beheld Bertrand le Noir advancing with the prisoner, and followed by half a dozen of his armed retainers.

"So, we are well met, Ivan, at last," he exclaimed, in a tone of fiend-like exultation. "Thou art standing upon the verge of eternity, and thy guards only wait a signal from me to hurry thee to thy doom."

"And yet that doom may not be so near as thou thinkest," answered the robber, with his usual cool indifference. "I knew what I had to expect from thy vengeance, and have not quailed at it."

"Perhaps then thou expectest to escape me even now?"

"To speak the truth, I do."

"Then must it be by a miracle, for nothing else can rescue thee from death."

"The miracle I speak of will show itself ere long," answered the undaunted robber. "Nay, doubt me not, for I have been in as great emergencies before now, and yet I stand here to tell thee I fear thee not."

"Why, man, the gallows is already erected, upon which thy worthless carcase shall be swung."

"The gallows may be erected," replied Black Ivan, "but again I tell thee it will not have its victim."

"Are his bonds made secure?" whispered the knight to Bertrand le Noir; "art thou sure he is so bound as to prevent the possibility of his escape?"

"None can rescue him," answered the other, "unless it be his old familiar friend, the devil."

"Hear me," cried Ivan, who had watched them with an eye of scorn during this brief conference. "Ye tremble, both of ye, I see, lest I should yet find the means to cheat the gibbet of its expected prey. My words have struck ye with terror, and now let me once more warn ye that I shall not only escape, but that I shall live to witness the shameful end of both of ye."

" 'Tis false !" roared the knight, furiously, "thou shalt not elude the grasp of him who glories in having brought thee to this fearful pass.— One moment more, if I give but the word, will be your last, and who, think you, is there to snatch from me the prey I have made my own ?"

"Upon that subject," answered the robber, scornfully, "I shall remain silent. Let it suffice thee that I am well content to see matters proceed to the last extremity, because even then, I feel assured, you will behold the utter frustration of all your hopes."

"Humph !" ejaculated Sir Gaston ; " 'tis well that thou canst so well console thyself at a moment of such extremity as this. Yet again, I, thine enemy, do warn thee that thy days are numbered, and that after a few brief minutes have passed away, I shall triumph in the accomplishment of thy fatal doom."

"And I," answered the Outlaw, with indifference, "do again tell thee that I feel no terror at thy threats. I have, ere now, shown thee the advantage of a light pair of heels, and shall do so once more as thou wilt find out before long."

"Vain boaster, thou art mistaken this time, at all events," exclaimed the knight. "I have taken precautions to prevent the frustration of my design, and thy men must be reckless of life indeed were they to attempt thy release at the hazard of their own persons."

"Why, as for that," replied Black Ivan, "there is not a man among them who would not shed the last drop of his blood in defence of his leader. I have tried them on other occasions, Sir Knight, and therefore can speak with confidence of their faithfulness and zeal."

"Then you acknowledge," cried Sir Gaston, "that it is through them you hope for deliverance from death ?"

"I acknowledge nothing," answered the robber. "Thou hast said I have but a few minutes to live, and, therefore, wilt thou soon learn the means by which thou wilt soon be cheated of thy prey."

Sir Gaston de Neville was enraged at the indifference with which his threats had been received, though he endeavoured to conceal as much as possible the vexation that was growing at his heart. Bertrand le Noir observed the anger that was rapidly growing to a height, and fearing lest the victim should indeed escape as he had boasted, he approached his master, and whispered softly in his ear :—

"Pardon me, Sir Gaston, but this is no time to waste in hesitation ;— Ivan is bold and resolute ;—his men love him for his recklessness of danger, and we shall lose our promised victim unless immediate orders are given to swing him from yonder gibbet."

"Thou art right, Bertrand," answered the Templar ; "too long already has the execution been delayed, and, therefore, do I now charge thee to hurry this business to a close. Let him be taken hence, and I will myself be present to give the word that shall for ever rid the world of the man I hate."

"Do I hear rightly ?" exclaimed Bertrand ; "would you run the risk of being present when there is every reason to suppose that a desperate encounter may take place with those who seek to rescue him ?"

"I have said it," answered Sir Gaston. "My determination is not to be changed by anything thou canst say ; nor would 1 lose this satisfaction, even though I might be certain that my own death would instantly follow."

"Nay," said the other, "let me entreat ——"

"Peace, sirrah!" interrupted the knight; "thou hast received my commands, and any farther delay will render me, from henceforth, thy sworn enemy. To your duty, Bertrand, and let me not have to chide thee again for unwillingness to do my bidding."

Bertrand le Noir saw that any further remonstrance would be made in vain, and hurrying off towards the prisoner, he commanded him to proceed forthwith towards the place of execution. Nor did Black Ivan appear to be at all moved by his order, but turning once more towards Sir Gaston, he said, in a tone of triumph:—

"I go, Sir Knight, but not as you expect to death. Now is your time for exultation, but presently we shall see who has the most reason to congratulate himself."

"Lead him to death!" roared Sir Gaston, in a paroxysm of rage;—"drag him hence, I say, and, should any attempt be made to rescue him, remember that I shall be the foremost to resist their efforts."

With these words the retainers closed around the prisoner, and thus guarding him on every side, he was conducted to the place where the gibbet had been erected for his execution. Ivan, however, was unmoved by the sight of the preparations that had been made for his exit from this world, and having glanced a look of contempt at the instrument of death, he turned round, and perceiving Sir Gaston de Neville close at hand, exclaimed in derision:—

"I perceive, Sir Knight, you have not been sparing in providing for me the means of quitting this world with all honour. The gibbet, methinks, is somewhat the loftiest, and therefore will it be the better for sustaining the carrion remains of him who has caused it to be erected."

"Proceed with your task, fellows," roared Sir Gaston, stung to fury by the coolness of the prisoner. "Let the rope be placed round his neck, and when I give the word, see that not another moment remains between him and eternity."

At these words Black Ivan was conducted beneath the gibbet, and being placed upon a stool the cord was fixed, and everything immediately afterwards declared to be in readiness for the last act of the tragedy.— Even now, however, the Knight Templar could not forbear giving loose to the exultation that filled his soul, and advancing yet nearer to the wretched man, he exclaimed with a hoarse laugh of derision:—

"Ho! ho!—what say you now, Ivan?—Are you not deceived in your expectations of release from death?"

"Not in the least," answered the other, unmoved by his perilous situation. "I feel that my hour is not yet come, and that it is thou and not I who at this moment stands in the greatest peril."

"Indeed! where then is thy help to come from?"

"Where I have most reason to expect it," answered the robber; "even from those who have sworn to yield up their own lives rather than see me perish!"

"From thy band of desperadoes then thou lookest for aid?"

"I do."

"Then is thy hope a most vain one," replied Sir Gaston, "for nearly all thy men were destroyed in the attack I made upon them a few days since."

"So thou believest," returned the other, "but thou wilt learn, ere long, that there were many absent at the time from the cavern, who will not fail to gather near this spot upon the first news that reaches them of their leader's peril."

"And even if they did so," retorted Sir Gaston, "have we not enough present to resist any attack they may be fool-hardy enough to make?"

"Not against the desperate men who have the courage to place them-selves under my command," answered the Outlaw. "Thou mayst boast of having three to one, but the gallant fellows I command, glory in having the odds against them, because it serves as a spur to goad them on to greater exertions."

"Let them but venture to show themselves," exclaimed Sir Gaston, confidently, "and they shall learn at length that they are not doomed always to prove victorious."

"At any rate," answered Ivan, "I fear nothing for the result;—you are equally confident, and it now only remains to see which will be in the right."

"By heavens ! I have no fear about it," cried Sir Gaston.

"Dost thou not indeed ?"

"I do not," returned the other;—"and yet I have detected thine eyes wandering towards yonder green copse, as if from that point was to come the assistance thou so confidently expected.—Say, am I not right in my conjecture ?"

"That," answered the Outlaw, "is a secret I can hardly be expected to divulge. It is sufficient that you treat my warnings with contempt, and that I express my readiness to be turned off, whenever you may think fit to give the word of command."

"Oh, thou shalt not have to wait much longer for that," answered Sir Gaston. "I have now triumph enough in the torture I know thou feelest, and it is, therefore, my intention to close thy earthly scene, by giving the signal your executioner so anxiously awaits."

"Beware how you give it then," exclaimed Black Ivan, in a prophetic tone ;—"beware, I say, for whenever the signal is given, it will be for thine own destruction."

"I care not," returned the knight, haughtily;—"your threats have no influence upon me, and thus do I consign thee to thy doom of death."

Saying this, Sir Gaston de Neville addressed a few words to the exe-cutioner, who, with alacrity, began to set about the task for which he had been engaged. In a few minutes everything was in readiness, and as the last part of his duty, he was about to kick away the stool upon which the malefactor stood, when an arrow, whistling through the air from the little wood hard-by, struck him to the heart, and with a groan of mortal agony, he sank dead at the feet of the very man he was in the act of hurrying into eternity.

At this sight, an involuntary cry of terror and dismay burst from the assembled retainers, and, in spite of the commands of their imperious master, the whole of them commenced a most precipitate retreat towards the castle gate, which they had no sooner entered, than it was closed again, to prevent any pursuit from their unseen enemies. Thus were Sir Gaston, and his attendant, Bertrand le Noir, left to the mercy of their foes, and, so completely had they been taken by surprise, at this unexpected desertion of their own party. that they were surrounded by a large body of the robbers, who had rushed from the thicket, before they had time to devise any plan for their own safety. At the same instant, too, Black Ivan was released from the cords that bound him, and ad-vancing towards the knight, who had so lately boasted the power he possessed over him, he exclaimed exultingly :—

"Now, Sir Gaston de Neville, will you not confess that I am a better prophet than you were lately willing to believe ? Said I not that my turn for triumph would come, and have not my words proved true ?"

"Villain !"—cried the outraged knight, "thou hast gained an advan-tage over me I admit. I am now helpless and in thy power, nor will I utter one word that may be construed into a request for pity or mercy from thee."

"Why, then, thou hast said well," answered Black Ivan, "for, to confess my mind to thee, it is my intention to deal out the same doom, that but a few minutes since you had intended for me. I have bitter cause to send thee to thy long account, and rely upon it, I will not give thee a chance of ever again placing my neck in the jeopardy it has just been released from."

"I do not ask it," answered Sir Gaston, sullenly;—"I feel that my sand of life is well nigh run, and my only request is that you will command your archers to despatch me with as little delay as possible."

"Nay," returned Black Ivan, "thou art not to die so honourable a death as that, Sir Knight. The gallows was considered good enough for me, since it has been prepared for its deadly work, it shall not be removed until it has borne the body of him who ordered it to be erected."

"How!—wouldst thou hang me like a common felon?"

"Aye," answered Ivan, sternly;—"is it not a doom that thy many crimes have richly merited?"

"Nay, I implore thee, consider of this," cried Sir Gaston, in despair. "I ask not for mercy, but that thou wilt grant me the death becoming a soldier."

"Say rather the death justly merited by a villain," answered the Outlaw. "Remember, thou hast provoked me to this retaliation, and I am resolved to have no more pity upon thee, than thou hadst before we had changed situations."

"Bertrand le Noir," whispered the knight to his attendant, who stood close by, "thou hast heard the ignominious fate to which I am doomed by this ruffian. Thou at least has had no cause to charge me with tyranny, and therefore do I now ask thee to do me one last favour."

"Name it," answered the attendant, "and I pledge my word to fulfil your command whatever it may be?"

"Stand nearer then, lest they overhear us," he continued, "I care not about dying, my friend, but would escape the shame of perishing upon yonder scaffold."

"Curses light upon the cowards that fled from us on the first appearance of danger!" muttered Bertrand; "had they but stood firm, our enemies would not now have had the gratification of threatening us with a fate they themselves so justly merit. However, it is vain to repine now;—we are in the hands of reckless men, and must submit to their decrees."

"Never!" returned Sir Gaston. "I will yet cheat them of their promised vengeance, and thou, good Bertrand, must be the friend to aid in my design."

"If it be to fight our way through the throng of ruffians that surround us, I will stand by thee to the last."

"Nay, we are unarmed, and such an attempt would be madness," answered Sir Gaston. "Yet there is one way, and thou alone canst aid me in it."

"Name the means, and I will obey thee."

"Thou seest yonder man," whispered the knight, "who holds his pike trailing upon the ground?"

"I do."

"Would it not be easy to snatch the weapon from his hand?"

"Nothing easier," answered Bertrand, "and having possessed myself of it, thou wouldst have me clear a passage for our escape, through the crowd that hems us in?"

"Nay, I would have thee plunge the weapon into my body, and thus release me from the ignominious death these fellows meditate."

"How!" cried Bertrand le Noir, with suppressed horror; "wouldst thou have me murder the master I have so long followed and loved?"

"Thy love," answered the knight, "will but be shewn in thine obedience to my orders. Thou hast heard what they are, and I will now ask thee for the last time, whether thou wilt become my executioner, or see me hung up like a dog to yonder gallows?"

"I—I—will do thy bidding," stammered the other, after a brief struggle with his feelings. "In prosperity I have followed thee through all the perils of battle, and I will not now refuse to obey thee even though thy commands are such as I shudder to execute."

As he spoke these words, he made a sudden rush upon the robber who had been pointed out by his master, and having succeeded in wresting from his grasp the pike he held, turned back, and was in the act of plunging the weapon into the bosom of Sir Gaston de Neville, when three or four of the bandits rushing forward, arrested his arm, at the very moment when the point of the instrument was about to enter the knights heart.

"How now!" exclaimed Black Ivan, darting through the thickest of the throng;—"is this the way the gibbet is to be cheated of its expected prey?"

"If thou hast any mercy in thy breast, I pray thee give me a soldier's death," cried Sir Gaston, imploringly. "It is all I ask, and surely you will not carry your vengeance to any further extremity?"

"By your commands," replied the Outlaw, "yonder gibbet has been erected;—I, it is true, was to have been the unfortunate victim, but chance has kindly turned matters in my favour, and, therefore, it remains for me to decide as to what death you shall meet. Hanging was considered good enough for me, and, therefore, do I now award thee the same ignominious punishment."

"Aye, aye," shouted the bandits,—"let him be hanged by all means!"

"Away with him, then," exclaimed the Outlaw. "Drag him to the place of execution, and see that ye delay not the task, or he may chance to escape, as I have done."

This order was no sooner given, than the knight and Bertrand le Noir were seized upon by the foremost of the mob, and conveyed by main force to the foot of the gallows. At that moment, however, a flight of arrows, from the castle, came hissing through the air, and at the same time, a mounted party of the knight's retainers were seen galloping up to the spot. In numbers, they more than trebled those of the robbers, and as several of the latter had been severely wounded by the last discharge, an immediate flight towards the thicket was commanded. At first, it was determined to take Sir Gaston and Bertrand with them; but, as this was certain to be attended with fatal consequences to themselves, the bandits, at last, resolved on leaving them behind, and then commencing their retreat to the copse, they there waited for their foes, determined either to maintain their ground, or perish on the spot.

But Sir Gaston de Neville no sooner found himself safe among his own followers, than he began to consult with Bertrand, as to the policy of following his desperate adversaries to a place where they had so great an advantage over him. After some deliberation, therefore, it was determined that they should return to the castle, without pursuing the robbers at present, and orders having been given to that effect, they hastened back with the knight, whose life had been so nearly forfeited to the vengeance of Black Ivan.

CHAPTER XXIV.

have been scorned,—persecuted,—wronged;—
The world hath been mine enemy, and foes
Have multiplied against me though I know not why."

THE MOOR.

It was a source of deep humiliation to Sir Gaston de Neville, that he who had doomed Black Ivan to a death of infamy, should at length have fallen into the power of the very man he had thought to triumph over. The narrow escape that he had had instead of calling forth his gratitude to Heaven for so signal an interference in his behalf, served only to render him the more inveterate against the Outlaw, and if any consolation he could be said to have, it was in the resolution he formed to take ample vengeance on the very first occasion that offered.

On the day following, the events narrated in the last chapter, the knight was suddenly interrupted in the midst of his gloomy reflections, by the entrance of Bertrand le Noir, who, after offering many apologies for the intrusion, informed him that a monk had just presented himself at the castle gate, requesting permission to visit the Jewess, who, he had heard, was confined in one of the dungeons, and, for whose conversion to the Christian religion, he expressed the utmost anxiety. Sir Gaston heard the request with an expression of scorn, that he could not conceal, but at length, having weighed the matter over in his mind, he enquired whether the monk belonged to the neighbouring monastery, or was one of the

No. 16

wandering friars, whose visits at the mansions of the great and powerful were more frequent than welcome.

"That," answered Bertrand, "is a question that I am unable to reply to, seeing that the holy father wears his hood so as to conceal his face. I was a little inquisitive to be sure, but he took pretty good care to prevent my being gratified with a sight of his countenance."

"And does he say that his only motive for seeing Rebecca is the welfare of her soul?"

"That he says is his only object."

"Then let him be gratified," answered Sir Gaston. "Say to him that he has my permission to visit her dungeon, but, at the same time, warn him to convince her that longer to resist my overtures would be madness."

"I go, Sir Gaston, and if the holy father gives not a good account of his mission, let him look to it, for there is a foul ditch on the outside of the castle walls, and he will be like enough to make acquaintance, unless he makes good use of his opportunity."

"Stay, Bertrand," exclaimed the knight, as his attendant was about quitting the room;—"upon second thought, I will see this girl first myself. She hath been obstinate, and I am anxious to know whether the ordeal she has to go through to-morrow, has had any effect upon the foolish resolution she had formed."

"Then the monk," returned Bertrand, "must amuse himself as well as he can for the present, in the buttery?"

"Even so," replied the knight, "and let it be your task to see that the holy father wants for nothing. Set your choicest viands before him, and, above all things, let there be no stint of wine, for these reverend men would sooner pardon any other omission, than that of hospitality."

"I will make it my care to see that he wants for nothing," answered Bertrand, and hastening from the chamber, he was soon on his way to join the friar, with whom he intended to join the companionship of a bottle.

When Sir Gaston de Neville was left alone, he began to make preparations for his meditated visit to Rebecca, and having lighted a lamp, he proceeded through a secret door in the pannel, which conducted him to a steep flight of steps, down which he made his way, and from thence, along a narrow passage, to the cell in which his hapless victim was immured. For a moment or two, however, his resolution wavered as he stood at the door of her dungeon, but, at length, summoning his usual determination, he removed the heavy fastenings, and entered the dreary abode of her who he had resolved to destroy.

As he stepped in, Sir Gaston perceived by the faint rays emitted from his lamp, that the Hebrew Maiden was seated on the heap of straw which had been placed in lieu of a pallet, and that her face was buried in her hands, as if in the depth of her sorrowful meditation, she was still unconscious of his close proximity. At last, however, he placed his hand upon her shoulder, and as he did so, she started up with terror, fleeing at the same time to the farther corner of the cell, as from some hateful fiend, whom she abhorred."

"Maiden," exclaimed Sir Gaston, in the softest tones of friendship that he could assume, "I am here once more to offer my services to thee, ere it be too late. You are in danger, and the love I bear you, prompts me to make one more effort for your rescue."

"I ask no favour from you," she replied, coldly. "Begone, and let me perish here in peace."

"Come, come, lovely Rebecca," answered the knight; "recollect yourself, and ask your heart whether there is indeed no favour that you would ask?"

"None," she replied,—"none from thee, proud knight, unless it be to implore thy mercy for my poor old heart-broken father. He hath never injured thee, and it would be some consolation to me, to know that his last few remaining days were suffered to be passed without further cruelty and oppression from thee."

"You wrong me, Rebecca," cried the knight. "I bear no malice against your father, nor have I, to my knowledge, done ought to injure him."

"What!" she exclaimed, indignantly, "hast thou not robbed him of his child—the only comfort of his declining days?—Hast thou not done this, and yet thou canst say thou never harmed him!"

"His daughter's obstinacy has produced the evil she complains of," answered Sir Gaston. "Had she complied with my earnest prayers, I had never sought to make her mine by force."

"Monster!" exclaimed Rebecca, indignantly, "thou hast come, it seems, to mock my misery and despair!"

"Then be wise in time, and exchange your present misery for future happiness," he replied. "Say that you will return the love you have so often scorned, and upon the instant you shall be restored to liberty."

"I scorn your offer with contempt," answered Rebecca. "Here it hath pleased you to bury your unoffending victim, and so far is her soul from being terrified by your oppression, that she now gladly takes the opportunity of telling you, that no tortures you can inflict, will ever prevail upon her to abandon the paths of virtue and innocence that she has been taught to love."

"And yet," replied Sir Gaston, "time may serve to alter that resolution. Here you are beyond the power of all earthly aid, and unless you consent to the terms I have proposed, other means will be resolved to that at present you know not of."

"You have come then to threaten me to submission?"

"Nay, I am here to tell which you know not of," he replied. "Your father has made application to the king for your deliverance from my custody."

"Ah!" cried the maiden, "then there is yet one gleam of hope."

"You are mistaken," answered Sir Gaston, with fiend-like triumph. "I have charged you with the robbery of my diamond, and in the absence of all proof of your innocence, my story is believed."

"Villain!—villain!" cried Rebecca, in accents of horror.

"Oh," he replied, with indifference, "you can call me whatever names you please, since the advantage I have gained has been a sufficient recompense. The king, as I have told you, believes the charge I have brought against you, and you would have been condemned to be burnt at the stake, had it not pleased his majesty to command that you should go through the trial by ordeal, in order to satisfy him and others of your guilt."

"Lost! lost!" cried Rebecca, burying her face in her hands, and bursting into a flood of tears.

"Why, this is well," exclaimed the tyrant in a tone of exultation. "I have at last succeeded in touching thy heart with fear, and presently I shall have the satisfaction of hearing thee submit to my own terms."

"Never!"

"Then thou wilt perish!"

"I can welcome death with joy and thankfulness," she replied, firmly;

"even torture itself, rather than become the loathsome wretch thou seekest to render me."

"Well, we shall see how all this affected fortitude will end," replied the knight, sarcastically. "At a little distance off, death loses his terrors, but when he approaches nearer, we begin to discern horrors that were not visible before. Such will be the case with thee, proud girl, and thou wilt yet gladly save thy life at any sacrifice."

"Thou knowest me not, Sir Gaston," she replied; "I have been taught to love virtue and honour above all other things;—the lesson has not been thrown away, and I will prove to my father that his anxious warnings have been carefully stored away in the inmost recess of my heart!"

"Nay," exclaimed Sir Gaston, "this is the idle boasting of one who has not deeply meditated upon the consequences of her obstinacy. Thou hast some hours before thee to think of the matter, and I doubt not, to-morrow, thou wilt yield, rather than endure the perils of the trial by ordeal."

"Thou shalt find that I will remain unmoved."

"What! hast thou no terrors then?" asked Sir Gaston :—"art thou so utterly destitute of feeling, that no feelings of alarm can be awakened in thy bosom?"

"Thy threats," she replied, calmly, "are at least insufficient to effect thy evil designs."

"And your father," resumed the knight,—"have you thought of his sufferings;—of what he must endure through your fatal obstinacy."

"My father," she replied, "will be resigned to anything, so that I forget not the precepts he hath taught me."

"But he also may perish through the wilful folly of his child."

"No, no!" she cried, wildly,—"you do not—cannot mean that a helpless old man—one, who is so innocent, shall suffer, because his daughter hath offended you!"

"We shall see," answered the villain ;—"you are resolved to thwart me, it seems, and it will be a subject for after consideration, whether or not he is made to suffer through your wayward conduct."

"I see," exclaimed Rebecca, wildly,—"you wish to terrify me into submission. This is some trick, for base and hardened as your heart is with crime, you would not dare to put your power against a poor old man who never injured thee."

"Nay, then, I promise thee I *will* do it," answered Sir Gaston, who began to hope that he might succeed in thus operating upon her terrors for the old man. "Thou hast it in thy power, girl, to save him, and a single word from thee will do it."

"Aye, Sir Gaston de Neville," she replied, "but that word shall never be spoken by me! He would curse me were I to utter it, and from that moment would he cast me off as unworthy of his love. Proceed, therefore, with your cruelty;—send me to the fearful ordeal you have spoken of, and then let the fire blaze around me that your own motive hath served to kindle!"

"This is madness!" exclaimed the Templar, bewildered by her firmness of purpose. "I thought to have found thee capable of reasoning, and now, even the last chance of saving you, fades away for ever."

"Let it fade," she replied ;—"my soul is firm to the purpose it has formed, and I can cheerfully submit to the death you have designed for me."

"Then prepare yourself for the ordeal you have to go through to-morrow."

"I am prepared," answered the maiden.

"Nay, but reflect," cried Sir Gaston, imploringly,—"thou canst not pass through it unscathed, and then thou wilt be adjudged to die at the stake."

"How knowest thou that I cannot pass through the ordeal in safety?" she demanded. "Will not the God of my father's watch over, and protect the innocent from the base designs of her enemies? Thinkest thou because my religion differs from thine own, that I shall be deserted in the hour of need?"

"I will not stay now to argue that subject with thee," answered Sir Gaston. "At present, I must leave thee, but there is a holy father of our church within this castle, who has asked permission to visit and prepare thee for the great trial thou hast to undergo. I will send him to thee, and may his efforts prove serviceable to one who so much need his aid."

Upon this, the Knight Templar retired from the dungeon, leaving our heroine, more resolved than ever to endure any sufferings, rather than yield herself to a villain, who she now more than ever execrated. It was not long, however, that she was suffered to remain in solitude, for presently afterwards the door of her cell was again heard upon its hinges, and, on directing her gaze that way, she perceived a figure advancing wrapped in the sombre habit of a monk. Vexed at this interruption, she turned away, but at the same moment her arm was taken hold of, and on looking round, she perceived, to her astonishment, that the friar's gown had been thrown aside, and that it was a woman who stood before her. At this discovery, a cry of mingled surprise and alarm escaped her, and starting back a pace or two, she demanded the reason of this intrusion, and the motive of the visit.

"Hush, girl, or we shall be overheard," exclaimed the other. "In me you behold a friend, who has risked much in your behalf, and one who will venture more, rather than suffer her benefactress to become the prey of her enemies."

"Thy voice is familiar to me," cried Rebecca, "and the professions thou hast made assure me that I am in no danger from thee. Say then, who art thou?"

"Meg of Finchley."

"Ah!—she who they call the Wierd Woman of the Heath?"

"The same;—yet still will I be thy friend. Thou wert kind to me, when I must have perished, but for thine aid, and I would now return the service thou hast performed, to her who was cast forth and persecuted by a heartless world."

"I remember thee," answered Rebecca, "and yet our acquaintance was so brief, that I should scarcely have expected thou wouldst have run this risk in my behalf."

"Nay, I owe my life to thee," she replied, "and the debt can only be paid by gratitude. I heard the rumour of thy having fallen into the hands of Sir Gaston de Neville, and from that moment have been devising the means for thy rescue."

"Alas!" sighed the Hebrew Maiden, "shouldst thou be detected, thy life will be the forfeit of thy generous zeal in my cause."

"It may be so," replied the woman,—"and yet I shall not regret the effort I have made. To rescue thee, I put on the garb of a friar, and in that disguise, gained ready access to the castle of thy gaoler."

"It is in vain to think of rescue now," answered Rebecca, in a tone of deep dejection. "Here I am constantly guarded by the minions of Sir Gaston de Neville, and in a few hours more,—as he hath himself just told me,—my career of wretchedness and misery will be closed by death."

"I have heard it all," exclaimed Meg;—"the king has been imposed upon by the artful tales invented by this recreant knight, and you are condemned to die. One alternative, however, remains, and by that you may be saved from the death your enemy has plotted to bring about."

"It is useless to fill me with hopes that never can be realized," answered Rebecca. "I am prepared to meet my doom, and hail, with joy, the near approach of that moment, which will release me from the persecutions I have so long endured."

"Nay, girl," cried the old woman,—"thou must not abandon thyself thus tamely to thy fate. It is decreed that thou shalt go through the trial by ordeal, and therein lie the hopes I entertain of thy safety."

"What safety can there be for me?" asked Rebecca, reproachfully. "Few, I have been told, can pass the ordeal, and should I fail to satisfy my accuser of my innocence, I shall be immediately condemned to perish miserably at the stake."

"Never!" exclaimed Meg;—"there is at present, every certainty of thy escape, if thou wilt but follow the counsel I am about to give thee."

"Thou wouldst advise me to make a mad attempt to escape from this castle."

"Girl," replied the Wierd Woman, "thou art mistaken. To flee from the castle would, indeed, be madness, since it would not only serve to convince thy foes of thy guilt, but would render thy father an object for Sir Gaston's persecution. Besides, thou wouldst soon fall into their clutches again, and perhaps tortures would be added to the other punishments they have in store for thee."

"What means, then, do you propose?" asked Rebecca.

"Listen to me, and you shall learn. From inquiries that I have made, I find that the ordeal you have to undergo, is that of boiling water. You will have to plunge your arm into a vessel filled with the scalding liquid, and should you be able to endure it for the space of five minutes, without flinching, it will be taken as a manifestation of your innocence, and your immediate release will be the consequence."

"Alas!" cried Rebecca, in despair, "is this the only hope you can offer me of escape. The agony of such an ordeal it will be impossible to bear, without giving tokens of the pain I suffer, and instead of establishing my innocence of the charge, I shall afford only a plain proof to my persecutors that I am guilty."

"Thou hast not heard me out, girl," answered the Wierd Woman. "In this little box is contained an ointment, the preparation of which is known only to myself. Before thou art taken from hence, to-morrow, to undergo this ordeal, thou must rub thine hands and arms with it, so as to leave no part untouched. The power it possesses, is so miraculous that it will enable thee to plunge thine arms into the boiling fluid without feeling even the least sensation of pain."

"Dost thou indeed speak the truth, old woman?"

"Aye, as heaven is my witness!"

"Hast thou ever seen its virtues proved?"

"I have tried it myself," she replied, "and found it to possess the virtue I have told thee of. Take it then, and rely with confidence on the result of thine ordeal."

"I will not refuse thy gift," answered Rebecca, taking from her hand the small box which she held out. "That it is meant in kindness I have no doubt—though, to confess the truth, I have little faith in the miraculous powers you have stated it to possess."

"Fail not to use it as I have directed," exclaimed the old woman— "and I will answer for it with my life that thou wilt pass through this trial unscathed. Thy countenance will exhibit no pain, and that alone will be taken as a sufficient proof that heaven has interfered to manifest thine entire innocence."

"Is it possible," cried Rebecca, "that jugglery can be so mistaken?"

"Thou wilt find it so, maiden."

"But even should I be declared acquitted of the crime laid to my charge," exclaimad our heroine, "shall I not still be left to the villainous practices of Sir Gaston de Neville."

"Nay, from that moment thou wilt have protection from the king," replied Meg of Finchley.

"And will that, think you, be sufficient to guard me against the designs of mine enemy?"

"There is every reason to suppose it will," answered the old woman. "At any rate, Sir Gaston will be careful how he proceeds, for should he be detected in practicing against thy future peace, it will be at the risk of incurring the king's fiercest wrath."

"And that, perhaps," sighed Rebecca, "in the madness of his revenge, he will scarcely think about."

"At all events," answered the woman, "you will have the protection of your father, who being aware of the malignity of your enemy, will not fail to take every precaution to prevent your again falling into his hands."

At this moment footsteps were heard approaching the dungeon door, and ere Bertrand le Noir could enter, the monkish garb was again put on, and the conversation turned to another subject. In answer to his surly enquiry whether their interview was almost over, Meg bowed an assent, and then following him silently from the dungeon, she left Rebecca to meditate alone upon the extraordinary object of the visit she had received, and the probable results that would ensue from it.

CHAPTER XXV.

"Wilt thou not yield to me,
And by compliance overcome the fate
That else must crush thee?"—THE WRECKERS.

AT an early hour on the following morning, our heroine arose from her wretched straw bed, and having first of all offered up her earnest prayers to heaven for assistance to go through the severe trials of the day, she next applied the ointment to her hands and arms in the manner that had been directed by the Wierd Woman of the Heath. That done, she seated herself and waited with patience and resignation until the arrival of the gaoler, who was to conduct her to the palace where the ordeal had been appointed to take place. At length footsteps were heard approaching—then followed the heavy clanking of chains as they fell with a crash to the ground, and the next moment Bertrand le Noir— looking more ferocious than usual—presented himself before her.

"Now," he exclaimed, sulkily, "are you ready to go with me, or has your fortitude so far forsaken you as to alter your opinion with respect to my master's liberal offer?"

"If you would know whether I prefer infamy to accepting this opportunity of clearing my innocence," she replied, "I at once declare my readiness to accompany you to the place of ordeal."

"That is to say you prefer a certain and horrible death to the offer Sir Gaston has made you?"

"I do."

"Then more fool you, that's all I know about it," answered Bertrand. "As the mistress of my noble master you may live in splendour and affluence; but by this obstinacy of yours, peril and danger will quickly gather round you, and, when too late, you will repent the folly that has urged you to so foolish a resolution."

"Nay," she replied with composure, "I can gladly welcome death, since that alone can release me from a villain whom I loathe and detest."

"Nonsense—he offers you fairly enough, don't he?"

"On the contrary," answered Rebecca, "were I to yield to his infamous proposals, I should for ever become the scorn of all the virtuous of my own sex."

"And what of that?" demanded Bertrand le Noir; "is not scorn more easily endured than torture? Besides, if you think fit to give way in this manner, Sir Gaston will soon remove you far from those whose opinions you seem to stand so much in awe of."

"Alas!" cried Rebecca, "could he remove me, think you, from the opinions of an afflicted heart?"

"Yes, to be sure he could," replied the ruffian; "that is if you would on'y make up your mind to look at things differently to what you do now. So far, you have taken a view only of the dark side of the picture, but if you would only turn your gaze on the fairer prospect for a short t me, your folly would become so plain as to overcome all ridiculous scruples."

"Nothing will ever induce me to become the wretched outcast he would make me," exclaimed our heroine, with more than even her usual tone of determination. "I am threatened, as you know, with torture and death, yet can I endure both with resignation rather than sell myself to such a foul monster of iniquity as he is!"

"Of course, you will do as you please," replied Bertrand le Noir, doggedly. "I am sent here to lead you to the place of ordeal, and if I have said anything to affront you it was because I would rather see you accept terms that would make you happy, than madly throw away your life for the sake of a few scruples."

"Nay, then, lead on whithersoever you please, for my resolution is finally and irrevocably made."

"Will you not see Sir Gaston de Neville before you go forth from his castle?"

"Wherefore should I do so?"

"That he may use all the arguments in his power in order to prevail upon you to avoid death by yielding to the chief desire of his soul."

"I will not see him," answered Rebecca, resolutely; "the sight of him is hateful to me, and I would fain leave this world at least in peace with him."

"And cannot you do that after another interview with him?"

"I think not."

"And you can look forward to the ordeal without fear?"

"I can."

"Yet it may prove the means of hurrying you to a brief and igno-

minious end," exclaimed Bertrand le Noir. "Should you give sign or token that the ordeal is more than you can endure, the king will instanly command you to be led forth to execution at the stake."

"Be it so," she replied, unmoved by the threat intended to be held out by the ruffian. "Thus far I have been enabled to regard my doom with firmness, and it is not its near approach that will terrify me to submission."

"Perhaps," sneered Bertrand, "you expect a miracle to be vouchsafed for your preservation?"

"I expect," answered the Hebrew Maiden, "that protection which is always given to the pure and helpless. The God whom I serve has never yet forgot his faithful people, nor will he do so now when heavenly aid is so much required for an oppressed and persecuted Hebrew."

"Psha!" exclaimed the ruffian, "it is idle to expect it, and therefore I would advise you to make up your mind for the worst. The ordeal by boiling water is no trifling thing to bear, I can tell you; you will be required to plunge your arm to the very shoulder in the scalding fluid, and should the least flinching—the most trifling distortion of a muscle—it will at once be taken as a proof of your guilt; and, since it will appear that heaven has deserted you, there will not be the faintest hope of mercy from those who will then alone have the power to grant it."

"Nor shall I ask for it," she replied, proudly! "if my judges are not satisfied with my innocence, I can yield myself up to death without a murmur."

"Is there no way to convince you of your folly?" cried Bertrand le Noir, with evident vexation.

No. 17

"None," she replied; "lead on, and you shall see that I feel no fear for the result of this day's trial."

Finding that all argument would be in vain, the fellow now conducted her from the dungeon, and, having led her through a long and dreary subterranean passage, they at length began to ascend a flight of steep and broken steps, that terminated in one of the lower apartments of the castle. Here, Sir Gaston de Neville was anxiously waiting her arrival, and no sooner did she appear before him, than he advanced eagerly towards her, and demanded whether she had thought better of the proposition he had made. But Rebecca was unmoved by his presence, and as his eye shrank beneath her proud gaze, she replied:—

"The victim of your tyranny appears at the summons of him who would be her destroyer. She is, however, still unsubdued in spirit, and boldly defies her enemy to put his threats of torture into execution!"

"Rash girl, reflect!" exclaimed the knight, earnestly. "Remember, you are alone and unprotected in the hands of one who is accustomed to have his slightest commands obeyed."

"If I am alone and unprotected," answered Rebecca, unmoved by his threats, "it is the greater reason why I should claim your generosity. It is said that you have reaped honours in the field of battle, and yet, you would stain the glory you have achieved, by trampling upon a poor, and almost unfriended girl."

"That is because thou hast obstinately refused to listen to my entreaties," answered the knight. "I have sought to exalt thee to a state of greatness, equal to mine own, and thou rejectest my prayers with scorn."

"You have heard my determination, Sir Gaston," she replied: "and therefore, I hoped this interview, at least, would have been spared me."

"But," exclaimed the knight, "I would yet save you, unless your obstinacy interposes to prevent the mercy I would exert."

"Your follower," she returned, glancing towards Bertrand, "has already received my positive answer. He, I suppose, was desired to exert himself in his master's behalf, and let him now tell you, that I have declared my resolution to endure any sufferings, rather than yield myself to disgrace and infamy."

"She prefers death, Sir Knight," cried the retainer, "and since she is so reckless, it is my opinion that she ought to be humoured for once."

"Silence, sirrah!" exclaimed Sir Gaston, vexed at this interference, and then, addressing himself once more to his captive, he earnestly entreated her to save her life by the means he had so often proposed.

"Never!" she replied, firmly; "from heaven I have received fortitude enough to face the terrors with which you have attempted to scare me; I feel confident that I shall not be deserted in the great hour of my troubles, and in that assurance, am ready to depart for the place of ordeal, whenever you shall think fit to order my departure."

"Girl!" cried the knight, "thou hast not weighed the consequences of this step with sufficient care. Recollect, I charge thee, that the ordeal thou hast to endure, is one thou canst not hope to escape unscatched; many have been tried by it—have failed in proving their innocence, and afterwards suffered a prolonged and painful death."

"It may be as thou hast said," she answered, with unshaken resolution. "I may fail, as others have done, and should such be my fate, you shall see that I have fortitude enough to endure even the worst inflictions my enemies can heap upon their victim."

"Is it possible," exclaimed Sir Gaston, "that one so young and delicate, can regard death with the indifference we should, in vain, look for from even the boldest and most reckless of men!"

"My own innocence is the shield that protects me in this instance," answered our heroine. "You have charged me with being concerned in the crime of robbery, and I have denied it; proof, however, of my innocence, I have none, and therefore, I now rely with confidence on the goodness of Heaven, to rescue my name from eternal disgrace."

"Hah!" ejaculated the knight, with contempt, "it appears, then, that you really expect the interposition of some miracle in your behalf."

"And if such a thing were not possible," she asked, "why is the trial by ordeal offered me?"

"Aye, aye," returned Sir Gaston, "wert thou a Christian, there might indeed, be some chance of escaping the perils of this fearful trial."

"Blasphemer!" cried Rebecca, with scorn; "thou thinkest then God, who rulest over Christians and Jews alike, will desert one of his people, because she happens to differ from thee in certain points?"

"I do; and thou wilt find that it is so, maiden, when the moment of trial arrives."

"Well," she exclaimed, "my confidence in the hope of mercy, is not extinguished by anything thou canst urge in thine own opinion. Each day serves to prove that our people are not so abandoned by their Maker as you imagine. In no instance do we receive marks of displeasure; nor canst thou, vain as thou art of thine own creed, prove that we are to become the sport of all those who choose to tyrannize over and oppress us."

"Well, well, girl," cried the knight, when he found there was very little chance of frightening her into submission, "it seems that we are but wasting time in this idle parley. Thou art bent upon thine own destruction, I see, so it only remains for us but to proceed to the palace, where King Richard waits to give judgment between thee and myself."

"Thou hast already heard that I am ready," she replied, with undiminished firmness; "lead on, therefore, and may I, presently, meet with more mercy than thou and thy myrmidons seem disposed to yield me."

Sir Gaston de Neville deigned no reply to this, but motioning to his attendants, they shortly afterwards quitted the castle in procession, a strong guard having been placed round the prisoner, in case any attempt should be made to rescue her, in their way to the palace.

CHAPTER XXVI.

"Now thou must be mine,
Unless high Heaven, by some miracle,
Should interpose between us."—MARIANNE.

"WHITHER art thou going to, old man?" demanded one of the royal archers, of Isaac of Tadcaster, as he was endeavouring to make his way through one of the palace gates; "whither, I say, art thou going, with this haste, as if thou wert entering thine own *hostelrie?*"

"To the king!—to the king!" answered the old man, in a voice trembling with emotion. "I would see him on a matter of life and death; nay, I must see him, or my heart will break with agony."

"*Must* see him!" ejaculated the archer, with surprise; "come, that's rather bold too, considering that thou art a Jew, and he a Christian king."

"In such a time as this," cried the old man, "I can scarcely be expected to wait for ceremony; my daughter,—my daughter, my beloved, my only child, is in peril of her life, and I would plead for her, where alone earthly justice is to be looked for."

"Indeed," retorted the other, "and so, because your daughter happens to have got into trouble, you expect me to run the risk of my own ruin, by suffering you to make your way into the presence of our good King Richard.

"He will pardon me,—I know he will,—because my case is urgent," cried Isaac, with anxiety. "Pity me, friend,—I implore thee pity me, and let this purse of silver reward thee for the good office."

"Hah!—wouldst thou bribe me?" exclaimed the man, with mock indignation, but at the same time weighing the money in his hand, and then securing it in his belt. "Knowest thou not, old man, that I am placed here as a guard over royalty, and that, should I be found out serving thee as thou desirest, I should meet with a certain, and not very pleasant sort of death?"

"I am aware there is some risk," answered Isaac, "and therefore did I offer thee some recompense in money."

"Which is bad salve for a stretched neck," retorted the other.

"Nay, it surely will not be so bad as that, even though the service thou dost me should be found out?"

"By the beard of St. George, I should have nothing less to look for," returned the other, gazing anxiously around, to see whether anybody was observing them. Finding, however, that the place was quite clear, he continued; "however, it's not every man that can refuse a bribe, and, as I don't set myself up to be better than my neighbours, I'll e'en accept your present, and hear what you have to say. You say your daughter is in trouble, so now tell me who she is, and where she happens to be at this moment."

"You have heard that a Hebrew Maiden is this day about to submit to the ordeal, to clear herself from a crime brought against her by a foul and recreant knight, called Sir Gaston de Neville."

"Aye, aye, I have heard of her, sure enough," replied the archer. "Everybody is speaking of it, and, between ourselves, there are few people that don't think her guilty."

"Then they do her a most foul wrong," exclaimed Isaac, with startling vehemence; "she is innocent, I tell thee, and I would see the king, to implore his intercession for one who is persecuted and hunted down by her enemies."

"Nonsense, old man," retorted the other; "who, think you, would be at the trouble of injuring one of thy despised tribe?"

"It is because we are despised," answered Isaac, "that we are thus harrassed and oppressed. Sir Gaston de Neville professes to have fallen desperately in love with my child, and in revenge for her having rejected his infamous proposals, he has charged her with a crime that may end in her destruction."

"But the king is to be her judge," answered the man; "he is just towards all his subjects, whether they be Jews or Christians, and therefore, she is certain to have a fair hearing, and a proper sentence."

"Nay," exclaimed Isaac, "I would see him, and on my knees entreat that mercy, which he will himself hope for, on that dread day when he must stand before the judgment seat of his Maker. It is seldom that the grey hairs of age do not make some impression, and something whispers in my heart, that my supplications will not be unheeded."

"I can't do it, so there's an end of it," replied the soldier. "It's as much as my life is worth, I tell you, and a poor fellow like me cannot be expected to act against the orders he has received from his superiors."

"Would you know, then," cried Isaac, "that a helpless maiden must perish because her father may not be permitted to approach the person of royalty ?"

"I would like to do her an act of kindness, certainly," replied the other, "but then, it must not be at the expense of my own neck. Yonder, however, comes the procession, so I'll tell you what you may do :— force your way in with the crowd, and if I see you, there won't be much fear of my driving you back."

"Thanks, friend,—a thousand thanks, even for that trifling indulgence," cried the old man, fervently clasping his hands in gratitude. "I will follow your counsel, and should my efforts succeed, depend upon it, I will not forget to add a further reward upon one, who is not altogether deaf to the prayers of a heart-broken father."

By this time the procession had reached the gate, and as it passed in, the aged Hebrew adopted the advice he had received, and mixing himself with the crowd behind, contrived to gain admittance, without attracting the notice of those who would have driven him back. From thence they crossed two or three court-yards, and then entering a spacious saloon, discovered the king seated beneath a canopy of state, where he was impatiently waiting to comence the business of the day. On a given signal, Rebecca was placed before him, and immediately afterwards, Sir Gaston de Neville stepped forward, and saluting the monarch, exclaimed :—

"Gracious sire, I am here by your command, to confront the girl, whom I have charged with being in league with Black Ivan, the Outlaw You see her before you, and I now ask for that justice, which is never denied to the meanest of your subjects."

"You shall have it, Sir Gaston," answered the king, "but first you must declare whether no circumstances have arisen since our last interview, that may serve to throw a more favourable light on this unfortunate business."

"Nothing, sire," replied the knight ;—"indeed I am more convinced than ever, that she must know more of the robbery than she at present chooses to admit."

"It is false!" exclaimed Isaac, unable to express the strong emotion that shook his soul.

"Hah!" cried the king, "who dares to interrupt the solemnity in which we are engaged. Speak some one, and say who it was that gave the lie to the answer ?"

"May it please your highness, it was yonder Jew," replied Sir Gaston, pointing to Isaac, who by this time, had thrust himself to a foremost place in the crowd. "He is the father of the girl, and is thus bold in asserting the innocence of one who he knows to be most guilty."

"Well, well," exclaimed the monarch, "'tis natural enough that a parent should step forward in behalf of his child !—So, hark'ee, Jew, you are pardoned for this once, but let us not hear your voice again until you are called upon to give your evidence in her favour."

"I will endeavour to obey your majesty's commands," answered the old man, submissively, "and yet it is hard to hold one's peace, knowing as I do, the vile motives that have instigated yonder craven knight to——"

"Peace, I charge you!" interrupted the king, angrily; "and remember, Jew, that, being here upon sufferance, you will be turned out, unless you bridle that slanderous tongue of yours." "And now, Sir Gaston, he continned, addressing himself to the knight, resume thy charge boldly, and I pledge my royal word to administer fair and im-partial justice between the accuser and the accused. Dost thou still de-mand the full vengeance of the law upon this unfortunate girl, unless she can satisfactorily prove her innocence?"

"I do."

"Then I have no alternative but to grant thy request," resumed King Richard. "Thou canst certainly insist upon it, though methinks it would have showed a more forgiving spirit hadst thou been less greedy in thy cry for retribution."

"Your majesty then," exclaimed Sir Gaston, "thinks proper to take part with the accused. But, perhaps, that may easily be accounted for, seeing that a pretty face and a pair of sparkling eyes are not without their effect, even when justice calls for a rigid enquiry."

"Thou art insolent, Sir Knight," cried the king, fiercely;—"it seems thou presumest on the favour I have hitherto shown thee, and that I am to be bearded by a subject, even within the walls of my own palace."

Sir Gaston de Neville began to perceive that he had gone too far, and knowing as he did the hasty temper of his royal master, he began to draw in a little, and with a bland smile, he replied:—

"Pardon me, sire, if I have been betrayed into more warmth of feeling than was courteous towards one who I am bound to love and reverence. The truth is, however, I have sufficent cause for complaint against this girl, and I feared lest she should escape the punishment she so justly merits."

"And me, truly, and upon thine honour," exclaimed the king; "hast thou not some private cause for the animosity thou hast betrayed against this Hebrew Maiden?"

"Private cause!" reiterated Sir Gaston, with affected surprise.

"Aye"—returned the monarch—"that is to say hast thou not been struck with her beauty, and wouldst therefore make the proposals that she may have rejected with scorn."

"Your majesty judges me too severely."

"Perhaps I may," replied Richard, "and yet in fairness towards the accused, I must hear her version of the story." Then addressing him-self to Rebecca, he continued:—"thou hast heard, maiden, the charge that hath been brought against thee by Sir Gaston de Neville. He, it seems, has lost a valuable diamond which was stolen from him by that desperate Outlaw, Black Ivan, and within a short time afterwards the precious gem was found in thy possession. This is the accusation, and thou hast now to answer the charge."

"Alas! sire," cried our heroine, "what can a poor unfriended girl say, when one so powerful as Sir Gaston de Neville has resolved upon her destruction? I am innocent, my liege, and that is the only reply I can make to him."

"Has thou no evidence to bring forward in support of thy denial?" asked the king.

"My father, sire," answered Rebecca, glancing towards the place where the old man stood. "He will not forsake his child, though I fear there is little chance of his evidence being received with favour."

"If I may be permitted to speak," interrupted Sir Gaston, "I should say this old man ought not to be believed on his oath.—He is a Jew, my liege, and therefore will not care what he says against those who profess a creed different to his own."

"Nay, in that respect, I must differ from you," returned the king,

sharply. "The people you speak of, have been already too much oppressed by those who mis-call themselves Christians, and I am resolved
to protect them whenever I see that they are deserving of my care."

"Then your majesty will make many enemies by so doing," replied
Sir Gaston, instantly;—"hitherto it has been customary to discourage
these unbelievers, and yet now it seems they are to be exalted above us."

"In that respect I shall allow no one to dictate to me," exclaimed the
king. "You will therefore drop this subject, Sir Gaston, and permit
the old man to say what he knows towards the unravelling of this
mystery."

Upon this, Isaac of Tadcaster reverently advanced towards the throne
and throwing himself upon his knees, earnestly implored mercy for his
daughter.

"She is innocent, sire! indeed, indeed she is!" exclaimed the old
man, in an agony of terror. "The jewel which this knight has charged
her with stealing, was brought to my house by one who afterwards
turned out to be Black Ivan. Imposed upon by an artful look that he
had mounted, I purchased the diamond of him, and instantly placed it
upon the hand of my daughter for safety. At that juncture, the robber
was traced to my house by Sir Gaston and his followers—the ring was
found in her possession, and for motives which he well understands, she
has been accused as an accomplice of that hardened and sinful man."

"Your majesty," cried Sir Gaston de Neville, "this is but a subterfuge to rescue his daughter from the punishment she so well merits.—
No one saw Black Ivan go to the house of the Jew; the house was
searched all over, and as no trace of him was to be found anywhere about
the place, there is every reason to suppose the story you have just heard
is a falsehood."

"Have you any proof to bring forward?" asked his majesty of the
Jew; "or can you, in any way, satisfy us that you became possessed of
the diamond in the way you have described?"

"My servant, Jonah," answered the Jew, "can add his testimony to
what I have said."

"Why that would be bringing one Jew to support another in his
falsehoods!" exclaimed Sir Gaston, peevishly.

"Is the man present?" asked the king, without paying any regard to
these latter words.

"He is not, my gracious liege," replied Isaac; "indeed I had much
difficulty to obtain admittance here for myself, and one so humble as he
is, would have been driven away as though he had been some dog or
heathen."

"To our shame, it must be acknowledged, there is some truth in what
thou hast said, old man," exclaimed the king. "However, I have a duty
to perform here between the prisoner and her accuser, and I cannot object to any means being tried by which the truth may be satisfactorily
brought out."

"Then let her go through the ordeal according to the form prescribed
in such cases," returned Sir Gaston. "It is a test that I have a right
to demand, and your majesty has been graciously pleased to promise
that my desire shall be complied with."

"It shall, Sir Gaston," replied the monarch, "though—to say the
truth—I think your conduct harsh in the extreme, and most sincerely
do I hope that she may receive assistance from heaven to carry her
safely through the perils with which she is threatened."

"Your majesty mistakes me," answered the knight, with hypocritical submission. "I ask only for justice, not for any unnecessary harshness towards the accused."

"My liege," cried Rebecca, whose faith in the nostrum that had been given her by Meg, inspired her with more boldness to endure the trial than she would otherwise have felt; "my liege, I fear not to undergo the ordeal demanded by my accuser. I am ready to submit to it, and even ask for that public proof of my guilt or innocence."

"Art though mad, girl!" cried the king with astonishment; "knowest thou not that none have ever been able to endure the torture of boiling water, and that shouldst thou fail, thy instant doom will be inevitable."

"I am aware of all that," she replied, "yet am I, at the same time, convinced, that innocence will not be forsaken by the Supreme Power that I worship! I am ready to submit myself to the ordeal, and all I ask for, in case I pass through it safely, is, that I may be snatched from the hands of this knight, who has so unceasingly sought my destruction."

"Thy wish shall be granted," exclaimed the king, "but say, is there nothing more thou wouldst ask for?"

"I would ask protection for my father, should I perish," she replied. "He is old, and little able to endure the wrath of man, that hunts so many of our tribe to destruction."

"Fear not, maiden," answered the monarch, in a voice of kindness and compassion;—"he shall be protected, and woe unto those who seek to injure him after I have sworn to become his friend."

"Your majesty's kindness cheers and consoles me amidst all my afflictions," cried Rebecca, bursting into tears;—"and yet," she continued, blushing,—"there is one other, for whom I would claim protection from his enemies."

"Who is he, maiden?"

"One Reuben Grenard."

"Hah!—thy lover, I suppose;—nay, thou needst not blush, girl, for he also shall share my protection even though it be against his powerful rival, Sir Gaston de Neville, himself."

"Your highness is rather hard upon me," muttered the knight, confounded by these words; "I came not here to supplicate for vengeance, but for justice, and I believe all who now stand around your throne, will unite in declaring that, as a loyal subject, I have a right to demand it."

"Well, man, and thou shalt have it," exclaimed the king; "have I not sworn that thou shalt, and does not the maiden herself, express her readiness to submit to the ordeal thou hast demanded? You see she shrinks not from the trial, and that, in my opinion, argues no little in favour of her innocence."

"Your majesty, then," muttered Sir Gaston, smarting under the sarcasm with which this was uttered, "imagines, of course, that I have brought a false charge against her?"

"That remains to be proved, Sir Knight," retorted the king.

And then motioning to some of his attendants, they immediately departed, shortly afterwards, however, returning, and bringing with them the huge caldron, containing the boiling liquid, and beneath which was a furnace, to keep the liquid at the requisite degree of heat.

"Now, maiden, stand forward," exclaimed Richard;—"advance towards the caldron, and ere the ordeal commences, declare whether thou art still resolved to endure the trial and the consequences to which it may lead."

I am prepared," [she replied, to submit to anything that may prove my innocence of this foul charge."

"Oh, heed her not, my liege!" exclaimed her father, alarmed at the danger in which his child was involved—"she raves, and considers not the fatal doom that may be the result of this vain mockery."

"Hear the blasphemer!" cried Sir Gaston de Neville;—"he dares to call that a mockery which the laws have instituted for the securing of justice."

"It is not blasphemy that I utter," returned the aged Israelite, "but the terror a father suffers on behalf of his unfortunate offspring. We are none of us proof against pain, and yet if she flinches from the torture you are about to inflict, it will be construed into an evidence of her guilt."

"I am ready to submit to it, father," she replied, with a calm and unmoved countenance. "Forbear, therefore, I entreat of you, to intercede any further for me, and you shall be convinced, that, in a cause like this, I can exert a degree of firmness that you expect not from me."

"You hear, Sir Gaston," exclaimed the king, reproachfully;—"she is willing to endure the torture you would inflict, and now it remains only for yourself to say whether mercy shall not be extended towards the accused."

"Your majesty will do as you please," answered the knight, sullenly, "but, for my own part, I am not at all changed in the purpose that brought me here. I would have justice, and if it is to be withheld from me, let others of your subjects learn the chance of reparation they are to look for on applying to the highest authority."

"You are insolent, Sir Knight, and presume too much on the kindness

No. 18

I have thus far shown you!" cried Richard, chafed with anger at these taunts. "However, let that pass for the present;—the maiden feels confident in her own innocence, and even demands the test you are so anxious to administer."

"Nay, most gracious king, heed her not, I implore you!" exclaimed the time-worn Israelite;—"she is rendered desperate by the cruelty of her enemies and knows not what she says."

"It seems then," muttered Sir Gaston, "that I am to be refused satisfaction for the wrong I have endured, I am to be robbed and the guilty are to escape punishment."

"Stay!" exclaimed Richard, peremptorily, as the knight was about to quit the court; "the trial is a most severe one it must be admitted, yet there is no alternative, and she must submit to it. Advance, maiden, and bare your right arm to the shoulder."

Rebecca, without exhibiting the least appearance of fear, did as she had been commanded.

"Now, girl," demanded the king, "art thou prepared?"

"I am, sire."

"Then plunge your arm into the boiling cauldron, and if, when I have given the signal to withdraw it, you have betrayed no sign of pain or suffering, you will be adjudged innocent and ordered to be discharged without further stain upon your character."

Instantly did our heroine obey, and so powerful was the antidote she had applied, that after placing her limb in the scalding fluid, she was enabled to stand with as much composure as if nothing whatever had occurred. At this, even her worst enemies shouted out "a miracle!"— "a miracle!" and Sir Gaston de Neville himself gazed upon her as though a being of another world was standing before him. He was, in fact, struck mute with astonishment at what appeared to him nothing less than the interference of Divine Providence to thwart his evil designs against her, and he was unable to give utterance to a word until after the king had broken the silence which had followed the exhibition we have alluded to.

"Now, Sir Knight," exclaimed Richard, with exultation, "what sayest thee to the charge so unjustly brought against this maiden? Wilt thou not, at least, acknowledge that that suspicion has been injurious and unfounded?"

"I know not what answer to make your majesty," replied Sir Gaston, with hesitation. "It certainly appears singular that she has had the firmness to withstand so much pain, and yet it is evident that she must have been aided by the power of witchcraft, or never could she have cheated us as she has."

"Hah! I understand thee well," cried Richard, angrily;"—"having been defeated in one of your charges you would now seek to bring another against her! But look, Sir Gaston, and convince yourself—does not the water boil and bubble whilst her arm remains in it? and is not that a direct answer to the unjust accusation you have brought against her?"

"I admit there is something singular in all this," replied Sir Gaston de Neville, "yet still, do I remain unconvinced of her innocence. Your majesty says, she has successfully passed the ordeal, but I would now ask you to command her to withdraw her arm in order that we may see whether some cheatery has not been practised to circumvent me."

"Comply with his request, girl," cried the king, "and convince this unbeliever that thou art fairly entitled to thine acquittance from the crime laid to thy charge.,'

The Hebrew Maiden did as she had been commanded, and after submitting her arm to the careful examination of Sir Gaston, he was compelled to admit that he was not able to discover any trick that would have wrought the wonder he had witnessed.

"Then you own yourself fairly convinced at last?" exclaimed King Richard, with satisfaction.

"I do, my liege."

"Heaven be praised for the great mercy it has this day vouchsafed to show me," cried the aged Hebrew, falling upon his knees in the fulness of his gratitude. "My child has escaped the snares of her enemies, and she will be again restored to the arms of her now happy father."

"Aye, thou mayest take her with thee, old man;" returned the monarch;—she is free, and never more can she be charged again with the crime of which she has been so miraculously acquitted in the sight of those who were most resolute in declaring her guilt."

Isaac waited for no second bidding, but taking the hand of his daughter, he bowed respectfully to the king and assembly, and left the place. As for Sir Gaston de Neville. he gazed after them with a countenance expressive of the mortification he felt, which being perceived by the king, the latter exclaimed :—

"You now perfectly understand me, Sir Knight; the maiden who has just now left us, is, from this time forth, to be free from any further persecution on account of a charge which has been disproved in the presence of her most inveterate foes. Remember, she is no longer to be the sport of fortune or your malice, as it is my firm resolution to punish with the utmost severity any further attempts that may be made to injure her."

Sir Gaston de Neville merely bowed in reply to this, and without again venturing to encounter the angry glances of his sovereign, he motioned to his followers, and left the royal presence, heartily cursing, in his own mind, the chance that had thus deprived him of his meditated revenge.

CHAPTER XXVII.

NEVER, in the whole course of his life, had Isaac of Tadcaster felt so happy, as he did when returning home with his fondly cherished treasure, who had been so unexpectedly rescued from a fate that had appeared to him inevitable. Rebecca, however, soon explained to him the means by which she had been enabled to endure the ordeal she had undergone; and then, for the first time, did he recollect the words of Meg of Finchley, whose promise to assist her, he had quite forgotten, as a thing that was utterly impracticable. Now, however, he remembered all that had passed between them, and as her words had been fulfilled, he resolved to reward her in any way she might think fit to insist on. As he uttered this determination, a hand was laid upon his shoulder, and, turning round, he beheld the very person of whom he had been speaking.

"What!" she exclaimed, "do you start at the presence of one who has so recently proved herself your friend?—am I, indeed, so terrible that even you, old man, cannot look upon me without fear and apprehension?"

"Nay, you mistake me," answered Isaac ;—"it was not fear that made me start, but the suddenness of your appearance, at a moment when you were so little expected to be near at hand."

"I have followed close at your heels," she replied,—" ever since you quitted the palace-gate. In fact, I felt anxious to leave the result of the day's trial to your daughter, but her being suffered to return home with you, assures me that my wishes in her behalf are accomplished."

"They are," replied Isaac, in accents of joy, " and, from henceforth, my gratitude is due to you, after heaven, for her escape from a horrible death."

"There is no need to talk of gratitude to me, old man," exclaimed Meg, "since what I have done is only in return for the kindness I have received from her. When I must have perished by the way-side, she came like a ministering angel to my relief, and from that time I vowed to return the service whenever an opportunity should offer for my doing so;—that chance has been given me, and so far I am happy, but never will the debt be entirely cancelled, whilst I have the power to render her any assistance."

"Let me hope there will be no further need for it," exclaimed Rebecca, earnestly. "I have happily escaped one imminent danger, and surely Sir Gaston de Neville will no more attempt to injure me."

"You know him not, madam," replied the old woman, with emotion; "he is not to be easily daunted, when once he has set his mind upon any object; and defeat, in this instance, will only serve to render him the more desperate in future."

"But will he not fear the king's anger?"

"To a man, utterly regardless of consequences as he is, that will prove but a slight protection to her," replied Meg. "I have watched the evil of his ways for many a year, and therefore can assure you that he will not be daunted by what has taken place."

"Alas!" cried Isaac, "will he then again seek her destruction?"

"There is but too much reason to fear he will," answered the Wierd Woman;—"he possesses to love the maiden, and though his intentions are not honourable towards her, he will never give up the pursuit whilst a chance remains of accomplishing his base designs."

"Suppose then, I immediately consent to her union with Reuben Grenard?" exclaimed the old man. "In him she will have a husband and protector, and surely then, she will no longer become the object of this base knight's persecutions?"

"You grievously mistake the villain," answered the woman, "if you suppose her marriage would effect any change in his determination. As the husband of your daughter, Reuben Grenard, would soon be marked out as an object of vengeance, and there is every reason to suppose the most fatal consequences would ensue. In fact, the destruction of both would be aimed at, and thou, who know Sir Gaston de Neville, cannot be at a loss to guess how his efforts would terminate."

"Yet still," exclaimed Isaac, after a moment's reflection, "I cannot but rely upon the love of justice professed by the king. He has warned the knight how he persecutes one who has been cleared of the foul charges brought against her, and his own life would probably be forfeited should he act in opposition to the royal command."

"Be warned in time, I entreat you," cried the old woman;—"your daughter is still in peril, I say, and let that be sufficient to put you upon your guard against the designs of a heartless libertine. Besides, there is another whose evil practices you have no less reason to dread;—has not Black Ivan given you proof that she is not safe whilst he remains at liberty, and think you he will ever give up the pursuit whilst a single chance of success remains?"

"Alas!" sighed Rebecca, "it seems then, that I have only escaped death this day to become the sport of fortune."

"That remains to be seen," replied Meg; "that you have thus far eluded the snares laid for your destruction should inspire you with better hopes."

"Then why do you seek to fill our minds with apprehension?" asked the aged Israelite.

"Because," answered Meg, "I would endeavour to warn you in time. There is danger, I repeat, and it behoves you, as her father, to guard over, and watch incessantly, to defeat the intentions of the wicked. Of Sir Gaston's designs you have already had sufficient example, and let that teach you to doubt him for the future."

"But you spoke also of Black Ivan," returned Isaac. "Speak, woman, I implore you, and say whether you know of any fresh project that he has formed?"

"I merely judge him by his former acts."

"Then, perhaps we have no real ground for alarm after all," exclaimed the old man. "As an Outlaw, he cannot venture to shew himself too openly, and surely we may guard against his base intentions towards my daughter."

"He is a desperate man," answered Meg, "and has given proof ere now, that he can be rashly bold whenever he has fully resolved upon the accomplishment of any project. Already he has had Rebecca in his power, and though she escaped from him at a moment when all hope appeared to be lost, it ought rather to warn you that he is an enemy, requiring all your vigilance to guard against."

"Would that I had perished this day, when my enemies were so eagerly thirsting for my blood!" cried Rebecca, in accents of despair. "I have escaped one great danger, it is true, but it seems that I am to live in continual dread of the machinations of my enemies."

"At any rate, madam," replied Meg, "this yielding to despair, will not serve to extricate you from troubles, that require all your fortitude and caution to avoid. It was to put you upon your guard, that I came forward at this time, and yet it appears that my well-meant efforts have done more harm than good."

"Pardon us, my good woman," interposed the Jew, "if our terrors make us appear ungrateful for the kindness you have extended towards us. We are well aware of your generous motives, and will do all in our power to deserve the pains you have taken in our behalf."

"I require no thanks," she replied, "since my best reward will be the certainty of seeing you safe over the dangers that at present crowd upon you. Sir Gaston will not fail to put immediate projects into execution for your ruin, and even should he not succeed, you will still be in peril from the Outlaw, Black Ivan."

"Shall I remove to some distant part of the kingdom?" asked Isaac, scarcely knowing, in his despair, what plan to devise for his daughter's safety.

"That," answered Meg, "would, I fear, rather injure than serve you, for the emissaries of your foes will even be upon the watch, and you would be followed in whatever direction you might think it advisable to flee. Besides, the further you were from London, the less hope would there be of a rescue, since, in all probability, the king would never hear of the new act of oppression."

"You think, then, we shall be safer if we remain in our old habitation?"

"Aye, if your daughter will remain there for a time, without venturing forth," replied the old woman, "neither Sir Gaston de Neville, nor his rival, Black Ivan, will, I should imagine, dare to drag her from thence by violence, and should you discover that they are forming plans for taking her away, an application to the king will obtain for you the royal protection, which will be sufficient to deter them from the evil they intend. However, we have now nearly reached thy house, and I will therefore take my leave with an understanding that we shall meet again should I chance to learn any intelligence that may be of importance to thee."

Without waiting for any further thanks, Meg hurried away, and al. most at the moment she did so, Reuben Grenard was seen approaching them, to congratulate his beloved mistress on the narrow escape she had had from the machinations of her enemies.

CHAPTER XXVIII.

"Treason doth lurk in darkness,—
But drag it from its murky hiding place,
And lo! how hideous, foul, and venomous
The monster then appears!"—STEINBACH.

NOTHING could have been more mortifying to Sir Gaston de Neville than the triumphant acquittal and subsequent release of Rebecca from the bondage in which he intended she should have passed the remainder of her days. His soul was tortured with a thousand conflicting passions when he thought of the opportunity that had been thus lost, and in the desperation of the moment, there is no crime he would have hesitated to commit in order to avenge himself for the disappointment he had been made to endure. Nor was his confidant and adviser, Bertrand le Noir, backward in urging him to resort to further violence, rather than tamely suffer himself to be defeated; he even went so far as to counsel the secret assassination of the maiden, now that all hopes of obtaining her had vanished, and offered to perpetrate the deed with his own hands, whenever he might receive his master's commands to do so.

But Sir Gaston, however well he might have been pleased with the ready zeal of his follower, was too careful of his own safety to yield compliance to this proposition without mature consideration, and it was not till two or three days after this conversation had passed between them that he gave a decided negative to the sanguinary plan that had been suggested, at least, he would not consent to it, he said, until the design would be carried into effect without fear of involving himself in any share of suspicion.

"Were we to proceed to violence," he exclaimed, "the king would at once regard the act as mine, and thus I should not only lose his royal favour, but the chances are that I myself should be involved in difficulties from which it would not be very easy to escape. Richard is a chivalrous prince, and in the defence of a female, whether she be Jew or Christian, he would sacrifice even his best friends in revenge for any wrong that might be inflicted."

"But," answered Bertrand, "there is no occasion to let him even suspect that you had any hand in the affair. Give but your consent and I promise that, before this time to-morrow, the girl shall no longer have it in her power to annoy and vex you."

"Thou wouldst remove her by some act of violence?"

"I would—my dagger will prove a sure remedy in this case, and you will at least be spared the mortification of seeing her become the prize of another."

"Again, I tell thee, Bertrand, the king's suspicion would be immediately directed towards myself. Already has he warned me that his heavy anger would follow any further attempts against the maiden, and even in the presence of his gaping courtiers hath he insulted me by alluding to what he calls my dishonourable love for Rebecca of Tadcaster."

"I know he has," answered Bertrand le Noir, "and had I been in your place, his royal dignity should not have screened him long from my wrath."

"Hah!" exclaimed the knight, startled by these words of his follower—"what meanest thou, Bertrand?—surely thou wouldst not counsel me to break out into open rebellion against the monarch I have sworn fidelity to?"

"I counsel nothing that may be against the conscience of my noble master," answered the retainer, with hypocritical submission. "I merely say what I would do were I in his place, and leave him to act upon the hint as he may think proper."

"Bertrand!" exclaimed Sir Gaston de Neville, "these words of thine have served to revive thoughts that once filled my brain, and which I had hoped were now banished from my mind for ever. Yes, I acknowledge to thee that the king's interference in my pleasure, has more than once inspired me with thoughts of vengeance, and that it has been with no little difficulty that I have managed to curb my fiery impatience thus long."

"And why have you done so?" asked Bertrand, venturing to act further upon this hint. "Has he not interfered to thwart you in an affair that lies nearest to your heart—and shall a subject suffer wrong patiently, because it pleases his royal master to act the tyrant?"

"Thou art right, Bertrand," exclaimed the knight, impatiently. "I have thought seriously upon this matter, and more than once have persuaded myself that I should be justified in openly rebelling against him."

"Nay, why run so useless a risk?" demanded the retainer. "Open rebellion may bring you to destruction; and, therefore, I say it would be madness, seeing that vengeance may be more safely procured by acting with secrecy and caution."

"Thy words are dark, Bertrand," cried the knight; "that thou entertainest some deep design, thy words have made manifest, and therefore do I now command thee to declare the purpose of thy soul."

"Thou wilt not be angry with thy servant, if his zeal prompts him to utter that which may be abhorrent to thine own feelings?"

"I promise thee I will not be angry; nay, more, thou shalt be forgiven whatever may be the nature of the proposition thou hast to make."

"It is enough, and I take thee at thy word," returned Bertrand le Noir. "Know then, that thou art not alone in thy dissatisfaction at the conduct of King Richard; he has many enemies, and his death would give joy to more of his subjects than thou mayst perhaps think."

"Aye," answered the knight, "but he is young, and the chances are that he will live long, contrary to the hopes of those who would not be sorry to get rid of him."

"And yet," returned the other, in a subdued whisper, "he is not proof against the knife of an assassin!"

"Villain!" cried Sir Gaston, startled by these words of his dependant, "dost thou dare breathe thy thoughts of treason in the ear of one who is sworn to protect the life of his sovereign, even at the price of his own blood!"

"Nay, thou art angry with me, I see," exclaimed Bertrand. "I have been mistaken in supposing that thou didst desire satisfaction for the wrongs thou hast received."

"Why wilt thou madden me?" cried the knight, rapidly pacing up and down the chamber. "Is it not enough that I have been made the sport of fortune, but thou must remind me of the king's interference in my affairs? Thou knowest I would gladly seek vengeance, though not by the base means thou hast proposed."

"Pardon me, Sir Knight," returned Bertrand, "but I said it was not necessary thou shouldst have any hand in the affair I have hinted at,— Thou shalt be free from the crime—as thou callest it—and I will myself undertake to do the deed which shall release 'England from the rule of her present monarch."

"Wouldst thou indeed risk thy life by murdering him?"

"I would."

"But hast thou reflected that shouldst thou be discovered thy life would be the forfeit?"

"I have thought of all, and yet am willing to run the hazard in so good a cause."

"Dost thou call the cause a good one," asked Sir Gaston, "when the only motive that impels thee is vengeance for a private wrong?"

"That is not the only cause," answered Bertrand le Noir. "The king, however popular he may be with the common herd of his people, is not liked by the generality of his subjects. He is imperious in his conduct towards them, and if occasion of dissatisfaction be required, it is to be found in the favour he has been pleased to shew towards the Jews. Hitherto, our monarchs have taken part against the whole race, but he has thought proper to shield them whenever there have been any differences between the descendants of Abraham and our own people."

"If that," exclaimed Sir Gaston, "is the only cause for rebellion against him, I shall continue to serve him faithfully, though I must needs say, my heart is not very earnest in his behalf."

"Then I will no longer seek to prevail upon thee," replied Bertrand, in a tone of disappointment. "I thought thou wert sensible of the wrongs thou hast endured, in respect of this maiden, and my zeal for thee made me speak more freely than perhaps I ought. There is one thing, however, to be said—Richard is not without enemies, and unless he looks well about him, the assassin's dagger may reach his heart ere many more days have passed over him."

"Bertrand," exclaimed the knight, sternly, "thou speakest in words that are not to be mistaken; thou hast hinted that the barons are ripe for revolt, and that the king's life is in danger, not only from rebellion, but from the hands of private malice."

"I have told thee nothing more than the truth," answered Bertrand. "Prince John, our monarch's brother, is anxious to seize upon the reins of government, and he wants not for plenty of friends to aid him in his designs."

"Hah!" cried the knight, "by heaven! my thoughts have more than once turned towards John. I know him to be ambitious of sovereign power, and the mortification I have endured from Richard Cœur de Lion, has made me think of his pretensions with more favour than I otherwise should. The prince, I have thought, would not interfere with the pleasure of his subjects, and for that reason I have sometimes wished the throne were occupied otherwise than it is."

"And so it would be, were the present occupant removed," answered Bertrand le Noir. "Besides, John is well known to be the sworn enemy

of the Jews, and it is, therefore, certain that from him you would find no opposition, should you think fit to carry off this Hebrew Maiden by violence."

"Nay," cried the knight, "urge me no more at present upon this subject. Already do I feel half tempted to lend my aid towards substituting one monarch for another. My own private feelings strongly urge me to the step thou hast thus darkly hinted at, and perhaps upon mature reflection, I may become a convert to thy designs. Prince John—once on the throne of England—would naturally favour those who took part in his cause, and thus I might not only elevate myself to a condition of high honour, but this maiden must become my prize, in spite of any obstacles that may be thrown in my way."

"Then, I may reckon on thee as a friend to the prince?" exclaimed Bertrand le Noir.

"Sirrah!" returned the knight, haughtily, "I have not yet said so much, that thou shouldst set me down for a rebel against my king.— True, I have cause for feeling angry with him, but it may take some time before I can make up my mind to break the oath of allegiance I have sworn to him. In some instances Richard has proved a kind and indulgent monarch, and, for the kindness he has done me, I would fain forget his interference between me and this Hebrew Maiden."

"How canst thou forget that which there is so much cause to remember?" asked Bertrand, resolved not to lose an opportunity of bringing the knight to his own way of thinking. "Did you not accuse her, upon what appeared to be clear evidence, of having been concerned in the robbery of your diamond? and has she not been pronounced guilty of the crime by the lips of King Richard himself?"

No. 19

"She has," answered the knight, "but there was no help for it. She passed the ordeal unharmed, and, therefore, the king was bound to hold her innocent."

"Yet I would wager my life there was some foul jugglery in it all," exclaimed Bertrand. "The girl must be leagued with fiends, for in no other way can I account for her having endured a torture that was never before known to fail in compelling suspected criminals to acknowledge the crime charged against them."

"Psha!" muttered Sir Gaston, "canst thou suspect the king of being in league with a Jewess?"

"Why, to confess the truth," replied Bertrand le Noir, "there are more improbable things in the world than that; King Richard's heart is not proof against the glances of a black-eyed damsel, and I have had my suspicions that the reason of his opposing you in this affair, is, that he hopes, by depriving you of the Jewess, to obtain her as a prize for himself."

"Hah!" vociferated the Templar, "did I think there was any truth in that surmise, I would no longer hesitate to enter the ranks of the king's enemies."

"Why, then, I can tell you there is no doubt of it," answered the retainer; "nay, it has been remarked by those most about the court, that Richard is evidently smitten with the charms of the Hebrew girl.—Whenever she has been present, his eyes were detected wandering towards her, and therefore, doubtless, he has his own reasons for interposing the royal authority to prevent your depriving him of a prize he himself hopes to carry off."

"By heavens!" exclaimed the knight, furiously, "should that suspicion be confirmed I will no longer hesitate to become his deadly foe."

"In which case," observed the other, "you will admit the expediency of putting him quietly out of the way."

"I would."

"And I might, perhaps, be permitted to have the honour of releasing England from the dominion of a tyrant."

"I said not so," returned the knight, eagerly, "in fact, were it discovered that a retainer of mine was engaged in the deed, suspicion would immediately light upon me, and perhaps ruin would fall upon and crush me ere I was aware of the impending danger."

"Why, then, I have another method to propose" answered, Bertrand le Noir. "You remember that in our last encounter with Black Ivan's brigands we took a prisoner who has been surnamed by his associates, Ranulph the Avenger. That man is now a captive in one of your dungeons, that his disposition is sullen and ferocious, I have had an opportunity of proving, and all that is required to make him your faithful adherent is to grant him an instant and unconditional release from captivity."

"Humph!" muttered Sir Gaston, "and thus give him an opportunity to repay upon myself any cruelty that you may have thought proper to inflict upon him during the course of his captivity."

"I will answer for his fidelity with my own life," replied Bertrand. "Against you he entertains no malice, but towards the king he breathes nothing but vows of hatred and revenge."

"And wherefore," asked Sir Gaston de Neville, "does this ill feeling on his part arise?"

"From some wrong inflicted upon him by King Richard," answered the retainer. "He fought with him in Palestine, I believe, and for some trifling crime was chastised and degraded in the sight of all those comrades among whom he had gallantly fought and bled. Be that as it may, however, it seems that he returned to England shortly afterwards, when, smarting under the injuries he had received, he joined the band under the command of Black Ivan, resolving, at some time or other, to avenge himself in the blood of his royal oppressor. In fact, his imprisonment at this moment is only grievous to him because it prevents the execution of the vow he has made ; and, no doubt, if you give him his liberty, one of the earliest uses he would make of it, will be to rid us of a monarch that we dislike."

" Let him be set free;" exclaimed Sir Gaston, " see that he is instantly released from his dungeon, and, if he thinks fit to accept of it, he may have a place in my household for the present.'

" Your order shall be obeyed, Sir Gaston," answered the retainer, inwardly chuckling at the success which had thus far attended his scheme. " I will away to set the captive free ; and, to-morrow, he shall attend you to the hunt when you accompany King Richard;—perhaps he may then find an opportunity to let fly a strong arrow at his majesty,—but, at all events, if he happens not to succeed, then, I dare say, it will not be very long before he makes way for Prince John to ascend the throne."

Upon this, Bertrand le Noir hastened from the presence of his master, who he left meditating upon the dark deed that had been contemplated and was now about being put into execution.

CHAPTER XXIX.

" Hear and believe me :—when thine arm is raised
Strike to his very heart !—strike fearfully,
Or we ourselves shall perish."

LORENZO.

LITTLE did the gallant King Richard dream of treason when with a light and bounding heart he set out on the morning that had been appointed for the chase. Indeed, never before had he met his nobles with more confidence than on the present occasion, and towards Sir Gaston de Neville, in particular, did he address himself, endeavouring, as he said, to rouse him from the melancholy in which his soul seemed to be absorbed.

It was a gallant and glorious sight to see the king thus nobly attended ride forth to the chase, which, in those days, formed one of the chief ornaments even of the highest in the land. And abundant, too, was the sport which rewarded them on this occasion, keeping them in constant exercise until a late hour in the day, and which so occupied their attention that none of them thought of giving up the pleasures of the chase until the black masses of clouds above threatened to burst forth into a storm of more than usual violence. Occasionally, the lightnings flashed forth with tremendous vividness, and then followed the roaring thunder, commencing, apparently, at a distance, and then rolling and swelling towards them until it burst over their heads with such terrific reports that seemed to rend the very heavens in twain.

At the commencement of the tempest most of the barons were absent from the king, nearly all of them having followed a noble stag, unmindful of the storm which was threatening above them. Richard, however, was prevailed upon by some of the nobles who remained about him,— amongst whom was Sir Gaston de Neville, to retreat with as little delay as possible, and to apply for shelter at the first place, however humble it might be, at which they should arrive. Accordingly, away they all rode at their utmost speed, nor did they attempt to restrain the impetuosity of their steeds until they reached a number of detached houses, before one of which the king suddenly halted.

"By St. George!" he exclaimed, dismounting, and giving his impatient charger to the care of the first groom that approached; "by St. George, but we are likely to find a kindly welcome here, after the hard ride we have had. In this place lives an honest Jew, and, doubtless, the worthy man will gladly give us the brief shelter we so much need."

"Are you aware, gracious sire," asked Sir Gaston de Neville, "that in this house dwells the father of the girl I lately accused of robbery?"

"But you forgot to add," observed the king, "who so satisfactorily proved her innocence of the charge! Yes, yes, Sir Gaston, I remember the house well, seeing that the last time I was in the neighbourhood, some of your villainous retainers had set fire to the place, by way, I suppose, of purging it, for having given shelter to a Jew."

"Your majesty's memory is good," returned Sir Gaston. "Indeed, I had hoped, that ere this, you had forgotten an affair of so little importance."

"By my hallidome, this is treating a serious affair rather lightly!" exclaimed the king. "Burning a man's house about his ears is no such trifle either; nor was I likely to forget an act which, for its baseness, deserved my severest displeasure. However, I am not reproaching you with it now, so here let the matter drop; for the rain, I see, will soon be coming down in torrents, and I would rather obtain shelter from the much-despised Jew than ride home to the palace with a wet doublet."

"Then I, for one, must beg permission to take leave of your Majesty for the present," answered the knight. "The girl, Rebecca, is doubtless within, and I have more reasons than one to avoid seeing her who I still believe is guilty of knowing more about the robbery of my diamond than she is willing to admit."

"A very wise resolution too," exclaimed the king, "who knows what alarm your presence might occasion to a poor girl who has already felt so large a share of your persecution. So, go your way, Sir Gaston, and, to-morrow, if thou wilt come to the palace, I will myself tell thee the sort of reception I have met with."

"At any rate," answered the knight, "I will leave two of my retainers at your service. Both Bertrand and Ranulph are faithful to their master, and, doubtless, they will prove equally zealous towards their king."

"I will accept your offer, Sir Gaston," answered Richard. "These men shall be my especial guards whilst I remain, and should they prove faithful to me, their services shall not go unrewarded."

"Doubt them not, my liege," exclaimed Sir Gaston. "They understand their master's commands well, and I am much mistaken if they act otherwise than in strict accordance with my wishes."

As he said this, the knight exchanged a meaning glance with his two retainers, and, perceiving that they perfectly understood him, he quickly disappeared, followed by all the rest of his usual retinue. As he rode off, the king advanced towards the door of the Jew's house, where he found the old man and his daughter already waiting to receive and welcome him to their hospitable roof.

"I am come to thee, Isaac, as a beggar," said the king, as he entered the house of the aged Israelite. "The truth is, that these storms are no respecters of persons, and having been fairly caught, I am under the necessity of craving shelter until the violence of the tempest has passed away."

"Your majesty," answered Isaac, "could not have applied to one among your subjects who would more cheerfully respond to the calls of hospitality, even had the applicant been of far inferior degree. As it is, however, I am proud of the honour which has thus been vouchsafed to one so humble as myself."

"Nay," smiled the king, "the honour has been conferred upon thee by mere accident, or thou never wouldst have had to bestow the duties of hospitality upon Richard of England. As it is, however, I am obliged to thee, and in return, whatever favour thou mayst ask shall be freely granted thee."

"I am an old man," answered Isaac, falling upon his knees before the king, "and, therefore, have nothing to ask for myself. Yet, there is one, who, without me, would be utterly friendless, in a world where the unprotected are trampled upon and oppressed."

"I think," returned the king, glancing his eye towards Rebecca, "it requires no wizard to guess who it is for whom you would solicit my favour and protection. Your daughter is not without enemies, and you would ask my watchful care to preserve her in the event of any further attempts being made against her peace?"

"Such, gracious sire," replied the humble Israelite, "was indeed, my most anxious desire. As a father, I feel for the helplessness of her situation when I am called away, and naturally do I look to your highness for aid, should she unfortunately ever need it."

"She shall have it, Isaac," exclaimed the king; "you have my royal word for it, and knowing as I do, the chief enemy she has to contend with, I shall keep upon him a strict watch, to see that no further violence is offered to the daughter of my present hospitable host. So now, old man, clear thy moody brow, and if thou hast any refreshment in the house, let it be speedily placed before me, for by my crown I swear, the exercise I have this day had, has given me a keen appetite for the enjoyment of any coarse fare your larder may afford."

"My daughter has already anticipated your majesty's wishes," said the Jew, as Rebecca, at this moment, began to place before the royal guest the produce of an adjacent closet. "Thou hast it, sire, with a welcome, and all that I have now to ask of thee is, that thou wilt stay beneath my roof for the night, seeing that the storm increases in violence, and ere it altogether ceases, it will be too late to return to your palace with safety."

"Thy offer is accepted with many thanks, old man," exclaimed the king. "Having a roof above my head, it would be unwise to venture forth to-night, and, therefore, will I become thy guest till morning. But, remember, I require not any fuss to be made about my sleeping; I am a soldier, hardy and inured to all things, so that a few rushes upon the floor will afford me a luxury that has often been denied me in my campaigns abroad."

While this conversation was taking place between Isaac and his royal guest, Bertrand le Noir and Ranulph the Avenger, were engaged in another apartment, in an earnest conference upon the traitorous design they had in contemplation. At first, it was determined to assassinate the king on his way home, and when that was done, to effect their escape amidst the confusion that would be sure to ensue. The darkness of the night, too, was favourable to the murderous project they were engaged in, and the villains were congratulating themselves upon the expected result of their treason, when news was brought them that the king intended sleeping there, and that he would not return to the palace until daylight on the following morning,

This change in the arrangements somewhat startled the conspirators at first, but being once more left to themselves, they shortly afterwards concocted another plot, which offered them even greater facilities than the former one for executing, with more safety to themselves, the san. guinary deed in which they were engaged. To Bertrand le Noir belonged the odium of this new suggestion, and no sooner had it entered his mischief-working brain, than, approaching nearer to his companion, in crime, he inquired in a low tone of voice, whether he had courage enough to perpetrate the contemplated deed beneath the roof where they now were.

"Hah!" exclaimed Ranulph, "what is it thou sayst?—Have I courage, indeed!—why to be sure I have, so out with thy plot, man, and thou shalt find that I will not hang back, when revenge is to be accomplished."

"Aye, so I thought," returned the other, "so thou must prepare to slay the king as he sleeps to-night."

"Perdition!" muttered the other, "that is a cowardly way of doing the business, however."

"'Tis a safe way, and, therefore, the better for us," answered Bertrand. "Besides, thou wert not wont to be so squeamish, my friend, and surely the remembrance of thine own wrong will not fail to urge thee on to satisfy thy revenge."

"And yet ——"

"Nonsense, man!— if you hesitate, the chance may be lost for ever. Now is the time or never, and if you refuse the present opportunity, the reward promised by Sir Gaston de Neville, will be given to one less scrupulous than yourself."

"Aye, aye, so I suppose," returned the ruffian; "the work of blood must be done, and who so fit for the office as one who still smarts under the injuries he has received? I have sworn to satisfy myself for the disgrace I was made to endure, and, therefore, you may command me, Bertrand, even though it be to murder a man in his sleep."

"Then I may depend upon you?"

"You may."

"Why that's well said, Ranulph," exclaimed the other, with exultation. "In truth, the job is not difficult of execution, and when Richard is dead, you will have nothing to fear from the vengeance of his successor, who will be rather inclined to reward, than punish the man who has opened the way for him to the throne."

"Humph!" muttered Ranulph, "it may be all very well to talk about the gratitude of his successor, but I am not one of those who can pin their faith on princes. Once let John have his turn served, and the man who has raised him to the throne may go to the devil."

"Methinks you are rather severe in your judgment upon Prince John," exclaimed Bertrand le Noir. "That he is not very scrupulous about trifles must be admitted, but in an instance like the present, he will scarcely fail to pour his royal favours upon one who has so greatly served him."

"True,—but, perhaps he may exhibit his royal favour, as you call it, by sending me to the gallows."

"Nay, if you fear that, the safer way will be to leave England, and thus escape a doom so unworthy of your deserts. There are places abroad where you may live happily enough, and especially as you will receive a good round sum from Sir Gaston de Neville, for the service you have promised to do him."

"Why, as to that, one place is the same as another to a desperate man like me," answered Ranulph. "At any rate, England will be no home for me, after my revenge has been accomplished, especially, as on getting over to Italy, I can easily join a band of brigands, and pass the remainder of my life amongst comrades that will not turn their backs upon me because my hands happen to be stained with the blood of a fellow-creature."

"True," replied Bertrand, "your resolution is a wise one, and you may depend upon my services towards getting clear off from this place. You shall remain concealed in the castle of Sir Gaston, if any stir should be made about the matter, and when all is quiet again, I will put you safely on board the first vessel that sails for an Italian port. So now, what say you to executing the deed I just now proposed?"

"I have already answered that question," replied the ruffian. "The king's doom is sealed, even though he had a hundred lives!"

"You will stab him then, to-night, as he sleeps?"

"I will," exclaimed the other, "but, first of all, you must tell me how it is to be accomplished; the chamber he sleeps in will be guarded, and I may have no opportunity of passing the attendants that are placed there for his protection."

"Nay, in that instance," replied Bertrand, "we have nothing to fear. We shall ourselves be placed on guard, and when all is quiet, you can enter the chamber, and stab him without fear of discovery. That done, you can escape by the window, so that it will appear as if the assassin had entered that way, and thus all suspicion will be directed to some other channel."

"Hush!" exclaimed Ranulph; "some one comes this way. Speak not another word,—I understand all now, and will perform my task to your satisfaction.—Again, I say, be silent, for, unless my ears deceive me, footsteps are approaching yonder door."

Then, turning the conversation to some other subject, the regicides affected to be engaged in discussing topics of no importance, during which they were interrupted by the entrance of the king's page, who came to announce to them that his royal master had retired to his chamber, and that the duty had been allotted to them of guarding him during the night. This intelligence was received with satisfaction by the two villains, who had thus been plotting against the life of the monarch whom they had been appointed to guard, and rising from their seats, they each emptied a cup of wine to give them courage, and, hastening from the room they had occupied, proceeded to occupy the post that had been assigned them.

But, in spite of all their attempts at secrecy, there was one who had been a terrified auditor of the conversation that had taken place between the conspirators. That person was Rebecca, who happening to enter an adjoining apartment, had been struck by the low earnest tone in which the men spoke, and as some of the words they had uttered filled her soul with suspicion of their dark motives, she listened still more eagerly, and in a short time learnt the horrible truth, that a scheme had been devised, by murdering the king beneath her father's roof. Horror-struck by their words, it was with difficulty that she could restrain herself from giving utterance to her horror, but having overcome this feeling, she again listened, and being then fully satisfied that the king's life was threatened with immediate danger, she summoned all her fortitude and silently left the place where she had overheard them, resolving in her own mind to peril all in the defence of her sovereign's life; still, however, she determined to keep the secret even from her father, and no sooner had the king entered his sleeping chamber,—where he had thrown himself, dressed as he was, upon his couch,—than she followed through a secret door, and concealed herself behind the tapestry, waiting with breathless anxiety until she should be called upon to rush forward to his deliverance.

Nor had our heroine to remain long in suspense, for scarcely had she satisfied herself by his deep and heavy breathing that the king was sound asleep, than footsteps were heard softly stealing across the floor, and at the same moment the light which he bore in his hand discovered to her the features of the assassin as he glared round the apartment in search of his unsuspecting victim.   Rebecca could scarce forbear screaming with affright as she beheld the guilt-marked countenance of the villain, and she was about to dart forward from her place of concealment, when her hand rested upon the king's battle axe which he had placed there against the wall,—as was his usual custom,—in case of any sudden emergency. Thus armed, her fears were in some degree allayed, and grasping the weapon firmly in her two hands, she determined to remain quietly where she was until the moment should arrive when her assistance would become necessary.

At length Ranulph approached close to the couch on which lay the sleeping king, and having made sure of his deadly aim, he raised his dagger high in the air, when Rebecca rushed forward, and poising the pond'rous axe above her head, would have struck the ruffian dead at her feet had he not at the instant perceived his danger and stepped hastily aside to avoid the fate that otherwise would have sealed his doom for ever.

"Help!—murder!—treason!—help!" cried the terrified maiden, agonized by the perils with which the king was still threatened, and at the same moment Richard, starting from his couch, seized the ruffian by the throat, at the very moment when he was preparing to revenge himself upon her who had thus unexpectedly frustrated his murderous design.

"Hah! villain, what dost thou in my chamber, at this hour of the night?" exclaimed the monarch, almost lost in wonder and astonishment. "Speak, sirrah, and explain yourself, or, by the heaven above us, you have not another five minutes to live!"

"Take your hand from my throat, and I'll answer you," gasped the almost choking ruffian, struggling violently to disengage himself from the powerful grasp of his adversary. At this juncture, Isaac of Tadcaster and a number of the king's attendants hurried into the chamber, to which they had been directed by the loud shrieks of Rebecca, and no sooner did they perceive their sovereign in danger, than rushing to his rescue, they seized hold of Ranulph, who they would instantly have sacrificed upon the spot, had not their royal master commanded them to desist.

"Hold!" he exclaimed, in a voice of thunder; "hold! I command you; and you, villain, whoever you are, declare freely, and without equivocation, why you have thus made an unprovoked attack upon my life?"

"Your majesty is mistaken," answered Ranulph, in a voice of assumed humility; "I am not the villain you take me for, nor should I have ventured to enter this chamber, had not my suspicions been awakened by noises proceeding from it, that convinced me some foul play was meditated for your destruction."

"Indeed!" exclaimed Richard, incredulously; "then, if I understand rightly, you would have me believe that you came hither to serve me?"

"Such, gracious sire, was the only motive that drew me from the place where I had been stationed as one of your guards."

"Humph!" cried the king, "then, being innocent yourself, who is it you accuse of having a design against my life?"

"Yonder girl, sire."

"Hah!—the Hebrew Maiden!—speak, villain,—is it Rebecca of Tadcaster, that you charge with the guilty intention of murdering me in my sleep?"

"She alone is guilty of the foul crime," answered the ruffian, with an unabashed countenance. "Nay, if proof be wanting, her hand still grasps the weapon with which she was about to commit the deed, when I hastened to your rescue, and prevented a blow that was aimed at the life of my sovereign."

"False villain, thou liest!" cried Isaac, maddened by the accusation that had thus been brought against his beloved child.

"It is indeed false," exclaimed Rebecca, throwing herself imploringly at the feet of the king; "he it was who came hither for your destruction, and too surely would his traitorous design have been accomplished, had not fear nerved my woman's arm to frustrate a blow aimed at your life."

"Both accuse each other, and both strictly deny being the guilty party," observed the king, after a few moments consideration. "At present, the affair is involved in the deepest mystery, but never will I rest satisfied until the truth is discovered."

"Alas!" cried our heroine, in accents of despair, "am I then suspected of being concerned in a crime, that I would have sacrificed my own life to prevent?"

"Your majesty," exclaimed Isaac, with terror,—"my daughter is innocent,—indeed,—indeed she is innocent!"

No, 20

"I am willing to believe she is," answered the king:—" and yet, since they were both found in my room, at this hour of the night, it is necessary that she explains more fully, than she has hitherto done, the motive that brought her here."

"That I will readily do," answered Rebecca, " the truth is, sire, I, by chance, overheard a conversation between this man and Bertrand le Noir, in which your name being mentioned, I was induced to listen,—they spoke, however, in low tones, but from the few words I gathered, it was evident that a plot was formed against your life, and that the crime was to be committed without delay. Inspired by terror, I came here through a secret door behind the tapestry, and scarcely had I satisfied myself that you were still safe, when this man stole into the room, and making his way towards your couch, was in the act of striking the fatal blow when I interposed to avert the dreadful crime. Happily, I succeeded, but, being detected in his villainy, he would now shield himself by charging me with being here, for the purpose of committing a deed that my soul shudders at."

"I believe thee, maiden," exclaimed the king, "and now, villain, what hast thou to say why death should not be the award of such a rank traitor as thou art?"

"I have nothing to say," answered Ranulph, gloomily. " Thou believest that I am guilty ; and, therefore, it would be in vain to say anything, when prejudice set so strongly against me."

"If thou art obstinate, we will wrest the truth from thee, by means of the torture," exclaimed Richard, fiercely. " Confess then, the motives that have led thee to meditate this crime, and if thou hast any comrades to share thine ignominy, I may be induced to extend my mercy towards thee in return for the trifling service thou hast it in thy power to perform."

"I ask not, nor will I receive any favour from thee," answered the other, sulkily. " Already hast thou injured me, and thou canst only add to other wrongs by sending me to an ignominious punishment."

"Hah ! by heaven I know thee now !" exclaimed the king,—" thou art the man, Ranulph, whom I dismissed from the army in Palestine, for conduct that was alike unsoldierly and dishonourable. Thou hast brooded over what passed between us, and thy attempt upon my life to night was in revenge for what thou doubtless considerest an act of tyrannical oppression."

"I shall make no reply to thee," answered Ranulph ; " that of which thou speakest, cannot now be remedied ; and, therefore, the only favour I ask, is that my death may follow the sentence as quickly as possible."

" Nay, thou shalt be tortured first, to extort the truth from thee," cried the king. " Besides it appears from this maiden's narrative, that thou hadst an accomplice in the crime, and it is, therefore, my command that he also shall be brought before me. Go, some of you, and bring hither Bertrand le Noir, who, I have reason to believe, can throw much light upon the conspiracy, if the rack will only serve to make him open his lips."

At this command, two of the attendants left the room, for the purpose of arresting the other culprit, but in a short time afterwards they returned, declaring that he was nowhere to be found, and from the fact of one of the casements being left open, there was every reason to suppose he had effected his escape, as soon as he found that the treasonable plot had miscarried. At first, the king was greatly chafed at this, but quickly recovering his composure, he said :

" It is my command that the prisoner we have taken, shall be narrowly watched to prevent his serving us the same slippery trick, that has been practised by his comrade in iniquity. Guard him well, and in the morning he shall be carried before our Chief Justiciary, who will have the task of sifting this matter to the bottom. And now, friends, to horse and away, for should Bertrand le Noir have an opportunity, he will not fail to seek further means for accomplishing the crime that has been thus far happily frustrated."

In an inconceivably short space of time, the horses were brought to the door, and having thanked the Jew and his daughter for their hospitality, and commanded them to appear on the morrow before his Chief Justiciary, he mounted his impatient steed and rode off, followed by his retinue and the prisoner, whose limbs, by this time, had been securely bound to prevent his escape.

CHAPTER XXX.

> " To the torture with him !—
> Make him confess his motives and accomplices,
> That we may know the foe, whose secret aim
> Is thus against our life."
>
> THE DOOMSTER.

AT an early hour on the following morning, Ranulph was conveyed from the strong room, in which he had been placed for security, to the court of the Chief Justiciary, whose duty it was to institute a rigid inquiry into a conspiracy, that had nearly terminated so fatally to the king. It was in vain, however, that the person, into whose custody he had been given endeavoured to draw from him a confession of the crime he was charged with, or the names of those who were with him in the atrocious act he had sought to commit. Ranulph maintained an obstinate silence upon that subject, and the only words he could be prevailed upon to utter, were those of defiance towards those into whose power he had fallen, and an expression of utter contempt for any means that might be put in practice, to draw from him any acknowledgment that might serve to involve in the accusation that had been brought against himself.

Shortly after his arrival in the court, the Chief Justiciary took his seat, and previous to the commencement of business, the king entered the arena of justice, taking his seat upon the right hand of Ralph de Glanville. Things being thus arranged, the prisoner was brought forward, and asked if he was willing to purchase mercy from his sovereign, by a full acknowledgment of every thing connected with the disobedient act which had been so signally frustrated.

"I have already said all that you will be able to get from me," replied the prisoner, with an air of cool indifference to his fate.

"Do you acknowledge your crime?" asked De Glanville, the Chief Justiciary.

"I confess nothing," answered the other; "the king knows well enough that I charge another with the crime that is now laid against me, and since my word is discredited, it would be in vain to repeat the accusation."

"My lord," exclaimed the king, interposing, "it is true that he has declared another to be guilty of the heinous offence against our person. He says Rebecca, the Hebrew Maiden, was the person who meditated my destruction, but circumstances are sufficiently strong against him, to prove that he most foully wrongs her, and that she is wholly innocent of any design such as he would bring against her."

"You have only her 'word against mine," answered Ranulph; "we were both found in your chamber at the same instant,—both of us were armed, and I would ask who can safely condemn me, since there is as strong suspicion against her as against myself?"

"Have we any evidence to prove which of them was the intended assassin?" asked the Justiciary.

"The girl herself," answered the king, "has declared that she over-heard a conversation between the prisoner and another person, who, for the present, has escaped. In that interview it was agreed between the two, that I was to be murdered, and it was to save my life that she en-tered the chamber, where she was afterwards found as this man has said."

Rebecca was now ordered to stand forward and relate all that she had overheard on the night previous; this she did, with so much clearness and precision, as to convince every person in the court that she was not only innocent, but that the king owed his life to her intervention.

"And now," said the Justiciary, when her narrative was ended, "you have heard, prisoner, the simple recital of this girl, whom you have so basely sought to destroy by an accusation that might have ended in send-ing her to an ignominious death. Her story, there is no reason to doubt, and I, therefore, now call upon you to confess your crime, and by a full discovery of your accomplices, to earn, perhaps, the mercy of your sovereign, whom you would traitorously have destroyed."

"I have nothing to confess," answered Ranulph, unmoved by the peril in which he stood. "No motive has been urged against me for making so mad an attempt, and, therefore, it may be presumed that I am innocent."

"Nay, thou hadst a motive," exclaimed the king; "revenge, for sup-posed injuries, had long been rankling in thy heart. Long ago, I dis-honoured thee most deservedly, and there are witnesses to prove that thou hast sworn to be revenged."

"And if I did swear to revenge myself upon your majesty," replied Ranulph, "it follows not that I must be guilty in the present instance. Besides, I have had opportunities before now of gratifying my revenge, if I had been so bent upon it as my enemies believe."

"You still persist, then, in denying the crime?"

"I do, my lord."

"And you will not acknowledge to us who else is concerned in this dastardly attempt upon the king's life?"

"I have said that I am innocent," replied Ranulph, determined not to be thrown off his guard, "and, therefore, cannot have accomplices as you seem to suspect."

"Prisoner," exclaimed the Justiciary, "it is in vain that you deny your guilt; we have sufficient proof that you are the person who trai-torously sought the king's life, and, therefore, the heaviest punishment of the law will be inflicted, unless you choose to purchase the royal cle-meney, by making a full disclosure of every thing connected with the affair."

"I ask no clemency of the king," cried Ranulph, with his usual dar-ing. "I am not terrified at death, so you can e'en send me to my doom with as much speed as you please."

"Nay, sirrah, we must have the truth first," answered De Glanville; "it is necessary, for the king's future safety, that we probe this affair to the very bottom, and, therefore, if you remain obstinate in your refusal to confess, it will be my duty to order you for immediate torture, so that we may 'extort, by pain and violence, that which you persist in withholding."

For an instant, a death-like paleness overspread the prisoner's countenance, but quickly subduing the temporary fear that had seized him, he replied with all his former boldness:—

"Your threats of torture, my lord, will not obtain for you the confession you so much desire. I can bear even the rack without a groan, but you shall not make me swerve from the resolution I have formed."

"Sir Gaston de Neville," exclaimed the king, as he perceived that person entering the court, "you have, doubtless, heard of the cowardly attempt that was last night made upon my life. One of your domestics is charged with having instigated this man to commit the crime, and I, therefore, crave your aid to bring the guilty parties to justice."

"Your majesty knows my zeal in your service," answered the knight, with as much calmness as he could assume. "As a soldier I have fought and bled for you, and, as a faithful subject, I will do all that in me lies to bring your intended assassin to justice."

"In that case," exclaimed the king, "let Bertrand le Noir be brought forward, that he may hear the accusation we are prepared to prove against him."

"Bertrand, my gracious liege, is nowhere to be found," answered the Knight Templar. "He has not returned to my castle, and I fear his absence is only to be accounted for by the occurrence of some accident."

"Art thou sure he is not concealed in any part of thy strong fortress?"

"I am quite certain of it, your majesty; every part of it has been strictly searched, without success."

"Nevertheless," rejoined his majesty, "I am convinced the villain has sought refuge somewhere within your fortress. In fact, no sooner had the project against my life been frustrated, than he deserted the post he was in charge of, and since all clue to him has been lost, there is but little doubt that he has retreated to the place I have named."

"Then your majesty believes that I would give shelter to one of your enemies !" exclaimed Sir Gaston, in a tone that was intended to express a feeling of indignation.

"Nay !" cried the king, "I do not profess to understand your secret thoughts, Sir Knight. All that we know, at present, is, that a retainer of yours is strongly suspected of being engaged in a plot against my life, and, since the honour of Sir Gaston de Neville is implicated, I shall certainly expect from him all the assistance in his power to bring a well-deserved punishment upon the guilty parties. Let this be done and the current of my regal favour shall not be stopped."

"But your majesty will surely pardon me," exclaimed the templar, "if I declare it to be my firm conviction, that Bertrand le Noir is in no way concerned in the scandalous outrage that has taken place."

"At any rate," answered Richard, in a tone of sarcasm, "your follower is lucky in having a master whose confidence in his worthiness is so unbounded."

"Judge him," returned the knight, "by his former good character. That he is brave, I know full well, and, therefore, I have ventured to suggest to your majesty that he may lie at present under an unjust suspicion."

"Then, why has he concealed himself, if he were really conscious of his innocence?" asked Richard. "Flight has injured him in the estimation of my friends, and now, methinks, he must tell a plausible tale indeed, if he expects to reverse the opinions we entertain of him."

"Pardon me, your majesty," exclaimed Sir Gaston, "but it is possible that you may have wronged him by these suspicions. That he is present absent, certainly excites suspicion; and yet, I have my doubt whether, or not, he may not have been assassinated."

"That, Sir Gaston," interposed the justiciary," is scarcely credibl seeing that an act of such violence could not have been committed with out some trace being left of the foul deed."

"Nor do I positively make the charge," returned the knigh haughtily.—"It is, however, certain that he is at present missing, an the only way I can account for the circumstance, is, by supposing tha he has fallen beneath the poniard of some secret assassin."

"My liege," cried Rebecca, kneeling before the justice seat, "thi is but a subterfuge to shield the villain from the just punishment of hi crimes. I, myself, heard him plotting your death with the prisoner no before you, and it is certain, that he effected his escape at the momer when he found that his base designs were frustrated."

"Hah!" exclaimed Sir Gaston, fiercely, "dost thou, minion that tho art, dare to bring so heinous a charge against those who are the king' most faithful subjects?"

"It remains to be proved that this maiden has spoken falsely of thos she charges with meditating my death," answered the king —"So fa as we have gone in this enquiry, her evidence is unshaken, and, t speak the truth, I am satisfied that thy retainer will not be found so inno cent as thou seemest to imagine. His absence, at this moment, confirm my suspicion, and, by all the saints in Heaven, he shall not escape m wrath, if once he is found guilty of the cowardly act laid to his charge.'

"Believe me, sire, he is not guilty," exclaimed the knight, earnestly "To me, he has ever proved himself a faithful and attached follower and I can answer for him with my life, that he would rather aid tha plot against one whom his master so dearly reverences."

"Perhaps," said Richard, "it would be better to have less confidend in a man whose actions have brought him under our strong suspicion We will, however, let this subject drop for the present, and return t the examination of this prisoner, who so obstinately refuses to purchas our mercy by a full confession of all the accomplices who were engaged with him in this treason. Proceed, my Lord Justiciary, and question the man further upon the crime for which he has been brought before us.'

"Ranulph," exclaimed the judge, "you have heard the evidence in support of a charge that affects your life. The king is merciful to those who confess their crimes, and, in his name, I offer you life and liberty, in consideration that you make a full disclosure of all you know about this late attempt against your sovereign."

"My lord," replied Ranulph, "you speak to a man who is weary of life, and who is, therefore, willing to lay it down whenever the king shall command it."

"But you forget, sirrah," retorted Glanville, "that it is usual to apply torture, where delinquents are obstinate."

"Torture," answered the ruffian, with disdain, "will fail to extort from me one word, when my soul is resolved, as it is in the present in-stance. I have not failed to see that the rack has been prepared to do its office upon me, yet I shall not flinch, even though it may please my tormentors to tear me limb from limb."

"Dost thou, then, refuse the proffered mercy his majesty would bestow upon thee?"

"Thou hast heard me declare it."

"Wilt thou still deny that thy motive in entering the king's chamber was to slay him?"

"It would be in vain to deny it any longer," answered the prisoner. "Such, I confess, was my intention, and I only regret that I was prevented by yonder girl, from putting my intentions into execution."

"Wretch!" exclaimed Ralph de Glanville, "dost thou regret the interposition of Heaven, that hath prevented thee from becoming a murderer?"

"It has not prevented me from being guilty of murder," answered the ruffian.—"These hands are not free from the stains of human blood, and, perhaps, the first use I might make of freedom, would be to destroy all those who now so eagerly seek my destruction."

"Thou hearest him, my lord!" cried the king, breaking in upon the silence that followed this declaration; "thou hast heard him declare his unquenched thirst for blood, and it, therefore, behoves us to prevent the execution of his meditated revenge. Let him be placed upon the rack, and if he thinks fit to confess who his accomplices are, we will spare his wretched life, on condition that he passes the remainder of his days in hopeless captivity."

"Let him be placed upon the instrument of torture!" cried the judge, motioning to some of the men who surrounded the prisoner. "He shall feel the torture we have the power to inflict, and if he perishes beneath it, his blood be upon his own head—not on ours."

At these words, Ranulph the Avenger was seized in the herculean grasp of two of the men, but before they could force him to the place of punishment, he broke away from them with a violent effort, and snatching a battle-axe from the hand of one of the soldiers, he rushed towards the place where Rebecca was standing, and, raising the ponderous weapon in his arms, he was about to fell the maiden to the earth with a deadly blow, when Reuben Grenard, throwing himself madly forward, struck aside the instrument of destruction, and at the same moment the villain was dashed with tremendous violence to the earth. All this had passed in the space of an instant, and so electrified were the spectators at the suddenness with which it had taken place, that not a word was uttered, except a cry of horror, until the king, starting from his seat, commanded the prisoner to be immediately secured and placed upon the rack. While this was doing, he made his way to the spot where Rebecca had fainted in the arms of her father, and undertaking to support her himself, conveyed her to a seat beside the one he had just quitted. At this act of royal condescension a murmur of surprise ran through the assembled multitude; some, indeed, there were, who would have expressed their indignation at the king's attention being thus bestowed upon a daughter of Israel, but while they were yet uttering their astonishment, a groan of mortal agony broke upon their ears, and looking round, they beheld the prisoner stretched upon the rack, whilst four executioners, with their levers, were straining his limbs until they were almost ready to start from their sockets. Still, however, the wretched man seemed resolute to maintain his secret inviolate, and still the tormentors continued their hateful labour, until it was evident that the prisoner must soon sink under the dreadful tortures he had been doomed to endure. Then, and not till then, did the Chief Justiciary interfere to put an end to the exhibition for the present, and when Ranulph had, by his orders, been placed, nearly fainting, in a seat before him, he demanded in a peremptory tone, whether he would now make the required confession of his accomplices.

A languid shake of the head was the only answer the exhausted culprit could give.

"Your majesty perceives," exclaimed the judge, " that the prisoner is

still obstinate. He has heard the merciful terms that have been pro.
posed, and madly rejects them."

"At all events," answered Richard, "he has suffered enough at pre.
sent;—let him now be carried back to his cell, and perhaps, upon re.
flection, he may be induced to reveal a secret he at present so obstinately
persists in withholding from us. A skilful leach shall attend upon
him, in order to assuage the tormenting pangs that have been produced
by his own wilful silence. Away with him, and when he is sufficiently
recovered, he may be again brought before me, that we may see whether
by a confession, he will not spare himself a repetition of the torture he
has this day suffered."

Having given these commands, the king delivered the now recovered
Rebecca to the arms of her father, and then, followed by his guards,
quitted the court, in which he had witnessed a scene that had turned
his heart sick.

CHAPTER XXXI.

"Sure this is haunted ground,
Where ghosts and shrouded spectres keep carouse."
THE MAID'S REVENGE.

ALARMED at the turn which affairs had taken against him, Sir Gaston
de Neville hastened back to his castle, where, shutting himself up in his
solitary chamber, he gave way to the current of uneasy thoughts that
were rapidly passing through his mind. That the king suspected him
of favouring the ambitious designs of Prince John, was sufficiently
clear, and that which most served to increase his terror, was the fear that
Ranulph the Avenger would, after all, be forced to confess by whom it
was that he had been instigated in his recent attack upon the king's life.
Hitherto, it is true, the ruffian had maintained the secret inviolable, but
he was threatened with a renewal of the torture, and it was scarcely to
be expected that he would endure more, when he could readily purchase
the royal pardon by denouncing those who had entered into a league for
the speedy destruction of their sovereign.

Terrified with these thoughts, the knight resolved to visit his chief
adviser and counsellor, Bertrand le Noir,—who, in spite of his repeated
declarations to the contrary,—was concealed in one of the secret dungeons of the castle, until circumstances should favour his escape from
England. From this ruffian, he hoped to obtain a scheme by which he
might avoid the perils that at present environed him, and, he was about
to proceed to the cell for that purpose, when an unexpected intruder
appeared before him, in the person of Black Ivan, the Outlaw.

"Ivan!" he exclaimed, startled with mingled terror and surprise,
"what means this unlooked-for visit from one whom I have every reason
to rank among my enemies?"

"Psha! I am no enemy to thee, man," retorted the robber, quickly;
"we are rivals in love, it is true, but that is an affair which may be soon
settled if you will only take the piece of advice I am come to offer."

"What advice hast thou to give a man who neither seeks nor requires it?"

"Give up all further idea of the girl, Rebecca, and thou wilt change
me from an inveterate foe into a fast and faithful friend."

"When I have need of thy friendship," answered the knight, with

scorn, " it will be time enough to make terms such thou hast proposed. At present, however, I scorn thy offer, and, therefore, bid thee hence, lest I call for assistance, and have thee thrown into a dungeon for thy pains."

" Tush, man !" retorted the other, " threaten me not, for I heed not thy words any more than I do the idle wind. I am above thy malice, and can defy thee to do thy worst."

" Art thou not at this moment in my power?"

" Had there been any danger," answered the robber, " I should not at this time be standing before thee. My person is here perfectly safe, and I can defy thee to do thy worst ; warning thee, however, that any attempt to prevent my free passage from your castle, will be followed by pains and penalties that you at present little think of."

" Am I to be threatened beneath my own roof?"

" It is not my design to threaten thee, Sir Knight," replied Ivan ; " I would merely warn thee, lest, by a hasty act, thou shouldst entangle thyself in difficulties it will not be easy to escape from."

" What, if I give the word," asked Sir Gaston, " is to hinder thee from falling into the hands of my vassals ?"

" Thy vassals know the value of their own lives, and, therefore, will make no attempt against mine," replied the robber, in a tone of indifference. " It is true, thou mayst slay me, but, so surely as thou dost, thou wilt henceforth be a marked man to my comrades, and neither thou nor thy followers will escape the vengeance of those who will be ever ready to avenge the fall of their leader. This I speak not as an idle threat, but as a warning that will be surely and terribly accomplished."

No. 21

"Well, well, I wish not to harm thee," returned the knight, "neither thy life nor liberty is sought by me, and I would only prevail upon thee to leave this place before thou hast incurred danger by letting my dependants see thee here. They have vowed thy destruction, and ——"

"Oh, I fear them not," interrupted Ivan, "I entered your castle secretly, and can leave it in the same way, whenever my business with thee is finished."

"What dost thou want with me?" asked the knight.

"I have already said," returned the other;—"we have been rivals in love, and I would know whether thou wilt resign all future pretensions to the Hebrew Maiden?"

"Assuredly not, at thy bidding," answered Sir Gaston de Neville, resolutely. "I love the wench too well, to give her up, whilst there is a chance of making her mine."

"I tell thee there is no chance for thee," cried Black Ivan, with emotion;—"the king will not fail to keep a watchful eye upon thine every motion, and since report says he has fallen desperately in love with the pretty Jewess himself, the chances are that he will soon find means to rid himself of his rival, should he appear likely to prove a serious obstacle in his way."

"I tell thee, sirrah," exclaimed the knight, "Richard dares not play the tyrant with those who, like myself, have power enough to resist him. His brother John has friends among the barons, who would not be sorry to have an opportunity of seeing the throne differently occupied to what it is at present."

"Humph!" cried the robber, "and you, I suppose, are one of those *honourable* men who would involve the nation in ruin, for the sake of placing a heartless tyrant like Prince John upon the throne of England?"

"Hush!" whispered Sir Gaston, "I said nothing of the sort;—in fact, I only meant to convince you that the king stands too much in awe of his barons to incense them by interfering in their pleasures. Besides, I believe the report touching his love for the Jewess, to be utterly groundless, and, consequently, I have little to fear from any anger on his part, should I succeed in carrying her off, as I have so long designed."

"By St. Nicholas! thou shalt never do so while I live," exclaimed Black Ivan, striding impatiently towards his rival. "I have resolved that no obstacle shall oppose me, and woe unto those who wilfully throw themselves in my way, after they have received this warning. Beware, Sir Knight, I again say, for terrible shall be my wrath shouldst thou dare venture to excite it. Farewell, then, for the present, and should we ever meet again, let it not be as enemies, as thou dost value thy life!"

And having given expression to this threat, the robber directed his steps towards the door, through which he disappeared before Sir Gaston de Neville had sufficiently recovered from his surprise to follow him. When at length, however, he did so, no traces of his late visitor remained, and pondering upon the mysterious manner in which the bandit entered and quitted the castle, he hastened on with a troubled soul, until he had reached the secret dungeon, which was at present occupied by the fugitive, Bertrand le Noir. As he entered, the ruffian was lying on the heap of straw that served him as a bed, but no sooner did he hear the well-known voice of his master calling to him, than starting up, he joyfully approached his unexpected visitor.

"By St. George! Sir Knight, but this is a consolation that I had scarcely looked for," he said, in an accent of gratitude. "'Tis true I have found a shelter from those that would hunt me to death, but I expected not that my master would himself come to visit me in my solitary dungeon."

"I come to ask thy advice, Bertrand," answered the knight. "Richard, as thou knowest, has escaped the death we intended for him, and having got Ranulph in his power, there is but too much reason to fear that he will compel him to confess who are his accomplices. I am thus placed in great danger of my life, and, therefore, it remains for you to suggest some method by which to escape the peril that otherwise may involve me in ruin."

"Canst thou not escape to France, where thou mayst find a secure asylum for the remainder of thy days?"

"That," answered the knight, "were easily enough done, but by following such a course, I should confirm the suspicions that have already been excited against me, and thus dishonour would for ever afterwards be attached to the name of Sir Gaston de Neville."

"Why there thou sayst truly enough, Sir Knight," replied the other; "they will be sure to say thy flight is caused by a consciousness of guilt, and as the king is just now getting together all the money he can for the prosecution of the war in Palestine, it is not unlikely but he might sell thine estate towards the enrichment of his treasury."

"In that case, some other plan must be thought of to turn away from ourselves the peril that at present threatens us," observed Sir Gaston. "Say, then, art thou still willing to hazard something in the prosecution of a scheme that has so far proved unsuccessful?"

"In plain words," exclaimed Bertrand, "thou wouldst know whether I will again venture to aim at the life of this Richard Cœur de Lion?"

"That is indeed my meaning," answered the knight. "Say thou wilt do so, and I will procure thine immediate liberation from this gloomy and cheerless abode."

"Nay, pardon me, Sir Knight, for methinks there might be too much danger in that."

"Not if you follow my advice;—I would have you escape from hence, to join the band of Black Ivan, the Outlaw. There thou wilt find a secure asylum, and in a short time thou mayst devise some scheme by which to rid ourselves of King Richard. His brother will then ascend the throne, and our reward ——"

"Will be the gibbet!" exclaimed a hollow, sepulchral voice, and on looking in the direction from whence the sound came, they perceived the same apparition of an armed warrior, which had so greatly alarmed them before. Bertrand le Noir was so terrified at this, that he sank upon his knees, but the knight rushed with frantic speed towards the terrible object which at the moment glided away, and was no more to be seen. Horror-struck at what he had beheld, Sir Gaston hastened back to his retainer, who by this time had sunk upon the ground in a swoon, and having ineffectually tried to restore him, he hurried out of the dungeon, and repaired to his own private apartment, where he might in solitude think over the mysterious circumstance that had thus unnerved him.

CHAPTER XXXII.

"Say, beldame, can thy devilish arts discover
The secret of my fate?—Canst thou foretell
The joy or woe that is to come?" THE WANDERER.

RACKED with uneasy thoughts, Sir Gaston de Neville continued to pace his chamber, until the rapidly increasing shades of evening reminded him that something must be immediately done towards securing his own safety. In this emergency he thought of Meg of Finchley whose supposed necromantic powers had given her a fame that had often reached his ears, but which, till the present moment, he had never thought of, except as an idle rumour, utterly destitute of foundation. Now, however, he resolved to test her abilities by visiting her cabin in disguise, and thus learning from her own lips whether she could satisfy him as to the fate that awaited him. This project was no sooner thought of than a resolution was formed to put it into immediate execution, and summoning his favourite squire, Julian, he desired him to saddle his swiftest horse with as much secrecy as possible, in order that no one in the castle should be aware of his absence.

"Does my honoured master intend to ride forth at night unaccompanied?" asked Julian, with surprise.

"I do," answered the knight; "the business I go about requires secrecy and caution, and, therefore, do I for this once dispense with the services even of my faithful Julian."

"But the danger you run ———"

"Will not deter me from pursuing the course I have chosen to adopt," interrupted the knight impatiently. "I am aware that foes may lurk in my path, but it is to strengthen myself against them that I make this secret journey. To-morrow I shall know my doom, and if fate declares against me, I shall at least be prepared for the worst."

"Your words fill me with terror, Sir Gaston," cried the squire, earnestly;—"you allude to hidden perils, and surely if there is danger, it is the more necessary that I should not be left behind, whilst you are left to the vile arts of your adversaries."

"Thy faithfulness and zeal pleases me well," exclaimed the knight, gratefully;—"I know thy love for me, Julian, but be assured thy presence near me will not be required to night. I am not going to travel very far, and the disguise I am about to assume will effectually protect me from those who may have a design against my life."

"Nay, pardon me, but I would again entreat, that I may be allowed to follow you, in case ———"

"Again I tell thee," interrupted Sir Gaston, "that it may not be. I shall be well armed, Julian, and, therefore, thy presence will be rendered needless."

"Then may the saints protect thee, my noble master," cried the squire, despondingly, "for knowing thy recklessness of danger I cannot but fear that some harm will this night befal thee."

"None can happen," answered Sir Gaston,—"if thou wilt but prove faithful to the secret of my being absent from the castle. No one must know of it, and, therefore, two hours hence, thou must be waiting at the southern postern, to give me admittance when I return. So remember to keep my injunctions faithfully, and I will not fail to reward thee according to thy deserts."

"May I not again entreat thee to let me bare thee company?"

"Not unless thou wouldst seriously offend me, Julian;—thou hast thine answer, and I expect to meet with thy ready compliance. Away then,—saddle me my swiftest steed, and lead him to the postern, I have already named where I will meet thee, as soon as my disguise has been completed."

Thus commanded, it was in vain for Julian to offer any further remonstrances, and having received a few more instructions, he reluctantly quitted the apartment to put into execution the orders of his master. Sir Gaston then proceeded to an adjoining chamber, where he attired himself in a garb of more humble appearance, than that which he usually wore, and having carefully armed himself in case of any sudden emergency, he descended a private staircase, that led towards an unfrequented part of the castle. As he reached the court-yard, he directed a hurried gaze around him to see whether his steps had been watched, but finding that all was quiet, he moved rapidly forward, and passing through the portal, found Julian waiting there with a steed, according to the orders he had received. Here a few words passed between them in a low whisper, and when the squire had received the necessary instructions, Sir Gaston sprung upon the back of his impatient charger and in a few moments, both the horse and his rider, were out of sight.

"What can all this mighty secret portend?" thought Julian to himself, vexed at the want of confidence exhibited by his master, and burning to know the nature of that business, which required more than usual caution on the part of Sir Gaston de Neville. "He was not wont to be so mysterious in his affairs, and by the Virgin, I will sift the matter to the very bottom, but what I'll know the reason of his leaving the castle thus strangely, at this unusual hour of the night."

"And so will I, Julian," exclaimed Edith, who at this moment advanced from behind a buttress, which had hitherto concealed her from his view. "I should like to know what mighty business hath taken our master forth to-night, and I am no true woman, if I worm not the secret out before I am many hours older."

"Ha!" cried the squire, with surprise, "hast thou been watching us then, girl?"

"Why, to be sure I have," she replied, archly. "We females, you must know, Julian, have an utter abhorrence of all secrets, and as this happens to be one of importance, I am the more determined to find it all out."

"But tell me, Edith," cried the squire, "how in the name of all that is singular, did you contrive to learn that Sir Gaston was going to take this evening excursion?"

"By making a proper use of my ears to be sure, you simpleton," she replied, archly. "I heard my master cautiously creeping down the back stairs, and guessing something curious was going on, I watched him across the court-yard, and then followed on tip-toe till I managed to conceal myself behind yonder buttress, where I overheard ——"

"Just as much as amounted to nothing at all," laughed Julian, placing her arm within his, and leading her towards the castle.

"Why there, I must confess," she replied, with good humour, "you have exactly guessed the amount of all the information I contrived, with so much trouble, to gather. Sir Gaston seemed determined that I should not be the wiser for anything he might say, and thus I am obliged to look to you for a revelation of this mighty mystery."

"Why, then, my dear girl," answered Julian,—"I am afraid your curiosity is doomed for a long time to go unsatisfied. Our master is never very fond of making confidants of those about him, and on this occasion he appears to have been more than usually reserved towards me."

"Are you quite sure, Mr. Innocence, that you know nothing about this affair?"

"Quite sure."

"If I thought you were deceiving me, I would never ——"

"Hold, Edith," interrupted Julian, playfully,—"no rash vows, my dear girl, or perhaps you may go the length of saying you will never fulfil your pledge of becoming my pretty bride, unless I tell you more than Sir Gaston has thought fit to entrust me with."

"I don't know that I shall, sir," she replied, with a semblance of anger; "you are too fond of keeping secrets, and, to my thinking, that is an offence deserving the severest punishment."

"Nay, Edith, there you are unreasonable. In this matter, I am as much in the dark as yourself, and yet you expect me to tell what I really know nothing about."

"Are you certain that you can form no idea of the business that has taken Sir Gaston out to-night?"

"I tell you again that I have not the least idea."

"Why, then I have," she replied, and then, whispering in the ear of her lover, she whispered : "depend upon it, Julian, the knight is after no good; there is mischief going on, or I am no true prophetess, and if he succeeds in his wickedness, I know of one poor girl that will heartily wish herself out of the world."

"Indeed!—and who is she?"

"Rebecca, the Hebrew Maiden!"

"Nay, then, I think you are wrong for once, dear Edith," exclaimed the squire; "our master took the road towards Highgate, and thou knowest that the Jew's house lies in a direction exactly opposite."

"Well, and may he not turn off when he gets a little way from home?" asked Edith.

"He might certainly, but, had that been his object, he would have taken some of his retainers with him, in case of any resistance being offered. Besides, I think his love begins to grow cooler in that quarter, and that he will no longer risk the anger of King Richard, now that he knows what an interest he takes in the girl's fate."

"Aye, aye," answered Edith, "he is artful enough to conceal what he means, but I know enough of Sir Gaston to distrust him the more when he is most quiet. Depend upon it, he has not given up the idea of making the girl his, and you will find that I am right before many hours more pass over our heads."

"Nay, you wrong him;—Sir Gaston de Neville is headstrong in his passions, but I cannot believe he is so base as you would make me believe."

"Say, rather, that you flatter him," cried Edith;—"that he is headstrong, I know, and, more than that, he will not let trifles stand in his way, when once he is resolved to accomplish his infamous designs. This I know of him, and, therefore, do I now distrust him."

"But has it never occurred to you, that your prejudice may have done him wrong?"

"It now occurs to me," answered Edith, tartly, "that you are a great goose, for taking so much pains in behalf of a very worthless master. Have we not seen how he has persecuted that unfortunate Jewess, and is not that enough to prove that I have spoken truly of him?"

"True," replied Julian, "he has acted harshly towards Rebecca, but then, you must recollect, that she belongs to a race whom all men persecute alike."

"Then more shame for them, that's all I know about it," cried Edith, warmly.—" But, however, be that as it may, we all of us know that Sir Gaston has accused her of being concerned in the robbery of his lost diamond, and, though everybody else believes her to be innocent, he still persists in his charge, and will never rest satisfied, until he has frightened her into becoming his mistress."

"Well, well," cried the squire, "I see you are prejudiced against Sir Gaston, so, with your leave, we will now drop the subject for a far pleasanter one. You know, Edith, how often you have promised, one day or other, to become mine, and I would take the present opportunity to ask when the happy day is to be."

"Fie, Julian! how unawares you take one," cried the girl, with provoking earnestness.—"I declare, now, if I had been born with such sentimental things as nerves, I should have gone off into hysterics, at the suddenness with which you have thought proper to pop the question."

"But, being above affectation," rejoined Julian, "I hope you will give a plain answer to a plain question."

"Well, then, will a dozen years hence be too early, think you, Julian?"

"A dozen hours, I would rather say."

"Nay, methinks you are in a vast hurry, sir, to encumber yourself with the chains of matrimony."

"But, remember, love," retorted Julian, "the chains are silken ones, and, therefore, easily worn."

"Such," retorted the damsel, "is ever the language of you lovers. You are all ready enough to risk the wearing of them, but when once you become husbands, the load of these said silken chains become intolerable, and, in your hearts, you curse the hour that converted you from a gay bachelor into a sage Benedick."

"And is that," asked Julian, "your opinion of all our sex?"

"Of a great portion of them it certainly is," she replied.—"However, I see you are not very highly flattered with the pictures I have drawn, and, therefore, to make some amends, I will candidly admit, that some men are very passable sort of creatures, and that you, sir, are not among the very worst of them."

"Good!—then I may hope that, ere long, you will have compassion on my present forlorn condition?"

"Humph!—perhaps I may."

"Then I may hope that our wedding day will not be postponed for any very long time?"

"Mercy! how the creature teazes a poor girl," cried Edith, playfully. "However, as you have taken upon yourself the part of my father confessor, I suppose I may as well make a clear conscience of it, by admitting that I will not keep you in suspense longer than may be absolutely necessary."

"Say that our union shall take place in a week, a month, or a year, and I will be satisfied."

"Why, then, I name the longest time you have mentioned," said Edith, sportively ;—"but, mind, you must be upon your very best behaviour all the time, or I shall discard you for ever."

"Agreed!" exclaimed Julian, snatching a kiss from her pouting lips, "and thus I seal the bargain, fair maiden."

"And thus I witness it, saucy varlet," she replied, dealing him a smart box on the ear, and then scampering off with the nimbleness of a frighted fawn. Julian took this as a hint to follow, but his pace was far inferior to hers, and when at length he found that all further pursuit would be in vain, he returned to his own room, happy in the thought that the playful damsel was now pledged to become his bride.

But we must now return to Sir Gaston de Neville, who we left at the moment he quitted his castle, to pursue his way to the humble cabin of Meg of Finchley. The darkness which had begun to set in before he left home, rapidly increased as he proceeded onwards, until all became enveloped in gloom, so intense that he could scarcely see beyond the head of the horse on which he rode. Consequently, he was obliged to move forward at a slow and wearisome pace, rendered doubly irk-some by his anxiety to reach the place of destination. Presently, the clouds, which had been gathering in the east until they had reached the zenith, began to throw forth their forked flames, followed by the bel-lowing thunder which seemed to shake the earth to its very foundation. The lightning, however, served in some degree to guide him on his way, and urging his steed onwards, he at length reached the desolate place, on some part of which, unknown to himself, stood the solitary hut of the aged woman he was in search of. But now he was more perplexed than ever, for having quitted the main road, there was no pathway to guide him, and he was just about to abandon his search in despair, when his horse suddenly started back as if from terror by the vivid glare of the lightning's flash, he discovered the aged and hag-like form of a woman, standing beneath the leafless branches of a blasted tree, that stood directly before him. Taken by surprise, the knight could scarcely sup-press a cry of horror, and he was about to turn his horse's head in another direction, when the old woman, leaping forward, seized the bridle with one of her hands, and uttering a demoniac laugh, exclaimed, a voice that scarcely seemed human :—

"Thou art welcome, Sir Knight, to the lone spot that owns me for its queen. I have been looking for thee these last two hours, and I had almost began to fear that the terrors of the storm had driven thee back to thy castle."

"Thou hast mistaken me, woman," answered Sir Gaston, anxious to maintain his incognito; "I am no knight, neither have I a castle as thy words imply."

"Nay," she replied, "'tis in vain you seek to deceive me, I know Sir Gaston de Neville, and more than that I have expected him to pay a visit to my poor hut for purposes which he best understands."

"Hah !—thou art Meg of Finchley, then ?"

"I am."

"To confess the truth, then," he replied, "I am, indeed, here to con-sult thy art relative to my future doom. Say,—wilt thou accept my gold as a reward for that I ask of thee ?"

"I will."

"Then lead me to thy hut, old woman, for I would gladly obtain shelter from a storm I have already been too long exposed to. Lead the way, and thy services shall be amply repaid."

In obedience to this mandate, the old woman conducted the steed across the heath until they reached the ruined cabin of the prophetess, before the door of which, Sir Gaston alighted, and his horse having been tied to the trunk of a wide spreading tree, he followed his aged con-ductress into the dilapidated apartments within. Here, on a sign being given by his mysterious hostess, he seated himself, and being fully occu-pied with his own thoughts, remained silent until recalled to recollection by the hollow voice of the ancient sybil.

"Attend to me, Sir Knight," she said ;—"thou hast come to consult me as to thy future destiny. Thou wouldst know whether success or defeat shall attend thy dark plotting, and thus, in some degree, will throw thyself in the power of a stranger."

"I do so," answered Sir Gaston, "but my necessities are great, and therefore am I compelled to trust myself in the hands of a stranger,—perhaps to one who may prove an enemy."

"Dost thou doubt me then ?"

'I do not.'

"In that case, thy confidence shall not be abused," she replied;—"true, I am no friend to thee, Sir Gaston de Neville, but having entered my poor cot without hesitation, I will not betray thee."

"Thou knowest nothing," answered the knight, sullenly, "of which thou canst take advantage. Thus far, I have not even alluded to the business that brought me hither, and therefore am I safe from harm."

"Dost thou think then that I know not thine errand?"

"If thou dost, it is almost even more than I do myself," answered the knight; "I came hither to consult with thee on many things, none of which thou shalt know until I have thy solemn promise of secresy."

"Which I could either keep or break according to my humour," she replied, with scorn. "Nay, I wish thee not to explain thy motive for paying me this visit, since, without another word being uttered by thy lips, I can tell thee each purpose upon which thou art most anxious to speak."

"Prove that," exclaimed the knight, "and I will give thee credit for the marvellous things I have heard of thee."

"In the first place, then," she replied, "thou wouldst know whether thine attempts, against a certain Hebrew Maiden, will be ultimately crowned with success."

"Ha!—thou art not very wide of the mark there, I confess, old woman," exclaimed Sir Gaston, startled by hearing her speak upon that subject. "I love the girl, as thou art, perhaps, aware, and if thou can'st truly tell me that I shall succeed in making her mine, a handsome reward shall repay the service."

"May curses light upon the gold that was accepted for such a ser-

No. 22

vice!" cried the old woman, scornfully. "No, Sir Knight, the girl is too much at thy mercy already, and it is now some consolation to me that I have it in my power to tell thee she never shall be thine."

"How!" exclaimed Sir Gaston, plucking forth his dagger threaten. ingly, "dost thou dare to taunt me with the frustration of my hopes?"

"Aye, and glad am I to have it in my power to tell thee so," cried Meg, exultingly. "The maiden thou persecutest is virtuous,—she scorns the base proposals thou has made, and having heaven on her side, will yet be able to thwart the villainy of him who would oppress where he ought rather to become a generous protector."

"At another time," exclaimed the Knight Templar, "these insolent words of thine would have cost thee thy life. As it is, however, I for. give thee, on condition that thou wilt answer my questions fairly and honestly."

"I have already spoken honestly," she replied; "my words are those of truth, and hereafter thou shalt bitterly acknowledge them, unless, from henceforth, the maiden is released from all further persecution."

"Oh, I fear not thy threats," he replied sullenly, "in battle I have braved death, and surely, after that, it will not be much to endure with patience the idle brawling of a woman's tongue."

"Be warned in time," she replied, scarcely heeding the latter words of the Knight Templar. "What I speak is for thine own advantage, for in spite of all thy artifices, the maid's good fortune will preserve her from the snares of the libertine."

"Psha! can she resist force if once I resolve to carry her from her father's protection?"

"Thou wilt find that thine efforts are too puny when directed against female innocence," replied the old woman. "Heaven will not desert her while the dark designs of the seducer are being directed against helpless purity."

"Well, well, a truce to this subject," exclaimed the knight, endea. vouring to conceal his chagrin. "I came not to ask thee questions about the maiden, but rather to inquire whether an enterprise I am engaged in will prove successful or otherwise."

"Thy questions shall be answered in a few minutes," she replied, and drawing a circle on the floor, she traced therein several cabalistic cha. racters accompanied with adjurations, not one word of which reached the ears of the knight. This done, she desired him to step in the magic circle, and then extinguishing the lamp repeated other conjurations in low and muttered tones. At the end of these, an intense circle of light ap. peared against the opposite wall, in the midst of which figures soon be. came perceptible. Upon examination, Sir Gaston could perceive one that represented himself standing in the presence of another, bearing the exact similitude of King Richard. Upon the sovereign's counte. nance sat anger and disdain, and, on a signal being given, the figure that represented himself, was dragged forth by the guards from the presence of the king.

Then a change succeeded, and Sir Gaston beheld a scaffold erected in an open place, upon which kneeled the same figure which had just been removed from the king's presence. In a few moments it rose, staggered towards the block, and laying his head upon it, awaited the blow from the uplifted axe of the executioner!

On this the agitation of Sir Gaston de Neville became so violent that he could no longer control himself, and rushing from the circle in which he had been standing, he hastily quitted the hovel of the old woman, and throwing himself upon the back of his steed, set forward on his return home, with all the haste he could urge it to. On reaching the southern postern, he was received by Julian, according to previou commands, and muttering a few words that were unintelligible to hi auditor, hurried into the castle, where he shut himself up, resolving to be no more disturbed until he had resumed some of that serenity which had been so marvellously disturbed.

CHAPTER XXXIII.

" Hunt and pursue the villain to his den,
  And see that he escapes not.   A thousand crowns
  Shall be the rich reward of him who takes
  The monster dead or living."

THE FLORENTINE.

RELIEVED for a time, from the persecutions of Sir Gaston de Neville, and feeling secure in the protection of the king, our heroine began to forget the miseries she had gone through in the brighter visions that were opening before her.   Black Ivan, too, had forborne to annoy her with his hateful suit, and as her marriage with Reuben Grenard was fixed to take place at no very distant period, she now regarded her misfortunes as ended, and looked forward to pass the remainder of her days in peace and quietness.

Her father, however, was less sanguine in this hope than herself;— he had seen the persecutions to which his race was subjected, by rapacious men, thirsting for their hard-earned gold, and though the protection afforded by the king, gave them temporary security, it was well known that the people regarded his act with dissatisfaction, and were only waiting for an opportunity to recommence their oppressions, which there was every reason to fear would burst forth with redoubled violence, whenever their present restraint should be removed.   Rebecca heard these prophetic warnings of her father with uneasiness, but her own youthful hopes soon served to revive her confidence, and relying upon the generous guardship of King Richard, she fondly imagined that the persecutions, predicted by her father, would never be revived.

One evening, a few days after the events related in the last chapter, Rebecca was seated at the casement, watching the glorious sun, as he sank in majesty towards the western horizon.   At that moment her soul was absorbed in a thousand pleasureable emotions, but chiefly was she thinking of Reuben and her father, whose return she was anxiously awaiting, as the former had been absent three days, on 'a mission of some importance, with which he had been trusted by Isaac of Tadcaster.   Indeed the period of their expected arrival had already passed, and she was beginning to grow uneasy at the delay, when the dark shadow of a man was seen crossing the path just beneath the window.   At first she was rather startled at this, but quickly banishing her fears, under the supposition that her father and Reuben had returned, she sprang from her seat, and was rushing forward with a joyful cry, when the door was violently thrown open, and instead of those she loved, she beheld the grim figure of Black Ivan, as he strode with rapidity into the room.   Starting back with affright, the maiden would have screamed aloud in her terror, but in an instant the robber was by her side, and seizing her roughly by the arm, he exclaimed, in a hoarse whisper :—

" Silence, girl, or your fate is this moment sealed for ever. Speak not a word, but follow me without hesitation."

" Villain! I will not follow thee!" cried Rebecca, summoning all her fortitude. " Leave me, I say, or my cries shall bring assistance when least expected."

" Wouldst thou have thy father's hearth stained with human blood?" demanded the robber fiercely. " Wouldst thou, I say, cause murder to be committed, when, by remaining passive, the deed may be avoided."

" If it is my life only that is in peril," she replied, firmly,—" I will resist even to the very last. Thou art hateful to me Ivan, and gladly would I perish, rather than fall into the hands of one so loathed as thou art."

" Nay, *thy* life is safe, girl," answered the robber,—" because I have resolved to make thee my own. I am now here to carry thee off to my strong hold, and should any one interpose,—even though it were thy father himself,—my dagger's point shall drink his heart's blood. Now, therefore, thou knowest my purpose, and it remains for thee to decide whether bloodshed shall follow or not."

" Monster!" cried the trembling maiden,—" wouldst thou slay an old man, who never injured thee, and whose grey hairs should be his protection!"

" Aye, marry would I," answered Ivan, in a tone of indifference.—" Grey hairs have very little influence with a desperate man like myself;—and as for his never having injured me, that I regard as nothing, seeing that he would not hesitate to betray me into the hands of my enemies, if he had but the opportunity of doing so. Thus thou seest, I am under no obligation to him on the score of good wishes, nor should I be disposed to show him mercy, if his presence here should happen to place me in jeopardy."

" Oh, in mercy leave me!" cried Rebecca, throwing herself at the feet of the robber. " Quit the place, I implore thee, and in my father's name I promise thee any sum of money that he may have it in his power to bestow."

" Psha! I want not his money, and if I did, would it not be easy to help myself without making any favour of it? I tell thee, girl, it is thyself I want;—I have run a great risk in coming hither to carry thee off, nor will I leave the place unless it be in thy company."

" Monster!" cried Rebecca, " I will not go with thee unless thou takest me a bleeding corse. Stab me to the heart if thou wilt, but thou shalt not drag me from this place, unless my cries for assistance should prove unavailing."

" Girl! this is madness!" exclaimed the robber, somewhat disconcerted by the firmness she displayed ;—" by thine obstinacy, thou riskest, not only thine own life, but those who may venture to thy assistance. I am bold and reckless as thou well knowest, nor will I be robbed of my fair prize, whatever sacrifice may be made in obtaining it."

" Let me entreat thee to spare me!" cried Rebecca, in an agony of terror ;—" that I love thee not, thou well knowest, and, therefore, do I humbly, upon my knees, implore thee, to have mercy upon a defenceless girl. Renounce thine ill-placed and hopeless love, and my father will reward thee for it, even to the utmost of thy demands."

" I tell thee it is in vain to ask my forbearance," exclaimed Ivan, resolutely. " Money will not recompense me, nor will I except the wealth of a whole kingdom in exchange for thee. So, girl, thou hast now my final answer, and, therefore thou wilt see the utter uselessness of urging me further upon that subject."

"Then thus will I make a last effort to escape the fate thou hast doomed me to," cried Rebecca, starting from the humble posture she had assumed, and darting with inconceivable swiftness towards the door. In this attempt, however, she was frustrated by the robber, who, throwing himself between her and the place she was fleeing to, seized her in his arms, and was preparing to carry her from the house, when Isaac, rushing in, snatched the almost unconscious girl from his arms, and retreating a few paces, boldly defied the brigand to advance another step, for the purpose of regaining the prize he had so unexpectedly lost. For a moment or two, Black Ivan stood as if he had been petrified, but presently recovering from the surprise into which he had been thrown, he hastily drew forth his poinard, and brandishing it threateningly in his hand, exclaimed in a voice almost choked with rage:—

"Hark'ee, old man, thou hast dared to deprive me of a prize that I have ventured life itself to obtain. For that I could find it in my heart to strike thee dead at my feet, and that I have not done so, thou mayst thank the circumstance of thy being the father of her I love. But remember, Jew, I am no longer to be trifled with;—resign the girl to me, or, by the heaven above us, I will no longer answer for thy safety."

"Villain!" cried the old man,—"thy threats are unheeded by one to whom life would be valueless, if deprived of the only tie that renders existence desirable. I fear not thy dagger, nor will I resign my daughter to thine arms, whilst strength remains in me to resist the heartless libertine in his designs against the innocent."

"Fool!" exclaimed the brigand, fiercely,—"then hast thou spoken thine own doom!"

And with these words he strode towards the aged Israelite, into whose bosom he was about to plunge his uplifted dagger, when Reuben Grenard, rushing into the chamber, caught the descending arm, and in an instant wrested the instrument of death from his grasp. Infuriated at this, Black Ivan drew his sword, and was in the act of sacrificing his rival to his boundless rage, when Simon Snout, the constable, followed by a number of the neighbours, hurried tumultuous into the house, calling upon the robber, in the king's name, to surrender. Ivan, however, regarded them with a look of contempt, and knocking two or three down, who stood in the way of his retreat, hastened towards the open window, where he paused for a few moments, to gaze upon the motley throng, all of whom, he well knew, had too much regard for their own lives to venture within reach of his sword.

"Now," he exclaimed, tauntingly, "who is there among ye that will attempt to prevent my exit from this place? Are ye not cowards, thus to suffer one man to set ye at defiance? Shame on ye all, that not one will venture a little to obtain the large reward that has been offered for the capture of Black Ivan, the Outlaw!"

"Have at him, boys!" shouted Simon Snout, the constable, "on to him, and, remember, a purse of gold will be distributed among all that are engaged in capturing him. Follow me, lads, and the prize is ours!"

Simon Snout, however, had reckoned without his host, for none of his companions were at all inclined to follow him, and as he advanced to capture the robber, he received a blow on the head from the haft of Ivan's sword that sent him reeling to the floor. Upon this, the Outlaw sprang from the window, followed by the courageous mob, all of whom were willing enough to join in a pursuit when there was no very manifest danger to themselves. There trouble, however, was in vain, for the agility of Black Ivan soon left them at a considerable distance behind, and they were at length compelled to give up the chase, exhausted by the speed they had exerted, and disappointed of the golden harvest they had thought to reap in the event of his capture. Neither Isaac nor Reuben could lend any assistance in following the robber, for Rebecca had fainted from terror and agitation, and required all the care and attention they could bestow.

CHAPTER XXXIV.

" Wilt thou, by one bold act, perform a deed
That shall preserve us from the doom we dread
And place us both in firm security ?"

THE ORACLE.

FEARFUL of learning the full extent of King Richard's indignation towards him, Sir Gaston de Neville refrained for some time from going to court, lest an open rupture should break out between him and his royal master before his own projects were ripe for execution. That his treacherous designs were in hourly danger of being exposed by Ranulph was certain, and equally certain was it that his enemies would not relax the tortures they were daily inflicting upon him, whilst there was a chance of forcing him to a confession that should implicate all who were engaged in the plot which was to destroy Richard Cœur de Lion, and place on the throne, instead of him, his brother, the weak but ambitious Prince John. Every moment, indeed, the danger which threatened the Knight Templar, became more and more apparent, and, as his friends were not yet ready to strike the decisive blow, he began to entertain thoughts of leaving England for awhile, under pretence of joining the army on the continent which was being collected for the avowed purpose of being sent for the deliverance of the Holy Land from the hands of the Pagans, who had long held dominion there."

But in the midst of these conflicting thoughts, news reached Sir Gaston de Neville, in the solitude of his castle, that active preparations were making for the king's coronation at Westminster, and that the 3rd of September had been fixed upon as the day whereon that solemnity was to take place. This was a source of fresh inquietude to the knight, and being greatly perplexed how to act, he hastened to the dungeon of Bertrand le Noir, from whom he hoped for counsel and assistance to relieve him from his present difficulties.

"Bertrand," he exclaimed, upon entering the gloomy hiding place of his vassal, " I am now come to tell thee that it is time thou shouldst leave this dungeon to become once more useful to me. The dangers which, until lately I have regarded as being distant, are now pressing closely upon me, and, unless instant measures are adopted to counteract the coming evil, I shall fall, dishonoured, with the hateful name of traitor to my king and country."

"How can I aid you?" asked Bertrand, sullenly. "Am I not obliged to hide myself, lest I fall into the hands of those who would have no mercy were they once to lay upon me their infernal claws."

"Thou must leave this place, Bertrand."

"Indeed !—and wilt thou insure my safety if I do so?"

"Psha !" ejaculated the knight, peevishly, " what danger hast thou to dread that I do not participate in? Is not my life in as much danger as thine own, and thinkest thou I would endanger thee when the same ruin threatens to involve us both ?''

" Well, I'll take thy word for it then," answered Bertrand, gloomily. "Say what it is thou wouldst have done, and I will perform the service, even though I chance to fall in the execution of my duty."

"Why, that was spoken like thyself—so now listen to me:—thou dost remember what I said to thee touching Ranulph, the Avenger; we have much to fear from him, Bertrand, for should he, after all, be forced into a confession, thou knowest we should both be implicated in the crime of treason, and that a death of shame would be the result."

"True," exclaimed Bertrand, in a tone of indifference; "such a fate would assuredly befal us, and yet, methinks the shame would fall heavier upon thyself than it would upon me."

"Such a fate I would avoid," answered Sir Gaston, "nay, it must and shall be averted, or with my own hands will I wrap this castle in flames, and bury myself beneath its ponderous ruins."

"Didst thou not say just now," asked the other, "that it is possible to save ourselves without thus madly rushing into destruction?"

"I did," returned the knight, "but it depends solely upon thyself whether my plan can be accomplished."

"Ah!" cried Bertrand, "I begin to see how it is; I am to leave this place and commit some desperate deed, by which we are both to be released from danger. Excellent! i'faith,—most excellent."

"Well, well," retorted the knight, in a tone of evident disappointment; "I see how it is, misfortune hath made thee selfish, and thou no longer wishest to serve him thou wert once proud to call thy master."

"Nay," answered Bertrand, "I have not yet heard the project thou hast in hand for me. Besides, to confess the truth, the armed apparition that has been seen by us both, two or three times already, seems sent as a warning for us to depart from the wickedness of our ways."

"Psha! thou hast become a coward, Bertrand."

"Had any but thyself told me so," answered the retainer, fiercely,— "I would have dashed him at my feet, and trampled him into the very dust."

"Hah!—is that meant as a threat!" cried Sir Gaston. "Wouldst thou triumph over me, because, at this moment, I happen to stand in need of thy services?"

"Thou hast ever found me faithful and diligent to execute whatever task was imposed upon me," answered Bertrand, in a voice of greater humility. "For years past I have been in thy service, and till this moment never heard a word of reproach such as has now been uttered."

"Thou hast never merited my anger till now," replied Sir Gaston;— "on the contrary, I have, on all occasions, found thee most faithful to my interest. However, let us now forget what has passed, remembering that the safety of both of us depends upon our continuing firm and upon one point. I have, as thou knowest, fallen under the displeasure of the king, and unless my fears greatly deceive me, Ranulph will not much longer maintain the secret upon which depends our future safety."

"Is there any reason then to suppose that he will confess our share in the intended revolt?"

"We have every thing to fear," answered the knight. "It is said that he has already betrayed an inclination to confess; and should he do so, the cause we have engaged in will not only be lost, but our own lives will be sacrificed to the fury of King Richard."

"I'faith, master," exclaimed Bertrand, "it seems then that we stand in some peril at present. Our lives are scarcely worth a week's pur-

chase, and yet, so far, thou hast offered no suggestion by which to extricate ourselves from the dangers we have so much reason to apprehend."

"Hear me then," cried Sir Gaston; "the prisoner, Ranulph, the
Avenger, must be secretly destroyed!"

"With all my heart," returned the other; "and yet it is easy to say
he *must* be destroyed, without giving a hint how or in what way it is to
be done."

"There is, I confess, a difficulty in the way," answered Sir Gaston,
"but, as thou well knowest, nothing is impossible to men who are once
resolved. With care, access may be obtained to the prisoner's cell, and
then thou knowest how the rest is to be accomplished."

"Humph!" muttered Bertrand, "then, from what I can gather, it
seems pretty certain that I am to have the honour of performing this
very notable service."

"It was to ask thee, that I came hither," answered the knight,
eagerly. "I know, Bertrand, thy perseverance and contempt of danger,
and having long had proof of thy zeal in my behalf, I have resolved to
commit this affair to thy hands."

"Then I am coolly to assassinate a poor creature who has never
harmed me?"

"If thou dost not, we both shall perish," replied Sir Gaston. "It is
reported that the king's coronation is to take place on the third of next
month, and, on that occasion, all prisoners will be set at liberty who
may think fit to confess their misdeeds, and denounce those who were
concerned in them. Among others, Ranulph will receive the offer of
freedom, and I must acknowledge that I fear him, in this instance, more
than I ever feared anything before in all my life."

"A very fair reason why he should be put out of the way," exclaimed Bertrand, "though, still I do not see so clearly how he is to be
got rid of quite so easily as thou seemest to imagine. Of course, a constant guard is kept over his dungeons, and therefore I may look in vain
for an opportunity to obtain access to it, for the purpose of getting rid
of the prisoner."

"It must be done by means of a disguise," replied Sir Gaston, after a
brief pause. "Monks are constantly admitted to his cell, and thou hast
only to assume the holy garb to render thy success certain. '*Pax vobi-
scum*' pronounced at the door, will prove thy passport to the interior of
the prison, and then thou hast only to say thou comest to urge the prisoner to confession, and thou wilt be speedily conducted to his presence."

"But will they leave us together?"

"Most assuredly they will. It is usual to leave prisoners with their
ghostly advisers, and I need not tell thee how necessary it will be to
take advantage of the opportunity thus afforded. A dagger may be
concealed beneath thy monkish garb, and when most the prisoner is off
his guard, strike thy weapon to his heart with so sure an aim that he
shall die without a groan to warn his keepers of what has befallen him."

"'Tis a coward's way of doing the business after all," muttered Bertrand le Noir, with evident dissatisfaction.

"At least," retorted his master, "'tis the only way left to save ourselves from destruction. We must either consent to rid ourselves of
Ranulph in the way I have proposed, or make up our minds to fall like
traitors through being over scrupulous when necessity urged us to adopt
this course."

"Well, be it as you have said," answered Bertrand, though not without reluctance. "I am in a pretty plight either way, and since I must
either slay this man after the fashion you have hinted at, or become a

victim to the king's resentment, I shall 'choose the former course. You may, therefore, rely upon my attempting the deed, and should I chance to fall into the enemies hands, I can endure any torture they may think fit to apply rather than betray who it was that set me on to perform this deed."

"Art thou ready to go about thy task without further delay?" asked the knight eagerly.

"This moment, if it pleases you to command it," answered Bertrand le Noir. "I am now ready, and perhaps the sooner the thing is done the better."

"Follow me then to the eastern turret," exclaimed Sir Gaston, delighted at the eagerness manifested by his dependant;—"follow me, I say, and I will supply thee with the garb of a friar, belonging to the late Father Francis, the last religious instructor that ever found a home beneath this roof. Hist! tread gently as we pass along, for these old walls send forth echoes over the whole building, and it would scarcely be advisable to let a third party know the business that we have now in hand."

Silently, Bertrand le Noir followed the footsteps of his master, and after passing through a number of narrow passages, they began to ascend a lofty flight of broken steps, so dilapidated and worn, as to render their progress both difficult and dangerous. At length, however, they reached a door, that yielded with a slight push and immediately afterwards, Bertrand discovered that they were in an apartment of octangular form, lighted only by small loop-holes, and bearing pretty evident traces of having been recently used for the purpose of a prison. This was one of the portions of the castle which he had never before seen, and he was about to enquire why he had been taken there, when Sir

Gaston stooping, picked up a friar's habit which was lying upon the ground, and handing it to Bertrand, he said :—

"This is the disguise I told you of ;—put it on, and with a dagger concealed beneath, you may safely execute the deed you are commissioned to perform. But again let me warn you against exhibiting any symptoms of trepidation, for so surely as you do that, you will excite suspicion, and thus perish through your own folly."

"I will not fail to obey your injunctions," answered Bertrand, holding forth his hand to take the offered garb, but no sooner had he done so, than shrinking back with terror, he exclaimed, trembling :—

"Holy Mother !—what is this I see !—there is blood upon the friar's gown, and that accounts for the reports I have heard of his having come unfairly by his death !"

"Peace, fool !" cried Sir Gaston, eagerly ;—"Father Francis was an officious, meddling priest, and no favourite in this castle. His death was sudden, as all have heard, and if he met a violent end, the matter concerns neither you nor I.—So quick !—put on the cassock and effect your escape from the castle whilst you can do so with safety."

Bertrand said no more, but obeying the mandate of his imperious master, he armed himself with a dagger, which he concealed beneath the holy garb in which he was disguised, and then following Sir Gaston down another flight of steps, descended into a quadrangle, seldom visited by any of the domestics. Having crossed this, he passed through a small postern, and then hastening his steps, directed his way towards the prison in which Ranulph was confined.

CHAPTER XXXV.

"I charge thee flinch not when the moment comes
To favour thy design."   MARCO.

TORTURED in mind as well as in body, Ranulph's determination to maintain his secret began at length to give way, and reflecting on the sufferings he had endured, and the agonies that still awaited him in the event of his still remaining obstinate, he resolved to make a full acknowledgment of his crimes, as well as of those who had leagued themselves for the destruction of the king. By so doing he knew that his life would be spared, and which was of still more consequence, that he would escape a repetition of the tortures that had already reduced him nearly to the verge of the grave. To be sure he had not yet been promised his liberty, but, with returning strength, he thought it possible to effect his own release, when by again joining the band of Black Ivan, the Outlaw, he would place himself beyond the danger of falling a second time into the hands of his enemies.

During the time that he had been in prison, the tortures had been several times applied ; each application being more severe than the former one, it being the design of his tormentors to force from him a confession, even though he should die under the cruel infliction he was made to endure. In fact, they began to see that terror had at length taken possession of his soul, and exulting in the probable success of their plans for extorting from him the truth, they pointed out to him the folly of remaining obstinate, seeing that he must either perish or make the required confession. Then, upon partially recovering from the effects of the torture, they would send priests to him to convince him that resistance was a most henious offence, and that since the king's life was endangered, it was absolutely necessary to make a full confession, in order that the enemies of his sovereign might be punished, as a warning to all who plotted his destruction.

At first, Ranulph paid very little attention to the counsel thus given, but at length, when his sufferings had been increased to an insupportable pitch, he began to manifest less resolution than had formerly been exhibited, and from that circumstance, it was imagined that it required but little more to bring him to their purpose.

It was at this period that Locksley, the gaoler, was sent to him for the purpose of ascertaining what probability there was of making a speedy confession. The man who had been thus commissioned, commenced his task by appearing to be much concerned for the sufferings of the prisoner, and with many professions of kindness and consideration, he urged him to make a clear conscience by revealing all that he knew of the transaction in which he had been engaged. But, Ranulph, though he had resolved to confess every thing, was not yet prepared to make the required disclosure, and looking sternly at his gaoler, he said with all his wonted resolution :—

"It is in vain, Master Gaoler, that your master's send you here to preach the advantages I shall receive by doing as they would have me. By this time they have seen that I am not to be forced against my inclination, and to speak the truth, I have not yet determined whether or not I shall purchase my life by denouncing others."

"Tush! this is madness," retorted the gaoler; "remember what you have suffered, and worse tortures remain if you continue obstinate."

"Aye, that's were it is," exclaimed Ranulph;—"you think to frighten me into submission, but such a course, I can tell you, may only serve to defeat its own ends. I have, as you are aware, borne much.—I may almost say without flinching, and think you I cannot endure more if my mind is made up to die with the secret locked up in my own heart?"

"Perhaps you can do so," replied the gaoler, "but I should think you a very foolish fellow to suffer the torture when it can be so easily avoided."

"Humph,—but when a man is sworn to secresy, it is by no means easy to convince himself that he is doing right to break the oath he has taken."

"Well, but the king has strong suspicions as to who his enemies are, and all that is required of you is to confirm them. Besides, innocent persons may chance to suffer for an act they never thought of, and it therefore becomes your duty to denounce those who are really criminal."

"You have got your lesson perfect enough, I see," exclaimed Ranulph, in an accent of scorn. "Your master's have instructed you well, but all your arguments will fail to convince me till I have thought more seriously upon the subject."

"Nay, let me persuade you," cried the gaoler, "to waste no further time in idle consideration of this matter. In truth, Ranulph, orders have been sent down that you are to be tortured again to day with greater severity than before, and as it was doubtful on the last occasion whether or not you would recover from the effects, there is but too much reason to fear that this time you will not survive the infliction."

"Well, in that case, death will be most welcome," answered the prisoner. It is but to suffer once more, and then my persecutors have no further power over me."

"But, remember how easily you may avoid it."

"I do remember it, but have not yet made up my mind to turn traitor to my cause, Besides, I have cause for deep enmity with the king, and as I have failed in my attempt against his life, I care not how soon I perish."

" Psha! the king will be grateful to thee if thou wilt but do him this one service."

" Ah!—he would be kind enough to grant me my life, on condition that the remainder of my days shall be passed within these walls."

" On the contrary, he will reward and liberate thee."

" But what if I doubt him?—What if I think him treacherous, and unlikely to keep a promise?"

" King Richard's honour," exclaimed the gaoler, " is never doubted; he is lavish in his generosity towards those who do him a service, and believe me, thou wilt not regret the moment when thou wert prevailed upon to confess."

" Be that as it may," answered Ranulph, " I have not yet made up my mind what course to pursue. You may, therefore, leave me, and when your masters ask you what success you have met with, tell them that Ranulph, the Avenger, is yet unsubdued in spirit as he was ere he entered as a captive, the dungeon of his foes. Tell them, that in spite of his sufferings, he can still feel a triumph in the certainty that his enemies possess not the power to subdue his stubborn spirit."

" Art thou determined then, not to confess?"

" I have not said that I will not," replied Ranulph, " but I will not be forced to do so until I think fit."

" And supposing thou dost so, when shall we know thy determination?"

" When next they take me to the rack," answered Ranulph.

Finding the prisoner thus obstinate, the gaoler withdrew without further remark, leaving the prisoner utterly unmoved by the conversation that had taken place between them. Presently afterwards, however, Lockley returned, bringing with him Bertrand le Noir, who, in the disguise of a friar, had obtained permission to visit the captive, in the hope that his exhortations might prove successful in the effort he had promised to make to prevail upon the prisoner to confess.

" Here is a holy father come to offer thee the consolations of religion," exclaimed the gaoler. " He will tell thee better than I could, the duty of submission, and most heartily do I pray that his efforts may prove successful."

And with this Lockley retired, leaving the captive and supposed friar to confer together in privacy. Ranulph, however, seemed not to be best pleased with his visitor; he rose and paced uneasily up and down the cell, and then suddenly pausing and looking fiercely towards the other, he said, sullenly:—

" Wherefore hast thou come to annoy one who needs not thy services? Art thou also in league with my tormentors to render more wretched the last few hours that may remain to me?"

" Hist!—utter no exclamation of surprise, and thou shalt know who I am," whispered Bertrand. " Thou lookest on me with amazement, yet, I tell thee it is no enemy that stands in the presence of Ranulph the Avenger."

" Hah!—who art thou, then?"

" Behold!" exclaimed Bertrand, and throwing back the hood that had hitherto concealed his features, he advanced a step or two nearer, and grasping the arm of the prisoner, continued in a low tone: " Beware, Ranulph, how thou givest utterance to thy surprise; I have come to visit thee, and perhaps, concert measures for thy escape."

"*Perhaps!*" exclaimed Ranulph, "dost thou hesitate, then, in contriving the rescue of him who has risked so much, and whose peril is occasioned by listening to thy counsel. Out upon thee for a false friend, who it had been better never to have seen than to be thus deserted in my necessities."

"Nay, Ranulph," answered the other, "thou hast not yet heard me out;—I tell thee I have come to serve thee, but I must first know whether thou hast faithfully kept the secret, upon which hangs the life of my master, Sir Gaston de Neville."

"I have."

"Art thou sure no hint hath escaped thy lips, by which he may be suspected?"

"Not a word:—hitherto I have defied the torture they have applied to me. I have been torn nearly limb from limb, Bertrand, yet have I endured all, rather than break the oath I have so solemnly taken."

"Why that is well," answered Bertrand le Noir; "I am glad to hear of thy firmness, and the more so as I happen to know that a design was on foot to assassinate thee, if it should appear likely that thou wouldst denounce the enemies of King Richard."

"Art thou in earnest, Bertrand?" exclaimed the prisoner, with mingled rage and astonishment. "Can it be possible that there is any truth in the damning words thou hast uttered?"

"I tell thee, I have spoken nothing but the truth," answered the other. "Nay, I see nothing so very surprising in it, either, since self-preservation is the first thought with all of us. Sir Gaston's life would be endangered, were his plots against the king to be discovered; and, for my own part, I can see nothing very surprising in his seeking to circumvent any evil that may be designed against thee."

"By Heaven's, Bertrand," exclaimed the prisoner, "I now begin to see through the motive of thy visit;—thou, villain, as thou art, hast been entrusted with the bloody deed of ridding thy master of this danger."

"I confess, thou hast partly guessed my errand," answered Bertrand; "and yet, matters are not quite so desperate as you appear to think. Pledge thy word not to reveal this secret, and not only will thy life be safe, but measures shall be instantly set on foot to obtain thy deliverance."

"You trifle with me, Bertrand," exclaimed Ranulph, impatiently. "I have already been tortured till the nature within me is well nigh exhausted. So far, I have maintaind the secret,—my pledge is unbroken, though, to confess the truth, I have had thoughts of acknowledging everything before this day closes upon me, rather than endure the torture with which I am again threatened."

"For thine own sake, I would advise thee to pause ere thou resolvest upon betraying thy secret. I would save the from death, Ranulph, but my master's honour is far dearer to me than my own existence, and should their be occasion for it, this hand shall destroy thee, ere the fatal secret is betrayed."

"Villain!—I see thine aim now," cried Ranulph, trembling from excess of rage. "Thou hast come hither to assassinate me, because thy master's life is in my power. He hath moved thee to this; but let him not think to triumph over me, for even with a single word of mine, his messenger shall not live to return with the story of my death."

"Tush!—how canst thou prevent it?" demanded Bertrand, in a tone of exultation;—"thou art unarmed, whilst I possess a weapon that with one blow will lay thee breathless at my feet."

"There, it must be confessed, thou hast some advantage over me," exclaimed Ranulph;—"yet, still I am not utterly harmless, since, were I once to pronounce thy name aloud, I'll answer for it, enough would rush in upon thee to prevent the execution of the deed for which thou wert sent."

"And, if I thought thou wouldst do so, thy life would not be worth a single instant's purchase;" retorted Bertrand le Noir, snatching forth his poniard and preparing himself for the worst. "Thou see'st, Ranulph," he continued, "that I have not ventured hither unarmed, and the first indication I perceive of thy intention to betray me, will be the signal for thine own death."

"Be it so," retorted the other, with scorn; "I have been for some days past living in hourly expectation of death, and I know not that I could at any time die more cheerfully than when I know that thine own fate will be sealed shortly afterwards. Here, a single word of mine, will make thee a prisoner as well as myself, and, by all the fiends in hell, that word shall be spoken even though it should be my very last !"

"This then to thy heart !" exclaimed Bertrand, rushing forward and plunging his weapon full into the body of his antagonist. So sudden indeed, was the attack, that Ranulph had not time to guard himself against it, and with a heavy groan of agony he sank deluged in blood at the feet of his assassin. This accomplished, Bertrand replaced the poinard in his girdle, and having once more concealed his face beneath the hood of his friar's garb, he hurried from the scene of death towards the entrance of the prison, where Locksley was anxiously waiting his return, to know how he had prospered.

"Well, holy father," he exclaimed, "how hast thou left the prisoner? Hath he listened to thy words of wisdom, or is his heart still hardened to persist in his obstinacy ?"

"I have left him quieter than thou hast ever seen him before," answered Bertrand, with affected humility. During the conference, I have particularly strove to convince him of the necessity of making a full and ample confession, and, I doubt not, that when thou seest him again, thou wilt acknowledge that I have saved thee much trouble."

"Dost thou think he will confess, holy father ?"

"I believe thou wilt not have to torture him again, my son," answered Bertrand;—"he has already had enough of the rack, and, henceforth, thou wilt be spared the pain of witnessing his agonies. In fact, thou mayst do with him as thou wilt, for he will no longer resist thee."

"Thou hast worked a miracle, holy man," cried the gaoler, "and I long to go and see my prisoner, now thou hast so wonderfully overcome his obstinacy. So, farewell, and heaven speed thee on thy way."

"Benedicite ! my son," muttered Bertrand, and leaving the prison, he hurried onwards with all the speed he could. Presently, however, he heard a cry of alarm raised from behind, and knowing by this that the assassination had been discovered, he threw aside his religious garb, and urging his way with all speed took a bye-path which he knew led towards the retreat of Black Ivan, the Outlaw.

CHAPTER XXXVI.

"Oh, whither shall I fly !—where hide me from
The foes, whose cries of vengeance follow me
Where'er I go ?"

THE FRATRICIDE.

BERTRAND LE NOIR continued his rapid flight for about an hour, without daring to pause for a single instant lest, by so doing, he should give his pursuers an opportunity of gaining upon him. That they had followed him some distance, he was certain, from the loud cries of vengeance that reached his ears, and it was more than probable that some of them were still after him, though they were now silent ;—this, however, he thought might be in order to render his capture the more certain, and suspicious as he was, he determined to throw away no advantage to favour those from whom he had not a shadow of mercy to expect. At length exhaustion compelled him to slacken his speed, and then listening intently for a few seconds, he pretty well satisfied himself that he had thus far succeeded in distancing his pursuers, who, by this time, had, doubtless, given up in despair all hopes of capturing him. Thus released from some of his anxiety, he had now an opportunity to look around him, in search of some trace, by which he might hope to find the robbers' retreat. To his disappointment, however, he found that he had now reached the midst of a widely extended heath, where not a house was to be seen around him ;—here and there were patches of low underwood, but, save these, not a place of refuge presented itself where he could rest himself after the exertion he had undergone.

Thus situated, he resolved to seek concealment, for the present, in one of these small thickets, and making his way towards the nearest of them, he was about to enter it, when a ruffian started forth, and presenting a cross-bow at him, commanded him to halt, under pain of instant death. Of course, a mandate thus seconded, was not to be resisted ; and, pausing, instantly, waited with fear and trembling while the man advanced towards him.

"Who art thou, sirrah ?" exclaimed the ruffian ;—"speak, or thou wilt have a shaft through thy heart, before thou art many seconds older."

"I am Bertrand le Noir," answered the other ;—"a wanderer upon this desolate place, and looking for a sheltered spot wherein I may rest myself.

"Ho ! a traveller !—thou hast money then, which must be transferred from thy pouch to mine."

"I have but a few silver pieces," answered Bertrand, "but they, if it is thy will, shall become thine."

"Sensibly spoken, i'faith !" retorted the other ; "and so thou has only a few silver pieces, eh ?—Art sure, sirrah, that thy purse contains no stray gold coin that might make it better worth my while to rob thee ?"

"I have no more than I have said," replied Bertrand. "I am poor, and need concealment from my enemies, and, if I mistake not, thou belongest to the band of whose leader I am now in search."

"Hah !—wouldst thou see Black Ivan ?"

"I would."

"Dost thou know him ?"

"A little."

" And are thy purposes fair ?"

" Perfectly so ;—I have told thee I am pursued by my foes, and my only motive for seeking the retreat of Black Ivan is to claim his powerful protection."

" Wilt thou become a robber on condition that I take thee before our leader ?"

" Most willingly;—in fact, I am a proscribed man, and the only alternative that remains, is to join the band of your gallant leader."

" But what surety canst thou give, that thou hast not come as a spy to betray us ?"

" None " answered Bertrand, " beyond my bare word; I am, however, as thou seest, alone, and should I have falsely represented myself, it will be easy to punish me, as such an act of treachery would justly merit."

" Well, thou speakest fairly enough, certainly," returned the robber, after a brief pause. " To be sure, thou art alone, and therefore the danger in taking thee to our stronghold is not great. But I warn thee, that if thou shouldst give occasion for the slightest suspicion, thou wilt be poniarded with as little mercy as if thou wert a dog."

" I am content to take my chance," replied Bertrand; " lead me to your chief, and I am assured he will not deny me the shelter I request."

" Perhaps you know something of him then ?

" I have seen him."

' And where ?"

" In the castle of Sir Gaston de Neville."

" Aha !" cried the robber, " that says very little in favour of your meeting a cordial reception from Black Ivan."

" He surely would not punish me for having been the faithful friend and follower of his rival !" cried Bertrand with half suppressed fear.

" Why that," answered the robber, will depend entirely upon circumstances. If our chieftain thinks you would make a useful member of his band, he will forget his animosity against your master, and admit you among our ranks. If, however, he should suspect that you have been sent here as a spy to watch, or perhaps betray him, you would be hung up on the nearest tree as a terrible example to all others who would seek the destruction of Black Ivan, the Outlaw."

" My motives are fair and honourable towards him," answered Bertrand, " and I am content to risk my life to his generosity."

" Well, you know best about that," exclaimed the ruffian, " so if you choose to run the risk, after the warning I have given, follow me, and I will presently lead you into the presence of our captain."

And, so saying, they moved onwards in profound silence, reaching another thicket where Herbert, the second in command under Black Ivan, started up from the ground, and angrily demanded of his comrade why he was taking a stranger so near to their secret haunt.

" Because he is fool-hardy enough to seek an audience of our noble captain," answered the fellow. " I have sounded him pretty well as to the reason of his being in our neighbourhood, and finding that he was flying from justice, I thought there could be no great harm in taking him before our chief."

" Thou hast done wrong, then," exclaimed Hubert,—" for in our master's present humour, it is likely enough he will order both of you to be put to death. Thou knowest that he has ordered that no strangers shall be suffered to approach within two miles of our retreat."

" True, but this man, it seems, is no stranger."

"Answer me, fellow," cried Hubert, addressing himself fiercely to the new comer;—"who art thou?—Speak, for thy life depends upon thine answer."

"I am Bertrand le Noir——"

"Ha!—the seneschal of Sir Gaston de Neville?"

"I was so, but I have been compelled, by circumstances, to quit his service."

"And what is thy object in coming hither?"

"To enrol myself among the band of Black Ivan!"

"Are thy designs fair towards us?"

"They are;—in fact I have no choice left, since I must either seek refuge here or fall into the hands of those who thirst for my blood."

"Well," replied Hubert, "that certainly affords some warrant for the honesty of thy purpose."

"Then, being thus far satisfied, wilt thou take me into the presence of Black Ivan?"

"Why, to speak truth, I must do so," answered Hubert;—"thou hast trespassed within the forbidden bounds, and must, therefore, be taken before our chief. He will set in judgment upon thee, and if thou givest not a good account of thyself, thy life will be forfeited."

"I fear nothing from Ivan," exclaimed Bertrand le Noir;—"he will protect me, I know, and from this day I shall become your comrade."

"Well, it may be so," answered Hubert, "and, for my own part, I have no wish to frighten you;—but I happen to know Black Ivan has no very great partiality for your late master, and if he should chance to take it into his head that your are come here as a spy he will not hesitate much about ordering you for immediate execution."

"I am no spy," exclaimed Bertrand, earnestly. "I am a fugitive from those who seek my life, and surely your captain will not refuse shelter to one who thus throws himself upon his protection?"

"Well," returned Hubert, "prove that you are deserving of his generosity, and I have no doubt it will be extended to you. But understand me;—our leader is not to be imposed upon by artful tales;—he will sift everything to the very bottom, and should you fail to satisfy him, I have told you what will be the consequence."

"I am willing to run the risk," answered Bertrand. "In my case I am threatened with danger, and I may as well meet death through his means, as from those who I know would show me no mercy."

"What crime hast thou committed, that thou hast been obliged to run so hastily for thy life?"

"I have conspired against the life of the king, and having failed in my object, have lost the protection of those who could and would have sheltered me."

"Humph!" ejaculated Hubert, "that, at least, will not obtain for thee much pity from Black Ivan. He is no traitor to his king, nor do I believe he will give shelter to one who has plotted against Richard Cœur de Lion."

"Will he then abandon me to my fate?" cried Bertrand, in an accent of despair.

"Nay, you needn't be afraid of that," replied Hubert, with indifference; "you have thought fit to venture thus near our retreat, and if Ivan does not order thee to be executed, he will send thee to one of the dungeons of our strong fortress, where thou wilt be vigilantly watched to prevent the possibility of thy escape."

"And wherefore should he do this?"

"To guard against thy betraying our present abode, to be sure," answered the ruffian. "Once already the troops have succeeded in dislodging us from our retreat, and, therefore, it is high time that we take care to prevent the repetition of such a disaster.—But what is this I see?" he continued, glancing at the dress of Bertrand le Noir;—"thy clothes are soiled and spotted with blood!"

"They—they are," stammered Bertrand, scarcely knowing how to answer.

"The marks are fresh, too," continued Hubert;—"by heaven, man, thou hast not long since committed a murder!"

"Nay, it was in self-defence," answered the other, confused by this unexpected charge;—"I was closely pursued, as I have already told thy comrade, and as no other way presented itself by which I might secure my escape, I turned,—grappled with my assailant, and slew him."

"Oh, well, that's all fair enough," exclaimed Hubert;—"when a man is pressed, anything is excusable; though, to tell you the truth, Black Ivan is rather particular in selecting his band, and never yet did a deliberate murderer find any encouragement or protection from him."

"I am not a deliberate murderer," answered Bertrand; "what I have done was in self-preservation, and was, in fact, forced upon me, by the circumstances in which I was placed."

"Aye, aye," replied Hubert, "our chief will see to that, you may rest assured, so now, as we are no great way from our place of destination, you must submit to have your eyes bandaged, in order to prevent any possibility of a discovery taking place. Nay, friend, you seem to object to being blindfolded;—perhaps you suspect that we mean you some foul play?"

"No," answered Bertrand, with hesitation;—"I was merely thinking that the precaution is unnecessary;—in fact, that as I am among strangers, it would be giving an opportunity for despatching me under an unfair advantage."

"Oh, you needn't be afraid of that," exclaimed Hubert;—"we are honourable men here, I can assure you, and that you will find out if ever you should have the luck to become one of our band."

Bertrand was about to offer some further remonstrance, but at that moment the ruffian he had first made acquaintance with, stepped behind him and threw a bandage over his eyes, which was secured before he had the power to offer any further resistance. This done, the robber, each of them, took hold of a hand, and he was thus led onwards uncertain as to which way he was going

---

CHAPTER XXXVII.

> " What means that awful voice?
> Whence comes it?"
>   THE SANCTUARY.

AFTER proceeding some distance, the robbers turned first on this side, and then on that, occasionally making a complete circuit, in order to deceive Bertand, both as to distance and the direction he was going. Then he had to ascend what appeared to be a lofty flight of steps, after which they walked some distance, on what appeared to be a level surface, and then descending another flight of steps, that seemed to be as lofty as the others, they walked onwards at a more rapid pace, till at length they suddenly came to a pause, and then the bandage being removed from his eyes, Bertrand perceived he was standing in a large gothic hall. In the midst of this was an immense table, along each side of which were seated a number of the robbers, whilst, on an elevated chair at the head, sat Black Ivan himself, like some regal personage in the midst of his vassals and dependants. As Bertrand gazed around he heard a murmur of dissatisfaction from the assembled brigands, but ere they could break out into a more open demonstration of their anger, at the presence of a stranger, the chief himself rose, and addressing himself to Hubert, enquired who the prisoner was, and why he had been brought to their retreat.

"He calls himself Bertrand le Noir, and——"

"Hah!" interrupted the brigand,—"that name alone is sufficient to convince me that he has come hither on no friendly errand to ourselves. He is a follower of Sir Gaston de Neville, and therefore do I command you to drag him forth to the forest, where he shall be hanged upon the branches of the first tree we come to, as a warning to all other foes who may come hither to entrap us."

"Hear me, Ivan," cried Bertrand, almost maddened by his terrors;— "I am no enemy of thine, but an unfortunate man, who has just escaped one perilous adventure to find himself involved in another."

"What proof canst thou give, sirrah, that thine intentions are not hostile to us."

"I have no proof," answered Bertrand, " unless, indeed, it is to be found in the fact of my being seen in the neighbourhood of your retreat. Had I entertained any treacherous thought, I should have taken care to avoid running into a danger like this."

"Thou dost deny then having come hither as a spy to betray us to our ever watchful enemies?"

"I do deny it;—I came hither as an unfortunate fugitive, to claim your protection in the hour of need."

"If that, indeed, be your only purpose," replied Black Ivan, "I shall be disposed to pause before I proceed to pass judgment. Our band requires strengthening, and we are willing to receive a few staunch and daring spirits, but none will be admitted into our society who cannot satisfactorily convince us that their designs are not hostile."

"Let your oath be adminstered," answered Bertrand, "and I will take it without hesitation,—nay, more, I swear that a more faithful comrade shall not be found in the whole band than I will be."

"But what if thou shouldst be despatched on any service against thy former master?" cried Black Ivan. "Wouldst thou still remember thine oath, and, at my command, plunge a dagger to his heart?"

"Art thou likely ever to employ me to execute such a deed?" asked Bertrand, with alarm.

"Why, possibly I may," replied Ivan, indifferently; "thou knowest well enough that I bear no good will towards thy late master, and it is, therefore, likely enough that I may, one of these days, take it into my head to put an end to the rivalry that at present exists between us. In that case, I should require the assistance of some one who knows every secret part of the castle, and who is so well fitted for the task as thyself?"

"I—I—I scarcely know how to answer you," stammered Bertrand, completely taken by surprise. "As a comrade, however, I would not forget the oath to obey my chieftain in all things, nor is it likely I should refuse to do even the deed you have named."

"Your reply must be more directly to the purpose," exclaimed Ivan, resolutely; "we can admit no half promises here, but must know you will bind yourself by our oath to do whatever you are bid."

"I will," replied Bertrand, finding that no equivocation would now serve him. "I have already told you that I am driven by circumstances to seek concealment amongst your band, and having once done so I shall be compelled to remain a brigand for the remainder of my life."

"Aye, aye, captain," exclaimed Hubert, "the fellow says truly enough there, for if once he should take it into his head to turn honest again, there would be little chance of escaping the gallows. In the first place, he has been engaged in a plot to take the king's life; and, in the second, he has committed a murder ——"

"Ah!—a murder, sayst thou?" vociferated the robber chief; "then is it to shield himself against the consequences of that crime that he has come to seek shelter and protection here?"

"I was on my way to join you," answered Bertrand le Noir, "when the event occurred of what this man speaks."

"Didst thou slay thy victim for the sake of possessing thyself of his money?"

"I did not;—in fact, he was pursuing me during my flight, and I turned upon him for self-preservation."

"Why, that makes all the difference," replied Ivan, "for in such a case it was, perhaps, thy only alternative. Men call Black Ivan cruel and blood-thirsty, but they know him not, or they would give him credit for a better heart than that; indeed, it is my chief care to prevent my followers from committing murder in all cases where their own personal safety will not suffer by their humanity."

"And yet," exclaimed Bertrand, "it is scarcely a moment since you asked whether I would hesitate to assassinate Sir Gaston de Neville."

"I did, but it was only to try thee."

"Then thou hast no intention to execute so terrible an act of vengeance upon him?"

"Why, at present he is safe," replied Ivan, "but I cannot say how long he will be so, unless he gives up all idea of robbing me of the girl I have set my heart on. He is my rival, as thou well knowest, and if my patience should be taxed too far, there is reason to fear I may be compelled to rid myself of him by means of violence."

"Pardon me, captain," interrupted Hubert, "but you hinted just now that this man should be hung up to the branches of one of the trees in the forest. I would now know whether execution is to be done upon him, for I see our comrades here are looking forward anxiously to a treat that they have not enjoyed since ——"

"Peace, Hubert," interrupted Ivan;—"at present, it is my command that no violence is offered to him. If he is indeed sincere, we may, perhaps, admit him to our band, but we must first satisfy ourselves that he has not come among us for any evil purposes."

"If I thought he had," exclaimed Hubert, drawing forth a poniard, "I would, without mercy, strike him dead at your feet."

Upon this, a murmur of approbation ran amongst the assembled brigands, and when all was again quiet, Ivan thus addressed them :—

"You are aware, comrades, how unceasingly I have watched over your interests from the first moment when I was chosen to fill the office I now hold. Your interest has ever been my care, and if, on the present occasion, I have resolved to spare the life of this man, it is that we may make of him a useful member of our band. That he is brave, I have had frequent opportunities of witnessing; and if we can but be assured of his good faith, I know he will prove a valuable acquisition to our numbers."

"Aye, aye," muttered several of the band, "but how are we to be assured of that?"

"How was I assured of the honour of any of you till you had been tried?" demanded Black Ivan. "And yet we have never had a traitor among us, nor one that would not die in defence of his captain and friends. At any rate, we will administer the oath to Bertrand le Noir, and then, if, at the end of three days, we find nothing against him, he shall go out with some of you and have an opportunity of manifesting the degree of zeal he feels in our cause."

"But in the meantime," observed one of the band, "he may escape and betray us to our enemies."

"Then be it your task to watch him," exclaimed Ivan. "Be you his guard, and if he escapes from us, you shall answer for it with your life."

"Believe me, I have no thought or wish to leave you," answered Bertrand. "It was my own voluntary act to come hither, and here I will remain if I have your permission to do so."

"Let him be sworn as one of our brothers," exclaimed Black Ivan; "he shall take the oath, and should he afterwards break it, the consequences will be his own immediate death."

"But what if he escapes and avoids the doom?" asked the same voice that had put the former question.

"He may escape for a time," replied Ivan, "but sooner or later he must meet the doom to which all traitors to our band are subject to."

At this juncture, Hubert advanced to adminster the oath, but ere he had commenced the ceremony, a brigand rushed breathless into the hall.

"Brothers," he exclaimed, "I call upon ye for vengeance! One of our band has been foully murdered, and his blood cried aloud upon us for retribution!"

"What mean these words?" cried Black Ivan, rising hastily from his seat;—"speak, sirrah, and end our doubts at once by explaining the meaning of thy words."

"I have just heard," replied the brigand, "that Ranulph, the Avenger, has been murdered in the prison to which he had been sent after his unsuccessful attempt on the life of King Richard."

"Hah!—Ranulph murdered, sayst thou?" exclaimed Ivan, in a voice almost choked with rage. Ranulph, our gallant friend and comrade, for whose escape we had just formed so safe a plan."

"It is even so," replied the other; "he was found stabbed to the heart, and unfortunately the assassin contrived to escape before the murder was discovered."

"By heavens the villain shall be hunted out, even if he has sought refuge in the uttermost corner of the earth!" exclaimed Black Ivan, fiercely. "I will, myself, never rest until the assassin has been made to pay, with his own blood, the price of our comrade's life."

"It must be some one belonging to the prison," observed Hubert;—"perhaps the gaoler himself, and if so, it shall not be many hours before he feels the vengeance he has called down upon his own head."

"The gaoler, I believe, is innocent," replied the other; "at least so I should suppose from the information I have been able to gather. It seems that the assassin obtained admittance to his cell in the disguise of a friar, and having committed the hellish deed, he left the place without any suspicion having been raised as to the cowardly act he had committed."

"And is there no clue to guide us," asked Black Ivan, "by which we may discover who it was that entered the cell disguised as you have said?"

"None whatever,—Ranulph was speechless when discovered, and died shortly afterwards without being able to describe who was his murderer."

"But he obtained admittance, you say, as a friar?" exclaimed the chief of the robbers."

"He did."

"Now then," said Black Ivan, addressing himself sternly to Bertrand, "I would ask whether you happened to have heard anything of this bloody deed before you came here to ask our protection?"

"Nothing whatever."

"Humph!—you knew, however, something, I believe, of the man that has been thus foully murdered?"

"Certainly,—he was engaged with me to procure the king's death."

"And fell into the hands of justice whilst you contrived to escape."

"He was unfortunate in that respect, it must be acknowledged," answered Bertrand. "I, however, was not to blame for securing my own safety, seeing that if I had been taken, it would not have made his fate any better."

"Well then, I will now ask you a plain question," exclaimed Black Ivan; "was not yours the hand that struck the dagger to poor Ranulph's heart?"

"Are you serious in asking such a question?"

"I'll have a clear and straight forward answer to my question; "was it not your hand, I again ask, that struck the fatal blow —— ?"

"N—n—no—certainly not," stammered the affrighted Bertrand le Noir.

"And yet," exclaimed Ivan, "I could almost take it upon myself to swear that you know more of this damnable affair than you think fit to acknowledge."

"And why should you believe me capable of the deed?"

"Because," replied the chief, "you had your own purposes to serve. Ranulph had been tortured, and there might have been reason to fear that he would at length be compelled to confess who were his accomplices in the late attempt against the king's life."

"But who says," asked Bertrand, "that the noble knight, my master, had anything to do with the conspiracy?"

"I say so," replied Ivan; "nay, if there should be need for it, I can prove the charge. Therefore, I say there is sufficient ground to suppose that he dreaded an exposure from the lips of Ranulph, the Avenger, and that he employed you as the guilty instrument that was to commit the murder."

"Let him die then," vociferated every voice.

"Aye, blood for blood is fair play," answered Black Ivan. "That our comrade has been murdered, is most certain, and it now only remains for us to discover who was the assassin; at present, suspicion points towards Bertrand le Noir, and, unless he can prove his innocence, he shall die within an hour."

"It is impossible to prove my innocence," exclaimed Bertrand;—"but again I declare the deed was none of mine."

"Liar!" vociferated a hollow voice at the other end of the hall.

"Hah!—there is an invisible witness against thee," cried Black Ivan. "Thou hast heard thine asseverations of innocence denied, and thy cheek grows pale with conscious guilt?"

"This is some trap to ensnare me," exclaimed Bertrand, in an agony of terror. "If there is any one present who is prepared to charge me with this crime, I pray you to bring him forward."

"Go, Hubert," said the chief;—"haste to the other end of the hall, and bring forward the man whose evidence we require to establish this caitiff's guilt."

Hubert proceeded as he had been directed, but in a few moments afterwards he returned, declaring that though all present had heard the voice of denunciation, no one was able to say from whence it came. This announcement created a visible alarm among all present.

"Thou seest, Bertrand," exclaimed Black Ivan, "that there is more against thee than belong to this earth. An invisible agent is present, and through his evidence I do adjudge thee to immediate death."

"Mercy!—mercy!" cried the culprit, convulsively;—"give me a short time, and I shall be able to prove that this charge is utterly without foundation."

"I will not grant thee an instant," replied Ivan. "Thou hadst no mercy on thy victim, nor shalt thou have any from us. Ranulph was our comrade, and terribly will we avenge his fate."

"I have been charged falsely," exclaimed Bertrand le Noir. "The voice thou hast heard, is some trick to urge thee on to vengeance, and all I ask of thee, is time to disprove the accusation brought against me."

"I tell thee there is no trick in it," answered Ivan; "the voice thou hast heard proceeded from a supernatural agent, and from that evidence alone I do adjudge thee to die for thy crime."

"Shall we hang him like a dog as he is?" asked Hubert, advancing in readiness to bear off the prisoner,

"No," answered Ivan, "his doom shall be more sudden ;—this ¡
be the scene of his punishment, and thou, thyself, shalt be his ex
tioner."

"Cheerfully,—thou wilt have him hung then from one of you
rafters."

"No,—take this axe, Hubert, and when I give the signal, by ç
ping my hands three times, let the instrument of death do its work.

"And yet, such a fate is far too good for the murderer of our c
rade."

"Nevertheless, sirrah, it is my will, and see that thou performes
Advance, Bertrand,—lay thy neck across this stool, and if thou hast
prayers to offer up let them be said quickly, for thou hast not many n
minutes to live !"

With these words, the captive was forced to the place appointed
his doom, and the ruff was taken from his neck, and Black Ivan
in the act of giving the concerted signal, when the mysterious voice
again heard.

"Hold !" it exclaimed ;—"let not your judgment be too sudden
spare your prisoner for a few days, and then, if he confess not his cri
let him suffer the death he so justly merits."

"Hubert," cried the robber chief, "you have heard the words of
invisible witness ;—let him be obeyed, and to you do I consign the ¡
of the prisoner, until we have seen whether he will confess throu
whose means it was that he murdered our comrade."

Against this command there was no appeal ; Bertrand was theref
released for the present from his perilous situation, and having b
conveyed to a dungeon, he was there left to ruminate alone upon
mysterious events that had brought him to his perilous situation.

CHAPTER XXXVIII.

"I come in the king's name
To bid thee to the royal presence ;—nay, refuse not,
For I am armed with power, and will use it
Should need appear."

THE BONDSMAN.

NOTWITHSTANDING the tender care bestowed upon Rebecca by h
father and lover, after the failure of Black Ivan's last attempt to car
her off, it was some time before she recovered from the effects of t
terror, which had for a period deprived her of all recollection. By a
by, however, she became conscious of the presence of those she love
and then, as the remembrance of all that had passed flashed upon h
mind she convulsively grasped the hand of her father, and, in piteou
accents, implored him to protect her from the evil practices of her unr
lenting persecutors.

"I will, I will, my child," exclaimed the old man, endeavouring
conceal the emotion that shook his soul,—"already thou hast seen th
the hand of Heaven is outstretched for thy preservation, and all th
mortal can do to accomplish thy safety shall be tried whilst life is giv
me."

"I know it will," cried Rebecca, gratefully,—"and thou, too, Reube
Grenard,—thou wilt not suffer them to execute the base design of tea
ing me from thee for ever ?"

"Rather would I perish than lose the beloved object of my earthly adoration," exclaimed the younger Israelite, in a tone that denoted firmness and resolution. "Thou hast heard my vows, Rebecca, and though thine enemies relax not in their endeavours to accomplish thy destruction, yet I will ever be ready to thwart their designs."

"Thou shalt have a husband's right to do so," said Isaac, breaking the pause that had followed these last words ;—"yes, my children, I will no longer delay my consent to thine immediate union, and unless thou, Rebecca, wouldst postpone the happy day, I declare, that at the end of a week, thou shalt become the bride of Reuben Grenard."

"So soon, dear father?" cried the blushing girl.

"Aye, my daughter," he replied, "why not? Thy lover is worthy of the prize I am about to bestow upon him, and when once thou art his bride the persecutions of thine enemies will cease for ever."

"Alas! dear father, I fear not," answered Rebecca. "I, perhaps, shall no longer be the object against whom their malice will be directed, but will they not turn all the might of their disappointment and revenge upon their successful rival?"

"And if they do," replied Reuben, "I shall not shrink from the duty I shall then have taken upon myself, to protect thee even at the hazard of my own life. But let us hope that you anticipate dangers which never may threaten us; Sir Gaston de Neville has already sworn to procure my destruction, and since he has thus been foiled in accomplishing his designs let us hope that Heaven will yet protect us from his foul arts."

"Yet there is another that we have to fear," answered Rebecca, timidly; "Black Ivan, as we have seen, follows the impetuous torrent

No. 25

of his will, and even though I become thy bride, he will not cease to pursue me until I am utterly in his power."

"Thou forgettest, child," exclaimed her father, "that the laws will protect thee from the vile arts of such men as those we speak of. King Richard is a just and righteous sovereign, and never will he suffer one class of his subjects to be oppressed by another, even though, one be a Jew and her enemy a Christian."

"But the people murmur against the favour he has shown our race," answered Rebecca. "They are dissatisfied at the protection that has been bestowed upon us, and even Richard, powerful and gallant as he is, dares not tempt his subjects too far lest they break into open rebellion."

"In that case, then," exclaimed Reuben, "it will be necessary that our own people adopt means for our own protection from the rabble that assails us. We are numerous, and why, therefore, should we not take up arms for our own protection?"

"Because the time has not yet arrived," replied Isaac;—"at present, we must bow our necks to the yoke; it is the will of Heaven that it should be so, and therefore it becomes our duty to submit yet a little longer."

"And if we do so," exclaimed Reuben, "have we not a right to expect the forbearance of those who are opposed to us in religion?"

"Their own creed should teach them to love all mankind as their brethren," replied Isaac; "they boast, indeed, that it does so, and yet a day never passes without some act of violence being perpetrated against a people who never interfere with them. Still, I say again to thee, let us not rashly quarrel with them, but rather seek to allay their fury by meekness and submission."

"You speak as an old man," exclaimed Reuben, "and therefore your words carry with them a weight that I cannot resist. I will yield myself to your advice, and may Heaven reward us with its assistance against the oppressors who have so long trodden us beneath their feet."

"Then," cried the old Israelite, "is is understood that your nuptials with Rebecca will take place at the expiration of a week?"

"Need I declare," exclaimed the lover, rapturously, "how happy your words have made me?"

"But why art thou silent, my child?" asked the father, anxiously;— "thine eyes are full of tears too, and thy downcast looks seems to say that thou art not anxious to change the state in which thou hast thus long lived."

"Pardon me, dear father," cried the maiden, throwing her arms affectionately round the neck of her parent. "Pardon me for appearing thus averse to thy will, but the thought of leaving thee, even though it be with my dear Reuben, fills my soul with sadness and despair."

"Nay, girl," exclaimed the old man, "thou shalt not quit the roof that has sheltered thee from infancy to womanhood. This house is large enough for all our purposes, and never will we part until death removes me from this world of trouble and turmoil. So cheer thee, and look forward with hope to happier times."

Rebecca was about to reply, but ere she could do so, Jonah entered the room, to say that Hugh Tiptoft, the captain of the royal archers, was at the door, on a message from the king, and desired an immédiate audience. This message filled the heart of Rebecca with new cause for dread, which being perceived by her father, he took her hand, and in a tone of encouragement, said :—

"Be not alarmed, my child, but recollect that we have nothing to fear from Richard. He is our friend, and I dare venture to assert that his officer comes on a message rather peaceful than otherwise."

"Shall I bring the man in?" asked Jonah.

"Aye,—but stay,—does he come alone?"

"No,—he is accompanied by a small party of his archers."

"Ah!" cried Rebecca, "then his errand here is not so peaceful as you just now anticipated!"

"That we shall see," answered her father;—"at present, however, I see no cause to suspect danger, since it is not unusual to send a small body of the military, whenever the king desires to communicate with his people. Besides, were violence intended, Hugh Tiptoft would not have waited thus long at the door when he could so easily have forced an entrance in spite of any resistance of ours to prevent him."

"I am to bring him in, then?" said Jonah, though not without a slight manifestation of fear.

"Certainly," answered the old man, "but if it may be so, I would have him admitted alone. See, however, that his men are well provided for in the battery, and let it be thy care, Jonah, that thy master's name, for hospitality, suffers not, through any niggard conduct of thine own."

Thus commanded, Jonah departed, and in a brief space of time afterwards, returned with Hugh Tiptoft, who he had no sooner ushered in, than, taking his own departure, he hastened away to fulfil the duties of hospitality imposed upon him by his venerable master. On the other hand, the captain of the royal archers, seemed fully aware of his own consequence, and seating himself with all the familiarity of an old acquaintance, he exclaimed authoritatively :—

"I am commissioned by the king, old man, to require your immediate presence at the palace. You, of course, know that such a command is imperative, and it is therefore to be hoped that I shall not have to use force in the execution of my duty."

"The king's commands," answered Isaac, "have ever been my law, and in the present instance I shall obey them cheerfully. But you speak of using force, most noble captain,—surely King Richard has seen no cause for treating me with harshness?"

"His majesty is the best judge of that," replied Hugh Tiptoft, in a tone of indifference, "I am but his servant, and you, as a subject, have but to obey, without question as to his motives for sending me on this message."

"Tell me, I implore you," cried Rebecca, whose terrors was now roused to the highest pitch, "is there any danger to my father, or have we the king's word for his safety?"

"You have heard my errand, and I can tell you nothing more," answered the captain of the archers.

"Did the king seem angry when he sent you?" demanded Reuben Grenard, to whom the suspicion of some lurking danger had communicated itself.

"You can satisfy yourself, young man," answered Hugh Tiptoft, "for I have also orders to convey you to the palace, in case you happened to be here."

"Hah!" exclaimed the aged Israelite, with perturbation that he could no longer conceal, "then there is some charge against us, and perhaps our lives are in danger."

"Why, for that matter," replied the captain, coldly, "you ought to be the best judge whether there is any grounds for a charge, such as you speak of. For my own part, I am only a servant to his majesty, and, of course, know nothing of the secrets, that do not concern me."

"Oh, keep us not in this dreadful suspense," cried Rebecca, trembling with emotion ;—" pity us, I implore thee, and if it is in thy power, assure us that the danger we apprehend is groundless."

"Well," exclaimed Hugh Tiptoft,—"since a pretty girl has asked me the question, I can no longer hold out. So do not look quite so frightened, my dear, for, between you and I, something strikes me, that neither your father, nor this youngster, have anything to fear just at present from the king."

"Perhaps you are certain that no danger threatens them ?" she said, anxiously.

"Come, come, my girl, you must not press me too far upon that subject," answered the other, more good-naturedly. "I have already told you more than I had any business to do, and if I open my mouth too much, it may chance that I shall get into a scrape, that it won't be very easy to get out of. So now, having done thus much for you I would fain ask a reward for my services."

"Name it," she replied, "and if it be a reasonable one, you will find my father no niggard, I can promise you."

"Nay, your father, perhaps, will refuse the reward I ask."

"Why this hesitation ?" asked the old man ; "if thou hast aught to ask, let the request be made, and——"

"You will refuse me."

"Perhaps not," returned Isaac ;—" so be brief, man, and I will be equally prompt with my reply."

"Well, then, old man, all I ask for my civility is, that I may be permitted to take a chaste salute from those pouting coral lips of your daughter."

"Hah !" vociferated the Israelite, " wouldst thou insult the maiden, with thy coarse ribald jests ?"

"Upon my life, it was no jest, old man," answered the captain, with his usual cool effrontery. "The girl is pretty, and where is the man that can boast of being proof against such beauty as hers."

"Peace, sirrah !" exclaimed the father, indignantly ;—" thou hast insulted her enough, already,—and I command thee, utter not another word, that shall bring into her cheeks the crimson blush of shame."

"Nonsense !" retorted Hugh Tiptoft; "you cannot be churlish enough to refuse me so trifling a favour as that I have asked ?"

"Add not to the insult thou hast already offered," cried Isaac, resolutely. "My daughter is no wanton upon whom to practice thine illtimed ribaldry, and therefore I charge thee speak no more upon a subject so offensive as this."

"You refuse my poor request then ?"

"I do."

"Then here goes to take the kiss," exclaimed Hugh Tiptoft, and he was hastening towards the maiden for the purpose of putting his threat into execution, when Reuben Grenard, who had hitherto been a silent observer of what had taken place, rushed fiercely upon the libertine, and seizing him with the strength of a giant in his arms, hurled him, with all the force he could muster, to the further end of the room. Enraged at this interference, Hugh instantly snatched forth his sword, and would have plunged it into the body of his antagonist had not Rebecca foreseen his intention in time, and throwing herself upon the bosom of her lover, thus offered an effectual screen against the weapon of the incensed soldier. Fortunately, too, Hugh's anger soon evaporated, and once more sheathing the sword which had been so vengefully plucked forth, he said, with affected carelessness :—

"Egad, young fellow, you may congratulate yourself upon a narrow escape from death. I, however, war not against woman, as it was impossible to slay the guilty without first killing the innocent, I thus defer the punishment I had meditated to some better opportunity."

"Let me entreat thee to think no further of this matter," exclaimed the old man, earnestly, "Reuben did but his duty in repelling thy rudeness, and if thou hast a spark of honour in thy bosom, thou wilt not seek to revenge thyself upon one who, after all, performed but a duty that he owed to the mistress of his affections."

"Well, answered Hugh Tiptoft, "for the present, at any rate, he is safe; your presence, as well as that of this reliever of distressed damsels, is now anxiously looked for by the king, and I dare not tarry longer in the execution of my errand."

"Are we to go with you as prisoners?" asked the elder Jew.

"Not unless you refuse to obey his majesty's commands."

"Which," answered Isaac, "neither Reuben or myself are likely to do."

"In that case," replied Hugh Tiptoft, "my gallant archers can return to their quarters as soon as they please. They merely accompanied me hither in case you should prove refractory, but as there are no symptoms of anything of that kind, you will now please to set forth with all despatch, and I will content myself by following at a short distance, just to see that you play no slippery tricks by running away instead of obeying the king's absolute commands."

In such a case as this, there was, of course, no alternative, and bidding a hasty adieu to Rebecca, who they implored to support herself with all the courage she could till their return, they set forth on their way towards the palace of King Richard.

CHAPTER XXXIX.

" Speak, stranger, and reveal your mystery ;
    Say why thou com'st thus suddenly upon me,
    To fright me with thy presence."
                                        LUSIGNON.

UPON being left to herself, Rebecca gave way to the racking suspicions that filled her soul, as to the motives that could have induced the king to send for her father and Reuben without notice of his intentions. Used as she was to treachery, she could not divest herself of a fear which assailed her that some scheme was in progress against them, and that they had only been drawn away from home in order that she might be left unprotected, whilst others would be at hand to carry into execution some plan that had been formed for her destruction. Full of these fears, she was about to summon Jonah to her presence, but as she rose from her seat to do so, the door of her apartment slowly opened, and the figure of an aged female advanced towards her. Rebecca would have called loudly for the presence of the domestics, but the old woman evidently perceived her intention, and placing her finger upon her lips, she made signs for her to remain silent, and then approaching yet nearer to our heroine, said, in a low tone :—

"Hush, girl, or I am lost! breathe not a word above a whisper, for should I be discovered, a gloomy dungeon, nay, perhaps a horrible death, will be the doom of the terrified being who now throws herself upon your compassion."

"Who and what art thou?" asked the terrified maiden.

"It matters little to thee who I am," answered the old woman, "and it must satisfy thee to know that my life is forfeited whenever chance should throw me into the hands of my enemies."

"Art thou come to ask for concealment?" asked Rebecca, startled by the mysterious manner of her visitor.

"I ask for nothing but that thou wilt remain quiet," answered the old woman. "Thou seest one who comes on an errand of pity, and who has risked thus much in order that she may serve a wretched creature in her last dying agonies."

"Ah!" exclaimed Rebecca, with terror, "what meanest thou by these words of fearful import—speak to me—answer me quickly, I beseech thee, and say who it is that stands thus upon the very threshold of eternity?"

"One whom thou hast served before," answered the old woman;—"nay, to keep thee no longer in suspense, Meg of Finchley,—she whom thou call the Weird Woman of the Heath,—is now at the point of death, and having something on her mind nearly touching thine own welfare, she cannot die in peace until the story is told to thyself."

"Where shall I find her?" asked Rebecca, shocked at the news she had just heard.

"In a wretched hovel, scarcely half a mile from hence," replied the mysterious visitor. "I found her by the road-side in a fit, and having known something of her in former days, conveyed her to the place where she now lies, and have 'tended upon her until I received her request to come hither in search of you."

"Is she in immediate danger?" asked Rebecca, anxiously.

"So much so," replied the old woman, "that it is almost doubtful whether she will survive my return."

"Then hasten back," cried our heroine, "and say that I will visit her immediately after the return of my father."

"Nay, thou must not defer thine errand of pity even for a single moment," exclaimed the other, earnestly. "I tell thee she has something of the greatest importance to reveal, and thou knowest not the feverish anxiety with which the poor dying creature waits for thy presence."

"It is impossible to go at present," returned Rebecca; "my father is now from home, and if thou wilt describe the place where I may find the unhappy creature, I will hasten to her immediately upon his return."

"It will be too late," cried the old woman; "death cannot be delayed even for a single moment, and unless thou goest with me at once, the secret will die with her for ever."

"It is impossible that I can leave at present," answered Rebecca,—"my father will not be absent much longer, and should he find me from home at his return, he will be terrified lest some evil has befallen me."

"Nay, think not of that at such a moment as this," exclaimed the woman. "Recollect a dying fellow-creature makes it her last request that you will visit her, and it would be inflicting a heavy disappointment were you to neglect her injunctions."

"Stay, then," cried Rebecca, "till I have told Jonah that I am going out and shall return again shortly."

"That must not be," answered the other; "none must know of thy departure but myself."

"Ah! then perhaps some treachery is intended!"

"Psha! why dost thou think so?" demanded the old woman. "Is it an uncommon thing for dying people to express a wish to see those they most respect in their last moments?"

"What, then, needs all this secresy?" demanded Rebecca; "if thy purposes are fair, why should not I leave word at home where I am gone to with thee?"

"Beware!" answered the other, "I have already told thee I am in danger from those that would gladly deliver me into the hands of avenging justice. Should it be known that you are gone to the hovel where Meg of Finchley lies at the point of death, others would follow us there, and I should be betrayed into the hands of those who seek my destruction."

"Then leave me for the present," cried our heroine, "and I will follow immediately after my father's return home."

"That I cannot do," replied the other, "for I swore to the poor gasping wretch I left behind, not to return to her without thee. My word is pledged, I tell thee, girl, and fallen though I am, I will not break it to one who is standing upon the verge of eternity."

"But I will follow thee anon," cried Rebecca; "I will but wait to see my father on his return, and then hasten to join thee wherever thou shalt direct. Say then, where thou art to be found, and thou shalt see that I will keep my word."

"It is in vain to urge me," replied the woman; "I am resolved, and am not to be moved by any arguments thou canst urge."

"And yet a few minutes since, thou saidst thy life would be in danger shouldst thou be seen."

"I did so, and spoke the honest truth."

"Then why remain here to expose thyself to danger?" asked Rebecca. "My father may chance to know thee, and should he be acquainted with any crime thou hast committed, his sense of justice will compel him to order thine immediate arrest."

"And should he do so," answered the other, "I would not answer for his own safety an hour afterwards. I am persecuted, and hunted down, girl, yet there are those who would revenge me, should I fall in the manner you have mentioned."

"Dost thou threaten woman?"

"I do but warn thee of the consequences that would follow, in the event of my falling by treachery."

"Then here let our conference end," exclaimed Rebecca; "I have all along doubted thee, but now I feel assured that thou comest here the messenger of evil deeds."

"Nay, there thou wrongst me," returned the other, earnestly. "I came hither on an errand of kindness, and my motives are misconstrued even by her whom I would most have served."

"How am I to know that thou art not an enemy?" asked our heroine.

"By the fact of my venturing here, when by so doing I may sacrifice my own life."

"And how wilt thou satisfy me that thou art commissioned to bear the message thou hast delivered?"

"Follow me, and thou wilt be convinced of it," replied the old woman. "Meg will tell thee that she it was who sent me on this errand, and then, perhaps, thou wilt do justice to one who has risked so much in thy service."

"But if this is a snare, I shall never see her whose name has even now been made use of."

"I tell thee, girl, thou hast no snare to fear from me," exclaimed the woman. "I have come to deliver a message as I received, and it now only remains for yourself to say whether you wilt go with me or not."

"Well, then, I will rely upon the honesty of thy purpose," answered Rebecca, after a pause of short duration. "I will accompany thee though, to confess the truth, I would gladly wait till the return of my father."

"And thus spoil all by thine own obstinacy," cried the other, with bitter emphasis;—"however, thou knowest best, and, therefore, I leave it all to thyself."

"It shall be even as thou hast said," replied our heroine; "if Meg is indeed dying, as thou declarest, it is a duty I owe to a fellow creature to visit her in this extremity of danger."

"Thou hast said well, girl," cried the old woman, in a voice of half suppressed exultation. "Meg told me thy heart was easily acceptible to pity, and thou knowest not how it will joy the poor old soul to see thee. I dare venture to say that she has a secret to tell, well worth the hearing, and, therefore, the sooner we take our departure from hence the better."

Whilst the mysterious visitor was thus speaking, Rebecca attired herself for walking out, and as soon as her simple toilet was completed, she directed the woman to lead the way with all the expedition she could. But the other paused, ere she obeyed this mandate, and once more approaching our heroine, she replied :—

"Be cautious how you leave the place, or we shall be discovered; no one must observe our departure, and, therefore, I again warn you to step lightly towards the door, lest any prying eyes should chance to be directed towards us. So now follow me, girl, and I will lead you ere long to the place I have spoken of."

Without making any reply to this, our heroine cautiously left the room, and treading closely in the footsteps of her conductress, she was soon on the outside of the house, from whence they directed their way towards a lane, which, at that period, led over what forms at the present time, the eastern suburb of London. For nearly a quarter of an hour they continued their way in silence; and then turning down another lane more obscure even than the former, they, within a few seconds afterwards, found themselves standing in front of a wretchedly delapidated hovel, the tottering fragments of which seemed to threaten its immediate destruction. Here the old woman paused for an instant, and then beckoning to her companion, entered the low doorway, which stood ready open for their reception.

CHAPTER XL.

"Alas! 'tis thine to triumph o'er me now,—
    To bring me to thy feet an humble supplicant
    For mercy from a foe that I despise."

                                        LORENZO.

THE gloomy and desolate appearance of the only room belonging to the hut, inspired the heart of our heroine with the most melancholy forebodings, and her first impulse was to effect her retreat with all possible despatch, lest some new act of treachery had been devised against her. The old woman, however, perceived what was passing in her mind, and

throwing herself suddenly between the affrighted girl and the door, she peremptorily desired her to remain where she was.

"Ah!" cried Rebecca, in a voice that betrayed the agony which wrung her soul, "am I then deceived, and entrapped into the snares of my enemies!"

"Peace, girl!" exclaimed the old woman, pointing to what appeared to be a human form huddled up on a heap of straw in one corner of the the wretched chamber;—"yonder lies the person you come hither to see. Behold her helpless condition, and then believe, if you can, that mischief is intended you."

"If it is really Meg of Finchley," cried our heroine, gazing earnestly towards the spot indicated, "why does she not speak to confirm the truth of what you have said!"

"Probably because she has lost the power of utterance," answered the other. "She was growing weaker and weaker when I left, and I dare say the poor soul can now only converse with you in whispers."

"But she does not even make a sign that she recognises me," returned Rebecca, doubtfully.

"Thou art wrong, girl," exclaimed the old woman;—"see—she waves her hand, as if she would have thee approach. Go nearer to her, wench, and receive the last words of a poor expiring fellow-creature."

"I dare not!" murmured Rebecca, shrinking back with horror, and burying her face in her hands.

"And why dost thou not dare?"

"Because something assures me that I have been deceived."

"Nay, why these unjust suspicions?" demanded the old woman, angrily. "Have I not brought thee hither thus far in safety, and

No. 26

wouldst thou now leave the place without executing the errand of charit
that brought thee hither?"

"Woman!" exclaimed Rebecca, firmly, "if thou dost indeed speak th
truth, afford me some proof that I may rely upon the words thou has
spoken."

"I can give you no further proof," answered the other; "you hav
ventured thus far with me, and it now only remains for you to hear th
communication yonder poor wretch is so anxious to make."

"Then, do you go to her," said Rebecca; "say that I am here, anc
if she then expresses a wish to speak with me, I will no longer hesitat
to approach."

"And while I do so," replied the old woman, "you will make th
best use of the opportunity that offers, by effecting your escape fron
yonder door."

"Nay, you wrong me by such a suspicion."

"Well, be that as it may, I shall not obey your bidding in this case,'
answered the other. "So now go to the suffering wretch, and, les
there should be any secret passing, I will go and stand outside the door
until your conference is ended."

And so saying, the hag took her departure, leaving our heroine ful
of doubt and terror, as to the result of an adventure to which she had s
foolishly trusted herself. At length, however, she resolved to effect he
escape, if it were yet possible to do so, and she was about to make
rush towards the door, for the purpose of carrying this design into effect
when a rustling amongst the straw caused her to turn her head in tha
direction, and as she did so, instead of seeing the attenuated form o
Meg of Finchley, she beheld the hated figure of Sir Gaston de Neville
A loud scream of terror followed this fatal discovery, and she was pre
paring to rush distractedly from the hovel, when the heartless libertine
darting forward, seized her in his arms, and uttering a malignant laugl
of derision, exclaimed:—

"Whither so fast, my pretty one?—What! wouldst thou flee fron
me, after all the pains I have been at to secure a prize I have so much
desired?"

"Villain! release me, I command you!" gasped the struggling girl
in vain trying to escape from his loathed presence. "Let me go, Sir Gas
ton de Neville, or my cries shall bring to my assistance those who know
how to punish treachery like thine."

"Aye, aye," exclaimed the recreant, "storm away, my dear; vent al
your indignation, and when you have done, I will tell you what brough
me hither."

"Alas! I know that already," sobbed his victim in accents of de
spair; "you came to entrap me into your toils, and care not by wha
treacherous arts your infamous designs are accomplished."

"And whose fault is it that I have thus stooped to make thee mine by
deceit?" asked Sir Gaston de Neville. "Have I not sought by every
means in my power to obtain thee by fair means, and with thine own
consent?"

"And if I have refused to listen to thee," answered Rebecca, scorn
fully, "was it not because thy propositions were such as no virtuou
woman should listen to?"

"Not if they are prudes like thyself, girl," returned the knight
"however, I have at length succeeded in getting thee once more into
my power, and by the heaven above us, we part not on such easy term
as we have done before."

"Am I then to remain a prisoner in this wretched hovel?" asked our heroine, in despair.

"No," replied Sir Gaston, "thou shalt be better lodged than that, I promise thee. I had thee brought hither, in order the better to deceive those who will shortly be searching for thee, but it is now my intention to convey thee to my castle, where thou wilt occupy the apartments formerly assigned to thee."

"Oh, Sir Knight, in pity let me go!" cried the alarmed maiden; "release me, and thou shalt ever have the prayers of one who can pardon the treachery that has been practised."

"Psha! I care not for thy prayers, girl," exclaimed the knight, scornfully; "say thou wilt freely become mine, and I promise thee return, every luxury that wealth can bestow."

"Thou knowest I cannot be thine," she replied.

"And wherefore, most obdurate maiden?"

"The difference of our religions forbids the union," she replied.

"And is that the only obstacle?"

"It is not; I am already, as thou well knowest, betrothed to another."

"Then that other must be content to lose thee," answered Sir Gaston, with indifference to her appeal. "The weak must yield to the powerful, and, therefore, Reuben Grenard,—for such, I believe is the name of your lover, must e'en be content to look out for some other bride."

"Wretch!" exclaimed Rebecca, indignantly, "dost thou then believe that I will ever consent to be thine?"

"I care not whether thou dost or not," answered the other, unmoved by her tears and reproaches! "at present, the advantage is mine; thou art in my power, girl, and it will be my own fault if ever thou contrivest to escape, as thou didst on a former occasion."

"But there are those," replied Rebecca, "who will never relax from their exertions until they have obtained the retribution thy crimes so justly merit."

"Tush! thou speakest of thy father and this Reuben Grenard, my rival for thy love! They, thou sayst, will raise a cry of vengeance against me, but let them beware, for I have the means to crush them like reptiles beneath my feet!"

"But the king knows thy crimes, Sir Knight, and from him, at least, we may obtain that justice which it would be in vain to expect from thee."

"The king, girl," answered Sir Gaston, "knows better than to interfere with his more powerful subjects. Prince John, his brother, aspires to the throne, and should the present sovereign displease his barons, it would not be long before he found himself deposed and driven from the country."

"Ha!" exclaimed Rebecca, "dost thou acknowledge thyself then to be a traitor to thy king?"

"To thyself, I hesitate not to say it," answered the knight, "because there is little fear of thy ever having an opportunity to betray my secret. Richard, however, suspects me not at present, and perhaps, I may never take part against him, unless he unwisely interferes to disgrace me, for having taken thee from home against thy will. But come, we are wasting time, and thus giving an advantage to those who will soon, I have no doubt, be searching for thee."

"Oh, let me again entreat thee to have compassion upon a poor helpless maiden," cried Rebecca, fondly hoping, in her despair, that she might yet prevail upon him to release her. "Remember, I implore you, that I have been foully deceived in being brought hither, and reflect upon the agony that would rend your own heart, were a daughter of yours placed in a situation similar to this."

"I will think of nothing but the accomplishment of my purposes," answered Sir Gaston de Neville, resolutely. "Thou hast hitherto foiled me, girl, and now I swear that all thy prayers for mercy shall be disregarded."

"Where is the woman that brought me hither?" asked Rebecca, gazing round her in despair; "let her be summoned to thy presence, and perhaps, her entreaties, coupled with my own, will not be thrown away, even upon the stern heart of Sir Gaston de Neville."

"She is gone," answered the knight; "when thou wert brought here, her mission was ended, and, therefore, she has wisely taken her departure from the place."

"Ah!" groaned the despairing Jewess, "then every hope has indeed forsaken me?"

"Thou mayst well say so," replied Sir Gaston, "for thou art now so completely in my power, that no earthly assistance can aid thee. In a short time thou wilt be within the walls of my strong fortress, and then I may bid defiance even to the king himself, to obtain thy deliverance."

"Monster!" cried our heroine, summoning all her energy, "dost thou not dread the vengeance of heaven, for this base outrage upon the helpless victim of thine unbridled passion?"

"Girl!" exclaimed the other, contemptuously, "I dread nothing, when my own will directs me."

"And yet," she replied, "thou art one of those, who, not long since, fought in Palestine for religion."

"Nay, I fought for glory," he exclaimed; "strife is my favourite element, and my restless soul is never so easy as when I am engaged in scenes of blood and warfare, at present, I am constrained to live in inglorious repose, and since no other game offers itself, I have resolved to pursue the enterprise in which I am now engaged."

And I, unhappily, am your victim."

"Aye, if you can call it an unhappiness to be loved by one who has ample wealth for you to share."

"I seek not wealth," she replied; "in humility I have been brought up, and all I ask is, to be permitted to pass the remainder of my days with those amongst whom I have lived."

"But since I have willed it otherwise, you must e'en submit," answered Sir Gaston, and stamping his foot three or four times violently upon the ground, he was quickly joined by some of his dependants, who, rushing into the hovel, threw a cloak over the head and face of the maiden, and then hurried her from the place. Thus muffled up, it was impossible for her to call out for assistance, and, nearly fainting, she was conveyed to the castle of Sir Gaston de Neville.

CHAPTER XLI.

"I warn thee, man, of dangers that are near;—
Of deeds suggested by the busy brains
Of foes, who seek thy blood."

THE MALEDICTION.

IT is now necessary that we follow Isaac of Tadcaster, and Reuben Grenard, who, accompanied by Hugh Tiptoft, proceeded to the royal palace at Westminster, and shortly after their arrival there, were ushered into the presence of the king. Uncertain of the object for which they had been thus summoned, they now threw themselves at the feet of the sovereign, remaining there until commanded to rise from the lowly position they had taken.

"Isaac," exclaimed the king, "it pleases me not, to see reverend age, like thine, stooping thus humbly, even at the feet of thy prince. I have sent for thee, because I have matter of deep import to confer about, and would save thee, if possible, from the wrath of those who would hunt thee and thy tribe to destruction."

"Your highnesses consideration deserves my best thanks," answered Isaac, with humility.

"Nay, I would but prevent the mischief with which thou art threatened," replied the king. "Evil men have invented falsehoods to excuse the violence they meditate, and I have sent for thee to warn thee of the danger that lurks in thy path, even when thou dost least expect it."

"If I am myself the only object of men's rancour, I am content to abide the worst," answered the old man, bowing his head meekly to his bosom.

"But I tell thee, man, thou art not doomed to be the only sufferer on this occasion," retorted the king. "Thy whole tribe, not only in London, but throughout my dominions, are looked upon with jealousy, and distrust. A general massacre is intended, and I, therefore, warn thee of it in time, that thou mayst escape while there is yet an opportunity."

"Are thy subjects then so little under control," asked the Jew, "that thou, their acknowledged and lawful sovereign, cannot repress so foul an act as that thou speakest of?"

"I can punish the guilty, *after* the crime has been committed," replied the king, "but that will be of little service, when the mischief shall have been done. Nay, more, I have issued a proclamation, commanding my people to abstain from all violence against their Jewish brethren, yet they may disregard my injunctions, and execute the vengeance they have pledged themselves to take."

"Surely, then," exclaimed Isaac, "they must have some new charge to bring against our persecuted race?"

"On the contrary," replied the king, "the accusation has been made before, though never with so much virulence as on the present occasion. They say the Jews are extortioners, and hoarders of gold and silver, and, attributing the poverty of the nation to their means, are about to take summary revenge, alike upon the innocent and the guilty."

"But your highness knows that these charges are false," exclaimed Isaac with increasing confidence. "*You*, at least, are aware that they are brought against us by men who hope to profit by our destruction."

"I am aware of it," replied the king, "and have taken the earliest opportunity to put thee on thy guard against the ruin that threatens thy people. A rising will shortly take place for the purpose of carrying these designs into effect, and, amidst the exasperation that will follow, I fear that neither old age, nor the helplessnes of childhood, nor yet the weakness of the gentler sex, will find pity from the ruthless destroyers."

"Pardon me, your highness," interposed Reuben Grenard, "but, knowing this, is it not in your power to command the military to defend us?"

"The military," answered the king, "are of the same opinion as the rest of my people. They have been taught to regard all Jews with distrust, and I fear no reliance is to be placed upon them, even though they were sent out for your protection."

" Then," exclaimed Isaac, " it appears that we are doomed to become the prey of infuriate madmen."

" I fear so," replied the monarch, " unless you take speedy means to save yourselves."

" You would recommend us then to flee the country ?"

" I would."

" And thus leave for ever the homes that have sheltered us from child-hood !"

" Even so," answered Richard ; " for that seems to me the only way left to save your tribe from destruction."

" Then I, for one," answered the aged Israelite, " will prefer abiding my doom, whatever it may be."

" And I," said Reuben Grenard, in a tone that showed his resolution. " If our enemies are resolved upon our destruction, flight will not save us from the evil they meditate against us."

" But I charge ye both to remember," exclaimed the king, " that it is not yourselves only that ye have to think of. Both of ye have those whom ye would be sorry to yield tamely to destruction, and, there-fore, I again implore ye, to consider well ere ye consign all to the fierce vengeance of misguided men."

" If your majesty," answered Isaac, " will consult the annals of our tribe, you will find it written that the Jews have ever been most jealous of the honour of their wives and daughters. Instances are recorded of sacrifices being made at which the blood thrills with horror. Yet ne-cessity urged them on, and I doubt not in the present instance you will see that if we are doomed to perish, it shall not be ingloriously."

" Canst thou protect thy women from insult ?" demanded King Rich-ard ; " remember the violence to be expected from an enraged multitude, and then consider whether it will not be better to take prompt measure to secure thy safety."

" Our women," answered Isaac, " have little to fear from the brutal conduct of which you speak."

" Hah ! dost thou then believe that thou hast the power to check the evil passions of reckless men ?"

" Alas ! sire," exclaimed the elder Israelite, " I know the brutal nature of the men thou speakest of too well, to expect mercy at their hands."

" And dost thou not think of thy daughter's honour ?"

" I do, but will take means to prevent her becoming a prey to such hateful monsters."

" Thou hintest darkly, old man," exclaimed the king. " How, I ask thee, canst thou save thy child from a fate I thought thou wouldst have shuddered at ?"

" By plunging a dagger to her heart with my own hand !"

" Hah !" exclaimed the king ; " do I understand thee rightly—wouldst thou, indeed, destroy the life of a maiden whom thou hast said thou lovest ?"

" It is my love for her that would prompt the deed," answered Isaac, warmly. " From infancy to womanhood I have watched her with the affection that a father only knows. I have regarded her as the chief prize of my existence, and rather than see her live to become the victim of a villain's lust, I would send her gentle spirit before me to stand in the presence of that Maker who knows and understands all hearts."

" But such a fatal deed," observed the king, " may be avoided by ac-cepting the advice I have given thee."

" It is impossible to accept it, my liege," answered the Hebrew ; " our hearts are centred in our homes, and few are there, I believe, who would consent to be driven forth into the world penniless, and without a resting place."

"And yet, even that, I should have thought is preferable to encountering the dangers I have warned thee of."

"Your majesty," replied Isaac, "will, I hope, pardon the obstinacy of an old man, whose days are now well nigh numbered. I feel grateful for the warning I have received, and if I have refused to take advantage of it, it is because I know that there are few belonging to my tribe who would consent to be driven forth from country and home merely because a lawless robber rises to persecute them."

"But the riches, said to belong to the Jews, have tempted them to form this detestable plot against thee," answered the king. "Say, then, will it not be better to escape with thy treasures than to remain and lose all thou hast,—life, fortune, friends—nay, thy very children?"

"I grant that it is a fearful sacrifice to make," exclaimed Isaac of Tadcaster, "and yet I see no probability of avoiding it. If we were to carry the little treasure we possess on board ship, the fact would quickly become known, and thus we should only be briefly postponing the evil hour your majesty wishes us to avoid."

"Still," observed the king, "there is a chance that some of you might escape."

"Perhaps so," replied Isaac, "and let those that are timid try to save themselves. I, however, am old; my life is not worth a single thought, and even if it were, I would risk it, rather than be driven forth a homeless wanderer."

"And thy daugher," cried the king, earnestly, "must she also perish because of her father's obstinacy?"

"Name her not, your majesty, I entreat!" exclaimed Isaac, in an agony of grief. "She is the sole prop of my declining days,—the one fair treasure that I value far beyond the price of gold or silver. When I think of the sufferings she may be doomed to undergo, my heart bleeds for her, and sometimes I pray Heaven to take her to itself, ere I die, that I may be assured of her escape from the base men who have sought her destruction."

"You speak of Sir Gaston de Neville and Black Ivan?"

"I do, your majesty,"

"But they, I believe, have ceased the persecutions thou hast complained of?"

"Latterly they have," answered Isaac, "but I fear they only wait till a favourable opportunity arrives to carry their villainous plans into execution."

At this moment, voices were heard near the door, and immediately afterwards, Hugh Tiptoft entered, and throwing himself at the feet of his sovereign, announced that Jonah had just arrived in search of his master, with intelligence, that Rebecca had suddenly disappeared, and that fears were entertained lest she had again fallen into the hands of one of her former persecutors. To describe the agony of the old man, at this news, would be impossible; for an instant or two, he stood dumb and motionless, gazing with a look of frenzy upon Reuben Grenard, who was also speechless through the intelligence that had just been brought them. At last, however, the old man fell upon his knees before the king, and in broken accents, implored his intercession for the recovery of his lost child.

"Thou shalt have all the aid I can give thee, Isaac," answered the

monarch, "but first it will be necessary to ascertian whether she h
really been taken away by either of the persons you suspect."

Then addressing himself to Hugh Tiptoft, he commanded him to brii
in Jonah, who was no sooner placed before him, than he was interr
gated as to any light that he could throw upon the cause of his youi
mistress's sudden and unexpected disappearance from home. But tl
terrified serving-man was too much confused to give any explanatii
just then, and after a good deal of stammering and stuttering, he w:
obliged to confess that he could not offer anything in the shape of :
explanation.

"Villain!" exclaimed the distracted father, "why didst thou n
better guard the precious treasure I left in thy charge?"

"I—I—I—knew—nothing—nothing at all of her leaving the place
stammered Jonah. "She left without saying a word about going ou
and—and—"

"How knowest thou that she is gone then?" asked the old man in
petuously."

"Because a neighbour afterwards told me that he saw her walkin
away with a strange female."

"Hah!" exclaimed Isaac, "it was some fiend employed to lure h
from home. You hear, my liege," he continued, addressing himself
the king, "our persecutors are again at work to tear her from the arn
of her doating father, and I have lost the precious jewel that aloi
makes life of value to me."

"Be calm, old man, and listen to me," said Richard, compassionatel
"I have hither interested myself in your behalf, and if you think fit
trust this affair to my hands, I promise not to relax in my endeavoui
till I have either restored the girl, or punished those why have dared 1
take her from thy care."

"Your highness will pardon me," replied Isaac, "but a father can ei
trust this affair to no one but himself. Reuben and I, will go forth i
search of her, and if I find the villain who has betrayed her, I will the
throw myself upon your kindness, and implore the infliction of a pui
ishment, such as the crime merits."

"Thou hast my royal word, old man, and I will not break it, eve
if the wrong-doer were my own brother."

"But we know not, yet, which way Rebecca went" exclaime
Reuben Grenard, anxiously interposing at this moment. "She may nc
be far off, and it may still be in our power to overtake her."

"What direction did she take?" asked the king, of Jonah, who stoc
trembling by the side of his master.

"Towards the eastern suburbs of the city," replied the person ad
dressed."

"And was no one with her but the old woman you have before spoke
of?"

"Not that I have heard."

"Did anybody follow in pursuit?"

"A few neighbours only," replied Jonah, "but I know not with wh:
success, as I hastened hither to let my master know the misfortune tha
has happened to him."

"Then thou knowest not but she may have been rescued, and is, per
haps, at this moment, at home?"

"I cannot say, my liege," replied the man, "but as half an hour ha
passed, since she went away, I am afraid there was little chance of be
being overtaken."

"Alas!" groaned the old man, "there is no likelihood of it! She is now in the hands of her cruel foes, and I fear there is no chance of saving her from destruction."

"Nay," exclaimed the king, "yield not to despair till thou knowest the worst. She may merely have been called out to visit some sick friend, and in that case she will be at home before thou arrivest there thyself."

"It is in vain that I try to think so," answered Isaac, in a mournful tone. "That she has enemies I know but too well, and, doubtless, one of them, taking advantage of my absence, has stolen the lamb from her fold."

"Is there any one," asked the king, "whom thou hast reason to suspect more than another?"

"One of two persons I am certain it is," replied the old man. "Either Sir Gaston de Neville, or Black Ivan is guilty of this cruel outrage."

"Then the former shall be summoned to my presence without delay," exclaimed King Richard, hastily; "he at least shall be made to give a direct reply, though the other, I am sorry to say, is beyond my reach, unless, indeed, we happen to get him once within our grasp."

"I will myself follow the robber to his lurking place," cried Reuben Grenard. "Once, already, I have stood face to face before the ruffian, when not a soul was by to befriend me. By the aid of heaven I then contrived to escape from him, and the life that was then preserved cannot be better devoted than in making one more attempt to rescue my betrothed bride from his custody."

"Rash boy!" exclaimed Isaac, with emotion, "thou shalt not venture thyself again within that villain's reach. He would slay thee, wert thou to follow him, and perhaps after all, my child is in the power of Sir Gaston de Neville."

"That, at least, shall be tried, ere he is much older," said the king; "so return to your home, old man, and prosecute your enquiries as best you may. For my own part I will not waste a single moment, and should I discover aught of thy daughter, thou shalt receive a message from me forthwith. And now let me persuade thee to look to thine own safety according to the warning I gave thee when first thou camest hither. Let thine whole tribe look to it, for again I say that a storm is about to burst forth that will be beyond my control."

So saying, the king took his departure, and immediately afterwards Isaac and Reuben, followed by Jonah, slowly left the audience chamber, to return to that home which had been rendered desolate by the departure of the unfortunate Rebecca.

CHAPTER XLII.

"I pray thee to take pity on me :—
Release me from this thraldom, I entreat,
And I will bless thee!"

ZARAH.

It was some little time after Rebecca's arrival at the castle of Sir Gaston de Neville, that she became conscious of where she was, but upon recovering from the stupor, in which she had fallen, she at once recognized the apartment in which she was, and if anything were needed to convince her that she was not mistaken, it was the presence of Edith, the female domestic who had attended upon her during the period of her last imprisonment there. The kind consolations offered by the girl, had at length the effect of restoring her to a slight feeling of confidence, and bursting into a flood of tears, she threw herself upon the neck of the only being she could hope to receive commisseration from in the stronghold of her betrayer.

"Well, lor, Miss, who'd ever have thought of seeing you back to this dismal place!" exclaimed the girl, in a tone that betokened pity for the unfortunate being who thus clung to her as it were for support and assistance. "I'm sure, for my own part," she continued, "I was glad enough when you managed to make your escape last time, and it grieves me to the very heart,—that it does,—to see you brought back again against your will."

"Alas!" sighed Rebecca, "better had they borne me to my grave, than to this abode of crime and infamy!"

"Now don't talk about the grave, dear madam, pray don't!" cried Edith; "this castle is bad enough to be sure,—and for that matter, so are most of the folks that live in it, but then you may happen to get out of it as you did once before, and if you should be lucky enough to do so, I'll be bound you would take care not to let Sir Gaston find you out a third time."

"It is impossible to avoid him," answered Rebecca, sorrowfully. "The evil passions of that man are not to be controlled, and I fear that, having again got me in his power, he will keep so strict a watch upon me, that I shall not find another opportunity to escape from him."

"But you forget," answered the girl, that there is one in the place who pities, and would help you if she only knew how."

"Thou alludest to thyself, Edith?"

"Aye, of a verity do I."

"For thy kindness to one who is almost a stranger to thee, I thank the girl," exclaimed Rebecca, ardently. "With a friend near me, even though it be a helpless female, I feel somewhat more assured that the licentiousness of my persecutor will be repressed."

"Depend upon it, Sir Gaston shall not fail to know what my opinion is upon the subject," replied Edith;—"he has heard a good deal of truth from me already, and it shall go hard but he learns a good deal more unless he takes my advice and mends his ways."

"Nay," I would have thee be cautious how thou offended him," cried Rebecca, earnestly. "He is of a fierce and malignant temper, and I dread the effects of it, shouldst thou offend him by too much freedom of speech."

"Oh, but he knows that I don't care a fig for him," replied, Edith with indifference. "Sir Gaston may rave and storm as much as he pleases, but with all his passion, he knows better than to say a great deal to me."

"And why," asked our heroine, "should he be afraid of saying more to you than any body else?"

"For this simple reason," answered the loquacious girl; "he is aware that I know more than he would like to have repeated, and as a woman's tongue is not to be controlled when once it is set going, he has good reason to fear that I shall let the cat out of the bag, and then heaven help him, I say! for no one knows what might be the end of it."

"But others," observed Rebecca, "I should suppose know of those things as well as yourself?"

"To be sure they do," replied the attendant, "but then Sir Gaston has taken care to bribe them well, and make it their interest to keep his secrets. There was one, however that was not exactly to be depended upon, and, would you believe it, the poor fellow suddenly disappeared, and has never been heard of since!"

"Indeed!" exclaimed Rebecca, shuddering at the suspicion that crossed her mind, "and what inference, may I ask, was drawn from that circumstance?"

"Why what else should the people about him think, but that the man was murdered?"

"Murdered!" cried our heroine, shrinking back with horror.

"Yes, murdered," answered Edith; "Sir Gaston de Neville is by no means particular, when his own interest is concerned, and between ourselves, it is reported that many others have gone out of the world unfairly through his means."

"Nay," cried Rebecca, "let us hope that these reports are without foundation."

"You may hope what you please," retorted the girl, "but people's thoughts ain't to be checked in that way, and so our master must lie under the suspicion till he chooses to prove his innocence. Then there was his brother, who, I believe, I told you about the last time you were here,—there was a deal of mystery in that affair; and, to make short of a long story, the castle is haunted by an armed spectre, who takes it into his head to appear every now and then to frighten us all out of our wits."

"Depend on it, Edith," returned our heroine, "all the reports respecting the appearance of a spectre, are founded in superstition. I have heard of it before, but never gave heed to the idle story, knowing as I do, that there is scarcely an old castle where similar rumours are not prevalent."

" Well, but this armed knight as been seen by nearly every body in the place," answered Edith, sharply. "Even Sir Gaston himself does not deny it, though it must be confessed he gets into a terrible passion if any body ventures to speak a word to him upon the subject."

"Then, of course, the subject is never mentioned to him?"

"Very few would like to run the risk, I believe," replied Edith, "though I was once bold enough to tell him that the apparition had been seen the night before by some of the people about the castle."

"It was a hazardous experiment to say the least of it," observed Rebecca.

"So I found it," answered the other, "for I never shall forget the terrible passion master threw himself into, as soon as he heard what I had got to say. He stamped and swore like a madman—then he drew his poniard, and I thought he was going to stab me outright, but I suppose he thought better of it, for all of a sudden he ordered me out of the room, taking care, however, before I went, never to mention the subject to any body, under pain of his severest displeasure."

"And yet," observed Rebecca, "you have now broken his commands, by telling the whole story to me !"

"Ah !" replied Edith, "that's because I'm such a bad hand at keeping a secret. But, bless your soul, its not to you alone, that I have mentioned it, for there is not a person that is willing to listen to me but what I have informed of it."

"And if Sir Gaston heard of your imprudence ——"

" He would get into a towering passion again, I dare say," interrupted the girl ; "but I can't help it if he does, for there's something so satisfactory in telling these very great secrets, that makes amends for all the risks one happens to run."

" It seems then," sighed Rebecca "that you fear him not as I do?"

"Bless you !" cried Edith, "I don't care a rush for him, and I believe he knows it too pretty well by this time. Besides, I happen to be in possession of too many other secrets to make it safe for him to offend me, so I do pretty well as I like here, which is the only thing that makes the place at all bearable. But hush !—I hear Sir Gaston's footsteps coming this way, so as I have no very particular wish to see him just at present, I'll take my leave of you for a short time, and return again as soon as I know he has left you."

Rebecca would have intreated the girl to stay, and be present at the dreaded interview, but Edith was not to be prevailed upon, and as she took her departure by one door, Sir Gaston de Neville entered by another, and striding hastily towards the trembling victim of his ill-used power, he demanded whether she was yet more reconciled to a fate which it was no longer in her power to avail.

"Sir Gaston de Neville knows the hatred I bear him," answered Rebecca, firmly, " and, therefore, it is needless to enquire whether I am reconciled at finding myself his prisoner."

"Prisoner !" exclaimed the knight, with affected surprise. " Dost thou indeed believe thyself a prisoner, when it is love alone that has prompted the step I have taken."

"Nay, Sir Knight," she replied " had you really loved me, I had not been torn thus ruthlessly from my home. That my heart was given to another was well known to you, and yet, in defiance of every feeling of honour, you have taken me from the protection of my father."

"And if I have," answered Sir Gaston, "it is that you may find protection in my arms."

"Again I tell you, Sir Knight, that I utterly scorn your professions."

"Then again I tell you," retorted Sir Gaston, that if persuasion fails to convince you of your own folly, it only remains for me to teach you that my will is not to be rejected with scorn."

"'Tis a brave deed," cried Rebecca, with scorn, "to threaten one whom you have rendered thus powerless!—Methinks thy knighthood might be better employed in the field of battle, than in thus warring against a helpless woman!"

"Hah! dost thou taunt me, girl."

"Nay, I do more," she replied, "I loathe and abhor thee, as I should the venomous serpent that I might find in my path. From the first thou hast been my bane—my curse—and each hour of thy life proves more and more the deep and lasting cause that there is for my boundless hatred."

"By St. George, fair maiden, thou knowest how to scold," exclaimed Sir Gaston, somewhat abashed by her vehemence; "and yet I warn thee that it would be better for thee wert thou to betray less of the shrew, where these ill-humours can do thee no service."

"Why then do you keep me here against my will?"

"Because it is _my_ will and pleasure," he replied. "I have tried to conquer thine aversion by every means in my power, and since they have failed, it is now time to have recourse to subtler methods; by deceit, girl, I have succeeded in decoying thee to my snare, and having succeeded so far, no argument that you can use shall prevail upon me to give up my prize."

"You forget, Sir Knight," she replied, "that King Richard has already expressed his determination to befriend the helpless object of your persecutions, and when he learns that you have acted thus in defiance to his commands, he will not fail to manifest his displeasure towards a disobedient subject."

"King Richard has no right to control my actions," answered Sir Gaston de Neville, haughtily, "and he shall now learn that I have spirit enough to reject his interference in this matter. Besides, thou belongest to a race that has no right to look for support from a Christian king, and were Richard to interfere further in thy behalf, he would soon bring upon himself the dislike of nearly the whole nation."

"And yet," exclaimed Rebecca, "you call these people Christians!"

"I do, for if they persecute thy race, is it that they may thereby strengthen and support thine own religion."

"Do we not worship the same God?"

"Perhaps thou dost, but still thou art not Christians."

"If we were," replied Rebecca, with bitter sarcasm, "we might, like Sir Gaston de Neville, commit crime with impunity."

"Girl!" exclaimed the knight, impatiently, "I will argue no longer with thee upon this subject. It is sufficient for my purpose that I now have thee safe in my custody, and it will be my own fault if ever thou leavest this castle again."

"Perhaps not," she replied, "and yet I can still defy thee to prevent my escape."

"How! dost thou defy me, girl?"

"I do!"

"Then thou hast yet to learn the impossibility of quitting this place," answered Sir Gaston. "Every gate and avenue will be strictly guarded, and death shall be the reward of those who may negligently suffer thee to carry thy threats into execution."

"Nay," she replied, "I do not mean that I will attempt to flee from the castle, but, should there be no way to escape thy violence, my own hands shall rid me of a life that is rendered burdensome to me by captivity!"

"So!—thou wouldst become thine own slayer, wouldst thou?"

"Aye, any thing to escape from a villain such as thou art!"

"Thou mayst call me villain, girl," he exclaimed, "but the triumph is mine, and I can patiently listen to thy wild ravings. Here thy friends cannot penetrate, and whilst they are madly seeking for thee, thou art far beyond their reach."

"Hast thou no pity, Sir Gaston," cried Rebecca, overwhelmed by her peril, and bursting into a flood of tears:—"dost thou not think of my aged father's sufferings, and of the broken heart that will be caused by thine own cruelty."

"Thy father would have had no pity upon me," answered the knight, in a tone of utter indifference, "had he known that his refusal to give thee to me would have caused my death. He would have scorned the Christian even as I scorn him now, and, therefore, thou hast little right to expect mercy from him who has had so much trouble to get thee in his power."

"I tell thee again," replied Rebecca, "that I was betrothed to another, and, therefore, his pledged word could not be broken. Thou knowest that my heart was engaged to Reuben Grenard, and yet, disregarding the honour thou dost so much boast of, I have been persecuted, and torn from those I most love in the world."

"And if I have persecuted thee, girl," answered Sir Gaston de Neville, "thou hast to blame thine own beauty, which tempted me even in spite of myself. At first I strove to conquer the mad passion that had taken possession of my heart, and had nearly succeeded in effacing thine image from my memory, when chance again threw thee in my way, and I loved thee more than ever. Still I would have subdued my passion, but finding that it was impossible to do so, I, at length, resolved to let no obstacle stand in my way, and from that time, as thou well knowest, I have not ceased in my endeavours to obtain thee by every means that ingenuity could devise.'

"And wilt thou still persevere," asked Rebecca, urgently, "in wronging one who has never injured thee by word or thought?"

"Nay, girl," he replied, "if thou art wise, thou wilt submit with patience to thy destiny. I tell thee I love thee to madness; this castle shall become thy home—thou art, from henceforth, its mistress, and I will become thy willing slave."

"I will hear no more!" exclaimed Rebecca, resolutely; "thou art immoveable from thy purpose, and loathing thee as I do, I bid thee leave me."

"Not till thou hast promised to look less unkindly upon me," replied Sir Gaston, with hypocritical servility. "Say only that thou wilt take time to reflect, and I will not only leave thee to thyself for the present, but will even wait any reasonable time for your final answer."

"Thou hast it already," replied Rebecca, impatiently. "I have told thee I can never regard thee otherwise than as the destroyer of my happiness, and no consideration can ever move me from the decision I have given."

"But a few days may serve to soften the bitterness of thy present feelings," answered Sir Gaston de Neville. "At any rate I will prove to thee that I am not quite so bad as thou believest, and will therefore grant thee a week for the consideration of the offer I have made thee."

Rebecca was about to return a scornful reply to this proposition, but ere she could give utterance to the words, a retainer approached to announce that Hugh Tiptoft had arrived at the castle on a message from the king. Sir Gaston at once knew that Richard had been again informed of Rebecca's disappearance from home, and his first impulse was to refuse admittance to the messenger. Upon consideration, however, he changed his mind, and having given orders to that effect, Hugh was immediately afterwards introduced to him.

"So!" he exclaimed, "thou comest, I see, from the king, who, doubtless, has some mighty affair in hand, since he has chosen so discreet a messenger on the occasion."

"His majesty," replied Hugh Tiptoft,—"has sent me hither to command your immediate presence at the palace."

"Indeed! then perhaps thou knowest the occasion of this sudden humour of our gracious king?"

"I was not bid to tell thee more than I have already said," answered the captain of the archers."

"Humph!" ejaculated the knight,—"thou art a mysterious conveyer of messages at any rate. Thou tellest all that is bidden thee to say, and, of course, no nothing further."

"Except under *peculiar* circumstances," replied Hugh Tiptoft, with an expressive gesture.

"Hah!—I understand thee, now," exclaimed Sir Gaston, flinging a purse of gold, which the other dextrously caught in his hand, "We shall begin to know each other better, presently, I see, and perchance thou canst now divulge a little more than was just now convenient?"

"I can tell thee, Sir Knight," replied the other, "that the king is in no good humour with thee."

"Indeed! and pray what fresh cause of anger has good King Richar found against me?"

"It is reported,—and I see not without foundation," answered the other, glancing towards Rebecca,—"that thou hast again stolen the daughter of Isaac of Tadcaster, notwithstanding his majesty's express commands, that thou wouldst cease to annoy her."

"And does his majesty suppose," asked Sir Gaston de Neville, "that I will submit to his dictation in an affair like this?"

"I know not what you may feel inclined to do," answered Hugh Tiptoft. "All I can say is, that I have been charged to command your immediate presence at court, and further, my advice is that you fail not to obey it."

"That is a matter that must be left to my own opinion," exclaimed Sir Gaston. "That the girl is here, you may perceive, but it is extremely doubtful whether I shall deliver her up, even at the command of England's king."

"Then, of course, you are prepared to take the consequences?"

"I am," replied the knight; "so let them be what they may I shall t shrink from them."

"Let me advise you not to commit yourself by too great rashness," cried Hugh Tiptoft; "his majesty's anger may fall heavily upon you, and it would be wiser to avoid than to court it."

"Perhaps it would," answered Sir Gaston, after some hesitation, "so return to King Richard, and say to him that I am at present at one of my castles in the north."

" And that the Hebrew Maiden is here ?"

" Nay, sirrah !—say that thou couldst hear nothing of her, but th thou believest I have had no hand in taking her away."

" But how can I reconcile so great a falsehood to my conscience ?"

" By accepting this other purse of gold." said the knight, suiting th action to the word. " Take it, my friend, and if you perform your pai well, I will not fail to double the reward."

" Nay, tell the king that I am here against my will," cried Rebecc: who had hitherto been a silent auditor of this conversation ;—" tell hir that I am in the hand of a villain, and that I implore his immediat aid to effect my release."

" Heed not her ravings, but obey me," exclaimed Sir Gaston, takin Hugh's arm, and leading him to the door. " Tell the king that you coul not find me ;—say that to him, my friend, and perhaps in a few days may visit him at the palace."

With this, Sir Gaston de Neville left the room with the royal mes senger.

CHAPTER XLIII.

" Make a clear conscience by confession,
    Say all thou know'st, and in return I'll give
    Both gold and liberty."

THE FUGITIVE.

IN an agony of suspense, Isaac and Reuben passed the whole of the night of Rebecca's disappearance in watching and devising plans for rescuing her from the villain who had thus artfully decoyed her from home. For a long time, however, they were without any clue by which they might hope to bring the crime home to the guilty party ; but at length the attention of the old man was attracted to something that was lying upon the floor, and picking it up, he discovered it to be a silken purse, with the initials of Sir Gaston de Neville richly embroidered in the centre. This was sufficient to confirm the suspicions that had been already formed, and being thus satisfied that she was again in the hands of the Knight Templar, the next thing to be considered was the means that should be employed to release her from the power of the libertine. Burning with rage against his unprincipled rival, Reuben Grenard insisted upon im- mediately hastening to the castle of Sir Gaston de Neville, and demand- ing the immediate restoration of his betrothed bride, but the venerable Israelite would not hear of a proposition so fraught with danger to one whom he now regarded as a son.

" No, Reuben," he exclaimed, " thou shalt not leave me to undertake so desperate an errand as this. Sir Gaston owes thee a mortal grudge, for standing between him and the object of his base passion, and he would surely slay thee, wert thou thus madly to throw thyself in his way."

" Wouldst thou have me remain inactive, then, at such a time as this ?" demanded Reuben, impatiently. " Shall I rest quietly, and know that my loved Rebecca is in peril ?"

" Hear me, rash boy !" exclaimed the old man, almost choking with emotion. " If I refuse to let thee go on this errand, it is because I value thy life far beyond my own ;—my long pilgrimage of life is nearly ended—and, therefore, I choose to take this risk upon myself preferring

to perish in defence of my daughter, so that thou who art younger, and better able to cope with this villain, may still be left to avenge her cause."

"But Sir Gaston is as inveterate against thee, as he is against myself," answered Reuben.

"I know he is," returned the other, "and he may, perhaps, slay thee in his passion, shouldst thou venture alone into his presence."

"Death has no terrors for me," exclaimed Reuben, firmly. "But, thy daughter, think of her sufferings, wert thou to perish by the hands of this villain."

"I have thought of all," replied the old man, "and no danger that I may run, shall deter me from making one last effort for her rescue. I know the fierce passions of this man, Reuben, and can willingly dare them in a cause like this."

"But why not suffer me to go?" asked Reuben, imploringly. "My life would be in no more danger than thine own, and, even if I should perish, thou wouldst be left to a well-merited punishment upon my assassin."

"I have already told thee why I will not consent to it," answered the old man. "I would save thee from destruction, and for the sake of doing so, will cheerfully lay down my own life."

"Thinkest thou, old man, I could endure existence, embittered as it would be with the reflection, that thou hast fallen, where I alone ought to have been the victim?"

"Nay, boy," replied Isaac, "it may not be so bad as we have anticipated. That Sir Gaston de Neville is fierce and blood-thirsty, we have but too much reason for knowing; yet, my grey hairs may save

No. 28

me from his fury, and, perhaps, my prayers and entreaties may soften a heart that never yet knew pity."

"Believe, rather," exclaimed Reuben, "that the tiger would release his prey, than that Sir Gaston de Neville will yield up the unfortunate girl whom he has thus pursued."

"Still there is the king to appeal to," replied the old man. "Richard has proved himself a zealous friend to our cause, and Sir Gaston de Neville knows full well that life, fortune, and honour, are in the hands of his offended sovereign."

"He has known that long since," answered the younger Jew, "and yet has he ventured to risk all by disobeying the king's commands. He is fully aware of the great risk he runs by thus persecuting thy daughter, and yet, in spite of all danger, he has now carried her from the house of her father."

"Aye," replied Isaac, "but the day of retribution will come anon."

"Not, I fear, till it will be too late."

"Then let me not waste another moment," exclaimed the old man, impatiently. "I will away, Reuben, and with the first dawn of daylight, demand admittance to the presence of this haughty Knight Templar."

"And if thy demand is granted," answered the other, sorrowfully, "thou wilt never be permitted to leave his castle again with life."

"In that case," cried the agonized father, "I shall be spared the grief of beholding my beloved child the mistress of a villain."

"Oh, let me again implore you to relinquish this fatal project," exclaimed Reuben Grenard, yet more urgently; "let the task be given to me, and I swear either to bring back Rebecca to her father's arms, or perish in the attempt."

"It is in vain that you seek to prevail upon me," answered the other, resolutely, "for my mind is made up to the course I have chosen, and no persuasions shall ever move me from it. The discovery of this purse has confirmed the suspicion that I had formed, and now that I am certain where she is, I will hasten to her place of concealment, even though death stood before me in all his terror."

Reuben was again about to urge his request, but, at that moment, his eyes rested upon an object outside the window, and, upon looking yet more intently, he perceived that an old woman was closely observing them. In an instant, therefore, and without waiting to explain the motive of his sudden exit, he rushed from the room, and directed his rapid footsteps towards the place where he had seen the female. To his utter disappointment, she was no longer in sight, and he was about to return in disappointment to the house, when a rustling amongst some bushes close by, attracted his attention, and darting towards the place, he seized the trembling object of his anxious search. In vain did she implore to be released; Reuben was firm in his determination to sift into the motives of her presence near the house of his benefactor, and dragging the resisting female by main force, he once more presented himself before the astonished Israelite.

"Behold, sir," he exclaimed, "a spy, who, for some reason which she shall explain, has been watching us through yonder window. I detected her in the act, and believing that she must have some motive for lurking about your house at this hour of the night, have brought her in, that she may be examined as to the reason of her visit.

"I had no motive, indeed I had not," cried the woman, with terror.

"Didst thou come hither by chance, then?" asked the elder Jew, sternly.

"I did."

"Why, then, were you watching us through the window?"

"Seeing a light as I passed," she replied, "I entered the wicket, and had only just approached the casement, when this young man caught sight of me."

"And is it usual for thee," asked Isaac, "to be wandering about at this late hour of the night?"

"It is not," she replied.

"Then, why were you so on the present occasion?"

"Because,—because," stammered the woman, "my mind was ill at rest, and, as I could not sleep, I rose from my bed, and wandered forth to seek ——"

"Well, to seek what?" exclaimed the old man, observing her hesitation.

"This purse!" she cried, darting forward, and snatching from the Israelite's girdle the very purse he had just before found. "This was what I sought," she continued, "'tis mine, and now, having explained the object of my coming hither, I demand to be once more set at liberty."

"Hag!" exclaimed Isaac, fiercely, "thou shalt have no liberty till thou hast explained how that purse became thine."

"When you have shown by what right you ask that question, I will answer it."

"Woman!" cried the old man, "the torture, if nought else can do it, shall wrench from thee the truth!"

"The torture will fail to effect thy purpose," she replied, with perfect indifference. "I have told thee all I mean to reveal, and it will be at your own peril to keep me longer here."

"The purse," exclaimed Isaac, "which thou hast claimed, is not thine own."

"Indeed!—and how knowest thou that?"

"Because it is marked with the initials of Sir Gaston de Neville."

"Ha! I knew not that!" muttered the old woman to herself, and then perceiving that her countenance was closely watched, she resumed, with more composure:—"It is as you have said,—the purse bears upon it the initials of Sir Gaston, and little wonder is there in that, seeing that he himself gave it me not long since."

"Did he so?" cried the old man; "then, having thus far explained thyself, perhaps thou wilt now say for what service it was given?"

"I shall deign no further reply," she answered, haughtily.

"Wilt thou say how it was that this purse happened to be lost in my house? I see the question rather puzzles thee, but since, it is evident thou hast been here in my absence."

"I have not been here," she replied, doggedly.

"In that case, then," answered Isaac, "the purse does not belong to thee."

Thus convicted, the woman stood confounded for some few seconds, but at last, recollecting herself, she said :—"Again, I tell thee, it is mine ;— Sir Gaston de Neville gave it me, and having lost it by some mischance, I came to look for it."

"You say it was given to you by Sir Gaston?"

"Aye, I do say so."

"And what service was to be performed for the gold that is contained in it?"

"Upon that subject," she replied, "you have no right to question me."

"I have," exclaimed the old man, with eagerness ;—"my daughter has been stolen from me this very night, and the admissions thou has made, convince me that thou hast had some share in robbing an unhapp father of his child."

"What proof hast thou to maintain such a charge as this?"

"The purse thou claimest being found in my house, is a sufficient evi dence that you must have been here."

"Try her by the offer of a bribe," whispered Reuben to the old man —"gold seems to be her idol, and she may, perhaps, be induced to con fess her share in this business."

"Thou art self-convicted, old woman," exclaimed Isaac, taking th hint that had just been given; "and it is in my power to give thee int custody, for aiding in carrying off my daughter. I, however, offer the fair terms,—here are ten pieces of gold, in consideration that thou wil confess where the girl is whom thou hast basely taken from her home.'

"And, if I accept thine offer," returned the woman, "wilt thou promis not to prosecute me further in this matter?"

"I give thee my word thou shalt be at liberty to depart, when thou hast told all thou knowest."

"Give me the money, then," she exclaimed, eagerly holding forth he almost fleshless hands. "Let me have thy bribe, and I will do th bidding."

"Take it," cried the old man, "and now tell me whether it was no Sir Gaston de Neville who employed thee to decoy away my child?"

"It was."

"And didst thou take her to his castle?"

"No, he was waiting at a hovel hard by, and having fulfilled my par of the affair, I went my way."

"Did she go willingly with thee?" asked the father, anxiously.

"She did."

"Hah!" cried the old man, in accents of despair, "then the villai has at last succeeded in prevailing upon her willingly to forsake all tha she once held dear!"

"Nay, you accuse her wrongfully," answered the woman. "I im posed upon her by an artful tale, or she never would have consentee to leave your house. She believed that Meg of Finchley was dying in wretched hovel hard by, and went thither, expecting to hear the last re velations of one who she was made to believe had an important secret t discover."

"Then," cried the old man, exultingly," she did not voluntarily for sake her aged parent, to become the paramour of a villain she has alway treated with so much scorn."

"No," answered the woman, "to do her justice, she would not hav left her home had it not been that she gave credit to my story about Me of Finchley."

"Wretch!" exclaimed Isaac, fiercely, "then, thou couldst lend thysel for a paltry bribe, to become the guilty instrument for procuring the de struction of a helpless girl!"

"Heap not your reproaches upon me!" cried the old woman; " have told you all fairly enough, and if you are satisfied, I will now tak my departure, according to the promise you made before I confessed m share in this business."

"Go, then," exclaimed Isaac;—"yet, ere thou leavest me, say wher thou mayest be found, in case thy evidence should be hereafter required.'

"I have no dwelling place in particular," she replied; "mine is wandering life, and, it is, therefore, impossible to say where I may be foun to-morrow."

"You can leave us," exclaimed the elder Israelite, "and shouldst thou ever find it in thy power to serve me by any further revelation, wait upon me, and thy services shall be amply requited."

Without waiting to make any reply to this, the woman now hurried away, glad enough to escape from the awkward situation in which she had just found herself. As she left the room, Isaac again turned his thoughts to the best means that could be adopted for rescuing his daughter from the castle of Sir Gaston de Neville. Still he resolved to entrust the task to no one but himself, and, in spite of Reuben's remonstrances, he prepared immediately to set forth for the accomplishment of his design. By this time, the first gleam of day-light began to illuminate the eastern horizon, when, taking his staff in his hand, and bidding farewell to Reuben Grenard, he set forth to accomplish the hazardous task he had undertaken.

CHAPTER XLIV.

"Wilt thou not listen to an old man's prayers,
Or heed the cry of one who comes for justice?—
Hear me, my lord!—in mercy hear me!"

NORNA.

IT was scarcely light when the aged Israelite left his home to go in quest of his lost child, and oppressed as he was with the heavy infirmities of years, it was sometime after sun-rise that he stood before the darkly frowning portal of Sir Gaston's castle. With an anxious eye he surveyed the various towers that rose before him, in hopes that he might chance to see Rebecca at one of the numerous windows; but in this expectation he was disappointed, for not a moving figure was to be seen, except a few sentinels, whose heads was just perceivable above the battlements. It was evident, therefore, that the inmates had not yet quitted their beds, and knowing that it would be useless to summon the warder just at present, he continued to wander round and round the walls in a vain expectation that he might chance to catch a glimpse of his unfortunate captive child. At length sounds began to reach him, denoting that some at least were stirring, and then returning to the principal entrance, he shortly succeeded in rousing the man who was in charge of the gate, and who, after much growling, and muttering, admitted him inside, though resolutely refusing to intimate his arrival to Sir Gaston until his usual time of rising.

"Why should I disturb him for the sake of an unbelieving Jew?" asked the fellow, in a surely tone;—"besides, its more than my place is worth to do it, and I'm sure I'm not going to be turned away just to satisfy your whims."

"But, my business with him is most urgent," exclaimed Isaac, as tears of anguish started from his eyes.

"Can't help that," retorted the warder. "Orders is orders, you know, and I mustn't go against them."

"Will it be long before he rises?" demanded the old man,

"Can't say," replied the other, "but you will know if you've only got patience to wait."

"At least," exclaimed Isaac, persevering in his questions, "you can perhaps tell me whether a young female was brought in here last night."

"I know nothing about it," replied the warder; "we servants have got no eyes nor ears for anything but our master's service."

"But, if a stranger should arrive here, you must, of course, know of it?"

"Yes, but I am not obliged to tell you, am I?"

Finding it was in vain to expect any other answer than such as he had already received, Isaac threw himself upon a bench, and gave way to the racking thoughts that tortured his soul. The warder, however, took no heed of the poor old man, but having arranged sundry little matters, he took his departure, leaving Isaac to continue his mournful ruminations alone. In this solitude the Israelite remained for nearly two hours, at the end of which time the man, in a worse temper, if possible, than before, returned, and desired him in no very courteous terms to follow him.

"Whither are you about to take me?" asked the afflicted Hebrew.

"To Sir Gaston, to be sure," returned the fellow, gruffly; "that's where you want to go, ain't it?"

"It is; but I would know whether he takes it ill that I am thus early in my visit."

"Why, for the matter of that," retorted the other, "he's not in the very best of humours, I can tell you. At first he bade me say that he would not be seen, but when I told him I believed you came here something about a girl, he altered his mind, and ordered me to take you before him directly."

"'Tis well!" muttered the old man, with something of satisfaction.

"For my own part," returned the warder, "I should think it anything but *well* to be ordered before him in the precious humour he's now in. He smiled grimly when he found who it was that wanted him, and, between ourselves, Sir Gaston never smiles but when there's mischief in the wind."

"Well, well, it matters not, so lead me to him at once," said the old man, and rising from the seat on which he had thrown himself, he followed the warder through a number of passages and quadrangles, until they reached what appeared to be the principal part of the castle, when entering a noble doorway, they soon after reached the apartment in which the knight was anxiously awaiting the hapless father of the unfortunate Rebecca. Having conducted him thus far, the warder retired, and then Sir Gaston looking threateningly towards the venerable man before him, demanded the object of his visit.

"I come, Sir Knight," replied the Israelite, "to entreat your compassion towards one who has been deeply injured.—My child—my loved Rebecca hath been basely stolen from me, and having good reason to know that she has been brought to your castle, I have ventured to follow her hither, and to implore that you will immediately restore her to me."

"I tell thee, Jew, thy child is not here," exclaimed Sir Gaston, boldly venturing on a falsehood.

"It is useless to deny it," answered the Hebrew. "I have obtained information upon which I can rely, that she was brought here last night by yourself."

"Ha! and who has told thee that?"

"The woman who assisted you in decoying her under false pretences from home."

"Thou liest, old man!" roared the Templar, fiercely; "this is some invention of thine own, and by St. Hubert thou shalt be made to suffer for it, ere I have done with thee."

"Thy threats, Sir Gaston de Neville, will not intimidate me, answered the other, firmly; "I am here to prosecute a righteous cause, and, if thou refusest to deliver up my child, I care not how soon it may please thee to put me to death."

"Thou shalt be tortured, villain, for thine effrontery," exclaimed the knight, yet more fiercely. "What! am I to bearded with impunity in my own castle, and that, too, by a vile Jew, whom, as a Christian knight, I ought to have slain long ago."

"Thou hast done worse," answered Isaac, "for thou hast stabbed me to the heart, and yet leavest me to writhe in the torture thou hast inflicted."

"Thou shalt be tortured more ere I have done with thee," cried the enfuriated knight. "I'll order thee to be thrown into the cauldron of boiling oil, and thy flesh shall be cast forth to become the food of dogs."

"Nay," exclaimed Isaac, "thy threats cannot intimidate one who is reckless of life, since she who was dearer than existence itself has been torn from him."

"Again, I tell thee," exclaimed the knight, "I know nothing of thy daughter."

"And again, I tell thee, that thou dost!" replied Isaac, unmoved by the anger of the Templar. "The woman I have spoken of, has confessed the share she had in the plot,—and if anything were wanting, to prove the truth of her words, it is to be found in the fact of her having claimed a purse, which, in her confusion she dropped in my house."

"A purse!" exclaimed Sir Gaston, "and what, pray, can that have to do in fixing any of the blame upon me?"

"Thine initials are embroidered on it," answered the Jew,—"and I have since learned that it contained the bribe with which thou didst prevail upon the woman to assist you!"

"Hah! and how knowest thou all this?"

"Because I used the same means as thou didst. I also tried the effect of a bribe upon the woman, and, yielding to her thirst for gold, she related the whole particulars, by which thy crimes have been discovered."

"Thou hast said enough!" roared the infuriated knight;—"I have been bullied by a Jew in my own castle, and it shall go hard but I will be revenged for it."

"Do with me as thou wilt, Sir Knight," answered the Jew,—"torture me to death by slow degrees, nay, practice upon me all the cruelties thou canst devise, and I will die without a murmur, so that thou wilt but release my daughter from this castle."

"Never!" vociferated Sir Gaston, thrown suddenly off his guard.

"Hah! thou dost acknowledge then, at last, that she is in thy hands!" cried Isaac, with startling earnestness.

"It is no longer requisite to conceal the fact," answered Sir Gaston. "Thou art now my prisoner, and I will take care that thou never again quittest this castle, to blab of secrets that might place my honour in jeopardy."

"Do as thou thinkest proper," replied the Jew,—unmoved by the dangers that surrounded him; —"keep me, as thy prisoner, here if thou wilt, but let me warn thee, ere thou dost so, that it will be at thine own peril if thou dost;— Reuben Grenard knows of my coming hither, and, if I return not by a certain time, he will apply to the Justiciary for a power sufficient to search thy castle."

"And if they do so," answered Sir Gaston, "their search will prove a vain one, for I have dungeons that will defy the strictest search, and amongst those thy daughter and thyself shall be concealed, until all danger is over."

"Shall my child be with me?" asked Isaac, eagerly.

"No," replied the knight, "thou shalt be separated, for I will show no indulgence to those who have thus dared to set my power at defiance."

"Let me entreat thee not to separate us" cried the old man, earnestly;—"my life is in thy hands, and I care not how soon thou takest it, but do not—do not, I implore thee, separate a father from his beloved child."

"'Psha!" replied Sir Gaston, contemptuously,—"dost thou expect mercy from me!"

"Scarcely," replied Isaac, "and yet I know that even the most ferocious, can be magnanimous at times."

"Expect it not from me, then," exclaimed the Templar, fiercely.—"Howl to the winds if thou wilt, or sooner will they heed thy words, than myself."

"Spare, oh, spare my child!" cried the agonised father.

"I will spare neither, now that they are in my power," retorted Sir Gaston; and then stamping furiously upon the floor, he immediately summoned three or four of his retainers, to whom he gave a few hurried orders, and immediately afterwards the old man was forced from the apartment and conveyed to the cheerless dungeon that had been assigned him.

As soon as Isaac had been borne from his presence, Sir Gaston rose from his seat, and paced uneasily up and down the room for some time. At length, however, a new thought struck him, and hurrying away, he proceeded towards the chamber occupied by the unfortunate Rebecca.

CHAPTER XLV.

"Anon, and I will briefly tell thee all
The fearful secrets of this prison-house;—
List, then, and hear them."

LORENZO.

LITTLE anticipating the dangerous situation of her father, our heroine was occupying herself with embroidery, in the hope of thus keeping from her mind the remembrance of her captivity; and the numerous other afflictions with which she was now visited. For a wonder Edith was absent from her; but, as if to make amends for this, Adrian, the youthful page of Sir Gaston de Neville, entered the room, in order to chase away, by his presence, the melancholy reflections with which he supposed the beauteous captive must be oppressed. Perceiving, however, that Rebecca was busily engaged at her employment, he was about to retire in silence, when the voice of the maiden, like some powerful spell, drew him to her side.

"Stay, Adrian," she said, "thou wouldst speak with me, I dare say, and sorrow has not yet made me so selfish that I would send thee away till thou hast executed thine errand."

"Nay, lady," he replied,—"I came but to bear thee company till Edith shall arrive;—this castle is a cheerless place to those that are

compelled to abide in it, and, seeing that thou art almost always in tears, it seems that thou art no willing guest within the walls of my master's strong-hold."

"I am not," she answered; "nay, I would cheerfully exchange places with the most wretched beggar, to be once more free from the power of your imperious master."

"Hast thou any hopes of escaping from hence?"

"None," answered Rebecca;—"I am resigned to the will of heaven, but, should there be occasion for it, I have yet some means left by which to preserve my honour from the contamination it is threatened with."

"Thou knowest him not," exclaimed Adrian, "or thou wouldst be less confident of thwarting him. He is firm in his resolutions whether they be for good or evil, and since thou hast once escaped from him, he will watch thee with a vigilant eye, to prevent thy flight a second time."

"But I have a week given me to consider his propositions," replied Rebecca;—"and in that time, heaven may interfere to release me from the accursed power of this villain."

"I pray that it may be so," exclaimed the page, fervently;—"my heart feels for thy distress, and I only wish that I were older and stronger for thy sake."

"Wouldst thou exert thyself in the behalf of one, whom all people of thy religion treat with scorn?"

"Aye, lady," he replied, ardently;—"my heart can feel for the distress of a female, whether she be Jew or Christian, and my sword,

No. 29

were I able to use one, with effect, should ever be ready to protect her against the evil machinations of her enemies."

" I thank thee, boy, for thy good intentions, at any rate," cried Rebecca, with a smile of gratitude ;—" there is some consolation in knowing that I am not without friends, even in this cheerless fortress, and should I die here,—as it is not improbable,—my last prayers shall be offered up for those, who pity and would assist the oppressed Israelite."

" Believe me, lady," exclaimed Adrian, " I pity all who happen to fall into misfortune."

" Indeed ! then I fear thou hast but too much occasion for the exercise of thy compassion."

" There, thou art right, maiden," answered the youth, " for in this place are many captives besides thyself; and if good intentions were of as much service, as good deeds, they should soon be exerted in thy behalf. Nay, this very morning one of thy tribe arrived at the castle,— and from what I have been able to gather, the poor old man has but little chance of ever leaving the place alive."

" Ah !" cried Rebecca, with terror ; " dost thou know who this old man is thou speakest of ?"

" I know nothing more than I have told thee, lady," answered the youthful page.

" Canst thou describe him to me ?" asked Rebecca, whose soul was racked by the most tormenting supicions.

" I cannot," answered the other, " and for this very sufficient reason: —I have not yet had an opportunity of seeing him."

" How knowest thou, then, that such a person has thou speakest of is now within the castle ?"

" Because," answered Adrian, " it is the subject of general conversation amongst the knight's retainers. I have heard them speaking of a venerable Jew, who came here for some purpose or other, and as he is now clossetted with Sir Gaston de Neville, it is a very great chance that he ever gets his liberty again, unless, indeed, he consents to pay a heavy ransom for it."

" If thou dost indeed pity me, as thou sayest," cried Rebecca, " thou wilt quickly obtain for me all the intelligence thou canst. My heart is filled with a thousand terrors, and something seems to assure me that the old man thou speakest of is my father !"

" Nay, maiden," exclaimed Adrian, with compassion, " thou tormentest thyself with fears that, perhaps, after all, are utterly without foundation. There are thousands of old men, belonging to thy tribe, besides thy father, and, therefore, I would counsel thee to look only on the favourable side of the picture, till thou art convinced whether thy fears are founded in truth or not."

" I will try," answered the maiden, " and yet it can only be on condition that thou wilt speedily make all the inquiries thou canst, and inform me of the result."

" Thou mayst rely upon me," exclaimed the page, with earnestness.

" I will take thy word for it," answered Rebecca, " and yet, shouldst thou have deceived me by a pretended zeal in my behalf, my confidence will have been reposed in thee in vain, and I may find an enemy where I once fondly hoped to have found a friend."

" Nay," cried the youth, warmly, " you do me an injustice by these suspicions."

" And if I do," replied Rebecca, " the fault lies with the world in general; I have, alas! met with disappointment everywhere, and, therefore, it is little to be wondered at if I now distrust even thee."

"And yet," exclaimed Adrian, "there is one captive in this castle who could prove to thee that my promise made to an unfortunate fellow-creature is ever held sacred. She, at least, knows my faithfulness, and though I have hitherto been unable to effect her release, I have often visited her cell by stealth, and cheered many an hour that would otherwise have been passed in solitude and grief."

"But, perhaps," observed our heroine, "this female may possess a claim upon thee that I do not; she may have made an impression on thy youthful heart, and thus obtained a zealous friend where I might in vain hope to find one."

"I love her," replied Adrian, ardently, "but not in the manner thou suspectest. In fact, she is much older than myself, and is already a wife."

"Alas! then," sighed our heroine, "she also, like myself, I suppose, has gained the hated love of Sir Gaston de Neville, and having rejected his unhallowed suit, has been enclosed in one of his gloomy dungeons, as a punishment for having dared to treat his base propositions with the scorn they merit."

"Nay," exclaimed the page, "it would make thee hate my master more than ever if I told thee who she is."

"That is impossible," replied Rebecca; "already my soul scorns him as much as it is capable of doing, and, therefore, nothing that thou canst tell me will increase the bitter loathing with which I regard him."

"What wilt thou say," asked the page, "when I tell thee that she of whom I have spoken is the unfortunate and persecuted wife of Sir Gaston de Neville?"

"His wife!" cried Rebecca, with unfeigned horror.

"Even so," answered Adrian; "she is now a captive, and I fear must remain so during the remainder of her days."

"Villain!" exclaimed our heroine, vehemently.

"Aye, so I call him myself," answered Adrian, "and, yet, what is the use of that, when I see the poor creature pining away her life in hopeless captivity?"

"Has she been long a prisoner?" asked Rebecca.

"Five years."

"So long!" exclaimed our heroine, "and with what crime is she charged, that her punishment is thus heavy?"

"I have never heard of anything against her," replied Adrian; "but I believe he grew tired of her because she was much better than himself. Be that as it may, however, she was thrown into a dungeon, as I have told you, and there she now lies, without any chance of her regaining her liberty again."

"And, is there no one in the castle," asked Rebecca, anxiously, "who would risk his life to release this unfortunate lady from the cruelty of her imperious lord?"

"The circumstance," replied Adrian, "is known to scarcely any of the retainers. Two or three only of those that may be depended on are in possession of the secret, and they are so devoted to the knight's service, that she has little to hope from their friendly interference in her behalf."

"If the secret has been so closely kept," asked Rebecca, how is it, that thou, a mere youth, art in possession of it."

"Because," replied the page, "chance enabled me to overhear a conversation between Sir Gaston de Neville and Bertrand le Noir;—they were speaking of the unfortunate Lady Alicia, and being induced to listen further, I ascertained that she was a prisoner, and even learnt the part of the castle where she was confined."

"And thou hast from that time visited the unfortunate captive in her dungeon?"

"I have," replied Adrian; "shortly afterwards I managed to obtain possession of the key when Sir Gaston was not aware of it, and the armourer, who is my best friend in the castle, soon furnished me with a counterpart of it, by means of which, I have since been enabled to visit the dungeon whenever I could do so securely. In doing so, however, I am obliged to be very cautious, lest a discovery should take place, by which I should in future be prevented in supplying her with many luxuries, of which Sir Gaston would deprive her."

"You take her food, then?"

"Aye, and wine, too, whenever I can get it," answered Adrian. "It forms a good substitute for the bread and water with which she is daily furnished by the knight's orders, and I am amply rewarded by the gratitude of one whom I would willingly perish to save."

"Noble youth," cried Rebecca, with enthusiasm, "thy generosity charms me;—and yet," she continued, after a pause, "I would now ask thee, how it is that the Lady Alicia has been so long immured in a dungeon without exciting some enquiry amongst her friends?"

"Because they believe her to be dead," answered Adrian.

"Which rumour," observed our heroine, "has, of course, been spread abroad by Sir Gaston himself?"

"It has," replied the page; "in fact, a mock funeral was got up, and Bertrand le Noir, with two or three of the other retainers as worthless as himself, were ready enough to swear that the Lady Alicia had died of a contagious disease, that rendered her immediate and private burial necessary."

"Then, knowing as thou dost," said Rebecca, "the falsehood of these reports, how is it that thou hast never, up to this time, contradicted them?"

"Lady Alicia forbade me to do so," replied Adrian. "She has no vindictive feelings against her husband, and would rather endure the sufferings she does, than bring disgrace upon him."

"But thou, at least," exclaimed our heroine, "hast no such scruples to prevent thee publishing his crimes to the world, and thus rescuing thy lady from the unjust punishment she is subjected to."

"Why, to tell you the truth," answered Adrian, "I have more than once thought of doing so. But then I know that Sir Gaston de Neville is most vindictive in his nature, and the chances are, that he would order her to be murdered by some of his people if he found there was any chance of his crimes being brought to light."

"Perhaps thou art right, good Adrian," cried our heroine; "the Lady Alicia's life depends upon thy prudence in this respect, and I can readily excuse the conduct I was about to condemn. However, you have greatly interested me about this hapless lady, and if thou art, indeed, earnest in thy desire to serve me, thou wilt not refuse the request I am about to make."

"Nay," answered Adrian, "I must first know what it is."

"I would go with thee to the cell of the Lady Alicia," replied the Hebrew Maiden; "we are companions in misfortune, and, perhaps, the occasional society of one of her own sex may serve to lighten some of those moments that she is doomed to pass in imprisonment."

"Wouldst thou indeed visit her?" cried the page, anxiously.

"Aye, if thou wilt but aid me to do so."

"I will, then," exclaimed Adrian; "yes, lady, I pledge my word to do so; but at present I cannot name the time when you can accompany me, lest we should happen to be discovered. And now, lady, I must leave thee, for I hear the footsteps of Sir Gaston approaching, and if he suspects us in the least, means will be taken to prevent our future meetings."

So saying, Adrian disappeared through a secret pannel behind the tapestry, and within a second or two afterwards, the Knight Templar entered the apartment, wild and disordered from his recent interview with Isaac of Tadcaster.

"Now, Rebecca," he exclaimed, "I am come to urge upon you once more to accept the terms I have offered. Nay, it is in vain that you turn from me with contempt, for in this castle, at least, I am master, and, therefore, there is little need for me to become a beggar for thy mercy."

"Hast thou forgotten thy promise so soon?" asked our heroine, reproachfully. "Yesterday thou didst grant me a week for consideration of thy proposals, and yet now thou comest to demand an instant reply!"

"I do," he exclaimed, imperiously, "and insist upon having it."

"And I," answered Rebecca, unmoved by his frantic gestures, "shall hold you to the pledge you have given. A knight's word, Sir Gaston, is seldom forfeited—and never, without bringing foul dishonour on him who breaks it."

"But the promise," replied the Templar, "was given to a Jewess, and, therefore, is not binding to my conscience. Had it been given to a Christian, indeed, I should have regarded it as more solemn and imperative."

"Like a recreant knight as thou art, thou dost equivocate!" cried Rebecca, with more than her usual fortitude. "I, at least, did not hesitate to take the word of a Christian, and I will hold thee to it in spite of the dishonourable subterfuge thou wouldst lay hold off."

"Psha!" exclaimed the Templar, disdainfully; "it is in vain that thou heapest these reproaches upon me, for I am proof against all thou canst say to deter me from the execution of my purpose. Thou art in my power, girl, and even though a legion of fiends come to aid thee, I would still make thee mine."

"Thou shalt not!" cried Rebecca, in a tone of determination.

"Humph!" muttered Sir Gaston, "perhaps thou thinkest again to effect thine escape from hence?"

"Nay, Sir Knight," she replied, "I know thee too well to expect such an opportunity as thou hast spoken of. Whilst thou canst help it, I know there is no chance of my ever quitting the dreary walls that now surround me; I know thy fierce, lawless temper too well to expect mercy from thee; and yet my case is not hopeless, whilst friends are left to lay before the king a disclosure of the dark crimes thou hast committed against a helpless girl."

"Tush!" retorted the knight, "have I not told thee before, that I fear not the interference of King Richard? He may, doubtless, have his own reasons for wishing to deprive me of the prize I seek, but he will find it no easy matter to snatch thee from my strong grasp."

"False knight!" exclaimed our heroine, "has he not commanded thee to molest me no more?"

"He has," returned the other, "but, thinkest thou I will obey the orders even of King Richard, in an affair that he has no right to inter-

fere in?   Besides, thou hast not yet answered the accusation I brough
against thee respecting my lost diamond, and seeing that it was foun
in thy possession, girl, I have a right to hold thee as my prisoner til
thy guilt or innocence is proved."

"Then, why not give me the opportunity at once?" asked Rebecca.—
"Already I have gone through the trial by ordeal, and, as heaven, o
that occasion, clearly indicated my innocence, I have now a right to de
mand that liberty of which thou hast again deprived me."

"Oh, thou mayst preach of thy rights," exclaimed Sir Gaston d
Neville, with a malicious grin of triumph, "but it remains with mysel
whether I choose to part with thee now that thou art in my power."

"Am I to understand, then, that thou hast resolved to hold me thy
captive?"

"Thou art."

"Then, beware of the vengeance that will yet surely fall upon thee!"
she cried, wildly; "beware, I say, for baseness such as thine will neve
be suffered to triumph against the innocent and helpless."

"Nonsense, girl!" exclaimed the knight, "why dost thou persist in
holding out threats that I despise and laugh to scorn? Thou wouldst terrify
me into giving up the prey I have secured, yet thou knowest not th
man thou hast to deal with, or thou wouldst save thy breath to a better
purpose."

"If thou dost still believe me guilty of having any share in stealing
thy diamond," she replied, "I am willing to undergo any trial in orda
to prove my innocence to the world. Nay, stab me to the heart if thou
wilt, and I will thank thee for the blow that robs me of a life which is
now hateful to me."

"Psha! exclaimed the knight, "one live beauty is worth a million
dead ones. I love thee, wench, and therefore will not slay thee;—at
least, I will not do so unless thou shouldst hereafter become a burden
to me."

"Wretch!" cried our heroine, indignantly, "thou dost triumph now,
but, beware, lest the ruin that is preparing, is not ready to fall down
upon and crush thee."

"Oh, rave on, girl!" returned the knight, in a tone of withering contempt; "give free utterance to all thine invectives, and when thou hast
done, I will tell thee of something that thou knowest not yet of."

"Say what thou wilt, villain!" she exclaimed, "for thou canst not
heap more misery upon me than that which I endure."

"There thou art wrong, wench," returned Sir Gaston, "for since i
last saw thee, fortune has thrown in my way one whom thou wilt grieve
to know is my prisoner."

"Ah!" cried Rebecca, in an agony of terror; "what new horror
awaits me?—Speak, Sir Knight, I implore thee, and end at once the
fearful doubts that distract my brain."

"Humph! thou dost acknowledge then, at length, that thy brimfull
cup of sorrows will yet contain another drop?"

"Oh, ease my tortured heart, I implore you!" cried our heroine, de-
liriously;—"speak, Sir Gaston, who is it that hath now found a prison
in thy stronghold?"

"Thy father, girl!"

"My father!" shrieked Rebecca, distractedly, and reeling, she would
have fallen to the floor, had not Sir Gaston caught her at the moment in
his arms. The thought of the old man's peril, however, soon restored
her, and clasping her hands fervently, she cried in piteous accents:—

"Oh, spare him!—spare him, I implore thee!—Remember he is old —very old, and that he, at least, has never done anything to bring upon him thy burning wrath."

"It is in vain that you plead for him, Rebecca," answered the knight; "he is my prisoner, I tell thee, and will remain so until thou consentest to the terms I have proposed."

"Monster!" exclaimed the indignant girl, "wouldst thou then make a father's liberty dependant on the sacrifice of his daughter's virtue?"

"I tell thee, Rebecca," answered Sir Gaston, "it is in vain to urge me further upon a subject like this. I have long sought an opportunity to get thee in my grasp; hitherto thou hast successfully eluded me— but now thou art rendered powerless, no prayers—no entreaties of thine, shall ever move me from my purpose."

"Wilt thou murder him?" cried Rebecca, wildly.

"Why, no," answered the Templar, "I will not take his life, because, at present, my doing so would not, in any way, forward my designs. It will, however, rest with thyself whether I do so at a future opportunity; and, remember, should I be driven at last to that alternative, thou wilt have to reproach thyself for his death."

"Grant me, then, the time you have already promised me," cried Rebecca, in the height of her despair, and eagerly grasping at any chance of deliverance, however trifling it might be. "Give me a week for deliberation, and at the end of that time I will return the answer."

"And why should I do so?" asked Sir Gaston, coldly; "why should I give thee even a moment's time, when I have it already in my power to enforce thy submission?"

"Thou hast promised me," answered Rebecca, "and there are few men who would willingly forfeit their pledged word. Remember, Sir Gaston, I am thy captive, and having taken care to prevent my escape, the favour I have asked is surely not too much."

"But thou hast once contrived to effect thy retreat," exclaimed Sir Gaston de Neville, "and, I suppose, if the truth were known, thy only motive for asking this delay is, that thou mayst have another chance of escaping."

"Nay, I have no chance now," she replied; "on the former occasion Black Ivan aided me; but now, even if I could do so, I should hesitate to leave behind me a father, whom you would sacrifice to your blind fury."

"Well," exclaimed the knight, after some deliberation, "there may be some truth in that, to be sure. Thou wilt not like to leave the old man, I dare say, so perhaps I may yield to your entreaties; though, observe me, girl, I do not bind myself to do so."

"May I then see my father?" asked Rebecca, earnestly.

"Thou shalt, girl," replied Sir Gaston, "and that, too, without delay. I will order him to be brought into our presence, and, perhaps, his entreaties may induce thee to save thy life, even though it may be at the sacrifice of thine honour."

With this, he stamped upon the ground, as a signal to those of his attendants who were waiting for him without, and who promptly attended the bidding of their haughty master. A few words served to explain the service he required them to perform, and then hastily quitting the room, they proceeded to the dungeon occupied by the unfortunate Isaac of Tadcaster.

CHAPTER XLVI.

" A father's feelings will not be controlled,`
When danger threatens those whom most he loves ;
You have my answer, sir ;—no more of this !"

THE BETROTHED

THE brief imprisonment endured by the venerable Israelite, had been passed in the most tormenting reflections,—not so much for any fear that he felt on his own account, as for his unfortunate daughter, who, now, more than ever, was thrown entirely upon the mercy of her inexorable enemy. Rendered helpless as he was, the only hope that remained, lay in the exertions of Reuben Grenard, whose ardent love for Rebecca would, doubtless, spur him to put forth all his energies for her release. Upon this point Isaac was certain ; but then it was equally certain that Sir Gaston de Neville was now more than ever watchful over his helpless victim, and that even force would not avail, should it be exerted to rob him of his fair prize.

" The only alternative, therefore, that remained, was to petition to the king once more, in behalf of the captive Rebecca ; to expose the treachery that had been used to entice her from home, and then to point out to the sovereign the absolute necessity of immediate steps being taken for her deliverance. Yet, even this plan presented many obstacles to its successful termination ; King Richard was constantly surrounded by those powerful barons who were the principal enemies of the Jews, and whose voices would be immediately raised against any measures being adopted by which a Christian knight might be disgraced for the share he had had in carrying off a girl, who, after all, belonged only to a race of people whom it was the pleasure of their unjust persecutors to trample into the very dust beneath their feet."

Isaac foresaw all these difficulties, and his heart yielded to the despair which they engendered. He now felt that he had acted imprudently in trusting himself to the power of a crafty enemy, like Sir Gaston de Neville ; and feeling but too well assured that all was lost, he threw himself upon the miserable pallet with which his dungeon was supplied, and gave free vent to the black despair, which pressed like a heavy load upon his tortured heart.

He had not, however, remained long in this state of grief, when the removal of heavy chains and bars attracted his attention, and turning his head in the direction from whence the sounds came, he perceived the two men who had been sent by Sir Gaston, the foremost of whom carried a lighted lamp, the flame of which, threw upon the frowning walls of the dungeon a sickly glare, which served to render the place the more frightful. Isaac was startled by the ferocious appearance of the men, and believing that they were sent by their master for some deadly purpose, he started from his recumbent posture, and, looking earnestly in their countenances, demanded whether it was the will of their tyrant master that he should now pay the penalty of his life for having ventured to ask the liberation of his child.

" I tell you what it is, old fellow," exclaimed Arnold, in reply,—"its all very well for chaps like you to find fault with our master, but if you had not been fool enough to come here bothering him about your daughter, you might have been at liberty at this moment."

" Aye, aye," rejoined Raymond, the other ruffian, " its all very well

for you to find fault with Sir Gaston, but let me tell you, he's got more mercy in him than I have, or you should not live another moment to make a fuss, just because he happens to have carried off a wench that he has taken a fancy to."

"If thou art sent to murder me," cried Isaac, in despair, "let thine errand be done quickly."

"Oh !" exclaimed Arnold, "you needn't be in such a hurry to die, old gentleman. Your time is not come yet,—more's the pity !—and all I hope is, that our master will not be long in deciding upon it, and that I may have the job of putting you out of your misery whenever it may be."

"Well," muttered Raymond, "you needn't be so greedy about it, at any rate; those things don't happen every day, and I should like to have the pleasure of helping to put an unbelieving Jew out of the way,"

"It seems, then," exclaimed the old man, without paying much attention to the words of the ruffians: "it seems, then, that you have not been sent to murder me ?"

"Murder you !" growled Arnold, "why what the deuce put such a foolish notion as that into your crazy head ?"

"Your master's well known blood-thirsty disposition, and your own evil looks," answered the Jew.

"Well, that's a compliment, at any rate!" exclaimed Arnold, sulkily. "However, we won't quarrel with you about that just now, so make yourself easy, old boy, and follow us as quickly as your legs will carry you."

"Where would you take me to?" asked the Israelite, with hesitation.

"Where !—why to the presence of Sir Gaston, to be sure."

No. 30

"I will not go with you, then," exclaimed the old man, drawing back, and betraying his repugnance.

"Nonsense!" growled Arnold, "you don't mean to say that we are to have the trouble of carrying you?"

"You have heard me," answered the Hebrew;—"I refuse to go with you, and, therefore, you can return to your master with my message."

"Psha!" exclaimed Arnold, scornfully ;—"you won't go, eh?"

"You have had my answer.—Sir Gaston has thought fit to send me to this dungeon, and I wish not to leave it until it may be his pleasure to restore me to that liberty which he has so unjustly deprived me of."

"Well," exclaimed Arnold, "you seem pretty obstinate, at any rate; but what will you say, when I tell you that Sir Gaston has sent for you at the request of your daughter?"

"My daughter!"

"Aye,—she wants to see you,—and our master, who is a good easy gentleman enough,—sent us to bring you into his presence."

"Lead me thither, instantly!" cried the old man, eagerly; "lead me thither, I say, that my old eyes may once more gaze upon the beloved form of my child."

"Ha! ha! ha!" shouted the heartless ruffian, "I thought we should bring you to something like reason at last! And so you will go to see this wench, though you refused to stir when you fancied it was only to meet Sir Gaston!"

"Is it not natural," exclaimed Isaac, "that I should wish to see my daughter? Has she not been torn from me by ruffian force, and think you I can resist taking perhaps the last opportunity I may ever have of seeing her in this world?"

"And whose fault is it if you do not see her as often as you like?" demanded Arnold. "All you've got to do is to persuade her not to be so plaguy obstinate, and my life for it, you will not only have your liberty, but the girl will be made a lady of?"

"Peace, sirrah! and insult me not by such words as those!" exclaimed the old man, passionately. "My daughter's honour is far more dear to me than life or liberty, and never will I yield my assent to her becoming the profligate mistress of thy cruel master."

"In that case, you must take the consequences upon your own head," answered Arnold. "I've tried what good words would do with you, and since they are of no avail, you had better go at once to Sir Gaston, and tell him as much as you have just now said to me."

"Now, for my part," interposed Raymond, "I should just set you down as an obstinate old fool, that would throw away a good chance when it offers."

"You have my answer," exclaimed Isaac, firmly; "and I, therefore, know the fulfilment of your orders; lead me to the presence of Sir Gaston de Neville, that I may have the satisfaction of once more seeing my daughter, and urging her to preserve her honour, even though it may be at the sacrifice of her life."

"If you take my advice, you will keep your tongue quiet upon that subject," returned Arnold, with a sneer of contempt; "Sir Gaston is not blessed with one of the most patient tempers, and if you say only half as much as you have to us, the chances are that you will not live to return to this place."

"Such threats," answered Isaac, "will not deter me from the duty I owe to my child."

"Do you love her?" demanded the ruffian.

"Love her!" cried the old man, with a burst of affection;—"aye, sirrah, better,—far better than my own life! It is because I love her so dearly, that I prefer her honour to all else that the world contains."

" Then you would rather, by your own obstinacy, condemn her to perpetual imprisonment within these walls ?"

" It is useless to urge me further upon this subject," exclaimed the father, indignantly. " If you have been sent hither to prevail over my scruples, I desire you to return without delay, to Sir Gaston, and tell him that no persuasion,—no threats he can hold out shall ever induce me to regard his suit otherwise than with abhorrence."

" I tell you we have not been sent to interfere at all in the matter," answered Arnold; " it's only our good nature that has prompted us to try what we could do to persuade you to your own good, but since you seem so obstinate about the matter, why things must take their own course, and then you'll have only yourself to thank for whatever may happen."

" My trust is in heaven, not in man's aid," cried the aged Hebrew, in a tone of resignation ;—" but if she must fall, it shall not be through the interference of her father."

" Then come along with us," exclaimed Arnold, snatching up the lamp which he had placed upon the floor during this conference ;—" we, at least, have done our best to save both you and your daughter from further violence. You, however, are determined to sacrifice the girl by your own obstinacy, and as that is the case, the sooner we take you before Sir Gaston de Neville the better."

Having expressed himself thus, Arnold led the way with his light, and followed closely by the Jew, they slowly proceeded through innumerable narrow passages to a lofty and winding flight of steps, leading from the deep subterranean caverns to a portion of the castle which was but little used. On emerging once more into the day-light, they pursued their way through a low Saxon doorway, which led towards the apartments usually occupied by Sir Gaston de Neville.

CHAPTER XLVII.

" Dost thou refuse my tempting offers, girl—
My wealth,—my castle for thy dwelling place,
And all the pleasures gold can purchase for thee?"

THE SOLDIER'S BRIDE.

IT was with a faltering step that Isaac entered the apartment in which sat Sir Gaston de Neville, but it was in vain that he cast an eager glance round the room in search of her who was the object of all his care and anxiety. The knight watched the old man with a feeling of fiendish exultation, and having satisfied himself with the contemplation of the misery he had occasioned, he said :—

" I have sent for you, Isaac, to see whether you still remain determined to oppose my wishes with respect to your daughter. Both, as you are aware, are now in my power, and let that suffice to convince you, that I wish not to act hastily while there is a chance of prevailing upon her to accept the offer I have made."

" I can perfectly understand your motives," replied the old man, with marked emphasis ; " having me in your power, you believe that I am to be terrified into submission, and that to save myself, I will become the base pander to my daughter's shame."

"Nay," answered the knight, haughtily; "I need not any assistance from you,—Rebecca, thanks to my own ingenuity, is now out of your reach, and when ent eaties have entirely failed, I can triumph even in spite of you."

"Art thou a man or fiend?" exclaimed Isaac, whose rage could no longer be controlled.

"I am, at least, thy master," replied Sir Gaston, with perfect coolness. "Even thy life is at my disposal, and, therefore, I caution thee against spurring me on to violence by further insults!"

"Take my life, if thou wilt!" cried the Hebrew, throwing open his vest, and baring his bosom;—" here is my breast, Sir Gaston de Neville, —strike to my heart, if thou wilt, but in mercy to an old man, spare, oh, spare my child!"

"Ho!" vociferated the knight, insultingly; "thou canst stoop to supplicate me, canst thou?—But 'tis well, thy stubborn heart begins to yield, and presently thou will begin to see the madness of attempting to frustrate me."

"Never!" cried the old man, resolutely;—"were it my last word, it should be uttered in the execration of the villain who seeks to triumph over a weak and helpless girl."

"Let it be even as thou wilt," answered the Templar; "I thought by this time thou wouldst have seen the folly of thy resistance, and that thou mightst have purchased liberty by giving me thy daughter. It seems, however, that thou art still madly obstinate, and, therefore, thou mayst return to thy gloomy dungeon, which now will close upon thee for ever!"

"Nay," exclaimed the Israelite, "thy threats terrify me not, for I am old, and thou canst not much shorten the days that otherwise would have fallen to my share: a prison, Sir Knight, has no terrors for me, since liberty would be dearly purchased at the cost of a maiden's fame."

"Thou art still determined to oppose me, then?"

"I am."

"Bear him away, Arnold," exclaimed the knight, beckoning to his two ruffians, who were waiting his orders at the further end of the chamber. "Replace him in the dungeon from whence you brought him, and when that is done, return hither, for I have further need of your assistance."

"Hold!" cried the old man, imploring;—"but for one single moment, hold!—I was brought here under a promise of seeing my daughter, Rebecca;—grant me then but one last interview with her, and I will repine at no misery it may afterwards be your pleasure to inflict upon me."

"Hah!" exclaimed Sir Gaston, with a malicious grin of exultation; "so! thou wilt stoop at last to ask a favour of me, for all that thou hast refused to lend thy voice in aid of my suit to thy daughter! Thou wouldst see her old man, wouldst thou?"

"I would," answered the Jew,—"that is, Sir Gaston, on condition that thou wilt ask no favour of me in return."

"I must not expect thee then to say a word in my behalf?"

"Thou must not."

"Then the favour is all to be one side?"

"It may be so," answered the Jew, "but it will most likely be the last I shall ever ask of thee. Let me see my child, and when that interview is over, thou mayst deliver me over to death as soon as thou pleasest."

"Well," exclaimed the knight, after some hesitation, "I have been thinking of thy request, and as there is nothing particularly unreasonable in it, I shall grant it."

"For that, at least, thou shalt have my thanks."

"Stay, old man," interrupted the knight;—"I was saying thou shouldst have the interview thou hast asked for, but it must be on one condition ; thou must see her in my presence, or not at all."

"Agreed."

"And remember thou must not attempt by word or sign to express the disapproval of her accepting the liberal offer I have made."

"I will endeavour to obey you even in that," exclaimed the old man, tremulously ;—"and yet," he continued, "it is hard for a father, even by silence on one subject, to give his child reason to suppose that he will sanction her departure from the paths of virtue."

"Well, thou canst do as thou pleasest," answered Sir Gaston ; "I wait but to know whether you will see your daughter on the conditions I have named. Refuse them, and thou shalt return to thy dungeon, never more to meet her whom thou dost profess so to love."

"I agree !" cried the old man, eagerly.

"In that case, then, thou shalt behold her ;" answered Sir Gaston, striding towards a door at the further end of the apartment, and returning almost immediately afterwards, leading Rebecca by the hand. "She is here, old man," he resumed, "and having fulfilled my promise, I shall expect you to be equally strict in the observance of your own."

These words were unheard by either Rebecca or her father, who, locked in each others arms, were lost to all thoughts, save those of the momentary happiness that had been vouchsafed them. From this pleasurable dream they were, however, quickly awakened by the stern voice of Sir Gaston de Neville, who, as he forced Rebecca from the embrace of the old man, commanded his retainers to bear away the prisoner to the dungeon from whence they had brought him. These words roused the Hebrew Maiden from the torpor that had come upon her senses, and rushing madly forward, and throwing herself upon her knees at the feet of the libertine knight, she wildly entreated for compassion upon her poor oppressed father.

"Spare him ! Sir Gaston, spare him ! I implore you !" she exclaimed, frantically. "He is old, very, very old, and the cruelty thou wouldst inflict will hurry him to that grave to which he is fast approaching."

"Thou askest mercy," retorted Sir Gaston, unmoved by her earnest intreaties, "and yet can refuse it to me, when I have so often implored it. I seek thy love, girl, and am rejected with scorn ; yet *thou !*—thou, who hast spurned me as if I had been a dog, canst now throw thyself at my feet, to ask mercy for this old man."

"I do," answered Rebecca, rising proudly from her humiliating posture. "I have asked mercy for my aged father, but none for myself. I fear not thy dungeons, Sir Gaston ; nay, I could endure torture with pleasure, could I but know that my sufferings had purchased the liberty of this old man."

"Well," replied the knight, "thou knowest, girl, the conditions upon which alone he can obtain his freedom. Give me thy heart, and the moment thy promise is uttered, Isaac shall be permitted to return home."

"Girl ! heed him not !—heed him not !" exclaimed the old man, earnestly. "Think not of me, for I fear no punishment that he may have the power to inflict upon me ;—treat his solicitations with the scorn they merit, and doubtless, ere long, assistance will arrive when least expected."

"Indeed !" cried Sir Gaston de Neville, with scorn ;—"it seems, then, that thou hast not yet abandoned the foolish hope that assistance from thy friends may avail thee."

"I place no reliance but in heaven!" answered Rebecca, meekly; "the real one I look for aid, and seldom does villainy like thine triumph, without receiving its just reward. But it is not my own safety, Sir Gaston, that I now regard; I can see only the misery thou seekest to heap upon an old, and broken hearted man, whose only crime against thee, is, that he would save a beloved child from destruction,"

"Nay," exclaimed Sir Gaston, "I have deeper cause for hating him than that. He it was that went to the king; publishing my deeds, and seeking to bring odium upon me, because it so happened that I had fallen desperately in love with a girl who thought fit to despise the generous offers I made. He sought to ruin me with my sovereign, girl, and for that alone. I owe him the full vengeance he now will feel!"

"What I did," answered Isaac, "was provoked by thine own base conduct."

"Is it so base then to love a maiden whose beauty I could not resist?" demanded Sir Gaston de Neville.

"Oh, call it not love, Sir Knight!" cried Isaac, bitterly; "thine was a baser feeling, and one that would have degraded the object of thy mad passion to the lowest depths of shame."

"How knowest thou that?—might I not have married her?"

"Never!" exclaimed the old man;—"the haughty Knight Templar, proudly calling himself a Christian, too, would hardly mate himself with the humble daughter of Isaac the Jew."

"But," exclaimed Sir Gaston, "were she inclined to turn Christian, I would yet make her my wife."

"That, Sir Knight, will never be!" cried Isaac;—"my child has been brought up to reverence the religion of her forefathers, and sooner would she suffer any martyrdom that cruelty could devise, than become an apostate from the creed she has followed from infancy."

"Thou knowest not that, old man," answered Sir Gaston; "converts have been made before now, and it is not impossible but that the exertions of our priesthood might have been crowned with success."

"Never!" cried Rebecca, with indignation. "Thine own actions, Sir Gaston de Neville, are alone sufficient to deter me from changing my religion."

"What!" he exclaimed, "not on condition of becoming my wife?"

"Nay," exclaimed our heroine, "hast thou not one wife already?"

"Hah!" vociferated Sir Gaston, stamping furiously; "what means this insolence?"

"It means," answered the maiden, firmly, "that your villainy has not been kept so secret as you imagined. Rumours are abroad that your wife, who was reported to have died ten years ago, is now a prisoner in one of your castles."

"'Tis false!" roared Sir Gaston, fiercely, "I have witnesses who can prove that they were present at her funeral."

"Thou mayst have witnesses," replied Rebecca, unmoved by his violence, "but will they obtain credit when it is well known that their master will not hesitate to stoop even to perjury to conceal his own evil deeds!"

"Who has told thee of this story?" demanded the knight.

"I have heard it commonly stated abroad," answered our heroine, afraid lest she should involve Adrian in a dilemma; "people do not hesitate to speak openly about it, and many even venture to express a hope that condign punishment will fall upon the villain who could thus sacrifice his helpless wife."

"Then, do they accuse me most unjustly," cried Sir Gaston, endeavouring to conceal his confusion; "it is well known to nearly everybody about the castle that the Lady Alicia died of a contagious disorder, which rendered an immediate and private funeral necessary. The world believed the truth of the story at the time, and yet now it seems that a report has been raised by those dastardly enemies who seek my ruin."

"It is your own conduct, Sir Gaston de Neville, that has raised up the enemies you complain of," exclaimed Isaac, interposing. "People grow weary of your tyranny, and, it therefore, is but natural that they should now recur to events that have passed away and might otherwise have died in utter oblivion."

"Thou believest this story, then?" cried the knight, angrily.

"How can I refuse credence," asked the Jew, "knowing, as I do, that crime is a part of your nature. In your mad career, you stop not for anything, and remembering, as I do, the circumstance of your marriage—the reported disagreements that took place between the Lady Alicia and yourself, and your own evil propensities—it is almost impossible to doubt that you are guilty."

"Villain!" cried Sir Gaston, rushing forward, and grasping the old man firmly by the throat; "thou shalt perish for having given utterance to thy base falsehoods;—thou, doubtless, hast been the means of propagating this falsehood, and my own hand shall avenge the dishonour thou wouldst bring upon me."

"For mercy's sake, spare him!" cried Rebecca, hastening forward as she saw the danger with which her father was threatened; "save him! —save him! I entreat."

"He shall die!" vociferated the knight, still more fiercely; "his own tongue hath urged me to the deed, and no persuasion of thine shall prevail on me to forego my vengeance!"

"Then this to thy heart!" cried Rebecca, wildly, and snatching a poniard from the knight's belt, she aimed a blow that would surely have proved mortal, had he not, at the moment, moved his arm, and thus averted the fatal direction the blade would, otherwise, have taken. As it was, however, Sir Gaston received so severe a wound, that he sank exhausted to the floor, ere either of the retainers could fly to his assistance. The alarm thus created, brought a number of domestics to the assistance of their master, and there is no doubt Rebecca would have fallen a victim to the fury of the ruffians, had not the knight exerted his little remaining strength to command them to desist, until he should give further orders as to what should be done with her. He then desired to be conveyed to his own bed-chamber, which order was speedily complied with; whilst Arnold and Raymond dragged away the Jew from the embrace of his daughter, and immediately hurried him to the dungeon from whence they had brought him. As for Rebecca, the scene which had just passed, had wrought so powerful an effect upon her mind, that sinking upon a couch, she was, happily, for some time, unconscious to the troubles that afflicted her.

CHAPTER XLVIII.

"In that dark hour when dire affliction comes,
Then Friendship best displays itself."—THE PILGRIMAGE.

How long she had remained in her fainting fit, Rebecca knew not, but on recovering her senses, she perceived that Edith was anxiously

employed in tending upon her; and remembering the scene of terr
that had taken place, she eagerly enquired whether the wound she ha
inflicted upon the knight was likely to prove mortal.

"Oh! bless your heart, no," replied the girl; "wicked fellows, lil
Sir Gaston, generally contrive to get over what would kill any bod
else. A skilful leech has just examined his wound, and he says th
though master has lost a great deal of blood, there is not the least dan
ger to be feared."

"Heaven be thanked for that!" exclaimed Rebecca, fervently.

"Well!" cried the girl, with amazement, "you are the strange
creature that ever I came near in all my life. First of all, you try t
kill Sir Gaston, and then you are almost out of your wits for joy be
cause it's likely he'll recover to torment you again."

"The act was done in a moment of desperation," answered Rebecca
"I saw that my father's life was in danger, and, maddened by my terro
I committed a deed, against which, my soul now revolts with horror!"

"And why, pray, should you think anything at all about it?" aske
Edith; "I'm sure you have no great reason to respect him, and if h
had happened to have died, you would most likely have been set a
liberty."

"Nay, that is unlikely," answered our heroine; "had the knigh
perished by the hand of a Jewess, there is no telling where the mischie
would have ended;—my own life would have been forfeited to the out
raged laws of the country, and every Hebrew in the land would hav
been persecuted for an act performed by one of their tribe."

"Why, there's something in that, to be sure," replied Edith, "an
yet, after all, who could have blamed you for saving your own father froi
being strangled before your face. Sir Gaston, I am sure, ought to b
very thankful that he was prevented committing a murder, even thoug
he may have lost some blood by it."

"But my father," cried Rebecca, despairingly, "is still left to th
fierce vengeance of this base knight; they have dragged him again t
his dungeon, and perhaps the first orders given by Sir Gaston, will b
to despatch him in retaliation for the wound he has received."

"Nay, child, I don't think you have much to be afraid of, on tha
score," exclaimed Edith, in a tone of encouragement. "The king ha
I know, sent here to command the appearance of Sir Gaston at court
it is something about you, I have no doubt, so that our master mus
mind what he is doing, or he may chance to get into a scrape that i
won't be quite so easy to get out of again."

At this moment they were interrupted by the arrival of Adrian, who
came with a message from the knight, requiring her immediate attend
ance in his chamber. This was a command anything but agreeable u
Edith, but as there was no choice left, she contented herself by mutter
ing her dissatisfaction, and bustled out of the room in no very goo
humour.

"And now, Rebecca," said the young page, as soon as they wer
alone, "I have come to tell you that there is no longer any obstacle ii
the way of your seeing the Lady Alicia, whenever you may think fit
I have prepared her for seeing you, and it is impossible to describe her
joy at the prospect of once more being permitted to associate with one o
her own sex."

"Yet, she will hate me," cried our heroine, "when she learns tha
the love of her guilty husband has been bestowed on me."

"Nay, I have told her all," answered Adrian; "I explained to hei
the persecutions you have endured through your refusal to accept the
terms of Sir Gaston de Neville."

"And did she not execrate me for robbing her of that love which she has been so unjustly deprived of?"

"On the contrary," replied the page; "she wept at the recital of your misfortunes, and offered up her earnest prayers to heaven, that you might have the means given you to escape from the dangers with which she is surrounded. Nay, more, she implored me to aid you by every exertion in my power, and to try whether nothing could be devised by which to secure your escape from the castle."

"And does she know that her husband had nearly perished by my hand?" asked Rebecca, earnestly.

"I have concealed nothing from her."

"And did not that fill her soul with hatred against one who had so nearly become her murderer?"

"She shuddered when I told her the story," answered Adrian, "but after a pause, she seemed to reflect upon the situation in which you were placed at the moment, and frankly acknowledged that had she been in your place, despair would have prompted her to the same deed."

"And knowing all these things," cried Rebecca, "she is still willing to permit me to visit her?"

"She is."

"Oh, how my heart throbs for the moment of our interview!"—exclaimed our heroine, passionately; "her sorrows have aroused a deep interest in my heart, and cheerfully would I change places with her to restore the unfortunate Alicia to liberty."

"Ah!" exclaimed Adrian, "I knew you would be just the companion she would like to have,—grief has visited both of you, and in each other's society, you will learn to forget the past in the rapture of the

No. 31

present moment. As for the Lady Alicia, I know you will love her from the instant of your first meeting,—her gentleness of spirit will be sure to warm your heart towards her, and sad as captivity is, it will be lightened by the occasional visits I shall be enabled to obtain for you."

"Generous boy!" cried Rebecca. "thy kind zeal in behalf of an unfortunate mistress, assures me that I have found a friend in whom I can implicitly rely."

"Believe me, lady, you may," answered the page; "in truth, I pity you, and would do anything in my power to serve one whom misfortune has almost overwhelmed."

"Wilt thou befriend my father in the same way?" asked Rebecca, anxiously;—"wilt thou visit him in his dungeon, and assure him of his daughter's present safety?"

"I will do my best to serve him," answered Adrian, "but I fear it will be impossible for me to gain admittance to his dungeon,—I have no means of obtaining the key belonging to it, and I fear neither Arnold nor Raymond, who are entrusted with his safe keeping, will allow me to see a prisoner whom Sir Gaston has ordered to be kept in the strictest solitude."

"Are the men you speak of, incapable of doing a kindness, even though, in doing so, they should act against the orders of a tyrannical master?" asked Rebecca.

"I cannot say much for their good temper in general," answered Adrian, "though, to be sure, I have nothing to complain of, seeing that they usually treat me with more kindness than they ever show to any body else in the castle. I have sometimes thought I was a bit of a favourite with Arnold, for on one occasion I saved him from the wrath of Sir Gaston, and from that time, the fellow has been uncommonly civil."

"Perhaps, then," observed the maiden, "he may be induced to relax some of the severity he has been ordered to exercise towards my unfortunate father."

"At any rate I will try him," answered the youth, ardently. "I will see Arnold by-and-bye, and over a cup of Rhenish wine, I will endeavour to find out whether or not his heart is made of penetrable stuff."

"But will he drink, think you?" asked the Hebrew Maiden.

"Drink! aye, like a toper; both Arnold and Raymond are rare lovers of good living, and I'll answer for it, that by the time they have drank a pint or two, they may be prevailed upon to do almost anything, except suffer their prisoner to escape."

"If they will but soften the rigour of his imprisonment, it will be something," cried Rebecca, rejoiced at the prospect there was of obtaining better treatment for her father; "he is old, and unable to bear up against the severity with which Sir Gaston de Neville would treat him."

"Well," exclaimed Adrian, "I only wish I knew of any way to get him out of this dismal place; and yet, I do not know that that would be of much service to him, seeing that Sir Gaston would take care to have him brought back again before he had enjoyed his liberty many hours."

"I ask only a mitigation of his sufferings," cried the maiden; "obtain but that for him, and, I doubt not, he will, ere long, be released from this place."

"Do you really think so?" asked Adrian, eagerly.

"Nay, I feel certain of it."

"And on what ground, may I ask?"

"The king will hear of his detention," answered Rebecca, "and when he learns this further violence that has been practised by Sir Gaston, he will take instant measures to procure his release from the power of his inveterate foe."

"But will the king take the same pains to take *you* from Sir Gaston de Neville?"

"I think he will," she replied, "but if he does, it can only be to throw me into a prison on a charge of having attempted to take the life of Sir Gaston de Neville. That I shall be condemned, too, is most likely, and, in that case, the poor Jewess, who has dared to raise her hand against a Christian knight, will hardly be suffered to escape a less penalty than death!"

"You don't mean to say that they would go so far as that?"

"Aye, boy, they would though," she replied; "I have enemies enough to urge such a doom, and, doubt not, they would exalt in having an opportunity to send one of a race they despise to meet her fate on the public scaffold!"

"Well, but the knight is not slain," answered Adrian, "and surely they will not punish you so severely when it is known that you stabbed him only when there was no other chance left of saving your father from death."

"That will not be held as any excuse for an unfortunate Jewess," she replied; "had the act been committed by a Christian, it is possible mercy might have been exercised."

"Still," returned Adrian, "matters are not quite so desperate as you seem to fancy; Sir Gaston professes to love you, and, in spite of this little affair that has just taken place, he will rather do anything than part with you. Nay, since he has recovered from the stupor that followed the loss of blood, he has done nothing but rave about you, and denouncing the fiercest vengeance against all of us, in case we suffered you to escape from the castle. Then he speaks of the beauty of his captive,—laments the difference of religion that forbids his union with her, and vows that if she would only become a convert to Christianity, that he would wed, and make her the sharer of his rank and fortune."

"He thinks not, then," cried Rebecca, bitterly, "of the wretched wife whom he has doomed to hopeless captivity."

"Why, even if he does ever think of the Lady Alicia," answered Adrian, "it is only as of one whom he hates, and for whose death he is most anxious."

"Did he not mention her name in the delirium you were just now speaking of?" enquired the maiden.

"Not that any of us heard," replied Adrian; "he muttered a good deal, to be sure, that we could not understand, and it seemed that his thoughts were wandering to some very painful subject, for he groaned most heavily, and by the violent shuddering of his frame, it was very evident that something was terribly torturing him."

At that moment, one of the menials came to announce to Adrian, that Sir Gaston required his immediate presence in his chamber; he was, therefore, compelled to take his departure, though not without first of all arranging to return as soon as ever the dusk of evening had set in, when, if nothing hindered him, he was to convey her to the cell of the Lady Alicia.

CHAPTER XLIX.

" Nay, scorn me not, girl,
   For spite of ev'ry power,
   I'll make thee yield the slave of love and me."

Anon.

Absorbed in thoughts, of a thousand different hues, our heroine was so utterly lost in contemplations, upon the past and future, that she heard not the footsteps that were approaching her, nor was she conscious that her privacy had been intruded upon, until a well-known voice whis-pered in her ear,

" May I ask, lady, the nature of the anxious ruminations that appear to be just now occupying your brains?"

Rebecca startled from her seat as these words were uttered, and with a faint scream, she cried:

" Black Ivan!—how cam'st thou hither, and with what dreadful pur-pose?"

" I come hither," he replied, carefully, "through yonder secret door, and the purpose of my visit was to perform the same kind office I once did before."

" Thou wouldst release me, I suppose?"

" That, maiden, was the errand that brought me here."

" And then convey me to thy secret haunt, to become the companion of thy base bandit followers."

" Oh!" exclaimed Ivan, " if that is any grievance, matters may be very easily arranged otherwise; I can take thee where thou wilt have no other companion than an old woman, who is too deaf to hear thee, and too sulky to enter into any conversation. So thou wilt not quarrel much, and thou shalt occasionally be gladdened with my presence."

" It seems, Ivan, that you came hither to mock my despair," cried Rebecca, reproachfully. " I am already oppressed and bowed down by the weight of my affliction, and now thou dost visit me to offer liberty upon terms which thou well knowest I will never accept."

" And why shouldst thou not accept them?" asked Black Ivan, haughtily;—" am I not as well-favoured as Reuben Grenard, and shall I submit to see so fair a prize carried off by him, without making an effort to secure it for myself?"

" Leave me, Ivan!" cried the maiden, in a peremptory tone,—" leave me, I say, ere thou compellest me to call for aid, against an insolent intruder."

" If any come to interfere with me," exclaimed the robber, fiercely,— " it will be the last time they will ever have an opportunity given them to spoil sport. I am not in the castle of my enemy unarmed, as you may perceive, nor shall I fail to use sword and dagger, against all who may have the temerity to venture within my reach."

" Wouldst thou murder those who come to aid a helpless woman?" asked Rebecca, with scorn.

" Aye."

" Then art thou as bad as report hath painted thee!" cried our heroine, with indignation that she could not suppress.

" I care not for what report may say of me," answered Black Ivan; —" people may say that I am a robber,—and they are right,—for my necessities have compelled me to assist myself, by occasionally helping a neighbour, when I happen to know that he is possessed of more than is absolutely necessary for his subsistence. Thus far, girl, I am certainly guilty, yet never did I commit murder, unless driven to it, in order to preserve myself from falling into trouble."

"Again I entreat thee to leave me," cried Rebecca, earnestly.— "Some one may suddenly break in upon us, and I dread thy violence, should any attempt be made to capture one upon whose head a heavy price is set."

"Let no one attempt to take me," replied Ivan, "and I will engage to leave this place as quietly as I entered it. Unobserved, I came hither through one of the private posterns, and since it seems so easy to come in or go out of this castle, I have made up my mind to offer you liberty, on condition that you will consent to accompany me."

"Never!" exclaimed Rebecca, indignantly;—"here I know I am in peril;—yet bad as my situation is, I will not change it to become the companion of such as thou art."

"Oh, thou mayst be as scornful as thou likest, girl," retorted the robber;—"thou canst rail, for 'tis a woman's privilege, and I would not deprive thee of the pleasure it affords. There is, however, one thing that I would caution thee against!—do not, by thine obstinacy, make me thine enemy, for so surely as thou dost so, I will bear thee off in triumph, in spite of any resistance that may be offered."

"That may yet be tried," answered Rebecca,—"for wert thou to put thy threat in into execution, I could quickly bring to my rescue more than enough to punish thy mad temerity. Thou seest, therefore, that I am not to be terrified into submission, even though it be Black Ivan himself that has come to war against a helpless woman."

"I do not war against thee," answered the robber, somewhat awed by the resolute manner in which she had spoken;—"I came to release thee from the hands of Sir Gaston de Neville, and love, alone, has prompted me to the act."

"How knowest thou I was here?" demanded our heroine.

"From one of my fellows," answered Black Ivan, "who chanced somehow or other, to pick up the information. I learnt also that thy father is in captivity here, and it will be thy fault if I make not a bold effort for his rescue."

"That is impossible," exclaimed Rebecca, "for he is confined in one of the deepest dungeons of this castle, and I fear no effort can ever snatch him from the arts of the tyrant, Sir Gaston de Neville."

"Psha! I tell thee, girl, thou hast no cause to despair," replied the robber chief;—"agree to become mine, and thy father shall be released within a few hours."

"I will make no promise," cried Rebecca, "yet I would know how it is possible to carry off my father, who is so carefully guarded as to forbid all hope of ever rescuing him from the living tomb in which he is buried?"

"But it so happens," replied Ivan, "that I have at this time, as my prisoner, the favourite retainer of Sir Gaston de Neville. This man shall be offered as a ransom for thy father, and if the knight dares refuse my terms, I will hang his caitiff follower on the nearest tree I can find, and afterwards send the carrion to Sir Gaston, as a hint of what he may himself expect, should chance at any time throw him in my way."

"Wouldst thou murder one who cannot help himself?" asked Rebecca, with a shudder.

"I would," replied Black Ivan, "and with tolerable justice, too, I think, seeing that it is in the power of his master to save him if he thinks fit."

"My father needs not such help as that thou hast proposed to give him," cried Rebecca. "He is now beyond any aid that thou canst give him,—and it is, therefore, in vain that thou wouldst prevail upon me to flee with thee, under a pledge which would surely be broken."

"And dost thou remember," exclaimed the robber, "that by remaining here, thou wilt fall a victim to thine own rash obstinacy? Sir Gaston de Neville is not the man to relinquish his prey, when once his eye is fixed on it, and ere many days have passed away, thou wilt regret the folly that has urged thee to reject the offer I have made."

"At present," replied Rebecca, "I have nothing to fear from the violence of him thou speakest of."

"How knowest thou that, girl?"

"Because he his now confined to his couch, in consequence of a wound inflicted by my hand."

"How?—hast thou had the courage to attempt the life of Sir Gaston de Neville?"

"I have, but it was not till the villain was in the act of slaying my father. Rendered desperate by the danger that threatened a parent, I thought not of the consequences that might follow the act, but snatching a poniard from his girdle, I aimed a blow at his heart, which must have proved mortal, had he not raised his arm, and thus received a wound which, happily, is not mortal."

"Then is thy situation worse than ever," exclaimed Ivan;—"Sir Gaston will not easily forgive the injury thou hast done him, and the time during which he is confined through the effect of thy blow, will be passed in forming fresh projects against thee and thy father."

"I care not, even if it should please him to consign me to an ignominious death," answered Rebecca. "I fear but for my father, and he, alas! is, like myself, in the power of one who knows not mercy."

"Then why not flee from him, girl?"

"With thee!"

"Aye,—why not with me? I can afford thee a secure retreat, where the malice of thy foes would fail to find thee. I could shield thee, Rebecca, and would part with thee only at the expense of my own life."

"And my father," answered the indignant girl, "might be left to linger out his few remaining days in hopeless captivity!"

"Nay, have I not already promised to do all in my power to obtain his release?"

"Thou hast, but thy efforts would be useless," she replied;—"besides, I know my father's feelings too well to act against them, for he would spurn me like some loathsome reptile, were I to barter my honour as the price of his liberty."

"But I will wed thee, girl,—thou shalt become my wife."

"The wife of a robber," she exclaimed, indignantly.

"Aye,—thou mightest do worse, I can assure you;—I am wealthy, Rebecca, and having no great partiality for the life of a bandit, I would resign the office I hold among my brave companions, and retire with thee to some foreign land, where the rest of our lives might be passed in happiness."

"I have told thee before, Ivan," replied Rebecca, "that my heart is already given to another:—I am betrothed to Reuben Grenard, and never will I consent to break faith with one whose love has been so long and severely tried."

"Dost thou reject all the offers I have made thee, then?" demanded Black Ivan, fiercely.

"I do, and therefore entreat that you will now leave me under a promise never to see me again."

"Leave thee!" cried the robber; "thinkest thou I will depart without thee, after the trouble I have taken to gain admittance here, for the purpose of carrying thee off? No, girl!—there may be some danger in making the attempt, but let what may happen, I will hazard everything rather than quit this place without thee."

And then advancing hastily, and stretching forth his arm, he would have seized upon our terrified heroine, had she not at the moment started back, and uttered a scream that was heard, even in the remotest parts of the castle. Yet this did not deter the robber from executing the project that had brought him thither, and muttering aloud his bitter curses, he again advanced for the purpose of seizing upon his intended victim. This time, however, she was preserved by the sudden rushing in of a number of Sir Gaston's domestics, who perceiving only the terror of our heroine, flew to her assistance, and thus afforded an opportunity of escape to the robber chieftain. In fact, Black Ivan soon saw that there were enough to overpower him, in case of any resistance being offered, and taking advantage of the momentary confusion that had ensued on the first irruption of the domestics into the room, he slipped aside the secret pannel, which, on a previous occasion, had been so serviceable to him, and disappeared before anybody thought of securing him. When, however, Rebecca had recovered sufficiently to explain the cause of her loud outcries, they began to curse their stupidity, for suffering the escape of a man, for whose capture, a large sum of gold had been offered. But it was in vain to grumble now, for Black Ivan had doubtless fairly got the start of them, and resolving to keep a better look out for the future, they retired, leaving Rebecca to the care of Edith, who by this time had arrived at the scene of tumult.

CHAPTER L.

"I tell thee, sirrah, none shall hinder me,
For I have sworn to make the treasure mine,
And death itself, e'en, should not turn me from it."
THE VENETIAN.

THE scream that had been uttered by Rebecca, was heard by Sir Gaston de Neville, who, starting from the torpor in which he had been lying, inquired of his page the cause of the fearful outcry that had just burst upon his ears. But Adrian knew no more than himself, though he felt alarmed lest any new danger had befallen Rebecca, and rising hastily from his seat, by the bed side of his suffering master, he inquired whether he should go and ascertain the reason of the cry of terror, which they had just heard.

"Aye, do, good Adrian," answered the knight, in a voice rendered feeble by exhaustion;—"haste thee, boy, for the tones seemed to be those of the Hebrew Maiden, and I fear some harm hath happened to her."

" Shall I tell her, Sir Knight, that you would see her ?" asked Adrian, " or wouldst thou rather defer the interview till another time, when thou wilt be better able to converse with her."

" I will not see her at present," answered the knight, languidly;— " this wound makes me fretful, and I might, perhaps, reproach her for the blow she struck."

" And yet, after all," exclaimed the page, " she is not, I think, so much to blame for what she did ;—her father's life was threatened, and there are few who would not have done as she has, if they were placed in the same situation."

" I have made every allowance for that," replied Sir Gaston ;—" and on one condition, can freely forgive the sufferings she has caused me. Tell her this from me, and urge her, if you can, to accept the offer I have made."

" I will deliver your message," answered Adrian, retiring from the room, but at the same time mentally resolving to have no share in prevailing upon her to become the paramour of his imperious master.

For some time after Adrian's departure the knight lay as still and silent, as if death had already claimed him as his prey. Gloomy thoughts were passing through his mind, and fresh projects were forming, by which he might succeed in his base designs against the peace of a vir- tuous maiden. He was resolved to allow no obstacles to interpose, and imagining that if kinder treatment were given to her father, it would have some effect towards softening the angry feelings with which she re- garded him, he beckoned to Arnold, who was now in attendance upon him, and inquired what had been done with Isaac of Tadcaster after the recent interview. A grim look of savage delight spread over the coun- tenance of the fellow, and chuckling at the idea of tortures which he hoped would be inflicted upon the helpless old man, he replied,—

" He is now in his dungeon where we conveyed him, immediately after you received the wound that we all of us thought mortal. He thought that we were going to kill him at once, I believe, but we told him that you had not given any orders yet, and that, no doubt, he would have to suffer a great deal more, before you would think fit to put him out of his miseries."

" Then thou hast done wrong, Arnold," replied the knight ;—" the old man must be better treated, or all the pains I have taken to secure that girl, will be thrown away."

" Why," exclaimed Arnold, with surprise, " you would not shew any mercy to an unbelieving Jew ?"

" Obey me, as you value my future favours," answered Sir Gaston;— " let him be removed to a better chamber, than the cheerless one he now occupies, and see that his food is less coarse than that which he has hitherto been supplied with."

" And all this kindness," cried the fellow, " is to be shewn him, I sup- pose, because he has been the principal cause of his daughter's obstinacy. Besides, hasn't the wench tried her best to take away your life, and are they to be rewarded for it, as if they had really been doing you some great service ?"

" I have my own reasons for it," answered Sir Gaston; " and you will, therefore, obey me, unless you would bring upon yourself the vengeance you would induce me to take on them."

"Oh, it shall be done, of course, since it is your command," an- swered Arnold, submissively. " The Jew shall have the best chamber

in your castle, if that's all, only it must be confessed I expected he would have been put upon the rack instead of having all this civility shown him."

"Thou knowest me not yet, I can perceive, Arnold," exclaimed the knight;—"if severity would have answered my purpose, I should not have failed to exercise it to the utmost. I have, however, discovered that the girl resents the imprisonment of her father, and will never regard me but as a monster, until the old man is released from his dungeon."

"And my life on it," exclaimed the ruffian, "she will not think a bit the better of you when all this is done."

"Why dost thou think so?"

"Because it seems that she fancies some one a great deal better than she does you," answered the other, bluntly.

"That may be, but he is poor."

"True,—yet he belongs to her own tribe, and, therefore, will be preferred to a Christian knight."

"Had she been still at liberty," answered Sir Gaston, "it is likely enough that she would have accepted him instead of the more splendid offers I have made her. Now, however, she is a captive in my hands, and it must be our care to prevent her ever again seeing this Reuben Grenard."

"Yet, suppose he should contrive to enter your castle in disguise?—How would you have me act then?"

"Slay him without mercy!" cried Sir Gaston, endeavouring to raise himself, but falling back again through exhaustion.

No. 32

" Humph !—then you would not shew the same kindness to him that you will to the old man ?"

" He is my rival," murmured the knight, " and, were he dead, my chances with Rebecca would be all the better.   She might, then, perhaps, listen to me, which I fear she never will whilst any chance remains of becoming his.   But list!—Adrian returns, and I would learn from him the cause of the cry we just now heard."

As Arnold retired to the further part of the chamber the page advanced towards the bed-side of his master.

" Well, boy," cried the knight, with anxiety, " hast thou discovered the meaning of the piercing scream that just now roused me from the lethargy into which I had fallen?"

" I have," answered Adrian ;—" it seems that the Hebrew Maiden, —your captive, —has been visited by Black Ivan, the Outlaw,— who ——"

" Hah !" exclaimed the knight ;—" Black Ivan in my castle !—then, of course, he has been secured, and is now in my power ?"

" On the contrary," replied Adrian ; " it seems that he has somehow or other, most unaccountably escaped, and though a strict search has been made, no one as yet been able to discover him anywhere about the castle."

" Idiots !" exclaimed the Knight Templar, furiously ;—" did they not know the reward they would have received for his capture, and the anxiety I have always expressed to get that man into my power."

" Nay," answered the page, " I believe it was no fault of theirs that the fellow managed to escape.   All their attention was needed by Rebecca, who, it seems, was nearly fainting from terror, and whilst they were occupied in attending upon her, Black Ivan took the opportunity to make his escape."

" He must still be somewhere within the castle walls," cried Sir Gaston de Neville.   " It is impossible that he can have passed the sentinels, and I shall yet have the villain in spite of all his efforts to elude me."

" I fear that is unlikely," answered Adrian, " for from what I can gather from Rebecca, it seems that he contrived to enter the place without being seen, and if that is the case, it is quite as likely for him to escape the same way."

" Some post must have been left unguarded, then," exclaimed the knight ;—" see that every part of the walls are doubly manned, and let orders be given to slay Black Ivan, whenever he may venture to shew himself in this place again."

" I will do your bidding, Sir Gaston," replied the page ; " and yet it strikes me that Black Ivan is too cunning to fall quite so easily as you imagine.   He always goes well armed ; and, from what I have heard, is well able to cope with any half-dozen of your stoutest men."

" We shall see," answered Sir Gaston ,—" at any rate a large reward is offered by the king for his apprehension, and I will double the sum whenever the ruffian is either slain or made my prisoner."

" That, at all events, will serve to sharpen their wits," cried Adrian ; " and yet," he continued, " Ivan knows pretty well the sort of reception he is likely to meet with here, and, I'll dare be sworn, he shews not his face again till he can do so with tolerable safety,"

" But Rebecca,—is she recovered ?"

" Oh, yes," replied the page ;—" she has got over the terror the fellow threw her in, and is now attended by Edith, who, I dare say, will not leave her again in a hurry."

"If I understood you rightly, boy," exclaimed Sir Gaston, "the robber made an attempt to carry her off by violence?"

"He did,—not, however, I believe, till he had used all the arguments he could to persuade her that it would be far better to fly with him than remain here as your prisoner."

"And she refused to accompany him!" cried the knight, in a tone of triumph;—"that, at least, goes far to prove that she would rather trust herself with me, than with the man who would thus have carried her off under the plea of preserving her from the power of Sir Gaston de Neville.'

"That may be," replied Adrian, "and yet, to speak the truth, her opinion about you does not seem to be much altered at present. She shudders whenever your name is mentioned before her, and entreats every body about the place to prevent, if possible, her ever seeing you again."

"Aye, boy," exclaimed Sir Gaston, evidently mortified at the freedom with which the youth had spoken; "she may at present feel indignant at the means I took to bring her here; but that is a feeling which will soon wear off, and when she finds that her father is no longer treated with severity, gratitude will prompt her to behave with more courtesy to the man who has the power, if he chooses to exert it, of destroying the old Hebrew by the slowest, and most agonising tortures. She is well aware how completely I command their destinies, and will pause ere she risks her father's life by any farther obstinacy. But I grow faint, Adrian, and the pain of my wound prevents my continuing this conversation at present. You will, however, see Rebecca, and whenever an opportunity occurs, speak for me, and urge upon her the prudence of waving all those scruples that have hitherto interfered to frustrate my designs. Do that, Adrian, and when you are old enough, I will bring about the union you so much desire with Edith, and furthermore I will bestow upon the girl a dower that shall render her a match worthy of the proudest in the land."

Adrian made no reply to this, but seated himself in silence by the bedside to watch his master, and tend upon his every want. Sir Gaston slept uneasily, yet he woke not from the terrible dreams that haunted his imagination, and as the dusk of evening gradually approached, our young page began to make preparations for attending Rebecca as he had promised, to the dungeon of the unfortunate Lady Alicia.

CHAPTER LI.

" Theirs was a dark and solemn pilgrimage,
Through places unfrequented and obscure,
Where darkness reigns triumphant."

IMOGENE.

As the shades of evening slowly gathered around, Rebecca began to grow anxious for the arrival of the young page; the time appeared to be longer too than usual, and when, at last, the darkness had reached its highest pitch, she despondingly lit her lamp, in the full belief that something or the other had occurred to prevent her intended visit to the persecuted Alicia. With increasing uneasiness she waited another half hour, at the expiration of which period, she heard light footsteps in the corridor, and glancing towards the further end of the chamber, she perceived the figure of Adrian advancing on tip-toe, and holding his finger to his lips, as a caution for her not to speak too loudly, for fear of being overheard.

"You have thought me a long time coming, I dare say," he said, "but care is necessary to avoid any discovery of this meeting taking place. At present, Sir Gaston has not the slightest suspicion that I know anything of her ladyship's hapless plight, but if he thought I was aware of a fact so dangerous to himself, he would take care to prevent its going any further, by taking instant measures for silencing me."

"He would, perhaps, order you to be secretly assassinated!"

"Why, no, not quite so bad as that, I fancy, replied Adrian, "but he would take care to shut me up, so as to prevent any indiscretion of mine from getting him into trouble."

"I see!" cried Rebecca, shuddering;—"he would send you to one of those dark cheerless dungeons which are already nearly filled with his unfortunate victims."

"That he would do to a certainty," answered the page, "so all I have got to do, is to avoid the danger by keeping the secret as close as possible."

"Have you ever told anybody else of it?" asked our heroine.

"I have not whispered it to a soul besides yourself," replied Adrian. "Somehow I fancied I could trust you, and believe me, I have no fear that my confidence will be misplaced."

"By me, at least, it never shall be mentioned," answered Rebecca. "Unfortunately, I know too well the blind and impetuous fury of Sir Gaston de Neville;—his cruelty chills my blood whenever I think of it; and sooner would I endure any torture, than reveal that which would bring upon you the full weight of his terrible displeasure."

"I know it,—I am sure of it!" exclaimed Adrian, fervently; "not, however, that I fear the anger of the knight on my own account, but the Lady Alicia would miss the only kindness that is now done her, and left once more to the solitude of her cheerless cell, she would feel more than ever the cruel severity with which she is treated by her husband."

"And you think, Adrian, that the visit I am about to make will not prove an unwelcome one?"

"On the contrary," he replied, "I know she is even now expecting you with the greatest anxiety."

"Then let us not lose another moment," cried Rebecca; "I am quite ready to follow, when you think proper to set forward on this visit to your afflicted lady."

Without another word Adrian now took up the lamp, and silently motioning Rebecca to follow, he proceeded across the room, and raising the tapestry, discovered a door which had hitherto escaped the observation of our heroine; this readily yielded to a slight push, and passing onwards, they found themselves in a spacious chamber, that appeared to be unoccupied for some years, as the furniture was covered with dust, and the place altogether presented a most wretched and neglected appearance.

"This," said the page, was Lady Alicia's favourite sitting-room, ere she fell under Sir Gaston's displeasure;—here I have often sat with her for hours, and watched the tears as they chased each other down her wan cheeks; for she was unhappy long before Sir Gaston threw her into the wretched dungeon she now occupies, and I have since thought that most likely the poor dear lady had a notion of what was about to follow."

"You must have been very young at the time you speak of," observed Rebecca, gazing sorrowfully upon the desolate scene around her."

"I was not more than twelve years old at the time," answered the page, "but young as I was, I could not help pitying the poor lady, when I saw that she was so unhappy;—she saw that she had outlived the regard of her husband, and I believe would gladly have died, rather than experience the coldness and neglect he treated her with."

"And did she never remonstrate against his unjust treatment?"

"Never;—on the contrary, she tried to appear cheerful whenever she was in his society. On being left alone, again, however, tears would once more come to her relief, and thus her days were passed in misery and solitude, such as I verily believe no other poor creature ever had to endure."

"Lead on," cried Rebecca, earnestly, "the place fills my soul with the most mournful reflections, and I would gladly escape from a scene that reminds me of such unmerited sufferings."

Adrian obeyed, and opening another door, they entered a passage, at the further end of which was a flight of steps, down which they proceeded, till they reached a spacious vaulted apartment, which appeared to have been hewn out of the earth, the roof being supported by massive pillars, down which the damp trickled in thousands of tiny streams; the light, too, grew more dim from the foulness of the atmosphere, and for some time it was feared they would be left in darkness. As they proceeded, however, a current of fresh air from some unseen aperture rendered the place more free from noxious vapours, and by the time they had reached the further extremity of the vaults, they felt entirely relieved from the pain and oppression they had experienced. Here they paused to rest themselves for a few minutes, and then once more resuming their way through a door on the right hand, they reached another series of caverns, less horrible in appearance than those they had already passed through, and finding a stone seat in one of them, they seated themselves whilst they considered how it would be best to proceed.

"The way we have come," said Adrian, "is both further and more difficult than the one I usually take; I had reason, however, to know that Raymond was lurking about the other vaults, and, therefore, I have brought you this way in order to avoid meeting with him."

"Can he have any suspicion that we are going to visit the Lady Alicia?" asked Rebecca, with alarm.

"I think not," replied the page; "he likes to be officious, however, and by way of obtaining favour from his master, affects a great deal of zeal in his service."

"Had we not better return?" asked our heroine;—"we may be discovered, and then all will be lost!"

"At present," answered Adrian, "I see no reason for retracing our steps; in this part of the castle, at any rate, we are safe, for none venture hither, on account of rumours that are afloat that the place is haunted by evil spirits. Even Sir Gaston himself, if he were well enough, would not visit these dungeons for fear of seeing sights that his guilty conscience makes him tremble at."

"But may we not chance to meet with Raymond lurking about the door of Alicia's dungeon?" demanded our heroine, trembling with apprehension; "if his suspicions have been excited as you seem to believe, he may lie in wait for us, and discover a secret which would prove most fatal in its consequences."

"He is too great a coward to venture alone," replied Adrian, "and his companion, Arnold, is, I know, safe enough in Sir Gaston's room.— We are, therefore, tolerably safe, and I think may venture to proceed as soon as you have sufficiently rested yourself."

"Hark!" cried Rebecca, starting from her seat with terror that she could not conceal; "what sound was that, Adrian, that came echoing through yonder dreary caverns?"

"Nothing that we need be at all alarmed at," replied the youth, smiling at her fears; "a legion of bats have been startled by the appearance of our light, and are trying to make their escape from their usual place of retreat."

"Are you sure of that?" asked Rebecca, whose terrors were not to be easily allayed.

"I am quite certain of it," returned the youth; "this is not the first time I have visited this place, and, on each occasion, I have heard the same sounds. Sometimes I have seen a few of the stragglers, and, therefore, by this time, I am quite convinced as to what sort of customers we have to deal with."

"Then they," observed Rebecca, "are, doubtless, the only evil spirits that have scared away Sir Gaston and his followers."

"They have nothing worse to fear, depend on it," answered the page. "I have often thought so, but it would not have been prudent to explain away their terrors, since, in that case, I should often have lost an opportunity of visiting poor Lady Alicia. This way, I am always certain of being able to pass without interruption, and, therefore, I have allowed their superstitious terrors to remain uncontradicted. But come, all seems quiet now, and we have yet some distance to go before we reach the place we are in quest of."

Somewhat recovered from her terrors, Rebecca now followed her youthful conductor through several more dreary vaults, each of which appeared to have been used for the imprisonment of unfortunate captives, as huge staples and chains were fixed in the walls, each seeming to tell its tale of wretchedness and despair. Rebecca shuddered as she beheld these emblems of tyranny and mis-used power; and passing quickly forward, she endeavoured, as much as possible, to avoid a sight that filled her young heart with grief.

In this way they continued to proceed without scarcely venturing to look around them; but, at length, their course was impeded by a huge stone, which fell from the roof almost at their feet, threatening them with instant destruction had they been only one step further in advance. Terrified, they paused and gazed with horror, on the huge fragment before them, and whilst thus occupied, their terrors were increased to the highest pitch, by observing, at no great distance before them, the same grim form of the armed apparition, which, on several other occasions, had presented itself before the inmates of the castle. With a cry of terror, Rebecca sank, almost fainting, in the arms of her youthful companion; and when Adrian again turned his eyes in the direction where the figure had stood but a moment before, the place was vacant, and not a vestige of the mysterious visitant was anywhere to be seen. Summoning all his resolution, therefore, he now began to assure our heroine that her fears were groundless—that they had been terrified without cause,—and, in proof of his assertion, he directed her attention towards the spot, where, but a few moments before, the horrible phantom had met her view. It was in vain, however, that he sought to convince her; she was too painfully convinced that her fears were too well founded, and though she forbore saying anything more upon the subject at present, she was still certain that her worst terrors had been realized. At Adrian's solicitation, however, she hurried with him from the scene of her alarm, and after passing through two or three more of the subterraneous chambers, they arrived at a door, which, her conductor informed her, communicated with the dungeon of Lady Alicia.

CHAPTER LII.

" Oh, despair not thus, I pray thee, but rely
 On him whose life shall cheerfully be spent
 To do thee service."

THE REVOLT.

ENTERING the cell with a slow and noiseless step, they were unnoticed by her they came to visit, who was kneeling before a crucifix
placed upon a rude oaken table, and before which was burning a lamp,
by the dim light of which, they could, with difficulty, see round the
cheerless apartment of her who had once been mistress of the castle.—
Rebecca would have retreated from a scene like this, had not Adrian
motioned her to remain where she was, and almost at the same moment
the poor captive, rising from her knees, perceived the presence oi those
who had thus come to console and comfort her.

Alicia, however, betrayed no emotion upon discovering them, for the
religious offices in which she had been engaged, had served to calm her
usually perturbed spirits; and, smiling upon the new comers, she welcomed them to the only portion of the baronial mansion which she could
now call her own.

"Dear lady," exclaimed Adrian, advancing, and leading the Hebrew
Maiden towards his imprisoned mistress. " I have brought, according to
my promise, a fellow prisoner, whose society, I hope, will often serve to
beguile some portion of your time of its tedium. You will find in her a
companion worthy of your friendship, though I could have wished your
introduction to each other had taken place anywhere else than in this
wretched abode of misery and despair."

"Maiden," cried Alicia, tenderly, "thou hast risked much in thus
coming to visit me, and I am, therefore, the more indebted to thee. We
will be friends, even though it be in adversity, and thus the monotony
of our lives will be relieved in spite of those who would plunge us into
the lowest abyss of despair."

"Let us rather look forward to the happy moment that shall favour
our escape from this abode of wretchedness," answered Rebecca, as she
kissed the hand which had been extended towards her; "the power of
the wicked doer will not last for ever; and, even in this strait, I do not
doubt but that we shall be freed from the power of him who thus holds
us here against our will."

"At all events," interrupted Adrian, "you shall have my aid towards
getting your liberty. Sir Gaston, it is true, has taken every precaution
to prevent your escape; yet, his people may not always be as watchful
as they are at present; and, rely on it, whenever the time comes I will
not fail to make the best use of it."

"Does Sir Gaston talk of leaving the castle?" asked the Lady Alicia,
anxiously.

"At present," answered the page, "there are good reasons why he
should remain here."

"He is ill, then?"

"He is."

"Dangerously?"

"No; not dangerously, my lady," answered Adrian; "at least, so
said the leech, when he left him scarce an hour since."

"Boy!" exclaimed the Lady Alicia, "how is it that you told me not
of your master's illness before?"

"Because it came upon him suddenly, since last I saw you."

"Nay," cried Rebecca, "why should we disguise the truth? Sir Gaston, dear lady, has been wounded,—and—and—mine was the hand that dealt the fatal blow!"

"Ah!" cried Alicia, "do I hear aright? my husband's life has been aimed at, and thou now comest to tell me that the act was committed by thyself."

"Hold! my lady, I entreat you," exclaimed Adrian, earnestly;—"blame not this poor maiden, for the deed was executed without premeditation, and at a moment of desperation that might well have excused her, even had his life paid the forfeit of his baseness."

"He is in no danger, you say?"

"He is not, my lady;—in fact, from what I have heard, it seems likely that he will be able to leave his bed in the course of to-morrow or the next day."

"'Tis well," cried Alicia; and then addressing herself to Rebecca, she said :—"pardon me, madam, for the momentary anger I felt on learning the act which had well nigh deprived me of a husband ——"

"And a tyrant!" interposed Adrian.

"Peace! boy," exclaimed the Lady Alicia, "and speak not thus of one who,—though his treatment to me has been harsh and cruel,—is yet my husband. I have loved him—nay, love him still, and in spite of all that has passed, should bitterly have regretted the blow that sent him to another world, with all his crimes unrepented and unforgiven."

"Nor am I less rejoiced than yourself at the escape he has had,"—cried Rebecca; "necessity and the madness of despair, must be my excuse for turning the poniard against his breast; and, therefore, I throw myself upon your kindness for that pardon which I scarcely dare to ask for."

"You have it, girl, for I can well imagine the agony that must have wrung your soul, when you beheld the deed your own hand had accomplished."

"Be that as it may," observed the page, "it will afford Sir Gaston time to reflect upon the wrongs he has inflicted upon others, and, perhaps, to repent them. Besides, if he had died, he could not but have confessed, at his last moments, that his fate had been most justly provoked; each day he grows more and more tyrannical, and now that he has got this poor maiden's father in his power, there's no saying where his cruelty will stop, unless she consents to become ——"

"Peace—Adrian!" interrupted Alicia, angrily; "that thy master is unhappily governed by evil passions, is, unfortunately, true, and yet it becomes not thee to speak thus of one who, with all his faults, has been a generous friend to thee. However, we will now change this subject; thou say'st this maiden's father is, at present, a captive within this castle?"

"He is, my lady."

"And confined in a dungeon?"

"He was;—but, for some reason or other, orders were not long since given that he should be provided with a better apartment than the miserable dungeon he has been occupying."

"For that, at least, I thank Sir Gaston!" exclaimed our heroine, fervently.

"Ah!" cried Adrian, "that is just what the knight expected. He saw, well enough, that you were indignant at the cruelty inflicted upon your father; and so he now tries what a little kindness, administered to the old man, will effect upon the daughter. It is a deep scheme, to

be sure, yet, methinks the plan will not succeed quite so well as he expects."

"Let him but release my aged parent," exclaimed Rebecca, ardently, "and I care not then how soon death comes to release me from this misery that has bowed my spirit to the very dust."

"He will—be assured he will," cried the Lady Alicia. "He can bear no ill will against your father, and his imprisonment, therefore, will not last beyond a few days at farthest."

"Alas!" sighed Rebecca, "you forget that we belong to a race persecuted and despised."

"Aye, and most unjustly are they persecuted," exclaimed Alicia, with generous warmth. "I have seen much of the people to whom you belong; have observed their patient endurance of the wrongs heaped upon them, and believing them to be worthy of different treatment, have ever felt for them as for brethren unjustly enduring the tyranny of those who unjustly condemn them to persecution."

"Would that other Christians would think so to," cried Rebecca, with tears of gratitude. "Unfortunately, however, a Jew is made the mark for scorn;—the laws protect us not, and we fall unpitied by those who hunt us to death like dogs!"

"It is only by the worthless," replied the Lady Alicia, "and from them, even those who profess themselves Christians are not safe. Thou hast seen to what I am doomed by a husband, and surely, even thy people cannot but acknowledge that my sufferings have been fully equal to any that have been inflicted upon themselves."

No. 33

" I only wish I was older and stronger, for your sake," exclaimed Adrian, with generous warmth.

" And why do you wish that?" asked Alicia.

" Because, in that case, I would demand your liberty."

" Which demand," answered the lady, with a sigh, " would be rejected with scorn."

" Very likely," replied the page, " but, in that case, I would challenge Sir Gaston to single combat."

" And thus risk your life for one who is quite unworthy of this generous attachment."

" There, my lady, I differ from you," exclaimed Adrian; " nay, I feel so warmly interested in your fate, that more than once I have entertained serious thoughts of declaring to the world, the fact of your being still alive, and the unjust imprisonment you have been subjected to, by one who is altogether unworthy of you."

" Do not, I implore, you!" cried the Lady Alicia, earnestly; " the exposure would bring ruin and disgrace upon my husband, and, in that case, liberty would be rendered utterly valueless."

" Yet, remember, dear lady, the hopelessness of your present situation," exclaimed Rebecca, earnestly. " Already you have suffered years of imprisonment, and since the world, by an artfully contrived tale, believes you to be dead, I fear nothing but an exposure of your husband's infamy can ever restore you to that society from which you have been torn."

" I will endure the worst, rather than consent to disgrace Sir Gaston de Neville, by giving utterance to my complaints," answered the suffering wife, mildly, yet with firmness. " It is reported that I am dead, and since people have ceased to make inquiries about me, I will cheerfully pass the few remaining years of my existence in this dungeon, rather than inflict disgrace upon one whom I have not yet entirely ceased to love."

" Will you, then, escape," asked Adrian, " if I provide the means to get you out of this dreary place?"

" Not," answered Alicia, " if, by so doing, I should risk the reputation of Sir Gaston de Neville. I should soon be recognized, were I once to quit this place, and thus the history of the wrongs I have endured would be made known, and my husband's reputation sacrificed."

" Aye, and very justly so, in my opinion," answered the youth; " however, there is a way to avoid it, if you think fit to adopt the plan I will propose."

" Alas! it is impossible," sighed Alicia.

" Nothing is impossible, when people are but resolved," answered the page. " In fact, it will be easy enough for you to escape over to France, and from thence you can travel to Switzerland, where, in a snug cottage by one of the beautiful lakes, you may pass the remainder of your life in freedom. I have saved money enough to take us there, comfortably enough, and when once we are safely there, Sir Gaston will be glad to make you a liberal allowance, on condition that you remain there under some other name."

" You speak like a rash, headstrong boy, as you are," exclaimed Lady Alicia, charmed at the generous interest thus manifested in her behalf. " Immured as I am in this dungeon, and with every gate carefully watched by Sir Gaston's retainers, how is it possible that I can ever hope to make my escape from this castle?"

" Simply," replied Adrian, " for the reason that where there is a will there is a way. In fact, if proof be wanting, Rebecca can tell you that she has herself once contrived to escape from the castle, though an unfortunate circumstance has once more brought her under the power of Sir Gaston de Neville."

" Is it true," asked Alicia of our heroine, " that you have ever found means to elude the vigilance of your captor ?"

" Adrian has, indeed, told you truly," replied Rebecca ; " yet, I must not conceal the fact, that my escape was entirely owing to the assistance of one who chanced to know of a secret outlet."

" And who might your conductor have been ?"

" Black Ivan."

" Ah! I remember the name well," cried Alicia ; he was the leader of bandits, and a price was set upon his head by the government."

" Yet, in spite of all that," replied Adrian, " he still continues to levy contributions upon all those of his majesty's subjects who chance to fall in his way. A score of times, at least, has he been put into prison ; yet, somehow or other, he has always contrived to escape, and continue his depredations with the same success as before."

" And was it to such a man as that," asked Alicia, " that a young and timid female entrusted herself ?"

" Why, what else could she do ?" retorted the page ; " the truth is, no other way offered, and had she refused, a second offer might not very soon have presented itself."

" But what," inquired the Lady Alicia, " has all this to do with the subject we were speaking of ?"

" I was going to tell you," replied Adrian, " that if one person had it in her power to escape from this infernal castle, there is pretty good reason to hope that others may meet with the same piece of luck. Now, it so happens that I know the way as well as Black Ivan does, and, therefore, it only remains for you to say whether you will take the first chance that offers to set yourself at liberty ?"

As Adrian finished speaking, the door behind them swung heavily upon its hinges, and closed with a loud noise that made them start with terror. It seemed, indeed, but too evident that some one had been listening to the preceding conversation, and, resolving to ascertain the truth of this surmise, Adrian snatched the lamp from the table, and rushed with frantic haste to the spot from whence the sound came. Nothing, however, was seen to confirm this suspicion, and having searched everywhere that it was possible any one could have concealed himself, he returned to the dungeon, declaring the result of his labours, and his conviction that the door must have been closed by the violence of the wind. Still, he conceived it necessary that he and Rebecca should return without loss of time, and bidding a hasty farewell to the Lady Alicia, they took their departure, locking the door carefully, and leaving every thing as nearly as possible in its former state.

It was with some difficulty that they succeeded in retracing their steps through the subterranean vaults, but, at length, Adrian left his trembling companion in the place from whence they had started, and then hurrying off to his own chamber, he threw himself upon his couch, to dream of those happier days which he anticipated would fall to the lot of those for whom he was so earnestly interesting himself

CHAPTER LIII.

" Think not to escape me,
For since thy folly brings thee to my snares,
I'll make thee captive, as I have thy friends."
THE CASTELLAN.

ON the morning following the events just narrated, Sir Gaston de Neville woke refreshed from the sleep into which he had fallen, and, as very little fever now remained, his medical attendant ventured to declare that by the next day he might safely leave his couch, and attend to his ordinary occupations. These were happy tidings to the knight, and he was just felicitating himself upon so speedy a recovery, when Stephen, one of his most attached dependants, entered the room to announce that Reuben Grenard, and a stranger, who was with him, had just arrived at the castle, to request an audience. At this intelligence, Sir Gaston's countenance brightened with fiendish exultation, and, anxious to learn who the stranger was, he inquired of the retainer whether he had ever seen the person before.

" Why, that's more than I can tell," answered Stephen, " for the fellow seemed to be ashamed of showing his face; and when he saw me looking at him, he held his head down, so as to conceal his countenance in a huge cloak that he wears."

" There may be some treachery in this," exclaimed the knight, after a few moments' silence; " Reuben Grenard bears me no very good will, and it is not unlikely that this is some plan to take vengeance for my having deprived him of his bride."

" We shall see about that," answered the man, " but, at all events, you can have plenty about you to prevent anything of that sort. For my own part, I have a dagger at your service, and it shall not be long before it finds a sheath in the fellow's heart, if I only see the least chance of treachery."

" Nay, you must be cautious how you act," exclaimed the knight, " for I have already enough blood to answer for, without shedding any more unnecessarily. You will, however, watch their actions narrowly, and should you see occasion, I shall not be angry at your ridding me of an enemy. Go, therefore, and bring them with all speed into my presence."

" Will you see them both," demanded Stephen, pausing suddenly, as he was about to leave the room.

" Aye, both of them," answered Sir Gaston;—" we will know their errand, and I am much mistaken if this Reuben ever finds his way out of a place he seems so anxious to enter."

In obedience to these commands, the man took his departure, and in the course of a few minutes, returned with the young Israelite and the man of whom he had spoken. It was in vain, however, that the knight endeavoured to see the countenance of the mysterious stranger, for he still kept his face carefully concealed and placed himself in a part of the room, where the deep shadow aided in protecting him from the inquisitive glances of Sir Gaston de Neville.

Occupied in endeavouring to discover who the other visitor was, Sir Gaston was silent for some few minutes after they came into the room. —At length, however, his thoughts recurred to the triumph he had achieved over Reuben Grenard, and turning towards him, he said, exultingly :—

" So, young man, it seems you have come to beard the lion in his den;—you are here, doubtless, to make enquiries after the Hebrew Maiden, who, they say, has left home to bestow herself upon some more worthy lover."

" I came to entreat the release, not only of Rebecca," answered the other, " but of her father, who, it seems, thou hast thought fit to detain in your castle, though he came hither merely to ask the restoration of his daughter."

" And who has told thee that I know anything of either of them?" asked the knight, haughtily.

" My own heart tells me so," answered the young man.

" Indeed!—then it seems that your heart has, on this occasion, misled you."

" Nay, I have further grounds for suspicion," replied Reuben;— " you have ever sought to tear her from home, and knowing the recklessness of your disposition, there is every reason to believe that you have brought her hither by violence."

" Well, proceed, sir," exclaimed the knight, endeavouring to stifle his rage;—" proceed, young man, and when you have quite done, perhaps, I may think it worth my while to answer you."

" I have already told you," answered Reuben, " that I have every reason to believe that the maiden is now within your castle;—nay, I am very certain that she is, and, therefore, am I come to sue humbly for her release."

" Sue to the rocks, and they will yield to thee as soon as I shall," replied Sir Gaston, haughtily. " At present, I am master of your destiny, and it shall go hard, but I will now revenge myself upon him who has dared to place himself in my way as a rival."

" Your threats intimidate me not," exclaimed Reuben, boldly;—" I am come to demand the liberty of those you have unjustly detained in custody, and if it is your will to throw me, also, into a dungeon, I can endure your tyranny without giving utterance to a single murmur."

" We shall test this boasted bravery, young man," exclaimed the knight, wrathfully. " At present, you will be detained here as my prisoner; but should the girl ever become mine, upon the terms I have proposed, it is likely that both you, and the old man, will find favour from him, who, you say, has ever acted the part of a persecutor."

" Do you, then, still persist in asserting that the girl and her father are not at this moment beneath your roof?"

" Ask me no questions," exclaimed Sir Gaston, " for I will not answer you."

" At any rate, then, you dare not deny it!"

" Say, rather, that it is not worth my while to answer one like thyself," replied the knight, haughtily. " Here, at least, I am master, and it is, therefore, my pleasure to order thee and thy friend, yonder, to be thrown, without further delay, into separate dungeons."

" Do with me as thou wilt, Sir Knight," cried Reuben, " but do not, I implore, extend your tyranny towards yonder stranger, who has not spoken one word to give thee offence."

" It matters not," returned the Templar;—" he came hither with thee, and must, therefore, suffer for his impertinence in prying into affairs that concern him not."

" But, first of all," exclaimed Stephen, advancing from the place where he had taken his stand;—" I would order the fellow to let us see his face;—he seems ashamed to be looked at, and I dare venture to swear, that he has good reason enough for keeping himself concealed."

" You had better pause ere you proceed to violence," cried Reuben, stepping between the stranger and the retainer. " He has reasons, as you say, to avoid a discovery, and being well armed, he will not submit to your insults, without amply avenging himself for them.— Beware, then, I say, and do not rouse the anger of one, who accompanied me hither, only that he might protect me from your lord's tyranny."

" How ?" muttered Sir Gaston, fiercely, " has he then dared to come hither only to interfere between me and any degree that I may think fit to pronounce ?"

" Such, Sir Gaston de Neville," answered the young Israelite, " is the only motive that has induced him to accompany me,"

" Then he is a Jew, like thyself ?"

" Nay, thou art mistaken," returned the youth ;—" he, whom thou see'st yonder, is a Christian ;—one who hates tyranny, and whose arm is ever ready to strike those, who dare to oppress the weak."

" Well, then, we shall shortly put his boasted gallantry to the test," answered Sir Gaston, with a sneer. " He has been mad enough to enter my castle gates, on an insolent errand, and, by heaven, he shall not depart from this place again with life."

" Shall I take the fellows to their dungeons ?" asked Stephen, advancing in readiness to obey the expected assent of his imperious master.

" You may," answered Sir Gaston ;—" and hark you, sirrah; to your especial keeping I entrust them, and should either succeed in effecting an escape, your own life shall answer for your carelessness !"

" Oh, you needn't fear me," exclaimed Stephen, and stepping towards Reuben he was about to seize hold of him, when the stranger stepping hastily forward, commanded him to desist.

" Hah !" cried Sir Gaston, fiercely, " who art thou, who thus dares to interfere between me and my pleasure. Speak, sirrah, or on the rack thou shalt presently be made to confess all I desire to know !"

" Then have thy will," answered the stranger, in a voice well-known to the startled knight, and throwing aside the cloak, which had hitherto concealed him, he discovered the noble form of Richard Cœur de Lion !

A cry of terror burst from the lips of Sir Gaston, as he recognised the person of his sovereign, and throwing himself back upon his pillow, he remained some few moments incapable of giving utterance to the excuses he was desirous of making.

" So it seems, exclaimed the king, at length breaking the silence, " that I was not expected to become a guest in the castle of my very *gallant* knight, Sir Gaston de Neville."

" Indeed, sire, I looked not to be thus honoured," cried the Templar, with perturbation.

" I can believe thee, Sir Gaston," answered Richard, in a tone expressive of the anger he felt ;—" hadst thou believed me to be so near, thy conduct towards this young man would have been more courteous."

" Nay," exclaimed Sir Gaston, " perhaps an explanation may serve to restore me to the royal favour, which it seems I have so unhappily lost."

" It may, answered the king; " and yet I am at a loss to conceive how thou canst make it appear to me that thy conduct has been otherwise than most cruel and unjust."

" Is he not a Jew ?"

"He is; and, therefore, as belonging to a persecuted race of men, should have received thy protection."

"Does our Christian king then counsel me to encourage one who is an unbeliever?"

"I would that all men be allowed the free exercise of their own conscience," replied the king, firmly. "That this man differs from us, is no fault of his own;—he follows but the ancient religion of his forefathers, and surely, as Christians, we ought not to persecute those who hold fast to a faith, in support of which they are content to endure the revilings and ill-usage of those who would hunt them to death."

"Then your majesty," exclaimed Sir Gaston de Neville, "would have me set at liberty the man who has ever crossed my path of happiness!—But for him, I should long, ere this, have been blessed with the possession of her whose love I now vainly endeavour to obtain."

"Answer me one question," retorted the king;—"is not the girl betrothed to this young man?"

"So it is reported."

"Then ought not that to protect her from the addresses of a man that she can never love?"

"Your majesty forgets," replied Sir Gaston, "that love is not to be easily controlled. I have tried to forget her, but all has been in vain, and, therefore, seeing that she is but a Jewess, I have had recourse to other means, in order to obtain possession of my promised treasure."

"You acknowledge then," exclaimed the king, "that she is now an unwilling visitor beneath your roof?"

"I have acknowledged nothing," replied Sir Gaston, turning pale with the rage he was trying to conceal.

"Do you then deny that she is here?" asked the king.

"I do."

"Oh, believe him not, my liege," cried Reuben, earnestly; "he knows she is here, and, furthermore, that her poor old father is also a prisoner, until she agrees to the vile terms that have been proposed."

"Slave!" exclaimed the enraged knight, "dost thou dare then to charge me with having told a deliberate lie!"

"Thou hast heard him, Sir Gaston," interposed King Richard "and judging from previous circumstances, it must needs be confessed that there are fair grounds for believing that the maiden is, at this moment, under thy roof."

"Does your majesty, then, join in this suspicion of a loyal and true knight?"

"To speak my mind truly, I know not what to think," answered the king. "A charge has been brought against you, and instead of answering it with direct proof of your innocence, you content yourself with merely asserting that you know nothing about her."

"And is not my word to be taken, as well as that of yonder stripling?" demanded the indignant knight.

"Aye, truly is it," answered King Richard, "and yet, Sir Knight, I would gladly have something more than thy bare word to assure me that she is not here."

"Will your majesty be pleased to go through my castle, and convince yourself?" demanded Sir Gaston de Neville.

"Why, not just at present," answered Richard, "for, to confess the truth, I have seen several of thy retainers, whose grim looks assure me that I should not be very safe in their company. At all events, I am not inclined to trust myself with them, and, therefore, will decline your offer for the present."

" Does your majesty believe, then, that I have those in my service who could meditate a thought of treason against the person of their sovereign ?"

" I have told thee that I like them not," answered the king, quickly, " I could see treachery in their eyes, and, between ourselves, I believe it will be safest to postpone the search, until thou art able to accompany me."

" Which will be in the course of two days," replied Sir Gaston; " by that time I shall be able to leave my couch, and if your majesty will honour me with a visit, I well myself accompany you over every part of my castle.   Then, at least, you will acquit me of the crime of which I am, at present, suspected; and, perhaps, from thenceforward I may re. gain some of that confidence and esteem which, it appears, your majesty has lately withdrawn from me."

" That will depend on circumstances," answered the king.

" Will not my former loyalty be sufficient ?"

" Aye,—that is, Sir Knight, provided that I see reason to believe in thy sincerity."

" Hast thou any reason to doubt it ?"

" I fear I have but too much;—report says that thou art one of those who hast joined my brother, Prince John, in an attempt to depose me; —nay, I have good proof that rumour, in this instance, is not to be doubted, and I, therefore, warn thee that many eyes are constantly watching thine actions, and, that the first step thou takest, will lead to thine own utter ruin."

" Nay, your majesty wrongs me by these suspicions."

" It is to be hoped I do," answered he king; " at any rate, I will freely confess my error, should I see reason to believe that thou hast been traduced."

" On the word of a knight," exclaimed Sir Gaston de Neville, " thou hast been imposed upon : that I have enemies about the court is certain, but if the opportunity is given me, I will not only clear my name from reproach, but, at the same time, cover my enemies with confusion."

" And wilt thou promise, for the future, to be less severe in thy con- duct towards the Hebrews ?"

" Certainly, if it is your majesty's wish."

" In that case, you will commence by immediately restoring to liberty Isaac, of Tadcaster, and his daughter, Rebecca."

" Have I not declared that I know nothing of them ?"

" You have," answered the king, " yet this young man persists in as- serting that they are both within your castle, and as he offers proof in support of his charge, I cannot be satisfied till you have fully and freely answered him."

" Hah !" exclaimed the knight, wrathfully, " is it then expected that I am to answer an accusation brought against me by a Jew ?"

" Certainly, if thou wouldst clear thyself."

" Then I am content to be under thy suspicion," cried the Knight Templar, with an ill-suppressed sneer.   " That I have fought bravely for thee in the field, thou canst not deny, and yet, my character is to be blasted by one whom all Christians ought to hold in scorn."

" Thou art wrong," answered Richard, " for no *true* Christian would ever seek to injure a fellow creature, because he happened to differ with him in religion.   This man speaks fairly enough—he complains that thou hast wronged him and those he most loves, and, sworn as I am to administer impartial justice between all my subjects, I came hither with him in disguise, in order that I might protect him should any violence be offered against him."

"Had your majesty deigned to inform me of your intended visit,"—replied Sir Gaston, "I should have made preparation to receive you with the honour becoming your exalted rank. As it is, however, I may have been betrayed into some warmth by this Jew's insolence, and, therefore, do I humbly crave your pardon."

"On one condition," replied the gallant king, "you shall obtain both pardon for the past, and my favour for the future."

"A most tempting offer, truly," exclaimed Sir Gaston; "but may I now ask the nature of the condition your majesty would propose?"

"You must promise never again to molest this poor fellow."

"Let him keep his distance, and I promise he shall have no further cause to complain of me."

"I think I can answer for him in that respect," answered Richard Cœur de Lion. "At all events, I know that he is not very ambitious to intrude upon thee, and, therefore, we have good reason to suppose that he will not again intrude upon you unless foul persecutions should induce him to beard the lion in his den."

"My word is passed!" exclaimed the knight, "and he may depart in the full assurance that I shall no longer seek to punish his insolence as it deserves."

"And Rebecca and her father?"

"I have already said that I know nothing of them," answered Sir Gaston, "and surely my word may be taken in an affair where my honour is so deeply implicated?"

"For the present, at any rate, I will take your word, Sir Gaston," exclaimed the king, with bitter emphasis. "In two days, however, in accordance with your own invitation, I will either come myself, or send

No. 34

some trusty messengers to search every corner of thy castle; thus I shall be convinced, and upon the result will depend your future fortune."

So saying, the king beckoned for Reuben Grenard to follow him, and passing through the great baronial hall, he quickly found himself once more surrounded by a numerous band of his attendants, who had been ordered to wait for him on the outside of Sir Gaston de Neville's castle.

CHAPTER LIV.

"Some cunning method must be now devised
    To cheat these meddlers, who, with foolish zeal,
    Would interpose to rob me of my treasure."

                                        MUZIO.

ALL the remainder of that day and the following night, Sir Gaston lay pondering over in his own mind a thousand various plans by which to thwart the king in the search he was about to institute throughout the castle. That Rebecca should not be lost to him he was determined, let the consequences be what they might; but how to deceive Richard when next he made his appearance at the castle, was a question that required deep and anxious consideration.

At length, on the day after the events recorded in the preceding chapter, Sir Gaston de Neville commanded Stephen, who was now his chief agent in the absence of Bertrand le Noir, to attend upon him, and receive some important instructions he had to give him, in an affair that required all his skill to perform with success. Upon Stephen making his appearance, all the other domestics were commanded to leave the room, when the Knight Templar, raising himself as well as he could, enquired if he was certain that both Rebecca and her father were still safe in his custody. This question seemed rather to puzzle Stephen, who, wondering at the motive that had induced the question, replied, that he had every reason to believe that they were now in their separate places of confinement.

"When did you see them last, sirrah?"

"Scarcely two hours since, Sir Knight," answered the other, trembling with alarm.

"And have you never entrusted them to the care of any other person?"

"Never."

"Does any other person have access to them?"

"No one except Adrian, your page."

"Hah!" exclaimed the knight, "that boy has too tender a heart to suit my purpose. He softens too readily at a tale of woe, and I fear whether he may not be induced to make some rash attempt to aid that girl in escaping from my castle."

"If he did," muttered Stephen, "I'll answer for it his life would soon pay the forfeit of his rashness."

"And where would be the use of that?" demanded the knight, angrily. "It should be our object to prevent mischief, not to punish the perpetrators of it when they have done the worst."

"Do I understand, then, that you wish this Adrian to be safely disposed of?"

"That will depend upon his power of injuring me," answered the knight; "if I thought there was any danger to be apprehended from him, I would not hesitate, for a single moment, to give orders for his death."

"Why, for that matter," exclaimed Stephen, "the young fellow seems to be quiet enough, and I should think there is not much deceit in him, —unless, indeed, these Jews should happen to tamper with him, and promise a large reward for any service he may feel inclined to do them."

"Your quiet water is sometimes the deepest," cried Sir Gaston de Neville; "for my own part, I have always, till now, had a most favourable opinion of the youth; but, of late, he has shown symptoms of dislike in my service, and I begin half to suspect that it would not be a very difficult task to make him a traitor to his master."

"You mean so far as assisting this Isaac of Tadcaster and his daughter to escape, after the trouble you have been at to make them your captives?"

"I do not know that he would do so, Stephen," answered the knight, "but I would take precaution in time to prevent his doing me any mischief."

"Then, why not remove your two Hebrew prisoners to one of your other castles in the North of England?"

"I have been thinking of doing so," answered Sir Gaston, abruptly; "in fact, I had made up my mind to send them away, only that I knew not how to get them out of the castle without attracting notice, and thus convicting myself of a falsehood, after having solemnly declared to the king that I knew nothing of the persons he came to search for."

"Yet it may be managed," exclaimed Stephen, "by entrusting the job to a few of your most faithful dependants."

"How many are there about me that I could depend upon," inquired the knight, anxiously.

"More than half of those who have the honour to serve you," replied Stephen; "you shake your head with doubt, but I know the men, and can vouch for their fidelity."

"Are they proof, think you, against a bribe, should one be offered by the king, for the discovery of the place in which the captives are about to be confined?"

"I should think so," replied the other; "but, if you wish to make quite sure of them, I would promise double the amount of any reward that may be offered by the other side."

"Be it your task, then, to see that this arrangement is carried into effect," exclaimed Sir Gaston de Neville, well pleased at the zeal with which his retainer entered into all his plans; "make whatever promises you please in my name, and I will not fail to carry out your intentions."

"But, I must first know whither it is your pleasure to have them conveyed?"

"To my castle in Yorkshire."

"And when?"

"This very night."

"I will not fail, depend on it."

"See that you do not, or your life may answer for it," exclaimed Sir Gaston. "And harky'e, sirrah;—let the old man be taken away an hour or two before the wench, lest attention should be drawn towards them, and our project fall to the ground."

"I was thinking of something of the kind myself," replied Stephen; "for they would be sure to make a fuss if they happened to see one another, and thus all our pains would be thrown away for ever."

"You understand me, then?"

"Perfectly, Sir Gaston."

"Yet, there is one thing I had forgotten to tell thee,—the old man may, perhaps, raise an outcry, when he gets on the outside of the castle walls, and I would, therefore, have you caution him before-hand, that the least noise will be the immediate forerunner of his own death."

"And shall I keep my word, if he is obstinate enough to cry out for assistance?"

"Aye,—stab him to the heart, Good Stephen, and afterwards hide his body in the castle-ditch, where, though many may seek, none will ever be able to find him."

"It shall be done;—but, what are we to do with the girl in case she should happen to make any outcry?"

"Let her be gagged, and hurried away with all speed," replied Sir Gaston de Neville; "horses will be in readiness for you in the thicket hard by, and it will be your own fault if you do not put at least a dozen miles between yourself and London, ere you have been mounted an hour."

At this juncture Adrian entered, who, advancing to the bedside of the knight, said:—

"I come, Sir Gaston, to ask a boon for one, who, I believe, you are not very likely to refuse."

"How is this, boy," exclaimed the Templar; "if there is so little doubt upon the matter, what need is there for thy coming to ask me at all?"

"Because I was bid to come hither by a female, and you have ever taught me that gallantry is one of our first duties towards the fair sex."

"Upon my word, but thou art an apt scholar; however, thou mayest deliver thy message, upon telling me by whom thou art sent hither."

"I come, Sir Knight, from Rebecca, the Hebrew Maiden."

"Hah!" exclaimed Sir Gaston, "what favour has she to ask of one whom she has ever treated with scorn?"

"She craves permission to have an interview with her father."

"Indeed!—then I fear I shall be compelled to refuse the first boon she has ever thought proper to crave."

"Must I, then, tell her that so simple a request is denied?"

"Peace, boy!" exclaimed Sir Gaston, vehemently, "and dare not to bandy words with one who will order thee to be scourged like a dog, if thou art insolent. Peace, I say, and return to Rebecca with a refusal of her request."

"Shall I tell her why you refuse?"

"Aye, you may tell her that I will grant no favour to her while she maintains her haughty conduct towards me. Say that I regret the being compelled to act thus harshly, and that it remains with herself to define the limit of the captivity at present endured by herself and her father."

"I will obey your commands," answered Adrian, with a look and tone expressive of scorn.

"Do so; but before you go, hear the advice I am about to give you:—it has not escaped my notice, that you have of late grown more and more insolent towards me; this I have not hitherto resented, sir, but I warn you, from this moment, to be more circumspect in your behaviour. Remember, sirrah, that I am your master, or I may so far forget myself as to administer a punishment that will hang like a curse to thee for the remainder of thy days."

"I will not forget your injunctions," replied the page, with a suppressed sneer; "henceforward, you shall find me meek, humble, and subservient;—at least," he continued to himself, "till I can find an opportunity to escape from a tyrant that I despise."

"That boy must be narrowly looked after," exclaimed the Knight Templar, as the page took his departure; "he appears to have wormed himself into some of my secrets, and it only needs confirmation of my suspicions to put an end for ever to all chance of his betraying them."

"Think you he knows anything about the Lady Alicia ——"

"Silence, villain!" exclaimed Sir Gaston, furiously; "why dost thou mention a name that is never breathed even by myself?"

"Simply because I forgot myself," replied Stephen; "and yet, having so far broken the ice, perhaps it would be as well that we talk over a subject that may prove of the greatest consequence. Again, therefore, do I ask whether you have any suspicion that the youngster knows of the Lady Alicia being still alive?"

"I think he does not," replied the knight, after a little hesitation.

"You are not sure of it, then?"

"I am not; but it seems likely that he is ignorant of the fact, seeing that, if he knew anything about the secret, it would have been revealed long enough since."

"And is that the only ground of your present security?"

"It is;—but why are you so anxious to know my thoughts upon this subject?"

"Merely," replied Stephen, "because I feel an interest in the affair, and should like to be satisfied. The secret of Lady Alicia's being alive, must be kept profound, or, neither you or I are safe for a single instant."

"By heaven!" exclaimed the knight, anxiously, "you speak as if there was good reason for supposing that Adrian really knows of Lady Alicia's imprisonment! Speak, knave, what cause hast thou seen for believing that our lives are thus placed at his mercy?"

"I do not say that he knows anything about it," replied Stephen, "but, if Adrian does not, I am convinced that somebody else does."

"Hah! and why dost thou think so, fellow?"

"Because she never eats the bread and water that I daily take to her dungeon," answered the man, doggedly, "and that, I consider a pretty good proof that she must get food from some other quarter."

"Have you ever seen anything to confirm your suspicions?" asked Sir Gaston de Neville, with anxious curiosity."

"Never;—in fact, she is wise enough to prevent detection, though I hope some day or other, to find out who the unknown friend may be."

"Thou hast watched, of course, Stephen?"

"I have;—day and night have I watched near her dungeon door, but whilst I have been there, not a soul has ventured to make his appearance."

"And you keep the dungeon door locked?"

"Yes, but I have thought it possible that false keys might be made, and if that has been done, why there, you know, is an end at once of the mystery."

"If it should be as you have said," exclaimed the knight, gloomily, "there must have been a want of watchfulness, and I shall not fail to inquire into, and punish all those who are to blame in the matter."

"But I have done all I could," replied Stephen, whose anger began to be roused by this threat; "I have taken the pains to watch her ladyship through many a weary day and night, and surely, if they contrive to cheat me after all that, the fault is not mine."

"Well, well, Stephen, I meant not to blame you," exclaimed the knight, in a milder tone, "it must be confessed that I felt vexed at hearing that the secret of Lady Alicia's being still alive was likely to be spread abroad, but since you seem to have done all in your power to avert the mischief, I can look over the past, on condition that you watch carefully the motions of this Adrian."

"Trust me for that," answered Stephen, "and I'll warrant that you will not be disappointed in the end. I am not over partial to this page of yours, and nothing would give me greater pleasure than to have an opportunity of paying off some of my old scores."

"Humph!" muttered Sir Gaston; "I have been thinking whether we may release ourselves of the evil, by sending him away from the castle as soon as possible."

"It would, doubtless, be well to get rid of him," answered Stephen, gruffly, "but who can say that he will not blab more than either you or I should like to be known?"

"True," replied the knight, "we may be in his power;—circumstances may have put him in possession of the fact relating to the Lady Alicia, and, as the king happens to be in no very good humour with me, at present, the chances are that I should be disgraced and ruined, without hope of ever reversing the royal doom."

"What say you to shutting the boy up in one of the dungeons?" demanded Stephen; "it is one way to quiet a foolish, chattering tongue, though, between ourselves, I know of another that would be still more effective than that."

"What mean you, Stephen?"

"That a poniard should silence him for ever!"

"Villian!" groaned the knight, "wouldst thou then, tempt me to the commission of another crime?—Must I murder one, whose youth should be his best protection against the assassin's steel?"

"All that may be very true," answered Stephen, "but your own safety demands that the sacrifice should be made; and you pretty well know the consequence if these idle scruples are suffered to interfere."

"But the youth was entrusted to my care by a dying father," exclaimed Sir Gaston, struggling violently with his feelings; "I promised to watch over and protect him as if he were my own son, and I will do so, in spite of any danger I may be threatened with."

"Well, then," replied Stephen, "if you won't put him out of the way, so as to make sure work of it, let him be shut up for a time, and I'll answer for it, a little wholesome restraint will not be thrown away upon him."

"I will think of it, sirrah."

"Nay, let me rather advise you to act without wasting time in thinking. For my own part, I always act on the spur of the moment; and then, you know, if repentance does happen to follow, it comes when the mischief cannot be remedied."

"At present, we have got quite enough on our hands, without adding to it, by hurling destruction upon a poor defenceless boy;—there is Rebecca and her father to be looked to, and my orders have been already given to convey them away from the place before morning."

"I know it," answered Stephen, "and since the task has been entrusted to my care, you may depend upon its being rigidly obeyed. Within an hour, the old Jew shall be on his road, and when he is far enough advanced, I and two or three others will follow with Rebecca."

"You must deceive her though, as to the purpose of her removal, or she may raise an outcry, and thus, not only secure her own rescue, but expose me to the anger of Richard Cœur de Lion."

" Nay, never fear, Sir Knight," answered Stephen, " for I have been use to affairs of this kind, and it will go hard, indeed, if I do not prevail upon her to accompany me from the castle with as much willingness as if she was going to the altar with your rival, Reuben Grenard."

" Fulfil that promise," exclaimed Sir Gaston de Neville, " and your reward shall be great. I am resolved not to lose the girl again, and will grudge no amount of gold to those who may lend their assistance towards conveying her to a place of greater security."

" Upon that understanding, then, I take my departure," returned Stephen, " I will now see to the removal of Isaac of Tadcaster, and when that is done, my next visit will be paid to his daughter, who, I dare answer for it, will not be very unwilling to accompany me."

" At the same time, however," exclaimed Sir Gaston, sternly, " you will remember that my orders are, to use no more violence than may be absolutely necessary. Recollect, sirrah, that your life will depend upon the prudence with which you execute this task."

" Oh, I'll take care, Sir Gaston, never fear," answered the ruffian, not very well pleased at the threat which had been thus held out; " I love the fair sex so well, that I would not harm one of them,—unless, indeed, she took it into her head to raise an alarm, and then, you know, a man must be a little desperate, or he finds himself in trouble before he is aware of it."

With these words Stephen gloomily turned away and took his departure, leaving Sir Gaston to reflect in solitude on the difficulties into which his own wayward designs had plunged him.

CHAPTER LV.

" Prepare, I say, for thy departure hence,
For I have stern commands to execute,
And needs must do them."

THE COMBAT.

ISAAC of Tadcaster, as we have before had occasion to observe, was removed from the miserable dungeon he had at first been made to occupy, to one of a better description, and where his wants were supplied with more liberality than before. He was, however, aware that this had been done, not so much from any kindness towards him, as from a hope that better treatment might, in the end, soften his resolution, and prevail upon him to prevail upon his daughter to yield, rather than any longer make an enemy of one who had it in his power to bestow upon her almost unlimited wealth.

Such, he knew well enough, was the intention of his persecutors, but Sir Gaston de Neville had calculated wrong when he supposed that a father was to be prevailed upon by any means he could adopt, to sacrifice a child whom he loved, even though his own life might depend upon it. In fact, Isaac of Tadcaster was more determined than ever to support his child in her virtuous rejection of the knight's suit, and often did he prostrate himself upon the floor of his prison, to implore the aid of heaven to strengthen him in the resolution he had formed.

It was during one of these, when the Jew was engaged in intense prayer, that Stephen entered the room, immediately after his interview with Sir Gaston de Neville; half ruffled by what had just passed, he came in no very good humour, and perceiving the old man kneeling with his forehead resting upon the ground, he demanded with a sneer, what fool's antics he was now playing off. Isaac slowly raised himself, and folding his arms across his bosom, said, submissively :—

"I was doing that, friend, which, I fear you never think of;—offering up my earnest prayers to the Maker of the Universe, for strength to endure the trials which I, in common with all mankind, must endure in my turn."

"Indeed!—then, perhaps, you will be the better disposed to listen to what I have to propose?"

"If it is a message from thy master, I will hear it with patience," answered the old man, "though I will not promise obedience to his commands."

"He offers thee liberty," replied Stephen, "on condition that thou wilt exert thine influence with Rebecca, in his behalf."

"Sir Gaston de Neville knows already that it is in vain to urge me," exclaimed Isaac, firmly. "I have told him that I prefer my daughter's virtue far beyond my own life, and it is, therefore, useless for him thus to trouble me with messages that I shall continue to treat with the scorn they merit."

"Fool!" exclaimed the ruffian, "you recollect not, then, the anger you will bring upon yourself by this blind obstinacy."

"Oh, I forget not into whose hands I have fallen," replied Isaac, with indifference. "I am aware that I have no mercy to expect from Sir Gaston de Neville; but he shall, at least, find that I can firmly endure any torture he may think fit to inflict, rather than yield a consent which would render my child the loathsome outcast I so much dread to think of."

"Well, of course, obstinate people must be suffered to go on as they please," retorted Stephen; "we cannot, perhaps, force you into compliance, but, since you choose to be so rash, I have now to inform you that your place of residence is to be changed for a castle of Sir Gaston's down in Yorkshire."

"Be it so," replied the Jew, meekly;—"doubtless, I shall soon be forgotten, and he can then order me to be assassinated without fear of discovery."

"You believe him, then, to thirst after human blood?"

"I do, indeed."

"You do him an injustice, old man," exclaimed Stephen, warmly; "the knight whom I have the honour to serve, is passionate in his admiration of the fair sex;—nay, he is not very easily turned from any purpose that he has formed, but he will not shed the blood even of an enemy, unless he is driven to it as a last resource."

"I ask him not to spare me," exclaimed Isaac, "but to pity a helpless girl, who has never wronged him."

"Never wronged him, eh?—has she not rejected all his proposals with scorn, and think you he will easily forget that, old man?"

"I know not," replied the Jew, in accents of despair;- "I have had reason to discover that his heart is scarcely human, but at the same time, I place my confidence in the humanity and generosity of the king."

"Then do so no longer," answered Stephen, "for Richard was here yesterday to demand your restoration, and having failed in discovering you, it is scarcely likely that he will again trouble himself upon the subject."

"Nevertheless, I do not despair," cried Isaac, earnestly;—"Reuben

Grenard is still happily at liberty, and I know him too well, to doubt the exertions he will make for the liberation of those he loves."

"Psha!" ejaculated the ruffian, "he has already done all he could, and having failed in it, there is very little reason to fear that he will ever attempt anything of the kind again. In good truth, Jew, the rash youth had very nearly found his way to one of our dungeons;—aye, and he would have done so, too, had not King Richard been at hand in disguise to help him out of his scrape."

"And is he now safe?" demanded the old man, with intense agony; "hath he escaped from this den of infamy, where wickedness triumphs over the virtue it seeks to undermine?"

"Oh, yes, the young fellow is safe enough, if that affords you any consolation," answered Stephen, gruffly; "he went off with the king, but I would have him take care of himself, for Sir Gaston de Neville has vowed vengeance against him, and I'll answer for it, will not be very long before he pays off all old scores."

"And if he does so," replied Isaac of Tadcaster, "the king will find no very great difficulty in guessing who the aggressor is."

"Perhaps so, but the king has quite business enough upon his hands, without interfering with the differences that have sprung up between one of his bravest knights, and a parcel of Jews."

"But his love of justice," replied the old man, "will prompt him to take part with the weaker side, against the powerful oppressor;—he hath hanged a knight before now, because he committed an act of violence upon one who was without protection."

"True," answered Stephen, sneeringly;—"he did on one occasion hang a knight; but he, upon whom he executed that summary act of vengeance, happened to possess but little influence in the state, and, therefore, his death was not regarded much. It is, however, different in the case of Sir Gaston de Neville, whose power is greater than that of any other knight in the kingdom, and whose friends are therefore to be dreaded, should they see occasion to rise for vengeance in behalf of one of their order."

" And who are the friends of whom Sir Gaston can boast?" demanded Isaac, contemptuously;—" by all good men he is shunned, and those only adhere to him, who are either as worthless as himself, or who have joined with him in a treasonable league to dethrone the king, and place his brother John at the head of this great nation."

" Hah! where didst thou hear this, villain?"

" From those who have been careful watchers, though fortunately unsuspected by those whose every movement they have narrowly scanned."

" And they have hinted these suspicions to the king?"

" Nay, that I will not assert. In fact, I believe they prefer keeping a careful watch themselves, to becoming informers."

" But they intend to tell King Richard all these things, so soon as it may be their interest to do so?"

" Aye, if there is no other way to save their monarch from the evil designs of his enemies."

" Wilt thou tell me the names of those who have made themselves thus busy in this affair?"

" Never!"

"Then the rack shall force the secret from thy lips."

" Nay, torture will effect no good for thee," answered the venerable Israelite;—" I would merely warn Sir Gaston de Neville that his evil deeds are not quite so secret as he perhaps imagines."

" Villain!—thou shalt suffer for this!" exclaimed Stephen, and clapping his hands, the room was instantly filled by a number of the knight's retainers, who were waiting without, in readiness for the moment when their services should be required. At the same moment a dozen poniards were gleaming in the air, and Isaac of Tadcaster would speedily have fallen a prey to their ungovernable fury, had not Stephen peremptorily commanded them to desist."

" Put up your weapons, fellows," he exclaimed, " and attend to the orders I am about to give;—this man is to be instantly conveyed from the castle; you will find horses in readiness at the thicket, and having once mounted, you will ride off with all speed to Danby Castle, whither I shall shortly follow you with the Hebrew Maiden. So, now away, fellows, and see that your duty is performed with zeal and faithfulness."

" But, if he makes any outcry," observed one of the retainers, " what are we to do then?"

" Gag him, and if that is not sufficient, let your poniard find its way to his heart!"

In spite of all remonstrances, Isaac was now securely bound with cords, and being thus rendered incapable of offering any resistance, he was borne away from the chamber, and from thence across the court-yard, towards the place where it was said horses would be found in readiness for them. Once or twice he raised his feeble voice for assistance, but a violent blow on the head at length deprived him of all consciousness for the present, and in that condition he was carried onwards, and mounted behind one of the men on the swiftest and strongest steed that could be found.

In the meantime, Stephen hurried away from the chamber, and procceded to that which was occupied by Rebecca, who he found bathed in tears, and bitterly lamenting the cruel chance that had thus thrown her into the power of a ruthless enemy. For a second or two Stephen paused to observe with exultation the agony of his fair captive, and then advancing further into the room, he said, with evident satisfaction :—

"So, at last I find thee in tears, do I, maiden?—You now begin to regret your folly in having rejected the offer of Sir Gaston de Neville, whose anger having been once excited, threatens to hurl ruin and destruction upon thee and thy father."

"It was not for that I wept," answered Rebecca, with forced composure;—"I just now sent to entreat your imperious master to grant an hour's interview between me and my father, yet it has been denied me, as too great a favour for a child to ask."

"It has been refused because thou hast so long maintained thy foolish obstinacy," replied Stephen; "if thou wouldst find favour in the eyes of my master, yield without delay to his earnest entreaties, and I'll answer for it, you will have no further harshness to complain of."

"Did he send thee hither on this errand?" demanded the Hebrew Maiden, glancing scornfully towards the ruffian.

"I cannot say that he did," replied Stephen; "but knowing him as I do, I thought it would only be kind on my part to tell you how you may best gain favour from my master."

"Indeed!" cried Rebecca; "then, having thus far executed your charitable intentions, perhaps you will leave me, for solitude is the only favour that I am now permitted to enjoy."

"You do not wish, then, to have an interview with your father?" exclaimed Stephen.

"Alas!" she replied, "words cannot express how grateful I should feel, were I permitted to see him, even were it but for an instant."

"Well," retorted the other, "have patience, and I dare say your wish will soon be gratified."

"Canst thou tell me when?"

"No, but I dare say it will not be long; though between ourselves, wench, you have a long journey to go before you can meet the old man."

"Ah!" exclaimed Rebecca, misinterpreting his words, "what mean you, sirrah?—Is my father murdered then, for I fear by your manner that something terrible has befallen the poor old man."

"Well, you have no cause to fret about that just yet," answered Stephen, with a grin of satisfaction. "The old fellow is not dead yet, though, perhaps, it may depend upon yourself whether his days will last much longer."

"Will they kill him, then!" cried Rebecca, in a voice husky with terror.

"That's more than I can tell you," replied Stephen; "however, if you think fit to accept Sir Gaston's proposals, I dare say the old man will not only be set at liberty, but the chances are, that he will have wealth heaped upon him, besides passing the remainder of his days unmingled with care."

"Peace, villain!" exclaimed the Hebrew Maiden—"peace, I say, and never dare again to broach a subject so abhorrent to my soul. That I have no mercy to expect from the vindictive Sir Gaston de Neville, is but too certain; yet I can bear death, even though he comes accompanied with his worst horrors, rather than become the hateful wretch he would make me."

"Oh, it's all very well to talk in this way," replied Stephen, "but

I'll be bound you will think better of the affair before you have left this castle any long time."

"Am I, then, going to leave this place?"

"To be sure you are;—I am here to conduct you from the place—horses are waiting for us at no great distance off; and what is more, your father is by this time some few miles on his journey."

"Ah!" sighed Rebecca, "we are to be separated then?"

"Nay, there you are wrong," answered Stephen.

"Why, then, are we to be removed from hence?"

"Because it is supposed you are not quite so safe here, as is to be wished," replied the ruffian. "In fact, maiden, it seems the king has a notion that you and your father are confined in this castle, and he is coming to-morrow for the purpose of ascertaining whether there is any truth in the supposition."

"Alas!" cried the Hebrew Maiden, "then we are to be removed, in order that the king may be deceived into a belief of Sir Gaston's innocence."

"Exactly so," replied Stephen; "and, in my opinion, a very capital plan it is, too.—By so doing, my master will completely satisfy the king that the charge against him is a false one; and as it will be imagined that you have fled somewhere else, of course your best friends will, from that moment, set you down as a light-o'-love and a wanton."

"Oh, villain! villain!" groaned Rebecca," and canst thou then exult in the downfall of one who never injured thee?"

"I can; for though thou hast never injured me, thou hast spurned my master's offers, and, as a faithful servant, I am bound to resent the act."

"Will not the promise of a large reward induce thee to become my friend?"

"Why that, girl, will depend entirely upon the amount."

"Rely upon it, sirrah, the sum bestowed shall be worthy of thine acceptance."

"Canst thou not say how much it will be?"

"I speak in my father's name," replied Rebecca, "and yet I can promise thee a thousand crowns on condition that thou wilt undertake to convey me and my aged parent to a foreign land."

"Humph!" answered Stephen, "but it so happens that I can gain two thousand crowns by serving my master faithfully in this matter. He shall know the offer thou hast made, and I am much mistaken if I make not a good day's work of this."

"I ought to have known better than to trust you," cried Rebecca, disgusted at the treachery of the villain she had confided in; "and yet," she continued, "thou canst not injure me much, either, since the same power will protect us from the perfidy of those who seek the destruction of the innocent."

"Do you, then, expect to get off so easily?"

"I know not," replied the maiden; "hope is the chief balm of the afflicted, and you cannot deprive me of that which supports us all, even to the very verge of the grave."

"Well, of course, you can think what you please," answered Stephen, "though, between ourselves, you are leaning upon a broken crutch that will soon bring you to the ground. However, I have no more time to spare in useless parley; your father is now some distance on his journey, and unless we follow instantly, we shall have but little chance of overtaking him before he reaches the castle, which, for the present, is to be your place of captivity."

"Alas!" sighed Rebecca,—"whither, then, are you about to force us?"

"To the knight's strong fortress, in Yorkshire!" answered Stephen: "there, at least, you will be safe, for a time, and if it's any consolation to know it, Sir Gaston will follow us, in the the course of two or three days."

"When,—oh, when will my persecutions end!" cried Rebecca, bursting into a flood of tears.

"At the same moment that your own obstinacy ends," answered the hardened ruffian.

"Then that will never be."

"Why, then, you must take the consequences of your own folly," exclaimed Stephen ;—"now, for my own part, I can't see any occasion for making such a fuss about nothing,—the knight has made you a fair offer enough, and if you had been wise you would have saved him the trouble he has been at in this affair."

"I would rather perish, than yield to his base proposals," cried our heroine, resolutely ;—"nay, had he one spark of honour in his bosom, he would, long since, have ceased to pursue one, who has rejected him with the scorn he merits."

"And, why should he do so, my pretty lass?" demanded the fellow, with insolent freedom. "Sir Gaston de Neville is not used to be crossed in any project that he has formed, and it is, therefore, hardly likely that he will suffer you to thwart him, when he has you already in his power."

"Alas! I am in his power!" cried Rebecca, dejectedly. "And yet," she continued, with more resolution, "there is one way left to escape, and, horrible as it is, I will not hesitate to adopt it."

"Really,—well, upon my word, you are a bold lass, though, between ourselves, I think you have about as much chance of escaping as you have of flying. However, the thought may serve as a pretty toy, to amuse your mind with ; so continue in the enjoyment of it, my dear, till Sir Gaston joins us at the place whither we are going."

"And where I shall not have one friend near me!" sighed the almost heart-broken girl.

"Nonsense!" retorted the other ;—"you forget that your father is already on his way to the castle. To be sure, you will not be indulged with meeting each other, very often, nor will he be able to render you much assistance, but then there will be a great consolation, you know, in having the old man so near you!"

"Leave me!" exclaimed Rebecca ;—"leave me, I say, and do not add to the bitterness, with which my cup is filled!"

"'Psha! leave you, eh!" returned the other ;—"no, no, my girl, I have my duty to perform yet, so just throw this veil over your head, and follow me without noise,—for if a word is spoken as we pass, it may, perhaps, cost you your life."

"Be it so," replied Rebecca, unmoved by the threat ;—"slay me, if thou wilt, for rather would I perish, by the most cruel tortures than become the mistress of this recreant knight!"

"I'll hear no more!" exclaimed Stephen, wrathfully ;—"already have I wasted too much time in this useless parley, and now thou shalt go with me, even though the fiend of hell, were to interpose himself in thy behalf!"

And so saying, he threw the veil over the head of his terrified victim, and raising her in his arms, bore her with speed from the chamber. One faint scream only escaped the lips of Rebecca, upon being thus suddenly seized upon, and then, overpowered by her terrors, she sank fainting in the arms of her gaoler.

CHAPTER LVI.

" See'st thou yon cloud of dust ?—
We are pursued, Anselmo, and I fear
Our case is hopeless."

THE SICILIAN.

How long Rebecca had remained in this state of insensibility, she knew not; but on recovering, she found that she had been placed in a litter, which, being raised upon the shoulders of four men, was borne along with the greatest rapidity. Her first impulse, upon making this discovery, was to call aloud for help, but, on reflection, she was but too certain that she was surrounded only by enemies, and, consequently, that any appeal made to them would be in vain. In this state of despair, therefore, she offered up an earnest prayer to heaven for assistance in this, her utmost need, and imploring, at the same time, protection for her aged parent, whose only crime consisted in the natural zeal he had manifested to deliver an only child from the cruel persecutions of an enemy.

Somewhat re-assured by this, she now ventured to look around, and by the bright moonlight, ascertained that they were conveying her across a lonely heath, where not a house appeared in view, and all appeared desolate and blank, as her own hopeless fate. Presently, however, there was a commotion among the people that surrounded her; then they came suddenly to a halt, and they whispered among themselves, pointing occasionally on one side, as if from that point they expected an imme-diate attack. Nor was it long before our heroine became aware of the cause which had led to this confusion among her enemies, for presently afterwards the distant galloping of horses was heard, and as they ap-proached nearer and nearer, so did the alarm increase throughout the party who held her in captivity.

" Why do you stand loitering here?" at last demanded Stephen, fiercely, advancing towards the trembling cowards under his command; " advance, I say, or by all the saints in heaven I will lay the first skulk-ing villain that refuses, dead at my feet."

Alarmed at this threat, the men were about to obey him, though with evident reluctance, when the advancing horsemen,—as if antici-pating their design,—wheeled round, and dashing across the heath, entered the road at a point not many hundred yards in advance of them.

" By St. George, we are foiled, lads!" exclaimed Stephen, who had observed this movement with uneasiness ;—" these fellows, whoever they are, seem determined not to let us escape, so the best way will be to stand prepared to meet them as enemies, and give them a warm reception, if there should be need for it."

In an instant every sword was drawn, and the men, drawing them-selves up in front of the litter which contained Rebecca, stood resolutely expecting the arrival of those, who, by this time had nearly approached them at a furious gallop.

" Hold, there!" exclaimed the leader of the advancing party, whose voice immediately betrayed him to be no other than Black Ivan, himself;—"hold, I say, or, by St. Nicholas, the patron of thieves, I will order my men to cut every one of you down."

"Hah!" exclaimed Stephen, "is it Black Ivan that thus interrupts the servants of Sir Gaston de Neville, when they are on their way to execute the commands of their master?"

"It matters not to me whose servants ye are," answered the robber, carelessly. "We are out for a moonlight ride, and we seldom stand particular when we meet a traveller, even though it might be the king himself."

"But we are poor men and have no money."

"Oh, I care not for that," replied Ivan, "since I dare say your master will give a liberal ransom for the restoration of his servants;—think you not that he will, good Master Stephen?"

"That is more than I can answer for."

"Well, we shall see," returned the robber, "for when once ye are all safely stowed away in my stronghold, I shall send a message, informing the knight of your situation, and declaring my intention to deliver ye all up to death, unless he thinks fit to send me so many crowns for your release."

"Then take that for your pains!" exclaimed Stephen, suddenly raising his arm, and aiming a blow with his poniard at the breast of his adversary. The intention was, however, foreseen by Black Ivan, who, reining his steed back a step or two, struck, with his broad-sword, the poniard from Stephen's hand, and sent it flying through the air with the force of an arrow that has just parted from the bow.

"Villain!" he cried, fiercely, "I have frustrated your intention, and it is now my time to seek for blood! And yet,"—he continued, checking himself, "why should I seek to revenge myself upon such a base cur as thou art! No; thy life is safe for the present, but beware how you again tempt me, or even thy worthlessness may not save thee from a well merited punishment."

"Why do you interrupt us in our way, then?" demanded Stephen, sulkily.

"Because it is my will and pleasure to do so," answered Ivan, "and that ought to suffice for any one who has not the power to prevent me. Besides, I heard that Rebecca, the Hebrew Maiden, is in thy company, and I brought my men hither to aid in taking her from thee."

"Hah!" exclaimed Stephen, "how didst thou know she was with us?"

"Oh, easily enough," replied Black Ivan;—"the fact is, we took her father prisoner scarcely half an hour since, and from him and his attendants we learnt that you were close behind with the girl."

"Oh, tell me of my father!" cried Rebecca, from the litter;—"tell me of him, I beseech you, or I shall go mad with terror."

"Nay, there is no occasion for that, maiden," replied Ivan, "for he is quite safe in my retreat; and having heard that you and your guard were likely to be this way so soon, we set off immediately to see whether we could not offer our services in your behalf."

"If you, indeed, mean us well," cried Rebecca, earnestly, "you will immediately release both me and my father from the bondage we have endured."

"And why should I do that, my pretty damsel?" asked the robber, advancing towards her;—"have I not been at some trouble to rescue you from the hands of these fellows, and shall I so easily yield up the pleasure I anticipate in your society?"

" If there remains one spark of generosity in your bosom, I pray you set us at liberty."

" Why, as for generosity," answered Black Ivan. " I have, perhaps, as good a share of that commodity as most people ; but here is a difficulty that I cannot very easily overcome, for if I set you at liberty, I deprive myself of the reward I so greatly covet."

" Nay, then," she cried, " I implore you to give freedom to my poor aged father,"

" Aye, perhaps I may indulge you so far, maiden," replied Black Ivan. " Prisoners are rather in our way, when they happen to be of the rougher sex, so, provided he thinks fit to pay a handsome price in good broad pieces of gold, he may go his ways as soon as he pleases."

" He will not accept your offer," cried Rebecca ; " for freedom will be valueless to him, unless I am permitted to share it with him."

" Well," retorted Black Ivan, " if he is such a fool as to refuse a good offer, it is no fault of mine. He ought to think himself lucky at getting off at all, without expecting that I shall part with his daughter, who I have so long endeavoured to make my own."

" Methinks, Ivan," exclaimed Stephen, " you have forgotten the superior claim that has been urged for this maiden, by Sir Gaston de Neville, my master. He loves the girl to madness, and I need hardly tell you that he will severely retaliate, should you dare rob him of his destined prize."

" Sir Gaston had better tell me that to my face !" replied Black Ivan, with a contemptuous sneer. " He would, perhaps, like to trust himself within my reach, just now, that I may have it in my power to pay off some of the long standing score of hatred there is between us."

" Nay, thou hast little cause to boast," answered Stephen, " for more than once already thou hast been a prisoner in his castle, and had he done as I would have advised him, thou wouldst not have had it in thy power at this moment to boast thus."

" At any rate, I have not to thank him for my liberty," exclaimed Ivan, fiercely.

" True, but had he slain thee, he would have got rid of an enemy, whom he has so much reason to dread."

" He might so," replied the robber, " but had he destroyed me, he would have had more enemies to deal with than he could have managed. I have fifty stout followers under my command, and there is not one among them but would have vowed deadly vengeance against him for slaying their chieftain. Yet, why should I boast of what it is in my power to do, since a dozen, at least, of his followers are now my prisoners, and it shall go hard, indeed, but I have him also before he is many hours older."

" Thou canst not," exclaimed Stephen, " for he is at this moment confined to his chamber, by a wound that he has lately received from the hand of this maiden."

" Hah !" vociferated Black Ivan, " do I hear aright ? has Rebecca so far cast aside her womanly fears, as to seek the death of her captor ?"

" I did," answered the maiden, timidly raising her eyes, and glancing towards the robber ;—" in a moment of frenzy I aimed a blow at his heart ;—aye, and I would do so again, if no other way offered itself by which to escape from the hands of a villain."

" Thou speakest boldly, girl," exclaimed Black Ivan, " and methinks I can detect something like a threat against myself. I shall, however, be better prepared for thee, and, therefore, thou mayst make up thy mind to submit to thy doom without hope of rescue,"

"Unless it be through Sir Gaston de Neville," answered Stephen ;— "he will, no doubt, collect his vassals together, and ere three days have passed away, they will seek thee, and then, woe to the villain who has thus dared to rob him of his heart's dearest treasure."

"Let Sir Gaston come when he will," replied Ivan, "and I'll warrant he finds us not unprepared to give him a warm reception. Already I owe him the deepest hatred, and let him but once throw himself into my power, and he shall feel the heavy vengeance that his wrong will inflict."

"Wilt thou hear one proposition that I have to make?" asked Stephen.

"I will."

"Then let the quarrel be decided this moment."

"Aye, if thou wilt tell me how it is to be done."

"I am considered a skilful swordsman," answered Stephen, "and, therefore, in that respect, am a match for thee. I would, therefore, propose that we instantly engage in single combat, and I swear never to yield until thou hast either slain me, or I have laid thee dead at my feet!"

"A very pretty proposition, truly!" exclaimed Ivan, haughtily ;— "and so thou wouldst have me waste my prowess upon a worthless menial like thyself."

"I am, at least, equal to a robber," retorted the other.

"Hah! dost thou bandy words with me, villain?"

"Have I not a right to demand a combat with thee?" exclaimed Stephen. "Thou say'st I am thy prisoner, and I would fain know whether thou hast the power to enforce thy boast."

No. 36

"Let me take the task upon myself, captain," cried Hubert, advancing, and placing himself immediately in front of the person he designed to engage with. "I, perhaps, may be a match for the fellow, and if he really wants to fight, I'll give him an opportunity before he is many minutes older."

"Thou shalt do no such thing, Hubert," exclaimed the robber chieftain ; "the fellow is my prisoner, and he and his companions shall go back with us to our retreat, where they will remain either till they are ransomed, or —"

"Or what ?" demanded Stephen, eagerly.

"Till it is my pleasure to order your execution !" answered Black Ivan ;—"aye, you may look amazed, but so surely as that you now stand before me, I shall give orders to have you despatched, together with the whole of your companions, unless Sir Gaston de Neville thinks proper to send your ransom within three days from this time."

"Wilt thou also give me my liberty on condition of receiving a large sum of gold ?" asked Rebecca, anxiously.

"Nay, that is a bargain that I cannot agree to," replied Ivan ;—"thou art a prize far dearer to me than gold, silver, or jewels ; and, therefore, thou must be content to remain with me, and in return, thou shalt be mistress over all I possess in the world."

"I will rather perish !" cried our heroine, firmly.

"Come, come, girl," he exclaimed, "it is useless to resist, now that thou art in my hands ;—besides, thou shouldst have a husband, wench, and what matters it to thee who it is, so that thy future days are passed in happiness ?"

"I cannot love thee," answered Rebecca, recoiling with horror;— "nay, I have deep cause for cursing the fatal moment when first we met, and never will I give my hand to one whom my heart loathes as a monster of iniquity."

"Psha ! thou wilt think differently of me by-and-by, depend upon it."

"Never !" she exclaimed ; "a deep and lasting hatred has taken possession of my heart ;—I know thee for a villain, whose hand is crimsoned with human blood !—thy life has been passed in crime, and rather than submit to link my destiny with thine, I would undergo the most horrible tortures thy malignant heart can invent."

"And yet," replied Black Ivan, coolly, "in spite of these heroics, thou shalt be mine."

"Never !" exclaimed a voice from behind, and the next moment Isaac of Tadcaster, rushing forward, threw himself between the robber chief and his daughter; "never shall she be thine, while a father's arm is strong enough to prevent so hateful an union !"

"How is this !" demanded Ivan, fiercely ;—"how hast thou escaped from those into whose custody thou wert given ?"

"I thought of my daughter's peril," answered Isaac, "and resolved to lose no opportunity that might arise to save her from thy villany. Thy ruffians would have forced me to thy abode of crime and infamy, but chance favoured me, and slipping off unperceived, I was directed towards this spot by hearing thy voice in conversation with those by whom thou art surrounded."

"And what good wilt thou do now that thou art here ?" asked Ivan. "Thinkest thou I will relinquish my hard-earned prize, merely because an old man comes to demand her release ?"

"If thou hast the least feeling of human nature in thy heart, thou wilt not reject my prayers," replied Isaac.

"But suppose I do not boast of possessing the virtue thou speakest of?" retorted the robber;—"suppose I do not choose to hear thy prayers, what power is there on earth to compel me?"

"Nay, I will appeal to thee as a man," cried Isaac, throwing himself at the robber's feet;—"on my knees I implore thee to liberate a helpless maiden, and thus earn for thyself the prayers and blessings of those whose gratitude will know no bounds."

"Psha! what care I for gratitude?" exclaimed Black Ivan, sullenly; "it is but a worthless coin to one like me, and, therefore, not likely to be accepted in exchange for one so young and beautiful as Rebecca."

"Alas!" sighed our heroine, "hast thou no pity for the unfortunate; no mercy for her who calls upon thee in her helplessness?"

"None!"

"Then again I tell thee that I never will be thine," she exclaimed, vehemently; "thou hast heard my vow, Ivan, and never will I break it."

"Well, we shall see that, at any rate," answered the robber, with affected carelessness; "at present, I allow thee to rate and scold as much as thou likest, but thy licence will quickly be over, or I shall marvel greatly at the folly which permits thee to use thy tongue thus glibly."

"Nay, again do I implore thee to have mercy upon us!" cried the aged Israelite, in piteous accents.

"It is in vain you ask me, for I am not to be thus easily moved from my purpose."

"Yet, consider,—the maiden loves thee not."

"That," answered Ivan, "I care little about."

"Besides, her religion forbids an union such as the one you propose."

"Nonsense, old man!—you talk to one who entertains no such scruples as those you have mentioned. My will is the only law I ever follow, and having once made up my mind upon this subject, thou wilt find it no easy matter to turn me from it. Besides, what matters it to thee who has her, seeing that she has two lovers, one of whom must, and will triumph over the other?"

"Thou art mistaken," replied Isaac, "for neither thyself, nor Sir Gaston de Neville, shall ever tear away from me a jewel that I esteem beyond all price."

"How cans't thou help thyself, old man?"

"Heaven," answered the Hebrew, "will not desert us in our hour of need."

"Indeed! how is it, then, that both thou and thy daughter are at this moment in my power?"

"It is for a purpose," replied Isaac, solemnly, "that neither thou nor I can see into. For the present, it is true, we must yield to the storm that has overtaken us, but, be assured, the moment is not far distant when thy evil machinations willl be signally defeated."

"Dost thou dare prate to me of defeat?"

"I dare do so," answered the Jew, "and thou wilt soon be compelled to acknowledge the truth of what I have uttered. We are not forsaken, though at present thou hast obtained an advantage over us, and we are made to feel that we are in thy power."

"It is useless to parley further with thee," exclaimed Black Ivan, sternly; "I have told thee that the girl shall be mine, and no power shall thwart me in my will. I, therefore, make thee a fair offer, give me thy daughter, old man, and thy instant liberation from captivity shall follow."

"Urge me not," cried Isaac, "for liberty without my child, would be a curse, heavy, and unendurable. I can suffer death this moment, if it is thy will, without giving utterance to a single murmur, but never will I basely surrender my daughter to one who I know to be a villain!"

"Thou art resolved, then, to sacrifice both thyself and her?" exclaimed Black Ivan.

"Aye, if refusing to bestow my Rebecca on thee will do so, I am resolved," answered the Israelite.

"Then blame me not afterwards," cried the robber, "for I have offered thee fair terms, and thou hast wilfully refused them. I would have given thee liberty, hadst thou but thought fit to prevail upon her to accept the offer I have made, and now, having rejected my proposition, thou must e'en take all the blame upon thine own shoulders."

"Fiend!" exclaimed the old man, bitterly, "why dost thou torment thy victims thus cruelly?"

"Because I would still endeavour to prevail on thee to accept my terms before it is too late."

"It is in vain to urge me," answered Isaac, resolutely; "my daughter's honour is far dearer to me than all other earthly considerations, and I will die to preserve it from a ruffian such as thou art."

"We shall see how far thy boastings will avail thee, old man," answered Black Ivan, writhing under the torture of his own passion;— "thou forgettest that Ivan is now the master of thy destinies, and that I have the power to enforce that which I have condescended to solicit."

"If it is thy pleasure to slay me," exclaimed Isaac, "let the mandate be issued at once, for I would not live to see my child become a prey of the monster who has hunted her into his snare."

"That," replied the robber, "will be matter for future consideration; at present you and Rebecca will go with me to my retreat, and, perhaps, I may afford you one other chance of saving your own life, on condition that you accept the terms I have proposed. So now onward, my men, and see that our prisoners are taken care of till my further pleasure is known."

With this, they pursued their way towards their retreat, leaving Black Ivan, who, after pausing for a few moments, shortly followed them, whilst his mind was busily engaged in forming plans for future operation.

CHAPTER LVII.

"Who art thou, that crossing thus my path,
  Doth fill my soul with terrors, such as ne'er
  Before did haunt me?"

THE RECLUSE.

COMPLETELY occupied with the reflections that hurried through his teeming brain, Black Ivan was so throughly lost in the rushing torrent of his thoughts, as to be unconscious of the presence of the Wierd Woman of the Heath, until she suddenly sprang directly in his path, uttering at the same time a wild and frightful laugh, that rang in the robber's ears like a sound from hell.

"What ho!" she exclaimed, exultingly; "Black Ivan, thy presence here gives me joy, for I have that to tell thee which I know will madden thee with rage."

"Avaunt!—leave me, thou accursed imp of darkness!" cried the robber, with a gesture of impatience.

"Oh, thou mayst call me what thou wilt," answered Meg of Finchley; "I am but too much used to the railings of mankind to feel mortified at any terms of reproach that may be heaped upon me."

"Wilt thou leave me, hag?"

"Aye, when mine errand is accomplished, and not till then, even at the bidding of Black Ivan, the Outlaw."

"What wouldst thou with me?"

"Thou shalt know anon, if thou wilt follow me."

"Whither?"

"To yonder lightning-riven oak," answered the old woman, pointing in the direction she alluded to; "thou canst see it plainly, even by this fair moonlight, and thou must go with me thither, for I have a sight to show thee there, that has just now filled up my cup of misery to the very brim."

"Another time, and I will go with thee."

"Nay, another time will not do, for ere many hours have passed, I must see that the earth hides from all eyes the object I must now show thee."

"Shall I be doing thee any service by going with thee?"

"Thou mayst, perhaps, be able to point out the villain that committed the cruel deed I complain of."

"Woman!" exclaimed Black Ivan, "why dost thou not explain thyself, for I have yet to learn in what way I have ever done thee an injury?"

"Go with me, as I have said," cried Meg, impatiently, "and thou shalt see if I have not cause for complaint."

"Well, well, lead the way, and I will follow thee," returned Ivan, wearied by her importunities; "take me to the spot thou hast named, old woman, but remember, there must be no treachery, no ambuscade about the place, for I am well armed, and will have no mercy upon any that may chance to fall in my way, should their designs be to destroy me."

"Thou hast nothing to fear," exclaimed Meg; "thou wilt see no one there,—at least none that will have the power to injure thee."

"Hah! what meanest thou, woman?" cried the robber, startled by the peculiar tones in which these latter words were spoken; "who is it, then, that thou art so anxious for me to meet?"

"Come with me and thou shalt see."

"Nay, answer me, woman;—is it some fearful apparition that thou art about to summon from the grave?"

"No," she replied, sorrowfully, "it is one whom the grave has not yet closed upon."

"It is some enemy, then?"

"Again, I say," cried Meg, "come with me, and thou shalt see why I desire thy presence yonder."

Ivan hesitated for a moment or two, as if irresolute, and then waving his hand impatiently for her to proceed, he followed across the heath in the direction towards which the old woman had directed his attention. In about a quarter of an hour they reached the blighted oak, and on casting his eyes towards the ground, he discovered, beneath the leafless branches, an object that appeared like a human form, sleeping under a cloak that was spread over it. The robber was startled at this, and believing that he had been betrayed into the hands of an enemy, he drew his sword, and was about to plunge it into the body of his supposed foe, when Meg, rushing towards him with a scream, earnestly implored him to refrain from the act he meditated.

"Hold!—I entreat you, hold!" she cried, earnestly, "and do not thus cruelly mutilate one who has no longer the power to injure thee."

"What meanest thou, woman?" demanded Black Ivan, fiercely;—"speak, explain this mystery, or my sword shall reach the villain's heart!"

"Nay, I again implore thee to hold thy hand," cried Meg, more earnestly than before; "I tell thee thou hast nought to fear from him who lies at thy feet, for the malice of his enemies has already done its worst towards him."

"Woman! why dost thou keep me in this suspence?" cried the robber, fiercely; "explain this mystery, or my threat shall be fulfilled."

"Behold, then!" exclaimed Meg, throwing aside the cloak, and discovering the ghastly, bleeding form of a corpse; "behold, Ivan, the enemy thou dost dread so much; thou seest him dead at thy feet, and yet thy limbs tremble as if some fiend of darkness had suddenly presented himself before thee."

"Hag!—what is the meaning of this?" demanded Ivan, fiercely;—"whose bleeding form is this thou hast brought me hither to behold?"

"That of my grandchild," she replied, with a burst of grief.

"Thy grandchild!"

"It is."

"By whose hand has he fallen?"

"By that of Hubert, thy friend."

"Hah! and when was the deed perpetrated?"

"This morning."

"Yet, surely there was some cause for it, woman?—the youth came, perhaps, as a spy to betray us into the hands of our enemies?"

"He came hither by my orders," replied Meg;—"I knew, by the power I possess, that danger threatened the Hebrew Maiden, and the boy thou seest dead before thee, come to see if he could not aid in rescuing her from the peril into which she has since fallen."

"Then he has deserved the fate he has met," exclaimed Black Ivan; "if he came to rescue Rebecca from my hands, he has but received the reward his foolish interference so justly merited."

"Dost thou, then, exult in the deed of blood thy murderous comrade has perpetrated?"

"I tell thee he deserves his fate," answered Black Ivan. "Had he been slain without cause, I would have punished his slayer even though it were Hubert, who I esteem far beyond all the rest of my band."

"Am I not, then, to have vengeance against the murderer?" asked Meg, in accents of mingled rage and reproach.

"Thou hast heard me, woman," answered the robber, haughtily;—"the boy tempted his fate, and thou beholdest him before thee a victim to his own rashness."

"Then let Hubert beware!" exclaimed the old woman, in a voice of thunder; "let him beware, I say, for even though he were to take refuge before the altar, he should not cheat me of the revenge that fills my heart!"

"What!" cried Black Ivan, "is the life of Hubert to be threatened by a woman?"

"Aye," she replied, "and by one who will never abandon her design until the villain has paid the fearful penalty of his crime. I now gaze upon the mangled remains of all that I most loved upon earth; the blood that is now oozing from his wounds, calls aloud upon me for vengeance, and the cry shall be answered before many hours have passed away."

"If I thought thou wouldst carry thy mad threat into execution," answered Black Ivan, " my poniard should at once deprive thee of life.—Remember, hag, thy words may kindle up my rage, and, with a single blow, I can prevent the mischief thou speakest of."

"Do it, then," exclaimed the old woman, unmoved by threats of the robber; "let thy dagger find my heart, for in so doing, thou wilt send me to join the soul of him who lies stretched before thee."

"Art thou so eager, then, for death?"

"I am, for the villain, Hubert, has robbed me of all that my heart once held dearest."

"The youth sought his death, and has found it," answered Ivan.—"He came here to thwart me of the prize I intended to make, and if he has fallen, the blame rests only with himself."

"Roland only sought to aid the helpless against the evil designs of the powerful and wicked," replied Meg; "he would have rescued the Hebrew Maiden from her persecutor, but villainy triumphed, and I am left in my old age to mourn the loss of one who was more to me than all the riches of the world."

"And what reason has he for seeking to assist this girl in escaping from me?" asked Ivan.

"Gratitude."

"Gratitude!"

"Aye;—Rebecca has been kind to me, when every body else would have suffered me to die for want of assistance. She has watched by me when I laid on a bed of sickness, and I should have died, had it not been for the care with which she tended on me. From that time she has never ceased to do me all the services that lay in her power, and, therefore, it is not to be wondered at that my poor grandson should have risked his life in defence of one who has done so much for her who had ever been to him as a mother."

"How know you," demanded the robber, "that he fell by the hands of Hubert?"

"Because I saw the fatal blow struck," answered the old woman, shuddering; "I had a fearful prognostication that some evil was about to befal him, and with frantic speed I followed to warn him of his danger. As I approached this place, I saw him engaged in conversation with the murderous ruffian; I raised my voice, urging him to fly without loss of time, but alas! I was too late, for the assassin's poniard was instantly raised, and ere I could throw myself upon my knees at the villain's feet, his steel had entered the heart of my poor boy, and he sank with a groan of agony to the earth. Another, and another wound followed, whilst I stood transfixed with horror to the spot; but, at last, frantic with rage, I darted forward, and clutching the murderer by the throat, should instantly have avenged the death of my boy, had he not shook me off with a giant's strength, and stretched me almost lifeless upon the ground."

"And most justly wert thou served for thy pains," exclaimed Black Ivan, scowling grimly upon her. "Thou didst try to strangle him, and it would have been but fair had he left thee dead, instead of giving thee a chance of doing him a mischief hereafter."

"Let him take care of himself," returned the old woman. "for I have vowed to revenge this boy's death, and I will never relax my endeavours until I have kept my word! Hubert has rent my heart in twain by this cruel blow, and he shall die for it."

"Woman!" muttered Ivan, between his clenched teeth, "thou mayst consider thyself lucky that I have not silenced thee, ere this, with my poniard. I, however, warn thee to seek no further for revenge, for so surely as thou art found lurking about in this neighbourhood, thou wilt become the victim of thy madness."

"I care not for thy threats, Black Ivan," she replied, scornfully, "for life is no longer of value to me, since all that I loved most dearly is gone before me."

"Well, thou hast been warned," exclaimed the robber, "and since the accomplishment of thy revenge will not bring back thy boy to life again, I would fain persuade thee to forget thy griefs, and to pardon him of whom thou so bitterly complainest."

"Never!"

"Thou art resolved, then, to brave my anger?"

"I am, for I regard it only as the idle wind which blows upon without harming me."

"And yet it may happen that a tempest may arise, through thy madness, that no power of thine own can put a stop to."

"Thou wouldst fright me if thou couldst, Ivan."

"Nay, I would only show you the folly of carrying this affair any further," he replied. "There is the youth thou so much regrettest;—the life-blood has left his heart, and all thy prayers and lamentations will not serve to restore him. Therefore, I say, submit with patience to thy destiny, and if gold will be any recompense for the anguish thou hast endured, I will not fail to supply thee most liberally with it."

"Gold!" exclaimed the old woman, bitterly; "dost thou think, then, that my grief can be assuaged by the same filthy dross that has tempted thee to sin and crime."

"You refuse my offer, then," exclaimed Ivan. "Well, well, I will leave you for the present, to reflect upon the matter, but once more, I charge you, as you value your own life, to abandon all further thoughts of vengeance from your heart.—Remember my words, old woman, for much depends upon it."

Upon this, Black Ivan took his departure, when Meg, overpowered by the feelings that struggled in her heart, sank upon the dead body of her grandson, in which situation she remained until long after the sun had risen on the following morning.

CHAPTER LVIII.

"Your pleadings are all vain,
For you do speak to one who never felt
The force of pity."

THE WRECKER.

WHEN Isaac and Rebecca were conveyed back to the robbers' retreat, Hubert gave orders for them to be immediately conveyed to seperate chambers, where they were to be carefully guarded, until the pleasure of Black Ivan should be made known. This was a severe blow to both the father and daughter, who, in spite of the misfortune that had befallen them, still cheered themselves with the consolation of each other's society, at least for the present. Now, however, it seemed that even that gratification was to be denied them, and, surrounded as they were by robbers, there was, indeed, but too much reason to fear that some terrible violence was intended. Addressing himself, therefore, to Hubert, who acted as chief in the absence of Black Ivan, the old man earnestly implored that he might be per-

mitted to remain with his daughter, whose terror had been excited in the highest degree by the perilous situation in which she now found herself. But the ruffian was deaf to these entreaties, and spurning the old man with his foot, he said :—

"It is useless to ask favours of me, Jew, for I am one of those that scorn thy tribe, and who, were it in his power, would, with one blow, destroy the whole of thy hated race."

"And wherefore shouldst thou be so uncharitable?" demanded Isaac. "Are we not thy fellow-creatures, and in every respect as good as thyself?"

"Humph!" growled Hubert, "perhaps, in your own opinion, you may be so; but in mine, you are not worthy to breathe the same air with us. However, be that as it may, it's useless to ask any favours of me, so away with you to your dungeon, and I'll see presently where I can stow away this wench, till Black Ivan returns to us."

"I implore thee to have pity on us," cried Rebecca, earnestly; "we are here among strangers, and I should die with terror to be left alone amongst men whose lawless habits I have always trembled even to think of."

"Indeed!" retorted the robber, "and so, I suppose, you think us very terrible fellows."

"So much so," answered our heroine, "that I would gladly give all I possess in the world to be once more set at liberty."

"Then, let me advise you to make up your mind to remain with us all the rest of your life," exclaimed Hubert, grinning with savage delight; "our captain, you must know, has taken a wonderful fancy to you, and he is not the man, as you will find out, to give away a chance, when once it's thrown in his way."

"Let him beware how he tyrannically holds us in his power," cried the Israelite, firmly; "let him beware, I say, for King Richard has befriended us on former occasions, and he will not desert us when he hears that we have fallen into the hands of Black Ivan, the Outlaw."

"Ho, ho!" shouted the robber, with derision, "and so you really expect that the King of England will think it worth his while to trouble himself about two such little folks as you and your daughter?"

"I speak from former experience," answered Isaac; "the monarch, although young in years, has already proved himself to be the father of his people, and never does he hear a tale of oppression and cruelty, but he hastens to punish the evil-doers."

"Aye," answered Hubert, "but you seem to forget that it is not always very easy to do it."

"In this case, at any rate," observed the Jew, "it will not be very difficult to punish the guilty oppressors of our unhappy race. He has long intended to crush the band which owns Black Ivan for its head, and when he learns that my daughter has been made your captive, he will dispatch a party of his soldiers to destroy those who have, in too many instances, proved themselves a scourge to the country."

"Why don't you hack the old scoundrel down?" exclaimed one of the ruffians, advancing with a drawn sword, as if for the purpose of executing the threat he had hinted at. Rebecca, however, saw the intention of the robber, and, giving utterance to a loud scream, she threw herself forward, imploring the villain to have mercy upon her father.

"Spare him! oh, spare him!" she cried frantically, "or, if a life must be sacrificed, let mine suffice to satiate your blood-thirstiness."

"Why, as for that matter," replied Hubert, striking the weapon out of his comrade's hand, "we shall do as we like about it, though, for the present, the old man is safe enough, seeing that we very seldom do anything here, without first of all having our captain's orders for it."

"He is an old man," sobbed the maiden, in the anguish of her heart, "and it would be cowardice to strike one who has not the power to protect himself."

"Aye, aye, that may be all very true," replied Hubert, "but we very seldom keep useless people in this place, and, sometimes, when we find them in the way, we get rid of them in the shortest way we can."

"Thou shalt have all we possess in the world on condition that his life is spared."

"Well, that's something to be sure," replied Hubert, "but, I dare say it will depend on how much he is able to offer us, whether he is let to go or not."

"I will not give a single piece of gold for my liberty, unless thou, my child, art permitted to depart with me from this den of infamy."

"Then you will be very likely to die for your obstinacy," exclaimed Hubert, gruffly.

"Alas!" cried Rebecca, "is there, then, no way by which we may escape from the toils in which we have fallen?"

"None that I know of," replied the robber, carelessly. "In fact, you have no choice now, but to become the bride of our noble chieftain, and, in case of your accepting his offer cheerfully, I think I can undertake to promise that your father will be allowed to take his departure as soon as he pleases."

"Let not Black Ivan imagine that any circumstances shall force me to accept his terms," cried Rebecca, firmly.

"Then, I suppose you would rather see the old man die, than save him by becoming the mistress of this band."

"I would save my father at almost any sacrifice," replied our heroine; "I would die for him, but never will I become the bride of a robber."

"Ah! you are too particular by half."

"It is in vain that you pursue us thus," exclaimed Isaac, again interposing; "we are already resolved, and if assistance should not arrive, as I expect it will, we can perish together, without a murmur at the injustice which has doomed us."

"Upon my word, old gentleman, you seem to treat the matter very coolly."

"I do, for though you may have succeeded in placing my body in bondage, you have not yet subdued my spirits, or compelled my soul to bow down before the tyranny you would exercise. At present, you triumph; but beware, for a time may soon arrive when you will be as fallen as I am now."

"Aye, aye, it's all very well to talk in this way," exclaimed Hubert, "but when our captain returns, he may, perhaps, teach you that his power is not to be despised."

"He will imprison me, I suppose, in this retreat of his."

"Aye, or may-be he will order both you and your daughter for instant death."

"Well," answered the Jew, with resignation, "come when it may, death will be welcome, since it will save us from the foul dishonour meditated by your villainous leader."

"Come, come," growled Hubert, "we can't hear this sort of language against our captain, you know. He is is a fine, noble fellow, and there is not one under his command, but would shed his last drop of blood in his service."

"Yet, again do I say that he is a villain!" answered Isaac, "or he would not thus have hunted down with persecution the unfortunate victim of his impure passion."

"Psha!" muttered the robber, "who is there, I should like to know, that can conquer Love, when once the urchin thinks fit to take possession of the heart? For my own part, I love all the gentle sex dearly, and if the captain should think fit to give up his chance, I don't mind standing in his shoes."

And, with these words, he threw his arm round Rebecca's waist, and was about to salute her chaste lips, when Black Ivan himself made his appearance, and, darting forward with the fury of an enraged tiger, he snatched away the trembling maiden, and at the same moment aiming a tremendous blow at his lieutenant, he sent him reeling and tottering like a drunken man to the further end of the chamber. In an instant, the discomfitted robber snatched forth his dagger, and would have taken speedy vengeance for the insult he had received, but the countenances of his comrades betokened anything but commisseration with him, and, therefore, returning the weapon at once to its sheath, he smoothed his ruffled brow, and said, with forced sauvity:—

"Methinks, captain, you were over hasty in this salution of yours;— the girl and her father were brought here according to your own desire, and I was only going to lead her to the chamber she is to occupy, when you rushed upon us, and treated us in the unceremonious way that our friends just now witnessed."

"Thou may'st think thyself fortunate to have escaped with life," replied Black Ivan, fiercely. "I came hither angry with you, and the first thing that met my eyes was your insolent treatment of the maiden whom I had entrusted to your care."

"Angry with me, captain!"

"I was."

"And wherefore, I pray?"

"Because thou hast this day slain the grandson of Meg of Finchley."

"Well," retorted the ruffian, "and if I have done so, it was his own fault. He came hither to do you and all of us an evil turn, and, there. fore, I thought there could be no great harm in preventing the mischief he intended."

"But, by so doing," answered Ivan, "thou hast raised an implacable enemy in the person of old Meg."

"In that case, then," exclaimed Hubert, "we must serve her as we did the boy. Let me have the dealing with her, and I'll warrant there's not much harm will come from the old beldame."

"What!—wouldst thou shed more blood?"

"Aye, captain, an ocean of it should it seem to be necessary."

"Hubert," exclaimed the chief, "I would now be alone;—retire with thy comrades to the refectory, and I will myself undertake the task of conducting Isaac and his daughter to their separate chambers. The other prisoners I shall leave here, and remember, if any of them escape, you and your comrades will have to answer for it."

"Fear not but your orders will be obeyed," answered the lieutenant, with a grim smile;—"they shall be safe enough, and if I catch any one of them trying to slip off, my sword shall quickly prevent a second attempt of the same kind from being made."

"Aye, aye, spare them not," exclaimed Black Ivan;—"have no pity on the rascals, if they try to escape, for I have resolved to have a handsome ransom for them from Sir Gaston de Neville, and not a man must be suffered to depart from hence, till I have received every coin of the gold I intend to demand."

With these words he took Rebecca by the hand, and beckoning with his sword for her father to follow, he left the chamber, for the purpose of conveying them to the apartments which had been set aside for their use.

On his departure, Hubert took all necessary precautions for the security of their other captives, and having done this to his satisfaction, he retired with his comrades to enjoy themselves in a grand carouse.

CHAPTER LIX.

"Shall we not seek for liberty,
Since one bold effort will release us all
From our accursed foes?"

THE SIEGE OF RHODES.

IT was some time after Stephen and his companions had been left alone, ere any of them ventured to speak, lest their voices should arouse the suspicions of their captors, to the design which each of them secretly meditated of effecting their escape from captivity. At length, however, Stephen was the first to speak, and in a voice scarcely above a whisper, he inquired of them whether they felt inclined to run the risk of their lives in one desperate attempt to leave the place, ere the robbers entertained any suspicion of their designs.

Of course, his question was answered with an unanimous assent, and having thus assured himself of their co-operation, the next question to be considered, was the means by which their escape was to be accomplished.

"The task we have set ourselves," observed Stephen, in continuation, "is by no means an easy one, though I doubt not we shall succeed if you only proceed in the affair with proper caution; the rascals are, doubtless, resolved upon watching us pretty closely; but, presently, the fumes of the wine they are drinking, will have mounted into their heads, and our best opportunity will be afforded by the sleep which will naturally follow the deep carouse in which they are now indulging."

"But how are we to proceed?" demanded Wilfred, who was, perhaps, the least sanguine of all;—"at present, our hands are confined by the means of these cursed cords, and it will be in vain to make any effort to release ourselves from this place unless we are each able to grasp a weapon for our defence, in case the villains should happen to fall upon us unawares."

"Art thou beginning to be afraid already?" demanded Stephen, angrily.

"Why, as for being afraid," answered Wilfred, "I am, perhaps, as bold as yourself in this affair, only I should like to make sure before we set about the task we have taken on ourselves. I say, again, we ought to be armed, or our cause is hopeless."

"Well," exclaimed the other, "and do you not see weapons in abundance at our service?"

"I do, Stephen, but of what use are they, while our wrists are thus secured with cords?"

"Aye, aye, where, indeed?" murmured the rest, who began to foresee that their case was desperate.

"Nay, do not ask me!" cried Stephen, out of patience at the alarm that had thus seized upon them;—"I have already hinted that I despair not, and you shall soon see that I have good reason for my confidence."

With these words he mounted the table and placing the cords that bound his wrists over the flame of a lamp that hung suspended from the ceiling, he quickly disengaged himself from his bonds, and then leaping once more to the floor, he said, in a tone of exultation:—

"You see how easy it is to execute a task that appeared so difficult to yourselves. I am now able to wield a sword, and by all the saints in heaven, I will not fail to make good use of it, should our enemies happen to throw themselves in our way."

"But how are we to assist you?" demanded Wilfred; "our hands are still bound and you will fare but badly alone, should all the robbers se upon you at once."

"Aye, but thus I give you each the same advantage that I myself possess," answered Stephen, and without further hesitation he, with his sword, cut through all the bonds, and thus gave them so far an opportunity to secure their flight from the strong-hold of the robbers. This done, they immediately armed themselves with such weapons as happened to be lying about, and then, addressing themselves to Stephen, offered to put themselves under him on condition that he would conduct them with all speed from the place of their captivity. This he promised to do, but suddenly recollecting himself, he said:—

" There is one thing, my friends, we had nearly forgotten;—the Hebrew Maiden and her father are still in the power of these robbers, and I, for one, dare not return to Sir Gaston de Neville, unless we take back with us those who were entrusted to our care."

" Art thou mad ?" demanded Wilfred, sullenly ; " wouldst thou throw away an advantage merely for the sake of releasing those we have no reason to care for."

" Nay, if you grumble," exclaimed the other, " make your way from hence the best way you can. I, for one, am determined not to go without the Jew and his daughter; so now, as you know my mind upon the subject, every man may be at liberty to do as he pleases."

" But know you not that the robbers are now at carousal," asked Wilfred, " and that the slightest noise will bring them all upon us ?"

" I know,—or, at least, I judge, that, by this time, they have all fallen into a deep sleep," replied Stephen. " Their wild clamour has suddenly ceased, and, therefore, there is little doubt but that we may search for the two prisoners without fear of being discovered."

" Black Ivan led them through the very room where the revellers are," observed Wilfred.

" Well, and what if he did ?"

" Why, does it not naturally follow that we must go through the chamber where these ruffians are ?"

" Very true," answered Stephen, " but if all the robbers happen to be asleep,—as from their silence, I suspect they are,—what is to hinder our passing among them, without fear of being discovered ?"

" At any rate," observed one of the men, " there is a chance that some of them will be awake, and, in that case, we shall pay dearly for our folly."

" 'Psha !" growled Stephen, sullenly, " then all I can say about it is, that those who are afraid had better look to their own safety at once.—I, however, mean to run the risk, for I would rather perish in this way, than meet Sir Gaston, without being able to produce the Jew and his daughter."

" If Sir Gaston is so anxious to get hold of them, again," observed another of the retainers,—" let him come here and do the business we have objected to."

" Perhaps you will have no objection to tell him so, yourself?" cried Stephen, fiercely :—" he will, no doubt, be well pleased at the great zeal exhibited by his servants, though, to confess the truth, I have a notion the man that tells him so, will never again have an opportunity to desert him in the hour of need."

" Then you would persuade us," said Wilfred, " to run the risk we are all so much afraid of."

" You have heard what I had to say," replied Stephen, " and, therefore, every man can do as he pleases."

" Then I," said Wilfred, " shall certainly take my departure without running any further risk of meeting death from these robbers."

" And so shall I," exclaimed all the rest.

" Well, you can do as you please," cried Stephen, " but if you all choose to sneak off in this way, I will find means to punish you for it before you are many minutes older."

" You will !"

" Aye, as surely as the threat has been uttered," replied Stephen, resolutely. " So now, you understand clearly what I mean, and the first movement that ye make to leave this place, shall be to meet a fate that ye would all flee from."

"How!—are we then threatened?" cried Wilfred.

"You are," answered the other, "and if you do not take care, my threats will be accomplished sooner than may be expected by those that know my usual resolution. Nay, the moment I see any attempt made to escape from this place, I will rouse the sleepers in yonder chamber, and ye will then learn whether it would not have been better to follow the advice I have given."

"You are a pretty fellow, Stephen, ain't you?" exclaimed Wilfred, angrily;—"and so you would betray your friends into the hands of these robbers, merely because they do not think fit to join you in a mad adventure that would be sure to cost them their lives."

"The truth is, you are in peril either way," returned Stephen. "Follow your own inclinations in this affair, and I will deliver you into the hands of these ruffians, but if you think fit to do as I have said, there is a fair chance of getting off without being discovered by these drunken revellers."

"But," observed one of the men, "we must expect to have a fight for it, should the rascals discover us before we get clear off from the place."

"Well, and you have arms in your hands, in case of such an emergency," replied Stephen. "There are eight of us to fight against these fellows, and the deuce is in it, if we do not prove more than a match for fifty men that are drunk and stupified from the effects of the wine they have drank."

"But——"

"Nay," interrupted Stephen, "I'll not have another word that you have to say about it; so make up your minds at once, and then I shall know what to do in the matter."

"It's in vain to say any more," said Wilfred, "so lead the way as soon as you please, and I can answer for my companions that they will follow wherever you may think fit to take them."

Upon this, Stephen advanced alone towards the door, for the purpose of reconnoitering a little, previous to taking a more decisive step, and having convinced himself that all the robbers were asleep, he returned on tip-toe to his companions, assuring them there was no danger if they only used the least precaution, and then bidding them follow him, weapon in hand, they passed through the chamber in which lay the sleeping bandits, and from thence proceeded to a passage, on each side of which were numerous apartments, all of which they searched, without discovering those for whom they had risked so much. At length, however, they entered the one in which Isaac of Tadcaster was watching the approach of morning; at the moment of their approach, the old man turned his head towards them, and believing that it was a party of the robbers sent to murder him, he fell upon his knees, imploring them to let him have one more interview with his daughter before they put him to death.

"Follow us in silence, or you perish!" exclaimed Stephen, holding his sword's point at the bosom of the terrified Jew;—"follow us, I say, for your child's life depends upon your promptly obeying my commands."

"And who art thou," demanded the old man, "who thus comes to me at this dead hour of the night?"

"Dost thou not know Stephen, the retainer of Sir Gaston de Neville?"

"I do recognize thy voice now," replied the Hebrew; "yet still am I at a loss to divine the reason of thy visit to me."

"We are here to save both thee and thy daughter."

"Indeed!—why 'tis scarce an hour since I saw thee and thy comrades in the hands of Black Ivan and his band,"

"Thou didst, but we have liberated ourselves from the bonds that held us, and have now come hither to offer the same advantages to thee and Rebecca."

"I will not accept thy assistance," answered the old man, resolutely.

"Thou wilt not?—Dost thou remember in whose hands thou hast fallen?"

"I remember all," replied Isaac;—"I am a prisoner to Black Ivan, the Outlaw, and may expect to pass the remainder of my days in hopeless captivity."

"Then why not go with us," demanded Stephen, "and secure that liberty of which you may else be for ever deprived?"

"Because," replied the Israelite, "I should only be exchanging one kind of captivity for another. Sir Gaston de Neville has long been practising his arts against the honour of my daughter, and never again will I trust her in his power whilst I have life to prevent it."

"You forget, then, that Black Ivan is his rival in love?"

"I have not forgotten it," replied the Jew, "but why should I seek to release her from one danger, merely for the sake of plunging her into another. Both are equally villains, and since we have escaped from Sir Gaston, I will not take a step by which to fall into his hands again."

"Then art thou irrecoverably mad, old man," exclaimed Stephen, impatiently. "I tell thee she is in greater danger here, than she would be in my master's castle, for it is not long since I overheard a conversation, in which it was agreed that the nuptial rite between Rebecca and Black Ivan should take place early to-morrow morning."

This was a falsehood, but Stephen saw that nothing would answer his purpose so well as by exciting the terror of the old man, and in this instance, at least, he had judged with tolerable correctness. Isaac was, indeed, alarmed for the safety of his beloved daughter; and immediately forgetting all the other perils to which he might expose her, he said eagerly:—

"I know not, sirrah, whether thou art deceiving me or not, but my child's safety is far beyond any other consideration, and, therefore, do I yield to the proposition thou hast made."

"You will accompany us, then?"

"I will; but whither wouldst thou lead me?"

"To thy daughter's apartment; knowest thou where we can find it?"

"She is in the room adjoining this," answered the old man; "I heard the villains take her there immediately after they had left me here; and, I was thinking, at the very moment when you arrived, whether there was no way by which I might obtain a brief interview with her."

"You shall have one now, old man, if you will but follow us," answered Stephen; "but there is one thing I must warn you of though; we have not much time to spare, just at present, for fear of being disturbed by the robbers, so be content with merely bidding her to go with us, and I promise you shall have as long an interview as you like, when once we get thoroughly clear from this place."

The Jew signified his assent to this proposition, and accompanying the men, he led them immediately to the chamber occupied by Rebecca, who they found in tears, and bitterly lamenting the cruel fate that had thus hunted her into the snares of one of her most vindictive enemies. At their approach, however, she started from the ground, upon which she had thrown herself, but perceiving that her father was among them, she threw herself upon his neck, and gave fresh vent to the sorrows that afflicted her young heart.

"Alas! why have they brought thee hither?" she cried, in accents

of despair: "is it for a last interview, ere they drag thee to thy doom ?"

"Hush, my child!" whispered the fond old man, " we have come to give thee liberty."

"Liberty !" she cried, joyfully, "are we, then, to be henceforth free from those who have hitherto persecuted us ?"

"I know not, my child, whether we shall be quite free," answered Isaac, "but to remain longer here, would be to ensure thy future misery, for Black Ivan has sworn to wed thee, and to-morrow morning is to unite thee to him for ever. It is on that account that I have come to prevail upon thee to flee from a place that is so unfit for my Rebecca."

"Oh, delay not a moment, I implore you!" she cried, distractedly; "lead me from hence, dear father, for my soul is already sinking with terror and apprehension."

"Yet, there is one thing I have not yet told thee," exclaimed the old man; " these men thou see'st with me are the servants and retainers of Sir Gaston de Neville, and if we leave this place with them, it must be to return to the castle of the Knight Templar."

"Ah !" cried Rebecca, with alarm, "is there, then, no alternative by which to escape this second peril ?"

"None, girl," answered Stephen, interposing; " you must either return with us from whence we came, or, to-morrow will see you the bride of Black Ivan, the Outlaw !"

"That will never be!"

"You will go with us, then ?"

"Nay, I must reflect, ere I accept your terms."

No. 38

"Yet, remember,—if you reject my offer, nothing will prevent your becoming the wife of a robber."

"Thou art wrong, sirrah, for death will I prefer to becoming the bride of a villain such as he is."

"But he will not suffer thee to escape that way," exclaimed Stephen; "Ivan is well aware that you like him not, but he will take care to prevent your falling by your own hand."

"He cannot," replied Rebecca, firmly.

"Be not too sure of that," cried Stephen, "but accept the offer that has been made thee, and escape from hence, ere it is too late."

"How can I hope to escape from hence," demanded the Hebrew Maiden, "when so many have been set to watch over and guard us?"

"Aye, but those who were to look after us are now fast asleep," replied the other. "They have emptied the wine-cup in honour of their captain's nuptials, and at this moment, they are buried in a slumber so profound, that we need not be afraid of disturbing them."

"Is this true, that I hear?" she demanded of her father.

"It is," he replied.

"And is it with your consent, that we make this effort to escape?"

"I certainly came here to prevail upon thee, my child," answered the Jew, with hesitation; "I felt that thou wert in danger, and, like a drowning mariner, have seized upon the first object that offered, to rescue thee and myself from peril."

"Then I will follow thee," said Rebecca, without any further hesitation; "yes, I will go with thee, even though it is with every certainty of falling into the hands of Sir Gaston de Neville."

Taking the arm of his daughter, Isaac now silently followed Stephen and his companions from that portion of the place in which they had been confined, and, passing through the refectory where the robbers were still sleeping, they succeeded in reaching the narrow passage that formed the only entrance to the stronghold. They then cautiously removed the fastenings that secured the door, but scarcely had they effected this, and thus gained the exterior, when one of the robbers, who had been left as sentinel, started up from the ground, and, ere he could be prevented, he raised a bugle to his lips, and raised an alarm that was echoed from a hundred points around them. In an instant the ruffian was struck down and disarmed, but the mischief he intended was already done, and, ere they could effect their retreat, a vast body of the robbers came rushing forth, and the fugitives would have paid dearly for their attempt to escape, had not the same signal that had alarmed the brigands, attracted to the spot a party of the royal guards, who had been sent forth by command of King Richard, for the purpose of rescuing the Israelite and his daughter, who, it was reported, had been sent secretly away by Sir Gaston de Neville.

The conflict that now ensued was long and severe, but, at length, the robbers began to yield to the superior numbers and force of their adversaries, who, pursuing the advantage they had gained, followed them to the very gates of the castle, which Ivan and his band succeeded in entering, and immediately closing them, so as to prevent the further advance of those who had already given full proof of the ardour that inspired them.

Knowing that it would be in vain to make any further attempt against the impregnable walls of the castle, the guards immediately desisted from the attack, and, placing Isaac and Rebecca in the midst of their ranks, they set forward on their return to London.

CHAPTER LX.

"Were it in my power,
I would exterminate thy race accursed,
And blot them out for ever."
THE HINDOO.

BAD as the roads were, in those far distant days to which our narrative belongs, it was by no means an easy task to make their way across the few miles that intervened between our travellers and the metropolis. To Rebecca, whose delicate frame was nearly exhausted by the fatigue she had already endured, the journey was one of extreme difficulty, and she must have fallen by the wayside, had not the captain of the guard perceived her distress, and dismounted from his horse to lift her on the saddle before him. This done, Isaac seemed to be relieved of half his anxieties, and, walking close by her side, he endeavoured, by cheerful conversation, to divert her thoughts from the gloomy anticipations that still oppressed her soul.

"We are now safe, my child," he said, in answer to an observation she had just made relative to the series of ills that had lately befallen her; "those who surround us are friends, and, therefore, I beseech thee to look forward with hope and gratitude."

"Alas! my father," she replied, "why should I hope for rest, seeing that my enemies are many, and that they are determined to hunt me to destruction?"

"Be not ungrateful to that power which has so often preserved thee from peril," exclaimed the Israelite. "Already hast thou experienced the goodness that is ever watching over thee, and thou may'st rely on it, after all the care that has been bestowed upon thee, a better fate than thou expectest is in store."

"You say wisely, old man," observed the captain; "the girl has had some narrow escapes, and you may take my word for it, that the king will take good care she gets into no more of these troubles."

"And yet, methinks," exclaimed Stephen, gloomily, "his majesty might be better employed, than in wasting his time for the sake of an unbelieving Jewess."

"Richard is a just king," answered the other, with warmth, "and extends his protection to all his subjects alike, whether they happen to be Jews or Gentiles."

"By which conduct," returned Stephen, "he has lost the respect and confidence of those he ought to depend upon for support."

"Aye, you allude to your master, Sir Gaston de Neville, and other discontented nobles," replied the captain, with a sneer. "These are the men for whom his majesty is to perform an act of injustice, by suffering the more helpless portion of his subjects to be harassed and oppressed."

"What!" exclaimed Stephen, "dost thou, then, dare to say aught that may throw shame and dishonour on my noble master? Upon one who has fought and bled for his king and country, and who has spent the best years of his life in a foreign land to uproot the infidels who have so long infested the Holy Land."

"King Richard values him as a gallant knight," answered the captain, "but knowing, as he does, the unjust persecutions to which he has subjected this poor maiden, he cannot but feel angered at an act that cannot be excused."

"''Psha!—what is it to him if my master happens to fall desperately in love?"

"Nothing, if the love was an honourable one," replied the other;—"but, as it is well known that he has no intention of wedding the maiden, there is ample cause for interfering in her behalf."

"And for which kindness," exclaimed Isaac, fervently, "he has obtained the prayers and blessings of —"

"A Jew!" interrupted Stephen, with a sneer.

"It may be as thou hast said," answered the old man, in a tone of mild reproach. "The king has extended his royal protection to a daughter of Israel;—he has saved her from the snares of a libertine, and the deed will, perhaps, redound as much to his honour, as if he had performed the same kindness towards the daughter of a Christian knight."

"Thou art insolent, old man!"

"On the contrary,—I speak the truth, and if that offends thee, it is no fault of mine."

"Aye, aye," retorted Stephen; "I see how it is,—the king's misplaced kindness hath made thee over bold, and, by and by, I suppose, we shall hear of thy people claiming equal rights with the followers of the Cross!"

"And why should we not?" demanded the old man;—"are we not men like yourself?—natives of the same soil on which we live, and shall privileges be granted to one class of the human race, whilst another is to be ground down with cruelty and oppression?"

"Humph!—upon my life, things are beginning to come to a pretty pass!" growled Stephen;—"you talk, old man, as if you were to have it all your own way, but, take my word for it, in spite of the king's foolish kindness, thou wilt never live to see the equality of which thou speakest."

"Perhaps, not," answered the Israelite, "and yet the thing of which I have told thee will one day or the other happen. Ages, perchance, may roll away, ere we break our present bondage;—but the time will come, when men will grow wiser, and better than they are at present;—prejudice will then disappear like a mist from before the sun, and the Jew will be admitted to an equality with his fellow men."

"'Tis well thou canst console thyself thus easily," exclaimed Stephen, "since it may serve to dispel some of the sufferings thou hast yet to undergo."

"Sufferings I have still to undergo!" cried the old man.

"Aye, and not only thyself, but thy daughter."

"Thou hintest darkly," returned Isaac, endeavouring to conceal the anxiety occasioned by these words. "Thy lips have given utterance to a threat, and I would, therefore, ask thee the nature of that peril thou speakest of?"

"I will tell thee, then," answered the other:—"thou canst not have forgotten the affair of the diamond stolen from my master, and afterwards found in the possession of thy daughter?"

"I do—I do—" replied the old man, with emotion;—"the jewel was said to have been stolen by Black Ivan,—of whom I purchased it,—without having any suspicion of his having become possessed of it dishonestly."

"That is your version of the story," answered Stephen. "My master, however, is not to be so easily convinced of your innocence, and since Rebecca has thought fit to thwart him at every turn, he will now insist upon having the matter sifted to the very bottom."

"He has already done so," exclaimed Isaac; "my daughter has submitted to the ordeal, and, according to that fearful trial, has been pronounced innocent."

"There must have been some trickery in it," answered the other;—"thy child has practised witchcraft, or never could she have passed unscathed through the ordeal of boiling water."

"Alas!" cried Rebecca, who had hitherto been a silent listener to this conversation, "to what further persecutions am I to be driven to, through the vengeance of my enemies?"

"Oh, don't talk about persecutions," exclaimed Stephen, "because all suspected persons,—whether Jews or Christians,—are obliged to submit themselves quietly, whenever a charge is brought against them. Besides, your father still keeps possession of the diamond ring, and——"

"I bought it at its full value," interrupted the Israelite, "and, therefore, I have every right to keep the jewel, until the sum I gave has been offered in exchange. Sir Gaston knows that I have made him the first offer, but he refuses to buy it, hoping, no doubt, that the law will compel me to restore it without compensation."

"Nay, the king will be thy judge," exclaimed the captain of the guard, interposing; "he best knows the affair as it stands between thee, and will administer impartial justice, so as to satisfy both parties with his decision."

"He will not be impartial," answered Stephen, "for I can answer for it, he will not hand this Jew and his daughter over to the executioner,—for having been found in the possession of a jewel that has been stolen."

"It would be most unjust were he to do so," returned the officer, "for it has been already proved, that though the diamond ring was found on this maiden, yet it had been purchased by her father without any suspicion of its having been stolen."

"In proof of which we have only his bare word."

"And why should not mine be taken, as well as that of thy master?" demanded the old man.

"Because thou belongest to a people who would say or swear to anything."

"A most unjust charge, truly!" cried Isaac, with honest indignation; "and yet it is only a small portion of the falsehoods and evil things said of us, by those who glory in being the persecutors of a people they have long despised."

"Dear father," exclaimed Rebecca, "restrain your anger, I beseech you;—at present, it is in vain that we assert our innocence of the cruel charges that are being constantly brought against us;—bigotry and intollerance are the feelings of the age we live in, and useless, therefore, is it to speak to men, whose enmity we cannot easily remove."

"Girl!" exclaimed the Israelite, sternly, "wouldst thou, then, see me lie down to be spurned and kicked at, by those who treat us with scorn and contempt?"

"Ho! ho!" shouted Stephen, with derision, "here is a brave Jew, truly!—A fellow that,—if he had his own way,—would, I dare say, head an insurrection, for the purpose of exalting his own people over the heads of us Christians!"

"Our tribe seek not to exalt themselves," replied Isaac, with humility;—"all we ask, is to be made equal to our fellow creatures, and, when that is done, it will be seen that we are not unworthy of the tardy justice dealt out to us."

"Well, if every body was of my way of thinking," exclaimed Stephen, " every Jew should be put out of the way, to make 'room for their betters. However, be that as it may, you have no friend, I can tell you, in Sir Gaston de Neville, so either make up your mind to let him have your daughter upon his own terms, or be prepared to see her once more given up to the tender mercies of the law."

" Not whilst there are men, who will not see oppression, even though a Jew may happen to be the unfortunate victim," replied Isaac. " I know there are many, like yourself, who would rejoice at the torture inflicted upon any of our people, but, heaven be praised for it! we are not yet so fallen, but that we may hope for protection from one, who has the power to defend us."

" Aye, aye," sneered Stephen, " you reckon largely upon the kindness of King Richard, but, at the same time, you must not forget that his own will must not be consulted in these matters. He has powerful barons to please, some of whom are not so blind to their own interests, but they may transfer their allegiance from him to his brother, Prince John, who, it seems, is ready to accept the throne, whenever it may be offered to him."

" Hah!" exclaimed the captain of the guard, " does treason, then, set in from that quarter?"

" Nay, I speak only from hearsay," stammered the other, who began to see that he had gone too far. " It is, perhaps, an idle report which I was induced to repeat, just to convince this old man, that he and his accursed race, are not quite so secure as they may believe."

" Well, well," exclaimed the officer, " we have now reached the royal palace, but, remember, I shall seek an early opportunity to inquire whether there is any truth in the hint you have given, about his Highness, Prince John."

" There is none," replied Stephen, vexed at the communication he had thus thoughtlessly made. " I spoke without knowing what I said, and sorry should I be, if any word of mine should happen to throw disgrace upon one who deserves it not."

" At any rate," cried the captain, " this is not the first time that it has been rumoured Prince John has designs against his brother. Nay, more,—it has been whispered that he is secure of Sir Gaston de Neville's assistance, in case of an opportunity occurring; and, therefore, I shall feel it my duty to inform my royal master of the words you have just spoken."

" You would ruin me, then?"

" Aye, and gladly, too, if thou art really guilty of being privy to a plot against the king," answered the officer. " However, at present, thou may'st take thy departure with thy fellows, and when thou see't Sir Gaston, warn him of his danger, for, be assured, I shall not fail to tell the king what I have heard, who will, of course, act as he thinks fit. So, farewell to thee, and, if thou art wise, abandon, for the future, the society of those, who would depose our rightful sovereign for the sake of placing a usurper upon his throne."

Having given utterance to these words, the officer conducted his party into the palace, leaving Stephen and his friends to continue their way towards the castle of Sir Gaston de Neville.

CHAPTER LXI.

" If there be treason in the land,
We'll quench it in the blood of all those traitors,
Who dare to rise against us."

THE INVASION.

EARLY as it was in the morning, when our party arrived at the royal palace, King Richard was already stirring, and no sooner was a message conveyed, informing him of what had occurred, than betaking himself to the usual audience chamber, he desired the persons to be conducted into his presence. From his chief officer he learnt the affair that had taken place between his guard and the robbers, and having learnt the manner in which Isaac and his daughter had been rescued, he desired the former to relate how it was that he had again 'fallen into the hands of Black Ivan.

" My liege," answered the old man, " I have been made a prisoner of, by Sir Gaston de Neville, because I went to him as a suppliant, in behalf of my daughter. For some days I was his captive, and then, wishing to place me where there would be less chance of my escape, he sent me, under a guard, for one of his castles in the north. On our way, however, we were intercepted by Black Ivan, the Outlaw, and shortly afterwards, my daughter, who had been sent to follow me under another escort, also became a captive to the robbers."

" And how did you contrive to escape ?"

" Through some of Sir Gaston's men, who were made prisoners at the same time with ourselves. They succeeded in getting us out of the robbers' retreat, but an alarm being given, there is every reason to believe we should again have been taken, had not your guard made its appearance, and rescued us, by compelling the robbers to seek refuge within their own walls."

" Then, after all, you have been prisoners to Sir Gaston de Neville ?" observed the king, after a pause.

" We have, my gracious liege."

" Then the false knight lied, when he told me that neither thou nor thy daughter was beneath his roof ?"

" He did," answered the aged Israelite ;—" both I and my child have been his prisoners ever since the evening he prevailed on her to leave home under a false pretext."

" By heavens, he shall dearly answer for this !" exclaimed the king, wrathfully ;—" he has deceived me once, and having at length detected him, he shall feel that I have the power to punish, as well as to reward."

" Let him not be punished for anything he has done to us," cried the Jew, earnestly. " If he hath wronged us, I can forgive him, and all I ask is, for protection for Rebecca and myself."

" Which never can be obtained," answered the king, " except by showing him that all my subjects shall be alike protected against the tyranny of their foes. Hitherto, Sir Gaston de Neville has found me only anxious to reward him for the services he performed for me in the Holy Land. Now, however, he hath proved himself unworthy of my regard, and from this time forth, I cast him from my heart, unless he will undertake to swear that you shall never more be subject to his cruel persecutions."

"Your majesty," interposed the captain of the guard, "has, indeed, heavy cause of complaint against Sir Gaston de Neville."

"Hah!—how knowest thou that?" demanded the king.

"From the lips of one of his own followers," answered the officer.

"But can the man be depended on?"

"In this instance, I should suppose he may," replied the other, "the fact escaped him unawares, and afterwards he would have turned it off."

"And what says the man?" demanded King Richard.

"Enough to prove that there is a plot to raise Prince John to the throne, and that Sir Gaston de Neville is deep'y implicated in it."

"Indeed!—I have heard something like that before," exclaimed the king, angrily. "Sir Gaston has been observed to shun me, when we have chanced to meet, and from the frequent and secret interviews he has lately had with my brother, I fear there is more truth in this than was at one time inclined to believe."

"The serpent must be crushed," observed the officer, in reply, "or it will sting the royal hand that has fostered it. That a traitorous scheme is in progress, I feel certain, and never will I rest satisfied until the infamous affair is fully dragged to light."

"Let us be cautious in what we do," replied the king, "or we may do an injustice to the knight whom you accuse. At present, we have no clear evidence against him, and all that we have heard may be nothing more than the malice of certain enemies who seek his destruction, in order to rise upon the ruin they have made."

"Yet, even allowing that he may not be engaged in any treasonable projects against your majesty," replied the officer, "there is enough to prove him guilty of evil practices towards this old man and his daughter. They have been the victims of his arbitrary power, and would have fallen long ere this, had it not been for the generous protection afforded them by their sovereign."

"For that," exclaimed the king, "Sir Gaston de Neville must answer and that too, without further delay. It will, therefore, be your business to summon him before me, instantly, and if he gives not a good account of this affair, he shall answer for it in a way that he little expects."

"Again," cried the Israelite, "I implore your majesty to let this matter rest where it is. That I have been cruelly wronged, it is true but already we have many enemies, and should any stir be made in this business, our lives, perhaps, may be made to answer for it."

"Who, think you," exclaimed King Richard, "will dare to harm you whilst under my protection? Do not my subjects know that I am terrible in my vengeance, as well as in the field of battle, and that those who seek to injure thee or thy daughter will thereby bring upon themselves wrath as sudden and destructive as the lightning?"

"They know it, my liege," replied Isaac, "yet would I fain prevent that which would be sure to raise against you a host of enemies. Sir Gaston de Neville is surrounded by a host of partizans, and, if what we have heard is true, they are only waiting for such an opportunity as this would afford, to raise in this country a civil war, which would blaze from one end of the country to the other."

Before the king could reply to this, one of the royal archers approached to announce that Sir Gaston de Neville was waiting without to learn whether the king would grant him the favour of an audience. This intelligence seemed to excite the king's rage to the utmost, and pacing angrily up and down the apartment, he desired the knight to be instantly admitted.

"I will now charge him with the treason," he exclaimed, fiercely, "and

by the heaven above me, unless he can satisfactorily clear himself of the crime urged against him, I will deliver him over to an ignominious doom, and afterwards give his body to be devoured by the wolves of the forest."

"Your majesty may have been misinformed by those who bear the knight no good will," cried Isaac, generously interposing in behalf of the man who had sought to injure him by every means in his power. "Treason may never have entered the mind of Sir Gaston de Neville, who, in spite of all his fault, I have ever regarded as one among the most faithful of your subjects."

"That shall, at least, be tried," exclaimed Richard; "I will roundly tax him with the perfidy, and should he falter, or change countenance, I will not fail to let him feel the vengeance he so justly merits."

As he said this, Sir Gaston, conducted by one of the attendants, entered the chamber, and, throwing himself upon his knees before the sovereign,

"My gracious liege," he cried, with the most abject humility, "I have come to crave an audience, for the purpose of assuring you that I am not the traitor people would make you believe me. I have enemies that wish to abuse the royal ear, and who would gladly seek my destruction, even by the invention of the basest falsehoods."

"What hast thou to say," demanded the king, "in answer to the charges of treason that have been brought against thee?"

"My liege, I utterly deny them."

"Humph!—thou hast no wish, then, to elevate my brother, Prince John, to the throne I at present occupy?"

"I should deserve death by the most dishonourable means," exclaimed Sir Gaston, affecting the greatest indignation that such a suspicion should have been harboured against him. "Nay, I have ever proved myself

No. 39

amongst the very foremost of your majesty's loyal subjects, and am again ready to prove my zeal in the cause of my royal master."

"Thou speakest fairly enough to my face," answered the king, "and it is possible I may have wronged thee, by listening to the report of men who may be thine enemies; yet, for all that, thy conduct has been unworthy of thy knighthood, and I now tell thee that a continuance will bring upon thee my severest displeasure."

"To what," asked the knight, with pretended surprise, "does your majesty allude?"

"To your repeated acts of tyranny towards a poor Jew and his daughter."

"Ha! does your majesty think it worthy of your high dignity to declare yourself the friend of that outcast tribe?"

"A king," answered Richard, sternly, "if he is worthy of his high station, will suffer no portion of his subjects to be trampled upon by another. The Jews, humble and meek in spirit as they are, have ever proved themselves loyal to the monarch, and good members of society."

"But do they not, on the other hand," asked Sir Gaston de Neville, "grind us to the very earth by their unjust extortions?"

"Not to the extent they are charged with," answered the king, severely. "The Israelites are oppressed without cause; we make them a mark for all kinds of injuries and insults; we deny them the same privileges that are granted to other persons, and yet wonder that they seek to enrich themselves by the only means left them. If a spendthrift wants money, does he not apply to a Jew, and though the interest charged may be considered usury, is it to be wondered at, since many of their debtors are not very scrupulous when the day for payment arrives?"

"I know it is in vain to argue with your majesty upon this subject," exclaimed Sir Gaston; "and I shall, therefore, only observe, that, though my own conduct towards Isaac, of Tadcaster, and his daughter, may have appeared harsh, yet, it has been provoked by the treatment I have received from others of their tribe."

"And so," cried the king, "you would make them suffer for injuries inflicted by others!"

"My liege," answered Sir Gaston, "you judge me too harshly; I love the girl, Rebecca, and it is her own fault that I have been constrained to use violence, in order, if possible, to make her mine."

"But you are aware that her heart is already engaged," exclaimed the king; "that she is, in fact, betrothed to a youth belonging to her own people, and that her father has been pleased to grant his consent to their union."

"I have heard something of the kind," answered the Knight Templar; "but, even if there is any truth in it, I see no reason for desisting from a pursuit like this. The girl is mistress of her own actions, and if my efforts to prevail over her scruples should be successful, I see no reason why my actions should be called in question."

"Perhaps, then," observed Richard, sternly; "it is a matter of no consequence if you offend your king, by persisting in a course that he considers most dishonourable, and utterly unworthy of a sworn knight."

"Your majesty knows that I would rather forfeit anything in the world than your esteem," exclaimed Sir Gaston de Neville. "In war, I have bled in behalf of the monarch I serve; my sword is ever ready to leap from its scabbard whenever my country needs my services; and yet, now, because an artful Jew has been condemning me to your royal ear, I am to be cast off as one utterly unworthy of your future esteem or regard."

"Nay, you must not blame Isaac for this," answered the king, "for he has proved his generosity by only asking for protection, whilst he solicits my interference to prevent the execution of your evil designs. He is not revengeful, as you would have been able to convince yourself, had you been here a few minutes sooner than you were."

"Ha!" exclaimed Sir Gaston, malignantly; "it is, then, as I suspected —the hypocritical villain has been here before me to infuse into your majesty's ear his slanderous poison for my destruction."

"Again you wrong him," cried the king; "I have told you that he seeks to do you no injury; imploring only that I will throw around him and his daughter, the protecting shield of my authority."

"By which means," answered Sir Gaston, "he fills your mind with suspicions, that tend to render me less respected in your sight than I used to be."

"If such is the case," cried Richard, "you have an easy remedy for it in your own hands; promise to molest these people no more, and I will restore you to the same place, in my esteem that you formerly held."

"You ask of me that which is impossible," exclaimed the knight, after a momentary pause. "I have already tried to conquer a passion that I feel is ignoble, and having failed to do so, I must now yield myself to a fate that seems to be inevitable."

"You refuse my offer, then?"

"I refuse nothing that is requested by your majesty," replied Sir Gaston. "I merely tell you how impossible it is to eradicate love from the heart, and, therefore, throw myself upon your mercy, when I confess a weakness that is common, I believe, to all men."

"It is enough," exclaimed the king; "you are resolved, I see, to lose my favour, and I, therefore, command you to leave my presence, never to enter it again until you have learnt the duty you owe your sovereign."

"Let me implore your majesty to pardon him," cried Isaac, advancing from the further end of the room, where he had hitherto remained unobserved by the Knight Templar. "It is the request of an old man, and I trust will not be unheeded by one whose mercy is seldom asked in vain."

"Hah!" exclaimed Sir Gaston, "have I, then, been overheard by thee?—by the man that has, doubtless, come hither on no other errand than to seek my ruin."

"You have mistaken my motive for being here," cried Isaac, in a tone of humility; "I came but to seek justice for my daughter, and to implore his majesty's pardon for the injuries you have sought to inflict on her."

"For which I thank thee not, old man," exclaimed Sir Gaston de Neville; "his majesty is the best judge of the quarrel between us, and, doubtless, I shall obtain my pardon quite as soon on my own solicitation as on yours."

"May I, then, entreat you to spare my poor child, who has so long been the victim of your unjust persecutions?"

"That is a question I shall not answer just at present," replied the Templar, haughtily.

"Or, in other words," interrupted the king, "you would have him understand that he is still to be subjected to the arts you have so long practiced?"

"Your majesty has ever found me ready to obey in all things, wherein I knew it was my duty to do so," answered Sir Gaston, coldly. "In this case, however, I cannot see that any one has a right to interfere, even though it may be my sovereign who would lay his commands on me."

"It appears, then, that I am not to be obeyed."

"At present, I would that your majesty suffers this matter to drop," exclaimed the Knight Templar. "Perhaps I have expressed myself rather too warmly, but I have been taken by surprise in this instance, and must, therefore, crave a few days for consideration before I give my decided answer."

" Your request is granted," replied the king, and then addressing himself to Isaac, he said, " for the present, old man, you may retire—go home with your daughter, and remember, that if any fresh attempt is made to tear her from you, I shall hold Sir Gaston de Neville answerable for the act. Retire, I say, and may heaven shield you from all further persecution."

In obedience to this mandate, Isaac, of Tadcaster, bent humbly to his royal protector, and then slowly quitting the room, he proceeded to the apartment to which Rebecca had retired, and briefly informing her of what had taken place, left the palace with her on his return home.

On being left alone with Sir Gaston de Neville, the king remained silent for a few seconds, as if engaged in deep communion with his own thoughts, and then suddenly recollecting himself, he said, sternly,—

" It seems, Sir Knight, that the stories I have heard of thee are not entirely destitute of foundation. Thy conduct, even in the present interview, has already shewn that my authority is set at nought, and I would, therefore, hear from thine own lips the course of thy altered behaviour."

" Your highness has judged me wrong," exclaimed the Templar, endeavouring to subdue the haughtiness of his nature as much as possible.—"I might, perhaps, have felt mortified at hearing you express so much displeasure, with respect to the paltry affair between myself and the Jewess, yet, in all things that respect my loyalty, I remain unchanged and fervent, as ever I was in my life."

" It glads my heart to hear thee say so," answered the king, " and yet I cannot but confess that the report of your disloyalty has reached me from so many quarters, that I began to fear there was but too much truth in it."

" Then the evil practices of my enemies have not been without their ntended effect ?"

" I cannot but confess," replied Richard, " that circumstances have altogether conspired to strengthen the reports that have been raised to your prejudice. Your conduct towards this Hebrew Maiden, in defiance to my often-repeated commands, is of itself sufficient to convince me that my authority is utterly disregarded."

" I certainly have disobeyed you in that one instance," answered Sir Gaston de Neville, " but in doing so, I have only followed my inclination in an affair over which a man can scarcely be said to have control. The Jewess of whom you speak, attracted my notice long since ; I tendered her my love, which was haughtily rejected, and knowing that my power is absolute in almost all things, I have endeavoured to gain possession of her by means of force."

" Which was most unjustifiable," exclaimed the king, warmly, " seeing that you were absolutely rejected both by herself and her father."

" But being Jews," replied the Templar, " they can scarcely be said to be under the protection of the laws."

" Indeed ! and why, I pray, should such a distinction be made between any two classes of my subjects ?"

" That is a question," answered Sir Gaston, " that I have never taken the trouble to enquire into. It is sufficient for my purpose to know that such a distinction always has been made, and I have; therefore, offended no more than others have done before me."

" And so, for that reason, you would perpetuate a most abominable act of tyranny and injustice ?"

"Pardon me, sire, if I have offended you," exclaimed Sir Gaston de Neville, with pretended humility. "In truth, I knew not that you took so great an interest in these unbelievers; and, therefore, if I have erred in this case, it has been through ignorance of your wishes."

"Did you think, then, that I would encourage oppression by one class of men over another?"

"I never asked myself the question," replied the knight; "and yet, if I had, I should have thought that the monarch who fought so bravely against the Saracens, would scarcely hold out the shield of protection to the Jews, who are in no respect superior to them."

"In that instance, Sir Knight, we differ most materially," exclaimed Richard; "besides, all Jews born in the English territory, are my subjects—paying their share towards the support of my kingdom, and, therefore, naturally looking for the same fostering protection that is extended to all others who own my sovereign rule."

"And yet," answered the Templar, "I question whether four-fifths of your subjects would not raise their voices against such an opinion."

"When my acts deservedly give dissatisfaction to my subjects, they shall find that I am not unwilling to give a ready ear to their complaints," answered the king, proudly. "At present, however, I believe there are few who would dare to raise their voices against me, and those few had better beware how they rouse me to avenge myself for their perfidy!"

These words were uttered with an emphasis that could not be mistaken, and feeling their force, Sir Gaston turned pale, and with a faltering tongue said,—

"Your majesty, I hope, does not include me among those who are in danger of encountering your royal displeasure?"

"I am above disguise, Sir Knight," answered the monarch, with an angry frown, "and, therefore, will not deceive thee in this instance. You are now alone, and I do not hesitate to say, that I feel certain misgivings that your loyalty has been much shaken of late."

"Indeed, my liege, you wrong me."

"I hope I do," replied Richard, "and if I should hereafter find reason to alter my opinion, be assured that I will not fail to tell you so."

"What motive does your majesty think could ever urge me to become disloyal to my sovereign?"

"I know nothing of your motives, Sir Gaston de Neville," replied the king; "nor do I seek to enquire into a subject that, I must confess, affords me the severest pain. One thing, however, I am but too certain of, and that is, that you have lately sided with my brother, Prince John, who, it is but too evident, has designs upon my throne."

"Nay, your suspicions wrong me."

"Perhaps I may see cause to reverse the opinions I have formed," exclaimed Richard. "For the future, I shall narrowly watch your movements, and should it appear that my suspicions are correct, you will find me as resolute in pursuing you to justice as you have hitherto found me in heaping honours upon you for services that you have formerly done your country."

"It seems, then," cried Sir Gaston de Neville, in a tone of alarm, "that I have from some cause or other lost that esteem which I once held in your heart."

"For the present," replied the king, "I must confess that I hold you not so guiltless as I could wish. There are many reasons for my coming to this conclusion, and it must, therefore, rest with yourself to prove henceforth that your loyal attachment to myself is undiminished."

"But how is that to be done?"

"By being less in the society of those who I know to be my enemies," replied Richard. "Abandon their company without delay, and when I see that you are no longer plotting against him you have sworn faithfully to serve, I will again receive you as I have been used to do."

"I will endeavour to comply with your majesty's commands," answered Sir Gaston, and bowing stiffly he was about to retire, when the voice of the king made him pause just as he had reached the door.

"I had forgotten to say," exclaimed Richard, "that one part of my stipulation is that you offer no further violence either to the Jew or his daughter. Henceforth, you must resign all pretensions to the maiden, or our present parting will most likely be our last."

Sir Gaston de Neville again bowed, and quitting the room, he mounted the horse that was waiting for him at the palace gate, and rode off full of the dark thoughts that had been kindled in his busy brain by his late interview with Richard Cœur de Lion.

CHAPTER LXII.

"I have despatched a comrade in pursuit,
Who, faithful to my cause, will ne'er desert
The friend who trusts him."

MARIANNE.

WHEN Isaac and his daughter Rebecca arrived at home, after their interview with the king, they were met by Jonah, their faithful serving man, who, with a countenance depicting an equal share of fear and wonder, informed them that a stranger had called at their house during their absence, whose disappointment was expressed in no very gentle terms on finding that they were both out, and that the only person who was in charge of the place was unable to afford the slightest information as to when they might be expected to return. Indeed, poor Jonah seemed to attach no little importance to the affair, declaring that the man looked like a messenger from the infernal regions, and that he had no doubt in the world but that he had come upon some mischievous errand. Somewhat perplexed at this intelligence, Isaac paused for a few minutes in anxious communion with himself, and then finding that he was closely observed by his alarmed daughter, he affected to treat the matter lightly, and enquired of Jonah whether he could form no conjecture who the stranger was.

"Not I, upon my life, master," replied the man, "but by the airs he put on I should suppose he must be some very great personage, if he be not, indeed, Satan himself."

"Psha!" exclaimed Isaac, more petulantly; "'tis ever thus that your fears outrun your wits. The man, I dare say, was only some poor traveller, who, needing rest, applied here for shelter and food till he was able to resume his journey."

"Like enough," answered Jonah, "but be that as it may, you'll soon have an opportunity to convince yourselves, for as he left the place he said he should return again shortly to see whether you had come back."

"Why did you not ask him to remain here till our return?" asked Rebecca.

"For a very good reason," replied the cautious Jonah. "The fact is, he was quite a stranger, and as I thought master might have a little gold about the place that he wouldn't like to lose, I fancied there was nothing like being on the safe side, so I let him walk out, and when he's tired of the exercise he'll find his way back like a bad coin, I'll answer for it."

"But he may be the bearer of important news," cried Rebecca, with vexation.

"Not a bit of it," retorted the serving man, with an air of the utmost confidence; "he wanted to borrow money, I dare say, and if that's the case, there's not much fear but what we shall see him again before any of us are much older."

"Did he not mention his name?" asked the Israelite.

"No," answered Jonah, "he seemed to be remarkably close with me, as if he was afraid that I should be too 'cute for him. Not that he need have thought any thing of that kind of me, for master knows well enough that he's called me a fool many and many a time, so that I dare say there's some truth in it."

"You have done wrong at any rate, Jonah," exclaimed the old man, without heeding the latter words of his garrulous attendant. "The person, it is likely enough, had business with me, and I am much grieved that you have permitted him to depart previous to my return."

"But he said he should come back."

"That may be true," replied Isaac, "and yet, upon second thoughts, he may be inclined to distrust us, and thus I may lose a most important opportunity."

"Depend upon it there's no fear of any thing of the sort," answered Jonah, who began to be vexed that his own prudence had in this instance proved rather unfortunate. "The man seemed anxious enough to see you, I can tell you, and that being the case there can't be much doubt but that he will return here as he promised."

"How long has he been gone?" demanded Rebecca.

"Scarcely an hour."

"And how long did he say it would be before he returned?"

"He said nothing about how long he would be," replied Jonah; "but as I dare say he's only gone to satisfy the cravings of his appetite, it's hardly likely he will be much longer now."

"Did you observe which way he went?" asked Isaac.

"I did not; and a good reason there was for my not doing so, for the fellow looked so sternly at me that I thought it possible I might not live to deliver his message to you, if I took the liberty of looking too closely after him."

"It is evident that your terrors have misled you," exclaimed the Israelite, vexed at the stupidity of his domestic. "The man, I dare say, was harmless enough, and you have suffered your fears to deprive me of an interview that might, perhaps, have been of the greatest consequence."

"But," exclaimed Jonah, "if you'll take my word for it, he looked a great deal more like a cut-throat than any thing else that I can compare him to."

"So at least your folly would make it appear."

"Dear father," cried Rebecca, "had not Jonah better go forth to see whether the person he has spoken of is loitering anywhere in the neighbourhood?"

"There is no occasion for it, young lady," exclaimed a voice near the door, and at the same moment a tall, gaunt-looking figure strode into the apartment, and advanced to within a pace of where they were standing. "There is no occasion for your servant to put himself the least out of the way, for I have returned, you see, according to my promise, and it now only remains for your father to say, whether he will give a night's lodging to a poor devil who has been met by a part of the band of Black Ivan, and robbed of every coin that he possessed in the world."

"Poor fellow!" cried Isaac, with commisseration; "thy case is, indeed, a hard one, and deserves the kindness which an unfortunate man, like myself, can bestow. Make thyself easy, therefore, for my roof shall shelter thee till thou art able once more to resume thy journey."

" Well, that's kindly said, at any rate," exclaimed the stranger; "and as a proof that I do not scorn the hospitality even of a Jew, I will accept thy offer, and, if I feel myself comfortable, may, perhaps, remain with thee a week or two : by which time I hope to receive a further supply of money from my friends in the North of England."

" Master," whispered Jonah to the old man, " I know not what you may think of it, but this fellow's free and easy way serves only to confirm the opinion I had formed, that he is here for no good."

" Psha !" returned Isaac, in the same low tone, " what wouldst thou have me do? Wouldst have me turn him hungry and friendless from my door, when he tells me that he has lost all he had in the world by Black Ivan's band of ruffians ?"

" Oh !" exclaimed the serving man, " I shall say nothing, since it seems to offend you ; and yet, between ourselves, it would be best prudent to ask him his name, and whereabouts he comes from."

" So far I will take your advice," answered Isaac, and then addressing himself to the stranger, he said :—

" I mean not to offend you, friend ; but since I have received you thus far, in all confidence, it is fitting that I should know who it is that I have thus admitted as an inmate of my humble residence."

" A very prudent question, and one that I can have no reason for wishing to avoid," answered the other, quite at his ease ; " the fact is, old gentleman, I am called Ambrose Paston ; I left my native city of York eight days ago to search for a rich relation, who I have never seen, but who, they say, lives somewhere here in London, and on arriving at nightfall, yesterday, within a dozen miles of the termination of my journey, I unfortunately fell among robbers, as I before told you, who have stripped me of every article of value that they could lay their hands on."

" So far I am satisfied with your explanation," exclaimed Isaac; " though, to confess the truth, I cannot but think that you have acted with imprudence in thus coming up to London in search of a wealthy relation, who, after all the pains you have been at, you may never find."

" But what was a poor devil to do when he had nothing but starvation before his eyes?" demanded the other. " I struggled on against my difficulties as long as I could, and when I found that nothing else was to be done, I boldly made up my mind to take this long journey, collected together all the money I could, and set off, with a light heart, to tramp my way up to town."

" And on thy way hast lost all that thou didst possess."

" That's very true," replied the stranger; " but, then, I have found a friend in my adversity ; and as grieving is a fault which I am not much given to, I shall make myself perfectly contented here till something better happens to turn up."

" But," interposed Jonah, who was still suspicious of his master's guest, " you must take care not to wear out the welcome with which you have been received."

" Hold thy peace, Jonah, I command thee," exclaimed the old Israelite, angrily ; " dost thou not see that the poor fellow needs all our kindness, and yet thou wouldst throw a damp upon his spirits by hinting that he may intrude upon us too long."

" Oh," said Jonah, " I'll be dumb if my honest bluntness is likely to give offence to any body. I only thought it was as well to let him know

that this is no refuge for the idle, in order that he may set himself diligently to work to find out the friend he speaks of."

"That I shall do, depend on it," replied the guest. "Nay, I feel certain that I shall not have much trouble in finding my relative; and the chances are, that one night's lodging is all that I shall require from the hospitality of your master."

"If it should be a week or a fortnight, I shall not give it grudgingly," cried Isaac, warmly, "since it is no part of my nature to close my doors against those who require the little aid I can afford them. Make yourself, therefore, perfectly easy, and accept that which I have to bestow with the same freedom with which it is offered thee."

"You say," observed Rebecca, "that you have been robbed by the band of Black Ivan. Know you whether the leader himself made one of the party that you encountered?"

"That, maiden, is a question that I cannot answer," returned the stranger;—"in fact, I know not the person of whom you speak, though his fame has reached even the distant place from whence I come."

"Is the villain known so far off?" exclaimed Isaac.

"Aye, marry is he, old man," answered the other; "though, to speak the truth, people thereabouts do not regard him quite so unfavourably as you seem to do."

"Indeed!"

"Yes, you may take my word for it that the good folks of the north look upon him as a gallant spirit, that deserves to be better looked upon than he is. It is said, too, that he only plunders the rich; and he is so generous that he often spends all the booty he obtains in one day on some poor unfortunate who needs his assistance."

No. 40

"Aye, aye," exclaimed Jonah, "it's all very well for people at a distance off to praise him as a great man, but hereabouts we happen to know a
little too much of him, and master could, if he liked, say somthing to
convince you that he is as great a scoundrel as is to be found in all England."

"Does the knave speak the truth?" demanded the guest, with pretended
surprise.

"He does."

"Perhaps, though, you speak thus of him because he has somehow or
other injured you?"

"He has, and would have done so even further had not heaven preserved us from his evil practices."

"Perhaps he has robbed you?" observed the stranger.

"He tried to take from me that which is far dearer to me than gold
or jewels," answered Isaac. "Unhappily, he has seen my daughter,
affects to love her, and has on two or three occasions carried her off in
spite of her tears and supplications."

"But that is no proof of his being the bad man you represent him,"
exclaimed the other. "Few men can resist the influence of love,
and I suppose Black Ivan has only sought to possess himself of a prize
that is necessary for his own happiness."

"You take part with him then!" cried the Israelite, with astonishment.

"Not I,—I merely speak as a disinterested person, and as one who
would do justice to the motives, even of such a man as you represent this
Black Ivan to be."

"And I," answered Isaac, "speak of him as a father who he would have
wronged."

"Humph! but I suppose he would have married your daughter,"

"What! think you, then, that I would ever consent to my child becoming
the bride of a robber?"

"Why, certainly there is something to be said against that," replied the
other, checking himself now that he found he was going too far. "A
robber aint altogether the sort of husband that a father would choose for
his child, and yet there may be circumstances that would reconcile one
even to that."

"What circumstance do you allude to?"

"Merely that it is better for her to be the wife than the mistress of a
brigand."

Here the conversation was abruptly brought to a close by the entrance
of the housekeeper, who made her appearance with a substantial supper, to
which they all sat down, and immediately the subject was changed into
another channel. The stranger, by this time, had made himself quite at home,
rallying the Hebrew Maiden upon her downcast spirits, and praising the
good things before him, which, to do him justice, seemed to afford him the
highest satisfaction. At the conclusion of the meal wine was introduced,
and as the stranger become warmed with the generous liquor, he grew more
communicative upon former actions of his life. In the course of conversation he mentioned the name of Sir Gaston de Neville, who, it seemed, had a
stately castle in the neighbourhood from which he came, and of whom he
seemed very particular in his enquiries.

"I have heard," he said, "that the knight has another castle somewhere about London, and if I could only find him out, it would be the
means of providing me with another friend, which, situated as I now am,
would be rather desirable."

"Do you know anything of the person you speak of?" asked Isaac, inquisitively.

"Why, not much," replied the other;—"I once in the course of my life happened to do him a service, and was foolish enough to refuse the reward he offered me. Since that time, however, I have altered my opinion about those things, and if he would only recollect that I was the means of saving his life, perhaps he might be inclined to do something or other for me."

"You would visit him at his castle, then?"

"Perhaps I may," replied the other, "but I shall not make up my mind about that, just now, because I happen to be in very comfortable quarters, and may not be inclined to remove from them just at present."

"That's tolerably cool, at any rate!" muttered Jonah, whose feelings towards the stranger did not grow warmer, as they became better acquainted, with each other. "Here's a fellow," he continued, "that came like a beggar to ask for shelter, and now he talks of remaining here till he can find some more agreeable way of disposing of himself."

"What's that the fellow's muttering about?" demanded the guest, sternly.

"Nothing,—believe me, nothing, my good friend," answered the Israelite;—"Jonah has a habit of talking to himself, and you may take my word for it he was thinking of something else."

"Oh! well if that's the case, I shall say no more about it," exclaimed the stranger. "But I would just hint to him that my temper is not one of the most governable in the world, and if he mutters again, I may fancy that I am the subject of his thoughts, and in that case, I will not promise but he will get a sound drubbing, to make him know manners in future."

"How!" cried the Jew, with surprise, "do you,—the guest that I have invited to share my hospitality,—threaten my servant in presence of his master?"

"Tush, man! never be angry at a trifle like that," answered the other, with the most perfect composure. "Your servant and I shall understand each other better, I dare say, for this little explanation, and, therefore, he will know himself better than to insult the friend of his master a second time."

More wine was now produced;—the stranger drank deeply, and soon began to show that the fumes were getting into his head. At first he talked faster than he had been doing; then his voice grew thick and husky, and he was just going to throw himself back in his seat to enjoy a sleep, when the Jew beckoning to Jonah, whispered that he had better lead the stranger to his bed-chamber, where he might slumber off the potent effects of the wine he had swallowed. This was no sooner said than done; the stranger accepted the offered services of the menial with more civility than had been anticipated; and hiccupping forth a "good night," to Isaac and his daughter, he reeled from the room to that in which he was to sleep. In a few seconds Jonah returned to the presence of his master.

"Well," he exclaimed, "what think you of your guest, now?—Is he the sort of visitor that you would like to have invited to your house?"

"To be candid," answered Isaac, "I know not exactly what to say of him; he certainly is an extraordinary fellow, yet for all that, I see no reason at present to regret the hospitality I have shown him."

"Do you believe, then, the story he has told us about being robbed by Black Ivan's people?"

"I certainly do," replied Isaac; "nor can I see any reason for doubting it, seeing that people are daily in the habit of falling into the hands of that daring brigand."

"Well," exclaimed the servant, "in my opinion he has been telling a parcel of lies to hide the real purpose that has brought him to your house. Ah! you may start, master, and look as angry as you like, but in my opinion he is one of Black Ivan's men, sent here to make up the best story he can, and then to run off with your daughter on the first opportunity that offers."

"Ah!" cried Rebecca; "Jonah is right,—there is some fearful project plotting against me, and I am doomed, after all, to become the victim of Ivan's perfidy."

"Be calm, my child, and listen to me," exclaimed her father, imploringly; "this, depend upon it, is only some foolish notion of Jonah's, as no doubt I shall soon be able to satisfy you, and a very short time will serve to convince you that, villainous as Black Ivan is, he has nothing to do with the plot which has been surmised by this simple fellow."

"Well, if you think so," observed Jonah, "let us go together to his chamber; he is by this time fast asleep, and by searching among his clothes, I dare say we shall find that he has not only got more money about him than he chooses to acknowledge, but that he is armed, the better to enable him to carry his base designs against my dear young mistress into execution."

Trembling with apprehensions that had been excited by these words, the venerable Jew rose for the purpose of accompanying his faithful domestic, but ere he could leave the room, the door opened, and Reuben Grenard made his appearance.

"Boy!" exclaimed the old man, "thy presence never was more grateful to me than on the present occasion. I have need of thy counsel and services, for a stranger has sought shelter beneath my roof, from whom I begin to expect to meet with nothing but ingratitude for the services I would have done him."

"What dost thou mean?" asked Reuben, anxiously; "what stranger is it of whom thou speakest?"

"I know not who he is," replied Isaac; "but he says that he has just arrived from the city of York; that he has been robbed on his way by the band of Black Ivan, and being destitute in a strange place, he sought for, and obtained shelter in my house."

"Have you any reason, then, to believe that the story told you is false?"

"Nothing more than the fears of Jonah, which, to be sure, may after all prove without foundation."

"At any rate," interposed the person last named, "it would be wise to satisfy ourselves before we set down too quietly. Let us go into his room, and if I should be mistaken, I must be content to be laughed at all the rest of my life, for being alarmed when there was no occasion for it."

"Where is this stranger you speak of?" demanded Reuben Grenard, eagerly.

"In the next chamber, asleep."

"Are you sure that he slumbers?"

"There can be no doubt of it," replied Jonah, "for the fellow drank my master's wine till he could scarcely see, and just now reeled off to bed, in a state that leaves very little doubt that he is fast enough asleep by this time."

"Who do you take him for?" asked Reuben.

"Nay," replied the man, "that's a question that I cannot be expected to answer, seeing that I know no more of the fellow than you do yourself. I, however, fancy that he is one of Black Ivan's ruffians, sent here for some vile purpose, and, perhaps, if we do not take instant steps to prevent the mischief, he may carry off my young mistress before we have the power to prevent him."

"Villain!" exclaimed Reuben, furiously; "should this surmise of yours prove correct, he shall pay severely for the injury he would have inflicted."

"Hush!" whispered the old man;—"subdue your voice, Reuben, or we may be overheard, and our plans defeated. He is now, I dare say, asleep, and if we cautiously enter his chamber, we shall be enabled to satisfy ourselves whether these suspicions of Jonah's are correct."

"During my captivity in the robber's cave," exclaimed Reuben Grenard, "I had an opportunity of seeing every one of the villains forming the band of Black Ivan. I shall, therefore, be able to recognise the countenance of this man, should he, indeed, be one of them, and in the event of his being here on a treacherous errand, I shall not hesitate to take such instant vengeance as shall effectually prevent any further alarm from that quarter."

"Oh, have a care what you do, dear Reuben, for my sake," cried Rebecca, in an agony of terror. "This man, if he proves to be the villain you suspect, is, doubtless, well armed, and in that case, those who I love most dearly, will be sacrificed in a vain attempt to rescue me from the snare that has been laid for my destruction."

"Fear not for us, my child," exclaimed her father tenderly, endeavouring to assuage her terrors;—"we will be cautious in proceeding about this affair, and should our suspicions prove correct, Jonah shall be despatched for Master Simon Snout, the constable, who will instantly repair hither with a force sufficient to make him our captive. So now remain here quietly, and depend on it all will go well."

Having said this, the old man, accompanied by Reuben Grenard and Jonah, softly left the room, the latter bearing a lamp, the light of which he shaded with his hand, so as to prevent the glare from rousing the stranger from his slumber. With noiseless steps they entered the chamber, and having ascertained by the heavy breathing of the sleeper that he was unconscious of their approach, they with the same caution approached towards the couch, and then unscreening the light for a moment, revealed the features of the stranger. It was but a momentary glance that Reuben Grenard obtained, yet even that was sufficient, for starting back a pace or two, he whispered in the ear of Isaac that the man before them was no other than Hubert, the friend of Black Ivan, and the second in command over the band of brigands. At that moment, too, it was observed that the bandit was armed with a couple of poniards, one of which was stuck in his belt, whilst the other was grasped in his hand, as if in readiness should any occasion arise for requiring him to be on his guard. Convinced by all this, that not a single instant was to be lost; they now retraced their steps from the room, the door of which they securely fastened, to prevent his escape that way, whilst Jonah was despatched to Master Simon Snout, the constable, with a request that he would instantly come down with a sufficient force to capture one of the most daring of Black Ivan's band.

But Hubert was quickly aware of the dangerous situation in which he was placed, and starting from his couch, he first tried the door, which was, however, too well secured to permit his escape by that way. He then flew to the window, which was also fastened, and crossed with bars of iron; these, however, though not without some difficulty, he succeeded in removing, and throwing open the casement, was about to spring out, when he perceived the house surrounded by a number of persons, who had been collected together by the alarm that had been raised. These no sooner saw him, than a shout was raised by the people below, who called upon one another to keep a sharp look out, and not to suffer the escape of a man who was leagued with the terror of his country. Each moment, too, the mob kept increasing, and as Hubert saw his chances of escape momentarily diminish, he called fiercely upon the people warning them not to molest him in his flight, and telling them he was well armed, and would not fail to slay all that come in his way to oppose him. But the crowd was not to be intimidated by his threats, and gathering more closely round the place, they gave utterance to a howl of defiance, that showed but too plainly that he had nothing to expect but from his own resolution in overcoming the difficulty. Nor was it long before he had made up his mind as to the means he should employ in cheating them of their promised victory, and springing upon the window sill, he waved his hand imperiously, at the same time commanding them to disperse as they valued their lives.

"I am a desperate man, as you will some of you find to your cost," he exclaimed, furiously brandishing the poniard he held in his hand;—"my own life is in jeopardy if I remain here, and since flight alone can save me, I will fight my way through you, and slay all that come within reach of my arm."

But the people were not moved by his frantic gesticulations, and another yell from the mob showed that he had no chance left that way.

"You do but risk your lives needlessly," he again exclaimed, "I am sore beset by men that seek my destruction, and if I must perish, it shall be whilst carrying vengeance amongst those that would prevent my escape."

As he spoke thus, the constables followed by a mob of people, were seen approaching, and then feeling that no other chance remained, he was about to leap down to the ground, when he stumbled, and would have fallen had he not caught hold of the sill of the window, by which means he was left suspended without the power of recovering his former position. At last his strength failed him, his fingers could no longer support the whole weight of his body, and suddenly letting go his hold, he fell heavily to the earth. At this moment the mob rushed towards him with a cry of triumph, but ere a hand was laid upon him, he had again started to his feet, and clutching his dagger fiercely, he threw himself among the mob, wounding several persons, and thus intimidating others from advancing. This was the opportunity he wished for, and exerting all his speed, he continued to effect his escape in spite of the keen pursuit that was commenced after him.

CHAPTER LXIII.

" How now, good warder ;
Who hast thou there in close captivity ?
Speak !—whence comes he ?"

FULL of consternation at the fresh attempt that had been made by her persevering foes to tear her away frow the protection of her friends, Rebecca gave way to the terrors that again filled her soul, and for some time she was deaf to all the entreaties of her father and Reuben Grenard, who sought by all tender endearments to assure her that she was no longer in danger.

"The villain," exclaimed Isaac, " has happily been defeated at the moment when success appeared most certain, and knowing, as he does, that the officers of justice will be constantly on the alert for him, there is very little fear of his venturing here a second time to fulfil the base design which has been so signally defeated."

"Besides," interposed Reuben, " the people are now in pursuit of him, and he must have more luck than he deserves, if he contrives to escape from his hunters."

"Do not, I entreat you," cried Rebecca, " depend too much upon this being the last effort that will be made to get me into the power of this Black Ivan ; he is desperate in the prosecution of his evil courses, and never will he desist from his endeavours whilst there is a chance of following them up with success."

"Let him beware, then, of falling into the hands of those who have had but too much reason to hate him," exclaimed her father. "Let him beware, I say, for I will have no mercy upon him, should he but become the prisoner of those who will never relax in their endeavours until he is safely immured within a prison."

"Besides," continued Reuben, "his crimes have raised up enemies against him on every side, and the king, wearied with the continual complaints that have been made, has offered a large reward for his apprehension, that must eventually be the means of bringing him to that justice which he has thus long set at open defiance."

" And who, think you, will be rash enough to venture upon so hazardous an adventure?" asked Rebecca.

"I will myself make the attempt," answered her lover.

"You, Reuben!"

"Aye, why should I not," he asked, "when I know that it is the only chance of ridding you of a dangerous foe?"

"But your own life would surely pay the penalty of your rashness."

"And if it did," he replied, "I should die happy in the consciousness of knowing that I had, at least, done my duty towards her I have sworn to protect."

"My son," exclaimed Isaac, "this generous sacrifice must not be permitted. I know your noble heart prompts you to deeds of danger,—that you would yield up life itself for the protection of your affianced bride, yet I, who have some right to interpose my authority in this affair, do command you to abandon so perilous a design."

"And I also," continued Rebecca, "do entreat, by the love you bear me, that you will think no more of pursuing one who has sworn to accomplish your destruction."

"Rebecca, this is most cruel of you," exclaimed her lover, in a tone of reproach; "you know but too well the untiring zeal with which he has prosecuted his base designs, and if no steps are taken to frustrate him, I shall be doomed to see you fall a victim to his insidious artifices."

"Nay," cried Isaac, "you look only on the worst side of the question. Hitherto heaven has mercifully lent its aid to us, and, therefore, we have every reason to look forward with hope that we shall not be deserted in the hour of our utmost need."

"But you seem to forget," exclaimed Reuben Grenard, "that Black Ivan is not the only foe we have to fear. Sir Gaston de Neville is also to be ranked amongst our most implacable enemies, and, powerful as he is, we have but too much reason to fear that he will succeed in carrying off your daughter."

"What!" cried the old Hebrew, "when he knows that by doing so he will bring down upon himself the fierce anger of his incensed monarch?"

"And what cares he for that?" asked the young man; "Sir Gaston de Neville favours the ambitious views of Prince John, the brother of our king, and should their treasonable designs be accomplished, he will become one of the chief favourites about the court."

"But, at the same time, it must not be forgotten," observed Isaac, "that should they fail in driving King Richard from the throne, Sir Gaston will meet the punishment of a traitor, and thus we shall escape the persecution of one who we have even more reason to dread than Black Ivan himself."

"You think, then, dear father, that there is no longer any danger to be apprehended?"

"Nay, my child, I said not that," answered Isaac; "attempts may certainly be made to withdraw you from my protection, and yet, I have the strongest hope that, with a little care, we may frustrate them."

"That is," cried Rebecca, "if I remain a prisoner beneath your roof."

"There is a better preventive than that," interposed Reuben, "and one which will effectually prevent them from attempting any further violence."

"Explain yourself, good Reuben."

"Think not, then, that I am selfish in the proposition," he replied,— "and yet I would urge you, with all my heart, to permit our union to take place without further delay. Rebecca will thus have a protector, and her future life may pass without those cares and anxieties that have hitherto so incessantly been her's."

"I must have time ere I give you an answer on that subject," replied Isaac; "at present, you are both too young and inexperienced in the ways of the world, and though I have often looked forward to the period that should give my daughter to a worthy husband, I would rather that you both wait a year or two longer, in order that you may avoid those numerous shoals and quicksands upon which the happiness of but too many young people is unfortunately wrecked."

"And, in the time you may wish us to wait, my Rebecca may become the victim of either Sir Gaston de Neville, or his equally detestable rival, Black Ivan, the Outlaw."

"Nay, my son, have patience yet a little longer, and I will seriously weigh this matter over in my mind," answered the old man. "That I wish for your union with my child, you have long been assured, and if I now ask for a little delay, you may take my word for it that my motives are founded only in prudence and foresight."

"Urge my father no more, at present, I entreat you, dear Reuben," cried the Hebrew Maiden, earnestly; "let us abide his own time, and with the aid of heaven, we may yet defy the malice of those who, for the furtherance of their own base designs, have thus driven us almost to the verge of despair."

"It is your wish, then, that we tarry longer ere I claim the prize I have so anxiously sought after?"

"It is, Reuben."

"In that case," he replied, "I yield myself to your commands with resignation; and yet ——"

"Reuben," exclaimed the old man, "your willing submission fills my soul with gladness. Indeed I expected nothing less of thee, fondly believing, as I did, that in selecting thee for the affianced husband of a beloved child, I had chosen one to whose love and watchfulness I could safely entrust her. Circumstances have served to confirm the prudence of my choice;—and be assured that the delay that must take place, ere your nuptials are celebrated, shall be as brief as possible."

At this moment a great uproar was heard outside the house, and no sooner had Reuben Grenard opened the door to ascertain the cause, than Master Simon Snout, the constable, burst in, dragging with him a prisoner, whose form was completely hidden by a capacious cloak.

"I've done it at last, Isaac," exclaimed the constable, with an air of triumph; "the villain is now in custody, and if ever man earned a handsome reward for doing the state a service, I flatter myself that you see that identical chap before you."

"Meaning yourself, of course?" said the Jew, and then, having in vain tried to catch a glance at the prisoner's countenance, he continued:—"it appears to me that you have captured some one, Master Snout, but I am yet to be convinced that this person has ever sought to do me or my family any harm."

"What! do you suppose, then, that I have taken a man that has not been guilty of high crimes and misdemeanours against the laws of his country?"

"My father," interposed Rebecca, "does not doubt your zeal, good Simon, but seeing that your prisoner is so completely enveloped in the capacious cloak he wears, it is by no means easy to say whether he is indeed one of the people we have cause to complain of."

"And that, my young mistress," answered the constable, "I take to be a very sufficient reason for believing that he is the chap that lately escaped from your house. The very fact of his trying to conceal his face, shows that he is ashamed of his evil doings, and, consequently, that if I have not got Black Ivan himself in my clutches, I have, at least, taken one of his rascally comrades."

"Nay, that is not Black Ivan, I am very certain," cried Rebecca, carefully eyeing the proportions of the prisoner.

"Indeed!—and how can you tell that?" demanded the constable, with offended dignity.

"From the circumstance," answered Rebecca, "that he is neither so tall nor so stout as the notorious robber you speak of."

"Nonsense!—but I'll convince you, presently, that I am not mistaken," cried Simon. "I'll make him disrobe presently, and then you shall confess that I am not quite the fool you take me for."

"There you wrong me, good Master Snout," she replied; "I do not take you for a fool, though, in your own zeal in the discharge of your duty, I thought it possible you might have committed some mistake."

"You hear the girl," exclaimed the constable, appealing to the crowd of

No. 41

people that had followed him into the house; "she actually thinks I have made a mistake, and that this is neither Black Ivan nor one of his gang."

"Nor is she the only one that thinks so," cried Reuben Grenard, "for if the truth must be spoken, I should say that you have for once in your life been guilty of a very great mistake."

"Then, you are all a set of fools together!" exclaimed the constable, in high dudgeon. "Here have I been exerting myself for your good, and when I take the fellow prisoner, and bring him into your very presence, no one will believe but what I have made a mistake and captured the wrong man!"

"Be not offended at our want of faith, my good fellow," said Isaac of Tadcaster, "but answer me one question, and I may, perhaps, be convinced that we have wronged you."

"Well, ask the question, and if it is not an impertinent one I'll reply to it."

"What account, then, did your prisoner give of himself when you captured him?"

"Why, no account at all," replied Snout; "the fellow has been as dumb as a fish ever since we grappled him, and no threats of punishment have prevailed upon him to utter even a single word."

"That certainly appears rather suspicious," answered the elder Jew;—"and yet, upon second thoughts, he may have some reason of his own for not choosing to say anything till you have taken him before the sheriff."

"Then he shall not wait long for that," exclaimed Simon Snout, "for I mean to lock him up safe enough for the night, and, to-morrow morning, he shall go before the sheriff of Middlesex, who will, of course, send him to the Chief Justiciary, who will not be long about deciding what his fate shall be."

"Are you, then, so well able to read his fortune?" demanded the old man.

"I have just skill enough in the black art," replied the constable, "to declare that before the sun has set three times more, he will have ended his crimes upon the common gibbet."

"There thou art a false prophet!" cried the prisoner, casting aside the disguise, and, instead of some brawny ruffian, discovering the light form of a woman; "there thou art wrong, I tell thee again, for instead of going to the gibbet myself, it will be well for thee, scurvy knave as thou art, if I do not send thee to the stocks for interfering with honest folks, when they are travelling peaceably on the king's highway."

"Wh—wh—what's all this I see?" stammered the astonished Simon Snout. "Methought I had taken a robber prisoner, and lo! it turns out that I have only captured a foolish woman."

"The woman will not be *foolish* enough to let you go unpunished though, unless you fall down on your marrowbones and ask her pardon," cried Edith, for such was the person who had been thus unceremoniously dragged into the Jew's house. "I have been taken for a robber, and threatened with the gibbet; and, therefore, I think the least amends thou canst make, is to pray my forgiveness for the violence thou hast done me."

"Most magnanimous female I do most humbly pray you to overlook my offence," cried the constable, falling upon his knees. "I have indeed been guilty of a most foolish thing, and if you whisper my error abroad, it will bring upon me not only the laughter of my friends, but the sore displeasure of the sheriff, who will dismiss me from my office with shame and dishonour."

"Thou art forgiven, most worthy Snout," answered Edith, restraining herself, with difficulty, from laughing in his face; "my anger has been appeased, and, therefore, thou need'st not fear either the laughter of thy friends or the sore displeasure of the sheriffs. But let me dismiss thee with this piece of advice:—never, in future, be too certain of having the right person in custody, and especially be careful not to mistake harmless women for robbers, lest thou shouldst have thy face scratched for thy pains, which would be a pity, seeing that thou art really a very personable looking man, considering thine advanced age."

"Nay, I am but three score and five," answered the constable, rather indignant at the allusion that had been made to his years; "and, moreover, I am a widower anxious for a second wife, though heaven protect me from ever taking to my arms such a shrew as thou art likely to turn out."

"Come, come, we have had somewhat too much of this," interposed Isaac, and then addressing himself to Edith, he enquired how it was that she had fallen into the hands of Master Simon Snout and his assistants.

"Why, the truth is," she replied, "I wanted to see your daughter, and slipping on this disguise, I left the castle of Sir Gaston de Neville, when my evil fortune, as I thought it at the time, led me in the way of these men. They took me, it seems, for some criminal they were in pursuit of, and I was about to declare who I was, when I heard them talk of bringing me to your house. That was exactly the destination I wished to arrive at, and, therefore, holding my peace, they were kind enough to escort me here."

"I see," cried Rebecca; "you wished to see me, it seems, and, doubtless, upon some affair that deeply concerns myself?"

"You are right," answered the girl, "but what I have to say must not be spoken in the presence of these strangers. I would, therefore, have you take your departure, good Master Simon Snout, and do not forget the little bit of advice I just now gave you."

Muttering a few words that were not intended to be very complimentary, the constable and his followers took their departure, leaving Edith to relate the affair that had occasioned her present visit.

"The truth is," she said, "that fresh plots are forming against this young maiden; Sir Gaston, unawed by the threats of the king, has determined to make another desperate effort to get you within his castle, and I know his resolute nature too well to doubt that he will succeed, unless the greatest care is taken to prevent the evil designs he meditates."

"And hast thou risked the anger of thy master to do us this service?" asked the old man.

"Why, that there is some risk it cannot be denied," answered Edith,—"and yet, I should be unworthy the name of woman had I hesitated to give timely warning when a plot was in progress against one of my own sex. In fact, I have lost no time since I made the discovery, but, putting on the disguise you saw me in, I contrived to pass through the gates of the castle without being suspected by any of the warders."

"Do you know the nature of the plot against my child?" asked the old man, anxiously.

"Why, not exactly," she replied, "but I heard Sir Gaston tell one of his confidential followers that matters were now ripe for another attempt, and that this time the girl should be secured without any hope of rescue. Of course, that was enough to decide me as to what course I ought to pursue, and here I am, as you see, a willing messenger to put you on your guard."

"My good girl, I thank you for this zeal in the behalf of those who are persecuted by nearly all those that are opposed to them in religion. We have, indeed, had heavy trials to undergo, yet, with the assistance of heaven, I have still hopes that we shall not fall beneath the base attacks of our enemies."

",But it will also behove us," observed Reuben Grenard, "to take all the precautions we can to frustrate the evil designs of this heartless libertine. I will, myself, keep a strict watch upon the house, and none shall enter it who do not satisfy me that their errand is not a mischievous one."

"Alas!" cried Rebecca, sorrowfully, "in that case you will fall a victim to those who are reckless of all crime, so that they can but execute the base plots they have formed for my destruction. Doubtless, this time, Sir Gaston will come with a strong body of his followers, and, should they meet with resistance, your life will but too surely pay the penalty of your interference."

"Under such circumstances, death will be most truly welcome," exclaimed Reuben, ardently. "The Templar, proud and austere as he is, has too long trampled upon those that he conceives to be beneath him, but he shall yet find that one of the tribe he so much despises, will thwart him in the vile plans he has formed for the destruction of female innocence."

"My son," interposed the aged Israelite, "let not thy generous ardour carry thee too far in a case that appears to be almost harmless; remember, we have a powerful enemy to cope with, and he will hesitate at no crime to avenge himself upon all who would venture to interpose for the frustration of his base intentions."

"You seem to have formed a pretty just notion of my master's disposition," observed Edith, "and yet, for all that, I cannot help admiring the spirit of the young man; he don't like to see poor helpless women trampled on by a worthless fellow that has no more honour than Black Ivan himself, and if I might venture to give a piece of advice, I should say the best thing he can do, will be to keep a sharp look out after Sir Gaston, so as to prevent his carrying off the young woman."

"It would be madness to interfere, when no good can possibly result from it," exclaimed Isaac; "in fact, so convinced am I that his own destruction will be the consequence, that I most expressly forbid him to run any risk that we may hereafter have casse to regret."

"Then you would rather suffer your daughter to fall into the hands of my wicked master."

"Nay," answered the old man, "heaven is my witness how gladly I would lay down my own life for the preservation of my child's honour.— She is now the only prop of my age, and to see her dragged away from me would indeed be the heaviest affliction that could befal me."

"Then why," asked Edith, "refuse to let him keep a careful watch upon the man you have so much reason to dread?"

"It is because I love him almost as much as I do my daughter," answered Isaac; "he has been chosen by myself to be her husband and protector,—she loves him with all the ardour of maidenly affection, and to see him risk his life, when I know that all his efforts would prove of no avail, is an act that I neither can nor will encourage."

"Well, if you are determined not to let the young man do his best to save your daughter from the snares that are now being laid by Sir Gaston, it is not my business to say anything about it," retorted Edith. "I have, however, done my duty in coming to put you on your guard, and since you are now aware that he means to make another attempt to carry her off, I shall take my leave, without interfering any further."

So saying, she once more threw the cloak over her shoulders, and placing the slouched hat upon her head, so as to conceal her countenance as much as possible, she was about to take leave of them, when Reuben Grenard asked permission to see her as far as he safely could, towards the castle of Sir Gaston de Neville. An offer like this, was not to be rejected at that late hour of the night, and having taken farewell of the Jew and his daughter, she set forward on her return, accompanied by the young man who had so gallantly offered to escort her.

CHAPTER LXIV.

" Woman !—dost thou tell me truly ?—
Are we, then, threatened with a new-born peril,
When most we felt secure ?"

LORENZO.

PROCEEDING from the Jew's house as fast as they could, Edith and her companion arrived in the course of about half-an-hour, within sight of the castle, when the former, coming to a sudden pause, insisted upon being left to proceed the remainder of the way by herself. Against this, however, Reuben would have remonstrated, on account of the danger a young female like herself, might be exposed to ; but the girl was still resolute, and only laughed at the fears he had expressed in her behalf.

"As for danger, my good friend," she said, " I am too much used to that, every day of my life, to think much about that now, for Sir Gaston and his rough associates, are not, by any means, courteous to the females about them, and I have, more than once, had pretty broad hints that my life would not be very safe if ever they catch me whispering any secrets about what was going on."

"It is not within the castle, that I, at present, apprehend danger to you," replied Reuben ;—" but you have still some little distance to go, and there may be ruffians abroad, who will not suffer you to pass without an insult."

"You forget that my present disguise will mislead any one I may meet, as to my sex."

"You are resolved, then, to refuse my offer ?"

" For your own sake, I must," she replied ;—" we are now within sight of the castle, and should you be seen by any of our people, they would not hesitate long, about taking you before Sir Gaston de Neville, and then the consequences may be very easily guessed at."

"He would slay me, no doubt," exclaimed Reuben : " as my rival he bears me nothing but the most inveterate malice, and there is every reason to believe, that if ever I should fall into his hands again, it will be to meet the fate he has vowed shall be mine."

"You have nothing else to expect from him," replied Edith. " His hatred towards you is beyond all bounds, and never will he rest satisfied until he has executed the cruel designs he has formed against one who has had the temerity to thwart him in his hopes."

"And I will ever continue to do so," exclaimed the young man, resolutely. " Rebecca utterly detests the villain, who has sought, in so many ways, to tear her from the protection of an aged father, and knowing, as I do, the horror with which she regards him, I will oppose his arts by every means in my power, even though it may be the means of bringing upon myself that death, which he has vowed to accomplish."

" But should you perish," cried Edith, " the young Hebrew Maiden would be thrown entirely at his mercy."

" Not entirely," replied Reuben Grenard, " since her father would still be left to shield her from the arts of the libertine."

"And what protection, pray, can her father afford ?" asked the girl ; " he

is old and helpless, and belonging, as he does, to a race most unjustly abhorred, there are few who would put forth a hand to aid him against the
persecutions of a powerful knight, like Sir Gaston de Neville."

" You speak truly," answered the young man; " yet you forget that
King Richard, superior to the prejudices that exists among his subjects
against our people, has stepped forward in our behalf, and declared that his
severest displeasure shall fall upon the Templar, should he continue to
harass either the Jew or his daughter."

" And what cares Sir Gaston for that?" demanded Edith; " nay, as a
proof that he is reckless of the consequences, he is even now engaged in a
fresh plot to carry her off."

" Let him beware!" exclaimed a voice from close by the spot where they
were standing, and in another second, Meg of Finchley, turning the angle
of a ruined building, presented herself before them.

" Hah! you here!" exclaimed Reuben, starting with surprise;—" you
have been a listener to our conversation, and will, perhaps, earn a reward
from Sir Gaston de Neville, by telling him all you have overheard."

" You mistake me, young man," she replied, sharply. " I have, indeed,
overheard part of what has passed between you and this maiden, but never
will I earn the gold of Sir Gaston, by turning informer against the future
husband of Rebecca, the Hebrew Maiden."

" Why, then, have you followed us to this place?"

" To warn you of danger."

" Hah!—of what danger do you speak?"

" I am not permitted to explain further upon this matter at present,"
answered the old woman. " Let it suffice that Sir Gaston de Neville, resolving to be no longer foiled in his endeavours to obtain the maiden, has
now formed a fresh project which will be put into execution ere thou art
many hours older."

" I have heard something of this before," exclaimed Reuben, " In fact,
this person, from whom I was about to take leave, visited Isaac of Tadcaster this evening, for the purpose of putting him upon his guard against some
fresh schemes of this Knight Templar."

" And knowest thou the plan he will next execute?" asked Meg of
Finchley.

" I do not," answered Edith, " but from the secrecy of his frequent
consultations with those, who, no doubt, are to assist him in it, there is
every reason to fear the plot is skilfully devised, and will be successfully
carried into effect, unless precautions are taken to foil him."

" Let the maiden conceal herself for the present," suggested Meg.

" And where," asked Reuben, " can she flee, and be safe from the search
of her persecutor?"

" In my hut, on Finchley Heath," answered the old woman.

" And how are we to know," demanded Reuben, " that this is not some
plan of thine, to throw her in the way of Sir Gaston de Neville?"

" How!—dost thou suspect me of perfidy?"

" If my suspicions wrong thee, thou must pardon me, on account of the
many instances of treachery that I have already met with," answered
Reuben. " All the world seems to be arrayed against us as enemies, and,
therefore, it is little to be wondered at, that I regard thee among those, who
would betray us to an heartless villain."

" Never!" cried Meg, with great emotion;—" Rebecca has served me
more than once, and I owe her a debt of gratitude, that no act of mine can
ever wipe out;—besides, she has ever a kindly word for the poor outcast,
and think you I can betray her, when I know her to be my friend?"

" I will believe you, old woman," exclaimed Reuben, softened by the earnestness with which these words were spoken ;—" I have wronged you, Meg, and from this moment I will cheerfully accept your proffered services."

" Rebecca, then, shall come and live with me, till the tempest that threatens has passed away ?"

" That is more than I can promise," answered Reuben, " I will, however, mention your offer to the Jew, her father, and should he think well of it, I will, myself, conduct her to your abode without delay."

" It must be instantly," cried the Wierd Woman of the Heath, " or she will be lost !"

" Will to-morrow be too late ?"

" I almost fear it will."

" But may not Sir Gaston de Neville suspect her hiding place and fellow her thither ?"

" I can defy him, even if he should do so," answered Meg, with a triumphant smile ;—" he may visit my poor cabin, and yet, in spite of all his trouble, the maiden shall not be found."

" You have some secret hiding place ?"

" I have ;—and one that he is not likely speedily to find out. However, we waste time in useless parley, bring the maiden to me to-morrow night, and I'll answer for it, with my own life, that no harm shall befal her."

" Well, for my own part, I can see no objection to it," exclaimed Edith, who had been an attentive auditor to this conversation ;—" the offer seems to be a perfectly fair one, and though the place of refuge may not be a very tempting one, yet, any port in a storm, say I, and I dare say Rebecca will be of the same way of thinking."

" It must be so," cried Reuben ;—" at least, I promise to bring her to your solitary hut upon the heath, if her father does not absolutely forbid such a step."

" And that he will not do so, I feel assured," answered Meg. " Tell him that his daughter is in peril, from the schemes of this Knight Templar;—say, that nothing but instant flight can save her from his hellish designs, and urge him, as he loves his child, not to hesitate, but to commit her to my care till she can safely quit it again."

" I will tell him all you have said," answered Reuben,—" and will, myself, endeavour to urge him, should he seem not inclined to accept your offer."

" But how long," inquired Edith, " will it be necessary for her to remain stived up in the place you speak of ?"

" That is a question I cannot answer at present," replied Meg. " Possibly a few days may be sufficient, though I am inclined to think it would be more prudent for her to remain there until her father bestows her in marriage upon the young man. Then she will be safe from all further harm, since a husband's protection is the only shield that can ever save her from the foes that now harass her."

" Dear me," cried Edith, " how foolish the old man must be, then, not to let them marry at once."

" He, at any rate, does not think so," answered Reuben, " since it is scarcely an hour since he told us that we were too young to marry yet.— Such is his opinion, Edith, and it is not for me to dispute the point with one, who is about to bestow upon me so inestimable a treasure."

" Still, it seems very hard, that two young folks should be made miserable, because an old gentleman takes it into his head to be very obstinate."

" Heed not this giddy-pated girl," cried Meg, addressing herself to

Reuben, " but learn to bow with submission to the dictates of prudence.— Isaac, of Tadcaster, has lived long in the world, and if he withholds his consent to your union for the present, you may be assured that he has both reason and experience for the course he adopts."

" But, for all that," retorted Edith, " it is not very pleasant to have one's prospects blighted because one person thinks he knows a great deal more than any body else does. Besides, when they are married, Sir Gaston will hardly care to be running after another man's wife; and, upon finding that he has no further chance, he will give up the affair, and look out for some other young maiden."

" You will remember what I have said, Reuben," exclaimed Meg of Finchley ;—" prevail upon her father, if you can, to let her seek the shelter of my cabin, and, to-morrow evening, about this hour, I will expect her arrival."

So saying, she turned away, and passing round the ruin, as before, was almost instantly out of sight.

" Well, that's a curious sort of old woman, enough," exclaimed Edith, as the hag took her departure ;—" she pops in upon us, nobody knows how, and disappears in the same sort of way, for all the world as if she had dealings with a certain person that shall be nameless."

" It is said," replied Reuben, " that she practices the dark arts, but whether she does so or no, it is certain she possesses much humanity and a heart capable of prompting her to deeds of kindness."

" It may be so," answered Edith, " but if I was Rebecca, I would rather run any risk than be shut up in some dark place, where, I suppose, the light of day never enters."

" And yet if she can find safety there when it is denied her everywhere else, she would be foolish to refuse Meg's offer of shelter."

" Why, to be sure, there is something in that," cried Edith, " and so, having convinced me thus far, I shall now take my leave of you, as, by this time, it is Martin's turn to attend the principal gate of the castle, and as he has a sort of sneaking kindness for me, he will not make a fuss about my being out, in case he should happen to penetrate the disguise I have put on."

" Will you not suffer me, then, to go with you as far as the outer gate?" asked Reuben.

" You must not go another step with me," answered Edith. " Already you are near enough to be seen if any of the warders are upon the look out from the walls, and a shot or two from their cross-bows, would be pretty sure to rid Sir Gaston of a rival, for whom he entertains no very kindly feelings."

" Nay, but hear me —"

" Not another word," she cried, running away from him. " There may be other eyes upon us that we know not of, and if that is the case, you will hardly be suffered to reach home without encountering some of the emissaries of Sir Gaston de Neville. There are many among them who would gladly earn his favour by despatching Reuben Grenard, especially as the act would be followed with something handsome, in the shape of a reward."

" But are you certain of gaining admittance to the castle without interruption ?" asked the young man.

" I am quite sure of doing so," she replied, " if Martin happens to be at the gate. He thinks, poor fellow, that I do not regard him altogether with dislike, and in the vain hope that I may, hereafter, bestow myself upon him, he is so very civil, that I have often very great difficulty in restraining my tongue from telling him that he has no more chance of winning my love,

than he has of becoming sovereign of England. So, you see, there is no fear but I shall gain admittance to the castle easily enough, and, with that assurance, I now take my departure, though not without cautioning you, once more, to beware, lest Sir Gaston should contrive to carry off Rebecca when you might be least prepared for his attack."

With this, Edith, still wrapped up in the folds of her capacious cloak, tripped lightly towards the castle, leaving Reuben Grenard to return homewards, and concert with Isaac, of Tadcaster, on the best means for thwarting the new devices of their ever active enemy.

As for Edith, she, easily enough, gained access to the castle, and passing through the gate, she was hurrying across the court-yard, when Martin, whose suspicions had been aroused that all was not right, hastened after her, and plucking her by the cloak :—

"By your leave, good sir, you must return with me to the lodge"

Still Edith made no reply, but tugging lustily to escape from the warder's hold, endeavoured to pass on.

"Nay, it is no use to ride rusty with me, young fellow," exclaimed Martin ;—"I begin to suspect something is not right here, and I shall take you before Sir Gaston, who, if he finds any treachery going on, will be sure to order that you swing on the highest tower of his castle, within an hour after the sun rises to-morrow morning. So come along, for I am too trusty a follower of the knight's to let you escape in this way."

"Hush, dear Martin, for the love of our Lady !" cried Edith, upon thus finding that she was compelled to discover herself.

"Why, who, in the devil's name, have we here !" gasped the astonished warder, starting back, as if he feared that he had come in contact with

No. 42

some unearthly being. "Speak! and if thou bee'st some imp of Satan, take thy departure, and leave me in peace,"

"Why, Martin!" she cried, "is it possible that you do not know the voice of your own little Edith?"

"Edith!—why, surely, you don't say so!" exclaimed the warder, still doubting the truth of what he had heard;—"and yet," he continued, "it is like her voice, too,—and the figure and height, are just like her's,—and —but no—it's quite impossible, and this is some foul spirit come to do me some terrible mischief."

"I tell you, Martin, I am, indeed, Edith, in flesh and blood," she exclaimed;—"if you doubt my word, take my hand, and say whether I am a spirit or not."

"I'd rather not, thank you, till I'm quite certain that you are, indeed, the person you speak of."

"You will not take my hand, then?"

"Not till I am convinced that you are no spirit.

"Then let that convince you," cried Edith, dealing him a sound box on the ears that made him reel back;—"perhaps, sir, you will now acknowledge that I am the person I have before declared myself."

"Why, there's no doubting it now?" exclaimed Martin, rubbing his still tingling ears;—"I have every reason to believe that you are, indeed, Edith, but how the deuce came you to leave the castle, and what errand was it that took you forth at this hour of the night?"

"I left the castle," replied Edith, "because it was my will to do so, which, I take it, is a very sufficient reason; and the business that took me from home, was,—but no matter about that just now, Martin, for the truth is, I do not feel inclined to make you any farther confession at present, so prithee have patience, and, perhaps, I may tell you all the secret some other time."

"Tell it me now, Edith, if you love me," exclaimed the warder, half angrily;—"tell me at once, you jade, or I shall grow jealous, and suspect nobody knows what."

"Mercy, sirrah," cried Edith, "and pay what is it that you mean to suspect?"

"That you have been out to meet some rival of mine;—some paltry jackanapes, that I'll thrash within an inch of his life if ever he chances to come within my reach."

"Indeed!" retorted the girl, "and suppose there happens to be no rival in the affair;—don't you think, in that case, that you will look like a very silly booby?"

"Why then did you leave the castle, if it was not to meet some rascal that dares to be my rival for your heart?"

"I shall answer no impertinent questions, Martin," cried Edith, with pretended pique;—"I went on an errand of my own, and if that answer is not sufficient for you, why prithee go your ways, and never dare talk to me of love again as long as you live."

"Very well, Edith," exclaimed the warder; "you are determined to break my heart, I see, so good bye to you, and don't be surprised if in the morning you should happen to hear that poor Martin has hung himself in despair."

"Goodness!—why you are not serious, Martin?"

"Indeed but I am though."

"Well then I must relent a little, that's all;—the fact is, Martin, that I wanted to know whether you and I should be happy when we marry;—it was a odd thought, perhaps, you'll say, but be that as it may, I was determined to see Meg of Finchley,—the Weird Woman of the Heath, as they call her, and who it is said has uncommon skill in telling people their fortunes."

"Humph!" ejaculated Martin;—"and so you wish to make me believe that you have been all the way to Finchley."

"I don't wish to do anything of the sort, Martin," she replied, "for the truth is, I know you are a little bit too cunning to be cheated so easily as all that. In fact, I met her no very great distance from the postern gate, and, of course, I got from her all I wanted to know."

"Well, and what did she say?"

"Why, that you were one of the sweetest tempered creatures in the world, and that, as I am equally blessed in that respect, our marriage would be a happy one, and,—and —"

"Well Edith, go on."

"I cannot, Martin."

"And why not?"

"Because I have forgotten all that she told me besides."

"Nay," exciaimed Martin, "that is very unlikely;—"the fact is, she told you something else that was not quite so pleasant, and you wish to keep it from me."

"Well," replied Edith, "she certainly did say that you are of rather an inquisitive turn, and that one fault might be the means of disturbing our domestic harmony."

"The hag lies!" roared Martin, furiously.

"Upon my word I begin to think she does," answered Edith, haughtily, "for, as I said just now, she told me that you were blessed with a most excellent temper, and you have this moment convinced me that she knows nothing about it."

"Edith! do you want to drive me mad?"

"Indeed I do not, Martin," she replied, "but you would draw the secret from me, and now it seems that you are not best pleased with me for telling the truth."

"You should not have listened to her, then, when she began to talk of my faults," answered Martin. "It was all very well to listen with patience whilst she was describing my good qualities, but she deserves burning for a witch for daring to say that I am inquisitive, or that you and I shall ever quarrel with each other."

"Why you are quarrelling with me now, sir, and I'm sure that is a pretty good proof that the old woman knows something about her trade of fortune-telling."

"If ever Meg of Finchley comes here," cried Martin, "she shall be burned in the great court-yard, for daring to say a word against me!"

"And yet it seems," observed Edith, laughing, "that the poor old creature only spoke the truth."

"She has been setting you against me."

"Nay, there you wrong her, for the poor old soul only spoke of you as you really are."

"And the consequence is, that you will never consent to marry me," exclaimed Martin.

"I said not that," replied Edith;—"Indeed, there is no knowing what I may be foolish enough to do by and by, if you only promise not to tell anybody that I have been out of the castle to night."

"Well then, I do promise that I will not."

"In that case, I will permit you to live in hope," replied the light-hearted girl, and then bounding off, she entered the nearest door that presented itself to her, and proceeded to the housekeeper's room, where, luckily enough, no one was there present to perplex her with any more questions.

CHAPTER LXV.

" Again the apparition crossed their path,—
Stealing upon them with a noiseless step,
To frighten them with it's presence."

DON RAYMOND.

JUST at the time when Edith returned to the castle, Sir Gaston de Neville was closeted with Roland le Mark, one of his few confidential friends, and, indeed, since the absence of Bertrand le Noir, almost the only one of his numerous retainers with whom he thought fit to hold communion. It was evident that the knight was much disturbed at something or other, and yet it was some little time before he could prevail upon himself to give utterance to what he had to say. At last, however, pausing suddenly in the rapid strides with which he had been pacing the chamber, he looked intently upon the submissive follower, and asked cheerfully whether he was still faithful to the master he had so long served.

"As much so as I ever have been, Sir Gaston," replied the man somewhat surprised at the question ;—"and yet I cannot but marvel why you should now doubt me after the zeal I have ever shown in your service."

"I doubt thee not, Roland," answered the knight; "but friends are not always to be depended on, and knowing that many of my secrets have been laid open to thee, and would know how far I may rely on thee for the future ?"

"As much as ever you have," exclaimed Roland, "for rather would I sacrifice my life, than do ought to endanger him whom I am proud and happy to serve."

"I believe thee, my good fellow," cried Sir Gaston, "and though my question may have appeared abrupt to thee, it was only to satisfy myself of thy continued faith to me. Thou knowest of the share I have taken in the cause of Prince John, who I would gladly see seated on the throne that is at present occupied by his brother, and wert thou unfaithful to me,—nay, didst thou but utter a single word respecting the part I am taking, a death of shame would be my certain doom, and the name of Sir Gaston de Neville would go down to posterity with dishonour."

"You have nothing to fear from me on that account," replied Roland, "for I am myself concerned deeply in the conspiracy, and were I treacherous, torture and death would be surely mine."

"That is not quite so certain," answered the knight; "for they might offer thee life and liberty as the condition of thy faithlessness. It is against me that their vengeance would be directed, for already has the king shown his dislike to me, and from all I have heard, he only waits a fitting opportunity to bring me to an ignominious death."

"He must have proof ere he can do that," exclaimed Roland.

"A tyrant never wants proof," answered Sir Gaston ;—"besides, he has already told me that he suspects my loyalty to himself, and I know not how soon it may be his will and pleasure to hurl destruction on my head."

"'And the moment he did so," cried the retainer, "your friends would rise up in arms to avenge your cause. King Richard has enemies to deal with, who may yet prove too powerful for him, and I would have him beware how he commits violence against the powerful knight, Sir Gaston de Neville."

"He hath threatened me with his vengeance," exclaimed the other, "and has even interfered to wrest from me a girl upon whom I had set my heart. Even for that, Roland, I owe him retaliation, and, ere long, he will discover that the man he thus treats as he would a base minion, has it in his power to drive him from his throne."

"Are your friends ready to strike the blow?" asked the retainer.

"They are."

"May I ask whom, Sir Knight?"

"Relying on your fidelity," answered the Templar, "I will not hesitate to tell you a secret that at present is known only to the few principal persons concerned in the plot. The third of September is the day appointed on which the coronation of King Richard is to take place at Westminster, and during that ceremony, we shall have an opportunity to excite the mob, who may easily be prevailed upon to rise up against the sovereign whose guards and attendants may easily be overcome."

"And yet," observed Roland, "the time seems short to carry out such a project as you have spoken of."

"It is," answered the knight, "but every thing favours us, and I have little fear for the result. Richard is not popular with the rabble, in consequence of the favour he has showed the Jews, and we have only to remind them of this circumstance, to raise them in our behalf. The Hebrews are a despised race, and the people will not hesitate an instant if they are called upon to burn their houses, and massacre the whole tribe, so that not one shall be left to lament over the destruction of his bretheren."

"And yet," said Roland, "there is one among them that you would not willingly destroy."

"Aye, Rebecca must be saved at all hazards," answered Sir Gaston ;— "she must be made my captive previous to the day appointed for the coronation, and then it will be easy to save her from the general slaughter that will take place. Her father and lover must, however, perish, and then I shall secure a prize that I have long sought for in vain."

"And the king," exclaimed Roland, "is he also to die, if we succeed in overpowering his guards?"

"He must be taken alive, if possible," answered Sir Gaston de Neville, "and if we succeed in raising his brother John to the throne of England, it will remain for him to decide afterwards what shall be his doom. Richard, however, is of a bold and daring spirit, and as it is possible, he will fight desperately, let it be understood that he must be killed in the event of its being proved impossible to capture him."

"And what is to be the reward of him who either slays or makes him a prisoner?" demanded the other.

"One thousand pieces of gold," answered Sir Gaston ; "it is a tempting offer, Roland, and right glad should I be to know that the money has been earned by yourself."

"At any rate it shall be no fault of mine if I do not make the prize my own," exclaimed Roland ; "it is well worth the gaining, and, if I perish in the attempt, I shall, at least, have the satisfaction of dying in the faithful discharge of my duty to my master."

"Aye, and of serving Prince John," exclaimed the Knight Templar, "who, should you survive the skirmish that must take place, will reward your zeal most nobly. He has promised to give me a dukedom if we succeed in placing the crown upon his head ; and, as I shall always be near him, I will let slip no opportunity to obtain his royal favour for you."

"I ask no greater boon than for permission to live and die in your service," replied Roland. "As a boy, I was page to your mother ; and, as a man, I have followed you to the wars, where we have shared together the honours of victory. This has been my glory through life, and most cheerfully will I perish in any enterprise in which my master leads me on."

"I may depend upon thee, then?"

"Aye, you shall find me faithful even unto death."

"You will not hesitate, then, to assist me once more in capturing the Hebrew Maiden, and conveying her wherever I may choose to direct?"

"I will do your bidding, certainly, whatever it may be," answered Roland; "and yet, to confess the truth, I would rather war against men than women, for the latter rather need our aid than our enmity."

"Hah! you hesitate, sirrah!"

"Indeed, Sir Knight, you mistake me," answered Roland; "I own it is not altogether a pleasant task you would impose upon me, but, since it must be done, I am ready to obey whenever you think proper to command."

"You will assist then in carrying the girl off?"

"I will."

"But will you also promise to give no hint by which people may be led to suppose that I have had any share in the transaction?"

"I would rather my tongue should be cut out than turn traitor to my master," answered Roland. "Hitherto, Sir Gaston, you have found me faithful and zealous;—I have risked life and limb for you, and, therefore, it is rather galling to be suspected of treachery when my soul loathes even the very thought."

"I do not suspect you, Roland," replied the knight, "but you are aware that I am now in a situation of great peril. Upon you, for one, depends my safety, and it need not create much surprise that I am thus anxious to satisfy myself of your unfailing attachment. No one in my service knows so much of my affairs as you do, Roland;—my honour—nay, perhaps, my life itself—is thrown upon your mercy, and I seek but to convince myself that you will not betray your master when most he reposes in your fidelity."

"Here is my poniard," exclaimed Roland, throwing himself upon one knee and presenting the weapon to his master; "it has ever been used, Sir Knight, in your cause, and now that you seem to doubt my fidelity, I humbly implore you to plunge it into my heart, that you may hereafter have no further ground for suspecting me."

"Are you mad, Roland?" cried Sir Gaston, starting back from the weapon as though he had suddenly discovered a serpent in his path. "Are you mad, Roland, I ask, to bid me do an act which would be a reproach to me during the remainder of my existence?"

"I desire not to live after I have lost the confidence of my master," replied the other, gloomily. "If the zeal with which I have served you is not sufficient to convince you of the reliance that may be placed on me in future, I can resign into your hands that life which is devoted to your service."

"Come, come, Roland," exclaimed the knight, "rise, and learn, henceforward, to regard me rather as your friend than your master. From this moment I am convinced of your steady adherence to me, and never more will I give utterance to a doubt that seems so keenly to wound your generous spirit."

"I am content," replied the other, "and now, with your leave, I will hence and see whether instant measures cannot be taken for securing the Hebrew Maiden."

"Stay, Roland," exclaimed the knight, as his retainer was about to take his departure; "I have received intimation that my wife, the lady Alicia, is lying in her darksome cell ill, and, I believe, in some danger. She has requested to see me, and, as I hear she is not likely to survive much longer, I think of paying her a brief visit: you must accompany me, however, for the vaults are lonely and cheerless, and something of the coward creeps over me at the thought of meeting by myself the armed apparition, who, on several occasions, has presented himself to my view."

"Do you mean, Sir Knight, asked Roland, "to visit her ladyship immediately, or defer it till the morning?"

"It must be done without loss of time," replied Sir Gaston; "she is ill, I once more tell you, and glad should I be to witness her last dying pangs, that I may for ever be rid of one whose existence has of late years filled me with constant alarm."

"Aye," exclaimed Roland, "I have often wondered you took not your usual decisive measures in this case. People have long supposed her to be dead, and instead of keeping her confined in a dungeon all this time, I would, had I been you, have commissioned some trusty servant to despatch her. You might then have made yourself safe, instead of living as you have, in constant dread of a discovery taking place."

"Would'st thou have done the deed?"

"Aye—that is, if I saw no other way of making my honoured master secure."

"Why then didst thou never mention this notion of thine before?"

"I have done so," answered Roland, "at least, I have pretty broadly hinted at what I would recommend; but you made no reply to me, and I therefore supposed you were determined to let her live on in the misery you had doomed her to."

"Had I known thou wert to be depended on in this matter, the Lady Alicia should have ended her wretched existence long ere this," replied Sir Gaston de Neville. "However, it appears she is now ill and in some danger, and if heaven takes her to its mercy, I shall, at least, be spared the commission of one crime that would have hung upon my soul more heavily than all the rest."

"But this is not the first time she has been ill, and yet she still lives on," exclaimed the other; "even now she may recover, contrary to your expectations, and therefore would I counsel you to take such measures as will prevent her occasioning you any further uneasiness."

"What mean you, sirrah?"

"Nay, you are angry, good Sir Knight, and I had better say no more to excite your wrath."

"If thou wouldst not forfeit my regard, speak what thou meanest," said Sir Gaston, with vehemence.

"Thou wilt spurn me from thee, perhaps, if I do?"

"I pledge thee my knightly word to listen to thee with all patience," answered the Templar; "nay, I can already guess thy meaning, Roland—thou wouldst advise me to slay her during the visit I am now going to make to her dungeon."

"I would save thee that trouble, Sir Knight," exclaimed the ruffian; "I have my poniard with me, and if thou dost but say the word, it shall quickly find its way to her heart."

"Villain! thou dost almost tempt me to abet thee in thy cruel project of murder," cried Sir Gaston, enraged at the proposition: soon after, however, he grew more cool upon the subject, and, abruptly pausing in the rapid strides with which he had been pacing up and down the chamber, he said,—

"I have heard thy proposition, Roland, and was angered at it; more, perhaps, than I ought to have been, seeing that it was thy zeal that prompted the suggestion. Upon cooler reflection, however, I am determined not altogether to reject thy proposition, but to wait until I have seen the result of my interview with the Lady Alicia. Should she reproach me, thou wilt be at hand, and a signal will be sufficient to convince thee that I would have her instantly despatched."

"You will find me ready to obey your slightest order," replied Roland;

"a word or a look will do, and from that moment your prisoner ceases to live."

"Follow me, then," exclaimed Sir Gaston, snatching up a lamp and preparing to leave the room; "keep close behind me, Roland, and when I enter the dungeon, remain thou on the outside till I clap my hands thrice"

"I understand," replied Roland; "I am then to enter the cell and despatch my victim?"

"Not till I bid thee strike," cried Sir Gaston; "mark me, fellow! I would not rashly bid thee commit the murder, and perhaps even at the latest moment I may relent. Thou wilt, therefore, remain with the dagger in thy hand, and if I pronounce the word 'strike,' let thy blow be sure and her death speedy, for she has no more mercy to expect at my hand."

"Fear not but I will obey you, even to the letter," exclaimed Roland; and then, following his master, they proceeded together along the corridor, from whence a flight of steps led to the dungeons beneath the castle. Stealthily pursuing their way, for fear of being discovered by any one about the place, they at length reached the subterranean caverns, where even the light of the lamp they carried with them failed to illume the almost impenetrable darkness with which they were surrounded. Numerous doors, too, they had to open, which, turning upon their rusty hinges with a sharp piercing sound, like the lamentations of some unseen spirit for the crime they were going to perpetrate. Every now and then Sir Gaston and his companion started back aghast at the moans and other dismal sounds that met their ears; but, growing at length accustomed to this, they increased their speed until they found themselves standing near the door that led to the dungeon of the Lady Alicia. Here they paused, and whispered together for a few seconds; and then, having arranged matters between them, the Templar unlocked the heavy iron-bound portal, and, removing the bolts and bars with which it had been deemed necessary to secure the hapless prisoner, he entered the miserable chamber, leaving his ruthless companion on the outside, anxiously listening for the signal that was to give the Lady Alicia to death.

Nearly exhausted with illness and despair, the hapless captive was lying stretched upon her pallet of straw, and, with a small crucifix pressed to her lips, was silently praying for that death which she had so long sighed for in vain. She looked forward to it as a termination of her sufferings, and so absorbed was she in the thought of quitting a world of sorrows for one of joy and gladness, that she heard not the entrance of Sir Gaston until he had approached to the side of her wretched couch, and demanded why it was that she had sent for him. At the sound of his voice her eyes sparkled, as if lit up with sudden hope, and, gently raising herself, she said faintly,—

"Ah! my husband, you know not how happy it has made me to see that you have not quite forgotten me. I am now ill, even unto death, and perhaps a few short hours will rid you of one you have ceased to love for years."

"I come not to listen to your reproaches for what has passed," exclaimed Sir Gaston, sullenly; "you sent a message to me by the man that brings your daily food: and, gathering from his words that you were dying, I hastened hither to know whether you have any last request to make."

"I have but one," she replied, and that, I fear, you will not be inclined to grant."

"Name it," exclaimed the knight, "and, if possible, I will not refuse you."

"It is," answered the Lady Alicia, "that you will be pleased to order

my immediate removal from this place to one of the apartments in the castle. I would once more behold the glorious light of day, which for years has been denied me in this loathsome dungeon; and then, with the assurance of your forgiveness, I could die happy."

"You ask that which it is impossible I can grant," replied Sir Gaston; "It has been rumoured for years past that you were dead, and to grant your request would be to discover a secret that never must be known."

"And how have I deserved your unkind treatment?" demanded the Lady Alicia, mournfully; "was I not your constant and faithful wife, and did I ever give you cause for the hatred with which you at last regarded me?"

"Had I known that you intended to heap reproaches upon me, I would not have troubled you with this visit," exclaimed the knight, bitterly; "as it is, however," he continued, "you must change the subject, or I may be guilty of an act I would fain be spared."

"Ah!" groaned Alicia, "you threaten me, and I know there is some evil purpose in your heart."

"Alicia!" cried the knight, fiercely, "these are not the words with which I expected to be greeted by one who I understood to be dying. But you may urge me beyond bearing, and if you do, let your death lie at your own door."

"It is not to speak of myself," replied Alicia, "that I requested this interview;—I have reason to know that you have fixed your unhallowed love upon a Hebrew Maiden, whose virtue has hitherto successfully resisted all the attempts you have made for her destruction. I would speak for her, Sir Gaston de Neville, and implore you to have pity upon one who loathes the man who thus seeks her ruin."

"And how," asked the knight, impatiently, "do you chance to know

No 43

anything of this affair? You have been shut up for years past in this dungeon, and yet you speak to me on this subject as if you had been an eye-witness of all that has been going on."

"I know more about it than you suppose I do," answered Alicia; "and further, I can prophecy that you now stand upon the brink of an awful precipice, down which the slightest breath threatens to send you to destruction. Nay, you smile scornfully at my words; yet, rely upon it, Sir Gaston, they will be fulfilled, unless you take timely warning from her who trembles for your safety."

"To what do you allude?" asked Sir Gaston, struck by the earnestness with which she had spoken.

"To treason against your king, and conspiracy against the best interests of your country," she replied, solemnly. "Aye, you start, and wonder how I know all this; but I have had visions of fearful import, in which I have seen thee leagued with the discontented of the land, and making war upon the sovereign you have sworn to serve."

"Thy visions," replied the knight, "for once have not deceived thee: I am leagued against King Richard, but it is in favour of a prince who is better able to govern the country for the peace and happiness of the people."

"And yet," exclaimed the Lady Alicia, "the prince of whom you speak is doomed to fail in the mad enterprize you speak of. Richard is well beloved by his subjects, and few are there who will take up arms against one whose prowess in arms has made him the admiration of the whole world."

"And how knowest thou that, seeing that thou hast been a close prisoner in this cell from a period long before he came to the throne of England?"

"I heard it," she replied, "from the man that used to bring me my scanty allowance of food,—he, however, has not visited me of late, and the one who has taken his place is taciturn, and refuses to answer my questions."

"The fellow is in the right, and shall be rewarded for it," exclaimed Sir Gaston.

"And the one that was more kind to me?—surely, you will not punish him for displaying a little humanity to your wretched captive."

"He is beyond my power, or I know not but I should have sent him to pass the remainder of his days in a dungeon," replied the knight; "he is dead, Alicia; and, therefore, I am spared the necessity of punishing him for disobeying the strict commands I gave him. But I am wasting time in idle parley, Alicia; I came hither to know whether you had any communication to make, or any request to urge, ere you quit a world which has long been closed to you."

"I sought this interview," replied Alicia, "in the hope that I might succeed in changing your heart from the evil purposes upon which it is bent. I would implore you no longer to persecute the Jewish maiden, but to relinquish your designs, and then permit her to possess that happiness of which you have lately deprived her."

"Humph! and that is all you wished to see me about?"

"It is; and could I but accomplish my purpose, I could die content."

"Alicia," exclaimed the knight, "it is in vain you ask me to relinquish my hopes of making that girl mine. My whole heart and soul are bent upon this one object, and, were hell itself to yawn before me, it should not frustrate the design I have formed."

"Then," said the Lady Alicia, "art thou basely forsworn to me, thy lawful wife."

"Hah! dost thou dare to reproach me?"

"I do, and bid thee do thy worst! Let thy steel enter my heart, Sir

Gaston—murder me if thou wilt, for life has become such a heavy burden to me that I would thank thee with my latest breath for the good service thou hast done me."

"Nay, another shall strike the fatal blow," exclaimed the infuriated knight; and, clapping his hands three times, as had been arranged, Roland, grasping in his hand a naked dagger, looked enquiringly upon his master to know his pleasure.

"What wouldst thou have me do, Sir Gaston?" he demanded.

"Strike!" was the prompt and laconic reply.

Roland raised aloft the glittering blade, and was about to fulfil the dreadful mandate, when the door of the dungeon was thrown open with a terrific crash, and the armed apparition once more stood before them. Horrified at this sight, Sir Gaston and Roland uttered a yell of agony, and, as if blasted by what they gazed upon, sunk, in a state of total insensibility, upon the floor of the dungeon.

How long they remained in this state they knew not, but when they at length recovered, they found themselves involved in total darkness, for the lamp had been extinguished, and not a ray of light could be seen by which to guide themselves through the labyrinth of caverns through which they would be compelled to take their way on their return to the habitable part of the castle. To add to their consternation, too, it was discovered, on groping round the dungeon, that Alicia was no longer there!

CHAPTER LXVI.

"Escaped, say'st thou?
Then let pursuit begin, and woe to him
That fails me in this need."

THE MOSS TROOPERS.

To explain the mysterious disappearance of the Lady Alicia, it is necessary to inform the reader that no sooner had Sir Gaston and his attendant sunk with terror on the floor of the cell, than, with a powerful grasp, she was seized upon, and a cloak being thrown over her, she was conveyed with astonishing rapidity through the dark subterranean vaults of the castle. Terrified, she screamed loudly for assistance, but the exertion proved too much for her, and, fainting away in the arms of the person that carried her, she recovered not for some time afterwards; when, upon opening her eyes, she perceived that she was in one of the apartments belonging to the castle, and that she was attended by the faithful Edith, whose care had at length recovered her from the state of insensibility in which she had fallen.

"Edith!" she exclaimed, with surprise, "explain to me, I entreat, the mystery which on every side surrounds me. Tell me how it is that I now find myself under your care, when, but a short time since, I had given myself up as lost?"

"Indeed, my lady, I know not," answered Edith.

"Who brought me to this chamber?"

"That is more than I can tell," replied the girl. "I had secretly left the castle, and had succeeded in returning to this room without meeting any body except Martin, the warder, and just as I was congratulating myself on having tricked them all for once in my life, I was startled at hearing a loud knock at yonder door, and terribly frightened I was, you may be sure."

"And you had not the courage, I suppose, to satisfy yourself upon the subject?"

"For some time, it must be confessed, I was afraid to see who it was that had knocked so loudly, for they say the castle is haunted by an armed spectre, and thinking he might have taken it into his head to pay me a visit, I trembled so much that—"

"You torture me, Edith, with this long story," cried the Lady Alicia, impatiently; "have compassion on me, I conjure you, and explain, as briefly as you can, how and where you found me."

"Well, your ladyship," replied the girl, "you must know that after a little while, as all seemed quiet again, I began to grow more courageous, and so, creeping softly towards the door and opening it, I saw you lying insensible on the ground. At first, I could hardly believe my eyes, for I knew you were imprisoned in one of those horrible places beneath the castle. But, satisfying myself that you still lived, I exerted all my strength, and, carrying you into this room, set myself to the task of recovering you as well as I could."

"Fo which I owe you my eternal gratitude," exclaimed Lady Alicia, fervently. "And now, Edith, tell me if you saw any person besides myself when first you opened the door?"

"Not a soul, my lady."

"Then," cried Alicia, half aside, "he must have effected his retreat immediately after he laid me at the door."

"He! who does your ladyship mean?"

"The armed apparition."

"Horrible!" cried the shuddering girl. "You have seen him, then?"

"I have, Edith," replied Lady Alicia; "I have indeed seen the spectre you have been speaking of, and to that circumstance do I owe my life."

"How!" cried the astonished maiden, "do you indeed owe your life to a hobgoblin?"

"You shall hear my story," answered the Lady Alicia. "You are aware how long I have been imprisoned in a dark and cheerless dungeon by a husband who, for some reason or other, wishes me dead. This I have endured almost without complaining, because each day I thought he would come to visit me, and that then I should be able to prevail on him with prayers and entreaties to restore me again to liberty."

"Which was very unlikely, your ladyship, seeing that he has given out to the world that you were dead, and, to confirm the report, a mock funeral was got up, and the supposed Lady Alicia was buried with all the pomp that would have been observed in the event of her being really dead."

"I have heard so from Adrian the page," answered Alicia, "for he has secretly been my friend, and visited me when all the world beside seemed to have forsaken me."

"And did Sir Gaston never go to see you?" asked Edith.

"Very rarely," replied Alicia, "and even when he did, he always left me whenever I began to urge him on the subject of my release. At length, my patience became exhausted, and I resolved to adopt other means to see him; I made use of a falsehood, Edith, of which I am heartily ashamed, though it has proved the means of setting me at liberty."

"And who can blame you for it," exclaimed Edith, "seeing that by falsehood, he has succeeded in lulling the world into a belief of your death."

"Yesterday," resumed the Lady Alicia, "I sent him a message, saying that I was ill and at the point of death; my stratagem succeeded,—he came, —anxious, no doubt, to witness my last moments, and brought with him one of those attendants who are willing to commit murder, even should it be the command of his imperious master."

"Good heavens!" cried Edith, "did any body ever hear of such a cruel monster?"

"The result proved that I was not mistaken in the opinion I had formed," continued Alicia; "I spoke to Sir Gaston of the iniquities he has been guilty of, and urged him to repentance; my words, I suppose, stung him to the soul, for, on a signal being given, his ruffianly follower rushed into the dungeon, and was about to plunge his poniard in my breast, when the door was thrown back with a terrific crash, and the black phantom stood before us, in all his terrors. At that moment, the dagger fell from the assistant's grasp, and both he and his master fell to the ground, as if struck by the lightning's blast."

"Dreadful!" cried the horrified girl; "and you were thus left to the mercy of the grim spectre?"

"I have no recollection of what afterwards passed," replied Alicia, "except that I was snatched up from my miserable pallet, and borne along with inconceivable swiftness through the dark and mazy caverns of the castle. I screamed with terror, but my senses failed me, and I know nothing more till I found myself under your care."

"What a horrible situation!" cried Edith; "and yet, after all, the black spectre seems to bear you no ill will, since it was through his means that you escaped death."

"But only for a short time," sighed Lady Alicia; "Sir Gaston de Neville will soon discover me again, and either captivity or death will be my doom."

"Then the only way," replied Edith, "will be to escape from the castle as soon as you can, and if once the king hears the story of your wrongs, he will soon call your cruel husband to a severe account for his conduct."

At this instant they were alarmed at hearing some one at the door, and Lady Alicia had given herself up as lost, when the voice of Adrian served to allay their fears. He was immediately admitted, and when his first surprise, at seeing Lady Alicia, had subsided, he threw himself at her feet, congratulating her upon the escape she had had, and earnestly imploring her to take immediate steps for leaving the castle, ere Sir Gaston succeeded in discovering her retreat.

"I have seen him, your ladyship," he continued, "and a towering passion he is in at having been lost with Roland among the caverns of the castle. It was but little I heard, but I could gather that you had somehow or other, most unaccountably escaped, in consequence of the unlooked for appearance of the apparition, and that he and his attendant had been left to find their way out of the dungeon as well as they could. He spoke, too, in whispers to Roland, and telling him that you must be somewhere about the castle, bade him follow him in order that a strict search might be made through the place. They will soon be here, my lady, and I dread to think of your fate if once more you should fall into their hands."

"Alas! what will become of me?" cried Alicia, in despair; "who will befriend me in this sad hour of trouble?"

"I will, my lady," exclaimed Adrian, spiritedly.

"You!" cried Alicia; "but no, no, my good youth, your kindness would only lead you into trouble, and, perhaps, your own death might be the consequence of my selfishly putting your noble generosity to the proof."

"Ah, my lady!" cried Edith, interposing, "you know not how gallant Adrian can be, when a helpless female requires his assistance. He may be depended on, I know, and if you will but accept his services, he will yet save you from falling again into the power of Sir Gaston de Neville."

"Adrian has already proved his zeal in my behalf," answered Lady Alicia; "when all else had forgotten me, he came at the hazard of his life, to visit my dreary dungeon, and, but for him, I should, long ere this, have sank under the heavy load of misfortunes that pressed upon me. I can, therefore, rely upon the zeal with which he would serve me, and yet, never can I consent to bring upon him the fierce anger of one so vindictive as his haughty master."

"Nay, my lady," exclaimed Adrian, "let me entreat you to think better of this; remember, nothing but instant flight can prevent your being discovered, and, should you again fall into the power of Sir Gaston, I dread to think of the vengeance with which he would be certain to pursue you."

"I know my life would be sacrificed," replied Alicia, "yet would I prefer any death, however lingering it might be, to risking the life of one who would so generously hazard it in my defence."

"But Adrian might go with you," cried Edith, "and, in that case, he would not only be able to protect you from your enemies, but he would, at the same time, be safe from those who might feel inclined to punish him for aiding an oppressed mistress."

"Nay, it would not be prudent to be absent from the castle any length of time," replied Adrian, "because Sir Gaston would at once guess that I had accompanied my honoured lady, and thus he might, by and by, find a clue by which to trace to the place where we might find a refuge. Under these circumstances, I will content myself with seeing her ladyship to some secure retreat, and then return back to the castle before suspicion has been aroused by my absence."

"And a very good thought, too," exclaimed Edith, "for it will give your ladyship time to make up your mind how it will be best to act. For my own part, though, I should say the best plan will be to seek an interview with the king, who, they say, is the generous protector of all his subjects, and who will take means to prevent your suffering anything more from the tyranny and oppression of Sir Gaston de Neville."

"Heaven knows," cried Alicia, "I seek not to injure Sir Gaston, nor will I expose his cruelty to King Richard unless I should be driven to do so by his continued persecutions. He is my husband, Edith, and cruelly as he has treated me, I feel no desire to revenge myself by seeking to procure his ruin."

"And yet," observed the girl, "no man deserves less pity than the one you seem so anxious to shield."

"That may be," replied Alicia, "but, however worthless a man may be, it is not for his wife to announce his errors to the world, and bring upon him the execrations of his fellow creatures."

"You will not seek, then, to bring him to a well deserved punishment?"

"I would rather perish, girl," answered Alicia; "at least, nothing but the most imminent peril to myself should drive me to such an alternative."

"How, then," asked Edith. "can you ever hope to preserve yourself from his persecutions?"

"By entering a convent," answered Alicia; "there I may find that peace and quiet that has been so long denied me, and the remainder of my days may be passed in praying for a remission of my own sins as well as those of him who has cast me from his heart."

"But surely," cried Edith, "your ladyship would not retire from the world for ever?"

"I know not why I should not do so," answered Alicia. "I am but too well accustomed to confinement; and, therefore, the regions of a convent would appear like liberty to one who has suffered as I have. Indeed, girl, I have grown weary of life, and I cannot better pass the remainder of it than in offering up my gratitude to that Being who has never forgotten me even when I thought myself most forsaken by the world."

"But perhaps your ladyship may alter your mind about remaining all your life in a convent," replied Adrian. "I have been told they are sad dull places, and suited only for those who are really weary of the world."

"And, therefore, do I choose the life in preference to any other," exclaimed Alicia, pensively. "Deprived, as I am, of a husband's love, where can I find so much consolation as from the holy sisterhood, amongst whom I would seclude myself. From them I should learn resignation, and my future days would be passed in that peace which has been so long denied me."

"But," observed the page, "Sir Gaston may yet repent the cruelty he has exercised towards you."

"That, I fear, is most improbable," cried Alicia; "when he discovers my flight, he will become furious with rage, and no place but the sanctuary, afforded by a convent, will ever shield me from his search."

"And yet I would rather prevail upon you to throw yourself under the protection of the king," exclaimed Adrian; "he is ever attentive to the complaints of the humblest among his subjects, and even the highest of them tremble at the vengeance he takes upon those who dare to offend against the laws. It is for this reason, dear lady, that I would prevail upon you to seek his aid, and, take my word for it, your supplication would not be made in vain."

"Aye, my lady," cried Edith, "do take his advice, and tell the king how shamefully you have been treated."

"At present I have other thoughts besides those of vengeance," answered Alicia. "I am most gratified for my escape, and unless circumstances should drive me to it, I will never utter a word that shall publish to the world the long imprisonment I have endured in the dungeons of this castle."

"Then you are more forgiving than I should be under similar circumstances," answered Edith; "for my own part, I hate all tyrannical husbands, and if ever I should have the misfortune to be troubled with one, he should find out, to his cost, that I have a little more spirit than he might give me the credit of possessing."

"Hush!" exclaimed Adrian, with alarm; "footsteps are approaching this way, and we are lost."

"Nay," cried Alicia, "be under no apprehension, for I will myself take care that you suffer not for the kindness you have bestowed upon me. Sir Gaston may discover and drag me back to my dungeon, but he knows that neither of you had any hand in my escape, and, therefore, wrathful as he is, he will not seek to injure you."

"Your ladyship," exclaimed Adrian, "will not, surely, throw yourself into his power again, without making another effort to escape from the castle?"

"Alas!" sighed the hapless Alicia, "which way shall the hunted deer flee from her pursuers? There is no way open to me, and I must e'en submit patiently to my hard destiny."

"Stay!" cried Edith, "there is one way that I had forgotten till this moment;—here is a secret door, leading to a winding staircase, that conducts you to an outlet opening into the gardens. Night favours your escape, and, with Adrian's aid, it is yet possible to get safely from the castle before to-morrow's dawn."

"Quick!—quick, Edith, for the love of heaven delay not a moment!"— exclaimed Adrian, impatiently, and assisting her in searching for the spring lock; he at length touched it by mere accident, upon which the door flew open, and discovered a dark passage, at the further end of which they found the staircase which had been alluded to. By this time, Sir Gaston was heard knocking violently at the door, upon which, Edith returned alone to the chamber, and having secured the passage in which she had left Lady Alicia and Adrian, gave admittance to the knight and his retainer, whose appearance denoted no very good humour.

" Now, girl!" exclaimed the knight, fiercely, " where is the woman that has just escaped my vigilance? Where is she, I say, for if you dare to equivocate, Roland shall bear you to one of the dungeons, and never more shall you see the light of day."

" Perhaps," said Edith, without appearing to be in the least alarmed; —" perhaps, Sir Gaston, you will be kind enough to tell me what woman you mean, for, as I happen to be in perfect ignorance of what you are talking of, it will be impossible to give an answer to your question."

" Viper! you would deceive me!" roared the knight;—" you pretend ignorance, though I know you have both seen and spoken to the person I mentioned."

" Well," answered Edith, pertly, " since you know so much, Sir Gaston, there is good reason to suppose you are not ignorant of the rest. So, if any woman has been here, of course, you can tell, as well as I, which way she has gone."

" If Sir Gaston was of my way of thinking," exclaimed Roland, fiercely, " he would find a speedy remedy for this insolence."

" And if he was my way of thinking," retorted Edith, " he would not much longer keep in his service, such a black-looking, villainous ruffian as you are."

" Peace, girl, and answer me," exclaimed Sir Gaston, furiously. " That you know of this woman's escape, I am quite assured, and unless you choose to divulge so much as will lead to her discovery, I will order you to be dragged to one of the darkest dungeons belonging to my castle, where you shall pine in misery and despair, till the latest day of your life."

" Really, Sir Gaston, you ask of me more than I can possibly answer," cried Edith, who was not to be easily frightened by the threatening words of her master;—" you ask me about some woman that has escaped, as if I should know of such a thing, and not run and tell you of it directly."

" 'Tis false!" exclaimed the knight, vehemently; " I heard voices in this chamber as I approached it."

" Ah!" she replied, " but that was only me singing a song that was taught me by old nurse Goodram, when I was a little girl."

" If you take my advice, Sir Gaston," observed Roland, " I would recommend that she be instantly taken to the dungeon you spoke of;—that would bring her to her senses, I'll answer for it, and she'll soon find her tongue, and tell us all about the woman we are in search of."

" You are very kind, I'm sure, sir," returned Edith, sarcastically, " but I hope Sir Gaston is not quite such a brute as to lock up a poor young creature, just because she is not able to answer his questions."

" You still remain obstinate, then," cried Sir Gaston.

" Nay," she replied, " craving your knightship's pardon, it cannot be obstinacy, since I know nothing at all about what you have been speaking of. You say a woman has escaped;—who, and what is she that you make such a clatter about?"

" A mad woman," exclaimed the knight, " and, therefore, should she

happen to cross your path, believe not a word she utters. She will tell yon she is my wife, and that she has escaped, after being confined for many years, by my orders, in the castle."

"Dear me!" cried Edith, with well affected simplicity, "what a sad thing it must be, for a noble knight, like yourself, to be charged with such a dreadful crime!"

"Come, come, girl," exclaimed Roland, who fancied he could see through all this; "it's no use your pretending to know nothing about it. You have seen the woman we are in search of, and if you don't confess at once, I'll find out a way to force the secret from you."

"It's impossible for you to do that, when I've got nothing to tell," replied Edith, unmoved by his threats.

"Then she must be somewhere in the castle," whispered Sir Gaston to his attendant;—" she is, perhaps, lying concealed somewhere, and is only waiting for an opportunity to slip, unperceived, out of one of the gates."

"Then will she be greatly mistaken," exclaimed Roland, "for I have given notice to the guards, and they have strict orders not to suffer any person to leave the place, until they are satisfied who they are and why they are going out of the castle."

"You have done well, and if she is discovered through your means, I will not fail to to reward you nobly," answered the knight. "So now, as this wench either does not, or pretends not to know nothing of the person we are in quest of, we will continue our search, lest she should find means to slip by the guards, and thus defeat the labour of years." Then addressing himself to Edith, he continued; "beware, girl, how you tamper with one, whose anger is as terrible as the sweeping hurricane;—beware, I

No. 44

say, or you will repent, when too late, the deception you would practice on me."

With this threat, the knight and his attendant quitted the room, and no sooner had their last retiring footfall died away in the distance, than fastening the door by which they had retired, she once more gave admittance to Alicia and the page, who had been terrified witnesses of the conversation that had taken place.

"Now, my lady," cried Edith, " there is not a moment to be lost;—Sir Gaston and his cut-throat friend, are in full pursuit of you through the castle, and if day dawns ere you have quitted the place, I fear all hope of escape will have vanished."

"Alas!" sighed the Lady Alicia, " I fear there is no chance of escaping the search they are now making for me. I heard Roland tell his master, that he had given orders to the guards, not to permit any one to leave the place, without satisfying himself who, and what they are, and, therefore, nothing remains for me, but to resign myself once more to the destiny that will make me Sir Gaston's prisoner for life."

"Not if Adrian and I can help it, though," exclaimed Edith, with spirit;—" for my own part, I never give way to despair, and I'll answer for it, some way will yet be found to get you safely out of this hateful place."

"There is the eastern postern," observed Adrian, who had hitherto remained lost in thought;—" it is seldom used, and, therefore, never guarded, and, as I happen to possess a key that fits it, there is no doubt we may effect our escape, if we can but pass across the castle green, without being discovered."

"You hear that, my lady?" exclaimed the delighted Edith;—" I knew Adrian would not be long before he found a way to get you out of this difficulty, and you hear how cleverly he has managed it already. So, now, lose not a moment of the time that may be so precious to you, but proceed down the staircase I just now pointed out, and your guide will conduct you in safety from the place."

"That is," observed the Lady Alicia, with some doubt,—" if we can pass along, without being seen by any of the numerous persons belonging to the castle."

"There is not much fear of encountering any one, at this late hour of the night," answered Adrian;—" it is much past midnight, and few there are, who have not, long ere this, retired to their beds. The guards, too, are mostly stationed at the different gates, so that there is hardly a chance of encountering any of the difficulties that you seem to dread so much."

"But should we be so unfortunate," cried Alicia, " as to meet any one, I dread to think of the perilous situation it would place you in."

"Your ladyship need be under no fear on that account," replied Adrian, boldly;—" I am armed, as you see, with a dagger, and, believe me, I should not hesitate to draw it, were it found necessary to do so, in your defence."

"You are bold, for so mere a stripling!" cried the Lady Alicia, surprised at the courage displayed by her youthful champion.

" I can be bold," he replied, " when I see a woman become the victim of a man's tyranny. Besides, my lady, I aspire to all the honours of chivalry, and most unworthy should I prove, were I to stand passively by, and suffer you to fall into the hands of your enemies."

"Well," cried Alicia, " I thank you for your zeal, Adrian, and will accept the services you have so generously offered. Lead me where you choose, and I will follow, confident in the protection you have promised"

Edith now provided the unfortunate fugitive with such additional clothing as was required, and then, leading the way, lighted them down the spiral staircase, and conducted them to the door in which led into the gardens. Here she took leave of them, with a thousand good wishes for their safe departure from the castle, and gazing after them as they cautiously directed their way towards the eastern postern, returned once more to her own apartment, happy in the consciousness of having served, to the utmost of her zeal, one whose misfortunes had rendered her so great an object of pity.

We must now follow Alicia and her youthful champion, who, having ascertained that nobody was near, pursued their way in silence, until they reached the castle green. Here, however, they were startled by perceiving a figure, moving at no great distance off, and then pausing suddenly, they hid themselves in the deep shadow of the building that was nearest at hand. Still the figure kept advancing towards them, and as he approached, they recognized, to their unutterable horror, the stern features of Roland. Fortunately, however, he perceived them not in the dark place they had chosen for concealment, and to their great relief he passed on slowly, and with a heavy step, until he became lost behind an angle of the very building, beneath whose friendly shadow, they had found safety.

It was a moment of peril to them both, and most grateful did they feel at thus escaping it ; but Adrian knew there was no time to be lost, as the day would soon break, and whispering to the trembling Alicia to be of good heart, he once more led the way, and, crossing the castle green, at length reached the postern, from whence he expected to leave the place. Nor were his anticipations formed in vain, for, luckily, no one was near to guard it, and, in a few seconds, he, to his inexpressible joy, conducted Alicia beyond the precincts of the castle. But even now, not a single instant was to be lost, and taking his way across the fields that lay beyond, he hoped to find some place, where he might provide her with a temporary shelter.

CHAPTER LXVII.

" Talk not to me of pity, sir,—
He is a Jew, and, therefore, we good Christians
Have no compassion on him."

DON RAYMOND.

IT was on the morning of the Lady Alicia's escape from the castle of Sir Gaston de Neville, that a crowd of idlers and other unworthy persons assembled in a field just at the northern outskirts of London, to consult on certain matters, which, to them, appeared to be of the utmost importance. In fact, a general feeling of dislike towards the Jews, had taken possession of the minds of the multitude, and in the plentitude of their wisdom, it was determined they should adopt measures either for driving them from the kingdom altogether, or, in case of their failing in that, to commence a general massacre upon a harmless and unoffending people. Nor were the poor and ignorant the only persecutors of that unfortunate race, for the rich took care to goad them on, alledging that poverty was produced by them, and that it behoved every man to seek instant retribution by first plundering, and then either murdering or compelling them to take to flight, whichever might seem most for the benefit of themselves. Moved by this tempting proposition, the people began to think they had a right to the spoils they expected to gain, and after a great many meetings had been held upon the subject, it had been agreed to meet in a body at the place and time specified at the beginning of this chapter. It was some time, however, before the business of the day commenced, and, at last, Simon Hyde, the tanner, erected himself aloft upon a stool, and most eloquently addressed himself to the multitude.

" Friends and countrymen," he said, " I think there is not a reasonable person present, who will not agree with me in saying that we are an ill-used and persecuted people. The king expects money and will have it ;—and where, think you, it comes from ?—why, from the pockets of a hard-working people to be sure, and I think I hear all of you exclaim with me; ' The more fools we, then, to put up with it so quietly.' And that we are fools, I think no man will be hardy enough to deny,——"

" To be sure we are !" shouted a dozen or two of voices from the crowd around him.

" Aye,—I knew you would agree with me," continued Simon, with conscious triumph in his greasy countenance ;—" the thing is so plain, that no one here, I should think, can doubt it for a moment. But it is not of the king alone that we have to complain, for the Jews are hoarding up the money that we ought to be earning, and the consequence of this is, that we must starve, whilst there is plenty in the land."

" Shame !—shame !" vociferated the mob.

" Aye," resumed Simon, " it is a shame, but we have it in our power to put an end to it, and if you will only follow me this day, I will put you in a way to get wealth, without having to work for it, and that, I take it, is a secret that every man here will be glad to learn."

" Aye, aye,—proceed, proceed !" shouted the eager crowd.

" Well, then," continued the orator,—" it is pretty well known that the Jews have got nearly all the money in their own hands ;—they are rich while we are poor, and I ask any sensible man among you whether we ought not to make them disgorge their ill-gotten gold, and divide it among ourselves ?"

" Nay, that would be a direct robbery, Master Simon," cried a voice, in the crowd, but he was quickly silenced by groans and shouts much after the manner that such things are done in this more advanced age ;—for mobs, in all ages, have been averse to hearing the truth, when it happens to tell against themselves, and, as a matter of course, the man who had ventured, in the present instance, to doubt the arguments of the speaker, would have been torn to pieces by the crowd, had he not beat a hasty retreat from the place. As it was, however, the people followed, and pelted him with stones, till they grew tired of the fun, and then they returned to hear further what Simon Hyde, the tanner, had to say.

" I am glad," he said, when the crowd had once more gathered round him,—" to perceive that you have the spirits of men in you, and that you are not to be misled by what is said by a simpleton like him that interrupted me. I was telling you, I believe, that the Jews have all the money, and that all we hard-working people have none. That, I believe, is about the plain state of the case, and now I would ask whether we ought to starve, while there's so much gold locked up in the fellows' coffers ?—Why, to be sure we ought not, and if you are all of my way of thinking every man here shall have his pockets crammed full, before we are many hours older."

" Well, then, speak out, and we'll follow you," exclaimed one from the mob ; "tell us what you mean, Simon, and I'll answer for it there aint a man among us that will stand very particular about trifles."

"Well, then, to come at once to the point," continued the orator, "I propose that we go together in a body, and attack the houses of all the Jews, in and about London.—Does that meet the views of every man present?"

"It does;—bravo!—bravo!"

"And after attacking the houses," resumed Simon, "I further propose that we help ourselves to all that we can lay our hands upon.—Is that also agreed upon?"

"To be sure it is!—excellent!—capital!" roared the mob, in perfect extacy at the idea of plunder, and never once thinking of the injustice they were about to commit.

"And having taken from them their ill-gotten gold," continued Simon, "it will be perfectly right and just, that we burn down their houses, and massacre the whole tribe, men, women, and children. There is no one here, I should suppose, who will say there can be any harm in that?"

"None!—none!" roared the multitude, for even the thought of blood was palatable, so long as all that was shed belonged to the persecuted Israelites.

"Then, as you are all agreed upon the subject," exclaimed the principal speaker,—"I suppose you will not refuse to follow me. I will be your leader, and, if I am not mistaken, we shall go to bed richer men than we rose this morning."

"The truth is, Master Simon," said a man, who had hitherto taken but little part in the business, "that we all like your plan well enough, but as there may be some danger in it, perhaps it would be quite as well to be certain whether or not, the soldiers will not be sent out against us. The king is said to favour the Jews, and all that take a share in this business will be likely enough to answer for it in a way they won't like."

"You are a coward, Dickon!" exclaimed the orator who had spoken so much; "you are a coward, I say, and afraid because you take it into your head there's danger. You speak of the king, too, as if we cared a bit about him;—he may be as friendly to the Jews as he likes, but we—the people of England—are powerful in our numbers: and if he offends us, there's his brother, Prince John, and we can put him on the throne whenever we think fit. He is a good fellow, and has no respect for Jews, unless it is, indeed, to wring some of their gold from them whenever he happens to find his own exchequer running low. Why it was but last week that he tortured old Lazarus, the goldsmith, till he almost died; and then the rascal confessed that he had concealed his money under a pavilion in the garden. For once the rascal spoke the truth—the coin was found, but he died within two days afterwards, from the effects of the torture."

"And he was rightly served for his pains," cried one of the crowd, "for he ought to have given up his gold as soon as it was demanded. But these Israelites are obstinate fellows, and think they have a right to be protected the same as we have."

"They shall have fire in their houses and steel in their hearts before this day's sun goes down!" exclaimed Simon, savagely. "I have long wished for an opportunity to wrest their gold from them, and now that we are all of a mind, we'll see if it cannot be done. We'll teach the fellows what it is to save money while we are starving; and as for King Richard, if he takes part against us, we'll—"

"You had better mind what you say about King Richard," exclaimed the plain-spoken man that had ventured to give an opinion before; "he is sudden and terrible in his wrath, and if he should happen to hear what you have said of him, he would order you to be hung up before your own door, as a warning to all other traitors in his dominions."

"Will any body silence that fellow?" cried Simon, who had a marvellous antipathy to all persons who in the slightest degree differed from him; "seize him, some of you, and let him be well ducked in the nearest horse-pond."

This very charitable hint would no doubt have been promptly acted upon, but the man was fully prepared for the worst, and brandishing a dagger over his head, he threatened to make mince-meat of the very first that dared lay a hand on him. Upon this the crowd shrunk back with astonishing alacrity, and he, like a very sensible fellow as he was, took the opportunity of making a hasty retreat before they had time to make a second demonstration of their hostile intentions. As every thing seemed likely to go his own way, the principal actor put it to his auditors whether he was not quite right in his view of the matter; and as the mob were very willing to acknowledge that he was, it was next proposed that they should proceed without delay to put their project against the unfortunate Hebrews into execution. It was further proposed and agreed to that no quarter should be shown the unoffending objects of their wanton attack, but that all should be slaughtered after they had made a full disclosure of where their supposed hoards of wealth were to be found. It was upon the suggestion of Simon Hyde, the tanner, that they were not to be slain until they had confessed where their money was secreted; and this he did, as he took care to explain, not because he would grant them a single hour of life, but that it would save them all a vast deal of trouble in hunting about for the much-coveted gold. At last, all was arranged among them, and Simon, placing himself at their head, marched with his motley troop to that portion of the suburbs where most of the Jews resided. As they proceeded on their way they were joined by a vast number of other idlers, so that, by the time they had reached their place of destination, the mob assumed somewhat of a formidable appearance. On reaching the street, however, another consultation was held, and silence having been proclaimed, Simon Hyde once more addressed himself to his motley crew.

"We are now," he said, "in the very midst of the tents of the children of Israel, and it only remains for us whose house we shall make the first attack upon. For my own part I care very little about the matter, but, since you have left the affair in my hands, I should propose that we begin with Isaac, of Tadcaster."

"Aye, aye," shouted the mob, "let's unkennel the old fox—let's burn him out with fire."

"Stop a moment, my friends, or you will spoil all," exclaimed the leader of the tumult; "Isaac must be summoned before us to give a true account of his wealth, and whereabouts he keeps it. No doubt we can easily frighten him into doing that, and when he has satisfied us so far, I shall leave him in your hands to do as you may think fit."

Hereupon a tremendous battering was commenced against the door of Isaac's house; and in a few moments the old man, supporting upon his arm his young and beauteous daughter, presented himself before the lawless assemblage.

"What is it you want of me?" he demanded; "why is my peaceful home thus attacked by men whose countenances assure me they come on no friendly errand?"

"We come to make you give up your ill-gotten gold," answered Simon, insolently; "so confess, old man, where it is, for you see we are strong in numbers, and it were best not to incense us by obstinately remaining silent."

"Perhaps," exclaimed Isaac, calmly, "you mean to take my life in case I refuse to obey your most unjust demands?"

"Aye," returned Simon, "that we do, to a certainty, old man."

"Your threats do not intimidate me," cried the Israelite, "for I am well stricken in years, and it matters little whether I die now or a few months hence. I would, however, ask one favour of you—my daughter stands before you, pale and trembling at the violence you threaten: spare her, I beseech you, and my life is your's whenever it pleases you to take it."

"He would bargain with us," exclaimed one of the mob, "as if he stood before us on equal terms. Let me cleave him with this battle-axe from skull-cap to brisket, and I'll answer for it his daughter will not be long before she tells us where to find the old man's money."

"Hold your tongue, Peter Sampson, and leave the settling of this point to me. Isaac is in my hands, and I dare say he knows pretty well by this time that I shall not hesitate to slay him unless he discovers his treasure."

"Here," cried the Israelite, pointing to his trembling daughter, who had thrown herself upon his bosom in an agony of terror, "here is the only treasure I possess in the world: harm her not, I beseech you, and an old man's prayers—albeit he is a Jew—shall ascend to heaven in your behalf."

"We want none of your prayers, Isaac," vociferated Simon Hyde;—"gold is all we desire, and if we have it not you die."

"No, no, no!" cried Rebecca, aroused by these words, and throwing herself upon her knees before the leader;—"spare him, I intreat, and if human blood must be spilt on the unholy altar of your avarice, let me be the sacrifice."

"Don't interfere with us, my girl," exclaimed Simon, "because our business happens to lie with your father, and if he don't choose to tell us what we have asked, he knows what he has to expect for it, that's all."

"What is it you would have of me?" asked Isaac, almost bewildered at the scene in which he thus found himself.

"What do we want?" reiterated Simon,—"why, gold, to be sure, and where should we go for it, but to those who have been laying up hoards of it for many a long year. I tell you, we are all half starving men;—our families are perishing for want of food, a famine wastes the land, and we that are needy, think that we have a right to satisfy ourself, as well as those who have riches. We want gold, I tell you, old man, and we will have it, too, or your life will not be safe for another five minutes."

"I have it not," cried the old man;—"I am poor, like yourselves,—very,—very poor!"

"It's a lie!" cried the leader of the mob;—"but it's always the canting, hypocrital cry of the rich whenever they would save their money. You have plenty, and we will not depart until we have received enough to satisfy us."

"In pity spare him!" exclaimed the terrified Hebrew Maiden,—"he is old and infirm, and the terror occasioned by your violence will surely kill him."

"Oh, we'll take care to save him the trouble of dying a natural death," growled Simon;—"we have not come here to be put off with excuses, and if he does not at once tell us where his money is, he shall presently receive the point of this dagger in his heart!"

"For mercy sake, I implore you to hold yet a minute longer!" cried the maddened Rebecca;—"and you, my father," she continued, addressing him earnestly,;—"you have heard the dreadful threats that have been given utterance to; they have said they will murder you, and in pity to your heart-broken child, I implore you to purchase life, even though it be at the expense of all you possess in the world."

"I tell thee, girl, I have no gold," exclaimed the Jew, alarmed lest her words should have convinced the ruffians that he was not so poor as he had represented. "I am needy like themselves, and, therefore, they must go elsewhere for the dross they would wring from me."

"You will not find it so easy to get rid of us, as you expect," cried Simon Hyde. "We are not to be put off in this way, so be quick about making up your mind, for if you are obstinate, we must e'en content ourselves of making you carrion for the crows, and after making that example, we shall see how many more of your tribe will will venture to put us off with the same excuses about their poverty."

"Leave us for a brief time," said Rebecca, imploringly, "and I will do my best to prevail on him; that is," she continued, suddenly checking herself, "if it is indeed in his power to bestow upon you the money you have demanded."

"At any rate," exclaimed Simon, "we have all made up our minds either to have his money, or send him to another world, where all his hoarded wealth will be of no use to him."

"Surely, surely, you would not murder him!"

"Indeed that we will, though, and, that too, before another minute passes over his head, unless he gives up all the money that by usury he has wrung from others."

"Away!" cried the old Israelite, determined to perish rather than yield up his darling treasure; "away! I tell you I have no money, I am poor; a beggar like yourselves."

"Well, then, it's no use wasting any more time with him," exclaimed the man with the battle-axe; "he seems determined to give us all the trouble he can, so here goes to make short work of it, and his blood be upon his own head!"

So saying, he raised the ponderous weapon, and was in the act of cleaving down the old man, when his arm was vigourously seized from behind, and, turning round, he perceived a youth and a lady, the former of whom it was that had so opportunely stepped forward to save the life of the aged Jew.

"What does this mean, sirrah?" cried the man, disappointed of the vengeance he had meditated;—"by the Virgin, you are over bold, young fellow, and I have a mind to serve you in the way I intended to have punished his obstinacy."

"If I had feared you," replied Adrian, for he it was that had thus interfered, "I should not have arrested your arm when you were about to slay a helpless old man. I, therefore, challenge you to throw aside your battle-axe, and if you have courage as well as ferocity to meet me upon more equal terms, I am armed only with a dagger,—do you content yourself with the same weapon,—for I see you have one,—and we will see whether you or I have the best of the conflict."

"Let us slay the insolent stripling!" cried the infuriated mob.

"Stop a moment," exclaimed Simon Hyde, "and let us see whether something cannot be done without shedding the youth's blood. He once saved my life in a street brawl, and I would do him the same service, if he will only take my advice, and leave this place while he can do so with safety."

"I ask for no favour," replied Adrian, haughtily.

"What do you mean to do, then?" asked the tanner.

"Remain where I am, to protect this old man and his daughter," answered the youth;—"aye, you may smile as grimly on me as you please, but stripling as you call me, I will make a hole through some of your jerkins, if an arm is but raised to do harm to either of these Israelites."

"By St. Mark! but you are over bold, young sir."

"And by St. George of England," answered Adrian, "you are all but sorry cowards to fall so lustily in a body upon one old man and a timid girl. Shame on you, I say, and disgrace cling upon your names for ever!"

"Hah!" vociferated Simon Hyde; "are we to be taunted thus by a beardless boy?"

"Down with him!" shouted the enraged mob.

"Nay, do not harm him, I conjure you;" cried the Lady Alicia, interposing to prevent any mischief that she saw would follow;—"and you, Adrian," she continued, addressing herself to the youth; "this rashness will serve no good purpose, and may involve you in the same peril that threatens those you would save from the fury of this lawless assemblage."

"Do you hear her?" exclaimed the man with the battle-axe; "she calls us a lawless assemblage, and shall we not teach her that we must be treated with more respect?"

"Cut down the youth first," cried Simon, "and when he is slain before her eyes, it shall be the privilege of any man that pleases to serve her in the same way."

Acting upon this hint, the ruffian again raised the ponderous axe, and this time Adrian would surely have fallen, had not a voice close by commanded the assassin to hold, and, instantly afterwards, Meg of Finchley threw herself between the page and his assailant. At sight of her the mob instantly shrank back, for she was regarded as a sorceress, and great was the terror inspired by her presence.

"What would you do?" she exclaimed, angrily;—"would you murder the youth, whose only fault is that he has had the boldness to interpose when he saw so many attacking these two poor unoffending creatures?"

"Why do you come between us, Meg?" demanded Simon, who alone

No. 45

was unawed of her ;—" know you not that he has had the hardihood to brave us with his insolence, and shall we not punish him as he deserves ?"

"Not while I am near to prevent it," cried Meg. "There shall be no blood shed this day, unless, indeed, it shall be his who shall dare to disobey my commands !"

"You hear that, comrades ?" exclaimed Simon, addressing himself to the crowd that surrounded him. "She, too, must come to brave us, and we must be fools, indeed, if we suffer a woman to mar our purpose."

"And yet," muttered a fellow near him, "there is not one among us that will dare to disobey her commands."

"Hah !—are all of you turned cowards ?"

"We are not cowards," answered the man, "and yet there is not one among us that would rashly bring upon himself the wrath of old Meg of Finchley."

"And what," exclaimed Simon Hyde, "if I myself strike the blow, and lay yonder stripling dead at my feet ?"

"In that case," replied the other, "you will make enemies of all that are now for you. Meg, they say, has dealings with the power of darkness, and there is no man here that would be rash enough to bring down her anger upon himself when it can be avoided."

"You hear what your comrade says ?" cried Meg, exulting in the influence she possessed ; "you are now powerless, Simon Hyde, and now I would advise you to return home, and attend to your own honest calling, instead of heading a mob, and going about to disturb the king's peace."

"And what," asked Simon, sullenly, "will follow, if I take not the advice you so kindly give ?"

"The gibbet."

"Hah !—does your knowledge in the black art, trust you so much, thou hag ?"

"It does, Simon ; and if you leave not this place quietly, it will not be many hours ere you acknowledge that my skill in foretelling events is not less correct than people give me the credit for."

"But these Jews," returned the fellow, somewhat intimidated by her words ; "are they not plunderers that draw to themselves all the wealth of the land ? Is it not through them that so many of us are starving? And shall we not rise up to put down an enemy of whom we complain ?"

"You complain against the children of Israel most unjustly," replied Meg ;—"they it is that are oppressed by those who falsely call themselves Christians. Grinding and cruel laws have been made against them, and yet they endure all without complaining. Nay, you persecute them without mercy, and because they seek, by the only means left them, to obtain a living for themselves and children, a cry of blood is raised, and they are to be slaughtered like wild beasts !"

"And if I have my will," said Simon, "not one of them within a dozen miles of this place, shall live to see the next setting sun !"

"You will not have your will, then," exclaimed Meg, in a tone of exultation, "for see !—yonder comes a body of the king's Royal Archers, and he who would save his own life, had better make his escape whilst there is yet time."

An instant glance was sufficient to convince the crowd that she had spoken the truth, and away they all scampered, each man caring only for his own safety. Many of them, however, was not fortunate enough to escape, for the soldiers pursued them through the streets, and when the chace was concluded, upwards of a dozen wounded were picked up, and conveyed to their homes ;—an example to all those who might henceforward feel inclined to break the laws by proceeding to open violence. Meg gloried in the turn matters had taken, and looking round her, she saw Adrian and Alicia standing close by, whilst Isaac and his terrified daughter were returning once more to the house. She, however, desired the two first mentioned persons to remain where they were, and then hastening after the others, prevailed upon them to remain, whilst she communicated a method she had thought of by which they might henceforth escape the cruel persecutions they had endured for so long a period. Isaac was at first reluctant, but being prevailed on by the entreaties of his daughter, he, at length, yielded, and Meg of Finchley commenced the generous task she had undertaken.

CHAPTER LXVIII.

"In me you see a wronged and injured man;—
One who has been the very sport of fortune,
And now accursed by all."

THE DISCARDED SON.

"It is not for me," she said, "to give advice to one whose experience in the world is fully as great as my own; but knowing the danger you run from the violence of your enemies, I came to see if I could not prevail on you to abandon your home, and seek, for a time, a more secure refuge, where the hatred of your enemies shall not discover you."

"I understand you," answered the old man;—"you would prevail on me to flee from the villains that haunt and persecute me?"

"I would."

"And yet it cannot be," replied Isaac;—"home is now almost the only solace of my old age, and to leave it would be to break the last link that binds me to life."

"But your daughter," cried Meg, "do you not think of her, and the dangers she is continually exposed to?"

"Ah!" groaned the Israelite, "that thought reminds me of all the miseries I have passed, and those I have yet to encounter. She has been hunted and persecuted like myself, and I fear her cup of sorrow is not yet full."

"Yet you can avoid much," answered the old woman, "by taking her to some place of safety."

"And where," asked the Jew, "am I to find such a place?"

"Beneath my humble roof," answered Meg. "Aye, you look surprised that shelter should be offered by one so poor and needy as myself. Yet I have a heart that can pity the unfortunate, and it will be your own fault if you and Rebecca do not find a home till better times arrive when you may come forth again without fear or danger."

"Do not urge my father upon this subject," cried Rebecca; "that he loves me I have had ample proof, but he also loves the once happy home of his youth, and I would not be the means of tearing him away from it."

"Peace, my beloved one," cried the old man, pressing his lips to her burning forehead; "peace, I say, for, however great the pang may be, it must and shall be made for you. Yes, Meg," he continued, addressing himself to the old woman, "I have conquered my own selfish feelings, and will accept the shelter you have offered us."

"You are ready, then, to follow me on the instant?"

"Not this moment," replied Isaac, with hesitation: "I have affairs to arrange ere I quit my home, and when they are completed, I will follow you."

" Your daughter, then, may go with me?"

" She may ;—that is if she objects not to it."

" Nay, father, I will not leave you," cried Rebecca ; "there is danger threatening you on every hand, and I will remain by your side constant in my love even unto death."

" Pardon me for interrupting you, fair maiden," exclaimed Adrian, advancing towards them at this period of the conversation, "but I have overheard all that has passed, and would add my voice to prevail on you to lose no time in accepting the offer that has been made. Your father will but remain behind a short time, and will then follow to the place where you are about to seek a refuge. Your own safety demands it, and I call upon you to obey the impulse."

" And who art thou?" asked the Jew, gazing with suspicion upon the young man ; " why dost thou plead so earnestly in an affair that concerns thee not?"

" I am a friend," replied Adrian, "and my only motive is to preserve your daughter from the dangers that threaten her."

" If I mistake not," observed Isaac, again eyeing him with a look of doubt,—" thou dost wear the badge of him who is the greatest of our foes."

" I am the page of Sir Gaston de Neville," answered Adrian, somewhat abashed at the suspicion such a circumstance must necessarily throw upon his motives.

" And as such," resumed the Jew, " likely enough to be our enemy; is it not so, young man?"

" Nay, be assured I am thy friend," replied the youth fervently. "I have long seen the cruel persecution with which the knight, my master, has pursued you, and, abhorring as I do his acts, I would fain serve thee all in my power."

" And how am I to know that thou dost indeed execrate the deeds of thy master?" asked Isaac.

" This lady," answered the youth, taking the hand of Alicia, " will vouch the truth of my words."

" Who is she?"

" One who it has long been thought was dead."

" Ha! you speak in riddles, boy!—explain yourself, or I will more than ever doubt your sincerity."

" Since it must be so," answered Adrian, " I will e'en let you into a secret that I would fain have kept.—She who now stands before you is the Lady Alicia, wife of Sir Gaston de Neville."

" Art thou sure," asked Isaac, of Tadcaster, " that this is no fabrication to deceive me?—The Lady Alicia was reported, years ago, to have died; the funeral ceremony was performed, and never, till this moment, have I heard that the story was made up to deceive the public."

" Yet so it was," answered Adrian; " this lady is the person we speak of, and is here to confirm my assertion."

" Do you so, madam?" asked the Jew.

" The page has spoken the truth," answered the Lady Alicia, " and yet, I could have wished he had said nothing about it, as, in spite of the harsh treatment I have received from Sir Gaston, I have no desire to publish his crimes against me. You will, therefore, let this secret remain locked in your own bosom, since, should it come to the king's ears, it may produce consequences to my husband that I would fain avoid."

" You have been kept a prisoner, then?" exclaimed Isaac, in a voice tremulous with emotion.

" Alas! I have."

"And was there no friend to enquire after or seek to obtain your deliver-ance?" enquired the old man.

"Had it been supposed that I was living," replied Alicia, "there are many who would have demanded my restoration to liberty. As it was, however, all supposed I was dead, and I was left to pine in the solitude of my own dungeon."

"And from that time, I suppose," observed the Israelite, "you have been kept a close prisoner?"

"So close," answered the Lady Alicia, "that during many years of the time, I saw no one but the stern gaolers, who were sent to convey my scanty allowance of bread and water. It was hoped, I suppose, that I should soon die under the heavy afflictions I was doomed to bear; but hea-ven was merciful to me, and inspired my heart with a hope that an end would one day or other come to my sufferings. Inspired by the thought, I bore up against all that I was doomed to endure, and at length came the hour for my release from darkness and solitude. A lucky chance gave me the long desired opportunity, and last night I escaped from my dungeon, though by whose means it was effected is at present involved in mystery."

"This young man, then," said Isaac, "had no share in procuring your release from captivity?"

"He had not," replied Alicia, "though he has long sought to do me the service you speak of. He, however, has befriended the poor captive when she thought herself forgotten by all the world besides, for he visited me in my cell, and brought me choice food and wine, when my only allowances was the coarsest bread and water, and that was frequently stagnant and filthy."

"How was it," cried the Jew, "that, having access to your dungeon, he did not apply himself diligently for your release?"

"It would have been a hopeless task," answered Adrian, "and had I been discovered, my own death would have been the consequence of my temerity, and thus the Lady Alicia would have been deprived of the only friend she had in her adversity."

"And whither," asked the Israelite, addressing himself to Alicia, "do you think of finding a hiding place from your husband? He will, no doubt, cause a rigid search to be made after you, and, should your place of retreat be discovered, it is to be feared his vengeance will prompt him to procure your immediate death."

"I know it," replied Alicia; "I am but too well aware of the cruelty I have to expect should I again unhappily fall into his hands, but where to find immediate shelter I know not. In a few days, however, it is my in-tention to enter a convent, there, at least, I shall find peace and quietude; for, harsh and reckless as he is, he would not dare to follow me into a sanctuary belonging to our holy church."

"It seems, then," interposed Meg of Finchley, "that, at present, you have no place wherein to find shelter and repose?"

"Alas! I have not," sighed Alicia.

"In that case," returned the other, "you will perhaps deign to accept the shelter my humble roof might afford you. In a cavern beneath my hovel you may rest secure from danger, for the place is known to no one but myself, and there will I keep constant guard in case Sir Gaston de Neville should chance to trace you to my house."

"I thank you for your generous offer," replied Alicia, "and will accept it with the same sincerity that it is offered. At present, it will not be in my power to make you any recompense, but the time I trust will soon ar-rive when I shall be able to raise you from the humble station you now occupy, to one that has been well earned by your hospitality to an unfortunate outcast."

" It would be in vain to offer me even the slightest return for the trifling benefit I may do you," replied Meg. "The world and I have long been at enmity, and never will I return to it, knowing, as I do, the evil passions that drive its people to the commission of crimes. In the solitude of my own hut I have lived happily enough, and there will I die, neither seeking for the pity of my fellow creatures, nor asking from them even the slightest favour."

" Perhaps you will think better of this ?"

" Never!" exclaimed the old woman; "my resolution is formed, and nothing will ever move me from it. But come," she continued, "it is now time that we set forward, for we have some distance to walk, and she who is to be the companion of your flight, is now ready to depart."

" What companion do you speak of?" enquired Alicia, who, till now, was unconscious of the arrangement that was previously made.; "who is it that is to accompany us?"

" Rebecca, the Hebrew Maiden ——"

" " Ah !" cried the Lady Alicia, with surprise; "she who I have heard has so long been persecuted by Sir Gaston?"

" The same;—you now behold her before you."

Rebecca shrank back as if she expected to meet the reproachful glances of the Lady Alicia, but the other, advancing, took her by the hand and said, kindly :—

" I can judge, maiden, by your looks, that you expect to hear nothing but anger from my lips. Be assured, however, that I have heard of the virtuous scorn with which you have ever treated my husband's reproaches, and that, even long ere I saw you, I wished to see you once, in order that I might assure you of the esteem your noble conduct has excited in my bosom. Already do I love thee as a sister, let us henceforth live as such."

" Can you, then, forgive me, dear lady," cried Rebecca, "the wrongs—though unwillingly—that I have brought upon thee ?"

" There is nought to forgive, girl," answered Alicia; "the fault was none of thine that thy beauty dazzled the eyes of Sir Gaston de Neville, nor can I think, without admiration, of the virtue with which you have held him in awe. Fate has, it seems, decreed that we shall become companions for a short time, and in that period, though we may be doomed to eternal separation, we will form a friendship that shall never perish whilst we live. What say you, old man," she continued, addressing herself to Isaac;— " will you permit your daughter to become the bosom friend of a Christian ?"

" Were all Christians like your ladyship," answered the Israelite, "our tribe would live in peace and happiness. You have honoured us by claiming the friendship of my child, and I feel but too happy in giving my consent to it."

" Come," exclaimed Meg of Finchley, interrupting them, "it is now time that we leave this place. Sir Gaston will, no doubt, send forth his emissaries in search of the Lady Alicia, and should they find her here, she will be borne off in spite of any resistance that might be made."

Thus urged, Isaac bade farewell to his daughter, promising to follow as soon as he could complete his arrangements at home, and immediately afterwards Meg led the way, closely followed by Adrian, who insisted on accompanying the females, lest any interruption should be offered them. It was a long walk for Rebecca and the Lady Alicia, but, encouraged by the page, they proceeded onwards, passing by the small village of Finchley, and pursuing what is now called the North Road, kept the highway, as offering fewer difficulties than they would have encountered had they gone by the nearer path that led across the fields. In this manner, they had accomplished somewhat better than half their journey, when the sharp clattering of a horse galloping before them, was heard, and directly afterwards a traveller was seen rapidly approaching them. Rebecca and Alicia would fain have left the road until the horseman had passed, for they both feared being seen, lest the rider should be one of Sir Gaston's retainers; but Adrian had already satisfied himself on that point, and scarcely had they somewhat recovered from the alarm into which they had been thrown, when a fresh source of terror arose, in consequence of its being discovered that the horseman was no other than Black Ivan, the Outlaw. It was, however, now, too late to seek for safety in flight, for, by this time, the robber chieftain had approached pretty near them, and, suddenly bringing his steed to a halt, he threw himself from the saddle, and advanced to meet them.

"By St. Nicholas, but this is an unexpected pleasure!" he exclaimed, on recognizing the Hebrew Maiden. "I was just despairing of ever seeing my pretty Rebecca again, and lo! she stands before me, like an angel just descended from heaven."

"Let us pass, sirrah!" cried Adrian, fiercely; "these ladies have placed themselves under my care for the present, and terrible though your name is to the multitude, yet am I prepared to defend them, should you offer violence."

"Ho! ho!—well crowed, my young cockerel!" exclaimed Black Ivan, scornfully. "By the mass, thou art a brave youth; though, methinks, somewhat too inexperienced to beard with one so renowned in deeds of arms as Black Ivan."

"Thou mayest vaunt of thy prowess," answered Adrian, boldly, "but meet me with equal weapons, and I will, at least, prove to thee that I am not so despicable an enemy as you may deem me."

"Well, to confess the truth, boy," exclaimed the robber, "I like thy spirit, and should be loth to do thee harm. Therefore, take my advice, and leave these ladies to the care of one who can and will protect them."

"Ivan!" cried Meg of Finchley, "thou hadst better leave us, or worse may come to thee;—hence, I say, ere I make thee tremble for the insolence thou hast offered us."

"Psha!—what can thy threats do?" asked the robber.

"Thou hast already felt my power, and shalt do so again, unless thou leavest us," exclaimed Meg. "Hast thou forgotten the spell I laid on thee once before, and how humbly thou didst come to implore me to remove it?"

"I remember something of the kind," replied Ivan, "and I also recollect what I would have done, had you been obstinate in the matter. I came to thee armed, Meg, and had there been occasion for it, thy heart and my dagger would have made so close an acquaintance, that I should never more have had cause to fear either thee or thy spells."

"A truce to this folly," interposed Adrian; "I have demanded a free passage for myself and these females, and should any further interruption be offered, it will be necessary that I exert force to compel you."

"Upon my word, you speak bravely, sirrah!" exclaimed Ivan, "however, as it is not my intention to converse further with thee, I will now ask the gentle Rebecca, and her lady companion, whether they will not prefer having for a guard one who is able to protect them from all interruption?"

"Let us pass on, I entreat you," cried Rebecca, earnestly. "We are now fleeing from the persecutions of Sir Gaston de Neville, and if one spark of generosity lingers in thy soul, thou wilt not delay us at the risk of being overtaken by our pursuers."

"Why, for that matter," returned Black Ivan, "thou knowest I have as little cause to like the Knight Templar as you have. We are sworn enemies, and should we chance to meet on such an occasion as this, I should exult in the opportunity it gave me of bringing him to a final account."

"Nay," cried Alicia, who had hitherto carefully concealed her face;— do not—do not harm him!"

"Holloa!" exclaimed the robber, "and who, pray, are you, who take so great an interest in the knight we speak of?"

"One," answered the other, "who bitterly regrets the moment that made her acquainted with him."

"Ah! I see how it is," returned Ivan; "you are one of the victims that he has deceived, and now, having found out that no faith is to be placed in his word, you have fled to bury yourself and your woes together, in some convent."

"Sir Gaston has deceived me," replied Alicia, "but not in the manner you appear to suspect. You are, however, right in guessing that I am about to enter a convent, where alone I can find peace, after the stormy years I have passed."

"But, perhaps," observed Ivan, "I may take it into my head to fancy your society in my retreat. We have a sad lack of females there, and Rebecca can tell you that our cavern is not so frightful a place to live in, as some folks may imagine."

"Villain!" exclaimed Adrian, "another proposition like that, and I will at least, do my best to avenge the insult you would pass on two unoffending females."

"Take my advice, and hold thy tongue, sirrah," cried Black Ivan, coolly. "I am but little used to be talked to thus by beardless boys, and, perhaps, I may not much longer be able to restrain my wrath, even though the object of it is scarcely worthy of a thought. And now, ladies," he continued, "I must e'en request that you will permit me to see you on your way."

"It is needless," replied Alicia, "for we are already near the place we are going to, and there is no fear of meeting with worse company than we have fallen into."

"You are pleased to be complimentary, madam."

"The truth, surely, need not offend you," retorted Alicia. "We have said that we require no further protection than that which we now have, and even though you may be a robber, that should needs be sufficient."

"But suppose my object should be plunder?"

"In that case, you would be grievously mistaken, as far as I am concerned," answered Alicia. "The truth is, I have just had the good fortune to escape from the dungeons of Sir Gaston de Neville, and ——"

"Hah!—by heaven, she speaks truth!" exclaimed Black Ivan, for the first time catching a glance of Alicia's countenance, and then suddenly altering his manner, he said, with more gentleness than he had hitherto used :—

"Forgive me, lady, if I have been guilty of unnecessary rudeness towards those whose sex should be their protection. I will, however, now request that which I before demanded—permit me to see you on your way, and I promise, on my word, to leave you whenever you think fit to command me."

"And my female companion," exclaimed Alicia; "will she also be free from your further insolence?"

"If it is your wish, she shall," answered the robber. "I love her, it is true, and have sought in vain to make her mine, but I am content even to resign her for ever, if it is at the command of the Lady Alicia."

"Ah!—you know me, it seems!"

"I do, madam."

"Where have we ever met before?"

"In your husband's castle."

"Indeed!—that must have been many years since, then."

"It was, lady, but I have not forgotten it, and as a proof how much I then esteemed you, I am even now ready to yield up Rebecca at your command."

"I remember not your features," exclaimed the Lady Alicia, after a brief, but keen glance at his countenance.

"That is likely enough, madam," answered Ivan, "seeing that those who have known me since you and I last met, do not recognise in Black Ivan one who they were formerly proud to rank among their most esteemed friends."

"May I not ask the name you were formerly known by?" asked Alicia, with some earnestness.

"At present that must remain a secret," answered Ivan. "That I have disgraced the name I bore, you are, of course, aware, and I would not publish to the world that which might bring shame on those I have loved."

"Then why not denounce at once the dishonourable profession you have adopted, and thus atone by your future life for crimes that have been committed?"

"It is impossible to do so, now," he replied;—"I am an Outlaw; the ban of my country is upon me, and who, think you, would henceforth asso-

No. 46

ciate with him, who has brought upon himself the execration of his fellow men ?"

"At any rate," observed Rebecca, "you might leave England, and in foreign climes obtain a place in society, from which, it appears, you have been driven in your own country."

"There are reasons why I should remain here," he replied. "I have a task of vengeance to fulfil, and until that is accomplished, I stir not from the land of my birth. For years I have watched my opportunity to put my scheme of revenge into execution, yet something or other has always happened to postpone the long wished-for hour of retribution."

"And is the person you so much hate within your reach?" asked Alicia.

"He is; and the only consolation I have yet had, is in the certainty of his being as much detested by all good men as myself."

"Then there let his punishment end," cried Alicia, "for surely he need endure no worse fate than that you speak of."

"Urge me no more on this subject," exclaimed Ivan, impatiently;—"I have already detained you too long, and now, if you will permit me, I will quietly walk my horse, and accompany you to the place where you are about to seek concealment."

"There is hardly any occasion for it," cried Meg of Finchley, "for they are only going to my house, and with the assistance of this young page, I shall require no more of your company."

"That is a plain way of speaking, Meg," laughed the Outlaw, "yet it is my pleasure to do so, and, therefore, it will be in vain for you to offer any further objection."

"You are determined, then, to go with us, whether we like it or not?" cried Adrian, provoked at the obstinacy of Ivan, though not quite so prejudiced against him as he was.

"To be sure, I am, young sir," replied the Outlaw, "that is if you have no particular objection to it?"

"Why, to tell you the truth, I would rather have your room than your company," answered Adrian. "However, as you seem bent upon it, perhaps the better way would be to submit with as good a grace as we can."

"A wise determination, truly," exclaimed Black Ivan; " so now, ladies, if you will accept the humble escort of a man who is not often so highly honoured, he is ready to go with you. Nay, it may be more necessary than you imagine, for there are rough fellows prowling about, and you might receive an insult from them, unless I happened to be present to give them a hint that you are to pass them toll-free."

Saying this, they all proceeded towards the hut of Meg of Finchley, and having, at length, reached the place, Black Ivan took his leave of them, and soon afterwards Adrian also left the ladies he had escorted thither, and returning to the castle of Sir Gaston de Neville, succeeded in avoiding another interview with the Outlaw of Enfield Chase.

CHAPTER LXIX.

" I will ne'er let them rest,—
But hunt them with stern hatred and revenge,
Down e'en unto the grave."
                              THE CALABRIAN LOVERS.

AFTER an unavailing search of some hours, the Knight Templar came to the conclusion that Lady Alicia must have found means to escape from the castle, and trembling at the consequence that might follow the discovery of his cruel conduct towards her, he began to form in his own mind a thousand schemes by which he might avoid the anger of King Richard. At one moment he even proposed to throw himself at the feet of his sovereign, and, after a full confession of his crimes and treason, implore forgiveness for them, under a pledge of thenceforth renouncing the evil practices which had involved him in so much danger. But he was by no means certain that the king would pardon one who had so often, and so greviously offended against the law of his country, and dreading lest his hope might fail him, he, at length, resolved upon leaving the country as soon as possible, and joining the army of the French king, which at that moment was on the eve of marching for Palestine. Still, however, he was determined to satisfy himself as to what had become of Alicia, and suspecting that the page had accompanied her in her flight, he resolved to go down to the house of Isaac of Tadcaster, believing it probable that they might have gone there to seek a temporary refuge. Without saying anything, therefore, even to his most confidential retainers, he left the castle in the morning unattended, and took his way towards the humble dwelling of the Jew. The period of his arrival there, was just after the mob had been dispersed by the timely arrival of the Royal Archers, and wholly ignorant of what had taken place, he knocked at the door of the Hebrew's house, and was almost instantly answered by the old man, who, startled at the sight of so unwelcome a visitor, hastily stepped back, and was about to retreat for security, when the knight in a more supplicatory tone than usual, entreated him to remain, and answer him one or two questions.

"And what," asked the old man, with hesitation, "can Sir Gaston have to ask of the victim of his persecution?"

"But little," answered the knight; "in the first place, I would know if you have seen ought of my young page, Adrian?"

"I have."

"Hah!—and he is now in your house?"

"He is not," replied Isaac;—"he passed by here about an hour since, and went away, I know not whither."

"Was he alone?" demanded Sir Gaston, eagerly.

"I believe so," answered the Jew, with some hesitation;—"but why do you ask me with so much anxiety?"

"Let it suffice," exclaimed De Neville, "that I have too much reason for putting the question to you. A female has also left the castle secretly, and I would obtain some clue by which to trace the fugitives to their place of retreat."

"Perhaps," returned the old man, with emphasis, "they had but too much reason for their fleeing from you."

"I tell you there was none," exclaimed Sir Gaston, scarcely able to restrain his rising anger. "They both left me without cause, and by heaven I will hunt them out, even though I may have to follow them to the uttermost boundaries of the world."

"And yet," returned the Jew, "you come to ask information from one who would rather shield, than say a word that might serve to throw them into the power of the tyrant, Sir Gaston de Neville."

"Dog of a Jew!" exclaimed the knight, wrathfully, "this insolence may cost thee dear.—Confess whither they are gone, or I'll tear the secret from thy heart with mine own hands."

"Your threats will but little avail with one who fears thee not," replied the Israelite, with firmness. "I am an old man, and can defy thee to do thy worst, since at most thou canst rob me but of the few days that remain to me in this world."

" But thou forgettest thy daughter," answered Sir Gaston ;—" she may yet fall in my power, and if she should, thou mayst take my word for it, she shall not escape me quite so easily as she has done before. She shall accompany me to foreign lands, whither I am about to go, and thou will be left to mourn over the fate of her thou dost so much love."

" Happily," replied Isaac, " my daughter is now beyond your reach."

" Thou liest, villain !" exclaimed the knight, vehemently ;—" this is but a subterfuge to cheat me of my prize, and I will search thy house for her, before I quit the place."

" That is a threat more easily uttered than put into execution," replied the old man, calmly ; " every one claims the privilege of excluding from his house those whom he does not approve of, and if ever you succeed in passing this door, it must be over the breathless body of him who now sets you at defiance !"

" Hah !—am I to be taunted thus by a vile Jew ?"

" The vile Jew, as you are pleased to call him, Sir Knight, is not to be intimidated by your threats," exclaimed Isaac. " He knows that he is under the protection of the laws, and that the Christian dares not trample upon a weak, defenceless old man, even though the subject of his wrath happened to possess a different creed."

" Thou art mistaken, sirrah," answered the knight, " for the people are ready to rise and slaughter thy whole tribe, whenever the time shall arrive for doing so."

" I am aware of it," answered Isaac, " for this morning a fierce rabble marched hither, and would have plundered and murdered me. Fortunately, however, some of the guards arrived, and the villains were dispersed, though not before some dozen or so of them were severely wounded."

" I heard not of this before," cried Sir Gaston, thoughtfully ; " but if thou tellest me the truth, it serves the villains right for making an attack upon thine accursed tribe before the proper hour had arrived. But, tell me, —who was it that led the rabble to the attack thou speakest of ?"

" I know him not," answered the old man, " but his followers called him Simon Hyde."

" And he, I suppose, like the rest, fled on the first appearance of danger?"

" He did, but being known, there is good reason to hope that he will yet be taken, and punished for his wanton attack upon those who have never injured him."

" Let them hang him for a base coward, knave as he is !" cried Sir Gaston, passionately.

" There is little doubt," observed the Jew, " but they will do so if he gives them the opportunity. He has caused the blood of his fellow-creatures to be spilt, and richly will he merit his fate for making so wanton an attack upon people that never harmed him by thought or deed."

" Dost thou call it nothing, then, to extort from us our gold, and to hoard it up when so many are starving for the want of it ?" demanded Sir Gaston. " Thy tribe has been the curse of the land, and never ought the people to rest satisfied until every Jew in England has been sacrificed."

" Fortunately for us, though," answered Isaac, " it so happens that King Richard is not inclined to favour one class of his subjects at the expense of another."

" For which," muttered the knight, " he may, perhaps, ere long, lose his crown."

" If I mistake not," observed Isaac, who had overheard this remark, ' you are one of those who would gladly assist in the deposing of one monarch for the sake of raising up another whose hatred to our tribe is but too well known. Prince John is the idol to whom you bow the knee ; but, be assured, Sir Knight, there are few besides thyself that will trust the destiny of this nation to the guidance of one who scruples not to break his promises whenever it may suit his purpose to do so."

"I came not here to bandy words with thee, old man," exclaimed Sir Gaston, impatiently; "my object is to seek after the runaways, and since there is good reason to believe—in spite of thy denying it—that they are concealed in thy house, I will not leave till I have thoroughly searched thy place."

"I have told you, Sir Gaston, they are not here."

"And I have said that I do not believe you," answered the knight; "I have ever found thee most forward in opposing my will, and this time, at least, I will prove to thee that I am not always to be thwarted as I have been. So, stand aside, old man, and suffer me to pass quietly into thy house."

"I have already told you," replied Isaac, "that you enter not with my free permission."

"Slave!" vociferated the other, "thine obstinacy will drive me to extremity."

"Aye, you may murder me, perhaps, but the fear of death shall not make me yield to your threats."

"I see how it is," exclaimed the knight, "thine intended son-in-law, Reuben Grenard, is in the house, and thou dost expect that his assistance will prevent the accomplishment of my purpose."

"Unfortunately, Reuben is not here, or the rabble that did lately make so wanton an attack upon me would have fared, most likely, worse even than they did."

"He, perhaps, acted wisely in keeping out of the way, when there was so much danger to him if he remained here."

"Reuben is no coward", answered the Jew; "he has, ere now, proved himself a match for his enemies, and will do so again should there be occasion for it. In truth, Sir Gaston, he is at present out on my business, but I expect him back every minute, and I would not have him meet you so near my house, lest, guessing your errand, he should teach you that even an oppressed Jew can rise against his enemies whenever there is a necessity to do so."

"Dog! I have endured thine insolence long enough," exclaimed the enraged knight; "stand aside, I say; for, if thou dost insist on opposing my entrance, I will grasp thee by the throat, and never quit my hold until thou hast paid the penalty of thy presumption with death."

"'Tis a vain boast, Sir Gaston," answered the old man, unmoved by the fury of his antagonist; "thou knowest that I am equally under the protection of the laws with thyself, and that my death would not pass unrevenged."

"Thus, then, do I defy thee, Jew," exclaimed the knight, rushing furiously upon his antagonist;—but Isaac was prepared for any sudden emergency, and slipping on one side, Sir Gaston missed his aim, and had nearly fallen to the ground. He, however, quickly recovered himself, and darting once more upon the object of his fierce wrath, he seized him by the throat, and would have strangled him, had not Reuben Grenard at that moment arrived, who, seeing the danger of his friend, threw himself upon Sir Gaston, and by main strength tore him from his victim.

"Murderer!" he exclaimed, hoarsely, "wouldst thou lay thine hands upon one whose age should have been his protection?"

"Villain!" cried Sir Gaston, almost choking with rage, "thy presumption shall meet its just reward. Thou hast foiled me for a moment, but beware of me, I say, for my rage is as remorseless as the sweeping tempest, which spares nought that comes within its reach."

"Nay, harm him not, I do beseech thee," cried Isaac, throwing himself between; "he did but interpose to save my life, and, therefore, I implore thee to offer him no further violence."

"Sir Gaston," exclaimed the youth, boldly, "will find that he has an enemy to deal with who fears him not. Too long already has he persecuted and trampled upon us, but it is now time that we rouse ourselves, and oppose, with all our power, the tyranny that would grind us into the very dust."

"And what, I prithee, can'st thou do?" asked the knight, scornfully.

"Resist force with force," answered Reuben. "Are not Jews men, like those that would play the tyrant over them,—and what should hinder them from taking up arms in defence of their lives and liberties?"

"By St. George of England, thou art over bold," exclaimed Sir Gaston, with a sneer of contempt; "it is something new for one of thy tribe to talk thus insolently to his master."

"Master!" cried Reuben, with scorn.

"Aye—does not the word please thee?"

"So little," replied the young man, "that had I but weapons equal to those thou dost carry, I would soon prove to thee that we are not yet so subdued as thou dost imagine."

"Truly, most gallant Jew, thou art a very champion amongst thy fallen race."

"Were but a few others inclined to follow my example," answered the young man, "thou shouldst not have it much longer in thy power to call us a fallen people. We have endured oppression too long, it is true, but even now it is not too late for us to shake off the fetters that have been placed upon us; and, perhaps, ere very long, we may prove to thee that we are not the abject slaves thou wouldst make us."

"Enough of this," exclaimed the knight, impatiently; "I came hither in search of two persons who have secretly left my castle; and had not this insolent old man opposed my wish to enter his house, he would not have had to complain of any violence on my part. Perhaps, however, you may be able to convince him of the folly of resisting me, in which case I will become thy friend rather than thine enemy."

"I ask not for thy friendship, Sir Knight," answered the youth, "nor would I purchase it at the price of giving up to thee those who have been so fortunate as to escape from thee."

"Thou dost acknowledge, then, that they are concealed in the house of this old man."

"I acknowledge nothing of the sort," answered Reuben, "for the truth is, I know nothing of the affair to which you allude. I have been from home some hours, and only hurried back on hearing a rumour that my master's house had been attacked by the rabble, and his life placed in jeopardy by the violence of his assailants. Fortunately, I arrived just in time to prevent an old man from becoming the victim of your rashness and intemperance."

"Say rather unfortunately," replied Sir Gaston, "since thine own life may be the sacrifice of thine interference."

"And cheerfully shall that sacrifice be made, if it should but prove the means of saving him from thy fury," answered Reuben. "I see, Sir Gaston, that my words are not palatable to thee—they smack somewhat too much of boldness to please thee; and knowing thy fierce nature as I do, it will be my care henceforth to be ever on my guard against thee."

"Thou shalt not escape me, though," exclaimed Sir Gaston, "for yonder comes a constable and his men, and thou shalt be dragged before the Lord Justiciary, who will teach thee better manners in future, by ordering thee to endure a little wholesome confinement."

And as he spoke, Master Snout and about a score of his followers approached the spot where they were standing.

"Sir Gaston," exclaimed the officer of law, "I have ventured to approach your illustrious presence, thinking my assistance might be necessary. These Jews begin to grow rebellious because the king has shown them some little favour; but if it is your will, I——"

"Your arrival was most opportune," interrupted the [knight; "I was myself about to chastise them in a way that they richly deserve; but, perhaps, it will be better that you take them into your custody, and convey them before Ralph de Glanville, the king's Chief Justiciary."

"Would you take both of us?" demanded Reuben, with an expression of surprise.

"You have heard my commands, sirrah," exclaimed Sir Gaston, addressing himself to the constable, and without appearing to take any notice of the young man. "I give them both into your charge, and see, therefore, that you execute your task diligently, or dread the punishment that will follow any act of favour that you may be weak enough to show towards your prisoners."

Reuben was about to resist the men who now stepped forward to lay hold of him, but Isaac at once readily submitted himself, and earnestly besought his younger companion to do the same.

"It is in vain," he said, "to offer resistance where numbers are so much against us. These men do but their duty in obeying the orders of the Knight Templar, and therefore, Reuben, I do conjure you to submit yourself quietly."

"What!" cried Reuben, "shall we tamely submit to this wrong because it is the will of our enemy to trample on us?"

"It would be in vain to contend against them," answered the elder Jew; "besides, Rebecca is now safe from her persecutor, and that being the case, I fear nothing that the tyranny of this haughty knight can inflict upon us. Submit then, boy, and I will answer for it that no harm befals us."

Reuben, though not altogether convinced, obeyed the suggestion of the old man; and when this was done, Sir Gaston, accompanied by three or four of the constables, entered the house for the purpose of searching it. In about a quarter of an hour he returned, more furious and disappointed than ever, whilst two of the men dragged between them poor Jonah, who was loudly complaining of the rough and unjust treatment he had been subjected to.

"Here's a pretty pass things have come to," he exclaimed, addressing himself to his master. "These fellows, not content with searching the house from top to bottom, must needs make me their prisoner, because they happened to find me in the place. But I'll not put up with it quietly, I can tell them; for I'll go and lay my complaint before the king, and I know he'll——"

"Peace, good Jonah, I command you," interrupted the old man; "thou see'st that I submit myself patiently, and, be assured, I should not do so, unless I felt satisfied that we shall find more justice from our judges, than from our accusers."

"Carry them, instantly, before the Justiciary," exclaimed Sir Gaston;—"lose not a moment, and I will, myself, follow you there immediately."

Saying this, he turned away, and immediately afterwards the prisoners were led away, and conducted to the court where Ralph de Glanville was sitting with the other officers of the crown. The chief Justiciary was busily engaged at the moment; but when the prisoners had been placed before him, he inquired of the constable the nature of the crime with which they were charged.

" May it please you, my lord," answered Snout, " they were given into my custody by Sir Gaston de Neville, on a charge of violently assaulting and threatening his life."

" Is he here to give testimony against them ?"

" I am, my lord," exclaimed Sir Gaston, who at that moment entered the court.

" I understand," resumed the Justiciary, " that you have a complaint to make against them. You have been assaulted I believe."

" I have, my lord, and come to demand justice at your hands."

" You shall have it ;—was any attempt made against your life ?"

" The younger one threatened me," answered Sir Gaston ; " and the old man treated me in a manner that no Christian could quietly endure from a Jew."

" The law will protect you, Sir Gaston," observed the Justiciary ;— " but, in the next place, I must know whether any provocation was given to them ?"

" None, whatever."

" What say you to the charge, prisoners ?" demanded the Justiciary.

" My lord," answered Isaac ;—" I deny it all. This knight has most foully wronged me on many occasions ; he has more than once carried off my daughter, and this morning he came,—I have every reason to believe, —to bear her away again. I refused to admit him into my house, when, springing upon my throat, he would have strangled me, had it not been for the timely arrival of this youth, who tore me from his deadly clutches."

" Is it true," asked the Justiciary, " that you sought to obtain an entrance to this Jew's house by violent means ?"

" I do not deny it," answered Sir Gaston,—" but I can show good reason for what I have done. This old man's daughter was found in possession of a valuable diamond, that was stolen from me ;—that she, herself, was the robber, I have every reason to believe, and yet the jewel is withheld from me, even though I have proved it to be my own pro- perty."

" If I remember rightly," observed the Justiciary, " the maiden you charged with the robbery, has submitted to trial by ordeal."

" She has, my lord."

" And was acquitted, in consequence of passing through it unscathed?"

" Aye,—but it was done by means of jugglery."

" Have you any proof that it was as you say ?"

" At present, I have not," replied Sir Gaston, " but if you will commit those three men to prison, I will undertake to find the girl within a week, and, in your presence, I will prove that she passed through the ordeal, by means of a trick imposed upon us."

" You hear that, old man," exclaimed the Chief Justiciary, addressing himself to Isaac of Tadcaster ;—" this knight undertakes to prove thy daughter guilty of the crime he charged against her ; art thou content to remain in goal till we can find the girl, who, it appears, has fled, to avoid a more rigorous examination ?"

" She has not fled, my lord," answered Isaac ; " I, myself, sent her away, knowing, but too well, the persecutions she would have to endure from Sir Gaston de Neville."

" Wilt thou produce her before us, in order that we may still further in- vestigate a charge that so nearly touches her character ?"

"Upon one condition, my lord, I will."

"This is most insolent!" exclaimed Sir Gaston;—"you hear, my Lord Justiciary;—the Jew would impose conditions on you!"

"I will hear him, Sir Gaston," said the judge, "and if he offers me good reasons, I may, perhaps, yield to him on this point. Now, Isaac of Tadcaster, name the condition you spoke of."

"It is merely that she shall have your protection against this man," replied the Israelite. "I know his artifices but too well, and this is only a device by which he hopes to draw her from the place where I have sent her for concealment."

"If that is the case, you shall have the protection you ask," replied the Chief Justiciary. "The girl shall be safe, but, remember, she must be brought into this court within a week, to answer whatever further charges this knight has to bring against her."

"With your leave, my lord," exclaimed King Richard, who at that moment presented himself at a door near the judgment seat, "I must put in my protest in this matter. I have heard from the adjoining apartment all that has passed, and prizing justice, as I do, beyond all else beside, I must declare against exposing this maiden to the evil practices of one who, I know, seeks her destruction. Nay, Sir Gaston de Neville, do not chafe and frown thus, I beseech you, for, by good fortune, I chance to know the unworthy motives that impel you to this course, and it is, therefore, my duty, as the people's guardian, to protect the weak against the artifices of the powerful."

"Your majesty wrongs me," cried Sir Gaston, biting his lips with vexation till the blood started from them.

No. 47

" I would be gladly convinced that I do so," answered the king; " but it unfortunately happens that I am but too well convinced of your perfidy towards those who are helpless."

" My liege!" exclaimed the knight, " those are strong words to use against one, who has never failed, when his duty to his king and country demanded his services."

" I know we owe thee something on that score," answered the monarch, —" but it follows not that you are to harass and oppress those who cannot protect themselves. You have long pursued and persecuted the Hebrew Maiden, and it is now time that something is done for her protection."

" Am I not also to be protected?" asked the knight, sullenly.

" Aye,—if you stand in need of it."

" I do, then, my liege," replied Sir Gaston;—" the girl in whose welfare you take so great an interest, has been charged with being in possession of a diamond that I have clearly proved belongs to me. I have charged her with being a party in the robbery, yet, by a mere piece of jugglery, she is suffered to escape without punishment."

" Dost thou call trial by ordeal, jugglery, Sir Knight?" exclaimed the king, indignantly. " Did she not submit herself by that most awful test, and has she not proved her innocence to the satisfaction of every one that was present on the occasion?"

" I, at least, am not satisfied with it," replied Sir Gaston; " she cheated us with some trick, and yet, because she happened to escape unharmed, her innocence is to be declared, in defiance of the oath I took, when first she was charged with the crime."

" And you," exclaimed the king, " would ruthlessly persist in hunting her to destruction?"

" I do but seek justice, my liege; and that, it appears, is to be denied me."

" How! are we to be insulted by a subject?"

" That *subject*," replied Sir Gaston, bitterly, " conceives that he has been wronged. I speak plainly, your majesty,—but when kings act with partiality, they must learn to submit to hear the truth, even though it comes from the lips of an inferior."

" Sir Gaston de Neville," interposed the Chief Justiciary, " this is not language that I may sit by and listen to quietly;—another such expression as that, and it will be my duty to send you into confinement."

" Nay, my lord, let him speak out as boldly as he pleases," exclaimed the king. " He has been defeated, when most he expected to come off victorious, and I can readily pardon words that have been provoked, at finding himself unable to hurl his vengeance upon those, who he thought might be so easily subdued."

" I know not," muttered the knight, " why your majesty takes so decided a part against me."

" Then I will tell thee," answered the king;—" it is because I am resolved to do my duty fairly between all classes of my subjects. Jews, as well as Christians, demand my care, and they shall have it, whenever I see a determination to hunt them down by means of tyranny. These people have been harassed and oppressed too long, and it is now time that I interpose my authority to prevent them becoming the prey of designing men."

" My liege ——"

" I will hear no more, Sir Gaston," interrupted the king;—" your complaint has not been proved, and these prisoners are discharged."

" Then will I seek elsewhere for justice!" muttered Sir Gaston de Neville, and turning abruptly away, he left the court, vowing vengeance against the king, and resolving to seek an interview with Prince John, who, he was aware, would be ready enough to enter into his views, whenever the time should arrive, for making an attempt to dethrone the present sovereign.

Isaac, and the two other prisoners, were now dismissed ; and, as he left the royal presence, Richard bade the old man be of good heart, and to rely upon him for that protection, which, as a subject, he had a right to claim.

CHAPTER LXX.

" See !—treachery is at work !—
The foul conspirators do meet alone
To ripen well their plots."

RINALDO.

BURNING with rage and disappointment, Sir Gaston de Neville hurried away from the court of justice, and proceeding immediately towards the residence of Prince John, he pondered deeply on the vengeance he had designed. He felt that he had been dishonoured, by the frequent reproofs he had received from the king, and becoming reckless of the consequences that might follow, he resolved to hazard any danger, rather than endure the consciousness of shame such as he now felt. From Prince John he was certain of receiving an ample reward for any aid he might give in placing him upon the throne, which was, at present, occupied by his brother, and as he would thus bring about the retaliation he so ardently desired, he would be serving two purposes, both of which he had long hoped to accomplish. Full of these thoughts he approached the palace of the prince, and as he was known to be one of the most esteemed amongst the friends of John, he was speedily admitted, and conducted to the apartment of the ambitious brother of his sovereign. At the moment of his arrival, the prince was busily engaged with several others of his adherents, but upon a hint being given that he wished to have a private audience, the others were ordered to withdraw, and he found himself alone with the person he had been so anxious to see. John received him with a hearty welcome, and being by this time quite alone, he, at once, eagerly demanded what had brought him so unexpectedly into his presence.

" Most gracious prince," answered the knight, " I came to learn when it will be your pleasure that we proceed with the plot that is in agitation, for placing the supreme power in your hands. The people are growing weary of your brother's rule, brief as it has been, and I have every reason to believe, that they wait only for the example we may set them to declare in your favour, and raise you to that eminence, your virtues so justly merit."

" Thou art a flatterer, Sir Knight," exclaimed the prince, smiling blandly upon his adherent ;—" and yet I know thine attachment, and the confidence I may place in thy great zeal for him, who only waits for an opportunity to reward thee, as thy services in his behalf may merit."

" Art thou ready to test my zeal, without wasting further time ?" asked Sir Gaston de Neville.

" I am," replied the prince ; " and if I have delayed acting upon the advice of my friends, it has been because I would not plunge them in the ruin that would follow the defeat of their plans in my behalf. It was on this consideration alone, that I have hesitated so long, but the moment I am convinced that all is prepared, I will place myself at the head of my followers, and endeavour to seize for myself the crown of my ancestors."

"The time is come, my prince," exclaimed Sir Gaston;—"the people are enraged at the favour that has been shown the Jews."

"But my brother has many friends, who will stand by him to the last," replied John;—"his gallantry in the field, has obtained for himself the love of all, who admire bravery in a leader, and among those we shall meet with opponents, more difficult to overcome, then you seem to expect."

"Many of them are dissatisfied with him on other points, though," observed the knight,—"and will declare for you, the moment a decisive step is taken;—they are men who have the good of their country at heart, and will not fail to join your standard, the moment it is unfurled."

"Have you spoken to any of them on the subject?"

"I have."

"And how many do you believe we may count upon?"

"More than half the nobility and chief men of the kingdom," replied Sir Gaston. "Their example will be promptly followed by the common people, and then our cause will be safe."

"How know you that?" asked the prince.

"From circumstances that are not to be mistaken," replied Sir Gaston —"I have, myself, taken the pains to sound the common people upon the subject, and the result has been most satisfactory. Their hatred to the Jews increases every hour, and it was only this morning that an attack was made upon them, which was, however, frustrated by the arrival of a body of the Royal Archers."

"The mob fled, then?"

"They did."

"In that case," exclaimed the prince, "I fear very little dependance is to be placed in them. By your own acknowledgment the people assembled together for a certain purpose, and yet no sooner do they see the first approach of danger, than they flee, like so many cowards as they are."

"Had there been any one to lead them," answered Sir Gaston, "the affair would have terminated differently. As it was, there was no one to set them an example, and fearing the armed men who made their appearance, their first thought was to seek for safety in flight; and dearly were they made to pay for their cowardice, for an immediate pursuit was commenced, and it is said many of the people were severely wounded by the soldiers of the king."

"Which will, of course, exasperate the common horde more than ever against their present ruler," exclaimed Prince John. "So far, we shall have benefited by what has taken place, though, I am still of opinion that it will be prudent to wait till we have seen on what we have to rely."

"King Richard already suspects our motives," observed Sir Gaston;— "and I fear delay will only give him time to be fully prepared for resisting us successfully."

"Has he an idea that you are favourable to me?"

"He has directly charged me with it."

" How is it, then, that he has not, ere this, taken measures for preventing the mischief he expects from you ?"

" I know not," answered Sir Gaston de Neville, " but I suppose he fears that any act of violence offered to me, will be resented by the populace, and thus hurry on the ruin he is so anxious to avoid. He, however, tells me he is only merciful in this matter, in consideration of the many services I have done my country, though I can scarce believe he would hesitate on that account."

" My brother is playing a deep game here, I see," exclaimed the prince; " he will suffer you to remain at liberty, but keeps a strict watch over your actions, so as to pounce upon you at the very moment when your projects seem ripe for fulfilment."

" And should he do so," cried Sir Gaston, " the consequences to himself will be more serious than he expects. The people will see that he persecutes a Christian knight, at the very moment when he is protecting the Jews ; and, when they become aware of that fact, their rage will know no bounds."

" Let it be understood, however," exclaimed the prince, " that my royal brother's life must not be sacrificed to the vindictive wrath of his enemies. It may chance that I come to the throne by the conspiracy, but if I do, and Richard should meet with violence, the first act of my reign shall be to punish those who are guilty of raising their hands against his life."

" And yet," exclaimed Sir Gaston, " whilst he lives, you will be in constant danger of falling by the same means that may cost him his royal crown. Friends will yet remain faithful to him, and no opportunity will be lost to restore him to his throne."

" I will consent that he is imprisoned for the remainder of his life," replied Prince John, " but that is the extent of what I will do for my own safety. Shut up from his few faithful adherents, they will soon cease to remember him, and in a short time my subjects will learn to pay me the same cheerful obedience that they have hitherto given him. Besides, I will begin my reign by a few acts, that will be sure to gain me the favour of the populace ;—the Jews shall be utterly exterminated, and if any chance to escape the fury of the multitude, their lives shall only be purchased on condition that they leave my dominions for ever. This will please the people, and secure their love for me."

" It will do much," answered Sir Gaston ;—" and I will take care that Isaac of Tadcaster shall be one of the very first victims, after which it will be no difficult task to make his haughty daughter submit to my terms."

" I have heard of your extraordinary passion for the girl," exclaimed Prince John, " but never has it been explained to me how you came to fall so desperately in love with one who belongs to a tribe you so vehemently hate."

" The current that is opposed, runs strongest," answered Sir Gaston ; " I have been foiled in my designs upon the wench, and though I cannot say that I love her, as I once did, yet there is such a thing as revenge for injuries received, and never will I cease from my endeavours, until I have brought ruin, not only upon Rebecca, but upon all those who belong to her hated tribe."

" Is this," asked Prince John, " the only motive you have for seeking the destruction of the Jews of England ?"

" It is not the only one," answered the knight ;—" it chanced that some time ago, I was robbed by Black Ivan, the Outlaw, of a valuable diamond; the jewel was shortly afterwards found in the possession of Isaac's daughter, and yet the king, your brother, refuses to bring the guilty parties to a well merited punishment."

"I remember something of this," exclaimed Prince John;—"I was hunting in Sherwood Forest at the time; but, if I was not misinformed, some notice was taken of your complaint, since I heard that the maiden was obliged to submit to the ordeal, through which she passed unscathed."

"It was a mere mockery of justice, your highness," answered Sir Gaston de Neville;—"the girl was certainly compelled to submit herself to the ordeal of boiling oil;—but she used charms and conjurations, and thereby escaped the doom that ought to have been her's."

"Have you any proof that she was aided by the powers of darkness?" asked the prince.

"Not at present," replied Sir Gaston, "though I hope soon to have all that may be required. One thing, however, is known—she had a secret interview with Meg of Finchley, a reputed sorceress, and there is every reason to suspect that it was through her means she passed so triumphantly through the ordeal."

"Has the hag been questioned on the subject?" inquired the prince.

"Not at present," replied Sir Gaston;—"I have frequently demanded that she should be seized and brought before the Justiciary;—but my request has been unheeded, and my enemies exult in their evil practices, whilst I am compelled to endure their insults that are daily offered me."

"You shall have justice, Sir Knight," exclaimed Prince John, after a pause, during which he paced anxiously up and down the apartment. "I will, myself, give orders for this Meg of Finchley to be taken into custody, and that you may be assured of having ample satisfaction, she shall be brought before me, and if I find her guilty on such evidence as you are able to bring forward, I will send her to the stake, where many a better woman has suffered before her."

"Your highness, I see, can feel for the wrongs I have been forced to bear," exclaimed the Knight Templar. "From you, I know, I can expect justice, and, therefore, have I thrown myself upon your protection rather than any longer serve a king who can see me wronged, whilst he shields those who are my enemies."

"Be it your task, then, to secure this hag," cried Prince John;— "let her be seized, and brought before me, and I will undertake to promise that you shall no longer have to complain of the wrongs you have spoken of."

"When will it be your highness's pleasure that I bring her here?"

"This very day, if it is in your power to lay hands upon her," replied Prince John. "Justice should not be delayed, even for a single instant, when it is in our power to [prevent it, and you have already endured too much from those who ought to have aided you."

"I will instantly despatch a party of my men to seize upon her," exclaimed Sir Gaston, overjoyed at the prospect of at length accomplishing his cruel scheme of revenge. "I know the lonely hut she dwells in, and will, perhaps, accompany my retainers, in order that no chance shall be given her to escape."

"Away, then," exclaimed the prince, "and when you have secured the witch, bring her without loss of time before me, and I will prove that I am not slow in fulfilling the promise I have made."

"Ere I go," cried Sir Gaston, "I would learn from your highness whether it is your pleasure to command that instant measures be taken for dethroning your brother? All is now in readiness, and I would humbly suggest that no delay should take place in a matter that requires the utmost promptitude."

"I promise that none shall take place, Sir Gaston," answered the prince; "I am anxious to fulfil the wishes of the people, and will immediately make preparations for carrying their designs into execution. It appears, however, that the king is suspicious of the plot that is in progress against him; and it will, therefore, be necessary to observe the greatest caution, lest we should be foiled at the very moment when everything seems most favourable to our views. A few days may remove some obstacles that I see in our way, and when that is done you shall find me as ready to aid in the design you have formed as your heart can desire."

"I am afraid the few days delay you speak of will ruin us," cried Sir Gaston; "in that time the king may gain more direct evidence of what is going forward among us; and in that case it is not difficult to foresee what will be the result to ourselves. A death of shame and ignominy would be the reward of those who have put themselves forward in this business, and your highness would be placed in confinement, most likely for the remainder of your life."

"That, Sir Gaston, is taking the most unfavourable view of the matter," answered Prince John. "I, however, have better hopes of success, if we only conduct ourselves with prudence. A few days can make no great difference, and at the end of that time you shall find me at the head of those men who are willing to risk their lives in my behalf."

"Since it is the will of your highness to postpone the affair," said Sir Gaston, "I would propose that we wait till the coronation of the king takes place. A great crowd of people will then be assembled to witness the ceremony, and by placing our own adherents in different parts, we may succeed in inflaming the minds of the multitude, and thus secure an easy victory over those who would oppose us. The king and his friends will thus be taken by surprise, and you may assume the royal command without difficulty."

"Your suggestion pleases me, Sir Knight," exclaimed Prince John; "the time you have mentioned is well chosen, and if we act with caution, there is no doubt we shall succeed to the utmost of our wishes. Thus far I agree with you; but let me again express my determination to punish those who may offer violence against the life of my brother."

"Your highness's wish shall be obeyed," replied Sir Gaston de Neville; "the king's life shall be spared, though I cannot help saying that the mercy which is thus extorted from us may prove the means of involving you in continual danger."

Whilst Sir Gaston was thus speaking, a servant of the king's approached, and throwing himself at the feet of Prince John, handed to him a paper, which was eagerly snatched from him, and hastily perused. The knight watched over the changing countenance of the prince, as his eyes glanced over the contents, and he could see that what he read filled him with rage that was almost uncontrollable. At length the prince rose abruptly from his seat, and commanding the bearer of the message to depart, said, when they were once more alone,—

"Sir Gaston de Neville, there has been some villany at work here! The king, it seems, suspects my loyalty to him, and after expressing his regret at the step he has found it necessary to take, commands me to leave London within eight days, and to quit the shores of England ere the expiration of a fortnight."

"Hah!" exclaimed the knight, "this is a bold step, indeed, my prince. Some traitor must have betrayed us, and thus nipped in the bud a scheme that must otherwise have placed your highness upon the throne of these dominions."

"Would that I knew the man to whom we owe this act of perfidy!"

cried the prince, fiercely; "but it is in vain to repine, for the secret is divulged, and no hope remains of carrying our designs into execution."

"Will your highness yield thus easily, because a trifling difficulty is thrown in our way?" demanded the Knight Templar.

"I am not willing to do so, certainly," answered John, after a short pause; "to be thwarted thus is but to make me more resolute than ever—and, could I see any way to accomplish our designs, I would treat the king's commands with contempt, and at once put myself at the head of those disinterested and faithful friends who are resolved to place the sceptre in my hands."

"'Tis well said, your highness," exclaimed Sir Gaston; "resolution can alone save us in this emergency,' and you will find your friends ready to assist in an enterprise upon which their hearts are so ardently fixed. All must now depend upon the vigour manifested by yourself; and, should you command us, we shall be ready at a moment's notice to make one desperate effort to seat you on the throne of England."

"We must first have a meeting amongst my friends," observed the prince, "and if I find them as zealous in the cause as you are, we will lose no further time in asserting my own right to the crown."

"Your friends, whom I found here just now, are waiting in the antechamber," said Sir Gaston. "They are equally as ardent as myself, and, I have no doubt, they will eagerly seize the opportunity they have so long desired."

"Bid them approach me," exclaimed the prince; "say I have business to confer with them about, and would see them instantly, to devise means for accomplishing their wishes in my behalf."

Sir Gaston de Neville was too well pleased at the errand that had been given him, to hesitate for a single moment; and immediately quitting the room, he returned in a few seconds, followed by the Earl of Albermarle, Lord Scroope, the Earl of Chester, Sir Walter Marsham, and Hugh Pudsey, Bishop of Durham. All these were most graciously received by Prince John, who, having expressed his confidence in their zeal, briefly opened the business for which he had summoned them to his presence.

"My lords," he said, " I have just received a communication from the king my brother, commanding me to quit England within a certain period. You well know how little cause he has for his harshness, and, relying upon your oft-expressed sentiments of love and attachment towards me, I now ask whether you are willing to assist me in repelling this most tyrannical decree?"

"I can answer for myself," replied the Earl of Chester, "and I believe your other friends are equally well prepared to act whenever you may please to command them. Said I not the truth, my lords?" he continued, addressing himself to those that surrounded him, "is there, I ask, any one among you who will withhold his support to Prince John now that it is required?"

"We are all ready to prove the zeal we have so often declared in favour of the prince," answered Lord Scroope.

And so said each of the others, except the Bishop of Durham, who, standing apart from the rest, maintained the strictest silence. This was observed by the prince, who, glancing somewhat sternly towards the prelate, said—

"How is this, my Lord Bishop?—I have ranked you amongst the foremost of my faithful adherents; and yet, now, when most your services are required, you stand aloof, and seem to regret the share you have taken in this business between myself and the king."

"As a churchman," replied the bishop, "I am compelled to remain

neuter whilst the struggle is going on. You have, however, my best wishes for your success, and whenever the time arrives that places you upon the throne of England, you will find me one of the first of your subjects to set an example of obedience to the people you will be called upon to govern."

"You are still favourable to the cause, then?" exclaimed the prince, earnestly.

"I am, my liege."

"You hear that, my lords," cried John—"the bishop will aid us by inducing the clergy to acknowledge my sway, and I know not but he may assist us as much, in his more peaceable way, as you will yourselves with the sword."

"At all events, your highness," exclaimed the Bishop of Durham, "you shall have no cause to reproach me with a lack of zeal in any way that I can be most useful. My profession is, however, one of peace, and, therefore, I cannot assist in a way that, under other circumstances, I could have wished."

"We take the will for the deed," answered Prince John;—"and now, my lords, having satisfied ourselves on this point, I would seek your counsel and advice respecting our future plans. I have already told you that the king has commanded me to quit his dominions within a limited time: he would act the tyrant with me, it seems; but, relying as I do upon your promises, I will resist his tyranny, even if, by doing so, I should lose my life."

"How long," asked the Earl of Chester "does he give your highness to quit the kingdom?"

"Fourteen days, my lord."

No. 48

" That is brief time for preparation, indeed," returned the nobleman ;— " his majesty seems to be aware that promptitude will prove his best safe-guard, and it will now be for us to show him that his tyranny is no longer to be borne with patience. I have five hundred followers, upon whose valour I can rely, and I undertake to bring them to your assistance when-ever they may be required."

" And I have an equal number," added Lord Scroope, " than whom a braver body of men do not exist in these dominions."

" I, also," rejoined the Earl of Albermarle, " can bring to your highness a troop of horse and foot, well armed and accoutred, and zealous in the cause of their master. Besides these, I can bring into the field a body of archers, well trained for service, and with such skill in the use of their weapons, that even the royal troops will not be able to stand against them."

" For my own part," added Sir Walter Marsham, " I cannot boast of the numbers that I can bring into the field ; but I have a few brave and faithful followers who will not disgrace their master's name by exhibiting cowardice in the hour of need. These I will lead in person, and when all is over, it shall not be said that Sir Walter Marsham was the least zealous in the cause of his prince."

" I am well pleased to find you all so ardent in my behalf," exclaimed John ; " and though, but a short time since, I felt loath to be precipitate in this affair, I now begin to think the sooner we commence the business the better it will be. Sir Gaston de Neville has also promised me considerable aid in this affair, and from what I already see, there is very little doubt but our efforts will be rewarded with victory."

" When is it the will of your highness that we strike the blow ?" asked the Earl of Albermarle.

" Within a few days, at the farthest," answered the prince. " Sir Gas-ton de Neville has proposed that we take advantage of the crowd that will be assembled to witness the coronation of the king. The opportunity will, doubtless, be a good one, and it, therefore, only remains for your lordships to say whether you agree with the proposition."

" I do, for one," exclaimed Lord Scroope, " for the ceremony is now close at hand, and we shall be able to bring about the overthrow of King Richard ere he can be aware of our intentions so as to frustrate them."

" Is it agreed, then, that we are to get everything in readiness by the day that has been mentioned ?" asked Sir Gaston de Neville.

" It is," answered all with one voice.

" And how," asked the prince, " shall I assure myself of [your faithful-ness and fidelity ?"

" We will bind ourselves by an oath," replied Sir Gaston ; " my lords," he, continued, addressing himself to those that stood around him, " you have heard his highness ;—he requires a test of our honour ;—is there any one here who will refuse so reasonable a request ?"

" We are willing to bind ourselves in any way that may appear necessary to the prince," replied the Earl of Albermarle ;—" we will take the oath, though I must needs say it is scarcely necessary, since we are all engaged in a cause that renders fidelity to each other imperative."

" At all events it will be more satisfactory to his highness," exclaimed Sir Gaston de Neville, " and, therefore, I, for one, am willing to pledge myself. My lords, let us lay our swords across that of the prince, and call heaven to witness the sincerity with which we have leagued ourselves with him."

These words were no sooner uttered, than each blade was bared, and the oath of fidelity to the prince was taken by every one present,—except the Bishop of Durham,—in the manner prescribed by the Knight Templar. The churchman was, of course, excused the performance of this military ceremony, but when the weapons were once more returned to their scabbards, he stepped forward, and addressing himself to the chief personage in the chamber, said :—

"My prince, you will, I am sure, pardon my apparent want of ardour in your cause ; but as a son of the church, it is my duty rather to maintain peace, than, by my example, to provoke war. That I will be faithful, however, I give you my honour, and the sacred calling I profess, will, perhaps, be the surest test that I am to be relied on. In the hour of peril I will be by your side ;—not, it must be admitted, with the sword, but with such advice as my experience in the world has given me ;—then, should success attend you, I may be of some use in aiding with my counsel in settling the affairs of the kingdom, so as to render the future government not only easy to yourself, but henceforth to the people."

"My lord bishop," answered the prince, " I am well pleased to hear you speak thus, your influence, well exercised, will do much towards establishing the peace of the country on a sure foundation, and, therefore, do I accept your pledge with the same sincerity that it is offered. And now, my lord," he continued, " we are so far agreed upon this matter, that the attempt to change the government is to be made on the day of my brother's coronation, I, myself, most heartily concur in the proposition, though, I fear, much blood will be spilt ere the king's friends will yield themselves to our force."

"They will find that we are no carpet knights," exclaimed Lord Scroope, " and having once drawn our swords for the purpose of dethroning the king, we will not sheath them again until our object has been fully obtained. Richard has too long insulted us by favouring the Jews at the expense of his Christian subjects, and we will now show him that we are no longer to be trampled on."

"And yet, my lord," cried Prince John, " it must not be forgotten that Richard,—whatever may be his faults, is my brother ; for my own part, I never can cease to remember that he is so, and, therefore, it is my imperative command that no violence be offered against his life. He may be taken prisoner, but when he is properly secured, my enmity against him will then cease for ever."

"Then will our labour be thrown away," observed the Earl of Albermarle, " for no prison will be strong enough to hold him, and should he escape, the fate of all those who have assisted your highness against him, will be sealed in blood. Nay, your own life will be sacrificed in his burning thirst for vengeance !"

"It may be so, my lord," replied John, coldly ;—" yet you have heard my commands upon the subject, and I warn none of you to act against them. Some of you, I see, look dark and frowningly upon me ; but I quail not at your anger, for rather would I hear you renounce my service for ever, than accept of a throne to which I had waded through the blood of my own brother !"

"Let it be as you please," answered Sir Gaston de Neville ;—" we are willing to abide by your commands, and will do so even though it may bring our lives into jeopardy. Your friends are faithful, my prince, though, perhaps, they feel some disappointment at the resolution you have just expressed."

"You have heard Sir Gaston de Neville ?" exclaimed the prince, addressing himself to the barons ;—" he says you are still faithful to my cause ; may I take his word in surety thereof ?"

"You may," answered every one present."

"I am satisfied," returned Prince John ;—" so now, gentlemen, I would wish to be alone with Sir Gaston for a brief period ;—leave me, and quit my palace separately, that none shall watch our movements, and report their idle rumours to the king.   I will see you here again to-morrow, and in the meantime will make all necessary preparations for the object we have in view."

Obeying this hint, the nobles prostrated themselves at the feet of the prince, and once more expressing their determination to remain faithful retired from his presence, leaving no one with him but Sir Gaston de Neville. For some few moments John remained thoughtful and gloomy, but recovering himself, at length, he said with some hesitation :—

" I scarcely know, Sir Knight, what to think of these haughty barons that have just left us ;—they are proud of their own power, and methinks it will require a strong hand, should I ever gain the throne, to keep |them in subjection."

" It would be a dangerous experiment to try," observed Sir Gaston; " they are powerful in the number of their followers, and I feel assured were any monarch to attempt either to curb them, or abridge their liberties, they would rise up as one man, and break down the kingly trammels that would restrain them."

" I may feel inclined to try them, though," muttered the prince, " for what would be the sovereign rule if only exercised as the haughty nobles might dictate. However, enough has been said on this subject for the present ;—you, Sir Gaston de Neville, will arrange everything for the important step we are about to take ;—succeed in it, and I will raise you to the highest place,—beneath myself,—in my kingdom."

" If I fail," observed the knight, " it shall be through no fault of my own ; I will bring zeal and loyalty to aid me, and should they fail, I will, at least, perish in the attempt that is made to exalt your highness to the throne."

" You may leave me for the present, Sir Gaston," said the prince; " I would be alone now, but do not fail to see me again to-morrow, when these barons make their appearance."

" I will not fail," answered the Knight Templar, retiring towards the door, and then advancing a step or two nearer to the prince. " There is yet one thing," he said, " that I wished to know your pleasure about ;— but, perhaps ——"

" Nay, do not hesitate," cried John, impatiently ;—" you have some request to urge ;—speak boldly, and if it is within my power, it shall not be denied thee."

" I spoke to you a short time since," replied Sir Gaston, " about an aged woman they call Meg of Finchley ;—she is a sorceress and through her means it was that Rebecca, the Hebrew Maiden, passed through the ordeal harmless."

" Ah !" exclaimed the prince ;—" I remember what it is thou dost allude to ;—I told thee I would myself witness her examination, and that she should be punished, if thou couldst prove thy charge."

" I can prove it, your highness."

" Then let her be brought before me with as little delay as possible," cried the prince ; " this very day if thou canst, for if she hath indeed wronged thee, it is fitting that justice should not be delayed."

" I will undertake to bring her here to-night," answered Sir Gaston ; " that is, if my doing so will not be considered too bold."

" Let it be at what hour it may, I will see her, " replied the prince ; " if I have retired to bed, command my servants to call me up, for thou hast ever been most active and persevering in my cause, and it is only fair that I should be equally on the alert to serve thee. So now, away, Sir Gaston de Neville, and remember I shall be ready to sit in judgment upon the woman of whom thou dost complain."

The knight, satisfied with this assurance, bowed, and retired from the chamber, and on leaving the palace of the prince, hastened homewards, in order to collect a few of his retainers to accompany him to the humble dwelling of Meg of Finchley.

As for the prince, he hurried himself in making all the preparations he could for the struggle he was going to make for the crown, and having at length wearied himself with perplexities that crowded upon his mind, he threw himself upon his couch, half resolved to abandon the enterprize, ere he had involved himself too far in the treachery he meditated against a brother.

CHAPTER LXXI.

"Sue not to me for pity ;—
My heart is steel, and I can hear unmoved
Your prayers and supplications."

THE CONVENT.

FULLY resolved to bring destruction upon Meg of Finchley, the knight returned to the castle, and selecting three of his most trusty followers, he informed them of the object he had in view, and commanded them instantly to mount their horses, and accompany him on his errand. He could perceive, however, that they had very little liking for the ignoble task he sought to impose upon them, for they had been used to war against men, and, therefore, it was not without some disatisfaction that they heard his orders to assist in capturing an aged female, [whose supposed dealings with the powers of darkness had long made her the terror of all who had chanced to hear her name. But Sir Gaston was not to be foiled thus; and telling them that he had a particular object to serve in desiring to make her his prisoner, he offered them a liberal reward in the event of her being brought to punishment, This answered his purpose admirably, for the fellows were not proof against the temptation of a bribe, and immediately assenting to his proposition, they shortly afterwards followed him from the castle, and took the road which led towards Finchley. Scarcely, however, had they left the suburbs of London, when a violent tempest came on, and as no shelter was to be found, Sir Gaston led them towards a wretched-looking hovel, situated at no great distance from the road they were travelling. At the door of this place they knocked for some time without receiving any answer, and Roland le Mark, by his master's orders, was about to force an entrance, when footsteps was heard within, and presently the door being opened, discovered the grim form of Bertrand le Noir. This sight rather startled even Sir Gaston, but quickly recovering himself, he advanced, and with more courtesy than he usually exhibited to inferiors, expressed his surprise at seeing the robber, who he had understood was captured, and lying in prison with little hopes of escape.

"Aye, aye, Sir Gaston," he replied, "you heard truly enough, then, for I have been in gaol, as you say, and, I believe, few, besides myself, would have found means to cheat the gallows of its victim. But my lucky star is in the ascendant, as old Meg of Finchley once told me, and keeping up a good heart, I looked out for the first opportunity that offered itself."

By this time the whole party had got into the hovel, and were seated round a blazing fire that Bertrand had made on the hearth. Luckily, some of Sir Gaston's followers were provided with flasks of wine, and when these

had been handed round, the robber once more went on with his narrative.

"I was saying," he resumed, "that I had made up my mind to keep a
sharp look out for the first chance that might present itself, and, as luck
would have it, on the day before it was ordered that I should hang for my
sins, the gaoler was taken ill, and an older man put in his place. Well,
the poor fellow came at the usual hour to bring my food, and seeing that he
was only armed with a dagger, I sprang upon him, and snatched the
weapon from its scabbard, and before he could utter a cry, plunged it
in his heart!"

"Horrible!" exclaimed Sir Gaston.

"Aye, it was a bad job to be driven to it," answered Bertrand, "but
what man, in his senses, would hesitate to save his own life at the expense
of another's? At least, I would not, and so, having despatched the old fellow, I rushed from my cell, and would have slain half a dozen other devils
that were pursuing me, only that they saw I was a desperate chap to deal
with, and they left me to make the best of my way. Of course, I was not
slow in taking advantage of the chance they gave me, and I kept on at a
smart pace till I reached the ruinous hovel where I have remained for the
last three days, feasting myself upon the poultry and other good things
that I manage to lay hold of at night, and resting myelf till I feel inclined
once more to join the band of Black Ivan."

"But suppose," said Sir Gaston, "I should conceive it my duty to order
my men to take you into custody as one of the robbers who have so long
harassed the neighbourhood."

"That you dare not do," answered Bertrand, with perfect composure.

"And why not, I prithee?"

"Because," answered the robber, "such an act of treachery would be
terribly avenged by Black Ivan. Your life would no longer be safe for a
single instant, nor would even your own strong castle prevent the entrance
of those who would vow your destruction from the moment that it was
known I had fallen by your means. Besides," he continued, "you have
received hospitality from me; I have given you shelter from the storm, and
there are few men, I believe, who would be such villains as to betray the
man who had been generous enough to serve them."

"Well," cried Sir Gaston, "I was only jesting with you, Bertrand; so,
now, if you have anything in the place worth eating, bring it out, man, for
I and these good fellows are in the humour to pay our best respects to your
larder."

"Here are some fowls," replied the robber, stepping into another room
and returning with a platter containing the articles he had mentioned.—
"You understand, however, that they were stolen; but, perhaps, your appetite is not so squeamish that they will eat any the worse for that trifling
circumstance."

There was, indeed, no hesitation on the part of any one present, and
when Sir Gaston had concluded his hasty meal, the robber once more entered into conversation.

"I have been telling your knightship," he said, "the adventures I have
met with, and my future views in life; now, turn and turn about is a fair
maxim all the world over, so, perhaps, you will inform me what it is that has
brought you out this way to day."

"We are going," replied Sir Gaston, "to search after Meg of Finchley;
the hag has too long been suffered to frighten the timid with her pretended
powers, and, therefore, I have resolved to put an end to them at once, by
putting her into just such a place as you have been lucky enough to escape
from."

"Poor devil!" ejaculated Bertrand; "and is it possible that a knight, and a soldier like you, should come forth with your retainers for the purpose of seizing upon a helpless woman?"

"The truth is," replied Sir Gaston, who began to feel rather ashamed of the part he had taken in the affair, "I have, myself, some cause for wishing Meg out of the way. There is, in fact, a little love affair in which I am engaged, and, therefore, I have determined to get rid of her by foul means since no other offer themselves. To this end I have come out, and if you think fit to earn a few broad pieces of gold, you have only to accompany us and they shall be yours."

"I thank you for your very liberal offer, Sir Gaston," answered the robber, sarcastically, "but though I don't boast of having more honour than should come to my share, I should feel ashamed of joining in such a business as this. What! cannot you find men to quarrel with, that you must needs war with a helpless woman, who, I'll dare be sworn, never harmed you?"

"She has harmed me," replied the knight;—"through her means the Hebrew Maiden got safely through the ordeal, and from that time I have vowed her destruction. We are now on our way to her cottage, and she must indeed be assisted by her friend, Satan, if she now escapes the punishment she deserves."

As Sir Gaston concluded, the casement was suddenly closed with great violence, upon which the whole party sprang from their seats, and, rushing to the door, sought to discover the cause of this interruption. No one, however, was to be seen, though one of the men stoutly swore he had seen a female figure dart into a thicket at no great distance off. Bertrand, however, only laughed at the whole affair, saying that the window had been blown to by a gust of wind, and that the story of the retreating female was nothing but the effect of imagination. But Sir Gaston was not to be so easily satisfied; and, bidding farewell to his entertainer, who still refused to accompany him, he led his men towards the copse, which they thoroughly searched, without finding any human being by which to confirm the assertion which had been made by one of the men. Still this did not alter his previous resolution, and he commanded his followers to give up their useless search, and to accompany him, without further delay, to the place inhabited by the Weird Woman of Finchley. Less than a quarter of an hour served to bring them to the place of their destination; and, knocking loudly at the door, they were, after some hesitation, answered by Meg, who, scowling angrily upon them, demanded their business with her.

"You will soon know what brings us here," exclaimed Sir Gaston, dismounting, and bidding his men follow his example—"we have come thus far in search of you, and it will go hard, in spite of your dealings with the fiends of hell, if we do not take you were you will at last receive the reward of your crimes."

"Of what crime do you accuse me?" demanded the old woman; "what have I ever done to make an enemy of Sir Gaston de Neville?"

"Hast thou not practised sorcery, thou hag?"

"So people say," she replied, calmly; "but it is false, and even if there was any truth in it, the crime would not have been greater than those that have been committed by him who now stands before me as my accuser!"

"Ha!" exclaimed the knight, "am I to be taunted, and by such as thou!"

"Even so, proud knight," answered Meg; "thy sins have brought thee to a level even with the meanest of the king's subjects, and, galling as it may be to thee, I again repeat that even if I am the sorceress people call me, thou art far worse."

"What knowest thou of me that thou dar'st say so much?" demanded the knight, fiercely.

"I know thee to be a villain!" she cried—"a black, heartless villain, who would destroy the maiden upon whom thou hast cast thine unhallowed love."

"You allude to the Jewish girl, Rebecca?"

"I do."

"And is that all thou canst say to my dishonour?"

"No," she replied—"thou hast a wife, despised and persecuted, because thou hast grown weary of the charms that first captivated thy young heart."

"She of whom thou speakest is dead."

"'Tis false, Sir Gaston—false as thine own heart! Thy wife lives,—nay, has escaped from the dungeon to which thou didst consign her many long years ago."

"Woman!—how didst thou know this?" demanded Sir Gaston.

"I have this day seen and conversed with her," answered Meg—"nay, more, I have pledged myself to see her restored to her right, and the act which does that, consigns thee to the hatred and execration of the world."

"Wilt thou endure this longer, Sir Gaston?" asked Roland le Mark;—"shall the woman rave thus, and not receive the reward she so richly merits?"

"Oh, thou mayst slay me if thou wilt," answered Meg; "strike thy dagger to my heart,—but know that the secret will not die with me. Others have learnt the story of Lady Alicia's wrongs, and the moment of retribution is near at hand! Thou hast said I am a sorceress, Sir Knight—shall I use the power thou say'st I have, and tell thy fate?"

"Hag!—I can endure thy taunts no longer!" cried Sir Gaston, drawing his sword, and preparing to rush upon his aged victim. At this critical juncture, however, a trap door opened in the floor close by, and Rebecca, followed by Lady Alicia, sprang into the room. The latter, however, fainted away on perceiving her husband; but the former, seeing the peril that threatened her protectress, rushed forward and threw herself between Meg and her furious assailant.

"Spare her—spare her!" she wildly cried; "she is old, and a woman, and surely you would not stain your sword with the blood of one so unable to protect herself?"

"Ha! have I found thee here, too!" he exclaimed, exultingly. "By St. George it was a lucky chance that brought me hither; and since we have met once more, it shall go hard if ever thou dost contrive to give me the slip again. Seize her, fellows, and some of you make prisoner of the witch, whom I will take another opportunity to punish for the insolence she has treated me with."

"And what," asked Roland, "shall we do with this other female, who, if my eyes deceive me not, is the Lady Alicia?"

"By heavens! you are right," cried Sir Gaston, gazing upon the pallid form of his still fainting wife—"it is Alicia, and, as good fortune wills it, she is once more in my power. Take care of her, Roland, and see that she escapes us not a second time."

"Aye," exclaimed Meg, "act the tyrant, Sir Knight, whilst it is yet in thy power to do so—convey her once more to the loathsome dungeon where so many years of her life have been spent in misery and despair;—take her there, I say, but ere you do so, learn from me that your tyranny has almost drawn to a close. A brief period of triumph only will be thine, and when thou hast received the punishment called down by thy crimes, the

Lady Alicia will live honoured and respected by all those who revere virtue and female constancy."

"Sir Gaston," cried Rebecca, earnestly, "do not, I entreat thee, again imprison thine unfortunate wife, whose only——"

"Peace, girl, for thy prayers are unheeded," interrupted the knight, passionately. "Thou, too, art luckily thrown in my way at the very moment when I was most uncertain where to seek thee; and yet chance, that has so often served me on former occasions, hath once more come to my assistance. Thou shalt away with us, Rebecca, and should'st thou remain obdurate to my prayers, a dungeon, such as has been the dwelling-place of Alicia, shall be the punishment of thine own folly."

"Place me where thou wilt," answered the Hebrew Maiden, "consign me even to death, if thou thinkest fit, but never shalt thou compel me to love thee."

"Be constant to that resolution, girl," cried Meg, "and thy reward is not far off. Let him confine thee in a dungeon, as he has threatened, for the period of his crimes will come ere long, and a shameful death be his just reward."

"Accursed hag, thou liest!" exclaimed Sir Gaston, furiously; "my days of triumph will yet be many, and my first revenge shall be to see thee dragged to the stake, where thou shalt be burnt as a witch in the presence of thousands of exulting spectators."

"Thou readest not my fate well," answered Meg, "or thou would'st see that destiny will never consign me to such a death as that thou hast spoken of. I am old—much older than thyself—yet shall I live to see thee meet the end of a felon."

No. 49

"Shall I not slay the witch, and thus give the lie to her predictions?" demanded Roland le Mark.

"Hold thy hand, sirrah, and dare not to strike until I give thee the word," exclaimed Sir Gaston, "I am a victorious conqueror here, and can well look over the angry words of an incensed woman, even though she may chance to sting me somewhat occasionally. I would have them all three live, that I may enjoy the triumph of witnessing the impatience with which they will endure the punishment I have in store for them."

"Again I tell thee," said Meg, "thou hast not long to live;—a brief time will bring about thy destiny, and in thy last hours thou wilt remember my predictions. Beware, I say, for thy days are numbered."

"And so should thy minutes be, thou hag, if I had my will," cried Roland, angrily.

"Ah!" cried Rebecca, "do not urge thy master to a crime so horrible. Look upon the grey hairs of her thou wouldst make thy victim, and if ever pity found a place in thy breast, let it now be awakened in behalf of one who never injured thee."

"But she taunts my master," answered Roland, "and that is a thing that no faithful servant can hear unmoved."

"There is no need for violence, in this case," replied Sir Gaston; "we have fairly traced the fugitives to their lair, and it will be my own fault if I make not the best of the advantage I have so [unexpectedly gained. It was a fortunate chance that threw them all in my way at one time; and you, who have so well assisted me, shall receive double the reward I promised on starting from my castle. To you, Roland, I shall consign them all for the present. Meg will, perhaps, receive speedy punishment for the insults she has heaped upon me, as I shall take her before Prince John, who has promised to attend to the charges I have brought against her, and to inflict upon her that punishment which she so well merits."

"Prince John knows not your villainy," cried Meg, "or he would pause ere he took thy word against me."

"But he believes thee, from common report, to be a sorceress," answered the knight, "and that alone will be sufficient to send thee to the torture. Thy limbs shall be racked, old woman, and if it will add to thy torture, I will myself be present to exult in the agony thou must endure."

"Say rather that I shall do so with thee," replied Meg, unmoved by his taunts; "the triumph thou dost speak of will be mine, and the last words thou shalt hear in the world will be those of exultation for thy fate."

"Woman, thou knowest it is impossible," exclaimed Sir Gaston; "art thou not in my power at this moment, and who shall deliver thee when once thou art delivered into the hands of justice? By heaven, I thirst for vengeance; and ere many days have passed over, I shall have the satisfaction of seeing at least one of my enemies punished as I could wish."

"Sir Gaston, be not thus revengeful against an old woman who has committed no crime against thee," cried Rebecca, throwing herself upon her knees before the knight. "Spare her life, and if it pleases thee to take mine instead, I will yield it up cheerfully, and thank thee for it with my latest breath."

"I tell thee, girl, I have another destiny for thee," exclaimed Sir Gaston, "thou shalt yet become my mistress, in spite of all thy prayers and entreaties; and as for Alicia, who lies fainting yonder in the arms of Roland le Mark, she shall be sent once more to her dungeon, until heaven, in its mercy, sees fit to release her from her earthly misery."

Having uttered these taunting words, the knight gave some general directions to his followers, and having placed the females on the saddles before them, they rode off in the direction for London.

CHAPTER LXXII.

" A heavy retribution fall on thee !
For thou hast ever aided those I hate,
And kept them from my wrath !"

LUDOVICO.

A SHORT time served to bring them nearly to the end of their journey, when, giving Rebecca and the Lady Alicia to the care of his men, the knight, with one retainer only, continued his 'way towards the palace of Prince John, the man having charge of Meg, who was now to be examined by his highness on a charge of practising sorcery against the subjects of King Richard of England. Passing through the City to Westminster, they reached the residence of the prince, and being admitted without hesitation, Sir Gaston was ushered into the presence of the king's ambitious brother, whilst his follower remained in an adjoining chamber to keep guard over the prisoner.

"So !" exclaimed John, " thou hast returned, Sir Knight, I perceive, and it is, therefore, scarcely necessary to ask thee whether thou hast succeeded in finding the old woman you accuse of exercising the black art."

" I have fulfilled my mission," answered Sir Gaston, " and the woman you speak of is now waiting your orders in the adjoining room."

" 'Tis well," cried the prince ; " and yet, methinks, thy time has scarcely been well employed, since, after all, thou hast but made captive an aged female, who it mattered not much whether she was suffered to be at liberty or not."

"Your highness has yet to learn that I have succeeded in this instance far beyond my hopes," answered the Knight Templar.

"What mean you, Sir Gaston de Neville ?"

"That I have discovered beneath her roof two females, of whom I have been anxiously in search. It appears she gave them shelter and conceal-ment, little expecting that I should so soon pay her a visit on an affair in which she is concerned."

"Who are the females ?" demanded Prince John.

"One of them is Rebecca, the Hebrew Maiden."

"Ha ! she has been unfortunate enough, then, to fall once more within your clutches."

"Say, rather, fortunately than otherwise," exclaimed the Knight Tem-plar, " since it will be the means of saving me a long search that I had made up my mind to make after her."

"Did you bring her away with you, Sir Gaston ?"

" I did, your highness."

"And she is now, I suppose, safe within your own castle ?"

" She is."

"And you do not intend to let her escape again if there are any means to prevent it ?"

" Never," exclaimed the knight, resolutely ; " I have had too much trouble already, and this time I will take care to keep her safe within the walls of my own strong fortress."

"You said just now," observed the prince, " that there were two females secreted in the hovel of Meg of Finchley—who, I pray, was the other one ?"

"One," answered Sir Gaston, " who had been prisoner in my castle, but who escaped from me a day or two since. She is mad, I believe, and, fear-ing that she might raise rumours against me, I have ordered a strict search to be instituted in every direction, so that she might once more be placed safely in my custody."

"What reports," asked Prince John, "can she raise that will be believed by the public? Sir Gaston de Neville surely need not feel alarmed when his own character is to be weighed against the falsehoods of a mad woman ;—does she accuse thee of the commission of any very heinous offence?"

"She declares herself to be my lawful wife."

"Indeed!—methinks that will be no easy task to prove, seeing that Lady de Neville has been dead many years."

"That is true, your highness," answered Sir Gaston; "but the common people are not well disposed towards me, and it is, therefore, to be feared they will believe her story, however improbable it may appear to those who have more reliance in my honour."

"And for this reason, then, it was, that you have kept her a close prisoner in your castle?"

"It was."

"Yet, in spite of all, she has found means to escape when you thought her secure."

"She has; but, I suspect, not without assistance," answered Sir Gaston de Neville. "I have a page, who, there is but too much reason to believe, has aided in getting her out of the castle; but I shall soon satisfy myself of that fact, and should my suspicions prove correct, he shall himself pass the remainder of his days in that hopeless captivity from which he sought to rescue her."

"And why should you be thus angry?" demanded the prince, "seeing that it will be so easy a matter to prove to the world that Lady de Neville has long since been dead, and that this woman is only some fanatic impostor of whom you know nothing whatever?"

"The assertion would be doubted by your royal brother, were I to make it," answered the Knight Templar; "you are aware of the prejudice he has formed against me, and were such a rumour as this to reach his ears, he would institute a strict inquiry, and thus bring upon me the attention of those enemies who have long sought to hurry on my destruction."

"Well, thou needst not think of thine enemies now," exclaimed the prince, "for our hour of triumph is at hand, and thou shalt rise far above the highest of those who hate thee. Then they shall have cause to envy thee, but let them beware, lest they bring upon themselves the ruin they seek to hurl on thee."

"And in return," answered Sir Gaston de Neville, "I will never fail in the duty and allegiance I owe to thee. When once thou art sovereign of these realms, I will be amongst the foremost of those who will ever be ready to draw the sword in thy defence."

"Since thou wert here," said Prince John, "I have seen one who is deep in my brother's secrets. From him I learn that Richard not only suspects our projects, but that he is privately occupied in taking steps to frustrate them even at the very moment when we may believe ourselves most secure."

"Does he know," asked Sir Gaston, eagerly, "that we have fixed the day of his coronation for the attack?"

"I do not think he has heard quite so much as that," answered the prince; "but, be that as it may, he is acquainted with a great deal more than I could have wished. He has commanded me, as you are already aware, to quit England ere the expiration of fourteen days, and unless we can bring matters to a conclusion before that time, there is every reason to fear that he will take measures to prevent all chances of my ever succeeding to the throne, even though he should die childless."

" But you are the next heir to the crown," answered Sir Gaston, " and, therefore, he has not the power, however good his will may be, to deprive you of your just inheritance."

" Not unless reports were raised against me," exclaimed John; " it appears, however, that people already believe that I should prove a tyrant, were I to obtain the sovereign rule of these fair dominions, and, should I not be able to disprove the falsehoods, there are few who will aid to raise me to the highest point of my ambition."

" It shall be my task to represent your character to the people in a far different light," answered Sir Gaston de Neville. " I will represent you as a virtuous prince, struggling against the unnatural enmity of your brother, and anxious only to find an opportunity to prove your honest zeal in behalf of a suffering people. I will tell them that King Richard only desires to get you out of the way in order that he may grind them beneath his feet, and that if they would save themselves from tyranny and oppression, it must be by placing themselves under your guidance. The people are easily led by a plausible story, and, if I have your permission to do so, I will undertake to place you upon the throne of England ere another month has passed over us."

" Dost thou think so ?"

" I am sure of it, your highness."

" But suppose you should have formed a wrong estimate of the people's disposition. Imagine them still loyal to the king : should we not, in that case, bring upon ourselves that punishment which there is now both time and opportunity to avoid ?"

" If your highness fears the consequences, it is time we should desist from our designs," answered Sir Gaston, emphatically.

" I understand you," exclaimed the prince; " you doubt my courage, and imagine that I would quietly submit to the imperious will of my brother, that would for ever banish me from the land of my birth. You believe I would submit to this without a struggle to defeat his intentions, even though I am aware that numerous friends are only waiting for the signal that shall bring them to my side."

" I doubt not your courage, my prince," replied Sir Gaston, " though it must be confessed I had some fear that you would hesitate to take up arms against a brother."

" Not after that brother has proved that he would act the tyrant over me," exclaimed John, sternly. " He has ordered me to go into banishment, and rather than submit to his will, I am prepared to adopt any plan of resistance that may be suggested by my friends. I have already told you as much before, and all I now ask of you is, to stand firmly by me until the great struggle between myself and the king is over."

" You have my oath to do so."

" I have," answered John, " and do believe thee true ;—on the other hand, rely upon the promises I have made thee; that thou shalt be rich and powerful beyond any of my other subjects, and that the chief patronage of the land shall be bestowed upon thee, so that thou mayst be regarded by the people as second to myself. Those are but some of the benefits I mean to heap on thee in the event of our plans being brought to a successful termination."

" It is understood, then," said Sir Gaston de Neville, " that our meditated attack is to take place on the day of King Richard's coronation ?"

" It is," answered the prince.

" In that case," exclaimed de Neville, " we shall avoid the suspicion that would otherwise be excited by the appearance of a large number of men being assembled in the street. Our first attack must be made upon the houses of the Jews, and should we succeed in that, it will be easy to over-power the king's guests, and make him our prisoner."

"But in case we should be defeated?"

"In that event," answered Sir Gaston, "there would be no evidence that we sought to harm any one except the Israelites, who are so hated by the people in general. None will know, except those engaged in the con-spiracy, that we intended ought against the king, and thus you will be permitted to leave the country, whilst I remain behind to form fresh plots that will enable you to return again ere many weeks have been passed in exile."

"Your plan is a good one, and shall be acted upon," cried the prince, after a moment's consideration. "I believe you to be faithful to me, Sir Gaston, and, therefore, do I place the utmost reliance in your honour and secrecy."

"Then, now, my prince," exclaimed the Knight Templar, "let me en-treat your aid in an affair that I have already told you gives me some un-easiness; the old hag I have mentioned has more than once been the means of thwarting my intentions respecting the Hebrew Maiden. She has thus brought upon herself my fiercest wrath, and since it is in your power to punish her, I claim your interference in my behalf."

"Let her be brought before me," said the prince; "and yet, ere she comes, let me tell you that my power does not extend quite so far as you may imagine. It is true, I may hear the charge you have to bring against her, and can represent the case to the Chief Justiciary, who will, no doubt, pay more attention to it than he would otherwise do. So far, I may be able to assist you, but it would be dangerous to give her up to punish-ment, when, by so doing, I should certainly bring upon myself that anger from the king, which it is my present interest to avoid."

"You will at least hear the charge I have to bring against her?" cried Sir Gaston, impatiently.

"I will," answered the prince; "let her be brought before me, and I will attend to your complaint."

Upon this Sir Gaston de Neville hurried from the chamber, and imme-diately afterwards, returned with Meg of Finchley, who he placed at some distance from the prince, and then taking his own station near the table, he commenced:—

"Your highness, this is the woman I charge with being a foul practicer of sorcery; leaguing herself with the fiends of darkness, in order that she may work her evil deeds against those who may offend her. I charge her with being a witch, and, therefore, one who is dangerous alike both to the king and to those who are placed beneath him."

"Thou hast heard what has been said against thee, woman," exclaimed the prince, "and now, if thou dost wish it, I will hear everything thou mayst have to say in reply."

"It is little I shall think it worth while to say," answered Meg;—"Sir Gaston de Neville, however, has just charged me with being a dangerous subject of the king's, and I would ask him who he conceives has most trea-chery at heart—he or myself?"

"You hear her, prince!" exclaimed Sir Gaston; "this is the way she ever treats those who seek to draw the truth from her; and, therefore, I suggest that the only way is to send her before the Justiciary, who, no doubt, will condemn her to the stake."

"What dost thou mean, woman," asked John, impatiently, "by charg-ing Sir Gaston de Neville with such a crime as treason?"

"I charge him with nothing more than I know to be the truth," answered Meg, firmly.

"'Tis false!" exclaimed the prince, "for there lives not a more loyal subject than he you so unjustly charge."

"It may be so," replied the old woman, "and yet I know his loyalty is not given to King Richard."

"Who is it given to, then?"

"To thyself, prince!"

"Hah!—another word like that, and thou shalt be dragged to the torture!"

"Thy threats are vain, and terrify me not," answered Meg, with the utmost composure. "That thou wilt do thy worst I know; perhaps thou mayst slay me! and yet, methinks that will be but poor satisfaction for the secret I have discovered, and which thou would have given the world not to have been known to me."

"'Tis false, hag!" exclaimed Sir Gaston, fiercely; "I am not disloyal to the king, nor would any, save a helpless woman like thyself, have dared to make such a charge to my face!"

"Thou mayst deny it," answered Meg, "but what I have said is known to the prince, before whom I now stand, as well as to myself."

"In that case," exclaimed John, "you charge me with being a party to an act of treason?"

"I do."

"Woman! this artifice shall not save thee," cried the prince, angrily.—"Thou knowest thou art in peril of thy life, and hast taken this means to preserve thyself. But I am not to be intimidated by thy words, knowing, as I do, that thou canst not say anything that will criminate me."

"You have heard my charge against her," exclaimed Sir Gaston de Neville, "and, therefore, do I now demand the justice you promised me. I have said that she is a sorceress, and that, by her arts, she preserved the Hebrew Maiden from the effect of the Ordeal, to which she had been condemned. The crime merits death, and I here demand her instant punishment."

"Let her be taken before the Lord Chief Justiciary," cried the prince; "he will fairly weigh the evidence produced, and should she be found guilty, she will not escape the punishment she so well merits. Nay, more, I will myself be present at the examination, and——"

"I understand your highness!" exclaimed Meg; "you will be there to influence the opinion of the judge against me; but, beware, I say, for the period of your own triumphant career is at hand, and ere many days have passed away, you will be far from the place that own your brother's sovereign rule."

"Ha! how knowest thou that?"

"I shall not tell thee how I know it," she replied, "but it may be sufficient for me to say that I am aware of the royal message you have received, commanding your immediate departure from England."

"Thou hast learnt this by thine accursed arts."

"I do know it, at any rate," replied the old woman, "and, therefore, I would again advise thee to make preparations for thine own safety; beware, I say, for the hour is at hand!"

"What hour dost thou speak of?"

"That upon which thy future destiny must turn; remain here, and thou wilt perish,—depart, and thou mayst live to repent the part thou hast acted against thy brother."

"Witch!—thou dost most foully belie me!" exclaimed the prince, fiercely. "I have acted no base part against my brother, the king, but would rather draw my sword, were it needed, for the punishment of those who dare rise up in enmity against him."

"Then let thy weapon reach the heart of Sir Gaston de Neville," cried Meg; "for that he is a traitor I am ready to prove,—aye, and I will do so if heaven spares me life but for a few hours longer."

"Hah!" exclaimed Sir Gaston, furiously, "then by hell thou shalt perish on the spot!"

Saying which, he rushed with his naked sword towards the defenceless object of his wrath, who would surely have fallen a victim to his rage, had not an armed man darted at the moment from behind the arras, and struck up the weapon at the very moment when it was within an inch or two of the woman's bosom. Enraged at this, Sir Gaston was about to turn his wrath against the intruder, when, to his astonishment, he beheld the well-known form of Black Ivan, the Outlaw! In an instant his weapon's point was lowered to the ground, and staggering back with amazement, he demanded, in an agitated voice, the reason of this unexpected interruption.

"Aye," exclaimed Ivan, carelessly, "I know my presence was not looked for; but the truth is, I chanced to hear of the violence with which you carried off this old woman and two others, who had sought a shelter in her house. That they were not safe in your hands I knew but too well, and tracing you along the road, I, by good fortune, obtained an entrance to this place, where I have lain quietly until I found it was necessary to interfere for the preservation of poor old Meg's life."

"Speak, villain!" exclaimed the prince, "and say how you gained admittance within my gates."

"When you learn to call me by less offensive names, I may, perhaps, answer you," returned the robber.

"Humph! is it expected, then, that I am to address a bandit as I would one of my own equals?"

"He who stands before you is not a robber by choice," answered Black Ivan; "the injustice of the world first drove him to seek revenge; he became leagued with desperate men, and is now what you behold him."

"A poor excuse for villany," muttered the prince.

"True," answered the fearless Outlaw, "yet there are villains in the world, who have not even so poor an excuse as that I have offered. However, you ask me how I gained admittance within your gates, and lest you should unjustly punish some poor devil for neglecting his duty, I will confess that I came in by none of your gates, but scaled the walls without observation, and gained yonder place behind the arras, without being suspected by a soul among your numerous dependants."

"The knaves should have seen and seized upon you," exclaimed the prince, with increasing rage.

"And if they had," answered Ivan, "what good would they have done by it? I am a desperate man, as I dare say you have heard before now; caring little for danger, and resolving to overcome all difficulties by the point of the sword; the truth is, then, that I should have slain the first man that offered to oppose me, and had others come to revenge his death, I would have placed my back against the wall, and thus have fought till overpowered by numbers. Thus, I might have perished, prince, but it would not have been till a dozen of your fellows had paid the penalty of their fool-hardiness."

"Leave the place, fellow!" exclaimed Sir Gaston de Neville; "leave us, I say, ere I may find it necessary to remove thee from the presence of his highness by force."

"Dost thou think, then," demanded the Outlaw, "that thou canst put thy threats into execution?"

"I will, at least, try to do so," answered Sir Gaston, fiercely.

"Hold! I command you both!" exclaimed the prince, on perceiving that they were about to engage in bloody strife. "And you, Sir Gaston," he continued, addressing himself to the knight;—"I desire you to put up your weapon, unless you would instantly see me become your foe. Here, at least, I expected to be free from the scenes of violence, and unless my command is instantly obeyed, I shall summon my attendants and give you both into their custody."

"You see, prince, how submissive I am," answered Black Ivan, instantly sheathing his sword;—"I came not to take the life of Sir Gaston de Neville, but to rescue an old woman who is in danger of falling into the snares he has artfully laid for her destruction."

"What is it to thee, if I think it necessary to rid myself of one who is in my way?" demanded Sir Gaston de Neville. "She has opposed my every wish,—nay, has given shelter to those I have sought after; and has even practised her magic art to serve the Hebrew Maiden, when condemned to undergo the ordeal."

"And are these the only reasons thou canst allege for persecuting a helpless female?" asked Ivan, scornfully.

"They are sufficient for me," exclaimed the knight, "and, by heavens! she shall not escape, even though all the fiends of darkness should come forth to oppose my will."

"It shall not be then whilst I am present," returned Ivan. "She has befriended Rebecca when she was in danger from thee, and, therefore, I owe her a debt of gratitude that cannot easily be paid."

No. 50

"Indeed!" sneered the knight, "and yet it is but a short time since you carried the wench off, and it was not without some difficulty that she effected her escape."

"All that I am quite aware of, Sir Knight," answered the Outlaw;— "I did take her off, and would have married her;—you, on the contrary, sought to make her your mistress, and, therefore, the brigand was more honourable than the Templar."

"She is now again in his power," cried Meg of Finchley; "he has this day carried her back to his castle, and she will become the victim of his lust, unless instant means are taken to deliver her from his power."

"You hear what is charged against you," exclaimed Ivan, addressing himself to the knight. "It is said the maiden is now in your castle, and that your designs against her are dishonourable;—now, answer me; shall she be instantly restored to her father's arms, or must I force you to perform an act of justice by means of violence?"

"Peace!" exclaimed Prince John, interposing;—"peace, I command thee both;—thou, Sir Gaston de Neville, art not bound to answer; and for this blustering bully, if he quits not my presence this instant, I will summon my followers to my aid, and command him to be thrown into one of the dungeons beneath my palace!"

"That thou darest not do!" answered the robber, in a tone of the utmost indifference.

"How!—dare I not perform my threat?"

"I again tell thee thou darest not do it."

"And why?"

"Because thine own life would pay the forfeit of thy temerity," answered Ivan, boldly;—"aye, thou gazest upon me with amazement, but again I tell thee thine own life would no longer be safe, wert thou to offer me the violence thy words bade me to expect. Remember, I have followers who would soon revenge any treachery that might be offered me, and it is not even thy princely title that would save thee from them, were they once to determine on your destruction."

"Insolent ruffian!" exclaimed the incensed prince, "am I to be thus bullied in my own palace?"

"Give but the word, your highness," said Sir Gaston, in a low tone, "and I will either slay, or drive him from your presence."

"Thou wilt find it difficult to do either," exclaimed Ivan, unmoved by the threats with which he had been assailed. "I have trusted myself, it is true, within the presence of those whose honour I hold not in much esteem; but I came not unarmed, nor shall I fail to make use of either sword or poniard, should I chance to find them needful for my own preservation."

"Leave us, fellow!" cried Prince John;—"we seek not to harm thee, and, therefore, thou art at liberty to depart from hence as soon as it may please thee."

"And glad enough you will be to get rid of me upon such easy terms," exclaimed the robber, with a smile of derision. "However, it does not suit my honour to go at your bidding like a slave; neither do I intend to depart, unless this *gallant* knight thinks fit to promise the speedy liberation of the Hebrew Maiden."

"Perdition!" cried the infuriated knight, "am I to make terms with a common robber?"

"Do not heed him, I charge you," exclaimed John, almost bursting with rage and mortification.—"Black Ivan, as you perceive, is now in my power;—I have guards at hand, and at my slightest signal, they will advance to make him a prisoner."

"Indeed!" said Ivan, smiling scornfully at the latter words. "I have been used to freedom all my life, and depend on it, I will not yield it up willingly. So now I crave permission for the departure of myself and this old woman, who must be the companion of my journey, since it chances that our way is nearly in the same direction."

"Hold!" exclaimed the prince; "Meg of Finchley remains here, to answer a charge that has been brought against her by Sir Gaston de Neville."

"Sir Gaston then must take another opportunity to get her in his clutches," replied Ivan;—"Meg goes with me, and whoever puts forth a hand to arrest our departure, may chance to lose his own life for his madness!"

With this, he led the old woman from the chamber, and left the palace of Prince John without receiving the slightest interruption. Neither the knight nor the prince attempted to follow them, but from that moment a resolution was formed between them for the destruction of Black Ivan the Outlaw.

CHAPTER LXXIII.

"Danger doth threaten you, my lord,—
Therefore I counsel an immediate sentence,
And instant execution."

THE HIGHLAND CHIEFTAIN.

THIRSTING for vengeance, Sir Gaston de Neville returned to his castle, and retiring to his own chamber, he gave orders for Roland le Mark to wait upon him instantly. Here alone, and unseen, he could indulge his rage to its fullest extent;—pacing with rapid strides up and down the apartment, and muttering words of fearful import. He had been defeated where triumph appeared to be certain, and resolving to be satisfied somewhere, even though it should be upon the innocent, his thoughts turned upon Rebecca and his unfortunate wife, who were both of them once more in his power. The Hebrew Maiden he had determined should never more leave the castle, but as for the Lady Alicia, he had not yet made up his mind respecting her, when Roland le Mark entered his presence.

"Sirrah!" exclaimed the knight, "I require your aid and counsel in an affair upon which rests, not only my happiness, but, perhaps, my very existence. You know my secrets, Roland, and can, perhaps, already guess which way my thoughts turn."

"I can," answered the fellow;—"you are placed in some danger by this woman you have brought to the castle;—you begin to find out that even a pretty face can bring mischief with it, and would now ask my advice as to the best way of preventing it."

"You are over bold in your speech, sirrah!" exclaimed Sir Gaston, angrily;—"but remember that though I may be somewhat in your power, I will endure no insolence!—you know my secrets, and, therefore, dare to encroach upon my forbearance;—yet there are means left to quiet thee, as thou well knowest, for this castle contains dungeons strong enough to hold thee, and if they should fail to answer my purpose, a dagger will prove my surest safeguard when all else deserts me."

"You are angry with me, Sir Gaston!"

"I am; and not without sufficient cause;—so decide, Roland, and tell me whether you mean to be my friend or foe?"

"Your friend, if you will suffer a menial like myself to so call myself."

"You will serve me, then, in any way that may appear necessary for the fulfilment of my plans?"

"I will."

"That is spoken like yourself, Roland," exclaimed the knight, in a tone of greater freedom. "Perhaps. I have been myself rather warm in this instance;—I have been angry, Roland, but, believe me, all shall be forgotten if I but find you true and faithful."

"You have never found me otherwise," answered the ruffian; "nay, when blood has been demanded, have I ever refused to shed it when called upon to do so by my honoured master?"

"I am aware of it," replied Sir Gaston; "you *have* done so, but it now remains to be proved whether you would serve me in the same way again."

"I would," exclaimed Roland le Mark; "that is to say, if it should be necessary for your own safety."

"It may be," answered Sir Gaston; "nay, at present I see no alternative, for there is one who must die, lest I, myself, fall into peril that may cost me both life and honour."

"May I ask who that intended victim is?"

"Aye,—the Lady Alicia."

"Your wife!"

"Say rather my bane, my curse!" exclaimed Sir Gaston. "For years past has she not been a perpetual source of danger to me; am I not in fear lest she should be discovered, and am I not justified in removing an object that I have so much reason to dread?"

"There is much in that, to be sure," answered Roland, "and yet, seeing that you have her again safe enough in this castle, I can't help thinking it would be as well to let her die a natural death in her dungeon."

"Have I not anxiously looked for her death for years past," cried Sir Gaston, "and does she not still live in spite of the hardships and privations she has been subjected to?"

"Yes, and that has puzzled me more than anything else;" replied Roland. "She has been immured in a close dungeon without a soul to speak to, and her food has not only been scanty, but of the coarsest quality. Yet she always seemed cheerful, and never uttered a complaint of the wretched fare that was given her. However, I have my own opinion upon that subject, for, depend on it, Sir Gaston, she has a secret friend in the castle, who not only visits her, but gives her better food than is provided by yourself."

"Hah!" exclaimed the knight, fiercely, "if I thought so, the man, whoever he is, should die!"

"I have no certain knowledge of the fact,". answered the ruffian, "but there seems to be pretty good reason to believe that I am not wrong, and in that case it will be for yourself to say whether the fellow should be watched and punished as he deserves."

"Is there any one that you suspect?" asked Sir Gaston, impatiently.

"There is."

"And who among my people would dare to act against my orders?" demanded the knight.

"The person I suspect is no other than your page, Adrian."

Sir Gaston's brow grew still more dark and gloomy at this disclosure, and for a minute or two he paced the room with rapid and irregular strides. At length, however, he again paused, and directed an inquisitive look towards his retainer, demanded what cause he had for suspecting the page.

"There are many reasons for thinking it is him," replied Roland, "but the chief one is that I have several times observed him gliding about the vaults and dungeons when he has not been aware that I was near. Once or twice he had a basket in his hand, and he then seemed to be coming from Lady Alicia's dungeon."

"And yet," cried Sir Gaston, reproachfully, "you neither stopped nor questioned him?"

"I did not," answered the ruffian; "in fact, I thought it as well to watch him further, and when I was quite certain about it, to inform you."

"There seems to be some probability in this," observed the knight,— "for it is certain that the youth left the castle and he has not yet returned."

"You are mistaken," answered Roland, exulting in the mischief he was making; "Adrian is now in the castle, and if it pleases you I will command his presence here, that you may question him closely upon this subject."

"Do so;" exclaimed Sir Gaston, and as the retainer left the room to obey this order, he threw himself upon a couch in that despair which a consciousnes of guilt is ever certain to bring with it. He now saw that his secret was known to more persons than he had expected, and fearing that a termination would soon come to his reckless career, he began to devise various means by which to postpone the dreaded hour. To rid himself of Adrian was a task of no great difficulty, but it would cost more blood, and steeped as he was in crime, he shrank from an act that filled him with dread. Besides, he was not yet certain that the page was in possession of the dreaded secret, and as the youth was the son of a friend who had died in battle at the very moment when he had flown to the rescue of Sir Gaston, he felt that to injure him would be to injure the memory of one he was so deeply indebted to. Perplexed with these thoughts, he had started frantically from his seat, when Adrian, accompanied by Roland le Mark, suddenly presented himself before him.

"So, boy!" he exclaimed, sternly, "you have at length returned to my castle, after an absence, that, to say the least of it, is most inexplicable. Where hast thou been, sirrah, and what business took thee away from the castle without first telling me of thine intention?"

"I went," replied Adrian, boldly, "because gallantry called me forth, and I have heard you say that a true knight should never be a laggard when woman demands his aid."

"True, boy," exclaimed the knight, "but thou hast also learnt that it is the duty of a page to submit himself cheerfully to the service of his master."

"Have you ever had cause to think I neglected my duty?" demanded the youth.

"So far I have believed thee to be most faithful to thy duty," answered Sir Gaston de Neville. "I have watched thy progress in feats of arms with much satisfaction; have seen thine increasing strength with almost a father's pleasure, and have heard people speak of thy progress in various games of chivalry, till I have almost wished thou hadst been a son of mine own. Think then, Adrian, what must be my grief at observing, as I have lately done, that thou hast forgotten thy duty to thy master, and given thy services to those who rank among his enemies."

"Has my honoured master cause for charging me thus?" asked

Adrian, wondering what he was alluding to, and trembling lest his secret interview with the Lady Alicia had been discovered.

"You shall judge for yourself, boy," answered Sir Gaston: "answer me, therefore, truly and honestly, whether you have not visited one of the dungeons in which a captive was confined, the knowledge of whose existence would bring ruin upon me?"

"I cannot deny that I have made such stolen visits," answered Adrian; "but as I have known the secret for some time past, you have assurance that I am not now likely to speak openly on a subject that would injure my master."

"So far, I grant thou hast been prudent," replied the knight, "but that does not prove that thou wilt always remain so; tell me, therefore, whether I am safe from treachery, or whether I must henceforth rank thee amongst my foes?"

"I will be faithful to him I serve," answered the youth.

"What warrant canst thou give me that thou wilt not betray me to those who would exult in my downfall?"

"My oath."

"I will demand no oath, but will take thy bare word for it," exclaimed Sir Gaston de Neville. "Promise me that thou wilt mention this affair to no one, and I shall rest satisfied."

"Do you allude to the Lady Alicia?"

"I do;—but how didst thou chance to know of her existence, or that she was confined in one of the castle cells?"

"Another time I will confess all to you," answered Adrian. "At present let it suffice that I did discover the secret, and that from the period I speak of, I have been almost a daily visitor to the place of her captivity. Thank heaven, however, she is now free, and I trust far beyond the reach of her enemies."

"Thou art mistaken, boy," exclaimed Sir Gaston, "for fortune has again thrown her in my way, and, at this moment, she is safe within my castle."

"Merciful heaven, shield and protect her!" cried Adrian, shocked at the intelligence. "I believed her free, and the first news I hear on my return, is, that she has once more fallen into the hands of those from whom she had fled."

"I have her now safe enough," ceied Sir Gaston, in a voice that betrayed the exultation he felt; "she is within these wall, and never more shall she leave them. Nay more, her life is in your hands, for by a single word you can doom her to immediate death."

"Ah! what means that threat?" exclaimed the page.

"It means," replied Sir Gaston, "that her life is safe only so long as you are prudent;—utter but a single syllable to any one, of her being here, and she shall die ere thou hast babbled my secret an hour!"

"I will be dumb," cried the terrified youth.

"Thou hast best be so if thou wouldst not doom her to death," replied the knight, fiercely; "thou knowest, Adrian, that I am sudden in wrath, and having told thee the conditions upon which her life will be spared, I leave thee to act henceforth as thou mayst think proper."

"Answer me but one question," exclaimed Adrian; "will the unfortunate lady be at liberty, or ——"

"Thou hast little right to question me thus upon my intentions," interrupted his imperious master. "I have already condescended to say more upon this subject than I intended to have done, and, therefore, I shall say nothing further to thee, than that I shall expect thy silence.— Tell no one of what thou knowest, or the Lady Alicia dies."

"I will not."

"It is sufficient," answered the knight; "I have said I will take thy word, so now leave us. Yet, let me tell thee one thing further,—thine own life as well as that of the Lady Alicia will depend upon thy prudence in this respect. Retire, boy, and leave us to ourselves."

Without venturing to give utterance to another word, Adrian withdrew from the chamber, leaving Sir Gaston and his confidential retainer to confer together on the next step that was to be taken in this pressing emergency. From the manner of the Knight Templar, it was very evident that his mind was ill at rest, now that he was aware how much he was in the power of the youth, and the uneasy glances of his eyes told the dark and terrible thoughts that were struggling in his bosom. Roland le Mark saw this, and having an old grudge to satisfy against Adrian, he began to urge his master upon the policy of ridding himself at once of the cause of his disquietude.

"It is plain," he said, "that you are now at the mercy of this boy; with a word he can bring foul disgrace upon your name, and, therefore, I leave it to yourself to decide, Sir Gaston, whether he shall live or die."

"Hah!" exclaimed the knight, startled by these latter words, "would thou prompt me to his death?"

"That is a matter," answered the ruffian, "that I leave to your own judgment. You know what to expect if he should happen to blab the affair, and there is only one safe way to prevent that I know of."

"Aye, you would murder him, and thus add another crime to the black catalogue of my sins."

"There's no occasion to be very squeamish about the matter," answered Roland; "the truth is, you are not safe whilst he lives, and as the stripling can't have many sins to answer for, I see no harm in putting him quietly out of the way."

"Tempter forbear!" exclaimed Sir Gaston, recoiling with horror from the proposed crime; "too long already have I listened to thee, and another word to bring me to thy foul purpose will convert me from a friend to an enemy."

"Oh, very well," cried Roland, indifferently, "if you don't mind what may happen from this, I'm sure I've no occasion to do so. For my own part, I have always expected to go out of the world with an hempen cravat about my neck, and the thought never gave me much uneasiness. But your *honour* is quite another affair, and I thought when I was making the proposition, that I was doing nothing more than my duty."

"I will hear no more," exclaimed Sir Gaston; "and mark me, sirrah, that boy's life must not be sought by thee under any consideration. At present I see no cause to fear anything from him: he has pledged his word to utter nothing that shall afford even the slightest hint of what has taken place, and even if there was cause to suspect him we have sufficient security in the dread he would feel at the consequences of his indiscretion. He knows I seldom break my word, and, therefore, he has every reason to expect that the life of Lady Alicia depends upon his silence."

"But as she contrived to make her escape from you," observed Roland, "it is likely enough that the secret is known by this time to a score or two of people. In that case, he will be an excellent witness against you, and there is no reason to doubt but he will be a very ready one."

"I know the youth better than to doubt him thus," answered Sir Gaston de Neville; "he has been with me from a mere child, and considering me, as he does, almost in the light of a parent, he would rather lose his own life than say ought that might, in any way, endanger mine."

"Well, confidence is certainly a very fine thing," exclaimed Roland, "yet, for all that it's sometimes abused, and I'm thinking it will be so in the present instance."

"Be that as it may, sirrah, I am content to run the risk," replied the knight, sternly. "At any rate, I will trust him for the present, and should anything arise to shake the good opinion I have formed against him, it will then be time enough to think of the alternative you have named."

"Just as you please, Sir Gaston," answered the ruffian, sullenly ;— "so, perhaps, while you about it, you will give me orders to set Lady Alicia and the Hebrew Maiden at liberty ?"

"How !" exclaimed Sir Gaston, "has it come to this, that I am to be subject to the sneers of a menial ?"

"I only thought," replied the fellow, "that as you are so mercifully disposed, you might think proper to order the liberation of all that happen, at this time, to be confined here."

"Understand me, Roland, and see that my orders are strictly attended to," exclaimed the Knight Templar ; "to your charge I have committed the care of both Rebecca and the Lady Alicia ; they must be carefully guarded, for, should they escape, your own life will answer for the neglect."

"There's no occasion for threats," muttered Roland le Mark ; "you have always found me mindful of my duty, and if either of them succeed in getting out of the castle, I will be content to forfeit my own life as a just punishment for my carelessness."

"Have you disposed of them as I commanded ?"

"I have ; they are both in the ante-chamber leading to the hall, which, being high from the ground, is the safest place I could put them in till I received your further orders."

"They are both together, then ?"

"They are, sir," replied Roland, "for, as each of them know the misfortunes of the other, I thought it could not matter much even if they did chatter to each other a little."

"I will visit them there," exclaimed Sir Gaston, after a brief time had been given for reflection. "I will see them, and Lady Alicia shall have the mortification of seeing that even in her presence I can bestow my love upon another."

"You are prepared, then, to bear reproaches that you might so easily avoid."

"What care I for her reproaches ?" demanded Sir Gaston ; "Lady Alicia has long since ceased to hold a place in my heart, and I can listen to the outpourings of her heart without feeling even the slightest pang or remorse. It will be some satisfaction to know that she suffers, and I can endure the rest without danger of showing even the slightest anger."

"And what," asked Roland le Mark, "do you intend to do with them after this interview ?"

"That," answered the Templar, "will depend upon circumstances.— I shall see how Rebecca conducts herself, now that she is again my captive ; it will be my care to point out to her the utter hopelessness of her escape, and the consequent impossibility that she can give her hand to my Hebrew rival ; nay, her father's life shall be spared only on condition that she yields to the terms I have proposed, and if all this fails, she shall be thrown into a dungeon, dark and cheerless as her own destiny, where she shall remain till her proud spirit is made to yield."

"And that it never will yield I feel pretty certain," exclaimed

Roland; "the girl is resolute, Sir Knight, and, in my opinion, even torture would not compel her to submit."

"We may have occasion to prove that at a future time," muttered Sir Gaston; "at present, however, it is my intention to try gentler means, but should she prove obstinate it will then be my turn to show the sternness of my nature."

"That," muttered Roland, "is the only cure for stubborn folks;—give them the torture, and if that don't bring them to their senses, it is time to give up the project in despair."

At this period a slight noise was heard behind an antique screen at no great distance from where they were standing; slight as it was, however, it did not escape the ears of Roland le Mark, who, rushing furiously towards the place, returned immediately afterwards with Edith, who, in spite of her cries and struggles, he dragged before her haughty master.

"What does this mean?" exclaimed Sir Gaston, angrily; "speak, girl, and confess what induced you to become an eaves dropper when I desired to be alone with my retainer? And mark me! let there be no equivocation,—no paltry subterfuge, or you will bring down a punishment that shall effectually prevent such insolence in future."

"Indeed,—indeed, Sir Gaston, I had no intention——"

"Speak to the purpose!" roared her master, fiercely; "tell me what brought you here, or by all the fiends in hell I'll lay thee dead at my feet with my poniard!"

"I will tell the truth,—indeed I will!—but—but—you terrify me so with your threats, that—that—I scarcely know what I say or do."

No. 51

"Why were you hiding yourself behind yonder screen?" demanded Roland le Mark.

"Not with any evil purpose, I assure you," replied the alarmed girl; "I came to look for Adrian, who, I was told, had returned to the castle, and finding you and Sir Gaston in this room, I was unable to get out again without being discovered, and so I ran behind the screen to wait till I could get away without any body seeing me."

"What did you overhear us saying?" demanded Sir Gaston, imperatively.

"Nothing——"

"Liar! thou art deceiving me," cried the enfuriated knight.

"I am not, indeed, sir," answered Edith, terrified lest he should put his threat of assassinating her into execution. "I was too far off to hear even so much as a single word, and I would have given the world to get away if I could have done it without being seen."

"She is telling you a falsehood, Sir Knight," exclaimed Roland, who was never so well pleased as when he was making mischief. "She has overheard more than she thinks proper to confess, and, if I was in your place, I would take care to prevent her babbling about it to the other servants in the castle."

"Come, come, girl, confess at once," cried Sir Gaston; "I know well enough that you cannot have been in that place without hearing some of our secrets, and when you have told all you know I will order your release, on condition that you promise never to repeat what you have now gathered from our conversation."

"I have told you the truth," answered Edith.

"It is impossible," muttered Roland le Mark; "woman's curiosity never could have resisted the opportunity of overhearing what passed, and if I was Sir Gaston I would either kill you at once to prevent mischief, or lock you up in one of the subterraneous vaults for the remainder of your days."

"But Sir Gaston is not so cruel to punish me for what I have never done," replied Edith, somewhat appeased at observing that her master took no notice of these suggestions. "He is too gallant, I'm sure, to lock up an unfortunate girl that has not heard a word of what passed between you."

"I am half inclined to believe her," whispered the knight, to his retainer; "she appears not to be aware of the presence of Rebecca and Lady Alicia in the castle, and if I was but assured of that, she should depart in peace rather than suffer my uneasiness to give her an idea that we were talking on a subject that requires so much secresy."

"As you please," returned the other; "but you appear to be in a forgiving humour to-day, and all I can say about it is, that I hope you will not afterwards repent it."

"I will run the risk, at any rate," answered Sir Gaston, and then turning towards the girl, he said, sternly:—"for this time, wench, you escape more easily than you had any reason to expect. You may leave us, but remember, your own life and safety will depend upon the prudence with which you act. It may be that you have overheard that which I would have a secret between Roland and myself, and if so let me caution you to keep it strictly to thyself, for your foolish babbling would soon reach my ears, and if I find my mercy has been misapplied, I will take such vengeance as shall prevent your offending me again.—And now, girl, away, and be guarded in every word you utter as you value your life."

Edith was too glad of the fortunate escape she had had to await a second bidding, and bustling out of the room, she mentally resolved to avoid all screens for the future. Sir Gaston de Neville watched her departure with a sullen frown, and then turning towards his retainer, he said :—

"I know not whether to believe that girl's assertions of ignorance or not; she has, however, thrown herself open to suspicion, and she must be carefully watched. Keep your eye upon her, Roland, and should there be the least cause to suspect that she intends to betray us, let her be instantly conveyed to a place of security, and I will afterwards decide whether she shall die at once or wear out the remainder of her days in hopeless captivity."

"I will obey your injunctions to the very letter," answered Roland le Mark; "the girl has once refused the offer of my hand, and I have vowed to have my revenge; chance has now thrown her into my power, and ——"

"Nay," interrupted Sir Gaston, "let it be understood that no private vengeance is to be satisfied in this instance; you must be well assured that she meditates betraying me, or never will I sanction any violence being offered."

"I will be careful to obey you," answered Roland, little pleased at these words;—"the girl shall be closely watched, and I promise not to interfere with her so long as she is prudent. So now, Sir Knight, I suppose you are ready to visit the two females that have been placed in durance till your further orders respecting them are known."

"I will visit them," answered Sir Gaston.

"Will you go alone, or shall I accompany you?" asked the retainer.

"You may go with me," replied Sir Gaston;—"at least, I would have you waiting outside the door in case I should have occasion for your services. I shall hear how my offers are received by them, and my future measures shall be taken accordingly."

"In your present excellent temper," exclaimed Roland, with an ill-suppressed sneer, "they may venture to oppose you as much as they please without fear of the consequences."

"Nay, you have judged me wrong there, sirrah," cried the knight, "for at this subject, at least, I am resolved. Rebecca must accept my offers, or she condemns herself to an endless imprisonment within these walls. Lady Alicia's fate is already pronounced;—she again enters her dungeon never to leave it, until death relieves her from her miseries."

With this Sir Gaston de Neville strode from the apartment, closely followed by the willing instrument of his crimes.

CHAPTER LXXIV.

"Will nothing move thee ?—
No vows, no prayers that I can make to thee ?
Must all then fail ?"

THE CONQUEST.

LADY Alicia and the Hebrew Maiden, as the reader is already aware, were conducted on their return to the castle to an ante-chamber, adjoining the great hall, where it was expected they would remain in safety till it was decided what should be done with them. For some time after their arrival there they remained silently absorbed in their own sorrows, but when Alicia at length turned from the window where she had been seated, and perceived the weeping companion of her captivity, she advanced towards her heroine, earnestly exhorting her to be of good courage, and to rely on Providence for protection under the accumulation of miseries that still continued to press upon her.

"It is in vain," she said, "to give way to grief, when all our energies are required to rescue us from the dangers into which we have fallen; it is our duty to seek means to relieve ourselves, rather than to fall for want of exertion, and, therefore, do I implore thee, dear maid, to forget your sorrows for a while, in order that we may plan some means by which to escape from the snares that have been laid for us by the ever-plotting Sir Gaston de Neville."

"Alas! dear lady," cried Rebecca, "I have endeavoured to look forward to hope till this moment. Now, however, I seem abandoned to my fate, and it would, therefore, be useless to struggle longer against a cruel destiny."

"What wouldst thou do then?" demanded Alicia.

"Die, lady!"

"Ah!—meanest thou by thine own hand?"

"No," answerd Rebecca, "that is a crime I dare not commit. I, however, pray for death, and most happy should I be were I but assured that the termination of my sufferings was near at hand."

"Dost thou forget thy father, maiden, and the grief thy death would bring upon his latter days?"

"I remember all, lady," answered the maiden; "but I am assured that he would rather look upon my breathless corse than know that I had died dishonoured."

"Thy virtue pleases me, girl," cried Alicia; "I feel deeply for thine unmerited sufferings, yet am confident that heaven will not desert one who so well deserves its protection."

"You speak kindly, madam," answered our heroine;—"more so than I could have expected from the followers of a religion which looks with scorn upon the fallen and humbled Jew."

"I regard not the religion," cried Lady Alicia, "so that the person professing it worships the same God that I do. Jews and Gentiles are alike acceptable to heaven, if they are but consistent in the offering of a pure heart. Thou hast proved thyself worthy of my love, and proudly will I acknowledge myself the friend of one so excellent in every virtuous principle."

"I would be glad to accept the generous offer of thy friendship," exclaimed Rebecca, "but, alas! I fear our companionship is doomed to be of short duration. Sir Gaston de Neville will not suffer us to remain much longer together, for you, I fear, are doomed to wear out the remainder of your days in a prison, whilst my fate is to be eternally hunted and persecuted by the man whose crimes I abhor, and whose professions of love I despise as much as I do himself."

"I intreat thee, girl, to be of good courage," answered Lady Alicia; "at present affairs may wear a dark and gloomy aspect; the fowler has ensnared his prey, and we see no help for ourselves in this sad extremity. Yet we know not what the future will bring forth, since all, for some purpose or other, is hidden in mystery and uncertainty."

"Dost thou think then, lady," asked our heroine, "that there is hope even in this hour of adversity?"

"For thee, there is," replied Alicia, "but for myself none. Sir Gaston knows that his honour depends upon this secret; he would have the world think I am dead, and to keep up the deception, he will confine me for life in a dungeon, from whence there will be little chance of escape."

"But your existence," observed Rebecca, "is known to a few, since you lately contrived to leave the castle."

"It is so," replied the lady, "but those to whom it is known, will scarcely venture to speak of it, lest they should bring upon themselves the fierce wrath of Sir Gaston de Neville. His rage would fall upon them like a consuming fire, and, therefore, will they conceal the fact of my existence, even though they might anxiously wish to rescue me from the perilous situation into which they know I have fallen."

"But there is one from whom we may hope better things," observed the Hebrew Maiden. "Black Ivan is aware of your existence, and deep as his crimes are, he has yet generosity enough to step forward for the rescue of injured innocence."

"And who, think you," asked Lady Alicia, "would give credit to the assertions of an Outlaw and robber? Besides, his own safety would be endangered were he to come forward even upon such an occasion as this, and in spite of his desire to punish Sir Gaston de Neville, who he hates for some cause or other, he will scarcely run so great a risk as this, which in all probability would cost him his life."

"In that case," observed Rebecca, "the only chance that remains in your favour is to elude the vigilance of those who guard us, and to escape before they again convey you to the dungeon, to which, I fear, you will be doomed."

"There is no possibility of getting out of the castle," answered the lady, discontentedly.

"Have you already forgotten, then, that you have once succeeded in effecting your own liberation?"

"I have not," she replied, "but then I was assisted by the faithful page, who, I now fear, has fallen into disgrace with his master for the service he did me. Adrian well knows every part of the castle, and he only is able to lead me through the mazes that would conduct me to liberty."

"Yet, if he lives," cried Rebecca, "I feel assured that he will risk life itself to rescue his beloved mistress from the cruel persecutions of Sir Gaston de Neville."

"Aye, if he lives!" returned Lady Alicia.

"Do you then believe that his generous zeal in your behalf has been punished with death?"

"There is too much reason to believe that such either has or will be his doom," sighed Alicia. "I know the fierce vindictive nature of my husband, and, therefore, cannot doubt that he will sacrifice him to his unbounded rage."

"Thus," exclaimed the maiden, "are all doomed to perish, who either excite the love or hatred of that fierce man."

"And it ever will be so," answered Alicia, "until heaven brings his headlong career to an end. Mischief is the idol of his worship, to which he bows down in adoration. Yet I have sometimes hoped that repentance might one day or other find its way to his bosom, and, that seeing the error of his sinful career, he would make amends for the wickedness of his past life. Now, however, I begin to think that hope is a vain one, and submitting myself to my cruel destiny, I have, at length, made up my mind to pass the remainder of my days in the lone cell to which his cruelty and tyranny condemn me."

"Thine, dear lady, is indeed a hard fate," cried Rebecca; "bearing him no hatred for the evil he has done thee, thou wert content,—in the event of thine escape,—to pass thy life within the walls of some holy convent, where, amongst the gentle sisterhood, thou mightest have forgotten thy persecutor, or only have remembered him to intercede with heaven in his behalf. But again has he got thee in his power, and from what thou hast said, I fear there is little hope of escaping him."

"There is none, girl," answered the lady, with resignation; —"I feel that I am rendered powerless, for those relations who would once have aided me, are now dead, and the few who at present know of my hapless condition, are prevented giving me assistance through knowing that the consequences of their interference would be fatal to themselves."

"Still," cried the Hebrew Maiden, "I think your escape from hence is not impossible. It is, at least, worth a trial, and if my poor services might be of use, they shall be exerted in your behalf, even though it might cost me my life."

"Indeed!" exclaimed Sir Gaston, who had been listening at the door to their conversation, and who at this moment abruptly made his appearance before them; "by my soul, girl, thou art largely endowed with generosity, though methinks thy kind intentions go faster than thy means."

"I was not aware," answered Rebecca, haughtily, "that though we are your prisoners, we were subjected to a listener!"

"Perhaps not, girl," exclaimed the knight, in a tone of indifference; "I can believe that you suspected not my being so near, or you would have been more guarded in your conversation with each other. However, it seems you would counsel her ladyship to escape, and anxious as I am to prevent unnecessary trouble, I will, at once, inform you that there is no hope whatever for any such mad project. Every avenue of the castle is well guarded, and orders have been given to the people at various gates not to allow any one to pass until it has been ascertained who they are, and what business takes them hence."

"Methinks, Sir Gaston," cried Lady Alicia, "your cruel taunts might have been spared on this occasion. That there was no chance of escape, I was well aware, and if there were, I should not have attempted it, seeing that you would have followed me wherever I might have gone, and I should only thus have aggravated the misery you have already heaped upon me."

"I tell thee, woman, as I have already told you before," exclaimed Sir Gaston de Neville;—"thou art a perpetual curse to me, for thy life yet lingers on, though I would gladly know thou wert in thy grave."

"Why dost thou not send me there, then?" demanded Alicia.

"Because my conscience," answered the Templar, "would tell me that the deed was murder!"

"True, but thou hast not hesitated to commit such a crime ere now, Sir Gaston."

"Hah!—dost thou tell me that to my face?"

"Thou seest I fear thee not," exclaimed Alicia;—"thy words fill me with no terror, though the time has been when they went to my heart like poisoned daggers. I have heard thee say how thou didst hate me, yet never hast thou told me the cause of that hatred."

"It is because thou art in my way," he replied;—"I have outlived whatever little love I might once have borne thee, and would see thee dead, that I might wed another, whose beauty is not on the wane as thine is. Nay, there is one who now stands beside thee;—a Hebrew Maiden, it is true, yet, as I am no great stickler for religion, I could overlook that difficulty, and make her mine, were no other obstacle in the way."

"Sir Gaston de Neville," cried Rebecca, "you have ere now heard me say how much I loathed and despised you; time has only served to increase my contempt, and the words I have just now heard, serve but to convince me that a fiend's heart has been centred in the frame of a human being."

"Humph! thy words are not over complimentary!"

"At least," answered the maiden, fearlessly, "they have the merit of being true."

"Peace! I conjure you," cried Alicia, addressing herself to Rebecca; "Sir Gaston will not heed thee; nor will the truth thou utterest serve to mitigate the fate he has already awarded against us. That he is fierce in his wrath I am, alas! a sad example, and that his passion is not to be subdued by difficulties, has been proved by the untiring zeal with which he has pursued thee, even though he knew the hatred with which thou hast ever regarded him. Answer him not, therefore, lest by so doing thou shouldst linger out thy days as I have done, in miserable captivity."

"Thy advice is good," exclaimed the knight, tauntingly; "the girl had better not thwart me, for thou canst tell her, Alicia, how little I regard the means when once I have an object in view. You have heard me, Rebecca, and now, once more I ask whether thou will accept the offer I have made."

"To become thy mistress?—never!"

"That is the same answer I have so often had before," exclaimed Sir Gaston. "Thou hast told me my intreaties were made in vain, and in reply, I have warned thee that thine obstinacy should yet be overcome;—again thou art in my power, rash girl, and I warn thee to provoke me no further!"

"I know I am in thy power, proud knight," cried Rebecca, "and yet I tremble not at thy impotent rage;—my life may, perhaps, be the forfeit of my resolution, but even the dread of that penalty will not terrify me to submission. Stab me to the heart, Sir Gaston, for there are none here to prevent the execution of thy hellish purpose!"

"Thou art bold, girl!" exclaimed Sir Gaston, bitterly; "and dost not hesitate to beard the lion even in his den. But thou knowest me not yet, or thou wouldst not tempt my anger by words that can only tend to thine own destruction."

"Thou wouldst not raise thine arm against a woman," cried the Lady Alicia, terrified at his words.

"Let her learn, then, to curb her tongue," muttered the knight. "Too long, already, have I endured her insolence, and it is now time that I seek to repress it. You have heard me, Rebecca," he continued; "I am not to be thwarted with impunity, and any further hesitation on thy part will be terribly revenged."

"If I am the only sufferer, I care not how soon you put your threats into execution," cried the maiden, undaunted by his menaces; "my life is now a weary load to me, and gladly would I lay it down to obtain that peace, which I have so long looked for in vain."

"Nay, it is not thy life I seek," answered Sir Gaston de Neville;— "thou must be made to endure tortures, far greater than any thou hast yet suffered; in a dungeon thou shalt pine away thy best years, and I will be the only visitor that shall ever come to see thee."

"_Thou_ my visitor!" cried Rebecca, shuddering.

"Yes, girl," he replied, "and each time I come to thy wretched cell it shall be to bring thee news that shall make thy heart bleed. I will tell thee of thy father's death through my means,—of his hoarded wealth taken away from him by my hands, and of the murder of Reuben Grenard, the puling idiot, who has dared to supplant me in thy heart.

These things, and more will I tell thee, Rebecca, until thou dost own that I can torture full as well as thou canst!" ₁

" Villain!" cried Rebecca, as soon as she could recover from the shock occasioned by these words,—" dost thou, then, dare to tell me thou wilt murder those I love, because my eyes cannot look upon thee without loathing ?"

" All this," answered Sir Gaston de Neville, " will be produced by thine own obstinacy ;—thou now knowest my designs, and it, therefore, remains for thee to say, whether the mischief I have sworn to execute, shall be perpetrated or not."

" And, in this way," cried Rebecca, scornfully, " thou dost expect to gain my love."

" I care not for your love," answered the knight ;—" become mine, and thou mayst hate me afterwards as much as thou pleasest. So now for thine answer, girl ;—wilt thou consent to my proposition, or must I execute my threats against those who I thought thou wouldst have saved even at any cost."

" Not at the cost of mine honour, Sir Gaston!" she replied ;—" take my life, if thou wilt, it is freely thine, but never will I forfeit the esteem of my friends, by yielding myself to a villain whom I so utterly despise !"

" Then, thou shalt hence with me !" exclaimed the knight, furiously, and he was advancing to seize upon his affrighted victim, when Lady Alicia, interposing, threw herself upon her knees, exclaiming in piteous accents :—

" Spare her, Sir Gaston, I entreat you ;—your violence terrifies her, and she knows not what she says. Leave her with me till to-morrow morning, and I will so far assuage her terror that she shall be prepared to answer you dispassionately."

" This is but a subterfuge to gain time," muttered the knight.

" The time gained is so brief, as hardly to be worth a thought," replied Alicia ;—" you see how you have disturbed her gentle spirit, and surely it is no great favour to ask for a few hours, ere she replies to your demands."

" Well," exclaimed the Templar, " for once, your entreaties shall prevail ; not, however, from any weak yielding, but that I wish to prove to her that I am not so destitute of feeling as you, perhaps, consider me to be. You shall remain together in this room till to-morrow, but remember, all hope of escape is vain, for a sentinel will be placed at the door, and another at the window, so that it would be useless to think of escaping from the power of the man who thus commands your destiny."

" Till the morning, then, we shall be free from interruption ?"

" You will, Alicia," he replied ;—" then, however, you will be conducted to your dungeon, and as for Rebecca, her fate will depend upon the determination she comes to after reflection."

And thus saying, he left the room almost as suddenly as he had entered it.

" Not an instant is to be lost, Rebecca," cried Lady Alicia, as soon as the knight had departed ;—" you have heard Sir Gaston's determination, and your escape must be effected at all hazards."

" Alas !" answered the Hebrew Maiden, " what chance is there of my leaving this place without discovery ? Sir Gaston has said that every avenue leading from it is guarded, and even if I could leave this room, which I see no chance of, it would only be to fall into the hands of some of his numerous hirelings."

"To remain here longer would be madness," exclaimed Alicia; "the attempt must be made, even if it should prove a vain one."

Rebecca was again going to urge the impracticability of an escape, when a low sound was heard proceeding from one of the walls of the apartment, after which the tapestry was observed to be violently agitated, and the terrified females were about to give utterance to their alarm in loud shrieks, when Adrian stepped from behind the arras, and, by the most importunate gestures, entreated them to be silent.

"Be not alarmed, dear ladies," he cried, "for even at the very moment when you believed yourselves abandoned to fate, I am here to aid your escape from the castle. Ah! you look surprised and incredulous, but the fact is exactly as I have related, and in proof of it, I have only to request that you will now accompany me, and I will either save you both, or fall like a hero in the attempt."

"Foolish boy!" cried Lady Alicia. "you know not the danger you run, by thus offering your assistance!"

"Oh, yes," answered the page, "I know pretty well what would be the consequence of being found out. Sir Gaston told me, not long since, that my life would answer for it, if I was discovered assisting you again, but I have learnt it is the duty of us males to protect helpless women, and I will do so in this instance, whatever may be the consequence of it."

"Leave us, Adrian," cried Rebecca, earnestly;—"leave us, I conjure you, for neither I, nor the Lady Alicia will seek to save ourselves at the risk of placing you in peril of your life."

"But allow me to say," answered Adrian, "that there is nothing so easy as to escape without discovery. I know the man that is placed as

No. 52

guard at one of the gates, and by means of bribes and plenty of drink I have prevailed on him to let me and a couple of friends pass him soon after dark."

"Does he know," asked Alicia, anxiously, "who they are that would accompany you?"

"Oh, no," answered the youth, "it would never have done to tell him that;—he believes they are a couple of male friends of mine, and to keep up the deception, I have brought these two large cloaks, and a couple of military caps, so that all you have got to do is to pass him without saying a word, and I'll be bound to get you both far enough from the castle before Sir Gaston de Neville is aware of the escape of his prisoners."

"It would be madness to attempt it," exclaimed Lady Alicia, "knowing, as we do, that, were the plan discovered, it must terminate in your own death."

"But there is no fear of its being discovered," returned Adrian;—"no one will ever suspect you in these cloaks, and as the night will be rather dark, and the sentinel cannot see very clear, thanks to the drink I gave him, there is no fear of your being recognised as two ladies that are trying to escape from the imprisonment they have been threatened with. Besides, even if we met with any interruption, I am not without weapons, and, depend on it, I should not fail to use them, if I saw there was occasion for it."

"It must not—shall not be!" cried Alicia, resolutely. "For your generous interest in our behalf, however, we thank you, and should an opportunity ever occur, depend on it, Adrian, you will find we are not unmindful of the noble sacrifice you would have made in our favour."

"Your ladyship," exclaimed the page, "does not mean to say that you would rather be shut up in a dungeon all your life than make your escape when it can be managed so readily?"

"Liberty, Adrian, would, indeed, be the most precious boon I could receive," answered the lady;—"most ardently do I desire it, but never will I purchase it at the risk of bringing you into peril."

"You have heard us, Adrian," cried Rebecca;—"it is our determination to remain here rather than endanger your life."

"And what care I for life, think you?" demanded the page, boldly;—"am I not looking forward to the time, when I shall be a knight like my my master,—though heaven forbid that ever I should possess a heart as black as his is. No, no, ladies, I am no coward, I can assure you, and, therefore, I again beg of you to think better of this affair. Follow me, and I will conduct you by yonder secret passage, to a part of the castle that is little used, and from whence it will be easy enough to reach the gate where the guard is placed that I have been speaking of. He will be sure to let us pass unchallenged, when he sees me with you, and once outside the castle walls, it will be our own fault if ever we suffer ourselves to come inside them again."

"For the present, at least, good Adrian, we must positively refuse your proffered kindness," answered Rebecca;—"that both of us desire liberty, you may be well assured: yet the hazard to yourself is, at present, so great, that we will remain here, rather than subject you to the same perils that threaten us."

"You will not go with me, then?" cried Adrian, with evident disappointment and chagrin.

"We will not," replied our heroine.

"Then all I can say about it is, that there is as pretty a plot spoilt as ever was concocted. Everything was done to make your escape certain, and yet when the moment comes, I find you determined to throw away the chance!"

"But only," replied Lady Alicia, " for the reasons I have already given you."

"Which, to my thinking," answered the youth; " are no reasons at all. If there is any danger it is mine, and I am quite willing to run it; for you two ladies there can be no excuse, seeing that if even you should be discovered, you cannot possibly be placed in a worse situation than you at present occupy. So, now, let me persuade you to put on these disguises, and, I'll answer for it, you shall find yourselves at liberty before you are another hour older."

"Urge us no more upon this subject," exclaimed Lady Alicia, "our resolution is made up as you have heard. Leave us, therefore, and another time we may, perhaps, gladly avail ourselves of your proffered aid."

Finding they were thus determined, the youth retired, terribly disappointed at the failure of his plan, and Alicia being thus left alone with our heroine, began once more to devise a scheme by which the latter should escape from the snares into which she had fallen.

CHAPTER LXXV.

> What art thou, that usurp'st this time of night,
> Together with that fair and warlike form
> In which the majesty of buried Denmark
> Did sometimes march?—by heaven! I charge thee, speak!
>
> HAMLET.

THE night wore away heavily, and the two captive females began to regret that they had not accepted the generous offer of assistance that had been made by the page Adrian. Upon cooler reflection, it appeared to them that there were not so many difficulties in the way as they had anticipated, and now that they perceived the hopelessness of their situation, they would have given worlds for such an opportunity as the one they had rejected. It was now, however, too late, and when, at about the hour of midnight, they heard a sentinel placed as a guard beneath their window, they gave up all idea of escape, and resigned themselves to whatever fate might be in store for them. Lady Alicia now reproached herself for being the cause of preventing the escape of her fellow prisoner, and gladly would she have assented to any plan that would procure the liberation of the Hebrew Maiden, even though she herself might be doomed to pass the remainder of her days in some cheerless confinement, that had embittered so many of the latter years of her life. Rebecca saw her grief, and at once conjecturing the cause, endeavoured to change the current of her thoughts :—

"You are thoughtful, my lady," she said :—" you now regret the determination you come to in rejecting the offer that was made to us just now by the faithful Adrian."

"I do," answered Alicia ;—" not, however, on my own account, but because by so doing, I have, perhaps, thrown an obstacle in your way, which may have the effect of making you a prisoner for life in this castle."

"And if such should be my fate," cried Rebecca," I will endeavour to bear it with patience and resignation."

"But will you not," demanded Lady Alicia, "sometimes curse me in your heart for having been the means of preventing your escape, when so fair a chance was offered?"

"Never, my lady." •

"Can you then forgive me, girl?"

"You have done nothing that needs forgiveness," answered Rebecca, soothingly. "The offer made by Adrian, was certainly tempting, but even if you had not refused it as you did, I should, myself, have rejected it, rather than have brought upon that noble boy the fierce wrath of his vindictive master."

"He would have escaped with us," exclaimed Alicia, "and thus would have found safety among our friends, even from the searching wrath of Sir Gaston de Neville."

"But on the other hand," observed the Hebrew Maiden, "had he fallen again into the power of his revengeful master, it would have been to meet a certain and terrible death. He would have been tortured to force a confession from him, and when he had told the secret motives that had induced him to befriend two persecuted women, the tyrant would have ordered him to instant execution, that he might thus deprive us of all further aid from that quarter."

The bolts that secured the door of this apartment were now heard gently grating, as if some one was trying to open it cautiously, and fully expecting to see one of Sir Gaston's emissaries, who had been sent to murder them, they clung frantically to each other, in the belief that the last moment of their existence had arrived. But in this they were deceived, for as the door opened, the faithful Edith presented herself to their view, carrying in her hand a basket full of provisions, which she had brought to them at no small risk to herself.

"Don't be alarmed," she said, cautiously stepping towards them;—"it's only me, and I'm sure I wouldn't frighten you, if I could help it, for all the world."

"Edith," cred the Lady Alicia, "that you are here to do us some kind service, I am well assured. I know the generosity that prompts your heart to aid the unfortunate, but, believe me, girl, I am grieved to see you thus plunging yourself into danger, when the consequences to yourself may be so terrible."

"Indeed, my lady, there is not the least reason to be afraid," answered Edith;—"I have taken care to make every thing safe, before I ventured on this errand, and as Sir Gaston has retired to his bed-chamber, and nearly all the inmates of the castle are fast asleep, there can be very little fear of interruption."

"But some of them may be disturbed," exclaimed Rebecca, "and in that case, my good girl, I fear you will be made to bitterly repent the kindness you seek to do us."

"Well," returned Edith, "supposing they should find out that I have got a heart not quite so hardened as their own, and that I can pity the distresses of my fellow creatures,—they can only kill me for it, or shut me up in a dungeon, and I shouldn't mind either of these things very much if I could only have the satisfaction of knowing that I suffered in a good cause."

"But we for whom you suffered," exclaimed Lady Alicia, "would have to endure the harrowing consciousness that all had been brought upon you through kindness to ourselves. Leave us, therefore, my faithful Edith, and hasten away whilst there is yet a chance of doing so without being discovered."

"Presently, my lady," replied the attendant.

"Nay, I would not have you remain with us another moment;—away, girl, or your kindness will meet a punishment that I dread to think of."

"Only let me stay while I tell you what has brought me here," answered Edith;—"in the first place, then, I have brought you such refreshments as I could find conveniently without disturbing those who, perhaps, would not have been quite so compassionate towards you;—here is part of a flask of wine, and some cold partridge, and some ——"

"Alas, Edith!" sighed the Lady Alicia, "we have little appetite for the good fare you have provided;—and yet we thank thee too, girl, since it proves that even the unfortunate are not without friends in the moment of need."

"You are not, my lady," answered Edith, "for I can tell you, Adrian is as much concerned for you both, as I am, and I cannot think how disappointed the poor fellow was, because you would not try to escape just now, when he had planned every thing so famously, that he says, there was no doubt but you would have got away without any one being the wiser."

"We owe him a heavy debt of gratitude for the zeal that prompted him to serve us, even at the hazard of losing his life," cried Rebecca, ardently. "It is not the first time he has proved how much he pities us, but we are not so selfish that we would suffer him to run the risk of Sir Gaston's displeasure, for aiding those who he has marked out as victims of his persecution."

"Ah!" observed the girl, "but Adrian is not to be frightened at the anger of his master;—he has a noble spirit, and will never hear of a female being in distress without doing the best he can to get them through it."

"You seem to entertain a high opinion of the youth," said Lady Alicia, smiling at the girl's earnestness, in spite of the grief that pressed upon her own heart. "He is a favourite in the castle, I suppose, and you, among the rest, must speak in his praise, at the hazard of leading people to imagine that you are actuated by love for the youth."

"Do you think, then," said the blushing girl, "that I could ever seriously fall in love with such a whipper-snapper fellow as Master Adrian?"

"You have given us pretty good reason to suppose so," answered Lady Alicia.

"But haven't I just called him a whipper-snapper?"

"Aye," answered Rebecca, "but we are not always to take people by their words. You, perhaps, are not very anxious that other persons should possess themselves of your secret, and, therefore it is easy to say he is a disagreeable fellow, or anything else you please, in order to deceive the world."

"Well," cried Edith, "there's no denying that there are worse creatures in the world than Adrian;—he's good tempered,—and he never thinks of danger if he can only serve a friend when he may happen to need his assistance. Sir Gaston knows how he hates oppression, and for that reason, I'm afraid, he is only waiting for an opportunity to get rid of him by foul means."

"It may be so," replied Lady Alicia, "but it must not be forgotten that Adrian is not only fully aware of his master's vindictive nature, but that he has also prudence enough to keep out of danger. He will keep a strict watch upon the actions of his master, and thus I hope the danger you apprehend may be avoided."

"Yes, yes," answered Edith, "he will keep a sharp look out, I dare say, my lady; he will not trust Sir Gaston out of his sight, but then

I'm afraid he will be running into danger the moment he happens to see that others require his assistance. As a proof of it, he would have persuaded you both to escape with him to-night, and if Sir Gaston had but have caught him at it, I'll warrant he would never have another opportunity to assist the unfortunate again."

"For which reason, Edith," interposed the Hebrew Maiden, "we thought proper to reject his generous offer. He urged us strongly to seize the opportunity for flight: declaring to us that there was no fear of a discovery taking place, as he had taken care to make every thing safe before hand, and that, consequently, we had every prospect of getting clear from the tyranny of his master. We, however, were determined that no selfish desire for escape should risk his life, and, therefore, you now find us so far reconciled to our fate, that we can await the future with composure, since there is one way still left by which we can deprive this haughty Knight Templar of the revenge he meditates."

"You don't mean to say you have found out a secret way to leave the castle whenever you please?" exclaimed the attendant.

"We do know of a secret passage beyond yonder tapestry," answered Rebecca, pointing towards the place where the page had so unexpectedly presented himself before them. "A door in yonder wall we have every reason to believe would lead us to liberty, should we think fit to run the chance of a discovery. At present, however, we do not intend to make the attempt, since I have resolved to perish by my own hands rather than submit to the insolence of Sir Gaston de Neville!"

"And the Lady Alicia?"

"Will also die, should no other alternative present itself."

"Dear! dear!" cried Edith, in alarm; "and is it after all to come to this, that you are both to perish in this horrid place rather than you would get any body into trouble for assisting you to get away."

"You have heard us, girl," answered Alicia, "and let it suffice that our resolution is not to be shaken. In case of my death, however, Adrian can still do me one last and important service. Bid him go to the Convent of Franciscans, and inform the head of that house that a female has expired, whose last wish it was to be buried in the chapel belonging to the convent. My request will be acceded to, and I shall thus have the consolation of knowing, in my last moments, that my body will be within the peaceful sanctuary, where, at one time, I had fondly hoped to pass the remainder of my days in humility and prayer."

"But, my dear, good lady," cried Edith, "you surely are not in earnest, when you talk about dying and being ——"

"I am serious, girl," exclaimed Alicia, solemnly. "Life has no longer any charms for one who has been the sport of fortune for these many long and weary years. This world offers no temptations to one who fears not to die, nor do I even care for liberty, could I but return to my dreary prison with the cheering certainty that by so doing I could secure this hapless maiden from the further tyranny of the unrelenting Sir Gaston de Neville."

"Nay, think not of me, I conjure you," cried Rebecca; "for myself I feel no alarm, since I am resolved to perish by my own hands rather than live dishonoured by him I loathe and execrate."

"But your father, girl, have you forgotten the anguish your death would cost an old man whose griefs have already proved so great and grievous a burden?"

"I have not forgotten him," answered Rebecca, "but I well know that he would rather mourn for the death of a beloved child than know that she had fallen dishonoured in her life."

"And your lover," added Lady Alicia; "I have heard you say that he is possessed of every virtue that can render man most estimable,—he loves, and yet you would rather take your own-life than seek to obtain your liberty."

"Reuben Grenard would soon be resigned were he to know that I died rather than prove false to him," replied the maiden. "Our race is unhappily but too much used to persecution from those professing a different creed, and knowing the persecutions I have endured from an implacable foe, he will soon cease to regret the fate of one to whom death will prove most welcome."

"Well," exclaimed Edith, "it's most surprising to me that people can talk so coolly about dying, when most folks have such a desire to live as long as they can. For my own part I never could bear the thought of leaving this world, seeing that——"

"Peace, Edith," interrupted Lady Alicia, "and do not again break in upon us, when our thoughts are thus solemnly occupied. Leave us, for awhile, and should you chance to hear that any fresh plots are in progress against us, return and give us the earliest information you can. You will then serve us, and it is not impossible but you may prevent the act of desperation, the mention of which just now filled you with so much alarm."

"If that's the case, I'll be off directly, my lady," returned Edith;—"so now I'll leave you to enjoy as well as you can the few things I was able to get together for your supper, and in the morning I will return again with something for your breakfast, since I do not suppose any body else will take the trouble to enquire whether you happen to be starving or not."

"You will be careful, girl, not to let any one know that you have found means to see us."

"You may depend upon that, my lady, seeing that if it was found out that I had been here, Sir Gaston would get into such a desperate passion that he would either kill me outright or I should be locked up for the rest of my days without ever having a chance of making my escape."

"You will now leave us, Edith," said Lady Alicia; "by remaining longer here, you will only be running a risk of bringing upon yourself the anger of Sir Gaston de Neville. He has ordered that we should be shut up here by ourselves, and the least departure from his commands will,—as you are aware,—frequently bring down upon the offenders his severest displeasure."

"I know it, my lady," answered the girl, "and so, as you wish it, I'll go directly, only, before I leave, I hope you and this young lady will promise not to be so rash as to think of killing yourselves in case Sir Gaston should take it into his head to be violent."

"In that respect, we shall be guided by circumstances," replied Lady Alicia; "of one thing, however, you may be very certain, and that is that we shall not, upon slight cause, commit an act of violence that never can be recalled. So now leave us, Edith, and should it happen that we never meet again in this world, let it be some consolation to you that we have escaped persecutions that were too great for further endurance."

Upon this, Edith unwillingly took her departure; after which there intervened a long silence between Alicia and our heroine, the former of whom at length, leaving the window from whence she had been trying to look, said:—

"I was in hopes the moon would, ere this, have aided us with light enough to ascertain whether there was any possibility of reaching the ground in safety. All, however, is still wrapped in the gloom of night, and we must, therefore, wait till the light of the rising sun favours us."

"Which," answered Rebecca, "will not be for some hours. Nor, indeed, do I see that even then it will avail us anything, for the place is carefully guarded, and not a single chance remains, since we refused the well-meant kindness of Adrian."

"Had we not done so," replied Lady Alicia, "the poor youth might have severely suffered for the generous zeal he manifested in our behalf. To tell you the truth, I was almost inclined, at one time, to accept his offer, but when I reflected on the probable consequences to himself, I at once rejected his offer, resolving rather to suffer myself than be the cause of misery to one who would have sacrificed so much in our behalf."

"The poor fellow, I am afraid, is already suspected by Sir Gaston," answered our heroine. "He has, on former occasions, manifested the interest he takes, and should the suspicions of the Knight Templar be confirmed, it will not be long before he takes measures to revenge himself upon the unfortunate object of his wrath. Thus, it appears, every chance of assistance is denied us, and the only thing that now remains for us is, to resign ourselves to our fate, and, if need be, to die rather than live to be any longer the objects of his cruel persecutions."

Scarcely had Rebecca done speaking, when a terrific flash of lightning burst from an overhanging cloud, and immediately afterwards followed a crash of thunder that made even the strong walls of the castle shake to their very foundation. Alarmed at the suddenness of this, the two females would have sought shelter in the remotest corner of the apartment, but ere they could do this, the tapestry was violently drawn aside, and again the black phantom stood before them, wrapped in flames, and assuming an appearance more horribly spectral than ever.— Uttering a loud scream, Lady Alicia sank fainting upon the floor, but Rebecca, collecting all the courage she could, was about to render whatever assistance was in her power, when the Armed Phantom, by a motion of the arm, seemed to command her to follow him. Overcome with terror, our heroine hesitated to obey, but perceiving that the mysterious figure grew more and more impatient, she at length mustered resolution enough to venture, and as the apparition turned away, she slowly followed it through the door by which it had entered the chamber. The passage along which she proceeded was dark, except when the swift lightning darted athwart the windows, revealing not only the place she was in, but the awful being that was solemnly moving at no great distance before her. Shuddering at the situation in which she found herself, Rebecca timidly pursued her way; now passing through a long range of apartments, and from the further extremity of these, ascending a flight of winding stairs that seemed to lead to an upper chamber of one of the turrets. Here she expected to find a termination of her labours, but, to her surprise, a secret door flew open, as if by magic, discovering an apartment beyond, lighted up with the rays of a solitary lamp, betokening that it was occupied. Somewhat re-assured by this, our heroine passed through the opening, and immediately found herself in a spacious apartment, in one part of which stood a bed, that appeared to be occupied. Wondering what all this could mean, she gazed round to satisfy herself, when the Black Phantom, gliding with a noiseless step, advanced to the bed, and, throwing aside the curtains, discovered the sleeping form of Sir Gaston de Neville! Terrified at thus finding herself in the presence of her worst enemy, Rebecca started back and would have fled screaming from the room, but the Phantom, with an expressive sign, commanded her to be silent, and, on turning

towards the door, she perceived that it was closed, and that thus her escape was rendered impossible. The alarm of the maiden was thus raised to the highest pitch, and she looked imploringly towards her unearthly conductor, but the grim spectre regarded her with a stern look, and pointing to a dagger that was lying unsheathed upon a table, seemed as if he commanded her to take it in her hands. Our heroine now believed that the apparition intended to warn her that danger was to be apprehended, and that she was to take this means for defence in case there should be any necessity to guard herself against the attacks of an insidious foe. Acting upon this impulse, she eagerly grasped the poniard, and as she did so, a loud crash was heard, lightning again darted through the chamber, and the Black Phantom disappeared in the same mysterious manner that he had at first presented himself before her.

Trembling with fear, Rebecca now gazed round to see whether there was any way by which she might effect her escape, but, at that moment, the knight started from his slumber, and perceiving the form of his intended victim, who still clasped the deadly weapon, he shouted loudly for assistance, and, having divested himself only of his armour on retiring to rest, he threw himself, with a sudden bound, from his couch, and seized upon the terrified girl ere she had time to seek for safety in flight. At this period, too, the door of the chamber was burst open, and Roland le Mark, followed by several of the knight's dependants, rushed into the room to the assistance of their master.

"You see," exclaimed Sir Gaston de Neville, "how narrowly I have this night escaped the death that was meditated by this enfuriated woman; behold! she has come armed for my destruction, and even now she grasps in her hand the fatal instrument with which my life was to have been sacrificed by her hellish fury!"

"Aye, aye," cried Roland, "here is pretty clear evidence of her guilty intentions; so now, since you have so narrowly escaped the fate she intended, we only wait your orders to carry her without delay to the torture chamber!"

"I am innocent of the diabolical designs charged against me," exclaimed Rebecca, shocked at the base motives that had been imputed to her; "I am innocent," she repeated, "and let me hear who dares charge me with entertaining an idea of slaying him who calls himself thy master!"

"This bravado will not do," returned Sir Gaston; your presence here at this late hour of the night, the hatred you are well known to bear me, and the fact of your being found with a weapon in you hand, all serve to prove that you came hither with the determination of satiating your revenge upon one who, instead of being an enemy, has ever sought to convince you that he is your friend."

"And how do you now seek to prove it?" demanded Rebecca, scornfully; "is it by accusing me of contemplating a crime that my soul abhors?"

"Why come you here?" asked Sir Gaston, "if it was not to slay the man you profess to hate?"

"My presence here," answered our heroine, "is involved in so much mystery, that I must confess I scarcely expect to find credence for my explanation. If, however, my word is to be taken, I solemnly declare that I never contemplated the foul crime that has been alleged against me."

"You speak of the affair being involved in mystery," exclaimed Sir Gaston de Neville, "but surely you will be able to tell me how it was that you found your way to this chamber?"

"I was guided hither by an armed apparition," cried Rebecca, shuddering at the recollection.

"Humph!" growled the Knight Templar; "a marvellous tale, truly; but one that will obtain little credit from those who laugh to scorn the idea of spiritual beings walking the earth. You speak of an apparition, girl, but how does it happen that I saw nothing, when I woke and discovered you standing near my couch with a poniard in your hand?"

"It vanished," answered Rebecca, "a moment before you were roused from your sleep."

"It must have been up the chimney, then," exclaimed Sir Gaston,— "for the door was fastened when these men arrived, and as a proof of it they were obliged to break it open ere they could obtain admittance to my chamber."

"Aye, this is a falsehood from beginning to end," cried Roland le Mark; "the tale is a most improbable one, and since she refuses to give a little better explanation of her motives for coming here, I propose that we give her a taste of the torture, just by way of letting her see that we are not to be trifled with."

"Your words do not terrify me," answered the Hebrew Maiden, with composure; "I am fully aware of the little mercy I have to expect from the ruthless fiends amongst whom I have fallen; yet, knowing that there is One above all, who watches over even the meanest of his creatures, I can resign myself to my fate without a murmur or reproach."

"Well," exclaimed Roland, "perhaps you may soon prove your firmness in a way you little expect. Sir Gaston has good cause to believe your designs against him were murderous, and though he once loved you more than you deserved, I should hope he will not be so tender hearted as to let you off without learning that he can punish the guilty as they deserve."

"Peace, Roland," cried the knight, "and do not interfere in an affair that concerns none but myself. You are aware," he continued, addressing himself to Rebecca, "that I now possess the power of life or death over you, and that your present situation is a hopeless one, unless your haughty spirit yields to the circumstances you are placed in. Choose, therefore, girl, whether you will now accept the terms I have before offered, and thus secure a life of happiness, or, by continued obstinacy, bring down the penalty I have the power to inflict?"

"I am not to be intimidated by the fear of death, Sir Gaston," answered the maiden, resolutely; "too long already have I been the victim of your continued persecutions, and, now, the greatest boon you could bestow upon me would be to put a period to those heavy afflictions that have made life a burden to me."

"You are still resolved to baffle me, then?"

"I am."

"Rash girl, you will bitterly repent this step!" exclaimed the knight, furiously; "you have yet to learn what desperation may drive me to, and, by heaven, you shall yet bow that haughty spirit even to the very dust."

"You know not with what a strong armour virtue encircles those who can resist the threats of villany," answered Rebecca, unmoved by these threats. "I have already proved that fear for my own safety can never oblige me to yield, and though you now threaten me with death, I can laugh your idle words to scorn, even though it should be your will to afflict me with the most cruel tortures that human ingenuity can invent."

"Perhaps there may be yet some vulnerable point," exclaimed the enraged knight; "your father and Reuben Grenard shall, ere long, be prisoners in the castle, and each day when I order them to be placed upon the rack, you shall be present to witness their agonies, and hear the curses they will heap upon her when obstinacy has brought them the tortures they are compelled to endure. This will try your boasted courage, and should it fail, you shall behold their execution, and then meet the same fate you have brought upon those you profess to love."

"Heaven will never suffer the innocent to fall thus, through the cruel malignity of the wicked," answered Rebecca. "I am not deprived of the blessed balm that hope gives even to the most wretched, and, therefore, I can calmly wait the moment when you intend to carry your base design into execution."

"Lead her away, Roland," exclaimed the knight;—"convey her to a place of safety, and in the morning I will give further commands respecting her. And mark me, 'sirrah, see that she escape you not, as you would avoid the fiercest wrath of one who will not fail to punish even the slightest omission of your duty!"

Rebecca, without making any further reply, followed the ruffian from the room, leaving Sir Gaston de Neville full of rage at the firmness with which she had rejected his offers.

CHAPTER LXXVI.

"Thou will find him merciful,
And shouldst thou prove thy charges 'gainst thy foe,
He'll do thee ample justice."

THE LAW OF DENMARK.

THE news was soon spread throughout the castle, that the Hebrew Maiden had made an attempt upon the life of Sir Gaston de Neville, and as few ventured to express a doubt upon the subject, the retainers wer loud in their denunciations against the unfortunate object of their sus picion. It was in fact, generally believed that the knight had only es caped death by a miracle, and with the exception of Adrian, there wa not one among the dependants who did not give full credit to the story The page, however, was resolutely opposed to them in this matter, an when he at length found that no argument would serve to alter th opinion they had formed, he began to laugh at the rumour, as one tha ought to be scouted by all who professed to be reasonable beings.

"Is it likely," he said, "that one so fair and gentle would seek t stain her hands with the blood of a fellow-creature. Is there a ma among you that can conscientiously declare it to be his belief that th Jews ever intended to raise a poniard against the life of our noble master?

"I don't know what you may believe about it," answered Roland l Mark; "but it so happens that I was the very first to enter the roor after Sir Gaston called for assistance, and I found him struggling wit the wench, whilst she still held in her hand the weapon she had intende to have struck him with."

"Aye, we all were witnesses of that," exclaimed a dozen voice together.

"Well," cried Adrian," and a great deal you were witness of, even i what you are speaking of is true. We all know,—do we not,—that Si Gaston has fancied himself desperately in love with the girl, and thoug she has told him plainly enough how much she abhors him, he still pe secutes the poor creature, till, I suppose, he has driven her almost mad.

"And so," observed Roland, "you mean to argue that she had right to seek his life!"

"I do not mean to argue anything of the sort, sir," replied the page "but I certainly do mean to say that if our master began to grow to violent, it was high time she should begin to think of protecting hersel Perhaps, no other alternative remained for her, and that being the cas she was completely justified in protecting herself, even though it migh be that she stabbed him to the heart."

"Well," observed Roland, "I should like Sir Gaston to hear you opinion upon this subject; he would, no doubt, feel himself highly flat tered, and, I dare say, you would be rewarded in a way you richly de serve."

"If you could give him a hint to that effect, there is no question abou it," exclaimed Adrian. "However, it seems you wish to fasten a quarr on me, and as I have no desire to come in closer contact with you, w will drop this subject before worse comes of it."

"Sir Gaston shall not fail to hear what you have said, boy," muttere Roland, fiercely; "it is as well he should know who are his enemie and as there can no longer be any doubt about you, I shall let him knot what you think of this attempt against his life."

"He is already aware that I hate oppression, and would take part with the weak against the strong," replied the youth. "He knows I am resolved to lend whatever aid I can to prevent his infamous designs, and I have long had reason to believe that he only waits an opportunity to overwhelm me with his wrath."

"Why, if that was the case, boy, he could have silenced you long enough ago."

"And so he would," answered Adrian, "only that he happens to have been under obligations to my father, who, I have heard, once did him an important service; and, to do Sir Gaston justice, he has, so far, treated me with tolerable kindness."

"Then why do you now take part against him?" demanded the other gruffly.

"I do not take part against him," answered Adrian, "but since it happens that he has been acting the part of a tyrant towards a helpless woman, it is high time that some one should interfere in her behalf. Not that I can do much good, perhaps, but since there's a parcel of ruffians in the castle that will not do their duty, I will take care to do mine, even if it should cost me my life."

"You talk pretty freely, young fellow," exclaimed Roland le Mark, "but, perhaps, we may, by and by, find means to change your tones a little. There are no ruffians, as you call them, in the castle, for if there had been, you would not have lived to call them by such a name again."

"I know of one, at any rate," observed Adrian, looking very hard at the last speaker, who understanding the allusion, had half drawn his dagger from its sheath, when a comrade interposed to prevent any further disagreement.

"Come, come, Roland," he exclaimed, "never let it be said that a mere boy had it in his power to make you angry;—and you, Adrian," he continued, "remember that you are speaking to those who are not used to hearing people's minds spoken too freely. We are, besides, friendly towards Sir Gaston de Neville, and if you say anything that calls his honour in question, it may so far provoke our wrath, that you may never have it in your power to offend again."

"In other words," observed Adrian, drily, "you are ready to cut my throat if I should have the hardihood to speak my mind freely."

"Why, perhaps you are not far out in your guess, young master," exclaimed the other. "At all events, you have had fair warning, and if that is not enough, you must take the consequences, that's all I know about it."

"And so," rejoined the page, "a poor girl is to be shut up in this castle, and if any one ventures to say a word in her favour, he is to have his throat cut for his pains!"

"Why, look you, Adrian," exclaimed Roland le Mark, who, by this time had got over the mortal affront he had received; "it must be allowed, I believe, that Sir Gaston de Neville is master of this castle, and that he has a right to do in it as he pleases. Well, allowing that it is so, what does all this come to?—that he has fallen in love with a pretty wench, and as she thought proper to treat him with contempt, he has found means to get her in his power."

"And by what right has he done so?" demanded the page.

"That is a matter," answered Roland, "that neither you nor I have any business to enquire into. Let it be sufficient for us, that she is here, and, seeing that the wench is only a Jewess, why should we trouble our heads at all about it?"

"Only a Jewess?" cried Adrian; "and is it possible that people, calling themselves Christians, should seek to oppress another class of persons, because they worship their Maker under different forms?— But I will not believe, Roland, that even you,—reckless as you are,— can uphold an act of tyranny upon such weak grounds as you have urged."

"Upon my life the boy speaks like a learned clerk!" exclaimed the ruffian, unmoved by the appeal; "he talks as if he pretended to know more than we do, and, in my opinion, we must take him down a little, or the place will hardly be large enough to hold him by and by."

"If you are wise, Adrian, you will hold your tongue," said a stander-by; "we are not used to arguments like yours in this place, for if we don't happen to agree readily upon certain points, we have a very speedy way of convincing our opponents. Every man wears a sword by his side, and he who is strongest and has most skill, generally succeeds in getting the best of the arguments."

"Aye," exclaimed Roland le Mark, "that's our way of settling knotty points; it's a convincing way enough of setting things to rights, and saves a great deal of trouble in the bargain."

"Would that I were older!" cried Adrian, fervently.

"And wherefore do you wish that?"

"Because I should then be able to convince you that there is one in this castle both able and willing to do battle in behalf of a defenceless woman."

"Ha! ha! ha!" shouted Roland; "why one would be almost inclined to think you have fallen desperately in love with the Jewess!"

"At all events," answered the youthful page, "I can admire her constancy and virtue;—she has withstood the temptations offered her by wealth, and even the threats of her persecutor have not compelled her to forget the vows of constancy and affection that she has given to another."

"Ah!—you speak of a youth called Reuben Grenard?"

"I do."

"Poor devil!" exclaimed Roland, "I would have him take care of himself, for he is in our master's way, and it may happen that he will one day or other, suffer for having dared to love the girl that is sought by Sir Gaston de Neville. It has long been proposed to put him out of the way, and I am much mistaken if our master delays much longer the only chance he has of curing the Jewess of her love for another."

"Surely Sir Gaston would not sanction a murder!" cried Adrian, in alarm.

"Psha! why call it by such an ugly name?" exclaimed Roland le Mark. "Murder is a word that I never like to hear uttered; it brings unpleasant recollections to one's mind, and is apt to make a man fancy all sorts of disagreeable things. Not that I have ever had anything to do with such matters, but, for all that, I don't like to hear the word used."

"It is a word of fearful omen to the guilty," observed Adrian.

"Come, come, young fellow, say no more about it," exclaimed the other;—"you know our notions about this affair between our master and the Hebrew girl; so join with us if you look to your own interest, for, depend on it, it will be a bad day's work for you, should Sir Gaston happen to find out that you take part against him."

"He is already aware of it," answered the youth.

"In that case, you have much to be thankful for," returned Roland, "for it is seldom that he fails to punish those that would thwart his views, in a way that prevents their ever doing so again. In other words, he gets rid of them, and I need not tell you in what manner."

"I am not afraid of him," said the page, "for I have already told you he had treated me with particular marks of his favour."

"That may be, young sir," exclaimed one of the men, "but our master don't happen to be burdened with a very large stock of patience, and, take my word for it, you will, one of these days, repent putting him out of humour. There are deep dungeons hereabouts, and nobody but himself knows how many poor devils are lying imprisoned in them."

"And yet," cried Adrian, "this is the master you can cheerfully serve! You know his tyranny, but have not the spirit to brook the bonds that bind you!"

"Why, for that matter," replied Roland le Mark, "I should like to see the man that would dare thwart him as you have done. It would be his first and last offence, I'm thinking, for it dont often happen that he gives a fellow an opportunity to displease him a second time. You, however, seem to be privileged to say and do just as you think fit, though, I warn you again, that those goings on will not last for ever, and so you may chance to find out before you are much older."

"You mean to say, then, observed the page, "that it will be dangerous for me to say a word in behalf of the unfortunate Hebrew Maiden?"

"That's just what I do mean."

"And even if it were so," continued Adrian, "think you I should be afraid to run the risk of his displeasure?"

"I don't know what you might be afraid of," answered Roland; "but I would not do it myself, for the value of all the jewels in the king's crown."

"And so the girl might perish for the want of one friend to stand forward in her defence?"

"Why, as for her perishing," retorted the other, "I don't see that we need concern ourselves much about that, as she is only one of the accursed Jewish tribe, and who is there, I should like to know, that would care to risk his own life for the sake of an unbelieving Israelite?"

"I would," answered Adrian; "aye, you may smile at me, Roland le Mark, but I have not yet learned to distinguish any great difference between Jews and Christians. We are all of us brethren;—worshipping the same Maker, and looking for the same reward after death shall have removed us from this world. Nay, I have seen many of this despised race of Israelites, whose virtues should have put to the blush many of those who profess themselves to be Christian."

"You are a fine champion in their favour, certainly," exclaimed Roland, with a sneer.

"I speak only as I have found them," replied the page. "They have long borne the ill-usage of the world with patience and meekness, and surely that of itself ought to be sufficient to secure our pity in their behalf.

"Well, think of them as you like," cried Roland, impatiently; "look upon them as persecuted and hardly used, but don't try to gain any friends for them among us; we all hate the whole tribe of them, and if we only had our own will in the matter, there would not be a Jew alive in the kingdom at the end of a week."

"It is useless then, to say any more upon the subject," exclaimed Adrian. "At first, it must be confessed, I thought I was speaking to men, but it seems that your unfortunate prejudice has lowered you to the level of brutes."

"Thank you for the compliment," retorted Roland le Mark, in no very good humour. "You have tried it on very hard to make us think well of these people, but you may take my word for it, that it will require more argument than you can bring forward, to convince us that Jews are equal to ourselves. So, good day to you, sirrah, and think yourself lucky if I do not report what has passed to Sir Gaston de Neville. He would not be best pleased to hear that you take part against him, and it's about a hundred to one that he took speedy means to convince you of the madness of endeavouring to cross him in love affairs."

With this, the retainers took their departure, leaving the page to ruminate alone upon the best means he could adopt to release Rebecca from the difficulties that pressed so heavily upon her. He knew, however, that individually he could render her no aid, and, as a last resource, determined secretly to visit the house of Isaac of Tadcaster, and to inform him of the situation in which his daughter was placed, so that immediate means might be adopted for her rescue. This resolution was no sooner formed than put in a train for immediate execution, and taking an opportunity to leave the castle unseen, he took his way towards that part of the suburbs which was then principally inhabited by the Jews. Wishing, however, to avoid observation as much as possible, he took a circuitous route, and it was consequently some time before he arrived before the humble dwelling he was in search of. Here he paused a few moments, ere he entered, and from the low sounds that met his ears, he discovered that those within were bewailing the fresh troubles that had befallen them. Unwilling to intrude upon their grief, he paused yet a little longer, but at length, raising the latch, he entered, and beheld a scene that filled his breast with sorrow. Isaac of Tadcaster, bowed down by his afflictions, was lying stretched upon his humble pallet, and Reuben Grenard was kneeling by his side, endeavouring to pour the balm of consolation into the ears of the grief-stricken old man.

" Be comforted," he said, " and place your dependence on that Power which chastens us for its own wise purposes. Rebecca is, at present, in great peril, but rely upon it, she will yet triumph over the evil machinations of our enemies."

The old man heard him, but replied not, except with groans and lamentations, and taking advantage of this pause, Adrian advanced towards them, saying,—

" Pardon me, friends, for thus intruding on you, at such a moment as this, but, trusting that I may serve thee, I ventured to come unbidden into your presence, that I might offer whatever aid it is in my power to give."

" Who is it?" demanded the old man, anxiously, but without directing his eyes towards the visitor. " Who is it, I say, who thus offers that which he has not the power to perform?"

' It is Adrian," answered Reuben Grenard, " the page of our unrelenting foe, Sir Gaston de Neville."

" Bid him depart, then," cried Isaac; " command him to leave the home his master has rendered desolate."

" You mistake the motives that brought me here," answered the youth. " I came hither as a friend, and am willing to sacrifice even life itself in your service."

" How say'st thou?" demanded Isaac; " thou wouldst deceive me, boy, for who ever heard of one, professing himself to be a Christian, who would bestow even a kindly thought upon the miserable and heavily persecuted Jews?"

" Nay, speak not thus harshly to the youth, interposed Reuben Grenard; "he has, ere now, proved himself to be our friend, and it would, therefore, be but just to hear the motives that have brought him here."

"I meant not to speak unkindly to the youth," answered Isaac, in a tone of greater kindness; "but grief has made me churlish, and I am alike to all persons, whether they be friends or foes. Speak, therefore, boy, and say what service thou wouldst do us."

"You are doubtless aware," answered the youth, "that your daughter Rebecca is now again in the castle of Sir Gaston de Neville?"

"I am, indeed!" groaned the old man.

"The fatal intelligence reached us some hours since," said Reuben Grenard, as the aged Israelite once more fell into a train of melancholy reflections; "we heard it from some of our friends, and we have been in vain trying to think of some method by which we may release her from the power of the base knight."

"May I ask," demanded Adrian, "what design you have formed to secure her rescue?"

"We have not fixed upon any, at present," replied the younger Israelite; "difficulties beset us on every side, and we were just beginning to despair, when you so unexpectedly presented yourself before us."

"There is no resource left," exclaimed Isaac, bitterly; "the evil ways of the wicked prosper, and it only remains for us to bow with submission to the affliction that has fallen on us."

"But it behoves you to make every effort to avert the destruction of your daughter's happiness," observed the page. "She is, unhappily, rendered powerless, and as you have still the means left you, it is necessary to exert them for her rescue."

"Think you, then," asked Isaac, despondingly, "there is any chance of aiding her escape from the castle?"

"I do not," replied Adrian, "but you can yet appeal to the king, who

No. 54

will not fail to exercise his authority to snatch her from the dreadful fate she may, ere this, be condemned to."

"Hah!" cried the old man, starting up from his couch, "your words fill me with a new dread!—What mean you, boy?—Is my child's life in peril?"

"It is."

"Of what crime is she now acused?"

"Of attempting to assassinate Sir Gaston de Neville."

"The villain most cruelly belies her!" exclaimed Isaac, in a paroxysm of terror. "My child is too gentle,—too good, ever to contemplate the murder even of her direst foe."

"She is so," replied Adrian, "and yet, what I have told you is the truth. Last night, by some means or other, she contrived to escape from the place of her imprisonment, and, strange as it may appear, was found in the chamber where Sir Gaston was sleeping. On being roused, he saw her standing near his couch with a poniard in her hand, and instantly giving an alarm, the room was soon filled with his retainers, who were thus made witnesses of the deed with which she is charged."

"This is some trick to secure her destruction!" exclaimed Isaac, in alarm at the news he thus heard;—"the villain finds that all other means have failed, and now he would bring her to an ignominious and undeserved doom!"

"Nay, give not way to despair," cried Reuben Grenard; "this is but another effort to destroy the innocent victim of this false knight, and, like all his other designs, will fail ere he can accomplish his wish."

"Would that I could think so," groaned the Jew, in the agony of his heart.

"Despair," exclaimed Adrian, "will but prevent the service you may yet effect in her favour. I have come to give you the earliest intimation of her danger, and, by using prompt means, she may yet be rescued from the dangers that surround her on every side."

"Thou say'st truly, boy," cried Isaac; "much depends upon my exertions, and I will instantly repair to the castle, and demand my daughter from the villain who has dared to tear her from me."

"In that," replied the page, "I fear you would succeed but indifferently; remember, old man, your grey hairs would obtain no favour from Sir Gaston de Neville, who, on finding himself likely to be frustrated, would order you to be thrown into one of his dungeons, and thus your daughter would be placed more than ever at his mercy."

"Wouldst thou have me remain inactive, when my child is in peril of her life?"

"I would not," replied Adrian, "but whatever steps you take must be conducted with caution, or all will be attempted in vain. The king will listen to the narrative of your wrongs, and from him alone must you expect the release of Rebecca."

"I will instantly seek an audience of him," cried Reuben Grenard; "he is ever accessible even to the humblest of his subjects, and, therefore, will not refuse the prayers I will urge to him."

"But even the sovereign cannot procure her liberty, now that she is charged with attempting the life of the Knight Templar," answered the page, despondingly.

"She is innocent!" cried Isaac, wringing his hands in despair; "my child never sought the blood of her enemy, and yet this fatal conspiracy may end in her destruction."

"Nay, wait with patience," said Adrian; "the charge that has been brought against her is easily made, but, depend on it, the king will not be satisfied until the strictest examination has been made to remove all doubt. He knows the evil that lurks in the heart of Sir Gaston de Neville, and, suspecting some treachery in the affair, will not be easily prevailed upon to regard her as being guilty of the attempted assassination."

"King Richard is as just as he is noble and generous," exclaimed Isaac; "he has ever proved himself to be the friend of the persecuted, yet, as Sir Gaston can at all times gain access to him, I fear he may be imposed upon by some artfully contrived tale, wearing the appearance of truth."

"Sir Gaston is out of favour at court, just at present," observed the page.

"That we are aware of," answered Reuben, "but he is not without friends, who are constantly about the king's person, and who will take care to report this matter in the most unfavourable light. We shall thus have many against us, and it is not difficult to foresee that their influence will prevail against those who are regarded with the most cruel prejudice."

"But," exclaimed the youth, "King Richard has proved himself to be a fair and impartial judge;—he is no enemy of the Jews, as you are aware, and whatever charge may be brought against Rebecca, will be carefully looked into before any decision is made."

"Think you then," demanded the old man, anxiously, "that the king will himself preside at her examination?"

"That will depend on circumstances," replied Adrian. "Unfortunately, she is now in the safe custody of Sir Gaston de Neville, and there is every reason to suppose that he will endeavour to be both judge and accuser, in this case. To prevent this, however, you or Reuben Grenard must see the king, and if the circumstances of the case are explained to him, he will order the examination to take place in his presence, and thus the knight will be foiled in his attempt to keep the affair secret."

"We will go to the palace together," exclaimed Isaac, "for the prayers and entreaties of an old man will not be urged in vain, when justice is the only demand he makes. Reuben, too, will be pleading for the life of his affianced bride, and, with such an object in view, he will scarcely fail to prove the injustice she is likely to endure, unless the royal authority is interposed in her behalf."

"May heaven reward your endeavours with success," cried the page, fervently.

"It will,—it will," exclaimed the old man; "my heart assures me that my application for justice will not pass unheeded, and Sir Gaston shall yet see that his cruel tyranny will not last for ever."

"But, in the meantime," cried Reuben, "she who is the object of our cares is a prisoner in the hands of her worst and most vindictive enemy."

"Not for long though," answered the page; "your interview with the king must not be delayed a single instant, and when your errand has been fully explained, an order will be sent to Sir Gaston, commanding him to surrender up the captive to the king's officers. She will thus be placed in safety, and no doubt the charge will be inquired into with as much speed as possible."

"Were I but assured that my daughter will be removed from the custody of Sir Gaston de Neville, I could rest satisfied," exclaimed the old man. "Away from him, she will be safe, and I could even resign myself to the cruel destiny that has so long harassed and oppressed me."

"Take my word for it," returned Adrian, "that all will turn out better than was expected. It has thus far been your fate to be afflicted with severe misfortunes, but a brighter prospect will, ere long, open before you, rendering your future life calm and contented."

"For my daughter's sake, I hope your prophecy will prove correct," replied the aged Israelite. "For her I would be content to give up the few remaining years of my life, and could leave the world without regret, on condition that I beheld my child wedded to the husband of her choice."

"All of which will be accomplished, depend on it," cried Adrian, gaily.

"You seem confident, young man," exclaimed the elder Jew.

"I am," replied the page, "for things have gone crossly so long, that I think there can be no doubt they are speedily about to change for the better. So, set cheerfully about the task you have undertaken, and rely upon it with confidence, that the moment of your daughter's deliverance from peril is near at hand."

"We will delay no longer," cried the old man, moving anxiously towards the door ;—"so come with me, Reuben, and let us away to the palace;— the king will not refuse to grant us an audience, and Sir Gaston de Neville shall yet find that retribution must follow the evil he has practised against us."

Bidding farewell to the page, the old man and his companion proceeded to the palace, leaving Adrian to return to the castle with the same secrecy that he had left it.

CHAPTER LXXVII.

"What errand takes thee forth ?—
Speak, sirrah, wilt thou ;—tell me where thou goest,
Or thou shalt move no further ?"

THE GLADIATOR.

HURRYING on towards the place of destination, the old man and his companion spoke but little of the important business that had thus suddenly called them from home. Their thoughts were, indeed, so occupied in the affair which just then drew their attention, that they were unconscious of the approach of a crowd of persons who were advancing towards them. Presently, however, they were roughly accosted by the fellow who led the mob, and raising their eyes from the ground, they beheld the huge and burly form of their old enemy, Simon Hyde, the tanner.

"Whither are you going, now ?" he demanded fiercely of them; "what devil's business are you on, that you are hurrying on as if there was mischief in the wind ?"

"And who art thou that dost thus rudely accost us ?" asked the old man.

"One that will not let you pass till his question has been answered," replied Simon Hyde.

"Ha !" exclaimed the Jew; "is not the highway free to me as well as to thyself ?"

"It is not,"

"And why ?"

"Because thou art a Jew, and, therefore, unworthy to tread in my footsteps."

"A most excellent reason, truly !" answered the old man; "and so two peaceful subjects of the king are to be driven from the common highway at the bidding of a bully like thyself !"

"Fair words, sirrah !" exclaimed the fellow, fiercely; "fair words, I say, or you and I may chance to quarrel, and in that case, I know who would have the worst of it."

"Coward !" cried Reuben Grenard, interposing himself between the old man and his assailant, "wouldst thou try thy strength against one whose years should be his protection?"

"Aye," retorted the blusterer, "or against thyself either, if it is thy wish to see how a good Christian would treat a dog of a Jew."

"Nay, let us pass quietly on our way," cried Isaac, dreading a contest in which he could foresee that his youthful companion would get the worst. "We have not interfered with thee, and, therefore, have a right to proceed without further interruption from thee, and thy blustering comrades."

"Come, come, no insolence, old man," exclaimed Simon Hyde, furiously. "Keep a civil tongue towards us, or we may give thee something for thy pains that will not soon be forgotten."

"Thou wouldst use violence, then, towards two unoffending passengers, who would have pursued their way without even bestowing a thought upon thee?"

"Aye, that would we," answered the fellow ;—"we are never very particular about these matters, and since you happen to be a brace of unbelieving Jews, I have a mind to amuse myself with a little sport at your expense. What say you, comrades,—shall we show these dogs what it is to be insolent to their betters?"

"Aye, aye," was repeated by a score or two of voices.

"There," continued the fellow, addressing himself to Isaac and his young friend, "you hear how willing they are to join me in a frolic, so now, answer whatever questions I choose to put to you, or you know the end of it."

"What wouldst thou know?" asked Isaac, alarmed lest they should execute the threatened violence.

"In the first place, we would know where you are going?"

"That," answered the elder Jew, "is a question that cannot concern thee;—however, since I am compelled to submit, I will inform thee that we are in our way to the palace."

"Humph!—to see the king, I suppose?"

"You have guessed our motives."

"And do you think his majesty will be troubled with a couple of pitiful fellows like yourselves?"

"I know not that he will," replied Isaac ;—"but he has on former occasions granted us interviews, and, therefore, do I hope we shall not be refused now."

"And supposing he should condescend to hold converse with you, what is the business you are so anxious to see him about?"

"It is upon a private matter," answered Isaac, "and, therefore, cannot concern thee to know."

"But as I choose to know it," exclaimed Simon Hyde, "it would not be safe for you to be obstinate about the matter. The truth is, however, that you are going to make a complaint against some one or other, and I should like to know who it is you would tell tales about?"

"I go to complain of Sir Gaston," answered Isaac. "He hath foully wronged me ;—hath stolen my daughter from me, and it is to obtain her release that I am about to seek the interference of King Richard."

"Indeed!" exclaimed Simon Hyde, with affected surprise, "and so a Christian Knight is not to do as he thinks proper, but up starts an insolent knave, like yourself, to mar his pleasures. But you shall be disappointed this time, old fellow, for unless you are content to walk back from whence you came, I and my comrades here will do something that will prevent your going to tell tales again."

"Let us pass without further interruption," cried Reuben Grenard ;— "move from our path, I say, or ——"

"Well," interrupted the ruffian, "or what were you going to say? Speak out, man, for though we are roughish chaps, we have no dislike to hearing a bit of truth, even though it may chance to come from the lips of a Jew."

"Heed him not, I intreat," cried Isaac, eagerly interposing to prevent mischief;—"do not regard any words that may fall from him, for he is nearly distracted at the peril that threatens my daughter, and gives utterance to words that I fear may create a quarrel between you."

"Ho, ho !" shouted Simon Hyde, " so he is the lover of the wench you are speaking of ?"

"He is her affianced husband," answered the old man ;—"I have long looked forward with pleasure to the period that was to unite them, and now when the marriage rites were about to be solemnized, she is stolen from me by the base arts of a heartless libertine, and I have but too much reason to dread that she will be doomed to death, unless I can speedily obtain an interview with the king, who, can alone save her from destruction."

"Well, I can't help that you know," returned the tanner, with indifference ; "Sir Gaston de Neville is a great man, and, therefore, has a right to fall in love with whoever he pleases ; nay, more,—you ought to think it a great honour that he has condescended to notice your daughter, for I can tell you it is not every Jewess that has the luck to gain the heart of such a man as Sir Gaston de Neville."

"He is a villain !" exclaimed the elder Israelite.

"It is well he is not present to hear you pay him so high a compliment."

"Would that he were here," cried Reuben Grenard, "for enraged as I now am, my hand should never quit its hold upon his throat until he lay a blackened and hideous corpse at my feet."

"Upon my life, young sir," exclaimed the other, "you speak as if the brave Sir Gaston would be nothing in your hands, if he and you happened to come to close quarters."

"I make no vain threats," answered Reuben ;—"but heaven knows I have received wrongs enough from him, and should an opportunity ever arrive, I will not fail to revenge myself for them."

"I would advise you to take care how you ever cross his path," retorted Simon, with a sneer. "Sir Gaston is not noted for possessing any extraordinary share of patience, and, depend on it, he will spoil your bragging if ever you come within arm's length of him. So return home with the old man, and instead of interfering any further in this affair, think about looking after your own safety, lest you should happen to be in the lion's grip when you least expect it."

"We will not return home till we have seen the king," exclaimed Isaac. "My daughter's life,—nay, more,—her honour depends on it, and rather would I meet instant death from your hands, than abandon the only chance that offers for her rescue."

"Well," returned Simon Hyde, "we shall see who will have his way in this affair ;—you have heard me say that you shall not pass, and that being the case, you might as well attempt to take heaven by storm, as to move me from what I have said."

"Nor will we be bullied from our purpose," exclaimed Reuben, resolutely ; "so stand aside, sirrah, and let no one dare to stretch forth a hand to prevent our passing onwards."

"Would you madly seek your own destruction?" asked Simon Hyde, stepping forward to prevent their going on.

"We are not to be frightened from our purpose by the blustering of a villain," replied Reuben, undauntedly. "An errand of importance has called us from our home, and be assured nothing that you or your comrades can say or do, will deter us from our design. And now, having thus explained myself, I desire that no further interruption may be offered us."

"Shall we quietly put up with this, comrades?" demanded the tanner, addressing himself to his motley associates.

"No,—no,—down with the Jews!—down with them!" shouted the excited mob.

"There," exclaimed Simon, "you hear what you have got to expect from them!—these fellows hate your whole tribe, as much as I do myself, and if I only gave the word of command, they would be upon you, like so many bloodhounds in eager pursuit of their prey."

"But you dare not give the word of command," returned Isaac;—"you dare not do it, I say, for so surely as either of us might be slain, so surely would you, as the leader of the mob, receive the reward of a murderer."

"Murderer!" exclaimed the ruffian, with scorn;—"do you call it murder, then, to take away the life of an unbelieving Jew?—Psha! I should get the praise of my fellow men for it, and even the king, much as he favours the Hebrew tribe, would not dare to interfere, when the voice of the whole nation would be raised against him."

"That is a point I shall not argue with thee," answered Isaac;—"at present, my object is to gain an audience of the king, and again I demand to be allowed to pass on my way without further interruption."

"The old man seems plaguy obstinate," said the leader, turning to the crowd, that was now pressing eagerly onwards. "He won't take advice, so, if he moves a step in advance, fall on him and this young fellow here, and prove to them, that we are not to be set at defiance, when once we have made up our minds to anything."

"Away with them both to the horse-pond!" shouted the mob, and the next moment both Isaac and Reuben were seized hold of, and would have been dragged from the place, had not a small party of men, whose tattered garments denoted them to be beggars, at that juncture rushed to the assistance of the Jews, and with their stout oaken clubs, laid about a dozen of the ruffians on the ground. As for Simon Hyde, he had contrived to escape with a smart blow or two, that made him wince with pain, and then advancing with a blustering air towards the leader of the rescuing party, he demanded, in an authoritative tone, who it was that had dared to interfere in behalf of the objects of his wrath. This the person addressed did not think fit to reply to at first, but observing that the mob which was led by Simon Hyde, was preparing to make an attack upon him and his little party, he said:—

"You have asked who it is, that has dared to interfere for the prevention of your unprovoked attack upon these two poor unfortunate Jews. Now, it is not convenient for me, at present, to answer insolent questions, and, therefore, the only reply I shall make, is that I have right on my side, and that I am ready again to interfere, should you be inclined to repeat your former violence."

"This is very pretty language from a beggar to a man like myself!" cried Simon Hyde, indignantly.

"Beggar as I am," answered the other, "it may be that I am, in every respect, more than your equal."

"How, fellow!"

"Aye, bully and bluster as you will," answered the other;—"try to intimidate me as you have these Jews, and in the end I may have to convince you that for once in your lifetime, you have met with a man that is more than your match."

"Send your poniard through his heart!" exclaimed a voice from among the crowd.

"I will, if he don't mind what he's about," replied Simon Hyde; and then addressing himself to the stranger, he continued :—"You talk, sirrah, with the confidence of one of the first barons of the land, but, perhaps, it may happen that, before long, I convince you of the madness of talking to a man like myself, that with a single word, could set all these ramping fellows upon you, like so many bull-dogs."

" I doubt it."

" And why should you ?"

" Because, by a single word, I could bring every one of your rascals at my feet."

" Who the devil are you, then ?"

" Your king !" exclaimed the supposed beggar, throwing aside his tattered cloak and hat, and discovering the noble and well-known countenance of Richard Cœur de Lion.

Upon this discovery a general consternation seized upon the crowd, which was still further increased, when the other imaginary mendicants also threw aside their disguises, and discovered themselves to be various noblemen attending upon their sovereign. Alarmed at the consequences that might follow their lawless violence, Simon Hyde and his comrades would have fled, but the king commanded them to remain where they were, and raising Isaac and Reuben, who had fallen upon their knees at his feet, he said :—

" You two, at least, have no cause to fear my presence, though it may have been unexpected. These other men, however," he continued,— " have well nigh committed an outrage, that would have cost them their lives."

" Aye, your majesty," cried Simon, in an altered tone, " we are all of us willing to confess our fault, but, indeed, it would never have happened had we known that you were so near."

" I dare say not," answered the king, smiling ;—" you believed yourselves quite safe in the act you were committing, and these unfortunate men were compelled to submit to your tyranny, because they happened to be seeking me, who alone was likely to redress their grievances."

" But, your majesty, they are only Jews."

" They are my subjects, and equally under the protection of the laws with yourselves," answered Richard, sternly. " I have already declared that none should harass or oppress the Jews, and yet in spite of all that, I have, myself, been a witness of the cruel persecutions with which you would hunt them from my dominions."

" If I have offended," replied Simon Hyde, " there are thousands of others in England, that are hourly doing the same thing. The fact is, the Jews are looked upon with hatred for the extortions which they practice upon the people, and nothing will ever satisfy your subjects till they are driven, one and all, out of the kingdom."

" Which shall never be done, whilst my hand sways the sceptre," exclaimed Richard. " So, now, mark me, fellows ; on the present occasion, I shall not seek to punish you for the violence you would have committed, but it is on condition that the Jews,—and these two in particular,—shall not be molested. Promise me this much, and you may depart."

" I promise it, since your majesty insists."

" And so do we all," murmured the crowd.

" In that case," said the king, " you may depart peaceably to your homes ;—but remember,—I shall keep a vigilant eye upon you, and should any man hereafter be brought before me, for an act of violence committed against these harmless people, I will punish him with a severity, that shall afford a wholesome example to all my other subjects !—So now depart, and do not forget the warning I have given you."

Upon this the mob suddenly left the place, and then Richard, addressing himself to the elder Israelite, said :—

"From what I have gathered, old man, it seems that you have fresh cause of complaint' against Sir Gaston de Neville. Speak fearlessly, and tell me what he has done, for it is not his rank nor wealth that shall shield him from my wrath, if he has done aught to wrong the helpless."

"My liege," answered Isaac,—" he has again taken my daughter, Rebecca, from me, and she is, at this moment, a captive in his castle!"

"By heaven, he shall be compelled to restore her, and that, too, without delay!"

"Nay, sire, I fear this time he can set even your authority at defiance," answered the old man.

"How!—what meanest thou?"

"That he has charged her with attempting to assassinate him," replied Isaac,—" and, under that plea, he now holds her as a prisoner in his fortress."

"In that case I may not be able to aid you," observed Richard, after a brief pause. " He must, however, be guarded in his conduct, for though she must necessarily be a prisoner for a time, I will punish him with the utmost severity, should he dare to take advantage of the helpless situation to which she is reduced."

"Your majesty can do us even a greater service," cried Reuben, diffidently.

"In what way?"

"By removing her from the custody of Sir Gaston de Neville," answered the youth.

"True," answered Richard ;—" she shall be taken from his castle, and

No. 5 E

placed under the care of those who will not abuse the trust confided to them. The charge, too, must be speedily brought against her, and should it appear that any conspiracy has been formed against the maiden, I will hurl the thunders of my wrath upon all those who have been concerned in this act of oppression."

"I believe," cried Reuben, "that it will appear she is wholly innocent of the crime brought against her. This is only an artifice to get her more completely in his power, and, at the same time, to revenge himself for the many times he has been foiled in his treacherous designs."

"I will, myself, see into the affair," said the king, "and if I find your suspicions correct, Sir Gaston shall rue the day that he concocted so foul a plot."

"If I may be permitted to plead for him," cried Isaac,—"I would entreat your majesty to be as generous, as you are well known to be just."

"Would you have your enemy escape the punishment he so well merits?" demanded the king, with surprise.

"All I seek," replied the old man, "is to secure my daughter from his further persecution; let but that be effected, and I will never harbour an unkind thought, of even the unrelenting Sir Gaston de Neville."

"That is generously said, at any rate," exclaimed Richard, "and yet I can hardly promise to let off so great a delinquent as the man we are speaking of."

"He may repent the cruelties he has committed against me," returned Isaac, "and, in that case, there will be little need to punish him further. My daughter's restoration is all I ask for, and if that one boon is granted me, I care not how soon death comes to relieve me of a load that has long been wearisome and oppressive."

"We must lose no time in compelling him to surrender the maiden into the custody of others," replied the monarch. "I would have a message carried to him instantly, but, unfortunately, I have no messenger to whom I could entrust the duty of conveying to him my commands."

"If your majesty will confide the task to me it shall be zealously executed," cried Reuben Grenard, eagerly.

"Hah!" exclaimed the king, "thou hast spoken well, boy; but art thou aware of the danger thou must incur through trusting thyself within the castle of thine enemy?"

"I know it well," answered the youth, "yet, with your majesty's permission, I will cheerfully run the risk, since it is to serve those I love so well."

"Reuben, this must not be," cried the old man, in alarm. "Sir Gaston de Neville has long wanted to get thee in his power, and should'st thou venture within his stronghold, it will be with little prospect of ever leaving it again. Remember, boy, he has already made a captive of her who was intended for thy bride, and, should I lose thee as well, the blow would be too heavy for endurance."

"I have nothing to fear from him," replied Reuben; "and even should I chance to meet the fate you seem to dread, I can endure it without a murmur, through the consciousness that whatever my sufferings may be, they will have been incurred for the sake of her for whose sake I would willingly lay down my life."

"Thy generosity pleases me, young man," exclaimed the king. "I have observed thy noble care for the maiden of thy love, and it shall be my task to prevent the occurrence of any mischief to thee. I will give thee a letter to convey to Sir Gaston de Neville, demanding that the girl shall be immediately given up, and warning him, as he values his own safety, to offer no violence to thyself. Nay, I will tell him that I shall expect thy return in two hours, and if, at the expiration of that time, thou dost not present thyself before me, I will send a troop of soldiers to his castle with orders to make him their prisoner."

"Alas! Reuben," cried the old Israelite, "I fear that my worst suspicions of thy fate are about to be realized. Sir Gaston will not let thee depart should'st thou once venture into his castle; and thus, in my old age, I shall be deprived of all those whom I most love."

"Thou art wrong there, Jew," exclaimed the king, "for the knight is well aware that my anger is not to be lightly thought of. He will dread my displeasure, and thus there is every reason to hope the young man will return after he has safely executed his undertaking."

The king then ordered his chamberlain to write a brief note to Sir Gaston de Neville, and having himself affixed the royal sign manual to it, delivered it into the hands of Reuben, with strict injunctions to lose no time in performing his errand. This the youth promised, and immediately afterwards they separated, the monarch taking the direction which led towards the palace, and the two Israelites proceeding by the road that led towards the castle of Sir Gaston de Neville.

CHAPTER LXXVIII.

"Take back this message, sirrah, to your liege ;—
Say, I am master here,—that I am firm,
And will not brook control."

THE SPANIARD.

THE elder Jew would gladly have accompanied the younger one into the presence of the Knight Templar, but Reuben would not listen to the proposition, uging the well-known violence of Sir Gaston, and the probability that he would be detained in order to compel the Hebrew Maiden to yield to the infamous terms she had thus far rejected with scorn. Isaac would not at first listen to these suggestions, but at length the entreaties of the other prevailed, and on arriving within view of the castle, he bade farewell to Reuben, offering up a hasty prayer to heaven for protection from the machinations of the man he was about to trust himself with. This done, he slowly retired, and Reuben hastening towards the principal entrance, demanded of the sentinal on duty to be immediately conducted into the presence of his master. Surprised at such a request, the fellow stared at the young man, and then seeming to recognize him, he said :—

"Sir Gaston is, at present, engaged, and you may think yourself lucky that he is, for something strikes me that if you trusted yourself in his presence, you would have good reason to regret the folly as long as you live."

"I ask for no opinion upon the subject," replied Reuben, sharply. "I am here on business of deep import, and even though certain death may await me, it shall not prevent the execution of the duty I have undertaken."

"Oh," retorted the other, "if you are determined to run into mischief it's no business of mine. Every one has a right to do as he likes, and yet I thought it a pity you should get into a scrape for the want of a friend to put you on your guard."

"How know you," asked Reuben, "that any peril threatens me?"

"Because Sir Gaston is not over partial to the man that is his rival in love."

"You are aware who I am, then?"

"To be sure I am," answered the sentinel; "you have been here before now, and, between ourselves, you were a lucky fellow to get off as you did. Sir Gaston has a speedy way of getting rid of his enemies, and if you had not got off as you did, it's likely you would never have troubled him much again."

"He would have murdered or imprisoned me," exclaimed Reuben. "I am aware, you see, of the means he usually employs to rid himself of those that are in his way, and yet, in spite of all that, I am willing to risk anything in behalf of one whose life is far more precious to me than my own."

"Ah!" exclaimed the fellow, with a leer, "I can guess what you're after now; you've come to see if anything can be done for the Jewish girl that's shut up in the castle; but it's all useless, for Sir Gaston has made up his mind as to what is to be done with her, and it ain't all that you can say or do that will ever persuade him to give her up."

"Perhaps not," answered Reuben, "but there are those before whom ven the haughty Sir Gaston de Neville must bow with submission."

"I don't know who they may be," exclaimed the man, "but even if you were the bearer of a message from the king, my master would think twice about it before he would tamely yield to his commands. He is powerful, as you well know, and having done some service in the wars against the Saracens, is not to be trampled upon by even the sovereign himself."

"Unfortunately," replied Reuben, "I have but too much reason to know that your master is reckless as well as cruel; he is the oppressor of the weak, and heeds not what sufferings he causes in the pursuit of his own lawless passions."

"You had better not let him know what sort of opinion you have of him," observed the man.

"He is already aware of it," answered Reuben; "he knows that I have vowed to revenge the injuries he has inflicted upon myself and those I love, and, no doubt, he will seek, by every means in his power, to rid himself of me."

"Then why venture here," demanded the sentinel, "when it is likely enough he will never suffer you to leave the place?"

"A desperate man looks not to such chances as you speak of," replied the other; "I have undertaken to become the bearer of a message to him, and, villain as he is, I have every reason to believe he will not dare to offer any violence against me on the present occasion. So I pray you lead me to his presence, for the affair that brings me here will not bear even the delay of an instant."

"And how do I know," asked the sentinel, "but my own life may be forfeited for suffering you to enter the castle?"

"There is no fear of that," answered Reuben, "for the message I bring is from King Richard, and, therefore, you cannot refuse to take me to him."

"But you may have some foul design against him."

"I give you my word I have not."

"Are you armed?" asked the sentinel.

"Not so much even as with a dagger."

"Humph! in that case I will admit you to him; but mind, if he should be angry with me for taking you into his presence, you must take all the blame upon yourself."

"I will," answered Reuben Grenard.

"In that case, all you have to do is to cross the court yard, and to enter yonder portal on the right hand; you will there find Adrian, the page, who, by the by, is in disgrace just now, but who will lead you to Sir Gaston.— You must then make the best story you can, for he will not be in the best humour at seeing you."

Following the direction given by the sentinel, Reuben passed on and found Adrian waiting in the entrance hall; the youth was somewhat surprised at seeing so unexpected a visitor; but having heard the nature of his errand, and finding there was thus a chance of releasing Rebecca from the unrelenting hatred of Sir Gaston de Neville, he at once cheerfully undertook to procure him the desired interview.

"I had begun," he said, " to fear that she was now utterly lost, for her persecutor had vowed never to part with her again, and nothing but this interference of the king could have saved her from either death or dishonour."

"Do you know where she has been placed for safety?" asked Reuben Grenard, anxiously.

"In an apartment near that occupied by Sir Gaston," answered the page. "She is confined there in order that any attempt to rescue her should fail, and I was just reflecting how hopeless her situation had become, when your arrival proved that there is still a chance left by which she may be restored to the protection of her friends."

"Nor were you, I dare say, the only person that thought so," exclaimed Reuben; "no doubt Sir Gaston believed that, as one of the Hebrew tribe, none would be found to take an interest in her behalf, and that thus her fate was sealed. He has yet, however, to see that King Richard will extend his royal protection to all his subjects alike, and that even the highborn knight is not to trample with impunity upon those whose rank places them in a lower situation."

"But you must be prepared to see the anger of my master excited to the highest degree," observed Adrian. " Hitherto he has been unchecked in his career of violence, and upon you, as the messenger of the king's commands, his anger will be sure to fall."

"I know what I have to expect," answered Reuben Grenard, "yet being reckless of all consequences to myself, I can endure his wrath with perfect indifference. He may confine me in a dungeon if he pleases, yet, should I be certain that Rebecca is at liberty, I can suffer imprisonment with patience and resignation."

"And her father," exclaimed the page, " is he also aware of the persecution he may have to suffer?"

"He is;—nay, I spoke to him on the subject as he walked with me just now towards the castle, and anticipating the wrath that would be sure to follow, he expressed himself well satisfied to bear all so that he could but be assured his daughter was placed beyond the reach of her persecutor."

"Perhaps," observed Adrian, " our fears have been needlessly excited; but knowing, as I do, that Sir Gaston is constantly surrounded by ruffians, who are ready to perform any villainous deed that may be proposed to them, I feared lest an attempt might be made upon the lives of both yourself and the old man."

"Sir Gaston will do as he thinks proper," answered the other; " he may rid himself of us by the violent means you have mentioned,—yet he must beware of the vengeance with which he will be pursued by the laws he would outrage. Disgrace, or, perhaps, an ignominious death would be sure to follow the violence we have been speaking of."

"The thought of that may certainly be in your favour," replied the page; " so now the only advice I shall give you, is to meet him fearless, and not on any account to let him imagine that you dread his anger."

"Of that you may be assured," exclaimed Reuben; " I have undertaken this task in the full knowledge of what may be the consequences, and, depend on it, I can stand unflinchingly in the presence of even the enraged

Sir Gaston de Neville.   But we waste time, and, therefore, I entreat you to conduct me to the place where I am to meet the author of all my afflic. tions."

"That I will do cheerfully," answered Adrian.   "You shall see him,— but, first of all, I must announce your arrival at the castle, lest, by too sud. denly appearing before him, his rage should drive him to some terrible ex. tremity.   Remain where you are, therefore, till my return, and, no doubt, he will grant the interview you desire."

Finding that Reuben assented to this plan, the page immediately took his departure, leaving the other to prepare himself for the meeting that was to take place.   In a very short time he was ready to go in the presence of his enemy; and, when Adrian returned with a message that the knight would see him, he immediately followed to the apartment where Sir Gaston de Neville was hurriedly pacing up and down, chafing and muttering his maledictions on the person who had thus dared to venture in his presence. Obeying his impatient signal, the page instantly retired, and being thus left alone with the young Israelite, Sir Gaston fiercely demanded why he sought an interview with one who had both the power and inclination to punish his presumption.   Reuben stood unmoved before the incensed Templar, and having heard him to an end, he said, unflinchingly:—

"I came here, Sir Gaston, to demand justice;—you have, by force, de. tained the daughter of Isaac of Tadcaster, and, unmindful of the danger I might run by thus throwing myself in your way, I have come to demand her immediate release."

"Indeed!" exclaimed the knight, "and suppose, instead of obeying your demand, I take it into my head to imprison you as well as the girl in whose favour you have thus foolishly interfered."

"That you dare not do, Sir Gaston de Neville."

"How!—am I then defied?"

"You are."

"Then you have sealed your fate, sirrah, for never again shall you leave this castle alive."

"I was aware," replied Reuben, coolly, "that you would threaten me, but, fortunately, I am now placed beyond the reach of your anger.   I defy you, Sir Gaston, and you will carry your threats into execution at your own peril."

"We shall see that presently," cried the knight, foaming with rage at this defiance.   "Here I am lord paramount, and at my slightest bidding, you will be conveyed to a dungeon, from whence you will have little hopes of ever escaping."

"And in that case," replied Reuben, "you will bring upon you the punishment your crimes have so long merited.   Nay, it is in vain that you look thus scowlingly upon me, for I am not so unprotected as you imagine, and any violence you may offer me will be the means of bringing upon yourself disgrace and infamy."

"We will see that," exclaimed Sir Gaston, preparing to give a signal that would bring immediate assistance; "you have too long bearded the lion in his den, and it is now time that I should teach you the madness of coming hither with your demands for justice, as you are pleased to call them."

"Hold!" exclaimed Reuben, "and do not summon your retainers to be witnesses of what is to pass between us."

"What mean you, sirrah?" demanded the knight, angrily.

"This paper will inform you better than I can," answered Reuben, handing the letter he was the bearer of.   "You perceive it is from the king, demanding the Hebrew Maiden to be delivered into the custody of his own officers, and warning you to offer no violence to the man who now stands before you."

"I see," exclaimed the knight, as he finished perusing the written document he held in his hands. "This does, indeed, purport to come from the king, but how know I that it is not a forgery, committed by yourself for the purpose of aiding in the escape of this girl?"

"Surely you do not deny the king's sign manual?"

"It is like it," answered Sir Gaston, "but you may return and tell him that I shall not obey the demand, until I am better assured of his having thus interfered in an affair he has no business with."

"In that case," answered Reuben, "you will soon be made to suffer for your obstinacy."

"Hah!—am I to be threatened again by an insolent Jew?"

"I threaten you not, Sir Gaston," answered the young man, "but the king will not be trifled with, and since he has pledged himself to see justice done to an injured girl, he will not be thwarted with impunity."

"But his majesty knows not that my life was attempted by the very person he now seeks to shield from the punishment she so justly merits."

"The king knows all," replied Reuben, "but, like myself, he is not inclined to place much faith in a charge that has most likely been made the more readily to procure her destruction. At present, he believes her to be innocent, and is determined to sift the affair to the very bottom, ere he gives credit to your assertions."

"It is true, and I can maintain it with the clearest evidence," answered Sir Gaston; "she was in my chamber armed with a dagger, and those who rushed in to my rescue saw her still grasping the weapon with which it was her design to have slain me."

"Your witnesses, Sir Knight," exclaimed Reuben, "may, like yourself, be inclined to assert any falsehood for the destruction of a helpless girl."

"Minion!—dare you charge me with falsehood?"

"I dare speak the truth, even though, by so doing, I offend a man of far higher rank than myself," answered Reuben.

"Beware how you enrage me!" cried the knight, furiously; "beware, I say, for it is in my power to pour down upon you such terrible wrath that you shall feel the effects of it as long as you live."

"Had I been afraid of that," answered Reuben, in a tone of extreme indifference, "I should not have taken this opportunity to present myself before you. That I am here, is sufficient evidence to prove how little I regard the anger of one I so utterly despise."

"Have a care, villain, how you provoke me!"

"I have already said and done enough to do so," answered the young Jew, "and yet, it seems, you fear to act upon the impulse of your own heart."

"Dost thou know, that at my bidding, I have people about me who would not hesitate to stop thine insolent tongue for ever?"

"I am quite aware of it, Sir Gaston."

"What hinders me, then, from ridding myself for ever of a hated rival in the love of the fair Rebecca?"

"Your own cowardice."

"Cowardice, sirrah!"

"Aye, art thou not afraid of the punishment that would surely fall on thee, wert thou to injure him who has been sent on a message from the king?"

"I fear nothing," answered Sir Gaston de Neville. "It is true the king has it in his power to hurl his anger upon all who may offend him, but Richard knows not how soon he may be driven from the throne, and it is only necessary that he should exhibit his tyranny towards me in the present instance, to secure his own downfall from the eminence on which he has placed himself."

"Is that the only message I am to take back to him?" demanded Reuben Grenard.

"I know not that I shall suffer you to depart at all," replied the incensed knight. "You have been most insolent to me, and it is not my custom to permit such things without punishing the parties guilty of them."

"I am not to be frightened by threats like these," exclaimed the youth. "I am sent hither by the king, and knowing that you cannot detain me here, I demand for the last time, whether it is your intention to deliver her up to those who will be sent by his majesty to convey her to some other place of secure custody?"

"The girl shall hear my answer as well as yourself," cried the infuriated knight, and opening a door that connected with another apartment, he returned immediately afterwards with Rebecca, who he dragged with violence into the room, and who would have rushed with a cry of surprise into the arms of her lover had she not been restrained by Sir Gaston de Neville.

"What!" he exclaimed, with a sneer, "would you even in my presence acknowledge the preference in which you hold yonder beggarly Jew?—Am I to be insulted and driven to madness by seeing thee encircled in the arms of one that I can crush whenever it is my will to be rid of him?"

"I had forgotten," answered Rebecca, "that I am here the slave and prisoner of a cruel tyrant."

"True,—thou art both my slave and my prisoner," exclaimed Sir Gaston, triumphantly. "Already I have taught thee to hold thyself as such, and if ought could serve to render more terrible the situation to which thou art reduced, I would strike thy lover with my poniard to the ground, and let him pour forth his blood at the feet of her who never can, or shall become his bride!"

"Monster!" gasped the affrighted girl.

"Nay, dear Rebecca, it is in vain you speak to him," exclaimed Reuben; "already has he proved the hardness of his heart, and it would be useless to reproach one who is destitute of all feeling."

"You speak truly," answered Sir Gaston, "for I have no feeling where my own interest is concerned. This girl is charged by me with making an attempt against my life;—I have proof to confirm my words, and she is here to deny the accusation if she can."

"Speak, dear Rebecca," cried the young Israelite; "you have heard the cruel charge brought against you, and though I do not believe him, yet would I gladly hear the denial by your own lips."

"Of what do you charge me, Sir Gaston?" she demanded, wildly.

"Of entering my chamber during the night time for the purpose of murdering me."

"That I most solemnly deny!"

"What! were you not found in my room?"

"I was."

"And you had a poniard in your hand?"

"It is most true; I had a poniard."

"For what reason did you steal into my chamber thus armed?"

"That I know not."

"How did you find your way there?"

"I was led thither by an apparition armed from head to foot."

"Nay, this is a most improbable story," exclaimed Sir Gaston; "it may do to frighten women and children with, but when the king hears of it, he will doubt the tale as I do."

"Even if he does," answered Rebecca, "I can most solemnly affirm that I speak the truth."

"Be that as it may, there is my accusation to be weighed against your declarations of innocence," cried Sir Gaston.

"Am I not to be believed then?"

"Certainly not, when the word of a knight is at stake. I have already told you that there are witnesses to prove your presence in the chamber, and even you do not deny being there with a murderous weapon in your hand."

"I do confess as much," answered the Hebrew Maiden; "but again do I affirm before heaven, that I never for a moment contemplated your death. I was guided thither by an armed apparition, who, pointing towards a poniard that was lying upon the table, bade me, by signs, to take it up. I did so, and as the spectre vanished from my view, you awoke, and detected me with the instrument of death in my hand."

"Humph!" ejaculated the knight, "and is that the best story you can invent, by which to account for a circumstance that seems fraught with suspicion?"

"It is the truth," answered Rebecca, "and, therefore, I need say no more upon the subject."

"You hear her, Sir Gaston," cried Reuben Grenard, earnestly; "she relates the affair in a manner that convinces me she speaks truly, and, therefore, am I convinced that the charge you have brought against her is unfounded."

No. 56

"It matters very little whether you are convinced or not," exclaimed Sir Gaston. "I, for one, can see plainly enough that the whole is an artfully devised story, and, therefore, shall I persist in my charge till the truth is discovered."

"At least," returned Reuben,—"you will obey the king's mandate, and send her, without delay, to the place appointed for her safe custody?"

"I know not that I shall part with her so easily," replied Sir Gaston. "The truth is, she is now my prisoner, and this may only be some plan to get her out of my hands."

"I would not accept of liberty on any terms," cried Rebecca, "but such as will wipe from my name the foul stain that has been cast on it. I have been accused of meditating a deed of blood, and never will I ask for freedom until something has been done to restore me to my good fame."

"Then you will ask that which it will be impossible to effect," retorted the knight.

"It is not impossible, Sir Gaston," cried Reuben Grenard. "True, you have done you utmost to crush an innocent maiden, by a most unjust charge, but the evil practices of the base do not always succeed, and I have yet a hope that she will be able to convince the world of the foul wrong you have sought to do her."

"What mean you, sirrah?" demanded the knight, writhing under the determination with which it appeared his rival would follow him up.

"I mean," answered Reuben Grenard, "that you have ever been her most bitter and resolute foe;—you sought to gain her love, and, failing in that, have done all in your power to force her to become the victim of your licentiousness. Happily, however, virtue has triumphed over vice, and now, since no other alternative remains, you would crush her beneath a false accusation, in the hope that she will, at length, be compelled to yield."

"And so she must," exclaimed the knight, "or there is a pretty fair chance that she will become the victim of her own wilful folly."

"Say, rather, of your cruel arts, Sir Gaston," cried Rebecca. "To you do I owe all the miseries that have been heaped, not only upon myself, but upon those I love. Your plotting brain has ever been at work to procure my destruction, and now, when every other hope fails, you bring forward this charge, in the expectation that I must either consent to your villainous propositions, or perish by an ignominious death."

"If I understand you, girl," exclaimed the knight, "you are still determined to thwart my wishes, even though, by so doing, you consign yourself to a death of shame."

"Better to die, than live in shame," she replied, fearlessly.

"You hear her resolution, Sir Gaston," observed the young Israelite;—"she is determined, as you may perceive, and I now ask whether you can longer persist in persecuting one who never injured you?"

"I shall answer no further questions," exclaimed Sir Gaston. "She is my prisoner, and I will not set her at liberty until she has been tried on the charge it is my intention to bring against her."

"Is that the answer I am to take back to King Richard?" demanded the young man.

"It is," replied the knight;—"or stay;—I would not act uncourteously towards my royal master, and, therefore, you may tell him from me, that the Hebrew Maiden is now safe in my custody, and that I will not part with her, unless it is the desire of his majesty to deprive me of a power I have a right to exercise."

"In other words," observed Reuben, "I am to tell the king you will not give up Rebecca, unless a force is sent to compel you to do so?"

"Nay," answered the Knight Templar, "I do not desire to offend the king, so you may tell him, that if he chooses to send a guard for her, she shall be sent away on condition that she is brought to speedy trial."

"I will convey your message," exclaimed Reuben, and he was about to advance, for the purpose of bidding a hasty farewell to Rebecca, when the knight interposed himself between them, and then giving his usual signal, the room was filled with armed retainers, who were immediately ordered to convey the youth beyond the outer portal of the castle. This was done without much resistance on the part of Reuben, and no sooner was he taken away, than our heroine was sent back to the chamber from which she had been fetched, there to await the coming of those, who were to take her to other and more secure quarters.

CHAPTER LXXIX.

"Tell thy proud master I defy his power,
And bid him quick prepare to meet a foe
He little dreams of."

VASSALDI.

IT would be impossible to describe the rage and mortification that took possession of the heart of Sir Gaston de Neville, upon finding that he was restrained from the acts of cruelty and oppression that he meditated. For some time after the departure of Reuben, he walked hurriedly up and down his chamber; muttering his heaviest curses upon all those who had, in any way, interfered to mar his plans, and vowing vengeance against all of them at the first opportunity that might arrive. Among others he recollected Adrian, and as that youth happened unfortunately to be within reach of his anger, he summoned Roland le Mark to his presence, and bade him instantly drag the page before him.

"The boy has, somehow or other, most unaccountably disappeared," growled the retainer, "and what is still worse, no one seems to have a notion where he is gone to."

"Escaped!" exclaimed Sir Gaston, wrathfully.

"I suppose so," answered the other;—"at any rate, we have been looking for him all over the castle, and as no one seems to know anything about him, it's most likely he got away while he could."

"He must be found and brought back, even though he has taken refuge in a sanctuary," exclaimed the knight. "That boy has forgotten the benefits he has received from me, and if I look not after him, he will bring upon me the ruin I so much dread."

"I will, myself, go in search of him," returned Roland; "the young fellow has given me cause to bear him no very good will, and, depend on it, I will lose no chance that may serve to bring him back to his old quarters."

"Are you sure he has left the castle?"

"There is every reason to believe so," answered the retainer; "at all events, we have not been able to see him anywhere about the place, and that being the case, it is most likely he left the castle as soon as he found that you knew of the part he has been taking against you."

"Perhaps, he is still in the place," observed the knight, scarcely heeding the words of his dependant. "There are many reasons why I should imagine that he has not left me, and I still think you will find him some-where within these walls."

" Can you give me an idea where it would be best to seek him?"

" That I can scarcely do," answered Sir Gaston, " and yet, were I to set about searching, the first place I should go to seek him in, would be the apartment at present occupied by my two female prisoners."

" I see," exclaimed Roland, " you think he has sought concealment with Lady Alicia and the Hebrew girl?"

" I do."

" Well, it's likely enough, and I'll go and seek him there, directly."

" Do, and return again with as little delay as you can."

" Bringing him with me, I suppose, in case I should happen to find him there?"

" Yes," replied Sir Gaston de Neville; " but you must offer him no vio-lence beyond what may be necessary to enforce my commands. The boy was entrusted to my care by a dying father, and if there is any possibility of rendering myself safe, without injuring him, I should be well pleased. One thing, however, you must recollect;—my commands are that you bring him before me, and I will then see whether something cannot be done to prevent his taking part against me."

" There is but one way of preventing him that I know of," growled Roland.

" How is that, sirrah?"

" By hanging him on the highest point of your castle," answered the ruffian. " You will thus rid yourself of a spy, and, at the same time, prevent others, by his example, from attempting to interfere in your affairs. It is an excellent remedy, and, I'll answer for it, will not be without its good effects."

" I have told you the boy must not be harmed," answered the knight. " I would save him if I can, but if he persists in working against me, I may, by and by, be induced to think more seriously on the hint you have just thrown out."

" You had better do so at once," observed Roland le Mark, " and thus save yourself all further trouble."

" No more of this, sirrah!" exclaimed the knight, angrily. " I have already given you your orders, and you will disobey them at your own peril. Remember, the boy must be brought before me, but no unnecessary violence may be used against him."

" And suppose he takes it into his head to resist?"

" In that case you are strong enough to conquer him."

" But he may try to effect his escape by running away."

" If he does, the consequences must fall upon himself," answered Sir Gaston. " I do not seek to injure the boy, in spite of all the provocation he has given me, but should there be reason to suppose that he intends to escape, I leave it to yourself to secure him in the best way you can. But, remember, any reward that I may give you for this service, will depend upon the care you take in obeying my injunctions."

" And suppose, if he attempts to run away, I should send a shaft from my bow, and kill him?"

" If it should be done in trying to prevent his escape, I will pardon you," answered Sir Gaston de Neville. " I, however, happen to know that you bear the youth no good will, and, depend on it, I will not fail to avenge his death, should I have reason to suppose it was wilfully caused."

" I shall observe your orders," replied Roland, in no very good humour at the strict injunctions that had been given him. " The boy shall be treated well enough, I warrant, but if he should happen to give me such an opportunity, as you have hinted at, I shall not fail to bring him down with an arrow, and as my aim is pretty sure, it's most likely he will never give either you or myself much trouble again."

With this he departed, leaving Sir Gaston perplexed and angry, at the difficulty in which he had thus been placed.

We must now, however, proceed to the apartment occupied by Lady Alicia and Rebecca, and where, as the knight suspected, Adrian was seeking temporary concealment; not that he regarded his own personal safety, but he knew that were he to leave the castle, they would not have a friend upon whom they could rely, and, therefore, he had resolved to make one more effort to prevail upon them to seek safety in flight. But his entreaties were in vain, and finding, at last, that they determined to trust themselves to fate, he began to devise other means by which he might rescue them from their perilous situation.

"If you are determined to remain here," he said, "I can see nothing before you but hopeless captivity; Sir Gaston is enraged at the many defeats he has sustained, and now that he has you safe in his grasp, he will take every precaution to prevent you leaving the castle."

"I know but too well what we have got to expect," answered Lady Alicia; "yet better is it that we should endure his tyranny than that you should suffer from his vindictive cruelty for having generously interposed to save us from the misery he seeks to inflict!"

"But I have freely volunteered my services," returned the page, "and, surely, under such circumstances, you will not refuse to oblige me by accepting my offer."

"You do but urge us in vain," cried Rebecca; "our resolution is fixed, and immoveable, and no consideration for ourselves will ever tempt us to purchase liberty at the expense, perhaps, of your life."

"Nay, you apprehend danger where none exists."

"Of that you will hardly be able to convince us," replied the Jewess;— "we well know the cruel nature of Sir Gaston, and dare not trust to his wrath should he suspect you of having aided us."

"Then I know but of one other way of releasing you," exclaimed Adrian.

"And that is by appealing again to the king, I suppose?" observed Lady Alicia; "the chance you speak of is, I fear, but a poor one, seeing that Sir Gaston has many places in the castle where he can conceal us, even though the strictest search be instituted."

"Besides," added our heroine, "the king has demanded that I shall be given up to the safe keeping of his own officers of justice; this Sir Gaston was unwillingly compelled to yield to, and, therefore, I have every reason to expect justice from those who are to enquire into the charges that have been brought against me."

".That may be very true," answered Adrian, "but flight would save you the pain and disgrace of a public trial."

"And it would also convince the world of my guilt," cried Rebecca;— "so you see the consequence that would follow any attempt to shun the enquiry, and, for that reason, I am resolved to abide the issue of a trial you appear to dread so much."

"But the Lady Alicia," exclaimed Adrian; "she has no chance of escape, unless she accepts the offer I have made."

"Imprisonment has no horrors for me," replied the hapless female he had spoken of; "I have endured it with patience for many a long weary year, and if it is the will of heaven to try me with affliction I can bear all without murmuring at the decree."

"You shall not be shut up in a dungeon though if I can help it," exclaimed the page.

"I must," answered Alicia, "for never will I expose my husband's conduct to the king, and who else is there that can aid me in this dark moment of despair?"

"One that you little think of," returned the youth.

"And has he the inclination as well as the power to do me the service you speak of?"

"He has."

"May I ask who this friend is?"

"Black Ivan, the Outlaw."

"Would you have me rely for assistance, then, on a man whose crimes have rendered his name the terror of all who are not as deeply steeped in crime as himself?"

"You wrong him, dear lady," cried Adrian, earnestly. "Black Ivan is not so bad as the world reports him; persecution and injustice have driven him to become the associate of men whom he would otherwise have shunned, and you have yourself lately seen that he is both willing and able to aid those who are oppressed."

"He did, indeed, do the best he could to conceal me from the search of my husband," answered Lady Alicia; "and from the kindness he manifested towards me, I augured that his heart was not so depraved as I had imagined."

"I also have received kindness from him," added Rebecca, "though there was a time when he made professions of love, which I could not listen to."

"Aye," answered Adrian, "but when he saw how you were persecuted by Sir Gaston de Neville, he generously gave up his suit, and sought, by every means in his power, to prove himself your friend."

"He did," replied the maiden;—"and, if money is any object to him, my father will not fail to reward him for the interest he has taken in my welfare."

"Yet it appears singular," observed Lady Alicia, "that a man who has been outlawed for his crimes should possess a feeling of honour that would be creditable to many of those who pride themselves upon the possession of every virtue."

"It certainly does appear strange," answered Adrian, "but I have my own opinion upon that subject. There is a great deal of mystery about Black Ivan, and I have sometimes thought it likely enough that he will turn out to be a man of consequence. At any rate his manners are not those of a ruffian, and as it is pretty certain that he has been driven to join a band of robbers through some injustice he has received, depend on it he will, by and by, startle the world by a discovery that no one expects."

"You spoke of him just now as the only one who can rescue me from this place," cried Lady Alicia, "and I would fain know what chance there is that he possesses the means of delivering me from bondage?"

"It is certain," replied the page, "that he takes an interest in your welfare, and as he knows a secret entrance to the castle, I am certain it will not be long before he finds means to effect your release."

"And, if I mistake not, you are about to visit his cave for the purpose of urging him to take the step you speak of?"

"That is indeed my intention."

"Hear me, then, Adrian," cried Lady Alicia; "it is my commands that you instantly abandon your hazardous scheme."

"For once in my life," answered the page, "I feel compelled to disobey your commands. Pardon me, therefore, my lady, when I declare that nothing shall prevent my executing a task upon which so much depends."

"Have you not reflected," asked Rebecca, "upon the consequences that would follow upon your detection?"

"I have; death may possibly be my doom, but I could bear that even under the most dreadful tortures, rather than abandon my mistress to her hapless fate."

"And what benefit would result from that?" asked Lady Alicia.— "Were you to perish through your generous efforts in my behalf, it would but add tenfold sorrow to those which already pass upon my aching heart."

"Aye," cried the page, "but your ladyship looks only at the worst side of the question. It is likely I may succeed in getting you from this place, and if I can but do that, my reward will be complete, even though I should have to suffer a lingering death."

"Let me have time to consider your proposition," exclaimed Alicia,— "and, perhaps, I may yet yield."

"I will not delay for a single moment," cried the page, resolutely; "it would be madness to do so, for Sir Gaston might hear of my intentions, and, in that case, all chance of your deliverance from hence would be lost."

"Nay, I ask you but to wait till to-morrow, and, by that time I will —"

At this moment Lady Alicia was interrupted by a noise at the door, and, at the same time, the voice of Roland le Mark was heard, cursing the locks that gave him so much trouble to turn. Alarmed at this unexpected visit, the Lady Alicia and Rebecca earnestly implored the page to seek some place of concealment, but the youth would not hear of such a proposition.

"No, no, dear ladies," he exclaimed, "the fellow shall find that I am not afraid of him. Here I am, and here will I remain, even in spite of the blustering ruffian that I suppose has been sent on some more of his master's dirty errands."

"This hardihood will cost thee thy life!" cried Lady Alicia, in a paroxysm of alarm.

"Oh, do not be afraid of that," returned the page; "I know the scoundrel well enough, and have ever found him to be a bully and a coward."

"But he may not be so," cried Rebecca, "when so mere a youth as yourself is opposed to him. Your strength is unequal to the task you would take upon yourself, and I can but too plainly foresee your death if you do not instantly hide yourself from him."

"I should be as great a coward as he is if I was to do that," answered Adrian, firmly.

"It is no act of cowardice for the weak to flee from the strong," exclaimed Lady Alicia.

"But I have yet to prove," answered the youth, "that I am not so weak, nor he so strong as you imagine. Besides, I am engaged in a good cause, and that alone is sufficient to make me a match for this heartless ruffian."

"Hark!" cried Lady Alicia; "he has at length succeeded in removing the chain that secured the door, and in another moment your escape will be impossible."

"I do not intend to attempt it," retorted the page, "so let the villain come when he will, he shall find that I am quite prepared for him."

As he spoke, the door was violently thrust open, and Roland, enfuriated at the obstacle he had met with, entered with even more than his ordinary ill-humour.

"So, young fellow, you are here as I expected," he exclaimed; "you have entered the chamber of the imprisoned females, but as it is evident you come not in at the door, I demand how you found entrance here."

"Your demand is made in vain," answered the page, "for even were Sir Gaston himself to ask the question, I should refuse to answer it."

"He will ask it, then," exclaimed Roland, "so instantly follow me to his presence."

"Nay, if I must go," replied the youth, with resolution, "it shall not be your task to take me there."

"How, you refuse obedience to the commands of our master?"

"Not when they are such as I can obey," replied Adrian; "it seems, however, that his rage has been kindled against me for some cause or other, and, therefore, I will refuse to appear before him unless he thinks fit to compel me by force."

"And that," exclaimed Roland le Mark, "I am authorised to use if it should be found necessary."

"You hear him, Adrian." cried Lady Alicia, in a tone of entreaty; "he has been desired to take you before Sir Gaston, and your further refusal will only subject you to the violence of this brutal ruffian."

"Your ladyship need not fear for me," returned Adrian, "I have already thought of a way to escape from this apartment, and the malice of this man shall not be gratified in the way he expects."

"Surrender, boy!" exclaimed Roland, advancing a step or two nearer; "surrender, I say, for if you attempt to escape, I shall be compelled to use violence."

"Keep where you are, fellow," cried Adrian, fearlessly; "keep off, I tell you, lest, being driven to desperation, I should bring you to closer quarters than you like."

"For heaven's sake, forbear!" exclaimed Lady Alicia.

"Would you have me yield quietly, then, to this ruffian?"

"I would not," replied her ladyship; "but you spoke just now of effecting your escape from hence. Waste not another moment, therefore, but leave the place where danger, and, perhaps, death itself threatens you."

"In this instance, you shall see how ready I am to obey you," answered the youth, and springing towards the open window, he stood ready to jump down into the garden beneath, and thus secure his escape from the castle. Ere he took the leap, however, he turned towards the enraged Roland, and in a tone of derision, said:—

"But a few moments since you boasted that I was in your power, and that you would forcibly carry me into the presence of Sir Gaston de Neville! You now see how little I have to fear from your threats, and, therefore, I charge you to return to your master, and tell him that his page, Adrian, tired of enduring his tyranny, has left his service, never more to return to it. Tell him this, Roland le Mark, and you can, if you please, add that I shall lose no time in endeavouring to procure justice for the Lady Alicia, who has so long been confined within the dungeons of this accursed place."

Unable to control his rage any longer, Roland poized his lance in his hand, and was in the act of hurling it with an unerring aim at the page, when Lady Alicia throwing herself between the ruffian and the object of his rage, so as to shield the youth with her own person, gave the latter an opportunity to jump down and effect his escape across the garden. The rage of Roland le Mark was now excited to the highest pitch, and he would have immediately followed in pursuit, but by the time he reached the window Adrian was no where to be seen, and thus all clue was entirely lost.

"May my curses light upon him for the trick he has played me!" exclaimed the ruffian when he discovered how completely he had been foiled; "he has escaped when most I thought him in my power, and I shall have to answer for it to Sir Gaston."

"'Tis well that it is so," answered Lady Alicia, "for otherwise the poor youth might have been condemned to wear out the remainder of his days in hopeless imprisonment."

"I care not what had become of him, so that I had not suffered him to escape."

"Nay, rather rejoice that he is at liberty," returned Rebecca, who had been anxiously watching from the window to see whether any traces of the fugitive were yet to be discovered.

"I should have rejoiced had he remained here," answered Roland, gloomily.

"He would have been mad to do so."

"Ha! I see how it is," exclaimed the ruffian; "this escape has been planned among you. You have plotted to set him at liberty, and I now bid you beware of the wrath you will bring upon yourselves! Sir Gaston shall know all, and heavy will be the vengeance he inflicts upon those who have dared rob him of his prey."

"I am willing to endure his wrath," answered Rebecca, without betraying the slightest symptoms of alarm.

"So am I," exclaimed Lady Alicia; "for my own part, I know well that imprisonment in a cheerless dungeon was to be my lot. I was content to endure it with patience, and should he now resolve to doom me to death, I shall regard it as an act of mercy."

"Speak, woman," cried the retainer, fiercely, "do you know where he is likely to flee for safety?"

"If I did, it is hardly likely I should set the bloodhounds on the track of their prey."

"But, by doing so, you might obtain favour with my master, and probably secure your own liberty."

"Which would be dearly purchased at the price you ask," returned Lady Alicia.

No. 57

"What!—do you throw away a chance that may never occur to you again ?"

"It is in vain you urge me further upon this subject," answered Lady Alicia. "That the youth has escaped, I must confess myself well pleased, and it is, therefore, hardly to be expected that I will say a word to throw him again into the power of your tyrant master."

"And you, girl," cried Roland, addressing himself to Rebecca, "are you also determined to remain silent on this subject, when you may make a good bargain for yourself?"

"I am."

"Remember how you are situated," exclaimed the ruffian; "here you are a prisoner; a heavy charge is about to be brought against you, and your fate will soon be sealed, unless you can by any means obtain the favour of Sir Gaston de Neville."

"I have already experienced his malice," answered Rebecca. "On a former occasion he charged me with being concerned in stealing from him a diamond ring of great price. I was publicly accused of it in a court of justice, and as publicly did I prove my innocence by going through the ordeal."

"Sir Gaston is not yet convinced of your innocence, though," cried Roland le Mark; "and even if he were so, there is another charge, far blacker than the one I spoke of. He accuses you of entering his chamber in the dead of night to stab him to the heart with a poniard that was found in your hand. There are witnesses who found you in the place armed as I have said, and, depend on it, you will not escape so easily on this occasion as on the last."

"The same Providence will still protect the innocent," answered Rebecca, meekly.

"But it is in your power to purchase both life and freedom," exclaimed Roland. "Nay, a single word may obtain for you the favour of Sir Gaston de Neville."

"I ask no favour of your master," replied Rebecca; "he has unlawfully detained me here a prisoner, and I rely upon the justice of the king for deliverance."

"But you can obtain it without applying to the king," answered Roland. "Confess where Adrian has fled to, and I will promise you immediate freedom."

"Never!"

"Then whatever happens will be your own fault," exclaimed the ruffian, and hastening out of the chamber, the door was again secured, and the two females were once more left to themselves.

CHAPTER LXXX.

" Let no one seek to do him injury ;
He must be safe amongst us, and his life
Be held as sacred as my own."

THE CAPTIVE.

As may be imagined, Adrian lost no time when once he found himself at liberty, and passing through the postern by which he had left the castle on several former occasions, he hurried across the fields that led towards the then insignificant village of Islington, on arriving at which place, he began somewhat to relax his speed as there was a tolerable chance that he would not be pursued. At any rate he had now got a fair start, and at a more moderate pace he proceeded on his way, resolving to call at the cottage of Meg of Finchley, whose aid he thought might also be of use in procuring the release of Lady Alicia from her present hapless situation.

It was some time, however, before he came in sight of the wretched abode he was in search of, but when at length he perceived it in the little hollow where it was situated, he was startled by hearing loud cries of distress issuing from the cottage, and flying with the speed of lightning, he entered it at the moment when the old woman was lying at the mercy of Herbert, the chief friend and companion of Black Ivan. In another moment the upraised dagger would have been buried in the heart of Meg of Finchley, but seeing her danger, the page rushed forward, and snatching the poniard from the hand of Hubert, thrust him violently to the further end of the chamber. This done, he raised the old woman, and, seating her upon a stool, stood prepared with the dagger in his hand, in case any attack should be made upon him by the robber.

"Coward!" he exclaimed, "is it against a helpless woman that you thus wage war?—Another moment and you would have had to answer for the blood of one whose age and infirmities should have been her protection."

"And who art thou," demanded the robber, fiercely, "who hast thus dared to interfere with me?"

"One who will ever aid the weak against the strong," answered Adrian, fearlessly. "Thou wouldst have murdered this woman had I not providentially been led hither to her rescue."

"Thine own life shall answer for it," exclaimed Hubert, fiercely. "I have been thwarted by thee, but it is strange to me if ever thou hast it in thy power to come again between me and my will."

"Thy threats I heed not," cried Adrian, fearlessly; "it is true I may not be able to encounter one of thy general strength, but I can die cheerfully when it is in the defence of those who need protection."

"Nay, thou needst not fear that I shall take thy worthless life," replied Hubert; "I would not stain my hand with thy blood, but thou shall go with me to the cave of Black Ivan, where thou wilt either remain a prisoner during the remainder of thy life, or perish by a death of misery and torture."

"I care not what befals me," answered the page;—"in truth, I was on my way to the retreat of Black Ivan, to confer with him on an affair of importance."

"'Tis false!" exclaimed the robber, "for thou wouldst never dare to seek the abode of him who is the terror of the neighbourhood."

"It is not the acts of Black Ivan that have made his name terrible," answered the youth, "but those of the men under his command. They have committed outrages out of number, and their chieftain bears the blame of them."

"Thou sayst right, boy," cried Meg, who by this time had recovered from the alarm into which she had been thrown. "Ivan is seldom cruel, and did he know the danger I have escaped from one of his band, he would speedily punish the villain as he deserves."

"Come, come, old hag," exclaimed Hubert, wrathfully; "thou hast had a lucky chance just now when my dagger was raised against thy life, and if thou art wise, thou will not tempt me again. Remember, I am soon moved to wrath, and it may happen that I do thee a mischief now before we part."

"Not whilst I stand by to prevent it," exclaimed Adrian, stepping between the old woman and the robber.

"Thou, boy!"

"I have said the word, sirrah," retorted the youth, "and am ready to prove that I am not so insignificant a foe as thou dost imagine."

"Perhaps that may be tried ere long."

"Peace, Adrian, and do not tempt thine own fate thus rashly," cried Meg, with terror. "Thou wouldst be nothing in a contest with this villain, and if thou dost provoke a quarrel with him, I should see my preserver fall by the hand of his enemy."

"Let the young fellow alone, will you?" exclaimed Hubert, gruffly. "He knows what he is about without any interference of yours, and if he will urge me to it, he must take the consequences of his own folly."

"That I am prepared to do," answered the youth. "I know thee to be a reckless seeker of blood, but even though I should be certain of meeting my death, yet would I make a resolute attempt to prevent thy violence against an old and helpless woman."

"Psha! why make such a fuss about Meg of Finchley?" demanded the robber; "she can die but once, and she may as well meet her fate now as any other time for ought I know or care."

"In what way has she injured thee?" asked the page.

"She has told me I am doomed to be hanged," answered the fellow, sullenly.

"And if she has," cried Adrian, "I should say that she has told thee nothing more than the truth."

"It may be so," replied Hubert, "but in this instance the truth had very nearly cost the hag her life."

"What!" cried the page;—"and was it for no greater cause that thou wert just now about to murder her?"

"Aye, and quite cause enough in my opinion," answered the ruffian. "I was wearied and hungry with a long walk, and called here to ask for rest and food. She, however, thought proper to revile me for the course of life I have thought it best to lead; and, in the end, she began her cursed predictions, telling me I am doomed to die by the hangman's hands."

"And you would have slain her for speaking what I believe to be the truth."

"Take care what you are saying, young fellow," exclaimed Hubert. "It is not always pleasant to hear the truth, and thou wilt, perhaps find, presently, that I am not to be taunted with impunity."

"What!" cried Meg of Finchley, "wouldst thou slay the young as well as the old?"

"Aye," replied the robber, "it's all one to me if people say things that are not agreeable to hear. I have a way of settling these things in an offhand way, and it may chance that I shall silence you both before I leave the place, unless you are a little more careful what you say."

"And if you carry your threats into execution," retorted Meg, "it is likely Black Ivan will call you to a severe account for it. He is not bloodthirsty like yourself, and if he hangs you up on the nearest tree, it will not be the first time he has made such an example for the benefit of those under his command."

"Next to himself, I am chief in command," returned Hubert, "and, therefore, I have little to fear from such a fate as the one you speak of.— Besides, I am quite as much liked among the band as he is, and, perhaps, a word from me might not only cost him his life, but, at the same time, place me at the head of my brave comrades."

"Hah!" exclaimed Meg of Finchley, "a word like that uttered in presence of thy chief, would cost thee thy life."

"Perhaps it might cost him his," retorted the other, with a sneer. "At all events, I am a match for Black Ivan himself, and he may rely on it, I would not lose my life without attempting something in my own behalf."

"Bloodhound!" exclaimed Meg, "thou wilt not much longer be suffered to go on in thine iniquity."

"Would'st thou urge me beyond bearing?" demanded the ruffian, threatingly.

"If thou likest not my words, depart ere I tell thee more that will prove unwelcome news to thee," cried Meg. "Remember, I can read thy destiny, and thou shalt know it, let it offend thee as it may."

"It will be at thine own peril then."

"Forbear," exclaimed Adrian, interposing to prevent any further quarrelling between them. "Too much anger has already passed between thee and it is now time that Hubert and I take our departure."

"Thou art determined then to visit the retreat of Black Ivan?"

"I am."

"'Tis well," responded the ruffian; "thou shalt go, boy, but not as thou didst expect. I will take thee as my prisoner to the cave, and I'll answer for it I can invent a tale that shall make thee rue the hour when thou didst set out on this rash enterprise."

"Thy words do not intimidate me," answered Adrian. "I left the castle of Sir Gaston de Neville with no other design than to see Black Ivan, and it matters very little to me whether I find my way to his presence as thy prisoner or as a voluntary visitor."

"Humph! so thou art in the service of the Knight Templar, art thou?"

"I am."

"That circumstance alone is sufficient to obtain for thee a reception thou little thinkest of," exclaimed Hubert. "The knight thou servest is my captain's most hated foe, and, therefore, thou hast little reason to congratulate thyself on what will follow thy mad enterprise."

"At any rate I am prepared for the worst," answered Adrian. "I can but lose my life in the cause for which I am about to venture into the presence of Ivan, and, should I perish, I shall, at least, have the consolation of knowing that it will be in the execution of my duty."

"A very comfortable reflection truly!" muttered the robber; "it is well for thee thou goest with so good a heart, for I can tell thee thou art not likely ever to escape from our retreat. To be sure, thou may'st be put out of thy miseries at once, which, between ourselves, I think is probable enough."

"Villain!" cried Meg of Finchley, "why dost thou taunt him thus?—The boy is ready to accompany thee, and I'll warrant he meets not so blood-thirsty a ruffian in Black Ivan as he has in thyself."

"Peace, old woman, and tempt me not to leave thee a corse upon thine own hearth!" exclaimed Hubert, menacing her, "I have already endured more than I usually do on occasions like this, but thou mayst urge me too far, and, in that case, thou wilt repent, when too late, that thou didst not take the advice I gave thee."

"Threaten her no more," cried Adrian, "for, despite the difference there is between us, I may yet be forced to try my strengh against thine."

"Humph!—a pigmy against a giant!" muttered the ruffian, with a grin of contempt.

"It may be so," replied the page, "but, in a good cause, heaven will aid the weak against the strong. Instances of the kind have happened ere now, and, if need be, I can enter on a contest with thee, full of confidence that I shall not perish by the hands of a villain such as thou art."

"Upon my word thou talkest wond'rous boldly," retorted the ruffian.—"Thou art not without a fair share of courage, I see, and as I respect valour, even though it may be in an enemy, I will not draw my sword upon thee until I know the pleasure of my captain. He may wish to have the pleasure of putting theé to death, and I would not deprive him of it merely for the gratification of my own wishes."

"Thou say'st well," interposed Meg of Finchley; "the boy is unequal to combat with thee, and it were better to take him to the retreat where Black Ivan will judge what had best be done with him."

"Perhaps you also would have no objection to go with us?" cried the ruffian.

"I would go," answered the old woman, "if, by so doing, I could, in any way benefit my preserver."

"Well then," retorted the other, "as I don't think you would be of any service, I shall leave you behind. And, harkyee, Meg, if ever you and I meet again, be careful not to tell my fortune quite so freely as you did just now, for men don't like to be reminded of the gallows, and I am none of the most patient when things are said that I don't like to hear."

"Come," said Adrian, "we have had enough of this, I am impatient to see your captain, and care not how soon we leave this place."

"Well, for once I will be indulgent enough to oblige you," answered Hubert; "so come along, and mind, if you make any attempt to escape, I shall slay thee as I would a dog.

With this they left the cottage of Meg of Finchley, and pursued their way across the heath without either of them breaking the silence that reigned around them. Hubert, however, kept a vigilant eye upon his youthful companion, and taking his way through a part that was least frequented, he at length reached a thicket of some extent, about the middle of which he thrust aside some bushes, and discovered a small aperture, through which he desired Adrian to pass, and then immediately afterwards followed him down a broken flight of steps, into a passage underground, that was lighted only by a solitary lamp that hung suspended from the ceiling. Along this place they proceeded some distance, and then a strong oaken door having been thrown open by Hubert, they entered a vaulted chamber filled with plunder, across which they made their way towards a more spacious apartment, in which were seated about a score of the robbers, enjoying themselves over their wine cups. At the head of the table was seated Black Ivan, who no sooner perceived the approach of Hubert and a stranger, than, starting up, he hastily approached them.

"How now, Hubert!" he exclaimed; "thou seemest to have a prisoner with thee; he is somewhat young, too, methinks, and, therefore, little worthy the trouble thou hast been at in capturing him."

"I know not that," answered the robber; "he tells me he was coming to seek thee, and I thought thou wouldst like to know what business can have induced him to visit the cave of Black Ivan and his associates."

"What answer dost thou make, boy?" demanded Ivan, addressing himself to the page; "few persons venture to seek me here, and I would learn why thou hast come where thou mayst encounter so much danger?"

"Thou dost not remember me, then?" exclaimed Adrian.

"I do not; and yet, now that I gaze upon thee again, I recognize one of the pages of Sir Gaston de Neville?"

"I am."

"Thy name?"

"Adrian."

"Ha!—the youth that made so bold an attempt to rescue the unfortunate Lady Alicia."

"I did so," returned the youth; "but, as you may remember, my efforts were thrown away; Lady Alicia is again in the hands of her tyrant husband, and, I fear, will never regain her liberty, unless a bold effort is made to assist her."

"I understand you," exclaimed Black Ivan; "the Lady Alicia is to be again the inmate of a dungeon, and you have come hither to ask my advice and assistance to deliver her from the hands of a cruel tyrant?"

"You have guessed my errand."

"So I thought;—and yet I marvel that one so young should throw yourself in the way of a man so dreaded as Black Ivan, the Outlaw."

"I thought of nothing but the danger that threatened a beloved mistress," answered the youth. "Besides," he continued, "I have seen that you are not the heartless ruffian that people report, and, therefore, did I seek you for your counsel and assistance."

"Thou shalt have both," answered the Outlaw, after a moment's deliberation. "I will assist thee in giving freedom to thine unfortunate mistress, though it must needs be at some peril to myself."

"I thought," observed Adrian, "you know of a secret entrance to the castle, and that her escape might be contrived without danger to yourself."

"I do know of such a means of gaining admittance," answered Black Ivan, "but you are, of course, aware of the malignant feeling entertained against me by Sir Gaston de Neville. For years past he has eagerly sought my life, and though I have frequently entered his castle, it has been in a disguise that was neither suspected by himself or those about him."

"And yet I have seen you there without disguise," observed Adrian.

"You have," replied the Outlaw, "but on such occasions I have run a risk greater than I ought. The knight would gladly get me in his power if he could, and, no doubt, he would then take care to prevent my ever intruding myself so near him again."

"Perhaps, then, it would be too hazardous to ask you to venture there again?"

"No," replied Black Ivan, "I have never shunned danger, nor will I do it in a case were my assistance is so much required. The Lady Alicia has too long suffered from the cruelty of this recreant knight, and even though it may be at the hazard of my own life, I will make another effort to set her free."

"When will you do so?"

"Perhaps, this very night."

"And shall I aid you?" asked the page.

"I think it would place you in too much danger," answered Ivan;— "that Sir Gaston would not fail to revenge himself on you I have every reason to know, for never yet did he fail to punish those, who could not look on, and approve of his villany."

"I care not for that," cried Adrian, fearlessly;—"let me but once see the Lady Alicia completely free from the tyranny of her remorseless husband, and I can willingly submit myself to any fate to which he may think fit to adjudge me."

"Nay, thou shalt not run so great a hazard," exclaimed the robber chieftain. Thy noble generosity pleases me, boy, and, depend upon it, thy mistress shall be set at liberty, if it is in my power to aid her. Thou hast done well in coming to me, and if thou hast need of a place of refuge from the search that will be made after thee, by Sir Gaston de Neville, thou shalt remain here as a guest, with free liberty to take thy departure whenever thou mayst choose."

"Do I hear aright?" exclaimed Hubert, with amazement;—"is the prisoner I have brought here to be treated as the friend of our captain?"

"He is," replied Black Ivan, "and more than that, Hubert, I charge thee to treat him as tenderly as thou wouldst my own son;—so let it be thy care to look after the youth, for if harm befalls him, I will revenge myself most heavily on thee."

" As you please, captain, but I think ——"

" Silence, sirrah, and dare not oppose my commands. I have told you what I expect, and if my orders are not strictly obeyed, it will be at your own peril."

" Of course, I shall do your bidding," answered Hubert, " but yet I can't help saying that it looks very much like treachery, when you come to think of it."

" What mean you by treachery?" demanded Ivan.

" I mean," replied the other, " that it's likely enough the boy has some reason that you don't think of for coming here."

" And why do you think so?"

" Because it's not very likely he would have sought out our haunt unless he meant to betray us to our enemies. People don't visit robber's caves for nothing, and I have heard before now of a whole band being destroyed, through believing such a story as this young fellow has just told you."

" Were I to be guilty of such an act of treachery," exclaimed Adrian,— " what chance of escape would there be for me. I am here in your power and must perish, should I ever commit the act you suspect me to have meditated."

" Aye, aye, that's all true enough," exclaimed Hubert, in reply ;—" we should have the satisfaction of rewarding you according to your deserts, and when that was done, our own fate would be sealed."

" There is no reason to doubt the youth," interposed Black Ivan. " He has ever been the friend of an unfortunate mistress, and, therefore, I am inclined to believe his motives, for coming here are not so unworthy as you suspect. At any rate, I shall afford him the shelter he requires, and, if it is in my power, will release the lady he speaks of from the danger that threatens her."

" Well," cried Hubert, sullenly, " of course, we are bound to obey your orders, and so there's an end of it. If I speak my mind pretty freely, it's because I think you are a little too easy in believing every one who tells a plausible story, and all I hope is, that this may turn out better than I had expected."

" For your opinion I have not much to thank you for," returned Adrian; " but that, perhaps, was to be expected, seeing that you could not forbear threatening even the life of a helpless old woman, who ought to have been rather an object for your pity than your vengeance."

" He speaks, captain," said Hubert, who saw the anger that marked the countenance of this, " of old Meg of Finchley, who offended me so much just now, that I was in the act of chastising her as she well merited when he came and rescued her from me."

" Say rather that I prevented you committing a cruel and cold-blooded murder," exclaimed Adrian.

" How is this, Hubert," demanded Black Ivan ;—" have I not told you over and over again, that Meg of Finchley was never to be harrassed by any of our band?"

" You have, captain," returned the other, " but flesh and blood could not bear the taunts she assailed me with."

" Where did you meet with her."

" At her own cottage."

" Indeed, and why went you there, sirrah?"

" To seek rest and refreshment."

" In return for which you would have taken her life!"

"Aye, but it was not till after she had told me that I was doomed to meet my death upon the gallows."

"Meg seldom foretells anything that does not come to pass," answered Ivan, "and I think, in this instance, her prediction is likely enough to be fulfilled."

"It was some such notion as that," exclaimed Hubert, "that made me draw my poniard on her. I was enraged, sure enough, and, if it had not been for the interference of this stripling, she would never have predicted evil against any one again."

"'Tis well that it happened so, at any rate," exclaimed Black Ivan, "for, had you slain her in defiance of my commands, your own life should have answered for it."

"What!—for killing a witch?"

"Aye, for she is, at any rate, harmless," answered Ivan. "She has long known of our secret haunt, and might have betrayed us to our enemies; and surely, her having failed to do so, should secure her from the injury you meditated."

"Well, I shall be careful to obey you in future," returned Hubert, "and as for this youth, he may remain here in safety for me, only let him mind not to give me cause for suspecting him of treachery."

Black Ivan now led Adrian to the table, and, having introduced him to the band as one that could be relied on, the interrupted banquet was renewed, and carried on till a late hour at night.

No. 58.

CHAPTER LXXXI.

" Here thou'lt find little mercy;—
For we, who are thy captors, scorn the world
And all its usages."

THE WANDERER.

AFTER a night of disturbed sleep, Adrian rose at an early hour on the following morning, and making his way to the scene of the last evening's orgies, he found several of the band, who, having indulged rather too freely in the juice of the grape, had fallen in a state of insensibility to the ground, where they were still lying, though the sun had, by that time, risen some height above the horizon.

Adrian had now an opportunity of observing the apartment, which, considering its subterraneous situation, was tolerably light and airy; it was evident, too, that the cave was a natural one, rendered more convenient and habitable by the ingenuity of its occupants. From this chamber, which was the principal one, four passages led to other apartments, chiefly occupied by the band as dormitories, and the entrances to which were so secured as to offer an admirable defence, in case their enemies should at any time succeed in forcing their way into the principal chamber. Around the walls hung various arms and accoutrements; the floor was strewed with boxes and chests of plunder, and in one corner were chained three enormous dogs, whose low growls of savage fury denoted that they would prove formidable opponents, in case they should be let loose upon an intruding foe. Altogether the scene was calculated to inspire a feeling of uneasiness in the mind of our page, and he was about to leave the place for the purpose of returning to the chamber from whence he had come, when a hasty footstep was heard advancing along one of the passages, and Black Ivan immediately presented himself before the youth.

"Thou art an early riser, I see," he exclaimed, "and might well set an example to these sluggards, whose brains are scarcely yet cleared from the fumes of last night's debauch."

"I was restless, and ill-inclined to sleep," answered the page; "even in my dreams I was troubled with the thought of the danger that threatened Lady Alicia, and, taking advantage of the silence that reigned here, I strolled from my apartment to obtain an uninterrupted view of your retreat."

"And what think you of it?"

"That it is exactly adapted to the purposes to which it is applied. It is scarcely possible that a stranger could discover a place where nature has done so much towards rendering it secure from observation."

"And as there are few that have been entrusted with our secret, we have but little to apprehend in that respect," answered Black Ivan. "Besides, treachery is always sure to meet its reward here, and if ever any one attempted to betray us, it would be at the expense of his own life."

"And that would benefit you but little," answered Adrian, "seeing that the mischief would be done, and your lives placed in jeopardy, before you could revenge yourself upon your betrayer."

"That I grant you," returned Ivan, " but the certainty of receiving the terrible punishment of his treachery, will always prove our best safe-guard. At any rate, we have hitherto found it so, and now we feel so well assured of our safety, that we scarcely ever imagine it possible that danger can come to us from that quarter."

"So it appears, from the soundness of these fellows' sleep," answered the page, glancing at the recumbent forms before and around him.

"Aye," returned Black Ivan, "the men sleep under a perfect consciousness of safety. They know how unlikely it is that their rest will be disturbed by the intrusion of strangers; and even if a party of the king's soldiers should chance to find their way among us, what could they do, think you, against us in our own stronghold?"

"That would depend on the numbers they might bring against you," replied Adrian.

"Numbers would not avail here," answered the robber. "We are well supplied with arms, as you see; our dogs yonder, would be let loose upon them, and they would prove formidable antagonists against any odds that might chance to be brought against us."

"You have no fear then?"

"Not the slightest, for you see how well we are prepared for any attack that might be made."

"I see that your fellows are now stupified with the effects of last night's carouse, and, in case of a surprise, I can perceive no hope of your successfully resisting a strong body of enemies."

"You shall see how soon I can rouse them," answered Black Ivan, and raising his bugle to his lips, he sounded the usual signal of danger. In an instant the robbers started from their sleep, and each man springing upon his feet, snatched forth his dagger, and stood ready for an attack. Perceiving, however, that there was nothing to fear, they sullenly retired to the further end of the chamber, sheathing their poniards, and growling one to the other at the trick that had robbed them of half their slumbers.

"The dogs seem displeased at having been so abruptly roused from their sleep," observed the robber chief to Hubert, who now stood before them. "They bend their brows upon me as if they would break into open rebellion against their leader; but let them beware, or I will yet find means to let them know who is master in the cave."

"The poor devils are sullen at being roused up so suddenly," answered Hubert.

"I did it only to try whether they were upon the alert," returned the captain. "I must depend upon them, and how can I do so, unless I sometimes try them when they least expect?"

"You have little to fear from any of your band, captain," answered Hubert. "They are all faithful enough, I'll warrant you, and I only wish I could say as much for those you take into your head to shelter, without knowing whether they may not mean to betray us."

"If your allusions are addressed towards me," exclaimed Adrian, "I can only say you have mistaken the motives that brought me here. I came to seek your leader's aid in the rescue of a hapless female, and, as I have his promise to do so, I am now willing to take my departure from the cavern whenever I am desired."

"I dare say you are," retorted Hubert; "and, no doubt, you have made up your mind to deliver us into the hands of our foes on the first opportunity."

"No more of this, sirrah!" exclaimed Black Ivan, angrily; "I have already told you that I am well satisfied of his honourable intentions, and those who do not think as I do, are at liberty to depart whenever they may think proper. I ask no man to stay here against his will, nor shall any one give utterance to a doubt, when I have declared the confidence I feel in his honourable intentions."

"Well," answered Hubert, "since it is your desire, I shall say no more about it.   One can't help one's thoughts, however, and they will not be much in favour of the young fellow you have taken such a great fancy to."

So saying, Hubert strode away with an air of dissatisfation, and, having left the presence of his leader, he quitted the cavern, and went forth in search of any passengers that might chance to approach that way. Black Ivan watched his departure with a look that denoted his displeasure, and then turning towards Adrian, he said :—

"That fellow is continually exhibiting a turbulent spirit, that I fancy will one day or other break out into open rebellion against me. But he must beware, for little dreams he of the vengeance that would follow any act of disobedience to his superior in command."

"It is he," answered Adrian, "who, by cruelty and oppression, has obtained for you a name that is regarded with terror throughout England. People blame you for his deeds, even though you know nothing of them till long after they have been committed."

"They may blame me if they please," exclaimed Black Ivan, "but they know not the wrongs and oppressions that have driven me to adopt the life of a robber. I have been deprived of my fair inheritance by a brother, and, whilst he revels in luxuries, I wander about the land, carrying with me the brand of a proscribed outlaw."

"Have you never sought for justice ?" demanded Adrian.

"I have," replied Ivan.

"And failed to obtain it ?"

"Aye, or you would not have seen me the wretched outcast that I am."

"Have you ever applied to the king ?" asked the page.

"It would be of little avail if I did," answered the robber chieftain.

"There I do not agree with you," exclaimed Adrian, "for it is said the king administers justice most impartially, and surely he would not refuse to restore you to the rights of which it seems you have been deprived."

"But I would rather avoid bringing about a disclosure that might serve to bring dishonour on any part of my family."

"And yet," observed Adrian, "you have yourself brought disgrace upon it by becoming a robber."

"True," answered Ivan, "but I have so contrived it at present, that no one suspects who I am."

"Not even the man that has wronged you ?" demanded the page.

"Even he," replied the chieftain, "has no suspicion that Black Ivan is the person he has robbed of his just inheritance."

"And was there no other way by which you might maintain yourself in honour ?"

"It was the only way by which I could hope to obtain revenge," answered Black Ivan. "In this disguise I have watched my oppressor for years ; chances have even offered themselves by which I might have destroyed my enemy, and yet I have suffered him to live on, hoping that he might repent, ere I completed the full measure of my vengeance."

"Is he in England ?"

"He is ;—but ask me no further questions, boy, on this subject," exclaimed Ivan. "'Tis one that I always avoid whenever I can, for the recollection of the wrongs I have endured fills my soul with bitterness and indignation. So now, to speak on the subject that brought you here ;—the Lady Alicia, it seems, is doomed to wear out the remainder of her days in hopeless captivity, unknown to all except Sir Gaston and the few he may have found it necessary to admit to his confidence ?"

"Such is his decree," answered Adrian, "and, therefore, did I venture to come hither, knowing that you would exert yourself towards effecting her release."

"I will, at least, try to release her," replied Ivan, "but we must first learn in what part of the castle it is his intention to keep her."

"That I can readily answer," returned the page, "for I heard Sir Gaston give directions to Roland le Mark to convey her immediately upon receiving his further orders, to one of the dungeons beneath the eastern tower."

"The eastern tower?—are you sure of it?"

"Quite."

"'Tis so far fortunate," muttered the robber chieftain; "to that part of the castle I can obtain ready access, and it shall go hard but I set his prisoner at liberty before she has been in her dungeon many hours."

"Ah!" cried Adrian, "you know not how happy it makes me to hear you say so. But a short time since, I feared her case was nearly hopeless, and now, I can already congratulate myself on the success of my mission to this cavern."

"Thou hast done well, boy," answered Ivan, "and the danger thou hast run in her behalf, was the reason why I so promptly determined to second your endeavours."

"Nay, the act requires no praise," cried Adrian, "for I should have been base indeed, to know that a female was in distress, and yet not put forth a hand to rescue her. For my own part, I could do nothing towards effecting her release, except come hither and prevail on you to aid me in frustrating the base designs of Sir Gaston de Neville."

"Thou hast done well, boy," exclaimed Ivan; "it was a bold and hazardous adventure, perhaps, to trust thyself with men of our reckless nature, yet, so well pleased am I with thy self-devotion in the cause of a helpless woman, that I again give thee my word thou shalt receive no harm from any of those men whom I command."

"If I had been afraid of them," answered Adrian, boldly, "I should have hesitated ere I ventured to trust myself among them. I, however, had confidence in you, and relying upon your protection, I fearlessly left my master's castle to visit the secret abode of Black Ivan."

"Thou shalt not repent the step thou hast taken," exclaimed the robber, "and, therefore, I again bid thee to rely upon him who seldom breaks his word, whether it may be passed for good or for harm. But hark!—I hear footsteps approaching from the entrance of the cave, and, if I mistake not, some of my fellows have returned, bringing with them a prisoner."

Ivan was right in his conjecture, for scarcely had he finished speaking, when Hubert and three or four of the robbers made their appearance, dragging between them a man, in whom Adrian quickly recognized the forbidding features of Roland le Mark. The fellow, however, did not appear to accompany them very willingly, for he made violent efforts to release himself, and on one or two occasions would certainly have broke away from his captors, had it not been for the iron grasp of Hubert, who was determined that his prisoner should not escape.

"Who is this fellow?" demanded Black Ivan, "and why have you brought him a prisoner before me?"

"It is Roland le Mark, noble captain," answered Hubert; "the rascal, it seems, has come this way in search of the youth I brought here yesterday, and as I thought it dangerous to let him wander about so near the entrance of our cavern, I made him my prisoner, and here he is to receive any judgment you may be pleased to pass on him."

"Why were you lurking in the neighbourhood of this place?" demanded Black Ivan, fiercely.

"Your man has already explained that matter," answered Roland; "he tells you I came in pursuit of a run-away page of Sir Gaston de Neville's, and I acknowledge that such was my errand here."

"It would have been better for yourself to have been less busy in the affair," exclaimed Ivan. "The boy you speak of has sought refuge in our cavern, and he shall have my protection, even though Sir Gaston de Neville brings all his force to wrest him from me."

"My master wishes not to interfere with you," replied the retainer, sullenly.

"Why, then, does his menial dare to pursue one who he ought rather to protect than betray?"

"That is a question I do not feel inclined to answer," replied Roland le Mark. "It will be sufficient for me to say that I expected to be rewarded for my zeal, but, having fallen into the hands of a band of ruffians, it is likely enough I may perish for my presumption."

"You are insolent, sirrah!"

"Order your men to let me depart, and you will no longer be troubled with my insolence."

"Rather order me to hang him up on the nearest tree we can find," suggested Hubert, whose rage was excited by the coolness of the prisoner.

"We will not act rashly in the affair," answered Ivan; "for perhaps the fellow may be induced by clemency to aid us in a little business I have in hand."

"You will get no aid from me," exclaimed Roland. "I came here in search of Adrian, and, having found him, demand to take him back with me to the castle of my master."

"By whose orders he would very likely be murdered," exclaimed Black Ivan.

"He would be severely punished, no doubt," replied Roland, with cool insolence. "Perhaps he might be shut up in a dungeon for the remainder of his days, but, if Sir Gaston only gives the word, I would not be long about ridding him of a young villain that would betray him."

"I fled," answered Adrian, "not to secure my own safety, but to preserve a helpless female from the tyranny of him who should have been her protector."

"Hah!" vociferated Roland, "and so it seems you have blabbed a secret that my master would not have had known for the world."

"He has told me nothing that I knew not of before," exclaimed Ivan. "I have long been aware of the base conduct of Sir Gaston de Neville towards an unoffending wife, who, unfortunately for herself, has outlived his affections. He would have murdered her, but for the dread of the punishment that would follow."

"And if he had done so, we should now have been safe," answered Roland. "I always advised him to put her quietly out of the way; but conscience would not suffer him to do that, and now the consequence is, that he may live to see and confess the folly of his humanity."

"I have long had my eye on Sir Gaston de Neville," exclaimed Ivan, "and had he followed your suggestion, I would have hunted him through the world, but he should have been punished for the crime."

"Indeed!—then are you a most humane cut-throat!"

"Call me what thou wilt, fellow," answered Ivan, unmoved by the insolence of his prisoner, "but thou shalt, at least, acknowledge that I am not an oppressor of helpless women. That I am a robber, is no fault of mine, seeing that I have been forced to adopt this course of life, in consequence of the baseness of a villain, who robbed me of my patrimony, and left me a beggar and an outcast."

"Aye, aye, fellows like yourself have always some excuse to make for their bad ways," retorted Roland, with a sneer.

"Shall this be borne!" exclaimed Hubert, impatiently.

"We can well afford to let him rail on," answered Black Ivan; "the fellow is now a prisoner in our hands, and I will take care to keep him here till Lady Alicia has been rescued from the bondage of her remorseless husband."

"I know not what you mean by Lady Alicia being the wife of my master," exclaimed Roland.

"Let it suffice, that I know sufficient to convince me that Sir Gaston de Neville is a villain."

"That is saying more than you would dare venture to say to his face."

"I have told him so, ere now," replied Ivan, "but he has never yet had the courage to meet me sword to sword for it."

"Humph!" exclaimed Roland, "it is hardly to be expected that he would disgrace his knighthood by challenging the captain of a band of robbers."

"The knave's insolence can no longer be borne," cried Hubert, furiously. "I have listened to this till my patience can endure no more, and, by St. Nicholas! another word of insult to my captain shall cost him his life."

"There is no occasion for it, Hubert," answered Black Ivan, with composure. "Here he cannot injure us, and it must now be our care to prevent his escape. Let him be closely watched, and if he attempts to regain his freedom, an arrow through his heart will save all further trouble on his account."

"Beware what you do," cried Roland le Mark; "beware, I say, for my master will soon suspect where I am, and depend on it, he will not fail to hurl his vengeance upon all those who now boast of claiming me as a prisoner."

"Sir Gaston will not venture here," answered Ivan; "and even if he should do so, we we will give him a reception that will be remembered to the latest day of his life."

"At any rate," exclaimed Hubert, "we have one of his fellows here, and if my advice was taken in the matter, he should swing on a tree by the wayside, as a warning to all other persons that might feel inclined to come prying in this neighbourhood."

"I'll tell you what it is, captain," cried Roland le Mark, who by this time began to entertain fears lest his imprudence had led him too far; "it seems to me that there can be very little use in our quarrelling about trifles, so, if you choose to let Adrian go back with me, I'll undertake to promise that not a hint shall be given by which anybody shall find out your secret haunt."

"Do you take us all for fools?" exclaimed Hubert, "that you think we are likely to let you go off on your own promises? No, no, we've got you now, safe enough, and I should think our captain would not risk the lives of all his band by letting you off like that."

"He shall be our prisoner until we have made all secure," answered Black Ivan.

"And Adrian," exclaimed the retainer, "what is to become of him?"

"He will remain here also."

"As a prisoner?"

"No; the boy has never sought to injure us, and I have reason to believe he will be of some service to me in an attempt I am about to make for the liberation of the Lady Alicia."

"What is that I hear?" cried Roland le Mark; "are you going to make an attempt to release a prisoner that my master has thought proper to place in confinement?"

"She is his wife," answered Ivan.

"'Tis false!—she is an impostor!" exclaimed Roland. "She of whom you speak, is not the wife of Sir Gaston de Neville."

"So thy master has taught thee to say," answered Ivan, "but we have proof to bring forward, when the proper time arrives, and, rest assured, I will never give up my object until the Lady Alicia is restored to the station from whence she has been so long driven."

"I tell you again she is not the wife of Sir Gaston," exclaimed the retainer. "The real Lady Alicia died many years ago, and was buried in the castle chapel, in the presence of hundreds of spectators."

"The funeral was a mock one to deceive the world," replied Black Ivan. "The ceremony you speak of was performed, but at the same moment the unfortunate Lady Alicia was languishing in the dreary dungeon to which the villany of her own husband had consigned her."

"Who told thee this?" demanded Roland.

"She who best knew the truth,—the Lady Alicia herself."

"'Tis false, for she of whom you speak has long since been mouldering in her grave."

"Nay," cried Ivan; "if you deny my words, here is one who is an evidence of their truth."

"Hah!—wouldst thou prevail upon Adrian to speak against his master?"

"I shall be obliged to do so, since all other means have failed," replied the chief of the robbers. "Nay, thy terrors tell me thou art privy to thy master's evil deeds, and, therefore, do I tell thee that thine own life depends upon the course you mean to pursue."

"What would you have me do?" demanded Roland.

"Confess thy villany, and thus make the only amends now in your power."

"Never!"

"Perhaps we may be able to cure this obstinacy," observed Hubert, holding up a rope which he had formed into the shape of a halter. "We have a short way of bringing people to their senses, you see, friend, and if you think proper to stand out, I shall presently have the honour to become your executioner."

"Do you think to frighten me?"

"It matters not whether I do or not," replied Hubert; "all I want is to make you promise to assist our captain in the way he has proposed, and if you won't do that, why we may as well save all further trouble by putting you out of your misery at once."

"Will you stand by," cried Roland, addressing himself the leader, "and see me murdered before your eyes?"

"You have nothing to fear from his threats," answered Ivan; "for the present, your life is in no danger, but I will not answer for my patience lasting much longer, unless you promise to reveal all you know respecting the barbarous conduct that has been pursued against Lady Alicia."

"I know nothing more about her than you have heard."

"You see how obstinate he is, captain," exclaimed Hubert; "the fellow is determined to stick to his lies, and, as he will only be an incumbrance here, I propose that we immediately sling him up to yonder cross-beam."

"So saying, he jerked the noose over the head of Raland, and it is likely enough he would have carried his design into execution, had not a bugle note been heard without, which immediately created the utmost confusion

amongst the whole band. Upon this, the rope was removed from the neck and arms of the prisoner, and when he was properly secured, two of the robbers led him away to the place usually employed as a prison. This done, Ivan desired his comrades to remain where they were in silence, and hurrying from the chamber, proceeded towards the secret entrance, for the purpose of ascertaining who the visitor was that had thus unexpectedly announced himself.

CHAPTER LXXXII.

" This villany too long hath been endured ;—
But now my anger hath been moved, and
By my soul the traitor falls !"

MARCELLO.

IT was with some impatience that the robbers awaited the return of their leader, and, in case of surprise, each man drew his sword, with a determination to defend the place to the last extremity. Adrian was a passive observer of all this, but circumstances soon convinced him that he was regarded with suspicion by the outlaws, who conferred together in low whispers, occasionally directing a searching glance towards him, and by various threatening gestures, betraying the vengeful thoughts that were stirring them to destroy him. He, however, maintained his firmness, and met their angry looks with a countenance that exhibited neither fear nor a consciousness of the treachery of which he was suspected. At length, whilst matters were in this state of uncertainty, the heavy tramp of footsteps again echoed through the vaults, and in another moment Black Ivan returned, ushering in two strangers habited in the garb of hunters, and whose appearance denoted them to belong to a superior class.

"Comrades," said Ivan, "I have brought among you two strangers, who need our hospitality. They are hunters, as you may see, who, having been carried away by the ardour of the chase, have lost their companions, and being much exhausted, after a night of useless search for their friends, need that rest and refreshment which we fortunately have it in our power to bestow."

"And who knows," muttered Hubert, "but this is some plan to betray us all to death?"

"Silence, sirrah!" exclaimed Ivan, "and learn to respect the commands of your leader."

"I always do so," answered the other, "when I am satisfied that he does his duty."

"Did you ever know me neglect it?"

"Perhaps not, but your disposition to believe every idle story you hear has more than once placed us in danger."

"I see," exclaimed the stranger who appeared to be the principal, "our motives are suspected; these men regard us as foes, and rather than breed dissension, we will go forth and seek shelter somewhere else."

"Craving your pardon," answered Ivan, "this must not be. I have myself invited you to partake of our hospitality, and feeling assured that it will not be abused, I must insist upon your remaining among us until you have so far rested yourselves as to be able to resume your journey."

"If the gentlemen have money about them, let us ease them of it," whispered Hubert to his captain.

"Another such proposition as that, and you are a dead man!" returned Ivan, fiercely. "They have entered this place in confidence, and they shall leave it without regret. Let the table be spread with the best fare our cavern affords, and see that the choicest wine is placed before our guests."

"As you please, captain, but ——"

"No hesitation, sirrah, but obey my orders with dispatch," cried the leader, peremptorily.

Thus commanded, Hubert could no longer resist without bringing upon himself the anger of his master, and having given the necessary directions to Maud, the table was soon spread with most excellent fare, to which the two strangers sat down with a zest that did honour to the good things placed before them. Whilst the guests were thus occupied, Hubert approached Black Ivan, and in a whisper inquired whether he knew who the persons were.

"I do," replied the chief.

"They are friends, perhaps?"

"Nay, they belong to too exalted a rank for that."

"The greater reason, then," observed Hubert, "why we should regard them with suspicion."

"If you knew them," answered the captain, "you would place as much confidence in them as I do."

"Why, then, observe so much mystery?—Tell me who they are, and perhaps I may be of your opinion."

"Another time I may indulge your curiosity," replied Ivan; "at present, it must content you to know that their high situation in life is enough to disarm all suspicion of treachery from either of them."

"This confidence will be our ruin, captain," growled the other. "We are at the mercy of these strangers, and if my advice were taken, they would not be suffered to leave the place till they have sworn to keep our secret."

"Which we are both willing to do," exclaimed the superior of the two visitors, who had overheard the latter words.

"You will pardon the suspicions of my lieutenant," returned Black Ivan, in a tone of apology. "He is ever inclined to think unfavourably of those who enter our secret haunt, and nothing that I can urge will convince him that you will not betray us."

"Well, perhaps he is right, after all," returned the person addressed. "Your lives are certainly placed at our mercy, and it is only fair that you should have some kind of pledge that we will never seek to harm you."

"What pledge can you give that will satisfy us?" demanded Hubert, gloomily.

"You spoke just now of administering an oath to us."

"True;—I did so, but upon second thoughts, that would be but poor security, if you are determined to deliver us into the hands of justice."

"How else can we satisfy your doubts?"

"By revealing your names."

"Come, come," interposed Black Ivan, "this must not be;—we have received these strangers as guests, and shall we now insult them with these doubts?"

"Your friend is not altogether wrong," exclaimed the stranger who had first spoken; "he has fair reason to regard us with suspicion, and since we have been so hospitably entertained, I think we can do no less than openly declare ourselves in the presence of your band."

"Nay, let me entreat ——"

"I am resolved, and, therefore, it is useless to oppose me," interrupted the other. "Gentlemen," he continued, "you behold before you your king."

"Richard Cœur de Lion!" exclaimed the robbers, as with one voice, and instantly every knee was bent in submission to the monarch.

"It is as I suspected, then," exclaimed Hubert; "we have received those into our confidence who will not fail to take an early opportunity to bring us to punishment!"

"Nay, there you wrong me, sirrah," cried Richard, with generous warmth. "I have found both rest and refreshment here, and may my right arm wither if ever I take advantage of a secret thus obtained. So, rise, all of you, and rest assured of your safety."

"Pardon me, sire," cried Hubert, with more humility than he had previously exhibited, "for suspecting one whose honour was never yet doubted."

"All is forgotten," answered the king; "it is my duty, I know, to punish all breakers of the law, but, in this instance, I will yield to gratitude. Overcome with fatigue, I have received your hospitality, and never shall it be said that King Richard tarnished the reputation he has gained in the wars, by a base act of treachery towards his entertainers."

"Long live King Richard!" vociferated the robbers, upon hearing these words.

"Aye, aye," exclaimed the monarch good-humouredly, "I thought we should be upon better terms when we became acquainted with each other. The truth is, I was at first half inclined to distrust you, but, after all, I find myself more secure now that you know who your visitor is."

"You are safe among us, sire," answered Black Ivan; "for, though our pursuits are lawless, there is not one among us who would not cheerfully fight in the cause of so illustrious a prince."

"Right nobly spoken, by St. George!" cried the king; "so now, let me prevail on you, Ivan, to relinquish this course of life, and I promise that both you and your followers shall be preferred in my army, according to your deserts."

"In anything else, your majesty's wishes shall be obeyed," answered the robber chief.

"How!—do you, then, reject my offer?"

"It is too late to change the course of life I have been compelled to adopt," answered Ivan.

"And why is it too late?"

"Because, with a character ruined and blasted as mine is, who is there that would associate with me? Is it not notorious that I have been the leader of a brigand band, and that alone is sufficient to render me an outcast from society."

"Besides," added Hubert, " we are all of us under sentence of outlawry, and our lives would be at the mercy of those who would exult in our downfall."

"The outlawry shall be reversed, if you will all yield to my suggestion," answered the king. "I have the power to do so, and, upon the word of a monarch, I promise you shall receive a full and free pardon for the past."

"The offer is a generous one," exclaimed Black Ivan, "but men who have lived by setting the laws at defiance, are not likely to forget their former habits."

"It seems then," observed the king, "that you prefer this sort of life to any other?"

"Necessity," answered the chief, "has compelled us to adopt it, and it is not easy to turn what the world calls honest. There are none that would take us by the hand with friendship, and even should we receive your majesty's gracious pardon, our crimes would be remembered, and ourselves shunned, as though our presence carried contagion with it."

"But have you forgotten," asked the sovereign, "that a period must come when the band will be routed and broken up?"

"We are all of us prepared for such an event as your majesty has spoken of," answered Black Ivan.

"In that case," continued the king, "you are also prepared to meet the ignominious death that is commonly awarded to malefactors."

"That," replied Ivan, "we are prepared to avoid."

"How can you do so?"

"By dying with our swords in our hands," answered the chief of the robbers. "We know full well the doom that would be the lot of those who might be taken, and there is not a man among us that would not rather die in his own defence, than yield himself a victim to the gallows."

"But I have told you how such a fate may be avoided," exclaimed the king; "You have this day done me a service, and, in gratitude, I would fain restore you to that society from which you have been banished."

"Under all circumstances, it is impossible to accept your majesty's offer," replied Ivan.

"Do all your followers say the same?"

"We do," shouted the whole band.

"In that case, I can only regret that you have deprived me of the power of serving you," answered King Richard. "And yet," he continued, fixing his gaze upon Adrian, who stood alone at the further part of the chamber, "there is one among you, I see, who appears not long to have joined your band He, at any rate, may accept the offer I have made."

"The youth belongs not to us," replied Black Ivan. "He came hither to obtain my assistance in behalf of an injured woman, and only remains among us till he can find a better place of safety for himself."

"If I mistake not," exclaimed the king, "this youth is Adrian, the page of Sir Gaston de Neville."

"It is, most gracious sire," answered the young man, advancing and throwing himself at his feet. "I am here, as Ivan knows, on an errand that involves me in much peril from the anger of my master, and I only remain here until I can find a better place of refuge."

"In that case, you may return with me to the palace," exclaimed the king. "In my service, you shall find the safety you seek, and perhaps, after a time, I may be able to soften the anger of Sir Gaston de Neville."

"That, sire, is a vain hope," replied Adrian, "for there is every reason to believe that I have offended him past forgiveness."

"It shall be tried, at all events," exclaimed the king, "so now, answer me, boy, and say whether you will enter my service, till we have learnt whether it will be safe for you to return again to the knight's castle."

"Most willingly, sire," replied Adrian, overjoyed at the prospect of quitting the robbers' cave.

"In that case, the bargain is concluded," exclaimed the king, "and you shall return with us to my palace. There, at least, you will be safe from the malice of Sir Gaston, and, doubt not, I shall be able to prevail on him not only to pardon any offence you may have committed, but to take you back once more to his favour and protection."

"Of that, I believe there is very little chance," answered Black Ivan; "the youth knows too many of his evil practices, and if once he gets him into his power again, he will not fail to punish him in a way that will effectually prevent his ever offending him in future."

"It seems, boy, that you are aware of some evil deed that has been committed by Sir Gaston," exclaimed the king. "I have long since been aware that he tyrannizes over those who are unable to protect themselves, and I would now fain learn from you whether he still persists in his designs against the Hebrew Maiden?"

"He does, sire."

"In that instance, I shall, at least, be able to thwart him," exclaimed Richard. "I have been informed that he now accuses her of having made an attempt upon his life, but, believing the story to be a mere fabrication of his own, I have given orders for her to be given up to my ministers of justice, from whom she may expect an impartial hearing. At any rate, he will not adjudicate in her case, and, if I am not greatly mistaken, she will be honourably acquitted of the crime alleged against her."

"I have heard that your majesty has interposed your royal authority in her behalf," answered Adrian, "and, therefore, I feel satisfied that she will have justice done her. There is, however, another female who he has imprisoned in his castle, and for whose deliverance I came to seek the aid of Black Ivan."

"Who is it you speak of?" demanded King Richard.

"Pardon me, sire," exclaimed the robber chief, "but, for the present, it is necessary that her name should remain a secret. I have long been aware of the injustice he has committed towards an unoffending woman, and if the affair is left to me, I will undertake to rescue her, and bring a well-deserved punishment upon the knight by whom she has been so foully wronged."

"Well," exclaimed the king, "I am content that it should be so; but, mark me, Ivan, it must be on condition that you do not take into your hands the punishment that is to be inflicted on him."

"I promise it," replied Ivan.

"In that case, I will ask no further questions at present," cried the king. "I will trust to you, but mind, I shall expect that no time is lost ere you carry your designs into execution."

"Not a moment," answered Ivan.

At this moment a great uproar was heard in one of the passages leading from the chamber in which they were assembled, and ere Hubert could leave the place for the purpose of ascertaining the cause of the noise, Roland le Mark rushed furiously into their presence, and snatching a dagger from the hand of one of the robbers, he was about to plunge it into the bosom of the king, when Adrian, throwing himself forward, arrested the fatal blow, and hurled the deadly instrument to the further end of the chamber.

"Villain!" exclaimed King Richard, "your design has been providentially frustrated, or your own life would have paid the penalty of your crime."

"He shall die for it!" cried Ivan, seizing the delinquent by the throat, and he was about to drag him away, when the voice of the king arrested his purpose.

"Hold!" he exclaimed, "and do not commit an act of violence upon one whose crime has been frustrated. My life has been preserved, and I will not prove my ingratitude by an act of unnecessary vengeance."

"Do you hear that, knave?" cried Black Ivan to his prisoner; "the king has saved your life for the present, but it will depend upon your own conduct, whether I shall ever let you leave our cavern as a free man."

"Humph!" muttered Roland, "perhaps you may not do so of your own free will, but Sir Gaston will soon guess what has become of me, and I warn you of his vengeance, should he ever come here to seek after me."

"He will not venture to approach the den of the tiger," exclaimed Black Ivan.

"You are mistaken," answered the fellow; "Sir Gaston de Neville owes you a grudge, and never will he rest satisfied till he has brought you to the dog's death you so justly merit."

"Hah!" exclaimed the infuriated chief, "it is well for thee that the king is present, or thy words would have cost thee thy life."

"Perhaps so," replied the other, with cool indifference, "but as my life is of very little consequence to me, I could willingly part with it, on condition that I knew thou wouldst be brought to the gallows."

"Another word like that, sirrah, and thou shalt die!" cried Hubert, raising his poniard threateningly.

"Nay, there shall be no bloodshed whilst I am present," exclaimed the king.

"Your majesty's commands shall be obeyed," answered the robber, stepping back and mixing with the crowd that stood around.

"And now, sirrah," said the king to Roland le Mark, "thou hast been assured of thy safety, and if thou hast any gratitude in thy heart, thou wilt assist us in releasing two females who are at this time the prisoners of thy master."

"There is no need of my assistance," replied Roland, sullenly. "Rebecca, the Hebrew Maiden, will be delivered into the hands of your majesty's officers, whenever it may be your pleasure to demand her. The other female I know little about, except that she is mad, and declares herself to be a person that died many years ago."

"Thou liest, villain!" exclaimed Black Ivan, furiously. "The woman has spoken nothing but the truth, and if it is necessary, she can bring forward proof that she is the person she has declared herself to be."

"Psha!" cried Roland, "my master declares solemnly, upon his honour, that she is an impostor, and surely his word will be taken in preference to that of a robber."

"I know not that," retorted Ivan, "for thy master has proved himself but a recreant knight, and his denial will not save him from the disgrace that awaits him. I can prove him to be a villain, and will not fail to bring down upon him the punishment his crimes deserve."

"No more of this, I charge you," interposed the king. "It seems that certain crimes have been laid against a knight, whose services in the defence of his country, should have made him respected and esteemed;—he is charged with cruelty and oppression, and, as it is but fair that he should have a chance to disprove them, I will give orders to have him summoned to my presence at the earliest opportunity. He will thus have the means to clear himself, and glad should I be to hear him disprove a charge that, at present, taints his name with dishonour."

"Here is one that has been his page," exclaimed Ivan, "and who can substantiate what I have said."

"Wilt thou do so, boy?" demanded the king.

"Not unless I am forced," answered Adrian.

"Wouldst thou suffer so great a criminal to escape for want of proof?"

"He was my master," answered the page, "and it is not for me to turn traitor to him."

"Thou art right, boy," returned the king, "and yet, I cannot imagine why thou hast escaped from the castle, if it was not to obtain redress for the many crimes he has committed?"

"My only motive," answered Adrian, "was to procure the liberation of one who, but for timely assistance, must wear out the remainder of her days in a wretched dungeon."

"But by so doing," returned the king, "you will expose him to the dangers that must follow an explanation of the conduct he has pursued."

"It shall be my constant endeavours to prevent that," answered the page. "I am aware of the danger your majesty speaks of, but if Sir Gaston yields ere it is too late, there will be no occasion for pursuing the inquiry further."

"Beware how you ever come within his reach again," exclaimed Roland le Mark, fiercely; "beware, I say, for should he chance to come across you, I can answer for it, he will never give you another opportunity to betray his secrets."

"The boy," returned Black Ivan, "has nothing to fear from your master; he is now to enter the service of the king, where he will be safe from all the schemes of his infuriated enemies."

"Not from the rage of a master that he is seeking to injure," replied Roland.

"He does not seek to injure him," exclaimed the king. "He would rather shield him, if it were possible to do so, and it will be Sir Gaston's own fault if he does not avoid the disgrace that at present threatens him."

"Well," exclaimed the retainer, "I care not what comes of it, so that I am not punished for the supposed faults of my master."

"Aid us in delivering the female we speak of from her persecutor, and you shall be set at liberty," exclaimed Black Ivan.

"And what if I refuse your terms?"

"You will then remain here for the rest of your life."

"Which is more mercy than you had any right to expect," added Hubert; "for, if I had my will, you should not live another hour after you had made up your mind to be obstinate."

"Well," cried Roland, "that's one way of frightening a man into being a traitor to the master he serves. But I am no coward, Ivan, and if you order me for instant execution, I shall die just as firm as I am at this moment."

"It seems, then," exclaimed the king, "that you feel no pity for the unfortunate female who has for so lengthened a period been the victim of Sir Gaston's cruel policy?"

"It is nothing to me," answered the fellow; "Sir Gaston has a right to follow his own humour in the affair, and it is not for me to refuse any office he may be pleased to give me. He has made me gaoler to the woman you speak of, and, though I have seen her sufferings these many years past, yet they never made any impression upon me, because I knew well enough my master had a reason for what he had done."

"Do you know his reason?" asked the king.

"I never gave myself the trouble to give it a thought."

"He says," observed Black Ivan, "that the female is mad, and I would ask whether you have ever seen anything in her conduct to prove that she is so?"

"I tell you," answered Roland, "the affair is no business of mine, and, therefore, I have merely obeyed my orders, without troubling myself with anything else. She may be mad for aught I know, and I dare say she is so, or Sir Gaston would never have thought of saying so."

"The fact is," said the king, "he has a reason for the conduct he has pursued towards her, and it may be convenient for him to raise reports that will serve to disarm suspicion. He, however, must now learn to obey my commands, for he may be assured that I will never rest satisfied until he has set his unfortunate captive at liberty."

"And that, I am convinced, he will never do," exclaimed Roland insolently.

"In that case, we must compel him by force," cried the king.

"Nay,—that you can never do."

"Hah!—will he defy me then?"

"I don't know that he'll do that," answered Roland; "but I do happen to know that there are people about him that would put her to death, rather than she should be set at liberty to be made a witness against him."

"You mean to hint, then," cried the king, "that he would not hesitate to commit murder?"

"I don't say that he would know anything about it," returned Roland, "but he has retainers who would slay the woman without giving him the trouble to give any orders about it. We can understand what will afford him satisfaction, and it's not a trifle that would prevent our earning his approbation."

"Your majesty hears him!" exclaimed Ivan; "the prisoner will be murdered, unless we take speedy means to snatch her from the grasp o her persecutor."

"Sir Gaston shall feel my rage, if he renders not a fair account of his unfortunate captive," answered the king. "I will myself inquire into this matter, and if I find your charges against him are true, I will not fail to visit him with the punishment he merits."

"It appears, then," exclaimed Roland, "that your majesty believes the falsehoods that have been told you by this robber?"

"I see no reason to doubt it, at present," replied King Richard.

"Then his word is to be taken in preference to that of a knight and a soldier!"

"Sir Gaston has only himself to blame for any doubt that I may throw upon his veracity," answered the king. "He has already in too many instances proved himself to be a tyrant over the helpless, and when I remember the injuries he has sought to inflict upon the Hebrew Maiden,

am more than ever convinced that he has treated his other prisoner in the manner that has been described. Nay, by your own confession, the woman is now deprived of her liberty, and has been so for many years past."

"My master," replied Roland, "has sufficient cause for what he has done."

"That I shall be better able to judge of hereafter," exclaimed Richard; "I will sift closely into this affair, and unless he can disprove the accusations brought against him, he will find, when too late, that he has lost the favour of his sovereign. So now, I will take my departure homewards, and you, Adrian, will follow me there with what speed you can."

"Will your majesty allow me to accompany you?" asked Ivan.

"I believe there will be no occasion for it," replied the king; "my attendant and I left our horses in a thicket hard by, and an hour's ride will bring us to the end of our journey. So, farewell, and when next we meet, may it be to hear from your own lips that you have determined to abandon a course of life that is ill adapted to you."

With this, King Richard and his attendant, guided by Ivan, left the chamber, and were shortly afterwards on their way towards London. The prisoner was then conveyed back to the place from whence he had so unexpectedly forced his way, and having given some general directions to his band, Black Ivan led the page from the cave, and without loss of time conveyed him to the palace of the king.

CHAPTER LXXXIII.

" She hath a tear for pity, and a hand
Open as day for melting charity;
Yet notwithstanding, being incensed, she is flint—
Her temper, therefore, must be well observed."

SHAKSPERE.

IMPATIENT at the long absence of Roland le Mark, and alarmed lest anything had occurred to increase his own danger, Sir Gaston strode with the
most painful anxiety up and down the armoury, to which he had repaired
immediately after the retainer had left. Guilt rendered him suspicious of
every event that he could not exactly account for, and, as the time
for Roland's return had long since passed away, he began to suspect that
he also had forsaken him, at a moment when danger threatened him on
every side.

Bitterly did he now curse the hour when he had yielded to his own evil
passions, and in the madness of his despair, he would have given half his
possessions to enjoy that esteem which he had so wilfully sacrificed in the
pursuit of pleasure. But he felt that it was now too late to retrieve his
errors, for none would believe his sincerity, and thus he would subject himself to the suspicions and sneers of those who placed no reliance in him.
This was more than his pride could submit to, and yielding to his baser
nature, he at last resolved to proceed in the course he had so long adopted.
Acting upon this determination, he left his chamber and proceeded to that
which for the present was occupied by Rebecca. But the maiden heeded
not his approach, for she was absorbed in her own melancholy reflections
when he opened the door, and it was not till his voice sounded in her ears,
that she was aware of the presence of her tyrant captor.

" What means this intrusion, Sir Gaston?" she said; " I was informed
that here I was to be left alone, until the time had expired when you demanded an answer to the shameless proposition you have made."

" Such was my intention, fair one," replied the knight, with forced gentleness. " I meant not to visit you till the end of the period that had been
named, but you must pardon the ardour of a lover, whose happiness rests
entirely upon the answer he may receive from the mistress of his heart."

" Thy words are a mere mockery, Sir Knight."

" There, maiden, thou dost most cruelly wrong me."

" What say'st thou!" cried Rebecca, indignantly; " dost thou dare to
stand boldly before me, and assert thou really lovest the despised Hebrew
Maiden?"

" I repeat," he exclaimed, " that never did I know what love was till I
met thee."

" Would we had never met, then," she replied, " for since that moment
peace has been banished from my bosom."

" That has been the effect of thine own blind obstinacy," answered Sir
Gaston. " I offered thee my heart, and a share of the fortune that is at my
disposal. This thou didst reject with scorn, and if my subsequent proceedings have seemed harsh, it is thyself only that is to blame for them."

" And why did I reject thy terms?" demanded Rebecca. " Were they
not such as you should have been ashamed to propose, or I to have accepted? Thou wouldst have made me the scorn and contempt of mankind,
and I have proved how much I esteem virtue by the fearlessness with
which I have braved your threats of death."

" Foolish girl!" cried Sir Gaston, " it is time thou shouldst reflect better on this matter. Remember, thou canst not escape my anger, and if that does not intimidate thee, turn thy mind upon thy father, whose death thou mayst have to answer for in another world."

"Ah ! wouldst thou murder him ?"

"That may depend upon the answer I am about to receive from thee, proud girl."

"Nay," exclaimed Rebecca, after a brief struggle with her own feelings, "even that threat shall not urge me to become the victim of thy evil passions. My father hath ever taught me to love virtue as a jewel far beyond all price, and he would load me with his curses, were I to yield myself to thee for the preservation of his life."

"But perhaps the old man may think better of it now," answered the Knight Templar. "He knows how powerless thou art in my hands; that I can deliver thee to death whenever I may feel inclined to do so, and that his own fate depends upon thy compliance with the terms I have proposed. These things should be well weighed in thy mind girl, and when thou hast carefully considered them, I anticipate thy answer will be very different to what it has hitherto been."

"It will never change, Sir Knight."

"Ha !—why art thou so sure of that ?"

"Because," she replied, "nothing can ever make me forget the perfidy of him who would tempt me to shame and infamy."

"In what has my perfidy consisted ?" demanded Sir Gaston.

"In many things."

"Perhaps," he exclaimed, "thou wilt be kind enough to enumerate some of them ?"

"In the first place," answered Rebecca, " I charge thee with rank perfidy towards thy wife. The Lady Alicia, having outlived thy affections, has been cast off and buried in a loathsome dungeon, whilst thou hast been rioting in the most boundless extravagance and licentiousness."

"By St. George, thou art candid enough, it must be owned," exclaimed the knight, affecting perfect ease, though, in reality, he was writhing beneath the torture she inflicted. "Thou hast taken me at my word, it seems, Rebecca, and yet, having spoken thy mind thus freely, thou seest I am not angry with thee. I can endure much from those I love, and, therefore, thou mayst go on with the catalogue of my crimes, without fear of exciting my wrath beyond bounds."

"Thou wouldst hear me further, then ?"

"Aye, proceed, girl,—proceed as far as thy humour carries thee."

"In the second place," she continued, " I have to accuse thee of gross perfidy against myself. Thou hast detained me here against my will,— made me thy prisoner, without one single reason to bring forward in excuse for thy tyranny. Thou hast sought by every means in thy power to gain my love, though thy wife was languishing in a dungeon, to which thou hast cruelly sent her, and when thou didst find that I still held thee in my scorn, thou didst seek to bring charges against me to ruin my fair name. All this thou hast done, Sir Gaston, and yet, in spite of thy base efforts, I still hold thee in the contempt thou deservest."

"It may be so, girl," exclaimed the knight, "but remember, I hold thee in my power, and thou mayst yet be compelled to yield to the terms I have offered."

"Never !"

"So thou sayst," he replied, "and yet, methinks, thou wilt ere long be compelled to be less obstinate."

"I shall never be less firm."

"Well," exclaimed Sir Gaston, "we will say no more upon this subject at present, but return to that we were just now speaking on. You have mentioned two instances of what you are pleased to call my perfidy, and I would know whether you have any further charges to make of the same nature?"

"There are many," she replied, "but for the present, I will content myself with naming one of them. I have before told thee that I am aware of the traitorous part you are playing towards our good king, Richard Cœur de Lion. Thou hast joined in a conspiracy to take away his life, and to set Prince John on the throne which would thus become vacant."

"Girl!" exclaimed the knight, quailing at these words, "thou dost, in this instance, accuse me falsely."

"Nay," she replied, "it is in vain that you deny my charge. I speak the truth, and heaven above can attest that I do not charge thee wrongfully."

"By whom hast thou been informed of this?"

"That is a question I cannot answer, since it would but bring the person under thy withering displeasure," answered Rebecca. "Let it suffice, however, that I do know of thy traitorous doings, and if thou darest me to the proof, I can explain all in presence of the king."

"Wouldst thou ruin me, girl?"

"Ha!—thou fearest me, then, proud knight."

"It is not that I fear thee," replied Sir Gaston de Neville, "but were such a report as that thou speakest of to reach the ears of the king, he would readily believe it, and I should be unjustly suspected of a crime I never meditated."

"The king," answered Rebecca, "already suspects that thou art leagued against him."

"He may do so, but his suspicions are unfounded."

"But a word from me," answered Rebecca, "will convince him that he has a traitor near him, of whom he must be aware. I can bring proof, aye, and will do so, unless thou dost not only set me at liberty, but also promise that my father shall no more be subjected to thy cruel persecutions."

"Thou askest more of me than I can grant," exclaimed Sir Gaston de Neville.

"And why canst thou not grant a request so just and easy of performance as this?"

"Because the king has demanded that thou shalt be delivered into his custody, until thou hast been tried on the charge I have brought against thee."

"Aye, thou hast accused me of an attempt to assassinate thee," cried Rebecca, reproachfully.

"I have, girl," he replied, "and seeing that thou wert found armed in my chamber, at the dead hour of night, and whilst I was sleeping, there is every reason to believe that my suspicions are but too well founded. Even Richard, bigotted as he is against me, must acknowledge that in this instance, I have not brought a false accusation against thee."

"Nor will the king judge partially," answered Rebecca; "he well knows the malice that prompts thee to seek my ruin, and depend on it, he will not condemn me without being well assured of my guilt."

"But thou wilt charge me, in revenge, with being concerned in a plot against his life?"

"I know not what revenge is," replied Rebecca. "I can feel that you have sought to injure me, and that you merit punishment, for having oppressed those who had it not in their power to protect themselves. I do not, however, seek to retaliate in the way you imagine, though I can readily guess how you would have acted, had our situations been reversed."

"On condition, then," exclaimed Sir Gaston, "that I do not press this charge against you, I need not fear that anything will be mentioned about the affair you spoke of?"

"I do not wish to bind you by any conditions, Sir Gaston," answered the maiden, "though your anxiety in this instance, proves that the charges I could bring against you, are well founded. I, however, ask your favour in behalf of my poor aged father, whom your past tyrannies have driven almost to the verge of the grave."

"Thy request shall be complied with," exclaimed the knight, "though, methinks, for one who professes so much loyalty to the king, it is rather singular thou shouldst make such a bargain, when, it seems, thou hast a strong suspicion that the life of thy royal favourite is in danger."

"Nor should I do so," replied Rebecca, "were I not well assured that Richard Cœur de Lion is too well protected by his faithful subjects, to be in much danger from thee. Besides, I shall myself keep a vigilant eye upon thine actions, and should I ever see real cause to apprehend immediate danger, it will then be time enough to denounce those who seek to rob him of life."

At this juncture an attendant entered to announce that the captain of the royal guard, with a party of archers under his command, had arrived at the castle and demanded an immediate audience with Sir Gaston. This, the latter at once knew, was the guard to whom Rebecca was to be given up, and, having subdued the rising anger that had well nigh choked his utterance, he desired that the officer should be immediately admitted to his presence.

"You see, girl," exclaimed Sir Gaston, when his messenger had departed, "to what a strait your obstinacy has reduced me; the king has withdrawn the confidence with which I was once honoured, and he has taken you from my custody, because he has been made to believe that you are not safe in the power of him, whose only fault consists in loving you too well."

"The fault is none of mine, Sir Knigot," answered the maiden, with conscious innocence; "I have been basely forced away from the protection of my father, and the king, well knowing the wrongs you have inflicted on me, has mercifully resolved to favour me with his royal protection."

"Which, in the end," muttered the knight, "may prove most unfortunate for both of you."

Rebecca was about to answer this half threat, when the door opened, and Hugh Tiptoft, the captain of the Royal Archers, entered the room. It was with difficulty that Sir Gaston could so far govern his rage as to speak with civility, but putting a curb upon his rising anger, as well he could, he said :—

"You are most welcome to the hospitality of my castle, though, between ourselves, I could have wished our royal master had sent you hither upon a more pleasant business."

"The affair can be easily arranged," answered the captain, "and I see no reason why you should regret the errand that brings me into your presence. But I see, you guess my errand, and are, of course, prepared to obey the king's mandate?"

"I am."

"Then my business is accomplished, and I have only to take the girl to a place where she will be securely kept until the day of trial arrives."

"In that matter the king will follow his own pleasure," answered Sir Gaston de Neville, coldly. "He has thought fit to demand a prisoner that was in my custody, and I know not yet that I shall risk the further displeasure of my sovereign, by demanding the justice that I once thought was to be fairly administered to all his subjects."

"It appears, then, you are not exactly satisfied with this arrangement?" exclaimed the captain of the archers.

"You will put what construction you please upon my words," answered Sir Gaston, haughtily. "The king knows that I have brought a charge of attempted assassination against the Hebrew Maiden, and he is also aware that it was my intention to prove that I had not accused her unjustly. He has, however, taken her out of my hands, and, therefore, I have little reason to expect that she will be found guilty of the charge."

"How!" exclaimed Hugh Tiptoft, "do you, then, suspect the king of partiality?"

"I suspect him of entertaining no favourable opinion of myself," answered the knight, gloomily. "I have served him faithfully in the field; —have fought side by side with him, when the battle raged the hottest;— have never failed in my duty when my country needed my services, and yet, now I am to be treated with open suspicion, because I accuse this Jewish girl of making an attempt upon my life."

"You judge the king wrongfully, Sir Knight," exclaimed Hugh Tiptoft; "he is not unmindful of the great services you have performed in behalf of your country, but, fearing lest you were about to do an act of injustice towards those whose weakness claims his pity, he has determined that the trial shall take place in his presence, so that the accused party may have a fair and impartial hearing."

"Which would have been the case," answered the templar, "had I been allowed to proceed in my own way."

"Alas!" sighed Rebecca, "there is too much reason to doubt that. Already I have endured tyranny and imprisonment at your hands, and you cannot deny that these measures have been taken against me in order to force me to consent to certain iniquitous proposals."

"Girl!" exclaimed Sir Gaston, "thou hadst better hold thy peace on that subject, or thou wilt draw down upon thyself a punishment thou mightest otherwise escape."

"Nay," cried Rebecca, "I am not so wholly in thy power as thou dost imagine. Some of thy most secret thoughts are known to me, and if I am urged too far, I may forget myself, and reveal that which will ——"

"Hold!" exclaimed Sir Gaston, furiously; "another word, and thou shalt never quit this chamber alive."

"Come, Sir Knight," cried the captain of the guard, "thou art menacing a helpless girl, who has no means of calling thee to account for it. If thou art angry, let it be vented upon me, and I'll warrant it will not be long before one of us is declared the victor."

"Knave!—wert thou sent hither to brave me thus in my own castle?"

"I was sent to take a helpless female from it," answered the other: "the king knew she was not safe in thy custody, and, therefore, has he commissioned me to come and bear her away to a place where she will be secure from thee."

"Indeed!—and supposing I should be in no humour to obey this command of the king's?"

"Why then I should call upon my followers, who crowd your court-yard, and the probability is that there would be bloodshed before my errand was perfectly accomplished."

"Do you forget that my men far outnumber yours?"

"I do not," answered Hugh Tiptoft, "but, at the same time, I know that they will not yield whilst one among my brave fellows lives to wield a sword."

"But by ordering the castle gates to be closed, you will all become my prisoners."

"I am aware of that also, Sir Knight, but at the same time, I know that you dare not execute the threat oou have just held out."

"Dare not, what have I to fear?"

"The king's displeasure."

"Humph!—that I have hazarded ere now."

"True, but it follows not that you will always escape the punishment of your temerity. King Richard has now grown weary of your continued opposition to his will, and, if I mistake not, you will bitterly rue any further acts that may excite his anger."

"By heavens! this insolence is not to be endured!" exclaimed Sir Gaston, fiercely, and drawing his sword, he called upon Hugh Tiptoft to decide their quarrel by single combat. Nor was the captain of the archers slow in answering this challenge, for instantly baring his glittering blade, he threw himself into an attitude of defence, and was awaiting the attack of his fierce antagonist, when Rebecca, terrified at the tumult that had thus suddenly broke out, rushed between the combatants, and earnestly implored them to desist. This appeal, however, had no effect upon Sir Gaston de Neville, whose rage had been excited to the highest pitch, and he was about to make a desperate attack upon his antagonist, when Bertrand le Noir burst into the room, and beating down their weapons, swore he would plunge his own sword into the breast of the first that attempted to renew the strife.

"How is this, villain?" exclaimed Sir Gaston, with mingled rage and surprise; "speak, how comest thou here, when I believed thee to be absent from my castle?"

"If you are a little cooler than you were, I'll unravel the mystery," answered the retainer. "The truth is, I have been lurking about the place for some hours, and seeing a party of the king's troops gain admittance, I began to think that all was not going on right. So taking an opportunity, I followed them, and lucky it was that I did, for the chances are that it was the means of saving both of you from death."

"Thou hast done wrong, sirrah," exclaimed the knight. "This knave here has well merited chastisement, and by heavens, he should have had it too, if thou hadst not come so inopportunely to save him from my vengeance."

"And what would have followed, if you had killed him?" demanded Bertrand le Noir; "why the king would have been incensed at the death of an officer that he had sent here for some purpose of his own, and you would not only have lost the favour of your sovereign, but it is not unlikely you would have fared somewhat worse than that."

"As for the favour of King Richard, that, I believe, is already lost," answered the knight, gloomily.

"You are mistaken there, Sir Gaston," exclaimed the captain of the archers. "His majesty is, doubtless, offended at your having oppressed certain of his subjects, who have been imprisoned in your castle upon charges that have never been proved. These wrongs he is determined to redress, and if you exhibit the least signs of repentance, he will be glad to grant his pardon, and take you once more into his favour."

"I ask neither pardon nor favour of King Richard," answered Sir Gaston de Neville.

"Well, in that matter you will please yourself," exclaimed Hugh Tiptoft, in a tone of indifference. "I have come here on an errand, and unless you have marvelously changed your mind within the last half hour, this maiden is to be suffered quietly to depart with me."

"My word has been given, and shall not be broken," replied the knight. "The girl may go with you, but tell the king from me, that I have a charge to bring against her, and that I shall expect justice at his hands."

"Fear not but you will have it," replied the officer.

"And you, girl," exclaimed Sir Gaston, addressing himself to the Hebrew Maiden, "remember it will depend upon yourself what course I shall pursue in this affair. Your father's life, as well as your own, will depend upon your silence, for should an incautious word escape, it will draw down upon you such vengeance as you justly merit."

"You need not fear me, Sir Knight," answered Rebecca; "I will be silent,—that is, so long as you do not seek to injure my father."

"Your father is at present safe, and, therefore, you may depart without fear on his account," replied Sir Gaston. "And now, let me advise you to think better of the proposal I have so often made, and which you have so obstinately rejected. You will now have time and opportunity to reflect on the advantages it will give you, and on my own part, I promise never to recollect the past unkindness with which you have thus far regarded my earnest suit."

"I will remember your words," answered the maiden, "though I do not promise to obey the rest of your injunction."

Here the interview ended, and Hugh Tiptoft led our heroine away to convey her to the Gate-house at Westminster, which, at that period, was used as a place of confinement for state prisoners. Sir Gaston watched their departure with sullen silence, and as they quitted the precincts of the castle, he motioned Bertrand le Noir to follow him into the armory.

CHAPTER LXXXIV.

"Better were I distract,
So should my thoughts be severed by my griefs,
And woes by strong imagination lose
The knowledge of themselves."

KING LEAR.

THE knight could not conceal the rage that was consuming him, and Bertrand le Noir could see plainly enough that he was meditating some terrible vengeance for the many disappointments he had encountered during the period he had been wasting in the pursuit of the Hebrew Maiden. But the retainer knew that it would produce no little mischief to himself, if he should venture to disturb the reverie into which his haughty master had fallen, and retiring to a distant part of the armoury, he affected to be deeply engaged in examining the numerous trophies that were ranged along the walls. Whilst he was thus occupied, Sir Gaston paced uneasily up and down the spacious chamber, muttering half-suppressed threats of vengeance, and cursing the fate that had hitherto thwarted every plan that he had formed for carrying his iniquitous designs to a successful termination. At length, he became weary of thus venting his ill-humour, he threw himself upon a seat, and calling for Bertrand to approach, inquired whether he was still willing to serve him as he had done before.

"I am, Sir Knight," replied the ruffian, "I have returned to your castle for that purpose, and am ready to die in any service you may think proper to give me."

"And may I depend on you as I did before you so suddenly left my castle?"

"You may," answered Bertrand, "and as for my leaving you so sud-

denly, the fault was none of my own, and I have taken the first opportunity to return to my old quarters. So now, Sir Gaston, you have only to give the word, and my poniard is at your command, even though you should bid me go and bury it in the heart of the king."

"Hah!" exclaimed Sir Gaston, "what put that fiendish thought into thy ever plotting brain?"

"I merely thought you bore King Richard no good will, and as I am not particular, I would put him quietly out of the way, if it was necessary."

"Thou hast tried it once, sirrah, and failed."

"I know it, but does it follow, that because I have failed once, I should do so again?"

"I see thy zeal in my behalf is as great as ever," exclaimed Sir Gaston; "thou wouldst risk thy life, Bertrand, were I to require the performance of some hazardous undertaking?"

"Why, to be sure I would."

"In that case, I will trust thee as I did ere thou didst leave my castle. I am in great need of some zealous friend, and, believing I can rely on thee, I will soon put thy promises to the test."

"And if I fail in giving thee satisfaction, hang me from the loftiest turret of your castle, as a warning to others not to undertake more than they can perform. So now, tell me the task I am to perform, and it shall be done, or never will I return to tell you of my own failure."

"Thou knowest," observed Sir Gaston, "how I have been baffled in the designs I had formed for the securing of Rebecca, the Hebrew Maiden; she has thwarted me at every turn, and though she has been several times in my power, yet, on each occasion have I been robbed of my prey, when

No. 61

most I felt myself secure. Thou hast seen how she was taken from me to-day, by command of the kin, and yet, I still hesitate to hurl upon him the vengeance I have meditated."

"Why do you pause," demanded Bertrand, "when, to my own knowledge, there are many like yourself, who have determined to get rid of this king, and place his brother upon the throne of England?"

"I can scarcely tell thee why I have hesitated," answered the knight, "but my friends seem scarcely ready yet; and many of them refuse to act until the deed can be accomplished without fear of a failure."

"And why cannot one man be entrusted to perform your intentions?" asked the ruffian.

"Because I have hitherto been unable to meet with a man whom I could trust in such an affair," andswered Sir Gaston. "You, however, I have every reason to believe, will faithfully serve me, and I will consider how the task may best be exenuted. In a day or two, I will speak with thee again upon this subject, and in the meantime do thou hold thyself in readiness to do my bidding."

"And why should there be any delay?" demanded the other. I am ready now, and, if you only give the word, I promise that King Richard shall not have many hours to live."

"Thou art too eager in this affair, Bertrand," exclaimed Sir Gaston de Neville; "remember, it is not the first time thou hast undertaken to despatch the king;—the first time thou didst fail, and be assured that he is now so well guarded, that it will be impossible to approach him near enough to do the deed we speak of."

"Humph!" muttered the ruffian, "it seems, then, that you want to take the life of Richard, and yet, have not resolution enough to give the word that would secure yourself from his interference in future."

"Peace, sirrah!" exclaimed Sir Gaston, "and learn to obey me without murmuring at the course I may think it most prudent to adopt. I have well weighed the chances in this affair, and, seeing that it cannot be done at present without involving more persons than myself in danger, I have resolved to wait yet a little longer;—a few days will, perhaps, remove all obstacles, and then thou shalt no longer have to reproach me with indecision."

"And in the meantime, what am I to do?"

"I will give thee a task, fellow, which will require all thy cunning and caution to execute. It will place thee in some danger, I must admit, but, if thou dost succeed, thy reward shall be worthy of acceptance."

"Come, there's a chance of doing something, after all; so now, Sir Knight, tell me what you would have done, and it shall be no fault of mine if I do not give a good account of myself, sooner perhaps, than you may expect."

"There is one," answered Sir Gaston, "who has often crossed my path, and frustrated me, when most I thought myself secure, He must be removed, and that speedily."

"He shall."

Canst thou guess who I mean?"

"Not exactly; but, were he my own brother, I would stab him to the heart, if it were your command."

"The man I speak of," replied Sir Gaston, "is Black Ivan, the notorious Outlaw."

"Hah;—an awkward customer to deal with, truly."

"He is," answered the knight, "I am aware of the difficulties you will have to encounter. but let me be rid of him, Bertrand, and ten thousaud crowns shall be your reward."

"Well, I will at least, try to earn your gold," exclaimed the ruffian; "the fellow has, it is true, baffled me several times already, but I may be too much for him yet, if I only set about my task with caution."

"You must, in the present instance, act with the greatest caution and secresy," answered Sir Gaston, "for should Ivan chance to see you, he will be sure to suspect that you have some design against him. He knows the hatred I bear him, and will at once guess your errand, should you be seen lurking any where about his usual haunts."

"Aye, aye," replied Bertrand, "I have got to deal with a cunning fellow, I know, and depend on it, I will not give him an advantage if I can help it. I will watch him as the hawk does her prey, and he shall die when least he suspects danger to be at hand."

"I will rely upon thy prudence."

"Thou mayst do so, Sir Gaston, for never yet have I failed thee when thou didst require my services. Besides, I myself bear no good will towards this Outlaw, for he has sworn to slay me on the first chance that offers; so, to make myself secure, I will put him out of the way as soon as possible."

"Take him alive, if thou canst," exclaimed the knight. "Bring him before me in bonds, and I will regard thy service more than if he should perish ere I have seen him again."

"I'll not promise to do that, Sir Gaston," answered the other, "because it so happens that he's a little too cunning to be trapped like a bird; besides, he is always armed, and you know as well as I do, that he can handle a weapon as well as any man throughout the king's dominions."

"There may be more danger, certainly, in taking him alive," returned Sir Gaston; "but if thou dost succeed in doing so, I will double the reward I have already promised. Bring him hither, so that I may speak with him, and thou shalt receive from me twenty thousand crowns."

"By'r our lady, a large sum that for capturing a robber!" cried Bertrand.

"It is, but I have a reason for wishing his life to be spared for the present, and, therefore, do thou my bidding without further questioning me upon the subject."

"I will," answered the ruffian, "but, perhaps you will allow me to ask what is to be done with him, in case I should be able to bring him here alive?"

"I am not yet resolved upon that subject," answered Sir Gaston;—"perhaps I may revenge myself by ordering him to meet an ignominious death upon a scaffold; or, perhaps,—which is most likely,—I shall throw him into one of my dungeons, where he shall pass the remainder of his days in hopeless imprisonment."

"You have tried that before," exclaimed Bertrand le Noir, "and yet he has somehow or other, always found means to escape when we least expected it."

"But this time, his limbs shall be loaded with fetters; his body shall be chained to one of the pillars of his dungeon, so as to prevent the possibility of his again escaping from my custody."

"Aye, we have thought it impossible before," returned Bertrand; "but he has managed to get clear off, and will do so again, if you are determined to keep him here as your prisoner, instead of putting him out of the way at once. Three or four inches of cold steel would make the thing certain, and save a great deal of trouble that you may otherwise have."

"Tush! thou knowest not the motives that urge me to this step, and, therefore, canst not judge what will be best to do."

"Very true, Sir Knight, but I know what Black Ivan is, and, therefore, have given my advice accordingly. He is not the man to remain here a prisoner, if he has only half a chance to get clear away from his gaoler, and you may take my word for it, that, in spite of all your chains and fetters, he would find means to set himself at liberty."

"Not unless he had some one to assist him in escaping."

"And that," observed the other, " is likely enough to happen."

"Hah! dost thou think there are traitors in the castle then?"

"No, but there is that black apparition that has so often made his appearance among us," answered Bertrand le Noir, "and I have sometimes thought whether Ivan was not indebted to the spectre, or whatever it is, for getting so clear away on former occasions."

"Psha!" exclaimed Sir Gaston, "why dost thou again mention to me that mysterious form, whose midnight visits have so often filled me with terror. Have I not bade thee be silent on the subject, and yet thou dost again remind me of that which I would fain forget."

"Well," replied Bertrand," I'll say no more about it, since the subject is a disagreeable one ; and so, by way of changing the conversation, perhaps you will tell me when I am to set about my task of searching after Black Ivan?"

"To-morrow."

"Humph! why delay it so long?"

"Because I have bethought me of other business that I have for thee to do in the meantime."

"Aye,—and prithee what is that?"

"First tell me," exclaimed Sir Gaston, "whether thou art willing to accept a wife of my choosing."

"That will depend upon circumstances," answered Bertrand, surprised at this unexpected question. "I am willing to oblige my master in most things, but this is putting my obedience to rather a severe test."

"Nay, submit to my command, and thou shalt have no reason to regret the step I have proposed."

"Is the lady young?"

"About thine own age."

"Fair?"

"I once thought her fairer than all the world beside."

"But, perhaps her beauty is now on the wane?"

"She is still handsome enough for so rough a knave as thyself," answered Sir Gaston.

"Well," exclaimed Bertrand le Noir," I begin to think matrimony will not be altogether disagreeable to me ;—so prithee, tell me the name of my future bride, and then——"

"Thou shalt know that anon, good Bertrand ;—and now, what sayest thou to the Lady Alicia, for she it is to whom I would see thee wedded."

"The Lady Alicia!" cried the other, with surprise.

"Aye,—is she not good enough for thee?"

"She is good enough, certainly, Sir Gaston, but seeing that she is your wife, it strikes me there is an obstacle in the way that we cannot very well get over."

"All can be contrived," replied Sir Gaston, " if you are disposed to rid me of one I have long ceased to love."

"I don't know that I should have any objection to take the Lady Alicia for a wife," answered the ruffian, "but it strikes me she would not be quite so willing to accept me for a husband. Besides, being already married, I do not see how you can bring this project to bear."

"That can be managed with less difficulty than you imagine," returned Sir Gaston. "She is a prisoner within this castle, and must remain so to the end of her days, unless I think fit to give her the liberty she has lost. On condition that she marries you, she shall be set free, and, as I intend to bestow upon her a liberal sum of money, you may take her to some foreign land where she may never be heard of again."

"Are you in earnest, Sir Gaston?" demanded the retainer.

"I was never more so in my life."

"But you must, of course, be aware that our marriage will not be lawful?"

"That," replied the Knight, I care nothing about. "I shall rid myself of her, and you must promise to take her where we shall never meet again."

"Well!" exclaimed Bertrand, "this is the most singular proposition I ever heard. However, you seem to be serious, and, if the Lady Alicia does not object to it, I see no reason why I should; so you may command me, Sir Gaston; but, remember, if she does consent to marry me, I must have a handsome allowance to support her with."

"You shall, Bertrand, but it will be on condition that you wed her without delay."

"Oh, for that matter, I am ready whenever you may think proper to command."

"Accompany me then immediately to her dungeon," replied Sir Gaston. "We will lose no time now that the thing is once resolved upon, and in the event of her becoming your wife, she shall be immediately set at liberty."

"And suppose she then takes it into her head to tell people of what has happened?"

"There is no fear of that," answered the Knight;—"I will bind her to secrecy by a terrible oath, and I know enough of her to be satisfied that nothing will ever prevail upon her to break so solemn a promise."

"Well!" exclaimed Bertrand, "I have scarcely been an hour in the castle, and already I have two as pretty affairs in hand, as any man need to wish for. In the first place, I have to hunt out a notorious outlaw and robber; and, in the next, I have to marry a woman that I have been acting the part of gaoler to, for I know not how many years past!"

"And for both of which services," replied Sir Gaston de Neville, "you will be liberally rewarded."

"Why, so they ought to be," answered the retainer, "seeing that I am running no little risk in your affairs. Black Ivan may chance to prove too much for me, and as for the wife you have chosen for me, she may chance to turn out a tartar, and, in that case, I render myself a miserable man for life."

"There is no fear of it," replied Sir Gaston;—the Lady Alicia will be grateful for the liberty you will be the means of obtaining for her, and as she must heartily hate me by this time, she will have little cause to regret the change that will have taken place."

"Well," exclaimed Bertradd, "at any rate I have made up my mind to do your bidding, so, at your earliest convenience, I will be ready to marry the lady; that is, on condition she does not object to it."

"She shall not object to it."

"That is more than you can promise, seeing that women can be obstinate when they take it into their heads."

"We will instantly go to her dungeon," answered Sir Gaston; "and as I intend to take my confessor, Father Francis, with us, the ceremony may be at once proceeded with."

With this, Sir Gaston left the armoury, followed by Bertrand le Noir, and having found the monk in the oratory, they all three proceeded towards that part of the castle in which was situated the entrance that led towards the dungeon. With the assistance of a lamp they succeeded in finding their way through the numerous vaulted passages, and, at length, reaching the cell where Lady Alicia was imprisoned, the bolts were removed, and the visitors entered, at the moment when the unfortunate captive was upon her knees, imploring the assistance of heaven to aid her in the terrible extremity to which she had been driven. At their entrance, however, she hastily rose from her attitude of supplication, and perceiving Sir Gaston among those who had so unexpectedly disturbed her, she enquired, meekly, the nature of the errand that had brought him into her presence.

"To know whether you have yet learned obedience," answered the knight.

"What do you come to ask me?"

"To release you from a hateful bondage that you have too long endured. Nay, to keep you no longer in suspense, Lady Alicia, I am here to know whether you will voluntarily become the wife of my retainer, Bertrand le Noir?"

"The wife of Bertrand le Noir!" cried Alicia, almost breathless with surprise.

"Aye, madam, I have spoken plainly, I believe; and now, having heard the object that brings us into your presence, I crave an immediate reply to my question."

"Am I not already your wedded wife?" demanded Alicia. "Are we not linked together in the sight of Heaven, and yet you demand that I should give my hand to another."

"Psha! I have long since grown weary of you," exclaimed the knight, fiercely.

"And yet you once swore to love me."

"True, and I did love you for a time; but that has now passed away, and I regard you only as a barrier to the happiness I might otherwise enjoy."

"I know not why I should have fallen under your displeasure, Sir Gaston," cried the lady, in trembling accents; "it seems, however, that you have long since ceased to love me, and the cruelty I have received at your hands proves how anxious you are to rid yourself of me by death."

"I do not seek to deny it, woman," exclaimed the templar; "I have eagerly looked forward to your death as the only means that offered for ridding myself of a curse; yet for years you have survived the hardships I have heaped upon you, and now I am resolved to end the uncertainty that has tormented and almost driven me to madness."

"You have no grounds for inflicting this cruelty upon me, Sir Gaston," cried Lady Alicia; "I have never given you cause to hate me, as you do, and yet I have been for years past the victim of your cruelty and injustice."

"I would that you had died under the cruelties you complain of," muttered the knight.

"I have prayed for death," she replied, "yet it was the will of Heaven that I should live to endure fresh tortures. I am weary of the sufferings I have borne, and thankful would I be to yield up an existence that has been embittered by so many sorrows."

"I come not to hear your complaints," exclaimed Sir Gaston; "my business you have already heard, and I must have an instant answer to my demand."

"You command me to become the wife of another?"

"I do, and you must obey me, or prepare to endure worse tortures than those hitherto inflicted."

"I can bear them all," she replied, firmly.

"How!" exclaimed the knight; "am I to be thwarted in my plans by one whose life is in my power?"

"I know my life is in your power," answered Lady Alicia, "but never will I consent to the base proposition you would wish me to accept."

"Beware, then, of the vengeance you provoke."

"Nay, my son," interposed the confessor, "do not give way to this unmanly violence. The Lady Alicia will reflect on this matter, and reply to it on some future occasion."

"Priest!" exclaimed Sir Gaston, "I ask no advice from thee, and thou hadst better hold thy peace, or never wilt thou quit those dungeons again."

"The Holy Father Confessor surely will not assist in forcing me to this unlawful marrige," cried Alicia, in despair.

"Father Francis knows too well that he dares not refuse my bidding," replied the knight;—"in this castle I am sovereign lord and master, and should he provoke me too far, it is probable he will be made bitterly to repent his folly."

"Besides," observed Bertrand le Noir, "he will be compelled to perform the marriage rites, seeing that I am not to be disappointed of a wife, and that I will strike him to the heart with my poniard if he betrays the least signs of hesitation and unwillingness."

"You have not yet heard the terms I come to offer thee, Alicia," exclaimed Sir Gaston de Neville, in a more subdued tone. "It has been long since evident that I love thee not, and surely the imprisonment thou hast suffered must, ere this, have taught thee the madness of resisting my will. Consent, therefore, to this union with Bertrand, and thou shalt have the liberty thou hast been deprived of."

"I will never consent to it," replied Alicia, firmly.

"Then I shall use force."

"Do, and Heaven's curses will light upon you for it."

"Nay, thou wilt not deter me by such threats as that," answered Sir Gaston; "I am resolute, as thou knowest; and let the consequence be what it may, I will see this ceremony performed before I leave the place."

"Oh, let me implore thee to recal those dreadful words," cried Alicia, in an agony of terror.

"Thou hast heard me, Alicia," exclaimed the knight, "and no prayers nor entreaties that thou canst urge shall change the fixed purpose of my soul. Thou shalt become the wife of Bertrand le Noir, and when that is accomplished I may once more taste of happiness."

"But dost thou not know that the marriage will be illegal?"

"I have thought of that, and prepared accordingly," answered Sir Gaston. "Once united to thy new husband, I will fearlessly confess to the world that thou art alive, and that I have imprisoned thee for purposes of my own, and which need not be explained. That done, I will obtain a dispensation from the pope, and thou mayest then become the lawful wife of Bertrand le Noir."

"Let me entreat thee, lady, to consent to this proposition," cried the confessor.

"Canst thou advise me to a step like this?" exclaimed Alicia, in a tone of severe reproach.

"Aye, since it is for thine own advantage, lady," replied the supple monk. "As it is, I see thee surrounded on every hand by dangers, and by taking this step thou wilt escape them."

"It is in vain to urge me further, priest," exclaimed Alicia, indignantly; "thou art leagued with those who would force me to this shameless act, and never will I listen to one who has so far forgotten his own sacred character as to advise a helpless woman to do that which she knows would be a crime in the sight of Heaven."

"If thou hast any regard for thyself, thou wilt not hesitate to do that which I can compel by force," cried Sir Gaston, impatiently.

"Besides," added Bertrand le Noir, "I cannot see why you should make so many objections to becoming my wife. To be sure I may not be quite so rich, nor so high in rank, as Sir Gaston de Neville; but then he has promised to bestow upon us a handsome sum of money, and I dare say you can manage to live more happily with me than you have done with him."

"I will never wed thee, Bertrand le Noir," answered Alicia, resolutely; "thou hast my answer, and let that content thee."

"Nay, if thou art obstinate, I shall be obliged to exert force to compel thee," exclaimed Sir Gaston. "I have told thee my will, Alicia, and thou knowest I am not to be defeated by the foolish fancies of a woman."

"Nor I," growled Bertrand le Noir.

"Yet the woman thou affectest to scorn, defies thee," answered the captive, resolutely.

"What!" cried the knight, "are my commands then, to be set at nought? By heaven this is no longer to be borne, and unless thou dost consent to this union with Bertrand within five minutes from this time, I will force thee to go through the ceremony I came here to witness."

"Oh, in pity spare me!" exclaimed Lady Alicia, falling on her knees at the feet of her obdurate husband; "spare me, I entreat, Sir Gaston, and do not bring down upon yourself the heavy maledictions of heaven for your share in this act of tyranny towards a helpless woman."

"Ha! I have humbled thy proud spirit at last, have I?" cried the knight, in accents of triumph; "thou dost, at length, plead to me for that mercy which thou wouldst never before deign to solicit."

"Nor would I do so now," she replied, "were it not to save thee from a crime that is alone sufficient to bring upon thee in another world, a punishment that I dread to think of."

"Psha! what is that to thee?" demanded the knight; "the crime, as thou dost call it, is mine, and thou hast nought to do with the consequences, even if they should be as terrible as thou hast imagined."

"Will nothing move thee to compassion?"

"Nothing that thou canst urge."

"Then heaven, be my shield!" cried Lady Alicia, in despair.

"I tell thee again, it is useless now for thee to call upon heaven," vociferated the Knight Templar. "Here thou art beyond all aid, and nothing shall prevent thy becoming the wife of Bertrand le Noir."

"Except death!" answered Alicia, rising from the humble posture into which she had thrown herself, and throwing herself with such suddenness upon the retainer, that she had plucked the dagger from his girdle ere he had time to prevent her. In another moment the weapon was upraised and would have been plunged into her heart, had not an awful peal of thunder at that moment broke forth, that shook the walls of the castle to their lowest foundation. Upon this, the poniard fell from the trembling hands of the captive, and sinking again upon her knees, implored pardon for the rash act she had so nearly committed. This interposition, however, had no effect upon Sir Gaston de Neville, who, raising her violently from the ground, commanded the priest to advance and proceed with the marriage ceremony.

"I will submit to no further delays," he exclaimed; "already has too much time been wasted in idle parley, and now the rites shall proceed, even though the great fiend himself should stand before us to forbid it."

Upon this, the retainer seized the hand of the terrified Alicia; the priest approached in obedience to the commands he had received, and the first

few words of the marriage ritual were pronounced, when another awfu crash was heard, and the door flying open with a tremendous sound disco-vered the form of the armed apparition. Aghast at this, all shrank back with terror, though still keeping their eyes fixed upon the fear-inspiring object that had interrupted the iniquitous proceedings. Still the figure ad-vanced slowly towards them, and with a motion of the hand, commanded them to depart, a signal that was instantly obeyed by Sir Gaston and his companions, who hastily left the dungeon, where Lady Alicia had fallen to the ground in a state of insensibility.

How long she had remained in this helpless condition the captive knew not, but on recovering from her stupor, she found herself in utter darkness. Then the remembrance of the dreadful scene she had witnessed rushed upon her bewildered brain, and in the madness of despair, she sprang from the ground to ascertain whether any means were left for escape. But to her dismay, she found that the door was locked, and then yielding to the terrors inspired by her hopeless situation, she threw herself upon a heap of straw that served her for a bed, and gave way to the agonizing thoughts that afflicted her.

CHAPTER LXXXV.

" The fatal time
Cuts off all ceremonies and vows of love,
And ample interchange of sweet discourse,
Which so long sundered friends should dwell upon."
RICHARD THE THIRD.

It is now necessary that we return to Rebecca, who, as we have seen in a former chapter, was conveyed from the castle of Sir Gaston de Neville,

No. 62

to the Gatehouse at Westminster, where she was to remain until the result was known of the charge that had been brought against her by the Knight Templar. Here, however, orders were given that she should receive every indulgence except liberty, for the king believed not the stories that had been circulated to her prejudice, and the only motive he had for sending her into confinement, was, that she should be safe from the machinations of her enemies, till after the trial had taken place.

To her surprise, therefore, she found every kindness and acccommodation that she could have desired, with liberty to range over the entire building, and to see any of her relations and friends as often as they thought proper to visit her. Under these circumstances, as may be imagined, her first wish was to see her father, and no sooner had this been made known, than a message was sent to Isaac of Tadcaster, informing him where his daughter was, and requesting his immediate attendance at the Gatehouse. This done, our heroine was shortly joined by Lestelle, the daughter of the gaoler, who, in a few words, informed the captive that she had been appointed by her father to attend upon her as long as she remained under his care. This arrangement was extremely gratifying to Rebecca, for she soon found that her new companion was just such a one as she would have chosen, and that she fully entered into the many and severe troubles with which she had been afflicted. Our heroine was, indeed, agreeably surprised at finding that she harboured none of those prejudices which at that period were entertained against the Jews, and having thanked her for the services that she had voluntarily tendered, she inquired whether they would be allowed to meet together as often as they pleased.

"Why, for that matter," replied Lestelle, "I believe we shall be under no restriction as to our meetings. My father has desired me to comfort you as well as I can, and, of course, if it is not disagreeable to yourself, I shall spend the greater part of my time in your society."

"And to whom do I owe this indulgence ?" asked Rebecca.

"To the king, I believe," answered the girl; "at least, Hugh Tiptoft told my father that you were to be treated with as much kindness as possible, and that any departure from the orders would bring down upon him the displeasure of his sovereign."

"Yet, for all that," cried the Hebrew Maiden, "I am to remain here a prisoner."

"You are," replied the other, "and a very good thing too, in my opinion. In this place, you will be safe enough from Sir Gaston de Neville, and that is more than could have been said, had you returned to the house of your father."

"I believe you are right, Lestelle," answered our heroine; "the Knight Templar has proved how ungovernable are the passions by which he is urged, and should I again fall into his hands, there is every reason to believe that he would convey me to some place where the vigilance of my friends would never discover me."

"And that," replied Lestelle, "is, no doubt, the reason why our good King Richard has thought fit to order your confinement in this place. Besides, it seems that Sir Gaston has brought some charge against you, and it would appear like partiality, if you should be suffered to go at large before the affair is thoroughly investigated."

"But," answered Rebecca, "I have good cause to know that the knight never intends to proceed with the charge he has thought proper to make against me, and in that case, I am likely to remain here a prisoner for life."

"There, I believe you are mistaken," cried the girl, "for the king's coronation is appointed to take place on the third of September, and I have heard my father say that it is usual on such occasions to set a certain number of prisoners at liberty. You will, therefore, have your choice of leaving this place, or remaining, though, to confess the truth, I think your safer way will be to stop till you are secure from all further persecution."

"Alas! when will that be?" sighed the Jewess.

"Very soon, unless I am wrong in my suspicions."

"What mean you, Lestelle?"

"Ah!" laughed the girl, "I know more of your secrets than you think for. Is there not a youth who is willing to marry you to-morrow, and when once you are his wife, will not the persecutions of this Knight Templar cease?"

"Perchance they would," answered the maiden; "but Reuben Grenard is young, and my father will not consent to our marriage taking place for some time to come."

"Then he is more obstinate than wise."

"Say rather that his years have given him experience that we ought to respect," answered Rebecca. "That my father loves me dearly, my whole life has borne witness to, and, therefore, it would ill become me to repine at a determination that is made solely for my own good."

"I dare say the old man means well enough," returned Lestelle; "but then his head may be filled with a great many ridiculous notions; and it certainly does seem strange that he should object to this marriage, when it would be so much to your own advantage."

"He does not object to it," answered our heroine.

"Very likely, but he wants to put it off, and that's almost as bad, to my thinking."

"My father has other reasons, that you are not aware of," replied Rebecca. "He tells me he is poor, and that we cannot prudently marry till he has saved enough to bestow on us a portion."

"Poor!" cried the other, with surprise; "why, surely he don't expect anybody to believe him?"

"He tells me so," replied Rebecca, "and it would ill become me to doubt the word of my parent."

"With all due submission, I doubt it though," exclaimed Lestelle. "Why, he has been known as the rich Jew, for years past, and if any of our Christian people want money, who do they apply to but Isaac of Tadcaster?"

"I know he is generally reported to be rich," answered our heroine; "he, however, denies it, and I have every reason to believe his word may be taken."

"You have never seen any of the hoards of gold, then, that he is reported to have saved?"

"Never."

"That's strange, too," observed Lestelle; "but I dare say he his cunning enough to keep his treasures out of sight, and by and by, when he dies, you will be agreeably surprised at the heaps of gold he has saved for you."

"Let us change this subject," cried Rebecca, with a languid smile at her companion's pertinacity. "You were saying, just now, that the king's coronation is appointed to be solemnized on the third of September, and that it is likely I shall be discharged from your father's custody on that occasion."

"Nay," answered the other, "it is quite certain you will, unless, indeed,

Sir Gaston de Neville persists in prosecuting his charge, and in that case, there is no saying how the affair may terminate."

" But I do not think he will carry this affair any farther," returned the Jewess. "He knows that I am aware of certain dark transactions in which he is engaged, and, conscious as he is of his own guilt, he will hardly venture to force me to declare that which would end in his own ruin, and the eternal disgrace of his name."

" Aye, in that case you are safe enough; but why not tell all you know, and thus save yourself from his future persecutions?"

" Because I would spare him from the inevitable destruction that must surely follow such a revelation."

" And why should you do so, seeing that his conduct towards you has been so cruel and unjust?"

" It is impossible to answer your questions," replied the Hebrew Maiden. "There are many reasons for my remaining silent on this subject, and one of them is, that I should involve others in the same ruin with himself."

" And, perhaps," answered the other, "they richly deserve it."

" That may be ; yet, as none of them have ever injured me, I cannot prevail upon myself to bring upon them that vengeance which would surely follow an exposure of their iniquitous designs. I have sometimes thought of doing so, Lestelle, but, upon reflection, have determined to remain silent."

" But, perhaps, some great danger is threatened to one who is unconscious of the designs of his enemies?"

" You have guessed rightly," answered Rebecca; " the greatest danger threatens one whose life I would willingly save at the expense of my own."

" Then, why stand quietly by, when a single word might avert the danger?"

" I have kept a vigilant eye upon the motions of the men I speak of," answered the Hebrew Maiden, " and, should no other alternative present itself, it shall then be my time to arrest the further progress of their designs."

Ere Lestelle could make any other reply, the door opened, and her father entered the room.

" I am come, maiden," he said, addressing himself to Rebecca, " to announce the arrival of visitors, and to know whether it is your pleasure to see them."

" Ah !—my father is one of them ?"

" He is, and the other is a younger man, who, if I am not much mistaken, you will be equally happy to see."

" Reuben Grenard ?"

" The same ; shall I admit them to your presence ?"

" Immediately."

The keeper of the Gatehouse departed on his errand, and Lestelle was about to follow, when the Jewess earnestly entreated her to stay.

" There will be nothing in our conversation," she said, " that we wish you not to hear, and it will be some consolation to my father and Reuben Grenard to see that I have one about me to relieve the solitude I should otherwise feel. They will be grateful to you, Lestelle, for the kindness bestowed upon one who is so dear to them both : and, believe me, should an opportunity occur, they will not fail to return it to the utmost of their power."

" And do you think, then," asked the girl, " that I will ever accept a reward for doing my duty? No, no, I am too happy that I have it in my power to render agreeable the period during which you must remain here, and, depend upon it, you shall ever find a faithful friend in your poor Lestelle."

At this juncture, Isaac of Tadcaster and Reuben Grenard entered the room, and the deep melancholy that seemed settled upon their countenances, showed how little they anticipated the comparative ease and security in which she was at present placed. After the first salutations were over, and whilst the aged Jew still pressed his child to his aching heart, she said :—

"You imagine, my dear father, that I am still a prisoner, and that my life is in peril; such, however, is no longer the case, for though I am necessarily confined here for a short time, yet I have found kind friends in my prison, whose affectionate care will render pleasant the brief period during which it will be necessary for me to remain here."

"Who are thy friends, daughter?" asked the old man.

"One of them, dear father, stands even now by my side."

"This maiden?"

"Yes; she has promised me her society, and I anticipate much happiness from it."

"Give me thy hand, girl," exclaimed the old man; "the touch will not contaminate thee, though there are many who would shrink from the grasp of a Jew, as if they believed he carried contagion about with him. 'Tis well, thou art above the prejudice of thy fellow people, and for thy kindness to my child, I will not fail to reward thee."

"Bless your heart, I want no reward for doing my duty," answered Lestelle.

"At least, you will accept my thanks?"

"Aye, for they cost nothing, and are equally valuable to those who are satisfied with having performed their task with zeal and fidelity."

"Such is not the feeling of the world in general," answered Isaac; "it is the nature of mankind to be selfish, and when an instance occurs of generosity such as you have displayed, it calls forth the gratitude of those upon whom it is conferred."

"Well, I declare," cried Lestelle, "to hear you talk so would make one believe nobody ever did a good-natured act before. But, see how happy the young folks are, Isaac; they are glad enough to see each other again, I'll warrant, and so, suppose you and I leave them together for a little while;—they have a great deal to say, I'll be bound, and I know, from experience, that it ain't at all pleasant to have other people present, when one's lover is saying a parcel of agreeable things."

"Nay," replied Rebecca, who had overheard these latter words, "neither Reuben nor myself wish you to leave us. We are happy in being permitted to see each other again, and ——"

"Have said all the fine things you had to tell, no doubt," interrupted the laughing girl.

"We have beeen speaking of the anguish we felt at the separation that has taken place between us."

"No doubt of it," answered Lestelle, "and have been promising yourselves days of happiness whenever the time comes for your marriage. And, by the by, Isaac," she added, addressing herself to the old man, "I have been saying to your daughter what a pity it is that there should be any delay in making them man and wife, since, after their marriage, there will be little danger of any further persecution from that terrible fellow, Sir Gaston de Neville."

"I have thought deeply and anxiously upon that subject," answered the aged Israelite, "and, though I should be glad to see the faithful love of Reuben rewarded as it deserves, yet, at present, it is impossible I can give my consent to their union."

"If it were not for being considered impertinent," cried Lestelle, "I should uncommonly like to ask what possible objection you can make to their immediate marriage?"

"Thou seemest to be a kind friend, and, therefore, will I indulge thy curiosity," answered the old man. "The truth is, I am not yet rich enough to bestow upon them such a portion as I wish, and, therefore, do I defer their union for the present."

"What is that I hear!" exclaimed the girl; "does Isaac of Tadcaster say he is so poor that he is unable to give his daughter a fitting dowry?"

"I have spoken the truth, girl."

"Upon my word, I can hardly believe you."

"Aye," replied Isaac, "that is because the world chooses to report me wealthy. But I am poor,—a very poor old man, and have not so much as a gold coin to give my child."

"I ask you for no money, sir," cried Reuben; "bestow upon me your daughter, and I will esteem the gift as far beyond any treasure you might give me."

"Foolish boy!—thinkest thou I could do that which would bring you both to beggary?"

"I am young, sir," replied Reuben, "and with the labour of my hands, could keep off the poverty you so much fear."

"Aye, aye," answered Isaac, "I have heard others say as much, but they have not been able to fulfil their intentions; their improvident marriage has brought ruin upon them, and, fearing lest my child should share a similar fate, I am resolved that you shall wait a little longer, ere I consent to grant the request you have so often urged."

"And, do you recollect," asked Lestelle, "that by delaying their marriage, you will give Sir Gaston de Neville another opportunity to carry his designs against your daughter into execution?"

"I have remembered it," answered the old man, "but, under present circumstances, they must be content to wait till a more favourable period arrives. At present, my child lies under an imputation of having attempted the life of the Knight Templar: she is now waiting her trial before the king, and till her innocence is made manifest, I will never consent to her becoming the wife of Reuben Grenard."

"But suppose Sir Gaston never thinks proper to carry on the prosecution he has threatened?"

"In that case," replied Isaac, "after a reasonable time has elapsed, I will petition the king for her release."

"And when you have done that, Sir Gaston will steal her from you, as he has done before, and the chances are that you will never hear of her again."

"My trust is placed in heaven," answered the old man, "for though the knight has hitherto triumphed over us, a period to his crimes will arrive, and vengeance light upon him for the many cruelties he has inflicted upon those who unfortunately fell within his power."

"And what says your daughter?" asked Lestelle, "is she also willing to give the knight another chance of taking her away nobody knows whither?"

"I willingly submit myself," replied Rebeccca, "to whatever decree my father may think fit to make."

"You hear her," exclaimed the old man; "she will obey me without a murmur."

"And for that very reason," answered Lestelle, "I should advise you to consider well before you take a step that may lead to much future misery. So, come, do not be hard-hearted, but consent to their being married as soon as she is released from this place, which, if I am not mistaken, will be before very long."

"Urge me no more, at present," exclaimed Isaac, "for this is a matter that will require more consideration than I can now give it. In a few days I will make up my mind; though, to speak the truth, I believe there is no chance of my agreeing to their union for some time to come."

"I will be content to wait your pleasure," cried Reuben, "though heaven knows how anxiously I look forward to the period that is to make your daughter my bride."

"Thou art a good and prudent youth, Reuben," answered the old man, "and thy patience shall not be taxed, in this respect, more than I can help. A few weeks more will enable me to ascertain what sum of money I can bestow upon Rebecca, and if by that time she is released from this place, I will offer no further obstacle to the accomplishment of thy hopes."

"Well," cried Lestelle, "if no better terms can be made, I suppose we must accept them."

"It will be no great tax upon their patience," answered the old Israelite, "and, perhaps, in reward for their obedience, I may give them an agreeable surprise."

"Ah!—do tell us what you mean, Isaac," cried the girl; "do tell me, there's a dear, good old man, or I shall positively die of downright curiosity."

"Nay, that would spoil the pleasure I anticipate, so you must e'en be content to wait till the proper time arrives."

"Then you must promise to make the time as short as possible, or I shall absolutely teaze you into telling me."

At this period a loud murmuring was heard in the streets, in which were mingled cries of vengeance and blood. Alarmed at this uproar, Lestelle was about to hurry out of the room for the purpose of ascertaining the cause of the disturbance, when she was met by Meg of Finchley, whose countenance was expressive of the greatest alarm.

"You must flee instantly from this place," she exclaimed, addressing herself to Isaac of Tadcaster; "the mob, inspired by Bertrand le Noir, and other mad partisans, have risen for your destruction, and having traced you hither, have sworn never to leave the place until you have been sacrificed to their vengeance."

"Why do they seek me?" cried Isaac, "what new cause has arisen for this fresh outrage?"

"I know not," replied Meg, "but from what I could gather, it seems that Bertrand has been set on to this by his master, in revenge for the trouble he has had with your daughter."

"But, why should the mob have joined in this cry for blood?" demanded the old man.

"Because they are easily excited to commit any act of violence," replied Meg. "Besides, you belong to a race despised and execrated by the ignorant rabble, and the knight, well knowing their prejudice, has sent his emissary among them with gold to pamper their avarice. He has distributed money amongst them, and by artful speeches, he has succeeded in raising their anger to the highest pitch."

"Dear father," cried Rebecca, "you are in peril here;—fly, then, I conjure you, or these bloodhounds will burst the doors open and tear thee piecemeal before my eyes!"

"Take Rebecca's counsel, I conjure you," exclaimed her lover; "it is yet possible to escape, and the delay of a moment may lead to the most fatal consequences."

"What!" cried the old man; "shall I effect my own safety, and leave my child to the fury of these lawless men."

"I will remain and protect her," answered Reuben.

"And thus lose your own life in a hopeless effort to save her's," exclaimed Isaac.

"Most willingly would I do so," replied Reuben, "if in my last moments I could but be assured of her safety!"

"There is yet time for all to save yourselves," exclaimed Meg of Finchley. "The mob has not yet surrounded the house, and, with the gaoler's assistance, you may get clear off before they have completely surrounded the place."

"It is impossible," cried Lestelle, who had been looking from a window that opened towards the rear of the prison; "the ruffians have not an avenue unguarded, and if I may judge from the earnestness with which they seem to be conferring together, I fear they are devising some means by which they may break into the place."

"Then do we commit ourselves to the protection of Heaven!" exclaimed Isaac, clasping his trembling daughter in his arms, and preparing himself for the worst. "We are again threatened by evil men, and they may, perchance, slay us, but they shall, at least, see that we can die with firmness."

"Would that we were armed," cried the younger Israelite; "nay, had I but a sword, these blood-thirsty villains should not enter yonder door till I had slain at least a score of them."

"It is in vain to resist them, boy," answered Isaac; "they are incited by rage and vengeance, and what, therefore, could thy single arm do against so great a multitude as now surround us?"

"The gates are strong," observed Lestelle, "and my father has several well-armed men under his command, who will not suffer these ruffians to break into this place for some time to come. In the meantime, assistance may be sent us, and the rabble put to the rout."

"That," replied Meg of Finchley, "is our only dependance. Yet, aid must arrive quickly, or I fear it will be too late."

"Hark!" cried Rebecca, with alarm, "they have commenced battering down the portals, and a short time will serve to throw us at the mercy of these bloodhounds."

"It will take them some time to break into the Gatehouse," answered Lestelle; "for an attempt was made not long since by a mob to liberate some prisoners, and, after all, they were obliged to give up their labour as useless."

"But in this instance," replied Isaac, "they are excited by vengeance, and perhaps they have assembled in greater numbers."

"That may be," answered Lestelle, "but, at any rate, the doors will stand half an hour's battering, and before the expiration of that time, I hope relief will be sent us."

"A ladle full of melted lead thrown from yonder window would send the villains flying," exclaimed Meg.

"True," replied Isaac of Tadcaster, "but even if we had such a remedy at hand, I should be loath to use it. The knaves have been misled by

artful villains, who seek our destruction, and if vengeance must fall, I would wish it to be upon those only who are most guilty."

"Hark!" cried Reuben; "that crash tells us but too surely that our enemies have succeeded in breaking down one of the barriers. They have forced an entrance, and in a few moments we shall be at the mercy of this lawless mob!"

"No," exclaimed Lestelle, who had been anxiously watching the crowd from a window, "our case is not yet hopeless;—a man has this moment thrown himself upon the leader of the rioters, and with herculean strength, has hurled him to the ground;—the rabble starts back with amazement at the boldness of the act, and some of them have even began to flee from the place in terror! And now,—yes, now I see a party of soldiers advancing; they come rapidly along,—and,—we are saved!"

Grateful for their deliverance, all of them fell upon their knees, and Jews and Christians mingled their grateful thanks to Heaven for the unexpected aid that had been sent them, when all hope seemed to have vanished.

CHAPTER LXXXVI.

"Such smiling rogues as these,
Like rats, oft bite the holy cord in twain,
Too intrinsicate to unloose.   KING LEAR.

WE must now introduce the reader to the rioters we have alluded to, but, previous to doing so, it will be necessary for us to return to Bertrand

No. 63

le Noir, who left the castle shortly after the alarm he had experienced from the appearance of the armed apparition, and the repulse he had met with from Lady Alicia, who had so firmly rejected the propositions that had been made by the imperious Sir Gaston de Neville. Enraged at the frustration of certain ambitious projects that he had formed, he was determined to vent his wrath upon some one, and, as a handsome reward had been offered by his master for the apprehension of Black Ivan, he resolved to seek the Outlaw, and, at least, make a bold effort to make him his prisoner. Full of these thoughts, he was hurrying onwards, when his name was pronounced, and looking round, he perceived a stranger standing within a deeply-shattered portal, at no great distance from him. Not recognizing the features of the man who had spoken to him, he was about to resume his way, when the other, advancing from his place of concealment, said in a voice of reproach :—

"Wilt thou pass me thus unheeded, Bertrand le Noir, when, for ought thou knowest, my business with thee may be of the utmost importance?"

"I know thee not," answered the ruffian, sullenly, "and, if the truth must be told, I have no wish to form an acquaintance with thee."

"That's plain, however," exclaimed the other; "and not over courteous, seeing that I have given thee no cause of offence."

"Perhaps, 'tis well for thee thou hast not," replied Bertrand le Noir;— "I wear a dagger, sirrah, and it may be drawn against thee, if I have much more provocation."

"Psha! thou art angry without cause, Bertrand."

"Hah!—again thou callest me by name!—speak, fellow, who and what art thou?"

"My name is Simon Hyde; by trade a tanner, and it will be thine own fault if thou and I are not firm friends, ere we part from each other. What say'st thou?—shall we shake hands, or wilt thou still distrust me?"

"I see no reason why we should know more of each other than we do at present," answered the other, gloomily; "I am on an errand of mine own, and would pass on without further interruption."

"But, perhaps I may serve thee."

"I shall not need thy assistance."

"That is more than thou canst be certain about," exclaimed Simon Hyde; "so, come, let us be a little less reserved, and I dare say we shall understand each other well enough presently."

"I tell thee, fellow," replied Bertrand le Noir, "I want no assistance that thou canst render me; besides, I would be alone, and yet thou dost press thy company upon me, as if I sought, rather than endeavoured to shun thee."

"Stay," exclaimed Simon Hyde, as the other was preparing to move onwards; "perhaps thou wilt join me in a little affair that I have on hand? Hast thou a fancy to hunt up a few Jews by way of sport?"

"It depends upon who they are," replied Bertrand.

"What say'st thou to Isaac of Tadcaster?"

"That I would like to unkennel the old fox, if I only knew where to light on him."

"Well, I can tell there where he is; I saw him and Reuben Grenard pass not long since, and something strikes me they have gone to see Rebecca, the Hebrew Maiden, who, they say, has been taken to the Gatehouse at Westminster."

"I have other game in view at present," replied Bertrand le Noir; "these Jews are no special favourites of mine, it must be confessed, but just now they must rest in peace till I have executed a task that has been set me by my master."

"Ah! I can guess thine errand, then; he has an enemy to get rid of, and thou hast undertaken to do it?"

"Thou art not far from the truth there."

"May I ask the name of the man who has been so unfortunate as to offend your master?"

"Thy question is rather a strange one, certainly," answered the retainer; "but since thou may'st, perhaps, aid me in searching after him, I will freely confess to thee that I am in pursuit of no less a personage than Black Ivan, the Outlaw."

"Indeed!" then something strikes me you will have a more difficult task than you expect. Ivan is too wary a bird to fall into the fowler's net; and if he should chance to guess your intentions, it is likely enough he will take such steps as will prevent your doing him this promised kindness."

"Perhaps so," replied Bertrand; "but at any rate the reward I am to receive for his capture is a handsome one, and I will not let it slip through my fingers if I can help it, so here's a chance for thee; assist me in taking the outlaw alive, and thou shalt have five hundred crowns for thy services."

"It's a bargain; I'll assist thee, Bertrand le Noir, and that, too, without claiming from thee the sum thou hast named."

"I see," exclaimed the other; "thou dost require from me some service in return?"

"Exactly so."

"And what may it be?"

"That thou wilt join with us in hunting out these Jews."

"It is a bargain," returned Bertrand; "but of course you can wait till we have laid this outlaw by the heels?"

"Nay, you are wrong there," answered Simon Hyde; "for these Israelites must be looked after first, and when that part of the bargain is finished, I will join you in hunting out that rascally Black Ivan."

"Can't you put off this affair of yours till to-morrow?"

"Not for a moment," replied the tanner; "I have a party of fellows ready to go with me down to the Gatehouse, and I shall want you to head one division of them, whilst I take upon myself the command of the other."

"Why you surely don't mean to make an attack upon the prison?" cried Bertrand, with surprise.

"Indeed, but I do, then," replied Simon Hyde; "we shall not be able to get hold of these fellows in any other way, and as I am determined not to let them escape this time, I have made such arrangements as will make every thing safe and certain."

"And what, pray," demanded Bertrand, "will you do with these Jews when you have them in your power?"

"That will depend on themselves," answered Simon Hyde. "If they are wise, they will purchase their lives with such a sum of money as I may think fit to demand."

"But the old man is obstinate, and loves his gold," replied Bertrand; "he is not to be intimidated so easily as you think; and, supposing he refuses to accede to your modest demand, how do you next propose to proceed?"

"Why, then, the chances are, that we shall knock out the brains of both the old man and his intended son-in-law."

"By which act," observed Bertrand, "you will earn the eternal gratitude of Sir Gaston de Neville. He regards these Israelites with no favourable eye; and should you, or any one else, rid him of Reuben Grenard, or Isaac, of Tadcaster, he may count upon receiving such a reward as will amply repay him for the deed."

" Why, in that case," exclaimed Simon Hyde, " it would be better to kill them both out of hand, than to waste time in trying to extort money from the old Jew."

" You agree to the proposal, then ?"

" I do."

" Then in that case I will instantly join you and your companions."

" Aye, I thought we should come to an understanding presently," answered the tanner; " the truth is, we can help each other more than you thought for at first, so follow me, and I'll take you to the place where our comrades are assembled, and then we can lead them to the Gatehouse, attack the prison on all sides at once, and carry off these Jews before any one has time to go and inform the soldiers of what is going on."

As he finished speaking, Simon Hyde conducted his companion down several narrow and little frequented streets, until they reached a small field, or enclosure, in the outskirts of London, and where a mob of perhaps a couple of hundred persons were assembled. At the moment of their arrival a fellow was addressing the crowd, and urging upon them the duty and propriety of exterminating the whole Jewish tribe, and so well had he succeeded in exciting them to acts of violence, that it was with some difficulty he was able to restrain them until the arrival of the man they had chosen to be their leader. No sooner, therefore, was he seen advancing, than a shout hailed his approach, and both he and Bertrand le Noir were received with an enthusiasm almost amounting to frenzy. At length, however, silence was restored, and then mounting upon the little eminence that had just been vacated by the former speaker, he addressed himself to his deluded followers."

" Friends," he exclaimed, " our cause is a good one, and, therefore, must succeed in spite of everything that may be done against us. We are now ready to march, and as you want another leader besides myself, I have brought with me Bertrand le Noir, who you all know to be of the right sort, and one that we may depend upon."

" Hurrah! Bertrand le Noir for ever !" shouted the mob.

" Aye," resumed the speaker, " I thought you would be glad to have him amongst us; he hates the Jews as much as any man here, and if he only has his own way in the matter, we shall soon get rid of the whole tribe of Israel."

" But shall we have their money when we've killed them ?" demanded a fellow, gruffly.

" Why, to be sure you will," replied Simon Hyde; " ain't we going for that purpose, and if any body resists us, we'll let them know that gentlemen are not to be deprived of their pleasure. We have sworn to have the lives of these accursed Jews, and who is there, I should like to know, that will break his word ?"

" None, none," shouted the rabble; " lead us on, Simon, and we'll soon let these Jews see that we are determined to have none of 'em in London."

" Stop !" exclaimed Bertrand le Noir; " does it happen to strike any of you, as it does me, that if we proceed much further in this affair, it's not at all unlikely that a few of us may chance to find our way to the gibbet ?"

" What! are you going to turn coward, Bertrand ?" asked the tanner, with a sneer.

" I don't call it cowardice to look forward a little when there's danger in the way," answered the retainer, sullenly. " This affair may happen to bring us all into a good bit of trouble, so those that have no wish to get into the scrape, had better return home before it's too late to repent."

" Perhaps," cried Simon Hyde, " you will be one of the first to follow your own advice ?"

"Perhaps I have as much bravery as yourself, for that matter, sirrah," replied the other. The counsel I give these fellows is nothing more than fair, and if they choose to adopt it, all well and good; if not, let them follow us to the Gatehouse, and we'll show them a piece of fun such as they have never seen before in the whole course of their lives. We will not leave one stone of the building upon another; and as for the Jews, they shall die, even though they clung to the altar for shelter and protection."

"Then let us waste no more time in idle words," exclaimed Simon Hyde. "Forward, lads, and we'll soon have gold enough shared among us to pay well for the little risk we may happen to be running."

The fellows now formed themselves into marching order, and, headed by Hyde and Bertrand le Noir, they left the place where they had assembled, and betook themselves across the fields, by a circuitous route, towards the Gatehouse at Westminster. Of their arrival there the reader has been already informed, and of the fierce attack commenced upon the building. It will also be remembered that the door was beaten down, and that Bertrand was to lead his ruffianly followers into the breach that had been thus formed, when a man sprang from among the crowd, and seizing the knight's retainer by the throat, hurled him furiously to the ground. For a minute or two Bertrand le Noir was completely overcome, but when he at length recovered, and perceived the dagger of his adversary gleaming before his eyes, his terror became unbounded, and in a voice tremulous with terror, he cried,—

"For the love of Heaven, Ivan, spare me! Slay me not, and I will do whatever you may think fit to command."

"Dare to breathe my name again, villain, and this blade shall, upon the instant, find it's way to your heart!"

"I will do anything you desire, on condition that my life is spared."

"Miscreant!" exclaimed Black Ivan, "and yet it is not five minutes since you were setting on these bloodhounds to murder the unfortunate Jews who chance just now to be beneath this roof."

"It is true," replied Bertrand, "but they are unbelievers in our holy religion, and surely you would not protect them from the fate they deserve?"

"And what dost thou deserve," demanded Ivan, "for having sought to injure those who never wronged thee?"

"There thou art wrong, Ivan," returned the other; "for, do they not rob us daily and hourly?—and shall we not, at length, revenge ourselves upon those who drain the country of its gold, and lay up stores of wealth, whilst we and our children starve for want?"

"Tush, man!" cried the outlaw, "thine argument will not bear thee out, for those thou dost at present seek to injure have never done aught by which to bring down upon themselves the fiery wrath of thyself and the brutal mob that has followed thee hither."

"Let them not hear thee," answered Bertrand le Noir, "or thou may'st repent calling them such scurvy names."

"What! dost thou think I fear the cowardly knaves that have followed thee on this gallant enterprise?"

"Thou may'st do so, should they happen to know the vile terms of reproach you cast upon them," answered Bertrand le Noir, threateningly.

"Hah! and if I fear them, why do I trust myself singly among them? There are something like two hundred men to one, and yet Ivan gives not a single thought to the danger thou speakest of. Nay, here I stand, with my foot upon thy prostrate form; thy people must know me by this time, and yet there they stand, gaping upon their fallen leader, and not one among them has courage enough to come forward and rescue the man that was to conduct them to such deeds of wonder."

"Let me rise," exclaimed Bertrand; "take thy foot from me, I say, or thou wilt presently find that they are not the base cowards thou hast taken them for."

"And supposing I release thee," cried Black Ivan, "wilt thou pledge thyself to lead these men away, and never to molest these Jews again as long as thou livest?"

"I will promise to prevail on these men to disperse themselves quietly; but I have yet to learn why thou dost desire me to leave these Israelites alone?"

"Did they ever harm either thee or any body belonging to thy family?"

"Perhaps not," answered Bertrand le Noir; "but it so happens that every one is crying out against their avarice and extortion; whilst others starve, they are growing wealthy beyond all bounds, and in a few years, if matters go on thus, the Hebrew nation will drive forth those who have a right to claim the soil upon which they have been born."

By this time, Bertrand had sprung upon his feet, and he was about to throw himself amongst his still hesitating followers, when Black Ivan, seizing him by the throat, commanded him to remain where he was on peril of instant death.

"It is in vain," he said, "to think of escaping me, sirrah, for now that you and I have met, there is a little affair to settle between us, that must be explained to my satisfaction. You would play me a scurvy trick, it seems;—that is to say, for the sake of a reward that has been offered by Sir Gaston de Neville, you would deliver me up to hopeless bondage."

"How knowest thou that?" demanded the trembling menial.

"It matters not to thee how I know it," returned Black Ivan. "The fact is as I have stated it, and thou mayest think thyself more fortunate than thou dost deserve, if I do not sacrifice thee to my just vengeance."

"Thou hadst better not do so," exclaimed Bertrand, doggedly.

"Indeed!—and why dost thou say so, sirrah?"

"Because those who witness thy violence, will not fail to revenge any violence that may be committed on me."

"Humph!—and so thou dost really believe that I value the interference of these fellows?"

"Aye, for thy liberty, if not thy life itself may chance to be in danger if thou givest cause for their anger."

"Tush! thy dependance is a vain one, if it is placed upon the curs that are now looking on whilst we are thus parlying," exclaimed Black Ivan. "These fellows hold my name in dread, and there is not one of them that would raise an arm against me even at the bidding of their doughty leader."

"Thou art mistaken," answered Bertrand le Noir, "for, relying as they do upon their numbers, it requires but a word from me, and thou wilt instantly be their prisoner."

"And if thou givest that word," exclaimed the outlaw, "it will be the last opportunity thou wilt ever have of doing me a mischief. Thou understandest me, sirrah, the least sign or signal given by thee, will procure thine own instant death."

"Which would be most fearfully revenged," cried Bertrand; "aye, thou may'st look doubtingly; but again I tell thee, villain, the least harm that befalls me, would be fearfully retaliated upon thyself by my comrades yonder."

"Hah!—thou thinkest, then, I am as unprotected here as thou at present seest me?"

"I know thou art powerless."

"If such is thine opinion," replied Black Ivan, "I have it in my power to convince thee to the contrary in a very few moments ; three blasts upon this bugle would be heard by my comrades, who are not far from home, and if once they should be let loose upon thy scurvy knaves, it would be no easy matter to stay their hands until every one of them had paid for thy treachery with their lives."

"Are thy people so near at hand, then?" demanded Bertrand le Noir, glancing uneasily around him.

"They are ; and, if thou doubtest me, I will convince thee of the truth of what I have said in a very few seconds."

"Nay, there is no occasion for it," answered Bertrand, by no means anxious that the assertion should be proved in the way proposed. "I can take thy word, Ivan, and, since matters have come to this pass, I am willing that you and I should come to some sort of terms."

"Thou may'st think thyself lucky," cried the outlaw, "that I am in no humour to exact any very hard conditions. I will, therefore, content myself with desiring that thou wilt withdraw thy followers from this place immediately, and that thou wilt no more persecute those unfortunate Jews who have but too long been harassed and oppressed by thee."

"I have but obeyed the commands of my master," replied Bertrand ; "for my own part, I have no quarrel with these people, and, since it is thy desire, I will withdraw my men instantly from this place."

"By your leave, I must have a word or two to say upon that subject," exclaimed Simon Hyde, approaching the two speakers. "I it was that brought down these men to attack the Jews, and we will not leave the place till our purpose has been fulfilled."

"How!—am I to be thwarted by a vile worm that I could crush beneath my foot?"

"Aye, aye," muttered the tanner, "its all very well to talk largely in this way, but the truth is, we know you to be Black Ivan, and before we part, the chances are, that we may make you talk in a little less bold key. There's a reward offered for your apprehension, and, if I don't lay you by the heels, say my name's not Simon Hyde, that's all."

"Fool!" exclaimed the outlaw, "you are but tempting your own ruin. I am not to be terrified by a prating idiot like thyself, so, if thou hast any regard for thine own life, hold thy peace before worse comes of this. I do not seek the blood of one so ignoble as thou art ; but thou must not urge me too far, lest in the suddenness of my wrath, I pluck forth my dagger, and stab thee to the heart."

"You hear him, friends!" cried Simon Hyde, addressing himself to his comrades ; "he threatens me with death, and yet there is not one among you to step forward in behalf of your leader."

"And they are prudent men for their pains," exclaimed Black Ivan, with a glance of peculiar meaning ; "they know I am not to be trifled with ; and who is there among them that will dare to stretch out a hand against me?"

"If they are all such cowards as to be afraid of one man, I'll do it my-self," cried Bertrand le Noir, rallying himself for a struggle, and then making a sudden spring, he would have fastened himself on the throat of the outlaw, had not the latter stepped on one side, and thus not only avoided the danger, but, at the same time, gave himself an advantage that he was not slow in making the best use of. In fact, Bertrand was himself thrown with fearful violence to the ground, and in an instant afterwards, his powerful adversary held him down with one hand, whilst with the other he flourished a dagger that seemed destined shortly to put an end to the existence of the prostrate retainer. Fortunately, however, for Bertrand, a shout was at that moment raised, that a party of soldiers had just been seen advancing towards them, and, as Ivan saw no time was to be lost, he quickly relinquished his hold, and directing a look of fury upon those who were pressing around, said menacingly,—

"For the present, this sprawling caitiff is safe from the vengeance he had well nigh brought upon himself. I have spared him, because my own life is threatened; but let him beware how we meet again, for so surely as we do, I shall not fail to remember that he has accepted a bribe to destroy me."

With these words, Ivan forced his way through the crowd, and then bounding forward with the speed of an antelope, he was immediately lost to view. By this time, the troop of soldiers had marched to the spot, the captain of whom advancing towards Simon Hyde, demanded who it was that had been the ringleader in the recent affray, and called upon him to assist in capturing all those who had acted most prominently in the attack upon the Gateway. But the tanner knew perfectly well that the less he said upon the matter, the better it would be for himself, and slipping away among the crowd, he left Bertrand le Noir to answer for him.

"The truth is," said the retainer, who, by this time, was well prepared with a falsehood; "that I know very little more about this affair than you do yourself. It seems, however, captain, that a parcel of riotous fellows have taken it into their heads to make an attack upon the Gatehouse, for the purpose of seizing some Jews who have lately entered it, and, if it had not been for me, the poor creatures would have been torn to pieces by the incensed populace."

"And you deny having had anything to do in this affair?"

"To be sure I do."

"Can you point out, then," asked the captain, "any one that was a leader in this riot?"

"I cannot, at present," answered the wily retainer, "but Black Ivan, the Outlaw, was here a few minutes since, and I rather think he had a great share in causing the tumult."

"Hah!—whither has he gone?"

"That's more than I can tell you, but he went in yonder direction, and if you instantly commence a pursuit after him, I have no doubt you will secure him, and the reward that has been offered for his apprehension."

Tempted by this thought, the captain gave the word of command to his men, and marched away in pursuit of Black Ivan, whose person they were determined, if possible, to secure. Nor was the mob slow in taking advantage of the opportunity that was thus offered, and in an incredibly short period of time, the space before the Gatehouse was as completely cleared as if nothing had occurred to disturb the tranquillity and peace of the neighbourhood.

CHAPTER LXXXVII.

"What fearful struggles agitate the soul
Of guilty men!—I have marked many such,
And oft have thought how fierce a fire must burn
Within their hearts." THE CONFESSIONAL.

IN despair at the defeat of every plan he had formed against the Israelites, Sir Gaston began to revolve fresh plans in his mind for the securing

a prize that had so often escaped him. To ensure success, however, he knew that the utmost caution and secrecy would be necessary; and, besides this, he determined to pretend repentance for the past, and to affect a friendship for old Isaac and his daughter, that was foreign to his heart. This conduct he was aware would lay him open to suspicion, but as he was well versed in hypocrisy, he believed that perseverance would eventually attain his object, and throw into his power the maiden upon whom he had so madly set his heart.

It was in the midst of cogitations upon this subject, when he was abruptly interrupted by the entrance of Bertrand le Noir, whose gloomy countenance betrayed the inward workings of his soul.

"How now, Bertrand," exclaimed the knight, "why hast thou returned thus soon, and with looks that tell me thou hast not been successful in thy mission?"

"I have been defeated again," answered the ruffian, fiercely, "the girl has again found friends, and slipped through my fingers, just at the very moment when I thought her most secure."

"Who dost thou speak of?"

"Of the Jewess."

"Hah!" cried Sir Gaston, "has she again escaped from our well-laid plans?"

"She has," answered the retainer, "and what is still worse, I fear we have now a worse chance than ever of bringing our plans to a successful conclusion."

"Perhaps," observed Sir Gaston, "thy plans were not carried on with sufficient caution."

"Nothing could have been better contrived," answered Bertrand le

No. 64

Noir, "I joined myself with a rabble that I found had vowed vengeance against the Jews, and we marched in a body to attack the prison where Rebecca and her father are confined."

"Well, and thou wert repulsed?"

"We were, Sir Gaston, and that too, at a moment when we had almost succeeded in effecting our object."

"Thou wert too long, perhaps, in considering the best method for conducting the attack?"

"There was no time lost," answered Bertrand; "in fact, we commenced an attack upon the gates of the prison, and had almost succeeded in breaking in, when I was seized hold of by a lusty arm, and hurled with violence to the ground before I had time to protect myself."

"How," cried the knight, angrily, "dost thou confess, then, that thou wert defeated by a single arm?"

"It is not to be denied," answered Bertrand; "but he who defeated me, seldom fails in overcoming all who have the hardihood to bring themselves under his displeasure."

"And who is it of whom thou speakest?"

"Of Black Ivan, the Outlaw."

"Hah!" cried the knight, fiercely, "has he again dared to interpose between me and my pleasure?"

"He has, indeed," replied Bertrand, "and not only did he prevent the execution of my purpose, but, as I said before, it was a mere chance that he did not deprive you of one of the most faithful and attached of your followers."

"Why did you not seize the fellow as I commanded?"

"That is easier said than done."

"But you have just said he was alone."

"True, and I might as well have been so myself, for all the good that was done me by the rabble scoundrels that only a few minutes before had been resolved to bring down destruction upon those Israelites. They seemed to have no wish to put the robber's prowess to the test, and no sooner did he make his appearance, than away they all started as if the devil himself had come among them."

"Cowards!" muttered Sir Gaston;—"and yet," he added, "I should have thought you were well enough able to have coped with him single handed."

"I have before told you that he threw me to the ground before I was aware of his being so near," replied Bertrand le Noir.

"Still thou hadst thy dagger, and a well-aimed blow would have finished the earthly career of this daring brigand."

"Hadst thou been in my place, Black Ivan would have triumphed in spite of daggers or swords either," answered the other sulkily. "Besides, he held me so firmly in his clutches, that a weapon was quite useless to me."

"It has ever been my curse to be surrounded by those who feel no interest in their master's business," cried Sir Gaston; "thou hast had a fair chance of capturing this outlaw, and yet, in spite of the large reward I offered for his apprehension, thou hast suffered him to escape."

"There was no help for it," replied Bertrand le Noir, "but, if I had been better supported, Ivan would not, at this moment, have been at liberty."

"And as he has escaped," observed Sir Gaston, "we may expect that it will not be long before he takes steps to revenge himself for the attempt you have unsuccessfully made against Rebecca."

"He must be quick about it, then," answered the retainer, "for I will yet find means to make him your prisoner."

"And suffer him to slip through your fingers, as you did just now," returned the knight, with a sneer; "you have had one good opportunity, and yet you come back to me with a lame story, that he has got clear off, though there were numbers enough present to have made his capture certain."

"Aye, you may reproach me now as much as you please," exclaimed the retainer, "but it shall not be long before I convince you that your reproaches are unjust."

"And how will you proceed in your proposed task?" enquired the knight.

"I will visit him in his own cavern."

"And by so doing, madly risk thine own life, without having a chance of succeeding in thy design."

"Not if I go cautiously about the business," answered Bertrand.

"Thy caution will be of little avail against one so cunning as Black Ivan."

"Yet he may be deceived, in spite of the cunning you speak of," answered Bertrand; "I will go to his cavern in the disguise of a monk, and, watching my opportunity, either slay or make him my prisoner."

"And dost thou think the garb of religion will save thee from the violence of the robber?"

"I have every reason to believe it will," replied the retainer; "it is said that Black Ivan pays uncommon reverence to the ministers of religion, and, therefore, I have good reason to hope that I shall receive better treatment than you expect."

"Perhaps so," replied Sir Gaston, "but have you considered the consequences if he should happen to discover the imposition you seek to practise on him?"

"I have thought of all that, Sir Knight," answered Bertrand, "and see no reason to fear that any mischief will befal me. I can play the part of a monk well enough to deceive even Black Ivan himself, and will either accomplish my errand, or perish in the attempt."

"But thou hast just failed when a much better opportunity presented itself."

"Thy reproach is a just one," answered the retainer; "yet the failure has only served to make me the more resolute, and this time I will perform my task with more care."

"Dost thou think, then, it will be possible to make him thy prisoner, surrounded as he will be by his band?"

"By watching my opportunity, even that may be effected," replied Bertrand; "I may, perhaps, have to remain in his cavern some days before the chance presents itself, yet my patience shall never desert me, and by maintaining my character of a monk, I shall at length be enabled to fulfil my errand successfully."

"Do so, and I will forgive thy recent failure," exclaimed the knight; "but, if thou shouldst again fail, it would be better for thee never to enter my presence again."

"There is little chance of our meeting, if I should fail in this instance," answered Bertrand; "Black Ivan hates me, as you are well aware, and if a discovery of my imposition upon him should take place, he would not give me a chance of returning to tell you of my discomfiture."

"The recollection of which," observed Sir Gaston, "will, of course, serve to make you the more cautious whilst you are waiting your opportunity?"

"I have no fear of a discovery taking place," answered the other, "for, in my youth, I was brought up in a monastery, and have learnt some of the tricks of these holy fathers; I can use their jargon when necessary; or, at least, quite enough to deceive these fellows, that I dare say know a great deal less of it than I do myself."

"You seem to be confident, at any rate," exclaimed Sir Gaston, "and, perhaps, may go through this task better than I expected; I, however, must again caution you to take him alive, if possible, as the chief part of my revenge will consist in my seeing him languish as a prisoner in one of my dungeons."

"If I can do so, you may be sure it shall be done."

"In which case," observed the knight, "your reward will be double that which I should give if you return with news that Black Ivan has been slain."

"Your promise has not been forgotten, I find," exclaimed Bertrand le Noir; "neither, I suppose, have you given up the idea of compelling the Lady Alicia to become my wife?"

"Thou hast judged rightly, sirrah," cried Sir Gaston; "the affair was broken off abruptly by the appearance of the armed spectre, but my resolution is yet unshaken, and I am now only waiting an opportunity to accomplish it, in spite of all her prayers and entreaties."

"Which opportunity," observed the ruffian, "I suppose you may wait some time for?"

"That will depend on circumstances," replied the knight. "I am, as you know, most anxious to rid myself of a wife whom I have long since ceased to love, and, depend on it, I shall lose no time in bursting the fetters that bind me to her."

"And I," exclaimed Bertrand, "am to be made your scape-goat?"

"How, sirrah! dost thou repent thy bargain?"

"Oh, not in the least," replied the other; "you have promised me a handsome sum for the sacrifice I make of my liberty, and I am content to relieve you of this burden. Besides, when once she is my wife, I can put her aside, as you have done, in case we should not happen to agree."

"Aye, or put her away altogether, if you think proper," answered the knight, in a tone of indifference."

"What! would you have me murder my wife?"

"Psha! what care I about it," exclaimed Sir Gaston; "she has been in my way long enough already, and it would occasion me very little grief to know that she had quitted this world for a better one."

"Then why not give me orders to despatch her, without wishing us to be married first?"

"I give no commands upon the subject," answered the knight; "you, however, know my humour well, and that I should not have been angry with you had news been brought me that the Lady Alicia was no more."

"We'll talk further upon this subject another time," exclaimed Bertrand, "for something strikes me it would be more agreeable to my own feelings to put her out of the way at once, than to marry the lady against her will. Wedlock is not exactly the state I should choose for myself, there is too much restraint about it, and as I was always a lover of freedom, you will, perhaps, have the kindness to give the word for me to put her ladyship out of her miseries."

"Villain!" cried the knight, fiercely, "dost thou not know that I will never give such a hint as you have spoken of?"

"Perhaps I ought to have known it," replied the other, sulkily; "and yet, if you are too great a coward to give the word of command, I don't see why I should be expected to commit a murder on my own account."

"Fool! thou knowest well enough that I would reward thee to thy heart's content."

"Aye," replied Bertrand, "I dare say you would not be sparing with your gold, but that is not all I require; I must be safe after doing this business, or I had better forego the reward you have been speaking of."

"What dost thou mean by being safe?"

"I mean," answered Bertrand le Noir, "that you, of course, wish to hold yourself harmless in this affair; in other words, that if ever it should be found out, I, and not you, should receive the punishment for the crime."

"It seems, then, sirrah, that you doubt my intentions towards you?" cried Sir Gaston.

"Very likely I may," answered the retainer, "and no wonder either, seeing that I know you are not very particular about who suffers, so that you contrive to escape."

"You are insolent, sirrah!"

"I speak nothing but the truth, at any rate," answered Bertrand; "however, you and I can get no good by quarrelling, for we know too much of each other's ways, and it might be dangerous to one, if not both, of us."

"Then say no more about it," exclaimed Sir Gaston de Neville; "each may be able to assist the other, but the moment we begin to disagree, it is impossible to say where the mischief will end. So now, as we, perhaps, understand each other all the better for this explanation, tell me how long it will be before you pay your promised visit to the secret retreat of Black Ivan?"

"In the course of a few days."

"And how do you intend to gain admission to a place that has baffled so many who have endeavoured to discover it?" asked the knight, doubtfully.

"It is not to be done without practising deception upon them," answered the ruffian. "I have said before that it is my intention to disguise myself as a monk, and as I happen to know pretty near where the entrance of the cave is situated, I shall throw myself on the ground, as if from illness, and there wait till some of the robbers chance to find me."

"And when they have done so," replied Sir Gaston, "they will leave you to your fate, as unworthy their care."

"There you are mistaken," exclaimed Bertrand; "I have already told you that Black Ivan pays all due respects to whatever ministers of religion fall in his way, and it would be more than the lives of any of his men were worth to pass heedlessly by, whilst a priest was in need of their assistance."

"You think, then, they would convey you, without loss of time, to the presence of the leader?"

"I am sure they would."

"And, supposing that to be the case, how would you next proceed?" demanded the knight.

"I should continue to feign sickness till a fitting opportunity offered to destroy or capture your rival. This would occur before long, and I have no doubt but I should return ere long with a good account of my mission."

"You are full of confidence, at any rate," observed Sir Gaston. To me, however, the adventure you have proposed seems to be anything but an easy one, and I should, therefore, be much surprised to see you return back to my castle in safety."

"It would surprise me more were I to fail in it," replied Bertrand. "This is not the first time within your own knowledge that I have gone on perilous errands, and you have always seen that, with the aid of a little cunning, I have come back victorious."

"Granted," replied Sir Gaston; "but in the present instance you have to deal with one more cunning even than yourself. Black Ivan knows there are many who seek to betray him into the hands of justice, and his suspicions are naturally excited against all strangers that fall in his way. He will at once see through your thin disguise, and, in that case, depend on it, his vengeance would not fall very lightly."

"Humph! you try to discourage me, it seems."

"On the contrary," answered the knight, " it is my wish that you should prosper in this enterprise; that I bear a mortal hatred against this outlaw, you are, of course, well aware, but, at the same time, I should be acting unfairly were I to suffer your departure, without pointing out the risk you must encounter."

"Why, for that matter," answered Bertrand le Noir, " I have run a far greater risk for much less profit than I am looking forward to on this occasion. Danger and I are old acquaintances, and I can look it in the face without much fear."

"I am satisfied," replied the knight, " and therefore you may take your departure with as little delay as convenient; do not forget, however, that the greatest caution is necessary, and that the least forgetfulness on your part will be certain to lead to the most fatal consequences."

Ere Bertrand le Noir could make a reply to this, Edith came running into the room, bearing traces upon her countenance of the greatest terror and excitement.

"Oh! Sir Gaston," she exclaimed, " such a disaster has just occurred. They have got the poor fellow at last, and are bringing him here, bound and fettered, as if he was some terrible criminal."

"Speak, huzzy; of whom do you speak?"

"Of whom should I speak, pray, but of poor Adrian, your faithful page?"

"Hah! have they, indeed, laid hold of the traitorous villain?"

"Traitorous villain!" retorted the girl; " why there is not a more faithful creature in your castle than poor Adrian."

"I ask no opinion from you," exclaimed Sir Gaston, angrily. "He has grievously offended me, and now that he is again within my reach, I will so punish him that he shall never have a chance of injuring me again."

"Ah!" cried Edith, " you surely cannot mean to hurt the poor fellow; he has never committed any fault, and the only thing that you can bring against him is, that he was kind to the poor lady you have shut up in a dungeon."

"And for that he shall meet the reward he merits."

"In that case," answered Edith, " you will bestow on him a handsome reward, instead of doing him an injury."

"Will you hold your peace, girl, or must I turn you out of the room?" exclaimed Bertrand le Noir; " the young traitor deserves to swing for what he has done; and if Sir Gaston takes my advice, he will order him to be hanged instantly."

"And if Sir Gaston was to take mine," cried Edith, " there is another in this castle who should meet exactly the same fate."

"I can guess your meaning, wench," exclaimed Bertrand, "and may take another opportunity to revenge myself."

"A truce to this folly," interposed Sir Gaston; and you, sirrah, haste and fetch this youth before me, that I may decide in what way it will be best to deal with him."

Cheerfully obeying such a command as this, Bertrand le Noir instantly quitted the chamber, leaving Edith to plead in behalf of her favourite page.

"Oh, Sir Gaston," she cried, earnestly, " do let me beseech you to have pity on this unfortunate youth. That he has offended you, I know, but remember, it was in the cause of humanity that he exerted himself, and that thought alone should be sufficient to ensure for him your pardon and forgiveness."

"What!" exclaimed the furious knight; "has he not attempted to set one of my prisoners at liberty?"

"He did," answered Edith, "but she is again in your power, and, therefore, he may be forgiven."

"I tell thee, girl, I will never pardon this last offence," replied Sir Gaston. "Ere now I have overlooked his meddling interference, for the sake of his father; I have seen that this boy was constantly plotting to defeat my plans, and yet he has escaped punishment that was richly deserved; his youth has hitherto preserved him from my wrath, but now I will make him bitterly repent the part he has thought proper to play in this affair."

Though hopeless of success, Edith was about to repeat her earnest entreaties, but ere she could do so, Bertrand le Noir returned with his prisoner, who he presented, bound as he was, before his imperious master.

"Now, Adrian," exclaimed the knight, "I find thee once more within reach of my vengeance, though thou didst seek protection even from the king himself. Thou art again within the castle of the master thou wouldst have injured, and I ask what mercy thou dost expect from him?"

"None," answered the youth, boldly.

"There thou say'st well," replied Sir Gaston; "but why dost thou not expect pity from one who, till now, has ever been to thee a friend and protector?"

"Because I had nearly foiled your plans."

"A most sufficient reason, truly, and one that shews thou art quite conscious of the magnitude of their offence."

"I knew not that it could be an offence to rescue an helpless woman from the hands of a cruel oppressor," answered the page.

"Hah! dost thou dare charge me with cruelty?"

"Ask thine own heart, Sir Gaston, if thou art not guilty of it."

"My own heart, sirrah, gives thee the lie!" retorted the knight, almost choking with rage.

"Ask thy conscience, then," replied Adrian, "and I am well assured thou must confess I did no more than my duty in endeavouring to give liberty to an imprisoned woman."

"But that woman has given me sufficient cause for the rigour I have adopted towards her," answered the knight, impatiently, "she has ever proved my enemy;—stands in my way when most I need her absence, and has even threatened me with exposure, should she again be set at liberty."

"There thou dost wrong her most foully," exclaimed Adrian; "for had she succeeded in effecting her escape, it was her intention to enter a monastery, and there end her days in that peace of which you have so long deprived her."

"And thus she sought to escape one species of imprisonment for no other purpose than to enter voluntarily upon another!" cried Sir Gaston, with pretended calmness.

"The one she knew to be unjust," answered the page; "but the other she could have endured with resignation, because she knew, that by entering a convent, she would relieve you of all fears, lest she might say anything to tarnish the honour of which you so proudly boast."

"Thou speakest falsely, boy!" exclaimed Sir Gaston, "for, instead of resolving to enter upon a life devoted to religion, it was her intention to throw herself at the feet of the king, and by an artfully devised tale, to bring upon me certain ruin."

"I know thou dost wrong her by such a thought, Sir Knight," replied Adrian, " and yet, even granting that such was her intention, it must be admitted she had received provocation enough to drive her to such an alternative."

"Boy! dost thou dare to bandy words with me ?"

" I dare speak the truth to thee."

"And dost thou remember what may be the consequences ?"

" I know," answered Adrian, unmoved by the fury of the knight, "that thou canst deliver me to one of thy ruffians for instant death. Nay, there is one standing at thy side, who, I am sure, would gladly obey your orders, were they to be such as I have just mentioned."

" The page is right enough, there," exclaimed Bertrand, who had observed the motions of the youth's eye ;—" he means me, and I care not how soon I receive your commands to despatch him."

" Be not impatient, Bertrand," answered the knight, "for it is not my intention just at present, to put your obedience to such a test. He shall live yet a little longer, but it shall be upon such hard terms, that he shall hourly call upon death to release him from his sufferings."

" Thy threats do but excite my scorn," cried Adrian, " for, let my sufferings be what they may, they will scarcely be felt, when I reflect that they are caused through my endeavours to give freedom to an unfortunate victim of thy tyranny."

" Beware how you urge me further," exclaimed Sir Gaston, " or I may order your instant death."

" Do so," retorted the page, " and you will, at least, deprive yourself of the happiness you anticipated in being a witness of the sufferings you just now threatened."

" Oh, heed him not, Sir Gaston," cried Edith, alarmed lest the youth should be ordered for immediate execution ; " he speaks rashly ; but, believe me, he means not what he says !"

" Peace, girl," exclaimed the templar, angrily ;—" peace, I say, or I may order thee to one of my dungeons, where thou wilt learn the folly of thine interference. Leave us, wench, or I will order Bertrand to drag thee from my presence."

" Art thou a man that thou dost war thus fiercely against helpless women and boys ?" cried Edith.

" If helpless women and boys provoke me, they must take the consequences of their own rashness," answered Sir Gaston ; " it is my fate to be crossed at every turn I make, and being at length excited to madness, I would have all beware, lest they bring upon themselves the consuming wrath that will destroy them."

" Nay," exclaimed Adrian, " let all your wrath fall upon me. I alone have offended you in this instance, and it is but just that I should bear the consequences. Deal with me as you please ;—either imprison or send me forth to instant death, but do not harm this poor girl, whose zeal in my behalf has thus drawn forth your anger."

" Oh, never heed him," exclaimed Bertrand ;—" the youth is far too bold in his speech ; and, if I may be allowed to give my advice, I should say put him out of the way with as much despatch as possible ; and, as for the girl, try the effects of close confinement upon her, and see whether a dungeon will not keep that restless tongue of her's a little more quiet."

" I shall take a brief space to consider what is best to be done," answered the knight. " In the meantime, you may convey him to a dungeon, where he will remain safe till I have decided what is to be done with him."

" And the girl ?"

" May have her liberty for the present," replied Sir Gaston, " but I would

have her make a good use of the clemency I have shewn her on the present occasion, lest I should be urged to adopt the advice you just now gave."

At a signal from Sir Gaston, the retainer withdrew to perform the errand he had been entrusted with, and once more the knight was left to the free indulgence of his own reflections.

CHAPTER LXXXVIII.

" Winding through devious passages, he finds
  Escape imposssible ; yet hope remains,
  And urges him still onwards."
THE SYBIL'S VOW.

CONSIDERING the circumstances in which he was placed, Adrian maintained a remarkable degree of firmness, and when his gaoler departed, leaving him in the solitude of a wretched cell, he took up the lamp with which he had been supplied, and began to make an examination of the place, in hopes of finding some opening from which he might effect his escape. This examination he conducted with the greatest care, but, in spite of all the patience that he had called to his aid, he was at length obliged to give up his object in despair.

Still, however, he resolved to maintain his fortitude for a continuance of those exertions that had been hitherto frustrated, and seating himself upon a stool, which was the only article of furniture that had been supplied him, he gave himself up to a consideration of the design upon which he had set

No. 65

his soul. Whilst thus engaged, his attention was directed towards a glittering object at some distance from him, and being impelled partly by curiosity, and partly by hope, he hastily snatched up the lamp, and with hurried steps, advanced towards the spot which had thus attracted his notice. Never before had a trifling circumstance occasioned so much curiosity as he now felt, and stooping to examine the substance that lay at his feet, he discovered that it was a steel breast-plate, the centre of which had been evidently perforated by the dagger of some assassin.

Here there was a subject for fresh reflection;—a murder had, without doubt, been committed within the very dungeon in which he was now confined, and when all circumstances were considered, there would be no hesitation in believing that the cruel deed had been committed at the instigation, and with the full knowledge of Sir Gaston de Neville. It was even possible that the murder had been perpetrated by the knight himself, for Adrian knew him to be cruel and vindictive, and in the event of his having a prisoner that he wished no one else to know of, it was quite certain that he would not hesitate to remove every source of danger, by destroying him with his own hands.

With fear and trembling at the thoughts that rushed to his brain, Adrian raised the fatal evidence of an unrevealed crime, and as he did so, his attention was directed towards another object that had hitherto lain concealed beneath the breast-plate; it was a dagger, the blade of which was stained with blood, and no doubt was the instrument with which the assassination has been committed! Aghast at the horrors that now crowded upon his mind, the page remained for some few moments totally absorbed in the melancholy reflections that circumstances had given rise to. He was irresolute how to act, when the thought struck him that the poniard might prove a useful implement by which to escape a place which had been the scene of so dark a tragedy, and hurrying towards the door, he began another careful examination to see whether he could not cut a hole in it sufficiently large to admit the passage of his body. For some time, however, his sanguine hopes were disappointed, and he was about to give up all further search as useless, when his hand came in contact with a part of the door, which was much decayed, and, therefore, offered but little resistance, even to the slight instrument with which chance had supplied him. The place thus discovered was near the ground, and, of course, more accessible than any other would have been, and being inspired with renewed hope, he set himself diligently about his task, and in less time than he had anticipated, removed a sufficient quantity of the crumbling wood to form an aperture quite large enough for him to pass through. This done, he listened for some time to hear whether any one was coming to visit the subterraneous vault of the castle, and having, at last, convinced himself that all was so far safe, he put the lamp beneath his cloak to conceal its rays, in case either Sir Gaston de Neville, or any of his retainers should chance to be prowling about. Then grasping his dagger with a firm determination to defend himself to the last, in the event of meeting with any one, he crept through the hole he had found, and immediately found himself in a dark vaulted passage, which, from its deep echoes, appeared to be of some length. For a moment or two, he stood irresolute whether to turn to the right hand or the left, but eventually trusting himself to chance, he turned sharply round, and proceeded with cautious steps, occasionally making use of his lamp to see what progress he had made, and whether there was any other path that was more likely to conduct him from the cheerless place in which he was entangled.

But it was some time before he reached the extremity of the passage into which he had emerged from his dungeon, and when he at length came to a termination of it, he found himself in a large vaulted chamber, around which were numerous doors connecting it with as many cells for the safe keeping of the unfortunate victims who had fallen under the displeasure of Sir Gaston de Neville. Had it been possible, the page would gladly have paused to aid in the deliverance of those who were confined in that part of the castle, but as there was little chance of his effecting any real service for them at that moment, he was about to pass on, when a low groan met his startled ear. This was enough for Adrian, whose generous sympathy was easily excited, and pausing to ascertain from whence the sound came, he shortly afterwards heard the groan repeated from one of the cells on his right hand. With the quickness of thought, he now urged his steps towards the spot which had been indicated, and by patiently listening at each door, at length convinced himself from which dungeon the sound came. It now, therefore, only remained for him to gain access to the unfortunate captive, and having, upon a careful examination, discovered that the door was only secured by chains on the outside, he soon removed the impediment, and stepping into the cell, discovered a female lying insensible upon the ground. Bitterly cursing the inhumanity of him who had thus subjected a woman to all the horrors of a dungeon, Adrian raised the female in his arms, and, as the beams of the lamp fell upon her countenance, he discovered the well-known lineaments of the unfortunate Lady Alicia de Neville!

Luckily, a jug of water was close at hand, and with the assistance of the cooling liquid, he was at length enabled to restore her to some consciousness that she was not altogether deserted in this sad hour of trouble and captivity. At first, however, Lady Alicia believed herself to be in the presence of her cruel gaoler, but soon the well-known voice of Adrian roused her from the dream of horror, and, in a faint voice, she thanked him for the generous care he had thus bestowed upon her.

"Nay, dear lady," answered the youth, "the poor service I have done you requires no thanks. I have only performed a duty; and now, if I can but release you from the hands of Sir Gaston de Neville, I shall be well satisfied, even though my own life might be sacrificed in the attempt."

"It is in vain to think of it," replied the captive, in a tone of the deepest melancholy, "fate has thrown me completely in the power of an unfeeling tyrant, and it is no longer of any use to resist my destiny."

"It shall be tried, at any rate," exclaimed the page, with generous warmth. "Too long already has Sir Gaston triumphed over an unprotected woman; and, young as I am, it shall be no fault of mine if I do not snatch from him one of the victims of his arbitrary power."

"And dost thou not remember," cried Alicia, "that thine own life would pay the forfeit of thy zeal?"

"I am prepared for all that he can do against me," answered Adrian; "I know he can deliver me over to death, as he has done with many others like myself; that he can torture me with the horrible implements he keeps for that purpose; but no consideration of anything that may befal myself shall ever deter me from making an effort to rescue you from his power."

"Your kindness overwhelms me, Adrian," cried the prisoner, bursting into a flood of tears; "it is seldom that I hear the voice of sympathy, and yet now, when I had given up all in despair, I still find one to cheer the desolation with which I am surrounded."

"Yet a brief time will serve to restore you to liberty," answered the page; "so cheer up, my lady, and I promise, ere another hour has passed away, to conduct you in safety from this cheerless abode."

"It is impossible," replied Alicia; "my limbs are no longer capable of supporting me, and I feel that to make any attempt at leaving this place would only involve you in that danger which I would fain avoid."

" My danger cannot be greater than it is already," exclaimed Adrian; " like yourself, I am a prisoner, and it only awaits the decision of Sir Gaston whether I shall be consigned to death, or pass the remainder of my days in hopeless captivity."

" Alas!" cried Lady Alicia, "then I can but too plainly see that your present danger has been produced by your zeal in my behalf."

" And even if it is so," replied the page, " it is no reason why you should regret the lucky chance that has enabled me to exert myself in your favour. I have already proved to Sir Gaston that you are not destitute of a friend, and he shall yet find that I have it in my own power to rescue you from his custody."

" It is impossible," exclaimed Lady Alicia, in accents of despair; " I am now unable to exert myself, even if my prison doors were thrown open, and, therefore, it is my earnest request that you escape whilst there is yet a possibility of doing so."

" Never!" cried Adrian, firmly; " for my own safety I care not; and if you refuse to accompany me, I will return to the dungeon I have just escaped from, and there abide my fate, whatever it may chance to be."

" This is madness, Adrian," exclaimed the Lady Alicia, endeavouring to rouse herself to exertion; " you do but seek to plunge yourself into danger, without a chance of doing me the service you design."

" Say that you will go with me, dear lady."

" It is impossible," she replied; " my limbs refuse to support me, and should I make the attempt, it would only be bringing upon you certain destruction."

" Which I am resolved to risk, rather than leave this place without you."

" Will neither prayers nor entreaties prevail on you to leave me to my fate?"

" Neither," replied Adrian; " in this instance I am resolute, and I will either escape with you, or share the perils with which you are threatened."

" At present," cried Lady Alicia, " I feel that my weakness throws a fatal barrier in the way of the project you have devised. I am overpowered by the miseries I have endured, and should sink from utter exhaustion long ere we could reach the confines of the castle."

" Suppose, then, we defer our escape till another day?"

" That would only be involving you in unnecessary danger." answered Alicia. " You said but just now that Sir Gaston was deliberating on the fate to which he will adjudge you, and by remaining here any longer, the danger I so much dread will be increased. Leave me, therefore, I implore you, and then my last few remaining hours will be passed in joy and thankfulness for your escape."

" I will never leave you, dear lady," cried Adrian, "until I have your promise to accept my assistance in leaving this place. Say, then, whether we shall seek liberty together, or perish miserably in these loathsome dungeons."

" Boy," exclaimed Alicia, " your obstinacy drives me to despair!— Heaven knows I seek not my own safety, and yet, if I refuse compliance with your generous wishes, I condemn you to a fate that I tremble to think of."

" Then you will consent to flee with me?"

" I would, if it were possible to do so without loss of time," replied Alicia; " I, however, feel that I am unable to do so at present, and, therefore, I again entreat you to seek your own liberty, and leave me to the fate which I no longer fear to think of."

"You have heard my resolution," answered the page, "and nothing you can urge shall ever shake it."

"Alas!" cried Alicia, "you will condemn me, then, to endure the horror of knowing that I am the means of bringing you to an untimely death."

"But it is in your power to avert it," answered the youth; "say that you will leave these dreary caverns with me, and I will be content; nay, postpone, if you please, the period of your escape, and I will wait with patience, however long it may chance to be."

"If it must be so," replied Alicia, "I will endeavour to rally myself by to-morrow. It is, however, not without much self-reproach that I consent to this proposition, and if anything should happen to you through the delay, I shall never cease to upbraid myself with being the cause of involving a generous friend in ruin."

"But at the same time," observed the page, "it may be some consolation for you to know that I had determined not to escape unless you accompanied me. Supposing, then, anything should happen to me, you can surely have nothing to reproach yourself with on my account."

"Had it not been for me," answered Alicia, "you might have been out of the castle long ere this."

"It is possible I might have been," replied Adrian; "but since a lucky chance threw you in my way, it would have been the basest species of cowardice to withhold my assistance where it was so much needed. I am now, as your ladyship is aware, in training for the honour of knighthood, and little should I deserve the distinction I aspire to were I to allow a helpless woman to perish when I had it in my power to assist her."

"Not less than I should deserve life, if it should be obtained at the risk of yours," answered the lady. "However, I have given my word to accompany you to-morrow, and loath as I am to endanger you, yet will I keep my word."

"For which I owe you all my gratitude," returned the page, respectfully pressing her hand to his lips. "Your concession, dear lady, has filled my heart with renewed hopes, and I will now return to my dungeon with the cheering consciousness that I shall be the means of rescuing you from this gloomy prison.

"And suppose Sir Gaston or any of his followers visit you there?" cried Alicia, "it would immediately be discovered that you had found a way to leave the place of your confinement, and your punishment, in all probability, would be nothing short of death."

"Nay, do not distress yourself on my account," answered Adrian, "for even if any of them should chance to visit me, I still think there is no fear of their discovering that I ever left my prison. The hole by which I effected my escape is so low down, that in the gloom of my dungeon it must escape detection; and, even if it should be seen, I will boldly avow the truth, and demand of my gaoler whether he would not have sought to escape had he been placed in the same situation."

"He will make no excuse for you, Adrian," replied Lady Alicia, "but in his zeal will inform Sir Gaston de Neville of the method you have taken to escape."

"And for which the knight can send me to meet my death," exclaimed the page, resolutely. "He may do so, lady, if he pleases, but he cannot make me regret that I sought to escape from the dominion of a tyrant."

"Thy words are bold, Adrian," cried Lady Alicia, "but let me entreat thee to curb thy tongue, if any evil chance should take thee into the presence of thy master. As thou knowest, he will not brook contradiction, and I dread to think of what may be the result shouldst thou anger him by reproaches for the past."

"I will bear your counsel in mind," answered the youth, "and for your sake endeavour to restrain the inclination I feel to hurl defiance in his teeth. The time, however, may yet come, when it will be in my power to bring a well-deserved punishment on him for the many crimes he has committed against the weak and powerless."

"Let us pursue this subject no further," exclaimed Alicia; "for the present I entreat you to leave me, and if nothing should occur to hinder your project, I will hold myself in readiness to accompany you to-morrow."

"I take you at your word," replied Adrian, again pressing her hand to his lips; "to-morrow I will punctually attend you, and if a bold heart will serve our purpose, I think I may safely promise to conduct you from the castle of Sir Gaston de Neville; so farewell, dear lady, and let your prayers this night ascend to Heaven for the safe accomplishment of our designs."

With these words Adrian hurriedly left the dungeon, and retraced his steps towards that which he had not long before quitted in search of freedom, but the task was by no means an easy one, for by this time his lamp had nearly expired, and its faint and flickering glare served rather to confound than aid him in his return to imprisonment. At length, however, he succeeded in finding the passage by which he had come, and then groping his way along for a considerable distance, he at last found the hole by which he had emerged from his cheerless cell. Entering, therefore, by the same aperture that had afforded him the means of escape, he extinguished his lamp, lest its feeble blaze should betray him, in case any one should chance to visit his dungeon. This done, he threw himself upon the straw that served him for a bed, and totally forgetting his own perilous situation, began to devise fresh schemes for affecting the escape of Lady Alicia.

He was thus occupied, when heavy footsteps were heard resounding through the arched caverns, and at once foreseeing that a visitor was coming, he feigned to be asleep, in hopes that he might thus disarm all suspicion as to the manner in which he had recently been occupied. Still the sounds came nearer and nearer, and at length he could hear the heavy chains and bolts as they were successively unfastened; then the door creaked heavily on its rusty hinges, and Adrian could see through his half-opened eyes, that his visitor was no other than the savage Bertrand le Noir, who, advancing, shook him roughly by the shoulder to rouse him from the slumber into which it was supposed he had fallen.

"Come, come, young fellow," he exclaimed, "you must jump up and answer me a few questions, or I shall drag you before Sir Gaston, who, I warrant you, will not be quite so easy with you as I am."

"What want you with me?" asked Adrian, pretending to wake from his sleep.

"What do I want with you?"

"Aye,—has your master sent you to despatch me?"

"No," replied Bertrand, gruffly; "he has given me no orders about that at present, though, perhaps, he may do so before very long. But I have something to ask, that I dare say you can answer if you like."

"Indeed!—what is it, I pray?"

"Come, Mr. Innocence, let's have none of this sort of nonsense, for it won't do with me, I can tell you. There is a large hole that has been made in your door, and as it is pretty certain it was not there when I brought you to this place, I should like to know whether you can throw any light upon the subject."

"If you ask me whether I made it myself," replied Adrian, "I at once candidly admit that I did."

"Soh!—and, of course, you did it with an idea of escaping from this snug little place?"

"Why else should I have taken so much pains?" asked Adrian, boldly.

"Very true," returned the ruffian, "and, since you have been so plain about the matter, perhaps you will be equally candid in admitting, that, after being unable to find your way out, you were obliged to return here and take whatever chances might happen to turn up?"

"You have exactly guessed it again," replied Adrian, who was glad to find any excuse, rather than say anything that might give a notion of his recent visit to the dungeon of Lady Alicia; "I thought to have escaped easily," he continued, "but losing myself among the intricacies of these subterranean vaults, I was compelled to return to the place I had left."

"Aye, aye, and so you are now convinced that it is not quite so easy to escape as you expected?"

"I am."

"But, perhaps, in spite of all that," exclaimed Bertrand, with a sneer, "you may be tempted to make another trial on the first opportunity that offers?"

"That is hardly likely," replied the page, "seeing that I had nearly lost myself before; and at one time, I began to fear lest I should perish for want of assistance."

"And, in my opinion, it would just have served you right if you had," retorted the ruffian; "however, I shall take especial care to prevent your serving me the same trick again, so make up your mind to remain where you are till Sir Gaston thinks fit to give further orders on the subject."

"Slay me at once," exclaimed Adrian, "and with my last breath, I will thank you for releasing me from the tyranny of your cruel master."

"Slay you, eh!" cried the other;—"no, no, young fellow, that would be more than my own life is worth. I have been ordered to bring you a fresh supply of bread and water, so I suppose Sir Gaston has not yet made up his mind what to do with you. Here is a pitcher of the pure element, and here a loaf of bread, so you see, however cruel you may think Sir Gaston, he has no intention to starve you."

"I care not what he does," replied Adrian, "so that he releases me from this horrible dungeon. Death I could endure with calmness, but to be unjustly deprived of liberty, fills me with rage that I cannot suppress."

"Psha! you have had nothing to endure yet, but if you wait a little longer, I dare say you will be tired enough."

"Wilt thou not kill me, then?"

"Certainly not, but I will put these fetters on you, and, perhaps, they may put a stop upon your rovings in future."

Saying this, he threw himself suddenly upon the page, and ere he could offer any effectual resistance, his limbs were securely bound by the ruffian.

"There," he exclaimed, when he had accomplished this feat, "I think that will do for the present, but if I should find out that you are up to any more of your tricks, I have a heavy chain outside that I will pass round your body, and secure you to yonder pillar. That I know will make you safe enough, though I don't wish to do it till I find nothing else will serve to keep you within bounds."

"You have no reason to be afraid of me now," answered Adrian, with feigned dejection;—"I have once failed in accomplishing my object, and you may depend on it I shall make no further attempt."

"I can tell you it will be better for you to remain quiet where you are," exclaimed Bertrand, "for, though I'm not naturally very harsh in my conduct towards prisoners, yet, if they do so happen to put me out of sorts, I've a way of my own that generally brings folks to their senses."

"You may trust me now," replied Adrian, "for having convinced myself that escape from this place is impossible, I shall rest satisfied to await the doom of your imperious master."

"Humph!" muttered the ruffian, "perhaps you would like me to tell him as much?"

"You can do so if you please," replied the page, "for, to speak my mind freely, I care not about his taking offence at anything that may chance to fall from my lips. Nay, so little do I regard his anger, that you may tell him, if you think proper, of the utter contempt in which I hold not only himself, but any punishment he may be inclined to inflict on me."

"Well, perhaps it may be as well for you to tell him that yourself," exclaimed the ruffian, "I have too often seen what mischief he can do when he gets into a passion, and as I don't feel at all inclined to get into a scrape on your account, I shall decline the honour you would confer on me."

"As you please," replied Adrian, "but, perhaps, it will not be too much to ask if you know what he intends to do with me?"

"I neither know nor care," answered Bertrand le Noir; "at present it seems he means to keep you here in captivity; but, if it should be his will to order you for execution, I shall perform his commands with the greatest pleasure and alacrity."

"I have every reason to believe you," exclaimed Adrian, "and now, as we seem to be on such perfect terms of confidence with each other, I would ask you one other favour."

"Ah, and what may it be, sirrah?"

"That you will remove these bonds from my wrists," replied the page; "they cause me a great deal of pain, and surely you cannot wish to add unnecessarily to my sufferings?"

"Ask me anything in reason, and may be I shall not prove very hard-hearted," returned the other.

"Is is not reasonable, then, to request such a trifling indulgence as the one I have mentioned?"

"It may not seem much to you," replied Bertrand, "but, if you should happen to escape through any neglect of mine, the consequences would not prove very pleasant to myself. So make yourself contented as well as you can, and I dare say the next time we meet, I shall be able to tell you what decision Sir Gaston has come to."

"Perhaps he may have resolved upon my death," cried Adrian.

"Very likely he may," returned the ruffian, in a tone of perfect indifference; "at present, I don't think he himself knows what he means to do, but if he should chance to take it into his head that your death will afford him more security, you may depend on it he will not hesitate a moment about what must be done."

"In that case," replied Adrian, "he shall, at least, see that I can meet my death with firmness."

"Depend on it, youngster, he'll not care whether you do or not," answered Bertrand le Noir; "he treats all these matters with perfect indifference, and being used to ordering people to be put out of the way, he'll scarcely bestow another thought upon you after the affair is over."

"Perhaps so," replied the page; "and now, since I have nothing further to say about myself, I would ask after one in whose fate I feel some interest."

"Hah! and who may that be?"

"The Lady Alicia."

"And what the deuce do you know about her?" demanded the ruffian, with surprise.

"I would merely ask whether she is at liberty?"

"She is not," replied Bertrand, "and since you contrived to find your way out of this dungeon, I am only astonished that you did not chance to stumble upon the one where she is at present confined."

"I feared she was again in danger," cried Adrian, alarmed lest his manner should give rise to a suspicion that he had had an interview with the Lady Alicia.

"And why did you think so?" demanded Bertrand, sharply.

"I had a dream," answered the youth, with trepidation, "and in my vision, I beheld the unfortunate victim of tyranny again languishing in a gloomy cell."

"Indeed! then, for once, your dream told the truth, for Lady Alicia is, at this moment, in a dungeon, and what is more, she never can escape from it, unless she consents to become my wife."

"Your wife!" cried Adrian, forgetting himself;—"she told me not of the fresh insult that had been offered her."

"Hah!" exclaimed the ruffian, "have you seen her then?"

"N—n—no!" stammered Adrian, and then quickly recovering himself, he added:—" I was speaking, Bertrand, of what passed in my dream, for methought I held a long conversation with her, yet she said nothing of a marriage with yourself having been proposed."

"And so you are fool enough to place reliance upon what was, after all, nothing but a vision?"

"I was, indeed, weak enough to do so," replied the page; " but everything seemed to be so real, that I could not help fancying we had actually met."

No. 66

"And so you might have done, if it had not been for your own blunder-ing," answered Bertrand; "she is shut up at no very great distance from hence, and all I wonder at is, that you did not, somehow or other, pounce upon the place where she is confined."

"Would that I had done so!" cried Adrian, anxious to mislead his gaoler as much as possible.

"And why, pray, do you wish to have met with her?" demanded the other.

"Because," replied Adrian, "the sight of her sufferings would have spurred me on to make greater efforts to escape."

"Come, that's candid, at any rate!" exclaimed Bertrand; "and so, as you have now pretty well relieved your mind by confession, I shall take my leave of you for the present. To-morrow, however, I shall see you again, and it may so happen, that I shall bring more certain news as to what Sir Gaston intends to do with you."

Upon this, the ruffian took his departure, and being thus left to himself, Adrian began to try whether it would not be possible to remove from his wrists the manacles with which they had been bound.

CHAPTER LXXXIX.

" Speak, slave, I charge thee!
Say'st thou they've fled?—escaped thy vigilance,
And gone thou know'st not whither?"

THE VICEROY.

THE task Adrian had taken upon himself, proved to be far less difficult than he had expected, for, with a very little exertion, he was soon enabled to remove one wrist from the bondage in which it had been placed, and in a short time afterwards, the other was equally at freedom. This done, he threw himself down to take that rest which he so much needed, for the labour of the ensuing day, and immediately sunk into a slumber as pro-found and calm, as if not a care or trouble rested upon his mind. At length, however, he fancied himself in the cavern of Black Ivan, and wan-dering about from one chamber to another, he reached one in which he be-held the Hebrew Maiden struggling with a ruffian, belonging to the robber band. Impelled by a desire to save her, he would have flown to her rescue, but some invisible hand seemed to hold him back, and in spite of all his efforts, he was unable to render her the aid she so much required. He then tried to speak, but his tongue refused him utterance, and in the midst of his despair, he still beheld the maiden struggling to release her-self from the grasp of the ruffian. At length, she broke away, when the villain drawing a dagger, was preparing to rush upon her, but, at that moment, the terrified girl threw herself upon her knees, and, in a voice of agony, implored him to have pity on her. This, however, the villain ap-peared to treat with contempt, and he was in the act of springing towards her, when Adrian, unable to endure any further controul, darted forward to her rescue. This served to rouse him from his slumber, and, on open-ing his eyes, he discovered that he was still in his dungeon, through a small aperture of which he could discern that day was just breaking.

Adrian now remembered the promise he had made to the captive Lady Alicia, and well knowing that their best chance of escape would be at that early hour of the morning, he immediately crept through the opening he had made in the door on the previous day, and hurrying along the passage as quickly as the darkness would permit, he at length reached the vaulted chamber that communicated with the dungeon, occupied by the unfortunate object of his search. It was not long before he succeeded in finding the right door, and opening it, he found Lady Alicia already awaiting his arrival.

"This is as I hoped to find you, my lady," exclaimed Adrian, as he approached. "Everything now favours us, and a little exertion will serve to place us beyond the reach of danger."

"Not beyond danger, Adrian," she replied, mournfully, "for even if we should contrive to escape from the castle, Sir Gaston will not fail to institute a search that I can scarcely hope to elude."

"Do you still despair, my lady?"

"What reason have I for hope?" she exclaimed; "have not I ever been the victim of Sir Gaston's base schemes, and shall I now look for safety when I know the determination with which he will endeavour to search me out?"

"Heaven will shield the innocent," answered Adrian; "for though you have hitherto suffered much from the vindictive rage of an oppressor, let us hope the time has now arrived when you will no longer be permitted to remain at his mercy."

"I have thought so ere now, and have been deceived," sighed the Lady Alicia.

"But you will be deceived no more," answered the page; "immediately upon quitting this place I will conduct you to the nearest convent, and, once safe beneath its roof, you may defy the power of Sir Gaston to drag you from it."

"Aye," replied the lady, "that is, indeed, the only refuge where I can expect to meet that peace which has been so long denied me, except, indeed, it be the grave, where all persecution ceases for ever!"

"I pr'ythee, lady, talk not thus sadly," cried Adrian; "happier times are now in store for you, and I feel assured that this is the last moment of your captivity, if you will only accompany me with a resolution to overcome any difficulties we may have to surmount."

"I am not without my share of firmness, as years of suffering will prove," answered Alicia; "yet there are times when tired nature fails, and we feel no longer able to sustain the load of care that oppresses us."

"I admit that it is so," exclaimed Adrian, "and yet it is our duty to endure without complaining; and since you have so long done so, I entreat your ladyship to bear up a little longer when I feel assured all will be well."

"I am resolved to do so," she replied, "and yet you cannot wonder that I feel wearied with the ceaseless persecution I have thus long endured."

"I do not, indeed," answered Adrian; "but as a period has at length arrived when you may expect a termination of your griefs, I would fain persuade you to summon up all your fortitude for any exertion that may be required."

"I am now prepared to endure all," replied the captive, "and am even willing to accompany you, though I feel assured in my own mind that some interruption from Sir Gaston will prevent our attempt to escape."

"And I, on the other hand," cried Adrian, "feel quite satisfied that we have only to exert ourselves a little, and all will be better than you appear to anticipate."

"Have you seen any of the people belonging to the castle?" enquired Alicia.

"Yes, my lady, Bertrand le Noir visited me shortly after my return to my dungeon, and finding that I had discovered a way to leave the cell, he took means, as he thought, to prevent my being able to do so again."

"Ah!" cried Alicia, "then we shall be watched, and our hopes of escape will be frustrated for ever!"

"I was myself afraid of it at first," replied the page, "but, upon reflection, I think Bertrand is so well satisfied of my safety that he will not trouble his head any further about me till he has received orders from Sir Gaston. Besides, at this early hour there will be no chance of our meeting with anybody, and by the time our flight is discovered we shall be safe enough from the pursuit of our enemies."

"I may be safe in the event of my reaching a convent," answered Lady Alicia, "but I fear you will be in danger of falling into the hands of those who seek your life."

"Not if I take care of myself," replied Adrian; "for after seeing you safe in your place of refuge, I will return to the palace of the king, where I shall find that security which elsewhere I should look for in vain. There Sir Gaston will not dare to follow me, lest he should bring upon himself the anger of an already indignant sovereign."

"Yet it appears," observed the lady, "that he has contrived to make you his prisoner, though you had thrown yourself under the protection of King Richard."

"Aye, but that was my own fault," returned Adrian; "for hazarding too much, I ventured from the palace, and scarcely had I done so, when one of Sir Gaston's retainers seized upon me, and I was dragged hither ere any one could come to my assistance. The consequences had nearly proved fatal; but if you can only command courage enough to follow me, I think we shall both be able to get clear off, and enjoy a laugh at those who thought we were so securely in their power."

"You may trust me, boy," exclaimed Alicia, "for I have resolved to make this one last attempt to escape, and I will exert myself to the utmost, rather than plunge you into danger by any weakness of my own."

"Then let us lose no further time, my lady," said Adrian; "daylight, I see, has now fairly set in, and each moment of delay will only serve to lessen our chances of escape."

Lady Alicia slightly bowed her head in token of assent; and as Adrian left the dungeon, she closely followed him, in the direction of a light that was seen faintly glimmering at a great distance off. Proceeding slowly, and with the utmost caution, the object towards which they were moving became gradually nearer and nearer, until they could at length see that the light was admitted through a breach in the wall, and from which they hoped to find a passage to the exterior of the castle; nor were they disappointed in this expectation, for, on stepping through it, they found themselves in one of the court-yards, on the opposite side of which was the portal that had been used by the page on former occasions when he wished to leave the castle secretly. Hurrying across the quadrangle, they found, to their infinite joy, that the door was unfastened, and eagerly making their way through it, they were once again beyond the precincts of their late prison.

Not a moment, however, was to be lost, and bidding his companion to sustain her courage yet a little longer, Adrian directed his steps across the fields, and, after half an hour's walking, arrived at the convent, in which he hoped to find a resting-place for Lady Alicia. His summons at the gate was quickly answered by the aged porteress, who no sooner heard the nature of their application, than she bade Alicia enter, assuring her that the abbess would gladly afford her the asylum she desired. Thus satisfied of her safety, Adrian took his farewell of the companion of his flight, and then, exerting all the speed he could, pursued his way towards the palace of King Richard, on arriving at which he was joyfully received by those who, suspecting into whose hands he had fallen, had given him up for lost.

We must now return to Bertrand le Noir, who, at an early hour in the morning repaired to the apartment of Sir Gaston, who he found had risen, and was impatiently pacing up and down his chamber as if unable to endure the conflicting thoughts that agitated his breast. As the retainer entered, he abruptly paused, and in a hoarse tone demanded what tidings he had now brought him?

"Nothing of much consequence," answered the other; "but as you had not last night decided what was to be done with your runaway page, I came here to learn your pleasure as to what is to be done with him."

"I have not yet made up my mind," replied Sir Gaston; "in truth, Bertrand, the subject solely perplexes me; for though my only safety lies in his death, yet there are circumstances that make me unwilling to resort to so violent an extreme."

"Well," exclaimed the other, "you know best, I dare say, but for my own part I can see no reason why you should be so unwilling to put him out of the way."

"I have my reasons for it, and let that suffice," returned Sir Gaston, sternly.

"Very well," retorted the other, "then if anything should happen, don't blame me for it, that's all."

"What mean you, sirrah?"

"I mean that if he should escape from us it will be no fault of mine."

"Psha! it is impossible he can find means to get out of this castle."

"Impossible as it may appear to you," replied Bertrand, "I have a notion that he means to try his best to escape."

"Ha! and how know you that?"

"Because I have discovered that he had already made one desperate attempt to break from his prison; and though I have secured him for the present, it is likely enough he will succeed if you are much longer in deciding about what is to be done with him."

"Explain yourself, Bertrand," cried the knight, impatiently; "in what way has Adrian endeavoured to elude our vigilance?"

"When I visited him last night," answered the other, "I found that he had made a hole in the door of his dungeon large enough to creep through. I taxed him with having tried to escape, and, to do him justice, he candidly admitted that such was the fact."

"How was it, then, that he was foiled?"

"Simply because he lost himself in the intricacies of the subterranean caverns," answered Bertrand. "He could not find his way out of them, and, I suppose, returned to his cell, in order that he might take another opportunity to give us the slip."

"And what means have you taken to prevent him?" asked Sir Gaston de Neville.

"I have secured his arms," replied the other, "and, for the present, I believe he is safe. How long he will remain so, however, I do not pretend to say, and, therefore, if you wish to get rid of any further trouble, the only safe way that remains is to dispatch him at once."

"I must think further ere I agree to your suggestion," exclaimed the knight. "Already I have enough crime to answer for, and the life of this youth must be spared as long as possible. And now, Bertrand, tell me of Lady Alicia;—is she still safe in your custody?"

"She is;—I visited her immediately after quitting the dungeon of Adrian, and found her more composed than usual."

"Aye," cried Sir Gaston; "perhaps she begins to reflect that it will be better to marry you than remain any longer a prisoner in this castle."

"It may be so," answered the other; "but somehow or other I fancy we shall have a harder task to convince her of that than you seem to think for. She don't appear to like me any better than she did; and you know when women take it into their heads to be obstinate, it's not a very easy task to make them change their minds."

" But she well knows that I no longer love her," observed Sir Gaston, " and surely the thought of that will be sufficient to bring her to our purpose."

" Perhaps she don't care whether you love her or not," replied Bertrand; " she knows she is your wife, and being tolerably resolute, the chances are, that she will refuse to release you in the way we have proposed."

" In that case, Bertrand, we must apply force to compel her."

" Ah! there you speak a little more to the purpose," cried the ruffian. " Force is your only remedy in this case; and if she will not become my wife by fair means, we must take a monk with us, as we did once before, and compel her to accept our terms."

" Have you already forgotten how we failed on the last occasion?" demanded Sir Gaston.

" I have not," returned the other; " we were interrupted by the armed apparition just as we thought ourselves most secure; but such a thing as that may never happen again, so at any rate it will be worth while to try experiment."

" And if we do," exclaimed Sir Gaston, " we may be interrupted in the same way. That terrible form is ever presenting itself to my view, and something tells me, Bertrand, that in one of its visitations I shall perish by a miserable end."

" Why you don't mean to say that you are going to grow chicken-hearted all of a sudden?"

" I tell you that form bodes no good," exclaimed the knight, with a shudder; " I have now seen it many times; and never does it appear but to mar some favourite project I have formed."

" Why its visits are certainly rather ill-timed," observed Bertrand le Noir; " but, perhaps, you have good reason to know why it is that you are so often troubled with the presence of this unwelcome guest."

" I do not," replied Sir Gaston, " for the form bears not the least similarity to any one that I ever knew in my life."

" At all events, he seems to take a wonderful interest in matters that don't concern him," answered the retainer; " and, if I was in your place I would——"

" Peace, sirrah, I command you," exclaimed Sir Gaston, impatiently "this subject is ever a disagreeable one to me, and I charge you, as you value my favour, never to mention it again in my presence."

" I will endeavour to obey you," returned the other; " and since you wish to have the conversation changed, perhaps you will tell me what I am to do with the two prisoners we have been speaking of?"

" The lady Alicia will remain where she is till I give you further instructions respecting her," replied the knight; " at present, it is my intention that she shall become your wife, in order that I may be fairly rid of her when the ceremony is to take place, I have not yet decided."

" And the page?"

" Will also remain in the dungeon until I have considered further what had best be done with him."

" In that case, you will not, of course, blame me if he should happen to escape."

" That, I should say, will be impossible," exclaimed the knight;—"you tell me he has been secured, and it is, therefore, most unlikely that he can get out of the castle."

"Aye," returned Bertrand; "but the youngster is as slippery as an eel, and glides out of one's hand before we can be aware of his intentions. He has served us the same trick over and over again, so that, to my thinking, there is every chance that he will not remain a prisoner here, if he has but the slightest opportunity afforded him to get clear away from us."

"I see how it is, Bertrand," exclaimed the knight; "you have taken a mortal hatred to the youth, and nothing but his death will ever satisfy you."

"Well," retorted the retainer, "you have as much reason to dislike him as I have, and yet you prefer saving his life, to making yourself safe by giving him up to my tender mercy."

"And why do you urge me so strongly to put him to death, but to satisfy your own longing for blood?"

"That I dislike the youngster, is not to be denied," answered Bertrand;— "I do hate him for his meddling and interference in matters that don't concern him. More than once I have found him watching me when I was about doing that which none but myself should have known; and, as I have found out that he is a spy, in my opinion, the sooner he is put out of the way, the better it will be for both you and me."

"We must do nothing rashly, sirrah," exclaimed Sir Gaston; " I have told you before that he was entrusted to my care by his dying father, and it would be an act of baseness, such as even I recoil from, to murder him as you have so often suggested."

"You must do as you please in the matter," replied Bertrand; "but, for my own part, I can see no reason why you should spare the life of a knave, merely because he happened to be entrusted to your protection by one that has been dead these many long years."

"It is my humour, sirrah," cried Sir Gaston; "and, therefore, I charge you to say no more about it."

"Well, you must be obeyed, I suppose," growled Bertrand; "but if you don't choose to hear what I have got to say, perhaps you will not refuse to go and visit him in his dungeon. You will then hear how lightly he speaks of the man who is so squeamish about taking his life; and if that will not stir you to do something desperate, I don't know what will."

"Your last suggestion I willingly accept," returned Sir Gaston; "so, lead on, and I will follow you to the place of his confinement."

Instantly complying with this order, Bertrand sullenly left the room, closely followed by Sir Gaston de Neville, and descending a flight of steps that led to the lower portions of the castle, they again began to thread those subterranean vaults in which so many of their fellow-creatures had been thrown at different times to linger out a wretched existence in hopeless captivity. Lighted only by a single lamp which was carried by Bertrand, they were obliged to proceed with extreme caution through the innumerable vaults that lay in their way, and it was, consequently, some time before they reached the dungeon which was just then the immediate object of their visit. At length, however, Bertrand removed the heavy bolts and chains with which the door was secured, and then entering the darksome cell, he discovered to his rage and chagrin, that the prisoner he expected to see was no longer a tenant of the wretched abode in which he had been left. For a moment or two surprise deprived him of the power of utterance, but at last, recovering himself a little, he exclaimed:—

"By all the fiends of hell, the young villain has escaped!"

"Escaped!" echoed Sir Gaston, wrathfully.

"Aye;—he is nowhere to be seen; and judging from these empty fetters that are lying on the ground, it seems he has found means to extricate himself from the bonds with which I thought I had secured him."

"Perdition seize thee for thy lack of care!" exclaimed the knight, furiously; "thou hast connived at his escape, Bertrand ;—nay, it is in vain to deny it, and thy life shall answer for thy treachery!"

"Ha! am I, then, suspected of favouring the escape of thine enemy?"

"I do more than suspect thee, villain!" cried Sir Gaston de Neville; "I feel assured that this is a contrivance of thine own, and should my suspicions prove correct, I will take care it shall be the last time thou shalt ever have it in thy power to play me false."

"I have never been false to thee, Sir Knight," answered Bertrand. "As I live, the page was securely pinioned when I left him last night, though how he has contrived to slip from his fetters, I am at a loss to explain. I can, however, solemnly declare that I know nothing of his escape out of this dungeon."

"That remains to be proved," exclaimed the knight, fiercely. "I shall not fail to institute the strictest inquiry into the affair, and, should I find you have deceived me, nothing short of death will satisfy my vengeance."

"I fear no inquiry that you can make," replied Bertrand; "for in this instance, at least, I am assured of my own innocence, and can defy you to prove that I am false."

"That we shall see, presently," exclaimed Sir Gaston; "so follow me, sirrah, to the dungeon of Lady Alicia, and let me see if thou hast taken as much care of her as thou hast of Adrian, my page."

Enraged at the suspicion that had thus been thrown on him, Bertrand le Noir rushed from the place, and pursuing his way along the passage we have before mentioned, reached the place to which his footsteps had been directed. To his utter confusion and dismay, the door of Alicia's cell was standing wide open, and the fatal truth rushed upon his mind. The other prisoner had also escaped, and there could be no doubt but they had left the place together. The fury of Sir Gaston de Neville now mounted to the highest pitch, and drawing his sword, he was about to plunge it into the heart of his retainer, when a thought struck him, that if the fugitives were ever to be discovered at all, it would be through the instrumentality of Bertrand; he, therefore, instantly sheathed his weapon, and assuming an air of more composure, declared that his forgiveness might be obtained, on condition of his finding and restoring the two prisoners to their former places of confinement. This Bertrand undertook to do, and they immediately returned to the upper part of the castle to devise means for the attainment of their object.

CHAPTER XC.

"I know each guilty secret of thy heart;
And knowing these, will turn them 'gainst thyself,
If thou dost not obey me."

THE SENATOR.

KNOWING, as he did from long experience, the sullen nature of his retainer, Sir Gaston knew that his better course would be to humour him into a belief that his anger had evaporated, and changing his manner, from extreme anger to an apparent forgetfulness of what had occurred, he soon lulled Bertrand into a belief that he had no longer to dread the fierce indig-

nation that had burst forth with so much fury. Thus satisfied, he proposed that he should go forth to ascertain whether any tidings could be heard of either of the fugitives.

"Thou may'st do so, Bertrand," answered the knight, in a subdued tone; "and, since no time is to be lost in making these inquiries, depart without delay, and see that thou dost return with news of the place of their retreat."

"I will," exclaimed Bertrand, somewhat softened by the altered demeanour of his master, "for, though they have contrived to make their escape from the castle, it shall not be long before they are brought back again, unless I am much mistaken."

"Dost thou want assistance?" asked Sir Gaston.

"It is likely I may," returned the other, "but as it will be as well to keep the thing as quiet as possible, I would advise that no more than one beside myself should be trusted in the affair."

"Thou hast said well," answered Sir Gaston, "and, as there is no one in the castle that I care to trust, I will myself go forth in quest of them. We will take different routes, and by carefully pursuing our inquiries as we go along, there is every reason to hope we shall succeed in our object."

"And suppose we catch them," asked Bertrand, "what course do you propose to pursue next?"

"That must be a subject for future consideration," replied the knight; "if we are fortunate enough to overtake them, they must be conveyed back to this place, and secured in some other part of the castle, from whence escape will be impossible. I will then consider what shall be done with them, and my decision shall be as prompt as you can desire."

"You know my opinion upon the subject," exclaimed Bertrand. "The page no longer deserves your pity, since there's no doubt that he has aided in the escape of Lady Alicia, and, therefore, I should recommend short work with him."

"I understand," cried Sir Gaston, thoughtfully; "you would have him slain as soon as he returns."

"I would not take the trouble to bring him back at all," answered the ruffian. "We have already had a pretty good specimen of the trouble he means to give us, and, to my thinking, the best thing we can do will be to plunge a dagger into his heart, whenever we may chance to light on him."

A dark frown gathered upon the countenance of Sir Gaston de Neville as he heard this suggestion, and even the stern nature of Bertrand shrank as he observed the tempest his words had excited. He knew well enough that it would be in vain to offer any palliatives just at that moment, and maintaining a dogged silence, he awaited the reply of his imperious master. At length, the countenance of Sir Gaston relaxed a little of its severity, and gradually the frown of anger was dissipated to give place to a feigned look of calmness.

"I have been thinking of what you said, Bertrand," he at last replied, " and though the hint at first excited my indignation, I have forgotten all that in the consciousness that your zeal for my welfare prompted the thought you gave utterance to. I know your anxiety to serve me, but you are also aware of my desire to spare the life of this stripling, and, therefore, I again tell thee no violence must be offered him, until you have received my further instructions."

"I understand," answered the ruffian; "you desire to nurse in your bosom the viper that is hereafter to sting you to death !"

"I will spare him so long as I can do so with safety to myself," replied Sir Gaston. "Let him but once again become my prisoner, and I will take such precautions to prevent his escape, that there shall be no further cause to fear any injury he may wish to do me."

"Yet, with all our caution," returned the other, "he has contrived to give us the slip, and, in my opinion, would do so again, even if we were to load his limbs with fetters, and chain him to the wall of his dungeon."

"That method shall at least be tried," exclaimed Sir Gaston. "Let me but once again get him into my power, and he shall find escape less easy than he has done before. I will hold him as my captive for the remainder of his life, but my present determination must alter greatly, ere I consent to the deadly alternative you have proposed."

"Then I shall say no more about it at present," returned Bertrand. " There is, however, another subject that I should like to hear your opinion about. I have been promised the Lady Alicia for a wife ;—to be sure she is married already, and that, with many people, might appear rather an awkward barrier to matrimony; but I am not over particular in these matters, as you know, and to prove that I am still your faithful servant, I am willing to accept the lady whenever it shall be your will and pleasure to command the ceremony to take place."

"And that shall be as soon as you have brought her back to the castle," answered Sir Gaston.

"And when the ceremony has been duly solemnized, I am to receive from your hands the sum of money agreed to on a former occasion?"

"By my honour thou shalt; that is to say, on condition that thou dost fulfil all my instructions."

"They shall be obeyed to the very letter," answered Bertrand. "I am to convey her abroad immediately after the marriage rites have been performed, and to take care that you never hear of her again ?"

"Aye, do that, and the gold I have promised shall be thine."

"Fear not, then," replied the ruffian, smiling grimly, "for if once I succeed in getting her safe out of England, thou shalt be safe from her for ever."

"Hah!" exclaimed Sir Gaston, "thy tone and look convince me thou hast designed to rid thyself of her by some foul and unfair practices!"

"Well," retorted the other, "and supposing it were so; does it matter how she is got rid of, so that you are never more troubled with her?"

"I would not have her murdered, villain!"

"Psha!" exclaimed Bertrand, "you have grown squeamish of late. The time has been when you thought less of blood than you do at present, but now your most dangerous foes are to live, because you happen to think it a crime to get rid of them. For my own part, I can see no harm in putting an enemy out of the way, when it happens to be necessary for one's own safety."

"Thou hast heard my commands, sirrah, and upon no other terms will I consent to trust thee with Lady Alicia."

"And yet, it is not long since that I heard you wish that some chance would rid you of her whose existence you declared was the chief cause of your disquietude."

"True," returned Sir Gaston, "but for all that, I do not wish to have her blood to answer for."

"Nor would you," replied the ruffian, "supposing I was to put her quietly out of the way, without informing you of my intentions."

"Bertrand," exclaimed the knight, "I will be urged no further upon this subject. You have heard my orders, and must be prepared either to obey them, or give up all further idea of obtaining the hand of Lady Alicia."

"Well," muttered Bertrand, "there's no accounting for the changes of people that don't know their own mind. A little while ago, you would have given the world to be fairly rid of a wife that you hate, and now, when there is as pretty an opportunity as any one need wish to desire, you shrink from the thought of a little blood, as if such a thing had never been shed before."

"Too much has been shed, of which I have been cognizant," answered Sir Gaston. "In the present instance, I may rid myself of her without the violence you propose, and never will I consent to the murder of one, whose helplessness should be her best protection."

"You wish, then, it seems," cried Bertrand, "to bestow upon me a wife with whom you have found it impossible to live happily?"

"Hah! dost thou taunt me, sirrah?"

"I speak the truth, Sir Gaston."

"Why then, it appears you already repent the bargain you were just now so willing to complete?"

"No," replied Bertrand, "I do not repent it, though, to confess the truth, I should have been all the better pleased to have disposed of the Lady Alicia after my own fancy. Our tempers may not agree, and in that case, I should, perhaps, feel inclined to get rid of an encumbrance in the best way that offers"

"Then our bargain ends here," exclaimed the knight; "so all I now demand of thee is, to go in search of the fugitives, and bring them back, as you value my future favour."

"But hear me, Sir Gaston ———"

"I will hear no more," interrupted the knight, severely; "you have received my instructions, and see that they are faithfully obeyed."

"And suppose I should happen to bring them back?"

"In that case, I shall confine them in separate cells, until I have m further arrangements for their safe custody. You have heard me, Bertrand, and, knowing as you do, that I am not to be trifled with, disobey me at your own peril."

The ruffian, who was well aware that it would be useless to offer any further remonstrance, took his leave, with a promise to exert himself to the utmost for the recapture of the fugitives, and immediately after his departure, Sir Gaston also left the castle, in pursuit of Adrian and the Lady Alicia.

Uncertain which way to go, the knight, without any fixed object for so doing, directed his way towards the royal palace of King Richard, but he had not proceeded any great distance, when he heard his name pronounced, and startled by the well-known voice that had addressed him, he looked up, and beheld Meg of Finchley standing within a few paces of the spot where he had come so suddenly to a pause. Furious at thus beholding one who he regarded as an enemy, he would have passed on without heeding her, but Meg foresaw his intention, and making three or four rapid strides towards him, she stretched forth her long bony arm, and held him firmly by the cloak.

"Stay, Sir Gaston," she exclaimed, "and listen to one whose words, as thou knowest, are not at all times to be scorned."

"I want to hold no communication with thee," answered the knight, angrily; "I, therefore, command thee to release me, ere I compel thee to do so with my dagger's point!"

"Humph! that would be an honourable deed for one who has taken the oaths of knighthood!"

"I have not sought thee, woman," he exclaimed, "and, therefore, thou dost but tempt me to a deed I should not otherwise have thought of."

"We do not part till I have fulfilled the errand that has prompted me to watch for thee," answered the weird woman; "thou hast ever proved a fierce and vindictive foe to those whom thou dost hate, and, fearing lest thou shouldst be the means of destroying one in whose safety I feel the greatest interest, I now ask of thee that mercy which it is so seldom in thy fierce nature to bestow."

"For whom dost thou plead, woman?"

"For Rebecca, the Hebrew Maiden."

"Ha! dost thou not know she is no longer in my power?"

"I am well aware that she is at present in the Gatehouse at Westminster," replied Meg. "So far, she is for a time safe, but you have charged her with attempting to assassinate you in your sleep, and until that accusation is either proved or abandoned, there is no chance of her obtaining that liberty of which she has been unjustly deprived."

"In this instance she has not been unjustly imprisoned," answered Sir Gaston de Neville.

"You still persist, then, in your charge?"

"I do."

"And what proof have you that she ever entertained an idea against thy life?"

"She was found, armed with a dagger, in my chamber, at the hour of midnight."

"That she denies not," replied Meg of Finchley; "but she solemnly declares that she was not there with any intention to take away your life."

"She will have a harder task than she expects to convince the judges of that," observed the knight. "My word will, at least, be taken against hers, and if that is not sufficient, I have at least a dozen witnesses to prove that she was found in my room as I have described."

"Yet was she innocent of any evil intentions towards you," replied

Meg. "I have her own solemn declaration to that effect, and will more readily believe her than one who has ever proved himself her enemy."

"You can believe what you please," retorted the knight, "but if her judges take my word, that will be quite sufficient for my purpose."

"Indeed! and have you reflected upon what will be the consequences, in the event of her being found guilty?"

"I have," replied Sir Gaston; "as a Jewess, and being convicted of an attempt against the life of a Christian, she will be first tortured, and then burnt at the stake."

"And knowing this," cried Meg, "you would remorselessly consign her to so horrible an end?"

"Does she merit anything better from me?" demanded the knight, fiercely; "has she not rejected my suit with scorn, and shall I now pity her, when I see that she is about to meet the death she deserves?"

"Thou callest thyself a Christian," exclaimed Meg, "and yet, would consign a fellow-creature to a horrible and ignominious death, because she has virtuously rejected the base propositions thou hast made!—Shame on thee, Sir Gaston, and may the world's scorn ever pursue thee for the baseness thou hast been guilty of!"

"Peace, woman!" cried the knight, fiercely, "and urge me no further, lest passion overcome me, and I sacrifice thee for thine insolent intrusion."

"Oh, thou canst not intimidate me by thy threats, false knight," exclaimed Meg, undauntedly. "I knew ere I came to meet thee, that my life would be hazarded, should I venture to speak the truth to one who dares not listen to it, lest his own conscience should reproach him for the evil of his ways. I am aware that thou wilt not scruple to slay an old and helpless woman, yet here I stand in thy presence, to tell thee to thy face that thou art undeserving the honour of knighthood that has been conferred on thee."

"Wilt thou not leave me, woman?" exclaimed Sir Gaston, trembling with rage. "I tell thee, hag, I seek not thy worthless life; but, if thou dost persist in thus heaping thine insults upon me, I may presently be urged by the blindness of my fury, to forget how utterly worthless and contemptible is the object of my rage."

"Strike when thou wilt," answered Meg, "thou shalt not see me shrink from the blow."

"Wilt thou not leave me, I say?"

"Not till thou hast promised to save the life of the Hebrew Maiden."

"What!—at thy command?"

"I do not command it," she replied, "but, if thou pleasest, I will ask the favour with all humility."

"Thou dost ask in vain," answered the the knight; "the girl has sought my life, and must take the consequences of her treacherous attempt."

"And hast thou forgotten thine own treacherous attempts upon her?" demanded the old woman.

"I know to what you allude," replied Sir Gaston, "but that has nothing to do with this affair. As the daughter of an accursed race, she has no right to claim the protection of the laws that were made for the government of Christians. She is an outcast from society, and, therefore, has been rather honoured than otherwise, by the preference I have shewn her."

"Sir Knight," exclaimed Meg, boldly, "thou art no true Christian to say so. The girl is virtuous, and I care not what religion she follows, since she has proved herself an honour to the sex to which she belongs."

"Away, thou canting hypocrite!" cried Sir Gaston, fiercely; "leave me, I say, or I may be driven to an extremity that I would fain avoid."

"Thy threats will not move me," she replied. "Death will soon be my lot, whether I receive it from thy hands or not.   I am willing to die, and in no cause could I better meet my fate, than in trying to serve a virtuous girl.   Say, then, that thou wilt spare thine unoffending victim, and thou shalt have my prayers and blessings, instead of my curses."

"I care for neither," answered Sir Gaston, with impatience.

"Thou art resolved, then, to hunt Rebecca to death?"

"Aye, if the law wills it so."

"If thine accusation is believed," replied Meg, "no power on earth can save her;—even the king must yield, in this instance, though I believe he would gladly save her, were it in his power to do so."

"Thou hast spoken truly," answered the knight; "she is indeed devoted to death, if I persist in urging my charge."

"And wilt thou persist in it?"

"Aye, as truly as that I now stand before thee."

"In that case," exclaimed Meg of Finchley, "thine own disgrace,—nay, perhaps thine ignominious death, shall speedily follow!"

"How!—dost thou threaten me?"

"I do, proud knight, and more, I will carry my threats of vengeance into execution."

"Psha!" retorted Sir Gaston, "thou canst never injure me."

"That we shall see anon," she replied, "for the evil of thy ways,—secret as thou hast kept them, are not unknown to me."

"Hah!—what dost thou know, woman?"

"That which will bring shame on thee!"

"I understand," answered the knight; "thou wilt invent a falsehood, in hopes that thou may'st thus save Rebecca by bringing odium upon myself."

"I will speak nothing but the truth of thee," she replied, "and that, I tell thee, will prove sufficient to bring shame and disgrace on thy name for ever."

"Woman!" vociferated Sir Gaston; "if thou knowest aught against me, tell me what it is, that I may be prepared to meet thy charges boldly."

"I will tell thee, since it is thy wish," answered the hag of Finchley. "Thou hast a wife, Sir Gaston de Neville; aye, a living wife, though the world, deceived by thy falsehood, believes her to be dead."

"Accursed hag!" exclaimed the knight, fiercely, "who is it that has told thee this most scandalous falsehood?"

"The secret has been too artfully kept to be told me by any one," replied Meg.   "I myself know it, and can prove my assertion, should there be occasion for it."

"'Tis false!" cried Sir Gaston, "for hadst thou known such a thing against me, thou wouldst long ere this have taken measures to obtain her deliverance."

"There may be reasons for my acting as I have done," replied the weird woman.   "I have my own motives for remaining silent thus long, but now the life of a fellow-creature depends on my speaking out boldly, and I will do so, let the consequences be what they may."

"And what," asked the alarmed knight, "will purchase thy silence on this subject?"

"Nothing but thy promise that Rebecca shall be set at liberty without delay."

"That is impossible," replied Sir Gaston, "for I have publicly made my charge, and am bound to carry it on to a close."

"I see, thou art madly determined, then, to rush upon thine own destruction?" exclaimed Meg.   "Thou fearest the exposure I can bring upon thee, and yet, so great is thy desire for vengeance upon this girl, that thou wouldst risk all to bring thy victim to death."

"Say that thou wilt prevail upon Rebecca to accept the terms I have proposed," answered the knight, "and I will then pledge my word to save her from the perilous situation in which she has fallen."

"Wouldst thou have me persuade her to consent to her own shame?" demanded the old woman.

"Thou art mistaken," replied Sir Gaston; "I have offered to share my fortune with her, and should she accept my terms, there will be little need for her to regard the sneers of an envious and harshly-judging world."

"And what, think you," demanded Meg, "would wealth be considered when weighed against the virtue of which every good woman is so justly proud? I know Rebecca well, and am convinced that she would rather perish by the most painful death that man's ingenuity can devise, than yield to proposals you have made."

"Then," answered Sir Gaston, sternly, "she must perish through her own foolish obstinacy."

"In which case," exclaimed the hag, "thou shalt not escape the just odium thy crimes have merited. I will pursue thee with the hatred of an enemy, and never will I lose sight of thee until I have brought thy proud and haughty spirit even to the very dust."

"This is only said to intimidate me," cried the knight, affecting an air of perfect indifference; "thou knowest nothing against me, and even if thou didst, who would believe thy word in opposition to my own? Thou wouldst be driven with disgrace from the court of justice, and I should not only succeed in bringing punishment upon Rebecca, but my name would be untainted by the foul reproaches thou would heap upon it."

"But what if I could tell the lady's name, and the circumstances of her long imprisonment in a loathsome dungeon?"

"Thou canst do neither."

"To prove that I can," answered Meg, "the name of thy deeply injured wife is Alicia."

"Such was, indeed, the name of my wife," replied Sir Gaston; "but she has been dead many years."

"So thou hast reported," cried the old woman;—"nay, a mock funeral was got up; but whilst the relatives of Lady Alicia was mourning her supposed death, she was pining in the wretched cell to which the cruelty and injustice of her own husband had condemned her."

"This is but a creation of thine own busy brain," answered Sir Gaston; "for she, of whom thou speakest, died, and was buried in a vault beneath the castle chapel at the time of which thou hast spoken."

"Perhaps thou wilt not object, then, to have the ground opened, and her coffin searched?"

"Woman!" cried the knight, "what put that fiendish notion in thy head?"

"Nothing," she replied, "but the certainty that thou hast been cruelly deceiving the world with a false report of thy wife's death. Nay, it is vain for thee to deny it, for, if compelled to do so, I will prove my assertion in the face of the whole world."

"And thou wilt not hold thy peace, unless I consent to act the coward's part, by refusing to appear against her who I have publicly charged with a crime of the highest magnitude."

"Thou hast charged her falsely, and, therefore, it will be to thy honour to abandon it at once."

"And on condition that I do so, thou wilt not whisper these suspicions of thine to a soul?"

"Hah! thy fears, Sir Knight, prove thy consciousness of the story I have told thee."

" It does not prove anything," replied Sir Gaston, in some confusion; " but knowing, as I do, how apt the world is to receive any slander that is uttered, I thought it better to accept thy offer, and let the affair drop where it is."

" Which can only be on condition that you promise not to press your accusation against Rebecca."

" I know not how I can make such a promise," answered Sir Gaston, " for the trial is appointed to take place to-morrow, and, if I fail to appear, it will at once be judged that I am absent through a consciousness of having falsely charged her with the crime for which she is to be tried."

" That may be easily avoided," replied Meg.

" How ?"

" By attending, and publicly stating before the assembled multitude, that you have reason to believe your first suspicions to have been unfounded," answered the old woman ; " you will thus secure her acquittal, and your own safety at the same time."

" But how can I be satisfied that you will keep the secret of which you say you have become possessed ?"

" By giving the Lady Alicia her liberty, you may secure yourself."

" The person you take for Lady Alicia, is already at liberty," answered Sir Gaston.

" She must have escaped lately, then ?"

" She has, accompanied by my page, Adrian, left my castle secretly, a few hours since."

" In that case," replied Meg, " you may depend upon my secrecy. I seek only to protect the innocent, and when that is effected, you have nothing more to fear from me. Remember, however, I rely upon your promise to abandon the unjust charge you have brought against her."

" I have already told you she has nothing to fear from me."

" At any rate," continued Meg, " I shall be at hand in case you should alter your mind. I will watch you narrowly, Sir Gaston de Neville, and, if you forfeit your word, I will instantly present myself to the Chief Justiciary, and relate the history of the Lady Alicia's wrongs. You will find me resolute, and so, for the present, farewell."

In an instant afterwards, Meg of Finchley had disappeared from his view, and pondering upon the perplexing adventure that had befallen him, Sir Gaston returned home without prosecuting his search after the fugitives.

CHAPTER XCI.

OTH. I'll know thy thoughts.
IAGO. You cannot, if my heart were in your hand ;
　　Nor shall not, whilst 'tis in my custody.
　　　　　　　　　　　　　　SHAKSPERE.

BERTRAND LE NOIR, who, it will be remembered, had set forth in search of the fugitives, was as unsuccessful as his master had been in obtaining any clue by which he might discover their place of retreat. He, however, felt certain in his own mind, that their first thought would be to seek refuge in the cave of Black Ivan, and, as he had already formed a design for the capture of the robber chieftain, he determined to return back to the castle, and provide himself with such a disguise as would not only secure him from all chance of discovery, but, at the same time, afford him

a fair opportunity of getting the brigand within the toils he had contrived for his capture. Indeed, he felt quite satisfied that everything would turn out exactly as he had planned; and, full of this thought, he was about changing his course towards the castle of Sir Gaston de Neville, when a figure, enveloped from head to foot in a capacious cloak, suddenly started from behind a ruined cottage, by which he was passing, and in a peremptory tone commanded him to stop.

"And who art thou who thus darest to arrest my footsteps?" demanded Bertrand.

"One who has both the power and the inclination to enforce his commands," answered the stranger.

"Indeed," retorted the other; "then for once thou hast met with one who heeds not thy commands. I am going on my business, and it will be at thy peril to delay me longer than I feel inclined."

"Wilt thou resist me, then?"

"Aye, even to the death!"

"Is thy life of so little value to thee, fellow?"

"I know not yet that it is risk by coming in contact with thee," answered Bertrand le Noir. "At any rate I wear a sword, and can use it with some skill, should there be need to draw it."

"Thou hadst better let it remain idle in its scabbard," exclaimed the stranger. "I, also, am well practised in the use of such weapons, and, as thou wouldst have but little chance were we to come in collision, it will be thy most prudent course to listen with patience to that which I have to say to thee."

"These threats move me not," answered Bertrand; "and since thou hast boasted of thy prowess, let us now seek to prove which is the better man."

No. 68

"Thou art rash," exclaimed the other, "and thy words might have tempted some men to punish thy temerity. I, however, am not so easily excited, and, therefore, I forbear taking an advantage that would end in thy death."

"Who art thou, vain boaster?" demanded Bertrand.

"One who seldom boasts of more than he can accomplish," replied the other, throwing aside his cloak, and discovering the gigantic form of Black Ivan. "Thou now seest who thine antagonist is, and it will, therefore, remain with thyself whether we finish our quarrel in the way thou hast proposed."

"I am not to be frightened from my purpose because Black Ivan happens to accost me in the king's highway," replied the other, with as undaunted an air as he could assume; "besides, I have long wished for an opportunity to meet thee face to face, and since the chance has now been afforded me, we will not part till one or the other has been compelled to bite the dust."

Whilst he was thus speaking, Bertrand le Noir flourished his sword, and threw himself into an attitude of defence, but the Outlaw eyed him with a look of ineffable contempt, and taking the first favourable opportunity that presented itself, he sprang upon his opponent, wrenched the weapon from his grasp, and threw it far away from him, ere the other could possibly prevent his design.

"Now what becomes of thy boasted prowess?" he exclaimed; "thou art defeated ere thou couldst put forth an arm in thine own defence, and it now only remains for me to punish thy temerity as it deserves."

"Strike, if thou wilt," answered Bertrand; "for, defeated as I have been by thee, I have no wish to return home with the news of my own disgrace."

"Hah!" cried the robber, "thy words do but confirm my former suspicions. Thou hast been employed by Sir Gaston de Neville to assassinate me, and hast been disappointed?"

"Sir Gaston did not desire thy death," answered Bertrand.

"For what other fate, then, was I to be reserved?"

"He would have made thee his prisoner," answered the other. "I was charged on no account to take thy life; but hadst thou fallen into my hands, he would have kept thee in hopeless imprisonment during the remainder of thine existence."

"And for which he, of course, would have rewarded thee to thy heart's content?"

"He would."

"Come," exclaimed Black Ivan, "thou art pretty candid, at any rate. I now know thy designs, and can, therefore, take means effectually to frustrate them."

"By slaying me, I suppose?"

"No," answered the brigand, "I am not a seeker after blood, though people have given me a character which I am far from deserving. I will prove to thee that I can be generous to my enemies, and, therefore, thou may'st depart homewards as unscathed as if we had never met."

"And dost thou make no conditions with me?"

"None; all I shall bid thee do is, to carry back my defiance to thy treacherous master. Tell him that I am his sworn foe, and that I am only waiting the first opportunity that offers to crush him beneath the just indignation he has provoked."

"I'll not undertake to be thy messenger," replied Bertrand.

"And wherefore dost thou refuse?"

"Because my own death would be the consequence," answered the ruffian. "I know the hasty temper of Sir Gaston de Neville, and I should surely perish were he to know that I had met with thee, and failed in the execution of the task I had undertaken."

"Bid him come forth himself, then," cried the robber. "Say I will meet him at any place he chooses to appoint, and that we will terminate this quarrel in any way he thinks proper. At any rate you may say, that I shall not shun him, and that if chance should ever happen to throw us together, I may no longer be able to control the rage his own conduct has inspired me with."

"He has done no more than other men," answered Bertrand; "all feel an equal desire to destroy Black Ivan, the Outlaw, and surely he has done but his duty in seeking to rid the land of an accursed pest."

"Thou art not over complimenting in thy speech, sirrah."

"At least you must acknowledge that I am plain spoken."

"Perhaps a little too much so," answered Ivan; "however, luckily for thyself, thou hast found me in tolerable good humour, and, therefore, I can permit free licence to thy tongue, even though it may somewhat gall me."

"For which," replied Bertrand, "I would not have thanked thee, had not my sword been wrested from me ere I was aware of thine intention."

"It is better for thee as it is, fellow," exclaimed the other; "I knew my own superiority both in respect of strength and skill, and as I do not seek to pick quarrels with those who are inferior to myself, I thought it better to deprive thee of the means that might have forced me to resist thy violence."

"Psha! if my life was in danger, the risk was my own, and thou hadst nothing to do with it."

"Dost thou grumble, then, at the mercy I have been induced to shew thee?"

"I do not thank thee for it," replied Bertrand, sulkily; "besides, we are now at odds, for, while I am unarmed, and at thy mercy, thou hast thy weapon to use against me whenever it may be thy pleasure to do so."

"In that case, I will speedily remove the cause of your suspicion," exclaimed Black Ivan, throwing his own sword as far from him as he could. "Now, at any rate, Bertrand, we are on perfectly fair terms, unless, indeed, my own strength of limbs is to be taken into consideration."

"That I am content to give thee the advantage of," replied the other, "if thou art inclined to try all, fall with me."

"If I thought there was a chance in thy favour, I would not refuse thy suggestion," returned Ivan; "but the truth is, I have no wish to harm thee at present, and, therefore, the best thing we can do is, to part on as good terms as we met together."

"If thou hadst no design against me, why did you present yourself before me?"

"Because I suspected thou wert bound on an errand of mischief, and sought to frustrate it?"

"Humph! dost thou know what brought me forth to-day?"

"I can form a pretty good guess."

"Perhaps you will explain yourself on this subject."

"Why, the truth is," answered Black Ivan, "your master has been again frustrated in his designs against those he sought to persecute. The Lady Alicia hath again escaped from his castle, and with her has departed the young page Adrian, whose only offence, I believe, consists in his having endeavoured to aid her in the midst of the difficulties with which she is surrounded."

"Hah!" cried Bertrand, "you speak of the Lady Alicia!—know you anything more of her, than that she was a prisoner in the castle of Sir Gaston de Neville ?"

"That is a question that I do not find it convenient to answer just at present," replied Ivan ; "I have my own reasons for keeping this affair secret so long as I have, but, in a little time, my evidence will be complete, and then let Sir Gaston beware, for he will find that he has a foe to deal with, that he little thinks of."

"And let me caution you to beware," exclaimed Bertrand ; "for the knight is furious in his wrath, and, should he have reason to suspect that you are plotting against him, he will not fail to take such speedy vengeance as will effectually prevent any danger that it may be in your power to do him."

"Tush ! what have I to fear from him ?"

"His burning vengeance."

"And that he will never dare to hurl upon me," answered Ivan. "Aye, you look doubtful and incredulous ; but, again I tell thee, Bertrand, that a word whispered in the ear of thy master, would so chill him with despair, that I should have little cause to fear his vengeance afterwards."

"Indeed ! and what, I pray you, would be the fearful word that is to produce an effect so miraculous."

"That, it will not be my present business to tell thee," replied Ivan ; "for a brief period longer, I must be content to endure the sufferings I have so long borne with patience and resignation ; but the end of my miseries approaches, and then shall Sir Gaston be utterly confounded with the disclosure I shall make."

"You know, then, something of this affair, about the Lady Alicia ?" cried the retainer.

"It is not of her I am at present speaking," replied Ivan ; "I am now alluding to injuries that I have myself endured, and which have driven me to become the wretched outcast you see me."

"You have long known Sir Gaston, I suppose ?"

"Nay, I have, perhaps, said too much already, and, therefore, we will speak no further about it," answered Ivan.

"Am I to understand, then, that you are secretly working to procure the ruin of my master ?"

"No, I will act openly," replied the other ; "he shall know his enemy in good time, though it may be in his power to avert the gathering storm."

"How can he do so ?" asked Bertrand.

"By rendering justice to those he has injured."

"Ah ! you mean the Lady Alicia ?"

"I certainly do mean her for one," replied Black Ivan ; "but there is another who has heavy wrongs that must be redressed at an early period."

"And that other ?——"

"Is myself."

"Indeed !—and how, I prithee, has my master injured thee so grievously ?"

"That thou shalt hear in good time," replied the robber ; "for the present, it is sufficient to say, that I have received injuries at his hands, and that I should never have been what I now am, but for the cruelty and injustice he has thought proper to inflict on me."

"He, also, complains of you, and, as it seems, not without cause," answered Bertrand le Noir. "It is not long since that you robbed him on the king's highway, and took from him,—besides gold, a diamond ring, which, for particular reasons, he would not have parted with on any consideration."

"And if I did do so," exclaimed Ivan, "let him blame himself for the occurrence; he, it was, that forced me to become what I am, and, therefore, he is the cause of the violence he now complains of."

"But, for which crime, your own life may yet have to pay the penalty," observed the retainer.

"It may be so," replied Ivan, with indifference; "my life may, certainly, be forfeited, but, let Sir Gaston de Neville beware whenever that moment arrives, for ere I die, the world shall know the villany of the man who first drove me to crime, and then punished me for it. It is not, however, for myself that I care, but the loss of the diamond ring has been the cause of much sorrow and misery to an unfortunate maiden who accidentally became possessed of the jewel, and, from that moment, has laid under the suspicion of having been concerned in a robbery of which she is entirely innocent."

"Had the girl been less obstinate," replied the retainer, "she would have made a friend instead of an enemy of Sir Gaston de Neville."

"Aye," answered Ivan, "but the sacrifice demanded was her virtue."

"True; and, if I remember rightly, there was a time when you, also, endeavoured by violence, to obtain possession of the girl."

"I plead guilty to the charge," answered Ivan; "struck by the remarkable beauty of the girl, I certainly did try to make her mine. Her virtue, however, subdued me, and, from that moment, I swore to defend her to the utmost of my power from the artifices of him who was not so scrupulous as I had been."

"And why should he be scrupulous?" demanded Bertrand le Noir; "the girl belongs to an accursed tribe, and, therefore, no one has any right to interfere in her behalf."

"At any rate, I have done so, and shall continue to exert myself in her favour," replied Ivan. "It seems, too, that he has now bethought him of another crime to charge her with, and to-morrow is the day appointed for her examination before the Chief Justiciary."

"And, if she is not burnt for it at the stake, I shall say there is no justice in the land for Christians," answered Bertrand le Noir. "We have already seen that the king favours the Jews, and it now remains to be proved whether Rebecca is to seek the life of my master without receiving the punishment her crime merits."

"But we know not yet that there is any truth in the charge that has been brought against her," replied Black Ivan. "At all events, it is more easily made than proved; and, therefore, the Chief Justiciary will do well to acquit her of the crime."

"It will not be well for the king if he does, though," exclaimed Bertrand le Noir.

"And what difference, I should like to know, can it make to King Richard?" demanded the brigand.

"It will serve to kindle the wrath that has for some time past been smothered," replied the retainer. "Cœur de Lion's unjust partiality for the Hebrews has given great offence to his subjects, and they only acquire such a confirmation as this to urge them into action."

"Humph! thy words infer that there is some foul treachery going forward?"

"That will depend upon the king himself," answered Bertrand; "let him punish these hated Jews, and the people will remain perfectly satisfied with his sway."

"But if he happens to be satisfied that the Jews are innocent of the crimes alleged, would you have him punish them?"

"There can be no reason to doubt their guilt, when such a man as Sir

Gaston de Neville comes forward to charge him with having attempted his life."

"The king, like myself, has no very high opinion of your master," answered Black Ivan. "He knows him to be revengeful and malevolent, and, therefore, he must be prepared with good evidence ere he can hope to have his story believed."

"And, why dost thou take part against Sir Gaston de Neville?" demanded the retainer.

"I have already told you that I have good cause for the enmity I bear him," replied Black Ivan; "at present, however, it is my purpose to keep my own secret; though, how long I shall do so will depend entirely upon the conduct he may think proper to pursue."

"Sir Gaston will not heed thine enmity," answered the retainer with a sneer; "he still has it in his power to betray thee into the hands of thine enemies, and he will do so whenever he finds that thou art preparing to do the mischief of which thou speakest."

"He will not know when to expect my vengeance," replied Black Ivan, "for it will come upon him at a moment when he is little prepared to avert the consequences of my fierce hatred."

"He himself best knows why he has so long deferred the punishment he had in store for you," exclaimed Bertrand le Noir. "That he will not fail in the object he has in view is, however, quite certain; and, therefore, I would not have you expect to escape the doom he has so long had in store for you."

"And in furthering of which," added Black Ivan, "he has had recourse to your well known cunning."

"I have already told you," replied the other, "that I have undertaken to lend my assistance in aid of the object he has in view. I have sworn to do my best to capture you, and being resolved to earn the reward that has been offered, I will either fulfil my intentions or perish in the attempt."

"For which kindness, I am much beholden to you," answered Ivan. "However, there is something to be said for your candour, and, therefore, to be equally plain, it is but fair that I should warn you against doing anything that may disturb the harmony that at present exists between us. You have seen how I have spared your life when it was in my power to have taken it, and be assured I feel no inclination whatever to stain my hands with your blood unless provoked to do so by some foolish act of your own."

"Well," exclaimed Bertrand, "there is one question I would ask and then we will part for the present. I am now in search of Lady Alicia and the page Adrian, who have found means to escape; and to tell you the truth I have a pretty strong notion that they have sought shelter and protection within your secret haunt."

"Thou art much mistaken," replied Ivan, "for I have seen nothing of them for some time past; if, as thou sayst, they have escaped, thou must look elsewhere after them, for it will but be labour in vain to seek the fugitives in my retreat."

"Dost thou know nothing of them?"

"I have said, I do not."

"But thou wilt not deny that thou art aware of the place of their retreat?"

"I deny knowing anything about them," answered Ivan.

"And yet," observed Bertrand, with surprise, "when we first met, thy words implied that thou knewest I was in search of them."

"Aye, but I had ascertained that beforehand."

"How didst thou do so?"

"I saw thy master, and from his lips gathered the information of which I have spoken."

"'Tis false," exclaimed Bertrand le Noir, "for never would my master utter such a confession to thee."

"I said not it was to me that he uttered it," replied Black Ivan.

"Hah! thou wert listening, then, where he was speaking in confidence to another."

"There thou art not far from right," exclaimed the brigand; "I saw thy master not long since in conference with Meg of Finchley; neither of them were aware of my presence, and wishing to overhear the subject of their conversation I slipped behind the projecting angle of a wall, and learnt as much as I had hoped to do;—at any rate, Sir Gaston is somewhat more in my power than he was previously, and it shall be no fault of mine if I do not take an advantage of it that he little thinks of."

"And do you also mind," exclaimed Bertrand, "or he will fall upon you with so much suddenness as to prevent any attempt at saving yourself."

"If he does so I will freely forgive him," replied Ivan, scornfully. "My eyes are on him when least he suspects it, and there is scarcely an important action of his life that I am not acquainted with."

"Thou hast spies on him, then?"

"Nay, I am my own spy, for I seldom trust another with the execution of a task that requires much secrecy or caution."

"Ha! dost thou often gain admittance to the castle without the knowledge of those that are posted to guard the gates?"

"Much more frequently than you imagine."

"Then the life of Sir Gaston is in continual peril from the presence of a deadly foe."

"Thou dost wrong me there," cried Black Ivan; "for, much as I hate thy master, I would not take his life in the cowardly way you imagine."

"Why, then, dost thou so frequently visit him in secrecy?"

"For a purpose of my own, which may hereafter be explained," answered Ivan. "At one time, however, I will confess my object was to visit Rebecca, for I thought she might be induced to love me, and that I should be happy in the possession of a prize I had so much coveted. That dream of hope, however, passed away; and when I found that she would never consent to be mine, I endeavoured to conquer my own feelings, and resolved to rescue her from the designs of Sir Gaston de Neville."

"By which means," exclaimed Bertrand le Noir, "you have incurred his everlasting hate."

"And what care I for that?" demanded the Outlaw; "I can return him hate for hate; and, perhaps, should we ever come to open war, he may feel that it was madness to excite my vengeance."

"But why should there be this enmity between you?" asked Bertrand le Noir; "would it not be better for you both to be friends, since you have the means to serve him, and he has gold enough with which to reward your zeal."

"Think you, then, I would ever take a reward from the man I rank as my chief enemy?"

"Yet there is no reason why you should be enemies," replied the retainer; "the wrongs you complain of may only be imaginary, and if you think proper to send a message by me, stating your wish to abandon the quarrel that is between you, I will undertake to promise you his future protection and esteem."

"Aye," answered Ivan, "there is no doubt he would be glad enough to avail himself of my services, if I was so weak as to plead for his favour. I, however, am little likely to do so, and, therefore, urge me no more to a course I never will adopt."

"Well, you can do as you like about it," returned Bertrand, "but if you don't choose to take my advice, perhaps you may acknowledge, ere long, that it would have been better to court the favour of the powerful Sir Gaston de Neville."

"Humph!" ejaculated the Outlaw, "I suppose you are alluding to the time when I am to be an unfortunate prisoner within one of his dungeons?"

"Which thou wilt be ere long," cried Bertrand, "in spite of the sneers with which you speak of such an event."

"And if so," exclaimed Black Ivan, "let it be thy task to keep watch and ward over me; for as surely as I should get into the jeopardy thou speakest of, I will find means to free myself from prison."

"Not if chains and bolts have the same power over thee that they have over others," replied Bertrand. "Shouldst thou escape after being once committed to my custody, nothing but my death would ever satisfy the wrath of Sir Gaston de Neville."

"Then refuse the charge he would confer upon thee," exclaimed the Outlaw; "for, again I tell thee, Bertrand, that never will I submit to the loss of liberty whilst I have strength left to obtain the blessed boon of liberty."

"But thou shalt be so guarded as to prevent every chance of escape."

"Aye, but thou hast yet to secure me in thy toils," replied Black Ivan, with contempt; "at present, there is little chance of thy succeeding in such an enterprise; and, even if such an attempt should be made, it may cost those dear who madly venture on it."

"The good fortune that has hitherto attended thee," cried Bertrand le Noir, "hath made thee vain; but, rely on it, a time will come, and in spite of all thy efforts, Sir Gaston will have thee in his power."

"Thou art a false prophet, for ere the knight can accomplish his purpose, he shall himself be made to endure the punishment his own crimes so justly merit."

"Of what crimes dost thou accuse the noble Sir Gaston de Neville?" asked the retainer.

"Of many," answered Black Ivan; "though, at present, it suits not my purpose to explain them."

"That," exclaimed the retainer, "is a cowardly way of bringing a charge."

"In your opinion it may be so," answered Ivan, unmoved by this insinuation; "I, however, have my own plans to work out, and, therefore, I shall use the caution necessary for securing the success of my own designs."

"Yet," cried Bertrand le Noir, "when I tell Sir Gaston, as I most assuredly shall, of the mischief you intend him, he will take effectual means to prevent the execution of your design."

"And suppose I now make thee my prisoner to prevent your fulfilling your threat?" exclaimed Black Ivan.

"In that case," replied the retainer, "I must endure my fate with what patience I can. Fortune, however, might still favour me, and, in that case, Sir Gaston would not fail to hunt you to destruction."

"He would come, I suppose, with a band of soldiers to make me his captive, in return for the violence offered to his retainer?"

"In all probability he would," answered Bertrand; "or, which is equally likely he would apply to the king and obtain his assistance to punish one who has long set the laws at open defiance."

"And in the event of his doing so," exclaimed the Outlaw, "I should be compelled to explain the villany that had driven me to the course that men now blame me for. This will not prove greatly to the credit of Sir

Gaston de Neville, and I feel assured that he would rather do anything than expose himself to the risk of bringing upon himself the scorn of his fellow men. So, now you can return to him, Bertrand le Noir, and relate the meeting we have had, and what has passed between us relative to any attempt that may be made to deprive me of my liberty."

Having thus spoken, Black Ivan retired from the place, and picking up the sword which he had thrown away, was shortly afterwards out of sight. The retainer was not long in following his example, and, having also recovered the weapon of which he had been deprived by his gigantic adversary, he left the place, and slowly returned towards the castle in Moorfields.

CHAPTER XCII.

" Nay, but he prated,
And spoke such scurvy and provoking terms
Against your honour,
That, with the little godliness I have,
I did full hard forbear him."

OTHELLO.

FIERCE and vindictive were the feelings of Sir Gaston de Neville when he returned home after his interview with Meg of Finchley, and found that he was likely to be thwarted in every plan that he had formed. That the Lady Alicia was now beyond his reach, he had every reason to fear. Adrian, also, had disappeared without a prospect of his being captured,

No. 69

and Black Ivan was still at liberty to execute the mischief he had so often threatened; all these things served terribly to perplex the knight, and it was with no little impatience that he awaited the arrival of Bertrand le Noir, upon the success of whose search, so much depended.   Never, however, did time seem to pass so heavily, and it was, therefore, with the greatest joy that he at length heard the heavy footstep of his retainer as he approached along the passage leading to the chamber in which he was sitting.

"Now, Bertrand," he exclaimed, as the man entered the room, "what news dost thou bring of those thou didst go in search of?   Hast thou traced them to their place of concealment?"

"No," replied the ruffian; "my search has been a fruitless one, for, scarcely had I commenced, when I was accosted by Black Ivan, who, by means of threats against yourself, succeeded in changing the purpose for which I set out."

"What!" cried the knight, reproachfully, "didst thou meet the robber, and yet fail in thy promise to capture him?"

"There was no help for it," answered Bertrand, "for, though I drew my sword, and dared him to single combat, he suddenly threw himself on me, and I was disarmed in less time than I have taken to relate the affair."

"Darest thou tell me of thy disgrace!" exclaimed Sir Gaston, fiercely, "or, am I to believe that thou hast been tampered with by the enemy, and that I have no longer a friend upon whom I may rely upon in the hour of need?"

"You may believe whatever you please of me," answered the retainer, sulkily; "hitherto I have been true and faithful to you, and yet, because I happen to have a defeat from this brigand, I am to be suspected of being unfaithful to the master I have sworn to serve."

"If thou hadst been faithful, Bertrand," exclaimed the knight, "thou wouldst have perished, rather than return with the news of thine own defeat."

"There was no help for it, I tell you," retorted Bertrand; "the robber possesses more strength and prowess than I do, and, therefore, it is not to be wondered at if I chanced to get worsted in an encounter with him."

"But, it seems you yielded without striking a blow for your own preservation."

"I did; but he came upon me so unexpectedly that I was not aware of his intentions."

"How!—couldst thou meet Black Ivan, and yet doubt that he meant to take advantage of thee?"

"When we first met, he was disguised, and I knew him not," replied Bertrand; "in fact, I was not prepared for such an encounter, and when, at length, he suddenly threw aside his cloak, I was disarmed before I had an opportunity to recover from my surprise."

"How was it he spared your life,—knowing, as he well does, that you are among the fiercest of his enemies?"

"It was not from any merciful consideration, I believe," replied the retainer; "but, as he wished a message to be conveyed to you, he chose to make me the bearer of it."

"What message has the villain dared to send me?" demanded Sir Gaston de Neville.

"He threatens you with his vengeance," answered the other.

"Indeed! then the sooner we meet the better."

"I should rather counsel you to avoid him," replied Bertrand le Noir. "He speaks of some important secret that he is in possession of, and threatens to disclose it, unless you refrain from all further persecution of the Hebrew Maiden."

"Hah!" cried Sir Gaston; "then it is evident he is in league with Meg of Finchley, for I met the hag not long since, and she, also, threatened me with her wrath, unless I would consent to abandon the charge that has been brought against her."

"And do you intend to obey the warning?" demanded Bertrand le Noir.

"That is the subject that sorely perplexed me at the moment you entered this chamber," answered the knight; "I have sworn that Rebecca made an attempt upon my life, and now to hesitate in proving my charge will be construed by the world into a consciousness of having accused her through motives of revenge."

"It may, indeed," exclaimed Bertrand, "and yet, of the two evils, it will be best to choose that which offers the least mischief to yourself."

"And thus," muttered the knight, "spare the girl who have ever treated me with coldness and disdain."

"Why, that is mortifying enough," returned Bertrand, "but, still your plans may only be deferred for a little time, since, by laying quietly on the watch, you may soon find another opportunity to carry them into effect."

"That I am afraid is hardly likely," exclaimed Sir Gaston, "for I myself may be watched by those who take so great an interest in her safety, and thus I shall be foiled in every hope that I have formed."

"Do you begin to depair, then, already?"

"Is there not enough to make me do so?" cried the knight; "have I not been foiled in every instance where I believed success most certain; and why should I now look forward with hope, when fate has so often declared against me?"

"Because a more fortunate turn may now take place in your behalf," answered Bertrand le Noir; "hitherto you have had to combat against an adverse fate; but, a brighter dawn will soon appear, and the vengeance you design shall be accomplished."

"What!" exclaimed the knight, "shall I encourage a hope with the threat of Black Ivan still ringing in my ears?"

"Black Ivan must take care of himself, or he will fall into a snare from which he will not find it easy to extricate himself," replied the retainer. "As an Outlaw, he is liable to be seized on every time he ventures from his secret haunt; and with the reward that has been offered for his apprehension, there is little doubt but we shall soon hear of his being captured."

"And yet you have yourself but just now suffered him to escape, when it would have been so easy to take him?" cried Sir Gaston, reproachfully.

"It was not quite so easy as you seem to imagine," answered the other. "My life was in his power, and would most surely have been sacrificed if it had not happened that he thought I might be useful in conveying his message to you."

"And, did he say anything about Lady Alicia?"

"He did."

"Does he know that she is my wife who has so long been reported dead?"

"That I know not," replied Bertrand; "but it seems that he charges you with having wronged him at some period of his life; and, if I may judge from his words, he is only waiting for the first favourable opportunity to retaliate the injury upon yourself."

"What does the villain mean by an injury?" exclaimed the Templar!— "I never knew him till within the last few months, and the only thing of which he has to complain is, that I confined him in one of my dungeons at a time when he had been declared an outlaw."

"It is not that he complains of," replied Bertrand, "for had it been so, he would not have made so great a secret of it.   He has, however, vowed revenge, and will surely carry it into effect, unless you consent to the terms he may think proper to propose."

" And those terms are, that I shall cease to prosecute my designs against those who have excited my anger?"

" So it appears," returned Bertrand ; " but, hard as it may be to submit, I think it would be advisable to do so, in order that he may be put off his guard till you have a chance of forming some certain plan for his destruction."

" Aye," exclaimed the Knight ; " such a design would be excellent, could I but depend on any one to aid me in its execution."

" Hah !" cried the retainer, " have I then forfeited the confidence you once bestowed on me ?"

" I have seen but too much reason to do so," returned Sir Gaston de Neville. " A few hours since I believed you faithful to your master's interests, and yet now you return home to tell me that Black Ivan has again escaped, though it was in your power to have taken him."

" It was not in my power," answered the other. " I have already told you I was taken by surprise, and that he disarmed me before I was able to defend myself against his unexpected assault."

" Had you been resolved to perform the service you undertook," replied the Knight, " you would have perished in an unequal combat, rather than return with the narrative of your own shameful defeat."

Mortified at the distrust which had thus been manifested, Bertrand le Noir could no longer restrain the fierceness of his anger and he was about to burst forth in a violent reply to the sarcasm of his master, when Edith ran into the room exclaiming,—

" Ah, Sir Gaston, there's a messenger from the king just arrived at the castle, with a body of archers at his heels, and he desires you to give him an immediate audience."

" Is it so !" cried the Knight, wondering what all this could mean;— " and, pray do you happen to know who the messenger is that has been selected to visit me on this important matter ?"

" I am not quite sure," replied Edith, " but I fancy it is Captain Hugh Tiptoft."

" And did he state the business he came on ?"

" Not to me, of course ; but if you wish to see the gentleman, I will show him in directly."

" I suppose there is no alternative," exclaimed Sir Gaston ; " so I will see him, lest the king should charge me with a want of courtesy towards his messenger."

" And shall I admit all the men that are with him ?" asked Edith.

" No ; they will remain in the court-yard till their captain again joins them," exclaimed the Knight. " You may return, Edith, to their officer, and say, that I am willing to see him, since he is the bearer of a message from my royal master. Bring him instantly, for I feel that the interview will be anything but a pleasant one, and, therefore, the sooner it is over the better."

Upon this command Edith left the room ; and Bertrand, once more approaching his master, asked, in a low tone, whether it would not be advisable to take the present opportunity to dispatch Hugh Tiptoft, who had so often proved himself an inveterate foe ?

" Nothing," he said, " would be more easy than to slay him in his present unprotected situation, and thus one enemy at least would be got rid of without much trouble or risk."

" The trouble," answered Sir Gaston, " would, I grant, not be much, but the risk would be far greater than I at present feel inclined to run.

The king would be sure to suspect that foul play had been practised, and though no proof might appear against me, yet should I bring myself under suspicion, and then my future life would be tainted with the foulest dishonour."

"You would rather endure his insolence, then," cried Bertrand, "than commission me to dispatch him with my dagger?"

"Why should I seek to take his life," demanded Sir Gaston de Neville, "knowing, as I well do, that it would certainly lead to my own destruction?"

"Not if the thing were well managed, Sir Knight."

"Manage it as thou may'st," replied Sir Gaston, "it is my command that no violence shall be offered to Hugh Tiptoft whilst he remains beneath my roof."

"But suppose his insolence should tempt me to strike," exclaimed the retainer, "am I to understand that your anger would follow the deed?"

"I can scarcely answer that question," replied Sir Gaston, with hesitation. "There are, certainly, bounds to patience, Bertrand, and, therefore, I will leave the matter so far in your hands. But, remember, should Hugh Tiptoft chance to fall, it must be your care to conceal the deed, and in the event of a discovery taking place, you must flee from England, so as to give me a fair pretence for charging you with having perpetrated the murder."

"I will do all that if there be need for it," replied Bertrand; "but, hist! I hear footsteps, and do you, therefore, prepare to meet your visitor with as much calmness as if there was no mischief in the wind."

Hugh Tiptoft now entered the room, and, after the usual salutations had passed, said:—

"I have been desired to visit you, Sir Knight, to know whether it is your intention to press this charge against the Hebrew Maiden, who has so unfortunately incurred your displeasure?"

"At present it is my intention to do so," answered Sir Gaston; "but as my determination is not irrevocable, I may, upon further consideration, be induced to let the affair drop for the present."

"By so doing," replied Hugh Tiptoft, "you will much please the king, who has taken an interest in the girl's welfare."

"Perhaps so," exclaimed the knight, "and yet I cannot imagine why his majesty should take so much interest in behalf of one who, he knows, has ever proved herself my determined enemy."

"That," answered the captain, "is a question about which I have no right to concern myself. You have heard the message I have been entrusted with, and it now only remains for me to say, that had you determined to prosecute this business further, it would have provoked the king to institute further enquiries into certain reports that have been spread against yourself, and which might have involved you in no little difficulty."

"That the king bears me no goodwill there is every reason to believe," exclaimed Sir Gaston; "but he has yet to learn that, though his subject, I am not yet a slave, and that in my own affairs I shall act as suits myself, without considering whether it pleases him or not."

"Perhaps you desire me to convey that message back to him?" cried Hugh Tiptoft.

"In that respect you will please yourself," answered the knight. "King Richard will not think worse of me than he does at present; and even if he does, it will make very little difference to one who cares neither for his favour nor his dislike."

"It is, then, as I suspected," exclaimed the officer, "you are an enemy of my royal master's, and a few more such words as those you have just uttered will compel me to arrest you on a charge of treasonable designs against your lawful sovereign."

"Nay, then, this shall prevent it," cried Bertrand le Noir, springing forward, with a drawn dagger in his hand, and making a blow that would have proved fatal, had not Hugh Tiptoft sprang aside at the moment, and caught the arm of the assassin.

"Villain!" he exclaimed, "you would have slain me, had I not been on my guard to prevent your treachery; but I am now aware of the evil designs of my enemies, and, with the assistance of my archers, who are below, I will convey both you and your master before the king, to answer for the foul deed you would have committed."

"Sir Gaston knows nothing about it," replied Bertrand le Noir; "the act was my own, and, if need be, I am prepared to answer for it."

"You shall do so," exclaimed Hugh Tiptoft, seizing the retainer in his grasp; but ere he could firmly lay hold of him, Bertrand, with a powerful effort, broke away, and rushed out of the room ere the other could sufficiently recover himself to pursue him. Seeing how vain it would be to follow the ruffian, Hugh Tiptoft turned his steps towards Sir Gaston de Neville, and said :—

"You have seen the murderous attempt that was made against me, and yet no attempt have you made to secure the villain; speak, therefore, and let me hear from your own lips whether I am to regard you in the light of a friend or an enemy?"

"That is a question which your own conscience may answer better than I can," replied the knight. "Remember, you came hither on an errand from the king, and yet would have seized me in my own castle for some few incautious words that chanced to fall from my lips."

"I should only have done my duty," answered Hugh Tiptoft; "and yet, for attempting that, your retainer would have slain me when unprepared for his attack."

"For which act of fidelity you can scarcely blame him," replied Sir Gaston de Neville. "The vassal is faithful to his master, and would have saved him when he believed there was danger."

"You uphold him, then, in his base conduct?"

"Nay, I do not say so," replied the knight; "and you heard his declaration, that I knew nothing of the attempt he so suddenly made. The act was his own, and I have no right to be further questioned about it."

"Why, then, since you do not applaud his conduct, was no effort made to secure him when he rushed from the room?"

"I am not bound to answer every impertinent question that may be put to me, nor will I do so, merely because you chance to be one of the king's officers."

"Perhaps, then," observed Hugh Tiptoft, "you may be more inclined to answer the questions of the king himself."

"It may be so," returned Sir Gaston, moodily; "though I can see no reason why King Richard should suspect that I had any share in this attempt against your life, since Bertrand le Noir has confessed that I had no knowledge of his intention."

"But I may still have my doubts," answered Tiptoft, "seeing that you offered me no assistance, and rather suffered his escape, than put forth a hand to arrest the flight of an intended assassin."

"And yet it is not to be much wondered at," exclaimed Sir Gaston, "when it comes to be considered that the man was provoked to make the attempt upon your life through hearing the threats you uttered against myself. Upon that consideration I certainly did not try to prevent his escape, nor would King Richard blame me if he knew all the circumstances of the case."

"It may be so," replied the officer, "so here the affair may drop for the present, on condition that you promise to surrender him up if any further notice should be taken of the business."

"I will not pledge myself to anything of the kind," answered Sir Gaston. "In fact, if the fellow has half the sense I give him credit for, he will have left the castle long before this time, in order that he may find safety in some place where the ingenuity of his enemies will never find him out."

"I see," exclaimed Hugh Tiptoft, "it is evident that you wish to shield him from the consequences of the crime he sought to commit."

"You may think of me as you please," replied the knight, "but your opinion will never make me betray the man who acted under an impulse, provoked by your own violence. He saw that you intended to betray me into the hands of the harpies of the law, for having uttered a hasty expression or two; and, knowing as I do, that he sought only to protect me from the threatened danger, I will still refuse to say aught that may throw him on the tender mercies of his enemies."

"We may have him yet," cried Hugh Tiptoft; "and if he does fall into my hands, I would have him beware of the consequences that will follow."

"It seems, then, that you thirst for his blood, instead of being thankful for the narrow escape you have had."

"I desire to see him punished for his perfidy," replied Hugh Tiptoft, "and am resolved to let no opportunity slip that may serve to effect my purpose. However, we will now return to the subject of my present visit. The king desires to know whether it is your intention to proceed any further in this affair against the Jewess; and, if I understand rightly, there is some chance, that, upon further reflection, you will abandon the prosecution against a harmless and unoffending girl."

"Upon one condition," replied Sir Gaston, "and, upon one only I will consent to let her escape unpunished."

"Aye, and what is that?"

"Simply that you promise to say nothing about what has passed here this day, and that no further proceedings shall be taken against Bertrand le Noir."

"How!" exclaimed Hugh Tiptoft; "would you prevail on me to suffer the escape of a man that has made an attempt upon my life?"

"Reflect a moment, and, perhaps, we may understand one another better," cried the knight: "you must not forget that you have just asked me not to press a similar charge against the Hebrew Maiden. She has made an attempt upon my life, and yet I am willing to overlook it on condition that you act with the same mercy towards my retainer."

"Well, there is some reason in what you have urged, and I will agree to it," replied Hugh Tiptoft; "you must, however, not fail to be at the court of the Chief Justiciary, to-morrow morning, in order to give your consent to the prisoner's discharge, and when that is done, I will not refuse to fulfil my part of the bargain."

"I will," exclaimed the knight.

"Then all is decided upon, and we will now part," replied the captain of the archers. "You must, however, be mindful of your promise, for, should any departure from it take place, I will not hesitate to declare all that has occurred since I have been in your castle."

With this, Hugh Tiptoft took his leave, and scarcely had he quitted the chamber, when Bertrand le Noir made his appearance from a secret door that opened behind the tapestry. His countenance betrayed considerable anxiety, and having carefully looked around to convince himself that no one else was present, he asked Sir Gaston what had taken place after his departure.

"Thou wilt be safe, I believe," he replied, "but thine own fool-hardiness had well nigh produced an effect that would have terminated in thine own death upon a gallows."

"Humph! I was aware of that," exclaimed Bertrand, "and it was the thought of that which made me retreat with so little ceremony after I had failed in my attempt."

"Why was thine arm so slow in the execution of its purpose?" demanded the knight, sullenly; "hadst thou used more despatch, the insolent slave would have met the fate he so justly merited."

"Nay, blame me not, good master," replied Bertrand le Noir, "for the fault was none of mine, I can assure you. The fellow's eye was too quick for me, and his hand was upraised in his own defence ere I could execute the purpose I had formed. And nearly had I suffered for it, too, for had he held me a little more firmly, the chances are, that I should have met the fate he intended."

"But, as it is, you are safe," exclaimed Sir Gaston, "for, at my request, he has promised that no further notice shall be taken of the affair."

"And how?" asked the vassal, "did you contrive to work so successfully upon his merciful consideration?"

"It was done without much difficulty," replied Sir Gaston. "The truth is, he came to know whether I intended to appear to-morrow against the Hebrew Maiden, and, as I saw there was an evident wish to shield her from the disgrace of a public trial, I offered to abandon my charge against her, on condition that nothing further was said about the attempt you had made against his life."

"And Hugh Tiptoft eagerly accepted the proposition?"

"He did; and since I have thus preserved you from the effects of your own intemperance, it is but fair that I should exact from you a promise to assist me in my designs upon those who have so long evaded my pursuit."

"You may depend on me, Sir Gaston," replied the retainer, "hitherto I have been faithful to you, and, rely on it, I will henceforth endeavour to prove my gratitude, for the services you have this day done me."

Upon this, the knight motioned for his vassal to follow him, and they proceeded together to another apartment in a distant part of the castle, where they could confer together upon the various topics, which, at that period, required their utmost serious consideration.

CHAPTER XCIII.

" A maiden never bold;
Of spirit so still and quiet, that her motion
Blushed at herself."

SHAKSPERE.

On the morning of the eventful day that had been appointed for the trial of the Hebrew Maiden, she arose at an early hour, and having offered up a prayer to Heaven for protection against the machinations of her enemies, became firmly confident that the result of the enquiry would prove favourable to her innocence. Much composed by the hope that now inspired her, she even longed for the moment of trial to arrive, and when her attendant, Lestelle, entered the room with her breakfast, she hailed her appearance with more than her usual animation. This was an unexpected

pleasure to the kind-hearted girl, and having arranged everything with her customary care and neatness, she inquired whether she felt able to go through the day's trial with fortitude and resignation.

"I do, indeed, dear Lestelle," answered our heroine; "for something assures me that I shall not be forsaken in the hour of my greatest need, and that the evil practices of my foes will either fall on themselves or else fail altogether."

"Well, I'm glad to find you so cheerful, at any rate," cried the attendant, "for, somehow, I thought to see you all tears and despair, and you cannot think how glad it makes me to see that you have strength of mind enough to meet the trial with firmness."

"It is because I have placed myself with confidence under the protection of heaven," cried Rebecca; "I have besought that aid of which I stand so greatly in need, and my heart assures me that my supplications have not been made in vain. The innocent have seldom occasion to tremble at the accusations of their foes, and I yet hope to thwart the evil designs of him who has sent me hither on a foul charge of attempting his life."

"Well, I don't wish to dishearten you," exclaimed Lestelle; "but we all know what a terrible fellow Sir Gaston de Neville is, and all I fear is, that he will so stick to the story he has told, that the judge will be forced to believe him whether he wishes it or not."

"That Sir Gaston will do so, I have very little doubt," answered Rebecca; "but the Chief Justiciary is an upright judge, and will not be led away because the prosecutor happens to be a great man, and the prisoner a humble Jewess. He will require proof ere he condemns me, and that Sir Gaston will be unable to produce."

"Be not too sanguine on that subject, dear lady," cried Lestelle, "for

No. 70

he is capable, I believe, of any crime, and will not hesitate to bring forward witnesses, who, at his command, would not mind perjuring themselves."

"Nay," exclaimed the Hebrew Maiden, "I am still confidant, notwithstanding the unfavourable opinion you have given."

"And if I have given it," replied Lestelle, "it was that you may not depend too much upon chances that may not be realized. It does not entirely depend upon the merciful disposition of the judge, but rather on the spirit of vengeance with which Sir Gaston seems to pursue you."

"It is not for myself that I care," exclaimed Rebecca, "but I know the misery that would be endured by my father and Reuben Grenard, in case I should be pronounced guilty of the charge, and, for their sake, I hope to escape the artful snares that have been laid for my destruction."

"Yet, as they are prepared for the worst, let us hope that the shock will not be so great as you anticipate," cried Lestelle.

"You, at any rate, seem to think I shall not escape scathless from this trial?" exclaimed Rebecca, with a vain attempt at cheerfulness.

"I have spoken my mind freely," answered Lestelle, "but, at the same time, I must acknowledge that your case is not without hope. The king is well known to be favourably inclined towards you, and, since his kindness may effect much, I think there may be a chance of your escaping the punishment so eagerly sought for by Sir Gaston de Neville. He, however, is not all-powerful in this case, and, consequently, if the charge should be made out against you, I fear the cruel nature of your prosecutor will prompt him to demand the full penalty of the law."

"Which would be death by torture."

"You have spoken truly, Rebecca," answered the other, "for it is decreed that any one belonging to the Jewish tribe who shall seek the death of a Christian, shall suffer the penalty of death by the most cruel tortures that can be inflicted."

Ere Rebecca could reply, the father of Lestelle entered the room, to announce that the hour of trial had nearly arrived, and that it would be necessary for them to take their departure shortly, in order that they might reach the court in time. The gaoler, however, spoke in a voice of commisseration, and seeing that the countenance of Rebecca turned deadly pale at the near approach of the hour of trial, he sought by every means in his power to inspire her with courage to sustain herself with fortitude.

"Do not," he said, "let your enemies see that you tremble to meet the foul charge that has been brought against you. They will exult in your terrors, and it is even possible that they may allude to it in support of the allegations they intend to produce."

"I will be firm," cried Rebecca, with more composure; "for if I trembled at the thought of the near approach of the moment of trial, it was not on my own account, but on that of those whose very existence may depend on the result of what will this day take place."

"You speak of your father and Reuben Grenard?"

"I do, maiden. Have either of them applied for permission to see me this morning?"

"Reuben Grenard has been here," answered the gaoler, "but only stayed a few moments, and then hastened back to your father."

"Alas!" sighed Rebecca, "does he, then, believe me guilty, that he failed to see me once more, ere I went forth to abide the issue of this day's trial?"

"He is more than ever confirmed in his opinion of your innocence."

"Why, then, did he go away without seeing me?"

"It was done out of consideration for you," replied the gaoler. "It seems he was fearful lest the interview should unnerve you, and that, consequently, you should appear before your judges as if with a soul borne down with a consciousness of guilt. In fact, it was at his request that I came to bid you be of good heart, since he feels convinced that those who have to decide upon your case, will act with fairness and impartiality, if you only remain sufficiently collected to answer whatever questions may be put to you."

"Was this, indeed, the opinion of Reuben Grenard?" cried the Hebrew Maiden.

"It was."

"Then I will endeavour to prove myself worthy of the kind esteem in which he still holds me," cried Rebecca, with re-kindled hope. "Yes, my friends, in spite of the difficulties with which I am beset, I will maintain my firmness to the last, and should it be my fate to perish through the evil machinations of my enemies, they shall, at least, see that I can die with fortitude and resignation."

"Let us hope it will not come to that," exclaimed the gaoler; "for my own part, I always look at the fairest side of the picture, and I see no reason to do otherwise in the present instance."

"I am glad to hear you say that, dear father," cried Lestelle, "for somehow or other, my own confidence began to give way, and I almost feared that this parting between Rebecca and myself would be for ever."

"Will you not, then, accompany me to the court of justice?" asked our heroine.

"I will, if it is your wish."

"It is my most earnest wish," exclaimed Rebecca. "Unless you are there I may be left without one friend to support me in the midst of my afflictions."

"Aye, aye, daughter," exclaimed the gaoler, "go with her, and see if you cannot assist in keeping up her spirits in the midst of the troubles she will be surrounded by. She will much need a friend, I am thinking; and, since you seem to regard her with so much affection, be as a sister to her, and I will love you all the better for it hereafter."

"A thousand thanks for your generous sympathy in behalf of one who thus greatly needs the kindness you have been pleased to bestow upon her," cried Rebecca. "Till now, I have rarely seen Christian charity extended towards the unfortunate of my faith; but, rely on it, should I escape this day's perils, I will never forget the kindness with which I have been treated by those into whose hands I have thus fallen."

"Why, the truth is," exclaimed the gaoler, "there are very few, I'm sorry to say, that have much compassion on people of your faith, if they happen to get into difficulties. I, however, could never see why one person's opinion should be better than another's, provided both endeavour to do what's right, and whether my prisoners are Jews or Gentiles, I shall always continue to treat them with as much kindness as possible, whilst they remain under my care. In this case, however, it is a helpless female that demands my pity, and do you think I could look upon my own daughter without hoping that she might find a friend, in case it should ever be her misfortune to get into such a dilemma as you have?"

"Again?" cried Rebecca, "must I pour forth my grateful thanks to you for ——"

"Nay, I want no thanks for only doing as I would be done by," exclaimed the gaoler; "so come, my lass, cheer up, for it is now time that we think of starting for the court where the trial is to take place."

"Is it far from hence?" asked Rebecca.

"Scarcely a stone's throw."

"Yet, even that," cried the maiden, "is too far to pass through the throng of idlers that will be assembled to gaze upon me."

"Nay, I have provided against that, by ordering a covered litter for your conveyance," answered the gaoler. "So now, if you are quite prepared, I am ready to attend you to the place of trial."

Again thanking him for the kind consideration he had exercised in her behalf, Rebecca now descended to the lower part of the prison, and having been assisted into the litter by the gaoler, she was accompanied by him and his daughter the short distance they had to go. At the door of the court-house she alighted, and was immediately conducted to the chamber of justice, where a crowd of persons had already assembled, in the expectation of hearing the long talked-of trial. It was some time, however, before Rebecca could raise her eyes to look around her, but when she, at length, summoned resolution to do so, she saw that Sir Gaston was not yet present, and the circumstance afforded her some slight hope that he might have relented the severity with which he had acted towards her. Lestelle, who had taken a place just behind her, now ventured to whisper an exhortation to maintain her firmness, and scarcely had she done this, when a bustle was heard in the court, and the Chief Justiciary advancing the next moment, took the raised seat exactly facing the prisoner. A death-like silence now prevailed for some few seconds, but this was at length broken by the judge, who inquired whether the prosecutor was present to substantiate the charge he had brought against the prisoner. This question was replied to in the affirmative, and the heart of Rebecca sunk with apprehension, as she perceived Sir Gaston de Neville enter from an open door, and proceed to the place appointed for witnesses. A low murmuring of many voices succeeded, and then came the dead silence that lasted until the Justiciary, addressing himself to the prosecutor, said:—

"It has been stated to the king, Sir Gaston de Neville, that you have certain charges to make against a young Jewess now at the bar; and his majesty, anxious at all times to do justice between his subjects, has appointed this time and place for the hearing. How say you, Sir Gaston?—do you still maintain that the girl hath sought to take away your life?"

The knight tried to speak, but failing in the effort, bowed his head in token of acquiescence. Then the Justiciary, turning towards Rebecca, said:—

"You are aware, I believe, of the heinous crime that has been alleged against you. The charge has been made by an honourable knight, and he is here to prove it, but, ere he does so, it is my duty to ask whether you confess the crime?"

"I do not," replied the maiden firmly.

"In that case," exclaimed the Chief Justiciary, addressing himself to Sir Gaston, "it only remains for you to state your charge to the court."

The knight, upon this, advanced a few paces, and was about to commence, when Meg of Finchley, forcing her way through the crowd, whispered in his ear a terrible denunciation, in case he violated the promise he had made her. At her voice, the countenance of the knight grew deadly pale, and turning away his eyes in another direction, he beheld Hugh Tiptoft, gazing menacingly upon him, as if threatening him with instant exposure, unless he forbore to carry the case any further. Utterly confounded at this, Sir Gaston trembled violently, and, instead of proceeding with his statement, he became so terribly agitated as to attract the attention of the whole assemblage. Even the Justiciary observed it, and, addressing himself to the prosecutor, desired him to proceed without any further delay.

"I must crave your permission for a few moments' consideration," replied Sir Gaston, in a faltering voice.

"How!" cried the judge, "have you not come prepared with your evidence against the prisoner?"

"I did," replied the knight; "but circumstances have since occurred to shake my belief in the girl's guilt."

"Indeed!—then, in that case, it will be my duty to discharge her from custody."

"Let me consider for a brief space," answered Sir Gaston, "for it is not impossible that I may yet proceed in the charge I have brought against her."

"If I may be permitted to have a voice in this affair," exclaimed Hugh Tiptoft, "I would say that the prosecution ought either to go on without delay, or the prisoner be acquitted for want of evidence."

"And why," asked the knight, "are you so anxious to hurry over an affair of this weight?"

"I wish not to hurry it," answered Hugh Tiptoft, "but I would be glad to know whether it is your intention to proceed further in this affair?"

"The business of the court must not be interrupted," exclaimed the judge, addressing himself to the captain of the Archers; "you, however, may have important evidence to give, and, in that case, I am now ready to hear you."

"How say you, Sir Gaston de Neville," demanded Hugh Tiptoft; "I have received permission to make my statement, and, therefore, it only remains for you to say whether I shall now proceed?"

"There is no occasion for it," stammered the confused knight; "I am inclined to have pity on the prisoner, and shall, therefore, proceed no further in this affair."

"I am rejoiced to hear it," replied the Justiciary, "but, since the charge has been publicly made, you must as publicly state your present belief that she is guiltless of the crimes for which she has been placed before me."

"And what," demanded Sir Gaston, "if I refuse to state my belief in her innocence?"

"In that case, the trial must proceed," observed the Chief Justiciary.

"And, in that case," exclaimed Hugh Tiptoft," I will now state what I know upon this subject."

"There will be no occasion for it," cried the alarmed knight, "for, since it appears to be necessary, I will declare that my suspicions against her were unfounded."

"In that case the prisoner is discharged without the slightest blemish on her character," exclaimed the Chief Justiciary.

A loud cry of joy now bust from the lips of Rebecca, and overpowered by her feelings, she would have sank upon the floor of the court, had not her father and Reuben Grenard, who, till that moment, had remained concealed, rushed forward and caught her in their arms. For some few minutes the maiden continued in a state of insensibility, but, at length recovering from her torpor, and perceiving that the court was yet crowded with spectators, the remembrance of her escape flashed upon her mind, and throwing her arms round the neck of her father, she gave free vent to the fullness of her joy.

"Aye, my child," cried the aged Israelite, thou art free, and I can again press thee in my arms, and without the foul taint that did of late environ thee.

"Who is this old man?" demanded the Chief Justiciary, surprised at the scene he witnessed.

"This girl's father," replied Isaac, proudly.

"Then do I congratulate you on the result of this day's business," exclaimed the judge; "your daughter is now at liberty to depart with you, and, for the future, you will have no cause to fear the enmity of your foes."

"I would that your words may prove true," cried the old man; "but, alas! I fear she will no sooner be at liberty, than the malice of our enemies will again be at work to complete the destruction that has for the present been foiled."

"There may be some present," exclaimed the Chief Justiciary, "upon whom my words may not be thrown away, and I caution them against any further violence, such as that which has been practised. From circumstances that have come out, it is pretty evident that the vilest motives have urged certain persons to acts of tyranny that had well nigh brought destruction upon an innocent maiden. These have, fortunately, been frustrated, and, from henceforth, I would caution these secret workers of mischief, that their actions will be watched with a jealous eye."

Sir Gaston de Neville knew well enough that these words were chiefly addressed to himself, and he would have burst forth into violent invectives against the person who had uttered them, had he not been well aware that by doing so, he would seriously injure himself. Writhing, therefore, under the reproof he had met with, he suppressed his indignation as well as he could, and subduing his voice so as to speak with apparent calmness, he said :—

"I know, my lord, that your words were chiefly addressed to myself, but conscious as I am, of not deserving them, their force is entirely lost on me. That I have charged this Jewish girl with a crime it is true, and equally true is it that I firmly believed she intended to take away my life. You have, however, since heard me declare, that I may have been in error; the prisoner has had the benefit of that declaration, and, therefore, it is time all further allusion to the subject should drop."

"Wilt thou promise never to persecute her again?" cried Isaac of Tadcaster, earnestly.

"Why should I promise anything of the kind?" demanded the knight, sullenly.

"That I may pass the remainder of my days in peace," answered the old man; "for months since, I have been constantly on the rack, lest my daughter should fall beneath their accursed arts, and now that she has been declared innocent of the crime she was charged with, I would know from your own lips, that, from henceforth, whether she will be suffered to pass her days in security and peace."

"Why dost thou fear me, old man?" asked Sir Gaston.

"Because thou hast ever been our enemy," answered the Israelite.

"I have never been so," exclaimed Sir Gaston; "it is true, I loved your daughter, and sought, by every means I could think of, to prevail upon her to look upon me with kindness. She, however, treated me with scorn, and then I sought, by other means, to obtain possession of the prize I covetted."

"Yet seeing that she loathed thine offers, why didst thou still resolve to persecute her with thy addresses?"

"Love is not to be so easily subdued as you imagine, old man," exclaimed Sir Gaston; "besides, she might have regarded it as an honour to be distinguished as she was by a Christian knight; nor did I expect to draw down your indignation for merely loving your daughter better than all the other maidens I have ever seen."

"Had thy love been honourable, thou mightest well have boasted of it," replied Isaac.

"Was it to have been expected then, that I would wed a girl belonging to thine accursed tribe?"

"Aye, it is well for thee to reproach us for the faith in which we were born," exclaimed the Israelite; "thou dost look upon us with contempt, and yet because a daughter of our tribe is fair, thou wouldst seek to win her by thy vile arts, and tear her from those who, knowing thy many crimes, have sought, by every means in thy power, to avert the danger with which she was threatened."

"Hadst thou not been so obstinate," returned Sir Gaston, "the persecution of which you complain, would never have taken place; I was, however, determined not to be thwarted, and hence the proceedings that have since taken place."

"If I may judge from thy words," cried Isaac, "thou hast not yet done with a pursuit that thou knowest is vain."

"I shall not afford thee any information on that subject," returned the knight, haughtily; "I will, however, tell thee, that if she will consent to the terms I have already proposed, I will——"

"Let me hear no more!" interrupted the old man, in a voice of indignation; "thou hast heaped injury upon injury on me, and now wouldst surpass all thy former crimes by making a base proposition to a father at which his soul revolts. Shame on thee for a false and reckless knight, and never again dare to make thine appearance before one whose tongue can scarcely forbear cursing thee for thy many crimes."

"Accuse him not, I entreat you, dear father," cried Rebecca, trembling with apprehension; "you know the vindictive nature of the knight, and, if he is provoked, we shall again have to endure those persecutions from which we have, for the present, escaped."

Urged by the supplicating accents in which these words were uttered, the old man bowed to the Chief Justiciary, and assisted by Reuben Grenard, led our heroine from the court. Sir Gaston watched their departure with a fury that he could scarcely restrain, and when they were no longer in view, he hurriedly left the place by another door, and pursued his way without knowing or caring whither he went.

CHAPTER XCIV.

> "Let him do his spite;
> My services, which I have done the seigniory,
> Shall out-tongue his complaints."
>
> SHAKSPERE.

It was some days after the trial and acquittal of Rebecca, that Sir Gaston de Neville received a message from Prince John, informing him that a meeting of the conspirators was to take place that evening, and requiring his presence for concerting a plan for the immediate overthrow of the present sovereign. This intimation had been expected for some time, for Sir Gaston knew that the traitorous design was intended to be carried into effect on the morning of the king's coronation, two days hence, and that it only required the arrangement of a few preliminaries to make sure of the daring plan that had for so long a period occupied their thoughts.

He was, therefore, fully prepared for the message he had received, and, enraged as he was at the disarrangement of all his previous schemes, he was well pleased at the near prospect that presented itself of revenging himself upon the person of the king for the disappointment he had been compelled to endure. No sooner, therefore, had the prince's message been delivered than he sent for Bertrand, his usual confidant on such occasions, to whom he speedily revealed all that had taken place, and the steps that were immediately to be taken for the deposing of one sovereign, and the placing of another upon the throne. Bertrand, daring as he was, listened with astonishment to the words of his master; but, having subdued his feelings a little, he at length enquired to whom the chief part of the design was to be given.

"That," replied Sir Gaston, "is not yet exactly decided upon. At present, I know not whether it is intended to take away the life of the king; but should such a step be rendered necessary, I believe there would be no great difficulty in finding a man firm and desperate enough to earn a noble reward by striking King Richard to the heart."

"Aye, I know who you mean," replied Bertrand; "I have ever been your scape-goat, and, I suppose, if any hazard is to be run, you will confirm on me the high honour of being the murderer of Richard Cœur de Lion?"

"Wilt thou refuse the task should it be the command of Prince John?" demanded the knight.

"Let Prince John take the danger on himself," exclaimed the other, sullenly.

"Come, come, Bertrand," retorted the knight, soothingly, "we must understand each other better, I see. Remember this is no common task you are called upon to execute; and if the deed is well done, John will be King of England, and, of course, your own path will be open to the highest honour a grateful sovereign can bestow."

"But it seldom happens," replied Bertrand, "that great people remember the favours they have received from their inferiors. Prince John, I dare say, would be glad enough to reach the throne by my assistance; but if I should chance to be seized on after perpetrating the murder of his brother, he would suffer the law to take its course, and I should thus be allowed to perish for the very act that had made him a king."

"And why," asked Sir Gaston, "do you think thus ungenerously of his highness?"

"Because I know that he would be compelled to punish the assassin in the event of his being discovered," replied the ruffian. "Were he to show me any mercy, the people would at once suspect him of being the instigator of the crime, and in his defence he would sacrifice me."

"You wrong him, Bertrand," exclaimed the knight; "believe me, you wrong him most foully; besides, he would be afraid of suffering you to perish, lest, in revenge, you should reveal the secret, which would be sure to publish his own share in the transaction."

"Why, there may be some truth in that, to be sure," answered Bertrand. "The prince would have a bad conscience against him, and he certainly might connive at my escape in order to save himself."

"In that case there can be no reason why you should hesitate to assist in an affair upon which so much depends."

"Why, I think there is a great deal of reason why I should take a little care of myself," exclaimed Bertrand le Noir. "It is true I might chance to escape with my life, but I should be compelled to pass the remainder of my days in banishment, and that's no very pleasant reflection for a man that has no wish to leave his own country?"

"You refuse, then, to take any part in this affair?" cried Sir Gaston de Neville.

"Why, it must be confessed I don't much like it," replied the retainer; "but as my refusal will be sure to draw down upon me your indignation, I suppose there is no alternative but to risk my life at your desire."

"You have decided well," exclaimed Sir Gaston; "and be assured that by so doing you will make me your firm and constant friend."

"Aye," replied the retainer; "but in case the mob should chance to fall on me after my attack upon the king, I should have little need of your favour or protection."

"Hah!" exclaimed Sir Gaston, "do you again waver?"

"No," replied the other, "I am not wavering; but when a man's life is placed in jeopardy, it's high time for him to look about. I have said that I will execute your commands; and, be the consequences what they may, I will keep my word."

"And you will find that I am not forgetful of mine," answered Sir Gaston. "Besides, in case Prince John should ascend the throne, I shall be high in his confidence and esteem, and, depend on it, I will not fail to obtain for you such a reward as your services deserve."

"Humph!" ejaculated Bertand, "and, perhaps, that may be a rope."

"Nay, you wrong me," answered the knight; "the reward I mean shall be an honourable one; you shall have a title of distinction, and your own lips shall name the sum that shall repay your services."

"The title," replied Bertrand le Noir, "would be of no value to me, and, therefore, I shall leave it to be bestowed upon some one more ambitious than myself; the gold, however, is a different affair, and you must not be surprised if my demand appears rather exorbitant."

"Whatever it may be it shall be given with an ungrudging hand," exclaimed Sir Gaston; "and now, having concluded this affair, tell me, I prithee, what you have done with respect to the fugitives you have been in search of?"

"At present, I have done little good," replied Bertrand. "In spite of
No. 71

all the pains I have taken, no clue can be obtained of the Lady Alicia; but from the information I got this morning from a man whom chance threw in my way, I have pretty well satisfied myself that Adrian has again sought shelter in the palace of King Richard."

" Indeed!" exclaimed Sir Gaston, with a grim look of exultation, " then the place will not remain a safe refuge for him much longer. The king will most assuredly fall, and then Adrian will once more be thrown into my power."

" And if he should," observed Bertrand, significantly, " of course you will take care to prevent his doing any more mischief?"

" I will," exclaimed Sir Gaston; for a long while I have endured his insolent interference in my affairs without punishing him as he deserves. Now, however, I can no longer regard him with favour, and your suggestions, therefore, shall be strictly acted on."

" Or, in plain language," returned Bertrand, " I may quietly dispatch him without risking your displeasure?"

" You may," answered the knight, hoarsely; " nay, should you chance, to meet him, let the youth meet his doom, without consulting me further upon the subject."

" Oh, you need give yourself any trouble about that now that I have your permission," replied Bertrand. " I owe the young fellow a grudge, and depend on it, you shall no more be troubled by him."

" 'Tis well," exclaimed Sir Gaston; " and yet, when I come to reflect, I almost wish it were possible to spare his life."

" Then the best way is not to reflect about it," cried the ruffian, bluntly; " these matters don't bear consideration, and, therefore, the less you think about it the better."

" But do you think there is also a probability of finding the retreat of Lady Alicia?" asked Sir Gaston. " She is now at liberty, and there is too much reason to fear that she will publish the history of her long imprisonment in this castle."

" Aye," replied Bertrand, " that's rather an awkward affair, to be sure, but a little caution may yet preserve you from the consequences of her escape. I will continue to keep a sharp look out for her, and if we should chance to meet, I will give you such an account of my proceedings as shall prevent your having any more to fear on her account."

" But she must not be murdered!" exclaimed the knight, in a tone that betrayed the greatest agitation.

" And why not?"

" Because it is my command," returned the other, fiercely.

" Oh, well, I am of course bound to obey you," replied Bertrand, " and yet I can't help saying that your pity is strangely misapplied in this instance."

" I would have no more blood to answer for," cried Sir Gaston, tremulously.

" And yet you have just now given me permission to make away with the page."

" True;" but he shall be my last victim," exclaimed the knight. " The life of Lady Alicia must be spared, but it shall be on condition that she either becomes your wife, or ends her days in hopeless imprisonment."

" In my opinion, then, she will prefer the latter alternative," observed Bertrand; " her ladyship appears not to hold me in much esteem, and it will require more force than persuasion to make her become the wife of your vassal."

" Perhaps," exclaimed Sir Gaston, " she will think differently when she finds that liberty will depend on her submission."

" I have no expectation of her yielding quite so easily as you seem to imagine," answered the retainer.

" And why do you think so?"

" Because she has contrived to escape two or three times already," replied Bertrand; " in spite of all the care that has been taken to keep her safely, she has managed to elude our vigilance, and for my own part, I can see no reason why she should not be able to outwit us again."

" But," observed the knight, " she will no longer have Adrian to aid her in any plot."

" No; but there is Black Ivan, who most unaccountably finds his way into the castle," replied the other. " He is a foe not to be despised; and so long as he lives there will be no certainty of keeping Lady Alicia in safety."

" Then why have you quietly suffered him to be so long at liberty?" demanded Sir Gaston, reproachfully. " It has been in your power more than once to make him my prisoner, and yet he is still at large to set me openly at defiance."

" And it is no fault of mine if it is so," answered the other, " for the truth is, the fellow is as cunning as the devil himself, and he contrives to slip through one's fingers just at the very moment when we think he is most secure."

" Thus far he has done so," exclaimed Sir Gaston, fiercely, " but a period to his insolence now draws fast to a close. Hitherto, no active steps have been taken to hunt him into our toils, but when Prince John comes to the throne, measures will be concerted that all his cunning shall not be able to save him from."

At this period the door was opened, and several retainers appeared, bearing, between them, a litter, which they placed in the middle of the chamber, and removing a cloth with which the whole had been carefully covered over, they exhibited the gory corpse of Roland le Mark, whose countenance was fixed in the stern rigidity of death. Sir Gaston started with horror at the sight that was thus presented to his view, and, in a voice almost choked with mingled surprise and rage, he demanded an explanation of the mystery.

" It is not much that we can tell you," answered one of the men; " but as we were lately passing through Hornsey Wood, our attention was attracted by groans of agony, and making our way towards the spot, we discovered Roland le Mark lying on the ground in the last agonies of death."

" Was he speechless?" demanded Sir Gaston.

" Not quite; but it was with great difficulty that we were able to make out what he appeared to be most anxious to explain."

" Did he say how he met with his death-wound?"

" He told us," replied the man, " that he had not long before encountered Black Ivan near the spot where we had found him; that he endeavoured to make him his prisoner; but that in the combat which ensued he had been mortally wounded by his adversary."

" It is as I suspected," exclaimed Sir Gaston, bitterly. " This is another of Black Ivan's acts, and it shall be his last, or I will myself perish in avenging this bloody deed."

There will be no occasion for you to risk your own life," answered Bertrand le Noir, " for we who are your faithful vassals will go forth in quest of the Outlaw, and never will we return till the villain has paid the penalty of his crimes."

" How am I to trust you?" demanded the knight, reproachfully; " ere now, you have promised me the same thing, and yet Black Ivan loves to heap fresh injuries upon me."

"That is no fault of mine," answered Bertrand; "I would have slain him ere now, but your commands were, that I should spare his life, and thus many opportunities have passed by when he might easily have been despatched."

"Let that be no longer an excuse," cried Sir Gaston; "the villain has now slain one of the most faithful among my retainers and nothing but his blood will ever satisfy me for the cruel deed. Remember, fellow, Black Ivan is to die, and he who brings me his head, shall receive a thousand crowns for his reward."

"It shall be done," growled Bertrand.

"How shall I be assured of it?"

"We swear it!" exclaimed Bertrand le Noir, and kneeling with the other retainers round the corse of Roland, they crossed their swords, and pronounced a solemn vow to accomplish the deed they had undertaken. This done, they rose, and were about to quit the presence of the knight, when Bertrand was commanded to remain, that he might receive a few more instructions ere he departed on his sanguinary errand. They were thus left alone together, yet it was some time before Sir Gaston could sufficiently collect his scattered thoughts to declare his further pleasure. At length, however, drawing near to Bertrand, he said :—

"You see how I am foiled by an accursed fate in every action of my life. Even now, Ivan has again triumphed over me, and yet I see no chance of bringing him beneath my vengeance."

"Why haven't we just sworn to slay him ?" demanded the other, with surprise.

"You have; but what dependence can I place in men who, for aught I know, may be purchased with the ruffian's gold. Ivan is reported to possess immense wealth, and he will be profuse in his promises of reward to all those who forget their fealty to me."

"And do you believe," cried Bertrand, "that there is a man in your service who would accept the gold of another to become a traitor to the master they have vowed faithfully to serve even with their lives ?"

"I have no confidence in any man," answered the knight.

"In that case you had better release us from our obligations and take others into your employ who may be more faithful."

"And those others," exclaimed Sir Gaston, "are as little to be relied on as yourselves. No, it is my fate to be disappointed at every turn, and for this once I will place my confidence in you; but remember, Bertrand, I shall watch you with a jealous eye, and should there be any want of zeal displayed, my fury shall fall upon you with such terrible certainty as to prevent my being deceived in future."

"Why is this warning to be addressed to me alone ?" asked Bertrand le Noir.

"Because I would have you caution all those who are engaged with you in this baseness," answered Sir Gaston; "besides, I have not been well pleased of late with your conduct, and doubting lest you should desert me after all your professions of good faith, I would warn you of the retribution which will be sure to follow in case my suspicions should prove correct."

"And so," exclaimed the retainer, "if we should chance to fail in this business, we are to be looked upon as traitors to our master's interest, and punished for it as if we were no better than dogs."

"Hah! dost thou dare to murmur, slave !"

"I dare remonstrate, when I hear myself unjustly suspected of perfidy," answered Bertrand.

"Prove that my suspicions are unjust and I will freely acknowlege myself in fault."

"And how," asked Bertrand, "am I to prove that to your satisfaction ?"

"By faithfully performing all that you have just now sworn to accomplish."

"You mean that we must either slay Black Ivan or bring upon ourselves your eternal wrath ?"

"Aye," replied Sir Gaston, "you have sworn to accomplish his death, and, therefore, I have a right to expect that you will not fail in my promise."

"There is little chance that we shall," answered Bertrand, "seeing that the reward you have promised is sufficient to secure the zeal of all who are engaged."

"I will take your word for it, in the hope that my confidence will not be abused," replied Sir Gaston.

"In that case you may rely on being rid of at least one of your enemies ere many hours have passed away."

"And yet we must not be too precipitate either," cried the knight; and, anxious as I am to revenge the death of Roland le Mark, yet his murderer must remain unpunished till the plot against the king has been brought to a conclusion. When that is done, we shall have an opportunity for completing the vengeance my heart so eagerly pants for."

"And the delay you have proposed may be the cause of entirely marring our plans."

"It will not be for any long time," answered Sir Gaston. "To-night, I shall know the exact plan that is to be adopted in our designs against the king; and when Prince John is safely placed upon the throne of England, we will turn our immediate attention towards the plans we have formed for the destruction of Black Ivan."

"Then I am to tell my comrades that they are to do nothing till they receive your further orders ?"

"Tell them to go forth in different directions and search after the Outlaw," replied Sir Gaston; "they may, perhaps, be able to meet with him, and, in that case, all further trouble may be avoided."

"Humph!" ejaculated Bertrand; "and so I am to lose all chance of getting the reward you have offered to the man that slays Black Ivan !"

"In the event of his being slain whilst you are engaged in my affairs, I will bestow upon you a sum of money to prevent disappointment," answered the knight. "You will, therefore, go and tell your comrades to lose no time, but to hasten forth without delay, and to continue their search until they have fully accomplished the business for which they leave the castle."

Dissatisfied at the arrangements which had been made, Bertrand le Noir hurried from the room; and Sir Gaston, glancing uneasily towards the corpse, which was still lying upon its bier in the midst of the chamber, shortly afterwards hurried away, to keep his appointment with Prince John and the other conspirators.

CHAPTER XCV.

" Let me see now
To get his place, and to plume up my will
In double knavery."
OTHELLO.

AT the hour that had been previously arranged the conspirators assembled together at the palace of the prince, and the utmost secresy was observed as they entered, lest the meeting together of so many persons should arouse the suspicions of those who might guess that mischief was afloat. As they gained the interior of the palace, they glided, like guilty traitors as they were, towards an apartment at the further end of the building, and where their consultation was likely to be carried on without fear of interruption. Each, as he entered the chamber, was warmly greeted by those who had already arrived, and, at length, all had assembled except Sir Gaston de Neville and the Bishop of Durham. The non-appearance of these two occasioned some surprise; but their apprehensions were soon quieted by Prince John, who at once explained the reason of their not being present.

"As for Sir Gaston de Neville," he said, "there is little doubt but he will speedily arrive. That he is warmly interested in our cause we all know; and, feeling as he does, a violent antipathy against King Richard, we cannot suspect him of repenting the share he has hitherto taken in our cause. The Bishop of Durham, however, is no longer to be depended on, for the proud churchman has an idea that we shall not succeed in our plans, and within the last hour I have received a message from him, declining all further share in the business that at present occupies our attention."

"If he is not a friend," exclaimed the Earl of Chester, "we must, perhaps, henceforth, rank him among our enemies."

"We have nothing to fear from him, my lord," answered Prince John; "for though he no longer acts with us, yet for his own sake he will be careful how he says anything that may prove him to have been an enemy of the king. The bishop is at the head of a wealthy diocese; and so well does he love the riches that are placed at his disposal, that there is little fear he will ever risk the royal favour by an acknowledgment that he has been guilty of encouraging treason."

"But," observed Sir Walter Marsham, "should Fortune favour us so far as to raise your highness to the throne of England, the bishop will stand a fair chance of holding his high office much longer."

"That will be a matter for after consideration," replied Prince John;— "the Bishop of Durham is a crafty schemer, and, perhaps, may be of more service than you seem to imagine. It matters not to him, I believe, what king happens to reign so that he can but remain in possession of his princely revenues; and should I treat him with favour, it will be the means of securing a powerful and influential adherent."

"But, on the other hand," exclaimed Lord Scroope, "his crafty nature may lead him to become an enemy, whose artifices will not easily be seen through. I have watched this haughty priest for a long time past; and though he had joined our party, I always distrusted him as one who would by and by bring destruction on our cause."

"He must be narrowly watched," observed the Earl of Chester; "and the moment we have good reason to believe that he is plotting against us, he must be put out of the way."

"My lord," cried Prince John, "would you commit murder on one of the sons of the church?"

"Aye, my liege, if we have reason to be satisfied that he intends to bring destruction on us."

"At present, he has given us no cause to suspect him," replied the prince; "to be sure he has deserted from our party, but I wish no man to act under compulsion, and his grace has most certainly a right to take which side he may think proper."

"That I am ready to grant," answered the Earl of Chester; "but should your highness fortunately succeed in this business, I would be among the first to counsel you to dismiss him from the high office he at present holds."

"Aye," exclaimed Sir Walter Marsham; "the Tower of London is a strong building, and sufficiently large even for the ambition of my Bishop of Durham."

"Your hint may not be thrown away," replied Prince John, with a meaning glance towards the last speaker. "At first, however, I will try what kindness and flattery will do for us; and should I find they are likely to be of no service, I may then be induced to see the effects of a little wholesome chastisement; the example may not be thrown away upon other churchmen, and thus I shall secure in my own interest a body of men who will have it in their power to do much towards securing the throne that is now the object of my ambition."

"A most excellent plan, truly," exclaimed the Earl of Chester; "but where, I wonder, is Sir Gaston de Neville all this time? He was to have been here half an hour since, and his absence at such an important moment gives rise to a suspicion that he may have followed the example of my Lord Bishop of Durham."

"My life on it you wrong him," cried Prince John; "nay, there is not a warmer or more zealous friend to our cause than Sir Gaston de Neville, and he who would whisper a word to his disadvantage belies him most foully."

"And yet," muttered the Earl of Chester, "princes are as liable to be mistaken in their opinions as are those of lower degree."

"Ha!" cried John, sternly; "hast thou any reason for these suspicions against Sir Gaston de Neville?"

"I have," answered the earl; "he has been treacherous towards King Richard and may be the same to thee."

"Why so hast thou, for that matter," retorted Prince John, "yet never have I suspected thine intentions."

"Thou hast had no reason to do so," replied the earl, "for I am here to my appointment, and, therefore, I can see no reason for thy suspicions."

"And so is Sir Gaston de Neville here to his appointment," cried Prince John, as the door flew open, and the Knight Templar presented himself before the assembled company. "We greet you well, Sir Knight," he continued, addressing himself to the last comer; "for though somewhat late in meeting your friends, there is yet sufficient room for any advice you may think fit to offer."

"Your highness honours me," replied Sir Gaston, with affected humility.

"Not more than your great zeal in our cause deserves," replied the prince. "I have long had reason to know that you were among those upon whom I can place the greatest reliance. Your detestation of my brother's rule fills me with confidence, and therefore do I chiefly rely on you in our present emergency."

"In that case," exclaimed the Earl of Chester, haughtily, "there can be little occasion for any of us that are now present to risk ourselves further in the cause of your highness."

"What!" cried the prince, "am I to be deserted by all because I respect the advice of Sir Gaston de Neville?"

"If his advice is better than our own, take it, and dismiss us without further ceremony," exclaimed the indignant earl; "for my own part I feel no anger at the preference shewn to Sir Gaston, but never will I consent to act under the commands of a man who I consider in every respect my inferior."

" Perhaps," whispered the Knight Templar, " your lordship would like to step into the court-yard, where we may have an opportunity of trying whether I am inferior to you in the art of swordsmanship ?"

" Another time I may favour you in the way you have proposed," answered the Earl of Chester, in the same low tone. " At present, however, we are engaged in the service of the prince, and our suddenly retiring would only cause them to follow us, and then our intentions would be defeated."

" Your lordship has found an admirable excuse, truly," muttered Sir Gaston.

" Hah !" vociferated the earl ; " dost thou doubt that my courage is not equal to thy own ?"

In an instant both their weapons were drawn, and three or four furious passes were made, when Prince John, rushing between them, struck up their glittering blades with his own sword, and in a voice of thunder commanded them to desist."

" Are ye both mad !" he exclaimed, as the two foes retreated a pace or two in obedience to his commands, " or would you by this ill-timed broil endanger the cause you have both promised to engage in ?"

" I did but seek to prove to his lordship," answered Sir Gaston, " that I am at least his equal in the use of the sword."

" And I," added the Earl of Chester, " was only going to prove that my courage was no more to be doubted than his own."

" You are both too warm," exclaimed Prince John ; " if there is a quarrel between you, this is no place to settle it in ; nor, indeed, should you now give way to those heats of passion when there is business in hand that requires so much caution."

" Your highness," answered Sir Gaston, " I acknowledge my fault, and crave pardon for it ; " I was, however, urged to it by my Lord of Chester, who, ere now, has taken other opportunities to insult me, by throwing out slurs that no man of honour can endure."

" Indeed !" exclaimed the earl ; " then be assured it will not be long before I again excite your anger in a similar manner."

" Forbear, my lord," interposed Prince John, " and remember that our cause may be deeply injured by this ill-timed quarrel."

" Will your highness inform us," demanded Chester, " how this hot blood is to be cooled ?"

" Aye, by shaking hands, and forgetting henceforth that any angry words have passed between you," replied the prince, " Come, my lord, and you, too, Sir Gaston de Neville, accept my mediation for this once, and let me see whether I may rely upon your obedience in future."

" I will not take his hand," answered the Earl of Chester ; " but since it is the wish of your highness, I promise not to proceed to any further violence until after the affair is concluded that is to place you upon the throne of England."

" It is enough," exclaimed the prince, and then addressing himself to Sir Gaston de Neville, he continued ;—" you have heard the promise of your rival. He will not break the peace any further at present ; and it now only remains for you to say that the truce will be sacredly observed on your side."

" It shall, my honoured prince."

" That is sufficient," exclaimed John, well pleased at the success of his attempt at peace-making, " I can rely with confidence upon your promises, and now, since this discord has ceased, let us proceed with the business which has called us together. You have heard, my friends, that the king's coronation takes place on the third of September ; two days only

intervene, and yet, short as that period is, the king must be deposed, and a successor found to occupy the vacant throne."

"And that occupier," observed Sir Walter Marsham, "shall be none other than yourself."

"None other," responded very voice in the room.

"Well, friends," cried John, with hypocritical reluctance, "if it is your wish, I will certainly accept the noble offer you have made ; but let it be remembered, that if I do respond to the universal request of the nation, it will be from no ambition of my own to climb to a summit so exalted as that you would raise me to."

"We are aware of it," answered Sir Gaston de Neville ; "the honour is none of your seeking, but is accepted purely for the benefit of my fellow-subjects."

"And now," exclaimed Lord Scroope, "perhaps your highness will condescend to inform us in what manner this affair is to be managed."

"I have told you," replied the prince, " that the change we seek to effect, must be executed on the day of my brother's coronation : he will then be unprepared for my sudden attack, and those who are engaged in the affair, may escape without danger."

"Is the king to be slain ?" demanded the Earl of Chester ; "you know the love I bear towards my brother," answered the prince, "and how unwilling I would be to consent to any act of violence that might deprive him of life. In this matter, however, I must throw myself entirely into your hands, and, if his life should be sacrificed, the crime will be none of mine."

"There is no help for it," exclaimed Sir Gaston de Neville, "for, should he be spared through any weakness of our own, the affair may, probably, terminate in our own ruin."

No. 72.

" Might he not be kept in captivity ?" demanded King John, with well dissembled concern.

" He might, answered Sir Gaston; " but, in the event of his escaping from prison, he would have little mercy upon those who were so considerate as to spare his life when they had it in their power to prevent all danger by despatching him out of hand."

" Sir Gaston de Neville speaks truly," observed Lord Scroope; " the king must die, or we know not how soon we may meet an ignominious death for the share we take upon ourselves in this plot against him."

" And what say you, my Lord of Chester ?" exclaimed Prince John.

" That I perfectly agree in the danger that would involve us in the event of our showing any ill-advised mercy on the present occasion."

" Hah !" cried the prince; " are you all bent upon spilling the blood of my royal brother ?"

" Necessity urges us to the course that has been proposed," exclaimed Sir Walter Marsham; " nay, your own life, my prince, would be more hazarded than that of any body else, and yet, from a mistaken notion of pity, you would save the life of him who would take the first opportunity that offered to send you to the scaffold, were he to escape from the imprisonment you have proposed."

" I see," cried Prince John, " we should all be involved in peril, and, therefore, no alternative presents itself but that he must e'en die !"

" You consent to it then ?" exclaimed Sir Gaston.

" Alas !" groaned the hypocritical John, " I am compelled by stern necessity."

" Know you of any one," asked Lord Scroope, " who would undertake to poniard the king on his way to the Abbey Church of Westminster ?"

" I do not," answered the prince.

" Leave that to me, and the affair shall be managed without trouble to any one," exclaimed Sir Gaston de Neville; " the task is hazardous, and requires to be performed by one who can be trusted."

" You know of such a person ?" exclaimed the prince.

" I do."

" Who is he ?"

" A retainer of mine, upon whose zeal I have relied on many former occasions."

" His name ?"

" Bertrand le Noir."

" Hah !" cried Prince John, I have heard the king speak of him as of one who had aided you in your attempts against the Hebrew Maiden."

" The king ever regarded him with dislike," answered Sir Gaston, " and Bertrand, knowing the suspicions that were entertained against him, has willingly undertaken the task of stabbing him to the heart."

" You have told him of our secret then ?" exclaimed the prince, with alarm.

" I have," answered the Knight Templar, " but you need not feel the least terror on that account; the man is trustworthy, and our secret is perfectly safe in his keeping."

" But may not self-interest urge him to betray us ?" asked the prince, whose suspicions had been aroused.

" Bertrand le Noir knows well enough that his own life would pay the penalty of any treachery that he might commit," replied Sir Gaston; " besides, he wishes the death of the king as much as any of us, and even without the prospect of a reward he would undertake the task I have spoken of."

"For which assertion we have only your own word," observed the Earl of Chester.

"And, if that is not enough," replied Sir Gaston; "I am willing to answer for my retainer's honour with my own life. He is bold and resolute, and, having once undertaken the duty, will go through with it even at the hazard of his own existence."

"And suppose," observed Prince John, "he should chance to fail in his object, he would then fall into the hands of the king's party, and an application of the torture would wring from him a full confession of the deed, and the names of those who have employed him."

"There is no fear of it," replied the knight, "for he is of a stern and stubborn nature, and no torture would ever make him confesss anything that might serve to implicate us as having any share in the plot."

"But, perhaps, an offer of pardon might induce him to save his own life at the expense of ours?"

"He values his own life at so small a price," replied Sir Gaston de Neville, "that I feel no hesitation whatever on that account; besides, the fellow has always been faithful, and there is no reason why we should suspect him on the present occasion."

"I think, my friends," exclaimed Prince John, "from the high opinion entertained of this man by his master, we can have nothing to fear from him. I, therefore, propose that we entrust him with the task, and in case any danger should threaten us, we will all be ready to flee from England at a moment's notice."

This was agreed to by every one present; and Sir Gaston being called upon to state the plan he had formed, thus proceeded to explain himself:—

"It is understood," he said, "that the king will proceed on horseback, attended by the principal officers of state, from the palace to the Abbey Church at Westminster. To show the confidence he reposes in the people, it is proposed that no soldiers shall be within a certain distance of him, and thus an opportunity will be afforded for reaching him without difficulty. This Bertrand will accomplish; his dagger will do its office; and in the confusion that will be sure to follow, he may easily effect his escape from the spot."

"All this appears easily enough," exclaimed Prince John; "but in case he should chance to be recognized as one of your retainers, the consequences may bc easily guessed."

"Bertrand le Noir has left my service some time," answered Sir Gaston, "and it is only within the last few days that he has returned. I may, therefore, disavow knowing anything about him, and thus the danger you apprehend will be easily got over."

"Let all be as you have said," cried Prince John, "for, since you are so confident of success, I am willing to trust all to your own management. Remember,—Bertrand le Noir is to hold himself in readiness for the appointed hour, and, should I mount the throne through his means, I will not fail to reward him in any way he may think proper to demand."

A knocking was now heard at the door, which being opened, one of the prince's attendants hastily entered to announce that Ralph de Glanville, the Chief Justiciary, had just arrived at the palace to demand an audience of the prince. Somewhat alarmed at this sudden and unexpected visit, John was about to hurry out in order to prevent the Justiciary following him to the scene of their late consultation, but ere he could do this, Ralph de Glanville, followed by a number of his officers of justice, entered the chamber.

"Your lordship's visit is most unexpected, though, I must add, most welcome," exclaimed Prince John, with much seeming cordiality.

"Your highness greatly honours me," was the grave reply of the Chief Justiciary; "though I doubt much whether you will not consider my hasty visit rather an unpleasant one."

"Is my royal brother ill?" asked John, assuming a tone of great concern.

"He is sick at heart," answered Ralph de Glanville; "for he has discovered that those he most trusted are least to be depended on."

"Indeed!"

"Your highness may well be surprised," returned the Justiciary; for 'tis indeed, a marvel that so good a king should have enemies, who, 'tis even said, are, at this very moment, plotting against his life."

"How!" exclaimed Prince John, concealing his own terrors as well as he could; "do I hear aright, or is this some vile report raised for the purpose of injuring some innocent person?"

"In the present instance," replied Ralph de Glanville, "I believe there is no reason to doubt the guilt of the suspected person."

"And who," asked the Earl of Chester, "are the men suspected of sharing in this plot against the king?"

"*You*, my lord, are one of them," cried the Chief Justiciary; "it was for you I came in search, and you are even now in my custody to answer, as you best can, the accusation that has been brought against you."

"My lord," cried the earl, "I have been most foully wronged by these suspicions."

"I trust it may hereafter appear so," answered Ralph de Glanville, "my present business, however, is to arrest you in the name of the king, my master, and you must, therefore, prepare for your immediate departure to a place of security."

"But, my lord——"

"I can hear nothing at present," interrupted the Chief Justiciary; "it has been my unpleasant duty to place you under restraint, but let us hope you will be able to prove your innocence so satisfactorily, that your acquittal will immediately follow."

"Is my lord of Chester the only person suspected of being disloyal to the king?" asked Prince John, anxiously.

"He is not," replied the Justiciary, with marked emphasis, "there are others as deeply implicated as himself, and the king well knows the names and rank of them all."

"Why does he not arrest the whole of the conspirators then?" demanded the prince.

"Because he has reasons which I am not at present able to explain further," replied the Justiciary; "he, however, hopes that this example will prove sufficient to deter the others from their purpose; and, in that case, perhaps, further proceedings against the Earl of Chester will be abandoned."

"Will you not tell me the names of the suspected persons?" asked Prince John.

"At present, I am commanded to keep the matter a secret," replied de Granville; "for the present, therefore, I take my leave of your highness, with a fervent wish that we may never meet again under similar disagreeable circumstances."

With this the officers closed round the Earl of Chester, and having deprived him of whatever arms he possessed, he was led away to the great astonishment and dismay of his late confederates. It was sometime, indeed, before Prince John could recover from the surprise into which he had been thrown; but, at length, arousing himself from the stupor that had come across his senses, he rose from the seat upon which he had thrown himself, and, addressing himself to his friends, said,—

" It seems that our plans have been discovered to the king ; and, judging from the language of Ralph de Glanville, it appears that our conduct will be so closely watched, that there will be little chance of our carrying the design we had formed to a successful termination."

" I differ in opinion from your highness," exclaimed Sir Gaston de Neville, who had been deeply occupied in thought, and was concerting other schemes for the fulfilment of their object ; " that the king suspected the Earl of Chester was evident, from the steps he has taken to prevent the mischief he was plotting. It is not, however, quite clear that we are suspected of being his accomplices, and, therefore, I propose that we go on with our plot as if nothing had happened."

" And thus run headlong into a dilemma," replied Prince John, " from which we shall not find it easy to escape."

" Had King Richard believed us equally guilty with the Earl of Chester," exclaimed Sir Gaston, " he would have ordered us all to be arrested together."

" I can see through his motive well," answered John ; " the king knows that I am concerned with you, and rather than bring so foul a disgrace upon his brother, he has commenced the arrest of one as a warning to the others of what will follow if they do not abandon their designs."

" If I understand you rightly, then," exclaimed Sir Gaston, " it is now your intention of giving up all further thought of securing for yourself the crown of England ?"

" How else," demanded the prince, " can I hope to save my faithful friends from the ruin and disgrace that will follow in the event of their being discovered in the midst of their designs ?"

" Your only safe course," replied the Knight Templar, " is to act with boldness and promptitude."

" But," exclaimed Lord Scroope, " if we should be detected meeting here again, we should be seized after the fashion of the Earl of Chester, and thus we should throw away the only chance of escape that has been left us."

" You mistake," answered Sir Gaston, " for our only chance of escape lies in the boldness with which we execute our plot. There will be no occasion for us to meet together any more until after the affair has been accomplished ; and, in the meantime, I will carefully instruct Bertrand le Noir in the method he is to pursue for the completion of our work. He may be relied on, and you will hereafter acknowledge that the task could not have been entrusted to better hands."

" We will take your word for the zeal and fidelity of your vassal," exclaimed Prince John, who had been deeply pondering on the knight's words ; " your scheme seems a good one, since we are to meet here no more till after the event, we all await with impatience until it has been carried into execution."

" Since your highness wills it so, I am content to agree with you," cried Sir Walter Markham ; " but in doing so, I must confess that I am not so completely satisfied with his fidelity as his master appears to be."

" And why," asked Sir Gaston de Neville, " should you doubt one for whose honour I have already said that I am willing to stake my own life ?"

" My reasons," answered Sir Walter, " may be explained in a very few words :—it seems that the king has somehow most unaccountably become acquainted with the plot that was going on against him ; you have revealed the secret to this retainer of yours, and who else is so justly open to suspicion, as a man whose poverty would prompt him to betray us for the sake of the reward that would be sure to follow his treachery ?"

"You have wronged him by your suspicions," exclaimed Sir Gaston; "the knave is honest in all matters where the interest of his master is concerned, and I can dare venture to affirm that he had no hand in the betraying of this secret."

"I believe Sir Gaston is right," interposed Prince John; "at least there is one other person who I think more likely to be the guilty party."

"Aye," exclaimed Lord Scroope, "and who may he be, your highness?"

"No less a personage than the Bishop of Durham."

"Aye," cried Sir Gaston de Neville, "he it is, I have no doubt, that we have to thank for the narrow escape we have just had. The haughty priest has thought proper to withdraw himself from our confederacy, and in order to make peace with his offended king, he has thus betrayed those with whom he formerly associated."

"I fear there is every reason to believe him guilty," observed Prince John; "at any rate, my first act on mounting the throne shall be, to institute a rigid enquiry into the affair, and if it should prove that he has indeed betrayed us, it is not his sacred character that shall shield him from my wrath."

"Were there no other arm willing to undertake the task," cried Sir Gaston, "my own should rid the world of so treacherous a villain."

"At any rate he will have but a poor chance if we trace the act to him," exclaimed Lord Scroope, "for his death would be a terrible one, that it might act as a warning to all who hereafter might feel inclined to act the spy upon their confederates."

"A truce to this subject for the present," interposed Prince John. "We will now separate till after the deed we met to discuss has been arranged; and should all go well, we will take instant steps for the discovery of the treacherous enemy. Should it happen, however, that Bertrand le Noir fails in his attempt, we will escape by different routes from London, and hurry over to France with as little delay as possible."

Upon this they separated with as much secrecy as they met, and within a few minutes afterwards the palace of Prince John was entirely cleared of the conspirators who had so lately assembled beneath its roof.

CHAPTER XCVI.

"This fellow's of exceeding honesty,
. And knows all qualities with a learned spirit
Of human dealings."

                                        SHAKSPERE.

It was in vain that Isaac endeavoured to assure his daughter that she had nothing more to fear from the violence of Sir Gaston de Neville, since the last trial she had gone through was sufficient to prove that all his former accusations against her had been founded in malevolence for the contempt with which she continued to regard his addresses. Still, however, she believed from former experience that he would not leave the object of his pursuit, and dreading lest, in the next attempt, he might carry her to some distant place to which she could never be traced, her heart sank with the most fearful forebodings; and, notwithstanding all the persuasions of her father to the contrary, she felt but too well assured that even the sacred protection of home would be disregarded by the man who, on so many previous occasions, had proved his utter disregard for the opinions of the world.

Reuben Grenard, too, endeavoured to prevail upon her to think no more of the past, but to look forward with confidence to the future; not but what he felt well assured that the nature of Sir Gaston would lead him to still further acts of violence and oppression, yet, trusting in his own powers of persuasion, he made one more effort to prevail on Isaac to consent to the immediate nuptials of himself and Rebecca. But the aged Israelite would not listen to him at that time, for he knew that his daughter would be as much an object of persecution after marriage as she had been previously to it. He, therefore, bade him have patience for a little while longer, telling him that a little time might serve to remove the difficulties which at present beset them, and even trying to persuade him to leave the house and not return to it again till he came to demand the hand of his betrothed bride. This, however, Reuben would not listen to, for he was resolved to remain where he was, that he might watch the actions of their enemies, and thus frustrate any designs which they might form for carrying off the hapless victim of their cruel arts.

It was on the morning after the meeting of the conspirators, that Reuben Grenard suddenly presented himself before the Hebrew and his daughter, and acquainted them with the report he had heard of a plot which had been formed for the assassination of the king, and the placing of Prince John upon the throne of England.

"In fact," he continued, "the conspiracy has been concocted by some of the chief men of the kingdom; and though great pains are taken to conceal the names, I have just learned that among them is our old enemy, Sir Gaston de Neville."

"Art thou sure," demanded Isaac, "that the knight has ranked himself amongst the foes of King Richard?"

"I believe," answered the young man, "there is no doubt of it; at any rate a report has been spread that the Chief Justiciary last night visited the palace of Prince John, and that he found the conspirators assembled together for the purpose of finally arranging their traitorous plans."

"And were they all arrested?" demanded Rebecca.

"Only one of them, as I hear," replied her lover; "but, no doubt, further arrests will take place unless the conspirators immediately abandon their blood-thirsty intentions."

"And who," asked Isaac, "was the person they arrested?"

"The Earl of Chester."

"Ah!" exclaimed the Israelite, "it has ever been suspected that the earl was no friend of our good king's. He has been frequently observed entering the palace of Richard's ambitious brother, and few, I believe, doubted the motive for which he went there."

"For the present," answered Reuben Grenard, "his mischievous designs have been put a stop to, and it is to be hoped that his arrest will prevent the fatal consequences that were anticipated."

"Be not too sure of that, Reuben," cried the Hebrew Maiden; "for something tells me that the discovery which has taken place will only serve to render them the more cautious in their actions."

"Perhaps so," answered Reuben; "but all their caution will not be sufficient to prevent their actions being known to those who will keep a vigilant eye upon them."

"If I mistake not," exclaimed Isaac of Tadcaster, "it is your intention to watch evil plotters?"

"I shall."

"I commend thy purpose," cried the old man, "though much I fear you will have little chance of succeeding in your generous object."

" Be that as it may," replied the other, " I will, at least, do my utmost for the preservation of the king's life."

" But do you know," enquired Isaac, " when the attempt you speak of is to be made ?"

" To-morrow," answered Reuben Grenard ; " as the king passes to the Abbey, where his coronation is to take place, an assassin will step forth from the crowd and aim his murderous steel at the monarch's heart."

" How hast thou learnt this ?" cried Rebecca.

" From one who is in the service of the prince," replied her lover ; " he watched with suspicion the arrival of the conspirators, and, listening at the door, overheard enough to prove that King Richard's life is in danger."

" And did he hear," asked Rebecca, " who was to be entrusted with the task of shedding the sovereign's blood ?"

" He heard the name," replied the young man, " but could not after-wards remember it."

" It was not Sir Gaston de Neville, then ?"

" No," replied Reuben, " but he had an indistinct notion that the man is one of the knight's retainers."

" Then my life on it," cried our heroine, " the villanous task has been given to Bertrand le Noir !"

" I have suspected as much myself," answered Reuben, " and it is my intention to look for him in the crowd, and to keep as near to him as I possibly can."

" Beware how you interfere, my son," cried Isaac, anxiously ; " the ruffian you have suspected is both cruel and resolute, and he will not fail to strike his weapon into your heart, should he be foiled through your means. Nay, think me not selfish in thus warning you of danger, but surely some other way may be found to save the king besides running the hazard of your own life."

" How else can it be done ?" asked Reuben.

" By warning the king in time of the treason that has been plotted against him."

" The warning would be thrown away," answered the young man ; " King Richard is already aware that there are men who seek his blood, but having given them a plain hint that he is not ignorant of their designs, he is willing to trust himself among his people, in token of the confidence he reposes in their loyalty and affection."

" In that case," cried the old man, " it behoves us to take the best mea-sures we can for his safety. I fear, however, lest harm should befal you, and would fain endeavour to prevail on you to think of some more safe way of shielding him from the threatened danger."

" I know of no other method," answered Reuben, " and, therefore, must needs run the risk which you are so anxious for me to avoid."

" And may I not accompany you, dear Reuben," cried our heroine, ear-nestly, " in order that I may share the peril you are about to encounter?"

" Nay," answered the young man, " if there is, indeed, danger, why should I not undertake this affair alone ?"

" Because it is my wish to share it with thee, dear Reuben," answered the Hebrew Maiden ; " nay, should'st thou die in the good cause thou hast undertaken, it is my earnest desire that we both perish together."

Scarcely had Rebecca finished speaking when a loud and impatient rap-ping was heard, and ere any one could hasten to see who it was that de-manded admittance, the door was burst open with a tremendous crash, and Black Ivan, breathless from the exertion he had used, presented himself before them.

"Be not alarmed, my friends," he exclaimed, "for my present visit bodes no mischief to any one here. I have been pursued, and took refuge in the first friendly place that chanced to offer itself."

"And what assurance have we," asked Isaac, "that thy visit is not an unfriendly one?"

"My own word, if thou wilt take it," answered the Outlaw. "I have told thee I was pursued; I have sought thy place for shelter; and, be assured, Black Ivan will never repay thy hospitality with base ingratitude."

"I will believe thee," replied Isaac; "for though I once ranked thee amongst our foes, thy conduct has since proved that thou canst be a friend to the unfortunate."

"Then thou wilt give me the shelter I ask?"

"I will:—but prithee tell me, Ivan, who it is that has thus compelled thee to seek for safety in flight?"

"Not one person, as thou may'st well imagine," replied the Outlaw. "In fact, I chanced to fall in with a number of Sir Gaston de Neville's retainers who were out, it seems, in search of me. The knaves were well armed; and, as ill luck would have it, I was less prepared than usual for an encounter with them. However, I was quickly surrounded, and finding there was no other chance of escape, I laid about me furiously; carved a way through the crowd with my trusty sword, and having left some half dozen of the knaves bleeding upon the ground, was fain to beat a hasty retreat from those who were determined to avenge the punishment I had inflicted on their comrades."

"And did they loose all trace of you?" demanded Isaac.

"Of that I am not quite certain," replied the Outlaw. "For some time, however, they came yelling after me like a pack of hungry wolves; but I

No. 73.

am used to being in such dilemmas; and, knowing the windings of the streets pretty well, I have led them such a dance, that I have a notion that they will not very easily trace me to this place."

"And if they should," exclaimed Isaac, "they will have some difficulty in finding you, for you are already tolerably well acquainted with the vaults to which yonder trap door leads, and whilst I engage them here in conversation, you will have a fair opportunity of making your escape from the place."

"Aye, aye," exclaimed Black Ivan, "leave me alone for taking care of myself, if the least chance in the world is given me. But tell me, old man, what is the meaning of the report I heard just before those fellows pounced upon me so unexpectedly? It was said that a plot against the king had been discovered, and that a nobleman has been arrested and sent to the Tower on suspicion of being concerned in it."

"It is all true enough," answered the aged Israelite; "last night the Earl of Chester was seized in the king's name, and, between ourselves, he was found in the society of those who ought to have been made partakers of his imprisonment."

"Indeed! and why were they suffered to escape?"

"Because," replied Isaac, "the king still bears an affection for one of them that little deserves it."

"I understand you, old man; Prince John is at the head of this unnatural conspiracy?"

"He is."

"And if I mistake not, Sir Gaston de Neville is as deeply employed in the plot."

"I have heard so."

"In that case," exclaimed the Outlaw, "I may have vengeance on him sooner than I expected. He has long been suspected by me, and it only required this information of yours to confirm my opinion."

"But," replied Isaac, "he is likely to escape the consequence of his crime, for the king is unwilling to publish the infamy of his brother, and, therefore, he is obliged to take no notice of those who are concerned with him."

"And yet, he has ordered the arrest of one of them it seems?"

"Aye," replied the old man, "but his motives may be easily seen through. He is in hopes that it will be a sufficient hint of their purposes being known, and that they will consequently abandon all further attempts against his life."

"And are his hopes likely to be realized, think you?"

"I am afraid not," replied Isaac; "at any rate there is every reason to fear that an attempt will be made upon the king's life to-morrow, and the chances are that it will prove but too successful."

"Not if I have the power to prevent it," exclaimed Ivan.

"You!"

"Aye, why should I not?"

"Because should you chance to be detected in the crowd, there are many that would be glad to seize upon you for the sake of the reward that has been offered for your apprehension."

"There may be," answered the Outlaw, "but by carefully disguising myself, it will be easy enough to prevent any such discovery taking place."

"And even if thou dost so," exclaimed Isaac, "thou may'st not be near the spot where the assassin stands ready to strike the fatal blow."

"I will accompany the procession from the palace to the Abbey," answered Black Ivan, "and by keeping constantly near the king, I shall be ready at all times to protect him from the murderous designs of his enemies."

"In that case," replied Isaac, "there is indeed some hope that the crime may be prevented. And now, Reuben," exclaimed the old man, addressing himself to the person he had named, "you have heard the determination of Black Ivan,—he has resolved to save the king's life, and, therefore, I can see no further cause why thou should'st risk thine own life in a vain attempt to save that of the king."

"It is in vain that you seek to turn me from my object," answered Reuben; "my mind is made up, and no consideration shall ever change it."

"And the young fellow is quite right," exclaimed the Outlaw; "he knows that two friends can do more than one, and I admire that spirit that urges him to protect the life of the king against the villanous designs of an assassin."

"I will keep near the ruffian," continued Reuben, "and the instant I see his arm raised I will rush forward and throw myself between him and his intended victim."

"Hah!" exclaimed Ivan, "it seems, then, that you know who the villain is that has been trusted to take away the life of King Richard?"

"There is every reason to believe," replied the young man, "that the ruffian is no other than Bertrand le Noir."

"Aye, the confidential friend of Sir Gaston de Neville?"

"The same."

"'Tis well you have told me thus much," exclaimed the Outlaw, "for Bertrand and I have a long score to settle, and it will be strange if we part before I have brought our affairs to a conclusion. Why, it is but a few days since that I spared his life when he was in my power, and little did I then think the mercy was bestowed upon one who, cowardlike, would seek to take the life of his sovereign at a moment when he was least suspicious of such treachery."

"Remember, Ivan," cried the aged Israelite, "we are not yet quite certain that Bertrand le Noir is the man who has undertaken this black affair. We, however, have reason to suspect him, and on that account Reuben was determined to station himself in the crowd, so that he might watch every action of the villain."

"Let him do so," answered the Outlaw; "he may thus be the means of averting the intended blow, and at the same time I will keep to my first intention of following the king throughout the whole procession. Thus he will be tolerably well guarded, and, between us both, it will rather surprise me if the rascal falls not into a dilemma from which he will not be able to get out of."

"Nay," exclaimed Reuben, "if the mob should happen to get hold of him he will be torn to pieces, and his limbs scattered in the air to become the prey of dogs and vultures."

"And what," asked Black Ivan, "will become of those who have instigated him to the deed?"

"They will, perhaps, be suffered to escape," replied Isaac of Tadcaster; "the king will not wish to make any stir in the affair, on account of the part his brother has taken in it; and, therefore, all who have joined him must, of course, be permitted to escape the punishment they so justly deserve."

"But it seems to be pretty generally known that Prince John is at the head of this conspiracy," observed the Outlaw.

"That is true," answered Isaac, "but I can undertake to predict that no further notice will be taken of it; because if one of them is brought to the block, it will necessarily follow that all must share the same punishment. In that case, Prince John must die, and that, worthless as he has proved himself, the king will never give his consent to."

"And so all are to be spared, to give them another opportunity of plotting against their sovereign?"

"Aye, it is so, indeed," replied Isaac; "and yet let us hope that the mercy they receive will not be thrown away upon them. At any rate, they will know that their every action will be closely watched, and that their chance of success will then be less than ever it was."

"Which will only serve to make them the more secret in their plottings against the king's life," observed Black Ivan. "I happen to know that the object of Prince John is to obtain possession of the throne; and, ambitious as he is, he will never cease to seek after it whilst a hope remains of placing himself at the head of this nation."

"Will no feeling of pity urge him to repent the evil practices he has employed against his brother's life?" cried Rebecca.

"John has no feeling that is not kindred with that of the wolf," answered Black Ivan. "His selfishness is well known; and that, together with his cruelty of heart, will ever render him callous to every thing that stands between him and the object of his ambition."

Just as the Outlaw had finished speaking a great clamour was heard in the street, and immediately afterwards a violent hammering was commenced against the door. In the midst of this uproar, however, the voice of Master Simon Snout, the constable, could be distinguished, demanding instant admittance to search for, and comprehend—as he was pleased to express it —a notorious villain and offender, who it was well known had found refuge there.

This was a sufficient warning to Black Ivan that his present place of shelter was no longer of service to him; and, whispering to Isaac, he asked him to open the trap door with as little delay as possible;—a request which was instantly complied with by the aged Israelite, who, pointing towards the opening in the floor, implored the Outlaw, by signs, to take his departure without further delay. Nor was Ivan slow in availing himself of the opportunity that presented itself for getting clear of his pursuers, and bidding them a hasty farewell, he instantly disappeared through the aperture which had been opened for his escape. This done, the trap was instantly lowered, and rushes having been strewed over it to conceal the place as much as possible; he next proceeded to open the door, grumbling all the time he was doing so, at the trouble that had been given him at that late hour of the night. His words, however, seemed to have no effect upon those who were impatiently waiting on the outside; and no sooner was the door thrown open than Simon Snout and four or five of Sir Gaston's retainers rushed into the house.

"Where is he?" exclaimed the constable;—"where's this flagracious villain that I've come here to comprehend?"

"I really don't understand you," answered Isaac of Tadcaster, with seeming surprise.

"Oh, you don't understand me, eh!" growled the man of law; "you're an ignoramus, are you, as we say in the classics; or, to speak plainly, in the vulgar tongue, a rank impostor?"

"I know not whether you have come here to insult me," exclaimed the venerable Israelite, "but if that is the only motive that has led to your visit, the sooner you leave my house the better I shall be pleased."

"Oh, indeed!—but supposing I don't choose to go till I have found the villain we have come in search of?"

"In that case," replied Isaac, "you may make up your mind to stay here for the remainder of your days."

"What!" cried the man of authority, "do you mean to tell me that the notorious breaker of the laws, Black Ivan, is not concealed somewhere in the interior of the inside of this here house?"

"I mean to tell you that he is no where about my premises," answered Isaac.

"Humph!—then you mean to consinuate that we are all as blind as moles?"

"That is a matter that I neither know nor care about," replied the Israelite. "You have heard me say that the person you seek after is not here, and that ought to be sufficient, unless you have any reason to doubt my word."

"And it strikes me there is pretty good reason for believing that you aint telling me the truth," retorted the constable. "Didn't we see the fellow bolt with all his speed towards your house, and didn't we then lose sight of him, and aint that quite enough to prove to us that the rascal is now in your house?"

"You may think as you please," answered the Jew, "but again I tell you the person you seek is not in my house."

"Well, we shall search the house," exclaimed the constable, "and if you've told us the truth we'll go away when that's been done, and trouble you no more about the matter."

"And that you will not find him I feel well assured," cried Reuben Grenard, who, with extreme difficulty, had restrained his passion during the preceding conversation.

"Indeed, Mr. Impertinence!" retorted Simon Snout, "and pray who asked you to interfere in this matter? Aint I his majesty's representative, and shall any body dare to confront me by talking just for all the world as if he was my equal?"

"If I have affronted you," replied Reuben Grenard, "it has been occasioned by your own utter ignorance and stupidity."

"You hear that, my friends!" cried Snout, turning towards his companions; "this fellow has called me villanous names, and if I don't trounce him for it, say I don't know what law and justice means."

"And if you preach here much longer I shall feel myself under the necessity of kicking you into the street."

"There again!" cried the constable;—"you hear him, sirrahs, and yet there aint one among you that attempts to knock him down for his insolence!"

"And they are wise for acting with so much discretion," answered Reuben, significantly;—"these men are better judges than yourself, seeing that they say little, and thus keep out of all danger."

"This is no longer to be borne," exclaimed the enraged constable; "I have been consulted and confronted beyond all bearing, and if I don't make you smart for this, young fellow, say my name aint Simon Snout."

"Come, come," cried Reuben Grenard, impatiently, "if you consider it your duty to search this house after the person you suspect to be in it, perform your office with despatch, and let us be rid of you with as little delay as possible."

"Oh! you want to get rid of me—do you?"

"Certainly I do," answered the young man; "for, to speak the truth, your presence is neither agreeable nor desired."

"Ah! that's because the guilty always tremble at the presence of us, officers," answered Simon Snout. "But, however, we don't want to stop with a parcel of infidels longer than we can help, so come along, my fine fellows, and help me to look over the house."

Upon this the constable bustled up stairs, accompanied by the retainers of Sir Gaston de Neville, and after they had searched every part of the house, not even omitting the closets and chimneys, they returned to the room where they had left Isaac and his family, to whom the constable acknowledged that his search had been a fruitless one.

"We hav'n't been able to find the villain," he said, with evident disappointment, "but, for all that, we're quite sure he came to the house, so if you've been playing any of your tricks to get him out of the way before we came, I'd advise you to look after yourself, for I'm a terrible fellow when I get into a passion, and, perhaps, you may find that out if you don't instantly confess what you've done with him."

"We have done nothing with him," exclaimed Isaac, alarmed at the significant glance the fellow cast towards his daughter; "we are innocent of any wrong against the king, and, therefore, I pray you retire from my house, now that you are convinced the object of your search is not here."

"Aye, aye," retorted the constable, "it's all true enough that he ain't here now, but will you swear, sinful old man, that you are,—that Black Ivan has not been in your house within the last hour."

"I will not deny it," replied the Israelite; "the person you have named was here, but he never harmed me in his life, and, therefore, I was not going to refuse him shelter when I knew he wanted it."

"Here's a pretty confession!" exclaimed Simon Snout; "the hoary-headed old villain confesses that he gave shelter to Black Ivan, and if that won't bring him to the gallows I don't know what will."

"How was I to know who he was?" asked Isaac; "the man applied for a little rest, and, of course, it was not denied; had you even presented yourself under similar circumstances, I dare say you would not have had the door closed in your face."

"Come, come, this story won't do," exclaimed the constable; "you must have known who he was, because it's not so long ago, remember, that I had the trouble of hunting him to the same place."

"Ah!" cried the Jew, "but my sight is not good, and I knew him not, and, therefore, if there was any fault, it was without design."

"Well, perhaps you may have to tell that story somewhere else," exclaimed Simon Snout; "at present, I shall take no further notice of it, but you must tell me which way the Outlaw escaped, or——"

"I can tell you nothing more than you have already heard," replied the Israelite; "the person you speak of remained here but a short time, and left the house only a few minutes before you entered it."

"Ah!" vociferated the constables, "if you had told me that at the time, we should have been able to overtake him."

"I am quite aware of that," answered Isaac, "and for that very reason I let you amuse yourself with talking till I had good reason for knowing he was beyond your reach."

"I have been bamboozled then!"

"You have."

"And for which you shall smart severely, you old cantankerous villain."

"You had better say nothing about it," answered the Israelite, calmly; "at present no one knows that you have been foolish enough to throw away a good chance of securing the Outlaw, and if you take my advice, you will keep your tongue quiet, instead of suffering it to publish an affair that cannot fail to bring upon you the laughter and jeers of your fellow men."

"Well," cried the constable, "something seems to tell me that I cut rather a contemptible figure in this affair."

"That is exactly my opinion," replied Isaac, "and, therefore, the best course you can pursue is, to let the matter drop, and if ever you should chance to be so near Black Ivan again, do not lose your time in talking, but go about your task in earnest, and I dare say he will easily be captured."

Burning with rage and mortification, the constable now dashed furiously from the house of the Jew, and closely followed by the men who had accompanied him in his search, he returned home, vowing vengeance against Black Ivan, and those who had aided in preventing his being taken when so good an opportunity had offered.

CHAPTER XCVII.

> "Wherefore this treachery
> Against a prince, whose mild, benignant rule
> Hath raised our land to greatness? Forbear, I say,
> And cease thine evil thoughts."
> THE CONSPIRATORS.

EARLY on the following morning, vast crowds began to assemble in the neighbourhood of Westminster, for the purpose of gratifying themselves with a sight of the magnificent pageantry that was to be exhibited in honour of the king's coronation. Few there were, indeed, who did not go to greet the sovereign with their loyal gratulation, though it must be confessed there were some,—such, for instance, as those who listened to the discontented speeches of Simon Hyde, the tanner, who thought the king too great a favourer of the Jews, whilst, in behalf of Prince John, they were ready to raise their enthusiastic cheers.

The crowd began to assemble at an early hour in the morning of September 3rd, 1189, the day appointed for the ceremony to which we have alluded. In fact, the whole line which the procession was to traverse was thickly thronged with an eager multitude, who, in spite of the tedious time they had to wait, contrived to maintain a tolerable degree of good humour in expectation of the treat that was in store for them.

But King Richard himself felt some misgivings that the day would not pass without the expected attack being made upon his life, and having attired himself by the advice of his friends in a shirt of mail, which was concealed beneath the rest of his clothes, he descended to the chamber from whence he was to step into the place reserved for him in the procession. By this time he had regained his usual spirits ; and, observing the heaviness of heart manifested by Sir Reginald Courtney, one of the most faithful among his friends, he playfully asked him why he appeared to be thus sorrowful on a day that was regarded as one of general rejoicing.

"My liege," replied Sir Reginald, "it is in vain to conceal from you the cause of my uneasiness. I am but too well aware of the treasonable designs entertained against you by a few discontented subjects, and much I fear, they may, this day, take advantage of the confusion, and attempt the execution of their evil purpose."

"Nay, never give way to thy fears, my good Sir Reginald," exclaimed the king, "for, depend on it, the knaves will not have courage to execute the infamous designs when they see me surrounded by thousands of my faithful subjects. Besides, it would be a weakness to betray fear at such a moment as this ; and, rely on it, he who has gained the title of the Lion-Hearted for his deeds in battle, will never be disconcerted because a few discontented men have plotted his destruction."

" Your majesty," exclaimed Sir Reginald, " will at least allow me to be near your person in the procession ?"

" If it is your wish, I shall not object to it," replied the king; " but by St. George, I see no reason to expect that I shall have need of thy loyal services."

" Would that I could think so," exclaimed Sir Reginald.

" Thou art strangely out of spirits, Sir Knight."

" It is because I cannot divest myself of the thoughts that your life will this day be placed in jeopardy," replied Sir Reginald, gloomily.

" And even were your anticipations well founded," answered the king, " there will, I hope, be loyal subjects enough about me to prevent the danger you so much fear."

" There are but few, I believe," exclaimed the knight, " who would not risk their own lives for the preservation of your majesty's; yet the hand of the assassin will be suddenly and secretly raised, and ere any one would interpose, the fatal steel may have performed its sanguinary purpose."

" Will nothing," cried the king, " remove this strange infatuation from your mind ?"

" Nothing, sire."

" But I tell thee again, I feel no fear."

" Your majesty never does," was the complimentary reply of the young knight.

" Hah," exclaimed the king, " art thou going to turn courtier that thou dost flatter me ?"

" I speak but the truth," answered Sir Reginald Courtney, " and that never yet gave offence to King Richard,"

" By St. George, thou hast fairly tied my tongue, or I would have told thee how I despise flattery," exclaimed the king, with a smile of good humour. " However, thou now knowest in what way I may be most easily offended, and as thou dost regard my favour, I would have thee avoid all such subjects for the future."

" It was drawn from me inadvertently, or your majesty should not have heard it," answered Sir Reginald Courtney. " However, to return to that which we were speaking of, I should be glad were it in my power to prevail on you to let some of your Archers surround you, in order to prevent the approach of any one whose intentions may be dangerous to your life."

" Why, that would look too much like cowardice on my part," replied King Richard. " I have never yet required any other guards than my faithful people, and to change my usual habits on the present occasion is a recourse that I cannot submit to."

" But never till now did you know that any plot had been formed to take away your life?"

" Nor can I believe there is so at this time," replied the king. " As you are already aware, I have ordered the arrest of the Earl of Chester, who I had reason to believe was among the most active of my enemies; and there is every reason to hope, that the capture of one of their number will strike such terror into the hearts of the rest, that they will abandon the design for fear of meeting the fate which has befallen their guilty associate."

" Had all been arrested at the same time," observed Sir Reginald Court ney, " your majesty would have had no cause to apprehend future danger."

" True; but you are aware of the reason why I have for the present forborne to prosecute this matter any farther?"

" I am; there is one among them whom every feeling of honour should ave prevented becoming your enemy. He you would not disgrace by

public exposure, and thus the others will share in the good fortune that favours the man in whose cause they have embarked."

"You are right, Sir Reginald," cried the king; "such are, indeed, the motives that sway me, and they are so insurmountable, that I can never be removed from my purpose."

"And yet," cried the knight, "I should think it possible to bring punishment upon the others? There are, for instance, my Lord Scroope, Sir Walter Marsham, and Sir Gaston de Neville, all of whom have plotted against your life, and who have no reason to expect mercy from the sovereign they seek to destroy."

"An opportunity may soon offer when I may retaliate on them the crimes they at present meditate," answered King Richard. "At any rate they may depend on it I shall watch them with a jealous eye, and should I find that my mercy has been thrown away upon them, I will not fail to pour upon their heads the burning wrath they have given rise to."

"And why give them a chance of carrying their traitorous designs further?" asked Sir Reginald. "There are men among them who deserve little consideration, and your only safe course is to deprive them of all further power to do you the injury they have plotted."

"Sir Gaston de Neville had better look to it," exclaimed the king, "or he will soon find that his scheming villany is doomed to come to a speedy and ignominious termination."

"His has ever been a busy and turbulent spirit," exclaimed the young knight, "and I have long suspected that he was ready to join with any traitors that might be in league against your majesty."

"Nor have I been blind to his crafty schemes for overthrowing my power," replied the king. "He has been my enemy because I would not
No. 74

countenance the tyranny he sought to exercise over some unfortunate Jews, and from that moment I could see that he was no longer to be depended on. Knowing, therefore, his readiness to enter into any plan that might be formed for my destruction, I kept a constant watch upon him, and when I saw that he was a frequent visitor to the palace of my brother, I knew that mischief was brewing in that quarter, and thus I discovered a plot that had almost terminated in my assassination."

" And even now I fear," exclaimed Sir Reginald, "that you are not safe unless some prompt measures are taken to secure yourself against any sudden attack that may be made in the course of this day's procession."

" Nay," replied the king, "your fears on the present occasion have been unnecessarily excited. Not but what I know there are men engaged in this plot who would not hesitate to do the deed you have mentioned; but at the same time I feel a firm confidence in my people, who would, I am sure, prevent any mischief that might be meditated against their sovereign."

" I am well satisfied of that, my gracious liege," answered Sir Reginald Courtenay, "and yet, in spite of all that, I cannot but feel a dread that this day will not pass over without the attempt being made by your enemies."

" Well," exclaimed the king, "if they should do so, the consequences must fall upon themselves. I would have shielded them from disgrace, but if they rush upon the ruin I would have averted, I shall have it no longer in my power to save them against the fierce wrath of the infuriated people."

As Richard concluded, the procession was completely formed; and, taking his place, he was quickly followed by Sir Reginald Courtenay, who was resolved to keep as close as possible to his royal master, in case his services should be required on any sudden emergency.

Leaving the king for the present, we will now conduct the reader to that portion of the line of procession where Simon Hyde, the tanner, and a numerous host of friends, had assembled to see the pageant. As usual, Simon was in high wrath against the king, and, after having waited some time impatiently, he whispered to one of the fellows that stood near him,—

" The king seems to be a long time before he makes his appearance, and who shall say that something has not happened that we should all be glad of?"

" Aye," replied the other; "it has been said that a blow will this day be struck, which will free England from a tyrant. Heaven send it may be true, and that the affair may by this time be over."

"Perhaps it may be so," returned Simon Hyde, "for in that case we should have one to rule us that would soon send those accursed Jews out of the land. They are the locusts that devour up all the goodness of the land, and till we are fairly rid of them, the country will never know the blessings of prosperity. They seem to bring heaven's curse with them wherever they go, and yet King Richard, for some reason or other, has always been friendly towards them."

" Aye, but their time has almost come," whispered the other; "for it has been proposed that our party shall this night make an attack upon their houses, and in that case a few thousands will be roasted in the fires of their own habitations."

" And who's to head the mob?" asked Simon Hyde.

"Why you, if you think proper."

" Have I been proposed by any of the fellows?"

"Oh yes, they all wish it," replied the man; "but they're almost afraid you won't have pluck enough to run the risk of leading them against the Jews."

"They are mistaken, then," exclaimed the tanner, "for I so hate the knaves that I would run any risk to put a few thousands of them out of the way. In short, I proposed something of the kind a short time ago, so it's hardly likely I should try to sneak out of it when there's such a good chance of paying off old scores with these Israelites."

"But how shall we make a beginning of the business?" demanded the other fellow.

"Why, by attacking the house of Isaac of Tadcaster, to be sure," replied Simon Hyde; "there's something like good generalship in that, I think, for Sir Gaston de Neville hates the old man, and has sworn the destruction of himself and all that belong to him. So that by beginning there, we shall secure the assistance of his retainers; and when the people see that we are going on without hindrance, thousands of others will be ready enough to join us; and I think, if we have any luck on our side, there will not be many Jews left to mourn the deaths of their countrymen, by the time the sun rises to-morrow morning."

"If I had my will, there should not be one of them escape," exclaimed the other; "I hate the whole tribe of Israel, and when once the affray begins, I'll prove myself to be among the most active of their slayers."

"Aye," answered Simon, "but you must be sure not to begin till we are all of us ready for the general attack. Any impatience would only serve to betray us, and instead of exterminating these Jews from the land, we should rush upon the very destruction we have been at so much pains to prepare for them."

"I'll mind all about that," replied the other; "and so tell me what is to be the signal for beginning the attack?"

"We must wait patiently till King Richard is disposed of," exclaimed Simon Hyde. "There is no doubt he will be slain long before, and when that has been done, we may go about our work without fear of interruption, in the midst of the confusion that will take place."

"Who is that fellow that I see muffled in his cloak and standing in front of the crowd?" asked the man.

"That," replied Simon Hyde, glancing in the direction that had been pointed out, "is Bertrand le Noir, a retainer of Sir Gaston de Neville, and one that is likely enough to make an attack on King Richard."

"I have heard of him," exclaimed the man: "report says he don't stand upon trifles whenever he has undertaken to do anything; and by the look of him, I should say he has something more to do to-day than to be an idle spectator of this pageant."

"You are right," exclaimed the tanner "the fellow looks frowningly; and if I may judge from his impatient glances towards the place where the procession is to come, I should say that there will be little chance of Richard's escape, if he has really made up his mind to rid England of her present sovereign. But hush! we must not speak too loud, or there may be some within hearing who would be glad to earn a reward by denouncing the plot before it has been executed."

"Hah! they come," whispered the other; "I hear music in the distance, and Richard approaches the destruction which he so little dreams of."

"You are right," answered Simon Hyde; "the procession advances, and yonder I see the first portion of it coming along the raised platform that turns round yonder street."

"And do you hear how the king is cheered as he passes through the crowds that have assembled to see him?"

"I do," replied the tanner, "and can scarce forbear smiling to think how soon all the joy may be turned into sorrow. And now, observe Bertrand le Noir—do you see how he thrusts aside his cloak, as if preparing to free himself from it on the instant when his opportunity arrives? By'r Lady! the knave looks firm enough in his purpose, and it will be miraculous indeed if he should fail in executing the task he has undertaken."

"How know you for certain," asked the other, "that Bertrand le Noir has taken upon himself the task you speak of?"

"Why his very looks," replied Simon, "would be enough to convince me of it, even if I had had no reason to have believed it before. Besides, he is the retainer of Sir Gaston de Neville, and all the world knows how little love is lost between King Richard and the Knight Templar."

"Yet, for all that," exclaimed the other, "it does not follow that Sir Gaston would assist in a plot for the murder of the king."

"Well," exclaimed Simon Hyde, "a few minutes will serve to prove whether I am right or wrong in the guess I have ventured to make. The king, as you may perceive, is now in sight, and Bertrand le Noir has stepped forward in advance of the crowd, as if he would be quite free whenever the moment for action arrives."

Some part of the procession had by this time passed them, and the king, mounted on a white charger, was seen at a short distance off unguarded, except by Sir Reginald Courtney, and a few zealous friends, who, on foot, surrounded him, in order to be in readiness should any attack be made upon the life of the sovereign. Nothing indeed could be more enthusiastic than the vociferous greeting of the multitude up to this spot, but when the king passed the place where Simon Hyde and his associates stood, a gloomy silence prevailed, which, however, was soon to be broken by an event which the reader may easily anticipate. In an instant Bertrand le Noir, who had been eagerly watching his opportunity, threw aside his cloak, and, rushing towards the platform, sprang upon it with the suddenness of an infuriated tiger, and, raising a dagger, which he firmly grasped in his hand, he was about to plunge it into the king's breast, when a person rushed from the crowd, and seizing the assassin by the arm, wrenched the weapon from his grasp in less time than we have taken to describe it. This done, he was in the act of striking the dagger into the heart of the villain, whose attempt had been thus frustrated, but, ere he could accomplish this piece of retributive justice, Bertrand contrived to break away from his hold, and leaping from the platform, he was soon concealed amongst the discontented followers of Simon Hyde.

Nothing could exceed the rage of the greater part of the assembled multitude, when it was known that the life of the king had been attempted, and had Bertrand le Noir fallen into their hands at that moment, there is little doubt but he would have been torn to pieces by those who regarded his act with abhorrence. But the king perceiving the confusion that had ensued, earnestly entreated the crowd to suppress their wrath for the present, assuring them that he had providentially escaped without the least injury, and adding a request that they would trouble themselves no further in seeking after the villain who had sought his life, as he himself felt no enmity towards the man, whose evil designs had been so signally defeated. After this exhortation, he commanded the person who had preserved him from the dagger of the assassin to be brought before him, but in reply he was informed that the man had disappeared, and was no longer to be seen among the crowd.

"Hah!" exclaimed the king, "does he then value our thanks so little that he would not stay to hear how highly we esteem the services he has this day done us?"

"There seems to have been good reason for his sudden retreat, my liege;" answered Sir Reginald Courtney, "for, if I mistake not, your highness owes your life to no other than Black Ivan, the Outlaw."

"Say'st thou so!" exclaimed the king; "Black Ivan has long laid under the bann of the laws, but, if thy suspicions are well founded, he shall rank high in my favour, and no reward shall be considered too great for the man who has thus rescued me from the dagger of an assassin."

"A proclamation to that effect," observed Sir Reginald, "would perhaps be the means of bringing him to your majesty's presence. He is aware that a price is set upon his head, and has, therefore, effected his escape, lest even a king's gratitude should be insufficient to shield him from the consequences of his former lawless life."

"My Lord Justiciary," cried the king, addressing himself to Ralph de Glanville; "you have heard my will upon this subject, and therefore be it your task to see that a free pardon is offered to Black Ivan, and a proclamation issued, commanding him with all speed to repair to my court, at Westminster."

"Your majesty forgets," observed the Justiciary, "that the man you thus favour, has long been notorious as a robber and a breaker of your laws."

"But I have not forgotten that to him I owe my life," answered the king. "But for him I should have perished by the hand of an assassin, and, therefore, it is my command that the proclamation be instantly sent forth and published throughout England."

"And shall no steps be taken to apprehend the villain that would have slain you?" asked Sir Reginald Courtney.

"I will consider further upon that subject," answered the king; and then addressing himself to Sir Gaston de Neville, who was sullenly standing at no great distance from him, he said:—"With you, Sir Knight, I wish to hold some conversation as shortly as possible, after the solemnities of this day are over. To-morrow morning I shall expect you at my palace, and perhaps you may be able to throw some light upon an affair that at present is involved in obscurity and mystery."

"I will obey your majesty," replied Sir Gaston, in a low, agitated voice, "though I marvel much how you can expect to learn anything touching this affair from one so loyal as myself."

"Your loyalty remains to be proved," whispered the king, with an angry frown. "However, I will rely upon your coming, and as our conversation will be strictly private, you have no cause to fear, unless certain suspicions I have formed should unfortunately prove to have been well founded. And now, my lords and gentlemen," continued the king in a louder voice, "we will on to the Abbey of Westminster, and may heaven shield me from all other designs, as it has the one I have just now so marvellously escaped."

Upon this, the procession moved on, and shortly afterwards the king entered the Abbey, where the solemnity of his coronation was performed in the midst of the thousands who had assembled to witness it.

CHAPTER XCVIII.

"I will hunt out these people,
And persecute them with my boundless hate
Till vengeance is appeased."

GLENGARRY.

IN consequence of the delay that had taken place, and the great length of the ceremony, it was nearly dusk before the whole of it was completed. In fact, many who had waited to see the return of the procession grew tired of standing longer in the streets, and gradually the crowd became so thinned, that Simon Hyde and his companions were enabled to advance within a short distance of the Abbey doors. The events of the morning of course formed the subject of their conversation, and it may safely be affirmed that there was not one among the discontented throng which acknowledged the leadership of Simon Hyde, who was not disappointed at the unexpected circumstance which had preserved the life of their king. Simon, however, was not without hope that the plot had only been deferred for a time, and had his courage been equal to his baseness, there is little doubt but he would have volunteered to slay the king on his return from the Abbey. Such at least was his wish, and he failed not to try whether there were any among his followers who would undertake a task which he was afraid to perform himself.

"I don't know whether you are aware of it, my friends," he said, "but there are some that I could mention, who would be well pleased were a man to be found who would rid England of this tyrant. Nay, they have it in their power to reward such a person as I speak of, and therefore, it only remains for any of you that are now listening to me, to declare whether you are inclined to try your fortune in the affair."

"It's all very well to talk about trying one's fortune," retorted one of the fellows, "but supposing we were to be foiled as the other fellow was this morning, what sort of a fortune would follow then, I should like to know?"

"Psha! you are a coward, Phil," exclaimed the tanner, "and it is not to such that I address myself."

"Then why don't you earn the reward yourself?" demanded the other; "the job is quite as easy a one for you as for anybody else, and as for the risk, it would be no worse for you than for me, or my comrades."

"Why, the truth is," replied Simon Hyde, "that I can serve you better with my head than my hands."

"Aye, and with your tongue better than either; you are a rare fellow to be talking, but the devil a bit do you ever run yourself into danger."

"What's that you are muttering about, fellow?" demanded the tanner, indignantly.

"I was saying," replied Phil, "that if talking would do any good, you might fairly rank amongst the best of us; but, if it should come to hard blows, I know well enough that Simon Hyde would be among the very first to look after number one."

"You judge me wrongfully, Phil, indeed you do," exclaimed Simon Hyde. "I may not perhaps be quite so rash as many that I could name, but, then, I know that it is absolutely necessary to have a leader in these cases, and as I have generally acted as such, among you all, with tolerable satisfaction, let us hope you will not accuse me of cowardice for merely seeking to preserve myself for the advantage of us all."

"And what good have we been doing all this time?" asked another the fellows. "We have been meeting together, and finding a great deal of fault, and yet for all that, we are now just where we were six months ago."

"Well, that's no fault of mine, at any rate," replied Simon, "I have been constantly telling you what to do, and now, when there's a fair opportunity of gaining eternal renown, there's not a man among you that will put forth his hand for the service of his country."

"Aye," retorted the other, "that's because its not quite certain whether the country would thank us for doing as you would persuade us. The king seems to me to have more friends than enemies, and, perhaps, when the mischief was done, we should find that there was a heavier reckoning to pay than we expected."

"But haven't I told you that there are some who have not only the power, but the inclination to reward us for striking the blow I have proposed?"

"Aye, you mean Prince John for one of them."

"I do, and you must, therefore, confess that there is a very good chance of our profiting largely by running the trifling risk I have mentioned."

"Well, then, why not let the risk be your own?"

"I'll tell you what it is, Phil," exclaimed the tanner, indignantly; "those that take the chief command in affairs, are always suffered to run the least risk, and very proper it is that it should be so, for suppose your leader should happen to be cut off by any accident, what then would come of the rest of you, I should like to know?"

"Why, for my own part," answered Phil, "I've a notion that we should get on quite as well without as with you. At any rate, a coward is of no use to any one, and so, as you have heard my opinion upon the subject, you can leave us as soon as you like."

"Do you hear that, my friends?" exclaimed Simon Hyde, turning round peremptorily to his companions. "I am called a coward to my face, and if that ain't enough to stir up the blood of a man, I don't know what is."

"Then why don't you prove him to be a liar?" asked one of the fellows. "Draw your dagger, Simon, and show him that you are not quite such a coward as he takes you to be."

"I would do so," replied the tanner, "but you must acknowledge that this is neither the time nor the place for a quarrel to be settled in."

"Then suppose we put it off till another opportunity," exclaimed Phil, with a sneer; "you don't seem to be in a hurry to settle the business, and so to oblige you, I'll give you a little more time to consider whether it will be better to fight, or give up all pretence to placing yourself at our head."

At this period a loud shouting was heard from the multitude that thronged round the Abbey doors, and presently afterwards a rumour spread around that some Jews had found their way into the church, and had thrown themselves before the king to make him rich offerings of gold and jewels. This was at once eagerly seized upon as an excuse to charge them with the contemplation of a treasonable design against the monarch, and in a few moments a cry was raised to seize upon the Jews, who had violated the sanctuary of the church, and a tremendous rush was made towards the doors for the purpose of laying hold of the offenders, and dragging them forth to punishment. In this design, they were, however, disappointed, for the heavy iron-bound portals were closed against them, and in spite of all their efforts to force them open, they were obliged to abandon their object in despair. This gave

Simon Hyde an opportunity to retrieve his lost character, and, bustling through the crowd, he exclaimed :—

"My friends, shall we, who are Christians, be shut out of the church, whilst a parcel of Jews have not only got in by means of fraud and deceit, but are protected, when we would punish them for their temerity?"

"Down with the Jews!" shouted a thousand voices, and at the same time as many caps were flung into the air.

"Will you follow me if I lead you on?" asked the tanner.

"Aye, aye, we will, we will."

"Then make towards the door, and burst it open," exclaimed Simon Hyde.

To do him justice, the tanner now endeavoured to recover his lost character, and he set himself to the work he had recommended, with a hearty good will. It soon, however, became evident that the door had been strongly barricaded within, and enraged by the discovery of this circumstance, the attack was kept up with a determination to effect the object they had in view. But they might have gone on till they had grown tired of the labour they had thus taken upon themselves, had it not been for the arrival of half-a-dozen smiths, who, with their ponderous sledge hammers, laid about them with such hearty good will, that in the course of a very short time, the wood work began to give way, and a sufficient aperture was formed, through which to thrust a youth, who immediately removed the bolts and bars, so that the doors could be thrown open for the admittance of the multitude. At this moment a tremendous rush was made into the body of the church; the poor, unoffending, though persecuted Jews, were seized upon and hurried to the exterior of the sacred edifice, where they were barbarously butchered, for no other crime than having presented their offerings to the recently crowned sovereign. This done, the mob next began to consult as to their future proceedings, and as Simon Hyde had taken a prominent part in the scandalous outrage, he was called upon to give his advice as to the course they should now adopt.

"Aye," he exclaimed, "you have at last found out, then, that I am of some service to you, and that my counsel is worth attending to."

"Come, come, we want no preaching, sirrah," cried a burley smith, "so either tell us what to do next, or hold your peace for ever."

"Well, then," exclaimed Simon Hyde, "I should say the best thing to do, will be to go without delay to attack the houses of all the Jews in London, and then slaughter the inhabitants."

"Aye," returned the smith, "the fellow advises us well; he recommends us to strike whilst the iron is hot."

"Which every smith should do, without being told by an ignorant tanner," retorted one of the mob.

"Hear him!" vociferated Simon Hyde; "here is a fool giving utterance to what he calls wit, when we have business of so much importance to get through."

"Never mind what he says, then," exclaimed Phil, "but attend to the affair we are consulting about. You recommend us to make an attack upon the Jews' quarter of the city, but are you willing to lead us, or are we to go by ourselves?"

"Why, I'll lead you, to be sure," cried Simon, encouraged by the vast crowd that he saw ready to accompany him. "I am one of those that hate the whole Hebrew nation, and, if you will only assist me well, I'll undertake to say there shall not be a score of Jews left alive in London in the course of another six hours."

"But remember," exclaimed Phil, "if you make any attempt to run away from us, my own sword shall cleave you from the shoulder to the hip. You know I am not used to break my word in these matters, and so you know what to expect."

"You have nothing to fear from me," answered Simon Hyde, "so now, as many of you as wish to gain eternal renown, follow me, and I will lead you to this glorious enterprise."

"Obedient to this command, the lawless mob drew themselves into a compact body, and following the footsteps of the man who had placed himself at their head, they quitted the neighbourhood of the Abbey, and passing along the outskirts of the city, approached that place where nearly all the Jews had taken up their habitation. As they came within sight of the place, they halted for a few moments, and Simon, addressing himself to them, said—

"My friends, we have now reached nearly the end of our march, and, as you see, the enemy is almost within reach. But you must now be silent, that we may fall on them unawares, for the darkness of night favours us, and, if we make good use of our advantage, there will not be one among these hated people that shall live to tell the tale of slaughter that is about to take place."

"But their cries," observed one of the ruffians, "will soon bring them assistance."

"We must not give them time to raise an alarm," exclaimed Simon Hyde, "our attack must be sudden, and half-a-dozen men will be found quite sufficient to attack each house."

"And are we to cut the throats of the inmates?" demanded one of the rabble.

No. 75

"That I'm afraid would take too much time," replied the tanner; "and I would, therefore, advise you to fall to with what speed you can, and when their houses are set fire to, let the Jews be prevented from escaping, that they may be roasted alive by the flames that have been kindled in their own dwellings."

"A most excellent plan," exclaimed Phil, who by this time began to give the tanner more credit than he had hitherto done. "By St. George, I should have pondered a long time, before I had thought of such a scheme as this, and I congratulate you, Simon, on your having for once in your life had a bright thought."

"Aye," retorted the tanner, "but presently the fires out yonder shall b brighter than the thought; so onwards, boys, and remember, not a Jew is to be left alive, nor a house standing."

Upon this they again marched forwards in a body, and immediately upon reaching the quarter inhabited by the Israelites, the mob separated into small parties, and instantly every house was so surrounded as to prevent the possibility of any escape. But this was only a prelude to the tragedy that was to take place, for, shortly afterwards, thick curling smoke was seen ascending in every direction, and then followed the cries of human creatures in distress, mingled with the crackling of burning timber, and the falling in of roofs where the destructive element had raged most furiously.

Whilst this was passing, Simon Hyde had proceeded towards the house of Isaac of Tadeaster, judging cunningly enough that if he could by any means secure Rebecca, he might receive from Sir Gaston de Neville a reward that would amply repay him for the service. Upon gaining admittance, therefore, he addressed himself to the trembling old man, and, in a surly tone, demanded the immediate surrender of his daughter.

"My child," replied Isaac, "is in her own chamber, whither she has flown to escape the violence of those who have made this unprovoked attack upon our people."

"Then you must bring her hither instantly," exclaimed the ruffian, "or the consequence of your refusal will fall heavily upon her."

"Villain! what wouldst thou do?" demanded the Israelite.

"That thou wilt quickly know without my being at the trouble of answering thee," replied Simon Hyde. "However, I will for once explain myself, and therefore I tell thee that unless the girl is surrendered to me in less than five minutes from this time, I will set fire to thy dwelling, and thyself and daughter, and all else that the house contains, shall be utterly destroyed."

"Wretch!" exclaimed Isaac, "thou darest not put thy cruel threat into execution."

"That you will see presently," answered the ruffian, "if my demand is not complied with."

"Why dost thou demand my daughter?" asked the old man, in despair.

"Ask me no questions, but answer those I put to you," exclaimed Simon, furiously.

"Thou wilt slay my child."

"No, I will save her life, if you only do as I have bid you," replied the villain.

"Save her, said you?"

"Aye, and that is no trifling favour," answered Simon Hyde, "seeing that all others belonging to her tribe are this night doomed to death."

"Aye," cried the old man, with terror, "for what dread purpose wouldst thou save her?"

"Why, if the truth be told," replied the ruffian, "I have an idea of conveying her to the castle of Sir Gaston de Neville. She will prove a marketable commodity there, and I shall, no doubt, receive a reward from the knight that will amply repay me for the extra trouble I shall have in the affair."

"Wretch!" exclaimed the old man, furiously, "and does Sir Gaston de Neville know of this? Is it he who has set thee on to perpetrate this most cruel and accursed act of thine?"

"Why, to tell you the truth," replied Simon Hyde, "the knight is not at all aware of what I have proposed. It is entirely a bright thought of my own; and between ourselves, I think you must be mad to yield your daughter to the flames rather than see her become the mistress of Sir Gaston de Neville."

"I will hear no more," exclaimed Isaac, seizing a burning brand from the hearth, and flourishing it threateningly at his antagonist; "too long already have I endured this insolence of thine, and now thou shalt either quit my house, or I will strike thee dead at my feet."

"Say you so, old man?" exclaimed the ruffian; "nay, then, if that's the case, it is high time that I should do something for my own protection."

And rushing as he spoke towards the venerable Israelite, he grasped him firmly round the body, and after a struggle of a few moments' duration, threw him heavily to the ground. Still, however, the old man was not quite subdued; and Simon Hyde, raising the piece of wood he had wrested from him, was about to aim a deadly blow at his head, when a loud shriek was heard, and Rebecca, wild with despair and terror, rushed frantically forward.

"Oh, spare my father," she cried, in piteous accents—"spare him, I entreat, and do not add the murder of an old man to your many other crimes."

"I want not to harm him, girl," replied the ruffian; "and since you have come just in the nick of time, I would know whether you will prefer going with me to remaining behind to be burnt in the fire that will soon consume this cottage?"

"Whatever my destiny may be," replied Rebecca, firmly, "I will not leave my father."

"Well, then, I suppose force must make you," exclaimed Simon Hyde, and seizing her in his arms, he was about to bear her from the place, when the door was suddenly burst open, and Black Ivan presented himself before the villain.

"Wretch!" exclaimed the Outlaw, as he snatched the almost fainting girl from his arms, "it is well thou hast not carried the girl away from her father's house; for hadst thou done so, thine own life should have answered for it."

"And who art thou," demanded Simon Hyde, "that dost interfere where thou art not required?"

"It matters not who I am," answered the other, drawing his dagger, and preparing for any sudden attack that might be made on him. "I am here to protect the helpless against the violence of a lawless set of villains, and I, therefore, give thee fair warning that thy own life will fall a sacrifice to my fury, unless thou dost instantly quit a place where thy presence is not required."

"Hah! I know you now, sirrah," exclaimed the tanner, as a sudden thought flashed across his brain—"thou art the Outlaw, Black Ivan, and we will not part till I have earned the reward that has been offered for thy apprehension."

"Indeed!—and dost thou know what will be the consequence of thy presuming to lay hands on one who scorns thee, as a foe too insignificant for his notice?"

"Humph!" exclaimed Simon Hyde, "you want to threaten me, I see—you would stab me, perhaps, with that ugly weapon of yours. But I'm not to be frightened quite so easily as you may think for, since I have only to raise my voice, and there's plenty of fellows outside that would rush in to my rescue."

"But not in time to save your life," answered Black Ivan. "The scoundrels, I dare say, would speedily come on hearing the alarm raised, but I should not be compelled to yield before many of them had paid the penalty of their own rashness."

"Why, what could you do against their numbers?" demanded the tanner, with a sneer.

"More, perhaps, than you imagine," answered the Outlaw. "At any rate, I must either fight resolutely or fall into the hands of my foes, and I should not fail to let them experience a little of that recklessness of danger that hitherto they have only heard spoken of as a rumour which was scarcely worthy of being credited."

"Aye," answered Simon Hyde; "but you forget that a price has been set upon your head, and that there are thousands who, like myself, would not mind running a little risk for the sake of earning a reward that would make a rich man of whoever may be lucky enough to lodge you in the hands of the king's officers."

"I tell thee, fellow," exclaimed Isaac of Tadcaster, who by this time had recovered himself sufficiently to comprehend the conversation that was going on—"I tell thee, fellow, thou art encouraging a hope that never will be realized. The king is aware that he has this day owed his life to the generous interference of Black Ivan, and a proclamation has been ordered to be immediately issued, promising a free pardon to Black Ivan for all former transgressions, and requiring him to present himself before his majesty, in order that his services may be rewarded as they deserve."

"Ha!" cried Simon Hyde, "is a ruffian like this to escape because he happens to save the king's life?"

"Such is the order of our noble sovereign," answered the Israelite. "He is as generous as he is brave, and will not suffer the righteous claims of Black Ivan to be treated with neglect, merely because he happens to have committed a few offences against a certain person, who, there is every reason to believe, was the cause of driving him to the lawless career he has since adopted."

"And so," exclaimed the tanner, "a robber is to escape because he happens, luckily enough, to have saved the king's life."

"It was not quite so much through luck, sirrah, as you seem to imagine," answered the Outlaw. "The truth is, I chanced to know that a conspiracy had been formed to assassinate the king this day, and it was with a determination to save his life that I ventured to trust myself in the midst of so many enemies. The result you are already aware of; and as I know the names of those who were engaged in the cowardly conspiracy, I would have them be cautious how they act in future, lest I should denounce them as villains and traitors."

"And do you also be cautious," answered Simon Hyde, "for in spite of the king's pardon, there are others who would willingly pay a handsome reward to the man who will rid him of you for ever."

"You speak of Sir Gaston de Neville."

"I do," answered the tanner; "you know how often he has vowed vengeance against the Outlaw, should he ever happen to fall in his way again, and there is a report abroad that at least five hundred pieces of gold will be the reward of that man who will slay him."

"And you, of course," cried Ivan, "would gladly earn the money you speak of?"

"There can be little reason to doubt it."

"Then why lose an opportunity so favourable as the present?" demanded the Outlaw. "Here I stand before thee! and if thou dost think I am better armed than thyself, say what arms thou wouldst like me to divest myself of, and I will cheerfully throw them away. So thou seest I am willing to place myself on equal terms with thee, and then we will see whether thou canst earn the reward from Sir Gaston de Neville of which thou hast spoken."

"Psha!" retorted the other, "dost thou think I am mad to run such a hazard as thou hast spoken of? No, no—there is not the least occasion for me to risk my life, and so I'll e'en wait till I have another opportunity to make sure of the prey I lie in wait for."

"Aye, you prefer lying in wait till you think I may not have it in my power to defend myself?"

"Why, I shall at least take care," answered the tanner, "not to throw away my only chances of success in this affair. Black Ivan has a name of cunning that few men can be a match for; and therefore he must expect to be met with an equal degree of caution."

"And pray what caution does it require," demanded the Outlaw, "seeing that thou hast a hundred or two of fellows outside, who would assist thee should there be need of their services?"

"Aye, but they may be cowards."

"There thou hast given them their true character," replied Ivan, "or they never would have followed thee to make this wanton attack upon the unfortunate Jews."

"The Jews deserve no pity from us," answered Simon Hyde; "they are unbelievers; and we, who are Christians, are bound to exterminate them from a land they have so long cursed with their presence."

"Your people are unjust to us," exclaimed Isaac of Tadcaster, in a voice of humility; "we seek but to be peaceable dwellers in your land, and yet you bring charges against us of crimes that we never contemplated."

"Aye, it's all very well to pretend this innocence," retorted Simon Hyde, "but we happen to know that your people contrive to get all the gold of the country into your own possession. We are poor, whilst you and your tribe hoard up your ill-gotten gains; and by and by, I suppose, we shall be obliged to bow down and submit to the accursed sons of Israel."

"We seek nothing of the kind," replied Isaac; "on the contrary, we comport ourselves with all humility, and are willing even to endure insults and injuries without murmur or complaint."

"You pretend to do so at present," answered the tanner, "but in my opinion you are only waiting a good opportunity to put your rascally plans into execution."

"Have we ever given thee cause to suspect us of such designs?" demanded the old man.

"I'm not here to answer a parcel of impertinent questions," replied Simon Hyde. "You know pretty well what I came for; and though I have been interrupted by this robber, yet, depend upon it, the evil day is only put off for a little while, so I would advise you to yield quietly, and perhaps your life may be spared through the mercy of Sir Gaston de Neville."

"What !" cried the Jew, with horror, "does he offer me life on condition that I will aid him in his base designs upon a daughter whom I love beyond all else the world contains ?"

"He does," replied Simon Hyde ; "and, in my opinion, the terms are too good to be rejected."

"Tell him from me, then," exclaimed Isaac, trembling with emotion, "that I am not afraid to die, and that the last moments of my existence shall be devoted to the protection of my daughter. Tell him this, sirrah; and moreover say to him, that if he will but spare my child, I will never cease to pray for one who has so much need of the intercession I have spoken of."

"And what, think you, Sir Gaston cares for your intercession ?" demanded the other ; "he is a Christian knight, who has fought in the sacred cause of religion, and therefore has little need for the prayers of an unbelieving Jew."

"And, truly, a very pretty specimen we have had of his boasted Christianity," exclaimed Black Ivan ; "we have seen him persecuting a helpless people, who have never given him the least cause of complaint; and, as if that were not enough, he has entered into a traitorous conspiracy to assassinate the monarch he is sworn to aid and protect against all enemies."

"I know nothing about that," answered Simon Hyde ; "the knight you speak of will pay me sufficiently well if I chance to do him a service, and therefore I will speak well of him till I can see cause to do otherwise."

"In that matter you will, of course, do as you like," replied Ivan; "but, since I have now an opportunity of doing so, I warn you never again to seek the injury of these people, who I have sworn to shield from the malice of their enemies. They are under my protection, sirrah, and I warn you that any injury which may be done them shall be fearfully avenged upon those who may be foolhardy enough to provoke my fierce displeasure."

"Aye," exclaimed the tanner, "but it shall be no fault of mine if you have an opportunity to carry your boastful threat into execution. At present you are safe, but perhaps the next time we meet you may have to acknowledge that Simon Hyde was too much even for the cunning and address of Black Ivan, the Outlaw !"

"And why," demanded the other, if you think that, "do you not make the best use of your present opportunity ? I am now alone, and you can, if you think proper, summon to your aid those valorous comrades who have summoned you here with the very creditable design of murdering a whole race of people, against whom no cause of complaint can be shown. Come, finish the business you have begun, and summon hither the ruffians that have accompanied you for blood and rapine."

"I am not to be so easily deceived," replied Simon Hyde, whose suspicions were aroused by the easy and composed manner in which the other had spoken ; "you have your band of desperadoes lurking about in the neighbourhood, and I suspect you would like to have an opportunity to bring them upon us, that we may fall into a snare that you have laid for our destruction."

"Come," answered Ivan, "I will be candid enough to confess that for once you have guessed pretty nearly the truth. My men, as you say, are concealed at no very great distance from this place, and three notes on my bugle will bring them to my assistance. So you see I am not quite so unprotected as you imagined, and that you have escaped death even at a moment when it threatened you most nearly."

"And perhaps even now," observed Simon Hyde, "they will fall upon me when I leave this place?"

"That will depend upon yourself," answered Ivan, "for there is not a man under my command who will seek to injure you unless they first hear the signal I have told you of. You may leave this house without fear, but, if you value your life, never interfere in matters that concern you not. Return to your home, Simon Hyde, and henceforward attend to your own proper business, instead of seeking to injure those who have never given you cause of offence."

"Aye, aye," retorted the other, gloomily; "it's your turn now to claim the victory over me, but, depend on it, my chance will come before very long, and then you will not have another chance of getting off so easily as you have on the present occasion."

"You threaten me, sirrah?" exclaimed Ivan.

"I do, but it will soon happen that I do more than threaten," retorted the other. "There is a reward to be earned that's worth the looking after, and much am I mistaken if the gold of Sir Gaston de Neville does not find its way into my pocket."

"Be not too sure of that," answered Ivan, quickly, "for it may happen, that instead of the reward finding its way into your pocket, my dagger may find its way into your heart; so be cautious how you proceed, or this affair will, in all probability, cost you your life."

"We will speak of this another time," answered Simon, moodily; "at present, it must be admitted, I have been foiled when I least expected it; and, therefore, I will now take my leave, with a promise to be better prepared for any future meeting that may take place between us."

With this, he turned sulkily away to rejoin his comrades, who by this time had been driven from the scene of their late mischievous attack upon the Jews. Ivan watched his departure with a sullen look of defiance, and then addressing himself to Isaac and his daughter, he bade them be of good heart, since they had now less to fear from the violence of their enemies than they had ever had before. He also assured them that he would be constantly on the watch to ascertain if further treachery was intended towards them, and departed with a promise to fly to their succour and protection, should his anticipations of their future safety prove unfounded.

CHAPTER XCIX.

" In what have I e'er wronged thee,
That thou dost league thyself in deadly hate
Against my life ?"

OLD PLAY.

WHEN the king returned to his palace after the ceremony of the coronation, his first thought was to send to his brother, Prince John, from whom he required an explanation of certain rumours that were spread abroad, touching his share in the conspiracy that had been entered into for his assassination. But the prince had already anticipated such a message, and, dreading an interview, until he had had an interview with his associates in crime, he sent back an excuse to the effect that he was ill in consequence of the traitorous attempt that had been made upon the life of his royal brother; and, with many expressions of deep concern, promised to hasten to the palace as soon as he had sufficiently recovered from the effect of the alarm he had experienced.

But King Richard was not to be deceived by the crafty devices of an enemy, who, he was well aware, had a design upon the throne which he himself at present occupied; and, sending for his faithful friend Sir Reginald Courtney, he solicited his counsel and advice, under the difficulties in which he found himself involved.

"You are aware," he said, "of the grounds upon which my suspicions rest, and of the little doubt that exists as to the share my brother has in the conspiracy that has been formed to take away my life. In my own mind his guilt is clearly established; and yet, could it be done with safety to myself, I wish to shield him from the consequences of his crime, and even to receive him once more to my favour and confidence."

"And is he aware of your majesty's gracious intentions towards him?" asked Sir Reginald.

"I believe not," answered the king; "at any rate, I have just now sent a message requiring his immediate presence here, and he has sent back an excuse, pleading illness for disobeying the command I sent him."

"It is most likely," returned Sir Reginald, "that he fears the consequences of his crime?"

"No doubt of it," answered Richard, "and yet, he little knows my heart if he thinks I would pursue my own brother with the vengeance he is conscious of deserving."

"Does your majesty mean to take no notice of a plot that had so nearly ended in your death?"

"Why, there is the difficulty in which I find myself placed," returned the king. "If I publicly notice the affair, I must bring my brother to a punishment that I would fain avoid; and, therefore, I was determined to speak with him privately upon the subject, and, after cautioning him of the evil consequences that must follow his further connection with these conspirators, to pardon him, on condition that he will henceforth abandon all designs against me."

"But does your majesty believe that your clemency will have the desired effect?"

"I am almost afraid to believe it will not," replied the king; "and yet, how can I act otherwise, seeing that the honour, and perhaps the safety of Prince John, must depend on the course I now adopt."

"Your situation, it must be acknowledged, is an extremely difficult one," answered Sir Reginald Courtney; "and yet, when you come to reflect on the dangerous league that has been formed against you, I can see no alternative except that of acting with promptitude and decision. Your safety rests upon it; and, therefore, I again entreat your majesty to lose no time in putting an end to a conspiracy, that, I fear, may prove too successful."

"Nay, I think there is little to be apprehended, since the failure that took place this day," replied King Richard. "At all events, we have foiled them in one instance, and I am inclined to think my foes will imagine it hardly safe to proceed further in the affair, now that they are aware that their evil practices are known to me."

"I am almost afraid that it will prove otherwise," answered Sir Reginald Courtney.

"And what ground have you for such a fear?" demanded the king, hastily.

"I think," replied the other, "that, finding themselves likely to fall into the snare they have laid for your majesty's destruction, they will only become the more desperate, and that they will strike the fatal blow when you and your friends are least prepared to expect it."

"In that case," answered the king, "it behoves us to keep a strict watch upon their actions; we shall thus guard against the danger we apprehend, and thus I may avoid the exposure of my brother, who has taken so guilty a share in the plot that has been formed for placing him upon the throne I at present occupy."

"But you will thus shield others who have less reason to expect your royal clemency."

"I am aware of my foes," answered King Richard, "and am well prepared to avert the evils they have so traitorously devised against my safety."

"Aye," replied Sir Reginald Courtney, "but they profess to be friends, and thus you are deceived into a confidence that I fear will, ere long, prove most fatal. Sir Gaston de Neville is among the most dangerous of your foes, and he, at least, should be secured, ere he has another opportunity to carry his designs into execution."

"Sir Gaston is well aware that his base intentions towards me are known," replied the king. "I spoke to him immediately after my escape from assassination, and the tone in which I spoke was alone sufficient to convince him that I knew he was concerned in the cowardly attack."

"And, for that very reason, there is the more danger to be appre-

No. 76

hended from him," answered Sir Reginald. "From this time, he will live in continual dread of meeting his deserts, and that will urge him to take immediate steps for the the accomplishment of a project which has just failed in so providential a manner."

"I shall soon be able to judge how far he may be trusted with safety," exclaimed the king; "he has my commands to attend here to-morrow morning, and I will then learn whether he will accept my pardon with gratitude, or still rank himself on the side of my enemies."

"Trust him not, my liege," cried Sir Reginald; "trust him not, I implore, for his word is not to be relied on. He will appear penitent, but it will only be to deceive you into a notion that nothing more is to be feared from him. I well know the hypocrisy of this arch traitor, and would still regard him with suspicion, even if he were to swear a renewal of that fealty which he has forgotten."

"Why, surely," exclaimed King Richard, "you would not have me doubt the solemn promises of a knight who has often exhibited his prowess in the field, and fought bravely for his sovereign?"

"Again, I say, do not trust him," cried Sir Reginald. "He has thus far deceived you by an appearance of loyalty, which has only been assumed as a blind to prevent your suspicions falling upon him. You have, at length, discovered his treachery, and believe me, to trust him further, will only be to favour the infamous projects he has in hand."

"I must not be too precipitous in this affair," answered the king, after a brief pause, "or I may chance to injure one whom I have no direct evidence against. True, I have long suspected him of being an enemy, but it is possible I may have wronged him by the thought."

"Nay," exclaimed the knight, "but there are others besides your majesty, who have suspected him."

"Perhaps so," replied Richard, "but they may have foully wronged him by the suspicion."

"And yet, that can hardly be," answered Sir Reginald, "seeing that the ruffian who attempted your life this morning, was one of Sir Gaston's retainers."

"Aye, that certainly does look suspicious," returned the king; "and yet methinks it would be going too far, were we to condemn the master unheard, for the acts of a villain who happens to be in his employ. The fellow may have been engaged by other parties; and, therefore, his attempt against my life was possibly unknown to Sir Gaston de Neville, till the cowardly act was so singularly frustrated. It is our royal pleasure, however, that a strict search shall be made after the ruffian, and perhaps the application of the torture will wring from him the secret of who it was that employed him."

"I have already given orders that a careful search shall be instituted after him," replied Sir Reginald. "The knave has hitherto had the good fortune to escape from us, but the reward I have offered for his apprehension will, I trust, be the means of placing him in our hands. He shall then be carefully questioned, and, my life on it, Sir Gaston will not prove so innocent of this crime as your majesty seems to imagine."

"Nay, it must be confessed, that I have my misgivings of Sir Gaston de Neville," answered the king, "though I am unwilling to condemn him unheard. I shall, however, have an interview with him in the morning, and I shall then be the better able to judge whether he is as guilty as we fear."

"And will your majesty trust yourself in the presence of a man of whose intentions we have so much reason to be afraid?"

"Certainly; I never yet hesitated to stand before even a dozen foes, and, surely, there is little reason why I should be afraid of meeting one."

"Aye," replied the knight, "but the one we are now speaking of, is so treacherous, that there is every reason to believe he will come armed to assassinate you."

"Hah! think you he is so monstrous a villain?"

"There is but too much reason to fear it," answered Sir Reginald. "I know him to be treacherous, and, therefore, would entreat your majesty to see him in the presence of some of your faithful friends."

"Which would look like cowardice," exclaimed Richard; "however, I can give you every credit for good intentions towards me, and, therefore, I will impose upon you the duty of remaining in the adjoining room with a dozen of our best spearmen. You will there overhear the conversation that takes place, and should I clap my hands, you may regard it as a signal that I require your prompt services to secure the knight."

"Your majesty may rely on it that I will not fail to be in attendance," replied Sir Reginald. "I will be there ere Sir Gaston de Neville arrives, and should there seem to be any peril, will not hesitate to secure him as my prisoner."

"But, observe me," added the king; "I shall not require your presence, unless you hear the signal of which I have spoken. It is likely he may be indignant at an accusation such as I have to bring against him, but you are not to make your appearance in the chamber until you have received my commands. This you will observe, as you esteem my future favour and regard."

"Since it is your majesty's command, I will, of course, obey it," replied Sir Reginald, "though I must still suggest that you are running a risk which ought to be avoided."

The king, however, was resolute in his determination; and having dismissed Sir Reginald Courtney, he shortly afterwards retired to his sleeping apartment, there to cogitate further upon the events of the day, and to devise other means for the frustration of a traitorous plan that he well knew was in progress against him. But these suspicions he was anxious to conceal from his friends, whom he feared would be too zealous in his cause; and choosing rather to rely upon his own judgment, he determined upon adopting a course that would be equally certain to foil the designs of his foes, and bring upon them as much punishment as he desired.

Leaving him for the present, we must follow Sir Gaston de Neville, who, haunted as he was with a guilty mind, passed a night of restless uneasiness that utterly deprived him of that sleep which tired nature so much required. It was, therefore, with a pale and haggard countenance that he rose on the following morning; and hastening to the Armoury he found there one of his retainers, from whom he learnt that Bertrand le Noir had secretly returned to the castle in the course of the night, and who had requested an audience with his master as soon as he quitted his chamber. This intelligence was most satisfactory to Sir Gaston, whose chief source of alarm had been lest his retainer should fall into the hands of any of the king's friends, who might induce him, by bribes or threats, to confess the whole affair, and thus implicate all the parties who had taken a share in the conspiracy that had been formed against the king. The news, therefore, removed a weight of anxiety from the heart of Sir Gaston de Neville; and dismissing the man with a liberal present, he desired him to send Bertrand le Noir with as little delay as possible. Nor was he kept waiting long in suspense, for within a few seconds afterwards a knock was heard at the Armoury-door, and immediately the person he was anxiously waiting for made his appearance.

"So," exclaimed the knight, "you have again foiled the blood-hounds that were in pursuit of you, I see. You have escaped the fate that I almost feared would befall you, and I have still a faithful servant left, upon whom I can rely in the hour of difficulty and danger."

"Yes," replied Bertrand, sulkily, "I have escaped, as you see, Sir Knight, but it has not been without much trouble; and as it seems likely I shall get poorly rewarded for all the risk I run, I have come to tell you that for the future you must find some one else that may be more inclined than myself to run the hazard of his life for nothing but empty promises."

"Why, how now, Bertrand!" exclaimed Sir Gaston;—"what means all this from one that I thought my friend?"

"Why it means that fine words don't fill an empty purse," replied the retainer. "In short, it means that I have run into danger to serve you, and now I must sneak out of the country in the best way I can, or risk falling into the hands of people that will not have much mercy if they should once lay hold of me."

"But there is no danger of your falling into their hands, Bertrand," exclaimed the knight, soothingly; "here you are safe, and, therefore, you have little reason to reproach me for what has unfortunately occurred."

"And how am I to know that I am safe?" demanded the retainer. "You care little who suffers so that you escape yourself, and, therefore, I am determined either to effect my escape from England, or purchase my own safety by revealing the whole secret of your treasonable plotting with Prince John."

"Villain! would you betray us?"

"Aye, for you have deceived me."

"In what have I deceived you?"

"Why, in not rewarding me for the services I have performed;—a dozen times, at least, I have risked my life for you, and yet I am still nothing more than the servant of the man who has urged me to run into danger."

"If that is your only complaint it shall soon be removed," answered Sir Gaston. "Here is a purse of gold that is well worth your acceptance, and the sum shall be trebled ere thou hast lived another week."

"Why this looks somewhat better," cried Bertrand, weighing the purse in his hand;—"this is, certainly, a more substantial way of rewarding a man; but still there is something else that I should like to be satisfied in before I say whether you have used me quite fairly or not."

"What is it thou wouldst know?" asked Sir Gaston.

"I would like to know how I am to be certain that you will not deliver me up to those who are even now in active pursuit of me?"

"Nay, you may be assured that I will keep you here in safety," answered Sir Gaston;—"my own life depends upon my doing so, since I could hardly expect you to keep faith were I to betray you into the hands of your foes."

"Aye, it's all easy enough to say so," replied the retainer; "but in the event of your securing your own pardon, there is little dependance to be placed in your thinking much of an humble individual like myself. Besides, there might be a certain condition made, that I should be given up to the tender mercies of my foes; and in that case I should have a poor chance of having my former services considered as a reason why I should escape the death I have deserved for being your dupe."

"You have mistaken me, Bertrand," exclaimed Sir Gaston de Neville; "your services can never be forgotton by me, and whilst I live you may depend upon having one friend who will never desert you."

"I may depend on you, then?"

"To be sure you may;—I sent for you to say that instant means must be taken for preventing the possibility of your falling into the hands of those who seek your life."

"And the only way of doing so," answered Bertrand le Noir, "is to give me an asylum in your castle till this affair blows off a little; in the course of time people will cease to trouble their heads about me, and then I may find an opportunity to escape without the fear of being taken."

"How many of my people know of your being in the castle?" asked the Knight Templar.

"Only the one that you just now spoke to," answered the ruffian. "I came in by stealth whilst the darkness of night favoured me, and was making my way towards the dungeons for concealment, when the fellow came suddenly upon me: in an instant I found that I was recognized, and drawing my poniard, I should have buried it in his heart, had not his well-known tones assured me that he was a friend, from whom I had nothing whatever to fear. In fact, I once saved the fellow's life, and in gratitude for the service, I believe he would willingly, at any time, lay it down to save me from danger."

"You think, then, he will not mention your presence here to any one in the castle?"

"I feel perfectly assured, Sir Knight, that he will keep the secret faithfully."

"In that case," answered Sir Gaston, "you have little cause for uneasiness. Here you may remain safe for the present, and I will myself take care that no one knows of your having sought a refuge within my fortress."

"And yet it appears to me," observed Bertrand, "that you are not altogether without a share of suspicion in this business. I have heard it whispered before now that Sir Gaston de Neville was no friend of King Richard's, and, depend on it, you run some danger of falling under the displeasure of your sovereign."

"I have had some uneasy thoughts upon that subject," answered Sir Gaston, "but cooler reflection encouraged me to hope that matters will not turn out so badly as I had expected. The king must be aware that his brother is at the head of this conspiracy, and he, therefore, cannot proceed against me without, at the same time, taking steps that will involve Prince John in the ruin that would crush me."

"But they are not upon the best of terms," replied Bertrand le Noir; "and, therefore, it is likely the king may take the first opportunity that presents itself, to get rid of a rival that aims at taking possession of the throne he now occupies."

"That," answered the knight, "would not be so easy an affair as you seem to imagine. Prince John has already many friends who are ready to rise in his behalf at any moment when they may be called upon to do so; and there are thousands of others who would follow their example, to rid themselves of a monarch whose partiality for the Jews has given occasion for much dissatisfaction. In truth, Bertrand, I should not be sorry to see a quarrel between the king and his brother, since there would then be a fair pretext for bringing the affair to a speedy issue."

"But which issue," observed the retainer, "might chance to place you in a very awkward situation."

"If so, I must abide by the consequences," replied Sir Gaston. "At any rate I have determined to place every thing upon the die, and if events should turn out differently to what I anticipate, I can perish without regretting the part I have taken in this affair. The king, as you well know, has never entertained the favourable opinion of me that I could have wished :—he has ever regarded me with an eye of suspicion and distrust, and it was partly in revenge that I, at length, resolved to side with Prince John, who I knew had long entertained a design to seizing the reins of government."

"Well," exclaimed Bertrand, "you will, of course, act as you think proper in this affair; but if you would adopt my advice ——"

"If I should humble myself at the feet of the king and ask pardon for my offences, and promise never to offend in future," interrupted the knight. " I his is the advice you would give, Bertrand, but sooner than follow it, I would risk the ignominious death that probably awaits me."

"I certainly should counsel you as you have said," answered the retainer; "and under all the circumstances, I think no safer method can be thought."

"Aye, aye, I know your thoughts as well as you do yourself," answered Sir Gaston de Neville ;—"you think that if I obtained my own pardon, that it would be easy to get you off without the punishment you are in fear of. But my mind is made up, and let the consequences be what they may, I will never seek a reconciliation with a king who I utterly hate."

"In that case then," replied Bertrand, "I shall expect you to find some way to get me out of the trouble I have got into through foolishly meddling with affairs that I had no business with."

"My word has already been given to that effect," exclaimed Sir Gaston; "for the present, however, you must remain here, and the first favourable opportunity that presents itself will be taken to get you out of England."

"And what assurance have I that you will do as you have promised?" demanded the retainer.

"My word," answered the knight, "which you know I never break even though it may be given to an inferior like yourself. I have told you that this place shall be a secure asylum against your enemies, and when the search after you has in some degree slackened, I will engage a ship to carry you abroad, where you will live safely and in luxury upon the sum of money it is my intention to bestow on you."

"Aye, now we begin to understand one another a little better," exclaimed Bertrand le Noir; "that, indeed, would be some recompense for the trouble and danger I have incurred in your behalf; and as I suppose you mean to be as good as your word, I shall rest satisfied till I have completed your bargain."

"Then here let our conference end for the present," answered Sir Gaston; "you will now go with me to occupy an apartment in the northern wing of the castle, which is shunned by all the foolish people through a rumour that that part of the building is haunted by an evil spirit. You, however, have no idle fears of that kind, and, therefore may safely abide there till an opportunity occurs to convey you abroad.'

"And how am I to obtain food?" asked the retainer.

"I will myself visit you twice a day," replied Sir Gaston, "and, therefore, you have nothing to fear on that score. It would, perhaps, be dangerous to entrust any one else with the secret, and ——"

"But one other already knows it," interrupted Bertrand, "and he may save you the trouble you are so considerate as to take upon yourself."

"I will trust no one," answered the knight; "in fact, it is my intention to tell him that you have left the place, and thus you will be more safe here than if your presence was known even to a friend."

Bertrand was about to reply, but the knight, with an impatient gesture, moved towards the door, and, pursuing his way through a long and winding corridor, conducted his retainer towards the chamber allotted to his use. At the entrance, however, Bertrand paused, as if suspicious lest some trick was about to be played upon him; but the apparent kindness of his master overcame these thoughts, and he stepped into the room, which he had scarcely done, when the door was violently slammed to, and the turning of the rusty key in the lock told but too plainly that he had suffered himself to be led into the snare that had been laid for him.

To describe the rage of Bertrand le Noir at discovering the imposition that had been practised upon him would be impossible. At first he vented his fury in loud curses and imprecations on the person who had thus cheated him; then he had recourse to prayers and entreaties; but finding none of these of any avail, he next began to look around, in order to see whether there was no way to escape. But in this he was doomed to be disappointed, for the door was of such immense strength as to defy his utmost efforts to burst it open; and the window, which he next examined, was at so great a height from the ground as to threaten him with instant death should he be fool-hardy enough to attempt an escape by leaping from it. Thus fairly baffled in every point, he, at length, threw himself upon the floor, and again gave vent to his rage in the most furious and horrible curses upon the man who had thus cheated him.

We must now, however, leave him for the present, and return to Sir Gaston de Neville, who, exulting in the success of his stratagem, hurried away from the place where he had left the retainer, in order to escape the heavy imprecations that were uttered against him. He, however, now felt himself more secure, since the only man who could betray him was safe in his custody; and having sought out the man who was aware of Bertrand's return to the castle, he told him that the fugitive had again left the place, with the intention of seeking a vessel in one of the ports, from whence he could make his escape to a foreign land. It was no very difficult task to make the man believe this; and having succeeded beyond his most sanguine wishes, he shortly afterwards left the castle to pay his much dreaded visit to the king.

This was, indeed, an interview that Sir Gaston had every reason to fear, for he knew that Richard was well aware of the conspiracy in which he was engaged, and there was much to be apprehended should the justly incensed monarch resolve to institute a rigid enquiry into the affair. He, however, resolved to put a bold face upon the matter; and as there was no positive proof against him now that Bertrand le Noir was kept out of the way, he began to entertain hopes that he might yet succeed in persuading the king of his own innocence. Somewhat revived by this hope, he approached the palace gates, where it appeared orders had been left concerning him, so that he no sooner presented himself than a page conducted him to the door of the chamber, where the king was anxiously expecting his arrival. But it was not without some misgiving that Sir Gaston stepped into the room, nor were his fears allayed when he observed the dark frown of displeasure with which his entrance was greeted.

" You are late with your visit, Sir Knight," exclaimed Richard; " I have been waiting your arrival these last three hours, and began at last to believe that you had so far forgotten your loyalty as to disregard the commands I gave for your appearance here this morning."

" Your majesty, I—I—"

" Nay, no stammering, Sir Gaston," cried the king; " but let me hear the plain truth. There are certain rumours abroad that you are not well affected towards us; and from circumstances that have lately occurred, I am grieved to say, afford some ground to fear that the report is not altogether groundless."

" And who," asked Sir Gaston de Neville, " has dared to breathe a word that would give rise to so foul a calumny?"

" I do not judge altogether from reports, Sir Knight," answered the monarch, gravely, " for there are other things that tend greatly to raise suspicions in my mind that I have not a very faithful subject in Sir Gaston de Neville."

" I do not understand your majesty."

" Nay, that is scarcely possible," replied the king: " for you are, of course, well aware, that a traitorous attempt was yesterday made against my life?"

" I was myself a witness of it," answered Sir Gaston, "and, therefore, cannot plead ignorance of the vile attempt you speak of."

"Oh," exclaimed the monarch, " I am quite aware that you could not attempt to deny some knowledge of the base outrage."

" True," answered Sir Gaston; " but though I saw the attempt that was made against your life, I had neither hand nor part in it."

" Indeed!—perhaps, then, you will also deny knowing anything of the villain who sought my death?"

" I do deny it."

" I thought so," answered King Richard, " and, therefore, that you shall no more plead ignorance, I now inform you that the attempted assassin was no other than your own retainer, Bertrand le Noir."

" The villain!" exclaimed Sir Gaston, with affected indignation; " but let me hope he has fallen into the hands of your majesty's officers of justice, and that he will receive the punishment he so well merits for his traitorous designs."

" And, if all traitors were to meet with their just reward," answered the king; " there are others whom I could mention that would not escape harmless."

" Perhaps so," replied the knight, with affected calmness; " but let me hope your majesty does not allude to any of those who are supposed to be your friends."

" It is to such that I allude," answered the monarch. " Nay, to speak more plainly on the matter, I have but too much reason to believe that you are engaged in this plot."

" I, my gracious liege!"

" Even so," Sir Gaston de Neville, " and, I believe, if need be, proof enough could be produced to convince the world that I have no wronged thee by this charge."

" Indeed I have been wronged by this suspicion," replied the knight but the working of his countenance showed that he felt severely the charge that had been spoken against him. " I have enemies, my liege

and they, probably, have given utterance to these falsehoods in order to ruin me in the estimation of my sovereign."

"I am not used to pay much attention to every idle rumour that is whispered in my ear," replied Richard, "and, therefore, you have little to fear from those who might seek to injure you in the way you have mentioned. There are reasons, however, for believing you guilty of conspiracy against me, and not the least evidence I have to produce is the fact of the attempt upon my life having been made by a favourite retainer of your own."

"The man is no favourite of mine," answered Sir Gaston ; "in fact, I quarrelled with him not long since, and he has left my service."

"And was that previous to his seeking my death on my way to the Abbey Church ?"

"It was."

"And has he not since then sought refuge within your castle ?"

"He did so, but I refused to give him the shelter he required, and he immediately left to go I knew not whither."

"How was it, then," asked the king, "that you did not secure him ?"

"I was unprepared at the time," answered Sir Gaston, with hesitation, "and he took his departure before I had recovered from the surprise into which I had been thrown."

"Your answers are all aptly prepared, I see," exclaimed the king, "but your confusion proves that you had no wish to bring the villain to punishment."

"Indeed, your majesty, I deserve not these suspicions," cried Sir Gaston de Neville, quailing under the questions that were thus put to him. "I am innocent of any evil designs against you, and if need be, will abide the issue of a trial."

No. 77

"Aye," returned the king, "it is well to speak thus boldly when you know that there are reasons why I desire to avoid a public trial."

"Those reasons may be known to your majesty," replied Sir Gaston, "but I do not presume to understand to what you are now alluding."

"Indeed! you know not, then, that at the head of this conspiracy is one, who I should last have suspected."

"Your majesty can mean no other personage than your brother, Prince John."

"I do," answered the king; "he has had the chief direction of this most unnatural conspiracy against me; and you, Sir Gaston de Neville, have aided him to the utmost of your means."

"And even if it were so," exclaimed the knight; "it seems that I am no worse than many others who have enlisted in the same cause."

"Aye," replied the king, "and they happen to rank amongst the chief of my subjects. I, however, know them, and as a proof that I make no idle boast, read over this list, and you will see your own name among the many others who are well known to be leagued against me."

"We have been deceived," cried Sir Gaston, starting with surprise, as he saw the parchment, on which were written the names and titles of his numerous associates; "we are betrayed by some villanous spy, and are now at the mercy of those who will gladly avail themselves of the opportunity to shed the blood of their enemies."

"You are mistaken, Sir Knight," answered the king, "for no further notice will be taken of this affair, if you and your fellow conspirators think fit to accept our royal pardon, and to become faithful subjects in future."

"I can make no promises of the kind," replied Sir Gaston, sullenly, "our secret is now divulged, and it is, therefore, hardly to be supposed that your majesty will ever place in us that confidence which we formerly enjoyed. Our actions would be watched by secret spies, and every proceeding would henceforth be regarded with suspicion and distrust."

"That will depend on yourselves," exclaimed Richard, "for I pledge you my royal word that all shall be buried in oblivion, on condition that you give me no further cause to suspect your designs."

"Aye," replied the knight, doubtfully, "such may be the case with your brother, but we, who are not allied to your majesty by blood, will shortly fall under your displeasure when least prepared to defend ourselves against the charges that may be brought against us."

"You refuse, then, to accept the mercy I have been disposed to offer those who have been leagued against me?"

"I do," answered Sir Gaston, sullenly.

"Am I then to regard you, henceforth, as an enemy seeking to destroy me?"

"That," replied the knight, "is a question that it may not be safe to answer. That I am now in your power I well know; but let the consequences be what they may, I now and for ever cast off the allegiance that once bound me to you."

"Hah! am I to be defied in my own palace?"

"I have spoken the truth boldly and fearlessly," answered Sir Gaston de Neville, "and, if that offends your majesty, you can send me to a prison, and from thence to the scaffold."

"That I do not seek your blood, Sir Knight," replied the king, "our present interview must have convinced you, that I have even offered you pardon on certain very easy conditions, and yet I still find you as resolutely as ever opposed to me."

"And good reason I have had for the course I have pursued," exclaimed the Templar, "even a trifling love affair, betwixt me and the Hebrew Maiden, was interfered with, and from the moment that I found you were in favour of the Jewess, I swore to take the first means that offered themselves for revenging myself. I then joined with those who I knew had formed a league for the purpose of driving you from the throne, and though we have hitherto been unsuccessful, I warn you that the moment is not far distant when we shall succeed in our design."

"This language is bold, and might tempt some to punish the traitor that uttered it," exclaimed the king; "I, however, desire not revenge, and, therefore, you may depart from me without hindrance. But, remember, Sir Knight, I may not always be disposed to endure your insolence, and the time may come when your life will answer for the treason that lurks in your heart."

"Come when it may," replied Sir Gaston, "you will ever find me ready to meet my death with firmness."

"You reject my offer of pardon, then, proud knight?"

"I do," answered Sir Gaston; "and now, as I suppose our conference is at an end, I will take my leave never to return here again unless it be to do the deed I have boldly avowed in your presence."

With these words the knight haughtily turned to leave the room; but ere he had reached the door, Sir Reginald Courtenay entered, with about a dozen spearmen, who, pointing their weapons at the Templar, formed so impassable a barrier, that his further progress was completely prevented. Supposing that he was now a prisoner, the knight directed a fierce glance towards the king, and, in a sullen tone of voice, said:—

"This, then, is the faith with which your royal word is to be kept; but a few minutes since it was declared that I was at liberty to leave the palace unmolested, and yet, it seems, your myrmidons were in readiness to arrest me at the moment of my departure."

"My word is not broken," answered the king; "nor are you, as you imagine, a prisoner."

"How is it, then, that I have been stayed in my progress from your palace?"

"That," replied the king, "is a question that can be better answered by Sir Reginald Courtenay, whose zeal for me has induced him to present himself before us without orders. You have, however, no violence to fear, and, as I said before, are at liberty to quit my presence whenever you may think proper."

"In that case I shall at once avail myself of your permission," answered the haughty Templar. "Again, therefore, do I say farewell; and better will it be for both of us if we never meet again."

With this, Sir Gaston de Neville strode haughtily from the chamber, leaving the king full of perplexity as to what course he ought to adopt, in order to prevent the mischief with which he was threatened. Sir Reginald Courtenay would fain have hurried after the Templar to bring him back, but the king would not listen to the proposition, and the young knight was shortly afterwards dismissed from the royal presence, with a command to set a double guard throughout the palace, and to keep a strict watch upon those whose intentions towards the king were with so much reason suspected.

CHAPTER C.

"What though he once hath escaped ?
A second time my snares shall compass him,
And then my aim is ended."

THE COURT PAGE.

IMMEDIATELY upon quitting the presence of his sovereign, Sir Gaston de Neville directed his steps towards the palace of Prince John, where, being well known, he was readily admitted, and conducted to the apartment where the ambitious prince was waiting impatiently to learn in what manner his ungrateful conduct towards the monarch was likely to be treated. It was, therefore, with considerable pleasure that he saw the approach of the Knight Templar, and pausing suddenly in his uneasy pacing up and down the chamber, he welcomed his unexpected visitor with more than his usual warmth.

"Thou hast come," he exclaimed, "to bring me the tidings I have been so anxiously waiting for. Say, therefore, and as briefly as thou canst, how I am likely to fare after the unfortunate defeat of our plan yesterday?"

"I fear badly enough, your highness," answered Sir Gaston. "At any rate, the king is aware of all our secrets, and, though he affects but little displeasure at present, I suspect a storm is brewing, that, when it bursts forth, will destroy us."

"Ha! does he know those who are his enemies?"

"He does, your highness;—nay, he showed me a written list, containing the names of all who have been concerned in this conspiracy."

"And was my name among the number?"

"It was."

"And thine own?"

"Was there also."

"In that case, our only safety lies in flight."

"Nay," answered Sir Gaston de Neville, "I believe there is less danger than you seem to apprehend. The king is rather mercifully inclined, and he promises that no further notice shall be taken of the affair, on condition that we enter into no further league against his life."

"And what answer didst thou give?"

"I told him that I would make no promise; for that I had, in fact, sworn to render all the assistance I could to drive him from the throne, and that I was determined to keep my oath, even though it should be the means of bringing me to the scaffold."

"And yet," observed Prince John, "in spite of all this, he suffered you to depart unharmed?"

"He did," replied the knight; "but the reason of his being so mercifully inclined is easily explained. He knows that he cannot punish the inferior agents in this conspiracy, without injury to him who has placed himself at their head; and, therefore, out of pure compassion towards your highness, he has suffered the affair to pass over without further notice."

"For which instance of his clemency, I scarcely thank him," replied Prince John. "There is, however, one thing in our favour; we may still go on with our plot, and when our next opportunity arrives, it shall not fail as it did in the former instance."

"It was, certainly, most unfortunate," exclaimed Sir Gaston de Neville, "and yet, I know not that the fault could be fairly attributed to any one in particular."

"Excepting thy blundering retainer," cried the prince. "He hesitated when the blow ought to have been struck, and thus an opportunity was given to arrest his arm."

"Aye," answered Sir Gaston, "and well would it have been for all of us, had the weapon been wrested from the grasp of the knave, and buried in his own bosom."

"Dost thou believe he will turn traitor to us then?"

"Perhaps he might, had an opportunnity been given him," answered the knight; "but, suspecting what might possibly happen, I have placed him in confinement, and never more will he have a chance of doing us a mischief that might terminate fatally to all."

"Thou hast done well, Sir Gaston," cried the prince; "and yet, perhaps it would have been the safer course to have delivered him over to the tender mercies of some of the ruffians in thine employ. They would have known how to deal with him, and thus we should have had nothing more to fear."

"But there are none whom I could have entrusted with the task you speak of," answered Sir Gaston.

"How is this?" exclaimed the prince; "art thou so ill served by thy people that there are none among them upon whom thou canst rely?"

"The truth is," answered the knight, "that Bertrand le Noir happens to be a favourite among them, and they would refuse to obey my orders were I to command them to perform the deed you speak of. I have, however, taken care to secure him in a part of my castle that is never visited; and as his presence is unknown, he will have little chance of receiving assistance from any of his friends."

"But he may find means to escape," observed the prince, "and a poniard would have effectually secured our future safety."

"I have already said that I know no one whom I could have trusted with the commission of the deed."

"And why," asked the prince, "couldst thou not have done it with thine own hand?"

"How!" exclaimed Sir Gaston, "wouldst thou have me become a shedder of human blood?"

"Come, come," cried Prince John, "these conscientious scruples of thine sit not well on thee. I have known thee ere now, but never did I hear thee scruple before when a service like this was required of thee."

"To tell thee the truth," replied the knight, "I have had a notion of this before. That the fellow may live to do us an injury I am much afraid, and if I could but make up my mind to commit the act you have spoken of, we should thus secure ourselves from the mischief he may contemplate."

"True, and therefore, since your own personal safety is concerned, I should think it would not be very difficult to remove the scruples that at present stand in your way. Your own life depends on your decision, and therefore I leave you to choose between your safety and the life of this ruffian."

"I have already determined upon it," replied the knight; "Bertrand le Noir shall perish by my hand!"

"Aye, now thou speakest somewhat more like thyself," exclaimed the prince, in a tone of encouragement. "The alternative, bad as it appears, must be adopted; and, therefore, the sooner it is put into execution the better."

"He shall die this very night!"

"And thou wilt do the deed thyself?"

"I will."

"Why, that is well said," exclaimed the prince, with a demoniac laugh. "You will thus render the cause a service, and from this time we have no fear of being betrayed to those we seek to destroy."

"But I," cried Sir Gaston, bitterly, "shall become a murderer."

"Aye, but it will be in thine own defence," answered Prince John;— "there is no help for it, you know, and, therefore, I see no use in regarding the thing in the light you seem to do. Besides, no one but myself will be aware of the deed; and, depend on it, I shall never speak of it, since I am, in some degree, concerned in urging thee to rid thyself of a probable foe."

"You have all to answer for," cried Sir Gaston; "for never should I have committed this act if it had not been at the instigation of your highness."

"Well, comfort thyself in that way, if it is thy will," exclaimed the prince. "Blame me in thine own mind if it will be any consolation to thee; and, at the same time, remember that I would not have hesitated to commit the deed half as long as thou hast, if I had been in thy place."

"Yet," answered Sir Gaston, "should our plot succeed, so that you gain the throne you strive for, it is not unlikely you will seek to rid yourself of those who know too much of this affair, and then, perhaps, you will bring against me this charge of murder, which would surely end in my ignominious death."

"Dost thou think me so cold-blooded a villain?"

"I know your highness's nature well," replied Sir Gaston, "and, therefore, do not hesitate to repeat that such an event as I have mentioned is likely enough to take place."

"In that case," exclaimed John, "thou hast been fool-hardy to join with one who is so little to be depended on."

"That," exclaimed the knight, "is an affair that it is now too late to think about. I have chosen my course, perhaps, more out of pique to the king, than any real regard for thyself; and having once taken up your cause, I am now resolved to go on with it in spite of all the dangers I may be threatened with."

"Well, well," cried the prince, "it would be folly for you and I to quarrel about trifles. We are both engaged in one cause, and though we may not have the most favourable opinion of each other, it is still necessary that we keep up our outward show of good fellowship, in order that no difference may be observed by those who are engaged with us."

"And in the event of your coming to the throne, as we anticipate," observed Sir Gaston de Neville, "I am to receive the rewards and honours that were promised when first I engaged to serve you."

"Thou hast the word of a prince for it," replied John, "and again I tell thee thou may'st rely on my faithfully keeping it."

"I will trust thee," exclaimed the knight.

"And I, with equal confidence," answered Prince John, "will rely on the promise thou hast given that Bertrand le Noir shall die."

"Thou may'st do so: for when to-morrow's sun rises, the fellow you have named shall have ceased to live."

So saying, Sir Gaston de Neville was going to leave the presence of John, but as he turned to take his departure the door opened, and a page entered, conducting in the Earl of Albermarle and Sir Walter Marsham.

"We came, my prince," said the former of these two personages, "to satisfy ourselves that your highness was safe from the adventure that had terminated so unfortunately. At the same time we take the opportunity to express our continued determination to assist, with our utmost zeal, in any fresh plan that may be devised for the overthrow of him who now sways the sceptre which it is our desire to see placed in your own hands."

"You have my warmest thanks, my lord, and you, too, Sir Walter, for this manifestation of your dutiful regard," answered the prince "That you were both faithful to me, I well know; but grieved am I to say, that there are some who feel inclined to desert me because our scheme happens to have failed in one instance."

"Let us know their names," cried the earl, "that we may henceforth shun them as traitors to the cause."

"I will save his highness the trouble," exclaimed Sir Gaston de Neville, "by declaring that I am one of the persons that have been alluded to."

"You! Sir Gaston?"

"Even so; I have somehow fallen under the displeasure of his highness, and now, I suppose, must lie under the imputation of being his enemy."

"Your future actions must prove whether you are so or not," answered John. "I, however, will not judge you too harshly, so that there is yet plenty of time to retrieve the character you have lost."

"May I ask what is the cause of this coldness between you?" asked Sir Walter Marsham.

"At present there is no occasion to enter further into the subject," answered the prince. "Our quarrel has for the present been made up, but whether we continue to be friends, will depend on Sir Gaston himself, who has promised to remove one principal cause of the disquiet that disturbs me."

"Which shall be done according to the promise I have given," replied the knight.

"In that case," exclaimed the Earl of Albermarle, "we may now proceed to arrange some fresh plans in the place of that which was so unexpectedly frustrated. The king, it seems, will make no further enquiry into the recent affair, and, therefore, we may now hope to succeed when next we make the attempt."

"And when," asked Prince John, "do you propose it shall take place?"

"On Thursday next."

"Hah! so soon my lord?"

"Why, it must be admitted the notice is short," answered the earl, "but for that very reason our design is the more certain to terminate favourable. The king will thus be taken by surprise, and he may be slain ere assistance can possibly reach him."

"And how know you," asked Sir Gaston de Neville, "that a favourable opportunity will present itself?"

"Because I have ascertained," answered the earl, "that on that day his majesty takes the diversion of hunting the stag at Enfield Chase. We will there assemble a large party of our friends, who may lie in ambush till their services are required, and upon a preconcerted signal, they may rush from their hiding place, and slay the king ere his friends can aid him."

"And is there no way," asked the prince, "by which I can obtain the throne but through the murder of my brother?"

"It is the only sure way," answered Sir Walter Marsham, "for should we fail in doing that, certain ruin would fall upon all who are in any degree connected with the affair. Remember, we have once escaped after our projects have been discovered, but should we be found again plotting for the king's overthrow, nothing will save us from meeting an ignominious doom."

"You mean to say, then, that our own safety will depend on destroying my brother?"

"It will."

"In that case there is no alternative," exclaimed Prince John, with seeming reluctance; "you see, my friends," he continued, "how unwilling I am that my brother's life should fall a sacrifice, but it appears that we should be endangered were we to adopt a different course, and, therefore, yield myself to the stern necessity of the case, by consenting that the deed we are contemplating shall be arranged by yourselves."

"And may we expect your aid in accomplishing it?" asked Sir Gaston de Neville.

"If it is the general wish of my friends, I will most certainly be present at the time and place appointed;" replied the prince. "I, however," he added, hypocritically, "would fain be excused so painful a trial of my feelings, since it cannot but be supposed that I most heartily deplore the necessity that exists for committing an act of violence against my own brother."

"His highness is in the right," exclaimed the Earl of Albermarle; "there are sufficient of us to perform this business without calling upon him for aid, and, therefore, I trust there are none among us who would so far overstep the bounds of natural feeling, as to require him to be present on the occasion we speak of."

"I am satisfied to let the matter rest in your hands, gentlemen," exclaimed Sir Gaston; "nor should I have made the proposition I have, if it had not been that his highness has just now counselled me to commit an act that I sought to avoid."

"How!" cried the prince, angrily, "art thou going to reveal that which passed in privacy between us?"

"I am not," replied Sir Gaston, "but I still had a hope that you would see the difficulty in which I am placed, and release me from the promise I have given."

"I will release you from nothing," exclaimed Prince John, "the safety of all of us depends entirely upon fulfilling your pledge, and, therefore, I expect you will not break your word."

"But it does not appear to me that we are in any danger from the person you allude to," returned the knight. "I have already told you that he is secure in my custody, and, therefore, none of us have anything to fear from him."

"And may he not escape, Sir Gaston, in spite of all the vigilance you may exercise?"

"It is impossible," answered the Templar: "the place where he is confined is well secured, and, being situated at a great height from the ground, he cannot venture to leap from the window without meeting certain death."

"From your conversation," observed Sir Walter Marsham, "I can understand something of the secret affair between you; it appears to be necessary that some person or other should be removed by a death of violence, lest he should have it in his power to mar our projects. Such at least seems to be the opinion of one, but the other appears to be anxious, if possible, to avoid the unnecessary death of a fellow creature."

"It is not unnecessary," exclaimed Prince John; "in fact, if the

than we speak of is suffered to live, we know not how soon he may obtain an opportunity to inform the king of all that has passed between us."

"Ha!" cried Sir Walter, "in that case, then, he must be one of those who have been in league with us."

"He knows more of this affair than I could have wished," returned the prince.

"You think, then, there is danger to be apprehended from him?"

"I am quite convinced of it."

"May I presume to enquire his name?"

"Bertrand le Noir."

"Why, as I live, that was the name of Sir Gaston's retainer, who made so fatal a blunder, when he might have made sure work of his victim."

"You are right, Sir Walter," exclaimed the prince; "it is the man you have mentioned, and I, therefore, ask you whether it will be safe to suffer him to live, knowing, as we do, that he may have a free pardon offered him on condition that he reveals our secret."

"Your highness is quite right in looking to our safety," observed the Earl of Albermarle. "This fellow will, doubtless, prove a traitor to us, and, therefore, I, for one, vote for his death, if no other alternative remains by which we may secure ourselves from the mischief he has it in his power to do."

"There is no other," answered Prince John, "and, therefore, I say again, this man must die."

"And I say," exclaimed Sir Gaston de Neville, "that having once

No. 78

pledged my word to it, I will not fail to do as I have said. Bertrand shall die, but let his blood be upon those who have forced me to shed it."

"The blame may rest upon me, if you will," replied Prince John; "the fellow has blundered in the task that he undertook, and, as there is every reason to suppose that he will take the earliest opportunity to save his own life at the expense of ours, it is no more than self-protection if we put him out of the way before he can do us the mischief."

"I have said already, that my promise shall be fulfilled," exclaimed Sir Gaston de Neville. "The fellow has little claim upon me for pity, and, as he is now safely lodged in an obscure part of the castle, I can visit him without giving rise to suspicion, and, when next we meet, I will give you proof that Bertrand le Noir has ceased to live."

"'Tis well, my good friend," replied the prince; "and, now, my Lord of Albermarle, it seems that you have concerted another scheme by which I may step upon the throne now occupied by my brother. You have, ere now, proved yourself most zealous in my cause, and, from the brief explanation you have already given, I think there is some reasons to hope that, on the present occasion, we shall not be disappointed as we were on the last."

"There is no fear of it, your highness," answered the earl, "I have already told you that the king hunts in Enfield Chase, on Thursday next, and, whilst a party of our friends surround him, it must be the duty of one of us who are now present, to stab him to the heart."

"Aye," cried the prince, "and who, I prithee, my lord, is to be the chosen one?"

"That must depend upon chance," replied the earl. "These two knights and myself must draw lots, and he upon whom the duty falls, must be sworn to execute his task faithfully."

"Agreed," exclaimed Sir Gaston; "I have already one murder to commit, but, should it fall to my lot to assassinate the king, you may rely on it I will not shrink from the duty imposed upon me."

Upon this, three slips of parchments, of different lengths, were cut and placed in the hands of Prince John, who held them whilst his associates in treason drew them out one by one; the drawer of the shortest it being previously arranged, taking upon himself the task of slaying the king. When all three had drawn, the slips of parchment were compared, and, as the one that had been taken by Sir Gaston de Neville proved to be the smallest, he, of course, was declared to be the person upon whom the lot had fallen.

"It seems," he said, "that fate has declared against me, and that, unwillingly though it may be, I am doomed to become the shedder of King Richard's blood. Such appears to be my destiny, and I will not shrink from it when the hour of trial arrives."

"Do you swear," demanded Sir Walter Marsham, "to plunge your poniard into the heart of the king?"

"Most solemnly I swear it."

"And, in case you should fail in your design and fall into the hands of our enemies, you will never betray by word or sign who it was that instigated you to attempt the deed?"

"I will be faithful," replied Sir Gaston; "but the king is already aware of the names of all who were engaged in the last transaction; so of course, in the event of my failure, he would be at no loss to conjecture who are engaged in the present plot against him."

"It would be but conjecture at the best," replied Prince John, "and I think I know him well enough to be convinced that he would suffer the matter to rest quietly, rather than expose me to the penalties which I might have to pay. At any rate I should not feel much alarm since he has already proved that he is not very anxious to pursue me with his wrath, though he knows how deeply I was concerned in the last plot against him."

"And you, Sir Gaston de Neville," exclaimed the Earl of Albermarle, "are, I suppose, ready to fulfil your promise, whenever called upon to do so?"

"I am, my lord."

"But may we rely on your faithfully discharging the trust confined to you?"

"I have already sworn to do so, and never do I break a pledge, however unwillingly it may have been given."

"On Thursday, then, you will be prepared to accompany us to Enfield Chase."

"Aye, at any hour of the morning it may be your pleasure to appoint."

"Your answers," exclaimed the earl, "are most satisfactory, and I entertain no doubt of the zeal and caution with which you will execute your task. We will, however, leave all other arrangements till a future opportunity, when we will have a meeting at your own castle, to consult further upon the subject. And now, your highness, having thus far decided, we will take our leave for the present, with a promise to exert ourselves in this business, so as to make your possession of the throne as soon as possible."

With this the three conspirators took their departure, and separating in the corridor, they left the palace by different doors, so as to avoid raising the suspicions of those persons who might possibly guess from the secrecy of their visit, that more treason was hatching against King Richard of the Lion's Heart.

CHAPTER CI.

" If I have an enemy,
Shall I not strike him dead to save myself
From further danger ?"

THE SANCTUARY.

SHORTLY after Sir Gaston had returned to his castle, he was met by Edith, who came running towards him with a countenance in which the utmost terror and consternation were depicted. For some few moments she was unable to give utterance to a single word, which so excited the wrath of her impetuous master, that in a voice of thunder, he desired to be informed the cause of her present agitation.

"Oh, Sir Gaston, "she at length ejaculated, "what ever is going to happen next? We have had horrors enough of all sorts, lately, but this one is—"

"Speak, girl," roared the knight; "what new piece of foolery have you come to annoy me with?"

"Ah! the ghost! the ghost!"

"What fresh madness is this?" demanded Sir Gaston.

"It's no madness, but the downright, real truth," answered the terrified girl.

"Do you speak of the armed apparition?"

"I know not what apparition it is," replied Edith, "but there has been the most horrible outcry in the castle that ever was heard, and it came from the northern tower, that everybody knows is haunted, and that no one will ever venture to visit if it was to a mine of gold."

These few words convinced Sir Gaston that the outcries she spoke of had been uttered by Bertrand le Noir, and wishing to encourage the belief, he merely replied that he had heard something about the place being haunted, and that the present horrible cries served to confirm the truth of the report.

"Ah!" cried Edith in reply, "but is it not dreadful to live in a place that is overrun with ghosts and hobgoblins? I declare I'm always being frightened out of my life, and some of these days I expect to be carried off to a certain place in a flash of lightning."

"If you have any terror of the kind," replied Sir Gaston, "you are at liberty to leave the castle whenever you may think proper to do so."

"I would take your advice if I could," exclaimed Edith; "but the truth is, I have no other home to go to, and what is a poor friendless girl to do under such circumstances as these?"

"Ask me no questions," returned Sir Gaston, "but either leave the place this instant, or make up your mind to keep these follies to yourself."

"It's not so easy as you think to keep such horrors as these to one's self," answered the girl. "The whole castle, I tell you, is swarming with ghosts and apparitions, and, if they will appear to quiet, harmless creatures, like myself, it follows naturally that we must speak of them, let who may be offended at it."

"Are the cries you speak of continued up to this time?" asked Sir Gaston de Neville.

"I don't know," replied the girl, "but I heard them plainly enough scarcely half an hour ago."

"And, I suppose," observed her master, "that you have been chattering all over the castle about an affair that has originated, very likely, in your own ridiculous imagination."

"Nay, I have not said a word about it to any one," replied Edith; "and that, too, for the very best of all possible reasons, for, just as I was running off to tell them all about it, I met you, and of course I was stopped before I could do any mischief?"

"Then, observe me, girl," exclaimed Sir Gaston, "speak not about it to any one, and, in return, I will bestow on you a purse of gold."

"I'll be as mute as a mouse, Sir Gaston," answered the girl, dropping a curtsey, on hearing of the promised reward. "I am discreet when there's any occasion for it, and can keep a secret as well as any woman in existence, so I'm sure I shall not go telling anybody of the ghost, nor of its sounding for all the world as if it was Bertrand le Noir, cursing and swearing like a madman."

"Bertrand le Noir!" exclaimed Sir Gaston, in a tone of the greatest alarm.

"Yes, indeed, sir. it was uncommonly like his voice," replied Edith; "and I've been thinking it's very likely to have been him for—"

"Fool!" roared Sir Gaston," knowest thou not that he is nowhere in the castle?"

"I have heard it said so," answered the girl; "and people think he may have been killed after his late wicked attempt upon the life of our good king; and, if he has been slain, its not at all surprising that his unhappy ghost should come to visit a place where it is said he has committed so many crimes."

"Whoever told thee that he had committed crimes beneath my roof?" demanded the knight furiously.

"Everybody says so," answered the girl, "and what everybody says, you know, must of course be true."

"In this instance it is not true," cried Sir Gaston, "and, if ever I hear such a report mentioned again, the person who utters it shall bitterly repeat the folly he or she has been guilty of. So observe me, girl, if ever you should hear such a rumour repeated, contradict it, and say, I shall not fail to punish whoever may give utterance to it."

"I will obey you in all things, Sir Gaston," answered Edith, "only, never ask me to go to that part of the castle where those horrible cries come from."

"You may be sure I shall not do that," he replied, "for the place has been shut up these many years past, and there is but one way of access to it, and that is known only to myself."

"But, surely," cried Edith with alarm, "you do not mean to visit it?"

"That is a question I cannot answer just at present," replied the knight; "but even if I keep away from the place, it will be from no idle terrors such as those that have just now sent you almost out of your wits."

"Ah!" returned the girl, "but you have not heard the sounds, or, perhaps, you even, bold as you generally are, would not be quite so venturous."

"You say the voice seemed to proceed from the northern tower, which has been closed for years past?"

"Yes, Sir Gaston."

"And did it appear to you as if the sound came from within the tower?"

"It did; and, lucky enough I thought of it, for, had the apparition contrived to get out, I perhaps might not have been here to tell the story."

"I will myself see to this," exclaimed Sir Gaston; "here is some mystery that I cannot fathom, and I will myself visit the place you have raised so ridiculous a report about."

"Oh, for goodness sake don't think of going there!" cried the girl with unfeigned alarm. "The ghost may be a very spiteful one, and may not be best pleased at being visited without an invitation."

"It matters not," replied the knight, "I never yet feared a mortal, and, therefore, it is hardly likely that I shall be afraid to meet a shadowy antagonist."

"You are determined to run the risk then?"

"I am."

"And what think you the people in the castle will say when they come to hear of it?"

"How! have you so soon forgotten my command? Did not I tell you scarcely a minute since, that this foolish story you have been telling me, must not be mentioned on any account?"

"Ah! I had forgotten that," replied the girl; "but it's hardly to be wondered at, either, for I'm sure I've seen and heard quite enough lately to drive what little sense I had out of my head."

"Be more discreet, then, in future," exclaimed Sir Gaston, "for, should I hear that you have been chattering about this affair, you will meet my severest displeasure. There are always enough idle stories about the castle, and I do not want to have another added for fools to talk over, and make their comment about."

"Why, to be sure, there's very little else talked of in the castle except ghosts and apparitions," replied Edith. "And then there's the armed apparition that they say has appeared to you, and—"

"Silence girl," exclaimed Sir Gaston, "and let me hear no more of a subject of which I have grown weary."

"Very well, sir," replied the girl, "but, supposing anybody else should have heard these sounds, what answer am I to make in case they should happen to ask me any questions about it ?"

"Appear ignorant of what they mean, and say you heard nothing of it."

"But that would be telling a great fib, and—"

"That you are now, no doubt, so well used to that, it will come naturally enough."

"Well, if I do tell any stories about it," returned the abigail, "the fault must rest with you that bade me tell them."

"Remember the reward I have promised, on condition of your complying with my commands."

"I'll remember all that," answered Edith, "but I am sure the money will be hard enough earned, considering that it's a woman you have asked to keep this mighty secret of yours."

"You have heard me," cried Sir Gaston, "and, therefore, I charge you to obey my injunctions. You must now leave me, Edith, and if you value your own safety, breathe not a word to any one of the foolish story you have just been relating."

Edith was about to reply, but the impatient waving of her master's hand warned the damsel that it would be dangerous to say anything more, and, hurrying out of the room, she went to the domestic's hall, where she was quickly surrounded by a number of the servants, who anxiously enquired whether she had heard the fearful sounds that had filled them with so much dread. But Edith was prudent enough to keep her own counsel, and assuming an appearance of the most perfect composure, she affected to laugh at their stories, assuring them that she she had come from the part of the castle they had mentioned, and that not the least sound had disturbed or given her alarm. With this, the other's were obliged to be satisfied, but none believed her, for it was deemed quite impossible that any one could be so deaf as not to hear sounds that had filled the whole castle with alarm.

We must now return to Sir Gaston, who, pondering on the words of Edith, began to revolve in his own mind certain projects that he had formed to remove the apprehensions that filled his soul with dread. That the sounds which the girl spoke of, had been uttered by Bertrand le Noir, he could entertain no doubt, but it proved to him that the presence of his retainer in the castle was in danger of being shortly discovered; it, therefore, became necessary that some steps should be immediately taken to avert such an unwished-for event, and recollecting the promise he had made to Prince John, he felt more convinced than ever that some method must be directly taken to prevent the probability of his escape, and the consequent exposure that would certainly follow. This served to fix his resolution ; and arming himself with a dagger, he hastened from the part of the castle where he then was, and proceeded towards the northern tower, where Bertrand was confined.

It was not, however, without some alarm that he approached the place of imprisonment, for he knew the resolution of the retainer, and, therefore, expected to meet with an antagonist who would not be easily overcome. But it was absolutely necessary for his own safety, that the attempt should be made, and preparing himself for a desperate struggle, he removed the bolts, and suddenly presented himself in the room occupied by Bertrand le Noir. In order, however, to put the prisoner off his guard, he assumed an air of more than usual composure, and stepping forward a few paces, said :—

"You see, Bertrand, I have not forgotten you, though, perhaps, my late singular conduct may have given rise to suspicions in your mind that I was about to play you false."

"What else could I think?" demanded the retainer, fiercely. "I was tricked into this place and made a prisoner, when I thought you meant to do me a service."

"And so I do, Bertrand, "answered the knight, with an appearance of the utmost sincerity. "I still intend to save you from the consequences of your late attempt on the king's life, and if you can endure confinement in this place for a little while longer, you will find me as good as my word."

"Why do you take such special pains then to lock me in this room?" demanded the other.

"For your own safety, to be sure," replied Sir Gaston; "I feared lest any one should enter this room during my absence, and, therefore, took the precaution, lest your being in the castle should be discovered."

"'Tis false!" exclaimed Bertrand; "this story might impose on others, perhaps, but I happen to know you, and can see that you say this only to cheat me into a belief that you have made me a prisoner only to insure my own safety."

"What other motive could I have?" asked the knight. "Have I not ever been a kind and indulgent master, and is it likely that I should now prove as treacherous as your suspicions lead you to imagine?"

"There is every reason to believe it," answered Bertrand; "you have served others in the same way before now, and I have always expected that my turn would come at last."

"You wrong me, Bertrand; on my soul you do."

"It is to be hoped I do, but it is not your own word that I'll take for it, though."

"Psha!" exclaimed the knight, "if I meant to serve you in the way you suspect, is it likely that I should have come alone to visit you?"

"There's good reason for it, perhaps," exclaimed Bertrand le Noir. "You are anxious that no one in the castle shall be aware of my presence here, and, therefore, it is hardly likely that you would have brought any one with you."

"Well, and even granting that it was so," replied Sir Gaston, "I should still have avoided presenting myself before the man I might have wronged."

"But you have come well armed, I see, and that is some proofs that you expected I was not to be fooled into a belief of your good intentions."

"True; I thought it likely enough that you would think me guilty of a gross deception, and knowing your hasty temper, I came prepared to resist any attack that might be made upon me. Now, however, I suppose you are convinced of my sincerity, and if you think fit to throw your own dagger from yonder window, my weapons shall immediately follow it, and thus we shall be placed upon a perfectly equal footing."

"I see your design, Sir Gaston," exclaimed Bertrand le Noir; "you would have me disarm myself first, in order that you may obtain an advantage over me, and thus rid yourself of one that you fear may have it in his power to injure you."

"Again you wrong me."

"Prove it then by being the first to throw your weapons from the window."

"Nay, in that case, I should throw myself completely into the power of a man who seems to be incensed against me."

"Then there the matter ends," exclaimed Bertrand; "for it appears that we equally distrust each other, and are not willing to give an advantage that might prove fatal. So let us both keep the arms we possess, and if it pleases you, we will decide this affair by trying who can make the best use of his weapons."

"How!" cried Sir Gaston, "dost thou think a knight could so far forget his own station as to enter into such a contest with his own menial?"

"The knight, then," answered the other, "should not have injured the menial he effects to despise."

"I have never wronged thee, sirrah," exclaimed Sir Gaston; "on the contrary, I have always preferred you before all others that are in my employ, and have even entrusted thee with secrets that are known to none but thyself."

"Aye," cried Bertrand, "and therein lies the secret of your present dislike to me. You know that I have it in my power to ruin you, and that a few words uttered by the despised menial you just now spoke of, would be the means of bringing your head to the block."

"You could do so, certainly," replied the knight, "but knowing you as I do, I believe there is little fear of your ever becoming so ungrateful."

"Ungrateful!" retorted the other, "and for what, let me ask, have you deserved my gratitude? Is it for placing me in the post of danger when the king was to be slain; or for now making me your prisoner, in order that an opportunity may be given for putting me out of the way, that you may be secured from future danger?"

"Nay, I have always trusted thee, Bertrand, and never hast thou yet deceived me."

"But it follows not that I should be such a fool any longer," answered the retainer.

"Hah! dost thou threaten me?"

"No; I merely wish to put you fairly on your guard, that you may be prepared for the worst."

"And by so doing," exclaimed Sir Gaston, "you may provoke me to take measures for preventing the fulfilment of the threat you have held out."

"In other words, you will keep me here as a prisoner till you have an opportunity of getting rid of me?"

"You are not very wide of the truth," replied Sir Gaston, "for you have been my prisoner for some hours, and there is nothing to prevent my keeping you here till I have thought of some other place to prevent the mischief you have threatened me with."

"You have been plain enough, it must be confessed," cried Bertrand, "and now, in return, I will be equally candid. You speak of keeping me here as your prisoner, but I tell you that your threat will never be fulfilled."

"Indeed!—and why so?"

"Because I will exert myself to the utmost to prevent you," answered Bertrand, resolutely. "That I have strength of limbs you have yourself acknowledged before now, and should I see any intention to lock me up again in this room, I shall not hesitate to thwart your cowardly measures in the best way I can."

"Villain! do you dare threaten me?"

"I dare do more than that if I am am once fairly driven to it," replied the ruffian.

"In that case," exclaimed Sir Gaston, "I will disarm thee with the only weapon thou hast."

And with these words, he rushed furiously upon Bertrand, who he held with a grasp that would have secured a man of less nerve and

strength; the retainer, however, soon released himself from the hold which the other had made upon his throat, and then raising the knight in his arms, he dashed him violently to the ground. But in an instant Sir Gaston again sprang upon his feet; the struggle between them was renewed with more fierceness than ever, and this time it appeared that the knight had gained the superiority, for after a short time, he wrested the dagger from the hand of Bertrand, and hurled it through the window. Enraged beyond all bounds at this, the ruffian collected all the strength he had to overpower his adversary, but in the attempt, his foot slipped, and they both fell firmly clutched in each other's grasp to the floor. And even then the struggle was maintained with unabated fury, till, at length, the knight obtaining a slight advantage, sprang upon his feet, and raising his dagger, would have plunged it into the heart of Bertrand le Noir, had not the other thrown himself on one side, and thus avoided a fate that seemed to be almost certain. In another moment he was upon his feet again, and then placing his back against the wall, he prepared himself to make one more desperate attempt to oppose the murderous attack of his exasperated foe.

"Sir Knight," he exclaimed, fiercely, "you have an advantage over me in possessing arms, whilst I am totally without them. I, however, warn you not to tempt a desperate man to do his worst, for if I must die, it shall not be without such a struggle as may likely enough to end in your own destruction."

"Then here let our contest end for the present," answered Sir Gaston; "the quarrel was provoked by yourself, but I can overloook the past, on condition that you will promise to be more grateful in future."

"Why, what want you now?" growled Bertrand.

No. 79

"Have patience, sirrah, and you shall find that I am not the enemy you took me for."

"Aye," replied the other, "you want time, in order that your next attack may meet with better success."

"I will promise to make no further attempts against you, on condition that you will listen patiently to the proposition I would now make to you."

"Well, proceed, then," exclaimed Bertrand; "but, remember, I shall be prepared if you intend to deceive me into a momentary belief of your sincerity."

"You have nothing more to fear from me," answered the knight, in softened accents. "The fact is, Bertrand, I would still serve you, in spite of the violence you have just been guilty of towards me. I would be your friend, and if you will but have a little patience, I shall be able to prove that you have fully wronged me by your evil suspicions."

"It will be a more difficult affair than you think for to convince me of that," replied Bertrand. "A few moments since you would have taken my life, if I had not had the good fortune to prevent you; and that, I take it, is a pretty good proof that no great dependance is to be placed in your promises."

"I was provoked, sirrah, beyond all further endurance, or I should not have sought your life," replied Sir Gaston; "however, all that is now over, and, therefore, I have only to desire that you will endure this imprisonment a little longer, and you shall soon have the liberty you require."

"Indeed!"

"You have my word for it, Bertrand."

"Your word is valueless," replied the retainer; "and I should not feel much inclined to take it, only that I happen to know that there is a better reason why I should not be afraid of you."

"And what reason is that?" demanded the knight.

"That you know your own life would be risked if you ventured to make another attack on me."

"How can that be," asked Sir Gaston, "when I am still armed, whilst you are without a weapon?"

"Aye, that may be true enough," replied the other, "but you don't seem to recollect what a desperate man will do when he finds his life is in jeopardy. If I must die, Sir Gaston, it shall not be alone, and so I warn you not to advance a single step nearer, as, in that case, I should spring upon you like an enfuriated tiger; and, should chance give me possession of your dagger,—which is probable enough,—I would at once secure myself by giving you to that death which I well know you have doomed me to."

The knight gazed upon the angry countenance of his antagonist, and a single glance assured him that the threat had not been idly made: he, therefore, retreated involuntarily a few paces, and holding his weapon so as to be in immediate readiness, said:—

"I have told you more than once, Bertrand, that you have nothing more to fear from me. You, however, refuse to believe me, and, as it would be in vain to lengthen this interview any further, I will now leave you, and take another opportunity to return when you are more cool than you are at present."

Seeing that Sir Gaston was slowly moving towards the door, Bertrand forgot the precaution he had hitherto observed, and stepping from the place where he had been standing, yielded up the slight advantage he had gained. This was instantly perceived by the knight, who, quickly turning round, made a furious rush towards the retainer, and would have buried the poniard in his breast had not the other closed upon him at the moment, and, with a desperate effort, hurled him once more to the ground. Enraged almost beyond control, Bertrand would have slain his treacherous opponent with his own weapon, but the thought of his own escape was just then uppermost in his mind, and grasping the throat of his victim, he held him so firmly that his head at last sank back, and he became insensible. Taking this opportunity, Bertrand determined to escape without delay, but as he was about to open the door for that purpose, he heard the voices of many people approaching, and who, he had no doubt, had been drawn thither by the loud outcries of the knight, when he found the imminent peril in which he was placed. Judging, therefore, that it would be impossible to escape that way, he next hurried to the window, from whence, dangerous as the attempt appeared to be, he determined to descend. Placing himself, therefore, on the outside, he slowly made his way down by means of the numerous projections in the wall, until he had performed rather more than half the perilous descent, when, his foot slipping, he was precipitated with terrible violence to the ground. For a few minutes he lay completely stunned from the effects of his fall; but, at length, reviving a little, he contrived, with extreme difficulty, to leave a place where he was threatened with so much danger.

CHAPTER CII.

" Tell me not of ghosts and apparitions,
    Such things there are not, and I'll prove it
    If thou'lt but follow me."

OLD PLAY.

WE must now follow Edith, who, on returning to the hall, usually occupied by the domestics, was assailed by a thousand questions as to the horrible noises that had just filled them with so much alarm. But, for a time, she was prudent enough to remember the caution that had been given by Sir Gaston de Neville, and, in spite of the number of queries that were put to her, she contrived for some brief period to persist in her assertions of utter ignorance upon the subject. At length, however, she could hold out no longer, and, in reply to old Jasper, the steward, acknowledged that she had heard the sounds he spoke of, and that, in her opinion, they could have proceeded from nothing else than a ghost.

"Ah!" exclaimed the old man, " that's just the opinion of all of us; we have said it must be an apparition or something of that sort; and, as the sounds came from the northern tower, there can be no doubt but this is some troubled spirit come to frighten us all out of our lives."

"You are right enough this time, Jasper," cried Edith, who, having broken the ice, was ready to tell all she knew about it; " the sound did, as you say, come from the northern tower, and pretty good reason I have to know it, for I was passing very near the place at the time, and there came such a groan that I nearly fell headlong down a flight of stairs in trying to make my escape."

"And did you see anything, Edith ?" asked Robert the Pantler, who had been an anxious listener to these words.

"See anything ?" asked the girl, with surprise, " do you believe that I was foolish enough to stop and make acquaintance with a ghost?"

"No; but I thought, perhaps, you couldn't help seeing it, for, sometimes, you know, they will place themselves before your eyes, whether you like it or not."

"Perhaps so," replied Edith, tartly; "but I can assure you I did not give it much opportunity this time; for, no sooner did I hear the noise, than I took to my heels, and when I got into the great hall, who should I happen to run against but master himself."

"Sir Gaston de Neville!"

"Aye, and looking as cross and glum as if something had happened to put him very much out of temper."

"Well," exclaimed Jasper, "and had he heard any of these terrible noises?"

"I don't know," she replied, "but he said he did not, though, I am more than half inclined to think he heard them, but would not acknowledge it."

"You told him all you knew, of course?"

"To be sure I did; and he seemed not half to like it, for he scowled more than ever, and looked as angry as if he thought I could help the ghost paying this unwelcome visit."

"And what did he say?" asked Jasper.

"Why, he enquired whether it was the black apparition that had frightened me; and when I told him it was not, he seemed more troubled in his mind than ever."

"Ah!" exclaimed the old man; "there are secrets in this castle that's perhaps well for us we know nothing about. I have heard that blood has been shed like water, and I happen to know, for certain, that many prisoners have been brought here that have never seen the outside of the place again."

"I know something of the kind," added Edith; "for, poor Adrian, who has been in such trouble lately, told me of a lady who has been confined in one of the dungeons for the last eighteen or twenty years, and it's only for assisting her a little that he's got into such terrible disgrace."

"Hush!" whispered Jasper, "if Sir Gaston should happen to overhear us talking of these affairs, we may all of us get into as much disgrace as Adrian has."

"Oh, there's no fear of that," replied the girl, "for, when I left our master, he was bent upon paying a visit to the northern tower, in order to convince himself whether I had been speaking the truth or not."

"Then, my life on it," exclaimed Jasper, "he must know something about it, or he would never venture to go to a place that we all believe to be haunted."

"I should not wonder in the least if you are right," answered the girl; "for, when I happened to say that the voice I had heard was very much like Bertrand's, he seemed terribly disturbed, and bade me not give a hint of the kind to any one."

"Which command," observed the old man, "you seem to have very carefully obeyed."

"How could I help it?" cried Edith; "haven't you all been worrying me out of my life? And should I have done so, think you, if I had not been quite certain that the secret is quite as safe in your custody as in mine?"

"Very true," answered Jasper, "I, for one, should say it will be quite as safe."

"Come, come, Mister Jasper, none of your sneering, I beg," retorted Edith, a little bit angry; "I can keep a secret quite as well as the rest of my sex, and ——"

"Aye, aye," interrupted the incorrigible steward, "there's no one here, I'm sure, that will doubt your being able to keep a secret as well as any of your sex can. That piece of credit we are all willing enough to give you; but, who ever heard, I wonder, of one of Eve's daughters that could help telling a secret?"

"If it was of any great consequence I could," replied Edith; "but as we are all concerned in this one, I thought everybody had an equal right to know it. Besides, Sir Gaston ought not to commit such shameful deeds as he does, and then there would be no occasion for him to be ashamed of their being made public."

"Let me again caution you to speak lower," exclaimed the old man. "Our master has spies about the castle, and if any of them should chance to hear what we have been talking about, he will send us to the dungeons, and look out for other servants who will be content to mind their own business without troubling their heads with his."

"The only spy that he would ever trust to," answered Edith, "was Bertrand le Noir, and he, you know, has never returned to the castle since the attempt was made upon the king's life. People do say that it was he who did it, and, if that's the case, I think it would not be very difficult to guess who it was that set him on to do the deed."

"You mean Sir Gaston?"

"Who else should I mean?" she asked; "don't we all know that he likes Prince John better than he does King Richard, and ——"

"You are wrong there, my girl," answered Jasper, "for our master cares for one just as much as he does for the other. To be sure, he favours the prince, but that's because he's out of favour at court; and, I suppose, he thinks Prince John would be sure to reward him handsomely, in the event of his coming to the throne. But all this, you know, is no affair of ours; we are but the servants of Sir Gaston de Neville, and if he acts wrong, we have no business to take any notice of it."

"And besides," interposed the pantler, "we are going altogether away from the subject of the ghosts that have been kicking up such a riot in the place. That's the affair that concerns us most at present, and so I was going to propose that we should go to the northern tower in a body, and see whether it contains an apparition or not."

"Psha!" muttered Jasper, to whom this proposition was anything but palatable; "you are a downright fool for letting such a thought enter your brains."

"A most prodigious fool!" chimed in Edith, to whom such a suggestion appeared to be very little short of sacrilege.

"Ah! you may call me what you will," answered Robert, "but it's always my plan to satisfy myself in cases like this, and if you are all too much of cowards to accompany me, I've a great mind to go there myself, and ——"

"You will have a greater mind to stay where you are," interrupted Edith; "you know you are a coward, Robert, and I very much doubt whether you would go with us, for all your boasting of what you will do."

"Ah!" cried Robert, "I see how it is, my girl, you are only angry with me because I have not popped the question before now; but never mind, Edith, it's not too late yet; and if you promise to leave off quizzing me, it's likely enough you will not have to wait much longer before I find courage enough to ask you to go with me to the altar."

"Ask me rather to go with you to the *halter!*" exclaimed the angry girl, "for, if it were to see you hanged for your impertinence, I would go gladly enough. Marry you, eh!—come, that's a tolerable piece of presumption considering you are only pantler in the establishment."

"Enough of this," interposed old Jasper, "for see how angry you have made him already, Edith, and maybe, presently, he'll be rash enough to swear that he will never ask such a little tartar to become his wife."

"In that case, he will spare himself the mortification of a refusal," replied Edith; "the fellow, I believe, has had a sort of sneaking kindness for me this long time past, and I am very glad of this opportunity of telling him a piece of my mind."

"Really," observed Jasper, "it's singular how the affair came round at all, for we commenced with speaking about ghosts and apparitions, and behold, it has turned round most marvellously to a quarrel between two lovers."

"He is no lover of mine, so don't think it," exclaimed Edith, indignantly; "to be sure, I have permitted him to speak to me, and have answered him civilly, and now, I suppose, he has the presumption to think that I am over head and ears in love with him!"

"Nay, but hear me, Edith ——"

"Silence, sir! and don't dare to speak to me!" she exclaimed, angrily. "I'm vexed with you, sir, and shall not have anything more to do with you."

How long this quarrel would have lasted it is impossible to say, but at this point it was suddenly broken off by an outcry so terrible that all started with alarm, and stared at each other as if demanding an explanation as to what could be the cause of the uproar. It was certain, however, that the sound came from the much-dreaded northern tower, and, of course, every one set it down at once as a fact that two apparitions must have met there together, and were quarreling who should keep possession of the place. Jasper was the first to recover himself, and, having gone to the hall door to satisfy himself, he returned to convince them that their suspicions were well founded, for that the sounds came from the northern tower.

"What it all means," he said, "I am at present unable to say; but if there are any here who are bold enough to accompany me, I will visit the place, and satisfy myself whether the uproar proceeds from an unearthly visitor or not."

"Why who else," asked Edith, trembling from head to foot, "do you suppose, but a ghost, would ever dare to venture into that haunted chamber?"

"By your own account, girl," replied the old man, "Sir Gaston left you not long since to visit that part of the castle. Amid the hubbub, I fancied I could distinguish his voice; and, therefore, I should like to go up, in order to see whether it was he, and whether we can render him any assistance."

"He was a fool to think of going there, and I told him as much," cried Edith. "I knew mischief would come of it, and now, perhaps he is sorry that he would not take my advice."

"It's no use talking of that now," exclaimed Jasper; "he may be in danger, and, if such is the case, it will be our duty to go and give him all the aid in our power. And hark! there's the noise again, louder than ever; so tell me who will go with me to see whether our master is in danger?"

"Not I, for one," said the huntsman, "for Sir Gaston has never been a very good master, and I'm sure he would not do as much for us if we were in danger."

"Nor I, for another," added one of the grooms, "for I see no fun in risking one's own life for the sake of preserving the life of a man that would not thank us for it."

"But surely you will not refuse to accompany me," cried Jasper, reproachfully.

"Well," exclaimed Edith, "I don't think it would be exactly fair to let an old man go alone; so I'll e'en run a little risk, and venture with you to the northern tower. We can take a survey of the place first, and if all should appear safe, we may, perhaps, go in and see what's going on."

"Why surely," cried the groom, "you are never going to be so rash as to run such a risk as this?"

"I should not have been obliged to do so," answered Edith, sharply, "if the men folks had not proved themselves to be such arrant cowards."

"We are not cowards," replied the man, "but the truth is, there's a great difference between cowardice and running a careless hazard that can do no one any service."

"You are mistaken," exclaimed the man; "for our master may be in danger, and it is our duty, whatever may be his crimes, to go to his assistance."

"Why he could expect no more from us," cried Robert, "if he was a kind and indulgent master, instead of being a regular tyrant over us. For my own part I can see no reason why we should go running after him, when it's likely enough we may be bringing danger on ourselves without doing him any good."

"Don't you hear those cries?" exclaimed Jasper; "they grow louder and louder; and I fear that even after all we shall be too late to render the assistance that is so much required."

"Well," muttered Robert, as he saw the old man hurrying away, "it would be a shame to let him go alone, so, if others will join me in it, I don't care if I make one of a party to keep him company."

Upon this several others volunteered their services, so that by the time Jasper and Edith had reached the bottom of the staircase that led towards the northern tower, they were followed by a sufficient number of persons to scare away all the ghosts that ever walked in Christendom. Rendered tolerably bold by this, they advanced up the stairs, and proceeded along a corridor; but there were many doors to force open as they went along, for the place had been closed up many years before, and no one knew of the secret means of access by which Sir Gaston de Neville usually visited that part of the castle.

At length, however, they reached a passage, at the end of which stood the much-dreaded apartment; and here the whole party paused to consult upon the best method of proceeding. Some were for one thing, and some for another, but they were pretty unanimous in one respect, which was, that they ought to be very careful before they ventured to enter a room which might disclose to them such horrors. Yet, as is frequently the case in such matters, the only woman in the company proved herself to be the most capable of giving advice; and, approaching the door, she listened for a few minutes, and then, returning to her companions, whispered that she had heard some one walking about the room, and, from the heavy sounds that accompanied the footsteps, she felt almost certain that it could be no ghost which had produced so much noise. This, however, was denied by three or four of her friends, who affirmed that there were very noisy ghosts in the world, and, as this might chance to be one of them, it was still necessary that they should proceed with the greatest caution. This counsel was not to be lightly rejected, and as there was still a disinclination to run more risk than was necessary,

Edith was again requested to listen, in order that they might be quite certain before they ventured to run any further hazard. This she accordingly did, and in a minute or two returned to inform them that the sounds she had previously heard had now entirely ceased, but that she thought she could distinguish the hard breathing of a man, as if some one inside was recovering from the effect of temporary strangulation.

This was anything but satisfactory to her auditors, but another consultation was held, after which it was decided that they should all advance in a body to the door; that Edith, as she appeared to be the boldest of the party, should be the first to enter the chamber, and the rest would be prepared to follow her in case their assistance should be required. Poor Edith was none of the bravest under ordinary circumstances, but here was a case in which the utmost exercise of her fortitude was required; and, summoning up all the resolution she possessed, she for the third time advanced towards the door, and throwing it open suddenly, so that her boldness should not have time to vanish, she beheld the apparently dead form of Sir Gaston de Neville lying on the floor. A faint scream escaped her as this object met her view, and running back to her companions, she related in a few hurried words the incident that had so much alarmed her. Then, seeing there was still some hesitation on the part of her friends, she assured them that she had seen nothing else in the room; upon which the others valorously came to a conclusion that there could not be much danger, and, plucking up what little share of courage they possessed, they forthwith followed Edith into the room, where they found Sir Gaston lying in the manner that she had described. Of course their first care was to ascertain whether he yet lived or not; and having satisfied themselves in this particular, they next applied themselves to revive him in the best manner they could. Fortunately, for their good intentions, it was not long before Sir Gaston gave tokens of returning animation, and shortly afterwards opening his eyes, he gazed wildly round the room, as if in search of some dreaded object. This was observed by the people that were assembled about him, and as it was inferred that he could be looking for nothing but the ghost, it was sagely set down as a fact that he had had a conflict with a supernatural being, and that his life had only been saved through the alacrity with which they had rushed to his assistance.

" Where is he?" exclaimed Sir Gaston, at length, with a shudder;— " where is he, I say? Bring him hither, that I may revenge myself for the violence he has committed."

" Poor fellow!" whispered Jasper to his nearest companion, " his brain wanders, and little reason is there to wonder at it, since, I dare say, the phantom came to him in some horrible shape."

" Will none of you answer me?" exclaimed the knight, angrily; " where, I say, is the wretch that has left me in this helpless condition? I command you speak."

" Who do you mean, Sir Gaston?" asked Edith.

" Who should I mean, girl, but Bertrand le Noir?"

" Heaven preserve your wits, good master!" cried old Jasper; " why, Bertrand le Noir has not been in the castle for the last two days."

" Aye, I had quite forgotten that," replied Sir Gaston, who was called to his recollection by these words. " Bertrand, as you say, was not in the castle; though, at the moment I recovered from that horrible lethargy, I fancied that he it was who had nearly caused my death."

" It was a ghost," exclaimed the pantler.

" Yes, yes, it was a ghost," repeated every one present.

This explanation of his recent adventure was perfectly satisfactory to

Sir Gaston de Neville, for he had no wish that the truth should be known, and it mattered not to him whether they believed his conflict had been with a ghost or a human being, so long as they were not aware of Bertrand having been so recently at the castle. Raising himself, therefore, from the ground, he spoke of his absent retainer as one whom he wished to see as soon as possible, as he wished to speak to him on business of the greatest importance.

"Some of you," he added, "must go forth in quest of him as soon as possible; but as we had a slight quarrel when last we parted, he may refuse to return. Say to him, however, that I have forgotten the past; and should he still refuse to accompany you hither let him be dragged here by force, since the affair I speak of will not brook even the most trifling delay."

"But," observed Jasper, "the task you have set us to do is not to be so easily performed as you may imagine. Bertrand le Noir is a most desperate fellow with his sword, and it is likely that those who endeavour to force him into your presence against his will would be made to pay dearly for their presumption."

"Am I to be obeyed, or not?" demanded the knight.

"Certainly," answered the old man: "but it is only reasonable that you should set us to do that which can be performed without danger."

"The danger is only in your own cowardly imagination," exclaimed Sir Gaston, impatiently. "Bertrand le Noir is not the desperado you have described him, but will cheerfully accompany you when he knows that it is my desire to see him."

"In that case," observed the old man, "there was no occasion for you to desire us to use force in the event of his refusal to come hither."

No. 80

"Hah! am I to be questioned by a vile menial?"

"I seek not to question you, Sir Knight," answered Jasper; "but, being unwilling to go forth on a dangerous errand like this, I would warn those about me to keep out of harm's way."

"And that they will scarcely do," exclaimed Sir Gaston, "if they dare disobey my commands in this instance."

"You desire us, then, to risk our lives when there is no real necessity for doing so?"

"There is a necessity," cried Sir Gaston, peremptorily; "the events of the last hour require clearing up, and he alone can do it to my satisfaction."

"Perhaps I may be allowed to ask one question?"

"Aye, but see that it be brief."

"There is a foolish notion among your domestics," said the old man, "that this part of the castle is haunted by evil spirits. As if in confirmation of these idle fears, strange noises have this day been heard, and on entering this chamber just now, we found you lying in a state of insensibility on the floor. It is possible you may have seen something to occasion this, and I would, therefore, know whether it is so or not?"

"It seems, then, old man," cried Sir Gaston, "that you are as superstitious as those who are younger, and have not had experience to guide them?"

"I am not superstitious," answered Jasper, "nor can I see any reason why you should refuse to answer a question that would set this foolish matter at rest."

"You presume, sirrah, on your age," cried Sir Gaston; "but be assured that it is neither your years nor grey head that shall save you from my wrath. Let him be seized, and we will soon see whether I am to be bearded thus by one of my own menials."

No one, however, offered to lay his hands on the old man, and the knight continued, more wrathfully than ever:—

"How is this?—Am I to be disobeyed by those who are the slaves of my will? Seize the hoary-headed villain, or I will strike some of you to my feet with this dagger."

"We are all of us willing enough to obey you when we can," replied Robert, who acted as spokesman for the rest. "That we are your retainers we know, but there is not one here who will be coward enough to raise his hand against an old man."

"Indeed!—then I may perhaps make you bitterly repent the insolence you have shown me. Seize him, I again command you, or the blood of some of you shall answer for this insolence."

"Be it so," replied Robert; "and if blood is your object, let mine be the first spilt, for I would rather perish than obey your present orders."

"Robert," whispered Edith, "I never liked you till this moment,—nay, I spoke sparply to you a short time since, but let that be forgotten, for you have now proved yourself to be worthy of my esteem, and I will never be angry with you as long as I live."

While this was passing, Sir Gaston strode fiercely up and down the room; but at length his fury became somewhat assuaged, and, pausing suddenly before his retainers, he said—

"I believe I was just now rather too severe to one whose age demands my respect. He is, however, forgiven; and let him, therefore, forget that I have ever uttered words that I now am sorry for."

"Aye," exclaimed Jasper, "I was sure you did not mean what you said, so here let the affair drop; and as for Bertrand, my comrades can, of course, do as they please about going in search of him."

"We will go," replied Robert, in behalf of his comrades, "but we will not undertake to bring him here by violence. Sir Gaston's message shall be delivered to him, and if that is not sufficient to answer the purpose, I am sure that anything we can do in the way of force will be in vain."

"I will be satisfied," exclaimed Sir Gaston; "go forth in search of him, and should you chance to meet, say that all is forgiven between us, and entreat him to return here, as I have an affair of the utmost consequence to consult him about. He will at once understand you, and, I doubt not, will readily obey my commands."

"And what if we should fail in performing our errand?" demanded Robert.

"In that case you must watch him carefully, in order to discover where he at present conceals himself. That done, I can take other measures to secure his return."

With this, Sir Gaston de Neville hastily left the room, to meditate in the solitude of his own chamber on various plans by which he might get Bertrand le Noir into his power, that he might take measures for putting so dangerous an enemy out of the way.

CHAPTER CIII.

"Where shall I fly to 'scape from pending death?
What refuge seek, to save me from the doom
That threatens to o'erwhelm me?"

OLD PLAY.

THE night had set in when Bertrand found himself on the outside of the castle, after his miraculous escape from death. Almost crippled with the bruises he had received from his recent fall, it was with extreme difficulty that he could move onwards; but the perils to which he was exposed left no alternative, and, bleeding as he was from numerous wounds, he slowly dragged his limbs forward, that he might search for some place where he might find concealment and rest till he was better able to resume his way.

Slowly as he proceeded, it was some time before he found any place that would afford him the shelter he required; but at length he saw by the moonlight a deserted hovel at no great distance off, and, exerting what little remaining strength he had left him, he with great difficulty succeeded in reaching the place where he might find the repose he so much needed. Here, throwing himself on the ground, he fainted from utter exhaustion, and for a time was unconscious of the anxieties and vicissitudes to which he was subjected. How long he remained in this situation he knew not, but on recovering from his temporary forgetfulness, he instantly became aware that other persons besides himself were present; and, after listening for a short time, he recognized the voices of Jasper and Robert, the two domestics of Sir Gaston de Neville. Judging, therefore, that they had been sent out in search of him, he remained quiet and motionless in the dark corner of the hovel where he was lying, for he knew that in his present weak condition he would be no match for them, and, consequently, that it would be madness to risk the consequences that might follow his discovery. Presently, however, they began to speak about him; and, listening with breathless attention, he was enabled to overhear the whole of their conversation.

"I don't half like this business that we have been set about," exclaimed Robert the Pantler. "There's a great deal of danger in it, and as I happen to be a peaceable man, I don't see why Sir Gaston should have sent me to look after a fellow that would no more mind cutting my throat than I should mind sticking my knife into a venison pasty."

"Aye, it's a mad affair after all," answered Jasper; "for we have been sent out on a fool's errand to look for a man that has gone nobody knows where. We may be within a short distance of him, or he may have taken himself off no one knows how far; and in either case all I know about it is, that I hope we shall not come within sight of Bertrand, who is too cunning to believe that Sir Gaston wants to see him for anything but mischief."

"And yet," exclaimed Robert, "to hear the knight speak, one would suppose that he had still the greatest friendship for his absent retainer."

"Aye," returned the old man, "but I have lived long enough in the service of Sir Gaston to be aware of his hypocrisy whenever he has any of his devilish objects in view. Why, I have known him smile upon the man that the next moment he was going to give over to one of his murderous associates."

"Like myself, then," observed the pantler, "you suspect that he means no good to Bertrand, in spite of all the fine words he has spoken about him."

"Why, I should think there's not much doubt about it," replied Jasper. "You saw what a passion he was in when we refused to go in search of the man, and how he afterwards turned when he found that his threats were of no use. These things we could not help noticing, and though he pretends to have made it up with Bertrand, it's only done to get him back again to the castle, that he may have his revenge on him."

"Aye, he would murder him."

"To be sure he would; for when once a man has offended him, he seldom fails to have full satisfaction. I have known him do so after years had passed away, and any one would have supposed the thing was forgotten."

"But Bertrand and he were always such excellent friends," observed the Pantler.

"That's true enough," replied Jasper; "but friends and enemies are all alike to Sir Gaston when once he has made up his mind to get rid of them. Besides, it is possible that Bertrand knows a little too much for him, and in that case he will be sure to meet his doom before very long."

"Ah!" exclaimed Robert, "that's the mischief of being taken into his confidence; for a time the knight is wonderfully thick with his friends but when he finds that he can either do without them, or they know too much of his secrets, they somehow or other disappear in a most mysterious manner, and are never heard of afterwards."

"In my opinion," observed Jasper, "the knight and his retainer have had a serious quarrel; in fact, Sir Gaston admitted as much, though he pretended that he had forgiven Bertrand, and only desired to see him again that he might speak to him on business."

"And a very pretty business it would turn out, I dare say," answered the other; "we, at any rate, should never know what it was all about, for the poor devil himself would not have an opportunity given him to tell any more secrets."

"That's very certain," replied the other; "as I said before, he has offended Sir Gaston, and from certain circumstances, I can pretty well guess the reson of his anger."

"Indeed!—then let me hear it."

"Why, you remember that after we found our master in the northern tower, the first person he enquired after was Bertrand le Noir?"

"I recollect he did."

"Well, there were strange noises heard there sometime previously, and every body said the place was haunted, and that the sounds come from some disturbed spirits."

"And which, by the by, is likely enough, Jasper."

"It is not at all likely," answered the other; "in fact, I have no doubt Bertrand was confined there, and that he it was who made such a hideous noise. Nay, I feel almost certain of it, for you may remember that Bertrand had been missing for a day or two, and that it was reported he had not returned to the castle since the attempt was made on the king's life, which he was reported to have had some hand in, though, of course, I know nothing certain about that."

"I had forgotten all about that," exclaimed Robert, "though now you mention it, the thing appears to be likely enough. Aye, it must have been Bertrand that we heard, and so there's an end of our marvellous ghost story."

"Well, then," exclaimed the old man, "since I have brought you to my way of thinking, perhaps you will now agree with me, that it's likely enough that Sir Gaston went to visit his prisoner, that a quarrel ensued between them, that they struggled together in mortal strife, and that Sir Gaston got the worst of it, which will account for the state in which we afterwards found him."

"It must be confessed you have made out a very plausible story, Jasper," returned the other; "but now I should like to know how you can account for the escape of Bertrand from the chamber."

"Aye," replied the old man, "that I confess is the most difficult part of the affair; for that he did not leave the place by the door, is very certain, for steps were heard in the room whilst we were in the passage. And as for making his escape from the window, it appears impossible that he could have done so, for had he leaped from it, he must have been killed by the fall."

"And yet it's quite certain he was not in the room when we entered it."

"Yes, yes, that's certain enough," replied Jasper, "and so we must be content to puzzle our brains about it till the truth comes out. At any rate, he must have run a great hazard, and, therefore, I should not be sorry if he escapes the search that is being made for him."

"But suppose we should happen to meet with him? you would not let him get off I suppose?"

"Why, no, it would never do for us to return the castle with an acknowledgment that we had seen Bertrand, and suffered him to escape; and so as we shall be two to one, I think we must do our best to take him back with us."

At these words, Bertrand, who had been eagerly listening to all that passed, gave himself up for lost, and throwing himself back upon the floor, he uttered a groan so loud and unearthly, that the two men started as if some horrible apparition had suddenly appeared before them, and without waiting to ascertain the cause of their alarm, they both rushed from the hovel, and scampered off as fast as their legs could carry them.

Finding himself thus unexpectedly released from the danger that threatened him, Bertrand with great difficulty raised himself from the ground, but weak as he was from loss of blood, he reeled, and would have fallen again, had not Meg of Finchley at that moment entered the hovel and caught him by the arm.

"You are in danger," she said, "and nothing but instant flight can save you from falling into the hands of your inveterate enemy."

"And how," demanded the other, "can I flee when my limbs are hardly able to sustain my weight?"

"I came not to counsel you how it was to be done," answered Meg, "but to tell you that in this place you are no longer safe."

"And why do you," asked Bertrand, "who have ever been against me, thus come to warn me of danger?"

"I saw you enter this place," she replied, "and was going to fetch assistance, in order that you might be secured. As I was departing, however, for that purpose, I observed the approach of the two men who have just left the place, and thinking you were certain to fall into their hands, I abandoned my own intentions as useless. I then approached the door, and overheard the conversation that took place between them, and when I found that you were a fugitive from the wrath of Sir Gaston, my heart turned towards you, and I resolved to exert what little strength I have to save you. They were, however, frightened by your groans, and I then entered to tell you that your only safety lay in immediate flight."

"And why," asked Bertrand, "have you so suddenly taken an interest in one who you previously so much hated?"

"I will briefly explain the reason," answered Meg; "the truth is, I thought there would now be a breach between you and Sir Gaston which would convert you into inveterate enemies. Hitherto you have ever been the willing instrument of his villanous designs, but now you have it in your power to obtain a pardon for all your own crimes, on condition that you bring him to a well deserved punishment."

"That may be true," exclaimed Bertrand, "but I must have time for consideration, ere I adopt that course."

"Well, at any rate," continued Meg, "you will no longer be the persecutor of the Hebrew Maiden, and it is at least to be expected that you will do all in your power to assist her against the future machinations of her enemies."

"Aye, so far I may indeed go," replied the other.

"Promise that you will do so," replied Meg, "and I think I can assure you of a safe assylum in her father's house till you have sufficiently recovered to escape."

"I do promise it."

"In that case, present yourself at Isaac's door, and I can answer for it, you will not be turned away."

"But may he not give me shelter in order to betray me into the hands of my enemies?"

"That he will never do," answered Meg; "the old man will treat you with kindness and hospitality, but let me warn you, Bertrand, never to abuse the favour he will do you. Be the protector of the old man and his daughter, and I promise you shall never have to regret the favour you will thus bestow upon me."

"Well, be it so," replied Bertrand:—"I am weary of the life I have led, and gladly take this opportunity to convince you that I am not the villain circumstances have made me appear to be."

"Then you will shield Rebecca from those who have so long been her persecutors?"

"I will;—but why, old woman, dost thou take so great an interest in that girl?"

"Because she was a friend to me when all the world besides would have suffered me to perish for want of common necessaries of life," answered Meg; "morning and night she was my constant vistor; when

I slept, she watched by my bed side, and left me only that she might the better administer to my wants;—this kindness I received from the hands of a Jewess, whilst Christians would have suffered me to perish from want."

"You have good cause then for the interest you have taken in their behalf," returned Bertrand; "and judging from their conduct towards you, I may hope to find there the rest and security I so much require."

"You have nothing to fear from them," answered the old woman, "and as the house of Isaac of Tadcaster is not far distant from hence, you may be able to reach it without much difficulty."

"It shall at least be tried," exclaimed Bertrand, staggering towards the door of the hovel; "I will throw myself upon their hospitality, and should it be denied me, I can but meet the fate that sooner or later must be mine."

Meg now assisted him part of the way, and when they came within view of Isaac's house, which was almost the only one standing since the late attack that had been made on the Jew's quarter,—she left him to pursue the remainder of the way alone. It was not, however, without much suffering and difficulty that the wounded man made his way towards the house; and, when he at length reached it, he fell heavily against the door, ere he could raise his arm to knock for admission. But fortunately for him, he had been heard by the inmates, and in a few seconds the door was opened by Reuben Grenard, who seeing a man lying in a state of insensibility, raised him in his arms, and bore his burden into the house without knowing who it was upon whom all this care and attention had been bestowed. On taking him, however, into the room where Isaac and Rebecca was sitting, the light fell upon the countenance of Bertrand le Noir, and the momentary start that was observable in all present, showed the alarm which the discovery had occasioned. Reuben, terrified at having introduced such a visitor to the house, would have conveyed him back to the place where he had found him, but the heart of the elder Jew was touched with pity, and motioning for him to be left where he was, he said:—

"It is an enemy that thus commands our assistance, and he must not be left to perish for want of that aid which we have it in our power to bestow. He is wounded, too, and base as his practices have been against me, there is little to fear from him in his present helpless situation."

Upon hearing this, Rebecca fetched such simple medicines as they happened to have in the house, and having administered these to the wretched man who had thus thrown himself on their humanity, he began slowly to recover, and gazing round the room with wonder and surprise, he at length seemed to recollect where he was, and to whom he was indebted for the care that had been bestowed upon him. In a faint tone, therefore, he thanked them for the kindness he had received, and at the same time bade them not to be alarmed at his presence, for that he had no evil designs against them.

"Aye," replied the elder Jew, "I was in hopes that in this instance our hospitality would not be abused, though we knew you for an enemy as soon as Reuben Grenard brought you into the room. Remember, we have saved you from perishing in the streets, and let that thought be ever uppermost in your mind, in case you should at any future time be employed to do us injury."

"I never had any ill-will towards you," answered the other; "nor should I ever have been your foe, but for the command of one I was bound to obey."

"Aye, Sir Gaston de Neville," exclaimed Isaac; "he has indeed ever been a bitter enemy to us, and the only wonder is that his base project have failed so signally."

"And you have yet to beware of him," replied Bertrand le Noir; "for even now he is plotting to carry your daughter away by violence, and well as his plans have been arranged, there is little doubt but this time they will prove successful."

"And will thou suffer my child to fall into a snare, when thou hast it in thy power to save her?"

"It is no business of mine," answered Bertrand, "to tell the secret of my master."

"Villain!" exclaimed Reuben Grenard, whose rage was not to be controlled; "wilt thou then receive the hospitality of this old man, and yet refuse to save his daughter?"

"I am not so great a villain as I have been," answered Bertrand le Noir; "nor yet can I reconcile it to my conscience to betray the man whom I have once saved. That which is past I shall not speak about, but if it will afford thee any consolation, thou mayest be assured that will myself watch over thy daughter's safety, and that she has little to fear from Sir Gaston de Neville so long as I am resolved to thwart his plans."

"May we depend on thy services?"

"Thou mayest."

"And what surety have we that thou art sincere in thy promises?"

"Aye, that is indeed the difficulty," answered Bertrand;—"my word thou wilt not take, and as for honour, I parted with it so long ago, that I have almost forgotten it except by name. I, however, tell thee in all sincerity, that I am no longer to be dreaded as thine enemy, and from henceforth I will serve thee whenever it is in my power to do so."

"I will take thy word," replied Isaac, "because I fancy I can see in thee a feeling of repentance for thy former misdeeds. But thou art thyself the best judge of thine own intentions, and, therefore, if thou hast come hither to deceive those who have served and will place their reliance on thy word, I leave thee to the heavy reflection that must some time or other follow thy crime."

"Thou mayest depend on me old man," answered Bertrand earnestly. "Thou seest me no longer as the retainer of Sir Gaston de Neville, but as one who has fled from his displeasure, and who is in danger of becoming the next victim of his vengeance."

"Ha! thou dost need a place of shelter then?"

"I do."

"Thou shalt find it here, then, for, though thou hast been our enemy, yet will I do my utmost to save thee from the fury of that insatiate man."

"But, dost thou remember," demanded Reuben, "that Bertrand is suspected of having been the ruffian who lately made an attempt upon the king's life, and that a large reward has been offered for his apprehension?"

"And would you earn that reward," asked the fugitive, "by giving up the man who has sought refuge in thy house from those who seek his death?"

"Never!" exclaimed the old man;—"gold is a tempting bait, but shall not prevail on me to yield thee up the fury of thy foes."

"Thou hast forgotten, then," continued Reuben, "that the fierce vengeance of the law is threatened against those who may in any way seek to shield Bertrand le Noir from the consequences of his crime."

"It is indeed a fearful risk," exclaimed Isaac, "and yet I cannot bring myself to turn a deaf ear to the reception of a fellow creature

And now, my daughter, what sayest thou—shall I give shelter to this man, or turn him from my door to meet a certain and ignominious death?"

"Nay, my father," cried Rebecca, "there is little need to ask me what to do in such a case as this; ask thine own heart, and I know it will not prompt thee to do a deed which thou would'st afterwards repent."

"Thou hast said well, my child," answered the old man; "my heart bids me give a welcome to the unfortunate, and Bertrand le Noir shall remain in concealment till the search after him has slackened. Then he may take his departure, and let us hope he will not prove ungrateful for the services we have done him."

"Thou hast no cause to fear me, Isaac," replied Bertrand, "though this stripling here would fain have persuaded thee to turn me forth from thy doors."

"Reuben did it but in his zeal for my welfare," cried the old man, anxious to excuse the suspicions of the other; "he was afraid lest I should run myself into danger, and only gave me a warning for which I am thankful to him."

"But how am I to know," asked Bertrand le Noir, "that he will not be the first to direct the officers of justice where to find me?"

"There are many reasons why he should not do so," replied Isaac, "but two will suffice for the present: In the first place I can answer for it he would not act with such treachery towards the man who had placed himself under my protection, and, secondly, he will know that, if he were to do so, it would be the means of bringing certain destruction upon myself and my daughter. For these reasons I know you are safe as far he is concerned, and, if you are still doubtful upon the subject, he will

No. 81

give his own word in addition to mine, that you have nothing whatever to fear from him."

"I will rely upon his honour," replied Bertrand; "and now having satisfied myself that I am safe, what is the protection you can offer me in case my pursuers should happen to trace me here?"

"There are vaults beneath this house," replied the old man, "that are known to few besides myself; yonder trap-door leads to them, and when once thou art there, thou mayst bid defiance to the utmost cunning of those who come in search for thee."

"But it may chance that they find it," exclaimed Bertrand, "and, in that case I shall have little hope of escaping them."

"The vaults are numerous, and many winding passages connect them," replied Isaac. "Nay, so cunningly is the place devised, that even if thy foes were to pursue thee there, thou wouldst easily be able to elude them."

"Thy words seem fair enough," cried Bertrand le Noir, "yet still must I question thee further. Thou dost propose that I shall seek concealment in the vaults beneath thy house, but how know I that thou wilt ever let me have my liberty again?"

"Thou hast the word of a man who never yet denied either friend or foe."

"Dost thou swear to release me from the place when all danger shall be over?"

"I do."

"In that case I will trust to thee. So lead me to the vault as soon as thou wilt, and should all turn out well, I will not forget to reward thee as soon as I am again safe."

The aged Israelite raised the trap-door, and was about to assist Bertrand le Noir down the steps, when a furious hammering was heard at the door, and several voices without demanded admission in the name of the king.

CHAPTER CIV.

"Thou hast sheltered one'
Whose crimes have made him odious to the laws,
And, therefore, shalt thou fall."

THE FEUD.

"HARK!" exclaimed the Jew, "we are in danger, and not an instant is to be lost. Descend the steps, and when I have closed the trap I will open the door to those who so clamorously demand it."

Bertrand, however, was so weak, that he was unable to do this as quickly as was necessary, and, ere he could reach the opening in the floor, the door was burst open, and Sir Gaston de Neville, followed by Simon Snout, and a numerous body of followers, rushed into the room. In an instant the knight recognized his fugitive retainer, and in a voice of thunder, he commanded Simon Snout to seize him; this, however, the officer of the law was by no means anxious to execute, as he apprehended there would be no little danger in attempting to arrest so desperate a fellow as Bertrand le Noir was reported to be, and the consequence was, that ere the constable had moved towards the object of their search, the retainer leaped across the chasm, taking care to close the trap door before any one could follow in pursuit. Sir Gaston was terribly enraged at this defeat, and addressing himself to Snout, he exclaimed wrathfully:—

"Villain! this is some base connivance on your part to save the fugitive from the consequences of his crimes. But he shall not elude me, so let some one instantly force open the trap door, and he who brings back Bertrand le Noir, dead or alive, shall receive a hundred crowns for his reward."

This offer answered the purpose for which it was intended; and, in a moment or two, the door being forcibly opened, a dozen fellows rushed down in pursuit of the fugitive. Simon Snout, however, had too great a regard for himself to run a risk that filled him with so much alarm, and, taking the opportunity that was offered by the bustle that ensued, he was sneaking out of the house, when Sir Gaston perceiving his intention, sprang forward like a tiger upon his prey, and brought the trembling constable back to the place from whence he had hoped to make a precipitate retreat.

"Thou shalt not stir from this spot," he exclaimed resolutely, "until we have ascertained whether the culprit has escaped or not. If we miss our object through thy cowardice, thou mayest rely on it I will so punish thee that thou shalt never again have a chance of offending in a similar manner."

"Pardon, great sir,—pardon, I beseech you!" cried the trembling constable, falling upon his knees and clasping his hands in an agony of terror. "If I have done wrong, I regret it most deeply, and—"

"If thou hast done wrong!" interrupted the enraged knight; "hast thou not thrown away a chance by thine own cowardice? Didst thou not suffer the villain to escape, though I told thee he had made an attempt upon my life, and that it was my determination to have him apprehended?"

"All that I admit, Sir Knight," answered Simon Snout; "but my own life would have been perilled had I followed as you desired, and should I not have been a fool to run so great a risk for so useless a purpose?"

"A useless purpose dost thou call it!" exclaimed Sir Gaston, "have I not said the villain sought to take away my life, and shall I not be revenged on a base menial who has dared to raise his hand against his master?"

"I know nothing about that," replied the constable; "my own life was in danger if I had followed him down that dark place beneath the house, and as my life is of some little consequence to the state, I did nothing more than was right in taking care of myself."

"I will see you rewarded in a way that you justly merit," exclaimed Sir Gaston de Neville, "and, as for this Jew, who has dared to give refuge and protection to the villain, he also shall experience my wrath, and bitterly shall he regret the part he has taken in this affair."

"Sir Gaston de Neville," replied the old Israelite calmly, "never needs an excuse when once he has resolved upon the destruction of one who he imagines has in any way marred the evil designs he has meditated."

"Dog of a Jew!" vociferated the knight, "hast thou not given shelter to a ruffian who made an attempt upon the life of good King Richard?"

"I waited not to think of that," replied Isaac; "for the man needed the little aid I had it in my power to give, and, therefore, I did not close my doors against him. If I have acted wrong in so doing, I am willing to endure the punishment due to so heinous an offence."

"Ha! thou mayest pass this affair over as lightly as thou dost please," replied the incensed knight, "but I swear to thee, old man, the humanity thou hast been pleased to show this day, shall cost thee dearly; I will myself inform the king of thy having harboured the man who so lately attempted his life, and it will be strange if thou dost not henceforth lose the favour and protection of me who, up to this period, has shielded thee and thy daughter from my designs."

"Thou dost intend, then," cried the old man, "to charge me with having afforded shelter to one who had no other place where he could find a refuge?"

"I shall charge thee," answered the knight, "with having afforded shelter and protection to a notorious and denounced traitor; this alone will be sufficient to bring upon thee the punishment of death, and until that has been accomplished I will never rest satisfied."

"Art thou still rooted upon my father's destruction!" cried Rebecca, with alarm.

"Thou knowest my determination, girl," answered Sir Gaston, "and when once I am resolved, it is not a little which will turn me from my plans."

"Alas! will nothing save my father from the cruel persecution of a vindictive foe?"

"Yes, girl," replied the knight, "thou hast it in their own power to preserve him from the fate thou dost dread."

"Ah! then I believe I can guess the thoughts that are now passing in thy mind."

"Thou mayest easily do so," replied Sir Gaston; "in truth thou must consent to be mine on the terms I have already proposed, and from that moment thy father will be safe from all further persecution."

"And thinkest thou," demanded the old man wrathfully, "that I will owe my life to the sacrifice of my child's honour?"

"In that thou wilt please thyself, Isaac," replied Sir Gaston, in a tone of indifference. "I shall not attempt to persuade thee against thy will, but thou must not forget, that, shouldst thou perish in thine own obstinacy, thy daughter will be left more than ever exposed to the designs I have formed."

"Villain! dost thou exult in the crimes that you should blush to mention?" exclaimed Isaac, trembling with emotion; "dost thou not fear the vengeance of offended heaven, when thou speakest thus of injuring those who have never given thee cause for the evil thou dost meditate?"

"Fool!" vociferated the Knight Templar, "what have I to think of, save the fulfilment of my own designs? Have I ever yielded to difficulties, or given up a favourite project, merely because it might chance to offend those whose anger I regard no more than I do thine own?"

"And yet," answered the old man, "thou wouldst not dare to say as much in the presence of the king."

"Father!" interposed the terrified girl, "do not, I implore you, increase the anger of one, whose enmity we have so much reason to dread. Sir Gaston de Neville is our most inveterate foe, and, deaf as he is to pity, we should at least endeavour to avoid bringing upon ourselves that rage which may only serve to plunge us still further in misery."

"Your father can do as he pleases about it," exclaimed the knight, haughtily; "he knows that I am not to be trifled with with impunity, and I, therefore, warn him for the last time, to desist from an opposition that can only terminate in his own destruction."

"I fear not for myself," replied the old man; "slay me, if you will, even under my own roof, but never will I consent to yield up my daughter, for the sake of preserving a life that is no longer of value to me."

"But, suppose Rebecca is left without a protector," cried Sir Gaston, "what is then to prevent her becoming my prize?"

"She will not be left without a friend," answered the aged Israelite; "the king, as thou well knowest, will not forsake an almost friendless maiden, and in him, at least, thou wilt have to encounter an adversary whose power far exceeds thine own."

"It may be so," replied the knight, carelessly, "and yet, it would not have been so, had the dagger of the man thou hast sheltered done its work with success."

"True," answered Isaac, "and few, I believe, are more disappointed at the failure of the treachery, than is Sir Gaston de Neville; who, as a sworn knight, was bound to protect, instead of plot against his sovereign."

"Hah!" exclaimed the Templar, furiously, "dost thou dare to charge me with a plot which has been so fortunately frustrated at the last moment?"

"I do," replied the old man; "and I believe the king is equally certain of the guilty share thou hast had in the crime that was plotted against him. It was thine own retainer that made the attempt upon his majesty's life, and it would be a task of some difficulty to make any one believe that thou wert ignorant of the murderous plot that was going on."

"Slave!" roared Sir Gaston, "dost thou dare to charge me with so heinous a crime as this?"

"I do," answered the Israelite, "and if thou dost accuse me of having given shelter to the assassin, I, in my own defence, will charge thee with being the instigator of his crime."

"Nay," cried Sir Gaston, somewhat alarmed at this threat, "I have not said that any notice would be taken of my having found Bertrand le Noir beneath thy 'roof. In fact, there shall be no notice taken of it, if thou wilt now deliver him up into my hands, without mentioning my present visit."

"I see thy meaning, Sir Knight," answered Isaac, with a sneer of contempt; "thou wouldst like to drag him away secretly to thy castle, because he knows more than is consistent with thine own safety. There thou wouldst have him privately murdered, and from that time, Bertrand le Noir would never more be heard of."

Sir Gaston's countenance betrayed the fury that these words had excited in his heart, and, for a moment or two, it seemed that he would have struck the old man dead at his feet. Presently, however, he assumed an appearance of calmness, and, affecting to feel no anger at the hint that had been thrown out by the Israelite, he said, with pretended good humour:—

"The truth is, old man, I have been much wronged by these suspicions of thine;—the man has certainly wronged me much;—nay, he would have slain me not long since, and I followed in pursuit of him. I do not, however, desire his death, and my only motive was to confine him for a short time in one of the dungeons of my castle, in order that he might have time to reflect on the heinousness of the crime he meditated. That done, I would have given him his liberty, on condition that he continued faithful to the end of his life."

"Perhaps so," replied the old man, "but having escaped, there will be no necessity for him to rely on a promise, that, it's most likely, would be broken."

"He has not escaped," cried Sir Gaston; "the villain is now beneath the vaults of your house, and he will be lucky indeed, to escape those who have gone in search of him."

"That we shall presently see," replied Isaac, "for, in my opinion, it will not be so easy to find him as you imagine, for the subterranean passages are numerous, and there is one way by which he may have escaped before your men had time to prevent him."

"And if he has," exclaimed the knight, unable to restrain his fury any longer, "you shall be made to feel what it is to offend one who has the means in his own hands to punish those who dare to thwart his will."

"Indeed!" retorted the Jew, "but, thanks to our good King Richard, the humble man is as likely to meet with the protection of the laws as those who are born in a higher station. Thou mayest slay me, Sir Knight, but if thou dost, the monarch will not fail to punish thee according to thy deserts."

"Hah! dost thou dare to taunt me, slave?"

"I tell thee only the truth," replied Isaac; "I am as well protected as thyself, and am not to be murdered in cold blood with impunity, merely because it happens that I am of a different religion to thyself."

"Say but another word, and I will burn thy house down, even though the king were to stand in our presence and forbid the act."

"Aye, do so," exclaimed Isaac, "and add one more crime to the many others that already stain thy soul."

Sir Gaston de Neville could no longer restrain his fury, and grasping his dagger firmly in his hand, he was preparing to make a deadly blow at the old man, when his attention was attracted by the sounds of many voices, and instantly afterwards the men he had sent in pursuit of Bertrand le Noir made their appearance through the trap door. One of them was bleeding from a horrible gash in his cheek, and so weak was he, that two of his companions were obliged to support him as he sank fainting upon the floor.

"What means this?" demanded the knight, as he perceived the wounded condition of one of his followers;—"speak, some of you, and tell me how this mishap has occurred."

"The truth is, Sir Knight," replied one of the fellows, "we have found that it is not so easy to find our way through the infernal, dark and winding passages that run under this house; the place is haunted, too, I believe, for whichever way we went, footsteps were heard just before us, and yet after all our search, nothing was to be seen but bare walls and zig-zag passages, that led nobody knows where."

"And have you been searching about all this time to no purpose?" demanded the knight, fiercely.

"Why," replied the other, "we have seen Bertrand le Noir, certainly, but he fought like a devil, and as you see, one of our comrades has got a wound that he is not likely to get rid of in a hurry."

"And was the blow inflicted by Bertrand?" demanded the Knight Templar.

"It was."

"You come to close quarters with him, then?"

"The wounded man did," answered the fellow, who had acted as spokesman; "but the place was so narrow that it was impossible for more than two to be engaged at a time, and when our comrade fell, Bertrand made the best use he could of the opportunity, and darting forwards, he sprang through an aperture that led in an upward direction towards the outside of the house."

"And did no one follow him?" demanded the knight.

"Yes, two or three of our most active fellows pursued him as quickly as they could," replied the man.

"Yet it seems they were not able to overtake him?"

"They could not, Sir Gaston, but that, I take it, was no fault of theirs, for Bertrand had been too nimble for them, and by the time they reached the open air, not a sign of the fugitive was to be seen."

"And so you have returned without bringing any satisfactory tidings of him?"

"There was no help for it," answered the other; "he stopped not to ask leave, and the passage, as I said before, was so narrow, that there was no chance of our being able to prevent his escape."

"S'death!" exclaimed Sir Gaston, "I am foiled, then, even at the moment when I made most sure of getting him into my hands."

"And lucky enough it was for the wretched victim of your furious rage," cried Isaac, delighted at the escape, even though he so much disliked the object of their present pursuit. "He is by this time far enough from danger, and should you ever chance to meet with him again, I trust he will be able to escape with as much ease as he has on this occasion."

"Hah! dost thou taunt me, Jew?"

"I do not," replied the old man, "and yet I exult in having been the means of rescuing one poor fellow from the fate you intended for him. He is now safe, and, therefore, I hope you will now quit a house in which your presence is no longer regarded."

"Old man," exclaimed the knight, fiercely; "this insolence of thine shall be terribly avenged; I will not leave thy house at thy command; at least, not until I have done that which shall deprive thee of the roof that has hitherto sheltered thee."

"Ah!" cried Rebecca, "for heaven's sake forbear, Sir Gaston, and do not threaten an old man, whose only crime consists in having protected an unfortunate creature, who, faint and weary from exhaustion, applied for a few hours shelter. This has been his only fault, and yet thou wouldst revenge thyself on him for it."

"Aye, girl, and I will do so, thou mayest depend on it," exclaimed the knight, fiercely. "I will have ample satisfaction for the insolence he has been guilty of, and thou shall away with me to the castle, even though the king himself stood in my path to forbid the act."

"Wretch!—thou wilt not dare carry thy base threats into execution," cried Rebecca, stepping back a pace or two, and eyeing him with a look of resolution. "I will myself resist thee even to death, and rely upon it, I am not without friends, who will aid a persecuted girl from the evil designs of an unjust persecutor."

"I am myself not wholly powerless," exclaimed her father, reaching down a sword from over the chimney piece, and placing himself between his daughter and the Knight Templar; "my arm has yet nerve enough to defend my child, and he who seizes upon her, shall have to do so by stepping over my breathless body."

"Nay, I have another fate in store for you, old man," retorted Sir Gaston de Neville; "you shall have neither house nor home to shelter you, for the place shall instantly be given to the flames, and from henceforth thou shalt wander a beggar through the world."

"Monster!" cried Rebecca, "base as you are, you dare not thus injure an old man whose grey hairs should obtain your reverence and respect."

"We will see that," exclaimed the knight; and, motioning to one of his followers, the fellow advanced cautiously behind Isaac, and having disarmed him in an instant, held him with so firm a grasp that there was no possibility of his breaking away. At the same time Sir Gaston advanced, and seizing Rebecca in his arms, was about to rush from the cottage, when the door opened, and Black Ivan, attended by a dozen of his stoutest followers, entered the room. In an instant the Hebrew Maiden was snatched from the knight, who, drawing a poniard, would have sprung upon his assailant: but Ivan was aware of his intention, and the weapon was wrested from his grasp ere the deadly purpose could be accomplished. This done, the fellow who had laid hold of the Jew was hurled from one end of the room to the other, and the robbers having placed themselves in such a situation as to prevent the escape of the knight and his followers, Ivan addressed himself to Sir Gaston.

"Again," he said, "I have been the means of preventing an act of violence and cruel oppression against those who have never injured you. I have warned you before that you have to fear my wrath, should it ever be urged beyond a certain boundary, and I now tell you again that should you injure the Jew and his daughter, it will be the means of bringing upon you that ruin and disgrace which is ready to fall upon you without even so much as an instant's warning."

"And who, pray, art thou," demanded Sir Gaston, "that dost pretend to possess so much power over me?"

"Who I am," replied Black Ivan, "matters little to thee at this present moment; that I know thee and the many crimes thou hast committed I can prove at any moment that it may be most convenient to me."

"In that case," exclaimed the knight, "why dost thou not do so at this moment? I am present to hear thy charge, and can deny it, I have no doubt, to the satisfaction of every person present,—unless, indeed, it should be the Israelite and his daughter, who, I suppose, are willing to believe any marvellous tale thou mayest take it into thy head to invent."

"I shall invent nothing," answered Ivan; "my secret will bear investigation, and whenever the proper moment arrives, thou shalt tremble at the revelation I have to make."

"Psha!" retorted Sir Gaston, "what care I for thy threats, or for the mighty mischief thou boastest it is in thy power to bestow? I can but smile at thy idle threats; and be assured the time is not far distant when I shall see thee receiving the punishment that is allotted to all others of thy lawless pursuits."

"Aye," replied Ivan, "it is well that thou canst pass the matter thus lightly, for thou knowest not the peril with which thou art threatened, and, therefore, canst console thyself with an assurance of safety. But again I bid thee beware, for nothing but an entire change in thy conduct can save thee from the destiny that ever follows evil actions."

"Humph!" muttered Sir Gaston, "and so I am to be threatened with the wrath of an outlawed bandit, unless I promise henceforward to cease loving the daughter of this aged Israelite?"

"That is not all," replied Ivan, "for there are other things thou must desist from, ere thou wilt be safe."

"Aye," muttered the knight, "I must pay homage to thee, I suppose, and promise to act in all time to come exactly as thou dost please."

"I want nothing of the kind," answered Ivan; "I only desire to protect the helpless from thy vile practices, and so long as that is done thou wilt have nothing further to fear from me."

"Indeed!" exclaimed Sir Gaston; "and so a knight who has served his country is to be dictated to by a ruffian who has been suffered too long to escape the gallows which he so justly merited."

"Ask thyself which has deserved the gallows most—thou or myself," retorted Ivan: "I have been driven by the villany of others to follow

course that my heart abominates; but thou hast no such excuse, since all thy crimes have been committed without any such incentives as have urged me to become the leader and associate of robbers."

"It is nothing to me whether you have been urged by injustice or not," answered Sir Gaston de Neville; "I speak of thee as thou art, and thou canst not deny that I have truly described thee when I said thou wert deserving of the gallows."

"But perhaps I may not meet my fate so soon as thou wilt thine own," replied the Outlaw. "At any rate, with all my bad qualities, I am not without a few good ones to counterbalance them, and that is saying more than thou canst say for thyself. I have never been the oppressor of women or old age, but have rather stepped forward in behalf of those who needed aid against those who sought to injure them."

"And a very honourable champion they have had, truly," answered Sir Gaston, with a sneer. "A robber sets up for moralizer, and a Christian knight is accused of crimes that the Outlaw would have shrunk from committing!"

"And the Christian knight, as he calls himself," retorted Ivan, reproachfully, "has not honour enough left to feel ashamed of the base part he has been acting."

"Hah! dost thou dare call my honour in question?"

"I do, Sir Gaston; and your recent attempt to carry off this maiden will fully bear me out in my assertion. There are other things which I could also mention, but this is not the time nor place to mention the subject further, and perhaps if you desist in future from oppressing these people, I may never say anything further about it."

"I ask no favour from you, nor will I grant any to the man whose

No. 82

insults I have too long endured," exclaimed the knight, haughtily. "S.
bring your charges against me whenever you please, and I will not only
triumphantly answer them, but afterwards bring upon you the punish
ment due to so notorious an offender."

"Take care, Sir Gaston, how you urge a desperate man to do tha
which he would fain avoid."

"Am I again to tell you," exclaimed the knight. "that I am prepare
for anything your malevolence may urge you to commit against me?"

"And am I again to tell you," answered Ivan, "that I have no privat
resentment to satisfy? Have I not told you that all will depend on you
future conduct? and yet you scorn my advice, with a determination t
rush headlong upon the ruin I would have prevailed on you to avoid!"

"If I do so," exclaimed Sir Gaston, "it is because I know there i
nothing that you can bring against me of which I have reason to b
ashamed or afraid."

"Yet anybody but yourself," answered Ivan, in a tone of bitter irony
"would be ashamed of having injured those who were unable to protec
themselves."

"We pardon him all that he has done against us," interposed Isaa
of Tadcaster, "on condition that he will henceforward desist from per
secuting us."

"Humph!" ejaculated the knight; "and so I am to make terms witl
an unbelieving Jew."

"I never yet heard," exclaimed Isaac, "that one class of person
had a right to tyrannize over another because their religion happen t
differ. Thou callest me an unbelieving Jew, but I will defy thee to sa
that I ever wilfully wronged my neighbour, or oppressed those who hap
pened to be beneath myself."

"How!" vociferated the knight, "is it not notorious that thine ac
cursed tribe have grown rich upon the spoils they have wrung fror
Christians?"

"It is a false accusation," replied Isaac; "thy people are apt to b
wasteful of their gold, and in their extreme need they come to us, wh
are less prodigal of our means. For the accommodation we expect inte
rest and security, both of which are frequently of little use to us; an
thou well knowest, Sir Knight, how often we are cheated out of our prin
cipal by those we have served. And yet we are accused of extortion.
if we grew wealthy upon that which makes your people poor."

"I am not going to argue that question with thee now, old man," ex
claimed Sir Gaston, impatiently. "I came hither in search of a vil
lanous servant whom thou hast sheltered, and aided to escape from th
punishment due to his crimes. For that thou art liable to be called to
severe account; and, rely on it, I will never cease my endeavours ti
thou and all belonging to thee have been made to feel the vengeance it i
in my power to inflict."

"And this," cried the old man, "I am to endure as a proof of yo'
Christian charity!"

"Take care what you say," vociferated the Knight Templar, "o
may bring you to the stake for uttering blasphemy against our holy
ligion."

"I am not speaking of your religion," answered Isaac, "but of thos
who falsely call themselves followers of it."

"Dear father," cried Rebecca, "it will be dangerous to speak furthe
on this subject. Sir Gaston de Neville looks eagerly enough to see hor
he may best ensnare us, and I fear he will gladly take the opportunit
to charge us with using words disrespectful to his religion."

"Why, I might do so, certainly," replied Sir Gaston, "but it so happens that I have already sufficient evidence to bring upon you the full resentment of the laws. You have given shelter to the man that attempted to assassinate the king, and afterwards, when I came to arrest the villain, contrived means for his escape. This is sufficient for my purpose, and, therefore, I now leave you to enjoy the pleasant reflection that in a short time you will have leisure to reflect on the folly that prompted you to reject the favourable terms that I was disposed to offer you."

With this Sir Gaston de Neville and those who had accompanied him left the house. Ivan followed them to the door, and, having watched their retreating forms till they were nearly out of sight, returned, and tried by every means in his power to console the father and daughter, and to assure them that they had very little to fear from their haughty persecutor.

"Let him do his worst," he said; "and I can venture to foretell that the mischief he can do will be very trifling. He may, perhaps, charge you with having given shelter to Bertrand le Noir, who lately attempted the life of the king, but King Richard knows full well who was the instigator of the crime, and he will hardly deign to listen to the man whose evil deeds have rendered him an object of suspicion and distrust."

"But he has again threatened my daughter," answered the old man: "he has vowed to carry her off, and I fear lest his artful stratagems should succeed against her."

"I will myself take care that he fails in that project," exclaimed Black Ivan.

"How canst thou do so?" demanded Isaac.

"By watching his actions narrowly," answered the Outlaw.

"But I fear," returned Isaac, "that even your watchfulness will prove of little avail against one whose wickedness of heart will prompt him to any crime."

"If thou art still afraid of him," returned Ivan, "there is but one way that I know of by which his schemes may be overthrown."

"And how is that?"

"Let thy daughter wed Reuben Grenard without delay, and she will be safe from her persecutor."

"If I thought so," answered the old man, "I would no longer withhold my consent to their immediate union."

"Take my word for it," exclaimed Ivan; "I never yet deceived thee, and therefore do I again urge thee to let the nuptials take place immediately.

"Dost thou consent to this, my child?" cried the old man, addressing himself to his daughter. "Wilt thou wed Reuben Grenard to-morrow, and thus take unto thyself a protector who will shield thee from this haughty oppressor?"

"I see she will," exclaimed Ivan; "the maiden blushes, but neither by word nor sign has she given any token that your proposition will be rejected. Let to-morrow see them united, and I'll answer for it one source of your disquietude will be removed for ever."

"And wilt thou," asked the old man, "be present at the ceremony?"

"I would most gladly have accepted thine invitation," replied Ivan, "had it not been that I have other business to attend to to-morrow which will require my presence elsewhere. The young folks, however, shall have my good wishes; and should they afterwards be annoyed by Sir Gaston de Neville, they shall find that I have not forgotten my promise to protect them against all their foes. So now, farewell, and when next we meet,'I trust it will be to congratulate you on your daughter's marriage with Reuben Grenard."

With this the Outlaw retired with his followers, and once more took his way towards their retreat in Enfield Chase.

CHAPTER CV.

" Repent thy crimes,
And, if thou wilt obey the words I speak,
Thy pardon soon shall follow."

ROLLA.

WHEN Bertrand le Noir effected his escape from the vaults beneath the Jew's house, he made all the speed he could to find some place of refuge, for he well knew that his pursuers would not suffer him to elude them whilst there was a chance of capturing him ; and, weak as he still felt from loss of blood, he yet strained every nerve to keep out of reach of those who he knew would deliver him up to Sir Gaston de Neville. It was not, however, that he cared much about life, for he had enemies, turn which way he might ; but he still hoped to be revenged on the Knight Templar for the treacherous part he had lately acted towards him, and so that he only managed to conceal himself until his own plans of retaliation were accomplished, he cared not how soon afterwards he met the fate which he was well assured would sooner or later be his.

Scarcely knowing whither he directed his flight, he at length found himself near some fields in the neighbourhood of Westminster, and being by this time overcome with fatigue and exhaustion, he threw himself down beneath a bridge, there to obtain that rest and repose which he so much needed. Here he obtained a brief forgetfulness in sleep, nor did he wake till morning's dawn, when the sound of human voices fell upon his startled ear ; and creeping yet closer into his hiding-place, he perceived three or four labourers proceeding to their daily toil in the fields. Fortunately, however, they passed on without knowing him, and when they were fairly out of sight, he once more ventured to leave his hiding-place, considerably strengthened and invigorated by the rest he had obtained.

Uncertain which way to go, he directed his way towards the Abbey of Westminster, the towers of which rose proudly above the trees ; and absorbed as he was in his own reflections, he heeded not the footsteps which were slowly advancing to meet him. But at last a well-known voice roused him from his reverie, and raising his eyes, he beheld Meg of Finchley, who, with extreme difficulty, was urging her way towards him.

"A fair good morrow to you, my son," she exclaimed ; "it is early, and yet I find you risen, and preparing, I suppose, to escape from those who are anxiously looking after you."

"I have had a narrow escape since we last met," answered Bertrand : "the knight traced me by some means or other to the house of Isaac of Tadcaster, and had it not been for some little resolution on my own part, I must have fallen into the hands of Sir Gaston de Neville."

" And have you any reason to believe," asked Meg, "that the Jew had any hand in betraying you to your enemy ?"

"None whatever," answered Bertrand ; "in truth, he received me with hospitality, and it was through his means that I contrived to escape from my pursuers."

"He is worthy, then, the protection I have given him," cried the old woman. "I have ever been his friend, when nearly all the world was opposed to him; but had he turned his back upon an enemy that was in distress, I would never more have troubled myself to take any interest in his behalf."

"You pity me then," exclaimed Bertrand; "and would save an almost friendless wretch from the doom that appears inevitably to threaten him."

"I certainly do pity, and perhaps may serve you," replied the old woman; "but it will depend upon yourself whether I exert the power I possess in your favour."

"What is it you expect of me?" demanded the other.

"That you will exert yourself to rescue those who are in danger from the artful machinations of Sir Gaston de Neville."

"That," answered Bertrand, "I willingly promise to do, if you will explain how it is to be done."

"I will do so by and by," she replied; "but I must first know whether you will assist in bringing down a just punishment upon Sir Gaston? You are better acquainted than any body else with the many villanies he has practised, and through you alone do I hope to bring him to a terrible account for all his crimes."

"You may depend on me," answered Bertrand le Noir; "but at the same time you must be aware that I cannot venture into his presence whilst he is so furiously enraged against me."

"I know all that," replied Meg, "and all that I require is, that you promise to assist me when the proper period for action arrives."

"May I ask," demanded the other, "whether you intend to proceed against him, or to serve those who he has been at so much pains to persecute?"

"That will entirely depend upon circumstances," replied the hag. "He may perhaps be prevailed upon to desist from further injuring those who have so long endured his tyranny, and in that case I shall see no further reason to trouble myself about him."

"And who is it you wish to serve?"

"The Lady Alicia, for one," answered Meg. "She is now, fortunately, in a place of safety, but I fear Sir Gaston will soon succeed in discovering the place of her retreat, and in that case she will not much longer be secure from his renewed tyranny."

"But I understood," replied Bertrand le Noir, "that she had sought safety in a convent, and if that is the case, he will not dare pursue her there."

"That may be all true enough," exclaimed the hag; "but Sir Gaston can easily invent falsehoods, and if he once discovers where she has fled to, I can answer for it he will soon have a story ready that shall serve his purpose, and compel the superior of the convent to give her up to his custody."

"And would that be done," asked Bertrand le Noir, "without some enquiry being made as to the truth or falsehood of his statement?"

"It is but too probable," answered Meg, "that the superior of the convent would be afraid to resist the demands of one so powerful as Sir Gaston de Neville. It is therefore likely she would be given up without hesitation, and in that case I fear there is every reason to believe the poor lady would be sacrificed to the deadly hatred of her bloodthirsty husband."

"And is it to save her that you require my assistance?"

"It is."

"Will you tell me, then, in what way I can render you the required assistance?"

"That must remain till I have thought of some plan," answered Meg. "Indeed, I have been considering whether it would not be running unnecessary risk to take the Lady Alicia from the convent till we are quite assured that Sir Gaston knows where to find her."

"True," exclaimed the other; "for our officiousness might be the means of throwing her into his power, and thus she would be plunged into the very danger you wish to avoid."

"I have thought of all that," replied Meg, "and have resolved to do nothing without giving it a careful consideration. The Lady Alicia must be saved at every hazard, and, therefore, if she should chance to fall into the hands of Sir Gaston de Neville, you must do your best to release her from peril."

"How is that to be done?"

"Easily enough," she replied. "You are acquainted with the secret of the knight's cruelty to her: you were her gaoler, and can reveal that which will serve to restore her to the rank and station from which she has so long been excluded. By your means, therefore, she may be restored to her rights; and on condition that you do this, I will exert myself to serve you."

"And what know you about the Lady Alicia?" asked Bertrand le Noir.

"In the first place I know she is his wife."

"Humph! and what else know you?"

"That she was reported to have died; that a mock funeral took place in order to impose upon the world, and that she was kept a close prisoner in one of the dungeons of the castle till she was fortunate enough to escape from his custody. All this I knew, and yet it is not sufficient to restore her without your aid."

"And why not, old woman?"

"Because," she replied, "Sir Gaston will deny that she is his wife; and it unfortunately happens that there are too many many persons in his employ who will not hesitate to swear that the Lady Alicia died as was represented at the time. My story, therefore, would not be believed, unless you, who were a party to the deed, were to give your testimony in favour of my assertions."

"Well," replied Bertrand, "I know not but I may do as you wish, on condition of receiving a handsome reward for the risk I may chance to run."

"You shall not have to complain of that," answered Meg, "for I can promise you not only gold, but a free pardon for any share you had in the transaction."

"And is that all I shall have to do?" asked Bertrand.

"It is not," she replied; "in fact there are two or three other affairs in which your testimony may be of the greatest service to the persons concerned."

"Indeed! and who are the persons you mean?"

"I know not that I am doing right in mentioning it just at present," returned Meg; "but you are, of course, aware that Sir Gaston de Neville had a younger brother who disappeared many years ago?"

"I have heard of it."

"Nay, you know more of it than you at present effect to do," replied Meg of Finchley.

"Well, perhaps I may; but what were you going to say about this brother that you were speaking of?"

"That he is still alive."

"The devil he is!"

"Aye, as truly as you now hear me tell you so."

"'Tis false, old woman."

"Again I tell you, he is alive," exclaimed Meg. "I, myself, conversed with him not long since, and, therefore, have reason to know that the person I have been speaking of is still in existence."

"Why then, if he is alive, and being the elder brother, has he not before come to claim the patrimony that is his by right of birth?"

"He has abstained from doing so for the kindest reasons," answered Meg. "He knows the awkward explanation that must take place, and, therefore, chooses to remain quiet, in the expectation that Sir Gaston de Neville may die first, and that he will then succeed to the property and title without wounding the feelings of one who little deserves so much consideration."

"Still I cannot believe you," cried Bertrand le Noir; "that my master had an elder brother, I am well aware, but he disappeared many years ago, and had he still been living, we should have heard of him long before now."

"I have told you why he has not revealed himself," replied Meg, "and let that be sufficient for the present."

"It must be some impostor," exclaimed Bertrand; "some adventurer, who, having heard the circumstance of a brother having disappeared, has now thought proper to come forward with a claim that will after all turn out to be a falsehsod."

"And why," asked Meg, "if that was the case, has he so long abstained from urging his claim?"

"That," answered the other, "you, who are, perhaps, in league with him can best explain."

"How! do you accuse me of entertaining a design wilfully upon Sir Gaston de Neville?"

"I know nothing about your motives," replied the other; "but it seems likely enough that you have received money from this fellow, whoever he is, and in that case there is no doubt you will do your best to palm him off upon the world as the brother of Sir Gaston."

"Man!" exclaimed the old woman, "I forgive you for the unjust suspicion, but do not, I charge you, imagine that Sir Gaston de Neville is secure. His brother has had an opportunity of watching him for many years past, and has refrained from making his own just claim by the thought of how much dishonour such a revelation might bring upon his name. If you value your own safety, therefore, I would advise you to quit a falling house, and attach yourself to a person who will have it in his power to reward you for any service you may do him."

"Tell me who he is," answered Bertrand le Noir, "and I will soon tell you whether it will be worth my while to put any faith in his promises."

"His name must not be revealed just at present," replied Meg of Finchley. "There are reasons why the secret should be strictly kept, and, therefore, let that be sufficient till circumstances will allow of further information being given on the subject."

"I know not that I can give any answer till I have learnt more about this mysterious affair," replied Bertrand. "Besides, I have only your word for it at present, and that is hardly sufficient to convince me that the lost brother of my master has returned."

"You are determined, then, not to assist in an affair when your aid may be of some consequence?"

"Why, I don't say anything positive just at present," replied Bertrand le Noir; "it may be to my own advantage to lend all the assistance I can, and, if it should turn out to be so, there is little reason why I should favour Sir Gaston de Neville, who I have every reason to believe would take my life if once he could lay his hands upon me."

"There is no doubt of his evil intentions towards you," answered Meg, "nor shall I hesitate to give him the necessary information where to find you if I observe any backwardness on your part to assist in the manner I have already spoken to you about."

"Hah! would you betray me, then?"

"That must depend entirely upon yourself," replied the old woman. "I have told you how it is easy not only to save your own life, but also to receive a handsome reward for any services you may have it in your power to perform. Choose, therefore, which way you will act, and I, for my own part, will afterwards proceed accordingly."

"But you will betray me if I do not happen to choose the side you have taken?"

"I may not betray you," answered the old woman, "but most certainly I shall not attempt to serve one who refuses the aid he has it in his power to give."

"In that case I suppose I must do as you wish me."

"If you do so, I am your friend," answered Meg, "but of course I shall expect you to enter heart and soul in the cause."

"You may depend on me if once I give my word to assist," replied the other.

"And then, with respect to the Jew and his daughter, I told you the last time we met that you must promise to protect them to the utmost of your power against the future persecutions of Sir Gaston de Neville. Since then, however, I have seen Black Ivan, the Outlaw, who tells me the maiden is to be married this day to Reuben Grenard, and thus, I believe, all fears on her behalf will soon cease to exist."

"And does Sir Gaston know of this?"

"He does not."

"So, indeed, I should imagine, for, had he a notion of it, he would not fail to take prompt measures to prevent this marriage of the Hebrew Maiden."

"And for that reason," exclaimed the old woman, "I would hve him kept in ignorance till after the ceremony is over. He will then cease to pursue her any further, and thus one great source of my uneasiness will be for ever removed."

"But by taking part against him," observed Bertrand le Noir, "I shall make a more inveterate foe than ever of Sir Gaston."

"Be not alarmed on that account," replied the hag of Finchley, "for a period has nearly arrived when he will be compelled to change his tone towards those he has been in the habit of acting the tyrant over. I am now watching him with a careful eye, and should he venture to go on any further with his baseness, it will be at the risk of bringing upon himself that ruin which has long been hanging over him."

As Meg finished speaking, one of Sir Gaston's retainers was seen advancing at his utmost speed towards them; at first, Bertrand would have turned and fled, for he well knew the object which had brought the fellow there; but resolution immediately prevailed over his fears, and, drawing a sword, with which he fortunately happened to be armed, he awaited the arrival of his foe with a firm determination to defend him-

self to the last, and to sell his life dearly, if, indeed, his opponent should chance to gain the advantage.

"Bertrand le Noir," exclaimed the fellow as he approached, "I have been sent by your master, Sir Gaston de Neville, to command your instant return to his castle."

"I own no man for master, now," answered the other, haughtily. "Sir Gaston and I have parted upon indifferent terms, and I am, therefore, not very likely to trust myself with one of whose perfidy I have, ere now, had pretty tolerable experience."

"You refuse to obey his commands, then?"

"I do; and you may return to him and say that I will never again venture within his castle walls whilst they own him as a master."

"Wouldst thou not think me mad, Bertrand le Noir," exclaimed the other, "to take so insolent a message to one of Sir Gaston's fiery temper?"

"I care not for his fiery temper, Raby, any more than I should for yours," answered the other resolutely. "He has once, within the last few hours, sought my life, and nothing shall ever tempt me to be fool enough to risk myself again under the same roof with one whose villany I have experienced."

"But thou canst not hope to escape him," exclaimed Raby, "his anger will impel him to hunt thee, even to the extremity of the earth, and his rage will be far greater against thee, than if thou wert to return according to the commands he has sent by me."

"I care nothing for the anger, so long as I can keep beyond his reach," answered the other.

"Besides," interposed Meg, "the knight has no further claim upon

No. 83

the services or obedience of his late retainer.   Bertrand le Noir is no longer his servant, and I should think he knows better than to trust to the word of one who never yet kept faith either with friend or foe, unless his own interest was concerned in it."

"And who, I prithee, art thou?" demanded Raby, "who hast thus dared to interfere in a business that concerns thee not?"

"One," answered Meg, "who happens to know thy master for a black and hardened villain.   Aye, thou mayest frown on me, man, but I speak the truth, and care not whether it pleases or offends thee."

"I have nothing to say to thee," exclaimed Raby, turning his back upon her, and addressing himself once more to Bertrand le Noir;—"my business is with you, and, therefore, do I ask you again whether you will obey the behest of your master, or take the consequence of a refusal?"

"That," returned Bertrand, "must depend upon circumstances, and, therefore, I ask in return what are to be the consequences with which you seek to frighten me?"

"One of the consequences" answered Raby, "will be, that I take you back with me by force, and the other may be that Sir Gaston de Neville will severely punish thee for daring to disobey his orders."

"Indeed! you think, then, that it is quite easy to take me by force into the presence of your imperious master?"

"I am sure of it; at least I know that I was never thine inferior in the use of the sword, and it is hard if I cannot now compel thee to surrender when I am sent on such an errand as this."

"Humph! but you forget Raby, that if we cross the weapons I shall be fighting for life and liberty, neither of which I feel inclined to give up without a desperate struggle.   Now, it may so happen, that you will fall, and, therefore, let me advise you to return to Sir Gaston de Neville with a message from me, giving him to understand that I will not again trust myself in his presence, unless, indeed, it will be with weapons in my hands, wherewith to guard myself against his treachery."

"And this," exclaimed Raby, "I am to understand for thy firm and unalterable resolution?"

"You may understand me as you please," replied Bertrand le Noir, with cool indifference; "I have spoken my mind pretty freely, and, if that is not sufficient, I stand here with a sword in my hand, and you can, therefore, try whether it is quite so easy to take me before Sir Gaston de Neville as you seem to imagine."

"I see," exclaimed the other; "you seek a quarrel to revenge yourself for an old grudge that has been between us."

"Hah! you remind me of our quarrel, do you?" exclaimed Bertrand, "nay, then, since you have done that, we will e'en settle the dispute now, with an understanding that no quarter shall be given.   I shall neither ask nor expect any, and, should'st thou prove the weakest in the conflict, be assured I will not spare thy life."

"Agreed!" returned the other, fiercely; "I accept thy terms, and gladly would I become thy victim rather than return to Sir Gaston de Neville with a confession that I had been conquered by a foe that I despise."

"Nay," cried Meg of Finchley, interposing between them, "let me implore you both to forbear; this quarrel it seems must end in blood if once thy swords are crossed, and, therefore, I entreat you, Raby, to return to the castle of your master, and deliver the message as it was given to you by Bertrand le Noir."

"Peace, old woman!" exclaimed Raby, "and interfere not with those who require not thy counsel. Leave us, I desire, for this is no place for one whose age and sex should impel her to leave a scene of blood and strife."

"I will not leave the place," answered Meg, "for, since you are both obstinately bent on each other's destruction, I will remain where I am, in hopes that the little skill I possess, may prove of service to him whose fate it is to fall by the sword of his adversary."

Before the old woman had done speaking, the angry combatants had crossed their weapons, and the combat commenced with the desperation of men who knew they had nothing to expect from the mercy of each other. For some time the fight was maintained with remarkable evenness on both sides, for their skill was as nearly equal as possible, and both of them were possessed of more than an ordinary share of courage. At length, however, a slight advantage was gained by Bertrand le Noir, who succeeded in inflicting a trifling flesh wound in the arm of his adversary, the effect of which was speedily seen in the diminished energy with which he resisted the assaults of his opponent. Bertrand also found that the victory would soon be his own, and, renewing his efforts with redoubled vigour, he at length succeeded in so far wearying the other, that he could scarcely offer any resistance to the attacks to which he was subjected. Seizing the opportunity, Bertrand made a furious rush forward, his sword passed completely through the body of his adversary, and Raby sank with a heavy groan to the earth.

Meg of Finchley now advanced to render what assistance she could to the wounded man, but her efforts were unavailing, for the tide of life was fast gushing forth, and, within a few minutes afterwards, the unfortunate fellow ceased to exist.

"Thou hast slain him, Bertrand," exclaimed the old woman, "and now let me advise thee to fly, ere thou art overtaken by other foes."

"Whither can I go that they will not follow me?" demanded Bertrand le Noir.

"Hasten to the sanctuary in the Abbey of Westminster," exclaimed Meg, "there thou wilt be safe, for none will dare to follow thee there, even though thou hast shed the blood of a fellow creature."

"He brought it upon himself," replied Bertrand, "for it was hardly to be expected that I would yield myself his prisoner, knowing as I did, that his master intended to give me up to death."

At this moment a number of persons were seen advancing at some distance off, and Bertrand, whose attention had been directed towards them by Meg, at once discovered that they were the knight's retainers, headed by Sir Gaston himself, who was urging them forward at their utmost speed.

"Delay not an instant if you would save yourself," she cried earnestly, "away to the sanctuary, and leave it not till you can do so in safety. The hounds are even now upon you, and, when they see the carrion lying on the ground, their fury will be redoubled, and you will hardly have time to secure yourself. Away, I say,—run for your life, Bertrand, and pause not till you have reached the place of safety!"

Bertrand le Noir required no second bidding, for, ere the hag of Finchley had uttered these last words, he darted away in the direction which led towards the Abbey of Westminster; nor did the old woman risk the fierce wrath of those that were advancing, and, making towards a small wood at no great distance off, she was soon beyond the reach of those whose fierce wrath she had so much reason to dread.

CHAPTER CVI.

" I care not for thy laws and usuages,
    He whom I seek for is a heinous wretch
    Who, having broke the laws, shall, therefore, suffer
    The penalty he merits."

THE FUGITIVE.

WITHIN a few minutes after Meg had left the place, Sir Gaston de Neville and his followers arrived at the scene of conflict, and the first object which met their view was the inanimate form of him who they had parted from not long since in life and health. The knight's rage was ungovernable when he saw the fate of his retainer, and addressing himself to them about him, he called upon them to revenge the death of their late comrade.

"You see," he exclaimed, "the fate that has befallen Raby, who set forward alone, in order that he might secure the villain who so lately made an attempt upon my life. This is another of Bertrand's deeds, and I now ask whether you will not hunt to death the wretch who has done this deed?"

"Aye, aye,—we will,—we will!" shouted a score or two of voices.

"And yet," observed old Jasper, who was among them, "I fancy there will be more difficulty in following him than you imagine; for I heard some of our comrades here say that they could see him hastening from this place towards the sanctuary at Westminster, and if he has once got there, it will be more than we dare venture to do to arrest him even though it be on a charge of murder."

"Peace, drivelling idiot!" exclaimed Sir Gaston, angrily, "and venture not to give thine opinion unasked upon a subject of this importance. Have I not found one of my retainers barbarously murdered, and shall I suffer the assassin to escape even though he has fled for shelter and protection to the sanctuary of which thou speakest?"

"I may offend, perhaps," cried Jasper "and yet, whether it happens so or not, I will speak my mind freely. It is not yet certain that Raby has been murdered by Bertrand le Noir; in fact, it is more likely that they engaged each other in mortal strife, and that he who we see lying breathless before us, received his death wound in a quarrel that was provoked by himself. Such, at least, is probable enough, and I think it but fair that we should suspend our judgment upon the affair till we have ascertained how it took place, and whether Bertrand le Noir is the cold-blooded assassin he has been represented."

"Will no one silence this pratling fool?" exclaimed Sir Gaston de Neville, half mad with fury; "send a poiniard to his heart, I say, and make him a companion for the lifeless corse that lies at our feet!"

"Aye, aye," replied Jasper;—"slay me as your master has commanded;—I have perchance spoken the truth, and, therefore it is mete that I should die for it. Here is my bosom bared for him who likes to slay an old man, nor will I shrink from the fate that has been awarded to me by a master whom I have faithfully served for many a long year. Strike, I say, and in pity let your daggers give me a speedy death!"

But there were none who would slay an old man whose grey hairs had obtained for him the respect of even the harsh retainers who followed Sir Gaston de Neville. The knight saw their hesitation, and knowing that a repetition of his cruel decree would only serve to render him odious to those who surrounded him, he assumed a calmer deportment, and spoke in a voice that betokened less anger than it had formerly done.

"You have done wisely," he said, "in not obeying the hasty commands of an over-excited man. I have no ill-feeling towards Jasper, whose long and faithful services have won for him my favour and protection, but he should be careful how he rouses the anger of one who is not accustomed to be governed by those who serve under him. The old man is forgiven, and I desire that this affair is immediately buried in oblivion."

"Is it still your pleasure, Sir Knight," demanded one of the retainers, "that we follow Bertrand le Noir to the sanctuary?"

"Aye, and that speedily too," answered the knight; "the villain has deeply injured me, and never shall I rest satisfied till he has paid the full penalty of his numerous offences against me."

"Would you break open the church in pursuit of the man?" asked old Jasper.

"Aye," answered the Templar, fiercely, "and drag him forth to punishment, even though he had taken refuge at the foot of the altar."

"But have you reflected on the consequences of such a step?" demanded the old man.

"I have, and no consideration shall ever induce me to give up my intention."

"Nay, think me not over bold, Sir Gaston," cried the aged retainer, "but suffer me once more to warn you of the danger you are running yourself into. By such a course as this you will bring upon yourself the fierce enmity of the churchmen, and never will they cease their persecutions until they have brought ruin upon him who has dared to violate the sanctuary of their sacred fame."

"Humph!" ejaculated Sir Gaston, "and what care I, think you, for the anger of men whose wrath I despise, and who it is in my power to crush should they become too insolent for further endurance?"

"You are interfering with their rights and privileges."

"Perhaps so; but if their rights and privileges were founded upon a better basis, I should not, perhaps, be disposed to interfere with them. As it is however they are disposed to offer a shelter and asylum to one who has openly violated the laws, and, therefore, I do nothing more than my duty in teaching these haughty priests that their power is no longer to be abused as it has been."

"But may not the people take up their cause," answered Jasper "and thus assist in bringing about that ruin which I am so anxious to avert?"

"Psha! I ask thee not to be anxious on my account," answered the Knight Templar, haughtily; "I am well enough able to defend myself against all who may be disposed to feel aggrieved at the course I am about to adopt, and so I would have them beware lest they plunge themselves into a quarrel that must terminate in their own overthrow."

"And perhaps in their own also."

"Sir Knight," interposed one of the men, "will you submit to be thus interfered with by one whose duty it is to yield himself to your will?"

"My honoured master," answered Jasper, "knows that I have only spoken in my zeal for his welfare;—he will at least give me credit for sincerity, and therefore, I still hope he may listen to the voice of reason in spite of the evil councillors by whom he is surrounded."

"I tell thee, sirrah," cried Sir Gaston, "it is in vain to speak to me upon this subject; my mind is made up, and even though the great

fiend himself were to oppose my project, I would not desist till the recreant Bertrand le Noir has been dragged from his place of refuge."

"Then the evil consequence I so much dread must follow," exclaimed
Jasper, in despair. "I would have given you such counsel as an old
man has to bestow; but you have scorned my advice, and you must e'en
fall as I have said."

"And if I do," replied Sir Gaston, "it shall not be before I have
taught these haughty priests a lesson that they will not be likely soon to
forget. I am not a foe to be trifled with, and I would have those beware
who may venture to interfere where they have no business."

"Pardon me, Sir Gaston," exclaimed one of the retainers, "but we are
wasting time when we should be actively engaged in dragging this
ruffian from his place of refuge. He may perhaps chance to hear that
we are about to follow him, and in that case he will leave his present
sanctuary to find an asylum in some other place where we may not be
likely to find him."

"True; we are indeed neglecting to make use of an opportunity that
so admirably serves us," replied Sir Gaston. "The villain must be
hunted to his lair, and that too before he finds means to set us at defiance."

"You are still resolved then," cried Jasper, "to pursue a course that
must end in your destruction?"

"I am, old man," returned Sir Gaston, "and therefore, if your timi-
dity prompts you to do so, go back to my castle, and await in safety there
till we return with news of Bertrand le Noir's capture."

"I will take advantage of your permission," replied the old man;—
not however from my cowardice, for you have ere now seen that I would
be brave in my master's service, but because you are at present engaged
in an act of violence towards the church which I have ever been taught
to respect and reverence. Such is the only motive I have for not following you on the present occasion, and, therefore, do I take my leave;
earnestly hoping that you may yet be induced to abandon a project that
must end in your own ruin."

With this Jasper turned away amidst the jeers of those who were less
scrupulous, and who now urged their master to lose no more time in
putting into execution the project he had formed. But the knight had
evidently been somewhat moved by the words of the old man, and it was
not till he had been pressed two or three times that he could resolve upon
the step he was to pursue.

"I would that the old dotard had held his peace," he at length said,
"for, to confess the truth, he has uttered words that fill my soul with
apprehension of danger."

"There is no danger," exclaimed the fellow who had acted as spokesman
on the occasion;—"the old man presumes upon his length of services for
a privilege to be as insolent as he pleases, though he must be aware that
Sir Gaston de Neville can have nothing to fear from those who may
think fit to grumble because a ruffian has been forcibly taken away from
the sanctuary."

"And yet there is some truth in what he has said," returned the
knight; "I shall be denounced as a monster by these howling priests,
who ever look with horror upon those who interfere with their privileges."

"You will abandon your designs then," muttered the man, "and
suffer Bertrand to escape in spite of the mischief you expect he may be
able to do you?"

"No;—by heavens he shall not elude me even though I pursue him to the very gates of hell!" exclaimed Sir Gaston, excited by the danger in which he would be placed if Bertrand le Noir should chance to disclose certain secrets of which he was possessed. "The villain would distroy me if he could, and why therefore should I not seize upon the present opportunity to rid myself of one whose existence may be fatal to my own?"

"Shall we to the sanctuary without further delay?"

"Aye," replied the knight, "waste not another moment in idleness lest the villain should escape. I will myself lead you to the place where he has sought for refuge, and let none dare shrink from the task he has thus taken upon himself, let the consequence be what it may."

All promised to follow Sir Gaston, who now conducted them towards the abbey, the gates of which they found closed against them. To break them open, however, was a task of no great difficulty, and then hurrying along the principal aisle, they reached the altar before which Bertrand was kneeling;—the sight of his offending retainer filled the heart of Sir Gaston de Neville with rage, and rushing forward, he would have grasped Bertrand by the throat to drag him away, had not the abbot at that moment interposed between them.

"Are ye men and Christians," he exclaimed, in a voice of mingled anger and reproach, "that ye have thus dared to violate the sanctity of the holy temple? Away, I command ye, or take the heavy anathemas of one whose prayers to heaven were never yet unheeded."

"I care not for your anathemas, holy father," retorted the knight, advancing as his followers shrank back with dismay; "I am here to capture a villain who has lately made an attempt upon the life of your king, and it will therefore be at your own peril to oppose me further in a duty that I have thus taken upon myself."

"Hast thou been sent hither by the king?" demanded the abbot, with surprise.

"I have not."

"Thou comest then to satisfy private revenge?"

"It may be so," replied Sir Gaston, "but that is a question which thou hast no right to ask."

"Ha!" cried the abbot. "dost thou dare to dispute my power and right in this place, where I am acknowledged by all to be the head and chief?"

"I deny thy right," answered Sir Gaston, "to interfere with one who comes to discharge his duty."

"Thou hast far exceeded thy duty," replied the abbot, mildly; "this place is a sanctuary for all, be the crimes what they may;—the laws never pursue them to this holy place, and I will not now permit thee to drag away this man even though he may be the henious criminal thou hast said."

"Thou shalt then answer for it to the king."

"That I am willing to do," returned the priest; "for King Richard is just, and never will he interfere with a privilege that has been allowed by all his illustrious progenitors. Besides, he has no right to meddle with the affairs of the church, and be the consequences what they may to myself, I will not permit this man to be dragged away from the altar before which he has thrown himself for protection."

"Indeed!—thou hast not considered then the consequences that may follow the obstinacy thou hast this day manifested?"

"Hear me, Sir Gaston de Neville," cried the abbot, resolutely; "if thou dost mean any mischief that thou mayest thyself do me, know that

I am perfectly at ease upon the subject. Thou art sanguinary and unjust I admit, but there are laws to restrain thy violence, and upon them will I rely for protection and succour."

"Humph!" muttered the knight; "it seems then I am to be defied by a priest, even though I am here to enforce the demands I have made?"

"My cause is just, sir," answered the abbot, "and, therefore, with the aid of Heaven, will I perish in shielding this man from the vengeance you meditated."

"But I tell thee, priest," exclaimed Sir Gaston, "he has attempted to assassinate the king, and was only prevented by a stranger who interposed to avert the deadly blow."

"I have heard it all," replied the old man, "and it is even said that he was instigated to commit the crime by one who ought to have been the last to turn his evil thoughts against the king. Thou mayest perhaps guess to whom I allude, and in that case I would advise thee to be less rancourous in thy pursuit of one who is not so guilty as he who urged him to the deed."

"Old man," exclaimed Sir Gaston, "I neither no nor care to whom you allude. My duty is to arrest this ruffian, and I will do so were fifty abbots to interpose themselves between me and my object."

"Thou wilt do so then at thine own peril," cried the abbot, placing himself between Bertrand le Noir and the enraged knight. "This man—criminal though he may be,—has sought the sanctuary which this place affords, and he shall be safe even in spite of thy threats and of the numbers by whom thou art surrounded."

"Dost thou beard me, old man?"

"I defy thy malice," retorted the abbot, "and, therefore, do I again bid thee depart, ere I am tempted to load thee with the curses thou hast so well merited."

"Psha!" exclaimed the knight, "and what thinkest thou does one like me care for the curses thou dost threaten me with. My whole life should have taught thee that I care not for priestly interference, and it may now, perhaps, only remain for me to slay thee by way of showing the world that I am above the weak superstitions that have prompted many a one to spare a foe merely because he chanced to wear the priestly garb."

"Thy words, Sir Knight, would lead me to suppose that my life would fall a sacrifice should I longer persist in protecting this man against thine evil designs?"

"Thou hast guessed my thoughts," returned Sir Gaston, "for be assured I shall not hesitate to shed thy blood should there be occasions for it."

"Aye, thou boasted because there happened to be so many armed men against one who is unarmed and defenceless."

"Nay," interposed Bertrand le Noir, "thou art wrong there, "for I, who have sought and claimed thy hospitality, am ready to sacrifice my life in thy behalf."

"Hah! say'st thou so, villain?" exclaimed the infuriated Sir Gaston de Neville;—"would'st thou dare to raise thine arm against the master thou hast sworn fealty to?"

"The master has already sought the life of his servant," retorted Bertrand, "and, therefore, it is to be expected that he no longer acknowledges himself bound to him. Besides, thou hast come hither to drag me away for the purpose of vengeance, and it is therefore time that I now turn against him who would sacrifice me were it once in his power to do so."

"And dost thou think," demanded Sir Gaston, "that I am to be

thwarted by my own vassal? By one who I have too long made my friend and companion, and who has, at length,—viper-like,—turned his venom against the hand that protected and nutured him? No, by heavens thou hast pronounced thine own doom, and were hell itself to yawn beneath my feet, it shonld not shelter thee from my burning veugeance."

"Peace, I charge thee, Sir Gaston," interposed the abbot; "remember the sanctity of the roef that at present covers thee, and do not bring upon thyself the further anger of that heaven which thou hast already so grievously offended."

"And who is it," demanded the knight, "that thus calls upon me to desist from a purpose which I have resolved to execute? Have I not said that my retainer shall be dragged away from the sanctuary he has claimed: and is a soldier to be thus frustrated by a feeble churchman, whose power he holds in the most utter contempt?"

"Attempt not the violence thou hast threatened me with," exclaimed the old man, "or thou mayest yet be made to feel that thy boasted strength will be as nothing against one who relies upon heaven alone for aid and protection."

"Thou hearest how he defies me," cried Sir Gaston, addressing himself to his followers, "and yet there is not one among you who has offered to step forward in order to strike him dead at my feet."

"The truth is, Sir Knight," exclaimed Michael, "we are all of us loath to raise our hands against a minister of our holy religion. The abbot claims a right to protect a criminal who has fled for safety to the sanctuary of his church, and it is not for us to interfere in a case like the present."

No. 84

"How, sirrah!" retorted Sir Gaston, "dost thou dare hesitate when I command?"

"At all other times," replied the retainer, "I am most willing to do all that a servant is expected to do for a master. I have served you faithfully and diligently for many years past, and never yet failed in the performance of my duty. Now, however, you ask too much, and it is therefore time that I should refuse when I see the danger that compliance would bring on me."

"Villain!" roared the knight, "thou shalt either obey me in this instance, or my own sword shall punish thee for thy disobedience and insolence."

"Hold, rash man!" exclaimed the abbot; "and dare not stain this edifice with blood that has been shed in this dispute. Here I hold sovereign sway, and it is my command that you instantly depart, leaving this man to enjoy in safety the sanctuary he has claimed."

"And so," cried Sir Gaston, bitterly, "you offer protection to a villain whose many crimes have long since deserved the punishment it is my present purpose to inflict."

"I do nothing more than obey the laws which offer a secure asylum to those who seek it at the foot of the altar," replied the abbot, mildly. "This man may have offended grievously, and I am inclined to believe he has, but thou art thyself not altogether blameless; and, therefore, I would have thee reflect upon thine own errors ere thou dost press too heavily upon those of others."

"Old man, beware how you urge me too far!" exclaimed Sir Gaston, fiercely. "I have already endured more from thee than I should from any one else, and having done so, I would fain advise thee to leave us; and whilst thou art engaged in thy pious offices, I will convey away the prisoner, whose numerous crimes well deserve the fate he will have to meet."

"But his crimes," replied the abbot, "whatever they may be, have been committed at thine own instigation."

"Hah! dost thou again dare to reproach me with having made this man what he is?"

"Ask thine own conscience whether I have accused thee unjustly," answered the priest. "Reflect deeply on my words, and if thou canst exonerate thyself, I will freely confess that I have most foully wronged thee."

"Psha!" exclaimed the knight; "and why should I follow thy advice when it is in my power to enforce the purpose that brought me hither? I have come to take hence a slave who has made an attempt upon my own life, as well as that of the king; and never will I leave your presence except with him as my prisoner."

"You have charged me wrongfully," cried Bertrand le Noir, "for whatever other crimes I may have been guilty of, I never yet have sought to take away your life. This you well know, and were it not that I wish not to expose you further, I could so explain this affair that the blame should rest rather upon yourself than upon me."

"Thou hast heard him!" exclaimed Sir Gaston to his retainers: "the villain, not satisfied with the crimes he has already committed, would now turn upon his master, to crush him beneath the vile accusations he would bring against him."

"It is in vain to contend against him at present, Sir Knight," cried Michael; "here he perhaps ought to be safe from the vengeance he has inspired you with, but the monks cannot keep him here beyond a certain time, and when once he is turned forth, it will be easy for some of us to lie in wait and make him our prisoner."

"It is in vain you seek to move me from my purpose," replied Sir Gaston de Neville, "for I have sworn to drag him from this place, and I will do so, in spite of all the priests in Christendom. Whilst he is at liberty my own life is continually exposed to danger; and let the consequences to myself be what they may, I will either take him hence, or leave him weltering in his own blood at the foot of the altar where he now kneels."

"Shall I not have the protection I have sought?" demanded Bertrand, appealing to the abbot, who yet stood between him and the knight; "am I to be sacrificed because a great man has come to claim me at your hands, or shall I receive the benefit that has been granted to far greater criminals than myself?"

"Thou shalt be safe, man!" answered the priest; "but I charge thee do not move, lest an advantage be given to thine enemies which I cannot avert."

"I will be trifled with no longer," exclaimed Sir Gaston, wrathfully; "already have we been delayed far beyond my patience, and now I call upon all my followers who would not be regarded as cowards to aid me in seizing upon the ruffian we came to capture."

At these words the retainers advanced in a body, but again they paused upon beholding the venerable abbot, who stood firm and unmoved at the danger with which he was threatened. Presently, however, one of them, who was bolder than the rest, sprang forward, and seizing the priest, hurled him with violence half across the chapel; and then, drawing his poniard, was in the act of rushing upon Bertrand, when a flash of lightning—probably attracted by the glittering steel he held in his hand—struck him to the floor, and in a few moments nothing remained of the retainer but a black and hideous corpse. This incident, sudden and awful as it was, struck every body with terror that it was impossible to suppress, and for a few moments every one stood motionless with surprise and horror, for none dared advance another step, lest he also should become the next victim of Heaven's displeasure. Even Sir Gaston, reckless as he usually was, stood speechless with terror for a brief period, but at length, suddenly recovering himself, he rushed forward and seized upon Bertrand le Noir ere the abbot, who by this time had recovered himself, could interpose his aid to rescue the criminal from the impending danger.

"Sir Gaston," exclaimed the old man, "I again implore thee to reflect ere thou dost commit a deed which thou may'st afterwards have to repent. Remember, this man is at present under the protection of the church, and if thou shouldst persist in forcibly carrying him away, it will be my duty to persecute thee for the crime of sacrilege, which will probably cost thee thy life."

"Oh, I am well aware of what may follow," answered the knight, scornfully, "and shall be quite ready to encounter any danger that you may have it in your power to bring on me. For all this I am prepared, but let the peril be what it may, I am fully resolved to take Bertrand le Noir with me, and to deal with him exactly as I may happen to think proper."

With this he motioned to his comrades, and in spite of the prayers and entreaties of the old priest, Bertrand was forcibly carried from the sanctuary, and from thence towards the castle of Sir Gaston de Neville.

CHAPTER CVII.

" Confess thou what thou knowest,
That I may pardon all thy great offences,
And set thee free."

THE BROTHERS.

CONFINED once more within one of the strongest dungeons of the incensed knight, Bertrand le Noir now gave himself up for lost. That he
had no mercy to expect he was well assured, for Sir Gaston was as cruel
as he was inexorable when once his malignity was aroused; and the
unhappy captive knew that he had too deeply offended ever to be forgiven by the man who was aware that he could reveal secrets, which, if
divulged, would be certain to bring upon him that punishment which he
so much dreaded to meet. Under these circumstances there was no hope
for Bertrand, and as the only alternative that remained, he resolved to
make a desperate attempt to escape from the miserable cell that had been
chosen as his prison. With this design he made a careful examination
of the place, but at length he was compelled to give up even this hope
as a vain one, for the dungeon was well secured in every part, the door
having extra bolts and bars placed upon it, and the window being situated at a height which precluded the possibility of his being able to reach
it. Added to this, fetters had been placed upon his limbs, so that he was
rendered almost helpless, even had there been less difficulties in his way.
Thus was he reduced to the very lowest depths of despair, and, throwing
himself upon the straw which had been provided for his bed, he gave
himself up to all the tortures which reflection brought to his mind.

Nor was Sir Gaston much less troubled than Bertrand, for he feared
lest any disclosures might be made affecting himself, and all his thoughts
were, therefore, directed towards the plan he should pursue in order to
extricate himself from a dilemma which threatened him with an exposure
that was likely enough to terminate in his own ruin and disgrace. At
one time he had resolved to liberate his retainer, on condition that he
took an oath never to divulge anything that might do him an injury;
but then upon reflection he knew that there were many who would strive
to obtain all they could from Bertrand were he to be set at liberty, and,
therefore, this plan was abandoned almost as soon as it had been formed.
He next thought of having him assassinated without delay, so that he
might thus get rid of a peril that would be continually haunting him;
but even that presented obstacles that he had not before thought of, and
after some further time had been spent in pondering over these various
difficulties, he at last determined to have him brought at midnight into
the torture-chamber, where, in the presence of two of his confidential
followers, he might interrogate him on certain subjects, and thus shape
out his future course accordingly. This seemed to be his safest plan, and
he therefore determined to adopt it in preference to any other.

Bertrand le Noir, as we have seen, had given up all hope of escape,
and in his despair had thrown himself upon the ground, a prey to those
agonized feelings which those only who have been placed in a similar
situation of difficulty can fully enter into. At length a sort of lethargy
stole upon him, from which he was aroused some time afterwards by
some one removing the heavy bolts and chains with which the door of
his dungeon had been secured. By this time his lamp had expired, and
the darkness with which he was surrounded served to fill him with a
dread lest some one had been sent to dispatch him. Presently, however,

the door slowly opened, and Michael entered the cell. Glancing cautiously round to see whether the prisoner was safe, and having assured himself of this, he next advanced, and commanded the captive to rise and follow him without delay. But the other hesitated ere he complied with this, and after a few moments of deliberation, he asked by whom he had been desired to undertake his present mission?

"I come by the desire of Sir Gaston de Neville," replied the other; "and, therefore, you, of course, cannot refuse to accompany me into his presence."

"But I do refuse," answered the prisoner; "at least, I shall not stir from hence till I know by whose orders I have been locked up in this dismal place."

"Humph!" growled the other, "that is a question that I should have thought you need scarcely have given yourself the trouble to ask. Sir Gaston brought you hither, and, of course, it was by his command that you have been thrown into this dungeon."

"You may take back a message from me, then," exclaimed Bertrand, "to inform him that I will not see him till he chooses to give me the liberty he has so unjustly deprived me of."

"It would be of little use my taking him such a message as that," replied Michael, seeing that he has you in his power, and can compel you to appear before him at any time that he may think proper. Besides, I rather think he is inclined to favour you, and so, of course, it would be madness for you to offend him at the time when his kindness is so much needed."

"I ask him for no favour," replied Bertrand, "neither will I accept of any from the man who I have any reason to believe smiles only that the blow may be the more certain whenever he takes it into his head to inflict it."

"There you wrong our master, Bertrand," answered the other; "for had he intended to harm you, how easy it would have been to do so in this place, where you could not have resisted."

"True; but I happen to know the deep artifices of Sir Gaston de Neville better than you seem to do," replied Bertrand. "There is some secret motive behind all this, or he would not show lenity to the man whose life he so lately sought, even before the holy altar of St. Peter's Abbey."

"And what motive could he possibly have for saving you at this moment?" asked Michael.

"I do not pretend to know all his thoughts," answered the captive, "but he is either afraid of his crimes being further looked into, or else he wishes to prevail on me to commit some other act that may serve for a time to keep off the dangers which are now so closely pressing upon him."

"Nay, you may wrong him," exclaimed Michael: "for, after all, his motives may be perfectly fair towards yourself; and, in my opinion, it is likely enough that you may now regain the favour you have lost for a little while. Sir Gaston, you know, has not always been your enemy, and there are, perhaps, good reasons why he should wish your future days to be spent in more harmony together."

"He has reasons for wishing it," answered Bertrand; "but I also have bitter cause to distrust him when he thus seeks to regain the confidence I once placed in him. For a time it is likely enough he might appear to forget the past, but should he ever find me off my guard, there is little to hope for from his mercy or consideration."

"You still doubt his intentions then?"

"I do."

"In that case," said Michael, "I have orders to take you before him by force."

"Ha!" exclaimed Bertrand; "and what if I oppose my force to yours? —Suppose I resist, shall I not have at least an equal chance with yourself?"

"Psha! your limbs are bound with fetters, and, therefore, your obstinacy would prove unavailing."

"But these fetters on my wrists," answered Bertrand, with a grim look of defiance, "may prove a useful weapon in case I should chance to need them."

"Aye," retorted the other, "but I have assistance near at hand; and with the aid of a few stout friends, you would stand but a poor chance against our united efforts to force you hence."

"True," replied Bertrand; "and it is likely that some of those fellows you speak of might chance to perish for their presumption in striving to force one whose will is opposed to their own. I am a desperate man, remember, and am not to be dragged into the presence of Sir Gaston de Neville against my inclination."

"And why are you so obstinate," demanded Michael, "when I have assured you that our master seeks rather to serve than to injure you?"

"Because I doubt his professions of friendship towards one whom I know he fears."

"Nay, if he fears you," replied the other, "there is the more reason to suppose that he will seek, by every means in his power, to gain your good will."

"Or rather," answered Bertrand, "he will seek, by the speediest means in his power, "to rid himself of one whose existence keeps his own in constant peril. I know him far better than you do, Michael; and for that reason I cannot but look with distrust upon any profession of friendship he may make."

"But you said not long since," observed Michael, "that it was likely he might want you to engage yourself in some affair or other that he has got on hand."

"I said it was probable, and still think he must have some such motive, or else he never would have pardoned what has taken place between us."

"Well, then," returned Michael, "in that case it would be madness to throw away a chance not only of saving your life, but of obtaining the favour which, but a little time since, you had so completely lost."

"The truth is," replied Bertrand, "I do not again choose to run the many risks I should have to do were I again to make myself the slave of his humours. The bonds that once united us have been severed, and I am now inclined rather to remain the object of his displeasure than again become the instrument of his vindictive temper."

"But should you prove obstinate," exclaimed Michael, "it is likely you may be made to repent that you threw away a chance of rescuing yourself from the miseries of this wretched dungeon."

"If it is his will that I remain here," answered the other, "I can resign myself to my fate without a murmur. The truth is, I have been used to see how others have been obliged to make the best of their misfortunes, and whether Sir Gaston thinks fit to order my immediate death or to keep me here for the rest of my life will matter very little to a poor devil that don't care how matters may go."

"Then, of course," observed Michael, "you will not refuse to follow me to the presence of Sir Gaston de Neville?"

"That will depend upon circumstances," answered Bertrand: "if I am to be forced there, I may, perhaps, give you all the trouble I can; but if you choose to treat me civilly, I'll go with all my heart, and hear what proposition the knight has got to make."

"In that case," replied the man, "I shall not attempt to compel you, though, as I said before, there is plenty of assistance close at hand, if it should be needed."

"Humph!—and am I to go before Sir Gaston with these fetters on my ancles and wrists?"

"You must; but I dare say you and Sir Gaston will soon understand one another, and then you will not have to endure these fetters much longer."

"Well, upon consideration, I believe it will be better to follow your advice; so lead the way, Michael, and I will judge for myself whether the knight is to be depended on."

Acting upon this hint, Michael again opened the heavy door of the dungeon, and proceeded into the passage, closely followed by Bertrand le Noir, who carefully observed every action of his guide, lest any treachery should be intended under the mask of friendship. The distance they had to go was considerable, but not a word was exchanged between them, for Bertrand's mind was fully occupied with his own thoughts, and he therefore pursued his way in silence, pondering deeply on the situation in which he found himself, and devising various schemes in case any trick should be intended by the artful Knight Templar. At length, they reached the top of a high flight of winding stairs, from whence they passed through numerous gloomy chambers, till they came to a door, before which Michael paused and rapped three times, as if for a signal to some one within. Then a voice—which Bertrand at once knew to be the knight's,—was heard, and the door being opened, they entered an apartment dimly lighted by a single lamp, which served to show that Sir Gaston was seated at a table, his head resting upon his hands, and his thoughts evidently occupied with the uneasy reflections that filled his mind. At the sound of their footsteps, however, he instantly roused himself, and directing a keen glance towards Bertrand, demanded whether the situation in which he found himself had served in any way to mitigate the angry feelings with which he had lately thought fit to regard him.

"That," answered the prisoner, sullenly, will entirely depend upon circumstances."

"Indeed!—it seems, then, that I am to make terms with a menial whose life is in my power?"

"Not so," returned the other; "I wish but to know whether it is possible you can ever regard your retainer with the same favour that you formerly honoured him with."

"Most assuredly I can; but first I must know that you are worthy of the esteem I would bestow on you."

"How am I to convince you?"

"By fairly answering whatever questions I put to you."

"Proceed then, and I will judge whether it be expedient or not to trust a man who has so lately dragged me from the sanctuary to which I had fled."

"And if I did so," replied Sir Gaston, "my conduct towards you has since shewn you that it was not your life I aimed at."

"I know not what your object was, Sir Knight, nor does it much matter to me; but I have been shut up in a dungeon ever since, and, therefore, I have reason to suppose that your intentions are not very favourable towards me."

"Your confinement was necessary, till I had matured my future plans," replied Sir Gaston. "I have, however, taken into consideration your former faithful services, and am now resolved to overlook the past, on condition that you promise henceforth to be as zealous in my cause as I have ever found you previous to our late differences."

"Ha!—you have more work, I suppose, that you cannot so well entrust to another?"

"Perhaps so," answered the knight, "and, surely, that thought alone should convince you of my good intentions, since I am again willing to trust my life and honour to you."

"I know how you can varnish and gloss over your designs," replied Bertrand, gloomily; "but there are other things to be considered, before we come to terms. You are aware that a reward has been offered for my apprehension, so that, of course, it will be impossible for me to leave your castle, unless I would madly run a risk which would end in my certain destruction."

"All that I know," answered Sir Gaston; "you cannot, at present, leave the castle, but events are now in progress that will tend to procure your speedy pardon, and when that has been obtained, you will be convinced, I suppose, of the good intentions I bear towards you."

"I understand," exclaimed Bertrand le Noir; "the plot is still in progress against King Richard, and when he is dethroned, I am to obtain a pardon from his successor?"

"Exactly so; everything has been satisfactorily arranged, and a short time is only required to bring our affairs to a successful termination. You will then obtain a reward from Prince John for your former services, and, from that time, a life of happiness awaits you."

"Aye, as usual, I see you are looking only on the most favourable side of the picture."

"I tell you, Bertrand, things must turn out exactly as I have said, and it will be your own fault if you do not at once take the opportunity that offers."

"And are you disinterested in the proposition you have made, Sir Knight?"

"Why, perhaps not altogether so; you will be required to afford whatever assistance you can, and your reward will be just what I have told you."

"But I can do nothing till I have the pardon you spoke of, and, therefore, my services will be of little benefit to any one till John has mounted the throne."

"I am aware of it," replied Sir Gaston; "and yet, there are many things in which you may be profitably employed. At any rate, you can disguise yourself and venture out during the night time, in order to mix among those malcontents who are willing to join us whenever our plans are properly organized."

"Or, in other words," observed Bertrand, "I may run my neck into a noose, and thus commit a species of suicide, for the sake of serving those who would not bestow a thought upon me when once their own turn was served."

"Do you doubt me, sirrah?"

"Unfortunately, I have had too many reasons to do so."

"Am I to understand, then, that you refuse to earn my pardon on the terms I have proposed?"

"And am I to understand," exclaimed Bertrand, "that the pardon you speak of is only to be obtained by making myself the slave to your will?"

"To be plain, sirrah," answered the knight, "you must either accept my terms or take the consequences of your own headstrong obstinacy."

"And what are the consequences of which you speak?"

"Death."

"Aye, I thought so," exclaimed Bertrand; "but you have yet to find that I am not without the means of defending myself against the treachery of an enemy. I am unarmed and fettered, it is true, but a desperate man may do much mischief, and, therefore, do I warn you that your own life would be hazarded were I to suspect that you meant any foul play towards me."

"Hah! am I to be threatened by my own vassal?"

"I make no threats that I do not mean to fulfil," replied Bertrand le Noir, doggedly;—"we are now alone, and therefore, tolerably equally matched, and should you make but one step towards me, the chains that now encumber my wrists should be converted into a weapon sufficiently fatal to ensure your death."

"Nay, we are not alone, sirrah," exclaimed Sir Gaston, "for suspecting that this interview might not turn out exactly as I wished, I have assistance close by to rescue me from the attacks of a ruffian."

So saying, the knight clapped his hands by way of a signal, and instantly the door was thrown open with a violent crash, and upon which a number of armed men, headed by Michael, rushed in, and, with upraised daggers, awaited the word that was to consign their victim to death. Sir

No. 85

Gaston, however, by a motion, desired them to retreat a few paces, and then addressing himself to Bertrand le Noir, he said :—

"You perceive, sirrah, that the advantage you boasted just now no longer exists. I am well prepared for any vengeance you may think proper to seek, and it now only remains for me either to dismiss these men or command them to rid me of an enemy from whose wrath I have reason to apprehend future danger."

"In that matter you can please yourself, Sir Gaston," answered the other; "for my own part, I care little which way you may decide, for life without liberty is scarcely to be desired, and I know not but I should prefer the speedy death you have hinted at to lingering out a miserable existence in the wretched dungeon I have just left."

"But it is still in your power," ecclaimed the knight, "to save yourself by accepting the terms I have proposed."

"I will not speak in the presence of witnesses," replied Bertrand;— "these men must be dismissed ere I speak further upon this subject."

"Leave us, Michael," cried Sir Gaston;—"for the present you may retire with these men; but be not far distant, for it may yet happen that I require your assistance against a sudden attack from this man. Remember the signal, and be in readiness to rush forward to my rescue should there be occasion for it."

Michael bowed low in token of submission, and immediately left the room, followed by those who were under his command.

"Now, Bertrand," exclaimed Sir Gaston de Neville, when they were once more left alone, "you have seen enough by this time to convince you that I am not so easily to be overcome as you imagined. I am well guarded, and it therefore only remains for you to decide without further loss of time whether we are henceforward to be friends or enemies."

"Why, the truth is, Sir Knight," answered Bertrand, "it matters so little to me upon what terms we stand towards each other, that I will e'en leave it to your own decision. There is however one thing I wish you to understand;—I will no longer undertake to place myself in situations of danger merely because you may escape the punishment due to the plots you contrive against others."

"I will ask you to do nothing of the sort," returned Sir Gaston;— "all I at present expect is, that you will act for me as a sort of spy, for I know there are many at this time plotting against me, and it is necessary that I should have some one in my confidence who will diligently exert himself to discover who are my foes, and what means they are taking to hurl ruin and destruction upon me."

"Humph!" muttered the other, "this is quite a new line for me to undertake; yet it may be possible that I can serve you in it, and, therefore, if you explain yourself further, it is not unlikely we may come to terms."

"In the first place, then," exclaimed Sir Gaston, "I have been told that you have lately been seen in conversation with Black Ivan, the Outlaw."

"Your information is correct enough there."

"And did he say anything about me?"

"A great deal."

"None of which was, of course, in my favour?"

"Very little, indeed, Sir Gaston," answered the other, "he spoke indifferently of you, and even went as far as to say that you are enjoying property and wealth that belongs to some one else."

"Hah!—and did he say who that person was?"

"Yes,—an elder brother."

"Psha!—why the elder brother he speaks of has long since been dead."

"Aye," answered the other, "Black Ivan said something about such a report having been circulated; but he declares that your brother is yet living, and ready to come forward at any time when it may be necessary."

"In that case why has he not shown himself long since?"

"The Outlaw explained the reason of it," answered Bertrand; "he says your brother was unwilling to come forward and create confusion during your life time, and that he has hitherto led a life of privacy, re-solving to await the period of your death, rather than expose one for whom he has some little pity."

"By my soul this is some rank impostor!" cried Sir Gaston, vehem-ently; "some villain who would raise a scandalous report against me, and yet has not the hardihood to come forward and substantiate his statement."

"It may be as you have said, certainly," replied Bertrand, "and yet it strikes me that you never had any good proofs that your brother had ceased to exist."

"The report was never contradicted," answered Sir Gaston, "and, if he had really been alive, it is hardly likely he would have remained quiet all this time, when a fair heritage was only awaiting the issue of a just claim?"

"That I know nothing about," replied Bertrand, "but the Outlaw seems to be very positive as to the correctness of his story, and I should say there must be something in it, or why did he make an assertion that could never be satisfactorily proved?"

"To suit some vile purposes of his own," replied Sir Gaston; "the villain has been among the most forward among my enemies, and now, he throws himself in the way of one of the retainers for the purpose of whispering slanders in his ear to the prejudice of his master."

"Aye," answered the other, "but that was because he happened to know of the quarrel we had had, and I suppose he thought to obtain in-formation that might serve to forward the views of this brother that he speaks of."

"And did he ask you any further questions?"

"Yes, he spoke of the Lady Alicia."

"Confusion! he knows then of the trick that was practised when I raised a report of her death?"

"He does," answered Bertrand le Noir; "the fellow deals with spirits of darkness, I think, for he spoke of affairs that I always ima-gined were known only to you and myself."

"Then something must be done to rid ourselves of so dangerous an enemy," exclaimed the knight; "the Outlaw must die, and that too, before he has done the mischief he meditates."

"Now, in my opinion," replied Bertrand, "it would be quite as well to leave him to his fate—a reward, as you are aware, has been offered for his apprehension, and, should he fall into the hands of the officers of the law, I'll answer for it he will have very little opportunity given to him to do you any further harm."

"But the villain may speak of things before his judges that would occasion so much trouble to contradict."

"You forget, Sir Gaston," answered the other, "that the accusations of a felon would have little weight against one who stands so high as you do."

"But I do not forget," exclaimed de Neville, "that he lately saved the king's life, and has since been pardoned by royal proclamation."

"And which pardon," added Bertrand, "he has rejected by not quitting the society of his lawless band ere this time."

"It is not too late for him to do so," answered Sir Gaston; "and then he can easily make what accusation he pleases against a man like myself, who has fallen under the displeasure of King Richard. Besides, there is that affair between myself and the Hebrew Maiden which the king has·so warmly taken up, and which—"

"You are still resolved to prosecute, I suppose?" interrupted Bertrand le Noir.

"I am, even though I should perish through it.

"Perhaps, then," exclaimed Bertrand, "you would like to hear a little piece of information that I could give you about this Rebecca, who has given you so much trouble?"

"I should; speak on, Bertrand, and, if your intelligence is of advantage to me, I will not fail to reward you for it to your heart's content."

"Release my hands and feet, then, from these bonds," answered the retainer, "and I will tell you all I know upon the subject. Nay, do not hesitate, for I give you my word not to make any bad use of my liberty, and, it is, moreover, likely enough that you will see reason to congratulate yourself for having given freedom to a poor devil that but a short time since you had made up your mind to put quietly out of the way."

"Well, I will trust to you," exclaimed Sir Gaston; and, selecting a small key from a bunch that he wore at his girdle, he quickly removed his fetters, with which his retainer had been bound.

"Now," he said, "you are free; I have placed reliance upon your word, and shall, therefore, expect that you will give me the information you have promised."

"It is, perhaps, rather too bad," exclaimed Bertrand, "because, what I am going to tell you will do an injury to old Isaac of Tadcaster and his daughter, who saved my life when I was perishing from want. You, however, have also saved my life, and, therefore, in gratitude I will tell you the secret I am possessed of."

"Proceed quickly, sirrah, for my patience will not endure much more trifling with."

"In the first place," cried Bertrand with perfect coolness, "I would know what time of the night it is?"

"Psha! what can that have to do with what you were about to tell me?"

"Much; so tell me the time, that I may know whether my information may be of service to you."

"It wants exactly an hour till midnight," answered Sir Gaston, looking at the hour glass which stood on the table beside him.

"Then, there is yet time to prevent the marriage."

"Hah!" what mean you by those words?" exclaimed Sir Gaston, eagerly.

"They mean," replied the other, "that the Hebrew Maiden is this very night to give her hand to Reuben Grenard."

"Villain! why was not this told before?"

"Nay, do not fly into such an outrageous passion," exclaimed Bertrand, "or I may, perhaps, tell you no more."

"Say you she is to be married to night?"

"I did; it is a whim of her father's that the rites should be solemnized at midnight, and, therefore, unless something is done to prevent it, you will lose all chance of gaining the prize you have so long sought after."

"By heavens she shall not be lost without one more effort to gain her," exclaimed Sir Gaston, starting from his seat and pacing hastily up and down the chamber. "I will immediately take a dozen of my followers to the house of Isaac of Tadcaster, and drag her away ere those irrevocable vows are uttered that give her to another for ever."

"In that case," observed Bertrand, coolly, "I would advise you to lose no further time in idle parley. The warden is yet to be won, since another hour has to elapse ere the marriage ceremony takes place."

"Will you accompany me?" demanded the knight.

"Nay, that is asking too much of me," replied Bertrand; "I have been villain enough to betray those who befriended me in the hour of need, but I will not make one of the party that is to tear her away from her father's arms at the moment when he is about to bestow her upon one who he has chosen for her husband. No, no, I will remain behind, and, though I refuse to accompany you on the present occasion, I dare say I shall not prove quite so particular should you hereafter need my services."

"Be it so," exclaimed Sir Gaston; "I will not press you further on this subject, but will go with those who I believe will not hesitate to aid me in bearing off my prize. I have sworn that none but myself should possess her, and were a legion of friends to rise up in her defence, I would persist in the task that now takes me forth."

With these words Sir Gaston de Neville rushed furiously from the room, and, directing Michael and the rest of his retainers, who were waiting in an ante-room to follow him, he left the castle and took his way towards the house of Isaac of Tadcaster.

As for Bertrand le Noir, he no sooner found himself left alone than, betaking himself to the chamber, which had been occupied by him in former times, he had leisure to reflect on the base part he had been playing towards those who had sheltered and protected him when no other place of refuge was open to receive him.

CHAPTER CVIII.

"What heaviness is this
That weighs upon my heart and fills my soul
With dire prognostics?"

TEMPTATION.

As the hour approached which was to consecrate the union of Rebecca and her lover, the heart of the maiden grew more and more heavy, for a consciousness of impending evil seemed to press on her mind, and, retiring to the solitude of her own apartment, she gave way to the tears that she could no longer suppress. Here she remained for some time undisturbed by any one, but at length a light step was heard advancing towards the room, the door opened, and her father presented himself before her.

"My child," he said, tenderly, "your absence has occasioned much grief to those whom most you love. I have looked long and anxiously for your return, and Reuben Grenard, though he has not yet ventured to enquire the cause of your abrupt departure, seems to believe that it is some slight insult shown to himself.

"Reuben Grenard wrongs me by the suspicion," cried the maiden, "for he knows how deeply I love him, and that no earthly consideration should ever induce me to forget those vows that have passed between us."

"Why, then, did you quit the room?"

"Because my heart was heavy, and I wished not to have it observed by those to whom I knew it would occasion much pain and suspicion."

"And why, my love, should your heart be heavy when you are about to bestow your hand upon him who has ever possessed your tenderest regard?"

"I can scarcely tell you why it is," replied Rebecca, "but my heart was heavy and oppressed, as if a forewarning had been given me that some terrible misfortune was about to happen."

"Nay, my child," cried the old man, "this is no time to think of perils that may have no foundation except in your own foolish imagination. A short period will see you the bride of Reuben Grenard, and from that time you will be in no further danger from those who have hitherto persecuted us with such unrelenting hate."

"And yet," sighed Rebecca, "I cannot but fear that something will happen to mar the peace you so fondly anticipate. My heart sinks with apprehension of some hidden danger, and seldom has it erred on former occasions when Sir Gaston de Neville has sought to carry me away by force."

"But I trust there is nothing to fear from him now," answered her father; "he will no longer seek to tear you from us when you have become the wife of Reuben Grenard; and even if he should do so, there are friends upon whom we could rely, and who would not fail to exert themselves in behalf of an injured woman."

"Alas!" cried Rebecca, "you appear to have forgotten altogether the fierce disposition of the knight we are speaking of. Sir Gaston has castles situated far away from this place, and should he convey me to one of them, there is little chance that I should ever be restored to those from whom it would be worse than death to part me."

"And dost thou still think, my child," exclaimed the aged Israelite, "that Sir Gaston de Neville will renew a pursuit which he knows is vain? Besides, I have heard that he has fallen under the displeasure of King Richard, and it is, therefore, scarcely to be expected that he will seek further to anger his sovereign by injuring one who has been honoured with his support."

"You think, then," cried Rebecca, "that we have nothing more to fear from him?"

"I feel well assured of it."

"Would that I could think it also!" sighed Rebecca. "It is, however, in vain that I try to convince myself that the fears which agitate my heart are without foundation. The more I ponder upon the subject, the more certain do I feel that villany is again at work against me, and that, ere another hour has elapsed, I shall, perhaps, be torn away from all that I most fondly love."

"Psha! this is a weakness that you should conquer," exclaimed Isaac of Tadcaster; "you are excited, my child; but depend on it you will hereafter own your folly, and laugh at the terrors that have thus found their way to your bosom. So come with me, dear Rebecca, and let us return to Reuben Grenard, who is alarmed at your absence, and fancies something very terrible has happened to you."

"Have patience with me, father, yet a little longer," cried Rebecca. "At present I am agitated, and Reuben could not fail to observe it were I to return just now."

"Reuben's wonder has been already excited," replied the old man, "and I fear he must think thee but a fickle wench thus to have shunned his society when so short a period intervenes between the present moment and that which is to make thee his for ever."

"I am sure he will not wrong me by his suspicions," answered the Hebrew Maiden, "for he knows that I love none but him; and if he feels somewhat surprised at present, the explanation I shall be able to give when we meet will fully satisfy any doubts that may have entered his mind."

"Thou hast every confidence in him, my child," exclaimed Isaac; "and I believe thou dost him nothing more than justice when thou speakest thus of him. I have myself watched him many a long year with the anxious eye of a father who is solicitous only for the happiness of his only daughter; and, believe me, I would not have given my consent to his marriage with thee unless I had been first well assured that he was well worthy the esteem with which I regarded him."

"And I," added the maiden, "have also observed him with sufficient care to convince myself that he merits the affection I have regarded him with. You will, therefore, I hope, acquit me of any fickleness in thus leaving him for a while; and now that I feel more composed I will return with you, and, with as much cheerfulness as I can assume, make all the amends in my power for the uneasiness that I may have occasioned him."

"Thou hast forgotten, then, the foolish fancies that just now weighed so heavily on thy mind?"

"Nay," she replied, "that I cannot promise thee, my dear father. "I will, however, endeavour to assume an appearance of my wonted confidence; and thus you will, I trust, give me some credit for appearing happy, when my heart is heavily laden with apprehensions of imminent danger."

"Thou art a good girl, Rebecca, and this is not the first time I have observed thy desire to lessen the uneasiness of others, even though it may cost thee the same pain. So come with me, for I hear the Rabbi has arrived, and it is now almost the hour appointed for the solemnization of thy nuptials."

Rebecca rose from her seat, and, taking the hand of her father, descended in silence to the lower chamber, where her return was gladly hailed by the lover, who, hastening towards his future bride, greeted her with an expression of joy and gratitude. The Rabbi then advanced, and leading her towards a seat near the table, which was to serve as a temporary altar, congratulated her on the approaching nuptials, and the protection it would afford her against the future machinations of those who had pursued her with such untiring persecution.

"Henceforth, Rebecca," he said, "thou wilt be safe under the protection of a husband who will guard thee as the treasure that is most dear and valuable to him. Thou wilt become the chief object of his care, and none, I venture to predict, will dare to injure thee without incurring the vengeance of one who will be ever watchful for thy happiness."

"Thou hast done me nothing more than justice in promising thus much in my behalf," exclaimed Reuben Grenard. "My life's blood shall willingly be poured out in her defence, nor will I ever cease to watch over the safety of her whose happiness is far dearer to me than my own."

"But thou hast forgotten, Reuben," cried the maiden, "that he we have to deal with is as vindictive as he is powerful, and that he has vowed never to relax his base endeavours until he has secured me in his snares."

"I am aware of all that, dearest Rebecca," answered the young man,

" yet I fear not the malevolence of a man whose power to inflict injuries is not equal to his inclination. Sir Gaston no longer possesses the friends that once used to flock around him : his crimes have converted almost all who formerly respected him into enemies, and those who would at one time have looked with apathy upon his evil practices against thee, would now be among the first to step forward in thy behalf."

" But he may tear me from thee, Reuben," sighed the maiden, "and would not that be a misery almost too great for endurance ?"

" Aye," exclaimed Isaac, " such is the foolish notion thou hast taken into thy head, my child. Thou dost fancy that he will bear thee away, even before the marriage rites are performed, though the Rabbi is at this moment ready to proceed with the service that is to make thee a happy wife."

" My father has said more than I could have wished," answered Rebecca, timidly. "However, as he has told thee thus much, I will now confess that such fears have indeed weighed heavily upon my mind."

" Then let them disturb thee no more," interposed the Rabbi, " for the power of Sir Gaston de Neville has passed away, and never again shalt thou endure tyranny from him who has hitherto so foully wronged thee."

" Make not too sure of that, holy Rabbi," cried Rebecca, " for in spite of the confidence thou wouldst inspire me with, I feel but too certain that this night will not see me the bride of Reuben Grenard. Nay, you know not the haughty Templar as I do, or you would not believe that he will ever cease his cruel persecutions whilst there is a chance of carrying his designs to a successful termination."

" And why, girl," exclaimed the priest, " dost thou think that even in the twelfth hour the plans of this wily knight will end in thy separation from those thou dost love ?"

" You will, perhaps, smile at my superstition," answered Rebecca, " yet will I confess that a dream has haunted me these three following nights, the purport of which was that a band of armed ruffians rushed into our cottage and tore me away from the altar at which we were standing."

" Hast thou faith in dreams, girl ?"

" I never had till now," replied Rebecca ; " but when the same vision has presented itself to me on three successive nights, it appears like a warning to put me on my guard against my enemies."

" Believe me," answered the Rabbi, " the dreams you speak of were caused by the anxiety with which you have thought over these things. The remembrance has left an impression upon your mind, and hence have arisen the visions of which you have spoken."

" You are right," exclaimed Isaac of Tadcaster ; " my daughter has too easily yielded to a weakness which at any other time she would have laughed at ; and even now I trust that it will not be long ere she is convinced that we have, in this instance, guessed nearer to the truth than she has herself."

" There, dearest Rebecca," cried her lover, tenderly, " thou hast heard the opinions of those whose experience render their words of value to us, who know not these things as well as they do. So, cheer up, my love, and rather look forward to years of happiness than thus give way to the despondency which at present fills your heart."

" Thou dost think, then, Reuben," cried the maiden, " that we have nothing more to fear from the malice of those who have hitherto been our inveterate enemies ?'

" I am quite confident of it."

"Would that I could think so, also," answered Rebecca; "I, however, still feel confident that my worst fears will be realized even, in spite of the confidence with which you kindly seek to inspire me."

"Then why not let the ceremony proceed at once?" asked Reuben, "we should thus defeat any attack that may be meditated against us, and, reckless as Sir Gaston is, he would hardly have the baseness to carry off one who had already become the bride of another."

"By doing so," replied Isaac, " I should but admit my own belief in the foolish terrors that have so much troubled my daughter."

"Thou hast said truly," answered the Rabbi; "it would, indeed, be proving that thou dost participate in these baseless fancies of hers, and, therefore, as the time appointed for the commencement of the ceremony has almost arrived, we will wait yet a little longer, and prove to her that she has given way to a weakness for which there was not even the slightest foundation."

"We shall see who is right, presently," cried Rebecca, "for though thou wouldst fain persuade me against the opinion I have formed, yet do I still believe that my predictions will after all prove correct."

"Nay, then," exclaimed the Rabbi, "thou dost believe the knight to be even worse than the world reports him to be."

"I have had bitter reason to know that he stops at no acts of wickedness when his own vile purposes are to be served," answered Rebecca. "Already has he carried me more than once to his castle, and that I have escaped him so often will but serve to strengthen his resolution against me. Sir Gaston is seldom foiled in his designs upon those who are weaker than himself, and, therefore, do I still think there is danger to be apprehended from him."

No. 86

"Perhaps the persecutions you have endured from Sir Gaston de Neville," observed the Rabbi, "have served to prejudice you against him even more than he deserves."

"Nay, in this instance," replied the maiden, "it is impossible for prejudice to go too far; his baseness is already well known to all the world, and believing, as he does, that I am almost unprotected, he will not fail even at the last moment to put his fell designs against me into practice."

"Then, now, let your apprehensions cease," interposed Isaac of Tadcaster, "for the hour appointed for the due solemnization of your nuptials has arrived, and a few minutes hence will see you the wife of Reuben Grenard. So, now let the rites begin, and thus shall my daughter obtain a protector who is well able to defend her against all foes who shall henceforth plot to injure her."

Obedient to this command the Rabbi took his place with the bride and bridegroom standing before him. Then addressing himself solemnly to those who were to perform the chief part in the ensuing ceremony, he pointed out the duties they owed to heaven, and the heavy responsibility they were thus about to take upon themselves. Having concluded his brief address, he was next about to proceed with the marriage ceremony, but scarcely had he commenced the first few words, when a tremendous uproar was heard without, and at the same moment the door being burst open, Sir Gaston de Neville, and at least a score of armed men, rushed in. Of course resistance against such superior numbers was in vain, yet Reuben Grenard fought boldly against his assailants, till a heavy blow from one of the ruffians laid him insensible on the ground. At that moment Sir Gaston advanced and seized upon the almost fainting Rebecca, who he bore away from the house, whilst a party of his retainers remained behind to prevent any alarm being given till he was beyond reach of pursuit. These, however, did not stay long, for no sooner did they imagine that the knight and his party were fairly beyond pursuit than, leaving the place, they hurried away with all speed, in the hope of rejoining their companions.

During this time, the aged Israelite had been diligently employed in endeavouring to revive Reuben Grenard, who had been stretched senseless on the ground by the blow which he had received in his vain attempt to preserve the maiden from those who had suddenly broke in upon the ceremony which, in a few minutes more, would have made her his wife. Nor were the efforts of the old man unavailing, for, scarcely had the ruffians quitted the house when he began slowly to revive, and gazing round the nearly deserted room, he enquired in a tone of alarm, for her whose safety occupied his chief thoughts.

"Where, where is Rebecca?" he cried, in a voice that betrayed the agony of his heart; "oh, tell me that she is safe, and I will bless thee even with my latest breath."

"Alas!" answered the old man, choking with the excess of his anguish, "she has been borne from us by the villains, who but a brief space since filled the house, and I, feeble as I am, had not the power to rescue her from the hands of Sir Gaston and his reckless associates."

"Let us not lose another moment, then," cried Reuben, impatiently. "We will follow and rescue her, or lose our lives in the attempt."

"Where shall we seek her?" demanded Isaac, almost distracted at the loss he had sustained.

"At the castle of Sir Gaston de Neville."

"I fear, my son," observed the Rabbi, who had hitherto maintained silence, "that your search will prove unavailing, for I observed that they took a road opposite to that which leads to the castle, and there is but too much reason to believe she has been conveyed to some place where you will in vain seek her."

"It was but an artifice to deceive us," replied Reuben; "she has been taken to the castle, and I will follow her thither let the consequences to myself be what they may."

With that the young man hurried towards the door, and was about to rush wildly forth, when the voice of Isaac arrested his hasty footsteps.

"Stay, Reuben," he exclaimed, "for it is not mete that thou should'st go alone when there is one other whose anxiety in her behalf is at least equal to thine own. I will accompany you, and, if there is peril, we will share it together."

"Nay, let me implore thee to abandon this design," cried Reuben, earnestly. "For myself I care not what danger I may run into, but thou mayest conceive what a heavy addition it would be to my suffering were I to know that thou must share them with me."

"Boy!" exclaimed Isaac, "thou knowest not the sufferings that rack a father's heart, or thou would'st not seek to prevail on him to remain inactive, whilst the fate of his only child is uncertain. I will go with thee, and before high heaven, I swear never to relax my endeavours till I have either rescued my daughter, or brought a heavy retribution upon him who has basely stolen her from the arms of a doting father."

Finding that all further remonstrance would be in vain, Reuben made no further objection, and, supporting the old man, he left the house in pursuit of the treasure that had been thus wrested from him. But the slow pace at which they were compelled to proceed, was most irksome to the impatience of the young man, which, being observed by Isaac, he exerted himself to the utmost, so that by the time they had reached the castle of Sir Gaston de Neville, he was almost exhausted by the efforts he had made. For a few minutes, therefore, he paused, and seating himself upon a stone, gazed upon the frowning walls, which, perhaps, imprisoned her who had been ruthlessly stolen from him. It was night, but the moon poured forth a rich flood of light that served to show every part of the castle with almost the distinctiveness of day, and scarcely could he refrain from uttering curses and imprecations upon the unhallowed fortress which had been the scene of so many crimes. At length, however, arousing himself, he again rose, and, taking the arm of his younger companion, advanced towards the principal gate, at which he knocked three or four times before the porter, who opened a small wicket, demanded who it was that had disturbed him at such an hour, and what business had brought him there.

"I would see Sir Gaston de Neville," answered the old man.

"Then you must call another time," retorted the fellow sulkily, "for he you seek is not at present in the castle."

"'Tis false!" exclaimed Isaac, "he is here, but thou hast orders to deny him."

"Beware what you say, old man," cried the porter, "for another word like that from thy lips, and thou wilt perhaps find thyself in the moat, ere thou art aware of it."

"Nay," answered the broken-hearted Jew, "I did not mean to offend thee. I have been robbed by thy master of an only child, and I am come hither to implore him on my knees to restore her to me."

"Hah! thou art the Jew, Isaac of Tadcaster, as folks call thee?"

"I am."

"Then take my advice and leave this place before worse comes of it," replied the porter, "for, if thou art found here, it is ten to one but thou wilt be made to repent having come hither on this errand."

"Hear me," exclaimed Reuben Grenard, who hitherto had taken no part in this conversation; "thou art already acquainted with the object that has brought us here, and, if thou hast the heart of a man, I implore thee to answer truly the question that has been asked."

"And what," asked the fellow, "am I to receive for the trouble you have already given me?"

"This purse," replied the old man, "it contains gold, which shall be freely thine, on condition that thou wilt tell me of my daughter."

"Give it me," exclaimed the porter, and stretching forth his hand from the wicket, he snatched the purse ere Isaac was aware of his intention. For a short time the man seemed busily employed in counting over the money, and, having satisfied himself of its contents, he muttered:—"Well, it don't contain any great deal to be sure, but I shall take your offer, such as it is, so you may ask what questions you please, and I'll answer them as far as I can."

"Thou hast said," cried Isaac, "that thy master is not at present in the castle?"

"Aye, I told you that before, so what's the use of putting such foolish questions as that?"

"Dost thou expect him to return to-night?"

"I do not."

"Canst thou tell me, then, where he is to be found?"

"Not I—people here say that he has gone to one of his other castles, and it's likely enough, if the girl you speak of is with him, for he would hardly be so foolish as to go where you would be likely to hunt him out."

"I fear so," groaned the Israelite, "but, perhaps, thou canst give me some clue by which we may find the place of his retreat?"

"Not I," muttered the other, "Sir Gaston has many castles besides this, so of course I can't tell you to which one he has gone."

"Cans't thou not give a guess?" demanded Reuben.

"I cannot," replied the porter; "besides, I have answered enough questions already, and I shall say no more about it, lest my freedom of speech should happen to get me into a scrape that it won't be easy to get out of again."

"Thou hast accepted my money," exclaimed Isaac, "under a promise to answer the questions I might put to thee, and yet thou dost now refuse to afford even the slightest clue that may serve to inform me where Sir Gaston is to be found."

"Why, as for your money, old man," replied the porter, "it was a free offering, and I was not going to be such a simpleton as to refuse it. Besides, I have answered as many questions as may be prudent, and I am not going to run the risk of Sir Gaston's displeasure, by talking about things that I have no business with."

"Tell me but where he is likely to be found," cried the old man, 'and I will ask no more of thee."

"Haven't I told you that I am not in the secret?" exclaimed the fellow, sulkily. "Sir Gaston de Neville was never in the habit of making a confidant of me, and I know my place too well to be prying into affairs that I have no business with."

"But," cried Isaac, in despair, "thou mightest surely have some pity on an aged father, who has been basely robbed of the dearest treasure of his soul."

"Humph!" ejaculated the other, "you are a Jew, and, therefore, I feel little pity for you."

"And yet thou callest thyself a Christian!"

"To be sure I do, and for that very reason I despise thee and all thy race."

"Unfeeling man!" cried Isaac; "yet once more do I throw myself upon your mercy, and ask of you to afford me even the faintest clue by which I may discover the retreat to which Sir Gaston has gone."

"I shall tell you nothing more," replied the porter, and slamming the wicket in the old man's face, he retired grumbling to his bed.

"It is in vain that we seek her here," exclaimed Isaac, in despair at the ill success that had attended him; "she is now lost to me for ever, and I care not how soon death came to release me from sufferings that are too heavy for endurance."

"Nay, do not give way to these melancholy thoughts," cried Reuben Grenard, "for there is yet hope, and never will I relax my endeavours to rescue Rebecca from the monster who has thus villanously carried her away. So come with me and seek that rest which you so much need, and to-morrow I will set forth never to return again until I have delivered her from the hands of Sir Gaston de Neville."

The heart of the old man was too full for utterance, and once more leaning upon the arm of Reuben Grenard, he returned to that house which had been rendered desolate and forlorn.

CHAPTER CIX.

" 'Twas he
Gave heat unto the injury, which returned,
Like a petard ill lighted, into the bosom
Of him gave fire to't. Yet I hope his hurt
Is not so dangerous but he may recover."
FAIR MAID OF THE INN.

AGITATED by the scene that had taken place, Rebecca was borne fainting from her father's house, and it was not till some time afterwards that she was again conscious of the new misfortune that had befallen her. On recovering, however, she found that she was on horseback with Sir Gaston who, with one arm round her waist, was supporting her, as they rode slowly onwards, accompanied by the knight's retainers. In a moment the thought flashed upon her mind that she had been forcibly dragged from home, and uttering a loud scream, she implored the assistance of any strangers who might chance to be within hearing. But her appeal was made in vain, for no one responded to it, and she was again about to call for assistance, when the voice of Sir Gaston de Neville grated harshly on her ear.

"Peace, girl," he exclaimed, "and make no more outcries that can avail thee but little, even if they should be heard by any who might be disposed to venture their lives in thy behalf. We are numerous, as you see, and well armed, and little chance would there be, even though a dozen stout fellows were to rush forward in thy defence."

"If thou hast any pity in thy bosom, I charge thee, hear me," cried Rebecca, roused to exertion by the perilous situation in which she found herself. "Thou hast ruthlessly torn me from my home, but even now it is not too late to make amends for the wrongs thou hast done me. Set me at liberty, Sir Gaston, and deeply as thou hast wronged me, I will never cease to pray for thee and bless thy name."

"Girl, thou dost plead to me in vain," answered the knight, sternly; "too long already have I been cheated of my fair prize, and now that she is once safely in my arms, nothing shall ever wrest her from me."

"Nay," cried Rebecca, yet more earnestly, "if thou hast no pity upon me, forget not the sufferings of my father, but relieve him of the dreadful agony he now endures by restoring to him the daughter of whom you have robbed him."

"Thy father never had pity upon me," answered the knight, coldly, "and, therefore, I see little reason why I should make the sacrifice thou dost ask."

"He never wronged thee."

"He has treated me with scorn and contempt," replied Sir Gaston, "and that is sufficient cause why I should now disregard the pain your absence may afford him."

"Dost thou forget his age?" cried Rebecca, "and shall not the sufferings of an old man obtain pity from one who calls himself a Christian knight?"

"I am not to be questioned thus," replied Sir Gaston, haughtily; "my will is the only law I ever obey, and, in this instance, thou shalt find that I can be as obdurate as thou hast ever been to me."

"I was not obdurate," answered Rebecca, "thou knowest that my heart was already engaged to another, and yet, in spite of all that, thou did'st continually annoy me with thine importunities."

"And did'st thou think," demanded the knight, scornfully, "that I was to be thwarted by a paltry rival like Reuben Grenard? Did he not know that I sought thee, and yet the knave persisted in standing between me and the object I aspired to attain."

"Reuben Grenard and I were betrothed when we were children," answered Rebecca; "we loved each other ere we knew the nature of the passion that had taken possession of our hearts—each year served but to increase our affection, and thou could'st hardly, therefore, expect him to give way when he saw me persecuted with the pretended love of a man whose intentions were dishonourable."

"Yet Reuben Grenard has incurred my anger," exclaimed Sir Gaston, "and now is he doomed to experience the pangs that I fortunately have it in my power to inflict."

"Thou dost exult, then, in the misery thou hast occasioned to one whose only fault has been that he was thy rival?"

"I do, girl."

"And dost thou believe I can ever regard thee with any other feelings save those of loathing and disgust?"

"I care not whether you do or not," answered Sir Gaston, in a tone of indifference; "you are now in my power, and the place to which I am about to carry you, will prove a secure hiding place from those who may feel disposed to seek after us."

"To what place, then," cried Rebecca, in alarm, "art thou about to convey me?"

"To my castle in Hertfordshire," replied the Knight Templar; "I seldom visit it, so that people will hardly think of my taking you thither, and, as a further security, the darkness that at present shrouds us, will effectually prevent all traces of the route we have taken."

"Alas!" sighed Rebecca, "is there no hope, then?"

"None whatever; this time at least I have you safely in my power, and I may defy those who, I suppose, will immediately make an ineffectual pursuit."

"Hast thou no pity for her you have thus wronged?"

"Ask thyself," replied Sir Gaston de Neville, "whether thou hadst ever any pity upon him from whom you now ask it?"

"I have ever been candid with thee," replied Rebecca, "I told thee from the first that my heart was given to another, and that I would not forfeit the word I had given him. Besides, thine intentions towards me were never honourable, and sooner would I suffer death by the most cruel tortures, than become the loathsome, abhorred wretch thou would'st make me."

: "And yet," retorted the knight, "thou mightest as well have done so, seeing that I can now treat with thee upon my own terms. Thou art far from those who would have aided thee, and no power in the world shall ever tear thee from the arms of him who glories in the triumph he has achieved."

"Nay," cried the maiden, "I may not be so friendless as thou dost imagine; the place we are now in is lonely, but my voice may yet reach the ears of those who will rush to protect me against the arts of a villain!"

And as she said this, Rebecca raised a shriek so loud and piercing that the retainers galloped nearer to their leader, urging him to quicken his pace, lest assistance should arrive ere they were prepared to repel it. But Sir Gaston was unmoved by their words, and, whispering to Rebecca, he commanded her to be silent, as he would rather slay her than she should fall into the hands of any persons who might hear, and come to her rescue.

"Let me advise you to gag her, Sir Gaston," exclaimed Michael, who had ridden close up to the side of his master. "The girl seems determined to make the best use of her tongue, and we shall get into some confounded scrape or other if her voice should happen to be heard by any one."

"You hear the advice that has been given by one of my retainers?" cried Sir Gaston, addressing himself to the maiden; "he counsels me to put an end to your screaming, and it may happen, if your voice is raised again, that I take means to silence you for ever."

"Ah! you threaten me with death!"

"I do; but it will depend upon yourself whether I carry the threat into execution or not."

"Your words, Sir Knight," answered Rebecca, fearlessly, "would not move me if I had reason to believe there was a fair chance of my voice being heard."

"You brave me then, it seems?"

"I merely warn you," she replied, "that no fear of death shall deter me from making an attempt to escape from the villain who has thus unlawfully made me his captive."

"I will try the effect of milder words, then," exclaimed Sir Gaston; —"let me entreat you, for your own sake, to remain quiet; for even if assistance should arrive, we are too numerous to be easily overcome, and rather than see you snatched away from me, I would bury my poniard in your heart, and thus revenge the injury which you seek to inflict upon me."

"And think you I fear death," asked the Hebrew Maiden, "that you thus threaten me with it?"

"Perhaps not," answered the knight; "but at any rate it will be some satisfaction for me to know that you can never more be rescued from the man you thus despise."

"And it will also be some satisfaction for me to know," replied Rebecca, "that I shall die instead of lingering out a life of misery beneath the roof that owns thee for a master."

"Ha ! am I defied—and by a woman, too ?"

"Hist!" exclaimed Michael, once more riding up to his master; "I heard sounds just now as of a body of horse advancing at some distance from us. We are, perhaps, pursued, and it, therefore, behoves us to take instant measures for our own preservation."

"Psha!" returned Sir Gaston, "it was nothing but the wind murmuring among the trees. I myself heard it, but knew at once from whence the sound proceeded."

"Don't make too sure that there is no danger," exclaimed Michael; "it has been heard by all of us, and the general opinion is, that we are pursued."

"And if it should be so," returned Sir Gaston, "are there not enough of us to defend ourselves ?"

"That's true enough," replied the man, "but we may chance to lose the girl if a bit of a skirmish should take place. Besides, they say that prudence is the better part of valour, and I thought you would rather avoid than seek a contest with these unknown pursuers."

"The only precaution I shall observe," answered Sir Gaston, "will be to proceed along the green turf, so that the sound of our horses' footsteps may not act as a guide to those you seem to dread so much."

"Had we not better gallop forward," asked Michael, "and thus distance our pursuers ?"

"What! basely fly when each man among us is well armed and prepared for a contest? If there are any here who, coward-like, shrink from meeting the foe, let him leave me, and, if necessary, I will encounter them by myself rather than seek for safety in flight."

"There are no cowards among us, I believe," answered Michael, " and the counsel I gave you was intended only to prevent the girl from being taken from us."

"Leave that to me," replied the knight, "and I will take care that no such mischance as you speak of shall occur. We may be pursued, as you have said, but it is hardly likely the foe is so well armed as ourselves ; and besides that, the darkness of the night will serve to shield us from their observation."

"But the moon shining upon our bright armour," answered Michael, " will be sure to betray us, long ere they reach the place where we are."

The sounds of approaching horsemen were now distinctly heard, and even Sir Gaston de Neville himself was forced to admit that there was now little doubt of their being pursued. He, however, treated the affair slightingly, and, spurring his charger on to the green turf, was quickly followed by his numerous retinue. For some few minutes they proceeded slowly and in silence, but it was evident, from the increasing noise behind them, that their pursuers were rapidly gaining upon them. At length the sounds were heard more to the left hand of the road they were taking and it thus became pretty evident that those who pursued them were taking a nearer path, so as to shorten, as much as possible, the distance between them. Sir Gaston was the first to observe this, and, urging his retainers to follow him, he galloped with all speed towards a part of the road which passed through a copse, in the shadow of which he hoped to avoid those whose object was not to be mistaken. It was not, however, through any fear that he did this, but his whole thoughts were occupied upon the means of preserving Rebecca from those who had followed to her rescue ; and he was determined to effect this object, even at the risk of appearing cowardly to his vassals. Upon arriving at this place he ordered a halt, and then, listening intently to every sound, he began to entertain a hope that he had succeeded in completely baffling those who

were in search of them. Addressing himself, therefore, to Rebecca, whose hopes of rescue had been excited to the highest pitch, he said, sternly—

"We are now, I believe, safe from those who came forth in search of you; at any rate, they have at present lost all clue, and I now charge you to remain silent, as you value your life. Remember, a word spoken above your breath dooms you to instant death by my hands."

"You need not fear me, Sir Gaston," she replied, "for I feel quite convinced that those who have come in search of me will not return till they have effected the object that has brought them forth. Be assured, Sir Knight, they are not far off, and that, perhaps, a few minutes may serve to release me from your hands."

"Thou art mistaken, girl," answered the Templar, in a tone of triumph, "for never shalt thou be rescued from me whilst I live. I have now torn thee from thy home, and the reward is even now at hand."

"Take, then, the reward you best merit!" exclaimed a voice from the copse; and scarcely were the words uttered when the sharp twang of a bowstring was heard, and at the same instant an arrow, passing through the joint of his armour, entered the breast of Sir Gaston de Neville. A cry of pain escaped the lips of the knight as he fell, wounded, from his horse to the ground: and Rebecca would also have fallen had not Black Ivan at the instant rushed from the shadow of the copse, in which he had been concealed, and caught her in his arms. As the retainers caught sight of him, they gallopped towards him with upraised battle-axes, for the purpose of avenging their leader, but ere they could effect this, they were held in check by about a score of Ivan's outlaws, who, stepping from the wood, stood with bended bows, ready to shoot the first who ad-

No. 87

vanced to carry this purpose into execution. At this sight a general alarm pervaded itself among the retainers, and two of them having dismounted and raised the wounded Sir Gaston upon his horse, they moved off with all the expedition they could use.

Overcome by the suddenness with which this had occurred, Rebecca swooned in the arms of Black Ivan. In a short time, however, she recovered her recollection, and, gazing round upon the harsh features of those who stood about her, she seemed lost in wonder at the situation in which she found herself. Ivan saw her perplexity, and, with as much gentleness as he could assume, assured her that she had nothing more to fear.

"You are now safe, Rebecca," he said, "for though there are many here who lead a lawless life enough, yet my commands are never disobeyed, and you will meet with the protection and temporary rest you so much require."

"Nay, I would return home without delay," exclaimed the maiden, anxiously. "My father and Reuben are in despair at their loss, and I must hasten back to relieve them of the agony they are suffering on my account."

"There is no need for it," replied Ivan, "for in our cavern thou shalt find a secure retreat; and whilst thou art under the fostering care of old Maud, our housekeeper, I will myself hasten to your father, and take to him the glad tidings of your safety."

"And why may I not accompany you?" asked Rebecca.

"Because thou art at present ill able to bear the fatigue," replied Black Ivan. "Besides, by going alone, I can reach your father's house with much greater speed, and he will be the sooner informed of your rescue from the hands of Sir Gaston de Neville."

Somewhat convinced by these words, the maiden acquiesced in the suggestion, and yet the timid glance she cast around showed that her mind was not altogether at rest. Ivan saw this, and immediately guessed the cause of her uneasiness.

"You are afraid of trusting yourself," he said, "with men such as those who now stand about us. There is, however, no cause for uneasiness, for they are faithful to their chief, and would die in defence of any one to whom I had offered shelter and protection."

"I will rely upon your word," answered Rebecca; "and now tell me, I beseech you, to what fortunate chance do I owe your arrival at a moment when I so much needed a friend to rescue me from the hands of Sir Gaston?"

"It would be too long a narrative to relate just now," replied Ivan, "and I will, therefore, content myself by saying that Meg of Finchley happened to be near the road-side when Sir Gaston and his party passed by. She saw you and heard your screams; and then, hastening off as fast as her aged limbs would permit, she came to give me information of the danger you were in. A few minutes served to get all things in readiness, and, quitting the cavern, we hastened to your rescue."

"But if I am not mistaken," cried Rebecca, "there were horsemen at one time pursuing us."

"It was us that you heard," replied the Outlaw; "for, pretty well judging what part of the road you must have reached, we turned down a nearer path, and were thus enabled to intercept the party of Sir Gaston de Neville. Arriving here before him, we dismounted from our horses, which are now secured at the other side of the wood; and then, secreting ourselves beneath the shadow of the trees, we were enabled to surprise the enemy when they were least prepared for the attack."

"And Sir Gaston?" exclaimed the maiden; "I remember he was wounded by an arrow."

"Aye—and which arrow," replied Ivan, "was directed by my hand. It was intended for his heart, but the armour he wore proved too tough for my purpose, and I believe it will be found that the wound is not mortal. It may, however, serve to confine him for some time, and during that period, I hope, he will repent the crimes he meditated against you. However, we are now losing time, and after conducting you in safety to our cavern, I will mount and ride off to your father, the bearer of a message that will carry joy to his almost despairing bosom."

With this Ivan led her through a winding pathway that passed through the wood, and then, taking the nearest road that led to the retreat, he left her in the care of old Maud, with a strict injunction to obey her as if she was mistress of the cavern. This done, he mounted a fresh horse, and rode off with all speed to bear home the happy news of the maiden's safety.

Maud, who remembered when our heroine had been compelled to become an inmate of the cavern under very different circumstances some months previously, was delighted to see her again; making all sorts of professions of her anxiety to please, and lauding the captain—as she called him—to the skies, as a man far above the station in which fortune had been pleased to place him. This praise was anything but unpleasant to Rebecca, who had lately received so important a service from him, and giving a sigh to the thought which pressed most closely upon her mind, she said, almost involuntarily—

"What a pity it is that he you have just been speaking of does not accept the king's pardon, and quit the society of men whose deeds have rendered them outcasts from society."

"Why, it is a pity, as you say," replied Maud; "but when you come to think of it, the matter is not quite so easy as it at first appears to be. The people he at present associates with dare not reproach him for the past, but it would be otherwise if he was to enter the world again; for, despite the king's pardon, there are few, I believe, who would ever look upon him as anything else than a robber. Besides, I believe he has reasons of his own for remaining as he is at present—at least, so say the people about him; and it is further said that he is only waiting till a good opportunity arrives to do something that will make people wonder a bit."

"You think, then, he means to abandon this course of life as soon as he can?"

"I am sure of it," replied Maud, "for the band have a pretty good notion of something of the sort, and they are already beginning to disagree among themselves as to who shall be his successor."

"Ivan has prepared them, then, I suppose, for something of the sort speedily taking place?"

"Not he, you may depend upon it," answered the old woman. "Ivan never speaks of his affairs to any one, and it is only from a few words which have dropped now and then that a notion of what he means to do has been gathered. Nor would it do for any one to give a hint that he suspects what's going to happen, for the captain will not brook interference, and it might cost a man his life if he made himself too inquisitive about matters that don't concern him."

"It is not known for certain, then," cried Rebecca, "that he intends to avail himself of the king's pardon?"

"Oh, no—nothing is known to a certainty," replied Maud; "but I happened to hear two of our men talking together the other day about the king's life having been saved by the captain, and they seemed to think that the pardon that had been offered him would prove a great bait, and that, most likely, he would accept of it before long. There seems, however, to be some reason, as I said before, for his not being in any hurry about it; so perhaps he may remain with us some time longer, and continue to govern the band, as he has done, with success, for a long time past."

"But," observed Rebecca, "the pardon may not be granted him if he does not accept it at once."

"You may depend on it Ivan has made sure of all that before he made up his mind about stopping here a little longer," replied Maud. "He seldom does things without first of all considering them well, and he has made sure work of it before he quite determined what to do."

"And yet," cried the maiden, "if he should happen to commit any fresh offence in the meanwhile, it will bar him from the royal mercy that has been offered."

"Yes," answered the old woman, "but Ivan is very quiet just now, and none of the band have been out upon any of their usual business since the day of the king's coronation. To be sure the men rather grumble at being suffered to remain in idleness, but the captain don't mind that a bit, and so he has given them orders not to commit another robbery till he has spoken further to them upon the subject."

"And do they never leave this cavern?"

"No," replied the old woman; "and a lucky thing it was for you that it was so, for when Meg of Finchley came here about a couple of hours ago, she found everybody in the place, and so all they had to do was to throw themselves upon their horses and gallop off in the direction she had told them of."

"And they arrived only just in time to save me," cried Rebecca; "another five minutes, and Sir Gaston would have succeeded in carrying me to his castle."

"The villain!—and so he still continues to persecute you as he used to do?"

"He does, and on this occasion he carried me off from my father's house at the moment when the sacred rites of our religion were about to bestow me for ever on Reuben Grenard."

"What! and did he steal a bride from the very altar?"

"He did," answered Rebecca; "and never should I again have seen those I love if it had not been for Black Ivan, whose fortunate arrival saved me from the hands of a villain."

"True," exclaimed Maud; "but in your gratitude you must not forget Meg of Finchley, who exerted herself so much to give timely notice of your danger. The poor old soul came running here almost out of breath, and not a step would she move from the place till she saw them fairly started forth to your rescue."

"She has left the place, then?"

"Oh, yes—Meg is uncommonly partial to the captain, and loves him almost as much as if he was her own son; but she likes not the sort of life he has been leading, and nothing could ever persuade her to come and live in the cavern, though the poor old soul has scarcely a roof to cover her."

"And being so poor," cried the maiden, "does Ivan give nothing towards her support?"

"He has tried to persuade her, as much as he could, to accept of money," replied the old woman, "but she will not accept of even the smallest coin, for she says it has been gained by dishonest means, and that she will never consent to support an existence upon the wages of crime."

"There must be some extraordinary connexion between them," observed Rebecca, "or the old woman would, ere now, have denounced one whose career she seems to hold in such utter abhorrence."

"Aye, there is something very mysterious," replied Maud, "that, I suppose, will one day or other be explained. Some say she knew him when he was not the sort of man that he is at present, and that she could, if she pleased, tell a story of him that would make some people look about them."

"Indeed!" cried Rebecca; "and have you any idea who those persons are that have so much reason to fear the revelations she has it in her power to make?"

"I have no notion at present," replied Maud; "but I dare say a little patience will serve to bring all the affairs to light, though I, old as I am, may not live to see it."

"Have you been long among these people?" asked Rebecca.

"Aye—it is now nearly nine-and-twenty years since I first became housekeeper to the horde."

"Then you were here before Black Ivan became chief of the band?"

"Oh, yes," answered Maud, "there have been several captains in my time, but there was not one of them that I could ever like as I have him."

"You can tell me then, perhaps, under what circumstances he was induced to become a robber?"

"Why, to tell you the truth, young lady," replied Maud, "I can throw very little light upon the subject. All I know is, that he was quite a young man when he first of all came; that he was very melancholy, and went moping about a good deal for a long time afterwards; that he was always looked upon as the bravest man in the whole band; and that when our last captain was killed in a skirmish with a party of travellers, Ivan was chosen to succeed him in the command. They then gave him the name of Black Ivan, from the darkness of his complexion, and though rather stern in his manner, I believe he is so well liked by the whole band that there is not a man belonging to it who wishes to see him throw up his command."

"And it seems," observed Rebecca, "that no exertions of the government have ever been able to break up the daring horde of which he is the chief."

"Why, the truth is," replied the old woman, "attempts are very rarely made to disturb them; now and then, to be sure, a bit of a stir has been made, when any robbery of any consequence has taken place; but when our folks find that to be the case, they lie quiet for a little while, and when the affair has pretty well blown over, they begin business again as usual."

"Do murders never take place among them?" asked Rebecca, with a shudder.

"Never," replied the old woman. "Such things used to happen occasionally in former times, but when Ivan was chosen to the command, he gave strict orders against bloodshed, and threatened such severe punishment to any man who should break his injunctions, that no one has ever since risked the shedding of his own blood by wilfully spilling that of another."

"Then, with the exception of his one great fault," cried the maiden, "Black Ivan is not so terrible a monster as people have represented him?"

"He is not," replied Maud, "and I can say this one thing in his favour—if he had not had the command of the band, a great many more crimes would have been committed than there have. He has restrained the men when they would have committed violence as well as robbery, and if it was for that one thing alone, he deserves the pardon that the king has offered him."

"'Tis a pity, then," exclaimed Rebecca, "that he has not, ere this, claimed the offer of mercy that has been made."

"Aye," answered the old woman; "but we know not yet what reason he may have for remaining quiet where he is. A little while may, perhaps, remove some difficulties that are in his way, and then he will leave the band, to mingle once more with society. But I am forgetting myself—you must be weary; and if you will follow me, I will light you to your chamber."

Rebecca was indeed fatigued; and though there was little chance of sleep visiting her eyes that night, she gladly accepted the offer of the old woman, and, accompanying her to a small chamber which had been allotted for her use, she was soon afterwards left to ruminate in solitude on the strange and trying events of the day. On one subject, however, her heart was at rest—her father and Reuben Grenard would shortly learn the news of her miraculous preservation; and, consoled with this thought, she threw herself upon the couch that had been prepared for her, and passed the remainder of the night in reflections that alternately raised and depressed her spirits.

CHAPTER CX.

"Say from whence
You owe this strange intelligence?
Speak, I charge you."

MACBETH.

ON returning home after their fruitless visit to the castle of Sir Gaston de Neville, the first care of Reuben was to prevail on the aged Israelite to take that rest which, in mind and body, he so much needed. At first Isaac resolutely refused the proposition that had thus been made by his younger companion, but at length he yielded to his earnest entreaties, and, throwing himself down upon the humble pallet which had been laid upon the floor, he soon sunk into a calm slumber, in which his cares and vicissitudes were, for a time at least, entirely forgotten. During this interval, Reuben Grenard sat down to watch over his friend, but his mind was occupied with the frightful occurrences of the day; and, agitated as he was by a thousand fears on Rebecca's account, he every now and then rose from his seat, and paced uneasily up and down the apartment.

Reuben had been thus occupied for some time, when his quick ear detected the sound of approaching footsteps at no great distance off; and wishing to avoid interruption, he placed the lamp in the fire place, so that its feeble light should not be seen through the shutters. His precaution was, however a vain one, for the sounds still continued to approach; and whilst he was deliberating whether to wake the old man, a low rapping was heard at the door, but Reuben maintained a death-like silence until the knocking became more loud and impatient; and then, resolving to satisfy himself as to who the visitor was, he softly approached the door, and in a low voice demanded who was there.

"A friend," was the immediate reply.

"Nay," answered Reuben, "I must know who and what thou art ere I give thee admittance."

"Black Ivan, the Outlaw."

"Ha!" exclaimed Reuben; "thy business?—comest thou here as a friend, or an enemy?"

"As a friend."

Reuben paused for a few minutes, irresolute how to act; but remembering that Ivan had, ere then, proved himself a valuable ally, he withdrew the bolts and bars with which the door had been secured, and the Outlaw entered the chamber.

"Thou wert distrustful of me," he said; "and yet I have come hither on an errand to do thee service. I have good news for thee, young man, and, therefore, I trust thou wilt excuse the somewhat unseasonable hour at which I have paid my visit."

"Alas!" cried Reuben, "thou hast come to a house of mourning: we are in deep affliction for the loss of Rebecca, who has been forcibly carried away at the moment when our bridal was about to be solemnized, and——"

"Thou need'st explain the affair no further,   .rupted Ivan, "for it is already known to me; and my present visit h   ) is to bring thee tidings of Rebecca."

"Ah!—is she safe?"

"She is; but thou must wake the old man, who, I see, is sleeping in yonder corner: he also will be rejoiced to hear of her safety—and not a word more will I say upon the subject till he is present to learn the good fortune that has rescued his child from the hands of a villain."

Overjoyed at the words he had heard, Reuben was quickly by the side of the old man, and, gently rousing him from his slumbers, he as briefly as possible acquainted him with the arrival of a visitor, and the object for which he had come. Startled by the hint which had been thus conveyed, Isaac hastily arose, and, advancing towards Black Ivan, implored him to explain, in as few words as possible, the intelligence of which he was the bearer.

"That I will do with all my heart," replied the Outlaw: "so, without further preface, I have the happiness to tell you that your daughter is at present in a place of safety."

"Heaven be praised for the mercy it has vouchsafed us in this our hour of trouble and affliction," cried the old man, fervently. "But say, —how was she saved, and to whom do I stand indebted for this great service?"

"It would be, perhaps, too long a story to tell the manner of her rescue," answered Ivan, "and it may, therefore, suffice to say that I was fortunately the means of saving her from a fate that seemed to be inevitable."

"You!" cried the father; "and are we indeed again indebted for her preservation to one whom all men have conspired to brand with every vice that can taint humanity?"

"It is even as I have told you," answered Ivan. "I, with the assistance of my men, saved her from destruction; and, guessing your anxiety on her account, I hastened hither to bring you the intelligence that has removed from your heart a heavy load of uneasiness."

"Thanks—a thousand thanks for thy generous interposition in favour of those who so much needed thy good services," cried the enraptured father. "But why," he continued, after a moment's pause, "why should I repay thy kindness with empty words, when it is in my power to reward thee with more substantial gold?"

"Thou may'st keep thy gold for those who are more avaricious than myself," answered Ivan. "What I have done has been amply repaid by the happiness it has bestowed upon those who have too long been oppressed, and, therefore, do I charge thee to say no more about rewards to one who neither asks nor requires them."

"And my daughter!" exclaimed the old man—"say, where hast thou conveyed her?—since it seems that thou hast not brought her back with thee."

"She is safe," replied Ivan.

"But where?"

"In my cavern near Enfield Chase."

"Ah!" groaned the father, "then she is still exposed to insult from the ruffians who——"

"Nay," interrupted Ivan, "thou must not condemn my followers till thou dost know them better. They are roughish in their way, to be sure, but being under my control, I can answer for it there is not one among them who, either by word or look, would dare to offend her."

"But in thy absence——"

"She is equally safe as if I was present in the cavern," replied Ivan; "besides, I have left her in the care of an aged housekeeper, who, I can answer for it, will protect your daughter as if she was her own child. So make your mind easy on that subject, and I pledge you my word that no harm shall befal her."

"I do believe thee," cried Isaac; "and now, being somewhat more assured on that subject, let me ask how it was that you were fortunate enough to rescue her, at a moment when I had given her up in utter despair?"

"I have told you that the story would be rather a long one," replied Ivan; "yet, as you are inquisitive upon the subject, I will be as brief as possible in my explanation. The truth is, then, I received intimation of her danger from Meg of Finchley; and having ascertained the exact road that had been taken by Sir Gaston de Neville, I ordered a party of my men to follow me, and we set forward to intercept them on their way. In this we succeeded almost beyond my hopes: your daughter was rescued, and, as I said before, has found an asylum in our secret abode."

"And what became of Sir Gaston de Neville?" enquired Reuben, anxiously.

"Why he, poor devil, fared badly enough, I believe," replied Ivan, "for an arrow, directed by a steady hand, entered his bosom, and he instantly fell bleeding from his horse. At that moment of confusion among his followers, I rushed forward to save Rebecca, and happily succeeded, though I had nearly paid with my own life for the ardour which had prompted me to throw myself thus unguarded into the midst of my enemies."

"And did you escape unhurt?" asked the old man, anxiously.

"Thanks to the promptitude of my men, I did," replied the Outlaw; "they saw my danger, and each man fitting an arrow to his bow, stood ready to discharge the fatal missiles upon the first who might have the temerity to advance against me. The knight's retainers shrank back at the peril they saw themselves placed in, and making the best use of the advantage that had thus been given me, I escaped with the fainting girl in my arms."

"And what," asked Isaac, "became of the knight and his followers?"

"Why, they retreated with all the speed they could," replied the Outlaw: "Sir Gaston de Neville was placed on horseback with a man to support him, and as we had effected the purpose we went upon, they were suffered to depart without further molestation from us."

"And had you an opportunity of judging whether the wound of the knight was mortal?"

"I paid little attention to that fact," answered Ivan, "but as the wound did not appear to be a very deep one, I should say that it is likely enough he may recover. At any rate it will be sufficient to confine him for some time to come in his castle, and, therefore, as I suppose your daughter will shortly be married to this young man, I think you may pretty safely congratulate yourself upon at length seeing a termination of your troubles."

"Then, now," cried Isaac, "let us instantly set forth, that I may see my daughter with as little delay as possible."

"Nay," answered Ivan, "with all allowances for a father's anxiety, I must protest against setting out just yet. At present it is dark, for the moon has now set, and as the roads are rugged, it will be impossible for one so aged as yourself to surmount the difficulties you would have to encounter."

"I can endure anything," cried Isaac, "rather than the torture of suspense."

"But I do not ask you to delay your journey for any long time," answered Ivan; "in a short time daylight will begin to appear, and, ere the sun rises, I will myself accompany you to the place where your

No. 88

daughter has found a refuge. I have a horse tied up at no great distance from hence, and thou shalt freely have the use of him whilst I and this youth will trudge sturdily by thy side."

"And why should we suffer the delay of even a single moment," asked the old man, "when I am ready to endure so much more for the sake of again folding Rebecca in my arms?"

"I have told you that it would be madness to make the attempt just yet," replied Ivan; "an hour can make very little difference, and, at the expiration of that time I promise to offer no further obstacles. Be content, therefore, with the certainty of your daughter's safety, and let that suffice till you again see her."

"Ivan is in the right," exclaimed Reuben Grenard; "with daylight in our favour we shall be able to get over the ground much more quickly, so that it will not be all the time lost if we delay a little longer the visit we are about to make."

"But I fear," cried the old man, "lest Sir Gaston should take second thoughts and send out a party of his men to search for her who has been so unexpectedly rescued from his grasp."

"Depend upon it Sir Gaston has got something else to think about," replied Ivan. "His wound, even if it is not mortal, will occasion him much pain and inconvenience, and during the confinement he will be obliged to submit to, there is good reason to hope he may think seriously of the foul injustice he has sought to do you."

"I fear there is little chance of that," exclaimed Isaac. "His disposition is naturally cruel and revengeful, and the remembrance of the disappointment he has been obliged to endure, will rankle in his heart, and make him more inveterate against us than ever."

"Why, in that case," answered the Outlaw, "I should have more to fear than yourself, since it is to me that he owes the disappointment you have spoken of."

"But he knows not of your retreat," replied Isaac, "and you have, therefore, only to keep yourself concealed there for a little while, and all danger will cease. Besides, the king has offered you a free pardon on condition that you abandon the course of life you have hitherto led, so that you can at any time claim the royal promise, and thus bid defiance to Sir Gaston de Neville, and the vile arts by which he may seek to hunt you to destruction."

"The pardon you speak of," exclaimed Ivan, "cannot at present be accepted on the terms that have been proposed—with a character notorious as mine unfortunately is, I should. be shunned were I at this time to venture into the society from which I have so long banished myself. In a little while, however, I may be enabled to explain the cause that drove me to adopt the course of life I have followed of late years, and when that is the case, I may, perhaps, obtain the pity and consideration of those who would now shun me with abhorrence."

"And why can you not enter into the explanation now, as well as at any future time?" asked Isaac.

"The reason will appear by and by, and that is the only solution of your question that I can give at present," answered the Outlaw; "let it suffice for you to know that I am not exactly what I seem to be, but that circumstances which I cannot explain further just now, drove me to despair, and in that moment I became the associate of robbers. Yet, even as Black Ivan, the Outlaw, it has been in my power to render services to my fellow men, which at some future time will, I hope, in some degree extenuate the step to which I was unhappily driven."

"By thy speech and manner," observed Isaac, "I should suppose thou wert born in a sphere far above that which you at present occupy."

"What I have been," replied Ivan, "thou wilt know ere long. At present it is my purpose to maintain the secret inviolable, but circumstances urge me on with irresistible violence, and, perhaps, ere I could have wished it, I may be compelled to declare myself, to the confusion and dismay of those who have driven me to become the companion and associate of robbers."

"Thy wrongs must have been great, indeed," exclaimed Isaac, "to force thee from thy natural station in society. Thou hast been disinherited, perhaps, foully robbed by those whom thou hast trusted, and, as a last resource, were driven to adopt the life of a robber?"

"Thou hast so far guessed rightly," answered Ivan.

"Then why dost thou not denounce the villain who has thus wronged thee?"

"The reason will be sufficiently apparent when thou dost know my history," replied the Outlaw; "that I have been grievously wronged, however, I again repeat, yet even those injuries would have been forgotten had I not received further provocation from the man who has made me what I am."

Whilst he was thus speaking, Reuben Grenard threw open the window-shutters, and admitted the first feeble light of the dawn, which was beginning to show itself in the east. Isaac hailed this sight with rapturous joy, since it assured him that a short time longer would serve to take him into the presence of his daughter.

"In half an hour," he said, "we shall be able to set out on our journey, and then shall I again behold her who has been so ruthlessly torn away from me."

"Hist!" exclaimed Reuben, "I see a figure stealthily approaching this way, as if anxious to avoid observation. Hah! it is a man as I suspected, and by his badge, I should take him to be one of Sir Gaston de Neville's retainers."

"What sayest thou?" cried Isaac, in alarm; "one of Sir Gaston's retainers, sayest thou, and creeping hither at this early hour in the morning!—Alas! then I fear there is more mischief brooding against us, and that the sum of our earthly misery is not yet complete."

"Nay, fear him not," exclaimed Ivan, "for the fellow seems to be alone, so that there can be little cause for apprehension. He perhaps comes on some apparently peaceful message from the knight—but trust not his fair words lest thou should'st fall into a snare from which it will not be easy to extricate thyself."

"He has just passed the window," cried the elder Jew, who was looking anxiously in that direction; "and hark! he now knocks at the door, and, by the impatience of his signal, I fear his errand bodes nothing but mischief to me."

"Then I will conceal myself in this closet," said Ivan, advancing towards the place he spoke of; "here I can remain unseen, and should any violence be offered, I shall be at hand to resent it in a way the villain little expects. Let him not suspect that I am here, and he will then fearlessly unburden himself of the message with which he has been charged."

So saying, Ivan stepped into the closet, and as soon as he was well secreted, the door was opened, and Maurice presented himself before the old man.

"Good morning, Isaac," he said, with the familiarity of an old acquaintance; "thou art up betimes, I see, for I warrant me thou art not often to be found sleeping when money is to be made."

"My thoughts were otherwise engaged, just at present," replied the Jew; "a villain has stolen from me my child, and I rose thus early that I might hunt him out and rescue her from his foul clutches."

"Aye, aye," answered Maurice, "I know all about thy loss, old gentleman; Rebecca was taken from you last night, and no doubt you think it one of the most unfortunate events that could have happened to you."

"I do, indeed," replied Isaac, affecting to be ignorant of her rescue by Black Ivan; "she was the only solace of my declining days, and yet thy villanous master has carried her where I never may be able to find her out."

"And for that thou canst hardly blame him," cried Maurice, "seeing that the wench has already given so much trouble, and would do so again, if she had but the opportunity."

"But I was in hopes," said the old man, trying to draw from Maurice the object of his visit; "I was in hopes, I say, that she might find means to escape him, and that you had come hither to see whether she had returned home."

These words rather startled the retainer, the motive of whose visit was exactly that which had been mentioned by Isaac; he, however, quickly recovered himself, and then forcing a laugh, he said :—

"Escape, eh! a very likely thing, indeed, that a woman should be able to escape when she is surrounded by such a number of men, every one of whom had orders to slay the girl rather than suffer her to give us the slip."

"If such was not the motive of thy visit, fellow, I pray thee tell me what is. Thou seest my daughter is not here, nor have I seen her since thy master, coward like, laid his hand upon a defenceless woman, who was unable to protect herself against his evil designs."

"Jew!" exclaimed the retainer, "be careful how you speak against Sir Gaston de Neville. Remember, he has it in his power to chastise thee, and will not fail to use it, unless thou can'st curb thy tongue, and teach it to utter less offensive expressions towards him."

"I speak," replied Isaac, "as a father who has been wronged by a villain, and if that offends thy master, let him make me restitution, and I will endeavour to frame my words so as to be more palateable to him in future."

"How can'st thou call it an injury," demanded Maurice, "when thy daughter has obtained the notice and regard of a man like Sir Gaston de Neville?"

"And thinkest thou," cried the old man, indignantly, "that I would ever consent to sacrifice my daughter's honour on the altar of pride? Tell thy master from me that he hath degraded himself beneath the lowest of those he affects to despise, and that I should consider it a disgrace even though he offered to make my daughter his lawful wife."

"Perhaps," observed Maurice, "such an offer as you have spoken of may not be so improbable as you may imagine; in fact, to speak plainly, Sir Gaston begins to think he has done you some wrong, and is willing to make all the reparation in his power."

"Indeed!"

"Aye; but what makes you so doubtful when I am delivering a part of the message I was charged with?"

"Because," answered the Jew, "I can never believe that Sir Gaston can be serious when he professes honourable intentions. I have known him long—too long to my own cost, and judging of his future conduct from his past, I should be unwilling to place the least reliance on his words."

"But you forget," exclaimed Maurice, "that your daughter's happiness may depend upon your present decision."

"My daughter's happiness is ever my first consideration," answered the old man, "but it so happens that I know she is not at present in the power Sir Gaston de Neville."

"There you are mistaken," exclaimed the retainer, "for she was taken away from this place before your own eyes, and not having returned, ought to be a convincing proof that she is still with my master."

"But suppose I have on good authority that she was rescued from him on their road to one of Sir Gaston's castles?"

"Hah!" exclaimed Maurice, "and who, pray, has been here to tell thee such a falsehood?"

"One whose word I would rather believe than I would thine own," answered Isaac: "one, in fact, who witnessed the transaction, and was, therefore, not likely to be deceived."

"Humph! and did he tell you more?"

"He did; he told me that Sir Gaston was wounded, and that his attendants carried him back to his castle in Moorfields."

"Confusion!" muttered Maurice, "what fiend can have been thus at work?"

"One that thou mayest dread to meet," answered Isaac; "nay, I charge thee, look to thyself, for thou knowest not how soon thou mayest have to answer to him for the deceit thou would'st now have practised on me."

"I can guess the name of thine informant," exclaimed Maurice, gloomily; "Black Ivan has been here, and it is from him thou hast learnt the story he has been pleased to trump up to suit his own purposes."

"I shall not tell thee who it is," replied Isaac, "but depend on it thou wilt know all sooner than thou mayest wish."

"That it is Black Ivan, I am certain," cried Maurice, "and, if so, I wish the villain were now confronted before me, that I might convict him of the lie he has spoken."

"Then have thy wish, sirrah!" exclaimed the Outlaw, as he stepped from the closet in which he had been concealed, and placed himself before the retainer. "Thou did'st want to see me, knave, and now behold, here I am to answer any questions thou mayest have to put."

"I—I—I have nothing to ask thee," stammered Maurice, utterly confounded by the suddenness with which this had taken place; "what I said was merely in jest, and—and—"

"No equivocation," interrupted Ivan, impatiently; "thou wert wishing to see me, I believe, and being willing to oblige thee, I am now ready to hear anything thou mayest have to say. Speak, therefore, sirrah, or instantly take thy departure, lest I should be tempted to chastise the insolence that thou hast dared to utter in this house."

Maurice waited for no second bidding, and rushing with all the haste he could from the house, he was soon far beyond the reach of the man who had so unexpectedly made his appearance before him. Ivan seemed to enjoy the fellow's alarm greatly, and as by this time it was broad daylight, he proposed to Isaac that he and his younger companion should accompany him without any further delay. This was a suggestion that they were both of them willing enough to accede to, and having secured the house against intruders, they set forth towards the place where the Outlaw had secured his horse.

CHAPTER CXI.

"——Come and see !—trust thine eyes.
A peaceful sign stands in the house of life,
An enemy, a fiend lurks close behind
The radiance of thy planet—O, be warned !"

COLERIDGE.

HAVING mounted Isaac on the noble steed which was impatiently awaiting the return of his master, the party set forward on their journey, taking the most unfrequented roads, till they arrived at Islington, where they came into the high road leading towards the little town of Barnet. For some time they had remained perfectly silent lest their voices should arouse any sleepers at that early hour in the morning, and thus afford a clue by which they might be traced to the retreat at Enfield Chase. The morning was clear and beautiful, and by the time they had proceeded a couple of miles on their journey, a few crimson streaks in the eastern portion of the sky told of the sun's approach, and of the commencement of another busy day. Yet even these glories, which at another time would have been hailed with rapturous delight, were scarcely regarded by our travellers, whose thoughts were just then bent upon other matters, and thus they passed onwards, speaking only at intervals, and then only a few words at a time. At length turning from the main road, they began to traverse a wild and desolate looking heath, with here and there a small plantation of trees, which, by their luxuriance, served to show yet more forcibly the poverty and wildness of those places which had not been thus favoured by nature. Onwards, however, they continued to move without heeding the scene by which they were surrounded, but at length as they approached a small copse, a sharp rustling was heard among the underwood, and, in another second, Meg of Finchley presented herself before them.

"We are well met," she exclaimed, addressing herself to Ivan; "I have been seeking you these two hours, and at last took my station here, knowing it is a path you often take on your return to the cave. I would speak to you, Ivan, and that, too, ere you proceed further on your journey."

"What is thy business, Meg?" demanded the Outlaw; "or stay, can'st thou not wait till I have more time and a better opportunity to speak with thee ?"

"That which I have to say to thee, will admit of no delay," she replied; "I would warn thee of danger, for the foe watches thee who is ready to strike the blow that will end in thine own destruction."

"Well," exclaimed Ivan, "if there is such danger as you speak of, let me know it, that I may be prepared to resist the attacks of my enemies."

"Come this way, then, and I will tell thee," replied the hag, plucking him by the sleeve.

"Nay, thou can'st speak openly before these persons," answered Ivan, pointing towards his companions; "they are friends, and I believe thou hast thyself, ere now, thought it worth thy while to interest thyself in their service. So speak boldly, woman, though much I doubt whether thou hast anything to tell me of which I need be much alarmed."

"Thou art in peril."

"From whom, I prithee ?"

"Sir Gaston de Neville,"

"That is impossible," replied Ivan, "for he is wounded, and will be unable to move from his couch for some time to come."

"But his brain will soon be working fresh mischief," answered Meg; "too often already hast thou failed him, and enraged as he is at the frustration of his plans, he will never rest satisfied till he has hurled upon thee the whole force of his vengeance."

"And how dost thou know this?" demanded the Outlaw.

"By the gift of prophecy," she replied, "besides, dost thou not know I am deeply learned in mystic lore, and that I can read the destinies of men with unerring certainty? Have I not foretold to thee many things that have afterwards come to pass, and wilt thou now hesitate to believe me when thine own safety depends upon the reliance you place upon my warning?"

"Thou sayest thou art certain that Sir Gaston de Neville is plotting mischief against me; can'st thou tell me how soon it will be ere the bolt is shot?"

"Aye; ere the sun has made his daily journey nine times more, thou wilt perish miserably, unless thou wilt heed the words I have this day spoken to thee."

"Indeed! and how, I prithee, am I to avoid the danger thou dost tell me of?"

"There are but two ways," replied the hag; "thou must either leave England for ever without delay, or take instant means to procure the punishment of Sir Gaston for the crimes he has committed."

"Both are alike impossible," exclaimed Black Ivan; "I will not leave my native land like a base coward, neither will I seek to injure the knight unless it should be in defence of my own life."

"And have I not already told thee," cried Meg, "that he will now plot thy destruction?"

"Aye, thou said so, I grant," replied Ivan, "but for all thy prophecies I must still think thou hast greatly magnified the danger. Sir Gaston is not at present able to leave his couch, and even if he could, I am watchful enough to protect myself against any designs he may have formed to serve his own purposes."

"Remember," cried Meg, "he has those about him who will gladly aid in any plot, however murderous it may be towards you; the knight, too, is smarting from the wound he last night received either from your hand, or one of your men, and the blood that has been shed will be fearfully avenged unless you take the counsel which I thus earnestly give you."

"If it be my fate to perish through his means," answered the Outlaw, "I can bow to it with submission. Life has no charms for me, and I know not whether it would not be better to die at once than linger out a miserable existence, scorned by all those who know me to have been the leader of a band of robbers."

"But thou mayest possess wealth," answered Meg, "if thou dost think proper to seek it. Gold is within thy grasp, and I need not tell thee that its possession will secure to thee more friends than thou really needest."

"True—but they would be hollow ones, and, therefore, little regarded by a man who scorns both the sycophant and the time-server. No, Meg, if I have friends, they must be such as would love me for myself, and not for the paltry gold that fortune may have bestowed upon me."

"And why shouldst thou not have friends such as thou speakest of?" demanded the old woman.

" Because this world will ever know me as the man whose name once carried terror with it."

" Well, but thou hast lately saved the life of the king, and a pardon for the past has been offered thee: yet thou dost not claim the offer of thy sovereign, and people now begin to think that thou canst not tear thyself away from the associates with whom thou hast been so long connected."

" The world wrongs me, then," answered the Outlaw; " for there is nothing I so much desire as to quit a life which has ever been hateful to me."

" Why, then, hast thou not done so ere this ?"

"Thou knowest the reason as well as I do myself," replied Ivan; " I have been wronged by one who should have been the last to persecute and oppress me; yet I have endured all with patience, rather than bring disgrace upon a name which has ever, hitherto, been sustained with honour."

" And does he deserve thy forbearance ?"

" Perhaps not, Meg; yet that is a question I have scarcely ever asked myself, for I am determined never to seek reparation for my wrongs unless circumstances should force me to do so."

" And is this thine unalterable resolution ?"

" It is; so now let us change this subject by bringing it back to that which we were first speaking of. You say I am in danger from Sir Gaston de Neville, and would counsel me either to fly or crush him by revealing certain events of his life that would bring upon him the scorn and execration of the world ?"

"Such is my advice," replied Meg; " and I see no reason why thou shouldst hesitate to do so, since he deserves neither thy pity nor regard. He has ever been thy foe, and even now would bring thee, if possible, to a shameful death."

" Let him try his worst," exclaimed Black Ivan, " for I fear no evil that he may feel disposed to work against me. In fact, he has ever found me to be an opponent over whom he could exercise no control; and perhaps that may be the cause of the burning hatred which he bears towards me."

" Make not too sure, lest he comes upon thee unawares," cried the hag; " he is artful as well as cruel, and will never give up his wicked designs till he has accomplished the vengeance that now rankles in his heart."

" But Sir Gaston de Neville has enough to do to look after his own safety," answered the Outlaw: " he is suspected by the king of a treasonable plot that has been formed to take away his life for the purpose of placing Prince John on the throne of England; the fact of one of his retainers being detected in the act of aiming a deadly wound against the king serves to strengthen the suspicion, and, therefore, it is likely his actions will be so closely watched in future that he may fall when he least expects it under the vengeance of those laws which, like myself, he has so long violated."

" And that he will do so I feel well assured," replied Meg; " but I fear there is too much reason to believe that it will not be till after he has succeeded in carrying out his designs against you."

" Psha !" cried Ivan, impatiently; " thy fears on my account, old woman, are groundless."

" Aye," she replied, " I thought my warning would be disregarded, even before I met thee. Yet let me again caution you, Ivan, to place no further reliance in the good fortune that has hitherto protected thee

from the machinations of a deadly foe. Thy encounter with him last night—the rescue of the maiden from him when he made so certain of carrying off his prize—and the pain of the wound from which he is suffering—will serve to render him more inveterate against thee than ever. Again, therefore, do I caution thee to avoid him as thou wouldst an envenomed serpent that lay coiled in thy path, ready to strike the fatal blow that carries death with it."

"Let him beware how he practices his evil deeds against me," answered Ivan; "his designs are known, and it will be my own fault if I suffer him to obtain an advantage whilst I am thus prepared for his attack."

"Thou wilt not quit England, then, to avoid a danger that threatens thee more and more every hour?"

"Why, that would be a coward's alternative!"

"It is the only one that promises thee safety."

"Perhaps so," answered the Outlaw; "yet, be the consequences what they may, I will not run from a foe whose power to injure me I utterly despise."

"Wilt thou, then, expose thyself to danger in spite of my repeated warnings?"

"I cannot expose myself much," replied Ivan, "for it is likely I shall keep close within the cavern for some days, to complete some business upon which I am at present engaged. Thou seest, therefore, I shall be tolerably safe without fleeing like a coward from a foe whose malice I despise."

"Why that, to be sure, may be something towards preserving thyself," answered Meg; "but the knight has a clue by which to find thy secret

No. 89

retreat, and it is but too probable that he will surprise thee there, and thus accomplish the villany he has designed."

"Thou hast forgotten, Meg," exclaimed the Outlaw, "that I shall be guarded by fellows as brave as any he can bring against me. They are well armed, too; and I'll warrant you there is not one among them but will sacrifice his life rather than suffer his leader to fall by such treachery as you have spoken of. And so, having, I hope, assured thee of the absence of all danger, I will now take my leave, with many thanks for the kindly interest thou hast taken in the welfare of a despised Outlaw."

Saying this he turned away, and once more joining his companions, pursued his way towards the cavern. Slowly as they proceeded, it was nearly two hours after their interview with Meg before they reached the place, but as they approached it, one of the robbers sprang forth from a bush, beneath which he had secreted himself, and, advancing towards Isaac, assisted him to dismount. This done, they preceeded by a circuitous path through a small wood, and, having threaded the mazes, which would have been a puzzle to any one less acquainted with it than Ivan was, they at length reached a spot where a huge stone was seen lying in a sort of ruin. Ponderous as it was, however, the Outlaw removed it without much difficulty, and discovered a rugged flight of steps, down which they slowly descended till they reached a vaulted passage, along which Ivan led them, with the aid of a few lamps that were thinly ranged along the roof, and threw a faint light, barely sufficient for the purpose intended. Quitting this, however, they entered a more spacious chamber, cut out of the earth, and supported by pillars so massive as to defy the immense superincumbent weight that rested upon them. From thence Ivan conducted them into a smaller apartment, which they had no sooner entered than a cry of joyful surprise was heard, and Rebecca rushed into the arms of her father.

"Oh, this is indeed a happiness!" she cried; "thus to behold you both again, when, but a few hours since, I, in my despair, gave up all as lost."

"My daughter," exclaimed the old man, "thy joy exceeds not mine or Reuben's, for we believed thee lost to us for ever. This, however, makes amends for all we have endured: Ivan has restored us to happiness, and never more, I trust, wilt thou become the sport of that fortune which has hitherto proved so cruel to us."

"No," cried Reuben, "the evil hour has passed away, and from this time forth, I trust, we may look forward to a brighter and more happy destiny."

"Of course," said Rebecca, "you know to whom I have been thus indebted for my rescue? Ivan, whose name was once so terrible to us, snatched me from peril, when, in my despair, I believed all hope was lost; and to him, therefore, next to heaven, is due the gratitude which fills our hearts."

"What I have done needs no thanks," answered the Outlaw. "The act has brought its own reward, and the only favour I shall ask for any service I may have done you, is, that you will remain here for a few days, to see whether Sir Gaston will take any further steps to hunt you out. It is true, his wound will prevent him from doing so himself, but he has agents who are ever ready to do his bidding, and it is likely enough that they will be actively engaged in trying once more to secure their victim."

This offer was accepted with gratitude, and having succeeded in this, Ivan led them to another chamber, where breakfast had been prepared by Maud.

CHAPTER CXII.

" Dire was the thought, who first in poison steep'd
The weapon form'd for slaughter--direr his,
And worthier of damnation, who instill'd
The mortal venom in the social cup,
To fill the veins of death instead of life."

ANON.

WHEN Sir Gaston de Neville was carried back to his castle, it was discovered that the wound he had received was of a much more serious character than had at first been imagined. Loss of blood, too, had rendered him nearly powerless, and on being conveyed to bed, a long fainting fit succeeded, during the continuance of which it was at one period imagined that he had expired. At length, however, to the surprise of every one, he began slowly to revive; but there was a marked change in his manner, for reflection now came upon his guilty mind, and the uneasiness that was visible on his countenance betrayed the anxiety with which he regarded the probable near approach of death. Observing this, Father Francis, his confessor, motioned for all present to retire, and then, approaching the couch of the sick knight, he enquired whether there was anything on his mind which he wished to be relieved of. This question appeared to startle Sir Gaston, and for a moment or two he regarded the holy man with a look of suspicion and distrust, but observing that they were entirely alone, he replied, in a low and subdued tone of voice—

"Thou hast well reminded me, father, of the last duty I may be called upon to perform. There is, indeed, much to confess, and more, I fear, than can be forgiven."

"Nay, despond not thus, my son," exclaimed the monk; "heaven is merciful to all those who are truly penitent. I, therefore, charge thee to make a clean heart, and when thou hast done that, I will intercede for thee with my prayers, and obtain for thee that pardon which we all so greatly need."

"Dost thou think, then, I can hope ever to be forgiven?" asked the knight, earnestly.

"There is, at least, reason to hope so," replied Father Francis. " I must, however, know the full extent of thy misdeeds; and when that is done, I will implore pardon for the evil thou hast committed. Proceed, therefore, immediately, and lose not another moment in hesitation and doubt."

"Not now, Father Francis," exclaimed the knight; " the wound may not prove so fatal as I have feared, and no confession shall ever pass my lips till every hope of life has passed from me."

"But thou may'st depend on me," replied the monk, "and never will I betray anything that may serve to bring the stain of dishonour upon thy name."

"It may be so," answered Sir Gaston; " and yet I will make no man the depository of my secrets till life is about to forsake me."

"And thou knowest not how near thou may'st be to that awful moment," replied the confessor. "Thy wound has placed thee in great jeopardy, and even thy physician entertains fears that thou wilt not survive it. Take, therefore, the opportunity that offers, and, by a full disclosure, manifest the penitence of thy heart."

"And may I expect no mercy, then," cried Sir Gaston. "except upon condition that I tell thee things which I had hoped never to have thought of again?"

"Unless thou art truly repentant," answered the monk, "thou hast no right to expect the mercy thou askest. To me thou may'st tell all without hesitation, for a priest never divulges that which is entrusted to him in confidence."

"And why," asked Sir Gaston de Neville, "dost thou thus press me with these questions?"

"Because," replied the other, "I have heard much whispering concerning certain things that have been alleged against thee."

"And thou believest all the idle stories that malignant enemies have invented to my prejudice?"

"Nay, you wrong me there," answered Father Francis, "for I am in hopes thou canst contradict the idle tales that men have circulated to the injury of thy fair name. For instance, it is not true, perhaps, that thy wife was imprisoned for years in a miserable dungeon, whilst a report was circulated that she was dead?"

"I will not deny it," exclaimed Sir Gaston, "since thou hast put the question so pointedly to me. The Lady Alicia was kept in confinement, as thou hast said; but she is now at liberty, and, therefore, that deed may be forgiven."

"But the liberty she enjoys was not voluntarily given by thee," answered the monk. "It is said she escaped from this castle, and that thou hast even meditated tearing her away by force from the holy refuge to which she fled for safety and protection."

"I confess that such was once my intention," returned Sir Gaston, "but when I found that she took no steps to bring punishment upon me for the past, I desisted, and meant that she should pass the remainder of her days in peace and quietness."

"So far thou hast done well," exclaimed the confessor; "and now, my son, let me ask another question of thee;—it has been told me that thou hast an elder brother living, and that all these fair possessions have been unjustly usurped from the rightful owner. Such is the story I have heard, and I would learn from thine own lips whether there is any truth in the assertion."

"Thou art asking me more than I can answer with safety to myself," answered the knight.

"I am only seeking to bring thee to confession, in order that thou may'st hereafter obtain pardon," exclaimed the monk. "At present, thy life is in imminent peril, and I would fain prevail upon thee whilst it is in thy power to do justice to those thou hast injured."

"Or, in other words," replied Sir Gaston, "you would worm yourself into my secrets for the purpose of afterwards denouncing me to the state as a criminal."

"There thou dost wrong me," answered the other, meekly. "Duty alone has prompted me to adopt this course; and the sacred office I bear might surely have protected me from the foul insinuation thou hast thrown out."

"Well," exclaimed Sir Gaston, "thou hast asked me if I have not an elder brother living at this time. To this I can only answer that I am not aware of it, though I must frankly acknowledge that such a rumour has reached my ears."

"And did the same rumour afford a hint where thy long-lost brother was to be found?"

"It did not."

"Nor hast thou, I suppose," asked the monk, "made any enquiries on the subject?"

"It was not my business to do so," replied Sir Gaston, "nor was it very likely that I would seek after one who, being found, would deprive me of almost all that I possess in the world. I have, therefore, taken pains to contradict the report of his being alive, and have even invented others to convince people that he perished many years ago."

"But I believe," observed the monk, "he is at this very moment in England."

"I have heard so, but never could give any credit to so improbable a story."

"Yet I believe it is almost certain that he is in this country," replied Father Francis, "and that he is content to remain in poverty and obscurity rather than, by a disclosure, bring shame and disgrace upon that brother who has seized upon his vast wealth."

"Hah!" exclaimed Sir Gaston; "thou speakest boldly, monk; but I warn thee to be cautious of thy words, lest my anger should burst forth and overwhelm thee."

"I am not to be terrified by thy threats, Sir Gaston de Neville," answered the confessor, firmly; "nor do I seek to raise the anger of one who is helpless; but I would bring thy heart to repentance, and urge thee to do justice whilst it is yet in thy power to do so."

"Or, in other words," answered the knight, "thou wouldst take advantage of my present helplessness, and insult me by the freedom of thy speech. But even now I am not quite powerless, as thou shalt find to thy cost, if I am provoked much further by thy words."

"Wouldst thou slay me for merely reminding thee of the justice thou dost owe a long-suffering brother?"

"I owe him no justice," answered Sir Gaston; "I always hated him for standing between me and the wealth that was to descend from our father. Circumstances have since then favoured me, and for years past have I enjoyed the rank and affluence I once thought was destined to be his."

"And have you no pity, then," asked the priest, "for one so nearly allied to you?"

"I have told you I hated him," answered Sir Gaston.

"Then he, at least, has not returned evil for the injuries thou hast inflicted upon him," exclaimed the monk. "For a long time past he has been content to remain in obscurity and poverty, rather than make a disclosure which would have brought ruin and disgrace upon a brother who deserved not his consideration."

"Beware how you urge me further upon this subject," cried Sir Gaston, fiercely. "And yet," he continued, "I see how it is—you have been set on to bring about a reconciliation, which I have sworn never to stoop to, and which no juggling priest like thee shall ever prevail on me to accept."

"You wrong me by the supposition that I have been engaged in this affair by your brother," answered Father Francis; "indeed, I have never seen him, that I know of, nor do I know in what place he has found shelter till the time arrives for declaring himself."

"He is an impostor," exclaimed Sir Gaston de Neville, "or, long ere this, he would have laid claim to the inheritance which I at present enjoy."

"It is pity for yourself," answered the monk, "that has induced him to remain quiet when a word would have restored him to the place you have usurped."

"Again I caution you to beware how you urge me too far," cried the knight, wrathfully. "I am not used to bear insults, nor shall a priest escape my vengeance because he pretends to more sanctity than his fellow men. I, therefore, command thee to depart, lest I call to my assistance those who would promptly obey my orders, even were they to doom thee to a death of violence."

"Thou would then add murder to the black catalogue of crimes already committed?"

"I seek not thy worthless life," exclaimed Sir Gaston, "but insolence cannot always be endured; and shouldst thou persist, it will be but a just punishment for the provocation thou hast given."

"I have only spoken the truth fearlessly," answered the confessor, "and if that has provoked thee, I must plead guilty to the charge. If I fall, however, I have the consolation of knowing that thine own fate is sealed, and that the world will not much longer be encumbered by a monster whose deeds have brought upon him the hatred and contempt of his fellow men. Thy wound will prove mortal, Sir Gaston de Neville; for though thou may'st linger for some time in torment, yet never again wilt thou have it in thy power to injure those who have too long been the victims of thy persecution."

"Accursed priest!" exclaimed the knight, "I shall at least live long enough to give thee up to death. Too much of this insolence have I already endured, and thou shalt not escape the punishment justly due to thee."

As Sir Gaston said this, he sprung from his couch, and, snatching up a sword from the table, was about to plunge it in the body of the monk, when his wound burst out afresh, and, fainting from exhaustion and loss of blood, he fell insensible upon the floor. Alarmed at the noise, a party of the retainers, headed by Michael, rushed into the room, and, seeing the helpless situation of their master, they quickly placed him once more upon the bed, and secured the bandage so as to prevent any further loss of blood. This done, the knight began slowly to revive, and, glancing anxiously round the room, he commanded the retainers to seize upon the priest, and keep him in close custody till they received further orders as to what should be done with him.

"Let him be carefully guarded," he cried, "for I have reason to believe that he meditated my death; and it is, therefore, only just that he should receive condign punishment for a crime that has been so fortunately frustrated."

"Why not lead him away to death at once?" exclaimed Michael; "the priest is no great favourite in the castle, and there's few, I believe, but would lend a willing hand to put him out of the way whenever it pleases you to give the word of command."

"I have committed no crime," said the monk, "and, therefore, Sir Gaston de Neville has no right to proceed against me in the way you have proposed."

"In this castle," exclaimed the knight, "I reign supreme, and no one will dare refuse to execute any orders I may think proper to give. At present, however, it is not my intention to inflict punishment, as I mean you to live a little longer in all the tortures of suspense. Your dungeon shall be the most loathsome that can be found, and my heaviest wrath shall fall upon those whose carelessness may afford you an opportunity to escape from the doom it is my intention to pronounce. You will, therefore, look to him well, fellows, and your reward shall be in proportion to the care with which you execute the orders I have given."

"And why am I to be thus subjected to your tyranny?" demanded the confessor. "Is it because I have spoken the truth too plainly, or that you may get rid of one who, knowing too much, is considered an enemy that ought to be speedily got rid of."

"I shall not bandy words with you," answered Sir Gaston; "so ask me no further questions upon an affair that has already brought you into so much danger."

"Sir Gaston de Neville," cried the monk, "for a brief space you are permitted to triumph over a guiltless man, but, take my word for it, heaven will not much longer suffer your iniquities to go unpunished."

"Bear him away!" exclaimed the knight, furiously; "let him be taken to his dungeon without delay, and see that my orders respecting his safety are strictly attended to."

"Give me instant death, and I will thank you for it," cried Father Francis.

"I have said that you shall live to endure the torture of suspense," answered the knight, "such is my will, and there is no one, I believe, in this castle who will dare to dispute it."

"And all this," murmured the confessor, "has been produced because I would have prevailed on you to repent the evil of your ways. But the thunder of heaven will soon burst on you, and whether I live or die, your fate is sealed, and a few more days will number you among the dead!"

"You may have prophecied truly there," returned Sir Gaston, "but I shall at least have the satisfaction of knowing that you will not escape the doom to which I shall adjudge you. The hours of both of us are numbered, and yet, brief though they may be, mine are more than your own. I shall see you perish, and then I care not how soon the term of my existence is completed."

"Repent, then," exclaimed the confessor; "repent, I say, or terrible will be thy punishment in the world to come."

"Let me hear no more!" cried Sir Gaston, "drag him away, and leave me to myself, that I may have leisure to reflect on the fate that is best fitted for him."

The monk yielded himself with submission, into the hands of his enemies, and directing a look of severe reproach towards Sir Gaston de Neville, he accompanied the retainers from the chamber. Left thus once more to his own reflections, the knight fell into a train of gloomy reflection, for he began to see that fate was working against him, and that even should his wound not prove mortal, he would be compelled to descend from his present haughty eminence, and give place to that brother whose inheritance he had usurped. Yet, where his brother was concealed, or when he would make his appearance, were questions that, though continually passing in his mind, could not be satisfactorily answered. From his recent conversation, too, with Father Francis, it was evident that many of his most secret actions were beginning to be talked about, and consequently he plainly saw that ruin and disgrace were fast approaching him. From this subject his mind wandered to Rebecca and her father, who had endured so much persecution from him, and yet had foiled him in every instance, however well his plans might have been laid. Still, however, he was determined to persevere, and imagining that they had taken refuge in the castle of Black Ivan, he resolved, if his wound permitted, to collect all his retainers together, and lead them against the Outlaw who had defeated his plans in so many instances. Thus he hoped to regain possession of the Hebrew Maiden, and if she still refused to listen to his suit, he determined to sacrifice both her and her father, by ordering their execution to take place with as little delay as possible. Thus would his vengeance be complete, and he cared not then how soon his own death might follow that of his unfortunate victims.

Sir Gaston was still indulging in these reflections, when the door opened, and Bertrand le Noir made his appearance.

" How now," he exclaimed, as the retainer advanced with an appearance of diffidence ; " what news dost thou bring me that thou hast come thus unbidden into my presence ?"

" I come, Sir Gaston," answered the man, " to inform you that the prisoner they just now took from hence, has made a desperate attempt to escape !"

" Hah ! and has he been secured again ?"

" He has, but he seems likely that he will try it again, and I ventured to come here in order that you may give further instructions respecting him."

" Let a guard be put over him," replied the knight, " and should he then escape my fiercest wrath shall light upon the villains that suffer it."

" I have placed a couple of men near the dungeon for that purpose," replied Bertrand. " They, however, seem to know what sort of fate will be theirs in case the prisoner should escape, and the consequence is, that they grumble and say the captive ought to be despatched at once, instead of giving them another chance by which their own lives would be sacrificed."

" Hah !" cried Sir Gaston ; " do the knaves dare to dictate to their master ?"

" They don't wish to dictate," replied Bertrand le Noir, " but, at the same time, they think that if the man is to die, the sooner the job is over the better it will be, since their own safety depends so much upon it."

" And what has their safety to do with it when my commands have been made known ?" demanded the knight. " Have I not said the prisoner shall linger for a time in suspense, and is my pleasure to be thwarted because these fellows will not take the trouble to guard him till I have decided upon his fate ?"

" I have no doubt the men will do their best," replied Bertrand le Noir, " but it appears that this confessor knows some of your secrets, and, if he should happen to escape, I fear the consequences to yourself would be most unfortunate."

" Why, there you speak more to the point," answered Sir Gaston ; " such an event would indeed involve me in some danger, and, therefore, I know not but what my own safety demands that he should be executed without delay."

" When shall he die ?" asked the retainer.

" This night, an hour after sunset."

" And by what method ?"

" Let him be precipitated from the loftiest ramparts of the castle," answered Sir Gaston. " At the hour appointed they must lead him to the place, and remember that you are there to see my orders strictly complied with. Thus I shall get rid of one babbling fool, whose tongue might have secrets that I should tremble to have known beyond the limits of my own castle walls."

" Does he know anything of the Lady Alicia ?" asked Bertrand le Noir ?

" He does," replied the knight ; " in fact he has been just now speak-

ing of her, and from that moment I resolved upon his destruction. He is ensnared, Bertrand, and even the priestly character that he supports shall not save him now that he is so dangerous to me."

"I will myself take care of that," replied the other; "so, rely on it this night shall remove all your fears from that quarter. The confessor shall find a way to heaven from the castle ramparts, and when that has been done, you may with more safety look after the Jewish girl, who has contrived to slip out of our fingers so many times when we thought her quite safe."

"Your words are fair, Bertrand," exclaimed the knight, "but how can I place dependance upon one who but lately had almost betrayed me?"

"Aye," answered the retainer, "but that was under circumstances of great provocation. I had been made your prisoner, and my life, even, had almost fallen a sacrifice to your violence. That, however, has all passed away now, and you may rely upon me with as much confidence as ever you did in your life."

"And will you assist me in recovering possession of this Jewish maiden, who, but a short time since, you would have protected against me?"

"I will," answered Bertrand, "though to confess the truth, I fancy there's very little chance of our succeeding, if, as we suspect, she has sought the protection of Black Ivan."

"Unless I am mistaken," returned the knight, "Ivan will not much longer boast an advantage over me. A plan for his defeat now occupies my attention, and should I recover from the effects of this wound, a week hence will serve to get everything in readiness. I will then place

No. 90

myself at the head of a strong body of men, and the outlaw shall either perish, or become my prisoner."

"But is it not true," asked Bertrand, "that he has obtained the king's pardon, for saving his life on the day of the coronation?"

"A proclamation to that effect was issued," replied Sir Gaston, "but he has not thought proper to take advantage of it, and he, therefore, still continues under the ban of outlawry. Besides, as a robber, all men should be armed against him, and I believe there are few people but would rejoice at seeing him brought to punishment."

"But the king——"

"Richard is not the monarch that I will ever swear fealty to," interrupted Sir Gaston de Neville, "and, consequently, it matters very little if he should chance to be displeased at my taking an active part against this outlaw. Besides, our plot is still going on, and could we but see Prince John upon the throne of England, my own fortune would be made, and no further chance would remain for those who are opposed to me."

"And does the Prince still encourage you to proceed with this affair?"

"He does; and when the proper moment arrives, will openly assert his claim to the crown. Thousands will then join his standard who now keep aloof from fear, and thus an easy victory will be achieved, in spite of the difficulties that at present seem to stand in our way."

"In my opinion, it will not be quite so easy as you expect," answered Bertrand. "The truth is, King Richard is greatly beloved by his subjects, and ever since our late attempt upon his life, they seem to regard him with even greater affection than before. Besides, it is thought Prince John would be likely enough to prove a tyrant, and that alone is sufficient to prevent his finding many friends."

"Prince John is no friend to the Jews," replied Sir Gaston, "and that circumstance will gain him many on his side, who, otherwise, would be apt to favour Cœur de Lion. Already the populace have shown their hatred of the whole Hebrew race, and the more Richard favours them, the more enemies will he make among the people."

"And yet," exclaimed Bertrand, "I almost wish you would keep clear of a plot that may bring destruction upon you."

"Nay," returned Sir Gaston de Neville, "my affairs can scarcely be rendered more desperate than they are at present. I am out of favour with the king;—my brother is said to be alive, and ready to claim the wealth I have so long held, and even my wife is now at liberty, and may publish to the world a story that would bring upon me the scorn of all those who profess to worship honour. Look which way I will, I see nothing but gathering clouds, and, ere long, the storm will burst and verwhelm me with destruction."

"And to avoid it," observed Bertrand, "you have hazarded yourself in the cause of Prince John, who, you expect, will protect you from all these fancied perils."

"I have his word for it," replied the knight.

"But the word of a prince is not always to be taken," cried Bertrand le Noir; "he will smile graciously enough upon you, no doubt, as long as he needs your services, but see him once firmly established upon the throne, and he would regard those who assisted him to it as no better than traitors to their late sovereign."

"You seem to have but an unfavourable opinion of the prince," observed Sir Gaston.

"I think of him now as I always have," answered the retainer. "I have myself perilled my life in his service, as you well know. In fact, at this moment I am denounced, and a price offered for my apprehension, on a charge of having made an attempt on the king's life. Yet, Prince John has never done aught to rescue me from the dilemma, and I might have perished before he would have put forth a hand to save me."

"You forget," replied Sir Gaston, "that he cannot interfere in the affair without bringing upon himself a suspicion that he was himself concerned in the business. The king already regards him with distrust, and should it be really known that he aspires to the crown, his high rank and near relationship to the sovereign, would not protect him from the consequences."

"And yet." exclaimed the other, "you would risk life, fortune, and honour, in the service of a prince, who, in my opinion, is not deserving of your regard."

"I have certainly undertaken to do so," answered Sir Gaston de Neville, "and, if this wound hinders me not, I shall yet prove that I am sincere in the cause. But how comes it, Bertrand, that you, who, a few days since aimed a deadly blow at the king's life, are now so changed in opinion that you can speak thus of the prince?"

"It is easily explained," replied Bertrand; "the truth is, I see much danger in the affair, and as I have no wish to meet the fate of a traitor, I intend to become loyal to the king, and thus obtain pardon for my former evil doings."

"And your first step, I suppose," observed the knight, "will be to denounce all those who have taken part in this affair against the king?"

"Not whilst my doing so would bring you into danger," replied Bertrand le Noir; "I have hopes, however, that you will change sides, and if that's the case, I think there can be no doubt the king will forgive the past, and take you into his favour in future."

"I would not accept his pardon upon any terms," exclaimed the knight, haughtily. "I have been wronged by him, and he has interfered between me and the Hebrew Maiden, when, but for him, she must have been mine."

"Why, to be sure, you have not much to thank him for on that account," answered the other; "his majesty was certainly rather angry at finding his commands were disobeyed, but I dare say all that has been forgotten long before this time, and, therefore, I should advise you to forget this Rebecca, who, after all, has caused you a great deal more trouble than she is worth."

"But I will never submit to be defeated," exclaimed Sir Gaston; "it is true that the love I once bore her is turned to hate, but there is yet vengeance to be obtained, and I will have it, even though I perished in the very act by which I sought it."

"It seems, you will run some danger in seeking her," observed Bertrand; "for if she and her father have taken refuge, as we suspect, in the outlaw's cave, they will not be captured without great risk. His men are resolute fellows, as we have had occasion to experience, and if he gives the command, there's not one of them but will die fighting in their defence, rather than surrender them into your hands."

"It seems then," exclaimed Sir Gaston, "that I must not expect your assistance when this attempt is made."

"Nay, I said not that," answered the retainer, "at your desire, I will put aside my own scruples, and I'll promise that there will not be one among your followers who will enter into the affair with more zeal than myself. Black Ivan and myself have an old grudge to settle, and I don't know but this opportunity would be quite as good as any other.",

"You will go with us then, as soon as my wound will permit me to leave the castle?"

"I will."

"And in the meantime you will not mention the subject to any one about the place?"

"Upon that you may rely."

"And touching this affair in which I am engaged against King Richard," continued the knight; "will you reflect upon it, and, if possible, give me your aid? Remember there is money to be made by it, and it will therefore, be worth your while to consider the matter well before you throw away so good a chance."

"But the money is not to be earned without running a very great chance," observed Bertrand le Noir. "Besides a reward has been offered for my apprehension, and should I happen to be discovered, there would be an end of the affair at once; I should die the death of a dog, and those that abetted me in the affair, would get off, perhaps, with suspicion."

"Why, where's the courage that I at one time thought you possessed?"

"My courage remains as firm as ever it was," replied Bertrand le Noir; "but experience has made me a little wiser, and I begin to see that there are men who will always keep out of danger themselves, whilst they get fools to do their dirty work. Prince John has ambition enough to aim at gaining a throne, but he has not the courage to appear in the affair. So, for my own part, I am not inclined to run a risk that may very likely end in my own death upon a gibbet."

"I suppose then," observed Sir Gaston, "that you do not mean to join me?"

"It is most likely I shall wish to keep myself out of danger," replied the retainer. "At any rate such is my present determination, whatever reason I may hereafter see to change it."

"Leave me, Bertrand," exclaimed the knight in a tone of displeasure; "I would now be alone, but let me once more caution you never to breathe a syllable of what has passed to any one. You will now prepare for the execution of Francis, and remember, an hour after sunset he is to be hurled from the highest turret of the castle. When that is done return hither to me, that I may know your task has been executed."

Bertrand le Noir made no reply, but instantly quitted the room, leaving Sir Gaston to ponder over the things which now occupied his attention.

CHAPTER CXIII.

Hear me, and mark me well, and look upon me
Directly in my face—my woman's face—
See if one fear, one shadow of a terror,
One paleness dare appear, but from my anger,
To lay hold on your mercies.

BONDUCA.

Upon leaving the presence of the Knight Templar, Father Francis was conveyed to a chamber at the top of the loftiest tower belonging to the castle, and where he was to remain a prisoner till the hour appointed for his execution arrived. Hitherto he had believed that his sacred character would preserve him from violence, but the grim looks and sullen answers of Michael at length dissipated the hope, and he began to entertain certain misgivings that his life would be sacrificed for the honest plainness with which he had reproved the vices of the imperious Sir Gaston. He then questioned Michael more closely upon the subject, but the fellow maintained a dogged silence, and merely hinting that he had better pass his time in prayer and repentance, he abruptly quitted the chamber, and with great care secured the door so as to prevent even the slightest probability of his prisoner's escape.

It now became evident to the confessor that no regard would be paid to his priestly character, and that unless he speedily made an effort for his release from captivity, a violent death would pay the forfeit of his temerity. Inspired by this thought, he instantly rose from the bench upon which he had thrown himself, and made a careful examination of the room, in order to see what chance of escape presented itself; but a brief space of time served to convince him that no hope of preserving himself remained, unless he could by any means contrive to remove the bars from the windows, and then lower himself to the ground. Rendered desperate by his situation, the monk exerted all his strength to tear away the iron stauncheons which impeded his design, but his feeble arm was unequal to the task he had taken upon himself, and he was at length compelled to abandon his object in despair. Yet even had he succeeded in removing the bars, the height of his chamber from the ground must have precluded the possibility of his escape, and with a heavy heart he again sat himself down to deplore the terrible fate to which his own honest zeal had hurried him. Occupied in these reflections a couple of hours passed away, at the end of which time he was roused by the sound of creaking bolts and bars, and when these had been removed, Michael again presented himself, bearing with him a basket of provisions, which he placed upon the table, and was about to retire without speaking, when the monk in an earnest tone demanded of him whether his fate had been decided on.

"It's no business of mine to answer a parcel of questions," replied the fellow; "Sir Gaston will do as he likes, I suppose, and whatever he thinks proper to order, we, of course, are bound to obey."

"Would you aid in the murder of a priest?" demanded the confessor.

"Aye, if the priest has been mad enough to interfere with things he has no business with," answered Michael. "It seems you have mortally offended the knight, and I, who am but a retainer, must obey his commands, whatever they are."

"Sir Gaston," cried the other, "will not surely dare to lay a hand of violence on one whose duty it was to check him in the career of crime he was following. I have done him no injury, and even if I had, he has no right to take away the life of a fellow creature."

"That's a reflection that will give him very little trouble," answered Michael. "The truth is he knows himself to be lord paramount in his own castle, and when once a person seriously offends him, he gets rid of him in the shortest way he can."

"Aye, by the murder of his victims?"

"You may call it murder, but *he* calls it justice," replied the other. "You have spoken your mind a little too freely to him it seems, to be a chance of your blabbing some of the secrets of the castle, it's natural enough that he should take the best means he can to prevent it. Besides there are plenty of priests in the world, and you would not be missed from among the number."

"But this crime cannot be kept long secret," exclaimed Father Francis, "and when the report comes to be spread that a monk has been slain he will meet that terrible punishment which he has but too long es. caped."

"And who think you will take up the affair ?"

"The king."

"You are deceived," answered the retainer, "for King Richard has enough to do to look after his own safety, without meddling in an affair like this. A single hour may be sufficient to see him driven from the throne, and in that case my master would find himself in high confidence with his successor."

"I am aware of the treasonable plot in which he is engaged," exclaimed Father Francis, "but he knows not the danger which would enthral him, even should Prince John succeed in gaining forcible possession of the crown. He would regard with distrust those who had taken part against their king, and his first act would be to rid himself of those whose next plot would be directed against his own person. I know the prince to be cruel and vindictive, and looking only to his own safety, he will crush the very men by whose aid he mounts to sovereign power."

"And if he does, it's no business of mine," replied Michael, with the utmost indifference. "I shall take care to keep myself out of danger, and it will matter very little to me who gets into trouble about it."

"You will not assist Sir Gaston then in his plots, should he recover from his wounds?"

"I will not."

"If I understand rightly, you do not consider yourself bound to obey all the commands of your master ?"

"Certainly not."

"And yet you will take away my life, in the event of his giving an order to that effect?"

"I would," replied the fellow; "but that's different altogether, for, as I said just now, there are plenty of priests in England, whilst there's only one king, and to lend a hand in putting him out of the way might get me into a dilemma that might be likely enough to cost me my life."

"It may happen," said the confessor, "that I have wronged him in the belief that he intends to take away my life. Fierce and vindictive as he is, it can hardly be credited that he will order my execution, for no other crime than the one I have been guilty of. I would have warned him against the evil consequences of his ways, and surely he cannot reward me for it with death."

"I can only say that it is his present intention to do so," replied the other. "Orders have been given to carry his design into effect, and tonight will be the last of your existence."

"Let him beware of the wrath that will follow," exclaimed the confessor; "heaven will not suffer the crime to go unpunished, and his own doom will quickly follow the execution of his iniquitous sentence."

"Perhaps so," answered the retainer; "but that can afford very little consolation, since it will not preserve your own life a moment beyond the time he has decreed."

"And when am I to die ?" asked the priest; "you said to-night, but surely he will give me more time than that to make my peace with heaven."

"Pshaw! what does a holy man like you want with more time?" asked Michael. "You, of course, are always ready to be called away at a moment's notice, and since you are so sure of entering heaven, one would think the sooner you cry quits with this world the better."

"All mortals are frail and erring," cried the confessor: and a few hour's preparation is not sufficient to obtain pardon for the faults of a whole lifetime."

"Humph! you want to gain a little more time then?"

"I do indeed."

"And how do you expect to get it?"

"Through your means," answered Father Francis;" go to him from me and say that the only favour I ask of him is, that he will suffer me to live another week."

"Do you think I am mad?" exclaimed Michael; "would you have me do that which would be sure to bring upon me the rage of Sir Gaston de Neville? No, no, it is my business to obey his orders, not to interfere with the will of a man that never brooks contradiction."

"Alas!" sighed the monk, "then I have no hope left?"

"Not the slightest," answered the other; "your doom has been pronounced, and therefore I would advise you to make the best use you can of the little time that remains to you in this world. Besides, it will soon be over, and I should think death can have but few horrors for a man that has spent his days in the service of religion."

"I ask but a brief time for prayer and repentance."

"And that," replied Michael, "you are not likely to get. Sir Gaston is a man that seldom changes a resolution which has once been made, and as he has reason to believe that your escape would get him into trouble, he will listen to no prayer for delay."

"Yet the time may come," exclaimed the confessor, "when he would give all he possesses for just as much grace as I now seek from him."

"Very likely," answered Michael, in a tone of indifference, "but I don't suppose he troubles himself with thinking much of that just now. He looks only to the present moment, and leaves that which is to come to chance. So now I'll bid you good bye for the present, and when next I come to pay you a visit, I suppose it will be for the last time."

"Will you not take my message to Sir Gaston?"

"I have already given you an answer on that subject," replied Michael, "and all you can say will not make me depart from my resolution. So farewell, and make the best use you can of the little time which is left."

And with this the retainer hurried away from the chamber, and having again carefully secured the door, he descended from the turret with as much unconcern as if the life of a fellow-creature had not been at stake.

Despairing of all success, Father Francis made one last effort to remove the bars from the window, but again his strength was found unequal to the task he had taken upon himself, and yielding to the agony of disappointment, he turned away with a heart sickening at the destiny against which not a single hope remained. At this moment, however, his ear caught a slight sound at no great distance off, and turning round he saw Edith advancing on tip-toe from the tapestry with which one portion of the chamber was hung. For a moment surprise suspended all power of utterance, and ere he could utter an exclamation of wonder, a signal from the girl admonished him to remain silent till he had heard her explanation.

"Holy Father!" she exclaimed, "be silent as you would save me from the terrible consequences of the step I have taken. No one knows of my visit to you, and should it be discovered, nothing short of death would be the punishment awarded to my temerity."

"Rash girl!" cried the confessor, "why have you thus run a risk which may terminate so fearfully."

"I came," she replied, " to warn you of the fate you have been doomed to meet."

"That I already know," he replied ; " Sir Gaston is thirsting for more blood, and I am to die to-night."

"Aye," she said, such is the stern decree, and nothing but prompt measures can save you from the hands of your relentless enemies."

"It is too late, my good Edith," he exclaimed ; "a few hours only intervene between life and eternity, and I see no hope of escaping from a place that has resisted all my efforts to get free."

"Do you despair then, Holy Father ?"

"I do ; unless, indeed, heaven should interpose its aid to rescue me from my great peril."

"And yet," she replied, " it is still possible to defeat the base plans of your enemies. Crime does not always triumph, and, in this instance, I believe you will see reason to admit that the machinations of the wicked bring with them their own punishment."

"Explain yourself."

" Hush !" she exclaimed in a whisper ! "you must speak in a lower tone, or we shall be discovered. I have come hither by stealth, and should it be known that I have visited you, my life would pay the forfeit."

"How," asked the confessor, "did you contrive to gain admittance to this chamber?—The door is still locked, and I have searched all round to see if there was any secret entrance by which I might effect my escape."

"My contrivance was extremely simple," she replied ; "I followed Michael just now, and whilst he was engaged in conversation with you, I slipped, unnoticed, into the room, and immediately concealed myself behind the tapestry. Unconscious of my presence, he retired, leaving me here, and I would now counsel you how to act under the trying situation you will soon be placed in."

"Heaven will reward you for the zeal that has thus urged you in my behalf," exclaimed the confessor. "I thank you for it with all my soul, Edith ; and yet, I cannot deceive myself so far as to believe that any chance of escape remains."

"You are mistaken," she replied, " for I have despatched a trusty messenger to Sir Reginald Courtney, the king's favourite, and through his means, succour will arrive in time to preserve you from the fate that threatens."

"Kind girl !" cried the monk, "and am I indebted to you for this generous interference in my behalf?"

"How could I do otherwise ?" she asked ; did I not know that the life of a fellow-creature was at stake, and should I stand idly by, when a word might save him ?"

"But your own safety has been hazarded in an effort to secure mine."

"That was an affair," answered Edith, " that I could hardly be expected to think of, when the necessity for exertion was so urgent. Had I hesitated a moment, the consequences must have been fatal to yourself."

"It is quite certain then," exclaimed the monk, " that the rage of Sir Gaston de Neville could only have been appeased by the death of his unfortunate victim ?"

"I myself heard him give orders for your execution this very night," she replied. "He suspects that it was your intention to betray some of the secrets you have heard at confession, and dreading the consequences which such a discovery would lead to, he resolved to save himself at the

expense of your blood. But his weakness will be foiled even at the very moment when all appears most safe."

"I cannot yet believe that anything can be done to save me," answered Father Francis; "it is true you have done much to carry your good intentions into effect, but Sir Gaston is not easily to be foiled, and I feel but too well assured that no assistance which may be sent will be of any avail."

"I am sure it will," cried Edith;—"remember those who are sent will come armed with the king's authority, and should Sir Gaston refuse to listen to them, he will be treated as a rebel to the sovereign, and in that case his castle would be taken from him by force of arms."

"But the knight is well prepared to sustain a siege," replied the confessor, "and those who may be sent by the king would he refuse admittance, till they could obtain it by a vigurous assault."

"And think you Sir Gaston de Neville would risk the fate of a traitor, in case he should fall into the king's hands?" asked Edith, with surprise.

"A desperate man will hazard much whilst there is a possibility of succeeding in his own plans," replied the monk. "He knows that under any circumstances, he has much to dread from the king's anger, and, perhaps, will choose to hold out to the last extremity, rather than yield to a fate which he has every reason to tremble at."

"Yet he must be aware that it will greatly increase the wrath of King Richard, should he dare lay violent hands upon one of the ministers of our religion."

"He has already braved the king's displeasure," answered the confessor, "and being suspected of leaguing with the enemies of his sovereign, it is hardly likely he will hesitate to carry his present design into execution. My

No. 91

fate has been pronounced, Edith, and I fear nothing will save me from the death he has resolved on."

"Woe to him, I say, if a hair of your head is injured!" cried Edith; "heaven itself would rise up against him, and hurl its fiercest lightnings upon the sacrilegious monster who would dare take the life of one who is the teacher of its holy doctrines. But I cannot believe,—reckless as Sir Gaston de Neville is,—that he will venture both body and soul in a crime that must bring with it its own awful punishment."

"Did you chance to hear," asked Father Francis, "the mode by which it is intended to finish my earthly cares?"

"I did," she replied;—"at dusk they are to take you from the chamber to the summit of the tower, and from thence they are to plunge you into the terrific abyss below. Your body would thus fall into the moat, and should it be found, a story would speedily be spread abroad either that you had committed suicide, or fallen in there by accident."

"And the accursed falsehood would readily be credited," exclaimed the father confessor.

"There is no doubt it would, had not I overheard the plot, and taken means to prevent it," replied Edith. "Now, however, it is known that your life is threatened, and should assistance unfortunately arrive too late, there will be some consolation in knowing that the wicked perpetrator of the deed will not escape the punishment he merits. His life will pay the penalty, and then perhaps the castle may come into the possession of some one who is more worthy the rank and wealth which has been so long disgraced by him who at present owns them."

"Have you ever heard," asked the confessor, "who it is that would become lord of this castle, in the event of Sir Gaston's death?"

"Why, to tell you the truth," she replied, "it is rather a dangerous subject to speak upon, and yet I have heard strange whisperings of late that Sir Gaston de Neville is but an usurper here."

"Hah! they say so, do they?" cried Father Francis; "and do they also guess who is the rightful owner?"

"I rather think that is a secret that no one has yet been able to get to the bottom of," answered the girl. "They say, however, that it is an elder brother, who has been unjustly deprived of his birthright, and that is likely enough, though why he has never come forward to make his claim is more than I can very well understand."

"His elder brother still lives," exclaimed Father Francis, "and only bides his own good time to come forward and assert his claim."

"And why," asked Edith, "is not the present as good a time as any other would be?"

"Because he does not wish to throw further odium upon a brother whose crimes have already brought him into the contempt of his fellow men," replied the confessor.

"True; Sir Gaston has met with more consideration than he deserves," cried Edith; "for my own part, I don't see that he has any claim to pity, seeing that he has never shown it to any one else."

"Such, at any rate, is not the feeling of the brother he has injured," exclaimed the confessor. "He can pardon the wrong he has endured, and has even suffered, much rather than plunge Sir Gaston de Neville further in the disgrace which is already attached to his name."

"And is the person you speak of in England?"

"He is."

"Anywhere near this place?"

"He is not far off, though I am forbidden at present to say anything which may lead to a discovery."

"But Sir Gaston is taking measures for your destruction," replied Edith, "and surely that alone would warrant you in any disclosure you might make."

"It is for the sake of him who has so long been deprived of his birth-right, that I maintain the secret," answered the confessor. "I am bound by a sacred pledge, and must not reveal who the brother is till necessity absolutely compels the revelation."

"And yet your life is threatened this very night," exclaimed Edith; "you may perish, and the important secret you possess die with you."

"In the event of my death," replied the monk, "the brother will himself come forward at the proper time to assert and substantiate his claim."

"Have you seen him lately?"

"I have."

"And is he living in poverty?"

"I may not tell you more," answered Father Francis.

"But suppose you escape the fate they intend for you," cried Edith, "would you not in that case seek revenge against Sir Gaston de Neville, by revealing all you know about his base conduct to a suffering brother?"

"Revenge is an evil passion, my daughter, and should never find a place in the human heart," replied the confessor. "Besides, the person who has been most injured is content to endure it without complaining, and why, therefore, should I mar the honourable intentions which have guided him through the trials he has endured."

"Well," cried Edith, "I would give my right hand only to know who the person is that you have been speaking of. I have been thinking over every one that I have ever seen, and among them all I cannot choose the man who is likely to be the brother of Sir Gaston de Neville."

"And yet a very short time might serve to clear up the mystery," replied the monk. "Sir Gaston is now suffering severely from the wound he received in his last attempt to carry off the Hebrew Maiden, and from present appearances, it is extremely probable that he will sink under it. Should that be the case, many hours will not elapse before the rightful owner makes his appearance."

"But has he witnesses to prove that he is the person he represents himself to be?"

"He has," answered the other; "all things can be clearly proved, and those who have to decide upon it will be able to do so in the course of a very brief examination."

"And is Sir Gaston himself aware that he stands upon such dangerous ground?"

"He is but too well aware of for his own peace of mind," answered Father Francis; "he knows the rightful heir is alive, and is in continual dread of his coming forward to make good his claim."

"In that case," observed Edith, "I only wonder he has not taken means to get rid of him. He has people about him who would not hesitate to take the life of his brother if he thought proper to give them the order."

"You say truly, my child," answered the monk; "but it most fortunately happens that he is not at present aware of the person from whom he has to apprehend danger."

"But he may find it out for all that," cried Edith; "and should he do so, the worst consequences may be expected."

"His brother is well aware of that," returned the monk, "and has taken good care to prevent any foul practices. Indeed, should he believe that any danger is to be apprehended, he would at once throw aside the mask, and hurl confusion upon the man who has in the first place robbed him of his patrimony, and would then take his life, for no other purpose than to conceal his former crime."

"You seem, Holy Father, to know a great about this affair of the two brothers?"

"I do, Edith," he replied, "and therein is the secret of the enmity borne against me by Sir Gaston de Neville. He knows I have it in my power to bring ruin and disgrace upon him; and it is through that knowledge that I may attribute the murderous design he has now formed against me. But let him take my life if he thinks fit, for all he can do will not save him from the discovery that must shortly take place."

"I only wish it was going to take place at once," cried Edith, "for then not only would the castle come into the possession of the rightful owner, but the poor Lady Alicia would be released from the melancholy situation to which she has been reduced by the cruelty of her husband."

Here the conversation was abruptly broken off, for the dusk of evening was approaching, and a sound was heard at the bottom of the staircase, which announced the arrival of the persons who had been appointed to carry into effect the doom which had been passed upon the monk. Edith now found that no time must to be lost, and that she must conceal herself again behind the tapestry, in order to avoid being seen by those who were coming to the chamber. Taking a poniard, therefore, from the belt that encircled her waist, she put it into the hands of the confessor, saying—

"Take this, holy father, and if need be, defend your life against the villains, who are hurrying this way to seek your destruction. Nay, shrink not from its touch, for though a man of peace, it behoves you to protect yourself from the attacks of villany. It may prove a friend to you in the moment of your greatest need; and my advice is that you hesitate not to strike it into the heart of him who first advances to hurl you from the ramparts. Remember my injunctions, and you may yet be saved."

Having uttered these words, she darted behind the tapestry, and scarcely had she sought this place of concealment, when the door again turned on its creaking hinges, and Bertrand le Noir, Michael, and three or four other retainers, entered the chamber.

"Now, old man," exclaimed Bertrand, harshly, "I have come to announce that the last hour of your life has almost come to a close. You must accompany us to the place appointed for your execution."

"By whose orders have you been sent on this cruel errand?" demanded Father Francis.

"By those of our master, to be sure."

"And by what right does he take upon himself to rob a fellow-creature of his life?" asked the monk.

"I didn't stop to ask him that question," replied Bertrand, with indifference. "All I know is, that he has given us directions what to do, and it would be more than my life is worth to disobey him."

"And because it is his command," exclaimed the old man, "you would lend your hand to the commission of a cold blooded and unprovoked murder."

"Come, come," cried Bertrand le Noir, "it's no use preaching to us, I tell you. We've got our orders what to do, and it ain't a foolish old priest that is going to frighten us out of our duty. So follow us quietly or some of these fellows will carry you to the place without much ceremony."

"I shall offer no resistance where it can be of so little service to me," answered the monk, calmly. "You have come, I see, fully prepared to execute the fiendish task, and if it is the will of Heaven, I must submit to it."

"There's no help for you, old man," exclaimed Bertrand, "and so it's better for you to do so. Besides, a fellow like you, that has passed his time in prayer and all that sort of thing, can have very little reason to be afraid of meeting death. It is but a leap from the battlements of the castle, and all will be over as comfortably as possible."

"I fear not death," answered the confessor, with composure; "but I deny the right of your imperious master to take away my life without a trial."

"You may deny what you please," exclaimed Bertrand; "but all you can say or do will have very little effect upon men who are not inclined to listen to you."

"We have no time to waste in talk," interposed Michael; "our orders are to execute this affair at dusk, and woe be to us if the time should pass without everything being fulfilled to the very letter. Our own lives would answer for it, and we should be fools indeed to run such a risk when we know the consequences."

"Hallo!" exclaimed Bertrand, stooping and picking up a female's slipper from the ground, "what, in the devil's name, have we got here? A shoe, by all that's mysterious; and, a woman's, too, so that it's clear enough it don't belong to the prisoner here."

All now turned their gaze towards the object which had attracted the attention of Bertrand le Noir, and a general wonder seemed to have seized them, as to how such a thing could have got into the room. That it was a female's slipper was, however, certain; and it, therefore, was evident enough that some one had found her way into the room since it was last visited by Michael, and that being alarmed at their approach she had fled, and in her haste had lost it from her foot. But, how any person could have gained access was the next wonder that occupied their attention, for the door was found exactly as it had been left by Michael, and it was, therefore, quite evident that she could not have obtained an entrance that way. Next the window was carefully examined, and as it was found impracticable for any one to have got in that way, they began to question the prisoner as to who his visitor had been; how she contrived to get in, and what had become of her."

"You have asked many questions," replied the old man; "but, for reasons of my own, I shall not answer them."

"Will you deny that this slipper belongs to a female?" asked Bertrand le Noir.

"I do not."

"Then tell me to whom it belongs, or we shall take means to force you to a confession."

"That you cannot do," replied the monk; "you may torture me on the rack, but not one word shall you force from my lips that may serve to injure the innocent."

"Ah!" exclaimed Bertrand, "you confess then that some one has been here, though you do not choose to say who it was."

"I confess nothing," answered the old man; "you have found something that you imagine proves I have had a visitor here, and you must prosecute the enquiry among yourselves, for not a word of explanation shall I condescend to give."

"You are insolent, old man," exclaimed Bertrand; "but you must not tempt me too far or I may apply the torture before we execute the task ordered by Sir Gaston de Neville."

"I can laugh your threats to scorn," replied the old man, calmly. "Torture me if you will, but your trouble will be thrown away, since nothing shall ever induce me to say a word more upon the subject."

"It matters not, Bertrand," exclaimed Michael; "for we have proof enough that some one or other has been here, and, in my opinion, the slipper is exactly like those that I saw Edith wearing this morning. That girl is always prying about, and I would lay a wager that it will turn out she has somehow contrived to get into the room."

"In that case she must be somewhere about," replied Bertrand le Noir; "so let a strict search be made, and if our suspicions prove correct, I would not be in her situation when she comes to stand in the presence of Sir Gaston de Neville."

Upon this they commenced an active search round the room, and one of the fellows throwing aside the tapestry, discovered Edith panting and ready to expire with terror at the perilous situation in which she found herself. She was not, however, suffered to remain long there, for Bertrand, seizing her by the arm, dragged her violently into the room.

"So, we have found you, huzzy, have we," he exclaimed, in a voice almost choked with passion; "and a very pretty day's work you will find you have made of it, when Sir Gaston de Neville comes to hear of what has been done."

"Indeed, indeed, I meant no harm," cried Edith, with alarm. "I knew Father Francis was confined here; and, knowing how little he deserves this cruel treatment, I came to bid him keep up his spirits, because I was sure Sir Gaston has too high a regard for his holy character to offer a pretence against his life."

"Then you are much mistaken," replied Bertrand, "for our master has given orders that he dies within an hour."

"And, I suppose," said the terrified girl, "he will now order me to die at the same time!"

"If he does it will be nothing more than you deserve," exclaimed Bertrand le Noir, "you have visited a prisoner without permission; and, no doubt, you will make it your business to chatter it to everybody you meet with. But that must be prevented at any rate, and the only way that I know of to stop a woman's tongue is to put her out of the way with as little loss of time as possible."

"Well, I care not for that," said Edith; "but though you may kill me—you cannot prevent the mischief that has been done before this time."

"What mean you, girl," exclaimed Bertrand; "surely you have not had the audacity to do anything that will bring Sir Gaston or ourselves into trouble?"

"I shall leave you to find out," she replied; "so now you may kill me as soon as you please: and, when that is done, look out for yourselves; for, as sure as you are standing there, your own turn will come before you are many hours older."

"Tell me what you have done," roared Bertrand, furiously; "tell me, I say, what mischief you have been making, or this dagger shall, in another instant, be sheathed in your heart!"

"Forbear!" said Father Francis, interposing himself between the ruffian and his victim; "forbear, I implore you, and shed not the blood of an innocent girl, whose only fault consists in her having pitied an old man that stands upon the very threshold of eternity."

"Peace!" exclaimed Bertrand, "and dare not to interfere in an affair that concerns you not. This girl, by her own confession, has done something to bring destruction upon us, and dearly shall she pay for it. Her life is forfeited, and she may be assured Sir Gaston de Neville will not fail to take the vengeance she so justly merits."

"Alas!" groaned the old man, "will he order her also to be murdered by his cowardly hand?"

"He'll order her to be dealt with so that she shall not have an opportunity to injure him any further," replied Bertrand. "She is an enemy too dangerous to live; and if she has thought proper to make a talking about one thing, there's no knowing what further mischief she may take into her head to do. There are many affairs that have taken place in this castle which it would not do to have known to all the world."

"She will not speak of them if she knows the consequences her imprudence would lead to," cried Father Francis; "you may depend upon it you will be safe let the secrets that are in her keeping be what they may."

"Aye, aye," muttered Bertrand, "they'll be safe enough, no doubt, because we shall take care to make them so. However, we have no time to talk about that now. So one of you fellows take the girl down stairs whilst we lead the old man to the ramparts, and finish the business we have undertaken."

Upon this Edith was immediately forced from the room, and then Bertrand and Michael, each taking an arm of the old man, dragged him up the narrow flight of steps that led to the roof of the turret in which he had been imprisoned.

CHAPTER CXIV.

" So stands the Thracian huntsman with his spear,
 Full in the gap, and hopes the hunted bear;
 And hears him in the rustling wood, and sees
 His course at distance by the bending trees,
 And thinks—' Here comes my mortal enemy,
 And either he must fall in fight, or I.' "

PALAMON AND ARAIDE.

HAVING reached the place from whence they intended to precipitate their unfortunate victim, the two ruffians released his arms, and stepped a pace or two back from him, as if to torture him with a view of the dreadful abyss down which they were presently about to hurl him. Bertrand gazed upon him, as if expecting to gratify himself with his terrors at the fate that was impending; but the confessor stood firmly erect, and, casting his eyes towards heaven, seemed to be earnestly imploring that mercy which man had denied him. Somewhat disappointed at this result, Bertrand broke in upon his meditations by demanding sullenly whether he was ready?

"Quite," was the brief and calm response of the old man.

"Humph!—and do you mean to say you feel no alarm at the near approach of death?" demanded the ruffian.

"None whatever," answered the old man: "my reliance is on heaven, and I can meet my fate without a murmur, or a wish to prolong a life which has already proved sufficiently burdensome."

"You mean to say, then," exclaimed his tormentor, "that death will be a release that you rather desire than otherwise?"

"I do not say that," replied the confessor, "but I expect, even in the eleventh hour, to be rescued from those who seek my life without any just cause."

"Nay," retorted Bertrand, "you cannot say that you have been condemned without cause. Your conduct towards Sir Gaston has provoked it all, and it is not to be wondered at that he has ordered your execution, seeing that there was every reason to fear that you intended to betray him."

"It may, perhaps, suit Sir Gaston de Neville to give that as his reason for murdering an infirm and helpless old man," answered Father Francis, bitterly. "He knows well enough that my death—secret as he endeavours to make it—must eventually be known to the world, and he has formed a plea which he thinks will satisfy the world that his actions have been compelled by my own conduct. But let him say or do as he pleases, the time is not far distant when he will suffer for the thousand tyrannous acts he has done against those who were helpless and at his mercy. Tell him from me to beware, for he will not much longer be permitted to murder and destroy as he has hitherto been doing for his own sport."

"You may depend upon it I shall not take him such a message as that," replied Bertrand le Noir. "I am not yet quite tired of my life, and shall, therefore, seek rather to win his favour than do aught that may in any way serve to excite his wrath against myself. He is not to be offended with impunity, as I dare say you have found out before this time, and as prudence is the best precaution, I shall e'en follow his instructions to the letter, and when all is over, I may expect to receive a reward from him for having been the means of ridding him of one of his enemies."

"I never was an enemy of his and he knows it," replied the confessor. "In this instance I may have spoken the truth a little too plainly, and he has taken the opportunity to make it an excuse for ridding himself of one he begins to grow afraid of."

"Why you don't mean to say," exclaimed Bertrand, "that a knight like Sir Gaston de Neville is afraid of a pitiful priest who is utterly powerless before him?"

"His own evil conscience is continually gnawing at his heart," replied the old man; "and knowing as he does the many crimes he has to answer for, it is not to be wondered at if he takes everybody about him to be his enemies. Nay, a word from me, and he becomes a beggar and an outcast."

"Indeed! then there can be little wonder that he is so anxious to get rid of you."

"It is not that alone that has prompted him to this deed," replied Father Francis, "but his own thirst for blood. All who offend him, either die or become his prisoners for life; and I, perhaps, ought to thank him for having chosen to put me out of my miseries at once."

"And yet death is not so pleasant a thing to most of us," observed Bertrand le Noir. "Look about you, old man, and tell me whether it is not better to live in this fair world, than to die and go you know not whither?"

"They alone fear death who have pursued a course of crime," answered the confessor. "You, doubtless, look forward to it with horror; but I, who have endeavoured to do all the good in my power, can regard the change as one that will bring me to happiness."

"You mean to say, then," exclaimed Bertrand, "that you are not afraid of the near approach of death?"

"I have no occasion to be so."

"Well, then, the sooner we bring the affair to a conclusion the better," cried the ruffian, and seizing Father Francis by the arm, he dragged him with the strength of a giant towards the edge of the battlements, down the dizzy heights of which the confessor cast an anxious eye in search of the succour of which Edith had given him hopes. Nothing, however, was to be seen, and wishing to gain some little time, he earnestly besought permission to address a few prayers to heaven ere he was hurried headlong into eternity.

"And what can a man like you want with prayers?" demanded the ruffian; "haven't all your life been devoted to that sort of thing, and do you believe a few more muttered over at the last moment can be of any service?"

"It may be of the greatest service," answered Father Francis, again looking anxiously in the direction from whence the expected assistance would arrive. "A few minutes cannot make any difference to you, whilst to me it may be the means of obtaining salvation."

"Well, go on, and be quick about it," exclaimed Bertrand le Noir. "And yet," he muttered to himself, "there may be some trick about it to gain time; but I'll keep a strict watch upon him, and should I see any chance of his escaping, I'll hurl him over the battlements with as little remorse as I would a dog!"

In the meanwhile, Father Francis had thrown himself upon his knees, and was apparently engaged in his devotions, though the truth was, his eyes were strained to pierce through the fast increasing shades of evening. At length, however, his ears caught the faint sounds produced by the trampling of horses at a considerable distance off, and he knew that could he but gain a little more time, he would be saved from the frightful death that threatened him. But Bertrand had also heard the sound, and his suspicions were instantly roused that a rescue was intended. He dreaded the fierce wrath of Sir Gaston de Neville in the event of his victim's escape through any delay on his part, and grasping the confessor by the arms he dragged him from the place where he was kneeling, towards the battlements, down which he was to be precipitated. But the priest was now urged by desperation, and exerting all the strength he possessed, he broke away from the hold of his antagonist, and, with the effort, brought Ber-

No. 92

trand to his feet. Thus released, he was about to rush down the stair by which they had ascended to the roof, but ere he could accomplish this, he was laid hold of by another of the ruffians, who, with many an oath, swore that this time nothing should save him from the doom to which he had been adjudged. It was in vain that the unfortunate man struggled to release himself from the hold of his new antagonist, for his little remaining strength had by this time nearly failed him ; and finding himself dragged with irresistible force to the edge of the fearful precipice, he bethought himself of the dagger with which he had been supplied by Edith. Under any other circumstances he would have shuddered at the thought of shedding the blood of a fellow-creature ; but self-preservation is a feeling so strongly implanted in our nature, that he yielded to the impulse, and having one arm at liberty, he snatched the poniard from the place where he had concealed it beneath his vestment, and with desperate force plunged it into the bosom of his foe. A loud cry of horror burst from the lips of the wounded man, who, falling across the battlements, close to which the struggle had taken place, was precipitated down the fearful height into the moat beneath. For an instant the utmost consternation and alarm succeeded, and then followed a cry for vengeance against the man who had thus preserved his life at the expense of that of one of their comrades. But the priest was well aware of what must be the result of his momentary triumph, and placing his back against a portion of the battlements, he flourished in his hand the still reeking poniard, and vowed to defend himself to the very last.

"Let no one approach me whilst I am thus armed," he exclaimed, furiously, "for I have not been the aggressor in this outrage, and if I must perish, it shall not be till your numbers have been thinned by this dagger. Back, I say, and tempt not a desperate man to shed more blood than has already been spilt in this affray."

" Are ye all cowards ?" cried Bertrand le Noir, addressing himself to the persons about him, " or is this one man to escape when there are so many to overpower him ?"

"It's all very well to say so," answered Michael, who had been among the first to shrink back ; " but who, I should like to know, would willingly hazard meeting the same fate that has befallen our comrade ? The old man seems more like a devil than a priest, and I, for one, shall take care to keep beyond the reach of his arm."

"Coward !" exclaimed Bertrand, furiously, "you will bitterly repent this when Sir Gaston de Neville hears that you have disobeyed my commands."

" Sir Gaston can but give me up to death," answered Michael, "and that I should be almost certain to meet were I to approach a desperate man that is guarded as this one is. We cannot approach him from behind, and the first that approaches is certain to become the victim of his own rashness."

" Then I must myself do that which you are all afraid of," said Bertrand. " One of our number has already fallen beneath his dagger, and thus do I hazard my own life to avenge the death of our friend."

With this, Bertrand le Noir sprang forward and endeavoured to put aside the poniard, but in his attempt to do this, he received a wound in the arm which compelled him to retreat a pace or two ; in a moment, however, desperation again urged him, and once more springing with fury towards the priest, he seized him by the throat, and in the struggle that ensued, they both came down heavily, rolling over and over, and each striving to obtain the mastery which was to save his own life. At length Bertrand succeeded in getting uppermost, and raising his poniard, he was about to plunge it into the body of his prostrate foe, when a messenger arrived with breathless haste, desiring Bertrand le Noir instantly to appear in the presence of his master.

"I will be with him in a few moments," answered the ruffian. "Say that I have but to despatch the priest, and I will obey his commands."

"The old man's life must be spared for the present," exclaimed the messenger. "It is Sir Gaston's command, and your own life will answer for it should he be disobeyed."

"Why, what new whim is this?" demanded Bertrand, sullenly; "but a short time since we were threatened with death if we suffered the priest to escape his doom, and now it seems we have our master's commands to spare him."

"There is but too much reason for what Sir Gaston has done," replied the messenger. "Soldiers have just arrived at the castle under the command of Sir Reginald Courtney, and it seems they have brought a message from the king that has filled our master with dismay."

"And this old man is to escape, though he has slain one of our comrades."

"For the present he must," replied the other; "but I dare say it will not be for long. So put up your dagger, Bertrand, and leave the old man in the care of some of these people while you go to our master."

"Well, I suppose it must be so," growled Bertrand, releasing the confessor, and springing upon his feet; "and yet it's a hard thing, too, to be obliged to spare him after the death of our comrade, and especially when, but for your arrival, he would have met his deserts from my hands. However, there's no help for it, and all I hope is, that Sir Gaston will soon give orders for his execution, and that I may have the carrying it into effect."

We must now go back to Sir Gaston de Neville, who, feeling his wound somewhat better, had risen from his couch to pace the room with slow and unsteady footsteps. From various circumstances that had lately taken place, he began to see that his career of crime and tyranny was fast drawing to a close, and all his thoughts were directed to the various means by which he hoped to postpone the much dreaded moment of his disgrace. He now bitterly regretted many acts of his past life, not, perhaps, because he saw the injustice of them, but because they had involved him in a degree of danger, from which he found it difficult, if not impossible, to extricate himself. The treasonable designs, too, of Prince John, in which he had taken so large a share, were growing more and more desperate every day, for even the king himself was aware of them, and no one knew how soon he might think it prudent to crush their plans, by ordering the arrest of some of the principal parties engaged against him. In that case, Sir Gaston knew that he would be among the first to meet the royal displeasure, and as Richard bore him no good will, there was every reason to suppose he would make an example of him by ordering his execution. This reflection filled him with uneasiness, and dreading the worst consequences, he made up his mind to flee from England as soon as his wound was sufficiently healed. Once safe in a foreign land he intended to offer his military services to the first potentate who might be willing to engage them, and to remain abroad till circumstances should render his return safe. This it seemed to him was his only present hope, and bitterly did he curse the accident which prevented the execution of his plan till at least some few days had passed away.

He could not but confess to himself that his ill-fated passion for the Hebrew Maiden had in a great degree served to accelerate his misfortune, and it was a subject of deep regret that, in spite of all his arts, she had succeeded in escaping the designs he had formed. It was now, however, too late to think of accomplishing his views with respect to her; and as he had all along dreaded lest his treatment of the Lady Alicia should come to the ears of the king, he had some thoughts of seeking a reconciliation with his deeply injured wife, and thus remove one of the charges which he knew would be brought against him. Yet his pride revolted from being the first to make the proposition; and after much consideration, he resolved to wait a brief space, and then to seek the interposition of some friend who would manage the affair for him.

Whilst Sir Gaston was still occupied in these thoughts, the day began perceptibly to draw in, and the approaching darkness reminded him of the fall to which he had adjudged the unfortunate confessor. He now began to regret that he had proceeded to such extremities, and had any of his retainers been present, he would have sent to countermand the order; but he feared it was too late, and whilst he was making an effort to go himself, the door of his apartment opened, and one of his attendants entered.

"Thou hast arrived just as I wanted thee," he exclaimed. "The priest whom I ordered to be cast down from the parapet must be saved. Hasten, therefore, and say that I would instantly have Father Francis brought before me."

"I believe it is too late to think of that now," replied the man; "he was taken from the chamber in which you ordered him to be confined, and by this time there can be little doubt he is lying dead enough in the castle ditch."

"This is most unfortunate!" cried Sir Gaston. "I would have spared his life, and the event that has just occurred may serve to plunge me yet further in the dilemmas that are so thickly closing round me."

"At any rate, neither Bertrand nor any of the others are to blame," retorted the man, "for they have acted by your orders, and to have disobeyed them would have been to bring down your heaviest displeasure."

"True," answered Sir Gaston; "and yet I cannot but wish he had come to consult me once more ere he executed that fatal command. Passion overpowered me, and I have consigned a fellow-creature to death, whom I would now willingly give half my possessions to save."

"He is but a priest," exclaimed the man, "and there are plenty more of that craft left if you have any wish to stock your castle with them. For my own part, I have always found them too meddlesome by half, and I was thinking you were of the same opinion, seeing that you gave one of them to death as an example to the rest."

"It is not from any respect I bear them," replied Sir Gaston de Neville; "but this affair will not pass unnoticed, and I already fear the consequences."

"In my opinion there is nothing to be afraid of," answered the retainer; "he is now safe enough in the castle moat, where I believe there is little chance of his being discovered; and, even if he should be found, who shall say that he came not there by accident?"

"But other charges of a serious nature have been brought against me," returned the Knight Templar; "and it will at once be imagined that he has been slain by my orders."

"Let them believe what they like while there is no chance of their bringing actual proof against you," replied the other. "In this castle you have no treacherous domestics, and I am convinced there is not a man who would say a word to fix you with the deed."

"Perhaps so," exclaimed Sir Gaston; "but it is impossible to feel easy when one's life is at the mercy of others. A bribe might make them turn against me, especially if they hoped to obtain their own pardon at the same time."

"Among the men folks I believe there is nothing to fear," answered the other,—" but there is at least one woman in this place who is hardly to be depended on."

"Aye—and who is that?"

" Edith."

" I thought so," exclaimed the Knight; " that girl has always been an object of suspicion, and I have believed that she only remained in my service in order that she might act as a spy upon every action of my life. But she shall be watched, and should anything occur to prove that our suspicions are correct, she shall be looked after in a way that will effectually put an end to any mischief she may intend me."

" If you wish to have any proof against her," answered the other, " we have lately discovered something that will convince you our suspicions are too well founded."

" Indeed!—what has she done now?"

" Been contriving, I have every reason to believe, the means for the escape of Father Francis."

" Hah!—art thou sure of this?"

" Quite positive."

" How dost thou know it?"

" Because we found her a short time since in the apartment of the prisoner."

"Who gave her admittance there?" demanded the knight.

"That I know not," replied the retainer; " but, if we may believe her own story, she took an opportunity of slipping into the room while Michael was visiting the prisoner, and concealing herself behind the tapestry, she remained there till the confessor was left alone."

"This must be enquired into," exclaimed Sir Gaston; " but does it appear that she made any attempt to set the prisoner at liberty?"

" We have not been able to satisfy ourselves about that at present," answered the other. " We afterwards discovered her by mere chance; in fact, a slipper had been left behind in her hurry to conceal herself when she heard us coming,—and upon searching the room, we found her concealed behind the tapestry, where, of course, she had overheard all our conversation; and, perhaps, the next thing she does will be to go and publish the whole affair to the world."

"Did you question her," asked Sir Gaston de Neville, " as to her motives for being there?"

" No; we asked her but few questions, thinking it would be better to leave that to you."

" Where is she now?"

" In the next room, where I left her till your commands are known upon the subject."

" Let her be brought before me," exclaimed the knight; " and should it appear that her motives were hostile to myself, instant measures must be taken to prevent the mischief she may intend."

Without waiting for a second order the man hastened from the room, leaving Sir Gaston full of alarm lest any fresh danger should occur through the circumstance of the girl's having obtained possession of the secret. Again, thoughts of blood passed through his mind, and he determined to have her instantly despatched, in case he should find reason to suspect that she intended to betray the fact of the confessor's imprisonment, and the fate to which he had been adjudged. In the midst of these reflections the retainer returned, accompanied by Edith, who he dragged, with some violence, into the room.

" Now, girl," exclaimed Sir Gaston, angrily, " it has been reported to me that you have been found prying into affairs with which you have no business. How is this, Edith? answer me, and speak truly, or bitterly will you repent any deceit you may seek to practice on me."

"You are angry with me, Sir Gaston," she replied; "and it would, perhaps, be better that you should question me upon this subject when your passion has a little cooled."

"I will have no equivocation, hussy," he exclaimed, still more fiercely; "speak, or you shall be sent to a dungeon, when you will have an opportunity to reflect upon the baseness you have been guilty of."

"I have been guilty of no baseness that I know of," replied Edith; "I knew Father Francis was in trouble, and took pity upon a man who is so good, that he has no enemies in the castle except those whose crimes have brought down his well deserved rebuke."

"Thou art insolent, girl," cried the knight; "for I know of none in my service, who either deserve or have received any censure from the holy father."

"Indeed!" retorted Edith, "then I, for one, know of several who deserve it; and if they have never been reproved, it must be because the monk kindly closed his eyes to their many and most hideous offences."

"This impertinence must be checked," exclaimed Sir Gaston de Neville, who with good reason imagined these shafts to be directed against himself. "I have already endured too much of it, and a repetition will bring upon you my heaviest displeasure. Now, answer me, Edith, what motive had you for visiting Father Francis, who has given sufficient reason for the severe measures I have taken against him?"

"I had no motive in particular," she replied.

"Had you not an idea that it might be in your power to assist him in escaping from the castle?"

"Indeed I had not," answered Edith; "for situated as his chamber was at the top of the northern turret, it was impossible to have escaped, even if the windows had not been secured with strong iron bars."

"But, perhaps, you were provided with false keys to give him liberty?" observed Sir Gaston.

"I had nothing of the kind," she replied; "when Michael went to visit his unfortunate captive, I took an opportunity of following him unobserved, and glided into the room without anybody guessing that a third party was there. The tapestry served as a place for concealment, and when Michael retired, I came forward and entreated Father Francis to be of good heart, for friends might make their appearance in his behalf when least expected."

"You did!—and what danger did you imagine threatened him, girl?"

"Death!"

"Hah!—and what reason had you for supposing the death of good Father Francis was intended?"

"Your own words, Sir Gaston."

"Beware, girl, how you trifle with me," exclaimed the knight, furiously; "your words imply that I had a design against the life of my excellent confessor."

"And so you had," answered Edith, fearlessly; "oh, you needn't look so black at me; for I am not to be terrified out of speaking the truth. I heard you give orders to some of your retainers, and to prove that I know as much as you do yourself, your commands were that he should be thrown down from the top of the tower where he was imprisoned."

"You hear how freely her tongue runs," whispered the retainer to Sir Gaston; "the girl is dangerous to you, and if it is your wish I will soon remove the cause of your uneasiness."

"It must be so," answered the knight; "and yet if there is any way to avoid it, I would rather spare her life." Then addressing himself to Edith, he continued, "It seems, girl, that you have formed a strangely mistaken notion as to my intentions towards the confessor. The truth is, I esteem him greatly, and would sacrifice my own life, were it necessary, rather than seek to do him an injury."

"Why, then," demanded Edith, "have you made a prisoner of the poor old man?"

"Merely as a slight punishment for some offensive words he spoke to me," replied Sir Gaston, with all the plausibility he could assume. "I was irritated at the moment, and adopted measures of severity that I have been sorry for."

"Indeed!" cried the girl, "then perhaps you will pledge your knightly word that he is at this moment living."

"For aught I know to the contrary he is."

"But you have good reasons for believing the contrary. Oh, Sir Gaston,—your changing countenance betrays you, and the poor confessor has been murdered!"

"Murdered!—nay, you are mistaken."

"If you would prove it, let me see him," cried Edith.

"You have my word for it," exclaimed Sir Gaston; "and surely that ought to be enough."

"Yet, for all that," she replied, "I will not be satisfied till I have seen him alive. I heard you give orders for the murder, and I know there is not one in your employ but would feel a pleasure in executing so fiendish a command."

"Can you endure this?" exclaimed the retainer, drawing his poniard, and anxiously awaiting an order to plunge it into her heart. "Her tongue will betray us, and bring ruin upon all who have been concerned in this affair."

"Peace, sirrah, and put up thy weapon till I bid thee pluck it forth," whispered the knight. "Retire to yonder window, and I will try whether she may not be prevailed on to keep this matter secret."

The fellow sullenly obeyed this order, and Sir Gaston, assuming as much composure as he could, again addressed her :—

"It seems, Edith," he said, "that you have taken into your head a notion that I meant to proceed to extremities with this old man, who has been fortunate enough to find so warm a friend in you; yet, believe me, girl, he is alive,—and in a few hours will be at liberty."

"Convince me that he is so," replied Edith, "and you will have no reason to be afraid of anything I can say."

'Nay, girl, I fear thee not."

"Your words and manner assure me the contrary," she replied. "Had you not thought I might mention this subject, you would not now have condescended to speak thus freely with me."

"Again you mistake my motives. I seek only to convince you that your suspicions have done me wrong."

"But my ears have not," answered Edith, "for I tell you I heard the words distinctly uttered that directed the execution of Father Francis at nightfall."

"Wouldst thou blazon this forth to the world, and thus bring upon me the suspicion of having entertained a thought against the life of a helpless old man?"

"I shall do so," she replied, "but not, perhaps, till I am certain] that my fears are well founded."

"Will a purse of gold prevail on thee to keep silence?"

"'Your castle full of gold," answered Edith, firmly, "would not purchase my silence, when once my suspicions have been confirmed by evidence."

"Beware, girl, how you refuse my offers," exclaimed Sir Gaston de Neville, forgetful of his former caution. "I would have spared thy life, had there been safety in doing so; but thou art obstinate, and it will be thine own fault if I am driven to the last fearful extremity."

"I understand you," answered Edith, "it will be necessary to conceal one crime by the commission of another, and I am to be the next victim of thy malignant passions."

Unable to restrain his fury any longer, Sir Gaston drew his sword with the intention of slaying her, but at that moment, the retainer who had stationed himself at the window, called out in a tone of alarm, that a large party of soldiers had arrived, and were then entering the gate, which had been left open by the terrified warder.

"Hah!" cried Sir Gaston, "then it is too late to bid them defiance. Doubtless, they have been sent hither by the king, and I am betrayed to death and dishonour."

"Shall I call your retainers together," asked the man, "and oppose these troops in the court-yard?"

"It would be in vain to do so," answered the knight; "they have gained an entrance to the castle, and it would but be throwing away lives that may be more profitably employed, should I hereafter need them."

"But should they find out the confessor's death ——"

"It may not be two late to prevent it," cried Sir Gaston, with eager haste; "fly to the northern turret with all speed, and should they not have fulfilled my commands, bid them let him live till they have further orders on the subject."

"And this girl?"

"Must be taken from hence till after I have learnt what has brought these soldiers to the castle. Secure her in some place of safety, and if an opportunity should occur, I will see whether she may not be prevailed on to maintain my secret inviolable. So now, away, for every moment wasted lessens the chance of saving the confessor's life."

Obedient to this command, the retainer left the room, dragging Edith with him, and having locked her in a chamber, he hurried up to the turret, where we have already seen he arrived just in time to save Father Francis from the uplifted dagger of Bertrand le Noir.

CHAPTER CXV.

"The rude ball rocks—they come, they come,
The din of voices shakes the dome;
In stalk the various forms, and, drest
In varying motion, varying vest,
All march with haughty step—all proudly shake the crest."

PENROSE.

ALMOST driven to madness by the dangers that were thickly crowding upon him, Sir Gaston, forgetful of the pain he suffered from his wound, strode with rapid steps up and down the chamber, and listening to each sound, as if it proceeded from the messengers of evil, whom he was momentarily expecting. At length, footsteps were heard ascending the stairs, and Godfrey, a favourite retainer, entered the room with terror and dismay marked in his pale countenance.

"Oh, Sir Gaston," he exclaimed, "it is all over with us, I fear. The castle is filled with the king's troops, and their captain desires to be intantly brought into your presence."

"Who is the captain?" demanded Sir Gaston.

"I know him not," answered Godfrey, "but some of his men called him Sir Reginald Courtney."

"He is a foe of mine, at any rate," exclaimed the knight, "and his presence here bodes me no good."

"I fear not, indeed, Sir Knight," cried the retainer. "At all events, they seem to have made the castle their home for the present, and I begin to be afraid that they have come on some heavy business from the king."

"Be it so," exclaimed Sir Gaston, with forced resignation. "I have long expected such a visit as this, and am, therefore, prepared for the worst; they may, perhaps, seek my life, but in that my enemies shall be disappointed, for rather will I perish by my own hand, than meet the ignominious doom to which their malice may adjudge me."

"If there is any danger," said Godfrey, "why not place yourself at the head of your faithful band, and drive these intruders far away from the walls they have dared to enter?"

"It would be in vain to do so," replied Sir Gaston, "besides, we are not yet quite certain that they come on a hostile errand, and I would, therefore, rather see their leader ere I decide upon the course I may think it necessary to adopt. Send this Sir Reginald Courtney to me, and should it be the king's command that I surrender myself to him, I may then call upon my faithful retainers to rescue me from the hands of my sworn enemies."

"Nay, be advised by me," exclaimed Godfrey, earnestly, "and do not

No. 93

trust yourself in the power of those who will be too glad of the triumph they have achieved."

"Obey my orders promptly, sirrah," cried the knight, angrily, "and let me see this captain, that I may know the nature of the message of which he is the bearer. I would not have him think that I am afraid to see him, which he will most assuredly think, if I refuse much longer to give him the audience he has demanded."

"You will, at least, allow some of your faithful servants to be in attendance here?" said Godfrey.

"Why, yes," replied the knight, "it may be as well to show the messenger from royalty that we do not receive him as a friend. A score of you may be present; but, remember, I require no interference unless any violence should be offered me."

"Your commands shall be obeyed, Sir Knight," answered the other, and with a humble obeisance, he went to convey his master's message to the captain of the royal troops. This interval was one of extreme pain and anxiety to Sir Gaston de Neville, who now for the first time yielded to the impulse of his own fears; there could no longer be any doubt as to the motive that had led to this unexpected visit, and anxiously as he desired to know the worst, he almost dreaded to meet the person who had been sent to him from the king. His thoughts then recurred to Father Francis, who had been the last victim of his tyranny, and all his hopes were centered in the chance that he had not fallen a sacrifice to the commands he had given respecting him; should he still live, there would be some probability that he might escape the punishment he so much dreaded, for he knew the king could forgive treason against himself, though it would be impossible to extend to him his royal clemency in case a murder should be proved against him. These thoughts troubled him exceedingly, and bitterly did he now regret the waywardness of his heart that had hurried him into acts which had thus involved him in a labyrinth of difficulties, from which he saw it would be almost impossible to extricate himself.

Whilst he was thus occupied, he was startled by hearing the measured tread of soldiers, as they marched along the passage that led to his chamber; and scarcely had he time to compose himself when Sir Reginald Courtney made his appearance, followed by his archers, who ranged themselves along one side of the room. Almost at the same moment an equal number of Sir Gaston's retainers entered by another door, and placed themselves immediately behind their master, in case he should find it necessary to call upon them for their assistance against his foes. Sir Reginald Courtney observed this, but for the present he took no further notice of it, and, approaching the Knight Templar, he said—

"I have been despatched hither, Sir Gaston de Neville, by my king, on an affair that I most sincerely wish had devolved upon other hands. You have long been suspected of treason, and our sovereign has now obtained proofs that have placed the matter beyond all doubt."

"The king can have no proofs against me," replied the Templar, haughtily. "That I have enemies about his royal person I am but too well aware, but even the worst among them can only support the foul charge with his own words."

"You are mistaken there," exclaimed the officer, "for we have letters of your own, in which you not only advise how certain measures shall be executed, but even the king himself is styled a usurper, whom it is necessary to slay, in order that another may ascend his throne."

"Indeed!" ejaculated the Knight Templar, incredulously; "and pray, Sir Reginald, where have you contrived to discover these precious documents?"

"In the palace of Prince John."

"Ah! has he proved false to his friends?"

"I believe it will turn out so in the end," replied Sir Reginald Courtney. "At present, however, he is placed in the same situation as yourself—a guard has been left to keep a strict watch over him, and he may, therefore, consider himself a prisoner during the king's pleasure."

"This is indeed strange news, Sir Reginald," cried the Templar, "and perhaps it will not be esteemed too great a favour to inform me upon what grounds the prince was suspected of being engaged in a plot against the king?"

"He has been suspected for some months past," answered Sir Reginald Courtney, "and every pains have been taken to withdraw him from a plot which it was clearly foreseen could end only in his own destruction. Nay, the king himself has told him that he knew all that was going on, and offered him pardon for the past on condition that he would become faithful to him in future."

"But the prince surely was not the first to betray a cause in which he took the principal part?"

"He was not," replied Sir Reginald; "in fact, you had a spy in the camp, and he it was who revealed the secret which has been the cause of my visit here to-day."

"Name him to me," cried Sir Gaston de Neville, hoarse with passion, "and, were it the last action of my life, I would lay the villain dead at my feet."

"At present," exclaimed the other, "you must remain in ignorance of that fact. My present business here is to arrest you on a charge of high treason, and place you in secure custody till a strict enquiry has been made into a charge that affects not only your honour and reputation, but your life also."

"The villain has basely lied," vociferated Sir Gaston de Neville; "I have never been disloyal to my king, and I will defy my worst enemies to prove the slander which they have uttered against me for their own evil purposes."

"Again I tell you we have your own handwriting to prove your participation in the affair."

"That may turn out to be a forgery."

"Nay," retorted the other, "that can hardly be, since many of the documents have your own private seal appended to them. I would myself gladly have believed them to be forgeries, and yet, truth to say, there is but too much evidence to convince the world of your guilt."

"I expected nothing else from Sir Reginald Courtney," exclaimed the Knight Templar, haughtily. "He has ever been among the foremost of my foes, and, of course, gladly seizes this opportunity to trample upon a fallen man."

"You wrong me, Sir Gaston," answered the other. "I never was your foe, nor should I have been here now on this unpleasant business had it not been that I was compelled to obey the orders of my king. And even now, I am anxious to occasion you as little pain as possible, by avoiding the publicity which might follow your arrest on so serious a charge."

"Indeed! then why, if you wished not to make the affair widely known, did you come here accompanied with so large a party of your military underlings?"

"There was no help for it," replied Sir Reginald Courtney; "there was reason to suppose you would resist my entrance to the castle if I had come with a smaller force, and my orders were to take you prisoner, without affording you the least opportunity to escape."

"And you have obeyed your orders well."

"I have done nothing more than my duty."

" Yet, for all that," answered Sir Gaston de Neville, "I am not so much in your power as you may believe. These men you see about me are faithful to the chieftain they have so long served, and were I but to pronounce one word, or make one motion with my hand, this chamber would be converted into a scene of blood and slaughter."

" And should it be so," replied Sir Reginald Courtney, "you would be the first victim to fall by your own madness. However, I come not to bandy words with you but to execute the orders of my sovereign; and whether you submit quietly or otherwise, I will never leave this place till I have executed the object that brought me here." And then turning to his soldiers, he said—"Prepare yourselves, my brave fellows, for the worst. Let your bows be bent, but not an arrow must be discharged till I give the word of command; and should it be necessary to resort to that, let your first mark be Sir Gaston de Neville."

" You need fear no violence on our part," exclaimed the Knight Templar, " for I would spare the blood of my faithful people, and will, therefore, submit to the will of him who has sent you hither. I am your prisoner, sir, and now, perhaps, you will deign to inform me where you found the papers which you are pleased to say connect me with this treasonable plot against the king ?"

" They were found among other papers in the possession of his Highness, Prince John."

" And are there any other persons connected with the affair besides myself ?"

" Several, and they are all in custody."

" Then," exclaimed Sir Gaston de Neville, "will some of the best blood in England flow upon the scaffold. The king had enemies even among the highest ranks in the kingdom; and had the discovery not taken place as it has, a few weeks would have served to place the prince on that throne which is now occupied by a tyrant and usurper !"

" Cœur de Lion is neither a tyrant nor usurper," said Sir Reginald, wrathfully. "The throne which he possesses is his by inheritance, and wert thou aught else than a self-acknowledged traitor, I would maintain his right against thy false assertions in single combat. However, I can well make some allowance for thy chagrin at thus beholding the overthrow of the base machinations in which thou hast been engaged against thy lawful sovereign."

" Richard was never an acknowledged sovereign of mine," replied Sir Gaston de Neville, haughtily. "I have endured much from him, and glad should I have been had it been in our power to drag him from the seat he has taken in defiance of the wishes of those he falsely calls his subjects. Thou may'st tell him this, for I am in his power, and I care not what becomes of me."

" It is madness to be thus reckless," answered Sir Reginald; "the king is merciful and considerate, and seeks not the blood of even his worst enemies. Learn, therefore, to think better of him, and he may even yet pardon the heavy offences thou hast committed against him."

" I ask him for neither favour nor mercy," replied Sir Gaston, sullenly; " he knows me for an enemy, and, if I had my liberty to-morrow, the first use I should make of it would be to use my utmost exertions to wrest from his grasp the sceptre he so unworthily holds."

" Wilt thou not take my counsel," exclaimed Sir Reginald Courtney; " and by contrition for the past make some amends for the mischief thou hast sought to do a noble and generous king ? He seeks not to injure thee, but, were it in his power, he will freely pardon the offences you are charged with, and even raise you to an eminence which at present you have no right to aspire to."

"Let him keep his honours for those time-serving slaves who desire them," answered the Knight Templar. "For my own part, I loathe and execrate him, and could I have seen him perish by the hand of an assassin, I could have met my fate with resignation."

"Thou art resolved, then," said Sir Reginald, "to accept no favour from your king?"

"I will take none from him," replied Sir Gaston; "even my life would be a curse to me were I to owe it to his mercy."

"Then shouldst thou perish," exclaimed the officer, "thy blood will be upon thine own head. Mercy will not be denied thee, but it would be granted upon certain conditions which thou wilt not find it very difficult to accede to."

"Aye, Richard, I dare say, would like to see me kneeling and cringing at his feet, like the other abject slaves who think fit to own his power. He would have me whine for mercy, and humbly acknowledge that I have merited a severe punishment for the part I have taken against him."

"King Richard asks no hard terms from thee," replied Sir Reginald Courtney; "all thy transgressions against himself he can freely pardon,—but the wrongs which thou hast done to others must be enquired into."

"Who have I wronged that he must needs interfere with it?"

"Many," answered the other; "it is said thy brother is wandering about in obscurity and want, whilst thou art enjoying the patrimony which is his by right. It is also reported, that thy wife is still living, though she was reported to have died many years ago, when a mock funeral ceremony was performed in the castle chapel, to give some colour to the rumour. Nay, more, she has been cruelly confined in one of thy dungeons, wearing out a life of wretchedness, which has been produced by thine own most unjust treatment."

"'Tis false!" exclaimed Sir Gaston de Neville, fiercely. "There is no such person in the castle as thou wilt convince thyself when thou hast searched it."

"I hope it may prove so," replied the other; "yet still thou wilt have to answer for the Hebrew Maiden, who has suddenly disappeared; and as neither she nor her father have been seen since, it is suspected that you have carried her off to some place where it will not easily be discovered."

"People may suspect what they please," cried the Knight Templar, with the utmost indifference; "but, by the Heaven above us, I know nothing whatever of the girl any more than you do yourself."

"And what has became of Father Francis?"

"I know nothing of him."

"Has he not been cast by thy orders from the battlements of thy castle?"

"Hah! who has told you this?"

"A message to that effect was brought to the palace about two hours since, and the king instantly despatched me hither to see if it might be possible to save his life."

"This, then, must have been the work of Edith," muttered the Knight Templar; "the girl has betrayed me, and her life shall pay the forfeit of her treachery."

Whispering to Godfrey, he commanded the girl to be instantly brought into his presence; and no sooner was this order obeyed, than, with a frown of anger, he exclaimed :—

"It seems, girl, that you have been acting the part of a spy upon me, and that I have been betrayed by one on whose fidelity I have placed the greatest reliance. My castle is filled with soldiers, and I am myself a prisoner, in consequence of the information you sent to the palace."

"I do not deny having done as you have said," answered Edith, calmly,

" but it was done to save the life of Father Francis, who had committed no crime worthy of punishment."

" She confesses it," whispered the knight to Godfrey, who was standing at his elbow. " She it is who has done all this mischief, and, therefore, do I now leave her in your hands; you understand me, sirrah?"

Godfrey made no reply, but drawing his dagger, he was in the act of striking it into his defenceless victim, when Sir Reginald Courtnay springing forward, interposed himself between them, and, with a blow, levelled the ruffian to the earth. All this had passed with the rapidity of lightning, and ere the other retainers could complete the work in which their comrade had failed, Edith was hurried to the further end of the apartment, where she was placed under the care of the archers. As for Sir Gaston, his countenance betrayed the fury which the frustration of his design had given rise to, and in a voice almost choked with rage, he demanded of Sir Reginald Courtnay why he had dared to prevent a punishment which the girl's conduct had justly merited.

" I have done nothing more than my duty," replied the other, " in protecting a helpless female against the cowardly attack that was made upon her life. She has done nothing more than her duty in endeavouring to frustrate the designs you had formed for the destruction of your confessor, and it will be at the peril of any one to attempt her injury, now that I have happily been the means of rescuing her from the fate to which your vengeance would have consigned her."

" She has accused me falsely," exclaimed the Templar, " for I have just been informed that Father Francis is in the next room."

" Will you send for him, that we may be sure that you are not still practising your deceit on us?"

" You have no right to doubt my word," answered the knight; " yet, to prove that I have spoken truly, you shall see him." Then addressing himself to Godfrey, who by this time had recovered from the heavy fall he had received, he commanded him to bring Father Francis into the room. This the ruffian prepared to do with evident reluctance, but seeing no alternative, he at length slowly departed, and, after a few minutes absence, returned with the confessor, who was nearly exhausted with the desperate exertion he had made to defend himself against the fierce assaults of his murderous assailant. The countenance of Sir Gaston de Neville somewhat brightened as he saw that the old man had escaped the fate to which, in the height of his anger, he had adjudged him, and turning towards the officer, he said:—

" You perceive how much reliance may be placed in the word of yonder girl. Her's was an artfully contrived plot to bring my enemies upon me, and yet she is suffered to escape the punishment she deserves."

" I will question the old man ere I give any opinion upon the subject," replied Sir Reginald.

" You can do so," answered the Templar, glancing entreatingly towards the confessor, " and, I believe, he will assure you that no evil has been practised against him."

" How say you, bold father?" demanded Sir Reginald; " have you any complaint to make against Sir Gaston de Neville?"

" As a Christian," answered the priest, " I can freely pardon all that has been done; but since the question has been put to me, I must declare that an attempt was just now made to assassinate me."

" And what were the means used?"

" They endeavoured to throw me over the battlments into the moat beneath;—but desperation lent strength to my nerveless arms, and with the assistance of heaven, I succeeded in preserving myself from destruction."

"And by whose orders was this done?"

"Sir Gaston de Neville."

"In revenge I suppose for some fancied injury you had done him?"

"I spoke my mind too freely, in endeavouring to prevail on him to amend his life," replied the confessor. "My words were perhaps too severe, and as I have happily escaped the peril I can now freely pardon the grievous injury he sought to do me."

"You have heard the old man," exclaimed Sir Gaston; "he has acknowledged that he feels no resentment for what has passed, and, therefore, no one else has any right to pursue this subject farther."

"But your intentions towards him are made no better, because he has pardoned the act that would have robbed him of life," replied the officer. "Besides, he is under no obligations to you, seeing that he owes his preservation entirely to his own exertions, when numbers were opposed to him."

"Was I then to know that I had an enemy," asked the Knight Templar, "and not make an effort to rid myself of him?"

"Not by murder, certainly!"

"You may call it by what harsh name you please," answered Sir Gaston, "but I call it nothing more than self preservation, which is allowable in all cases where there is good reason to apprehend danger."

"And what danger would you have been in from an aged man, whose religion would rather prompt him to do you a service, than urge him to commit an injury? But this is only one act of tyranny and oppression out of the many you have committed for the gratification of your own evil heart."

"Hah!" exclaimed Sir Gaston de Neville, "am I to be bearded then in my own castle?"

"The castle is yours no longer," answered Sir Reginald.

"Liar! who is there that will dare deprive me of it?"

"Oh, you may use what opprobrious terms you please," replied Sir Reginald Courtney, "for I can well endure them from one who is so far sunk in infamy as yourself. Call me what you will, and your words will be treated with the contempt they merit."

"Had I been differently situated," cried Sir Gaston, "you would not have dared utter such words to my face."

"And why not?"

"Because my sword should have avenged the insult you have heaped upon me."

"I have spoken nothing more than I should repeat under any circumstances," answered the other. "Your whole life has proved you to be unworthy the high station you have borne, and now the treason you have plotted against a generous king, ranks you beneath the very lowest of his subjects. These are my opinions of you, Sir Gaston de Neville, and should circumstances favour your liberation, you will find me ready to maintain my assertions with my sword."

"You can boast thus," replied the Knight Templar, "because you have good reason to suppose that I shall never again be at liberty. The king will, no doubt, take good care to rid himself of an enemy that he has just cause to fear, and if I would obtain my pardon, I would not stoop to ask it from one whom I despise."

"Yet you cannot bring forward one instance in which Richard Cœur de Lion has ever injured you by word or deed."

"At any rate he has never rewarded me in proportion to the services I have done him and the nation he governs," answered Sir Gaston. "Others have been raised to eminence without deserving the favour, whilst I, who have fought and bled for my country, have attained no higher rank than I enjoyed when I first took up arms."

"It has been your own fault," replied Sir Reginald Courtney. "The king has all along known you to be a foe, and it was hardly to be expected he would reward the man who was continually plotting for his overthrow. Had you been faithful to your king, he would not have failed to heap honours upon you according to your merits."

"And as it is," exclaimed the templar, "he will punish the man who has fought by his side, by sending him to meet an ignominious death upon the scaffold."

"You wrong him most foully," cried Sir Reginald, "for so far is he from desiring your death that he will grant an immediate pardon upon receiving satisfactory proof that you will become to him a true and faithful subject."

"Which I never will be whilst Prince John lives to claim my allegiance."

"In that case," exclaimed Sir Reginald, "you can have no claim to his mercy. I would that it had been otherwise, but you have yourself wilfully closed the gate of mercy ; and, therefore, I have only one course left to pursue. You must away with me as a prisoner, and if your wound renders your removal difficult, I will order a litter to be instantly prepared for conveying you to the Gatehouse at Westminster."

"Am I then to be imprisoned in a felon's gaol ?"

"You must remain there till the king's pleasure is further known," replied Sir Reginald. "Meanwhile you will have sufficient time before you for reflection, and I will hope you may see the madness of your course, and henceforth become a true and faithful subject to your sovereign."

"There is little chance of that," answered the Knight Templar.

"Nay, I trust you will think better of it," exclaimed Sir Reginald. "At all events do not make matters worse by further irritating the king, and perhaps in the course of time he may soften in his anger towards you. And now, Sir Gaston, if you have any favour to ask I am ready to hear it."

"I have none to ask for myself," he replied, "but I should be glad to know that my retainers will be suffered to remain in the castle till it is seen whether I shall ever be suffered to return to it."

"It is impossible that they should remain here," answered Sir Reginald Courtney ; "your long lost brother is expected to appear shortly to lay claim to the property you have unjustly usurped, and the king intends to hold possession till the person has proved the right which he is about to assert."

"There is no such person in existence," replied Sir Gaston, "he died many years since, and the best proof in my favour is that so long a period has been suffered to elapse without his having made his appearance."

"There may be a reason," answered the other, "which will satisfactorily account for the conduct he has thought proper to pursue. Let that, however, be as it may, you have forfeited all right to the estates by your treason ; and, therefore, the king will seize upon them in behalf of the rightful heir in case it should turn out that he is still living. But enough of this, we must now take our departure, and remember it will be your own fault if you remain much longer in disgrace."

With this Sir Gaston was assisted to remove by some of the soldiers, and a litter having been got in readiness for him in the courtyard, he was carried from thence to the Gatehouse, where the chamber used for state prisoners had been prepared for him.

CHAPTER CXVI.

It will have blood—they say blood will have blood,[1]
Stones have been known to move, and trees to speak,
Augurs and understood relations have
By maggot pies, and choughs, and rooks, brought forth
The secret'st man of blood.   SHAKSPERE.

Two or three days after the knight had been confined in the prison, it
was found that his wound had so far healed that a second removal could
be effected with perfect safety, and an hour having been appointed for
that purpose, he was taken to the king's palace, where his examination
was to take place before the sovereign, the Chief Justiciary, and
several of the other judges who had been ordered to attend. On this
occasion the accused maintained the same dogged firmness that had
marked his previous conduct, and the mildness with which the king
endeavoured to soften his enmity served only to urge him into still further outbursts of his treasonable expressions. He still asserted that
Prince John had a better claim to the throne than the royal personage
who occupied it, and called upon the king to resign the possession of
power to one who enjoyed the respect and confidence of so large a share
of the people. Yet Richard was unmoved by these expressions, for he
was not disposed to punish the man who he could not but acknowledge
had fought bravely for his country when most she needed his services;
and if it was on that consideration alone he would gladly have spared
him the disgrace which his own wilful conduct threatened to bring down
upon him. He reminded the prisoner of the oath of allegiance he had
taken upon his first coming to the throne, and asked him whether he had
not at present as great a right to it as he had at that time. But Sir

Gaston de Neville still asserted that he felt bound to maintain the cause of Prince John, and declared that if he had his liberty restored to him that moment, the first use he would make of it should be to embark once more in the same cause that had led to his present dangerous position. For death he manifested no fear whatever, asserting that he believed he had chosen a strictly honourable course, and that if he suffered for it, his last moments would be cheered with the consciousness of having done his duty towards the prince, whom, in his heart, he believed to be the rightful heir to the crown. It was in vain that they reminded him of the fact of the king being the elder brother, and that, consequently, he was the lawful sovereign of the nation he ruled over; for he still maintained that the people were almost unanimously in favour of Prince John, and that, consequently, he ought to have succeeded, since the peace and security of the kingdom depended on it. All this time, however, he seemed to forget that he was deeply interested in the success of the pretender, as he had been promised rank and emolument so soon as the business had been brought to a successful termination. This, indeed, was the secret spring that urged him to the desperate course he had taken, and which was now so likely to end in his own ruin and disgrace.

Yielding to the impulse of mercy, the king still endeavoured to prevail on him to accept of pardon, on condition that he would become a true and faithful subject; he pointed out to him the madness of the course he was pursuing, and informed him that even Prince John himself had given up the project in despair, renouncing all further right to the throne until it should come to him after the death of his brother, in the event that he should die childless; he also declared that a reconciliation had taken place between them, and that, consequently, whoever plotted henceforth to raise him to the throne would do so without his concurrence. Sir Gaston de Neville was still resolute in his own designs, and he even threatened the king with another attempt against his life should he ever have an opportunity offered him. Under these circumstances no alternative remained, and he was sent back to the Gate-house, under a hope that a few days' reflection might serve to alter his desperate resolution.

But the Knight Templar was not to be softened even by this kindness, and in the solitude to which he was left, he still turned his attention towards the object that had so long occupied it. He knew the desperate disposition of some of his retainers, and the fidelity with which they had always served him; and the thought of this assured him that some of them would soon find means to communicate with him, and, perhaps, procure his release from confinement. In that case it was his intention to ally himself with the lawless mob that owned Simon Hyde, the tanner, for their leader, and with their aid he thought it not unlike that he might be able to excite some thousands of the lower classes against Richard Cœur de Lion. Wild as this scheme was, it served to inspire im with hope; and though Sir Reginald Courtney frequently visited him for the purpose of ascertaining whether he was likely to accept the king's mercy, he still found him resolutely bent upon the purpose that had all along actuated him.

Leaving him for awhile we must now return to the robbers' cave where Isaac and his daughter were still under the protection of Black Ivan. In this place of security they had passed their time without meeting with any adventure worthy of particular notice, for the Outlaw had strictly forbidden any of his followers intruding upon them under any excuse; and, consequently, though dwelling among robbers, they saw little more of them than if they had been in their own house. A few days, however, after they had taken up their abode in this place, they were surprised at meeting with a most unexpected, though welcome visitor, in the person of Reuben Grenard, who had sought them out to relate certain events which had taken place during their absence from home. Isaac was much gratified at thus once more meeting with one who he so highly esteemed, and to Rebecca, the visit of her lover was still more gratifying, as she had entertained doubts and misgivings that some grievous harm had befallen him from the never-tiring persecution of Sir Gaston de Neville. At this interview, Black Ivan was present, and having suffered them to give full expression to the joy which this meeting occasioned; he enquired of Reuben whether he intended to remain in the cavern till all further persecution from the Knight Templar should cease.

"I believe that will hardly be possible," replied the young man; "for there are emissaries of Sir Gaston's abroad, and I have every reason to believe they are instituting a rigid search after her in every direction."

"Let them search as they will," answered the Outlaw, laughing; "and I think they will have very little chance of finding out the place of her retreat. Nay, even if they did, it is hardly likely they would venture to come into the lion's den, where they would be certain to meet with a reception that must prove anything but agreeable."

"But Sir Gaston himself would think very little about that," observed Isaac, "if ever he should happen to trace out where we have concealed ourselves from his persecution."

"Sir Gaston will never trouble us any more I believe," answered Reuben Grenard; "at least, there is not at present much chance of his seeing us, unless, indeed, he should by any means contrive to effect his escape."

"Escape!" said Isaac, with surprise; "what mean you, boy? has anything befallen the knight since our sojourn here?"

"He is now a prisoner in the Gate-house, at Westminster."

"Ha! his treason then against the king has been discovered?"

"It has; and, if the reports I have heard are true, he is likely to remain there some time, for he has refused the king's mercy, and declares his intention to seek his life should he ever chance to get his liberty again."

"Then if I was in King Richard's place," observed Ivan, "he should have no chance of carrying his threats into execution."

"But he is not prepared for death," cried Rebecca; "his life has been one continued course of crime, and I tremble to think of his being hurried into eternity with all his sins unrepented."

"Why, the truth is, my child," exclaimed her father, "I believe if he was to live for years it would only be to add other crimes to those he has already committed. Sir Gaston will not take warning by the past, and, therefore, I fear there's very little hope of his amendment. But, you have not yet told us, Reuben, the cause that has led to this event?"

"The king has obtained certain information of the plot that was going on against him," replied the youth; "and without giving any notice of his intention, he sent a party of soldiers to the palace of Prince John, with orders to seize upon all the papers they could find. This was done with so much success, that they brought away with them an immense number of documents relating to the treasonable plot, and among them were a great number of letters in the handwriting of Sir Gaston de Neville, and others who were engaged in the plot. They were all of them immediately arrested, and since then have undergone separate examinations before the king in council."

"And what has been the result?" asked Isaac.

"That all of them, except Sir Gaston, have accepted the king's offer of pardon, on condition that they will never again enter into any treasonable plot against him."

"Then the knight, I suppose," exclaimed Isaac, "will die the death of a traitor if he remains obstinate much longer."

"I believe his life will be spared, because the king is anxious to avoid all bloodshed in this affair," replied Reuben. "Such, at least, is the report, and as he has now been some days in prison, it seems likely enough he will have to remain there for the remainder of his days."

"Unless he contrives to make his escape," observed Ivan.

"It would be of little use to him if he did," answered the young man, "for he could hardly expect to leave England without discovery; and even if he attempted to seek concealment in any of his own castles, he would find them in possession of those who would speedily deliver him up."

"What mean you, my son?" asked Isaac; "have his estates been confiscated on account of the share he has had in these late treasonable transactions?"

"Partly so, I believe," replied Reuben; "but it said the king has received letters declaring that the elder brother of Sir Gaston is still alive, and that it is his intention shortly to appear and lay claim to the broad lands of which he has been so long and unjustly dispossessed."

"Is it known who this claimant is?" asked Ivan, eagerly.

"No one can even guess at it," replied the young man. "In fact, the whole affair is wrapped up in mystery, and there are some people who believe it to be a trick, and that after all no one will appear to make good the claim."

"I have heard something of this before," exclaimed Black Ivan, "and from what I was able to gather, I believe there is every reason to suppose the brother of Sir Gaston de Neville is still alive, and that he will come forward as soon as his arrangements are complete."

"But it will be no easy task for him to prove that he is the person he represents himself," observed Rebecca.

"I can see very little difficulty in that respect," answered the Outlaw. "There must be many persons living who will be able to recognise him, or there may be some distinguishing mark about his person that will prove him to be no impostor. In fact, if ever he comes forward, I have no doubt he will be able to convince the world of the truth of his statement."

"Yet supposing this brother to be living," said Isaac, "how can we account for his remaining in obscurity so long?"

"Ah!" exclaimed Ivan; "that I admit is a mystery which he alone can clear up. Doubtless he can give a very good reason for it, and all we can do, is to wait patiently till the time for the disclosure arrives."

"What says Sir Gaston to the rumour?" asked Rebecca.

"He affects to disbelieve it entirely," replied her lover, "and declares that his brother died many years ago. But so he said of his wife, yet circumstances have lately occurred to prove that the Lady Alicia still lives."

"And is it known where she has sought a refuge from her vindictive husband?" enquired Isaac.

"In a nunnery it is said," replied the youth; "at any rate, be where she may, Sir Gaston has never ventured to seek after her, thinking, I suppose, that it will be better to let her remain quiet than run the risk of forcing her to reveal a secret which would increase the odium which is already attached to his name."

"Yet, methinks that would have very little weight with him," exclaimed Black Ivan, "if he could only get a chance of putting her out of the way. Indeed, my only wonder is that he did not have her assassinated in preference to keeping her so long in confinement; it would have kept his secret safe, and he would have thus escaped some portion of the execration that now attaches itself to his name."

"It is indeed to be wondered at," cried Rebecca, with a shudder; "for it unfortunately happens that he is no stranger to blood, and, therefore, it was to be expected that he would have removed one of the chief causes of his disquiet. Her death might easily have been accomplished by means of those reckless men he has about him, and the deed being committed in the secret recesses of his castle would have remained undiscovered till long after death had put a period to his crimes."

At this juncture some one was heard approaching, and in another moment Meg of Finchley presented herself before them. Her countenance betrayed anxiety and alarm, and the agitation of her manner showed but too plain that she was the bearer of unpleasant tidings.

"I see," she said, hurriedly, "that my unexpected appearance among you has occasioned no little alarm."

"Speak, woman!" exclaimed Black Ivan, impatiently; "if you have brought us bad news out with it at once, that we may know the worst. What hast thou to tell us that agitates thee so much?"

"Sir Gaston de Neville has escaped."

"Hah! art thou sure of this, woman?"

"It is but too true," she replied. "Some of his friends have contrived to aid his escape from the Gate-house, and it is feared his first act will be to make another attempt on the life of King Richard."

"Nay," cried Isaac, "there must be some mistake in this, for surely his keepers would not suffer the escape of a criminal like Sir Gaston de Neville."

"It is true, I tell you," she replied. "Everybody is filled with wonder and alarm, for knowing his desperation, it is fully expected he will destroy all those who have ever taken part against him."

"We are lost!" cried Rebecca, with terror. "One of his first thoughts will be to hunt out for our retreat, and should he discover us, I dread the wrath with which he will seek to avenge himself for the past."

"Nay," exclaimed the Outlaw, "you can have little to apprehend from him whilst you remain here. This place he is not likely easily to discover, and even if he did, there are enough in this cavern to protect you against him and all the friends he may be able to muster. So cheer up, my girl, and make yourself quite easy, even if it should prove true that he has been able to break from his prison."

"And that it is true I can stake my existence," exclaimed Meg of Finchley.

"And pray which among his followers was it," asked Black Ivan, "that was willing to run so great a risk in behalf of his worthless master?"

"I know not his name," she replied, "but it seems he obtained admission to see him, and that they changed clothes, so that Sir Gaston was enabled to leave the prison whilst the other remained behind."

"And the man, of course, will not confess where Sir Gaston intends to conceal himself?"

"He will not," answered Meg; "they have tried him, I understand, with the torture, but the fellow remains steady to his purpose, and has declared his resolution to die rather than reveal the secret."

"Well, I like the fellow's honesty too," observed Black Ivan; "but for all that, I wish they could by any means prevail upon him to say where is master is to be found."

"There is no chance of his doing that," replied the old woman, "and so a large reward has been offered by the king to any one that will bring Sir Gaston before him dead or alive!"

"Would that I knew the place where he is lurking," cried Reuben Grenard, earnestly.

"And what could you do against a man who is famous for his prowess with the sword?" demanded the Outlaw. "No, no, boy, you had better remain quietly where you are, and I, who understand these matters better than yourself, will see what can be done towards finding out where the fugitive has fled to."

"Have you any notion," asked the aged Israelite, "where he may be found?"

"At present I have none whatever," replied Ivan, "but it strikes me it will not be long before I get a clue that will be of service to me."

"But he may leave England, and thus release me from all fears," observed Rebecca.

"He will not do that just yet, at any rate," answered the Outlaw;— "for some time to come, I dare say he will be close enough in his hiding place; leaving it only in the night time, and even then not till he is quite certain that no one is about. Sir Gaston will be wary enough, I warrant you, and it will be only by watching, and great caution, that we shall be able to discover where he has sought shelter from the pursuit that is made after him."

"At all events," observed Meg of Finchley, "those who have obtained protection in this place, must not think of leaving it till they are certain of being safe. To fall in with Sir Gaston now, would be to meet with certain death; and, therefore, I would caution you to remain in the cavern till all danger has passed away."

"But that may not be for months to come," cried Isaac, in a tone of doubt.

"There I believe you are mistaken," replied Meg, "for actively as people will be engaged in hunting after him, for the sake of the reward, he must either be taken before many days are gone, or seek refuge in a foreign land. In either case you will be safe, and then will be your time for leaving the place that at present offers you the security you could find no where else."

"I feel truly grateful for the kindness that has been bestowed upon us," answered Isaac,—"but ——"

"You are not altogether satisfied with the company that is to be found beneath the same roof," interrupted Ivan, good-humouredly; "but never think of that, old man, for though they may be roughish fellows in their way, I can answer for it there is not one among them but would fight ancle deep in blood for either you or your daughter, if I desired them. Besides, they have no great regard for Sir Gaston de Neville, I can assure you, for many a time it has been no easy task for me to prevent their making an attack upon his castle, and burning it to the ground, with all that were within its walls. On one occasion, he, with his own hand, slew one of their comrades, and from that time they have sworn to take revenge upon him at the first opportunity. So far I have been able to restrain them, but should they chance to meet him when I am not present, they will not fail to carry their design into effect."

"But you," exclaimed Isaac, "who have equal cause to hate him, seem to exert your authority to guard him from the danger that threatens him."

"I have more cause than you at present know of for hating Sir Gaston de Neville," exclaimed the Outlaw; "however, we will speak no further upon that subject at present; it seems he has contrived to escape from the Gate-house, and I will now leave you, whilst I endeavour to obtain some information concerning him. You, with your daughter, and Reuben Grenard, will remain here for the present, and perhaps when I return, it may be with news that will render your departure from hence safe. So farewell, and may your troubles find a speedy termination."

Upon this, Black Ivan having armed himself, took his departure from the cave, with the intention of making enquiries after the fugitive.

CHAPTER CXVII.

" Conscience may yet awake within his breast,
    And bring him to repentance;—I'll try him,
    And with fair promises of future favour,
    So urge him to my hope that he shall yield
    Obedience to my will."

THE REPROBATE.

ON leaving the prisoner, as he imagined safe in custody of the keeper of the Gate-house at Westminster, Sir Reginald Courtney hastened to the palace to acquaint his royal master with all that had been done. The zeal with which the youthful knight had executed his task, gave evident satisfaction to the king, who praising the promptitude with which he had acted, entrusted to him the somewhat difficult duty of prosecuting the affair to a close.

"I can foresee," he said, "that the stubborn knight will not yield to the mercy I would extend to him, and as it behoves us for our own safety, to keep him in close custody, you will place about his person a guard sufficient to prevent his escape."

"I have already done so, sir," answered Sir Reginald, "but I believe, wounded as he is, and faint from loss of blood, there is little fear of his making an attempt that must terminate in his defeat."

"I would not have you trust to that, Sir Knight," exclaimed the king, "for the templar has friends ready to aid him, and should he succeed in escaping, his first thought would be to seek my life. That I am no coward, you will allow, but Sir Gaston would resort to treachery, and who is there that can guard himself against the steel of a hired assassin?"

"The bitterness of his hate," answered Sir Reginald, "is not softened by time, for when I promised your royal clemency, on condition that he would swear allegience, he treated the offer with scorn, and boldly declared that he wished for life only long enough to wreak his vengeance upon his king."

"I know him to be revengeful," answered the monarch, "and care must be taken to prevent his accomplishing the crime he meditates."

"And if I may be permitted to offer a suggestion," observed Sir Reginald, "I should say the only means left to protect yourself is, by ordering his immediate execution."

"Nay," exclaimed the king, "I wish not to proceed to extremities till all other means fail. Sir Gaston and I have fought together in the same field, and as a gallant leader in the defence of his country, I must still feel some regard for him, even though he has since proved my enemy."

"Your majesty's clemency may be thrown away in this instance," answered the young knight. "I speak not out of enmity to Sir Gaston de Neville, but loving my king, as I do, I would apply any remedy that may best serve to foil the arts of a traitor."

"He may yet see his fault," cried Richard, "and in that case we may exercise our royal prerogative of mercy, without fear of the consequence."

"But his retainers," exclaimed the other, "will not forget that their master has fallen under your displeasure. One, at least, among them is of a wild and reckless temper, and having been once foiled in an attempt upon your life, he will take care on the next occasion to make sure work of it."

"You speak of Bertrand le Noir?"

"I do, my liege."

"Have no efforts been made to secure so dangerous an enemy?"

"A reward has been offered for his apprehension," replied Sir Reginald; "but the fellow is wary, and hitherto all search for him has proved in vain."

"Yet, doubtless he is to be found in the castle of Sir Gaston de Neville."

"It was thought so," replied the favourite, "and a strict search has been made for him, but without success."

"Were no unfortunate captives found in any of the dungeons?" demanded the king.

"But one—and she, it appears from her own account, had not been there many hours."

"Who is she?"

"Edith, a waiting woman, who gave offence to her imperious master, in consequence of the interest she took in the fate of the Father Confessor."

"Humph!" ejaculated the king; "he wars then, it seems, against women as well as men."

"He does, my liege, and there is every reason to believe that she would have perished had we not been fortunate enough to rescue her from his power."

"This girl may prove a witness against Sir Gaston," observed the king, "in the event of our proceeding to extremities."

"I have questioned her upon the subject of her master's manifold tyrannies," answered Sir Reginald, "but she is faithful, in spite of his cruel conduct towards her, and hitherto we have not succeeded in obtaining any information that will prove of importance."

"Does she know anything," asked the king, "of this brother of Sir Gaston, who is reported to be still living?"

"Nothing more than the rumour which we have all of us heard."

"It is a strange story," exclaimed the monarch, "and one that I can scarcely credit. Sir Gaston has held possession of the estates many years, under the general impression that his elder brother was dead; and yet, at the eleventh hour, we hear it reported that the real heir is living, and has been content to pass all this time in obscurity, for no

other purpose than a disinclination to bring disgrace upon the man who
has most injured him."

"Your majesty does not credit the story, then?"

"It is so improbable that I can scarcely do so," answered Richard.
"Not that I doubt the capability of Sir Gaston to act in the manner described, but that I think it most unlikely the other should have remained
in poverty and obscurity when a word would have restored him to the
right of which it is said he has been deprived."

"Yet the rumour has obtained much credit," answered the other, "and
even Sir Gaston himself feels uneasy whenever the subject is mentioned
before him."

"But, of course, he has not suffered a word to pass his lips that might
confirm the suspision?"

"He has not, my liege."

"Has he been questioned upon the subject?"

"Yes; but he remains obstinately silent, and there is reason to believe he will continue to keep his own counsel till the discovery has
taken place."

"And can no one guess who the person is, or where he has concealed
himself all this time?"

"That," answered Sir Reginald, "still remains involved in as much
mystery as ever."

"Humph!" ejaculated the king, "how, then, is it known that such a
person is in existence?"

"Through a woman they call Meg of Finchley."

"Aye, I have heard of her," exclaimed Richard; "she is reported
No. 95

to be possessed of supernatural powers, and the credulous are afraid of her.''

"She is regarded with dread, I believe,'' replied Sir Reginald Courtney; "but I believe a diseased brain is the only reason there is for accusing her of witchcraft. The old woman, however, declares that the rightful heir of the Neville estates is alive, and that she is ready to prove it whenever the proper time arrives.''

"Why has she not been taken into custody and questioned upon the subject?'' demanded the king. "The affair demands a rigid enquiry, and if I really thought there was any truth in it, I would myself take an active part in developing a mystery of such importance.''

"We wait but your majesty's commands,'' replied Sir Reginald, "and when they are issued, we will not fail to carry them into effect,''

"It is my desire that search be made after this hag,'' exclaimed King Richard, "and should she be found, let her be instantly brought before me, that I may satisfy myself whether there is any truth in her report.''

"Your commands shall be promptly obeyed, '' exclaimed the young knight; "though, with all humility, I would ask what reason there is for suspecting her tale to be nothing more than a fabrication?''

"She may be an enemy of Sir Gaston,'' answered the king, "or it is equally probable she has been bribed to spread this rumour by some hidden foe who is too cowardly to stand forward and make the charge himself.''

"Still, your majesty, I see no reason whatever for doubting this report against Sir Gaston de Neville. It is well known that his wife—the Lady Alicia—was confined many years beneath the dungeons of the castle, and, therefore, it is equally likely that he may have treated his brother in the same way.''

"Where is the Lady Alicia?'' enquired the king.

"I know not,'' replied Sir Reginald, "except that, on her escape from the castle, she sought refuge and protection within the walls of a convent.''

"Is there no way to find her?''

"Yes, sire, I believe Edith can tell us.''

"And where is the girl?''

"In the palace,'' replied Sir Reginald Courtney; "she seemed to be in great fear lest some of her master's retainers should take it in their heads to murder her, and I ventured to bring her here for present safety.''

"You have done well,'' answered the king. "Let her instantly be brought before me.''

In obedience to this command, the youthful knight hastened from the royal presence, and on being left to himself, Richard gave free scope to the thoughts that hurried through his mind. He would fain have believed Sir Gaston de Neville innocent of some portion of the crimes charged against him, and carefully avoided throwing out a word that might seem to Sir Reginald as if he believed the rumour that had lately been so extensively circulated. Still, in his own mind, he thought it likely enough that the templar had been urged by the united powers of avarice and ambition to deprive a brother of his birthright, and for that reason he determined to institute a rigid inquiry into the affair. Pondering deeply on this subject, he observed not the entrance of Sir Reginald and Edith into the room, till the voice of the former roused him from his reverie.

"The girl you spoke of is here,'' he said, "and awaits the commands of your majesty.''

"Come hither, girl," said the king to Edith, who stood abashed at thus finding herself in the presence of royalty. "I would ask you a few questions, but previous to doing so, I must say that I have no wish to terrify you into making disclosures that you may have any objection to. You have been in the service, I understand, of the Knight Templar, Sir Gaston de Neville?"

"Y-e-s, your high mightiness," stammered Edith.

"During your residence in the castle has any discovery taken place of a female, since reported to be dead?"

"Y-e-s."

"Nay," cried the king, good-naturedly, "answer me without fear. Who was the person you speak of?"

"They call her Lady Alicia."

"The wife, I believe, of Sir Gaston de Neville?"

"So I have understood."

"You are not able, then, to throw any further light upon that subject?"

"No, your majesty," she replied. "I was not born, I believe, at the time she was sent to the dungeon, and all I can say about it is, that they called her Lady Alicia."

"And after years of captivity she found means to escape from the wretched place she was confined in?"

"Thank goodness, she has!" exclaimed Edith, whose fear began to wear off as the interview proceeded. "She has got clear from the castle at last, and all I hope is, that Sir Gaston may never be able to find out where she is."

"Do you know the place of her retreat?"

"Oh, quite well, your majesty."

"Will you inform us of it?"

"That," she replied, "will depend upon circumstances. If I thought your highness meant no harm, I should not mind saying where she is, but it must be on condition that you don't tell her husband of it."

"You may rely upon that," exclaimed the king, smiling at her artlessness. "I would serve the unhappy victim of a husband's tyranny, and of course nothing can be done till we know where she is to be found."

"Well, if I thought that—"

"You may rely on the king's word," whispered Sir Reginald.

"In that case, your majesty," resumed Edith, "I don't mind telling you where the Lady Alicia is;—she has sought refuge in the convent near Hornsey Wood, and there she may be found whenever you may happen to want her."

"Sir Reginald," exclaimed the king, "I will entrust you with the duty of visiting this hapless woman, and informing her of the interest that her cause has excited in my bosom. Say I have vowed to see her restored to that station in society, and that it is my commands that she accompanies you here immediately."

"Your majesty shall be obeyed," exclaimed the young favourite, turning away to take his departure.

"Stay, stay," exclaimed Edith, "you must be careful what you say to her, or she will not obey even the commands of the king. Lady Alicia seeks not to injure her husband, bad as his conduct has been, and if she fancies any questions may be asked about him, she would not answer even though the torture were applied."

"The girl says well," observed Richard; "you must not let her suspect the business I require to see her upon, but merely say that having heard of her afflictions, I would endeavour to procure a reconciliation between her and her husband."

"I will be careful to obey your majesty's instructions," replied Sir Reginald Courtney, "and would now suggest that it is likely this girl may be able to throw some light on the rumour we have heard respecting the brother of Sir Gaston de Neville."

"You have heard what Sir Reginald says," exclaimed the king. "Do you know aught that may serve to clear away the mystery of which he speaks?"

"Indeed, your gracious majesty, I know nothing at all about it," answered Edith.

"You have heard, I suppose, such a rumour?"

"Oh, yes, everybody is talking about it," she replied, "and Sir Gaston has been looking glum ever since, for of course he would not like to be found out if he has been doing anything wrong, and—"

"Psha! to the point, girl! Do you know who the person is that may hereafter claim the inheritance at present enjoyed by Sir Gaston?"

"There is but one person that I think can be him," answered Edith, after a short pause.

"And who is that?"

"The armed apparition."

"The armed apparition!" exclaimed the king, vexed at the answer she had given.

"Yes, your majesty," she replied; "you may perhaps think me a very foolish girl for having such a thought, but for all that I don't think I am very far from the mark."

"And what," asked Richard, "is this supernatural visitant that you speak of?"

"A ghost," she replied, "that walks about the castle, and is always seen in black armour. Ah! your majesty, I've seen it many a time, and so have all the other people that are in the service of Sir Gaston."

"It appears, then, that you believe the brother we have been speaking of was murdered?"

"That's more than I can say, though it's likely enough," answered Edith; "be that as it may, however, the apparition seems to make itself quite at home in the castle, and as it knows every part of the building, I can't help thinking that if there really is a brother that's it."

"Psha! this is trifling," interrupted Sir Reginald.

"Not so trifling as you think for," exclaimed Edith, "nor would you think it a trifle I can tell you to be met every now and then by a ghost that don't seem to be very easy in its mind."

"This is some idle rumour, your majesty," observed Sir Reginald Courtney. "To the credulous every castle has a ghost, and this is nothing more than a report which owes its origin to the fears of those who are easily terrified by their own shadows."

"I only wish it would take it into its head to pay you a visit," cried Edith indignantly. "Everybody in the place has seen it, and everybody can't have been so much mistaken as you seem to believe."

"At any rate," exclaimed the young knight, "it is impossible to believe that it can be the brother of Sir Gaston de Neville, for had he taken the trouble to enter the castle at all, it would have been to claim his just inheritance, and not to frighten simple-minded people out of the little wits they possess."

"Have you any reason for supposing it to be the person we have spoken of?" asked the king.

"I have," she replied, "for if Sir Gaston's brother is alive, what better plan could he have hit on than to walk about the castle as an armed apparition? The visor always conceals its face, so that no better disguise could have been found, and as all people are afraid of ghosts, there was very little chance of any one making too many inquiries."

"The girl's suggestion is worthy our consideration," exclaimed the king, "and though incredulous at first, I now begin to think it will be worth while to pursue our investigation. You will, therefore, after bringing hither the Lady Alicia, visit the castle in Moorfields, and endeavour to find out the mystery that at present involves this affair."

"Your majesty may rely upon the zealous discharge of my duty," answered Sir Reginald. "I will do your bidding with all cheerfulness, though truth to say, I have little hope of making any discovery of importance."

"At any rate the inquiry is worth prosecuting with vigour," replied Richard; "for though at first I was inclined to treat this girl's story with discredit, yet upon second thoughts it does not seem unlikely that the long-lost brother of Sir Gaston would think of some such means to obtain admittance to the place he was about to claim as his own."

"Why then," asked the knight, "has he not before now made the claim and established his right?"

"That is a question not easily to be answered," replied Richard; "there may, however, be a good reason for it, and it is likely enough that he took the disguise which has been mentioned in order to avoid assassination."

"That's it, your majesty," cried Edith; "he knew well enough what sort of a fate he would have met in case of being discovered, and what better plan could he have thought of, than to appear as a ghost and frighten people so that they could not have the heart to make too strict an enquiry about him."

"Has the supposed apparition ever been known to speak to any one?" asked the king.

"Never," replied Edith; "and perhaps this is a very good reason why not, for whenever it makes its appearance peoply fly as if the old gentleman himself had come to pay them a visit."

"Are you aware whether Sir Gaston de Neville has ever seen it?" demanded his majesty.

"Oh yes, your highness," she replied; "he has seen it three or four times, and it has always contrived to pay its visits to him just when he has been going about something very bad."

"And did it seem to any one that he had any suspicion who it might be?"

"I should rather fancy he had not," replied the girl. "At any rate he never gave a hint of the kind, which is not to be wondered at, seeing that he has no wish for any one to have an idea that he believes the story about his brother. Besides, he knows the people about the castle are rather curious, and he was never very fond of making free with those about him."

"In what part of the castle did this supposed apparition usually confine itself?" asked the king.

"Nowhere in particular," she replied; "in good truth it used to wander about from one place to another, just for all the world as if the whole building belonged to it. And so it may for that matter, for it's not at all unlikely it may be the very person that has most right to be there."

"You will obey the orders I have given," exclaimed the king to Sir Reginald Courtney. "In the first place you will go and seek out the Lady Alicia, whose place of retreat has been revealed to us by this girl, and after you have brought her to my presence, you will proceed to the castle of Sir Gaston de Neville, where you may chance to discover a secret that I must needs confess interests me considerably."

"I will first of all order a strong guard to be placed round the Gatehouse, so as to preclude all possibility of his escape," returned Sir Reginald, "and when that is done, I will hasten to complete the remainder of the instructions I have received, and your majesty may rest assured that I will lose no time in bringing this affair to a successful termination."

"Let no chance be lost," exclaimed Richard Cœur de Lion, "for if the Knight Templar should be proved to have been guilty of the crimes laid to his charge, I will not fail to punish him according to his deserts. For all that he has done against myself I can freely pardon him, but he shall not escape his deserts if he should be proved that he has played the part of a villain to others."

"Has your majesty any further commands for me?" asked Sir Reginald Courtney.

"No, you now understand my intentions, and your speed will prove the zeal with which you enter into my service. So away, Sir Knight, and take back this girl to the place from whence you brought her, and give orders for her to be received into my household, until further directions are given respecting her."

Sir Reginald now left the room with Edith, and the king rising from his seat, paced up and down the room with all the uneasiness of a man upon whose mind business of the greatest importance is pressing. That Sir Gaston de Neville was guilty of crimes which merited the severest punishment, he was perfectly satisfied, but he could not forget the services he had done his country, and respecting him for his gallantry, he would have made any sacrifice, rather than see him meet an ignominious end. On the other hand, he saw that there was no reason to doubt the numerous charges that had been brought against him, and knowing as he did, the wrath which existed in men's minds, he foresaw that there would be no alternative but to satisfy the ends of justice, by giving him up to death. He, however, trusted that in an interview with Lady Alicia, he should be able to suggest some means or other for a reconciliation between them, and when that was done, it would be no very difficult task to prevail on Sir Gaston to restore his brother to the rights he had unjustly deprived him of. This effected, he would next interpose to obtain his promise never to molest Rebecca again, and then after extending his royal clemency to the traitor for all acts committed against himself, he hoped to restore the Knight Templar to some degree of favour and respect. While the king was thus occupied with thoughts of kindness, and benevolence, a slight noise aroused him, and Adrian the page entered the room with a quick and hurried step.

"How now, boy," exclaimed the king, "what evil tidings art thou now the bearer of?"

"My leige," cried Adrian, "they are full of danger and peril to yourself;—Sir Gaston de Neville has found means to escape from the Gatehouse."

"Hah!—then all the hopes I had formed in his favour are at an end," exclaimed Richard. "But art thou sure, boy, that this news of thine is correct?"

"I am quite certain of it," replied the page, "for the gaoler has just been here with the intelligence."

"Is the knave still here?"

"No, my liege," replied Adrian; "he left the palace immediately to go in search of the fugitive."

"Does he know how Sir Gaston contrived to effect his escape from prison?"

"At present he knows nothing for certain," replied Adrian, "but he fancies it must have been managed with the aid of confederates. Doubtless, some of his retainers have been lurking about till they found an opportunity to get him clear away from the place of his captivity."

"This is most unfortunate," exclaimed the king, "for I had formed plans to relieve him from the unpleasant situation to which his own crimes had reduced him, and now I fear he has madly plunged deeper into difficulties."

"The people are incensed against him," observed Adrian, "and should he be found in his lurking place, they will not fail to tear him to pieces."

"Is it guessed where he has fled to?"

"At present no one knows," replied the page, "but the keeper of the Gate-house has gone to collect a strong body of constables, and with their assistance, he intends to visit every castle belonging to Sir Gaston, in the hope that he has sought concealment in one of them."

"Their labour will be in vain," said the king, "for doubtless he will quit England without delay. With all his faults he is known to be a gallant knight, and in some foreign country he will seek employment for his arms. We shall be thus fairly rid of him, and let us hope he may yet retrieve the honour he has lost."

"I'm afraid there's but little chance of that, sire," answered the page. "I know his hot and impetuous temper, and never will he leave England till he has executed the full measures of his wrath."

"Nay," cried the king, "he will never be mad enough to remain where he knows a strict search will be instituted after him."

"In my opinion," replied Adrian, "he cares very little for life, now that he has gone so far in crime, and would die well content could he but ensure the vengeance that occupies his every thought."

"Nay, you wrong him, boy," exclaimed Richard;—"that he is haughty and revengeful, I know, but as a soldier, he will not risk dishonour by such a deed as you speak of."

"And yet," observed the page, "he has not hesitated to commit dishonourable actions ere now. His conduct towards the Hebrew Maiden; his cruel imprisonment of a faithful and unoffending wife, and his basely usurping the estates of his brother, all prove him to be as destitute of honour as he is of loyalty to your majesty."

"Thou hast brought a black catalogue of guilt against him," exclaimed the king, "and yet things are not so bad but they may be atoned for. His treason against myself, I can freely pardon, on condition that he does not repeat it, and the private injuries he has inflicted upon others, may be repaired through my mediation. In truth, I had just formed my own plans for effecting all this, when you arrived to inform me of his escape from prison."

"And his having fled from justice," observed the page, "shows that he dares not meet the accusers who would have come forward to prove his guilt."

"Thou speakest of him with rancour, boy."

"I speak only as I have found him, my liege."

"He once sought thy life, and now thou art glad to see his downfall."

"Indeed your majesty wrongs me by the suspicion," answered Adrian. "His offences against myself I think not of, but he has injured helpless women, and though I am not yet old enough to bear arms in their defence, yet am I right glad to see him punished for his crimes towards them."

"Thou hast spoken with some gallantry," exclaimed Richard, "and, therefore, I cannot be angry with thee. In future, however, I would have thee look with less prejudice on thy master's actions, for though criminal to a great extent, he may yet make amends, by returning to the path of virtue from which he has unhappily strayed. By my intercession, all may be made well, and I shall esteem it one of the fairest acts in my life, could I but succeed in recalling him to that honour which he has lost."

"I should be as glad as your majesty to see it," replied the page, "but I fear it is quite hopeless."

"At any rate," cried the king, "Rebecca shall be married to the husband of her choice, and thus one of his temptations will be removed for ever."

"That I shall rejoice at," replied Adrian, "but still there is the Lady Alicia, who has suffered years of imprisonment in a wretched dungeon, and though she has contrived to escape, it is only to find refuge within the walls of a convent, which, for all I know, is as bad as the other."

"He may be prevailed on to seek a reconciliation with his much injured wife," exclaimed the king. "At all events my best services shall be exerted to effect it, and in that case, he will make some recompense for the injuries he has inflicted upon her."

"I cannot doubt your majesty's zeal in a good cause," cried Adrian, "yet do I fear Sir Gaston de Neville is too stubborn to yield even to your generous suggestions."

"Nay, I have no doubt of it," replied the king, "and when that is done, there is every reason to hope Sir Gaston will restore his property to the rightful owner."

"And thus render himself a beggar."

"It shall be my care to reward him for any sacrifice he may make at my suggestion," answered the king. "I will myself bestow upon him lands fully equal to those he may give up, and thus I shall be the means not only of restoring him to the esteem of the world, but at the same time, I shall secure his gratitude for the future. However, my plans are not yet matured, and, therefore, I would be alone, boy, and shouldst thou hear of Sir Gaston's capture, be sure to hasten hither and inform me of it."

Upon this hint, Adrian left the royal presence to spread the news of the king's magnanimity, in thus overlooking the errors of his traitorous subject.

CHAPTER CXVIII.

"Ere long, thy trials shall be closed,
And peace and calm serenity shall shed
Upon thy future life that beauteous light,
That yet hath been denied thee."

ROLLA.

IT was a task of no great difficulty for Sir Reginald to find the convent in which Lady Alicia had found a place of temporary refuge, and on reaching the exterior walls, he left his attendants, and directing his way to the door, gave the usual summons for admittance. He was, however, obliged to knock three or four times before any one came to answer him, but, at length, he could hear footsteps slowly moving

within, and then a small wicket in the gate was opened, and a female of unprepossessing appearance demanded what he wanted.

"I wish to see the superior of the convent," he replied.

"The superior is at her devotions, and cannot possibly be disturbed," was the answer.

"Admit me, and I will wait till it is her pleasure to see me."

"Admit *you*, indeed!" cried the woman that had charge of the gate; "a very pretty scandal indeed, should I bring upon the holy sisterhood, were I to let a man into the convent."

"But I come on a message from the king."

"If you came on a message from the Pope himself, I would not let you into the place," replied the female.

"In that case, you will, perhaps, take a message from me to the Lady Abbess?"

"I don't know that," answered the portress; "I receive but little for my trouble, and I don't see why I should run of every fool's errand because he bids me."

"Nay," cried Sir Reginald, "do as I have asked, and this purse shall be your reward."

"That would be taking a bribe," exclaimed the woman, holding forth her bony hand to seize the prize;—"however, I will accept of it as an offering to the blessed saint under whose protection the convent is."

"You will tell the Abbess, then, that Sir Reginald Courtney has come from the king, to crave the favour of an interview on an affair of great importance."

"Shall I tell her the nature of your business?" inquired the portress, inquisitively.

No. 96

"No," answered the knight, "my message requires secresy, and, therefore, you will be content to deliver the message exactly as I have given it."

"But the superior may not be inclined to see you," replied the woman. "She will seldom be disturbed, and the chances are that she will refuse an interview."

"If she does so," replied Sir Reginald, "it will be at the hazard of offending the king, and he may, perhaps, be compelled to adopt stronger measures than a mere message."

"Holy Virgin!—why he would not injure us poor women, who are induced to spend their days and nights in prayers and vigils!" cried the portress.

"The king, my master, injures none who treat him with the respect due to his royal dignity," answered the knight. "He has been pleased to send me on an errand, and I must perform it with zeal ere I return."

"Well, well, you are obstinate, I see," cried the woman, "and I suppose your commands must be obeyed; but you will bear witness for me that I was not over anxious to carry your message to the Lady Abbess?"

"I can most conscientiously bear witness to that," exclaimed Sir Reginald, with a smile. "So, hasten to her, and that purse and its contents are yours, or the holy Saint's, whichever you may think proper."

Almost before he had finished this the portress had disappeared, and in a few minutes afterwards she returned, and opening the gate, desired the visitor to walk in. This Sir Reginald promptly obeyed, and when the gate was again secured, she, with a sign, bade him follow her; this he did, and passing through a long passage dimly lighted up with lamps, he was at length ushered into a room where sat the portly Lady Abbess, who had, apparently, just finished a substantial meal, instead of the devotions mentioned by the portress. Sir Reginald paid his obeisance, which were received with much dignity by the superior of the convent, who seemed to eye him with a look in which surprise and inquisitiveness were mingled."

"You have come, young man," she at last said, "on a message from the king?"

"I have."

"What, I pray you, are his commands?"

"I have no commands from him, Madam," answered Sir Reginald, "but he requests that you will deliver Lady Alicia de Neville into my hands."

"Indeed!" exclaimed the Abbess, with surprise; "Lady Alicia has sought shelter and protection beneath this roof, and far be it from me to refuse so poor a favour to one who needs a friend as she does."

"The king would also befriend her," answered the knight, "and it is for that purpose he wishes to have an audience with her."

"He cannot do it so securely as I can," replied the Abbess. "Within this sacred edifice the lady is safe, for none will venture to follow her, lest the denunciations of the church cling to him for ever."

"Nay," exclaimed Sir Reginald, "you are aware, I believe, of the differences that have existed between Lady Alicia and her husband. She has suffered much from his cruelty, but the king is about to use his influence in order to bring about a reconciliation between them."

"Which is a hopeless task," cried the Abbess, "and, therefore, would be better left alone. Besides, there is reason to believe she will take the veil, and in that case she will not require well the meant kindness of King Richard."

"You surely will throw no obstacle in the way when so much good may be effected ?"

"Heaven forbid, young man," cried the superior; "we are all of us erring mortals, but it behoves every one to do that which he conceives right. I will, therefore, order her to appear before us, and if she wishes to quit the shelter that has been given, I will promise to throw no obstacle in the way."

Upon this she called to one of the sisterhood who was in an adjoining apartment, and whispering to her, desired her to go to the cell occupied by Lady Alicia, and request her attendance. In a moment the ghost-like form of the nun slowly glided from the room, and as the door closed, the Abbess once more addressed herself to her visitor.

"You will tell the king," she said, "that I have bowed cheerfully to his commands, though they are against the strict rules which govern our sisterhood. The Lady Alicia will soon be here, and if it is in your power to prevail on her to quit this powerful sanctuary, I will say nothing which may induce her to adopt a contrary resolution."

"By so doing," replied Sir Reginald Courtney, "you will please his majesty, and may likely enough procure favours towards your establishment, such as are possessed by no other convent. The king is an ardent follower of our holy religion, and, therefore, you can have no fear that he will abuse the favour he has been induced to ask."

At this period Lady Alicia entered the room, and her appearance denoted that the change she had lately undergone for the better had not been without beneficial result. Her form had returned to its previous symmetry and grace, and her countenance had lost much of that care-worn expression that had marked it under less favourable circumstances. She started on perceiving a stranger in the room, and it was evident the person who took the message to her had said nothing further than that the Abbess required her presence.

"You are surprised, my daughter," said the superior, "at seeing that I am not alone; but there is nothing to apprehend, for the person you see here has come on a message to you from the king."

"From the king?" cried the other with surprise.

"Yes, lady," answered Sir Reginald; "his majesty has learnt your painful story, and is most anxious to lend what aid he can to restore you to your former station."

"That he cannot do," sighed Lady Alicia.

"Nay, you are wrong there, believe me," answered Sir Reginald, "for the interposition of a friend may do much towards making amends for the dark destiny that has been yours."

"What can he do?" cried Alicia, despairingly.

"In that he will be guided by yourself," replied the young man; "you have but to name your own wishes upon the subject, and King Richard will be prompt in carrying them into effect."

"Let him pardon my too guilty husband," cried Alicia, "and I will ask no more."

"That I believe he has already done as far as concerns any offences committed against himself," replied Sir Reginald. "Your husband's treasonable practices have been discovered, and instead of punishing him according to his deserts, the king is content to pardon him, on condition that he does full justice to those he has injured."

"And will Sir Gaston accede to these terms?"

"Of that we know nothing at present."

"Has the king seen him?"

"He would have done so ere now," replied Sir Reginald, "but he has, I hear, just escaped from the Gatehouse."

"He has been a prisoner then?"

"Yes, lady, but it was through his own mad folly that he has been so; Richard, in a message by me, offered him pardon on condition that he would henceforth become a loyal subject, but instead of that he returned an answer of defiance, and, as our only alternative, we were compelled to take him to the Gatehouse at Westminster."

"From whence," cried Lady Alicia, "I thank Heaven he has found means to escape."

"You seem glad that he has obtained his liberty, though it may be the means of involving yourself in fresh difficulty."

"I am indeed most sincerely glad of it," replied Alicia; "for though he has made me his captive for so many of the best years of my life, yet has my heart never ceased to regard him with affection."

"But he still hates you as much as ever," exclaimed Sir Reginald Courtney, "and I fear, should he chance to discover your retreat, he will find means to drag you from it in spite of the sanctity that should guard it from violence."

"Holy Virgin!" cried the Abbess, starting from the slumber she was indulging in; "surely you do not mean to say Sir Gaston de Neville will dare come here where there are nothing but helpless women to protect themselves!"

"I do not say he will do so," replied the young knight, "but he is fierce and vindictive, and would not hesitate were he ever to take it into his head."

"Heaven help us!" cried the superior with a shudder.

"Nay, I do not wish to alarm you needlessly," exclaimed Sir Reginald Courtney, "for though it is likely the knight would seek his wife here, I trust there are people enough that would come forward to aid the holy sisterhood."

"What would you advise us to do then?" demanded the Lady Abbess.

"I wish this long persecuted female to accompany me to the palace, where she will find shelter and protection till arrangements are made with Sir Gaston de Neville. A few days may suffice for that, and thus Lady Alicia's sufferings will at length meet with a happy termination."

"Alas!" she sighed, "I have long since abandoned that thought as utterly hopeless."

"And no wonder," observed Sir Reginald, "for a dungeon is but an indifferent place for comfortable reflections. However, affairs have taken a brighter turn, and a few hours more may serve to work marvels in your favour."

"But you say Sir Gaston has escaped," she observed; "and in that case it is most likely he has quitted England for ever."

"He certainly may have done so," replied Sir Reginald, "and if the surmise proves correct, it will save all parties a great deal of trouble. The king will have lost a worthless subject, and you will be free from one towards whom I apprehend you can entertain very little respect."

"I have already told you," answered Lady Alicia, "that I have never ceased to think of him with affection in spite of the hardships he made me endure."

"Your generosity has met with but a poor return," exclaimed the knight, "and yet I cannot but respect the goodness of heart that prompted you to forgive his injuries. However, you have consented to accompany me to the royal palace, and with the permission of the Lady Abbess, we will immediately take our departure from this holy sanctuary."

"The Lady Alicia," answered the superior, "is free to follow her own inclinations. These doors were opened to her at her own request, and should she wish it, the same asylum remains, if at any future time she requires it."

"We will lose no further time, then," exclaimed Sir Reginald. "I have a horse in readiness for you just without the convent gates, and half an hour's ride will serve to take us into the presence of the king. So your blessing, holy mother, and many thanks for the kindness with which you have received this unfortunate lady in your community."

A very brief period served to prepare Alicia for the journey, and taking an affectionate leave of the superior, she set out with Sir Reginald, and having passed through the convent gates, she was quickly mounted on the horse that had been brought for her accommodation. For a moment or two, her heart sank with apprehension lest she was again the victim of deceit, and that this was only a trap to get her once more into the power of Sir Gaston de Neville. Her companion, however, guessed her suspicions, and riding by her side, he over and over again assured her that she had nothing more to fear as she was now with friends.

At last they reached the palace at Westminster, where they dismounted, and entering the noble pile, a message was sent to his majesty, announcing their arrival, and requesting to know whether it was the royal pleasure to see them. This was conveyed to the king by one of the pages, who returned shortly afterwards with a command that they were to wait upon the king without an instant's delay. Accordingly, taking the hand of Lady Alicia, the youthful knight led her to the apartment usually occupied by his majesty, and where they found him anxiously waiting their arrival.

"By Our Lady! thou hast done mine errand both speedily and well," cried Richard, as they knelt before him. "I have ever found thee diligent in the performance of my commands, Sir Reginald, but this time thou hast even exceeded my expectations."

"It was an easy task, and without impediment," answered the young knight. "In fact, the Lady Abbess has proved her loyalty by the promptitude with which she furthered the wishes your majesty sent to her through so poor a channel."

"We will not fail to reward her for it," replied the king. "Her convent shall be enriched by a large donation, and privileges shall be granted to it equal to any other place of the kind in our dominions. And now, lady," he continued, addressing himself to Alicia, "I believe I see before me the injured wife of Sir Gaston de Neville?"

"I am the wife of Sir Gaston," she replied; "but I come not here to make complaints against one whom I have not yet ceased to regard with affection."

"Why, that is well said," exclaimed Richard; "for my wish is, that I may be able to affect a reconciliation between you."

"Your majesty will perhaps allow me to request that the remainder of my days may be passed within the peaceful walls of that convent which I have just left."

"I shall certainly oppose your wishes as little as possible," replied the king, "but having confessed that you have not yet learned to hate Sir Gaston, I was in hopes there might be a chance of bringing about a reconciliation."

"Sir Gaston, it is said, has escaped," observed Alicia.

"He has," replied the king; "but how did you hear it?"

"From Sir Reginald Courtney."

"Ah! and how knew you of it, Sir Knight?" exclaimed the king; "for when you left my presence to go on this errand it was not known to either you or myself."

"I heard it almost immediately after leaving the palace," replied Sir Reginald. "Indeed, I was almost inclined to go in pursuit, but having received your commands to fetch the Lady Alicia, I did so with a determination to go after the fugitive immediately upon bringing her into your presence."

"For the present that object must be abandoned," exclaimed Richard. "I will now confer with Lady Alicia, and it will depend on the result of our conference whether I seek after Sir Gaston de Neville, or suffer him quietly to make the best of his way out of my dominion."

"If the prayers of a heart-broken wife may prevail, let me entreat your majesty to permit his escape," cried the Lady Alicia. "He has done wrong, I know, but being deprived of the power of inflicting further injury, I trust your goodness will save him from further punishment."

"You are, of course, aware that he has plotted against my life?" said the king.

"I am," she replied; "but since you have providentially escaped the perils that threatened, I trust you will show your gratitude to Heaven by freely forgiving him."

"I have already done so," answered the king, "and well pleased am I to see a deeply injured wife pleading thus earnestly for the man who has so harshly treated her. He was pardoned all offences against me long before you came; but had it not been so, I could not have punished him after you had thus generously pleaded in his behalf."

"And are all his other offences forgiven?" asked Alicia.

"Not at present," replied the monarch. "In fact, it will chiefly depend upon himself whether I can again receive him into the favour with which I once regarded him."

"May I ask what your majesty alludes to?"

"Among other things, to his cruel and unjust persecution of an unfortunate Hebrew Maiden, whose beauty had made an impression on his heart."

"I have seen her," cried Alicia. "She used frequently to visit me when both of us were captives in Neville Castle."

"Indeed! And how happened it that you were permitted to see each other?"

"It was through the kindness of a page," cried Lady Alicia; "but poor Adrian suddenly ceased visiting my cell, and I fear he was slain on its being discovered that he had favoured the meeting between two hapless captives."

"You are mistaken," replied the king, "Adrian still lives, and is now beneath this roof."

"This news does indeed add to my present happiness," cried Alicia, "and most highly would I esteem the favour were I permitted to see him ere I leave the palace."

"Bid him come in, Sir Reginald," exclaimed the king. "The boy waits in the next chamber, and no doubt his joy will be as great as that of his former mistress."

The command was instantly obeyed, and no sooner did Adrian perceive the Lady Alicia, than falling at her feet, he gave way to the most extravagant expressions of joy and gratitude at her escape.

"This is indeed a happiness," he exclaimed, "for I feared Sir Gaston would discover the place of your retreat, and that ere now you had been taken back to the castle, and thrown into the dungeons from which you escaped with so much difficulty."

"And what reason had you for thinking so?" asked Alicia.

"Because on enquiring at the convent where I left you," he replied, "I was informed you had suddenly disappeared, and no one knew whither you was gone."

"That," answered Lady Alicia, "may be easily accounted for; soon after my arrival there, I was informed that Sir Gaston was making an active search after me, and fearing a discovery, I secretly took my departure, and sought a refuge in the place where Sir Reginald found me."

"And I trust," cried Adrian, "you are never going back to live in such a dreary miserable place?"

"That, I believe, will depend on circumstances," she replied; "at any rate, I have not at present any other home, and even if I had, I know not that I could do better than dwell within the peaceful walls of a convent."

"Nay," interposed the king, "here you may at least, remain till events prove whether Sir Gaston will be disposed to obtain pardon on the terms proposed. There is, however, one difficulty in the way, for it appears he has usurped the estates which belonged to an elder brother, and as that person is hourly expected to claim them, he will either have to comply, or submit to a violent expulsion."

"Alas!" cried Lady Alicia, "is there then any truth in the report that Sir Gaston has seized upon the property that by right belonged to another?"

"There is no reason to doubt it," answered Sir Reginald Courtney; "indeed, Sir Gaston himself does not deny that such a person may be in existence, and his agitation whenever the subject is mentioned, proves that he feels a consciousness of his own guilt."

"And who," demanded Alicia, "is the person he is accused of having thus wronged?"

"Aye, there lies the mystery," answered Sir Reginald, "for, though every one is quite positive the real heir lives, and is ready to come forward, there is not a person, I believe, who could name the person we have been speaking of. Edith, however, has made a random hit, which, in my opinion, is hardly likely to prove correct."

"And who do her suspicions point to?"

"Nay, you will but smile at her simplicity, when I tell you she believes the heir of Neville Castle and the armed apparition will turn out to be one and the same person."

"I remember the spectral form you speak of," cried Alicia. "It appeared before me on several occasions, and each time it was to save me from some pressing danger."

"Humph!—you also think, then, that the apparition will prove to be the heir so much spoken of?"

"I have every reason to believe that it is no spirit at all," answered Lady Alicia; "and, therefore, nothing can be more likely than it is the brother of Sir Gaston, who has taken upon himself that disguise, in order to avoid detection."

"Your opinion is exactly the same as my own," interposed the king; "I, of course, discredited the idle story of an apparition haunting the castle, and no sooner did Edith mention her thoughts upon the subject, than I became convinced of its correctness."

"And even supposing it should be so," observed Sir Reginald Courtney, "is there any one who would be able to prove the identity of this long missing brother?"

"That is at present uncertain," replied the king, "but, doubtless, the same Providence that has hitherto supported him in the hour of adversity, will aid in divulging the whole secret. Let the brother once be discovered, and there is no reason to fear but we shall be able to recognize in him the person he represents himself to be."

"But how," asked Lady Alicia, "are we to discover one whose motions have so often deceived us?"

"That, I believe, must be left to chance," replied King Richard. "It is said, however, that the person we are speaking of will appear to assert his claim whenever a favourable opportunity shall arrive."

"And a better one than the present could not possibly have happened," observed Sir Reginald.

"And why," asked the Lady Alicia, eagerly, "is the present opportunity so favourable?"

"Because Sir Gaston's guilt in other matters has been made to appear so manifest," he replied, "that no one will doubt the truth of that which at any other time would have appeared most improbable. The claimant will thus obtain a fair hearing, and thus we shall the more readily come at the truth."

"But why," asked Alicia, "if there is a brother living, did he not assert his claim before?"

"It was done, I believe," answered Sir Reginald Courtney, "from a wish not to expose a too guilty brother to a world which would execrate his crime. The motive has been a good one, and, therefore, we should not judge too harshly of the man who has been content to wait all these years for his just inheritance."

"Still," cried Alicia, "I must doubt that Sir Gaston de Neville has acted unjustly in the present instance. He is cruel and ambitious, but surely nature would not have suffered him to commit this foul injustice against his own brother."

"Your anxiety to advocate his cause, Lady Alicia," cried the king, "does honour to your heart. I myself discredited this story till lately, but now, it must be confessed, I begin to believe there is much truth in it. I have heard that the elder brother died under rather mysterious circumstances. Indeed, I believe no one could ever give a just account of where he expired, or of anything more about him than that he was dead and buried. Upon that, Sir Gaston took possession of the various castles and estates, and from that time, he has continued to enjoy them, though there were not wanting people to whisper strange rumours as to the right he had to take them."

"Yet, no one," observed Lady Alicia, "has till lately ventured to speak openly on the subject."

"It is true they have not openly spoken of the existence of this brother," replied the king; "for all that, men have never ceased to believe that the real heir would soon return to claim his inheritance. That moment has at length nearly arrived, and much as I should have wished to shield Sir Gaston, the only part I can take, will be to do justice to the heir."

"And Sir Gaston," cried Alicia, "will be crushed beneath the heavy accusations that are about to be brought against him."

"He has only to make amends to all whom he has wronged," answered the king, "and I will myself bestow upon him estates to make up for those he will lose. So, now, Sir Reginald Courtney, it will be your first care to provide suitable apartments within the palace for Lady Alicia, immediately after which, you will visit Neville Castle, to make

inquiries towards clearing up the mystery connected with the armed apparition."

Anxious as the young knight was to engage himself in a task of this nature, he soon carried into effect the former part of the king's commands, and having seen the Lady Alicia taken care of, he set forth towards dark,—accompanied only by one person,—for the noble residence of the Nevilles.

CHAPTER CXIX.

"Answer me, spirit,—say
Who art thou?—What's thine errand here?—and why
Thou dost appear before me in that shape
Of awful mystery?"

CONSCIENCE.

At the period to which our narrative belongs, nearly the whole of the intervening space between the royal palace at Westminster, and Moorfields, was an open country, with only a house here and there, to break the general monotony of the scene. Nor did they meet many persons on their way, for in that age people retired to their beds at an earlier hour than in the present days of luxury and dissipation, and it was only occasionally that they met some straggler who was directing his steps homewards. Sir Reginald Courtney was well enough pleased at the adventurous errand with which he had been entrusted, but not so was his companion Oliver, who, having but little of the

No. 97

spirit of chivalry about him, could see no use in visiting a castle for no other purpose than that of searching for an unearthly being, who, for aught they knew, might play them a scurvy trick for the trouble they had taken in hunting him out of his own quarters. Occupied with these thoughts, Oliver maintained a sullen silence as they rode onwards, which, being at length observed by Sir Reginald, he inquired whether he had entered unwillingly into the service he had undertaken.

"Why, to tell you a bit of my mind," replied the man, "I can see nothing but madness and folly in the affair we are going about. Ghost hunting was never a favourite amusement of mine, and all I can say about the matter is, that those who are fond of it, should not wish to drag other people into the dilemma."

"You go then unwillingly, sirrah?"

"To be sure I do," answered Oliver.

"Then why not have said so before we started, that I might have sought the assistance of some one with a better share of courage than you seem to have?"

"It would have been more than my life was worth to refuse the king's bidding," replied the other, "and as for courage, I don't think it shows any cowardice for a man to acknowledge his fear of unearthly spirits. Give me a human being for a foe, and I know what I've got to expect; but these apparitions are not to be combatted with mortal weapons, for it seems that a priest with a prayer or two, can sooner put them to flight, than a whole army of soldiers."

"Psha!—who has been filling thee with these foolish notions?"

"No one has done it," replied Oliver, "but my own sense tells me it is in vain for man to contend against spirits. They are mischievous foes, and he is a fool who would risk his life in hunting them out."

"Humph!—you are pleased to be complimentary!"

"Nay," answered the other, "present company, you know, is always excepted. Besides, one is apt sometimes to speak rather more plainly than one ought."

"It seems, Oliver, that you like not this errand of ours, and, therefore, before we go any further, I give you free permission to return."

"What! and leave you to go alone?"

"Better to do so," answered the knight, "than be accompanied by a man that is terrified even at the thought of having to encounter a trifling adventure like this. You understand me, Oliver; either summon up your courage, or leave me to pursue this enquiry by myself."

"That I'll never do, Sir Knight," exclaimed Oliver; "where you go, I'll follow, even if it should be to a certain place that ought never to be mentioned to ears polite. No, no, good master, I'm not a coward, though perhaps a little nervous when our business is with a hobgoblin."

"Psha!" exclaimed Sir Reginald, "this black phantom is no more a hobgoblin than either you or myself."

"Are you quite certain of that?"

"Almost so," answered the knight;" and at any rate I hope we shall return with news that will remove the mystery."

"And you expect then to find out that the armed apparition is a man of flesh and blood like ourselves?"

"Certainly."

"It's more than I do," exclaimed Oliver, "for I can see no motive that any man could possibly have for playing a prank like this. Besides, if there had been any trick in the affair, it must have been found out long enough ago."

"The alarm its appearance created was sufficient to prevent any discovery taking place," answered Sir Reginald. "Men are easily terrified into belief of supernatural agency, when they fancy they have ocular evidence of it, and as this supposed phantom has been seen by many persons, the report has gained confidence in spite of its improbabilty."

"Then you really don't believe anything about it?"

"I have told you I do not, and my present business is to discover the deception."

"Our Lady speed us!" cried Oliver, "for as sure as fate we shall both of us repent this business."

"If you think so, I again bid you leave me before we go any further," exclaimed Sir Reginald. "For my own part, I have no fear of going alone, and my only object of bringing you with me, was in case I might encounter living foes, who being superior in numbers, might overpower and slay me, whilst in the execution of the king's commands."

"I care nothing for mortal enemies," returned Oliver, "even if there should be three to one against us; but the gentleman from below in black armour is quite another affair, and if he should take it into his head to appear before us, I don't promise but I should run away from sheer terror. So now, as we have reached the principal gate of Neville Castle, perhaps your knightship will be good enough to say what I am to do?"

"We will dismount," replied Sir Reginald, "and having tied our two horses to yonder tree, demand admittance to the place in the king's name."

Upon this they both leaped from their saddles, and having secured their steeds in the manner proposed by Sir Reginald, he closely followed by his attendant, advanced towards the portal, and knocked lustily for admittance. The summons was, however, repeated without effect, and they began to grow impatient at the delay, when footsteps were heard within, and after the removal of sundry heavy bolts and bars, the ponderous gate was thrown open, and a man, closely wrapped up in a capacious cloak, and carrying a lamp in his hand, made his appearance, and demanded who they were, and what their business was. This question, however, was scarcely asked, when the light he carried streamed upon his countenance, and discovered the well-known features of the Outlaw. This recognition was anything but agreeable to the attendant, who, starting back three or four paces, exclaimed :—

"Black Ivan, by all that's terrible!"

"Aye," he answered, "it is Black Ivan ; and now perhaps you will tell me the motive that has led to this visit?"

"I have been sent hither by the king," replied Sir Reginald, "but little did I expect to encounter one whose life would be forfeited, were he to fall into the hands of his enemies."

"There is no fear of that," answered the other, with indifference, "for even if I should be taken,—which is not very likely,—I should claim the king's pardon, in consideration of having saved him from the dagger of an assassin."

"But you failed to accept the terms offered in the royal proclamation," replied Sir Reginald, "and having preferred the society of your own lawless associates, all further claim to his mercy has been forfeited."

"Well, well," exclaimed the Outlaw, impatiently, "it's hardly worth while arguing upon that subject just now, so, with your leave, I'll repeat the question I put to you just now :—What business has brought you hear at this hour?"

"I have told you I come in obedience to the king's commands."

"Humph!" ejaculated the other, sarcastically, "you have come, I suppose, with your *one* follower to take possession of the castle of Sir Gaston de Neville ?"

"At present," answered the knight, without heeding the manner in which these words were spoken, "the king has no intention to proceed to the extremities you have mentioned. He has heard, however, that a claimant is likely to make his appearance, and as it is suspected, that the armed apparition and the heir is one and the same person, I have been directed to make a strict search through the castle, in order that I may solve a mystery of so much importance. To my surprize, however, I find you here, though I should have imagined this was the last place you would think of visiting."

"I came here to seek Sir Gaston de Neville," answered the Outlaw; "and on gaining admittance to the castle, found it entirely deserted by all the knight's retainers."

"What ! are there none left to protect it ?"

"Not a soul," replied Ivan :—"I have wandered through a great part of it, and every apartment is deserted."

"What motive could they have had for this ?" asked the knight.

"That I know not for certain," replied Ivan, "but I suppose they have gone to one of the other castles, in order to escape the punishment that awaits a good many of them."

"Are there no prisoners in any of the dungeons ?"

"Not one,—I have searched them all, and have satisfied myself on that point."

"It seems you came here to see Sir Gaston," observed the knight;— "was there any reason to suppose you would find him here after his escape from the Gate-house ?"

"Why, I thought it was likely enough, but though I have gone through a great part of the castle, I have not been lucky enough to see anything of him yet."

"Will you tell me what reason you had for desiring to see him ?"

"Another time I may do so," answered Ivan, "but at present I can merely say that my business was chiefly to urge him to the performance of an act of justice."

"And could an Outlaw do this ?"

"Yes,—the Outlaw has but to whisper one word in his ear, and even the haughty Sir Gaston de Neville would yield to an imperative necessity."

"Your words are full of mystery," observed Sir Reginald : "yet, I suppose, you will afford me no further explanation just now on the subject I feel so deeply interested in ?"

"At present my principal object must remain a secret," answered Ivan, "though I do not mind telling you that two of the objects I have in view are,—firstly, that he will restore Lady Alicia to the place from which his cruel tyranny has driven her,—and secondly, that he will pledge his word that he will never more persecute the Hebrew Maiden."

"There is no fear that he will ever injure either of them again, I believe," replied Sir Reginald, "for Lady Alicia has now found a safe refuge in the king's palace, and as for Rebecca and her father, it is reported that they have fled to some place where he has hitherto been unable to trace them."

"If Lady Alicia is safe, I can answer for it the others are," exclaimed the Outlaw.

"Ha ! you know their place of concealment, then ?"

"I do,—in fact, they are at this time in my secret retreat, where none, Ibeli eve, will ever venture to follow them."

"How!—have they voluntarily thrown themselves under the protection of robbers?"

"They have, Sir Knight," answered Ivan; "and have hitherto seen no reason to regret their confidence. They seldom see any of the rough fellows that own my sway, and even if they did, the rogues know well enough that their lives would pay the forfeit, should they offer them any injury."

"You seem to have taken a great interest in their behalf," cried Sir Reginald Courtney, "and I cannot help thinking there must be some secret motive for it."

"The only secret," answered the other, "is that I detest the tyranny which is directed against the weak and helpless. Rebecca and her father belong to a race that is trampled on and despised without just cause, and when I saw the maiden about to become the victim of Sir Gaston's villanous designs I stepped forward in her behalf, and averted the evil that was meditated."

"And yet," exclaimed Sir Reginald, "one would hardly have expected so much from a robber."

"The robber is not so from choice, but necessity," replied the Outlaw; "he has endured wrongs from his fellow man, and in retaliation, took to the life you so loudly deprecate. I am a robber, but never yet have I been guilty of unnecessary cruelty, even towards a fallen foe."

"You have had cause, it seems, to complain of injustice from your fellow creatures?"

"Aye, heavy cause."

"May I know who has injured you?"

"It matters not," answered Ivan; "another time, should we ever meet together again, I may be better disposed to communicate more freely. But a truce to this;—you wish to go over the castle, and if you do not mind having me for a guide, I will myself conduct you."

"And my attendant?"

"Must remain here," answered the Outlaw:—"he seems but a timid fellow, and may do more harm than good should we permit him to accompany us."

Oliver heard this proposition with evident satisfaction, for though he did not much like the imputation of cowardice, yet to his thinking, anything was better than risking his life in what he could not help regarding as a very useless pursuit. He, therefore, contented himself with remaining where he was, and Sir Reginald Courtney, entering the portal, followed Black Ivan across she court-yard, and proceeded to the principal hall, the deserted appearance of which convinced him that the Outlaw had spoken truly, when he declared that the retainers had disappeared from the place."

"It is strange," he said, as he gazed round, "that not one should have been left behind to report any proceedings that may follow the downfall of this imperious owner."

"Why, the truth is they had good reason to suppose that it would be dangerous to remain here any longer," answered Ivan; "the knaves found that their master was in difficulties, and caring for nothing so much as their own safety, they have decamped, leaving everything to its fate."

"But what can have become of Sir Gaston himself?" asked Sir Reginald. "That he has escaped from custody, is quite certain, and I fancied his first place of refuge would be here."

"I thought so myself," answered Black Ivan, "but I suppose he expected his pursuers would not fail to to look for him here, and, doubtless, he has made the best use of his time by hurrying down to the sea coast, where he will readily meet with a vessel to carry him beyond the reach of danger. At all events he will take care to keep out of harm's way, till he knows how the king intends to proceed."

"His majesty is just now as much incensed against him," said the knight, "though, I believe, on certain conditions, he will not only restore him to his royal favour, but also bestow upon him lands nearly equal to those he will be compelled to give up to his brother."

"And does Sir Gaston know the gracious intentions of his majesty?" enquired the Outlaw.

"He does not, or I dare say he would not have escaped from prison as he has."

"Perhaps he will prove obstinate," exclaimed the other, "and refuse to acknowledge the brother you speak of."

"In that case," returned Sir Reginald, "he will for ever forfeit the king's regard, and force will be used to compell him to the performance of an act of justice."

"In other words," observed Ivan, "he will perish by the hands of the executioner, unless he relinquishes everything that he has wrung from the long absent heir."

"Such an alternative is not at all unlikely if he should prove head-strong," answered the knight. "Let us hope, however, that he may yield to stern necessity, and thus avert the dangers that at present threaten to crush him."

By this time they had reached the armoury, and as they were passing through towards an opposite door, their eyes lighted upon a steel gauntlet which was lying upon a table. The sight of this seemed to strike them both with surprise, for they well knew it to be one that was constantly worn by Sir Gaston de Neville, and the fact of its being there proved beyond a doubt that the owner had lately been there.

"This gauntlet," said the knight, "was on Sir Gaston's hand scarcely two hours before I heard the news of his escape. He has been here Ivan, and I dare say is still lurking somewhere about the place."

"The fox has been here and stole away as we approached his cover," exclaimed the Outlaw; "this he has left behind him in his haste to escape, but it will be hard if I do not contrive to find him now before I take my departure from the castle."

"But do you think he would remain in the place now that he knows of our presence here?"

"There's no doubt of it," replied Ivan; "for the building contains many conveniences for a man that wishes to play at hide and seek. Yet he may do his worst or his best, for I will find him in spite of all his efforts at concealment."

"Should we light upon him," observed the knight, "we must use no more violence than may be necessary for his re-capture. The king has been pleased to charge me with the execution of this duty, and I will obey him to the very letter."

"I have no more wish to slay Sir Gaston than you have yourself," replied the Outlaw; "nay, more, it is my determination to save his life, even though it might cost my own."

"And yet I fancied you had a motive for wishing to destroy him," cried Sir Reginald.

"Heaven forbid!" exclaimed the other. "His life I never sought, for had my wishes laid that way, he would long ere now have fallen by my hand. I would spare him, that he may have an opportunity to repent the crimes that ambition and his own uncurbed passions have led him into."

"You seem to entertain some regard for this man."

"I would spare him as far as I can," answered Ivan, "but his own mad career has compelled me to take an active part against him. I believe, however, he would not be quite so considerate towards me if I happened to be as much in his power as he is in mine."

"Perhaps he conceives there is ample ground for his hatred?"

"I know not how that may be," answered Ivan, "but we have ever watched each other with an eye of suspicion and distrust, and he hates me because I have foiled him in his base designs against Rebecca, the Hebrew Maiden."

"But I have heard," said Sir Reginald, "that you also persecuted her with your love at one time."

"I certainly did love the girl at one time," answered the Outlaw, "but when I found that her heart was given to another, I gave up my hopes, and lent what aid I could to assist her against the plots of Sir Gaston de Neville. Fortunately I succeeded, and hence arises his enmity towards me."

"You have assured me, however," cried the knight, "that in case you meet him, no violence will be offered beyond what may be necessary for his capture."

"That you may rely on, for I would rather save him from death than accellerate it."

"I will take your word for it," cried the knight, "and now tell me, Ivan,—for by your own admission you know every part of this castle,—did you ever see anything of this armed apparition that people talk so much about?"

"I have."

"And do you believe it to be a spirit or some human being that has assumed the disguise for purposes of his own?"

"That," replied the other, "is a question I am not at present prepared to answer. All in the castle, however, believed it to belong to another world, and even Sir Gaston himself is of that opinion."

"And yet," cried the knight, "I could wager my life it will turn out to be a deception."

"It may," answered Ivan, "but it remains for time to prove it. Your present business here is to penetrate the mystery, but I would have you be cautious, or you may pay dearly for trying to dive into secrets that concern you not."

"At all events," exclaimed Sir Reginald Courtney, "I shall execute my task boldly and without fear. My sword never yet failed me in the hour of need, and, should it be necessary to defend my life, I shall do so with a determination to sacrifice it rather than disappoint the expectations of the king."

"And so Richard feels an interest in this affair between Sir Gaston and his brother?"

"He does, and is resolved to pursue the inquiry to a successful termination."

"Perhaps I may be able to assist him," exclaimed Ivan after a short pause, "the affair rather interests me, and on one condition I will engage heart and hand in it."

"What is your condition?"

"That Sir Gaston's life shall not be hazarded."

"I have told you before," replied the other, "that the king has no ill-feeling towards Sir Gaston : nay, he has but to do the justice required of him, and I could almost undertake to pledge myself that he will imme- diately afterwards be restored to the royal confidence."

"Will his treason be forgiven?"

"That will entirely depend upon himself," answered the knight. "Sir Gaston has only to renounce all future connexion with Prince John and his partizans, and his past treason will be pardoned."

"How can you vouch for this?"

"From having heard his majesty utter words to the effect," replied Sir Reginald Courtney; "they have fought together in the same field, and Cœur de Lion frankly acknowledges that he has not a braver knight in his whole dominions than Sir Gaston de Neville."

"Nor one less likely to earn his forgiveness by an acknowledgment of his errors," observed Ivan.

"That," answered the other, "was in the height of his prosperity; but now his circumstances are changed, and having fallen under the royal displeasure, there is good reason to hope he will yield to the cir- cumstances that have so depressed him."

"And what is to become of the Lady Alicia?"

"She will be restored to that place in his affections which, through some unaccountable circumstances she lost," replied Sir Reginald Court- ney. "You smile doubtfully, but for my own part I see no improbabi- lity in it."

"That is because you do not understand the character of Sir Gaston de Neville as well as I do," answered Ivan. "He is not of a forgiving nature, and the man who could imprison his wife in the dungeons of this castle so many years, is most unlikely to regard her with any other feel- ings than those of bitterness and hate. On the other hand, Lady Alicia must look upon him as a cruel tyrant, and, therefore, under all circum- stances, I think it would be better that they never see each other again."

"But now, with regard to yourself, Ivan," exclaimed the knight; "how do you intend to act in the event of the king offering a free par- don for all your offences?"

"I shall accept it, of course."

"And for ever quit the society of your lawless associates?"

"Yes;" replied Ivan, "the fellows, like myself, are, I believe, growing tired of a trade that is no longer profitable, and it will be no difficult task to prevail on them to seek a more honourable employment in future. I have a considerable sum of money in the cave, and as I wish not to keep that which has not come over honestly into my possession, I shall divide it among them, under a promise that they will never again return to their old mode of living."

"And what do you propose doing yourself?" asked the knight.

"I shall not turn hermit you may be sure," he replied, "but as my arm is still vigorous, it shall wield a sword against the enemies of my country. Thus I may retrieve a character that is not quite so fair as it might have been, and should I fall in battle, people may perhaps forget my errors in the service I have done them."

"Upon my life, Ivan," exclaimed the knight, "there is a strange mix- ture in your nature that I cannot understand. In spite of your connexion with a band of lawless ruffians, there is honour still left in your heart, and had we a more favourable opportunity, I would ask to know the cause that first induced you to become the leader of these men?"

"The opportunity you speak of will arrive sooner than you expect," answered Ivan; "each hour serves to bring the crisis still nearer, when I shall throw aside the mask and appear before the world what I really am."

"Upon which," exclaimed Sir Reginald, "you will obtain the king's pardon for having saved his life on the day of the coronation. That was a fortunate circumstance for you, Ivan, and will procure for you both advancement and reward."

"Neither of which I require," answered the Outlaw. "However, as I have explained myself thus far, we will now proceed to execute the task that has brought us here. You will go in search of the armed apparition, and I to find Sir Gaston de Neville, who I am now certain has sought concealment in some part of the castle."

"I have undertaken the duty, and will endeavour to perform it," replied Sir Reginald; "but I am a complete stranger here, and it will be no easy task to find my way through the mazes and difficulties that everywhere surround me."

"You have but to keep straight forward, and your course is clear enough," answered the Outlaw. "A long range of apartments lies before you, at the termination of which you will find yourself in the eastern tower, from whence a flight of winding steps will lead you to the dungeons beneath this edifice. In that portion of the building the mysterious being you are in search of has most frequently been seen, and it is, therefore, likely enough you may not have your trouble in vain."

"But why need we part?" demanded the knight, as he saw the Outlaw preparing to leave him.

"Because it is necessary that we pursue our search in different parts of the castle," answered Ivan. "I know the place tolerably well, and can guess where it is most likely the fugitive knight may be found. So, now, let courage inspire you, and when next we meet, you will knowledge that the directions I have given were the means of leading to the discovery you are anxious to make."

"Will you not want the lamp?" asked Sir Reginald.

"No; I can find my way about here well enough," he replied, "but you, who are a stranger, will require the aid of a light. So, now, farewell for the present, and may you succeed to the full extent of your hopes."

Upon saying this, Ivan hurriedly left the room, and Sir Reginald, taking the lamp in his hand, prepared to commence the search in which he was engaged. With all his confidence, however, in the Outlaw, he could not help indulging a lurking suspicion that some treachery might be intended, and drawing his poniard, he moved slowly forward, keeping a vigilant watch on all sides, and resolving, should any attack be made upon him, to sell his life as dearly as possible. Thus intent upon his own defence in case of need, he passed through several chambers of such vast extent, that the feeble rays of his lamp were insufficient to penetrate the gloom with which he was surrounded. He, however, moved forward without dread, till at length the distance he had gone, convinced him that he had by some means or other missed the way which had been pointed out by Black Ivan. In this predicament he paused, uncertain which way to direct his steps, and yet unwilling to return to the point from whence he had set forth; it was in vain too that he thought of calling upon the Outlaw to come and aid him in this difficulty, for by this time he must be beyond the reach of his voice, and, therefore, trusting to chance, he moved forward, till he came to one of the walls, round which he groped his way to a door, from whence a few steps led into a lower chamber, which, judging by the hollow sound his footsteps produced, seemed to be of larger extent than any of the others he had passed through. He was now more puzzled than ever, and despairing of success, he had made up his mind to wait till the dawn of day to aid him, when a distant light was seen slowly approaching the place where he was standing. Believing this to be the Outlaw, he hurried forward to meet him, and his surprise may be more easily conceived than described, when he recognized, not the person he had expected, but the armed apparition he was in search of. For a minute or two he gazed in speechless astonishment upon the figure before him, but quickly recovering his usual firmness, he demanded whether it was a human being, or an unearthly being that had presented itself before him.

But the figure gazed upon him with a fixed look, and pointing towards the direction from whence he had come, seemed to bid him follow without fear.

"Ere I obey your commands," cried Sir Reginald, "I would know whether your intentions are friendly or otherwise?"

The apparition by a sign assured him that he had nothing to fear.

"Art thou a mortal like myself," asked the knight, "or do I indeed behold before me an inhabitant of another world? You reply not by word or sign, and, therefore, do I refuse to accompany you, lest I should be led into toils that may have been laid for my destruction."

The figure advanced a step, and by a sign, seemed to assure him there was no cause for suspicion.

"Wilt thou not speak to me?"

A motion in the head replied in the negative.

"Are thine intentions favourable towards me?"

The same silent answer assured him he might rely with perfect confidence.

"Whither would you lead me?"

The mysterious visitant pointed again in the direction from whence it had come, and seemed impatient at the delay. Sir Reginald, however, still had his doubts, and hesitating to consider what course he should adopt, he at length said:—

"My motive in visiting the castle was to see you, in order that a discovery might be made relative to the heir of this domain,—answer me, therefore, and say where we may seek the person we are in search of. Hah! you give no sign or token, and, therefore, do I believe you are the long-missing brother of Sir Gaston de Neville."

An impatient gesture was the only answer to this, and again the figure pointed in the direction he was to follow, and retreated backwards three or four paces, as if expecting he would obey a command thus significantly given. Still, however, Sir Reginald could not divest himself of a thought that some act of treachery might be meditated, and he paused to consider whether he should pursue this adventure any further, or by a decided refusal, terminate an adventure that it was likely enough might end in the much desired explanation. It was not cowardice that prompted him to this caution, for he was well armed in case of any sudden attack by an insidious foe, but he knew not into what trap he might be led, and willing as he was to sacrifice his life in a just cause, it was still necessary that he should act with prudence, until there was a certainty of bringing the affair to a certain close. Observing that the mysterious form still pointed in the direction he was to pursue, Sir Reginald again demanded whither it was about to lead him.

The phantom pointed downwards, as if they were about to visit the dungeons beneath the castle.

"And if I follow thee," cried the knight, "how am I to know that it may not be to danger? Nay, if thou wilt not answer me, at least raise thy viser, that I may see the face of him to whom I am about to trust myself."

But the figure again replied by a motion of the head, that signified its refusal to comply with this suggestion, and finding that no alternative remained, Sir Reginald came to the determination of accompanying his mysterious guide, let the consequences to himself be what they might.

"Thou hast refused to give any reply, that might serve to remove my doubt," he said, "and, therefore, I have reason to believe thine intentions towards me may prove treacherous. I have, however, a purpose to accomplish in visiting the castle of Sir Gaston de Neville, and in spite of all personal considerations, I will obey thy bidding. Lead on,—and should any evil be meditated against me, be assured, I will not perish till I have made a desperate resistance to my foes."

The apparition seemed not to heed these words, but gliding slowly onwards, led Sir Reginald through a long range of apartments, all of which, though evidently inhabited very lately, wore an air of desolation that seemed to throw a chill upon the heart of the youthful warrior. But his courage was not to be daunted by imaginary dangers, and looking cautiously around him as they passed along, he mentally resolved to sell his life dearly, in the event of his worst forebodings being realized.

In this way they continued to pass from chamber to chamber, without anything occurring to increase the suspicion of Sir Reginald Courtney, and on reaching the eastern tower, mentioned by Black Ivan, they began to descend a winding flight of steps, that being broken in many places, rendered the passage uncertain and dangerous. At length they reached the bottom, and pursued their way along a gloomy subterraneous corridor, on each side of which was a range of iron bound doors, that led to the various dungeons in which so many hapless victims had pined away their lives in hopeless captivity. Sir Reginald could not help shuddering as he reflected upon the misery of those whom tyranny had oppressed, and he was still meditating upon this melancholy subject, when the apparition suddenly paused before one of the cells, the door of which suddenly flew open at its touch, and discovered the cheerless gloom of the interior, faintly lighted as it was by the lamp which he held in his hand. Pausing for a moment, he saw that the figure pointed towards the dungeon as if directing him to enter, but a thought struck him that it might be intended to imprison him there, and for a moment he hesitated to take a step that might terminate in his imprisonment there for life. A little reflection, however, served to re-assure him that no such danger threatened him, and stepping fearlessly into the cell, he was startled at hearing a rustling among the straw that was lying heaped in one corner, and as he started back to defend himself, Sir Gaston de Neville presented himself to his view.

"Hah!" exclaimed the Templar, with a fiendish cry of joy, "we are well met, Sir Knight;—you have followed me to my place of concealment, and shall die for your temerity!"

"Sir Gaston de Neville," answered the other, standing upon the defensive, "should know me better than to imagine I am to be intimidated by his idle threats. I am not unskilled in arms, and since we have thus met, we will meet in deadly strife, and let heaven defend the right."

"Why hast thou come to seek one, who, whatever may be his faults, has never injured thee?"

"I have come," answered Sir Reginald, "by the command of him whose will I dare not disobey."

"Aye, the king has sent thee?"

"He has."

"Why did he not come himself?" demanded Sir Gaston, fiercely. "Was he afraid to meet the man he thus seeks to destroy?"

"Cœur de Lion, as thou well knowest, is a stranger to fear," answered the younger knight; "he has proved his valour in the field, ere now, and would not shrink from an encounter with thee, hadst thou not disgraced thyself by deeds of cruelty and oppression."

"And hast thou come to tell me this?"

"I am come to make thee my prisoner," answered Sir Reginald.

"Humph!—and was that thine only purpose?"

"No, I come in search of the armed apparition that report has said haunts thy castle."

"And of course thine errand has proved fruitless?"

"Not altogether," replied Sir Reginald;—"I have seen the phantom, and it is to its guidance that you owe my presence here at this moment. It led me to the spot, and having accomplished its purpose, has disappeared."

"Credulous fool!" exclaimed Sir Gaston, "dost thou also believe in an idle tale that should be credited only by women and children?"

"Thy words, proud knight, will not provoke me to anger," answered the other. "Nay, I would still be thy friend, and prevail on thee to purchase the pardon of thy royal master, by abandoning the evil ways that have marked thy life with shame."

"Shouldst thou be fortunate enough to escape my vengeance," cried Sir Gaston, "thou may'st tell him that I scorn to acknowledge the sway a usurper."

"Wouldst thou still further incense a king who seeks to do thee a service?" asked Sir Reginald.

"Dost thou call it a service to send thee here to my castle that thou may'st gather information to procure my ruin?"

"I came but to make enquiries about thy brother," answered the young knight; "it has been thought that he it is who personates the armed phantom, and I was desired to make enquiries into the truth or falsehood of that report."

"Well," exclaimed Sir Gaston, "and having seen this supernatural visitant, art thou any wiser than when thou did'st come here?"

"I must acknowledge I have not yet heard anything to clear up the mystery."

"Then having failed in thine errand, thou cans't return to the king with news of having seen me."

"Nay," cried Sir Reginald, "I go not unless you accompany me to the palace."

"Dost thou think I am mad?"

"I speak only for thine own good," answered the other. "The king seeks not to injure thee, but would remove from thee the foul reproach that at present clings to thy name."

"No more of this!" cried Sir Gaston de Neville fiercely. "Already have I listened to thee too long, and by heavens thy life will be put in fearful jeopardy if thou wilt not leave my presence without delay."

"Thy threats I care not for," exclaimed Sir Reginald: "duty is my own guide, and I will follow it in spite of the fury that I see kindling in thy soul."

"Then meet the fate thine own rashness has brought upon thee!" cried Sir Gaston, and rushing forward, he would have slain the object of his fury had not the other stepped on one side, and thus escaped a blow that was aimed at his heart. In another moment their swords were cast away, and each drawing his poniard, they sought by feints and stratagems to gain an advantage that would terminate in the death of his opponent. At last Sir Reginald sprang on his adversary with a sudden lunge, and seizing him by the throat, they both fell to the ground firmly clutched in each other's arms. In this struggle, however, Sir Gaston obtained the advantage, and as they were thus prostrate, he raised his dagger to strike it into the heart of his foe, when a violent blow from some unseen hand stretched him powerless and insensible on the earth.

CHAPTER CXX.

"But, if I live, his feigned extacies
Shall be no shelter to these outrages:
But he and his shall know that justice lives
In Saturninus' health; whom, if she sleep,
He'll so awake, as she in fury shall
Cut off the proud'st conspirator that lives."

How long Sir Reginald Courtney had remained in the condition he knew not, but when he at length revived, he found that it was broad daylight, and that he was in one of the apartments of the castle, with Black Ivan and Oliver anxiously applying themselves to the task of restoring him to animation. He still felt the stupifying effect of the blow he had received in the dungeon, but as his recollection gradually returned, and he thought of his death struggle with Sir Gaston de Neville, he enquired with great earnestness for an explanation of the cause that had led to his escape from a doom that appeared to be inevitable.

"You wish to know," exclaimed Black Ivan, "who it was that laid your enemy prostrate at a moment when the least delay would have been so fatal to yourself?"

"I do," replied Sir Reginald, "and yet upon reflection I know not who it could have been but you."

"You have guessed rightly enough there," answered the Outlaw, "but am I to understand that you saw not the person that interposed for your deliverance?"

"I did not," replied the young knight, "and yet I have a dim remembrance that by the faint reflection of the lamp against the wall of the dungeon I saw the shadow of the armed apparition."

"Nay, that would be impossible," exclaimed Ivan, "for I can answer for it there was no one present but myself."

"Art thou sure of that?"

"Quite positive."

"And the more I think of it," cried Sir Reginald, "the more certain do I feel that I am not mistaken."

"Humph!" retorted the Outlaw, "a shadow might easily deceive you, and the insensibility that followed will readily account for your labouring under this impression."

"Can you account to me," asked the knight, "for the death-like stupor in which it appears I have been so long lying?"

"That is readily answered," returned Ivan; "the blow that struck down your foe glanced upon your own head, and both you and Sir Gaston lay stretched at my feet in all the semblance of death."

"After which, it seems, you removed me to this place?"

"I did, and calling upon Oliver, your attendant, we have, after a little trouble, restored you to animation."

"And Sir Gaston?"

"Is, for aught I know, still in the dungeon where we left him," answered the Outlaw.

"And perhaps has perished from the blow that came so opportunely to save my life?"

"No," replied Ivan, "there is every reason to believe he had as good a chance of recovering as you had. At all events, he was still alive when I left him, and there is no doubt he will yet live to carry on his evil designs."

"Let him be instantly secured then," cried Sir Reginald, rising hastily from the couch upon which he had been laid. "Secure him, I entreat, Ivan, for whilst he is free the king's life is continually exposed to danger."

"Richard has not much to fear from him now, I believe," answered the Outlaw, "for the truth is, a careful watch will be kept to prevent his evil machinations from taking effect, and if any is to be apprehended, it is by those who have contrived to foil the plots his busy brain has engendered."

"To whom dost thou allude?"

"To all," replied Ivan, "who have in any way given him offence. The Israelite and his daughter, the Lady Alicia, nay, thou and myself must keep guard with a watchful eye, or we shall not fail to feel the deadly wrath of a man who cares not by what means he executes the vengeance of his soul."

"For myself I care not," cried Sir Reginald, "but for the sake of others something must be done to prevent the desperate practices of this bloodsucker."

"What wouldst thou do?"

"Seek the recreant knight in the dungeon where we left him," answered Sir Reginald, "and secure him ere he find means to escape again from our custody."

"That is easier said than done," exclaimed Ivan, "for, depend on it, if he has recovered from the stupor I left him in, he has contrived ere this to leave a place that no longer offers him the security he requires."

"And in that case," cried Sir Reginald, "who knows what crime he may commit ere this day comes to a close? He thirsts for blood, and never will he rest satisfied till he has accomplished some of the deeds he has long contemplated."

"But you forget," replied Black Ivan, "that should he be seen, there are many who would gladly capture him, even were there no reward in perspective."

"I have remembered all that," answered Sir Reginald, "yet rely upon it the Knight Templar will be careful not to trust himself where there will be danger. His first thought will be to fly to the place where his retainers are waiting till he joins them, and then I grant you he may very likely attempt some mad scheme that will terminate in his own destruction."

"It is by no means certain that he will succeed in escaping the vigilance of the many foes his cruelty has raised up against him," exclaimed the Outlaw, "and even if he should have the luck to do so, it will even then be very unlikely to have it in his power to do much mischief, since all are aware of him, and will take care to keep beyond his reach."

"I will seek him out, at any rate," cried Sir Reginald Courtney, "for his hand has been raised against my life, and I will not cease to hunt him out till I have either slain or once more placed him in the prison from whence he has found means to escape."

"Thou must promise not to seek his life," answered the other, "or, I can tell thee it is little help thou wilt get from me."

"And wherefore art thou thus mindful of one whom I thought was thine enemy?"

"He is my enemy," answered the Outlaw, "yet, it does not follow that I should seek his blood merely in satisfaction of my own vengeance. Nay, to speak the truth, I would rather hazard my own life in his defence, than stand idly by and witness the destruction of a man, who, in spite of his crimes, I would see come to repentance."

"These are strange words to be uttered by a robber!"

"Aye, it may seem so to thee," cried Ivan, "and yet, robber as I am, I never yet sought the blood of a fellow-creature."

"The world has much belied thee then."

"I am not the first that the world has wronged by false accusations," answered Black Ivan; "besides, I have led but a reckless, dare-devil sort of life, and it is natural enough that marvellous stories should be circulated to my prejudice. Some have pictured me as a monster of iniquity, and yet, I believe there is more real villany among those who profess a fair and unimpeachable character."

"There is a mystery about thee," cried Sir Reginald Courtney, "that remains to be explained."

"Not a bit," answered the Outlaw; "you see before you a man that has been much wronged, and who, as the only alternative, has been driven to deeds he never else would have dreamed of."

"How many years hast thou been connected with these brigands?"

"Judging from thine appearance," answered Ivan, "I should say more years than thou hast lived."

"And is it a course of life that thou hast followed from choice, or has necessity driven you to it?"

"I thought," answered the Outlaw, "my words had been sufficiently explicit upon that point. At any rate, let it now be understood that I did not voluntarily become what you know me to be."

"Then why not renounce the life," asked Sir Reginald, "and once more re-enter the honourable society from which thou hast been so many years excluded?"

"It is easy to ask such a question," exclaimed Ivan, "but let any man place himself in my situation, and he would soon find out how diffi-cult it is to retrace a few false steps. Nay, let me ask you,—who is there that would associate with Black Ivan the Outlaw?"

"Not if they knew thee to be the man," returned Sir Reginald, "but it would be easy to quit a part of the country where you are known, and by a change of name, deceive people into a belief that you are as honest as themselves. England has many places where you might remain secure enough, and even if there should be any danger of a dis-covery, you might soon remove to some other part, where, for a time, you might remain unknown to the world."

"And thus be hunted about from place to place," observed Ivan; "like a wretch that has no right to dwell in what part of the world he pleases. No, no, I must either be known for who and what I am, or the remainder of my life will be passed among those who for many a long year have been my comrades."

"And that may easily be," answered Sir Reginald, "for the king has published a proclamation, offering you a free pardon for saving his life from the hand of an assassin."

"I know it," exclaimed Ivan, "but there are reasons why I have not yet accepted the proffered clemency. At present, circumstances have prevented my doing so, but I am much mistaken if those obstacles will be in existence much longer. Each hour brings me nearer to the time when I may throw myself upon the king's clemency, and when the period arrives, I am much mistaken if people will not pardon my errors in consideration of the provocation I have received."

"For my own part," observed Sir Reginald Courtney, "I see not why the revelation might not be as well made at the present time as at any other. You would thus be relieved from the odium that at present attaches itself to your name, and the remainder of your days would be passed in that peace which seems hitherto to have been denied you."

"All will be done in good time," answered Ivan, "but no considera-tion shall ever induce me to alter my present plan. I am well content to remain in my present station yet a little while longer, and when a proper opportunity arrives, I shall not fail to seize upon it."

"Is there any way," asked the knight, "by which I can afford any assistance?"

"Just now, I see none," replied Ivan, "but, believing as I do, that the offer is made in all sincerity and kindness, I may, perhaps, hereafter call upon you to fulfil it."

"And, whenever that may be," cried Sir Reginald, "you may rely on it, you shall find a friend in the man whose life you have so recently saved."

"Psha! that was but a trifle, and cost me scarcely an effort," ex-claimed Ivan. "The truth is, I was not far off at the time, and hearing a bit of a skirmish between you and Sir Gaston de Neville, I thought it high time to interfere for the prevention of bloodshed. On entering the

cell, I found you both struggling upon the ground, and Sir Gaston's dagger raised for your destruction; of course, there was not much time for deliberation, and seizing hold of a bar belonging to the door, I, with one blow, laid your antagonist at my feet, and had very nearly, at the same time, finished your life. However, the event has turned out more luckily than I expected, and, therefore, let me now caution you never again to come in contact with Sir Gaston de Neville."

"Your caution is but thrown away upon me," replied the other, "for, let the consequences be what they may, I will never cease following him till he is again a prisoner."

"And are you thus inveterate against him only because he and you had that struggle together not long since?"

"Any private quarrel between us may be forgotten," answered Sir Reginald Courtney; "but I know him to be a dangerous enemy of the king's, and never will I give up my pursuit after him, till I am assured the life of my royal master is no longer in peril through his means."

"Thou mayest spare thyself all further trouble on that subject," exclaimed the Outlaw, "for I have taken upon myself the task to protect King Richard against the designs of his enemy."

"You will not go with me then, to see whether he is still in the dungeon where you left him?"

"Why, I don't mind doing that, on condition that you tell me your motive for wishing to go."

"It is merely to see whether he is there," replied Sir Reginald, "and in the event of our finding him, I would then promise to interfere no further with him, on condition that he gives his word to have no more to do with this treason."

No. 99

"Humph!" retorted Black Ivan, "it is hardly likely he will give any such pledge; yet, nevertheless, if that is thine only motive, I care not if I go with thee to search for him. But, remember, should any further quarrel take place between thee, it will be my part to interfere for the prevention of bloodshed."

"I pledge myself that no violence shall be offered, and should Sir Gaston seek to provoke a combat, I will rather incur his scorn, than break the word I have now given thee."

"Then will I rely on thee," exclaimed Ivan, "and if thou hast strength enough left, after the blow which laid thee prostrate, I am ready to act the part of thy guide."

"The blow has had no other effect than that of stunning me for the time," answered Sir Reginald; "I am now quite recovered, and can follow thee whersoever it is thy pleasure to lead me."

"And what," asked Oliver, with alarm, "is to become of me while you are gone?"

"You will remain here till our return," answered the knight, "we shall not be gone long, and it will be your task to watch lest any of Sir Gaston's retainers should be lurking about to rush upon us when we are off our guard."

"Why, as for that," exclaimed Oliver, "I care not a doit for any of the human beings I may chance to come across; but there is the black phantom to be thought of, and I should die with terror should that horrible form come in my way."

"Coward! do you shrink from your duty?"

"Aye, my good master," cried the fellow, "it's all very well to call me a coward, but where's the man, I should like to know, that has the courage to meet a spirit from the other world?"

"Psha! I have already told you this is no spirit."

"Then why didn't you satisfy yourself upon that point when you saw it not long ago?" asked Oliver. "There was a good chance lost, and as you can't prove it to be anything else than an apparition, I must, with all respect to yourself, decline the honour you have bestowed upon me."

"Then return home and await my arrival."

"What!—leave you here with a chance of losing your life in this gloomy castle?"

"I have no fear," answered Sir Reginald, "and, therefore, you need feel no apprehension for my safety. Away, sirrah, and should any one inquire about me, say that I am still in pursuit of the object that brought me here, and that I have still hopes of succeeding in it."

"You don't mean to send me away, Sir Knight?"

"Have you not heard my command?" exclaimed the other; "you have refused to stay in this chamber till my return, and, therefore, your services are no longer required."

"And if I have refused," answered Oliver, "it is because I have no fancy for meeting an apparition, that, for aught I know, may play me some confounded trick as a punishment for my presumption in remaining here. But though I like not that part of your commands, I am quite willing to accompany you through the vaults of the castle."

"The knave may be of service if he goes with us," observed Ivan to Sir Reginald Courtney, "for it must not be forgotten that there may be fellows lurking about the place, and in the event of our being suddenly surprised, we shall be the better able to resist our enemies."

"I care not how it is," answered the knight, "but judging from his terror just now, I must needs confess there is very little chance of his being of much use."

"You are mistaken there," exclaimed Oliver, "for though I may have an objection to face an apparition, you'll find that I'm no coward when a mortal foe stands before me. Only give me fair flesh and blood to fight against, and I'll answer for it you will not call me a coward again."

"It is possible you may be put to the test," observed Ivan, "so I would have you keep a good look out if you go with us."

"And go with you I will," returned Oliver, "for I would sooner meet twenty mortal enemies in your company than one immortal foe when I'm by myself. The very thought of it makes me shudder. Eigh! oh!—what was that? Did you hear anything make a frightful noise?"

"I heard nothing," replied Ivan, "but the echo of your own voice sounding through these deserted chambers."

"Come, come," exclaimed Sir Reginald Courtney, "we are but wasting time that may be more profitably employed; let us now descend to the vaults, and if Sir Gaston is yet there, we will either extort from him a promise to become a faithful subject of King Richard, or lead him once more a captive to the prison from whence he has contrived to escape."

"Either of which you may do," said Ivan, "but let it not be forgotten that I have obtained your promise to offer no violence against his life."

"And why, if I may be so bold," exclaimed Oliver, "is that man's life to be spared when all the world knows well enough that he ought to have been put out of the way long ago?"

"Ask no impertinent questions, sirrah," cried the Outlaw, "but whatever my motives are, you may rest satisfied that my reasons can be satisfactorily given to any one who has a right to demand it. In the mean time, Sir Reginald, you, I suppose, are content to restrain your curiosity till it may suit my purpose to enter into a more lengthened explanation?"

"All I wish for," replied the young knight, "is, that we may bring this affair to a speedy conclusion. Sir Gaston has much to confess, and, of course, we cannot expect to bring this affair to a close till he is again our captive."

"Then follow me," exclaimed Ivan, "and we will see whether he has yet left the castle, or is still lingering about in the hope of collecting his retainers together. If he is not here, we may expect that it will not be long before he makes a desperate attempt to restore himself to that proud eminence from which he has just been hurled."

"And the only chance he has of doing that," returned the knight, "is by joining Prince John, who, should he ever come to the throne, will hardly fail to reward the man who has run so many risks in his behalf."

"The prince is too closely watched to afford him an opportunity to do the mischief he contemplates," answered Ivan; "he is now known to be a traitor to his royal brother, and so sharply will all his actions be observed, that upon the least suspicion of any foul play he will find himself a prisoner, and at the mercy of the noble sovereign he has so basely sold. However, Sir Knight, we have no time to lose if we intend to look after Sir Gaston de Neville, so do you go before us with the light, Oliver, and should there be any danger, we will join you without the delay of even so much as a minute."

"But the armed phantom—"

"Psha! what need you fear the armed phantom, as you call it?" demanded Ivan, impatiently. "You have never done it any injury, and, therefore, can have no cause to imagine that it will present itself before us for no other purpose than to frighten a foolish fellow like you out of the little wits he posseeses."

Obliged to rest satisfied with this, Oliver now moved onwards, with slow and cautious footsteps, listening to each sound as he slowly moved forward, and continually looking about, to see if the much dreaded spirit of the Black Knight was anywhere within view. Nothing, however, occurred, and directed by Black Ivan, he continued to move onwards through a long series of deserted apartments till they reached the armoury, where all sorts of weapons in use at that day, and suits of mail, were arranged against the wall, so as to be in readiness at any time when there might be occasion for them. Here the Outlaw paused, and removing a table that stood in the middle of the room, discovered a large slab of stone, in which was fixed a ring for the purpose of raising it whenever it might be required.

"What are you now going to do?" asked Sir Reginald Courtney, as his guide stooped to take hold of the ring.

"To remove this stone," answered the person addressed; "so come, Oliver, lend me a hand, and we shall soon be able to find a shorter way to the part of the dungeons we want to go to than if we went to the eastern tower, so down that way."

Oliver assisted as he had been desired, and with more ease than he had expected, the stone was raised, and a dark, frightful-looking chasm disclosed to view.

"Now," said Ivan, "a flight of steps leads from here to the vaults below, and we shall soon find ourselves at the dungeon where we left Sir Gaston not long since."

"Methinks you seem to know the secrets of this castle much better than I should have thought a stranger could have done," exclaimed Sir Reginald.

"And yet there is nothing surprising in that," replied Ivan, "for I have passed many an hour in this place when no one suspected that I was within a dozen miles of it."

"Had you any motive for this?"

"Why, of course I had. Sometimes I came to aid unfortunate captives to escape from what appeared to be a hopeless confinement, but chiefly my visits were paid to the Lady Alicia, who few besides myself knew was a prisoner in the fortress, by the command of her own brutal husband."

"And were you never discovered here?"

"Very rarely," replied Ivan, "and even when that was the case, I had always a good excuse ready, and as most people had a notion that it would not do to resist me, I managed to get off much easier than might have been expected."

"And Sir Gaston," cried the knight, "did he never chance to see you here?"

"Sometimes," replied the other, "but more frequently I have been in the room with him when he has little suspected that so dangerous a foe was near him."

"And as a robber, were you never tempted to assassinate him for the sake of the plunder you might have obtained?"

"I have told you before," replied Ivan, "that I chose not the life I led from any liking I had to it; circumstances, however, compelled me to adopt some means for obtaining sustenance, and as I had never been used to work, I became what you and the world have long since known me to be."

THE LOST DIAMOND. 789

"But you must have had some object in thus entering the castle besides those you have told me of?"

"It was my will to do so," answered the Outlaw, "and as there was nothing to prevent it, I came and went exactly as it suited my own pleasure."

"You must have had a confederate among the domestics of Sir Gaston de Neville, or you could never have passed through the gates," observed Sir Reginald.

"There you are mistaken," replied Ivan; "the means by which I gained admission were unknown, yet I will now confess to you that there is a secret passage that runs beneath the moat, and by which I could obtain ingress at any hour of the day or night that I pleased. In this way I have had it in my power to relieve many an unfortunate who has been confined in these dungeons, and who would there have pined away a wretched existence had it not been for the assistance I was thus able to give them."

"And were the prisoners you speak of never missed?" asked Sir Reginald, with surprise.

"Oh, yes, their frequent disappearance was the cause of much wonderment at the time," replied Ivan, "but it was thought impossible that they could have escaped. Sir Gaston generally consoled himself with the thought that they must have wandered about among the dungeons till death put a period to the existence they had endeavoured to prolong."

"And," cried Sir Reginald, "it was in one of these cheerless abodes that the hapless Lady Alicia passed so many years of a life that was embittered by her husband's cruelty."

"Yes," answered the Outlaw, "and from this place she never would have escaped if it had not been for the page Adrian, who, under my instructions, found means to obtain her deliverance. She is now, however, in safety, and I trust will never again know the horrors it has been her sad lot to bear."

"At present," said Sir Reginald, "she has found a shelter in the king's palace, till it is known whether Sir Gaston de Neville can be prevailed upon to restore her to that station from which he has driven her. If he will do that, and pledge his honour to be true and loyal for the future, he will not only obtain the king's pardon, but even regain some of that confidence and esteem which he has lost."

"There is little chance, methinks, of Sir Gaston purchasing the royal favour in the way you have mentioned," observed Ivan. "However, we are but wasting time, so forward, Oliver, and by holding your light low down, you will see a flight of steps leading to the bottom of the fortress; but mind how you move, sirrah, for one false step will be sufficient to hurry you into eternity."

Thus cautioned, Oliver proceeded with all due care to descend through the aperture, and having secured his own footing, he paused to light his two companions down the perilous way that Ivan had thought fit to bring them. Luckily they reached the bottom in safety, and on arriving there, Oliver was directed by the Outlaw which way to go; but scarcely had he proceeded a hundred yards, when his foot struck against something on the ground, and he fell heavily on what appeared to be the body of an armed warrior. Terrified at this, the poor fellow uttered a cry of horror which soon brought the others to his assistance, who, upon examination, quickly discovered the cause of his fall. It was a complete suit of sable armour, the fashion and general appearance of which proved almost to a certainty that it was the same which had been worn by the armed apparition. This was a fresh cause of alarm to Oli-ver, whose terror could scarcely be restrained by Ivan, who tried to laugh him out of the fear that had thus seized him.

"You may deride me as much as you please, Ivan, "he said, as well as his agitation would permit him, "but all you can say, won't convince me against the evidence of my own senses."

"Psha !" exclaimed the Outlaw, snatching the lamp out of his hand, " let us have no more of this foolery ; it is time we go to seek after Sir Gaston, so follow me if your courage has not already been frightened out of you."

Upon this they went a few steps further, which brought them to the dungeon where the recent interview had taken place between the Temp-lar and Sir Reginald Courtney, but though a strict search was made all over the cell, no trace could be discovered of the object they were in search of."

"You see," exclaimed the Outlaw, "that he for whom we came to look is no longer here."

"Whither can he have gone ?" asked Sir Reginald.

"Far enough out of our reach by this time, I dare say," answered Ivan. "The truth is, he saw that his hiding-place had been discovered, and judging that a further search would be made after him, he has thought proper to decamp whilst it was in his power to do so."

"Nay," cried the knight, "it is likely he may have sought conceal-ment in some other part of the castle, and we will, therefore, continue our search till we have discovered the place of his retreat."

"It would be a waste of time to do so," replied Ivan, "for I am con-vinced he would know better than to remain where his speedy capture would be certain. So far our task has proved a vain one, and if you really wish to find the fugitive, your only way will be to look for him where he is more likely to have sought refuge."

"And where is that ?" asked the knight.

"That is a question which 1 am as unable to answer as yourself," re-turned Ivan. "It is likely, however, that some of his retainers may be found, and in that case we may hope to obtain a clue that will bring us to his lair."

"Are you sincere," asked Sir Reginald, "in your desire to serve me in this instance ?"

"Sincere !" exclaimed the Outlaw, " why what in the name of fortune could have put such a thought as that into your head ?"

"I scarcely know what to believe," replied Sir Reginald, "but I began to think you would rather favour the escape of Sir Gaston de Neville than assist in his capture."

"Well," replied the Outlaw, "it must be acknowledged I was not very anxious to accompany you here, nor should I have done so, had it not been that you pledged your word to abstain from drawing your sword against him."

"But why should you feel so much interest in behalf of such a tyrant as Sir Gaston de Neville ?"

"It would be too long a story to relate now, even were I inclined to gratify your curiosity," answered Ivan. "For the present, therefore, you must be satisfied with knowing that I have a reason for it, and in my opinion it is a very sufficient one."

"It would be useless, I see, to urge this matter any farther at present," exclaimed Sir Reginald Courtney, "but perhaps you will tell me whether it is your intention to assist me any farther in the search I have under-taken ?"

"On the conditions you have already made, I certainly will," replied Ivan. "The king, I believe, from what you have told me, is willing to pardon Sir Gaston on certain conditions, and as his life may thus be preserved, I see no way that I can more essentially serve him."

"But on the other hand," observed Sir Reginald, "it is by no means certain that he will accept the proffered mercy upon the terms that have been proposed."

"Nay, leave Sir Gaston alone for making a tolerable good bargain if it is once offered him," answered the other. "He is now driven to extremities,—his wealth confiscated, and his life forfeited, should he be mad enough to refuse the pardon which the king has it in his power to bestow. No, no, Sir Reginald, he will be glad enough to accept it, and thus save himself from the wreck and ruin that at present threatens him on every side."

"Yet even if he should do so," exclaimed the knight, "it is more than likely that he will again join himself with the enemies of the king, and plot against the life of the monarch whose mercy has saved him from destruction."

"He will know better than to do that," replied Ivan, "for should he be detected in any affair of that kind, he may be assured that nothing would save him from the vengeance he would in that case so justly merit. I, therefore, place every reliance in his prudence, and for that reason am quite willing to assist you in discovering the place to which he has flown for safety."

"Can you form any notion where he may be sought?" asked Sir Reginald Courtney.

"No more than you can yourself," replied Ivan, "but I should suppose it is a task of no very great difficulty, seeing that he will not dare show himself, and that we may consequently seek him in one of his other castles. The flight of his retainers from this place seems to confirm the notion, and as our presence here can be of very little service, we will now take our departure as soon as you please."

"Let it be instantly then," exclaimed Sir Reginald Courtney, "for I would now hasten to the king's presence, in order that we may receive his commands whether to seek the Templar in one of his other fortresses."

Upon this they all three hurried away to return to the habitable portion of the castle, but whilst they were proceeding through one of the subterranean chambers, a savage cry of triumph was heard, and at the same moment a man rushed forward with a poniard in his hand, which he was about to plunge into the heart of Sir Reginald, when his arm was arrested by the Outlaw. Alarmed by the outcry, the attendant with his lamp hastened towards them, and as the feeble rays of the light fell upon the ruffian, they recognized the well-known countenance of Bertrand le Noir!

CHAPTER CXXI.

Let strict enquiry be made,
To find the lurking place of this arch traitor.
Seek him in wood and tower, in dell and forest,
And should good fortune speed your enterprise.
Bring him before us.   THE CASTELLAN.

"VILLAIN!" exclaimed Ivan, at the moment this discovery took place, "you have been foiled in your murderous intention, and now your own life is at the disposal of those that you would have slain in cold blood."

"I know I'm in your power," answered Bertrand sullenly, "and since I have failed in the object I had in view, I deserve to meet any fate you may choose to award."

"And that will be death!" cried the Outlaw furiously.

"Nay, be not too hasty in your condemnation," interposed Sir Reginald Courtney, "for he may yet purchase life, on condition that he answers certain questions which I will put to him."

"I don't want any favour from you," exclaimed the ruffian doggedly. "I have been fool enough to throw away a chance, and I'll never beg for my life merely for the sake of dragging on a few more years of a miserable existence."

"You are not required to ask any favour," replied Sir Reginald, "for all we require is, that you will take us to the place where your master has sought concealment."

"Indeed! but suppose I know nothing about it?"

"You do know," answered the knight, "and surely you have been offered easy terms enough by which you may prolong an existence which your baseness has most justly forfeited."

"But I don't want to prolong it."

"In that case," said Black Ivan, "there is a very short way of bringing matters to a conclusion. You see this poniard, sirrah? and now will you answer the question that has been put to you?"

"I tell you I know nothing about what has become of Sir Gaston de Neville," replied the ruffian, shrinking back as he saw the deadly instrument pointed at his breast.

"You mean to declare then, that you have not seen anything of your master since his escape from the Gate-house?"

"I have said nothing of the kind."

"How long is it since you saw him?"

"About half an hour since."

"Where was he?"

"In this castle."

"Is he still here?"

"Why I should think not," replied Bertrand le Noir, "for he would hardly be such a fool as to remain in a place that is not likely to afford him the security he requires."

"Did he say where he was going?" asked Sir Reginald.

"He did."

"Then you have only to tell us where he is," said Ivan, "and your life will be spared."

"Do you think then I'll betray my master to his enemies, that I may save myself?" asked Bertrand.

"We are not his enemies," replied the Outlaw; "we seek him, it is true, but it is rather that we may serve than injure him."

"And yet," exclaimed the retainer, "it's not many minutes since I heard you talking together about making him your prisoner."

"Hah! you have been listening then?"

"I have," replied Bertrand, "and finding that you wanted to re-capture him, I drew my dagger, and rushing forward, should have slain the first man I encountered, had not my arm been seized at the very moment when I hoped to have carried my vengeance into execution."

"And a very lucky thing it turned out for you, that your design was frustrated," answered Black Ivan, "for had any one of us fallen, the others would have instantly retaliated, by laying you dead at their feet."

"Which would have been rather doing me a favour than otherwise," returned Bertrand, "for I am heartily weary of life, and care not how soon you rid me of it."

"Tush!" exclaimed Ivan, impatiently, "you have heard already that we don't want to harm you;—tell us where to find Sir Gaston de Neville, and you are free to go where you please."

"And what want you with my master?"

"Our object is to serve him."

"How can that be done?"

"Easily enough," answered Sir Reginald;—"the king is still willing to pardon him all the offences he has committed, and, on certain conditions, Sir Gaston may be restored to the royal favour."

"What conditions do you speak of?" asked Bertrand.

"Nothing but what may be easily acceded to," answered the young knight. "He will be expected to swear allegiance to King Richard, and to cease persecuting those whom he has hitherto injured and sought to hunt within his toils."

"And think you Sir Gaston de Neville will ever stoop to gain the favour of King Richard at the expense of humbling himself to the very dust?"

"If he is not utterly lost to all feelings of honour, he will do so," replied Sir Reginald Courtney. "It is never too late to repent of one's crimes, and surely there can be no degradation in Sir Gaston earning the royal clemency on condition that he returns to the path of virtue, which he has so long abandoned."

"Psha!" exclaimed the retainer, "and do you really imagine that Sir

No. 100

Gaston de Neville will become virtuous, as you call it, at the expense of gratifying his own pleasure?"

"It is the only way he can ever hope to raise himself to the eminence from which his own crimes have hurled him."

"Nay, there is yet another way," answered the ruffian.

"What is that?" demanded Sir Reginald.

"He can still side with Prince John, whose cause is not so utterly lost, as many people imagine," replied Bertrand, "and as there are thousands of persons at this moment ready to take up arms against the present king, it is by no means unlikely that we shall see one on the throne who will not fail to reward his friends far more liberally than Cœur de Lion is ever likely to do."

"But Prince John has seen the hopelessness of his cause," answered Sir Reginald, "and anxious only for his own safety, whatever may be the fate of his deluded followers, he has abandoned all claim to the throne till after his brother's death; so that Sir Gaston will only plunge further into difficulties if he persists in embracing so bad a cause."

"And what am I to understand from all this?" asked Bertrand.

"That it will be better to reveal to us the place where your master is confined, in order that we may point out the danger he is incurring, and prevail on him to reinstate himself in the favour of his sovereign, by doing justice to those whom he has injured for many a long year past."

"But how I to know," asked Bertrand le Noir, "that your motives are as friendly as you have declared?"

"Because as a sworn knight," answered Sir Reginald Courtney, "I would not pledge my word to an untruth."

"That may be all very well," replied the retainer, "but Sir Gaston de Neville was also a sworn knight, and he was never very particular in that respect, whenever his own interest happened to stand in the way."

"You don't seem much inclined to take our word for it," interposed Black Ivan, "and so as we are not very likely to come to terms, I'll finish this affair as briefly as possible, by telling you a piece of my mind. So now observe me, Bertrand le Noir,—you must either lead me to the place where Sir Gaston has sought a retreat, or you will stand a fair chance of having the point of this dagger in your heart."

"Haven't I told you before that I'm not afraid of death?"

"Aye, but that is a mere idle boasting," returned Ivan;—"you put on this indifference to deceive us, but I know well enough that you are as anxious to save your life as I should be to preserve mine if I was in a similarly awkward predicament. So speak, slave, or you die!"

"I'll tell you what it is," exclaimed Bertrand, who now began to flinch as he saw the determination of the Outlaw; "I'm a poor man, and life under such circumstances, would only be a useless prolonging of my miseries. So make me a handsome offer of a reward, and, perhaps, I may be induced to think better of it."

"Humph!—and so after all you will not object to sell your master for a sum of money?"

"The truth is," replied Bertrand le Noir, "my master has many times promised me gold on condition that I executed certain things for him to his satisfaction. This, I believe, I have done, and yet never have I received the reward he has been so liberal to promise."

"Why, this is a most marvellous change!" cried the Outlaw; "but a few minutes since, you were professing faithfulness and zeal to your master, and yet now we find you quite ready to betray him on certain pecuniary considerations."

"I am too poor to afford to be honest," exclaimed Bertrand; "one cannot willingly starve, you know, and had Sir Gaston de Neville consulted his own interest, he would have made me an offer that was worthy of my acceptance."

"Well," exclaimed Ivan, "and as he has not done so perhaps you will think it worth while to accept the present we may feel inclined to bestow upon you?"

"That will depend on circumstances," answered Bertrand le Noir ;— "What sum do you propose giving me?"

"Three hundred crowns, if that will be sufficient to satisfy your desires."

"Double the sum," exclaimed the ruffian, "and then, perhaps, I may feel inclined to do you this piece of service."

"Let it be given him," said Black Ivan, "and if he plays us false after that, it will be at his own peril. The knave knows me well enough, and he may make up his mind to die the death of a villain if he dares offer to mislead us."

"The sum you have named shall be yours, sirrah," cried Sir Reginald Courtney, "but I must know where your master is lurking for concealment, ere I part with even so much as a single coin."

"You won't trust me, then?"

"Not beyond my reach," answered the young knight ;—"so now tell me where the Templar is to be found, and you shall have the promised reward as soon afterwards as you think proper to come to my lodging in the royal palace at Westminster."

"And get arrested there for being such a foolish gull !" cried Bertrand le Noir.

"I will not deceive you," replied Sir Reginald, "nor have you any reason to believe it is my intention to do so. All I want is, that you tell the secret we desire to know, and when that is done, your reward is earned, and from that time forward, I shall never wish to meet you again."

"Come, come, sirrah," exclaimed Black Ivan, impatiently; "out with it at once, or I shall begin to grow weary of this delay, and put an end to it in a way you won't like."

"Well, then," answered Bertand le Noir, "you will find the Knight Templar at his manor house at Stratford; he left me not long since to go down there, and if you use speed, it is likely you will pounce upon him at a moment when he is little dreaming of danger."

"Have any of his people gone with him?" asked Ivan.

"I think not," answered the fellow; "for the place has been suffered to go to decay, and the servants were ordered to leave it a long while ago."

"Will there be much difficulty in getting admittance if Sir Gaston refuses to yield?"

"Not much," replied the other, "for it's a tumble down place altogether, and half a dozen men will be quite enough to get in, if they have only courage enough to run the chance of being cut down by Sir Gaston de Neville."

"I will myself be the first to enter the house," exclaimed the young knight, "and I dare say Ivan will not be far behind, when his services are most required."

"I shall not be able to join you in this instance," answered the Outlaw.

"You will leave me, then, to finish this affair by myself?"

"Take as many persons to assist as you please," cried Ivan; "but do not ask me to assist in the capture of this imperious knight; who, though

I have little cause to respect, shall never be captured by my hands. Besides, I must leave you now, for I have to return to the cavern, and bid farewell to the rough but faithful fellows who have for years past submitted themselves to my guidance."

"In that case," said Sir Reginald Courtney, "I will not urge you any further on this subject. I am shortly, however, about to see the king, and I hope to be the bearer of tidings that you have for ever abandoned a course of life that has rendered you the terror of your fellow-creatures."

"Why, yes," replied Ivan, "I believe I shall now try to make some amends for errors of my past career. It is true, there is no very heinous offence can be urged against me, for though I have plundered many in my time, the rich were always the sufferers, and whenever I saw honesty and poverty struggling together, I made it my business to render happier those who could not help themselves."

"Do you mean to leave England?" asked the knight.

"That will entirely depend on circumstances," replied Ivan. "At present, I see no obstacles in my way but such as may be easily enough removed, and should all go on as smoothly as I expect, I shall remain and spend the rest of my days in this country."

"And if you should not succeed?"

"In that event," replied the Outlaw, "I shall quit my native land, and join the troops in Italy, which are now assembling to march towards the Holy Land. I may thus make some poor recompense for any crimes I may have been guilty of, and should I perish in the field of battle, the world may, perhaps, soon forget my errors in the services I subsequently performed."

"But it is said," exclaimed the knight, "that King Richard is going to Palestine, and should that be the case, you will have an opportunity of joining his army. All the chief men of the nation have promised to accompany him, to attempt the restoration of Jerusalem, and great will be the reward of all those who take an active share in this great enterprise."

"Before anything is done," answered Ivan, "it will be necessary to attend to certain arrangements that may, possibly, lead to very important results."

"Is there anything to delay it?" asked the knight.

"Not much, at present," answered the other, "but it will depend principally upon the course pursued by Sir Gaston de Neville, whether it takes place now or at some future time. You, however, will shortly see him, and if he feels inclined to accept the pardon offered by the king, there is one ready to come forward with intelligence of his long lost brother."

"Who is the person you speak of?"

"Meg of Finchley."

"But may we place reliance in her word?"

"I see no reason to doubt it," replied Ivan; "especially as her words will be confirmed by circumstances that must effectually silence all scepticism."

"Has she been long in possession of this secret?"

"Aye, for many years."

"Why then has she never revealed a subject that was of so much importance?"

"Because she has been restrained by an oath," replied Ivan. "The old woman has with difficulty restrained herself from revealing the affair, but has so far been faithful to her pledge, through the hope she has indulged of the period not being far off when the revelation may be made."

"She has not been seen very lately," exclaimed Sir Reginald, "and, aged as she is, it is possible she may have paid the debt of nature at the very time when her evidence would have been of such essential service."

"The old woman still lives," replied the Outlaw, "and has a perfectly clear recollection of all the circumstances connected with the business we are speaking of."

"Why then does she suffer any delay?" asked the other.

"Why, because she acts upon the advice of those who knew better than herself." answered Ivan; "she has besides taken an oath to abide the proper time, and nothing will ever permit on her to break it."

"There is a mystery about all this which I cannot penetrate," exclaimed Sir Reginald Courtney; "however, I suppose the matter will be cleared up all in good time, and —"

"Perhaps much sooner than you expect."

"And *you*, I suppose, will have no small share in bringing about this much desired explanation?"

"Why, I dare say I may be able to throw some light upon the affair," replied the Outlaw, "at all events I shall not be far off, in case they should want me, and if I should have to confront Sir Gaston de Neville, it will be to tell him a secret, that at present, he has no idea of."

"Respecting his brother, I suppose?"

"Aye, and a good deal more besides that," replied Isaac.

"May I not enquire where the person is?"

"You will know all about that in good time," answered the Outlaw, "at present, secrecy is absolutely necessary, as the least exposure of our plans might serve to mar, if not entirely ruin them. You will, therefore, say nothing of what has accidentally escaped my lips, and I dare say a very brief period will be sufficient to remove the evil that at present obscures certain circumstances which are not just now quite ripe for a discovery."

"I don't know whether you have forgotten the argument you just now made with me," exclaimed Bertrand le Noir, in a tone that denoted no very large share of good nature; "I thought I was to go and find out the place where Sir Gaston is to be found, and yet no sooner is the bargain made than you seem to have given up the idea of it altogether."

"Nothing has been given up, sirrah," answered Sir Reginald, "but it was necessary that we should understand each other before we commence an undertaking where so much is at hazard. I am now satisfied that there is every probability of our being able to bring this affair to a most desirable conclusion, and whatever may be the result I shall not forget the promise I gave to obtain as much lenity as possible for Sir Gaston de Neville."

"And for me also, I hope."

"Aye, you shall not be forgotten," exclaimed Sir Reginald, "though Ineeds confess your acts have sufficiently villanous to bring down upon your head the full measure of vengeance that your crimes has justly merited."

"Psha! what great crime have I ever committed?"

"One act alone," replied the knight, "would be suficient to secure for you the fate that has befallen many a more deserving man than yourself. It was you who, on the day of the coronation, raised your murderous steel for the destruction of our good King Richard, who, had he consulted the wishes of his people would, long 'ere this, have sent you to meet an ignominious fate upon the scaffold."

"And no doubt such a doom would have been mine if they could only have laid hands upon me," exclaimed Bertrand. "I, however, chanced to know well enough the sort of kindness I had to expect from my enemies, and not being then tired of my life, I took a prudent course, and kept myself out of the way till the danger was over."

"But the danger is not over, as you will find out to your cost if you think to play us any of your scurvy tricks," observed Ivan; "remember, your offences have not yet been pardoned, and it will be in our power, at any time, to deliver you up to justice in the event of your deceiving us."

"There is no deception intended in the present instance," exclaimed Bertrand. "All I want is protection for myself, and as I have been promised that, I'll now take you to the place where you will find him. But, mind me,—he is desparate and will not be taken till he has offered a determined resistance against a power that he does not acknowledge."

"And even if he does so, it will not serve his purpose," returned Sir Reginald Courtney, "for what is his strength against that of the king's, who can crush him at any moment when he may feel disposed to do so. However, Richard wishes not to exercise his power tyrannically, and therefore the Knight Templar will receive every kindness from him, on condition, that he quietly resigns himself and promises, henceforth, to become a faithful subject."

"That is a promise that may be easily made," exclaimed Bertrand, "but who shall say how long it may be kept?"

"Why, surely," cried Sir Reginald, "you do not think him capable of breaking his word when once it has been solemnly given?"

"The truth is, you have driven him into a corner and he may be obliged to make a parcel of promises that he would never have thought of, if it was not for the sake of gaining a little breathing time. So he may remain quiet enough for a little time, but I for one have no great idea that it will last."

"Sir Gaston de Neville, may have committed many faults in his time, and which I believe no one will attempt to deny, but for all that, I cannot fancy that he will ever break his word after it has been solemnly pledged."

"I dont mean to say he would, in a general way," replied Bertrand le Noir, "but if you make people give promises against their will, it is not to be much wondered at afterwards if they happen to turn round and forget themselves."

"And if he did so," cried Sir Reginald Courtney, "my own sword should be the first drawn to punish such perjury. However, we will not believe it of him; so lead the way, and I will go with you to the Manor-house at Stratford."

Upon this they made the best of their way through the vaulted passages, and then ascending the flight of stone steps found themselves once more in the habitable part of the castle. From thence they proceeded across the court-yard, and passing over the drawbridge reached the place where Sir Reginald and his attendant had left their horses. Here Ivan took leave of them, promising to see the young knight again as soon as he saw that matters had grow ripe for the project he had in view. Sir Reginald and his attendant then mounted their steeds, with an understanding that Bertrand le Noir was to accompany them on foot; but they had not proceeded very far when a small party of armed warriors were seen galloping towards them, the leader of whom our young hero recognised as a friend and companion in arms. These, it appeared, had been sent out in quest of Sir Reginald by King Richard, who had grown uneasy at his long absence; but no sooner did the other learn the cause of his delay, and the probability of finding him at the Manor-house at Stratford, than he volunteered to accompany him thither, and thus make sure of Sir Gaston's capture. This having been agreed to it was further arranged that one of the men should dismount, in order that Bertrand might ride with them; and this having been carried into effect, they all of them set forth, headed by the Templar's retainer, who had undertaken to guide them on their way. In spite of the badness of the road, an hour served to bring them within view of the ancient edifice they were about to visit; and when they had arrived within bow-shot of the building, Bertrand suddenly reined in his steed, and pointing towards the Manor-house, said :—

"You see, Sir Knight, I have performed my part of the bargain; yonder is the place where you will find Sir Gaston de Neville, and now, I would ask, when I am to receive the reward you promised?"

"Perform all that you have undertaken," replied Sir Reginald, "and you shall have no reason to complain of any want of honour on my part. At present you have merely brought us to the place where Sir Gaston may have sought refuge; but you have to assist in capturing him ere you have any just claim to a reward for your service."

"Why, you wouldn't have me go into the place with you and run the risk of losing my life by the hands of my master?"

"There are enough here to protect you from his violence," answered Sir Reginald Courtney; "and even if it were not so, your presence among us would be required till we have brought this business to a close."

"Am I a prisoner, then?"

"You may consider yourself one for the present."

"Then you have broken your word, and I have been betrayed by the man I trusted."

"It is because I suspect you intend to betray us," replied the knight, "that I have come to this resolution. The truth is, you want us to enter the castle, and then means would be taken to prevent our ever leaving it again alive."

"Why do you think me capable of such treachery?"

"Because treachery has marked almost every action of your life," replied the knight. "Your anxiety to leave us at the moment we are about to enter the place proves to me that you intend us some mischief."

"How can one man harm so many of you?"

"It may easily be done if there are any of Sir Gaston's retainers in the mansion," answered Sir Reginald Courtney. "It is likely enough some of them are lying concealed there, and the moment the gates are closed upon us, we should find ourselves opposed by a superior number of foes, all of whom may be resolutely bent on our destruction."

"What is it you would have then?" demanded Bertrand, sullenly.

"You must enter the place with us," answered the knight, "and should my suspicions prove correct, you, at any rate, should be the first victim of your own treachery."

"Would you murder the man that you have brought here partly by bribery, and partly by compulsion?"

"You have come hither voluntarily, and in the expectation of receiving a reward for your services," answered the knight. "You have undertaken the business, and having gone thus far with it, I shall now insist upon your following it up till our mission is completed."

"In that case," said the retainer, "there is an end of our bargain; I have brought you here at some trouble and inconvenience to myself, but as you wish me to perform more than I undertook, I will now go my ways, and leave you to go on with the affair as well as you can."

"Villain!" exclaimed Sir Reginald Courtney, threateningly, "if you make one step to put that design into execution, my men shall send after you a flight of arrows that will effectually prevent your meditated designs against us."

"I have no designs," muttered the fellow.

"Nay, you cannot so easily deceive me," answered the young knight. "You know our numbers, and this place being sufficiently lonely for your purpose, you would ride off to bring a party of Sir Gaston's people for our destruction. Nay, it is in vain to deny it, and, therefore, I warn you as you value your life, not to make any attempt to leave us till you have my permission."

"I was a fool!" cried Bertrand le Noir, "to place my faith in a man who I might have been quite certain intended to deceive me."

"'Psha! it is you who have sought to deceive," exclaimed the knight, "and bitterly should we have rued our misplaced confidence, had we followed your advice, and trusted ourselves within yonder gates."

"You wrong me!" answered the retainer, with a hypocritical whine; "however, we will not speak further upon that subject just now, so tell me what I am next to do."

"You must enter yonder building alone," replied Sir Reginald, "and seek out your master, who you are to summon in my name to surrender himself a prisoner."

"Hah!" exclaimed Bertrand, "the place, I see, will soon be too hot to hold any of us! It is on fire, as you may see by yonder wreaths of smoke that are bursting through the roof and windows." *

Sir Reginald Courtney was soon convinced that the fellow had, in this instance, spoken the truth, for thick volumes of smoke were seen rising in all directions, and presently afterwards the flames darted up into the air, threatening certain destruction to all within their reach. At this juncture, the gates were thrown open, and Sir Gaston de Neville at the head of about a score of his followers, rushed out sword in hand, with a determination to cut their way through all obstacles that might oppose them. They were, however, fiercely assailed by those who had just arrived before the place, Sir Gaston himself making towards Sir Reginald Courtney, and singling him out as the object upon whom to vent the fury that was rankling in his heart. But the other was well prepared for the assault, sudden as it had been, and after a severe conflict, he succeeded in slightly wounding his antagonist, who, falling at his feet, called upon him to put an end to a life that had now become a burden to him. This, however, Sir Reginald refused to do, and beckoning to a couple of his attendants, they advanced with all the speed they could, and bound the limbs of the Knight Templar, in spite of the feeble resistance he still offered them. It was now evident, that the courage of Sir Gaston had completely forsaken him, for he saw that all his followers had been defeated, and that he must be carried a prisoner into the presence of his justly incensed sovereign.

Leaving the fire still burning furiously, Sir Reginald Courtney now called his people together, and mounting the Templar on a horse with one of his archers, they set forward again towards the Gatehouse at Westminster.

CHAPTER CXXII.

Wilt thou release him ?
Or must we, by force of arms, exert our strength
To rescue this our leader ?   Answer us, captain,—
For we are here assembled in our might,
And will not be refused.   THE REBEL.

THEY rode on together some distance in silence, for Sir Gaston seemed to be deeply mortified at the helpless situation to which he was reduced, and his thoughts were engaged in devising the means by which he might yet again effect his escape from those into whose power he had fallen. Sir Reginald Courtney saw that it would be useless to say anything more to him just then, and wishing at the same time to avoid any act that might appear to proceed from exultation at the advantage he had gained, he rode considerably in advance, trusting the safe keeping of the prisoner to those who had assisted in his capture. This did not pass unobserved by the Knight Templar, who whispering to the man who rode on the same horse with him, and to whom he was bound, inquired whether he was inclined to earn a large reward by doing him a favour?

"That will depend on what the favour is," replied the fellow.

"I would have liberty," answered the knight; "wilt thou aid me in obtaining it?"

"Humph!" ejaculated the other; "your wish is a natural one enough, but I see no way that I can assist you."

No. 101

"Hast thou a knife ?"

"l have."

"Draw it forth then," whispered the knight, "and cut the bonds which confine my limbs that I may escape from those who, for purposes of their own, seek to bring upon me ruin and disgrace."

"Aye, aye," exclaimed the man; "no doubt you would be glad enough to get clear away, but I am not going to risk my own safety for the sake of setting you free,"

"Hast thou forgotten that I have promised thee a large sum for thy services ?"

"I have not lost sight of that; but what good would thy gold be to me in case of its being known that I betrayed the trust imposed on me ?"

"Canst thou not escape with me ?" asked Sir Gaston.

"No, for there are plenty here to prevent it."

"Is thy horse an active one ?"

"Aye, he's pretty well for that," answered the man; "but why do you ask me the question ?"

"Because, by putting spurs to him we might gallop off and reach a place of safety."

"What! with two riders on his back ?"

"Hush! there is a listener close by," whispered Sir Gaston; "be silent for the present, and think well of the proposition I have just made to thee."

"What the devil are you both muttering about ?" growled one of the attendants, riding up to them. "Look well to your prisoner, Stephen, and remember if he escapes, it will be the worst day's work you ever did for yourself."

"Never fear about that," answered Stephen, "I know my duty, and if you do yours as well, Sir Reginald will have very little cause to complain of either of us."

"I did but ask him to release one of my hands," exclaimed Sir Gaston; "these thongs gall me, and surely my flesh is not to be lacerated by the bonds they have thought fit to put upon my limbs ?"

"I know nothing about that," answered the other, "but you are to be kept in safe custody, and the only way that I know of doing it is to bind you fast."

"Is it supposed then," asked Sir Gaston de Neville, "that I can escape when there are so many surrounding me ?"

"I dare say you wouldn't mind trying it if you had but the chance given you," retorted the soldier. "However, the distance we've got to go is not very great, and when you get into the presence of the king he can do as he pleases about trusting to your word."

"The king is my foe," answered Sir Gaston, sullenly, " and, therefore, I have little mercy to hope from him. I have offended him it seems, and am now made to suffer from his cruel tyranny and oppression."

"That I know nothing about," said the other, "but as this is the first time I ever heard King Richard called a tyrant, you will be kind enough to speak of him a little more respectfully in my presence."

"Hah! am I to be taunted by a slave like thee ?"

"It is always the fate of evil doers to be taunted by those that are not so bad as themselves," answered the man. "You have thought fit to take part with that traitor, Prince John; but I am a loyal subject, and as long as I am able to do so, shall throw up my cap and shout, long live our noble king—Richard of the Lion's Heart."

"Psha! I ask thee not to change thine opinions, friend," said Sir Gaston, "but my limbs are galled with these bonds, and I would fain have prevailed upon thee to relieve me of the pain that has been inflicted."

"You would have some of the cords removed?"

"I would."

"In order that you may have it in your power to escape from us, I suppose?"

"That would be impossible, seeing that I am surrounded by my guards."

"But it might be worth while making a desperate attempt to get your liberty," observed the man. "However, I'll speak to Sir Reginald Courtney about it, and if he has no objection, and gives orders to that affect, of course I shall be ready enough to obey him."

"Do not ask him any favour from me," exclaimed the knight; "he is my foe, and if he relieves me from these accursed bonds, it must be rather as a right that I claim from him, than an obligation done to me."

"I'll tell him, at any rate," muttered the other, not very well pleased at the haughty tone of the Templar, and riding forward, he whispered to Sir Reginald, who immediately checked his horse, and galloped back to the place were the captive knight was riding:—

"I understand," he said, "that you ask to be freed from your bonds, and I am willing to grant any favour or indulgence, on condition that you pledge me your word not to abuse it by an attempt to escape."

"Psha!" muttered Sir Gaston, "I never yet asked a favour from any man, nor shall I now stoop so low as to solicit an indulgence from a man whom I despise as much as I do him who now offers me what he is pleased to esteem a favour."

"You will please yourself in that matter," answered Sir Reginald Courtney, with equal haughtiness; "I would serve you in any way that will not interfere with my duty towards my royal master, but it must be on your promise not to escape from our custody."

"Let me remain as I am, then," cried the Templar. "I am galled both in body and mind, yet can I endure much more than this, rather than accept a favour from one who I despise as I do him that offers it."

"You regard me then as an enemy?"

"How else can I regard the man who hunts me to my own castle, and makes me his prisoner, though I am aware of no crime that should have brought me to this disgraceful condition."

"My present business is not to taunt you with what has been done," exclaimed Sir Reginald, "and yet, your words tempt me to remind you that your acts against the king have laid you open to a charge of treason."

"Let the king prove it," answered Sir Gaston, "and I will be ready to lay down my life, should he think proper to demand it. That I have long lain under his displeasure I am well aware, and I know, also, that I am indebted for his ill-will to certain persons, who, for their own private revenge, have rejoiced in having an opportunity to assist in crushing me. You, I know, are among them, and, therefore, do I refuse any favour, that, in your mercy, you may think fit to propose."

"I have never been your enemy," replied Sir Reginald. "It is true, I have seen, with deep concern, that you took part with Prince John in his base attempts to seize upon the crown of England, but beyond that, I have felt no enmity towards you. Nay, as a proof of it, I will order your bonds to be removed, that you may see that I can even now place reliance in your honour."

"Surely you won't trust him so far as that?" whispered the man who had previously spoken. "He is desperate, you know, and in his situation there's no telling what he may do for the sake of regaining his liberty."

"You will do as I have commanded," replied Sir Reginald. "Are we not twenty of us against one man, and shall we be afraid of anything he may be able to do?"

"Had it been any other man," replied the soldier, "I should not have thought anything of it, but Sir Gaston has so often proved himself treacherous on former occasions, that I should not like to trust him when once his hands are set free. Besides, he refuses to make any terms, and that I take it, is a pretty good proof that he intends mischief."

"You judge him too harshly," returned Sir Reginald Courtney, "and, therefore, do I again desire you to sever the bonds that confine his limbs."

"As you please, Sir Knight," answered the man, "but if you won't take my advice about the matter, what think you of the crowd of people I see coming this way?"

"I suppose they have merely come out of curiosity to see the prisoner conveyed to the palace."

"And yet," returned the other, "I see one among them that has always been considered a mischievous, discontented fellow."

"Who is he?"

"Simon Hyde, the tanner."

"Ha!" exclaimed Sir Reginald, "is that traitor among them? In that case it will, indeed, behove us to be cautious how we act. Let all the stragglers fall in, and form a compact body, and should any attack be made by these knaves, remember Sir Gaston de Neville, must not be suffered to escape on any consideration."

Scarcely had he done speaking, when a volley of stones was thrown among them, but fortunately without doing the mischief that was intended. Infuriated at this attack, the archers stood ready with their bows bent, but Sir Reginald Courtney, anxious, if possible, to prevent bloodshed, rode forward and placing himself at the head of his men, demanded of the rabble the reason of their making this unprovoked attack upon them.

"You have a prisoner that must be given up to us," replied Simon Hyde, who took upon himself to act as spokesman upon the occasion. "Surrender him and you may pass on without further hindrance."

"Indeed! and suppose we refuse to accede to this very modest request of yours?"

"Why, in that case," replied the fellow, "as we are provided with good stout clubs, we shall rescue him by violence; and, perhaps, a few of you may afterwards be sorry that you have not taken a fool's advice for once in the course of your lives."

"And know you that you are obstructing the servants of the king in the execution of their duty?"

"We own him for no king of ours," replied Simon Hyde; "he is a tyrant, and we have sworn to pull him down from his throne, and place Prince John there in his stead."

"Traitor! dare you speak thus to men who are loyal to their legitimate sovereign?"

"At any rate, we don't want to stand parleying here," exclaimed the tanner; "you know our object, and if you don't think proper to give up Sir Gaston de Neville, we shall soon find means to take him from you by violence. So come, make up your mind, for we can't stand losing our time here, whilst you are waiting for other people to come to your assistance."

"This insolence is not to be borne!"

"Oh, you'll have a good deal more to bear before we've done with you," replied Simon Hyde. "Ours is club law, you know, and you'll find that out to your cost presently, if there's any more delay in the matter."

"Retire, all of you, and leave me to my fate," interposed Sir Gaston de Neville, addressing himself to the mob. "I am at present in the hands of these hirelings of King Richard, and am content to wait with patience and see how far he will dare proceed against a man who sets his power and authority at defiance."

"Nay," cried Simon Hyde, "if they once take you before him, I'm afraid you will have very little chance of escaping with your life. We knew the bloodhounds were after you, and so I collected together as many of my comrades as I could, and we came out to see whether we could not contrive to rescue you."

"I want no man to risk his life for me," exclaimed the Templar, haughtily; "the king, it seems, for some reason or the other, wishes to get rid of me, and you see the sort of measures he has adopted to execute his tyrannical will. But even now I do not fear him, for should he spill my blood, there are plenty of bold spirits in England that will rise up to avenge my death upon the usurper."

"I see no use in waiting so long as that," cried Simon Hyde, "fo there's enough of us here to rescue you, and we will do it too, were the archers twice as numerous as they are."

"I would advise you to disperse, like true and faithful subjects of your sovereign," exclaimed Sir Reginald Courtney.

"And suppose we don't think fit to take your advice?"

"In that case I shall give orders to my men to disperse you," replied the knight. "We are less numerous than yourselves, it's true, but we are well armed, and should the word once be given, many who now stand around me, will lose their lives in a useless affray."

"You hear him," said the Templar, addressing himself to his terbulent friends; "he would be glad of an opportunity to shed your blood, and it is my request that you all return to your homes, without giving him the chance he desires."

"And what will become of you?" asked the tanner.

"That is a matter that gives me very little concern," replied Sir Gaston. "I am now beginning to grow weary of life, and as the tide of adversity has begun to set in, I care not how soon death brings oblivion of the past."

"Why you ain't going to turn driveller at last, are you?" demanded Simon, with a sneer.

"You ought to know me too well for that," answered Sir Gaston. "My enemies have made me their prisoner, and have bound my limbs with cords, but my heart is still as firm and unmoved as ever it was, and I can cheerfully die, rather than meanly stoop to ask my life of men who I utterly loath and despise."

"Sir Gaston," exclaimed the young knight, "you do us wrong in supposing that we are your foes. There is no one here, I believe, that seeks to injure you, nor does the king require you to be taken into his presence for any other purpose than that you may purchase his pardon by expressing contrition for the past, and thus secure for yourself his future favour and protection."

"Indeed!—and what will be the consequence of my spurning these very liberal intentions?"

"That is a question that I do not profess to have in my power to answer," replied Sir Reginald Courtney. "There are, however, several charges to be brought against you, and if any one of them is proved, it will be sufficient to procure your banishment from the country."

"And what has the king to do with my conduct, that he is thus to inquire into that which concerns him not?"

"Certain of his subjects complain of having received injuries at your hands," answered the young knight, "and he is, therefore, compelled to inquire into the charges they have brought; this can only be prevented by your changing the conduct you have hitherto pursued, and in that case, you will never hear anything more of that which is gone by."

"King Richard is very merciful, I dare say," answered Sir Gaston de Neville, "but I do not feel inclined to purchase his favour by any such sacrifice as that you have proposed. He has now got me in his power, and let him exert it as he may, for I will die, rather than meanly submit to prostrate myself before him."

"Aye, aye, Sir Gaston is right enough there," exclaimed Simon Hyde, "for why should he crouch at the king's feet, when he has so many fellows at his back ready to defend him the moment he chooses to give the word? No, no, down with the soldiers say I, and let every man of us perish, rather than see one of Prince John's best friends dragged away a prisoner."

"Am I again to warn you against violence?" cried Sir Gaston de Neville; "I have said that I am quite ready to go with these people to the palace, though I think they might have spared me the disgrace of dragging me there like a felon."

"A rescue! a rescue!" shouted the mob.

"Beware how you bring destruction on yourselves!" exclaimed Sir Reginald Courtney, "for the first man that offers to raise his hands against the authority of my royal master, dies upon the spot."

"You hear him!" cried the templar, appealing to the crowd of ruffians, "he has threatened death, and, doubtless, he will keep his word, should there be any here rash enough to hazard a tumult at so unfavourable a moment as this."

"What would you have us do, then?" asked Simon Hyde.

"Disperse with what speed you can, and wait for a more favourable opportunity to serve the cause in which you are engaged," replied the Templar.

"And why not go to work at once?" asked Simon; "there's enough of us here to overpower the few archers that are present, and when once you are set at liberty it will be easy enough to excite thousands of the people into joining us."

"I tell you, fellow, that such precipitation would but mar our plans, and lead to certain destruction," exclaimed Sir Gaston de Neville. "For my own part I can cheerfully submit to any fate that may fall to my lot, so that I do but feel a certainty of our cause eventually succeeding."

As the Templar finished speaking, a ruffian from the crowd, with a poniard in his hand, sprang upon the horse on which Sir Gaston was seated, and began to cut the cords with which his limbs were bound, and whilst he was thus occupied a general attack was commenced by the rabble upon the royal archers. One of the latter, however, perceived the fellow who was engaged in releasing the knight, and rushing forward, he, with one blow of his dagger, struck the fellow, mortally wounded, to the earth. This act served to excite yet further the rage of the mob, and so desperate grew the affray, that the soldiers were in danger of being sacrificed to the fury of the ruffians, who now seemed bent upon avenging the fall of one of their number. But the principal object of all was Sir Reginald Courtney, who was immediately surrounded by a dozen men, each of whom was resolved to sacrifice him to his resentment. For some few minutes the knight succeeded tolerably well in keeping them at bay; but so fierce was their attack that he was in momentary danger of falling beneath their numerous weapons, when a second party of the archers appeared in sight, and a cry was raised that struck terror among the rabble. In another instant they were seen flying in all directions, and with cowardly haste they ran away to avoid the consequences of their recent attack upon the king's guards.

Upon being joined by this reinforcement, the bonds were removed from Sir Gaston de Neville, as his escape was now considered impossible; and placing him in the midst of the archers, they all rode off at a brisk trot towards the place of their destination.

CHAPTER CXXIII.

Wilt thou repent the baseness of thy ways?
Make restitution for the grievous ills
Thou hast committed in thy long career,
Or must thine obstinacy incur
Our heaviest wrath?
THE AMBASSADOR.

ON reaching the palace, Sir Reginald Courtney and the Templar dismounted from their horses and entered the principal hall, from whence they proceeded to an apartment usually occupied by the pages when it was not their duty to be in attendance upon the king. Here they found Adrian, who Sir Gaston de Neville no sooner saw, than darting a look of fury toward him, he reproached the youth for having deserted his master and joined himself with those who were his most inveterate foes. Adrian, however, was not to be intimidated by the fury with which he was assailed, and regarding the knight with a firm and unflinching look, he replied that his flight had been produced by necessity, and that he must either have done so or remained where he was, with the certainty of falling under the vengeance of a fierce and vindictive master.

"I knew," he said, "that nothing short of my life would satisfy the anger which had been occasioned by assisting the escape of Lady Alicia, and not being willing to expose myself to your wrath, I sought the protection of King Richard, and have been at the palace ever since."

"Humph! and doubtless it is thine intention to become one of the witnesses against me."

"Fortunately," replied the youth, "I am spared the pain of appearing against my late master, for the king is ready to pardon all offences, and even to restore you to the favour which, for a short time, you had lost."

"And for which I thank him not," muttered the Knight Templar, contemptuously.

"Nay," said Adrian, "let me entreat you to think better of this, and to accept the offer of grace while there is yet time."

"I will have none of it," answered Sir Gaston, "am I not his prisoner; and having been thus far disgraced, shall I now humbly sue for a life that is no longer of value to me?"

"You are not required to ask for life," exclaimed the younger knight, "for that is already granted, without any condition. In return, however, it is expected that you will promise him your future allegiance, and do justice to those whom you have wronged."

"Indeed!—and is there any other act of humiliation that this merciful king of yours requires me to perform?"

"He asks for no humiliation," answered Sir Reginald Courtney; "but it having been reported to him that you have wronged certain persons, it is his desire that the complainants shall have justice done them."

"The Lady Alicia, I suppose, is one of my accusers?"

"On the contrary," replied the young knight, "she has sought, by every means in her power, to conceal the cruelties you have been guilty of towards her."

"How then, has Richard heard this story, which it seems has been reported to my prejudice?"

"From the mouths of many persons," replied Sir Reginald, "the story is now well known, and all parties unite in condemning the treatment she has received at your hands."

"Hah!—do people prate thus of my affairs?"

"They do."

"In that case I care not what fate I meet," exclaimed the Templar, "for up to this time I have fancied the affair might be hushed, and that it might be possible to keep that one action of my life a secret from the world. It is, however, published from mouth to mouth, and, as the world will be sure to condemn me, it matters not how soon I seek the oblivion of the grave."

"Would you rather die then, than live to repent the evil of your ways?"

"And why should I repent?" asked the Templar; "have I not hitherto acted freely and without restraint? and shall I now become a whining slave, passing my days in the bitterness of grief, and looking forward to the scorn of a world which I despise?"

"There is no occasion to regard the future in such a light as that," exclaimed Sir Reginald Courtney, "for it depends upon yourself whether you may not be restored to the royal favour, and in that case what need you care for those thoughts which people will not dare to give expression to?"

"Aye, but I believe there are other charges to be brought against me," answered the other, "and as I do not intend to refute them, of course the popular prejudice will go against me. And so let it, for I shall never stoop so low as to seek favour with the rabble."

"And yet," observed Sir Reginald, "it is not long since you had nearly owed your escape to the very class of persons you affect to despise!"

"True, but I solicited not their interference, and even did what I could to prevent their ill-timed violence."

At this period a page entered to announce that the king desired the immediate presence of Sir Gaston de Neville, who, accordingly accompanied by the other knight, left the apartment and proceeded to that where the monarch was waiting their arrival. On the brow of Richard might be observed a shade of anger which was seldom to be seen there, but no sooner was he aware of the Templar's presence, than banishing all appearance of wrath, he gently demanded whether he had come to

solicit pardon for the past, and promise to make restitution to those whom he had injured.

"When your majesty deigns to tell me by what right you thus question me, I may, perhaps be induced to answer," exclaimed the Knight Templar, haughtily.

"Hah! am I to be heard in my own palace, and by a traitor, too who it is in my power to crush?"

"I am not here to ask either favour or protection," replied Sir Gaston, sullenly; "your majesty sees me in your power, and should it be your will to send me to instant death, I can bow to your sentence without a murmur."

"Misguided man," replied the king, "will no kindness win thee from the evil of thy ways?"

"Nothing," answered Sir Gaston, "will ever make me love a monarch whom I regard only as a usurper!"

"Hah! dost thou dare tell me this to my face?"

"I have told thee so ere now by words," replied the knight, "and my actions have been sufficient to prove that my opinion has undergone no alteration."

"And why am I thus hateful to you?"

"Because you have listened to the tongue of envy when falsehoods have been whispered in your ear, and from the moment when I believed your favour was lost to take part with one who, should he come to the throne, would not forget the services I have done him."

"But dost thou not recollect that Prince John has long been suspected of having designs upon my crown, and that a word of mine would be sufficient to send him to prison for the remainder of his days, and thus end for ever the hopes you have formed of gaining his good?"

No. 102

"And were you to do so," exclaimed Sir Gaston de Neville, "it would lead to a civil war that might end in your own speedy dethronement. Aye, you look fiercely upon me, but I speak the truth, and you will find it so too, if any harm is done to me."

"Are you not my prisoner?"

"I am."

"And is not your life at my disposal?"

"It is."

"What then is to hinder me from punishing you according to your deserts?"

"Care for your own safety is the best safeguard I have," replied Sir Gaston, insolently, "you know I am not without friends, and my death by your commands, would be the signal for a rising taking place among those who have vowed to put Prince John on the throne of England. Nay, Sir Reginald Courtney has witnessed within the last hour how determined some men were to reserve me, and had they counted but a few more in numbers, it is likely your majesty would not have seen me at this moment before you."

"You acknowledge yourself there to be the head of a body of men that are traitors to their king and country?"

"I acknowledge only that I have friends, who would eagerly come forward to rescue me from the hands of those who seek my destruction," replied Sir Gaston;—"the men advocate what they conceive to be the right side, and though you may call them traitors, they would be regarded as good men and patriots should it happen that your brother contrives to obtain sovereign power."

"And thou hast forgotten thy former loyalty," cried the king, "to become an associate of men who openly declare themselves to be my sworn enemies?"

"If I do so," replied Sir Gaston, "it is because I have met with injuries from you which will never be either forgiven or forgotten while I exist."

"Your majesty hears him," exclaimed Sir Reginald Courtney, "and I would, therefore, ask whether it would be safe to let him go at large after the confession he has just made?"

"Kindness in this instance may do more than severity," replied Richard, after a pause of some few moments. "Sir Gaston de Neville and I have fought side by side in the same field of battle; we have shared the honours of victory together, and my own eyes have beheld him perform prodigies of valour that I can never forget. These things induce me to look over acts that are committed against myself, and in spite of his threatening language, I believe there is no reason to fear that he will ever seek to do me an injury."

"You then do me no more than justice," replied the templar, "for much as I dislike you I could not raise my hand for your destruction, even though I might be commanded to do so by one whose authority I hold to be far superior to your own."

"How was it, then?" demanded Sir Reginald Courtney, "that you not long since engaged in a plot to take away the life of King Richard of England?"

"I knew of the plot, certainly," replied the templar, "but mine was not the hand that was armed for the purpose of which you have thought proper to remind me."

"But your servant was the man who was to do the deed of blood," exclaimed the younger knight.

"Am I then to be accountable for the evil deeds of my servants?"

"Not in every instance," replied Sir Reginald, "but in this one the fellow has acknowledged that he never should have thought of the crime had he not been urged to its commission by yourself."

"Villain!" muttered the Knight Templar, "has he said that against me?"

"To do Bertrand le Noir justice," replied the king, "he was very cautious in his replies, and it was with extreme difficulty that we were able to obtain any information from him. When, however, he found that we did not intend to prosecute the business to any great extent, he opened his mind a little more freely, and we heard some few particulars that fully confirmed all the reports that had previously reached our ears."

"And am I to be condemned upon the evidence of my own servant?" demanded Sir Gaston de Neville;—"upon the bare words of a man whose poverty would induce him to say anything that you may wish your gold to purchase?"

"We have never sought to procure evidence from him," replied the king, "though it is well known he could give more than either you or I want. In fact, Sir Gaston, it is not your punishment I seek, but your departure from an evil course of life that has driven you to the very verge of destruction."

"Or, in other words, you wish me to become a faithful subject of your own, instead of vowing allegiance to your royal brother, Prince John?"

"I ask you not to do that which may be against your own conscience," replied the king, "but, surely, you must admit in this instance, that I have right on my side. Am I not the elder brother, and does not the crown, therefore, belong to me as a birthright?"

"It may so," answered Sir Gaston; "but as the people are generally inclined to favour Prince John, it ought to create no surprise that some are found who are willing to assist the common herd as leaders. I am one of those, and if your majesty thinks over the name of your nobility, you may reckon upon at least one half of them being favourers of your brother's cause."

"Let them come forward, then, fairly and candidly," replied King Richard; "let them say that they would rather be governed by John than myself, and I will cheerfully resign my crown and retire into that privacy and seclusion which have more charms for me than have all the glitter and tinsel of royalty."

"Your majesty," interposed Sir Reginald Courtney, "has already endured too much from the insolence of this knight. He is a rebel and a traitor, and I wait but your majesty's command to bear him away to prison."

"Is this to serve some private pique of thine own?" demanded the templar of the younger knight.

"I have no pique to serve," replied Sir Reginald, "but I would fain drive out from the country all those who would seek to disturb our present quiet. You are not satisfied with him who at present sways the destinies of this sovereignty, and, therefore, I would have thee so taken care of that no possibility should exist of your being able to injure him."

"Would that I were at liberty," cried Sir Gaston trembling with rage," and thy insolent words should have been checked long ere thou hadst said thus much. But I am restrained at present, or thou wouldst not have dared to taunt me as thou hast."

"Dared!"

"Aye, Sir Reginald, thou art a younger man than myself, but I can yet wield a sword as thou may'st find, should I ever get my liberty again."

"Peace, I charge you both !" exclaimed the king, interposing to prevent the continuance of this quarrel. "This subject has been already carried too far, and it is my command that no further notice is taken of words that have been spoken in haste and taken up in anger. Let all be forgotten, and if ye cannot part as friends, it is my desire that you shall not hereafter meet as enemies."

"Sir Reginald and I can never be friends," muttered the templar, sullenly.

"Never, whilst you are a traitor to your king," whispered the younger knight in his ear.

"Come, come, Sir Knights, we will hear no more of this," exclaimed the king, "and you, Sir Reginald, leave us for the present, and send hither the captain of the archers with a small body of his men to watch, lest Sir Gaston should escape ere the necessary enquiries have been made ?"

"Your majesty's commands shall be obeyed."

"And when you have brought the guard here," resumed the king, "you may fetch Lady Alicia, who I would see as soon as possible in order that her uncertainty may be brought to a speedy close."

Sir Reginald departed, and having despatched the captain of the archers to the king's presence, he went in search of the Lady Alicia, who was still an inmate of the palace.

CHAPTER CXXIV.

"Though an ill mind appear in simulation
And for the most, such quality offends,
'Tis plain that this, in many a situation,
Is found to further beneficial ends.— ORLANDO FURIOSO.

"I COME to bring your ladyship good tidings," he said as he entered the apartment. "Sir Gaston is once more a prisoner, and there is a fair prospect of affairs being brought to a more successful termination than was expected."

"And call you that good news," cried Alicia reproachfully, "which tells me that my husband is in danger ?"

"Sir Gaston has brought it all upon himself," replied the other, "and as for the danger you speak of, there will be none that I know of, unless he chooses to be obstinate and refuse the mercy that is offered to him."

"Will the king pardon his offences ?" asked the Lady Alicia, with eager haste

"It has been already offered."

"And does my husband refuse it ?"

"That is hardly known at present," answered Sir Reginald. "He persists in maintaining a sullen silence upon that subject, but for my part, I have no doubt he will gladly purchase the royal favour by swearing allegiance to his rightful sovereign."

"And what says he of me ?" demanded Alicia, "will he again receive me as his wife ?"

"Upon that point he is likewise silent," replied the knight. "He has been urged to do so, but will give no answer till he has had more time for reflection."

"Alas! he is obdurate then to the last!"

"He has been so thoroughly defeated," answered Sir Reginald, "that at present he seems to be completely lost in bewilderment. There is, however, little doubt that he will ultimately yield to the circumstances in which he is placed."

"But he can never sincerely love me after all that has occurred," cried Alicia; "the king's commands he may, perhaps, be compelled to obey, but the reconciliation cannot, I am afraid, be very sincere."

"Perhaps not," replied the other, "but self-interest may compel him to effect an outward show of kindness that has no real place in his heart. That, however, will be of little consequence, as whatever his inclination may be, he can never again practice upon the cruelties from which you have been so happily rescued. King Richard has himself taken the case in hand, and he is now sent for you, in order that arrangements may be made to secure you against all oppression in future."

"And where is Sir Gaston?"

"You will meet him in the king's presence; nay, do not tremble thus for I can safely pledge my knightly word you have nothing more to fear from him."

"It was not that which made me tremble," cried Lady Alicia, "but I cannot help dreading an interview with my husband under the circumstances in which we must meet."

"Yet it will be his own fault should the day pass over without receiving pardon from his majesty," exclaimed Sir Reginald Courtney. "Nay, so mercifully is the king inclined towards him, that he will bestow wealth and honours upon him, if he will only merit them by renouncing all future treachery against him."

"Which, I fear, the pride of Sir Gaston will never allow him to accept," cried Lady Alicia.

"In that case," exclaimed the knight, "either death or imprisonment for the remainder of his days will be his doom."

"Would the king consign him to death or imprisonment?"

"I see no help for it," replied the other; "for were Sir Gaston now at liberty, he would not hesitate to wage war against his sovereign. His word, however, will be taken, and he has only to promise allegiance, when his instant liberation would be granted."

"Has his majesty expressed such an intention?"

"He has, my lady, and Richard will not break his word, provided your husband is not too proud to accept his mercy."

"I fear he would rather perish than yield," cried Alicia; "he is a bold and fearless mind, which no peril can daunt, and I dread lest he should prefer any punishment rather than yield to the necessity that should urge him to submission."

"Yet adversity may have chastened his heart," exclaimed Sir Reginald, "and in that case, you may hope that he will not refuse the proffered mercy of his sovereign. Besides, he is now reduced almost to a state of beggary, for it is expected that his brother, who is the rightful heir to the property he has so long enjoyed, will disclose himself in a few days, and thus all the estates will pass away from your husband into the hands of the man who for years past has been content to endure poverty and seclusion, rather than expose a brother to the scorn and execration of the world. Nay, it is said he never would have come forward had it not been for the many crimes that have been committed by Sir Gaston de Neville."

" In poverty," cried Lady Alicia, "my husband's heart may be bound down to submission, and happy should I be to share with him the more lowly sphere it may soon be his lot to occupy."

" The king will take care that he feels not his mortification too severely," replied Sir Reginald; " but come, my lady, his majesty waits for us, and I must now entreat you to accompany me into his presence."

Lady Alicia made no reply, for her heart was saddened at the thought of meeting her husband under his present circumstances, and following Sir Reginald in silence, she was conducted to the royal chamber, when, throwing herself upon her knees before the king, she earnestly entreated his pardon for one whose conduct towards herself had been freely forgiven.

" Nay, lady," said Richard, assisting her to rise, "this posture of humility is not required in the present instance, for my own feelings towards Sir Gaston de Neville, prompt me to regard his abuse of power with some lenity. That he has erred, we all know, but the past may be forgiven, on condition that he amends his ways in future."

" He will,—he will," cried Alicia.

" That we shall presently see," exclaimed the king, and giving a signal to one of the officers in attendance, Sir Gaston was immediately conducted into the apartment. Alicia would have sprung forward to meet him, but the coldness of his look and manner repulsed her, and leaning for support on the arm of Sir Reginald Courtney, she gave way to a flood of tears, that she found it impossible to suppress. The king had observed his haughty movement with no little indignation, and scarcely curbing his anger, he said ;—

" I believed, Sir Gaston, that all enmity towards this unfortunate lady had ceased, and this interview has been brought about solely for the purpose of reconciling you to one who has endured injuries from you, and yet is willing to forget all, if you will bestow upon her that love she has so just a right to claim."

" Your majesty has me in your power," replied the templar, haughtily, " and in some things I know I must submit. But Lady Alicia possesses not my love, and, therefore, will I refuse to regard her otherwise than a stranger."

" How !" exclaimed the king, "wilt thou still heap injuries on one who has never given thee cause for this ill will ?"

" Let not that give offence, sire," cried Lady Alicia, " for my grief would only be increased were I to know that I was the occasion of thine anger. I seek but to remove the prejudice Sir Gaston has formed against me, and when that is done, I will retire within the peaceful walls of a convent, and pass the remainder of my days in prayers to heaven, for the forgiveness of those errors into which he has fallen."

" I ask no prayers from thee," exclaimed Sir Gaston; " thou may'st need them for thyself quite as much as him thou hast professed so much consideration for."

" Wilt thou be stubborn to the last ?" demanded the king.

" I will not be forced to do ought against my own inclination," replied Sir Gaston de Neville; " my present situation has been in a great degree caused through her, and I had hoped that we should never meet again in this world."

" Dost thou still bear malice towards her ?"

" No," he replied, " I bear her no ill-feeling, and all I ask is, that we may no more see each other. Let her retire to a convent, as she has proposed to do, and forget that she ever knew the man of whose conduct she complains."

"I had ventured to hope," cried Alicia, "that you would at least have uttered some few words of kindness ere we parted. But it seems I am still doomed to be the object of thine unmerited anger, and, therefore, will I now take my departure, with all good wishes for thy future happiness. Farewell, Sir Gaston, and should'st thou ever chance to remember me, let it not be with unkindness, for whatever misfortunes may have come upon thee, I have had no share in producing them."

So saying, she once more took the arm of Sir Reginald Courtney, and quitting the room, shortly afterwards returned to the convent she had lately left, and where the remainder of her days were passed in that calmness and repose which had been denied her through the earlier portion of her life.

The king watched her as she left the room, and anger kindled in his bosom as he observed the cold indifference with which Sir Gaston had thus parted from her whom he had cruelly oppressed, and who had generously pardoned the deep injuries she received.

"She whom it was thy duty to love, is gone from thee for ever," he exclaimed, "and yet thou canst look on without feeling for the sorrows thou hast wilfully produced."

"Upon that subject I will be no further questioned," exclaimed Sir Gaston, sullenly. "In this instance, at least, I can act as I think proper, and shall do so even at the hazard of drawing down the anger of your majesty."

"Thou art bold of speech, Sir Knight?"

"Not more than I would be in action, were I once more at liberty."

"Hah! I understand thee!—thou would'st still persist in the crimes which have produced thy downfall."

"I said not that," replied the knight; "events of late have much changed my heart, and were set at large, I should perhaps quit my native land for ever, to pass the remainder of my days in another clime."

"There is no reason why thou should'st do so," replied the king, "for thou shalt receive pardon and liberty on condition that from this time forward thou wilt become a true and loyal subject of thy sovereign."

"And of what value would pardon and liberty be to one who from having been possessed of wealth and power, must descend to poverty and degradation?" asked Sir Gaston de Neville. "My deeds too have been published to the world, and from this time forward I shall be regarded as a monster, whose crimes have made him unfit for the society of his fellow creatures."

"Thou art wrong," exclaimed the king, "for on certain conditions I will still continue to hold thee in my favour, and should'st thou show signs of repentance, there are few, I believe, who will be inclined to remember what is past."

"If I understand rightly," said Sir Gaston, "I may rely on your majesty's pardon, on condition that I promise never more to aid the designs of your brother."

"Such," replied Richard, "is my intention, and, therefore, thou knowest upon what terms thou may'st expect to render thy future days happier than those which are past away."

"The promise thou requirest can be easily made and kept," cried Sir Gaston de Neville, "for Prince John has seen how hopeless any attempt upon the throne must be, and wishing to spare those whose lives were endangered through their having advocated his cause, he has renounced all further claims on condition that your majesty will pardon all who have been concerned with him."

"I have heard something of this before, and am glad to hear it confirmed by thy lips," exclaimed the king. "Thou may'st, therefore, tell my brother that his request shall be granted, and all who have participated in his treason, are pardoned the offences they have committed."

"Then I am no longer a prisoner?"

"From this moment you are free," replied the king, "and let me hope you will henceforth retrieve your character by deeds of honour."

"Your majesty will hear but little of me from this time," replied the templar, "for I shall now quit England, and seek to obtain military honour in another country."

"And why not remain here?" asked the king.

"Because I cannot endure the poverty which now must fall upon me," answered Sir Gaston. "It is said that my brother is coming forward to lay claim to his estates, and I shall become a beggar."

"Nay, it shall be my care to prevent that," exclaimed Richard, "for thou shalt have gold and lands bestowed upon thee to support the rank thou hast obtained by thy bravery in the field of battle. Thy brother, it is true, will appear to make his claim, and thou wilt have to give up all, but thou shalt see that I am not unmindful of the sacrifice thou hast made."

"But it is not unlikely that the story of his being alive is a fabrication of my enemies," said the knight. "At any rate, he has long been spoken of as ready to come forward, and yet no one is able to say where he is, or when he will issue from his place of concealment."

"To-morrow," observed the king, "will prove the truth or falsehood of the reports we have heard. I have ordered a proclamation to be issued desiring him to appear before me in your castle in Moorfields; and in case of his failing to do so, the estates will continue to remain in your hands."

"And that he will not appear, I feel quite confident," answered Sir Gaston; "for had he been alive, as report says he is, he would have made his claim long ere this."

"Will you be present when we assemble to-morrow morning?" demanded the king.

"I will."

"We shall expect you there, and see that you fail not, for in the event of his not appearing to the proclamation, I shall formally re-instate you in the possessions that he is supposed to claim."

Then summoning Sir Reginald Courtney, he informed him that the templar was at liberty to depart whenever he pleased, he left the room to attend a council of the chief nobles of his kingdom.

CHAPTER CXXV.

Canst thou by thine art,
Tell me of things to happen?—Knowest thou my fate?
For I would learn the hidden mystery
That still involves the future.

THE BROTHERS.

THE day was fast drawing to a close, when Sir Gaston left the palace, and his thoughts being occupied with his recent interview, he wandered on without heeding whither he went, or reflecting that at that moment he had no home in which to seek a shelter for the night. At length, however, he reached the wild heath of Finchley, which he had nearly

crossed, when he was startled by hearing his name pronounced, and looking up, he beheld Meg, who, at a short distance off, was regarding him
with a scowl of the darkest malignity.

"What brings thee here?" she demanded; "would'st thou know thy
destiny, proud knight, that thou hast wandered thus far at this hour?"

"I would," replied Sir Gaston, "that is if it is in thy power to tell me
of the future."

"I can tell thee both of the future and the past," she exclaimed;—
"thou hast but just left the king, whom thou hast deceived into a belief
that from henceforth thou wilt become a faithful and loyal subject!"

"Hah!" cried Sir Gaston, "how knowest thou that I shall not keep
my word?"

"I have read it in the dark Book of Fate," she replied; "and well thou
knowest that thy heart is still as treacherous as ever it was towards the
king, who, forgetting the past crimes, would still take thee to his royal
favour."

"Had I done otherwise than dissemble," answered Sir Gaston de
Neville, "I should have passed the remainder of my days in a prison.
The king had me in his power, and, therefore, I had no alternative but to
assume the mask of hypocrisy, till circumstances shall enable me to secure that revenge for which my soul still yearns."

"Yet thou wilt never succeed in thy treachery," cried Meg, "for
thine own hours are numbered, and thou shalt perish even at the very
instant when thine arm is raised to slay thy sovereign."

"Hag!" exclaimed the templar, furiously, "how knowest thou that
I contemplate the king's death?"

"I have already told thee I have read it in the Book of Fate," she replied. "Thou hast plotted long and successfully, and now an end

No. 103

comes when the villainy thou hast contrived will be turned against thyself."

"What dost thou mean?"

"That thy death is not far off."

"Psha! thou art a false prophetess, for I shall live to see thee burnt for a witch as thou art."

"There thou art mistaken," exclaimed Meg; "but I have other business just now to talk to thee about; art thou prepared to yield possession of thine ill acquired lands to him who is about to claim them?"

"You speak of my brother?"

"I do."

"Art thou sure he is still alive?"

"I am, for 'tis scarcely half an hour since I parted from him."

"Then direct me where I can find him," cried Sir Gaston de Neville, "for I would fain prevent a public exposure of what has taken place, if the affair can be arranged between us."

"It is too late now," replied Meg, "for a proclamation in the king's name has been issued, desiring the claimant to come forward, and requiring him to do so to-morrow morning at your castle in Moorfields."

"That the king has himself told me," replied Sir Gaston, "but I still doubt whether the person you have spoken of will come forward. Nay, I am inclined to think that my brother has been dead many years."

"Have I not told you," demanded Meg, "that I saw him but a brief space since?"

"You said so," answered Sir Gaston, "but I am inclined to think your story has been invented to force me into yielding up that which I have long had undisputed possession of."

"I have spoken nothing but the truth," exclaimed Meg, "and if to-morrow morning you meet the king in the castle at Moorfields, you will there see the person you drove from his home, and whose life you have often sought through the aid of hired assassins."

"'Tis false, thou hag!" vociferated Sir Gaston de Neville, "for, should any one appear, I shall at once pronounce him to be a rank impostor."

"But he will have proofs to support his claim, and the king will not listen to what you say, unless he is convinced that the person has made an unfounded claim."

"Were he really in existence," said the templar, "it must be under an assumed name."

"Aye, thou art right there," replied Meg. "He has, indeed, assumed another name, or thou mightest have recognized him long ere now."

"We have met, then?"

"Frequently."

"Have I seen him of late?"

"You have."

"Well, it may be so," replied Sir Gaston, "for it is so many years since I saw my brother, and he was then so young that it is scarcely likely I should recognize him, even though we stood face to face."

"And thou art prepared to deny his assertions, when he comes forward to make his claim?"

"His claim will not be a just one," cried Sir Gaston, "and, therefore, I shall not yield possession of my rights unless he can clearly prove that he is the person he represents himself to be. I shall, however, have enemies enough there, whilst my adversary will be supported even by the king himself."

"Richard will not take part against him unjustly," answered the old woman; "and as for the enemies thou speakest of, to what dost thou owe them but to the cruelty and tyranny of which you have been guilty towards those who had not the power to protect themselves?"

"Who have I injured?" asked Sir Gaston.

"Canst thou ask that question, when thou knowest how many years the Lady Alicia pined within the darksome dungeon to which you had consigned her?"

"Lady Alicia has been set at liberty," answered Sir Gaston; "we have since been reconciled, and it is now by her own voluntary act that she has entered a convent to pass the remainder of her days in the gloom of a cloister."

"Where it is to be hoped she will be safe from the future persecutions of the monster that embittered the earlier portion of her days," cried Meg. "In that retreat she will be at peace, for there you dare not follow her."

"It is not my intention to do so," replied Sir Gaston de Neville, "for I hope never to see her again."

"And what say you of the Hebrew Maiden?"

"That I will possess her in spite of the outcry that has been raised in her behalf."

"Thou art mistaken there," returned Meg, "for Rebecca is now safe from your villainous art."

"Safe!—what mean you, woman?"

"That she has this day been married to Reuben Grenard, who will perish in his wife's defence, rather than see her become the prey of her treacherous persecutor."

"Hah!" exclaimed the templar, "then am I doomed to be foiled in every direction!"

"I thought the news of her marriage would gall thy heart," cried Meg, with exultation. "I was sure how bitterly you would feel the disappointment, and well pleased am I to see that you take it so heavily to heart."

"Thy triumph will be a short one then," returned Sir Gaston de Neville, "for, were she guarded by a legion of devils, I would find means to bear her to some place where none should be able to find her."

"And thus thou would'st again forfeit the regard of the king, who has so lately restored thee to his confidence?"

"I care not for that," answered Sir Gaston de Neville, "I have been foiled on every hand, and in this instance, at least, I will prove victorious."

"Have I not told thee that thy life is drawing near to a close, and—"

"Thou hast told me falsely then," interrupted the knight, furiously.

"That," replied Meg, "remains to be proved, and perhaps a few hours may be sufficient for the purpose. Be that as it may, however, the girl is married, and it will be at thine own peril to persecute her any further. Beware, therefore, I say, for thine hours are numbered, and thou knowest not how soon thou mayest perish in the midst of thy evil deeds."

"Nay," exclaimed Sir Gaston, "I have been told that this diamond ring which I wear upon my finger, possesses a magic influence that no harm can befal me whilst it remains in my possession."

"But the jewel has been once lost, and may be so again."

"True," replied the knight, "it was stolen from me by Black Ivan, and was afterwards found in the possession of Rebecca, the Hebrew Maiden."

"Whom you accused of having been concerned in the robbery."

"I did so," replied Sir Gaston, "in hopes of compelling her to accept the terms I proposed."

"And she rejected your terms with the scorn they merited."

"She did," answered the knight, "but my hour of triumph will yet come, and she shall be mine, in spite of all those who may seek to frustrate my design."

"That thou wilt never do," exclaimed Meg, "for virtue like her's ever has a protection that vice like thine cannot overcome. Thou wert boasting just now, too, of the ring which is to protect thee, but I warn thee that thou wilt lose it before thou returnest back to London."

"Hah !—and who is there shall take it from me ?"

"It is not a human being," replied Meg.

"Can I then be encountered by some supernatural foe ?" asked Sir Gaston, with amazement.

"No, but I would have thee beware of a raven, for thou wilt see one on thy way back, and the ring will be borne away by the bird, and given into the possession of him who claims from thee thy lands and castles."

"What jugglery is this thou speakest of ?" demanded Sir Gaston de Neville. "Wouldst thou have me believe that a bird can take from me that which I hold more precious than my life ?"

"All that I have said will happen," answered Meg. "Nay, more, thou wilt shed the blood of a fellow-creature, and the curse of Cain will be upon thee."

"Woman !" vociferated the Knight Templar, "beware how you urge me further with these fearful prognostications. Hitherto, I have refrained from depriving thee of thy miserable existence, but my patience is well nigh exhausted, and another word may tempt me to slay the prophetess of evil."

"Thy threats do not intimidate me," answered the old woman, "for even if thou wert to carry them into execution, it would but shorten my existence by but a brief period. I am old, and hurrying fast to the grave, Sir Gaston de Neville; yet, near as my own end is, thou wilt have quitted this world ere I do."

"Hag, thou liest !" roared the templar, and drawing his sword, he made a furious pass at her, which would have taken deadly effect had she not been aware of his intention, and slipped on one side ere he could effect his purpose. She then uttered a wild laugh of mingled scorn and triumph, and disappeared before he could repeat his attempt for her destruction.

Enraged at the defeat he had sustained, Sir Gaston de Neville now turned his steps towards London, meditating on the words he had heard, and plotting in his own mind how he should best carry his designs into execution. The intelligence of Rebecca's marriage with Reuben Grenard filled him with a fury that he could not control; yet, the more he reflected on it, the more determined was he to discover her, and by violence tear her from the arms of her husband. This thought filled his heart with savage delight, and he was still ruminating on the means he should employ for this purpose, when a dark form appeared before him, and in another moment he recognized the features of his retainer, Bertrand le Noir.

"We are well met, Sir Gaston," exclaimed the ruffian, in a tone of insolent familiarity. "I have been seeking for you ever since I heard that the king had ordered your liberation, and, being unable to discover whither you had gone, I was pursuing my journey without a hope of letting you know my demands."

"Demands!" exclaimed Sir Gaston, with surprise, "what demands have you to make on me?"

"Money," replied the other.

"Then you have asked me for it at a most unfortunate time," replied the knight, "for I am now reduced to my last coin, and, till to-morrow arrives, I know not what Fortune may do for me."

"'Tis false!" exclaimed Bertrand, "for you have gold, and I will have it before we part."

"Would'st thou rob me, villain?"

"No; I would only take that which thou hast promised."

"What have I ever promised thee, sirrah?"

"A reward for my services."

"Hast thou not had it?"

"I have not," replied the ruffian, "and even if I had, my present necessities require more, and I will have it too, or thy life shall be sacrificed."

"Wretch!—would you murder me?"

"Aye;—have I not committed murders ere now, at your command, and shall I not slay the man who has made me the villain I am?"

"Remember, Bertrand, I am armed, and thy baseness may urge me to slay thee in my own defence."

"I care not if I perish," returned the other, "for my life is now valueless to me, since I am obliged to flee from England, to save myself from those that seek to bring me to the gallows."

"Are the bloodhounds after thee?"

"They would be if they knew where I am to be found," answered Bertrand. "I have, however, contrived to slip away, and as I have no money to carry myself safely out of the country, I must apply to you for it, and in case of a refusal, take it by main force."

"I tell thee I have it not to give," replied Sir Gaston de Neville, "and even if I had, I would not bestow it upon one who demands it as thou hast."

"You forget, then, how often I have done things at thy bidding, that I would have shrunk from had I not been zealous in serving you to the utmost of my ability."

"That which thou hast done I have paid thee for most liberally," replied the knight, "and never will I submit to be intimidated out of money by a villain such as thou art."

"Which is the greater villain, thou or myself?" asked Bertrand le Noir, scornfully. "What has been done was at your bidding, and all the crimes that I have committed during my life, you will have to answer for."

"I shall have to answer for one thing more," cried Sir Gaston, furiously, "and that will be for slaying the wretch that had dared utter these words in my presence."

"That thou wilt hardly be able to do," replied Bertrand le Noir, in a tone of indifference, "seeing that I am armed as well as thyself, and will defend myself against thee to the very last."

"Psha!" exclaimed the templar, "why should we two quarrel, when it is still possible we may be able to assist each other? You are aware that I have obtained the king's pardon, and it will, therefore, be in my power to obtain the same boon for you."

"You would find that a more difficult task than you imagine," answered Bertrand; "for I have slain one of the royal archers, who was an especial favourite of Sir Reginald Courtney's, and he has obtained the king's promise to punish me for it with death. The officers of justice are even now searching for me, and should I fall into their hands, it is very little mercy I have to expect from them."

"How long ago is it since this happened?" demanded Sir Gaston de Neville.

"About two hours."

"And where?"

"Close by the king's palace."

"And a pursuit was immediately commenced?"

"It was, but I contrived to elude them, and went in search of you to demand money enough to carry me safely out of England. You were, however, no where to be found, and it is only a lucky chance that at length threw me in your way."

"Thou hast acted rashly in drawing thy sword against the life of one of the king's guard," exclaimed Sir Gaston, "and yet, despite the interference of Sir Reginald Courtney, I believe it will still be possible to obtain the royal pardon, if I solicit it."

"I shall not trust to your good offices in that respect," answered Bertrand le Noir.

"And why not, sirrah?"

"Because in the humour you are now, it is likely enough instead of trying to save my life, you would be glad to see me perish by the hands of the executioner. Aye, you may frown upon me, Sir Gaston, but I have spoken what I believe to be the truth, and shall place no faith in a man who, for more reasons than one, wishes my death."

"I can have no reason for such a wish," answered Sir Gaston de Neville, "unless it should afterwards appear that you are likely to do me an injury by speaking of things that are past and should now be forgotten."

"And would you not always be suspicious of me?" demanded the other.

"I should not," replied the Templar, "because I should know that you cannot say anything against me without at the same time implicating yourself."

"Well," growled the ruffian, "let that be as it may, I don't choose to run any risk at all about the matter. So either give me the money I have demanded, or take the death I have sworn to inflict with my own hands."

"Wretch! would you commit another murder in addition to those that already stain your guilty soul?"

"To be sure I would," returned Bertrand; "I have been used to that sort of work,—thanks to you for it,—and if you are added to the number of my victims, it will be nothing more than justice for the share you have had in putting other people to death."

"But I have told thee I have no money."

"That," retorted the other, "I must be convinced of before I believe the word of one who never scrupled to tell a falsehood whenever it was to serve his own purpose."

"Slave!" exclaimed Sir Gaston wrathfully, "leave me without the delay of another instant, or I will cleave thee in twain for the baseness thou hast been guilty of!"

"It remains to be proved whether thou hast the power to carry thy threat into execution," answered the menial, with provoking coolness. "At any rate," he continued, "I am not inclined to be frightened from my purpose, so you will either comply with my demand, or take the consequences of a refusal."

Unable any longer to endure the insolence of the ruffian, Sir Gaston de Neville unsheathed his sword, and sprang towards his victim with a cry of savage fury that showed the malignity by which he was urged. Bertrand, however, was not unprepared for this sudden attack, and the blow which had been aimed at him was parried, and in his turn, he rushed upon his antagonist with a degree of fury that could scarcely be resisted. But the knight was skilful in the use of his sword, and though less powerful than his antagonist, he contrived to avoid his deadly thrusts, and gaining a slight advantage, attacked him with such determination, that Bertrand began to yield from utter exhaustion. This was soon perceived by Sir Gaston, who was thus urged on to still greater exertion, till at length Bertrand received the sword of his adversary through his body, and with a loud cry of mortal agony the ruffian fell dead at his feet.

At this moment the templar remembered the words of Meg of Finchley, who had foretold that he would shed the blood of a fellow-creature ere he had crossed the heath, and gazing upon the prostrate body before him, he gave way to the reflections that crowded through his mind. Thus occupied, he was startled by a hoarse, croaking voice, that he knew could not have proceeded from any human being, and raising his eyes from the corpse, he saw a huge raven standing upon a fragment of rock, and gazing upon him with a look that filled his soul with horror. Again he remembered the words of the hag, in which she had said he should lose his ring by means of a bird of this description. As this thought struck him, he instinctively felt whether the jewelled ornament was still upon his finger, and, to his consternation, he discovered that it had fallen off during his combat with Bertrand le Noir. Filled with superstitious dread at the loss of his ring, upon the possession of which he always considered his safety depended, he began to search about for it round about the place where the combat had occurred; for some time, however, his labour was in vain, but at length he saw the precious relic sparkling in the faint moombeams, and overjoyed at the discovery, he was in the act of stooping to pick it up, when the raven, darting from the rock on which it had been standing, seized the ring in its beak, and flew away with it ere Sir Gaston could make an effort to interrupt its flight.

Deeply cursing an occurrence that seemed to threaten him with coming danger, the Knight Templar proceeded on his way, but he had not gone far ere he was met by Black Ivan, who taking him by the arm, demanded whither he was going at that hour of the night?

"I am out for my own pleasure," he replied, "and would rather have avoided than met with one who has been the means of frustrating me in almost every design that I have formed."

"Nay, be not sullen with me on that account, Sir Knight," exclaimed the Outlaw; "for if I have been the means of marring thy plans, I have thereby saved thee from much crime that would otherwise have been committed."

"If it had been committed," answered Sir Gaston, "I, and not thou, would have had to endure the punishment."

"Come, come, there is no occasion for a quarrel between us now," said Ivan. "I am no enemy of thine, for rather would I serve than do thee an injury."

"I ask for no service from you," replied the templar, sullenly. "My peace has been made with the king, and I am no longer in danger for anything that has passed."

"I am aware of all that," cried the Outlaw; "but do you know that a claimant will appear to-morrow to claim his inheritance from you?"

"A proclamation has been issued commanding the attendance of my

brother in the event of his being alive," answered Sir Gaston de Neville.
"It is, however, doubtful whether he will appear, and in that case I shall
resume my possession of the estates."

"Yet there are people," observed Ivan, "who say that your brother
Orlando is still alive, and that he will not fail to obey the royal proclamation."

"And even supposing that to be the case," replied the knight, "how
will he be able to prove that he is not an impostor, assuming a name he
has no right to?"

"That," exclaimed the Outlaw, "is a question that I cannot be expected to answer. All I know about it is, that your brother is expected
to present himself before King Richard, and should that be the case,
he must afford good proof of his being the person he represents."

"Which it is impossible he can do," exclaimed Sir Gaston.

"You seem to make yourself quite secure upon that point, Sir
Gaston?"

"I do, and may safely defy him to satisfy the king that his claim to
my estates is a lawful one."

"That, at any rate, we shall see when to-morrow comes," observed
Ivan.

"We—why, surely you do not mean to venture into the presence of
royalty?"

"And why not?"

"Because you are an outlaw."

"I have been one," answered Ivan, "but you forget that I received an
offer of pardon for saving the king's life, when a menial of your's made
a treacherous attempt upon it."

"I have not forgotten it," replied Sir Gaston de Neville; "and as
for the menial you speak of, the king is now quite safe from any attacks
from him in future."

"You have slain him?"

"I have. The villain sought my life just now, and in self-protection
I killed him."

"Then thou hast done well," exclaimed the Outlaw, "for Bertrand le
Noir was a villain, and thou hast saved him from a worse fate. However,
to return to what we were just now speaking of:—I intend to be present
to-morrow at the hour named in the proclamation."

"And think you a robber will be admitted into the presence of
royalty?"

"I am no robber now," replied Ivan.

"Humph!—you grew tired of that very honourable profession?"

"My motive for acting as I have need not be explained at present,"
answered Ivan; "let it suffice that I have quitted the band, and that
during my continuance in it I was never guilty of an act of cruelty, nor
did I ever permit those under me to rob those who were either poor or
unfortunate. I have also been the means of preventing much injustice
that you contemplated, and that reflection alone will be sufficient to console me for having leagued myself with men whose lawless acts I never
could do otherwise than condemn."

"And now you would turn moralizer?"

"I would become an honourable man," replied Ivan, "and that is
more than Sir Gaston de Neville desires to do."

"Hah! would'st thou taunt me?"

"Nay, I wish not to wound thee more than thou art already," exclaimed Ivan. "So mend thy ways as I have done, and thou shalt find
me a friend to thee through life, even though all else forsake thee."

"Psha! I want not thy friendship," cried Sir Gaston; "so go thy ways, and leave me to pursue my journey alone."

"Well," answered Ivan, "thou canst do as thou pleasest; so reflect on this matter at thy leisure, and when I meet thee to-morrow thou canst tell me whether my proffered friendship is still rejected. And, now, fare-well till we meet again."

Upon this Ivan hurried away, and Sir Gaston de Neville pursued his route, darkly ruminating upon the events that had recently occurred, and vainly endeavouring to assure himself that he had nothing to fear on the morrow.

CHAPTER CXXVI.

Last scene of all
Of this most strange, eventful history.
SHAKSPERE.

DURING the remainder of that night, Sir Gaston de Neville continued to walk about, for in spite of the hopes he endeavoured to fortify himself with, he could not feel quite at ease respecting the issue of the next day's events. Nor, in fact, had the once proud and imperious Knight Templar a place in which to shelter himself, for his castle in Moorfields had been taken possession of in the name of the king till it should be known whether the rightful heir would appear to make good the claim that had been

No. 104

put forward in his behalf; his house at Stratford, too, had been set fire to by his own hand, and all that remained of it was a heap of mouldering ruins. Nor had he at present one friend to whom he could apply among the number that were once ready to receive him with hospitality, and he now found himself homeless and friendless with despair and remorse gnawing at his heart.

At length morning dawned, and, fatigued as he was, he entered a deserted hovel in the suburbs of London, and throwing himself upon a heap of straw, he sought in vain to obtain a brief forgetfulness of his cares in sleep; but his mind was restless, and his body feverish, and, at the end of a couple of hours, he once more quitted the cottage, and instinctively directed his footsteps towards his castle, which he was now to behold in the possession of others. At any other time he would have been maddened with fury at an occurrence of much less magnitude; but, now his spirits were completely subdued, and knowing the utter helplessness of his situation, he awaited the issue with an appearance of composure, that, in his more prosperous days, he would have found it impossible to assume.

As he approached the castle, he saw many persons passing to and fro, from one of whom he learnt that the king and his retinue had arrived there about half an hour previously, and that he was now in the great hall, with a numerous assemblage of knights and nobles, who had accompanied him there to witness the important results which the day was expected to bring forth. This was gall to the heart of Sir Gaston, and he was turning away to quit a scene so painful to his feelings, when, remembering the promise he had made to the king, he changed his determination, and, entering by the principal gate, crossed the court-yard, and from thence made his way towards the place where he expected to meet those who were there to witness and perhaps triumph in his downfall.

At length, with slow and half reluctant steps, he entered the hall, and heard the murmur which his appearance there had occasioned. The king, who was one of the first to see him, sent one of his guards to desire that he would approach and take his place in the open space immediately fronting the elevated seat which he occupied. Sir Gaston silently obeyed this order, but scarcely had he made his way through the crowd, when, opposite to him, he beheld Isaac of Tadcaster, and his daughter, and her husband. The sight of these persons had a visible effect upon him, and he would have retreated to conceal himself among the crowd, had not the king called upon him to remain where he was.

"Sir Gaston de Neville," he said, "I can well conceive that your feelings must be deeply lacerated at what is now taking place before you; but I should be unworthy the high situation I occupy, were I to hesitate when called upon to adjudicate in an affair like this. It is said your brother Orlando is not dead, as has been reported, and that he will this day appear to make his claim to estates which you have most unjustly taken possession of."

"With all submission to your majesty," replied the Knight Templar, "it is yet to be proved whether I have acted with the injustice I have been charged with."

"For your own sake, I trust we shall see sufficient reason to acquit you of all blame in this matter."

"And that you will do so I feel convinced," answered Sir Gaston. "At any rate," he continued, looking round him, "there are enough here to witness my triumph or disgrace, whiche'er it may be; but I see some among them who I thought not to have met at a time like this."

"Who are they?" demanded Richard.

"Isaac of Tadcaster, Rebecca, and Reuben Grenard."

"With your majesty's leave," said Isaac, "we will retire, since our presence here gives offence to Sir Gaston."

"Nay, I command you to remain where you are," exclaimed the king. "The truth is, Sir Gaston, they have received a letter purporting to be from your brother, and desiring them to be present at this day's meeting."

"And they have gladly obeyed," muttered the knight, "since they may have the satisfaction of witnessing my downfall."

"Your downfall is not sought for," cried the king, "for the only object which has occasioned our assembling together is to judge impartially between you and the claimant. If he makes good his assertions, and proves to our satisfaction that he is the heir of your father, Sir Edward de Neville, it will be our duty to see him restored to his right. This he may perhaps do; but, if such be the case, it shall be my care to place you in a situation where you may achieve honour, and wipe away the stain you have brought upon your name."

"I repeat that the claimant is an impostor," exclaimed Sir Gaston, "and even if he should have the hardihood to appear, he will not be able to prove his right superior to my own."

"That may be," replied King Richard; "but it will be our duty to inquire strictly into the affair between both parties. I have no feeling to serve in the matter, and should this unknown claimant prove to be an impostor, I shall gladly avail myself of the power it will give me to restore you to the situation you have so long enjoyed."

"Has the party yet made his appearance?"

"He has not," replied the king; "at least, he has not thought fit to present himself before us."

"Nor will he ever do so," exclaimed Sir Gaston, gaining confidence from this circumstance. "He is well aware how easily his falsehood may be detected, and will not venture to appear in this assemblage."

"That remains to be proved," answered the monarch, "for he has not yet been summoned by our herald. When that has been done, if he fails to present himself before us, we shall regard him as a rank impostor, and restore you to the possessions we at present hold in obeyance."

"Then do I feel safe," exclaimed Sir Gaston de Neville.

"Let the herald advance," said the king, "and read our proclamation."

Upon this the herald approached, and the trumpet having been thrice sounded, he read as follows:—

"In the name, and by command of the king, Orlando de Neville is desired to come forward to substantiate his claims as the heir of Sir Edward, his father. If he obey not this proclamation, he will forfeit all right, and the estates will be given to the late possessor."

Again the trumpet sounded, and whilst all present were on the very tip-toe of expectation, a door, a little in the right of the king, flew open, and the armed knight strode forward till he had placed himself opposite the seat occupied by Richard Cœur de Lion, who demanded who it was that had thus intruded into their presence.

"The heir of Sir Edward de Neville," replied the Black Knight, as he raised his viser.

"Why, then," asked King Richard, "dost thou come before us with all this mummery?"

"He is an impostor," exclaimed Sir Gaston.

"Nay, that I deny," cried the other, throwing off his helmet, and quickly disengaging himself from his armour, he discovered himself to the astonished spectators as no other than Black Ivan.

"The Outlaw !—The Outlaw !" shouted a hundred voices.

"By your leave, gentlemen," he exclaimed, "I am no outlaw now, whatever I may once have been. You may remember that I saved the king's life, and the ban which drove me from society was removed."

"He speaks truly thus far," said the king, "but we have yet to learn how he will prove his right to deprive Sir Gaston de Neville of his estates."

"I am his brother, Orlando," exclaimed the other, "and am come to claim that which is my birthright."

"Thou canst not prove it," exclaimed Sir Gaston, fiercely, "for hadst thou been a brother of mine, thou would'st not have joined thyself with a band of robbers."

"I should not have done so," answered Orlando, "hadst thou not usurped my birthright."

"The past shall be forgotten," exclaimed the king, "and it now remains to be seen whether thou canst prove thyself to be the heir to these estates."

"I can do that," exclaimed a female voice from the further end of the hall, and, instantly, Meg of Finchley was seen making her way through the crowd towards the open space in front of the king.

"And who art thou?" asked Richard, as soon as she had taken her place before him.

"I am his nurse, your majesty, and can swear to him among ten thousand."

"How canst thou do that, woman?"

"By this red mark upon his wrist, my liege," answered Meg, pointing to the place.

"Hast thou any other proof?" demanded the king.

"There is one circumstance," replied Orlando, "but perhaps as it is connected with a superstition, it may scarcely be worth mentioning."

"Let me hear it."

"This morning," replied Orlando, "I found upon my table this diamond ring; it has been long in our family, and has been supposed to possess something of a supernatural charm. At all events, it has been constantly worn by those who possess our family estates, and the finding of it so unexpectedly this morning, seems to confirm the report."

"Do you know how it came there?"

"I do not," replied Orlando; "but I should inform your majesty that a raven was perched upon my window sill, and no sooner had I placed the ring upon my finger, than the bird flew away with a portentous croak that sounded to my ears almost like a cry of triumph."

"It was the raven that took it," exclaimed Meg of Finchley, "and the circumstance may be received as a proof that the person before you is the heir of the late Sir Edward de Neville."

"'Tis false!" cried Sir Gaston, in a paroxysm of rage. "I am the heir, and he who now stands forward as my rival, is a villain and an impostor."

"I am neither the one nor the other," replied Orlando, "and as a proof that I have not been prompted by mercenary motives, am now willing to retire into obscurity, on condition that you will recompense those whom you have oppressed."

"What!" exclaimed Sir Gaston, "and dost thou think I would cringe before one whom I despise as an outcast from the society he has outraged by his crimes?"

"My crimes," replied the other, "if fairly weighed in a balance, would be found far less serious than thine own. I was driven forth from my home, and compelled by stern necessity to become the associate of men who, in my heart, I loathed."

"And thou art pardoned," interposed the king, "in consideration of the service thou hast done me. To thee I owe the preservation of my life, when it was endangered by a villain who afterwards fled from justice."

"Your majesty alludes to Bertrand le Noir," observed Orlando; "he it was that attempted to assassinate you, but you have nothing more to fear from him, since I saw him last night lying at my feet a bleeding corse."

"Hah!" cried the king, "and was thine the hand to rid the world of the villain?"

"No sire, he fell by the sword of his late master."

"He would have slain me," exclaimed Sir Gaston, "and I killed him in my own defence."

"But thou hast many others to answer for," cried Meg of Finchley. "Bertrand knew too much for thee."

"Hag!" exclaimed the Templar fiercely, "dost thou dare taunt me with words like these?"

"I do, and will again tell the truth, should I feel myself in the humour to say what I know."

"Beware, woman," cried Sir Gaston, "lest, forgetting in whose presence I stand, I strike thee dead to the earth."

"Nay," she exclaimed, "I care not for thy threat; strike if thou wilt, for I am old and valueless, and it matters not how soon I find peace and quiet in the grave."

"Have then thy wish," roared Sir Gaston, and drawing a dagger from beneath the folds of his vest, he made a rush forward to sheath it in her bosom. Orlando, however, saw his design, and stepped forward to her rescue, when Sir Gaston turning all his vengeance, against the man who had thus supplanted in all the dearest objects of his ambition, raised the bared weapon in his hand, and was in the act of striking the fatal blow, when Meg rushing forward received the weapon in her breast, and with a piercing cry of agony sank dead upon the floor. At that instant some of the guards, at the king's command, sprang forward to capture the assassin knight, but ere they could do this he plunged the dagger into his own bosom, and with an exulting cry of triumph sank back into the arms of an attendant.

"Murderer!" exclaimed the king, "thou shalt be borne away to a dungeon from whence thou shalt never come forth till the hour appointed for thine execution."

"Thou mayest save thyself all trouble on that point," cried Sir Gaston with a fiendish laugh, "for death will ere long release me from the hands of those who would triumph in beholding my punishment and degradation. The blow I have struck is mortal, and in a few minutes I shall be beyond the reach of my enemies."

"Rash man!" exclaimed the king, "I would have saved thee from the consequences of thy many crimes, and yet thou hast chosen to fall ignobly by thine own hands. May Heaven pardon thee."

"Speak not of Heaven to me," groaned Sir Gaston.

"There is yet one question I would ask of thee," said the king; "dost thou acknowledge this person to be thy brother?"

"He is," replied Sir Gaston, who was now rapidly sinking through loss of blood; "I at first doubted that it was Orlando, but the mark upon his wrist confirms his assertion."

It was apparent to every one that the last struggle between life and death was approaching, and the horrible convulsions that distorted his countenance showed the inward workings of remorse and terror. Observing Rebecca among the crowd that was watching his last agonies, he uttered a groan of horror, and sinking back into the arms of the man that supported him, yielded up his guilty spirit.

Immediately after this, the king broke up the assembly, and, having formally restored Orlando to the possessions of his forefathers, he returned to his palace, full of sorrow for the tragical scene of which he had been a witness.

Orlando remained in the castle only long enough to attend the funeral obsequies of his brother and Meg of Finchley, who had died in his service; and then, leaving the home he had just acquired in the custody of a friend, he embarked for the Holy Land, where, by his bravery and example, he effectually wiped away the stain which recent events had cast upon his name.

Isaac of Tadcaster lived some years after this, and, though he still continued to complain of poverty, it was found upon his decease, that he had left immense wealth, all of which had been concealed in a secret recess in the vault beneath his house.

Of Lady Alicia, it is only necessary to observe that she found in the convent that peace and serenity which had been denied her when dwelling without its walls, and that upon the death of the Lady Abbess she was chosen to preside over the sacred establishment in which she had found a refuge.

Adrian, the page, had followed Orlando to Palestine, where, young as he was, he contrived to earn for himself some renown for the gallantry with which he fought in the numerous battles that ensued.

From the period when his plots had been discovered and exposed, Prince John had never given any further encouragement to those who were willing to advocate his unjust pretensions. He left London shortly after this, to pass his time in the quiet of a country house, nor could any of his former friends prevail upon him to join in any further plot for wresting the throne from its present possessor. At last, however, Richard Cœur de Lion fell in battle, and John, as the next heir, assumed to himself the crown of England.

THE END.